THE

KINDLY

ONES

THE KINDLY ONES

A NOVEL

JONATHAN LITTELL

TRANSLATED BY CHARLOTTE MANDELL

HARPER

An Imprint of HarperCollins*Publishers*

THE KINDLY ONES. Copyright © 2009 by Jonathan Littell. English-language translation copyright © 2009 by Charlotte Mandell. All rights reserved. Printed in the United States of America. No part of this book may be used or reproduced in any manner whatsoever without written permission except in the case of brief quotations embodied in critical articles and reviews. For information, address HarperCollins Publishers, 10 East 53rd Street, New York, NY 10022.

Originally published as *Les Beinveillantes* in France in 2006 by Éditions Gallimard.

Designed by Eric Butler

ISBN-13: 978-1-61523-576-6

For the dead

CONTENTS

TOCCATA

Oh my human brothers, let me tell you how it happened. I am not your brother, you'll retort, and I don't want to know. And it certainly is true that this is a bleak story, but an edifying one too, a real morality play, I assure you. You might find it a bit long—a lot of things happened, after all—but perhaps you're not in too much of a hurry; with a little luck you'll have some time to spare. And also, this concerns you: you'll see that this concerns you. Don't think I am trying to convince you of anything; after all, your opinions are your own business. If after all these years I've made up my mind to write, it's to set the record straight for myself, not for you. For a long time we crawl on this earth like caterpillars, waiting for the splendid, diaphanous butterfly we bear within ourselves. And then time passes and the nymph stage never comes, we remain larvae—what do we do with such an appalling realization? Suicide, of course, is always an option. But to tell the truth suicide doesn't tempt me much. Of course I have thought about it over the years; and if I were to resort to it, here's how I'd go about it: I'd hold a grenade right up against my heart and go out in a bright burst of joy. A little round grenade whose pin I'd delicately pluck out before I released the catch, smiling at the little metallic noise of the spring, the last sound I'd hear, aside from the heartbeat in my ears. And then at last, happiness, or in any case peace, as the shreds of my flesh slowly dripped off the walls. Let the cleaning women scrub them off, that's what they're paid for, the poor girls. But as I said, suicide doesn't tempt me. I don't know why, either—an old philosophical streak, perhaps, which keeps me thinking that after all we're not here to have fun. To do what, then? I have no idea, to endure, probably, to kill time before it finally kills you. And in that case, writing is as good an occupation as anything else, when you have time to spare. Not that I have all that much spare time;

I am a busy man, I have what is called a family, a job, hence responsibilities; all that takes time, and it doesn't leave much to recount one's
memories. Particularly since memories are what I have quite a lot of. I
am a veritable memory factory. I will have spent my whole life manufacturing memories, even though these days I'm being paid to manufacture lace. In fact, I could just as easily not write. It's not as if it's an
obligation. After the war I remained a discreet man; thank God I have
never been driven, unlike some of my former colleagues, to write my
memoirs for the purpose of self-justification, since I have nothing to justify, or to earn a living, since I have a decent enough income as it is.
Once, I found myself in Germany on a business trip; I was meeting the
head of a big lingerie company, to sell him some lace. Some old friends
had recommended me to him; so, without having to ask any questions,
we both knew where we stood with each other. After our discussion,
which went quite well, he got up, took a book down from his shelf, and
handed it to me. It was the posthumous memoirs of Hans Frank, the
Generalgouverneur of Poland; it was called *Facing the Gallows*. "I got a
letter from Frank's widow," he said. "She had the manuscript, which he
wrote after his trial, published at her own expense; now she's selling the
book to provide for her children. Can you imagine that? The widow of
the Generalgouverneur!—I ordered twenty copies from her, to use as
gifts. And I advised all my department chiefs to buy one. She wrote me
a moving letter of thanks. Did you know him?" I assured him I hadn't,
but that I would read the book with interest. Actually I had run into
Hans Frank once, briefly, maybe I'll tell you about it later on, if I have
the courage or the patience. But just then it would have made no sense
talking about it. The book in any case was awful—confused, whining,
steeped in a curious kind of religious hypocrisy.

    These notes of mine might be confused and awful too, but I'll do my
best to be clear; I can assure you that they will at least be free of any
form of contrition. I do not regret anything: I did my work, that's all;
as for my family problems, which I might also talk about, they concern
no one but me; and as for the rest, I probably did go a little far toward
the end, but by that point I was no longer entirely myself, I was off-bal-
ance, and anyhow the whole world was toppling around me, I wasn't
the only one who lost his head, admit it. Also, I'm not writing to feed
my widow and children, I'm quite capable of providing for them. No,
if I have finally decided to write, it really is probably just to pass the
time, and also, possibly, to clear up one or two obscure points, for you
perhaps and for myself. What's more I think it will do me good. It's true
that I have been in a rather glum mood of late. The constipation, probably. A distressing and painful problem, and a somewhat new one for

me; it used to be just the opposite. For a long time I had to go to the toilet three or four times a day; now, once a week would be a blessing. I've been reduced to taking enemas, a repulsive procedure, albeit effective. Forgive me for wearying you with such sordid details: but I do have a right to complain a little. And if you can't bear this you'd better stop right here. I'm no Hans Frank, and I can't stand mincing words. I want to be precise, as far as I am able. In spite of my shortcomings, and they have been many, I have remained someone who believes that the only things indispensable to human life are air, food, drink, and excretion, and the search for truth. The rest is optional.

Sometime ago, my wife brought home a black cat. She probably thought it would make me happy; of course she never asked my opinion. She must have suspected I would have flatly refused, so presenting me with the fait accompli was safer. And once it was there, nothing could be done about it, the grandchildren would cry, etc. But this was a very unpleasant cat. Whenever I tried to pet it, to show my goodwill, it would slip away to sit on the windowsill and stare at me with its yellow eyes; if I tried to pick it up and hold it, it would scratch me. At night, on the other hand, it would come and curl up in a ball on my chest, a stifling weight, and in my sleep I would dream I was being smothered beneath a heap of stones. With my memories, it's been more or less the same. The first time I decided to set them down in writing, I took a leave of absence. That was probably a mistake. Things were going well, though: I had bought and read quite a few books on the subject, in order to refresh my memory; I had drawn up organizational charts, detailed chronologies, and so on. But with this leave of absence I suddenly had a lot of free time, and I began thinking. What's more, it was fall, a bitter gray rain was stripping the leaves off the trees, and I was slowly overcome with dread. I realized that thinking is not always a good idea.

I should have known. My colleagues consider me a calm, collected, thoughtful man. Calm, certainly; but often during the day my head begins to rage, with the dull roar of a crematorium. I talk, I hold conversations, I make decisions, just like everyone else; but standing at a bar with my glass of Cognac, I imagine a man coming in with a shotgun and opening fire; at the movies or at the theater, I picture a live grenade rolling under the seats; in a town square on a public holiday I see a car packed with explosives blowing up, the afternoon festivities turned into carnage, blood filling the cracks between the cobblestones, gobbets of flesh splattered on the walls or smashing through the windows to land in the Sunday soup, I hear cries, the groans of people with their limbs torn off like the legs of an insect plucked by a curious little boy, the be-

wilderment of the survivors, a strange, earsplitting silence, the beginning of a long fear. Calm? Yes, I remain calm, whatever happens, I don't
let anything show, I stay quiet, impassive, like the empty windows of
burned-out cities, like the little old men on park benches with their
canes and their medals, like the faces of the drowned just beneath the
surface of the water, never to be found. I couldn't break this terrifying
calm even if I wanted to. I'm not the sort of man who loses his nerve
at the drop of a hat, I know how to behave. But it weighs on me too.
The worst thing is not necessarily those images I've just described; fantasies like these have lived in me for a long time, ever since my childhood probably, or in any case long before I actually ended up in the
heart of the slaughterhouse. The war, in that sense, was only a confirmation, and I have gotten used to these little scenarios, I take them as a
pertinent commentary on the vanity of things. No, what turned out to
be so disturbing, so oppressive, was to have nothing to do but sit around
and think. Ask yourselves: You, yourselves, what do you think of,
through the course of a day? Very few things, actually. Drawing up a
systematic classification of your everyday thoughts would be easy: practical or mechanical thoughts, planning your actions and your time (example: setting the coffee to drip before brushing your teeth, but toasting
the bread afterward, since it doesn't take as long); work preoccupations;
financial anxieties; domestic problems; sexual fantasies. I'll spare you the
details. At dinner, you contemplate the aging face of your wife, so much
less exciting than your mistress, but a fine woman otherwise, what can
you do, that's life, so you talk about the latest government scandal. Actually you couldn't care less about the latest government scandal, but
what else is there to talk about? Eliminate those kinds of thoughts, and
you'll agree there's not much left. There are of course other moments.
Unexpectedly, between two laundry detergent ads, there's a prewar
tango, "Violetta," say, and in a great surge you see the nocturnal lapping
of the river and the Chinese lanterns around the open-air dance floor,
you smell the faint odor of sweat on a joyful woman's skin; at the entrance to a park, a child's smiling face reminds you of your son's just before he started to walk; in the street, a ray of sunlight pierces through
the clouds and brightens the broad leaves, the off-white trunk of a plane
tree: and suddenly you think of your childhood, of the schoolyard at recess where you used to play war games, shouting with terror and happiness. You have just had a human thought. But this is a rare thing.
    Yet if you put your work, your ordinary activities, your everyday
agitation, on hold, and devote yourself solely to thinking, things go very
differently. Soon things start rising up, in heavy, dark waves. At night,
your dreams fall apart, unfurl, and proliferate, and when you wake they

leave a fine, bitter film at the back of your mind, which takes a long time to dissolve. Don't misunderstand me: I am not talking about remorse, or about guilt. These too exist, no doubt, I don't want to deny it, but I think things are far more complex than that. Even a man who has never gone to war, who has never had to kill, will experience what I'm talking about. All the meanness, the cowardice, the lies, the pettiness that afflict everyone will come back to haunt him. No wonder men have invented work, alcohol, meaningless chatter. No wonder televisions sell so well. I quickly cut short my leave of absence, it was better that way. I had plenty of time left to scribble, at lunchtime or in the evening after the secretaries had gone home.

A brief interruption while I go and vomit, then I'll continue. That's another one of my numerous little afflictions: from time to time my meals come back up, sometimes right away, sometimes later on, for no reason, just like that. It's an old problem, I've had it since the war, since the fall of 1941, to be precise, it started in the Ukraine, in Kiev I think, or maybe Zhitomir. I'll talk about that too probably. In any case, I have long since gotten used to it: I brush my teeth, down a little shot of alcohol, and continue what I was doing. Let's get back to my memories. I bought myself a stack of copybooks, the large ones, quadrille-ruled, which I keep in a locked drawer at my office. Before, I used to jot my notes down on index cards, also quadrille-ruled; now I've decided to start all over and forge ahead. I'm not really sure why. Certainly not for the edification of my progeny. If at this very moment I were suddenly to keel over, from a heart attack, say, or a stroke, and my secretaries were to take the key and open this drawer, they'd have a shock, the poor things, and my wife too: the index cards alone would be more than enough. They'd have to burn every last scrap quickly to avoid a scandal. It would be all the same to me, I'd be dead. And in the end, even though I'm addressing you, it's not for you that I am writing.

My office is a pleasant place to write, airy, sober, peaceful. White, almost bare walls, a glass cabinet for samples; and across from my desk a long bay window that looks out onto the factory floor. Despite the double-glazed glass, the incessant clatter of the Leavers looms resonates through the room. When I want to think, I leave my work table and go stand in front of the window; I gaze down at the looms lined up below, at the sure, precise movements of the workers, and let myself be lulled. Sometimes I go down and stroll among the machinery. The room is dark, the filthy windows are tinted blue, since lace is fragile and sensitive to light, and this bluish light soothes my mind. I like to lose myself for a while in the monotonous, syncopated clanking that fills the space, a metallic, obsessive two-step beat. The looms always impress me. They

are made of cast iron, were once painted green, and each one weighs
ten tons. Some of them are very old, they stopped being made a long
time ago; I have the spare parts made to order; after the war, electricity
replaced steam power, but the looms themselves haven't been touched.
I never go near them, to keep from getting dirty: all these moving parts
have to be constantly lubricated, but oil, of course, would ruin the lace,
so we use graphite, a fine black powder dusted over the moving parts of
the mechanism with an old sock, swung like a censer. It turns the lace
black and coats the walls, as well as the floor, the machinery, and the
men who supervise it. Even though I don't often get my hands dirty, I
know these great machines well. The first looms were British and a jealously guarded secret; a few were smuggled into France just after the
Napoleonic Wars by workers fleeing the excise duties. They were modified to produce lace by a man from Lyon, Jacquard, who added a series of perforated strips to them to determine the pattern. Cylinders
down below feed the thread upward; in the heart of the loom, five
thousand bobbins, the *soul*, are slotted into a carriage; then a *catch-bar*
(the English term has been carried over into French) grips and sets this
carriage swinging front to back, with a loud hypnotic clapping. The
threads are guided laterally, according to a complex choreography en-
coded within some five or six hundred Jacquard strips, by copper *combs*
sealed onto lead, and are thus woven into knots; a *swan's neck* carries the
rake up; finally the lace appears, gossamer-like, disturbingly beautiful
under its coat of graphite, slowly rolled onto a drum, fixed at the top of
the Leavers.

Work in the factory runs according to a strict principle of sexual
segregation: the men design the patterns, punch the strips, set up the
chains, supervise the looms, and manage the supply racks surrounding
them; their wives and daughters, even today, remain bobbin threaders,
bleachers, menders, taperers, and folders. Tradition runs strong. Our
tulle makers, up here, are something of a proletarian aristocracy. Apprenticeship is lengthy, the work delicate; a century ago, the weavers of
Calais came to work in buggies, wearing top hats, and called the boss
by his first name. Times have changed. The war ruined the industry,
despite a few looms kept working for Germany. Everything had to be
started again from scratch; whereas before the war four thousand looms
used to operate, today, in the North, only about three hundred are left.
Still, during the postwar boom, tulle makers were able to buy themselves cars before many a banker did. But my workers don't call me
by my first name. I don't think my workers like me. That's all right,
I'm not asking them to like me. And I don't like them either. We work
together, that's all. When an employee is conscientious and hardwork-

ing, when the lace that comes out of his loom doesn't need much mending, I give him a bonus at the end of the year; if someone comes to work late, or drunk, I punish him. On that basis we understand each other.

You might be wondering how I ended up in the lace business. Nothing particularly marked me out for commerce, far from it. I studied law and political science and received my doctorate in law; in Germany the letters *Dr. jur.* form a legal part of my name. Yet it must be said that circumstances played a part in preventing me from making use of my diploma after 1945. If you really want to know, nothing truly marked me out for law, either: as a young man I wanted above all else to study literature and philosophy. But I was prevented from doing so; another sad episode in my *family romance*—maybe I'll come back to it at some point. But I have to admit that when it comes to lace, law is more useful than literature. Here's what happened, more or less. When it was all over, I managed to slip into France, to pass myself off as a Frenchman; in all the chaos, it wasn't too difficult. I returned along with the deported, we weren't asked many questions. It must be said that I speak perfect French; that's because I had a French mother; I spent ten years of my childhood in France, I went through middle school there, then high school, preparatory classes, and even two years of university, at the ELSP, and since I grew up in the South I could even muster a Provençal drawl, but in any case no one was paying attention, it was a real mess, we were greeted at the Gare d'Orsay with some soup, some insults too—I should say that I hadn't tried to pass myself off as a camp inmate, but as an STO worker, and the Gaullists didn't like those too much, so they roughed me up a little, the other poor bastards too, and then they let us go, no Hotel Lutetia for us, but freedom at least. I didn't stay in Paris, I knew too many people there, and not the right ones, so I wandered around the countryside and lived off odd jobs here and there. And then things calmed down. They soon stopped shooting people, and then they didn't even bother putting them in jail anymore. So I started looking around and I ended up finding a man I knew. He had done well for himself, he'd managed the change of regime without a hitch; being a man of foresight, he had taken care not to advertise his services on our behalf. At first he refused to meet me, but when he finally realized who I was, he saw that he didn't really have a choice. I can't say it was a pleasant conversation: there was a distinct feeling of embarrassment to it, of constraint. But he clearly understood that we had a common interest: I, to find a job, and he, to keep his. He had a cousin up North, a former broker who was trying to start up his own business with three Leavers bought off a bankrupt widow. This man hired me as a salesman; I had to travel and find customers for his lace. This work exasperated me; I finally managed to convince him that I could be more useful to him in management. I did indeed have quite a bit of experience in that field, even though I could make even less use of it than of my doctorate. The business grew, especially in the 1950s, when I renewed my contacts in the Federal Republic and succeeded in opening up the German market for us. I could easily have gone back to Germany then: many of my former colleagues were living there peacefully; some of them had served a little time, others hadn't even been charged. Given my record, I could have resumed my name, my doctorate, claimed my veteran's and disability benefits, no one would have noticed. I would easily have found work. But, I said to myself, what would be the point? Law didn't really interest me any more than business, and I had actually come to acquire a taste for lace, that ravishing, harmonious creation of man. When we had bought up enough looms, my boss decided to set up a second factory, and he put me in charge of it. I have kept this position ever since, and will until I retire. In the meantime, I got married, rather reluctantly I must admit, but up here, in the North, it seemed necessary, a way of fitting in and consolidating my situation. I picked a woman from a good family; she was relatively good-looking, a proper sort of woman, and I immediately got her with child, to keep her busy. Unfortunately she had twins, it must run in the family, mine, I mean—one brat would have been more than enough for me. My boss lent me some money, I bought a comfortable house, not too far from the sea. And that is how the bourgeoisie finally made me one of its own. It was better that way. After everything that had happened, I craved calm and predictability above all. The course of my life had crushed the bones of my childhood dreams, and my anguish had slowly smoldered out, from one end of German Europe to the other. I emerged from the war an empty shell, left with nothing but bitterness and a great shame, like sand crunching in your teeth. So a life in keeping with all the social conventions suited me fine: a comfortable straitjacket, even if I often contemplate it with irony, and occasionally with contempt. At this rate, I hope someday to reach Jerome Nadal's state of grace, and to *strive for nothing except to strive for nothing*. Now I'm becoming bookish; another one of my failings. Alas for saintliness, I am not yet fully free of desire. I still honor my wife from time to time, conscientiously, with little pleasure but also without excessive disgust, so as to guarantee the peace of my household. And every now and then, during business trips, I go to the trouble of renewing some of my old habits—but mainly as a matter of hygiene, so to speak. All that has lost much of its interest for me. The body of a beautiful boy, a sculpture by Michelangelo, it's all the same: they no longer take my breath away. It's like after a long illness, when food has lost all taste; what then does it matter if you eat chicken or beef? You have to feed yourself, that's all. To tell the truth, there isn't much that has kept an interest for me. Literature, possibly, but even then, I'm not sure if that's not just out of habit. Maybe that's why I am writing these memoirs: to get my blood flowing, to see if I can still feel anything, if I can still suffer a little. A curious exercise indeed.

When it comes to suffering, though, I ought to know a thing or two. Every European of my generation could say the same, but I can claim without any false modesty that I have seen more than most. And also people forget so quickly, I see it every day. Even those who were actually there hardly ever use anything but ready-made thoughts and phrases to talk about it. Just look at the pathetic prose of the German writers who describe the Eastern Front: putrid sentimentalism, a dead, hideous language. The prose of Herr Paul Carell, for instance, a successful author these past few years. It just so happens that I once knew this Herr Carell, in Hungary, back when he was still called Paul Karl Schmidt and, on behalf of Ribbentrop's foreign ministry, wrote what he really thought, in vigorous, effective prose: *The Jewish question is no question of humanity, and it is no question of religion; it is solely a question of political hygiene.* Now the honorable Herr Carell-Schmidt has brought off the considerable feat of publishing four insipid volumes about the war against the Soviet Union without once mentioning the word *Jew*. I know this, I've read them: it was tedious work, but I'm stubborn. Our French authors, the Mabires and others like him, are no better. As for the Communists, they're the same, only from the opposite point of view. So where have they all gone, the ones who used to sing, *Boys, sharpen your knives on the sidewalk curbs?* They keep quiet, or else they're dead. We babble, we simper, we flounder through an insipid morass made of words such as *glory, honor, heroism*—it's tiresome, no one says anything anymore. Perhaps I'm a bit unfair, but I dare to hope that you understand me. The television bombards us with numbers, impressive numbers, in the seven-or even eight-figure range; but who among you has ever seriously stopped to think about these numbers? Who among you has ever even tried to count all the people he knows or has known in his life, and to compare that laughable number with the numbers he hears on television, those famous *six million*, or *twenty million*? Let's do some math. Math is useful; it gives one perspective, refreshes the soul. It can be a very instructive exercise. Be a little patient, then, and pay attention. I will consider only the two theaters of operations where I played a role, however minute: the war against the Soviet Union, and the extermination program officially referred to in our documents as

"The Final Solution of the Jewish Question," *die Endlösung der Juden-frage*, to cite that fine euphemism. On the Western fronts, in any case, the losses were relatively minor, a few hundred thousand here or there at most.

My starting figures will be somewhat arbitrary: I have no choice, since no one agrees on them. For the total Soviet losses, I'll stick to the traditional number, the twenty million cited by Khrushchev in 1956, while noting that Reitlinger, a respected British author, finds only some twelve million, whereas Erickson, a Scottish scholar who's just as reputable if not more so, comes to a minimum figure of twenty-six million; thus the official Soviet number neatly splits the difference, give or take a million. As for the German losses—in the East alone, that is—one can take as a starting point the even more official and Germanically precise number of 6,172,373 casualties between June 22, 1941, and March 31, 1945, a figure compiled in an internal report of the OKH (the Army High Command) that surfaced after the war, but one that includes both the dead (more than a million), the wounded (almost four million), and the missing (i.e., dead plus prisoners plus dead prisoners, some 1,288,000 men). So let us say for the sake of simplicity two million dead, since the wounded don't concern us here, including, thrown in for good measure, the additional fifty thousand or so men killed between April 1 and May 8, 1945, mainly in Berlin, to which we still have to add the roughly one million civilians believed to have died during the invasion of eastern Germany and the subsequent population movements, giving us, let's say, a grand total of three million German dead. As for the Jews, you have a choice: the traditional number, even though few people know where it comes from, is six million (it was Höttl who said at Nuremberg that Eichmann had told him this; but Wisliceny asserted that Eichmann had said five million to his colleagues; and Eichmann himself, when the Jews finally got to ask him the question in person, said somewhere between five and six million, but probably closer to five). Dr. Korherr, who compiled statistics for the Reichsführer-SS Heinrich Himmler, totaled up close to two million as of December 31, 1942, but acknowledged, when I discussed the matter with him in 1943, that his baseline figures were unreliable. Finally, the highly respected professor Raul Hilberg, a specialist in the matter and one who can hardly be suspected of holding a partisan stance, at least not in favor of the Germans, reaches, after a dense, nineteen-page demonstration, a final count of 5,100,000, which more or less corresponds to the opinion of the late Obersturmbannführer Eichmann. So let's settle for Professor Hilberg's figure, which gives us, to summarize:

Soviet dead . . . . 20 million
German dead . . . . 3 million
Subtotal (for the Eastern Front) . . 23 million
Endlösung . . . . 5.1 million
Total . . . . 26.6 million, given that 1.5 mil-
lion Jews have also been counted as Soviet dead ("Soviet citizens murdered by the German-Fascist invaders," as the extraordinary monument in Kiev so discreetly puts it)

Now for the math. The conflict with the USSR lasted from June 22, 1941, at 03:00, until, officially, May 8, 1945, at 23:01, which adds up to 3 years, 10 months, 16 days, 20 hours, and 1 minute, or, rounding off, to 46.5 months, 202.42 weeks, 1,417 days, 34,004 hours, or 2,040,241 minutes (counting the extra minute). For the program known as the "Final Solution," we'll use the same dates; before that, nothing had yet been decided or systematized, so Jewish casualties were for the most part incidental. Now let's average out one set of figures with the other: for the Germans, this gives us 64,516 dead per month, or 14,821 dead per week, or 2,117 dead per day, or 88 dead per hour, or 1.47 dead per minute, on average for every minute of every hour of every day of every week of every month of every year for 3 years, 10 months, 16 days, 20 hours, and 1 minute. For the Jews, including the Soviet ones, we have about 109,677 dead per month, which is 25,195 dead per week, 3,599 dead per day, 150 dead per hour, or 2.5 dead per minute, over the same period. Finally, on the Soviet side, that gives us some 430,108 dead per month, 98,804 dead per week, 14,114 dead per day, 588 dead per hour, or 9.8 dead per minute, for the same period. Thus for the overall total in my field of activities we have an average of 572,043 dead per month, 131,410 dead per week, 18,772 dead per day, 782 dead per hour, and 13.04 dead per minute, every minute of every hour of every day of every week of every month of every year of the given period, which is, as you will recall, 3 years, 10 months, 16 days, 20 hours, and 1 minute. Let those who smirked at that admittedly somewhat pedantic extra minute please consider that it is worth an additional 13.04 dead, on average, and imagine, if they can, 13 people from their circle of friends killed in 1 minute. You can also calculate the length of time it takes to generate a fresh corpse: this gives us on average a dead German every 40.8 seconds, a dead Jew every 24 seconds, and a dead Bolshevik (Soviet Jews included) every 6.12 seconds, or on the whole a new dead body on average every 4.6 seconds, for the entirety of said period. You are now in a position to carry out, based on these numbers, concrete exercises of imagination. For example, stopwatch in hand, count off 1 death, 2 deaths, 3 deaths, etc., every 4.6 seconds (or every 6.12 seconds, or every 24 seconds, or every 40.8 seconds, if you have a marked preference), while trying to picture them lying there in front of you, those 1, 2, 3 dead. You'll find it's a good meditation exercise. Or take some more recent catastrophe that affected you strongly, and compare the two. For instance, if you are an American, consider your little Vietnam adventure, which so traumatized your fellow citizens. You lost 50,000 troops there in 10 years: that's the equivalent of a little less than 3 days and 2 hours' worth of dead on the Eastern Front, or of some 13 days, 21 hours, and 25 minutes' worth of dead Jews. I obviously am not including the Vietnamese dead; since you never speak of them, in your books or TV programs, they must not count for much to you. Yet you killed 40 of them for every single one of your own dead, a fine effort even compared to our own, and one that certainly speaks for the value of technical progress. I'll stop there, we could go on forever; I invite you to continue on your own, until the ground opens up beneath your feet. As for me, no need: for a long time already the thought of death has been *closer to me than the vein in my neck*, as that beautiful phrase in the Koran says. If you ever managed to make me cry, my tears would sear your face.

The conclusion of all this, if you'll allow me one more quotation, the last one, I promise, is, as Sophocles said so well: *Not to have been born is best*. Schopenhauer has written roughly the same thing: *It would be better if there were nothing. Since there is more pain than pleasure on Earth, every satisfaction is only transitory, creating new desires and new distresses, and the agony of the devoured animal is always far greater than the pleasure of the devourer.* Yes, I know, that makes two quotations, but it's the same idea: in truth, we live in the worst of all possible worlds. Now of course the war is over. And we've learned our lesson, it won't happen again. But are you quite sure we've learned our lesson? Are you certain it won't happen again? Are you even certain the war is over? In a manner of speaking, the war is never over, or else it will be over only when the last child born on the last day of the war is safely dead and buried, and even then it will live on, in his or her children and then in theirs, till finally the legacy will be diluted, the memories will fray and the pain will fade away, even though by then everyone will probably have forgotten, and all this will have long gone to gather dust with all the other old stories, those not even fit to frighten children, much less the children of the dead or of those who wish they were, dead I mean.

I can guess what you're thinking: Now here's a truly bad man, you're saying to yourselves, an evil man, a nasty piece of work in every respect, who should be rotting in prison instead of wasting our time with the muddled philosophy of a barely half-repentant former Fascist. As to fascism, let's not confuse the issue, and as for the question of my legal responsibility, don't prejudge, I haven't told my story yet; as for the question of my moral responsibility, let me offer a few considerations. Political philosophers have often pointed out that in wartime, the citizen, the male citizen at least, loses one of his most basic rights, his right to life; and this has been true ever since the French Revolution and the invention of conscription, now an almost universally accepted principle. But these same philosophers have rarely noted that the citizen in question simultaneously loses another right, one just as basic and perhaps even more vital for his conception of himself as a civilized human being: the right not to kill. No one asks you for your opinion. In most cases the man standing above the mass grave no more asked to be there than the one lying, dead or dying, at the bottom of the pit. You might object that killing another soldier in combat is not the same thing as killing an unarmed civilian; the laws of war allow the one but not the other; as does common morality. A good argument, in theory, but one that takes no account of the conditions of the conflict in question. The entirely arbitrary distinction established after the war between "military operations" like those of any other conflict and the "atrocities" carried out by a minority of sadists or psychopaths is, as I hope to demonstrate, a soothing fantasy of the victors—the Western victors, I should specify, since the Soviets, despite all their rhetoric, have always understood what was what: after May 1945, having tossed a few bones to the crowd, Stalin couldn't have cared less about some illusory "justice"; he wanted the hard stuff, cash in hand, slaves and equipment to repair and rebuild, not remorse or lamentations, for he knew just as well as we that the dead can't hear our crying, and that remorse has never put bread on the table. I am not pleading *Befehlnotstand*, the just-obeying-orders so highly valued by our good German lawyers. What I did, I did with my eyes open, believing that it was my duty and that it had to be done, disagreeable or unpleasant as it may have been. For that is what total war means: there is no such thing as a civilian, and the only difference between the Jewish child gassed or shot and the German child burned alive in an air raid is one of method; both deaths were equally vain, neither of them shortened the war by so much as a second; but in both cases, the man or men who killed them believed it was just and necessary; and if they were wrong, who's to blame? What I am saying holds true even if you accept the artificial distinction between war and what the Jewish lawyer Lempkin baptized genocide; for it should be noted that in our century at least there has never yet been a genocide without a war, that genocide does not exist outside of war, and that like war, it is a collective phenomenon: genocide in its modern form is a process inflicted on the masses, by the masses, for the masses. It is also, in the case in question, a process segmented according to the demands of industrial method. Just as, according to Marx, the worker is alienated from the product of his labor, in genocide or total war in its modern form the perpetrator is alienated from the product of his actions. This holds true even for the man who places a gun to the head of another man and pulls the trigger. For the victim was led there by other men, his death was decided on by yet others, and the shooter knows that he is only the last link in a very long chain, and that he doesn't have to ask himself any more questions than does a member of a firing squad who in civilian life executes a man duly sentenced under the law. The shooter knows that it's chance that has appointed him to shoot, his comrade to guard the cordon, and a third man to drive the truck; at most he could try to change places with the guard or the driver. Another example, taken from the abundant historical literature rather than from my personal experience: the program for the destruction of severely handicapped and mentally ill Germans, called the "Euthanasia" or "T-4" program, set up two years before the "Final Solution." Here, the patients, selected within the framework of a legal process, were welcomed in a building by professional nurses, who registered them and undressed them; doctors examined them and led them into a sealed room; a worker administered the gas; others cleaned up; a policeman wrote up the death certificate. Questioned after the war, each one of these people said: What, me, guilty? The nurse didn't kill anyone, she only undressed and calmed the patients, ordinary tasks in her profession. The doctor didn't kill anyone, either, he merely confirmed a diagnosis according to criteria established by higher authorities. The worker who opened the gas spigot, the man closest to the actual act of murder in both time and space, was fulfilling a technical function under the supervision of his superiors and doctors. The workers who cleaned out the room were performing a necessary sanitary job—and a highly repugnant one at that. The policeman was following his procedure, which is to record each death and certify that it has taken place without any violation of the laws in force. So who is guilty? Everyone, or no one? Why should the worker assigned to the gas chamber be guiltier than the worker assigned to the boilers, the garden, the vehicles? The same goes for every facet of this immense enterprise. The railroad switchman, for instance, is he guilty of the death of the Jews he shunted toward the camp? He is a railroad employee who has been doing the same job for twenty years, he shunts trains according to a schedule, their cargo is none of his business. It's not his fault if these Jews are being transported from Point A, across his switches, to Point B, where they are to be killed. But this switchman plays a crucial role in the work of extermination: without him, the train of Jews cannot reach Point B. The same goes for the civil servant in charge of requisitioning apartments for air-raid victims, the printer who prepares the deportation notices, the contractor who sells concrete or barbed wire to the SS, the supply officer who delivers gasoline to an SP Teilkommando, and God up above, who permits all this. Of course, you can establish relatively precise degrees of legal responsibility, which allow you to condemn some while leaving all the rest to their own conscience, assuming they have one; it's even easier when the laws get written after the fact, as at Nuremberg. But even then they were sloppy. Why hang Streicher, that impotent yokel, but not the sinister von dem Bach-Zelewski? Why hang my superior Rudolf Brandt, and not his superior, Wolff? Why hang the interior minister Frick and not his subordinate Stuckart, who did all his work for him? A lucky man, that Stuckart, who only stained his hands with ink, never with blood. Once again, let us be clear: I am not trying to say I am not guilty of this or that. I am guilty, you're not, fine. But you should be able to admit to yourselves that you might also have done what I did. With less zeal, perhaps, but perhaps also with less despair, in any case one way or another. I think I am allowed to conclude, as a fact established by modern history, that everyone, or nearly everyone, in a given set of circumstances, does what he is told to do; and, pardon me, but there's not much chance that you're the exception, any more than I was. If you were born in a country or at a time not only when nobody comes to kill your wife and your children, but also nobody comes to ask you to kill the wives and children of others, then render thanks to God and go in peace. But always keep this thought in mind: you might be luckier than I, but you're not a better person. Because if you have the arrogance to think you are, that's just where the danger begins. We like to contrast the State, totalitarian or not, with the ordinary man, that insect or trembling reed. But then we forget that the State is made up of individuals, all more or less ordinary, each one with his life, his story, the sequence of accidents that led him one day to end up on the right side of the gun or the sheet of paper while others ended up on the wrong side. This path is very rarely the result of any choice, or even of personal predilection. The victims, in the vast majority of cases, were not tortured or killed because they were good any more than their executioners tormented them because they were evil. It would be a little naïve to think that way; allow me to suggest you spend

a little time in a bureaucracy, even the Red Cross, if you need convincing. Stalin, by the way, conducted an eloquent demonstration of my
argument, by transforming each generation of executioners into the victims of the following generation, without ever running out of volunteers. Yet the machinery of State is made of the same crumbling
agglomeration of sand as what it crushes, grain by grain. It exists because
everyone—even, down to the last minute, its victims—agrees that it
must exist. Without the Hösses, the Eichmanns, the Goglidzes, the
Vishinskys, but also without the railroad switchmen, the concrete man-
ufacturers, and the government accountants, a Stalin or a Hitler is nothing but a wineskin bloated with hatred and impotent terror. To state
that the vast majority of the managers of the extermination processes
were neither sadists nor sociopaths is now a commonplace. There were
of course sadists and psychopaths among them, as in all wars, and these
men did commit unspeakable atrocities, that's true. It is also true that the
SS could have stepped up its efforts to keep these people under control,
even if it actually did more in that line than most people realize. And
that's not easy: just ask the American generals what a hard time they had
of it in Vietnam, with their junkies and their rapists, smoking dope and
fragging their officers. But that's not the problem. There are psychopaths everywhere, all the time. Our quiet suburbs are crawling with
pedophiles and maniacs, our homeless shelters are packed with raving
megalomaniacs; and some of them do indeed become a problem, they
kill two, three, ten, even fifty people—and then the very same State that
would without batting an eye send them to war crushes them like a
blood-swollen mosquito. These sick men are nothing. But the ordinary
men that make up the State—especially in unstable times—now there's
the real danger. The real danger for mankind is me, is you. And if you're
not convinced of this, don't bother to read any further. You'll understand nothing and you'll get angry, with little profit for you or for me.

Like most people, I never asked to become a murderer. If I could
have, as I've already said, I would have gone into literature. Written, if
I'd had the talent, or else perhaps taught, at least lived in the midst of
beautiful, calm things, the noblest creations of the human spirit. Who,
of his own free will, aside from a madman, would choose murder? And
also I would have liked to play the piano. Once at a concert an elderly
lady leaned toward me: "You are a pianist, aren't you?"—"Unfortunately not, madam," I had to answer with regret. Even today, the
thought that I don't play the piano and never will play it suffocates me,
sometimes even more than the horrors, the dark river of my past carrying me through the years. I literally can't get over it. When I was a
boy, my mother bought me a piano. It was for my ninth birthday, I

think. Or my eighth. In any case before we left to live in France with that Moreau man. I had been begging her for months and months. I dreamed of being a pianist, a great concert pianist: cathedrals at my fingertips, airy as foam. But we had no money. My father had been gone for some time, his bank accounts (as I learned much later) were frozen, my mother had to fend for herself. But somehow she found the money, I don't know how, she must have saved up, or borrowed; maybe she even whored a bit, I don't know, it doesn't matter. She probably had ambitions for me and wanted to cultivate my talent. So on my birthday the piano was delivered, a fine upright. Even secondhand, it must have been expensive. At first I was dazzled. I took lessons; but my lack of progress quickly bored me, and I soon dropped them. Practicing scales was not what I had in mind, I was like all children. My mother never dared reproach me for my irresponsibility or my laziness; but I can see that the idea of all that wasted money must have gnawed at her. The piano stayed there, gathering dust; my sister was no more interested in it than I was; I no longer thought about it, and barely noticed when my mother finally resold it, most likely at a loss. I have never really liked my mother, I have even hated her, but this incident makes me sad for her. It's also somewhat her own fault. If she had insisted, if she had known how to be stern when she had to be, I might have learned to play the piano, and that would have been a great joy to me, a safe haven. To play just for myself, at home, that would have been a delight. Of course, I often listen to music, and I take a keen pleasure in it, but it's not the same thing, it's a substitute. Just like my male lovers: the fact of the matter, I'm not ashamed to say, is that I probably would rather have been a woman. Not necessarily a woman living and functioning in this world as a wife or a mother; no, a woman naked, on her back, her legs spread wide open, crushed beneath the weight of a man, clinging to him and pierced by him, drowning in him as she becomes the limitless sea in which he himself is drowned, pleasure that's endless, and beginningless too. But things did not turn out that way. Instead I ended up a jurist, a State security official, an SS officer, and then a director of a lace factory. It's sad, but that's how it is.

What I've just written is true, but it is also true that I have loved a woman. Only one, but more than anything in the world. Yet she was precisely the one I was not allowed to have. It is quite conceivable that by dreaming of myself as a woman, by dreaming of myself in a woman's body, I was still seeking her, I wanted to draw closer to her, I wanted to be like her, I wanted to be her. This is entirely plausible, even if it changes nothing. I have never loved a single one of the boys I slept with, I just used them and their bodies, that's all. Whereas with her, her love would have fulfilled my life. Don't laugh at me: that love is probably the only good thing I've ever done. All this, you're probably thinking, must seem a little strange coming from an officer of the *Schutzstaffel*. But why couldn't an SS-Obersturmbannführer have an inner life, desires, passions, just like any other man? There have been hundreds of thousands of us whom you still judge as criminals: among them, as among all human beings, there were ordinary men, of course, but also extraordinary men, artists, men of culture, neurotics, homosexuals, men in love with their mothers, who knows what else, and why not? None of them was more typical of anything than any other man in any other profession. There are businessmen who enjoy fine wine and cigars, businessmen obsessed with the bottom line, and also businessmen who hide obscene tattoos under their three-piece suits and go to work with a rubber plug up their anuses: all this seems obvious to us, so why wouldn't it be the same for the SS or the Wehrmacht? Our military doctors would find women's underwear when they cut open the uniforms of the wounded more frequently than you'd think. To state that I was not typical means nothing. I lived, I had a past, a difficult and burdensome past, but that happens, and I managed it in my own way. And then came the war, I served, and I found myself at the heart of terrible things, atrocities. I hadn't changed, I was still the same man, my problems had not been resolved, even though the war created new problems for me, even though those horrors transformed me. There are men for whom war, or even murder, is a solution, but I am not one of them; for me, as for most people, war and murder are a question, a question without an answer, for when you cry out in the night, no one answers. And one thing leads to another: I started out within the bounds of my service and then, under the pressure of events, I finally overstepped those bounds; but everything is connected, closely, intimately connected: to argue that if there had been no war I would still have resorted to such extremities would be impossible. It might have happened, but maybe not, maybe I'd have found another solution. You can never know. Eckhart has written, *An angel in Hell flies in his own little cloud of Paradise*. I always took that to imply that a devil in Paradise flies also in his own little cloud of Hell. But I don't think I'm a devil. There were always reasons for what I did. Good reasons or bad reasons, I don't know, in any case human reasons. Those who kill are humans, just like those who are killed, that's what's terrible. You can never say: I shall never kill, that's impossible; the most you can say is: I hope I shall never kill. I too hoped so, I too wanted to live a good and useful life, to be a man among men, equal to others, I too wanted to add my brick to our common house. But my hopes were dashed, and my sincerity was betrayed and placed at the services of an ultimately evil and corrupt work, and I *crossed over to the dark shores*, and all this evil entered my own life, and none of all this can be made whole, ever. These words are of no use either, they disappear like water in the sand, this wet sand that fills my mouth. I live, I do what can be done, it's the same for everyone, I am a man like other men, I am a man like you. I tell you I am just like you!

ALLEMANDES
I AND II

At the border they had set up a pontoon bridge. Just next to it, rising above the gray water of the Bug, the warped girders of the metal bridge the Soviets had dynamited lay in tangles. Our sappers had erected the new one in one night, we'd heard, and impassive Feldgendarmen, their crescent-shaped neck-plates reflecting the sun's glare, controlled the traffic with self-assurance, as if they were still back home. The Wehrmacht had priority; we were told to wait. I contemplated the big lazy river, the quiet little woods on the other side, the throng on the bridge. Then it was our turn to cross and right on the other side there stretched out, like a boulevard, the wrecks of Russian equipment, trucks burned out and crumpled, tanks ripped open like tin cans, artillery carriages twisted like straw, overturned, swept aside, tangled up in an interminable burned strip made up of irregular heaps running alongside the road. Beyond, the woods gleamed in the splendid summer sun. The dirt road had been cleared but you could see traces of explosions along it, big oil slicks, scattered debris. Then came the first houses of Sokal. In the center of town, a few fires were still gently crackling; dust-covered corpses, most of them in civilian clothing, blocked part of the street, intermingled with ruins and rubble; and facing us, in the shade of a park, white crosses topped with curious little roofs formed a tidy line beneath the trees. Two German soldiers were painting names on them. We waited there while Blobel, accompanied by Strehlke, our supply officer, went to HQ. A sweetish smell, vaguely nauseating, intermingled with the acridity of the smoke. Soon Blobel returned: "It's fine. Strehlke is taking care of the quarters. Follow me."

The AOK⋆ had set us up in a school. "I'm sorry," a little quarter-master in creased field gray said. "We're still getting organized. But they'll send you some rations." Our second in command, von Radetzky, an elegant Balt, waved a gloved hand and smiled: "That's no problem. We're not going to stay." There weren't any beds, but we had brought blankets; the men sat down on the little school chairs. There must have been about seventy of us. At night, we got soup with cabbage and po-tato, almost cold, some raw onions, and chunks of a black, gummy bread, which dried out as soon as it was sliced. I was hungry, I dipped it in the soup and ate it and bit into onions whole. Von Radetzky set the watch. The night passed peacefully.

The next morning, Standartenführer Blobel, our commander, gath-ered his Leiters together to go to HQ. The Leiter III, my immediate superior, wanted to type up a report, so he sent me in his place. The headquarters of the Sixth Army, the AOK 6, to which we were at-tached, had occupied a large Austro-Hungarian building, its façade gaily painted orange, enhanced with columns and stucco decorations, and riddled with shrapnel. An Oberst, who seemed to know Blobel well, received us: "The Generalfeldmarschall is working outdoors. Follow me." He led us toward a vast park that stretched down from the build-ing to a bend in the Bug, down below. Near a solitary tree, a man in swimming trunks was walking with long strides, surrounded by a buzzing cloud of officers, their uniforms drenched in sweat. He turned toward us: "Ah, Blobel! Hello, gentlemen." We saluted him: he was Generalfeldmarschall von Reichenau, the commander in chief of the army. His hairy chest, thrust forward, radiated vigor; embedded in the fat that, despite his athletic build, drowned out the Prussian fineness of his traits, his famous monocle gleamed in the sun, incongruous, almost ridiculous. Without stopping his precise and meticulous instructions he continued his jerky movements to and fro; we had to follow him, which was a little disconcerting; I bumped into a Major and didn't grasp much. Then he stood still to dismiss us. "Oh yes! One other thing. For the Jews, five guns are too much, you don't have enough men. Two guns per condemned man will be enough. As for the Bolsheviks, we'll see how many there are. If they're women you can use a full squad." Blobel saluted: "*Zu Befehl*, Herr Generalfeldmarschall." Von Reichenau

---

⋆ Since the author often neglects to explain the numerous terms of German military and administrative vocabulary, little known outside of specialized mi-lieus, we have thought it advisable to add a glossary and table of ranks at the end of the volume; we invite the reader to consult this.—Ed.

clicked his bare heels and raised his arm: "Heil Hitler!"—"Heil Hitler,"
we all replied in chorus before beating a retreat.
Sturmbannführer Dr. Kehrig, my superior, greeted my report sul-
lenly. "Is that all?"—"I didn't hear everything, Sturmbannführer." He
made a face and fiddled distractedly with his papers. "I don't understand.
Who should we take our orders from, in the end? From Reichenau or
Jeckeln? And where is Brigadeführer Rasch?"—"I don't know, Sturmbannführer."—"You don't know much, Obersturmführer. Dismissed."
  Blobel called all the officers together the next day. Early in the
morning, about twenty men had gone with Callsen. "I sent him to
Lutsk with a Vorkommando. The whole Kommando will follow in a
day or two. That's where we'll set up our headquarters, for now. The
AOK will also be transferred to Lutsk. Our divisions are advancing
quickly, we have to get to work. I'm waiting for Obergruppenführer
Jeckeln, who will give us orders." Jeckeln, an old Party hand, was the
Höhere SS-und Polizeiführer for southern Russia; all SS formations in
the zone, including our own, were subordinated to him in one way or
another. But the question of the chain of command continued to worry
Kehrig: "So, are we under the authority of the Obergruppenführer?"—
"Administratively, we're subordinated to the Sixth Army. But tactically
we receive our orders from the RSHA, via the Gruppenstab, and from
the HSSPF. Is that clear?" Kehrig nodded and sighed: "Not entirely, but
I'm guessing the details will become clearer as we go along." Blobel
flushed crimson: "But they explained everything to you in Pretzsch,
good God!" Kehrig kept his calm. "In Pretzsch, Standartenführer, they
explained absolutely nothing to us. They fed us some speeches and
made us exercise. That's it. I would remind you that the representatives
of the SD were not invited to the meeting with Gruppenführer Heydrich, last week. I'm sure there were good reasons for that, but the fact
is that I have no idea what I should do, aside from write reports on the
morale and behavior of the Wehrmacht." He turned to Vogt, the Leiter
IV: "You were there, at that meeting. Well, when they explain our tasks
to us, we'll carry them out." Vogt tapped on the table with a pen, ill at
ease. Blobel chewed the inside of his cheeks and stared furiously at a
point on the wall. "All right," he finally barked. "In any case, the Obergruppenführer is arriving tonight. We'll see about that tomorrow."
  This inconclusive meeting probably took place on June 27, since the
next day we were summoned to a speech by Obergruppenführer Jeckeln and my books affirm that this speech took place on the twenty-
eighth. Jeckeln and Blobel had probably told themselves that the men
of the Sonderkommando were in need of a little direction and motivation; late in the morning, the whole Kommando came to line up in the

school courtyard to listen to the HSSPF. Jeckeln didn't mince his words. Our job, he explained to us, was to identify and eliminate any element behind our lines that might threaten the security of our troops. Any Bolshevik, any People's Commissar, any Jew and any Gypsy could at any instant dynamite our quarters, assassinate our men, derail our trains, or transmit vital information to the enemy. Our duty wasn't to wait till he acted and then punish him, but to prevent him from acting. Nor was it a question, given the swiftness of our advance, of creating and filling camps: any suspect would be sent to the firing squad. For the lawyers among us, he reminded us that the USSR had refused to sign the Hague conventions, and that, therefore, the international law that regulated our actions in the West did not apply here. Certainly there would be mistakes; certainly there would be innocent victims; but that, alas, was war; when you bomb a city, civilians die too. At times it might be hard for us, our sensitivity and delicacy as men and Germans might sometimes suffer from it, he knew; we should triumph over ourselves; and he could only remind us of a phrase of the Führer's, which he had heard from his own mouth: *The leaders must themselves make the sacrifice of overcoming their doubts.* Thank you and Heil Hitler. That at least had the merit of frankness. In Pretzsch, Müller's and Streckenbach's speeches abounded with fine phrases about the need to be pitiless and merciless, but aside from confirming that we were in fact going to Russia, they had confined themselves to generalities. Heydrich, in Düben, during the departure parade, might have been more explicit; but he had scarcely begun to speak when a violent rainstorm broke: he had canceled his speech and gone off to Berlin. So our confusion wasn't surprising, all the more so since few of us had the slightest operational experience; I myself, ever since I had been recruited into the SD, did almost nothing but compile legal files, and I was far from being the exception. Kehrig took care of constitutional questions; even Vogt, the Leiter IV, came from the card files department. As for Standartenführer Blobel, they had taken him from the Düsseldorf *Staatspolizei*; he had probably never done anything but arrest asocials or homosexuals, along with maybe a Communist from time to time. In Pretzsch, they said he had been an architect: he had obviously not made a career of it. He was not what you would call a nice man; I found him aggressive, almost brutal with his colleagues. His round face, with his crushed chin and protuberant ears, seemed to be perched on the neck of his uniform like the naked head of a vulture, a resemblance even more accentuated by his beaklike nose. Every time I passed near him, he stank of alcohol; Häfner said that he was trying to get over a case of dysentery. I was happy I didn't have to deal with him directly, and Dr. Kehrig, who was forced to, seemed to suffer from it.

He himself seemed to feel out of place here. In Pretzsch, Thomas had explained to me that they had taken most of the officers from offices where they weren't indispensable; they had been summarily attributed SS ranks (that's how I found myself an SS-Obersturmführer, the equivalent of one of your lieutenants); Kehrig, an Oberregierungsrat, or government adviser, barely a month earlier, had benefited from his rank in the civil service to be promoted to Sturmbannführer; and he obviously had trouble getting used to his new epaulettes, as well as to his new functions. As for the noncoms and the troops, they came mostly from the lower middle class—shopkeepers, accountants, clerks, the kind of men who signed up in the SA during the Depression in the hope of finding work, and had never left it. Among them were a certain number of *Volksdeutschen* from the Baltic countries or from Ruthenia, gloomy, dull men, ill at ease in their uniforms, whose sole qualification was their knowledge of Russian; some could barely manage to make themselves understood in German. Von Radetzky, it's true, stood out from the rest: he boasted of knowing the slang of the brothels of Moscow, where he was born, as well as that of Berlin, and always seemed to know what he was doing, even when he wasn't doing anything. He also spoke some Ukrainian—he had apparently worked a little in import-export; like me, he came from the *Sicherheitsdienst*, the Security Service of the SS. His posting to the southern sector filled him with despair; he had dreamed of being in the center, of entering Moscow as a conqueror and *of striding across the Kremlin carpets*. Vogt consoled him by telling him we'd have fun enough in Kiev, but von Radetzky made a face: "It's true that the *lavra* is magnificent. But aside from that, it's a hole." The night of Jeckeln's speech, we received the order to pack our things and prepare to march the next day: Callsen was ready to receive us.

Lutsk was still burning when we arrived. A liaison officer from the Wehrmacht took charge of us to guide us to our quarters; we had to skirt the old city and the fort, the path was a complicated one. Kuno Callsen had requisitioned the Academy of Music, near the main square, at the foot of the castle: a fine, simple, seventeenth-century building—a former monastery that had also served as a prison, in the previous century. Callsen was waiting for us on the steps with some men. "It's a practical place," he explained to me as our equipment and our things were being unloaded. "There are still some cells in the basement, we just have to retool the locks, I've already started." For my part I preferred libraries to jails, but all the books were in Russian or Ukrainian. Von Radetzky was also walking around with his bulbous nose and his vague eyes, examining the decorative moldings; when he passed near

me, I remarked to him that there weren't any Polish books. "It's curious, Sturmbannführer. Not so long ago, this was Poland." Von Radetzky shrugged: "The Stalinists got rid of everything, as you can well
imagine."—"In two years?"—"Two years is enough. Especially for an
academy of music."

The Vorkommando was already overworked. The Wehrmacht had
arrested hundreds of Jews and looters and wanted us to take care of
them. The fires were still burning and it seemed that saboteurs were
keeping them up. And then there was the problem of the old fort.
When he was putting his files in order, Dr. Kehrig had found his
Baedeker and had held it out to me over the torn-open crates to show
me the entry: "Castle Lubart. Look, a Lithuanian prince built it." The
central courtyard was overflowing with corpses, prisoners shot by the
NKVD before their retreat, apparently. Kehrig asked me to go have a
look. This castle had immense brick walls built on earthen ramparts,
surmounted by three square towers; sentinels from the Wehrmacht
guarded the gate, and an officer from the Abwehr had to intervene so I
could enter. "Sorry. The Generalfeldmarschall ordered us to secure the
place."—"Of course, I understand." An abominable stench assaulted my
nose as soon as I went through the gate. I didn't have a handkerchief and
held one of my gloves over my nose to try to breathe. "Take this," the
Hauptmann from the Abwehr suggested, handing me a wet cloth, "it
helps a little." It did help a little, but not enough; even though I breathed
through my mouth, the smell filled my nostrils, sweet, heavy, nauseating. I swallowed convulsively to keep from vomiting. "Your first time?"
the Hauptman gently asked. I nodded. "You'll get used to it," he went
on, "but maybe never completely." He himself was livid, but didn't
cover his mouth. We had passed through a long vaulted corridor, then
a little quadrangle. "It's that way."

The corpses were piled up in a big paved courtyard, in disordered
mounds, scattered here and there. An immense, haunting buzzing filled
the air: thousands of heavy blue flies were hovering over the bodies, the
pools of blood, the fecal matter. My boots stuck to the pavement. The
dead were already swelling up, I gazed at their green and yellowish skin,
their faces gone shapeless, as if they'd been beaten to death. The smell
was vile; and this smell, I knew, was the beginning and the end of everything, the very signification of our existence. This thought filled me
with dismay. Little groups of soldiers from the Wehrmacht equipped
with gas masks were trying to disentangle the piles and line up the bodies; one of them tugged on an arm, which came off and stayed in his
hand; he tossed it with a weary gesture onto another pile. "There are
more than a thousand of them," the Abwehr officer said to me, almost

whispering. "All the Ukrainians and Poles they'd been keeping in prison since their invasion. We found women, even children." I wanted to close my eyes, or put my hand over my eyes, and at the same time I wanted to look, to look as much as I could, and by looking, try to understand, this incomprehensible thing, there, in front of me, this void for human thought. At a loss, I turned to the officer from the Abwehr: "Have you read Plato?" He looked at me, taken aback: "What?"—"No, it's nothing." I did an about-face and left the place. In the back of the first small courtyard, a door opened on the left; it led to some steps. In the upper floors, I wandered haphazardly through empty hallways, then noticed a spiral staircase, in one of the towers; at the top, one could access a wooden footbridge attached to the walls. From there, I could smell the odor from the fires in the city; it was far better, and I breathed deeply, then took a cigarette out of my case and lit it. I had the impression that the stench from the putrefied corpses was still stuck to the insides of my nose, I tried to chase it away by exhaling the smoke through my nostrils, but managed only to make myself cough convulsively. I looked at the view. Toward the back of the fort lay some gardens, little vegetable gardens with a few fruit trees; beyond the wall I saw the city and the loop of the Styr; on that side there wasn't any smoke, and the sun shone on the countryside. I smoked quietly. Then I went down again and returned to the main courtyard. The officer from the Abwehr was still there. He stared at me inquisitively but without irony: "Feeling better?"—"Yes, thanks." I tried to take an official tone: "You have an exact count? It's for my report."—"Not yet. Tomorrow, I think."—"And the nationalities?"—"I told you, Ukrainians, Poles probably. It's hard to say, most of them don't have any papers. They were shot in groups, you can see they did it in a hurry."—"Any Jews?" He looked at me with surprise: "Of course not. It's the Jews who did this." I grimaced: "Oh yes, of course." He turned back to the corpses and didn't say anything for a while. "What a mess," he finally mumbled. I saluted him. Outside, some kids were gawking; one of them asked me a question, but I didn't understand his language, I passed by without saying anything and returned to the Academy of Music to report to Kehrig.

The next day, the Sonderkommando set to work in earnest. One squad, under Callsen and Kurt Hans, shot three hundred Jews and twenty looters in the castle garden. In the company of Dr. Kehrig and Sturmbannführer Vogt, I spent my day in planning meetings with the military intelligence chief of the Sixth Army, the Ic/AO Niemeyer, along with several colleagues of his, including Hauptmann Luley, whom I had met the day before at the fort and who was in charge of counterespionage. Blobel thought that we were short on men and wanted the Wehrmacht to lend us some; but Niemeyer was categorical: it was up to the Generalfeldmarschall and his Chief of Staff, Oberst Heim, to decide that sort of question. During another meeting, in the afternoon, Luley announced to us in a strained voice that they had found ten German soldiers among the dead in the castle, horribly mutilated. "They were tied up and their noses, ears, tongues, and genitals were cut off." Vogt went up to the castle with him and returned with a waxen face: "Yes, it's true, it's horrible, they're monsters." This news created a stir; Blobel ranted through the hallways and then went back to see Heim. That night he announced to us: "The Generalfeldmarschall wants to take punitive action. Strike a strong blow, discourage those bastards." Callsen gave us a report on the day's executions. They had gone off without any snags, but the method imposed by von Reichenau, with just two guns per condemned man, had its disadvantages: if you wanted to be sure of your shot, you had to aim at the head rather than the chest, which caused splattering, the men got blood and brains in their faces, they were complaining. That led to a heated argument. Häfner shouted, "You'll see that it'll end up with a bullet in the back of the neck, like the Bolsheviks." Blobel reddened and pounded on the table: "Gentlemen! Such language is inadmissible! We are not Bolsheviks! . . . We are German soldiers. In the service of our *Volk* and our Führer!" He turned to Callsen: "If your men are too sensitive, we'll have schnapps served to them." Then to Häfner: "In any case there's no question of bullets in the neck. I don't want the men to have a feeling of personal responsibility. Executions will take place according to military method, and that's final."

I spent the next morning at the AOK: they had seized crates of documents when they captured the city, so I had to go with a translator and inspect these files, especially the ones from the NKVD, and decide which ones to deliver to the Sonderkommando for priority analysis. We were especially looking for lists of members of the Communist Party, of the NKVD, or other groups: many of those people must have stayed in town mixed in with the civilian population, to carry out acts of espionage or sabotage, so it was urgent to identify them. Around noon, I returned to the Academy to consult Dr. Kehrig. There was some agitation on the ground floor: groups of men were milling in the corners, whispering agitatedly. I caught a Scharführer by the sleeve: "What's happening?"—"I don't know, Obersturmführer. I think there's a problem with the Standartenführer."—"Where are the officers?" He pointed to a stairway that led to our quarters. On the way up, I met Kehrig, who was muttering as he came down, "This is insane, just insane."—"What's happening?" I asked him. He glanced at me gloomily and said, "How do you expect to work in such conditions?" He continued on his way. I climbed up a few more steps and heard a shot, the sound of broken glass, some shouts. On the landing in front of the open door of Blobel's bedroom, two officers from the Wehrmacht were pacing furiously back and forth in front of Kurt Hans. "What's happening?" I asked Hans. He gestured toward the room with his chin, his hands clenched behind his back. I went in. Blobel, sitting on his bed, wearing his boots but no jacket, was waving a pistol around; Callsen was standing next to him and trying without grasping his arm to direct the pistol toward the wall; a window pane had shattered; on the floor, I noticed a bottle of schnapps. Blobel was livid and spluttering incoherent words. Häfner came in behind me: "What's happening?"—"I don't know, it seems the Standartenführer is having a fit."—"He's gone nuts, you mean." Callsen turned around: "Ah, Obersturmführer. Go ask the gentlemen from the Wehrmacht to excuse us and come back a little later, all right?" I stepped back and bumped into Hans, who had made up his mind to come in. "August, go find a doctor," Callsen said to Häfner. Blobel was bawling: "It's not possible, it's not possible, they're sick, I'm going to kill them." The two officers from the Wehrmacht hovered in the hallway, rigid, pale. "Meine Herren . . . ," I began. Häfner pushed me aside and ran down the stairs. The Hauptmann squeaked: "Your Kommandant has gone mad! He wanted to shoot at us." I didn't know what to say. Hans went out behind me: "Meine Herren, I hope you'll excuse us. The Standartenführer is suffering a breakdown and we have to call a doctor. We will have to resume this discussion later on." In the bedroom, Blobel shouted piercingly: "I'm going to kill those shits, let me alone." The Hauptmann shrugged: "If that's what the senior officers of the SS are made of. . . . We'll do without your cooperation." He turned to his colleague, spreading his arms: "It's not possible, they must have emptied the asylums." Kurt Hans turned pale: "Meine Herren! The honor of the SS . . ." He too was bawling now. Finally I intervened and cut him off. "Listen, I don't know what's happening yet, but obviously we have a problem of a medical nature. Hans, it's no use getting carried away. Meine Herren, as my colleague was saying, it might be better for you to excuse us for now." The Hauptmann looked me up and down: "You are Dr. Aue, aren't you? Fine, let's go," he said to his colleague. In the stairway they met Sperath, the doctor from the Sonderkommando, who was coming up with Häfner: "Are you the doctor?"—"Yes."—"Be careful. He might shoot at you too." I stood aside to let Sperath and Häfner pass, then followed them into the bedroom. Blobel had put his pistol on the night table and was speaking in a broken voice to Callsen: "But you can see that it's not possible to shoot so many Jews. We need a plow, to plow them into the earth!" Callsen turned to us. "August, look after the Standartenführer for a minute, will you?" He took Sperath by the arm, drew him aside, and started whispering to him animatedly. "Shit!" Häfner cried. I turned and saw he was struggling with Blobel, who was trying to grab his pistol. "Standartenführer, Standartenführer, calm down, please," I shouted. Callsen came back and began speaking to him calmly. Sperath also came over and took his pulse. Blobel made another move in the direction of his pistol but Callsen deflected him. Sperath spoke to him: "Listen, Paul, you're overexerting yourself. I'm going to give you a shot."—"No! No shots!" Blobel's arm, flung up, hit Callsen in the face. Häfner had picked up the bottle and showed it to me, shrugging: it was almost empty. Kurt Hans remained by the door and watched without saying anything. Blobel let out almost incoherent exclamations: "It's those shits from the Wehrmacht that should be shot! All of them!" then started muttering again. "August, Obersturmführer, come help me," Callsen ordered. At the count of three, we took Blobel by the feet and under the arms and laid him down on the bed. He didn't struggle. Callsen rolled his jacket into a ball and slid it under his head; Sperath rolled up his sleeve and gave him a shot. He was already starting to seem a little calmer. Sperath led Callsen and Häfner to the door to confer and I stayed next to Blobel. His bulging eyes were staring at the ceiling; a little saliva was wetting the corners of his mouth, and he was still mumbling: "Plow the Jews, plow the Jews." Discreetly, I slipped the pistol into a drawer: no one had thought to do that. Blobel seemed already to have fallen asleep. Callsen returned to the bed: "We're going to take him to Lublin."—"Why Lublin?"—"There's a hospital there, for this sort of case," Sperath explained. "A madhouse, you mean," Häfner blurted coarsely. "August, shut up," barked Callsen. Von Radetzky appeared at the door: "What is this mess?" Kurt Hans spoke up: "The Generalfeldmarschall gave an order and the Standartenführer was ill, he wasn't able to bear it. He wanted to shoot at the officers from the Wehrmacht."—"He already had a fever this morning," Callsen added. He briefly outlined the situation to von Radetzky, along with Sperath's suggestion. "Fine," von Radetzky decided, "we'll do what the doctor says. I'll take him myself." He seemed a little pale. "As for the Generalfeldmarschall's order, have you already started getting organized?"—"No, we haven't done anything," Kurt Hans said. "Fine. Callsen, you take care of the preparations. Häfner, you'll come with me."—"Why me?" Häfner retorted, his face darkening. "Because," von Radetzky snapped with irritation. "Go get the Standartenführer's Opel ready. Take some extra gas cans, just in case." Häfner insisted: "Can't Janssen go instead?"—"No, Janssen is going to help Callsen and Hans.

Hauptsturmführer," he said to Callsen, "do you agree?" Callsen shook his head pensively: "It might be better if you stayed and I went with him, Sturmbannführer. You're in command, now." Von Radetzky shook his head: "That's why I think it would be better for me to go with him." Callsen still seemed doubtful: "Are you sure you shouldn't stay?"—"Yes, yes. In any case, don't worry: Obergruppenführer Jeckeln is arriving soon, along with his staff. Most of them are already here; I've just had a meeting with them. He'll take things in hand."—"Good. Because, well, you understand, an *Aktion* of this magnitude, for me . . ." A thin smile played over von Radetzky's lips: "Don't worry. Go see the Obergruppenführer, and start your preparations: everything will go fine, I guarantee it."

An hour later, the officers met in the main hall. Von Radetzky and Häfner had left with Blobel; he had started kicking when they put him into the Opel, Sperath had been forced to give him another shot while Häfner held him round the waist. Callsen began to speak: "Well, I think you're all more or less up to date about the situation." Vogt interrupted: "Could you perhaps go over it quickly?"—"If you like. This morning, the Generalfeldmarschall gave the order to undertake a retaliatory action for the ten German soldiers found mutilated in the fortress. He ordered us to execute one Jew for each person assassinated by the Bolsheviks; that is more than a thousand Jews. The Standartenführer received the order and that seems to have brought about a fit . . ."—"It's also somewhat the army's fault," Kurt Hans said. "They should have sent someone with more tact than that Hauptmann. And transmitting an order of this importance through a Hauptmann is almost an insult."— "We have to admit that this whole business reflects badly on the honor of the SS," Vogt commented.—"Listen," Sperath said acerbically, "that's not the question. I can tell you that the Standartenführer was already ill, this morning, he had a strong fever. The beginning of typhoid, I think. It definitely precipitated his breakdown."—"Yes, but he also drank a lot," Kehrig remarked.—"That's true," I ventured, "there was an empty bottle in his room."—"He had intestinal problems," Sperath retorted. "He thought that might help."—"In any case," Vogt concluded, "we're without a commander. And also without a deputy commander. That won't do. I suggest that while we wait for the return of Sturmbannführer von Radetzky, Hauptsturmführer Callsen take command of the Sonderkommando."—"But I'm not the highest-ranking officer," Callsen objected. "You are, or Sturmbannführer Kehrig."—"Yes, but we aren't operations officers. Among the leaders of the Teilkommandos, you're the most senior."—"I agree," Kehrig said. Callsen, his face tense, darted his eyes from one man to the other, then looked at Janssen, who turned aside before nodding his head. "Me too," Kurt Hans added. "Haupt-sturmführer, it's your command." Callsen remained silent and then shrugged: "Fine. As you like."—"I have a question," Strehlke, our Leiter II, said coolly. He turned to Sperath: "Doctor, according to you, what is the Standartenführer's condition? Should we count on his returning soon or not?" Sperath made a face: "I don't know. It's hard to say. Part of his affliction is certainly of nervous origin, but there must also be or-ganic causes. They'll have to see how he is when the fever goes down."—"If I understood you correctly," Vogt spluttered, "he won't be coming back right away."—"That's hardly likely. Not in the next few days, in any case."—"Maybe he won't come back at all," Kehrig snapped. A silence spread through the room. Obviously the same thought united us, even if no one wanted to give voice to it: it might not be such a bad thing if Blobel did not come back. None of us had known him a month ago, and we had been under his orders for scarcely a week; nonetheless, we had learned that working with him could turn out to be difficult, disagreeable even. Callsen broke the silence: "Listen, that's not all: we have to start planning our operation."—"Yes, but really," Kehrig went on vehemently, "it's absolutely grotesque, this busi-ness, it doesn't make any sense."—"What is grotesque?" Vogt asked.— "These retaliations! You'd think it was the Thirty Years' War! And also first of all, how are you going to go about identifying a thousand Jews? In one night?" He tapped his nose. "From sight? By examining their noses? By measuring them?"—"That's true," admitted Janssen, who hadn't said anything till then. "It's not going to be easy."—"Häfner had an idea," Kurt Hans laconically suggested. "We just have to ask them to drop their pants." Kehrig exploded suddenly: "But that's absolutely ridiculous! You're all out of your minds! . . . Callsen, tell them." Callsen remained somber but unmoved: "Listen, Sturmbannführer. Calm down. There must be a solution, I'll discuss it later on with the Obergruppen-führer. As to the principle of the thing, I don't like it any more than you do. But those are the orders." Kehrig stared at him, biting his tongue; he was obviously trying to contain himself. "And Brigadeführer Rasch," he finally blurted, "what does he have to say about it? He is our direct superior, after all."—"Exactly, that's another problem. I've already tried contacting him, but it seems the Gruppenstab is still on the march. I'd like to send an officer to Lemberg to report to him and request his in-structions."—"Who were you thinking of sending?"—"I was thinking of Obersturmführer Aue. Can you do without him for a day or two?" Kehrig turned to me: "How far are you with those files, Obersturm-führer?"—"I've already sorted through a large part. I need a few more hours, I think." Callsen looked at his watch: "It's already cutting it short if he's going to arrive before nightfall."—"All right," Kehrig decided. "In that case, finish up tonight and leave at dawn."—"Very well . . . Hauptsturmführer," I asked Callsen, "what do you want me to do?"— "Report to the Brigadeführer on the situation and the problem with the Kommandant. Explain what our decisions were and tell him we're awaiting his instructions."—"While you're at it," Kehrig added, "get some information about the local situation. It seems things are pretty confused down there; I'd like to know what's happening."—"*Zu Befehl*."

That evening, it took four men to carry the selected archives up to the offices of the SD. Kehrig was in a foul mood. "Come on, Obersturmführer," he growled when he saw my boxes, "I thought I'd asked you to sort through all that!"—"You should see what I left behind, Sturmbannführer."—"Maybe. We're going to have to borrow some more translators. All right. Your car is ready, ask for Höfler. Leave early. Now go see Callsen." In the hallway, I met Untersturmführer Zorn, another junior officer, who usually assisted Häfner. "Ah, Dr. Aue. You're lucky."—"Why do you say that?"—"Well, to be leaving. Filthy business, tomorrow." I nodded: "No doubt. Is everything ready, then?"—"I don't know. I just have to take care of the cordon."—"Zorn does nothing but complain," protested Janssen, who had joined us.—"Have you solved the problem?" I asked.—"Which one?"—"The problem of the Jews. How to find them." He laughed dryly: "Oh, that! It's very simple really. The AOK is going to print some posters: all Jews are requested to report tomorrow morning to the main square for forced labor. We'll take the ones who come."—"And you think there will be enough of them?"—"The Obergruppenführer says that yes, it never fails, it works every time. If not, we'll arrest the Jewish leaders and threaten to shoot them if they're not all there."—"I see."—"Ah, what a mess" Zorn sighed. "Fortunately I just have to look after the cordon."—"At least you're there," Janssen grumbled. "Not like that pig Häfner."—"It's not his fault," I objected. "He wanted to stay. It's the Sturmbannführer who insisted he accompany them."—"Right, exactly. And why isn't he here, then?" He looked at me darkly. "I'd also like to take a trip to Lublin or Lemberg." I shrugged and went to find Callsen. He was poring over a map of the city along with Vogt and Kurt Hans. "Yes, Obersturmführer?"—"You wanted to see me." Callsen seemed much more in command of himself than in the afternoon, almost relaxed. "You will tell Brigadeführer Dr. Rasch that Obergruppenführer Jeckeln confirms the army's orders and is personally taking control of the *Aktion*." He stared at me with calm eyes; obviously, Jeckeln's decision had taken a weight off his shoulders. "He also confirms my position as acting commander until Sturmbannführer von Radetzky returns," he went on, "unless the Brigadeführer has another preference. Finally, for the *Aktion*, he is lending us Ukrainian auxiliaries and a company from the Ninth Police Reserve Battalion. That's it." I saluted and went out without saying a word. That night, I stayed awake for a long time: I was thinking of the Jews who would be coming the next day. I thought the method adopted very unfair; the Jews of goodwill would be punished, the ones who might have come to trust the word of the German Reich; as for the others, the cowards, the traitors, the Bolsheviks, they'd stay hidden and we wouldn't find them. As Zorn said, it was a fine mess. I was happy to leave for Lemberg, it would be an interesting trip; but I wasn't satisfied with avoiding the *Aktion* that way; I thought something like that was a serious problem, but that you should confront it and resolve it, for yourself at least, and not run away from it. The others—Callsen, Zorn—wanted to wash their hands of it, or at least not assume responsibility for it: that wasn't right, to my thinking. If we were committing an injustice, we ought to think about it, and decide if it was necessary and inevitable, or if it was only the result of taking the easy way out, of laziness, of a lack of thought. It was a question of rigor. I knew that these decisions were made at a much higher level than our own; still, we weren't automatons, it was important not just to obey orders, but to adhere to them; yet I was having doubts, and that troubled me. Finally I read a little and slept for a few hours.

At four o'clock I got dressed. Höfler, the driver, was already waiting for me in the mess with some bad coffee. "If you like I also have some bread and cheese, Obersturmführer."—"No, that's okay, I'm not hungry." I drank my coffee in silence. Höfler dozed. Outside, there wasn't a sound. Popp, the soldier who was to serve as my escort, joined us and started eating noisily. I got up and went out to smoke in the courtyard. The sky was clear, the stars were shining above the tall façades of the former monastery, closed and impassive in the gentle white light. I couldn't see the moon. Höfler came out and saluted me: "Everything's ready, Obersturmführer."—"Did you take some cans of gas?"—"Yes. Three." Popp was standing next to the front door of the Admiral, looking awkward and content with his rifle on his shoulder. I motioned to him to get in back. "Usually, Obersturmführer, the escort sits in front."—"Yes, but I'd rather you got in back."

After crossing the Styr, Höfler turned off onto the road leading south. Signs marked the way; judging from the map, we had a few hours ahead of us. It was a fine Monday morning, calm, peaceful. The sleeping villages seemed scarcely affected by the war; the checkpoints let us pass without difficulty. To our left, already, the sky was growing paler.

A little later the sun, still reddish, appeared through the trees. Thin clumps of mist stuck to the ground; between the villages, large flat fields stretched out interminably, interspersed with copses and hills covered with dense, low foliage. The sky slowly turned blue. "The land must be good here," Popp commented. I didn't answer and he was silent. In Radziechow we stopped to eat. Once again, the roadsides and ditches were strewn with wrecked tanks, and burned isbas disfigured the villages. The traffic got thicker; we crossed long columns of trucks loaded with soldiers and supplies. A little before Lemberg, a roadblock forced us to pull aside to let some Panzers pass. The road trembled; whirlwinds of dust obscured our windows and slipped in through the cracks. Höfler offered Popp and me a cigarette. He made a face as he lit his own: "These Sportnixes really stink."—"They're all right," I said, "don't be so fussy." After the tanks had passed, a Feldgendarm approached and motioned us not to start up: "There's another column coming," he shouted. I finished my cigarette and threw the butt out the door. "Popp is right," Höfler suddenly said. "It's a beautiful countryside. A man could settle down here, after the war."—"You'd come settle here?" I asked him with a smile. He shrugged: "It depends."—"On what?"—"On the bureaucrats. If they're like the ones back home, it's not worth it."—"And what would you do?"—"If I could do anything, Obersturmführer? I'd open a business, like at home. A nice little cigarette shop, with a bar too, and maybe a fruit and vegetable stand, possibly."—"And you'd rather do that here than at home?" He banged the steering wheel sharply: "Well, I had to close the store at home. In 'thirty-eight already."—"Why?"— "Because of those bastards from the cartels, from Reemtsma. They decided we had to make at least five thousand a year, to carry their products. In my village, there are maybe sixty families, so, before you could sell five thousand reichsmarks' worth of cigarettes. . . . There was nothing for it, they were the only suppliers. I had the only cigarette store in the village, so our Parteiführer supported me, he wrote letters to the Gauleiter for me, we tried everything, but there was nothing to be done. It ended up in the commercial court and I lost, so I had to close up shop. Vegetables weren't enough. And then I got drafted."— "So there's no cigarette shop in your village now?" Popp said in his muffled voice.—"Well, no, that's what I said."—"In my town there never was one." The second column of Panzers arrived and everything started trembling again. One of the Admiral's windows had come loose and rattled wildly in its frame. I pointed it out to Höfler and he nodded. The column filed by, endless: the front must still be advancing at full speed. Finally the Feldgendarm signaled to us that the road was clear.

In Lemberg, chaos reigned. None of the soldiers questioned at the checkpoints could tell us where the HQ of the *Sicherheitspolizei* and the SD was; although the city had been captured two days before, no one seemed to have gone to the trouble of putting up tactical signs. We followed a large street almost at random; it ended up in a long boulevard divided in two by a mall and bordered with pastel-tinted façades prettily decorated with white moldings. The streets were swarming with people. Between the German military vehicles, cars and open trucks circulated, decorated with streamers and blue-and-yellow flags, teeming with men in civilian outfits or sometimes in scraps of uniforms, and armed with rifles and pistols; they shouted, sang, fired their guns in the air; on the sidewalks and in the park, other men, armed or not, cheered them, mixed in with impassive German soldiers. A Leutnant from the Luftwaffe was finally able to point me toward a divisional HQ; from there, we were sent to AOK 17. Officers ran up and down the stairways, came in, went out of offices, slamming doors; scattered, trampled Soviet files cluttered the hallways; in the lobby a group of men were standing with blue-and-yellow armbands on their civilian outfits, carrying rifles; they were talking animatedly in Ukrainian or Polish, I didn't know which, with some German soldiers wearing badges embossed with a nightingale. I grabbed hold of a young Major from the Abwehr: "Einsatzgruppe B?"—"They got here yesterday. They moved into the NKVD offices."—"And where are they?" He stared at me with an exhausted look: "I have no idea." He finally found a subaltern who had been there and told him to help me.

On the boulevard, the traffic crawled along at a snail's pace, then a crowd blocked everything. I got out of the Opel to see what was happening. The people were yelling at the top of their lungs and applauding; some had taken chairs from a café or some crates and were standing on top of them to get a better look; others were carrying their children on their shoulders. I made my way through the press with difficulty. In the center of the crowd, in a large cleared circle, a few men were strutting about in costumes stolen from a theater or a museum—extravagant outfits, a Regency wig with a hussar's jacket from 1812, a magistrate's gown bordered with ermine, Mongolian armor and Scottish tartans, a half-Roman, half-Renaissance operetta costume, with a ruff; one man was wearing Budyenny's red cavalry uniform, but with a top hat and a fur collar, and was waving a long Mauser pistol; all of them were armed with clubs or rifles. At their feet several men on their knees were licking the pavement; from time to time, one of the men in costume kicked them or hit them with the butt of his rifle; most of them were bleeding profusely; the crowd was screaming louder than ever. Behind me, someone started up a lively tune on the accordion; immediately, dozens of voices struck up the words, while the man in a kilt whipped out a violin on which, since he had no bow, he scraped out chords as on a guitar. A spectator pulled me by the sleeve and shouted at me excitedly, *"Yid, yid, kaputt!"* But I had already understood. I pulled away and went back through the crowd; Höfler, in the meantime, had turned the car around. "I think we can go that way," the man from the Abwehr said, pointing to a side street. We soon found ourselves lost. Finally, Höfler had the idea of asking a passerby: "NKVD? NKVD?"—"NKVD *kaputt!*" the man shouted joyously. With gestures, he showed us the way: it was in fact two hundred meters from the AOK; we had gone in the wrong direction. I dismissed our guide and went in to report. Rasch, they told me, was in a meeting with all his Leiters and some army officers; no one knew when he could receive me. Finally a Hauptsturmführer came to my rescue: "You came here from Lutsk? We've already been filled in, the Brigadeführer spoke on the phone with Obergruppenführer Jeckeln. But I'm sure your report will interest him."—"Good. I'll wait, then."—"No need, he'll be tied up for at least two hours. You should just go visit the city. The old city especially is worth seeing."—"The people seem excited," I remarked.—"That's certainly true. The NKVD massacred three thousand people in the prisons, before they decamped. And also all the Ukrainian and Galician nationalists have come out of the woods, or from wherever they were hiding, and they're a little worked up. The Jews are going to get it bad."—"And the Wehrmacht isn't doing anything?" He winked: "Orders *from above*, Obersturmführer. The population is clearing out the traitors and collaborators, it's none of our business. It's an internal conflict. See you later, then." He disappeared into an office and I went out. The gunfire coming from the center of town sounded like sticks of firecrackers on a holiday. I left Höfler and Popp with the Opel and headed on foot toward the main boulevard. Under the colonnade a jubilant atmosphere reigned; the doors and windows of the cafés had been thrown wide open, and people were drinking and shouting; people shook my hand in passing; a jovial man offered me a glass of Champagne, which I emptied; before I could return it to him, he had disappeared. Mixed in with the crowd, like at a carnival, men dressed in theater costumes were still parading; some were even wearing masks, amusing, hideous, ridiculous. I crossed the park; on the other side began the old town, entirely different from the Austro-Hungarian boulevard: here, it was all tall narrow houses from the late Renaissance, crowned with pointed roofs, their façades painted in various colors and long past their prime, enhanced with baroque ornaments carved out of stone. There were far fewer people in the narrow streets. A macabre poster filled the window

of a closed store: it showed an enlargement of a photo of corpses, with
an inscription in Cyrillic; I could only make out the words *Ukraine* and
Jidy, the Jews. I walked by a great fine church, obviously Catholic; it
was closed and no one answered when I knocked. From an open door
farther down the street came sounds of broken glass, blows, shouts; a little farther on lay the corpse of a Jew, his nose in the gutter. Little groups
of armed men wearing blue-and-yellow armbands were conversing
with civilians; from time to time they went into a house and there were
more noises, sometimes gunshots. Right before me, on the second floor,
a man suddenly flew through a closed window and came crashing down
almost at my feet in the midst of a rain of glass shards; I had to jump
backward to avoid the splinters; I distinctly heard the brittle snap of his
neck when he hit the pavement. A man in shirtsleeves and an officer's
cap leaned out of the broken window; seeing me, he joyfully shouted in
broken German: "Excuse me, Herr deutschen Offizier! I didn't see
you." My anguish increased; I passed around the corpse and continued
on in silence. A little farther, a bearded man in a priest's robe appeared
from a portal, at the foot of a tall ancient belfry; when he saw me, he
veered toward me: "Herr Offizier! Herr Offizier! Come, please come."
His German was better than that of the man at the window, but he had
a strange accent. He pulled me almost by force toward the gate. I heard
cries, wild shouts; in the courtyard of the church, a group of men were
cruelly beating some Jews lying on the ground, with clubs or iron rods.
Some of the bodies had stopped moving beneath the blows; others were
still twitching. "Herr Offizier!" the priest shouted, "do something,
please! It is a church, here." I remained by the gate, unsure; the priest
tried to pull me by the arm. I don't know what I was thinking. One of
the Ukrainians saw me and said something to his comrades, shaking his
head in my direction; they hesitated, stopped their blows; the priest
shouted a torrent of words at them that I didn't understand, then turned
toward me: "I told them that you were ordering them to stop. I told
them that churches are sacred and that they were pigs, and that churches
were under the protection of the Wehrmacht and that if they didn't
leave they'd be arrested."—"I'm all alone," I said.—"That's not important," the priest retorted. He shouted some more sentences in Ukrainian. Slowly, the men lowered their clubs. One of them addressed a
passionate tirade at me: I understood only the words *Stalin, Galicia,* and
Jews. Another one spat on the bodies. There was a long moment of uncertain wavering; the priest shouted a few words more; at last the men
abandoned the Jews and headed toward the gate, then disappeared into
the street, without saying a word. "Thank you," the priest said to me,
"thank you." He ran over to examine the Jews. The courtyard sloped

slightly, ending with a fine shaded colonnade roofed in green copper, built against the church wall. "Help me," the priest said. "This one is still alive." He lifted him up by the armpits and I took his feet; I saw that he was a young man, with hardly any beard. His head fell back, a stream of blood ran down his side curls and left a line of big shiny drops on the flagstones. My heart was beating very hard: I had never carried a dying man like this. We had to go around the church; the priest shuffled backward, moaning in German: "First the Bolsheviks, now the crazy Ukrainians. Why doesn't your army do anything?" In the back, a wide archway opened onto another courtyard and then the door to the church. I helped the priest carry the Jew into the vestibule and put him on a bench. The priest called out; two other men, dark and bearded like him, but in suits, emerged from the nave. He spoke to them in a strange language that sounded nothing like Ukrainian, Russian, or Polish. I followed the three men as they went out together, into the courtyard; one of them turned into a back alleyway as the other two walked back toward the Jews. "I sent him to look for a doctor," the priest said.— "What is this, here?" I asked him. He paused and stared at me: "It's the Armenian cathedral."—"So there are Armenians in Lemberg?" I said with surprise. He shrugged: "A lot longer than the Germans or the Austrians." He and his friend lifted up another Jew, who was quietly moaning. The blood from the Jews flowed slowly along the flagstones of the sloping courtyard and down toward the colonnade. Under the arches I could see tombstones sealed into the wall or set in the ground, covered with inscriptions in mysterious glyphs, Armenian no doubt. I went closer: blood filled the characters cut into the flat stones. I quickly turned away. I felt oppressed, at a loss; I lit a cigarette. It was cool under the colonnade. In the courtyard, the sun shone on the puddles of fresh blood and the limestone paving, on the heavy bodies of the Jews, on their suits of coarse cloth, black or brown, soaked with blood. Flies were buzzing around their heads and landing on the wounds. The priest returned near them. "What about the dead?" he asked me. "We can't leave them there." But I had no intention of helping him; the idea of touching one of those inert bodies filled me with revulsion. I headed for the gate, skirting round them, and went out into the street. It was empty; I turned left, more or less at random. A little farther on, the street came to a dead end; but to the right I ended up in a square overlooked by an imposing baroque church decorated with rococo ornaments and a tall columned gate, and crowned with a copper dome. I climbed the steps and went in. The vast vault above the nave rested lightly on thin cabled columns; daylight poured in through the stained-glass windows, shimmered on the wooden sculptures covered in gold leaf; the dark, polished pews stretched to the back, empty. In a little whitewashed side hall I noticed a low door of ancient wood set with brass fittings: I pushed it; a few stone steps led to a wide, low hallway lit by casement windows. Glassed-in shelves occupied the opposite wall, filled with religious objects; some of them looked ancient, wonderfully wrought. To my surprise one of the cases exhibited Jewish objects: scrolls in Hebrew, prayer shawls, old etchings showing Jews in synagogue. Books in Hebrew bore printers' marks in German: LWOW, 1884; LUBLIN, 1853, BEI SCHMUEL BERENSTEIN. I heard footsteps and raised my head: a tonsured monk was walking toward me. He wore the white habit of the Dominicans. When he reached me, he stopped: "Hello," he said in German. "Can I help you?"—"What is this, here?"—"You are in a monastery." I pointed to the shelves: "No, I mean all this."—"That? It's our museum of religions. All the objects come from the region. Look, if you like. Normally, we ask for a little donation, but today it's free." He went on his way and disappeared silently through the brass-fitted door. Farther on, where he had appeared, the hallway turned at a right angle; I realized I was in fact inside a cloister, closed in by a low wall, with windows set between the columns. A long horizontal display case caught my attention. A little lamp attached to the wall lit up the interior of the case; I leaned over: two skeletons were lying there intertwined, half emerging from a layer of dirt. The larger one, the man probably, despite the large brass earrings resting against his skull, was lying on his back; the other, visibly a woman, was curled up on her side, nestled in his arms, her legs over one of his. It was magnificent, I had never seen anything like it. I tried in vain to make out the label. How many centuries had they been lying there, intertwined with each other? These bodies must have been very old, they must have gone back to the most remote eras; the woman had probably been sacrificed and laid out in the tomb with her dead chief; I knew such practices had existed in primitive times. But this knowledge didn't change anything; despite everything, it was the position of rest after love, overcome, filled with tenderness. I thought of my sister and my throat tightened: she would have cried if she'd seen that. I left the monastery without meeting anyone; outside I headed straight, toward the other end of the square. Beyond that another vast square opened up, with a large building in the center, next to a tower, surrounded by trees. Narrow houses were squeezed around this square, fabulously decorated, each in a different style. Behind the main building an animated crowd was gathering. I avoided it and turned left, then went round a large cathedral, below a stone cross lovingly held in the arms of an angel, flanked by a languid Moses with his tablets and a pensive saint dressed in rags, raised over a skull and crossbones, almost the same emblem as the one sewn on my cap. Behind, in a little alleyway, stood a few tables and chairs. I was hot and tired, the café seemed empty, I sat down. A girl came out and spoke to me in Ukrainian. "Do you have beer? Beer?" I said in German. She shook her head: *"Piva nyetou."* That I understood. "Some coffee? *Kava?"—"Da."—"Voda?"—"Da."* She went back into the room and returned with a glass of water that I drank in one gulp. Then she brought me a coffee. It was already sweetened and I didn't drink it. I lit a cigarette. The girl reappeared and saw the coffee: "Coffee? Not good?" she asked in broken German. "Sugar. *Niet."—"Oh."* She smiled, took the coffee away, and brought me another. It was strong, without any sugar; I drank it while I smoked. To my right, at the foot of the cathedral, a chapel covered in bas-reliefs arranged in dark bands hid my view of the main square. A man in German uniform was walking round it, examining the intertwined sculptures. He noticed me and headed toward me; I saw his epaulettes, got up quickly, and saluted. He returned my salute: "Hello! So, you're German?"—"Yes, Herr Hauptmann." He got out a handkerchief and wiped his forehead. "Oh good. Do you mind if I sit down?"—"Of course not, Herr Hauptmann." The girl reappeared. "Do you take your coffee with or without sugar? It's all they have."—"With, please." I made the girl understand we wanted two more coffees, with sugar on the side. Then I sat down with the Hauptmann. He held out his hand: "Hans Koch. I'm with the Abwehr." I introduced myself. "Oh, you're from the SD? That's right, I hadn't noticed your badge. Very good, very good." This Hauptmann seemed mild and friendly: he must have been just past fifty, wore round glasses and was a little paunchy. He spoke with a southern accent, not quite Viennese. "You are Austrian, Herr Hauptmann?"—"Yes, from Styria. And you?"—"My father is from Pomerania, originally. But I was born in Alsace. Then we lived here and there."—"Of course, of course. Are you out for a walk?"—"Sort of, yes." He nodded: "I'm here for a meeting. Over there, next door, in a little while."—"A meeting, Herr Hauptmann?"—"See, when they invited us, they explained that it would be a cultural meeting, but I think it's going to be a political meeting." He leaned toward me as if to tell me a secret: "I was picked because I'm supposed to be an expert on Ukrainian national questions."—"And are you?" He flung himself back: "Not at all! I'm a professor of theology. I know a thing or two about the Uniate question, but that's it. They probably appointed me because I served in the Imperial army, I was a Leutnant during the Great War, so they must have thought that I knew something about the national question; but I was on the Italian front at the time, and in the Supply Corps too. It's true

that I had some Croatian colleagues . . ."—"You speak Ukrainian?"—
"Not a single word. But I have a translator with me. He's drinking now
with the OUN guys, in the square."—"The OUN?"—"Yes. You didn't
know they took over, this morning? At least, they took over the radio.
And they've delivered a proclamation, on the revival of the Ukrainian
state if I understood right. That's why I have to go to this meeting now.
The Metropolitan, I heard, has blessed the new State. It seems we're the
ones who asked him to do so, but I'm not sure."—"What Metropolitan?"—"The Uniate, of course. The Orthodox hate us. They hate Stalin
too, but they hate us even more." I was about to ask another question
but was suddenly interrupted: a rather plump woman, almost naked, her
stockings torn, emerged suddenly with a cry from behind the cathedral;
she plowed into the tables, stumbled, knocked one over, and fell at our
feet squealing. Her white skin was marbled with contusions, but she
wasn't bleeding much. Two strapping youths with armbands were
calmly following her. One of them spoke to us in bad German: "Excuse, Officers. *Kein problem.*" The other dragged the woman up by her
hair and punched her in the stomach. She hiccupped and fell silent,
saliva on her lips. The first one kicked her in the buttocks and she
started running again. They trotted after her, laughing, and disappeared
behind the chapel. Koch took off his cap and wiped his forehead again
while I picked up the overturned table. "They're real savages here," I
remarked.—"Oh yes, I agree with you on that one. But I thought you
were encouraging them?"—"That would surprise me, Herr Hauptmann. But I've just arrived, I haven't been filled in." Koch went on: "At
the AOK, I heard that the *Sicherheitsdienst* had posters printed and was
encouraging these people. *Aktion Petliura*, they called it. You know, the
Ukrainian leader? It was a Jew that assassinated him, I think. In 'twenty-
six or 'twenty-seven."—"You see, you are a specialist after all."—"Oh,
I've just read a few reports." The girl had emerged from the café. She
smiled and showed me that the coffee was free. In any case I didn't have
any local money. I looked at my watch: "Excuse me, Herr Hauptmann.
I have to go."—"Of course." He shook my hand: "Good luck."

     I left the old town by the shortest route and with difficulty made my
way through the jubilant crowd. At the Gruppenstab things were very
animated. The same officer welcomed me: "Oh, it's you again." Finally,
Brigadeführer Dr. Rasch received me. He shook my hand cordially, but
his massive face remained severe. "Have a seat. What happened with
Standartenführer Blobel?" He wasn't wearing a cap and his broad
domed forehead shone under the lightbulb. I briefly described Blobel's
collapse: "According to the doctor, it was due to fever and exhaustion."
His thick lips sketched a pout. He leafed through the papers on his desk

and took out a sheet. "The Ic from AOK Six wrote to me to complain about his remarks. Apparently he threatened some officers from the Wehrmacht?"—"That's an exaggeration, Brigadeführer. It is true that he was delirious, he was making incoherent remarks. But he wasn't after anyone in particular, it was just an effect of the illness."—"Good." He questioned me on a few other points, then signaled that the discussion was over. "Sturmbannführer von Radetzky is already back from Lutsk, he'll take the Standartenführer's place until he recovers. I'll have the orders drawn up, together with some other papers. For tonight, go find Hartl over in Personnel, he'll see to it that you're put up somewhere." I left and went in search of the office of the Leiter I; one of his subordinates issued me some ration coupons. Then I went downstairs to find Höfler and Popp. In the lobby, I ran into Thomas. "Max!" He slapped me on the shoulder and I was filled with a sudden flush of joy. "I'm happy to see you here. What are you doing?" I explained to him. "And you're staying till tomorrow? That's wonderful. I'm going to have dinner with some people from the Abwehr, in a little restaurant, a good one, apparently. You'll come with us. Did they find you a bunk? It's not the Ritz, but at least you'll have clean sheets. It's good you didn't arrive yesterday: it was a real mess. The Reds trashed everything before they left, and the Ukrainians came through before we arrived. We had some Jews clean up but it took hours, we didn't get to bed till morning." I arranged to meet him in the garden behind the building and left him. Popp was snoring in the Opel, but Höfler was playing cards with some policemen; I explained the arrangements to him and went to smoke in the garden as I waited for Thomas.

Thomas was a good friend, I was really glad to see him again. We had been friends for several years; in Berlin, we often had dinner together; sometimes he took me with him to nightclubs, or to famous concert halls. He was a bon vivant who knew his way around. And it was mostly thanks to him that I had found myself in Russia; at least the suggestion had come from him. But actually the story goes back a little further than that. In the spring of 1939, I had just received my doctorate in law and joined the SD, and there was a lot of talk of war. After Bohemia and Moravia, the Führer was turning his attention to Danzig; the whole problem was to anticipate the reaction of France and Great Britain. Most people thought that they wouldn't risk war for Danzig any more than they would for Prague; but they had guaranteed the western border of Poland, and were rearming as quickly as possible. I had a long discussion about it with Dr. Best, my superior and also somewhat my mentor at the SD. In theory, he said, we shouldn't be afraid of war; war was the logical outcome of our *Weltanschauung*. Quoting from

Hegel and Jünger, he argued that the State could reach its ideal point of unity only in and through war: "If the individual is the negation of the State, then war is the negation of that negation. War is the moment of absolute socialization of the collective existence of the people, the *Volk*." But in high places they had more prosaic concerns. Ribbentrop's ministry, the Abwehr, our own foreign affairs department, each evaluated the situation in his own way. One day, I was called in to see the Chief, Reinhard Heydrich. This was my first time and I felt a mixture of excitement and anxiety as I entered his office. Rigidly concentrated, he was working on a pile of reports, and I stood at attention for several minutes before he made a sign for me to sit down. I had time to observe him up close. I had of course seen him many times, during staff conferences or in the hallways of the Prinz-Albrecht-Palais; but whereas at a distance he presented the very embodiment of the Nordic Übermensch, up close he gave a curious impression, somewhat blurred. I finally decided that it must be a question of proportion: beneath an abnormally high, domed forehead, his mouth was too wide, his lips too thick for his narrow face; his hands seemed too long, like nervous algae attached to his arms. When he raised his little eyes, set too close together, toward me, they didn't stay in place; and when he finally spoke to me, his voice seemed much too high for a man with such a powerful body. He gave me a disturbing feeling of femininity, which only made him more sinister. His sentences fell rapidly, short, tense; he almost never finished them; but the meaning always remained crisp and clear. "I have a mission for you, Doktor Aue." The Reichsführer was dissatisfied with the reports he was receiving about the intentions of the Western powers. He wanted another evaluation, independent from that of the foreign department. Everyone knew that in those countries there was a strong pacifist trend, especially within nationalist or pro-fascist circles; but what was still hard to judge was their influence on the governments. "You know Paris well, I think. According to your file you were connected to circles close to the Action Française. Those people have acquired a certain amount of importance since then." I tried to get in a word but Heydrich interrupted me: "That doesn't matter." He wanted me to go to Paris and strike up again with my old acquaintances, to study the actual political weight of the pacifist circles. I was to use the end-of-term vacation as a pretext. Naturally, I was to repeat National Socialist Germany's pacifist intentions toward France to anyone who cared to listen. "Dr. Hauser will go with you. But you'll submit separate reports. Standartenführer Taubert will provide you with the necessary currency and documents. Is everything clear?" In fact, I felt completely lost, but he had caught me by surprise. "*Zu Befehl*, Gruppenführer," was all I could say. "Fine. Be back by the end of July. Dismissed."

I went to see Thomas. I was pleased he was leaving with me: as a student, he had spent several years in France, and his French was excellent. "What a face!" he said when he saw me. "You should be happy. A mission—they've given you a mission, that's all." I suddenly realized that in fact it was a godsend. "You'll see. If we succeed, that'll open quite a few doors to us. Things will start moving, soon, and there will be room for people who know how to seize the moment." He had gone to see Schellenberg, who was acting as Heydrich's main advisor for foreign affairs; Schellenberg had explained to him what they were expecting of us. "All you have to do is read the papers to know who wants war and who doesn't. What's more delicate is to gauge the actual influence of the various groups. And especially the actual influence of the Jews. The Führer, apparently, is convinced that they want to lead Germany into another war; but will the French stand for it? That's the question." He laughed openly: "And also in Paris you eat well! And the girls are beautiful." The mission went off without any obstacles. I found my old friends—Robert Brasillach, who was getting ready to tour Spain in a mobile home with his sister Suzanne and Bardèche, his brother-in-law, Blond, Rebatet, some others I didn't know as well, all my old comrades from my preparatory classes and my years at the ELSP. At night, Rebatet, half drunk, dragged me through the Latin Quarter to comment knowledgeably about the freshly painted graffiti, MENE, MENE, TEKEL, UPHARSIN, on the walls of the Sorbonne; during the day, he sometimes took me to see Céline, who had become extraordinarily famous and who had just published a second vitriolic pamphlet; in the Metro, Poulain, a friend of Brasillach, declaimed whole passages of it to me: *There is no fundamental, irremediable hatred between Frenchmen and Germans. What does exist is a permanent, implacable, Judeo-British machination to prevent at all costs Europe from reforming into a single unified Franco-German nation, as it was before 843. The whole Judeo-Britannic genius lies in leading us from one conflict to another, from one carnage to another, slaughters from which we regularly emerge, always, in an atrocious condition, Frenchmen and Germans, bled dry, completely at the mercy of the Jews of the City.* As for Gaxotte and Robert himself, who *L'Humanité* claimed were in prison, they explained to anyone who would listen that all of French politics were guided by the astrology books of Trarieux d'Egmont, who had had the good fortune to predict with precision the date of Munich. The French government—a bad sign—had just expelled Abetz and the other German envoys. Everyone was interested in my opinion: "Ever since Versailles has gone to the scrap heap of history, there is no more French

question, for us. No one in Germany has claims on Alsace or on Lorraine. But with Poland, things aren't settled. We don't understand what's
motivating France to get mixed up in it." And it was a fact that the
French government wanted to get mixed up in it. Those who didn't
credit the Jewish theory blamed England: "They want to protect their
Empire. Ever since Napoleon, that's been their policy: no single continental power." Others thought that on the contrary England was still reluctant to intervene, that it was the French General Staff that, dreaming
of a Russian alliance, wanted to attack Germany *before it was too late*. Despite their enthusiasm, my friends were pessimistic: "The French right
is pissing in the wind," Rebatet told me one night. "For honor's sake."
Everyone seemed glumly to accept the fact that war would come,
sooner or later. The right blamed the left and the Jews; the left and the
Jews, of course, blamed Germany. I didn't see Thomas much. Once, I
took him to the bistro where I would meet up with the team from *Je
Suis Partout*, introducing him as a university friend. "Is he your Pylades,
then?" Brasillach acerbically snarled at me in Greek. "Exactly," Thomas
retorted in the same language, modulated by his soft Viennese accent.
"And he is my Orestes. Beware the power of armed friendship." He
himself had developed contacts in the business world; while I was making do with wine and pasta in attic rooms crowded with excited young
people, he was eating foie gras in the best brasseries in town. "Taubert
will foot the bill," he laughed. "Why should we stint?"

   Back again in Berlin, I typed up my report. My conclusions were
pessimistic, but lucid: the French right was fundamentally against the
war, but had little weight politically. The government, influenced by the
Jews and the British plutocrats, had decided that German expansion,
even within the limits of its natural *Grossraum*, constituted a threat to the
vital interests of France; it would go to war, in the name not of Poland
itself, but of its guarantees to Poland. I conveyed the report to Heydrich; at his request, I also sent a copy to Werner Best. "You're definitely right, I think," Best said to me. "But that's not what they want to
hear." I hadn't discussed my report with Thomas; when I described its
contents, he looked disgusted. "You really don't understand anything.
It's as if you had just turned up from the backwaters of Franconia." He
had written exactly the opposite: that the French industrialists were opposed to the war because of their exports, and so the French army was
too, and that once again the government would bow before the fait accompli. "But you know very well that that's not how it's going to happen," I objected.—"Who gives a damn what will happen? How does
that concern us, you and me? The Reichsführer wants just one thing:
to be able to reassure the Führer that he can take care of Poland as he

intends. What will happen afterward, we'll deal with afterward." He shook his head: "The Reichsführer won't even see your report."

Of course he was right. Heydrich never reacted to what I had sent him. When the Wehrmacht invaded Poland, a month later, and France and Great Britain declared war on us, Thomas was posted to one of Heydrich's new elite Einsatzgruppen, and I was left to vegetate in Berlin. I soon understood that in the interminable *National-Socialist circus games*, I had gone seriously astray, I had poorly interpreted the ambiguous signs from above, I hadn't correctly anticipated the Führer's will. My analyses were correct, and Thomas's were mistaken; he had been rewarded with an enviable post doubled with chances for promotion, and I had been shunted aside: that was worth reflecting on. During the following months, I detected from sure signs within the RSHA, newly formed from the unofficial fusion of the SP with the SD, that Best's influence was waning, despite the fact that he had been appointed head of two departments; Schellenberg's star, however, was rising day by day. Now, as if by chance, around the beginning of the year Thomas had begun spending more time with Schellenberg; my friend had a strange and infallible genius for finding himself in the right place not at the right time, but just before; so that it seemed every time as if he had always been there, and that the ups and downs of bureaucratic precedence did nothing but catch up with him. I could have understood this sooner if I had been paying attention. Now, I suspected that my name remained linked with Best's, and thus equated with the labels *bureaucrat, narrow-minded lawyer, not active* enough, not *tough* enough. I could continue to write legal opinions, they did need people for that, but that would be all. And, in fact, in June the following year, Werner Best resigned from the RSHA, although he had contributed more than anyone else to its creation. At that time I volunteered for a position in France; I was told that my services would be more useful in the legal department. Best was clever, he had friends and protectors elsewhere; over the past few years, his publications had been evolving from the penal and constitutional fields to international law and the theory of the *Grossraum*, the "large spaces," which he was developing against Carl Schmitt in the company of my old professor Reinhard Höhn and a few other intellectuals; cleverly playing these cards, he obtained a post high up within the military administration in France. As for me, I was even allowed to publish.

Thomas, on leave, confirmed this diagnosis: "I told you what you did was stupid. Anyone who is anybody is in Poland." For now, he added, he couldn't do much for me. Schellenberg was the star of the day, Heydrich's protégé, and Schellenberg didn't like me, he thought I was uptight. As for Ohlendorf, my other support, he was having enough dif-

ficulties with his own position to be able to think about me. Maybe I
should go see my father's former directors. But everyone was a little
busy.

In the end, it was Thomas who started things going for me again.
After Poland, he had gone to Yugoslavia and Greece, from which he returned a Hauptsturmführer, decorated many times over. He always
wore a uniform now, as elegantly tailored as his suits had been before.
In May 1941, he invited me to dine at Horcher's, a famous restaurant
on the Lutherstrasse. "It's my treat," he declared, laughing loudly. He ordered some Champagne and we drank to victory: "Sieg Heil!" Past victories and victories yet to come, he added; had I heard about Russia?
"I've heard rumors," I acknowledged, "but that's all." He smiled: "We're
attacking. Next month." He paused to give the news all its weight.
"Good God," I finally let out. "There is no God. There's just Adolf
Hitler, our Führer, and the invincible power of the German Reich. We
are in the process of amassing the largest army in the history of humanity. We will crush them in a few weeks." We drank. "Listen," he finally
said. "The Chief is forming several Einsatzgruppen to accompany the
assault troops from the Wehrmacht. Special units, as in Poland. I have
reason to believe that he would positively welcome any talented young
SS officer who would volunteer for this Einsatz."—"I've already tried
to volunteer. For France. They refused."—"They won't refuse this
time."—"What about you, are you going there?" He gently swirled the
Champagne in his glass. "Of course. I've been posted to one of the
Gruppenstäbe. Each Group will direct several Kommandos. I'm sure
you could land a slot in one of the Kommandostäbe."—"And what exactly is the purpose of these Groups?" He smiled: "I told you: special
actions. SP and SD work, the security of the troops to the rear, intelligence, things like that. Keeping an eye on the military, too. They were
a little difficult, in Poland, a little old-fashioned; we don't want that to
happen again. You want to think about it?" Does it surprise you that I
didn't even hesitate? What Thomas was suggesting seemed only reasonable to me, even exciting. Put yourself in my place. What man of sane
mind could ever have imagined that they'd pick jurists to assassinate
people without a trial? My ideas were clear and strong and I scarcely
gave it a thought before replying: "No need. I'm bored to death here
in Berlin. If you can get me in, I'll go." He smiled again: "I always said
you were a good guy, that you could be counted on. You'll see, we're
going to have fun." I laughed with pleasure and we drank some more
Champagne. Thus does the devil expand his kingdom.

But I couldn't know that yet in Lemberg. Night was falling when
Thomas came to pull me out of my daydreams. I could still hear some

isolated gunshots, over toward the boulevard, but things seemed to have generally calmed down. "Are you coming? Or do you want to stay there gaping at the crows?"—"What's *Aktion Petliura?*" I asked him.—"It's what you saw in the street. Where did you hear about that?" I ignored his question: "Are you really the ones that started this pogrom?"—"Let's just say we didn't try to prevent it. We put up a few notices. But I don't think the Ukrainians needed us to start. You haven't seen the OUN posters? *You welcomed Stalin with flowers, we will hand your heads to Hitler as a welcome.* They came up with that one all by themselves."—"I see. Are we going there on foot?"—"It's right nearby." The restaurant was in a narrow street behind the main boulevard. The door was locked; when Thomas knocked, it opened a little, then opened wide onto a dark, candlelit interior. "For Germans only," Thomas smiled. "Ah, Professor, hello." The officers from the Abwehr were already there; aside from them, there was no one else. I immediately recognized the taller of the two, the one Thomas had saluted, a distinguished man, still young, whose little brown eyes sparkled in the midst of a large oval face, relaxed, open. He wore his dark hair a little too long, curled up at the sides in a very un-military way. I shook his hand: "Professor Oberländer. It's a pleasure to see you again." He stared at me: "We know each other?"—"We were introduced a few years ago, after one of your lectures at the University of Berlin. By Dr. Reinhard Höhn, my professor."—"Oh, you were a student of Höhn's! Wonderful."—"My friend Dr. Aue is one of the rising stars of the SD," Thomas slipped in maliciously.—"If he's a student of Höhn's, that doesn't surprise me. It sometimes seems as if the entire SD has passed through his hands." He turned to his colleague: "But I haven't introduced you yet to Hauptmann Weber, my adjunct." Both of them, I noticed, wore the badge embossed with a nightingale that I had seen that afternoon on the arms of certain soldiers. "Excuse my ignorance," I asked while we sat down, "but what is that insignia?"—"It's the symbol of the Nachtigall," Weber replied, "a special battalion of the Abwehr, recruited from the Ukrainian nationalists of western Galicia."—"Professor Oberländer commands the Nachtigall. So we're rivals," Thomas interrupted.—"You exaggerate, Hauptsturmführer."—"Not really. You came with Bandera in tow, we brought Melnyk and the Berlin committee." The discussion suddenly became lively. We were served some wine. "Bandera might be useful to us," Oberländer affirmed.—"In what way?" Thomas retorted. "His men are uncontrollable, they make proclamations all over the place, without consulting anyone." He raised his arms: "*Independence!* That's a nice one."—"You think Melnyk would do better?"—"Melnyk is a reasonable man. He wants the support of Europe, not terror. He's a politician, he's ready to work with us on the long term, and that leaves us more options."—"Maybe, but the street doesn't listen to him."— "Rabid idiots! If they don't calm down, we'll bring them to heel." We drank. The wine was good, a little rough but rich. "Where does it come from?" Weber asked, tapping his glass.—"That? The Carpathians, I think," Thomas replied.—"You know," Oberländer went on blithely, "the OUN successfully resisted the Soviets for two full years. It wouldn't be so easy to eliminate them. It's better to try to co-opt them and channel their energy. Bandera, at least, they'll listen to. He saw Stetsko today and it went very well."—"Who is Stetsko?" I asked. Thomas answered ironically: "Jaroslav Stetsko is the new prime minister of a so-called independent Ukraine that we haven't authorized."—"If we play our cards right," Oberländer went on, "they'll quickly back down." Thomas reacted sharply: "Who? Bandera? He's a terrorist, and he'll always be a terrorist. He has the soul of a terrorist. That's why all those maniacs adore him, too." He turned to me: "You know where the Abwehr found this Bandera? In prison!"—"In Warsaw," Oberländer added, smiling. "He was actually serving a sentence for assassinating a Polish government minister, in 1934. But I don't see any harm in that." Thomas turned back to him: "I'm simply saying he's uncontrollable. You'll see. He's a fanatic, he dreams of a Great Ukraine from the Carpathians to the Don River. He takes himself for the reincarnation of Dmitri Donskoy. At least Melnyk is a realist. And he also has a lot of support. All the old-time militants look up to him."—"Yes, but that's just the trouble: not the young. And you'll have to admit that on the Jewish question he isn't very motivated." Thomas shrugged: "We can take care of that without him. In any case, historically, the OUN has never been anti-Semitic. It's only thanks to Stalin that they've moved somewhat in that direction."—"That may be true," Weber quietly acknowledged. "But still there is a basis, in the historical link between the Jews and the Polish landowners." The dishes arrived: roast duck stuffed with apples, with mashed potatoes and braised beets. Thomas served us. "Capital," Weber said.—"Yes, excellent," Oberländer approved. "Is this a specialty of the region?"—"Yes," Thomas explained between mouthfuls. "The duck is prepared with marjoram and garlic. Usually it's served with a soup made with duck blood as an appetizer, but today they couldn't."—"Excuse me," I interrupted. "Your Nachtigall men, where do they fit in all this?" Oberländer finished chewing and wiped his lips before responding: "With them it's another thing entirely. It's the Ruthenian spirit, if you like. Ideologically—and even personally for the oldest of them—they come from a national unit of the old Imperial army that was called the *Ukrainski Sichovi Striltsi*, the Ukrainian Sich Rifles, you could say, a Cossack reference. After the war, they stayed here and a lot of them fought under Petliura against the Reds, and a little against us, too, in 1918. The OUN don't like them much. In a way they're more autonomists than separatists."—"Like the Bulbovitsi, too," Weber added. He looked at me: "They haven't shown their faces yet, in Lutsk?"—"Not to my knowledge. More Ukrainians?"—"Volhynians," Oberländer corrected. "A self-defense group that started up against the Poles. Since 'thirty-nine they've been fighting against the Soviets, and it could be interesting if we came to an agreement with them. But I think they keep more toward Rovno, and farther up, in the Pripet marshes." Everyone had started eating again. "What I don't understand," Oberländer at last went on, pointing his fork at us, "is why the Bolsheviks repressed the Poles but not the Jews. As Weber said, they've always been closely associated."—"I think the answer is obvious," Thomas said. "Stalinist power is dominated by the Jews in any case. When the Bolsheviks occupied the region, they took the place of the Polish gentry, but maintained the same configuration—that is, they continued to depend on the Jews to exploit the Ukrainian peasantry. Hence the legitimate anger of the people, as you could witness today." Weber hiccupped into his glass; Oberländer chuckled dryly. "*The legitimate anger of the people*. That's going a bit far, Hauptsturmführer." He had settled back in his chair and was tapping the table edge with his knife. "That's good for the onlookers. For our allies, for the Americans maybe. But you know as well as I do how that justified anger is organized." Thomas smiled amiably: "At least, Professor, it has the merit of involving the population psychologically. Afterward, they can only applaud the introduction of our measures."—"That's true, I have to admit." The waitress cleared the table. "Coffee?" Thomas asked.—"With pleasure. But quickly, we still have work to do tonight." Thomas offered cigarettes around while the coffee was served. "Whatever the case," Oberländer commented, leaning toward the lighter Thomas held out, "I'll be very curious about what we find when we cross the Sbruch."—"And why is that?" asked Thomas, lighting Weber's cigarette.—"You've read my book? On rural overpopulation in Poland."—"Unfortunately not, sorry." Oberländer turned to me: "But I imagine you have, with Höhn."—"Of course."— "Good. Well, if my theories are correct, I think that once we arrive in Ukraine proper we'll find a rich peasantry there."—"How's that?" Thomas asked.—"Thanks precisely to Stalin's policies. In a dozen years, twenty-five million smallholdings have become two hundred fifty thousand large-scale farms. The de-kulakization, I believe, especially the planned famine of 1932, was an attempt to find the point of equilibrium between the space available for the extraction of edible resources and the consumer population. I have reason to believe that they suc-ceeded."—"And what if they failed?"—"Then it would be up to us to succeed." Weber made a sign to him and he finished his coffee. "Gen-tlemen," he said, getting up and clicking his heels, "thank you for the pleasant evening. What do we owe?"—"Don't bother," Thomas said as he too got up, "it's a pleasure."—"It's our treat next time, then."—"Fine. In Kiev or Moscow?" Everyone laughed and shook hands. "My greet-ings to Dr. Rasch," Oberländer said. "We used to see a lot of each other, in Königsberg. I hope he'll have time to join us, one of these evenings." The two men went out and Thomas sat back down: "You'll have a Cognac? It's on the Group."—"With pleasure." Thomas ordered. "Say, you speak good Ukrainian," I said to him.—"Oh. In Poland, I learned some Polish; it's almost the same thing." The Cognacs came and we clinked glasses. "Tell me—what was he insinuating, about the pogrom?" Thomas took a while to answer. Finally he made up his mind: "But," he said carefully, "you keep this to yourself. You know that in Poland we had quite a few problems with the military. Especially about our special methods. Those gentlemen had objections of a moral kind. They thought you can make omelettes without breaking eggs. This time around, we took measures to avoid misunderstandings: the Chief and Schellenberg negotiated precise agreements with the Wehrmacht; they explained that to you, in Pretzsch." I nodded and he continued: "But still, we want to keep them from changing their minds. And for that, the pogroms have a huge advantage: they show the Wehrmacht that if the SS and the *Sicherheitspolizei* have their hands tied, there'll be chaos in their rear zone. And if there is one thing a soldier fears more than 'dishonor,' as they say, it's disorder. Three more days like this and they'll come begging us to do our work: clean, discreet, efficient, no fuss."—"And Oberländer suspects as much."—"Oh, that doesn't disturb him at all. He simply wants to be sure that we'll let him continue his little po-litical intrigues. But," he added smiling, "we will control him too when the time comes."

A strange guy, I thought as I was going to bed. His cynicism some-times shocked me, even though I often found it refreshing; at the same time, I knew that I couldn't judge his behavior by his words. I trusted him completely: at the SD, he had always loyally helped me, without my ever asking him, and even when I couldn't be of any perceptible use to him in return. I had asked him the question openly once and he had burst out laughing: "What do you want me to tell you? That I'm keep-ing you in reserve for a long-term plan? I like you, that's all." Those words had touched me deeply, and he had hurried to add: "In any case, smart as you are, at least I'm sure that you can never threaten me. That's already a lot." He had played a role in my entering the SD—that's also how I had met him; it's true that it had happened in somewhat peculiar circumstances, but one doesn't always have a choice. For a few years already I had been part of the SD's network of *Vertrauensmänner*, informants employed in all spheres of German life: industry, agriculture, bureaucracy, university. When I arrived at Kiel, in 1934, I had limited resources, and on the advice of one of my father's former directors, Dr. Mandelbrod, I had applied to the SS, which allowed me to avoid matriculation fees at the university; with his support, I had been quickly accepted. Two years later, I had gone to an extraordinary lecture given by Otto Ohlendorf on the deviations of National Socialism; afterward, I had been introduced to him by Dr. Jessen, my economics professor, who had also been his a few years earlier. Ohlendorf, it turned out, had already heard about me from Dr. Mandelbrod, with whom he was in contact; he rather openly extolled the *Sicherheitsdienst*, and recruited me on the spot as a *V-Mann*. The work was simple: I was to send reports, on what was being said, on rumors, jokes, the reactions of people to the advances of National Socialism. In Berlin, Ohlendorf had explained to me, the reports of the thousands of *V-Männer* were compiled, then the SD distributed a summary to the different branches of the Party, in order to allow them to gauge the feelings of the *Volk* and to formulate their policies accordingly. This replaced elections, in a way; and Ohlendorf was one of the creators of this system, of which he showed himself visibly proud. In the beginning, I found it exciting, Ohlendorf's speech had impressed me strongly, and I was glad to be able to participate in a concrete way in building National Socialism. But in Berlin, Höhn, my professor, subtly discouraged me. In the SD, he had been a mentor for Ohlendorf and for many others; but since then he had fallen out with the Reichsführer and left the service. He quickly succeeded in convincing me that working for an intelligence or espionage service stemmed from pure romanticism, and that I had much more useful ways to serve the *Volk*. I stayed in contact with Ohlendorf, but he no longer talked to me much about the SD; he too, I learned later, had his difficulties with the Reichsführer. I continued paying my dues to the SS and showing up for the parades, but I no longer sent in reports, and soon I ceased to think of the matter. I was concentrating on my thesis, which was somewhat daunting; what's more, I had developed a passion for Kant and was conscientiously boning up on Hegel and idealist philosophy; with Höhn's encouragement, I planned on requesting a position in a government ministry. But I must say that something else too was holding me back, private motives. In my Plutarch, I had underlined these sentences on Alcibiades one night: . . . *a man, judging by the outward ap-*

pearance, would have said, "'Tis not Achilles's son, but he himself; the very man" that Lycurgus designed to form; while his real feeling and acts would have rather provoked the exclamation, "'Tis the same woman still." That might make you smile, or grimace in disgust; now, it's all the same to me. In Berlin, despite the Gestapo, you could still in those days find whatever you wanted of that kind. Famous bars such as the Kleist-Kasino or the Silhouette were still open, and they weren't often raided, they must have been paying someone. Otherwise, there were also certain places in the Tiergarten, near the Neuer See in front of the zoo, where the Schupos rarely ventured at night; behind the trees waited the *Strichjungen*, or young muscular workers from "Red" Wedding. At university, I had had one or two relationships, necessarily discreet ones and in any case brief; but I preferred proletarian lovers, I didn't like to talk.

In spite of my discretion, I ended up running into trouble. I should have been more careful; after all, the warning signs were there to see. Höhn had asked me—quite innocently—to review a book by the lawyer Rudolf Klare, *Homosexuality and Criminal Law.* This remarkably well-informed man had established a surprisingly precise typology of practices, then, on their basis, a classification of offenses, beginning with *abstract coitus or contemplation* (Level 1), moving past *pressure of the naked penis on a part of the partner's body* (Level 5) and *rhythmic friction between the knees or legs or in the armpit* (Level 6), and ending with *touching of the penis by the tongue, penis in the mouth,* and *penis in the anus* (Levels 7, 8, and 9, respectively). To each level of offense corresponded a punishment of increasing severity. This Klare, it was obvious, must have attended a boarding school; but Höhn affirmed that the Minister of the Interior and the *Sicherheitspolizei* took his ideas seriously. I found it all rather comical. One spring night—it was in 1937—I went for a stroll behind the Neuer See. I watched the shadows of the trees until my gaze met a young man's. I took out a cigarette, asked him for a light, and when he raised his lighter, instead of leaning toward his hand, I pushed it aside and threw away the cigarette, took him by the back of the neck, and kissed him on the lips, gently tasting his breath. I followed him under the trees, walking away from the paths, my heart, as it does each time, beating crazily in my throat and temples; a sudden veil had fallen over my breathing; I unfastened his pants, buried my face in the sharp smell of his sweat, male skin, urine, and eau de cologne; I rubbed my face against his skin, his sex, and where the hairs thickened, I licked him and took him in my mouth, then, when I couldn't hold back any longer, I pushed him against a tree, turned myself around without letting him go, and buried him in me, until all time and grief disappeared. When it was over he quickly moved away, without a word. Exalted, I leaned on the tree, readjusted myself, lit a cigarette, and tried to master the trembling in my legs. When I was able to walk, I headed toward the Landwehrkanal, to cross it and continue toward the S-Bahn at the zoo. A limitless lightness carried each of my steps. On the Lichtenstein Bridge, a man was standing, leaning on the guardrail: I knew him, we had friends in common, his name was Hans P. He seemed very pale, distraught, and wasn't wearing a tie; a fine sweat made his face gleam almost green under the glum light of the streetlamps. My feeling of euphoria suddenly fell away. "What are you doing here?" I asked him in a peremptory, unfriendly tone. "Ah, Auc, it's you." His giggle bore a touch of hysteria. "You really want to know?" This encounter was growing odder and odder; I stayed as if transfixed. I nodded. "I wanted to jump," he explained, chewing his upper lip. "But I don't dare. I even," he went on, opening his jacket to reveal the butt of a pistol, "I even brought this."—"Where the hell did you find it?" I asked him in a muffled voice.—"My father is an officer. I nicked it from him. It's loaded." He stared at me anxiously. "You wouldn't like to help me, would you?" I looked around: along the canal, no one, as far as I could see. Slowly I stretched out my arm and took the pistol out of his belt. He was staring at me with a fascinated, petrified look. I examined the cartridge clip: it seemed full, and I shoved it back in with a sharp click. With my left hand I brutally seized his neck, pushed him up against the guardrail, and forced the barrel of the gun between his lips. "Open!" I barked. "Open your mouth!" My heart was pounding wildly, I felt as if I were shouting, though I was making an effort to keep my voice low. "Open!" I buried the barrel between his teeth. "Is that what you want? Suck it!" Hans P. was melting with terror, I suddenly smelt a bitter stench of urine, I looked down: he had wet his pants. My rage vanished immediately, as mysteriously as it had welled up. I replaced the pistol in his belt and patted him on the cheek. "It'll be okay. Go home." I left him there, crossed the bridge, and headed right, along the canal. A few meters farther on three Schupos appeared out of nowhere. "Hey, you there! What are you doing here? Papers."—"I'm a student. I'm taking a walk."—"Yeah, we know that kind of walk. What about him over there, on the bridge? Is he your girlfriend?" I shrugged: "I don't know him. He looked strange, he tried to threaten me." They exchanged a look and two of them headed at a trot for the bridge; I tried to walk away, but the third man took me by the arm. On the bridge, there was a commotion, some shouts, then gunshots. The two Schupos returned; one of them, livid, was holding his shoulder; blood flowed between his fingers. "That bastard. He shot at me. But we got him." His comrade gave me an angry look: "You're coming with us."

They took me to the *Polizeirevier* on Derfflingerstrasse, at the corner of the Kurfürstenstrasse; there, a half-asleep policeman took my ID papers, asked me some questions, and wrote the answers down on a form; then they told me to go sit on a bench. Two hours later they took me across the way, to the *Abschnittkommando* of the Tiergarten, the neighborhood's main police station. They led me into a room where a man who was badly shaved but dressed in a meticulously ironed suit sat hunched behind a table. He was from the Kripo. "You're in for it, young man. A man fired on a police officer and was killed. Who was he? Did you know him? They saw you on the bridge with him. What were you doing there?" Sitting on the bench, I had had time to reflect, and I stuck to a simple story: A doctoral student, I liked taking walks, at night, to meditate on my thesis; I had left home, in Prenzlauer Berg, to stroll along Unter den Linden then through the Tiergarten, I wanted to reach the S-Bahn to return home; I was crossing the bridge and this man had accosted me, he said something I couldn't catch, his strange behavior had frightened me, I thought he was threatening me and had continued on my way, then I had met the Schupos, and that was all. He asked the same question as the policemen: "That area is a well-known meeting place. Are you sure he wasn't your boyfriend? A lovers' quarrel? The Schupos confirmed you spoke with him." I denied this and repeated my story: doctoral student, etc. That lasted for a while: he asked his questions in a brutal, hard tone; several times he tried to provoke me, but I didn't let myself be intimidated, I knew that the best thing was to stay calm. I began to be bothered by a strong need and finally asked to go to the bathroom. He sniggered: "No. Afterward," and continued. Finally he waved the air with his hand. "Okay, Mr. Lawyer. Go sit in the hallway. We'll continue later on." I left the office and sat down in the entryway. Aside from the two Schupos and a drunkard asleep on a bench, I was alone. A bulb flickered now and then. Everything was clean, neat, quiet. I waited.

A few hours went by, I must have dozed, the dawn light was beginning to turn the windows in the entryway pale, a man came in. He was tastefully dressed, in an elegantly cut pinstripe suit with a starched collar and a pearl-gray knitted tie; on the lapel he wore a Party insignia, and under his arm he was holding a black leather briefcase; his jet black hair, thick, shining with brilliantine, was combed straight back, and although his face remained closed, his eyes seemed to be laughing as they looked me over. He murmured a few words to the Schupos on guard; one of them led him down the corridor and they disappeared. A few minutes later the Schupo returned and waved his stubby finger at me: "You there. This way." I rose, stretched, and followed him, struggling to hold back my urge. The Schupo brought me back to the room where I had been interrogated. The Kripo inspector had vanished; sitting in his place was the well-dressed young man, one arm with its starched sleeve resting on the table, the other casually hooked over the back of his chair. The black briefcase lay on the table near his elbow. "Come in," he said politely but firmly. He pointed toward an empty chair: "Please, sit down." The Schupo closed the door and I came and sat. I could hear the man's hobnailed boots clicking in the hallway as he left. The elegant, polished young man had a voice that was soft but barely hid its sharpness. "My colleague from the criminal police, Halbey, takes you for a Paragraph One-seventy-five. Are you a Paragraph One-seventy-five?" That seemed a genuine question to me and I answered frankly: "No."— "That's what I think too," he said. He looked at me and held out his hand over the desk: "My name is Thomas Hauser. A pleasure." I leaned over to shake it. His grip was firm, his skin dry and smooth, he had perfectly cut fingernails. "Aue. Maximilien Aue."—"Yes, I know. You're lucky, Herr Aue. Kriminalkommissar Halbey has already sent a preliminary report on this unfortunate incident to the *Staatspolizei*, mentioning your presumed involvement. It was addressed in duplicate to Kriminalrat Meisinger. Do you know who Kriminalrat Meisinger is?"— "No, I don't."—"Kriminalrat Meisinger directs the Reich's Main Office for the Struggle Against Homosexuality and Abortion. So he's in charge of the One-seventy-fives. He is not a nice man. A Bavarian." He paused. "Fortunately for you, Kriminalkommissar Halbey's report came across my desk first. I was on duty tonight. I was able for now to block the copy addressed to Kriminalrat Meisinger."—"That's very kind of you."—"Yes, it is. See, our friend Kriminalkommissar Halbey has formed suspicions about you. But Kriminalrat Meisinger doesn't care about suspicions, he cares about facts. And he has methods to obtain those facts that do not meet with complete approval at the *Staatspolizei*, but that generally turn out to be effective." I shook my head: "Listen . . . I don't really understand what you're talking about. There must be a misunderstanding." Thomas clicked his tongue: "For now, you're right. There seems to be a misunderstanding. Or perhaps rather an unfortunate coincidence, if you like, hastily interpreted by the zealous Kriminalkommissar Halbey." I bent forward, spreading my hands: "Look, this is all idiotic. I am a student, a member of the Party, of the SS . . ." He cut me off: "I know you are a member of the Party and the SS. I know Professor Höhn very well. I know perfectly who you are." Then I understood: "Oh. You're from the SD." Thomas smiled amiably: "That's more or less it, yes. Normally I work with Dr. Six, the replacement for your professor, Dr. Höhn. But for the time being I have been seconded to the *Staatspolizei* as assistant to Dr. Best, who is helping the Chief to draw up the legal framework for the SP." Even then I noted the marked emphasis with which he uttered the words *the Chief.* "So you're all doctors, at the *Sicherheitsdienst?*" I blurted out. He smiled again, a wide, frank smile: "Almost."—"And you're a doctor too?" He inclined his head: "In law."—"I see."—"The Chief, on the other hand, is not a doctor. But he is much more intelligent than we are. He uses our talents to reach his ends."—"And what are these ends?" Thomas knitted his eyebrows: "What are you studying, with Höhn? The protection of the State, of course." He stopped. I kept silent; we looked at each other. He seemed to be waiting for something. He bent forward and leaned his chin on one hand, tapping the manicured nails of the other on the table. Finally he asked in an annoyed tone: "The protection of the State doesn't interest you, Herr Aue?" I hesitated: "Well, I am not a doctor . . ."—"But you will be soon." A few more seconds of silence passed. "I don't understand what you're getting at," I finally said.—"I'm not getting at anything at all, I'm trying to help you avoid useless difficulties. You know, the reports you wrote for the SD, at one time, were quickly noticed. Very well written, to the point, nourished by a *Weltanschauung* whose rigor was unquestionable. It's too bad you didn't continue, but that's your business. Still, when I saw Kriminalkommissar Halbey's report, I said to myself that this would be a loss for National Socialism. I phoned Dr. Best—I woke him up, too—he agreed with me and authorized me to come here, to suggest to Kriminalkommissar Halbey that he curb his annoying initiatives. You understand, they're going to open a criminal investigation, as is necessary when a man dies. What's more, a policeman was wounded. At the very least you should in principle be called to appear as a witness. Given the location of the crime, a notorious homosexual meeting place, the case, even if I can convince Kriminalkommissar Halbey to moderate his zeal, will automatically be forwarded, sooner or later, to the services of Kriminalrat Meisinger. Then Kriminalrat Meisinger will take an interest in you. He'll start digging, like the coarse animal he is. Whatever the results are, it will leave indelible traces in your personal file. Now it just so happens that the Reichsführer-SS has a particular obsession about homosexuality. Homosexuals frighten him, he hates them. He thinks a hereditary homosexual can contaminate dozens of young men with his disease, and that all those young men will then be lost to the race. He also believes that inverts are congenital liars, who believe in their own lies—hence a mental irresponsibility that renders them incapable of loyalty, causes them to blab, and can lead to treason. Thus, this potential threat that the homosexual represents signifies that the question, for the Reichsführer, is not a medical question that can be remedied by therapy, but a political question, to be treated by the methods of the SP. He even recently expressed enthusiasm for the suggestion of one of our best legal historians, Professor and SS-Untersturmführer Eckhardt, whom you must know, to return to the old Germanic custom of drowning effeminate men in peat bogs. This, I would be the first to acknowledge, is a somewhat extreme point of view, and although its logic is undeniable, not everyone sees the matter in such an unequivocal way. The Führer himself, it seems, remains somewhat indifferent to this question. But his lack of interest on this subject leaves the field free for the Reichsführer, with his excessive ideas, to define the current policies. So if Kriminalrat Meisinger came to form an unfavorable opinion of you, even if he didn't manage to obtain a condemnation under Paragraphs One-seventy-five or One-seventy-five-A of the Penal Code, you could have all sorts of problems. It's even possible, if Kriminalrat Meisinger insisted, that an order for preventive custody be issued against you. I would be sorry about that, and Dr. Best too." I was only half listening because my need was overtaking me again, more violently than ever, but finally I reacted: "I don't understand where you're heading. Are you making me an offer?"—"An offer?" Thomas raised his eyebrows. "But who do you take us for? Do you really think that the SD needs to resort to *blackmail* for its recruitment? Come on. No," he continued with a broad, friendly smile, "I simply came to help you in a spirit of camaraderie, as one National Socialist toward another. Of course," he added with an ironic look, "we suspect that Professor Höhn is warning his students against the SD, that he must have discouraged you a little, and that's too bad. Did you know he's the one who recruited me? He has become ungrateful. If you ever changed your mind about us, all the better. I think if our work began to appear to you in a more favorable light, Dr. Best would be happy to discuss it with you. I invite you to think about it. But that has nothing to do with my actions tonight." I must say that this frank, direct attitude pleased me. I was very impressed by the uprightness, the energy, the calm conviction radiating from Thomas. It didn't at all correspond to the idea I had formed of the SD. But he was already getting up. "You'll go out with me. There won't be any objections. I'll inform Kriminalkommissar Halbey that you were in that area in the line of duty, and the matter will rest there. When the time comes you'll testify to that effect. That way, everything will be perfectly civilized." I couldn't stop thinking about the toilets; when the conversation ended, Thomas waited in the hallway while I finally relieved myself. I had time then to reflect a little: when I came out, I must already have made my decision. Outside it was day. Thomas left me on the Kurfürstenstrasse, shaking my

hand vigorously. "I'm sure we'll see each other again soon. *Tchüss!*"
And that is how, my ass still full of sperm, I resolved to enter the *Sicher-heitsdienst*.

The day after the dinner with Oberländer, as soon as I woke up, I
went to see Hennicke, the Group's Chief of Staff. "Ah, Obersturm-führer Aue. The dispatches for Lutsk are almost ready. Go see the
Brigadeführer. He's at the Brygidki Prison. Untersturmführer Beck will
take you there." This Beck was still very young; he was handsome, but
seemed to be brooding about something, harboring a secret anger. After saluting me he hardly said a word. In the streets, the people seemed
even more agitated than the day before; armed groups of nationalists
were patrolling, and traffic was difficult. There were also many more
German soldiers evident. "I have to stop by the train station to pick up
a package," Beck said. "Is that all right with you?" His driver already
knew the way well; to avoid the crowd, he cut off onto a side street,
which, farther on, wound along the side of a little hill lined with
middle-class houses, quiet and comfortable. "It's a beautiful city," I
remarked.—"That's normal. It is a German city, basically," Beck responded. I was silent. At the station, he left me in the car and disappeared into the crowd. Streetcars were discharging their passengers,
taking on others, setting off again. In a little park over to the left, indifferent to the commotion, several families of Gypsies were lounging
about under the trees, dirty, weather-beaten, dressed in colorful rags.
Others were standing near the train station, but they weren't begging;
the children weren't even playing. Beck returned with a little package.
He followed my gaze and noticed the Gypsies. "Instead of wasting our
time with the Jews, we'd do better taking care of those people," he spat
out viciously. "They're much more dangerous. They work for the Reds,
did you know that? But we'll deal with them." In the long street that
led up from the station, he spoke again: "The synagogue is here, right
next door. I'd like to see it. After that we'll go to the prison." The synagogue was set back in a little side street, on the left side of the avenue
leading to the center of town. Two German soldiers were standing
guard in front of the gate. The dilapidated façade wasn't much to look
at; only a Star of David on the pediment revealed the nature of the
place; there wasn't a Jew in sight. I followed Beck through the little
door. The main room rose up two floors, surrounded by an elevated
gallery, for the women no doubt; vivid paintings in bright colors decorated the walls, in a naïve but vigorous style, representing a great Lion
of Judah surrounded by Jewish stars, parrots, and swallows, and riddled
in places with bullet holes. In place of benches there were little chairs

with school desks attached. Beck contemplated the paintings for a long while, then went out. The street in front of the prison was swarming with people, a monstrous, cacophonic crush. The people were shouting themselves hoarse; women, hysterical, were tearing their clothes and rolling on the ground; Jews, on their knees, guarded by Feldgendarmen, were scrubbing the sidewalk; now and then a passerby kicked one, a rubicund Feldwebel barked, *"Juden, kaputt!"* Ukrainians frantically applauded. At the gate to the prison, I had to make way for a column of Jews, in shirtsleeves or stripped to the waist, most of them bleeding, who, flanked by German soldiers, were carrying putrified corpses and loading them onto wagons. Old women in black threw themselves on the bodies, ululating, then rushed at the Jews, scratching at them until a soldier tried to push them away. I had lost sight of Beck; I went into the prison courtyard, and there it was the same spectacle again, terrified Jews sorting through corpses, others scrubbing the pavement while soldiers hooted; from time to time one of them lunged forward, striking at the Jews with his bare hands or his rifle butt, the Jews screamed, collapsed, struggled to rise up and get back to work, other soldiers were photographing the scene, still others, laughing, shouted insults or encouragements, sometimes too a Jew didn't get up, and then several men would go at him with their boots, until one or two Jews would come to drag the body by the feet over to the side, while others had to scrub the pavement again. Finally I found an SS man: "Do you know where Brigadeführer Rasch is?"—"I think he's in the prison offices, over there, I just saw him go up." In the long hallway, soldiers were coming and going, it was calmer, but the green walls, shiny and filthy, were splattered with bloodstains, more or less fresh, and speckled with scraps of brain mixed with hair and bone fragments; there were also long trails where they had dragged the corpses, my boots stuck to the floor at each step. At the other end, Rasch was coming down the stairs in the company of a tall Oberführer with a chubby face and several other officers from the Group. I saluted them. "Oh, it's you. Good. I received a report from Radetzky; ask him to come here as soon as he can. And you'll report in person to Obergruppenführer Jeckeln about the *Aktion* here. Insist on the fact that it's the nationalists and the people who took the initiative. In Lemberg the NKVD and the Jews assassinated three thousand people. So the people are taking their revenge, that's normal. We asked the AOK to leave them a few days."—"*Zu Befehl*, Brigadeführer." I followed them out. Rasch and the Oberführer were having an animated discussion. In the courtyard, distinct from the stink of the corpses, rose the heavy, nauseating smell of fresh blood. Going out, I passed two Jews who were coming back in from the street under escort; one of them, a

very young man, was sobbing violently, but in silence. I found Beck
again next to the car and we returned to the Gruppenstab. I ordered
Höfler to get the Opel ready and find Popp, then went to get the dispatches and the mail from the Leiter III. I also asked where Thomas was,
since I wanted to say goodbye to him before leaving: "You'll find him
down by the boulevard," I was told. "Go look in the Metropole Café,
on Sykstuska." In the courtyard, Popp and Höfler were ready. "Shall we
go, Herr Obersturmführer?"—"Yes, but we'll make a stop on the way.
Go by the boulevard." I found the Metropole easily. Inside, clusters of
men were noisily talking; some, already drunk, were bellowing; near the
bar, officers from the *Rollbahn* were drinking beer and commenting on
the situation. I found Thomas in the back next to a blond young man
in civilian clothes with a bloated, sullen face. They were drinking coffee. "Hi, Max! This is Oleg. A very well informed, intelligent man."
Oleg got up and shook my hand eagerly; he actually looked like a complete idiot. "Listen, I'm leaving now." Thomas replied in French:
"That's very good. In any case we'll see each other soon: according to
the plan, your Kommandostab will be stationed in Zhitomir, with
us."—"Excellent." He continued in German: "Good luck! Keep up
your spirits." I nodded to Oleg and went out. Our troops were still a
long way away from Zhitomir, but Thomas seemed confident, he must
have had good information. On the road, I lost myself with pleasure in
the softness of the Galician countryside; we advanced slowly, in the dust
of columns of trucks and equipment heading toward the front; from
time to time the sun pierced through the long rows of white clouds that
scrolled across the sky, a vast roof of shadows, cheerful and calm.

I arrived in Lutsk in the afternoon. Blobel, according to von
Radetzky, wouldn't be returning right away; Häfner told us confiden-
tially that in the end they had left him in an insane asylum run by the
Wehrmacht. The reprisal *Aktion* had been carried out successfully, but
no one seemed too eager to talk about it: "You can count yourself lucky
not to have been there," Zorn whispered to me. On July 6, the Sonderkommando, still sticking to the advance of the Sixth Army, moved
to Rovno, then quickly on to Tsviahel or Swjagel, which the Soviets
call Novograd-Volynskiy. At each stage, Teilkommandos were detached
to identify, arrest, and execute potential opponents. Most of them, it
should be said, were Jews. But we also shot Commissars or cadres of the
Bolshevik Party, when we found them, thieves, looters, farmers who
were hiding their grain, Gypsies too, Beck would have been happy. Von
Radetzky had explained to us that we had to reason in terms of *objective
threat*: since unmasking each and every guilty individual was impossible,

we had to identify the sociopolitical categories most liable to cause us harm, and act accordingly. In Lemberg, the new Ortskommandant, General Rentz, had little by little succeeded in reestablishing order and quieting things down; nonetheless, Einsatzkommando 6, and then Einsatzkommando 5, which had come to replace it, had continued executing hundreds of people outside the city. We were also beginning to have problems with the Ukrainians. On July 9, the brief independence experiment came to an abrupt end: the SP arrested Bandera and Stetsko and sent them under escort to Cracow, and their men were disarmed. But elsewhere, the OUN-B started a revolt; in Drohobycz, they opened fire on our troops, and several Germans were killed. From that time on we began to treat Bandera's supporters too as an *objective threat*; the Melnykists, delighted, helped us identify them, and took control of the local administrations. On July 11, the Gruppenstab to which we were subordinated traded designations with the one attached to Army Group Center: from then on, our Einsatzgruppe was called "C"; the same day, our three Opel Admirals entered Zhitomir behind the tanks of the Sixth Army. A few days later, I was sent to reinforce this Vorkommando, while we waited for the rest of headquarters to catch up with us.

After Tsviahel the landscape changed completely. Now it was the Ukrainian steppe, an immense undulating prairie, intensively cultivated. In the fields of grain the poppies had just died, but the rye and barley were ripening, and for kilometers on end, the sunflowers, raised toward the sky, tracked the wave of the sun. Here and there, as if thrown haphazardly, a line of isbas in the shade of acacia trees or little groves of oak, maple, and ash broke the dazzling perspectives. The country paths were bordered with lindens, the rivers with aspen and willow; in the towns they had planted chestnut trees along the boulevards. Our maps turned out to be completely inadequate: roads marked did not exist or had disappeared; yet sometimes where an empty steppe was indicated, our patrols discovered kolkhozes and vast fields of cotton, melons, beets; and tiny municipalities had become developed industrial centers. On the other hand, whereas Galicia had fallen almost intact into our hands, here, the Red Army had applied on its retreat a policy of systematic destruction. Villages, fields were burning; we found the wells dynamited or filled in, the roads mined, the buildings booby-trapped; in the kolkhozes there were still livestock, poultry, and women, but the men and the horses had left; in Zhitomir, they had burned everything they could: fortunately, a number of houses remained standing among the smoking ruins. The city was still under Hungarian control, and Callsen was furious: "Their officers treat the Jews like friends, they have dinner with the Jews!" Bohr, another officer, went on: "Apparently some of the officers are Jewish themselves. Can you imagine? Allies of Germany! I don't even dare shake their hands anymore." The inhabitants had received us well, but complained about the Honvéd advance into Ukrainian territory: "The Germans are our historic friends," they said. "The Magyars just want to annex us." These tensions broke out daily in countless incidents. A company of sappers had killed two Hungarians; one of our generals had to go apologize. For their part, the Honvéd were blocking the work of our local policemen, and the Vorkommando was forced to lodge a complaint, via the Gruppenstab, with the HQ of the Army Group, the OKHG South. Finally, on July 15, the Hungarians were relieved and AOK 6 took over Zhitomir, followed soon after by our Kommando as well as Gruppenstab C. In the meantime, I had been sent back to Tsviahel as a liaison officer. The Teilkommandos under Callsen, Hans and Janssen, had each been assigned a sector, radiating out almost up to the front, blocked in front of Kiev; to the south, our zone reached that of Ek 5, so operations had to be coordinated, since each Teilkommando functioned autonomously. This is how I found myself with Janssen in the region between Tsviahel and Rovno, on the border with Galicia. The brief summer storms were turning more and more often into showers, transforming the loess dust, fine as flour, into a sticky mud, thick and black, that the soldiers called *buna*. Endless stretches of swamp formed then, where the corpses and carcasses of horses scattered by the fighting slowly decomposed. Men were succumbing to endless diarrhea, and lice were making their appearance; even the trucks were getting stuck, and it was becoming increasingly difficult to move around. To help the Kommandos, we were recruiting many Ukrainian auxiliaries, nicknamed "Askaris" by the old Africa hands; they were financed by the local municipalities using confiscated Jewish funds. Many of them were Bulbovitsi, those Volhynian extremists Oberländer talked about (they took their name from Taras Bulba): after the liquidation of the OUN-B, they had been given the choice between a German uniform or the camps; most had melted back into the population, but some had come to sign up. Farther up north, on the other hand, between Pinsk, Mozyr, and Olevsk, the Wehrmacht had allowed a "Ukrainian Republic of Polesia" to be established, headed by a certain Taras Borovets, erstwhile proprietor of a quarry in Kostopol nationalized by the Bolsheviks; he hunted down isolated units of the Red Army and Polish partisans, and that freed more troops for us, so in exchange we tolerated him; but the Einsatzgruppe worried that he was protecting hostile elements of the OUN-B, the ones whom people jokingly called "OUN (Bolshevik)" in contrast to the "Mensheviks" of

Melnyk. We also recruited the *Volksdeutschen* we found in the communities, to serve as mayors or policemen. The Jews, almost everywhere,
had been conscripted into forced labor; and we were beginning systematically to shoot the ones who didn't work. But on the Ukrainian
side of the Sbrutch, our actions were often frustrated by the apathy of
the local population, which did not inform on the movements of the
Jews: the Jews took advantage of this to move around illegally, hiding in
the forests to the North. Our Brigadeführer, Rasch, gave the order then
to have the Jews parade in public before executions, in order to destroy
in the eyes of the Ukrainian peasants the myth of Jewish political power.
But such measures didn't seem to have much effect.

One morning, Janssen suggested I come witness an action. That had
to happen sooner or later, I knew it and had thought about it. I can in
all honesty say that I had doubts about our methods: I had trouble grasping their logic. I had talked with Jewish prisoners; they told me that for
them, bad things had always come from the East, and good ones, from
the West; in 1918 they had welcomed our troops as liberators, saviors;
those troops had behaved very humanely; after their departure,
Petliura's Ukrainians had returned to massacre them. As for Bolshevik
power, it starved the people. Now, we were killing them. And undeni-
ably, we were killing a lot of people. That seemed atrocious to me, even
if it was inevitable and necessary. But one has to confront atrocity; one
must always be ready to look inevitability and necessity in the face, and
accept the consequences that result from them; closing your eyes is
never an answer. I accepted Janssen's offer. The action was commanded
by Untersturmführer Nagel, his adjunct; I left Tsviahel with him. It had
rained the night before but the road was still good; we traveled slowly
between two high walls of green streaming with light, which hid the
fields from us. The village, I've forgotten its name, was on the edge of
a wide river, a few miles beyond the old Soviet border; it was a mixed
hamlet, the Galician peasants lived to one side, the Jews to the other. At
our arrival I found the cordons already deployed. Nagel had pointed to
a wood behind the hamlet: "That's where it happens." He seemed nervous, hesitant; he too had probably never killed anyone yet. On the
main square, our Askaris were gathering the Jews, men of advanced age,
adolescents; they took them in little groups from the Jewish alleyways,
sometimes striking them, then they forced them to crouch down,
guarded by a few Orpos. Some Germans were accompanying them too;
one of them, Gnauk, was lashing the Jews with a horsewhip to push
them on. But apart from the shouting everything seemed relatively
calm, well ordered. There weren't any spectators; from time to time, a
child appeared in the corner of the square, looked at the squatting Jews,

then went away. "We need another half hour, I think," Nagel said.—
"Can I look round?" I asked him.—"Yes, of course. But take your orderly with you." That's what he called Popp, who ever since Lemberg
was always with me and prepared my quarters and my coffee, polished
my boots, and washed my uniforms; not that I had asked him for anything. I headed toward the little Galician farms, in the direction of the
river, with Popp following a few steps behind, rifle on his shoulder. The
houses were long and low; the doors remained obstinately closed; I
didn't see anyone at the windows. In front of a wooden gate coarsely
painted pale blue, about thirty geese were noisily cackling, waiting to go
back in. I went past the last houses and down to the river, but the bank
grew swampy, I climbed back up a little; farther on, I caught sight of the
woods. The air resounded with the throbbing, obsessive croaking of
frogs mating. Farther up, threading their way between soaked fields
where pools of water reflected the sun, a dozen white geese were walking in a line, fat and proud, followed by a frightened calf. I had already
had a chance to visit some villages in the Ukraine: they seemed much
poorer and more miserable than this one; Oberländer would be disappointed to see his theories demolished. I turned back. In front of the
blue gate, the geese were still waiting, watching a weeping cow, its eyes
swarming with clusters of flies. In the square, the Askaris were making
the Jews get into trucks, shouting and whipping them, though the Jews
were not resisting. Two Ukrainians, in front of me, were dragging an
old man with a wooden leg; his prosthesis came off and they threw him
unceremoniously into the truck. Nagel had walked away; I caught hold
of one of the Askaris and pointed to the wooden leg: "Put that with him
in the truck." The Ukrainian shrugged, picked up the leg, and tossed it
in after the old man. About thirty Jews could be crammed into each
truck; there must have been 150 in all, but we only had three trucks, so
it would take two trips. When the trucks were full, Nagel motioned me
to get into the Opel and headed toward the wood, followed by the
trucks. At the edge, the cordon was already in place. The trucks were
unloaded, then Nagel gave the order to pick the Jews who would go
and dig; the others would wait there. A Hauptscharführer made the selection, and shovels were handed out; Nagel formed an escort and the
group disappeared into the wood. The trucks had already left. I looked
at the Jews: the ones closest to me looked pale, but calm. Nagel approached and bawled at me sharply, pointing to the Jews: "It's necessary,
you understand? Human suffering mustn't count for anything in all
this."—"Yes, but still it does count for something." This was what I
couldn't manage to grasp: the yawning gap, the absolute contradiction
between the ease with which one can kill and the huge difficulty there

must be in dying. For us, it was another dirty day's work; for them, the end of everything.

Shouts were coming from the wood. "What is it?" Nagel asked.— "I don't know, Untersturmführer," a noncom said, "I'll go see." He went into the wood. Some Jews were shuffling back and forth, dragging their feet, their eyes fixed on the ground, in the sullen silence of dull men waiting for death. A teenager, crouching on his heels, was humming a nursery rhyme and looking at me with curiosity; he put two fingers to his lips; I gave him a cigarette and some matches: he thanked me with a smile. The noncom reappeared at the entrance to the woods and called out: "They found a mass grave, Untersturmführer."—"What? A mass grave?" Nagel headed toward the wood and I followed him. Under the trees, the Hauptscharführer was slapping one of the Jews, shouting: "You knew, you bastard! Why didn't you tell us?"—"What's going on?" Nagel asked. The Hauptscharführer stopped slapping the Jew and answered: "Look, Untersturmführer. We've discovered a Bolshevik grave." I approached the trench dug by the Jews; at the bottom, you could make out moldy, shriveled, almost mummified bodies. "They must have been shot in the winter," I observed. "That's why they haven't decomposed." A soldier in the bottom of the trench stood up. "It looks like they were killed with a bullet in the neck, Untersturmführer. NKVD work for sure." Nagel summoned the *Dolmetscher*. "Ask him what happened." The interpreter translated as the Jew spoke. "He says the Bolsheviks arrested a lot of men in the village. But he says they didn't know that they were buried here."— "These scum didn't know!" the Hauptscharführer exploded. "They killed them themselves, you mean!"—"Hauptscharführer, calm down. Have this grave filled in again and go dig somewhere else. But mark the place, in case we have to come back for an investigation." We returned to the cordon; the trucks were arriving with the remaining Jews. Twenty minutes later the Hauptscharführer, beet red, joined us. "We've come across more bodies, Untersturmführer. It's not possible, they've filled the forest." Nagel called a little meeting. "There aren't many clearings in this wood," a noncom suggested, "that's why we're digging in the same places as they did." While they talked, I gradually noticed long splinters of very fine wood stuck in my fingers, right under the nails; feeling around, I discovered that they went down to the knuckle, just beneath the skin. This was strange. How had they gotten there? I hadn't felt anything. I began to pull them out delicately, one by one, trying to avoid drawing blood. Fortunately they slipped out easily enough. Nagel seemed to have reached a decision: "There's another part of the wood, over there, it's lower down. We'll go try on that side."—"I'll wait for you here," I said.

"Fine, Obersturmführer. I'll send someone to get you." Absorbed, I flexed my fingers several times: everything seemed in order. I walked away from the cordon along a gentle incline, through tall weeds and flowers, already almost dry. Farther down began a wheat field, guarded by a crow crucified by its feet, its wings spread out. I lay down in the grass and looked at the sky; my soul spread calm and flat over the field, gently lazing out to the rim of the woods. I closed my eyes.

Popp came to find me. "They're almost ready, Obersturmführer." The cordon with the Jews had moved to the lower part of the wood. The condemned men were waiting under the trees, in little groups; some were leaning on the tree trunks. Farther on, in the woods, Nagel was waiting with the Ukrainians. Some Jews at the bottom of a trench several yards long were still throwing shovelfuls of mud over the embankment. I leaned over: water filled the ditch; the Jews were digging with muddy water up to their knees. "That's not a trench, that's a swimming pool," I remarked rather dryly to Nagel. He didn't take the remark too kindly: "What do you want me to do, Obersturmführer? We've hit an aquifer, and it's rising as they dig. We're too close to the river. But I'm not going to spend all day having holes dug in this forest." He turned to the Hauptscharführer. "Fine, that's enough. Tell them to get out." He was livid. "Your shooters are ready?" he asked. I understood that they were going to have the Ukrainians shoot. "Yes, Untersturmführer," the Hauptscharführer replied. He turned to the *Dolmetscher* and explained the procedure. The *Dolmetscher* translated for the Ukrainians. Twenty of them came to stand in a line in front of the trench; five others took the Jews who had dug, and who were covered in mud, and made them kneel along the edge, their backs to the shooters. On an order from the Hauptscharführer, the Askaris shouldered their rifles and aimed at the Jews' necks. But the count wasn't right; there were supposed to be two shooters per Jew, but they had taken fifteen Jews to dig. The Hauptscharführer recounted, then ordered the Ukrainians to lower their rifles and had five of the Jews rise again and go wait on the side. Several of them were reciting something in a low voice, prayers no doubt, but aside from that they weren't saying anything. "We should add some more Askaris," suggested another noncom. "It would go faster." A little discussion followed; there were only twenty-five Ukrainians in all; the noncom suggested adding five Orpos; the Hauptscharführer argued that they couldn't deplete the cordon. Nagel, exasperated, made a decision: "Continue as is." The Hauptscharführer barked an order and the Askaris raised their rifles. Nagel advanced a step. "At my command . . ." His voice quivered; he was making an effort to master it. "Fire!" The burst of shots crackled and I saw what looked like a red splatter, masked by the smoke of the rifles. Most of the men killed flew forward, face down in the water; two of them still lay there, huddled at the edge of the ditch. "Clean that up and bring the next ones," Nagel ordered. Some Ukrainians took the two dead Jews by the arms and feet and threw them into the ditch; they landed with a loud splash of water, the blood streamed from their smashed heads and spurted onto the Ukrainians' boots and green uniforms. Two men came forward with shovels and started cleaning the edge of the ditch, throwing clumps of bloody earth and whitish fragments of brain in to join the dead men. I went to look: the corpses were floating in the muddy water, some on their stomach, others on their backs with noses and beards sticking out of the water; blood was spreading out from their heads on the surface, like a fine layer of oil, but bright red; their white shirts were red too and little red trickles were flowing on their skin and in the hairs of their beards. They brought the second group, the five who had dug and five others from the edge of the wood, and set them on their knees facing the ditch, the floating bodies of their neighbors; one of them turned around to face the shooters, his head raised, and watched them in silence. I thought about these Ukrainians: How had they gotten to this point? Most of them had fought against the Poles, and then against the Soviets, they must have dreamed of a better future, for themselves and for their children, and now they found themselves in a forest, wearing a strange uniform and killing people who had done nothing to them, without any reason they could understand. What could they be thinking about all this? Still, when they were given the order, they shot, they pushed the bodies into the ditch and brought other ones, they didn't protest. What would they think of all this later on? Once again, they had fired. Now we could hear moans coming from the ditch. "Oh hell, they're not all dead," the Hauptscharführer muttered.—"Well, finish them off," Nagel shouted. On an order from the Hauptscharführer, two Askaris came forward and fired again into the ditch. The groans continued. They fired a third time. Next to them others were cleaning up the edge. Once again, a bit farther, ten more Jews were being brought up. I noticed Popp: he had taken a fistful of earth from the large pile next to the ditch and was contemplating it, kneading it between his fingers, smelling it, even taking a little in his mouth. "What is it, Popp?" He approached me: "Look at this earth, Obersturmführer. It's good earth. A man could do worse than live here." The Jews were kneeling down. "Throw that away, Popp," I said to him.—"They told us that afterward we could come settle here, build farms. It's a good region, that's all I'm saying."—"Be quiet, Popp." The Askaris had fired another salvo. Once again, piercing shouts rose up from the ditch, moans. "Please, dear Germans! Please!" The Hauptscharführer ordered them finished off, but the shouts didn't stop, we could hear men struggling in the water, Nagel was yelling too: "They shoot like lame idiots, your men! Make them go down in the hole."—"But, Untersturmführer . . ."—"Make them go down!" The Hauptscharführer had the order translated. The Ukrainians started talking agitatedly. "What are they saying?" Nagel asked. "They don't want to go in, Untersturmführer," the *Dolmetscher* explained. "They say there's no point, they can shoot from the edge." Nagel was red. "Make them go down!" The Hauptscharführer seized one by the arm and pulled him over to the ditch; the Ukrainian resisted. Everyone was shouting now, in Ukrainian and German. A little farther on, the next group of Jews was waiting. Enraged, the chosen Askari threw his rifle on the ground and jumped into the ditch, slipped, floundered among the corpses and the dying. His comrade went down after him, holding on to the edge, and helped him get up. The Ukrainian swore and spat, covered in mud and blood. The Hauptscharführer held out his rifle. On the left we heard several gunshots, shouts; the men from the cordon were shooting into the woods: one of the Jews had taken advantage of the commotion to cut and run. "Did you get him?" Nagel called.—"I don't know, Untersturmführer," one of the policemen replied from a distance.—"Well then go look!" Two other Jews suddenly dashed to the other side and the Orpos started shooting: one of them fell immediately, the other vanished into the woods. Nagel had taken out his pistol and was waving it around, shouting contradictory orders. In the ditch, the Askari was trying to press his rifle against the forehead of a wounded Jew, but he was rolling in the water, his head kept disappearing beneath the surface. The Ukrainian finally fired blind, the shot took the Jew's jaw away but still didn't kill him, he was struggling, catching on to the Ukrainian's legs. "Nagel," I said.—"What?" His face was haggard, the pistol hung from his arm.—"I'm going to go wait in the car." In the wood, we could hear gunshots, the Orpos were shooting at the fugitives; I glanced fleetingly at my fingers, to make sure I had taken out all the splinters. Near the ditch, one of the Jews started weeping.

Such amateurishness soon became the exception. As the weeks went by, the officers acquired experience, and the soldiers got used to the procedures; at the same time, one could see that everyone was searching for his place in all this, thinking about what was happening, each in his own way. At table, at night, the men discussed the actions, told anecdotes, and compared their experiences, some sadly, others cheerfully. Still others were silent; they were the ones who had to be watched. We had already had two suicides; and one night, a man woke up emptying his rifle into the ceiling, he had to be held down by force, and a noncom had almost been killed. Some reacted with brutality, sometimes sadism: they struck at the condemned, tormented them before making them die; the officers tried to control these outbursts, but it was difficult, there were excesses. Very often our men photographed the executions; in their quarters, they exchanged their photos for tobacco, or stuck them to the wall—anyone could order prints of them. We knew, through the military censors, that many of them sent these photos to their families in Germany; some even made little albums of them, with captions; this phenomenon worried the hierarchy but seemed impossible to control. Even the officers were losing their grip. Once, while the Jews were digging, I surprised Bohr singing: "The earth is cold, the earth is sweet, dig, little Jew, dig deep." The *Dolmetscher* was translating; it shocked me deeply. I had known Bohr for some time now, he was a normal man, he had no particular animosity against the Jews, he did his duty as he was told; but obviously, it was eating at him, he wasn't reacting well. Of course there were some genuine anti-Semites in the Kommando: Lübbe, for example, another Untersturmführer, seized the slightest occasion to rant against the Hebrews with extreme virulence, as if the whole of world Judaism were nothing but a vast conspiracy aimed at him, Lübbe. He tired everyone out with this. But his attitude toward the actions was strange: sometimes he behaved brutally, but sometimes in the morning he was overcome with violent diarrhea; he would report sick and had to be replaced. "God, how I hate those vermin," he said as he watched them die, "but what a filthy job." And when I asked him if his convictions didn't help him bear it, he retorted: "Listen, just because I eat meat doesn't mean I want to work in a slaughterhouse." He was transferred anyhow, a few months later, when Dr. Thomas, the replacement for Brigadeführer Rasch, purged the Kommandos. But increasingly the officers as well as the men were becoming hard to control; they thought they were allowed to do all sorts of things, unimaginable things—and this is probably normal, with this sort of work the boundaries get confused, grow vague. And then there were some who stole from the Jews, kept gold watches, rings, money, even though everything was supposed to be turned in to the Kommandostab to be sent to Germany. During the actions, the officers were obliged to watch the Orpos, the Waffen-SS, the Askaris, to make sure they didn't make off with anything. But officers too kept things. And also they drank, the sense of discipline started to unravel. One evening, we were billeted in a village, Bohr brought back two girls, Ukrainian peasants, and some vodka. He and Zorn and Müller started drinking with the girls and feeling them up, putting their hands under their skirts. I was sitting on my bed and trying to read. Bohr called to me: "Come take your fill too."—"No, thanks." One of the girls was unbuttoned, half naked, her flabby breasts drooped a little. This sour lust, this sagging flesh, disgusted me, but I had nowhere to go. "You're not much fun, Doktor," Bohr snapped at me. I looked at them as if I had X-ray vision: beneath the flesh I could clearly make out the skeletons; when Zorn embraced one of the girls it was as if their bones, separated by a thin gauze, knocked together; when they laughed, the grating sound burst forth from the jaws in the skulls; tomorrow, they would already be old, the girls would grow obese or, on the contrary, their exhausted skin would hang on their bones, their dry, empty teats would fall like a drained wine skin, and then Bohr and Zorn and these girls too would die and be buried under the cold earth, the soft earth, just like all those Jews mowed down in the prime of life, their mouths full of earth would laugh no more, so what was the use of this sad debauchery? If I asked Zorn that question, I knew what he'd say: "Just that: to have a little fun before I croak, nothing more, just a little pleasure," but I had nothing against pleasure, I too could take my pleasure when I wanted it, no, it was probably their terrifying lack of self-awareness, that surprising way of never thinking about things, good or bad, of letting themselves be carried along with the current, killing without understanding why and without caring either, groping women because they were willing, drinking without even seeking to be absolved of their bodies. That is what I didn't understand, but no one was asking me to understand anything.

In the beginning of August, the Sonderkommando conducted a preliminary cleansing of Zhitomir. According to our statistics, thirty thousand Jews lived there before the war; but most of them had fled with the Red Army, so no more than five thousand remained, 9 percent of the present population. Rasch had decided that was still too many. General Reinhardt, who commanded the Ninety-ninth Division, lent us some soldiers for the *Durchkämmung*, a fine but untranslatable German word that suggests a sifting-through. Everyone was a little tense: on August 1, Galicia had been reunited to the Generalgouvernement and the Nachtigall regiments had rebelled as far as Vinnitsa and Tiraspol. All the OUN-B officers and noncoms among our auxiliaries had to be identified, arrested, and sent along with the officers of the Nachtigall to join Bandera in Sachsenhausen. Since then, we had to keep an eye on the remaining ones, not all of them could be trusted. In Zhitomir itself, some Bandera supporters had assassinated two pro-Melnyk officials that we had put in place; at first, suspicion had fallen on the Communists; then we had shot all the OUN-B supporters we could find. Fortunately, our relations with the Wehrmacht were turning out to be excellent. The veterans of Poland were surprised at this; they had expected at best a grudging consent, but now our relations with the various headquarters were growing positively cordial. Often it was the army that took the initiative for actions; they asked us to liquidate the Jews in villages where acts of sabotage had taken place, as retaliation or because the Jews were regarded as partisans, and they turned over Jews and Gypsies to us to execute. Von Roques, the commander of the Rear Army Group Area South, had given the order that if the authors of some act of sabotage couldn't be identified with certainty, we should conduct reprisals against Jews or Russians, since we shouldn't arbitrarily blame the Ukrainians: *We must convey the impression that we are just.* Of course, not all the officers of the Wehrmacht approved of these measures; the older officers especially, according to Rasch, still lacked understanding. The Group was also having some problems with certain Dulag commanders, who were reluctant to hand over Commissars and Jewish prisoners of war to us. But von Reichenau, it was known, defended the SP vigorously. And sometimes, on the contrary, the Wehrmacht outdid us. The HQ of one division wanted to set up in a village, but there wasn't enough room: "We still have the Jews," their Chief of Staff suggested to us; and the AOK supported his request, so we had to shoot all the male Jews in the village, then regroup the women and children into a few houses so as to free up some quarters for the officers. In the report this was listed as a retaliation. Another division went so far as to ask us to liquidate the patients of an insane asylum they wanted to occupy; the Gruppenstab replied indignantly that *the Staatspolizei are not hangmen for the Wehrmacht*: "No interest of the SP makes this action necessary. Do it yourselves." (Yet, another time, Rasch had had some lunatics shot because all the hospital guards and nurses had left, and he thought that if the patients took advantage of this to escape, they would constitute a security risk.) What's more it looked like things were soon going to get worse. Rumors reached us from Galicia about *new methods*: Jeckeln, apparently, had received considerable reinforcements and was conducting much more extensive cleansings than anything that had been undertaken till then. Callsen, back from a mission in Tarnopol, had vaguely mentioned a new *Ölsardinenmanier* to us, but he refused to elaborate, and no one really knew what he was talking about. And then Blobel had returned. He was cured, and in fact seemed to drink less, but he was just as quarrelsome as ever. I now spent most of my time in Zhitomir. Thomas was there too and I saw him almost every day. It was very hot.

In the orchards, the trees bowed under the weight of the purple plums and the apricots; in the individual plots, on the outskirts of the city, you could see the heavy masses of pumpkins, a few ears of corn already dried out, some isolated rows of sunflowers, their heads bent to the ground. When we had some free time Thomas and I left the city to take a boat out on the Teterev and swim; then, lying under the apple trees, we drank bad white wine from Bessarabia and bit into ripe fruit, always within arm's reach in the grass. At that time there weren't yet any partisans in the region, so it was calm. Sometimes we read curious or amusing passages out loud to each other, like students. Thomas had unearthed a French pamphlet from the *Institut d'Études des Questions Juives*, the Institute for the Study of Jewish Questions. "Listen to this amazing prose. Article on 'Biology and Collaboration,' by a certain Charles Laville. Here it is. *A policy must be biological or not exist.* Listen, listen: *Do we want to remain a common polypary? Or do we on the contrary want to move toward a superior stage of organization?*" He read in French with an almost singsong accent. "Answer: *The cellular associations of elements with complementary tendencies are what have permitted the formation of superior animals, up to man. To refuse that which is now offered to us would be, in a way, a crime against humanity, as well as against biology.*" For my part, I was reading Stendhal's correspondence. One day, some sappers invited us onto their motorboat; Thomas, already a little drunk, had wedged a crate of grenades between his thighs and, comfortably stretched out in the bow, he fished them up one by one, took the pin out, and tossed them lazily over his head; the gushes of water thrown up by the underwater detonations splashed over us, while the sappers, armed with nets, tried to catch the dozens of dead fish that bobbed up in the wake of the boat; they laughed, and I admired their tanned skin and careless youth. At night, Thomas sometimes came to our quarters to listen to music. Bohr had found a young Jewish orphan and had adopted him as a mascot: the boy washed the cars, polished the officers' boots, and cleaned their pistols, but above all he played the piano like a young god, light, nimble, cheerful. "Fingers like that excuse everything, even being Jewish," Bohr said. He had him play Beethoven or Haydn, but the boy, Yakov, preferred Bach. He seemed to know all the suites by heart, it was wonderful. Even Blobel tolerated him. When Yakov wasn't playing, I sometimes entertained myself by jokingly taunting my colleagues, I read them passages from Stendhal about the retreat from Russia. Some of them took offense: "Yes, the French, maybe, they're good for nothing. But we are Germans."—"Certainly. But the Russians, however, are still Russians."—"Not at all!" Blobel blurted out. "Seventy or eighty per cent of the population of the USSR are of Mongol stock. It's proven.

And the Bolsheviks had a policy of deliberate racial mixing. During the Great War, yes, we fought against authentic Russian *muzhiks*, and it's true they were tough bastards, real bruisers, but the Bolsheviks exterminated them! There are almost no real Russians, real Slavs left. In any case," he went on without any logic, "the Slavs are by definition a mixed race, a race of slaves. Of bastards. Not a single one of their princes was really Russian, it was always Norman, Mongol, then German blood. Even their national poet was a negro *Mischling*, and they tolerate it, that's proof . . ."—"In any case," Vogt added sententiously, "God is with the German nation and the *Volk*. We cannot lose this war."— "God?" Blobel spat out. "God is a Communist. And if I ever meet him, he'll end up like his Commissars."

He knew what he was talking about. In Cherniakov, the SP had arrested the president of the regional *Troïka* of the NKVD, along with one of his colleagues, and had sent them to Zhitomir. Interrogated by Vogt and his colleagues, this judge, Wolf Kieper, admitted he had had more than 1,350 people executed. He was a Jew in his early sixties, a Communist since 1905 and a People's Judge since 1918; the other one, Moishe Kogan, was younger, but he was also a member of the Cheka and a Jew. Blobel had discussed the case with Rasch and Oberst Heim and they had agreed on a public execution. Kieper and Kogan were tried before a military court and condemned to death. On August 7, early in the morning, officers from the Sonderkommando, supported by Orpos and our Askaris, conducted arrests of Jews and gathered them together in the market square. The Sixth Army had made available a propaganda company car with a loudspeaker that wound through the streets of the city and announced the execution in German and Ukrainian. I arrived at the square toward late morning, accompanied by Thomas. More than four hundred Jews had been assembled and forced to sit down, their hands clasped at the back of their necks, next to the tall gallows put up the day before by the Sonderkommando drivers. Beyond the Waffen-SS cordon, hundreds of onlookers were flooding in, soldiers especially but also men from the *Organisation Todt* and from the NSKK, as well as many Ukrainian civilians. These spectators filled the square on all sides; it was difficult to clear a path through them; about thirty soldiers were even perched on the metal roof of a neighboring building. The men were laughing and joking; a lot of them were photographing the scene. Blobel was standing at the foot of the gallows along with Häfner, who had just returned from Belaya Tserkov. In front of the rows of Jews, von Radetzky was haranguing the crowd in Ukrainian: "Does someone have an account to settle with one of these Jews?" he asked. A man emerged from the crowd and kicked one of the seated men, then returned; others threw fruit and rotten tomatoes at them. I watched the Jews: their faces were gray, they looked anguished, wondering what was going to happen next. There were a lot of old men among them, but some quite young ones too. I noticed that in the cordon of guards were several Landsers from the Wehrmacht. "What are they doing here?" I asked Häfner.—"They're volunteers. They asked to help." I made a face. A number of officers could be seen, but I didn't recognize anyone from the AOK. I headed toward the cordon and questioned one of the soldiers: "What are you doing here? Who asked you to stand guard?" He looked embarrassed. "Where is your superior?"—"I don't know, Herr Offizier," he finally replied, scratching his forehead under his cap.—"What are you doing here?" I repeated.—"I went to the ghetto this morning, with my comrades, Herr Offizier. And then we offered to help out, your colleagues said yes. I had ordered a pair of leather boots from a Jew and I wanted to try to find him before . . . before . . ." He didn't even dare say the word.—"Before they shoot him, is that it?" I said sharply.—"Yes, Herr Offizier."—"And did you find him?"—"He's over there. But I haven't been able to speak to him." I returned to where Blobel was. "Standartenführer, the men from the Wehrmacht should be dismissed. It's not normal for them to participate in the *Aktion* without orders."—"Leave it, leave it alone, Obersturmführer. It's wonderful they're showing enthusiasm. They're good National Socialists, they want to do their part too." I shrugged and rejoined Thomas. He gestured to the crowd with his chin: "We should have sold tickets, we'd be rich." He snickered. "At the AOK, they call this *Executionstourismus*." The truck had arrived and was maneuvering under the gallows. Two Waffen-SS had Kieper and Kogan come out. They were in peasant shirts and had their hands tied behind their backs. Kieper's beard had turned white since his arrest. Our drivers placed a plank atop the truck's side, climbed up on it, and started attaching the ropes. I noticed Höfler standing apart, smoking glumly; Bauer, Blobel's personal driver, was testing the knots. Then Zorn also climbed up and the Waffen-SS hoisted up the two condemned men. They were placed standing below the gallows, and Zorn made a speech; he spoke in Ukrainian, he must have been explaining the sentence. The spectators were yelling and hissing, and he had difficulty making himself heard; several times he made gestures to silence them, but no one was paying any attention. Soldiers were taking pictures, pointing at the condemned men, and laughing. Then Zorn and one of the Waffen-SS placed the nooses around their necks. The two condemned men remained silent, withdrawn into themselves. Zorn and the others came down from the board and Bauer started up the truck. "Slower, slower," shouted the

Landsers, who were taking photographs. The truck moved forward, the two men tried to keep their balance, then they fell over, one after the other, and swung back and forth several times. Kieper's pants had fallen around his ankles; below his shirt, he was naked; horrified, I saw his engorged penis, still ejaculating. *"Nix Kultura!"* a Landser bellowed, and others took up the cry. On the posts of the gallows, Zorn was nailing signs explaining the condemnation; they stated that Kieper's 1,350 victims were *all Volksdeutschen and Ukrainians.*

Then the soldiers in the cordon ordered the Jews to stand up and march. Blobel got into his car with Häfner and Zorn; von Radetzky invited me to come with him and also took Thomas. The crowd followed the Jews, there was an immense commotion. Everyone headed outside the city toward what people called the *Pferdefriedhof,* the horse cemetery: a trench had been dug there, with thick beams stacked up behind, to stop stray bullets. Obersturmführer Grafhorst, who commanded our company of Waffen-SS, was waiting with about twenty of his men. Blobel and Häfner inspected the trench, then we waited. I was thinking. I thought about my life, about what relationship there could be between this life that I had lived—an entirely ordinary life, the life of anyone, but also in some respects an extraordinary, an unusual life, although the unusual is also very ordinary—and what was happening here. There must have been a relationship, and it was a fact, there was one. True, I wasn't taking part in the executions, I wasn't commanding the firing squads; but that didn't change much, since I often attended them, I helped prepare them and then I wrote the reports; what's more, it was just by chance that I had been posted to the Stab rather than to the Teilkommandos. And if they had given me a Teilkommando, would I too have been able, like Nagel or Häfner, to organize the roundups, have the ditches dug, line up the condemned men, and shout "Fire!"? Yes, certainly. Ever since I was a child, I had been haunted by a passion for the absolute, for the overcoming of all limits; and now this passion had led me to the edge of the mass graves of the Ukraine. I had always wanted my thinking to be radical; and now the State, the nation had also chosen the radical and the absolute; how, then, just at that moment, could I turn my back, say no, and at the end of the day prefer the comfort of bourgeois laws, the mediocre assurance of the social contract? That was obviously impossible. And if this radicalism was the radicalism of the abyss, and if the absolute turned out to be absolute evil, one still had to follow them to the end, with eyes wide open—of that at least I was utterly convinced. The crowd was arriving and filling the cemetery; I noticed some soldiers in bathing suits; there were also women, children. People were drinking beer and passing cigarettes around. I looked at a

group of officers from headquarters: Oberst von Schuler was there, the
IIa, along with several other officers. Grafhorst, our Kompanieführer,
was positioning his men. Now we were using one rifle per Jew, a bullet in the chest at the level of the heart. Often that wasn't enough to kill,
and a man had to go down into the trench to finish them off; the
screams resounded among the chatter and clamor of the crowd. Häfner,
who was more or less officially commanding the action, was shouting
himself hoarse. Between the salvos, men emerged from the crowd and
asked the Waffen-SS to trade places with them; Grafhorst didn't object
to this, and his men handed their rifles over to the Landsers, who tried
one or two shots before returning to join their comrades. Grafhorst's
Waffen-SS were quite young and, since the beginning of the execution,
seemed disturbed. Häfner began bawling one of them out, who at each
salvo handed his rifle over to a volunteer soldier and stood off to the
side, white as a sheet. And then there were too many shots that missed
and that was a problem. Häfner had the executions stopped and started
to confer with Blobel and two officers from the Wehrmacht. I didn't
know them, but could see from the colors of their collar patches that
one was a military judge and the other a doctor. Then Häfner went to
talk things over with Grafhorst. I saw that Grafhorst was objecting to
what Häfner was saying, but I couldn't hear their words. Finally Grafhorst
had a new batch of Jews brought over. They were positioned facing the
trench, but the shooters from the Waffen-SS aimed at the head rather
than the chest; the result was horrifying: the tops of their skulls flew into
the air, the shooters got pieces of brain splashed in their faces. One of
the volunteer shooters from the Wehrmacht was vomiting and his comrades were making fun of him. Grafhorst had flushed completely red
and was cursing Häfner; then he turned toward Blobel and the debate
started up again. Once again they changed methods: Blobel added some
shooters and they shot two at a time into the neck, as in July; Häfner
himself administered the deathblow when it was necessary.

The evening of that execution I accompanied Thomas to the Kasino.
The officers from the AOK were discussing the day animatedly; they
saluted us courteously, but seemed embarrassed, ill at ease. Thomas
started up a conversation; I withdrew into an alcove to smoke alone. After the meal, the discussions resumed again. I noticed the military judge
whom I had seen speaking with Blobel; he seemed particularly upset. I
approached and joined the group. The officers, I understood, had no
objection to the action itself, but to the presence of many soldiers from
the Wehrmacht and their participation in the executions. "If we give
them the order, that's one thing," the judge argued, "but as it is, it's inadmissible. It's a shame for the Wehrmacht."—"So," Thomas cut in,

"the SS can shoot, but the Wehrmacht can't even look?"—"It's not that, it's not that at all. It's a question of order. Tasks like this are disagreeable for everyone. But only those who have received the order should participate in them. Otherwise, all military discipline will collapse."—"I agree with Dr. Neumann," Niemeyer, the Abwehroffizier, said. "It's not a sporting event. The men were acting as if they were at the races."— "Still, Herr Oberstleutnant," I reminded him, "the AOK had agreed that this be publicly announced. You even lent us your PK."—"I'm not criticizing the SS at all, which is carrying out some very difficult work," Niemeyer replied, a bit on the defensive. "We did discuss it beforehand and we came to an agreement that this would be a good example for the civilian population, that it was useful for them to see with their own eyes how we are smashing the power of the Jews and the Bolsheviks. But things went a little too far here. Your men shouldn't have been handing their weapons over to ours."—"Your men," Thomas dryly retorted, "shouldn't have been asking for them."—"At the very least," barked Neumann, the judge, "we should raise the question with the Generalfeldmarschall."

The result of all this was a typical order from Reichenau: referring to our *necessary executions of criminals, Bolsheviks, and essentially Jewish elements,* he forbade soldiers in the Sixth Army, *without orders from a superior officer,* from attending, photographing, or participating in the actions. In itself that would probably not have changed much, but Rasch ordered us to conduct the actions outside the towns, and to set a cordon on the perimeter to prevent the presence of spectators. Discretion, it seemed, would henceforth be the rule of the day. But the desire to see these things was also human. Leafing through my Plato, I had found the passage of *The Republic* that my reaction in front of the corpses in the Lutsk fortress had brought to mind: *Leontius, the son of Aglaion, coming up one day from the Piraeus, under the north wall on the outside, observed, near the executioner, some dead bodies lying on the ground; and he felt a desire to look at them, and at the same time loathing the thought he tried to turn away. For a time he struggled with himself, and covered his eyes, till at length, overcome by the desire, he forced his eyes wide open with his fingers, and running up to the bodies, exclaimed, "There! you devils! gaze your fill at the beautiful spectacle!"* To tell the truth, the soldiers rarely seemed to feel Leontius's anguish, only his desire, and it must have been this that was disturbing the hierarchy, the idea that the men could take pleasure in these actions. Still, everyone who participated in them took some form of pleasure in them—that seemed obvious to me. Some, visibly, enjoyed the act itself, but these could be regarded as sick men, and it was right to ferret them out and give them other tasks, even punish them if they overstepped the bounds. As for the others, whether the actions repelled them or left them indifferent, they carried them out from a sense of duty and obligation, and thus drew pleasure from their devotion, from their ability to carry out such a difficult task despite their disgust and apprehension: "But I take no pleasure in killing," they often said, finding their pleasure, then, in their rigor and their righteousness. The hierarchy, obviously, had to consider these problems as a whole; the solutions could necessarily only be approximate or rough. *Einzelaktionen*, of course, individual actions, were rightly regarded as murders and were condemned. Berück von Roques had promulgated an interpretation of the OKW order on discipline, imposing a sixty-day confinement, for *insubordination*, on soldiers who shot Jews on their own initiative; in Lemberg, I had heard, a noncom had received six months in prison for the murder of an old Jewish woman. But as the actions became more widespread, it became increasingly difficult to control all their repercussions. On August 11 and 12, Brigadeführer Rasch gathered all his Sonderkommando and Einsatzkommando leaders together: besides Blobel, there were Hermann from 4b, Schulz from 5 and Kroeger from 6. Jeckeln came too. Blobel's birthday was on the thirteenth, and the officers had decided to throw him a party. During the day, he seemed in an even more execrable mood than usual, and spent long hours alone, locked up in his office. I myself was rather busy: we had just received an order from Gruppenführer Müller, the head of the Gestapo, to collect visual materials on our activities—photographs, films, posters, notices— to send to the Führer. I had gone to negotiate a small budget with Hartl, the administrator of the Gruppenstab, so as to buy copies of their photos from the men; he had started out by refusing, alleging an order from the Reichsführer forbidding members of the Einsatzgruppen to profit from executions in any way whatsoever; and for him, the sale of photographs constituted a profit. I finally managed to convince him that we couldn't ask the men to finance the Group's work out of their own pockets, and that we had to defray the expenses of printing the images we wanted to archive. He accepted, but on condition that we pay only for the photos of noncommissioned officers and soldiers; officers should reprint their photos at their own expense, if they took any. Armed with this agreement, I spent the rest of the day in the barracks, examining the men's collections and ordering prints. Some of them were remarkably accomplished photographers; but their work left me with an unpleasant aftertaste, and at the same time I couldn't take my eyes away from it, I was stunned. At night, the officers gathered in the mess, decorated for the occasion by Strehlke and his adjuncts. When Blobel joined us, he had already been drinking; his eyes were bloodshot, but he controlled himself and didn't speak much. Vogt, who was the oldest officer, presented him our best wishes and led the toast for his health; then he was asked to speak. He hesitated, then put down his glass and addressed us, his hands clasped behind his back. "Meine Herren! Thank you for your good wishes. Know that your confidence means a lot to me. I have to share some bad news with you. Yesterday, the HSSPF Russland-Süd, Obergruppenführer Jeckeln, delivered us a new order. This order came directly from the Reichsführer-SS and emanates, I want to emphasize this for you as he emphasized it for us, from the Führer himself." As he spoke, he winced; between phrases, he chewed the inside of his cheeks. "Our actions against the Jews will henceforth have to include the entire population. There will be no exceptions." The officers present reacted with consternation; several started talking at the same time. Callsen's voice rose, incredulous: "All of them?"—"All of them," Blobel confirmed.—"But look, that's impossible," Callsen said. He seemed to be begging. I remained silent; I felt a great coldness come over me; Oh Lord, I was saying to myself, now that too must be done, it has been spoken, and we'll have to go through that too. I felt invaded by a boundless horror, but I remained calm, nothing showed through, my breathing remained even. Callsen continued his objections: "But, Standartenführer, most of us are married, we have children. They can't ask us to do that."—"Meine Herren," Blobel snapped in a brutal but toneless voice, "this is a direct order from our Führer, Adolf Hitler. We are National Socialists and SS men, and we will obey. Understand this: in Germany, the Jewish question was able to be resolved, fully resolved, without excesses and in a manner in keeping with the requirements of humanity. But when we conquered Poland we inherited three million additional Jews. No one knows what to do with them or where to put them. Here, in this immense country, where we are waging a pitiless war of destruction against the Stalinist hordes, from the beginning we have had to take radical measures to ensure the security of our rear. I think you have all understood their necessity and efficacy. Our forces are not sufficient to patrol each village and at the same time wage battle; and we cannot allow ourselves to leave such treacherous, such sly potential enemies behind us. At the *Reichssicherheitshauptamt*, the possibility is being discussed, once the war is won, of gathering all Jews into a large reservation in Siberia or in the North. There, they'll be peaceful, and we will be too. But first we have to win the war. We have already executed thousands of Jews and there are still tens of thousands left; the more our forces advance, the more there will be. Now, if we execute only the men, there will be no one left to feed the women and their children. The Wehrmacht doesn't have the resources to feed tens of thousands of useless Jew females along with their brats. Nor can we leave them to die of hunger: those are Bolshevik methods. To include them in our actions, along with their husbands and their sons, is in fact the most humane solution given the circumstances. What's more, experience has taught us that the more procreative Eastern Jews are the original breeding ground from which the forces of Judeo-Bolshevism as well as of the capitalist plutocracy are constantly renewed. If we let some of them survive, those products of natural selection will be the source of a renewal even more dangerous for us than the present peril. The Jewish children of today are the saboteurs, the partisans, the terrorists of tomorrow." The officers were silent, glum; Kehrig, I noticed, was downing glass after glass. Blobel's bloodshot eyes glistened through the veil of alcohol. "We are all National Socialists," he continued, "SS men in the service of our *Volk* and our Führer. I remind you that *Führerworte haben Gesetzeskraft*, the Führer's word has the force of law. You must resist the temptation to be human." Blobel was not a very intelligent man; these striking sentences had certainly not originated from him. But he believed in them; even more important, he wanted to believe in them, and he was offering them in turn to those who needed them, those to whom they could be of use. For me, they weren't much use; I would have to work out my reasoning on my own. But it was hard for me to think about it; my head was buzzing with an intolerable pressure, I wanted to go to sleep. Callsen was fiddling with his wedding ring, I was sure he didn't realize it; he wanted to say something, but changed his mind. "A *Schweinerei*, this is a *grosse Schweinerei*," Häfner muttered, and no one contradicted him. Blobel seemed drained, out of ideas, but everyone could feel that his will was holding us and wouldn't let us go, just as other wills held him. In a State like ours, everyone had his assigned role: You, the victim, and You, the executioner, and no one had a choice, no one asked anyone's consent, since everyone was interchangeable, victims as well as executioners. Yesterday we had killed Jewish men, tomorrow it would be women and children, the day after tomorrow yet others; and after we had fulfilled our role, we would be replaced. Germany, at least, did not liquidate its executioners; on the contrary, it took care of them, unlike Stalin with his mania for purges; but that too was part of the logic of things. For the Russians, as for us, man counted for nothing; the nation, the State were everything; and in this sense we saw our reflection in each other. The Jews too had this strong feeling of community, of *Volk*: they mourned their dead, buried them if they could and said Kaddish; but as long as one single Jew remained alive, Israel lived. That, no doubt, was the reason they were our privileged enemies, they resembled us too much.

It wasn't a problem of humanity. Some people, of course, could criticize our actions in the name of religious values, but I wasn't one of them, and in the SS there must not have been many; or in the name of democratic values, but we had moved beyond what is called democracy in Germany sometime ago. Blobel's arguments, in fact, were not entirely idiotic: if the supreme value is the *Volk*, the people to which one belongs, and if the will of this *Volk* is embodied in a leader, then in fact, *Führerworte haben Gesetzeskraft*. But still it was vital to comprehend *within oneself* the necessity of the Führer's orders: if one accepted them out of a simple Prussian spirit of obedience, out of a *Knecht's* spirit, without understanding them and without accepting them, that is without *submitting* to them, then one was nothing but a sheep, a slave and not a man. When the Jew submitted to the Law, he felt that this Law lived in him, and the more terrible, hard, demanding it was, the more he loved it. National Socialism had to be that too: a living Law. Killing was a terrible thing; the reaction of the officers was a good proof of that, even if they didn't all draw the consequences of their own reactions; and the man for whom killing was not a terrible thing, killing an armed man as well as an unarmed man, and an unarmed man as well as a woman and her child, was nothing but an animal, unworthy of belonging to a community of men. But it was possible that this terrible thing was also a necessary thing; and in that case we had to submit to this necessity. Our propaganda repeated over and over again that the Russians were *Untermenschen*, sub-humans; but I refused to believe that. I had interrogated captured officers, Commissars, and I saw that they too were men like us, men who wished only good, who loved their families and their country. But these Commissars and these officers had caused millions of their own fellow citizens to die, they had deported the Kulaks, starved the Ukrainian peasantry, repressed and shot the bourgeois and deviationists of all stripes. Among them were sadists and psychopaths, of course, but also kind men, honest and upright, who sincerely wanted the good of their people and of the working class; and though they had gone astray, they were still men of good faith. They too were for the most part convinced of the necessity of what they were doing, they weren't all madmen, opportunists, and criminals like that Kieper; among our enemies too, a good and honest man could convince himself to do terrible things. What they were asking us to do now posed the same problem for us.

The next day I awoke distraught, with a sad rage stuck in my head. I went to see Kehrig and closed the office door: "I'd like to talk with

you, Sturmbannführer."—"What about, Obersturmführer?"—"About
the extermination order." He raised his bird's head and stared at me
through his fine-rimmed glasses: "There is nothing to discuss, Obersturmführer. Anyhow I'm leaving." He gestured to me to sit down.
"You're leaving? How's that?"—"I settled it with Brigadeführer Strecke-
enbach, with the help of a friend. I'm going back to Berlin."—
"When?"—"Soon, in a few days."—"And your replacement?" He
shrugged: "He'll come when he comes. In the meantime, you'll run the
shop." He stared at me again: "If you want to leave too, you know, that
can be arranged. I can go see Streckenbach for you in Berlin, if you
like."—"Thank you, Sturmbannführer. But I'll stay."—"Why?" he
asked sharply. "To end up like Häfner or Hans? To wallow in this
mud?"—"You've stayed till now," I said gently. He laughed dryly: "I requested my transfer at the beginning of July. In Lutsk. But you know
how it is, it takes time."—"I'll be sorry to see you leave, Sturmbannführer."—"Not me. What they want to do is insane. I'm not the only
one who thinks so. Schulz, from Kommando Five, broke down when
he learned about the *Vernichtungsbefehl*. He asked to leave right away,
and the Obergruppenführer gave his consent."—"You might be right.
But if you leave, if Oberführer Schulz leaves, if all the honorable men
leave, only the butchers will be left here, the dregs. We can't accept
that." He made a grimace of disgust: "Because you think you can
change something if you stay? You?" He shook his head. "No, Doktor,
follow my advice, leave. Let the butchers take care of the butchering."
"Thank you, Sturmbannführer." I shook his hand and left. I headed for
the Gruppenstab and went to find Thomas. "Kehrig is a sissy," he said
curtly when I had reported the conversation to him. "Schulz too. We've
had our eye on Schulz for a while now. In Lemberg, he let some condemned men go, without permission. All the better if he leaves, we
don't need men like that." He looked at me pensively. "Of course, it's
atrocious, what they're asking us to do. But you'll see, we'll get through
it." He suddenly grew even more serious. "I don't believe it's the right
solution. It's an emergency response, improvised because of the war. We
must win this war soon; afterward, we can discuss things more calmly,
and carefully think them through. More subtle opinions can be taken
into account. With the war, that's impossible."—"Do you think it will
last much longer? We were supposed to reach Moscow in five weeks.
It's been two months now and we haven't even taken Kiev or
Leningrad."—"It's hard to say. It's obvious that we underestimated their
industrial potential. Every time we think their reserves are exhausted,
they throw fresh divisions at us. But they must be reaching the end now.
And also, the Führer's decision to send us Guderian will soon open up

the front, here. As for Army Group Center, since the beginning of the month, they've taken four hundred thousand prisoners. And in Uman we're also surrounding two entire armies."

I returned to the Kommando. In the mess, alone, Yakov, Bohr's little Jew, was playing the piano. I sat down on a bench to listen to him. He was playing Mozart, the andante of one of the sonatas, and it brought a lump to my throat, deepening my sadness even more. When he had finished I asked him: "Yakov, do you know Rameau? Couperin?"—"No, Herr Offizier. What is it?"—"It's French music. You should learn it. I'll try to find some scores."—"Is it beautiful?"— "It might be the most beautiful thing there is." "More beautiful than Bach?" I considered the question: "Almost as beautiful as Bach," I acknowledged. This Yakov must have been about twelve years old, and could have played in any concert hall in Europe. He came from the region of Czernowitz and had grown up in a German-speaking family; with the occupation of the Bukovina, in 1940, he'd found himself in the USSR; his father had been deported by the Soviets and his mother had died in one of our air raids. He was truly a handsome boy: a long narrow face, full lips, black hair in untamed tufts, long blue-veined fingers. Everyone here liked him; even Lübbe left him alone. "Herr Offizier?" Yakov asked. He kept his eyes on the piano. "Can I ask you a question?"—"Of course."—"Is it true that you're going to kill all the Jews?" I straightened up: "Who told you that?"—"Last night, I heard Herr Bohr talking with the other officers. They were shouting very loudly."—"They were drinking. You shouldn't have been listening." He insisted, his eyes still lowered: "So you'll kill me, too?"—"Of course not." My hands were tingling, I forced myself to keep a normal, almost cheerful tone of voice: "Why would we want to kill you?"—"I'm Jewish too."—"That's all right, you work for us. You're a *Hiwi* now." He began hitting a key gently, a high note: "The Russians always told us that the Germans were mean. But I don't think so. I like you." I didn't say anything. "Would you like me to play?"—"Play."—"What would you like me to play?"—"Play whatever you like."

The mood within the Kommando was becoming execrable; the officers were nervous, they shouted at the slightest provocation. Callsen and the others went back to their Teilkommandos; everyone kept his opinions to himself, but you could see that the new tasks weighed on them. Kehrig left quickly, almost without saying goodbye. Lübbe was often sick. From the field, the Teilkommandoführers sent very negative reports on the morale of their troops: there were nervous depressions, the men often cried; according to Sperath, many were suffering from sexual impotence. There was a series of incidents with the Wehrmacht:

Near Korosten, a Hauptscharführer forced some Jewish women to undress and made them run naked in front of a machine gun; he took photos, and these photos were intercepted by the AOK. In Belaya Tserkov, Häfner had a confrontation with an officer from division headquarters, who had intervened to block the execution of some Jewish orphans; Blobel had to go down there himself and the affair went all the way up to von Reichenau, who confirmed the execution and reprimanded the officer; but it created quite a few ripples, and furthermore Häfner refused to inflict that on his men, and left the dirty work to his Askaris. Other officers did the same; but as the difficulties with the OUN-B persisted, this practice in turn engendered new problems: the Ukrainians, disgusted, were deserting or even committing treason. Others, however, carried out the executions without grumbling, but they shamelessly stole from the Jews and raped the women before killing them; sometimes we had to shoot our own soldiers. Kehrig's replacement hadn't arrived, and I was overwhelmed with work. At the end of the month, Blobel sent me to Korosten. The "Republic of Polesia," northeast of the city, was off-limits to us per order of the Wehrmacht, but there was still a lot of work in the region. The officer in charge was Kurt Hans. I didn't like Hans much—he was a foul man, moody; and he didn't like me, either. Still, we had to work together. The methods had changed, they had been rationalized, systematized according to the new demands. But these changes still didn't make the soldiers' work any easier. Now the condemned had to undress before execution, since their clothing was collected for the Winter Aid and the repatriates. In Zhitomir, Blobel had explained to us the new practice of *Sardinenpackung* developed by Jeckeln, the "sardine-packing" method that Callsen already knew. With the considerable increase in volume, in Galicia, as early as July, Jeckeln had decided that the graves were filling up too quickly; the bodies were falling any which way and got all tangled up, a lot of space was wasted, and so we were wasting too much time digging; so now the condemned, undressed, had to lie on their stomachs in the bottom of the trench, and a few shooters administered a shot in the neck at point-blank range. "I have always been against the *Genickschuss*," Blobel reminded us, "but now we no longer have a choice." After each row, an officer had to perform an inspection and make sure all the condemned were indeed dead; then they were covered with a thin layer of dirt and the next group came to lie down on top of them, head to foot; when five or six layers had accumulated this way, the trench was filled in. The Teilkommandoführer thought the men would find this too difficult, but Blobel didn't want to hear any objections: "In my Kommando, we will do what the Obergruppenführer says." Kurt Hans, in any case, wasn't too bothered; he seemed indifferent to everything. I attended several executions with him. I could now distinguish three different tempera-ments among my colleagues. First, there were those who, even if they tried to hide it, killed with sensual pleasure; I have already talked about them, they were criminals who revealed their true nature thanks to the war. Then there were those who were disgusted by it and who killed out of duty, overcoming their repugnance, out of a love of order. Fi-nally, there were those who regarded the Jews as animals and killed them the way a butcher slaughters a cow—a joyful or a difficult task, ac-cording to their humor or disposition. Kurt Hans clearly belonged to this last category: for him, the only thing that counted was the precision of the gesture, the efficiency, the output. Every night, he meticulously went over his totals. And what about me? I couldn't identify with any of these three types, but that was of little help, and if I had been pushed a little, I would have had trouble articulating an honest answer. I was still looking for one. Passion for the absolute was a part of it, as was, I realized one day with terror, curiosity: here, as in so many other things in my life, I was curious, I was trying to see what effect all this would have on me. I was always observing myself: it was as if a film camera were fixed just above me, and I was at once this camera, the man it was filming, and the man who was then studying the film. Sometimes that astonished me, and often, at night, I couldn't sleep; I stared at the ceil-ing; the lens didn't leave me in peace. But the answer to my question kept slipping through my fingers.

   With the women, the children especially, our work sometimes be-came very difficult, heart-wrenching. The men complained nonstop, especially the older ones, the ones who had a family. Faced with these defenseless people, these mothers who had to watch their children be-ing killed without being able to protect them, who could only die with them, our men suffered from an extreme feeling of powerlessness; they too felt defenseless. "I just want to stay whole," a young Sturmmann from the Waffen-SS said to me one day, and I understood this desire, but I couldn't help him. The attitude of the Jews didn't make things any easier. Blobel had to send back to Germany a thirty-year-old Rotten-führer who had spoken with a condemned man; the Jew, who was the same age as the Rottenführer, was holding in his arms a child about two and half years old; his wife, next to him, was carrying a newborn with blue eyes; and the man had looked the Rottenführer straight in the eyes and had said to him calmly, in flawless German: "Please, mein Herr, shoot the children cleanly."—"He came from Hamburg," the Rotten-führer explained later on to Sperath, who had then told us the story; "he was almost my neighbor, his children were the same age as mine." Even

I was losing my grip. During an execution, I watched a young boy dying in the trench: the shooter must have hesitated, the shot had hit too low, in the back. The boy was twitching, his eyes were open and glassy, and this terrifying scene blended into a scene from my childhood: with a friend, I was playing cowboys and Indians with some cap pistols. It was not long after the Great War, my father had returned, I must have been about five or six, like the boy in the trench. I had hidden behind a tree; when my friend approached, I leaped out and emptied my pistol into his stomach, shouting, "Bang! Bang!" He dropped his weapon, clutched his stomach with both hands, and fell down twisting. I picked up his pistol and handed it to him: "Come on, take it. Let's go on playing."—"I can't. I'm a corpse." I closed my eyes; in front of me, the boy was still panting. After the action, I visited the *shtetl*, empty now, deserted; I went into the isbas, dark, miserable dwellings, with Soviet calendars and pictures cut out of magazines on the walls, a few religious objects, coarse furniture. Certainly none of this had much to do with the *internationales Finanzjudentum*. In one house, I found a big bucket of water on the stove, still boiling; on the ground were pots of cold water and a washbasin. I closed the door, stripped and washed myself with this water and a piece of hard soap. I scarcely diluted the hot water: it burned, my skin turned scarlet. Then I got dressed again and went out; at the entrance to the village, the houses were already in flames. But my question wouldn't let go of me, I returned again and again, and that's how another time, at the edge of a grave, a little girl about four years old came up and quietly took my hand. I tried to free myself, but she kept gripping it. In front of us, they were shooting the Jews. *"Gdye mama?"* I asked the girl in Ukrainian. She pointed toward the trench. I caressed her hair. We stayed that way for several minutes. I was dizzy, I wanted to cry. "Come with me," I said to her in German, "don't be afraid, come." I headed for the entrance of the pit; she stayed in place, holding me by the hand, then followed me. I picked her up and held her out to a Waffen-SS: "Be gentle with her," I said to him stupidly. I felt an insane rage, but didn't want to take it out on the girl, or on the soldier. He went down into the trench with the child in his arms and I quickly turned away and entered the forest. It was a large, sparsely wooded pine forest, well cleared and full of soft light. Behind me the salvos crackled. When I was little, I often played in forests like this, around Kiel, where I lived after the war: strange games, actually. For my birthday, my father had given me a three-volume set of *Tarzan*, by the American writer E. R. Burroughs, which I read and reread with passion, at the table, in the bathroom, at night with a flashlight. In the forest, like my hero, I stripped naked and slipped among the trees, between the tall ferns, I lay down on beds of pine needles, enjoying the little pricks on my skin, I squatted behind a bush or a fallen tree, above a path, to spy on the people who came walking there, the *others*, the humans. They weren't explicitly erotic games; I was too young for that; I probably didn't even get erect then; but for me, the entire forest had become an erogenous zone, a vast skin as sensitive as my naked child's skin, bristling in the cold. Later on, I should add, these games took an even stranger turn; this was still in Kiel, but probably after my father had left; I must have been nine, ten at most: naked, I would hang myself with my belt from a tree branch, and let myself go with all my weight; my blood, thrown into a panic, made my face swell, my temples beat to the point of bursting; my breath came in wheezes; finally I would stand back up, regain my breath, and begin again. That's what forests used to mean to me, games like that, full of keen pleasure and boundless freedom; now, the woods filled me with fear.

I returned to Zhitomir. An intense agitation reigned at the Kommandostab: Bohr was under arrest and Lübbe in hospital. Bohr had attacked him in the middle of the mess, in front of the other officers, with a chair first and then with a knife. It had taken at least six people to control him; Strehlke, the Verwaltungsführer, had had his hand slashed, not very deeply but painfully. "He went mad," he said to me, showing me the stitches.—"But what happened?"—"It's because of his little Jew. The one who played the piano." Yakov had had an accident while repairing a car with Bauer: the jack, badly set, had let go, and his hand had been crushed. Sperath had examined it and declared it had to be amputated. "Then he's no good for anything," Blobel decided, and he had given the order to liquidate him. "Vogt took care of it," said Strehlke, who was telling me the story. "Bohr didn't say anything. But at dinner, Lübbe began taunting him. You know how he is. 'No more piano,' he said out loud. That's when Bohr attacked him. If you want my opinion," he added, "Lübbe got what he deserved. But it's too bad for Bohr: a good officer, and he's ruined his career for a little Jew. It's not as if there were a lack of Jews, over here."—"What's going to happen to Bohr?"— "That'll depend on the Standartenführer's report. At worst, he could go to prison. Otherwise, he'll be stripped of his rank and sent to the Waffen-SS to redeem himself." I left him and went up to my room to lock myself in, exhausted with disgust. I understood Bohr completely; he had been wrong, of course, but I understood him. Lübbe had no right to make fun of him, that was shameful. I too had grown attached to little Yakov; I had discreetly written to a friend in Berlin, for him to send me some Rameau and Couperin scores; I wanted Yakov to study them to discover *Le Rappel des Oiseaux, Les Trois Mains, Les Barricades Mys-*

térieuses, and all those other wonders. Now these scores were of no use to anyone: I don't play the piano. That night I had a strange dream. I was getting up and heading toward the door, but a woman was barring the way. She had white hair and wore glasses: "No," she said to me. "You can't go out. Sit down and write." I turned to my desk: a man was sitting in my chair, hammering away at my typewriter. "Excuse me," I ventured. The noise of the keys clacking was deafening, he didn't hear me. Timidly, I tapped him on the shoulder. He turned around and shook his head: "No," he said, waving toward the door. I went into my library, but someone was there too, calmly tearing the pages out of my books and tossing the gutted bindings into a corner. Well then, I said to myself, in that case I'll go to sleep. But a young woman was lying in my bed, naked beneath the sheet. When she saw me, she dragged me down to her, covering my face with kisses, wrapping her legs around mine, trying to unfasten my belt. It was only with the greatest difficulty that I managed to fight her off; the effort left me panting. I thought of throwing myself out the window; it was jammed, painted shut. The toilet, fortunately, was empty, and I hastily locked myself in.

The Wehrmacht had finally resumed its advance, and this was creating new tasks for us. Guderian was completing his breakthrough, attacking the Soviet armies in Kiev from the rear; his prey, as if paralyzed, wasn't reacting. The Sixth Army started moving again, and crossed the Dnieper; farther south, the Seventeenth Army was also passing the Dnieper. It was hot and dry, and the troops on the move raised columns of dust as high as buildings; when the rains came, the soldiers rejoiced, then cursed the mud. No one had time to bathe and the men were gray with dust and mire. The regiments advanced like little isolated ships on the ocean of corn and ripe wheat; they saw no one for days, and the only news that reached them came from *Rollbahn* drivers coming back up the line; all around them, flat and wide, stretched the vast earth: *Is there anyone living on this plain?* sings the knight in the old Russian tale. Sometimes, when we went out on a mission, we met one of these units; the officers would invite us to eat, happy to see us. On September 16, Guderian joined forces with von Kleist's Panzers in Lokhvitsa, 150 kilometers beyond Kiev, surrounding four Soviet armies according to the Abwehr; to the north and south, the air force and infantry began to crush them. Kiev lay wide open. In Zhitomir, since the end of August, we had stopped killing Jews, and the survivors had been regrouped in a ghetto; on September 17, Blobel left the city with his officers, two units from the Police Regiment South, and our Askaris, leaving behind only the orderlies, the cooks, and the repair gear for the vehicles. The

Kommandostab was to establish itself as soon as possible in Kiev. But the next day, Blobel changed his mind, or received a counterorder: he returned to Zhitomir to liquidate the ghetto. "Their insolent attitude hasn't changed, despite all our warnings and our special measures. We can't leave them behind us." He formed a Vorkommando under the leadership of Häfner and Janssen to enter Kiev with the Sixth Army. I volunteered and Blobel accepted.

That night the Vorkommando camped in a little deserted village near the city. Outside, the obsessive cawing of the crows sounded like babies crying. While I was lying on a straw-filled mattress in an isba that I was sharing with the other officers, a little bird, a sparrow perhaps, flew into the room and started careening into the walls and the closed windows; half stunned, it would lie on the floor for a few seconds, out of breath, its wings askew, before exploding again in another brief and futile frenzy. I thought it might be dying. The others were already asleep or else didn't react. Finally I managed to trap it under a helmet and release it outside: it fled into the night as if it were awakening from a nightmare. At dawn we were already on the move. The war now was just in front of us, we were advancing very slowly. By the roadsides the insomniac dead lay scattered, their eyes open, empty. The wedding ring of a German soldier gleamed in the early morning sun; his face was red, swollen, his mouth and eyes full of flies. The dead horses lay intermingled with the men, some, wounded by bullets or shrapnel, were still dying, they neighed, struggled, rolled furiously over the other carcasses or the bodies of their riders. Near a makeshift bridge right in front of us, the current carried off three soldiers, and from the bank for a long while we could make out the sodden uniforms, the pale faces of the drowned men, slowly drifting away. In the empty villages, abandoned by their inhabitants, cows with swollen udders were lowing in pain; the geese, horrified, were cackling in the little gardens of the isbas in the midst of rabbits and chickens and chained dogs doomed to die of hunger; the houses lay wide open, the people, overwhelmed with panic, had left behind their books, their framed prints, their radios, their quilts. Then came the outer suburbs of Kiev, ravaged by destruction, and then just after, the center, almost intact. Along Shevchenko Boulevard, under the fine autumn sun, the lush lindens and chestnut trees were glowing yellow; on Kreshchatik, the main street, we had to navigate between anti-tank barricades that exhausted German soldiers were clearing away with difficulty. Häfner liaised with the HQ of the Twenty-ninth Army Corps, and they directed us to the premises of the NKVD, on a hill above Kreshchatik, overlooking the center. It had once been a beautiful palace from the early nineteenth century, with a long yellow façade decorated with moldings and tall columns painted white flanking the main door, under a triangular pediment; but it had been bombed and then, for good measure, burned by the NKVD. According to our informants it used to be a pension for poor young virgins; in 1918, the *Soviet institutions* had taken over the building; since then, it had a sinister reputation, people were shot in the garden, behind the second *korpus*. Häfner dispatched a platoon to round up some Jews to clean and repair whatever could still be fixed; we set up our desks and equipment wherever we could, and some officers were already getting to work. I went down to army headquarters to ask for some sappers: the building had to be inspected, to make sure it wasn't mined; they promised me some for the next day. In the palace of young virgins, the first Jews were arriving under escort and beginning to clear away the rubble; Häfner had also confiscated some mattresses and quilts, so we wouldn't have to sleep on the bare ground. The next morning, a Saturday, I hadn't even had time to go inquire after my sappers when a formidable explosion echoed through the center of town, knocking out the few windowpanes we had left. Quickly the news spread that the citadel of Novo-Pecherskaya had blown up, killing, among others, the commander of the artillery division and his Chief of Staff. Everyone was talking of sabotage, delayed-action detonators; the Wehrmacht remained cautious, and didn't rule out the possibility of an accident caused by some badly stored ammunition. Häfner and Janssen started to arrest Jews, while I tried to recruit Ukrainian informants. It was difficult, we knew nothing about them: the men who presented themselves could just as easily be Russian agents. The arrested Jews were locked up in a movie theater on Kreshchatik; I was frantically cross-checking the information coming in from all over: everything seemed to indicate that the Soviets had carefully mined the city; and our sappers still hadn't arrived. Finally, after a vigorous protest, we were sent three engineers; they left after two hours without finding anything. At night, my anxiety bled into my sleep and infected my dreams: seized with an intense need to defecate, I ran to the bathroom, the shit pouring out liquid and thick, a continuous flow that quickly filled the toilet bowl and kept rising, I kept shitting, the shit reached up to below my thighs, covered my buttocks and scrotum, my anus kept disgorging. I frantically wondered how to clean up all this shit, but I couldn't stop it, its acrid, vile, nauseating taste filled my mouth, sickening me. I woke up suffocating, my mouth dry, doughy and bitter. Dawn was rising, and I climbed up onto the cliffs to watch the sun rise over the river, the dismembered bridges, the city, and the plain beyond. The Dnieper sprawled out at my feet, wide, sluggish, its surface covered with swirling green scum; in the middle, beneath the dynamited railroad bridge, stretched a few little islets surrounded by reeds and water lilies, with some abandoned fishing boats; a barge belonging to the Wehrmacht was crossing; farther up, to the other side, a boat was gathering rust on the beach, half aground, lying on its side. The trees hid the *lavra* and I could see only the golden dome of its bell tower, which dully reflected the coppery light of the rising sun. I returned to the palace: Sunday or not, we were overwhelmed with work; what's more, the Gruppenstab Vorkommando was arriving. They presented themselves in midmorning, headed by Obersturmführer Dr. Krieger, the Leiter V; with him were Obersturmführer Breun, someone named Braun, and Krumme, a Hauptmann of the *Schutzpolizei*, who commanded our Orpos; Thomas had stayed behind in Zhitomir, and would arrive a few days later with Dr. Rasch. Krieger and his colleagues occupied another wing of the palace, where we had already set things somewhat in order; our Jews were working nonstop; at night, we kept them in a basement, near the former cells of the NKVD. Blobel visited us after lunch and congratulated us on our progress, then left, back to Zhitomir. He wasn't planning to stay there since the city was already *judenrein*; the Kommando had emptied the ghetto the day of our arrival in Kiev and liquidated the 3,145 remaining Jews. One more number for our reports; there would soon be others. Who, I wondered, will mourn all these killed Jews, all these Jewish children buried with open eyes under the rich black earth of the Ukraine, if their sisters and mothers are killed too? If they were all killed, no one would be left to mourn them, and maybe that also was the idea. My work progressed: I had been sent some trustworthy Melnykists, they vetted my informants and even identified three Bolsheviks, including one woman, who were shot on the spot; thanks to them, I recruited some *dvorniki*, Soviet janitors who habitually informed for the NKVD but had no problem doing the same for us, in exchange for small privileges or for money. They soon identified officers of the Red Army disguised as civilians, as well as Commissars, Banderists, and Jewish intellectuals, whom I transferred to Häfner or Janssen after a quick interrogation. Häfner and Janssen for their part continued to fill the *Goskino 5* with arrested Jews. Since the explosion of the citadel, the city was calm, the Wehrmacht was getting organized, and the food supply was improving. But the searches had been overly hasty. Wednesday morning, the twenty-fourth, another explosion ripped apart the Feldkommandantur set up in the Hotel Continental, on the corner of Kreshchatik and Proreznaya Streets. I went down to look. The street was swarming with onlookers and idle soldiers watching the building burn. Some Feldgendarmen were beginning to collar civilians to help clear the rubble; officers were evacuating the intact wing of the hotel, carrying suitcases, blankets, phonographs. Glass crunched underfoot: for several streets around, the windows had been shattered by the force of the explosion. A number of officers must have been killed, but no one knew exactly how many. Suddenly another detonation sounded, farther down, near Tolstoy Square; then another huge bomb burst in a building opposite the hotel, projecting rubble and a cloud of dust onto us. The people, panicking, ran in all directions, mothers shouted after their children; German motorcyclists swarmed up Kreshchatik between the antitank obstacles, firing submachine-gun bursts at random. Black smoke quickly enveloped the street; fires had broken out everywhere; I was suffocating. Officers from the Wehrmacht shouted contradictory orders; no one seemed to know who was in charge. Kreshchatik was now blocked with rubble and overturned vehicles; the electric lines of the trolley buses, cut, dangled in the streets; a few meters away from me, the gas tank of an Opel blew up and the car caught fire. I went back to the palace; from above, the entire street seemed to be burning, and we could hear more explosions. Blobel had just arrived, and I reported the situation to him. Then Häfner arrived and explained that the Jews detained in the movie theater near the Hotel Continental had for the most part escaped in the confusion. Blobel ordered them found; I suggested it might be more urgent to have our quarters thoroughly searched again. Janssen then divided our Orpos and Waffen-SS into little groups of three and sent them into all the entrances of our palace, with the order to knock down any locked door, and especially to search the basements and attics. Less than an hour later, one of the men discovered explosives in the cellar. A Scharführer from the Waffen-SS who had served in the engineers corps went to look: there were about sixty bottlesful of gasoline, what the Finns called "Molotov cocktails" since their Winter War, apparently just stored there, but one couldn't be sure, we had to send for an expert. The news set off a panic. Janssen shouted and started whipping our *Arbeitsjuden*; Häfner, with his air of efficiency, barked out useless orders just to keep face. Blobel quickly conferred with Dr. Krieger and ordered the building evacuated. No fallback position had been planned, so no one knew where to go; while our vehicles were hastily being loaded, I hurriedly liaised with the HQ of the Army Corps; but their officers were overwhelmed, they told me to manage on my own. I returned to the palace through the fires and confusion. Wehrmacht sappers were trying to set up fire hoses, but the flames were gaining ground. Then I thought about the big Dynamo stadium; it was far away from the fires, near the *lavra* on the Pechersk Hills, and it wasn't very likely that the Red Army had gone to the trouble of mining it. Blobel approved my idea and directed the loaded cars and trucks; the officers set up in the abandoned offices and in locker rooms that still stank of sweat and disinfectant, while the men occupied the bleachers, and the Jews, brought under careful guard, were made to sit down on the grass. While our files, cases, and typewriters were unloaded and arranged, and specialists were unpacking the communication equipment, Blobel went to the Army Corps; when he returned, he ordered us to pack everything again: the Wehrmacht was assigning us some quarters in a former czar's residence, a little farther down. Everything had to be loaded up again; the whole day was wasted in moving. Only von Radetzky seemed happy at the commotion: *"Krieg ist Krieg und Schnaps ist Schnaps,"* he threw haughtily at whoever complained. By evening, I was finally able to begin collecting information with my Melnykist collaborators: we had to learn as much as possible about the Reds' plan; obviously the explosions were coordinated; the saboteurs had to be arrested and their Rostopchin identified. The Abwehr had some information about a certain Friedmann, an agent of the NKVD reportedly heading a spy and sabotage network set up before the Red Army's retreat; the sappers argued that it was just a matter of mines set in advance, with time fuses. The center of the city had become a hell. There had been more explosions, and now fires were raging all along Kreshchatik, from Duma Square to Tolstoy Square; Molotov cocktails, stored in the attics, were breaking in the heat, gelled gasoline ran down the stairways of buildings and fed the flames, which little by little were extending to the parallel streets, Pushkin Street on one side, then Mering, Karl Marx, Engels streets, all the way to the October Revolution Street, at the foot of our palace. The two TsUMs, department stores, had been stormed by the terrified population; the Feldgendarmerie was arresting many looters and wanted to hand them over to us; others had died in the flames. The entire population of the city center was fleeing, bent under bundles and pushing carts loaded with radios, rugs, and household appliances, while the babies squealed themselves hoarse in their mothers' arms. A number of German soldiers had mixed in with them and were also fleeing in complete disorder. From time to time a roof collapsed into a building in a huge clatter of rafters. In some places I was able to breathe only with a moistened handkerchief over my mouth; I coughed convulsively, spitting out thick globs of phlegm.

The next morning the Gruppenstab arrived, together with the bulk of our Kommando, headed by Kuno Callsen. Sappers had finally inspected our palace and taken away the crates of explosive bottles, and we had been able to go back to our premises in time to welcome them. A Vorkommando from the HSSPF arrived too and occupied the czar's residence that we had just left; they brought with them two Orpo battalions, which gave us considerable reinforcements. The Wehrmacht began to dynamite the buildings in the center of town to control the fires. Four tons of explosives had been found in the Lenin Museum, ready to detonate, but the sappers had managed to defuse them and buried them in front of the entrance. The new City Kommandant, Generalmajor Kurt Eberhard, was holding almost constant meetings, which representatives of the Group and the Kommando had to attend. Since Kehrig still hadn't been replaced, I found myself the acting Leiter III of the Kommando, and Blobel often asked me to accompany him or delegated me in his place when he was too busy; the Gruppenstab also conferred hourly with the men from the HSSPF, and Jeckeln himself was expected that night or the next day. In the morning, the Wehrmacht was still thinking of civilian saboteurs and had asked us to help search them out and repress them; then, in the course of the day, the Abwehr found a demolition plan of the Red Army, listing almost sixty objectives prepared for destruction before their departure. Engineers were sent to inspect and seemed to confirm the information. More than forty of the objectives were still waiting to explode, some equipped with wireless detonators, controlled from a distance; the sappers were furiously demining, as fast as possible. The Wehrmacht wanted to take radical measures; at the Group too, measures were being discussed.

On Friday the *Sicherheitspolizei* began its activities. With the help of information I gathered, 1,600 Jews and Communists were arrested during the day. Vogt had set up seven commandos for the interrogations— in the Dulags, in the camp for the Jews, in the civilian camp, and in town—in order to sift through the masses of prisoners and pick out the dangerous elements. I reported this during one of Eberhard's meetings; he nodded, but the army wanted more. The acts of sabotage continued: a young Jew had tried to cut one of the pipes set in the Dnieper by the sappers to feed their fire hoses; the Sonderkommando shot him, as well as a band of Gypsies caught rummaging around in an outlying neighborhood near an Orthodox church. On Blobel's orders, one of our platoons liquidated the mentally ill in the Pavlov Hospital, for fear they might escape and add to the disorder. Jeckeln had arrived; in the afternoon, he presided over a large meeting at the Ortskommandantur, which was attended by General Eberhard and staff officers from the Sixth Army, officers from the Group, including Dr. Rasch, and officers from the Sonderkommando. Rasch looked out of sorts: tapping on the table with his pen, he didn't speak, his somewhat vacant gaze straying distractedly over the faces surrounding him. Jeckeln, by contrast, was brimming with energy. He gave a short speech about the sabotage, the danger represented by the masses of Jews in the city, and the necessity to have recourse to the most rigorous possible measures of retaliation, but also of prevention. Sturmbannführer Hennicke, the Leiter III of the Einsatzgruppe, presented some statistics: according to his information, Kiev must at that time have been harboring some 150,000 Jews, permanent residents or refugees from western Ukraine. Jeckeln suggested, as a preliminary measure, shooting 50,000 of them; Eberhard warmly approved and pledged the logistic support of the Sixth Army. Jeckeln turned to us: "Gentlemen," he declared, "I give you twenty-four hours to prepare a plan for me." Blobel leaped up: "Obergruppenführer, it will be done!" Rasch spoke for the first time: "With Standartenführer Blobel, you can count on it." His tone held a rather marked irony, but Blobel took it as a compliment: "Absolutely, absolutely."—"We have to make a strong impression," Eberhard concluded, calling the meeting to a close.

I was already working night and day, and snatching two hours of sleep when I could; but to tell the truth, I didn't really contribute to the planning: the officers of the Teilkommandos, who weren't yet entirely snowed under (they were shooting *politruki* unmasked by Vogt's interrogators and a few suspects picked up more or less at random, but no more than that), took charge of it. The meetings with the Sixth Army and the HSSPF resumed the next day. The Sonderkommando proposed a site: west of the city, in the Syrets neighborhood, near the Jewish cemetery but still outside the inhabited zones, there were some wide ravines that would do well. "There's also a freight depot there," Blobel added. "That will let the Jews think we're sending them away to settle somewhere else." The Wehrmacht sent some surveyors to plot the land: based on their report, Jeckeln and Blobel decided on the ravine known as the Grandmother or the Old Lady, at the bottom of which ran a little stream. Blobel called together all his officers: "The Jews to be executed are antisocials, without any value, useless for Germany. We will also include asylum patients, Gypsies, and any other useless mouths to feed. But we'll start with the Jews." We studied the maps attentively; we had to position the cordons, arrange the routes, and plan the transports; reducing the number of trucks and the distances would save gasoline; it was also necessary to consider the munitions and food supplies for the troops; everything had to be calculated. For that we also had to decide on the method of execution: Blobel finally settled on a variation of the *Sardinenpackung*. For the shooters and the escorts of the condemned, Jeckeln insisted we use his two Orpo battalions, which visibly upset Blobel. There were also Grafhort's Waffen-SS and Hauptmann Krumme's Orpos. For the cordons, the Sixth Army placed several companies at our disposal, and they would supply the trucks. Häfner set up a depot for

sorting the valuables, between the Lukyanovskoe and the Jewish ceme-
teries, a hundred and fifty meters from the ravine: Eberhard insisted the
apartment keys be recovered and labeled, since the fires had thrown
twenty-five thousand civilians out on the street, and the Wehrmacht
wanted to rehouse them as soon as possible. The Sixth Army delivered
one hundred thousand cartridges to us and printed up posters, in German, Russian, and Ukrainian, on cheap gray wrapping paper. Blobel,
when he wasn't immersed in his maps, somehow found time for other
activities; that afternoon, with the help of the engineers, he had the
Cathedral of the Dormition dynamited, a superb little eleventh-century
Orthodox church in the middle of the *lavra*: "The Ukrainians have to
pay a little too," he explained to us later on with satisfaction. I discussed
this in passing with Vogt, since I didn't understand the sense of this action at all; according to him, it was definitely not an initiative of Blobel's, but he had no idea who could have authorized or ordered it. "The
Obergruppenführer, probably. It's his style." In any case it wasn't Dr.
Rasch, whom we saw hardly at all anymore. When I met Thomas in a
hallway I asked him furtively: "What's happening with the Brigadeführer? He doesn't look right."—"He's been arguing with Jeckeln. And
also with Koch." Erich Koch, the Gauleiter of East Prussia, had been
named Reichskommissar of the Ukraine a month before. "What
about?" I asked.—"I'll tell you later. Anyway he won't be around much
longer. One question, though: the Jews in the Dnieper, is that you
guys?" The night before, all the Jews who had gone to synagogue for
Shabbat had disappeared; their bodies had been found in the morning,
floating in the river. "The army has filed a complaint," he went on.
"They say that actions like that disturb the civilian population. It's not
gemütlich."—"And what we're planning is *gemütlich*? I think the civilian
population will soon have other things to worry about."—"It's not the
same. On the contrary, they'll be delighted to be rid of their Jews." I
shrugged: "No, it wasn't us. As far as I know. We're a little busy, right
now, we have other things to see to. And also those are not really our
methods."

On Sunday we put the posters up all over the city. The Jews were
asked to gather the next morning in front of their cemetery on the Melnikova, each with fifty kilograms of luggage, to be relocated as settlers
in various regions of the Ukraine. I had my doubts as to the success of
this ploy: this wasn't Lutsk anymore, and I knew that rumors had seeped
through the front lines about the fate that awaited the Jews; the farther
east we got, the fewer Jews we were finding; they were fleeing before
us now with the Red Army, whereas in the beginning they had waited
for us trustingly. On the other hand, as Hennicke pointed out to me, the

Bolsheviks were keeping remarkably silent about our executions: in their radio broadcasts, they accused us of monstrous, exaggerated atrocities, but without ever mentioning the Jews; maybe, according to our experts, they were afraid of weakening *the sacred unity of the Soviet people*. We knew, through our informants, that many Jews were designated for evacuation to the rear, but they seemed to be selected according to the same criteria as the Ukrainians and the Russians, as engineers, doctors, members of the Party, specialized workers; most of the Jews who fled left on their own. "It's hard to understand," Hennicke added. "If the Jews really dominate the Communist Party, they should have made more effort to save their brethren."—"They're clever," Dr. von Scheven, another officer from the Group, suggested. "They don't want to lay themselves open to our propaganda by too obviously favoring their own people. Stalin must also be counting on Great Russian nationalism. To keep power, they sacrifice their poor cousins."—"You're probably right," Hennicke said. I smiled to myself, but bitterly: as in the Middle Ages, we were reasoning with syllogisms that proved each other. And these proofs led us down the path of no return.

The *Grosse Aktion* began on Monday, September 29, on the morning of Yom Kippur, the Jewish Day of Atonement. Blobel had let us know this the day before: "They will atone, they will atone." I had stayed in my offices in the palace to write a report. Callsen appeared on the threshold: "You aren't coming? You know very well that the Brigadeführer gave the order that all officers should be present."—"I know. I'll finish this and then I'll come."—"As you like." He disappeared and I went on working. An hour later I got up, picked up my cap and gloves, and went to find my driver. Outside it was cold; I thought about going back in for a sweater, but decided not to. The sky was overcast; fall was advancing; soon it would be winter. I passed by the still-smoking ruins on Kreshchatik, then went up Shevchenko Boulevard. The Jews were marching west in long columns, in family groups, calmly, carrying bundles or backpacks. Most of them looked very poor, probably refugees; the men and boys all wore Soviet worker's caps, but here and there you could also make out a soft hat. Some were coming in carts drawn by bony horses, loaded with old people and suitcases. I had my driver make a detour, since I wanted to see more; he turned left and went past the university, then veered off toward the station by Saksaganskaya Street. Jews were coming out with their things from the houses and mingling with the stream of people flowing by in a peaceful murmur. Almost no German soldiers could be seen. On the street-corners these human streams merged, grew larger, and went on; there was no agitation. I drove back up the hill away from the station and rejoined the boulevard at the corner of the great botanical garden. A group of soldiers was standing there with some Ukrainian auxiliaries and were roasting a whole pig on an enormous spit. It smelled very good, the Jews passing by contemplated the pig with yearning, and the soldiers were laughing and making fun of them. I stopped and got out of the car. People were pouring out of all the side streets and coming to join the main flow, streams merging into a river. Periodically, the interminable column stopped, then started up again with a jolt. In front of me, old women with garlands of onions around their necks were holding the hands of kids with runny noses; I noticed a little girl standing between jars of preserves piled up higher than she. There seemed to me to be mostly old people and children, but it was hard to judge: the able-bodied men must have joined the Red Army, or else fled. To the right, in front of the botanical garden, a corpse lay in the gutter, one arm folded over its face; the people filed by alongside it without looking at it. I went up to the soldiers gathered around the pig: "What happened?" A Feldwebel saluted and replied: "An agitator, Herr Obersturmführer. He was shouting, exciting the crowd and telling lies about the Wehrmacht. We told him to be quiet, but he kept shouting." I looked at the crowd again: the people seemed calm, a little nervous maybe, but passive. Through my network of informers, I had contributed to spreading some rumors: the Jews were going to Palestine, they were going to a ghetto, to Germany to work. The local authorities put in place by the Wehrmacht had also done their part to avert panic. I knew that rumors of a massacre had also spread, but all these rumors canceled one another out; people must not have known what to think anymore, and so we could count on their memories of the German occupation of 1918, on their trust in Germany, and on hope too, *vile hope.*

I left. I hadn't given any directions to my driver, but he followed the flow of Jews, toward Melnikova Street. Still almost no German soldiers were visible; just a few checkpoints at the crossroads, such as at the corner of the botanical garden, or another one where Artyoma joins Melnikova. There, I witnessed my first incident of the day: Feldgendarmen were beating some bearded Jews with long curly sidelocks in front of their ears, rabbis possibly, dressed only in shirts. They were red with blood, their shirts were soaked, women were screaming, ripples ran through the crowd. Then the Feldgendarmen seized hold of the rabbis and took them away. I studied the people: they knew that these men were going to die, that was obvious from their anguished looks; but they were still hoping that it would just be the rabbis, the pious.

At the end of Melnikova, in front of the Jewish cemetery, some antitank barriers and barbed wire made the roadway narrower, guarded by soldiers from the Wehrmacht and some Ukrainian Polizei. The cordon started there; after this bottleneck, the Jews could no longer turn back. The sorting zone was a little farther on, to the left, in an empty lot in front of the immense Christian cemetery of Lukyanovskoe. A long red-brick wall, rather low, surrounded the necropolis; behind, some tall trees barred the sky, half bare or else still red and yellow. On the other side of Degtiarovska Street, a row of tables had been set up in front of which the Jews were made to line up. There I found some of our off icers: "So, it's already begun?" Häfner motioned his head to the north: "Yes, it started hours ago. Where have you been? The Standartenführer is furious." Behind every table was a noncom from the Kommando, flanked by an interpreter and some soldiers; first the Jews had to hand over their papers, then their money, their valuables and jewelry, then the keys to their apartments, legibly labeled, and finally their clothes and shoes. They must have suspected something, but they didn't say anything; in any case, the zone was sealed behind the cordon. Some Jews tried to argue with the Polizei, but the Ukrainians shouted, struck them, sent them back into the line. A stinging wind was blowing; I was cold and regretted not having brought my sweater; from time to time, when the wind rose, a faint crackling noise could be heard; most of the Jews didn't seem to notice it. Behind the row of tables, our Askaris were bundling the confiscated clothing into trucks; the vehicles set off for the city, where we had set up a sorting center. I went to examine the pile of papers, thrown in a heap in the middle of the lot to be burned later on. There were torn passports, workbooks, union or ration cards, family photos; the wind was carrying away the lighter papers, the square was littered with them. I gazed at some of the photographs: snapshots, studio portraits, of men, women, and children, grandparents and chubby-faced babies; sometimes a shot of vacation scenery, of the happiness and normality of their lives before all this. It reminded me of a photograph I kept in my drawer, next to my bed, in high school. It was the portrait of a Prussian family from before the Great War, three young Junkers in cadet uniforms and probably their sister. I don't remember where I found it, maybe during one of our rare outings, in a thrift store or a postcard shop. At that time I was very unhappy, I had been placed by force in that horrible boarding school after a major transgression (this all took place in France, where we had gone a few years after my father's disappearance). At night, I would examine this photo for hours on end, by moonlight or beneath the covers with a little pocket flashlight. Why, I wondered, couldn't I have grown up in a perfect family like that one, rather than in this polluted hell? The Jewish families in the scattered photos seemed happy too; hell, for them, was here, now, and they could

only lament the vanished past. Beyond the tables, the Jews in under-
clothing were trembling with cold; the Ukrainian Polizei separated the
men and boys from the women and little children; the women, children, and old people were loaded into Wehrmacht trucks to be transported to the ravine; the others had to go on foot. Häfner had joined
me. "The Standartenführer is looking for you. Watch out, he's really in
a rage."—"Why?"—"He's mad at the Obergruppenführer for imposing
his two police battalions on him. He thinks the Obergruppenführer
wants to take all the credit for the *Aktion.*"—"But that's idiotic." Blobel
arrived, he had been drinking and his face was glistening. As soon as he
saw me he began railing at me rudely: "What the hell have you been up
to? We've been waiting for you for hours." I saluted him: "Standartenführer! The SD has its own tasks. I was examining the arrangements, to
prevent any incidents." He calmed down a little: "So?" he grumbled.—
"Everything seems in order, Standartenführer."—"Good. Go up there.
The Brigadeführer wants to see all the officers."

I got back into my car and followed the trucks; at the end of the
road, the Polizei unloaded the women and children, who rejoined the
men arriving on foot. A number of Jews, as they walked, were singing
religious songs; few tried to run away; the ones who did were soon
stopped by the cordon or shot down. From the top, you could hear the
gun bursts clearly, and the women especially were starting to panic. But
there was nothing they could do. The condemned were divided into little groups and a noncom sitting at a table counted them; then our
Askaris took them and led them over the brink of the ravine. After each
volley, another group left, it went very quickly. I walked around the
ravine by the west to join the other officers, who had taken up positions
above the north slope. From there, the ravine stretched out in front of
me: it must have been some fifty meters wide and maybe thirty meters
deep, and went on for several kilometers; the little stream at the bottom
ran into the Syrets, which gave its name to the neighborhood. Boards
had been placed over this stream so the Jews and their shooters could
cross easily; beyond, scattered pretty much everywhere on the bare sides
of the ravine, the little white clusters were multiplying. The Ukrainian
"packers" dragged their charges to these piles and forced them to lie
down over them or next to them; the men from the firing squad then
advanced and passed along the rows of people lying down almost naked,
shooting each one with a submachine bullet in the neck; there were
three firing squads in all. Between the executions some officers inspected the bodies and finished them off with a pistol. To one side, on
a hill overlooking the scene, stood groups of officers from the SS and
the Wehrmacht. Jeckeln was there with his entourage, flanked by Dr.

Rasch; I also recognized some high-ranking officers of the Sixth Army. I saw Thomas, who noticed me but didn't return my greeting. On the other side, the little groups tumbled down the flank of the ravine and joined the clusters of bodies that stretched farther and farther out. The cold was becoming biting, but some rum was being passed around, and I drank a little. Blobel emerged suddenly from a car on our side of the ravine, he must have driven around it; he was drinking from a little flask and shouting, complaining that things weren't going fast enough. But the pace of the operations had been stepped up as much as possible. The shooters were relieved every hour, and those who weren't shooting supplied them with rum and reloaded the clips. The officers weren't talking much; some were trying to hide their distress. The Ortskommandantur had set up a field kitchen, and a military pastor was preparing some tea to warm up the Orpos and the members of the Sonderkommando. At lunchtime, the superior officers returned to the city, but the subalterns stayed to eat with the men. Since the executions had to continue without pause, the canteen had been set up farther down, in a hollow from which you couldn't see the ravine. The Group was responsible for the food supplies; when the cases were broken open, the men, seeing rations of blood pudding, started raging and shouting violently. Häfner, who had just spent an hour administering deathshots, was yelling and throwing the open cans onto the ground: "What the hell is this shit?" Behind me, a Waffen-SS was noisily vomiting. I myself was livid, the sight of the pudding made my stomach turn. I went up to Hartl, the Group's Verwaltungsführer, and asked him how he could have done that. But Hartl, standing there in his ridiculously wide riding breeches, remained indifferent. Then I shouted at him that it was a disgrace: "In this situation, we can do without such food!" Hartl turned his back to me and walked away; Häfner threw the cans into a box while another officer, the young Nagel, tried to calm me down: "Come now, Obersturmführer . . ."—"No, it's not normal, you have to think about things like that. It's his responsibility."—"Absolutely," Häfner growled. "I'm going to go look for something else." Someone poured me a glass of rum that I swallowed in one draught; it burned, and did me good. Hartl had returned and was pointing a finger at me: "Obersturmführer, you don't have to talk to me like that."—"And you didn't have to . . . to . . . to . . . ," I stammered, pointing to the overturned crates.—"Meine Herren!" Vogt barked. "Let's end this, shall we?" Everyone was visibly on edge. I drew away and ate a little bread and a raw onion; behind me, the officers were arguing animatedly. A little later, the superior officers had returned, and Hartl must have made a report, because Blobel came to see me and reprimanded me in the

name of Dr. Rasch: "In these circumstances, we must behave like officers." He gave me the order, when Janssen had come back up from the
ravine, to replace him. "You have your weapon? Yes? No sissies in my
Kommando, you understand?" He was spluttering, he was completely
drunk and almost out of control. A little later on I saw Janssen climb
back up. He threw me a dour look: "Your turn." The side of the ravine,
where I stood, was too steep for me to climb down, I had to walk back
around and come in from the rear. Around the bodies, the sandy earth
was soaked with blackish blood; the stream too was black with blood.
The horrible smell of excrement was stronger than that of blood, a lot
of people defecated as they died; fortunately there was a brisk wind that
blew away some of the stench. Seen close up, things were proceeding
much less calmly: the Jews who arrived at the top of the ravine, driven
by the Askaris and the Orpos, screamed with terror when they saw the
scene and struggled, the "packers" hit them with iron rods or metal cables to force them to go and lie down, even on the ground they kept
yelling and trying to stand up, and the children clung to life as much as
the adults, they'd leap up and start running until a "packer" caught them
and knocked them out, often the shots missed their mark and people
were only wounded, but the shooters didn't pay any attention and already moved on to the next victim, the wounded rolled over, writhed,
groaned in pain, others, silent and in shock, remained paralyzed, their
eyes wide open. Men came and went, they shot round after round, almost without stopping. I was petrified, I didn't know what to do.
Grafhorst came over and shook me by the arm: "Obersturmführer!" He
pointed his gun at the bodies. "Try to finish off the wounded." I took
out my pistol and headed for a group: a very young man was sobbing
in pain, I aimed my gun at his head and squeezed the trigger, but it
didn't go off, I had forgotten to lift the safety catch, I lifted it and shot
him in the forehead, he twitched and was suddenly still. To reach some
of the wounded, you had to walk over bodies, it was terribly slippery,
the limp white flesh rolled under my boots, bones snapped treacher-
ously and made me stumble, I sank up to my ankles in mud and blood.
It was horrible and it filled me with a rending feeling of disgust, like that
night in Spain, in the outhouse with the cockroaches, I was still young,
my father-in-law had treated us to a vacation in Catalonia, we were
sleeping in a village, and one night I got diarrhea, I ran to the outhouse
at the back of the garden, lighting my way with a pocket flashlight, and
the pit, clean during the day, was swarming with giant brown cockroaches, they filled me with horror, I tried to hold it in and go back to
sleep, but the cramps were too strong, there was no chamber pot, I put
on my big rain boots and went back to the outhouse, telling myself that

I could chase the roaches away with my foot and be quick about my business, I put my head through the door as I lit up the ground, then I noticed a shimmer on the wall, I pointed my flashlight at it, the wall too was swarming with cockroaches, all the walls, the ceiling too, and above the door, I slowly turned my head and they were there on the lintel too, a black swarming mass, then I slowly withdrew my head, very slowly, and went back to my room and held it in till morning. Walking on the bodies of the Jews gave me the same feeling, I fired almost haphazardly, at anything I saw wriggling, then I pulled myself together and tried to pay attention, but in any case I could only finish off the most recent ones, underneath them already lay other wounded, not yet dead, but soon to be. I wasn't the only one to lose my composure, some of the shooters also were shaking and drinking between batches. I noticed a young Waffen-SS, I didn't know his name: he was beginning to shoot any which way, his submachine gun at his hip, he was laughing insanely and emptying his cartridge clip at random, first shooting from left to right, then two shots and then three, like a child following the cracks in the pavement according to some mysterious internal topography. I went up to him and shook him but he kept on laughing and shooting right in front of me, I took away his submachine gun and slapped him, then sent him over to the men who were reloading the magazines; Grafhorst sent me another man in his place and I threw him the submachine gun, shouting, "And do it right, understand?!" Nearby, another group was being brought up: my gaze met that of a beautiful young woman, almost naked but very elegant, calm, her eyes full of an immense sadness. I moved away. When I came back she was still alive, half turned onto her back, a bullet had come out beneath her breast and she was gasping, petrified, her pretty lips trembled and seemed to want to form a word, she stared at me with her large surprised incredulous eyes, the eyes of a wounded bird, and that look stuck into me, split open my stomach and let a flood of sawdust pour out, I was a rag doll and didn't feel anything, and at the same time I wanted with all my heart to bend over and brush the dirt and sweat off her forehead, caress her cheek and tell her that it was going to be all right, that everything would be fine, but instead I convulsively shot a bullet into her head, which after all came down to the same thing, for her in any case if not for me, since at the thought of this senseless human waste I was filled with an immense, boundless rage, I kept shooting at her and her head exploded like a fruit, then my arm detached itself from me and went off all by itself down the ravine, shooting left and right, I ran after it, waving at it to wait with my other arm, but it didn't want to, it mocked me and shot at the wounded all by itself, without me; finally, out of breath, I stopped and started to cry. Now, I

thought, it's over, my arm will never come back, but to my great surprise it was there again, in its place, solidly attached to my shoulder, and
Häfner was coming up to me and saying, "That's enough, Obersturmführer. I'll take over for you."

I climbed back out and they gave me some tea; the warmth of the
liquid comforted me a little. The moon, three-quarters full, had risen
and hung in the gray sky, pale and scarcely visible. A little hut had been
put up for the officers. I went in and sat down on a bench in the back,
to smoke and drink my tea. There were three other men in this hut but
no one talked. Down below, the salvos continued to crackle: tireless,
methodical, the giant system we had set in motion went on destroying
people. It seemed it would never stop. Ever since the beginnings of human history, war has always been regarded as the ultimate evil. But we
had invented something compared to which war had come to seem
clean and pure, something from which many were already trying to escape by taking refuge in the elementary certainties of war and the front.
Even the insane butcheries of the Great War, which our fathers or some
of our older officers had lived through, seemed almost clean and righteous compared to what we had brought into the world. I found this
extraordinary. It seemed to me that there was something crucial in this,
and that if I could understand it then I'd understand everything and
could finally rest. But I couldn't think, my thoughts clashed with each
other, reverberating in my head like the roar of Metro cars rushing
through stations one after another, going in different directions on different levels. In any case no one cared about what I might think. Our
system, our State couldn't care less about the thoughts of its servants. It
was all the same to the State whether you killed Jews because you hated
them or because you wanted to advance your career or even, in some
cases, because you took pleasure in it. It did not mind, either, if you did
not hate the Jews and the Gypsies and the Russians you were killing,
and if you took absolutely no pleasure in eliminating them, no pleasure
at all. It did not even mind, in the end, if you refused to kill, no disciplinary action would be taken, since it was well aware that the pool of
available killers was bottomless, it could fish new men out at will, and
you could just as easily be put to some other use more in keeping with
your talents. Schulz, for example, the Kommandant of Ek 5 who had
asked to be replaced after receiving the *Vernichtungsbefehl*, had finally
been relieved, and it was said that he had landed a cushy job in Berlin,
at the *Staatspolizei*. I too could have asked to leave, I would probably
even have gotten a positive recommendation from Blobel or Dr. Rasch.
So why then didn't I? Probably because I hadn't yet understood what I
wanted to understand. Would I ever understand it? Nothing was less

certain. A sentence of Chesterton's ran through my head: *I never said it was always wrong to enter fairyland. I only said it was always dangerous.* Is that what war was, then, a perverted fairyland, the playground of a demented child who breaks his toys and shouts with laughter, gleefully tossing the dishes out the window?

A little before six o'clock, the sun set and Blobel ordered a break for the night: the shooters couldn't see anymore in any case. He held a quick meeting, standing behind the ravine among his officers, to discuss the problems. Thousands of Jews were still waiting in the square and on Melnikova Street; according to calculations, almost twenty thousand had already been shot. Several officers complained about the condemned being sent over the edge of the ravine: when they saw the scene at their feet, they panicked and became difficult to control. After some discussion, Blobel decided to have engineers from the Ortskommandantur dig entrances into the small ravines that led to the main one, and to have the Jews come in that way; then they wouldn't see the bodies until the last minute. He also ordered the dead to be covered over with quicklime. We returned to our quarters. On the square in front of Lukyanovskoe, hundreds of families were waiting, sitting on their suitcases or on the ground. Some had made fires and were preparing their food. In the street it was the same thing: the line stretched back to the city, guarded by a thin cordon. The next morning, at dawn, it began again. But I don't think it is necessary to continue the description.

By October 1, it was all over. Blobel had the sides of the ravine dynamited to cover the bodies over; we were expecting a visit from the Reichsführer, and he wanted everything cleaned up. At the same time the executions continued: Jews, still, but also Communists, officers of the Red Army, sailors from the Dnieper fleet, looters, saboteurs, officials, Banderists, Gypsies, Tatars. And then Einsatzkommando 5, headed now, instead of by Schulz, by one Sturmbannführer Meier, was arriving in Kiev to take over the executions and the administrative tasks; our own Sonderkommando would continue to advance in the wake of the Sixth Army, toward Poltava and Kharkov; so in the days following the Great Action, I was very busy, since I had to hand over all my networks and contacts to my successor, the Leiter III of Ek 5. We also had to attend to the results of the action: we had collected 137 truckloads of clothing, destined for the needy *Volksdeutschen* of the Ukraine; the blankets would go to the Waffen-SS for a military hospital. And then there were all the reports: Blobel had reminded me of Müller's order, and had put me in charge of preparing a visual presentation of the action. Himmler finally arrived, accompanied by Jeckeln, and that same day was pleased to address us. After explaining the necessity of wiping out the Jewish population, in order *to eradicate Bolshevism at the root*, he gravely noted that he was *aware of the difficulty of the task*; then, almost without transition, he revealed to us his concept of the future of the German East. The Russians, at the end of the war, pushed back beyond the Urals, could form a rump *Slavland*; of course, they would regularly try to return; to prevent them from doing so, Germany would set up a line of garrison towns and small forts in the mountains, entrusted to the Waffen-SS. All young Germans would be drafted for two years in the SS and would be sent there; of course there would be losses, but these small, permanent, low-intensity conflicts would allow the German nation *not to wallow in the weakness of conquerors*, but to preserve all the *vigor of the warrior*, vigilant and strong. Protected by this line, Russian and Ukrainian land would be open for German colonization, to be developed by our veterans: each one, *a soldier-peasant like his sons*, would manage a great, rich property; the labor in the fields would be provided by Slav helots, and the German would limit himself to administering. These farms would be placed in a constellation around little garrison and market towns; as for the frightful Russian industrial cities, they would eventually be razed; Kiev, a very ancient German city originally called *Kiroffo*, might however be spared. All these cities would be linked to the Reich by a network of highways and double-decker express trains, with individual sleeper cabins, for which special wide-gauge railways would be built; these vast projects would be carried out by the remaining Jews and war prisoners. Finally the Crimea, once the land of the Goth, as well as the German regions of the Volga and the oil center of Baku, would be annexed to the Reich, to become a vacation and leisure territory, directly connected to Germany, via Brest-Litovsk, by an express; the Führer, after finishing his great works, would come there to retire. This speech made a strong impression: clearly, even if to me the vision outlined evoked the fantastic utopias of a Jules Verne or an Edgar Rice Burroughs, there really was, elaborated in rarified spheres far above our own, a *plan*, a *final objective*.

The Reichsfürer also took advantage of the occasion to introduce to us the SS-Brigadeführer and Generalmajor der Polizei Dr. Thomas, who had come with him to replace Dr. Rasch as the head of the Einsatzgruppe. Rasch, in fact, had left Kiev on the second day of the action, without even saying goodbye: Thomas, as always, had anticipated events correctly. Rumors were flying: people speculated about his conflict with Koch; some said he had collapsed during the action. Dr. Thomas, who had the Iron Cross and spoke French, English, Greek, and Latin, was cast in a different mold: a doctor specializing in psychiatry, he had left his practice for the SD in 1934, out of idealism and National Socialist convictions. I quickly had occasion to get to know him better, since as soon as he arrived he began visiting all the offices of the Group and the Kommandos and talking individually with the officers. He seemed especially concerned with the psychological troubles of the men and officers: as he explained to us, in the presence of the Leiter from Ek 5 who was taking over my caseload, and of several other SD officers, it was impossible for a sane man to be exposed to such situations for months on end without suffering aftereffects, sometimes very serious ones. In Latvia, in Einsatzgruppe A, an Untersturmführer had gone mad and killed several other officers before he himself was shot; this case profoundly worried Himmler and the hierarchy, and the Reichsführer had asked Dr. Thomas, on whom his old specialty conferred a particular sensitivity to the problem, to recommend some measures. The Brigadeführer quickly promulgated an unusual order: all those who could no longer force themselves to kill Jews, either out of a sense of conscience or out of weakness, should present themselves to the Gruppenstab to have other tasks assigned to them or even to be sent back to Germany. This order gave rise to lively discussions among the officers; some thought that recognizing your weakness officially in this way would leave damaging traces in your personal file, and would limit any chance for promotion; others, on the contrary, declared they were ready to take Dr. Thomas at his word, and asked to leave. Still others, like Lubbe, were transferred without having asked for anything, on the advice of doctors from the Kommandos. Things were slowing down a little. For my report I had decided, rather than just delivering a stack of photographs, to make a display album. That turned out to be quite a job. One of our Orpos, an amateur photographer, had taken several rolls of color film during the executions, and also had the chemicals to develop them; I had some equipment requisitioned for him from a small photographer's studio so he could prepare prints of his best pictures for me. I also collected some black-and-white photographs and had all our reports dealing with the action copied on good paper, provided by the supply officer of the Twenty-ninth Corps. A clerk from the Stab wrote out captions and a title page in his fine official script, with *The Great Action of Kiev* as a title, and in smaller letters, *Reports and Documents*, with the dates. Among the specialized *Arbeitsjuden* kept in the new Syrets Lager, I unearthed an old leatherworker who had restored books for some Party offices and even made fancy albums for a conference; von Radomski, the camp commander, lent him to me for a few days, and with some black leather found among the confiscated goods, he bound the reports and the pages of photographs for me, in a cover embossed with the insignia "Sk 4a." Then I presented the book to Blobel. He was delighted; he leafed through it, went into raptures over the binding and the calligraphy: "Oh, I'd so like to have one too, as a souvenir." He congratulated me and assured me it would be given to the Reichsfürer, and even shown to the Führer himself; the whole Kommando could take great pride from it. I don't think he thought of this album as I did: for him, it was a trophy; for me, it was a bitter remembrance, a solemn reminder. I discussed it that night with a new acquaintance, an engineer from the Wehrmacht named Osnabrugge. I had met him in the officers' Kasino, when he had offered me a drink; he had turned out to be an interesting man, and I liked talking with him. I spoke to him about the album and he had this curious thought: "Every man must do his work with love." Osnabrugge was a graduate of a polytechnic university in the Rhineland, specializing in bridge construction; his vocation fascinated him, and he spoke eloquently about it: "You understand, I was trained with a sense of cultural mission. A bridge is a literal and material contribution to the community; it creates new roads, new links. And also, it's a beautiful thing. Not just to look at: if only you could understand the poetry of the calculations, the tensions and forces, the arches and cables, how it's all balanced by the play of mathematics!" He himself, however, had never built a bridge: he had drawn up some plans, but none had been realized. Then the Wehrmacht had sent him here to assess the bridge destructions carried out by the Soviets. "It's fascinating, really. Just as no bridge is ever built in the same way, no bridge blows up in the same way. There are always surprises, it's very instructive. But still, it pains me to see it. They're such fine works. If you like, I can show you." I accepted with pleasure; I had some free time now. He made an appointment with me at the foot of the largest of the destroyed bridges over the Dnieper, and I found him there one morning. "It's really impressive," he commented, examining the debris, hands on hips, motionless. This immense metal bridge with arches, built just under the cliffs of Pechersk, rested on five massive stone pillars; three whole spans were in the water, cut clean off by the explosives; across the river, two sections were still standing. The corps of engineers was building a floating bridge right next to it, with girders and wooden beams thrown across large inflatable boats; they had already reached almost halfway across. In the meantime, traffic was carried by means of barges, and a crowd was waiting on the bank, soldiers and civilians. Osnabrugge had a motor boat. We went round the pontoon bridge being built and he slowly drew alongside the twisted girders of the collapsed bridge. "You see," he showed me, pointing at the pillars, "there they even brought down the supporting arch, but over there they didn't. Actually it wasn't necessary, all they had to do was blow the load-bearing elements and all the rest would have come straight down. They overdid it."—"What about the pillars?"—"They're all good, except maybe the one in the middle. We're still checking it. Anyway we'll definitely rebuild it, but not right away." I looked around while Osnabrugge pointed out more details. At the top of the wooded cliffs, transformed by autumn into an orange-and-yellow blaze, with touches of bright red scattered about, the golden cupolas of the *lavra* were glittering in the sunlight. The city lay hidden behind it, and we couldn't see any houses on that side. Farther downstream, two other demolished bridges barred the river. The river flowed lazily between the half-sunken girders; in front of us, a barge loaded with peasant women in colorful scarves and sleepy soldiers calmly advanced. Contemplating the long seaweed undulating beneath the surface, I suddenly had a kind of dual vision: I could clearly see the seaweed and at the same time I thought I saw the bodies of Napoleonic hussars, in apple-green, bottle-green, or yellow uniforms, with cockades and ostrich feathers waving, drifting with the current. This was very intense, and I must have spoken the emperor's name, since Osnabrugge suddenly said: "Napoleon? I actually came across a book about Eblé before I left—you know, his chief engineer? An admirable man. Almost the only one, aside from Ney, who got his feet wet, literally, and the only one of Napoleon's superior officers who died, too. In Königsberg, at the end of the year, as a consequence of his bridge work over the Berezina."—"Yes, the Berezina, that's famous."—"We crossed it in less than a week. Did you know that Eblé had two bridges built over it? One for the men and one for the wagons, and the officers' carioles of course." We were heading back toward the shore. "You should read Herodotus," I said to him. "He has some fine stories about bridges too."—"Oh, I know, I know that." He pointed to the engineer's floating pontoon: "The Persians were already building on boats, like that." He made a face. "Better, probably." He left me on the shore and I shook his hand warmly. "Thanks for the expedition. It's done me a lot of good. See you soon!"—"Oh, I don't know. I have to leave tomorrow for Dniepropetrovsk. I have to examine twenty-three bridges in all, can you imagine! But I'm sure we'll meet again one of these days."

My birthday falls on October 10, and that year Thomas had invited me to dinner. At the end of the afternoon, some officers came with a bottle of Cognac to congratulate me and we had a few drinks together. Thomas joined us in a very good mood, raised a toast to my health, then drew me aside, shaking my hand: "My friend, I'm bringing you some good news as a gift: you're going to be promoted. It's still a secret, but I saw the papers at Hartl's. The Reichsführer, after the *Aktion*, asked the Gruppenchef to submit a list of deserving men and officers to him. Your album made a very good impression and your name was added to the list. I know that Hartl tried to oppose it, he never forgave you for your words during the *Aktion*, but Blobel supported you. You'd do well anyway if you went and apologized to Hartl one of these days."—"That's out of the question. He's the one who should apologize." He laughed and shrugged his shoulders: "As you like, Hauptsturmführer. But your attitude isn't making things any easier for you." I darkened: "My attitude is the attitude of an SS officer and a National Socialist. Whoever can say as much is welcome to criticize me." I changed the subject: "What about you?"—"What do you mean, me?"—"Aren't you also getting promoted?" He smiled broadly: "I don't know. You'll see."—"Watch out! I'm catching up with you." He laughed and I laughed with him. "That would surprise me," he said.

The city was slowly resuming normal life. After renaming the main streets—Kreshchatik had become Eichhornstrasse, in honor of the German general who entered Kiev in 1918; Shevchenko Boulevard became Rovnoverstrasse, Artyoma Street, Lembergstrasse, and my favorite, Tchekistova Street, a very common Gotenstrasse—the Ortskommandantur had authorized some private restaurants to open; the best one, apparently, was run by a *Volksdeutscher* from Odessa who had taken over the canteen for high-ranking Party officials where he used to work as a cook. Thomas had reserved a table there. All the customers were German officers, aside from two Ukrainian officials who were talking with some officers from the AOK: I recognized Bahazy, the "mayor" of Kiev put in place by Eberhard; the SD suspected him of massive corruption, but he supported Melnyk and von Reichenau had given his assent, so we had ended up withdrawing our objections. Thick velveteen curtains masked the windows, a candle illumined each alcove; we were given a corner table, a little set back, and brought some Ukrainian zakuski—pickles, marinated garlic, and smoked lard—along with some ice-cold honey-and-pepper vodka. We drank a few toasts while nibbling on the zakuski and chatting. "So," Thomas joked, "did you let yourself be tempted by the Reichsführer's offer—do you plan on settling down as a gentleman farmer?"—"I don't think so! Working the fields is not my line." Thomas had already moved on to the Great Action: "It was really hard, really unpleasant," he commented. "But it was necessary." I didn't want to pursue it: "What happened to Rasch, then?" I asked.—"Oh, him! I was sure you were going to ask me that." He pulled a few folded sheets of paper out of the pocket of his tunic: "Look, read this. But keep it to yourself, all right?" It was a report on the Group's letterhead, signed by Rasch, dated a few days before the *Grosse Aktion*. I quickly skimmed over it; toward the end, Rasch expressed his doubts that all the

Jews could be eliminated, and emphasized that they were not the only danger: *The Bolshevik apparatus is by no means identical with the Jewish population. Under such conditions we would miss the goal of political security if we replaced the main task of destroying the communist machine with the relatively easier one of eliminating the Jews.* He also insisted on the negative impact, for the reconstruction of Ukrainian industry, of the destruction of the Jews, and outlined an argument for the large-scale implementation of a Jewish labor force. I handed the report back to Thomas, who carefully refolded it and put it back in his pocket. "I see," I said, pinching my lips. "But you'll agree that he isn't entirely wrong."—"Of course! But there's no point in shooting your mouth off. That doesn't help get anything done. Remember your report in '39. Brigadeführer Thomas, now, had Parisian synagogues dynamited by French extremists. The Wehrmacht kicked him out of France, but the Reichsführer was delighted." The vodka was finished and they cleared things away; then they brought us some French wine, a Bordeaux. "Where on earth did they find that?" I asked.—"A little surprise: I had it sent to me from France by a friend. Can you believe it, they arrived intact! There are two bottles." I was very touched; in the present circumstances, it was really a fine gesture. I tasted the wine with delight. "I let it settle a while," Thomas said. "It's a change from Moldavian rotgut, isn't it?" He raised his glass: "You're not the only one celebrating your birthday, I think."—"That's true." Thomas was one of my few colleagues who knew that I had a twin sister; ordinarily I didn't talk about her, but he had noticed it at the time in my file, and I had explained everything to him. "How long has it been since you saw her?"—"Going on seven years."—"Do you ever hear from her?"—"From time to time. Not very often, actually."—"She still lives in Pomerania?"—"Yes. They go regularly to Switzerland. Her husband spends a lot of time in sanatoriums."—"Does she have any children?"—"I don't think so. That would surprise me. I don't know if her husband is even capable of it. Why?" He raised his glass again: "To her health, then?"—"To her health." We drank in silence; they brought us our meals and we ate, conversing pleasantly. After the meal Thomas had the second bottle opened and drew two cigars out of his jacket: "Now or with the Cognac?" I blushed with pleasure, but at the same time I felt vaguely embarrassed: "You're a real magician. We'll smoke them with the Cognac, but let's finish the wine first." The discussion turned to the military situation. Thomas was very optimistic: "Here, in the Ukraine, it's going well. Von Kleist is nearly at Melitopol and Kharkov is going to fall in a week or two. As for Odessa, it's a matter of days. But above all, the offensive on Moscow is smashing everything. Since Hoth and Hoepner linked up in Vyazma, we've taken another half a million prisoners! The Abwehr is talking about thirty-nine divisions annihilated. The Russians will never be able to bear those kinds of losses. And also, Guderian is already almost in Mtsensk and will soon meet up with the others. It was a real stroke of genius of the Führer's, to send Guderian here to finish Kiev, then send him back toward Moscow. The Reds didn't understand it at all. In Moscow they must be panicking. In one month we'll be there and after that, the war is over."—"Yes, but what if we don't take Moscow?" "We are going to take Moscow." I insisted: "Yes, but what if we don't take it? What will happen? How will the Wehrmacht spend the winter? Have you spoken with the supply officers? They have nothing planned for the winter—nothing at all. Our soldiers are still in summer uniforms. Even if they begin delivering warm clothing right now, they can never equip the troops properly. It's criminal! Even if we take Moscow, we'll lose tens of thousands of men, just from cold and sickness."—"You're a pessimist. I'm sure the Führer has everything planned." "No. the winter is not planned. I've discussed it, at the AOK, they don't have anything, they keep sending messages to Berlin, they're in despair." Thomas shrugged: "We'll find a way. In Moscow we'll find whatever we need."—"You can be sure the Russians will destroy everything before they retreat. And what if we don't take Moscow?"—"Why do you think we won't take Moscow? The Reds are incapable of resisting our Panzers. They put everything they had into Vyazma and we crushed them."—"Yes, because the good weather is holding out. But sooner or later the rains are going to come. In Uman, it's already snowing!" I was becoming heated, I felt the blood rising to my face. "You saw this summer what happens when it rains for a day or two? Now it'll last two or three weeks. Then the armies will have to stop too. And afterward, it will be the cold." Thomas stared at me sardonically; my cheeks were burning, I must have been red. "My oh my, you've become a real military expert," he commented.—"Not at all. But when you spend your days with soldiers, you learn things. And also I read. For instance, I read a book on Charles the Twelfth." I was gesticulating now. "You know Romny? Close to where Guderian made his junction with von Kleist? Well, that's where Charles the Twelfth had his headquarters, in December 1708, a little before Poltava. Peter and he were maneuvering with expensive troops, which they had to spare; they danced around each other for months. And then in Poltava Peter had a go at the Swedes and all of a sudden they retreated. But that's still feudal warfare, a war of feudal lords who care about honor and who especially fight as equals, so their war remains basically a courtly war, a kind of ceremonial game or a parade, almost theater, in any case not too deadly. Whereas later on, when the king's subjects, peasant or bourgeois, become citizens—when the State is democratized—then all of a sudden war becomes total and terrible, it becomes serious. That's why Napoleon crushed all of Europe: not because his armies were bigger or because he was a better strategist than his enemies, but because the old monarchies were still waging old-fashioned war, in a limited way. Whereas he had already moved beyond limited war. Napoleon's France was *open to talents*, as they said, the citizens participated in the administration, the State regulated, but it was the people who were sovereign; so that France naturally waged a total war, with all its forces put into play. And it's only when its enemies understood this and began to do the same thing, when Rostopchin burned Moscow and Alexander raised up the Cossacks and the peasants to harass the Great Army during its retreat, that the luck turned. In the war between Peter the Great and Charles the Twelfth, the stakes were small: if you lose, you stop playing. But when it's the entire nation that's waging war, it has to wager everything and up the ante over and over again, until total bankruptcy. And that's the problem. If we don't take Moscow, we won't be able to stop and negotiate a reasonable peace. So we'll have to continue. But do you want to know what I really think? For us, this war is a gamble. A gigantic gamble, which involves the entire nation, the whole *Volk*, but a gamble all the same. And a gamble is something you either win or lose. The Russians don't have that luxury. For them it's not a gamble, it's a catastrophe that's come crashing down on their country, a plague. And you can lose a gamble, but you can't lose when you're faced with a plague, you have to surmount it, you don't have any choice." I had delivered this whole speech rapidly, rapidly, almost without catching my breath. Thomas was silent; he drank his wine. "And another thing," I added heatedly. "I'm saying this to you, just to you. The murder of the Jews doesn't serve any real purpose. Rasch is absolutely right. It has no economic or political usefulness, it has no finality of a practical order. On the contrary, it's a break with the world of economics and politics. It's a waste, pure loss. That's all it is. So it can have only one meaning: an irrevocable sacrifice, which binds us once and for all, prevents us from ever turning back. You understand? With that, we leave the world of the gamble, there's no way back. It's the *Endsieg* or death. You and me, all of us, we're bound together now, bound to the outcome of this war by acts committed in common. And if we're mistaken in our calculations, if we've underestimated the number of factories the Reds have built or moved behind the Urals, then we're fucked." Thomas was finishing his wine. "Max," he said finally, "you think too much. It's bad for you. Cognac?" I began to cough and signed yes with my head. The cough continued, in fits, it was as if something heavy were stuck in my diaphragm, something that didn't want to come out, and I belched rather violently. I quickly got up, excusing myself, and ran to the back of the restaurant. I found a door and opened it; it led to an inner courtyard. I was seized with a terrible retching: finally I vomited a little. That helped somewhat but left me exhausted, I felt empty, I had to lean for a few minutes against a cart lying there, shafts in the air. Then I went back in. I went to find the waitress and asked her for some water: she brought me a bucket, I drank a little and rinsed my face. Then I returned to the table and sat down. "I'm sorry."—"Are you all right? Are you sick?"—"No, it's nothing, I just didn't feel well." It wasn't the first time. But I don't know exactly when it began. In Zhitomir, maybe. I had only vomited once or twice, but often, after meals, I was seized with these unpleasant and exhausting retchings, always preceded by a dry cough. "You should see a doctor," Thomas said. They had served the Cognacs and I drank a little. I felt better. Thomas offered me a cigar again; I took it, but didn't light it right away. Thomas looked worried. "Max . . . these kinds of ideas: keep them to yourself. They could get you into trouble."—"Yes, I know. I'm just talking about them to you, because you're my friend." I abruptly changed the subject: "So, have you picked one out yet?" He laughed: "No time. But it shouldn't be too difficult. The waitress isn't bad, did you notice?" I hadn't even looked at the waitress. But I said yes. "And you?" he asked.—"Me? Did you see the work we have? I'm lucky if I can sleep, I don't have any rest time to waste."—"What about in Germany? Before you came here? We haven't seen each other much, since Poland. And you're a discreet guy. You don't have a nice little *Fräulein* hidden away somewhere, who writes you long tearful letters, 'Max, Max, my darling, come back soon, oh how horrible war is'?" I laughed with him and lit my cigar. Thomas was already smoking his. I had certainly drunk a lot and I suddenly wanted to speak: "No. No *Fräulein*. But a long time before I met you, I had a fiancée. My childhood sweetheart." I saw he was curious: "Oh yes? Tell me."—"There isn't much to tell. We loved each other since we were little. But her parents were against it. Her father, or rather her stepfather, was a fat French bourgeois, a man of principles. They separated us by force, put us in boarding schools, far away from each other. She wrote me desperate letters in secret, I did too. And then they sent me to study in Paris."— "And you never saw her again?"—"A few times, during vacations, when we were around seventeen. And then I saw her again one last time, years later, just before coming to Germany. I told her our union would be indestructible."—"Why didn't you marry her?"—"It was impossible."—"What about now? You have a good position."—"Now it's too late: she's married. You see, you can't trust women. It always ends up like that. It's disgusting." I was sad, bitter, I shouldn't have been speaking about these things. "You're right," Thomas said. "That why I never fall in love. Anyway, I prefer married women, it's safer that way. What was her name, your sweetheart?" I made a cutting gesture with my hand: "It's not important." We smoked in silence, drinking our Cognacs. Thomas waited for me to finish my cigar before he got up. "Come on, don't be nostalgic. It's your birthday after all." We were the last ones there, the waitress was drowsing in the back of the room. Outside, our driver was snoring in the Opel. The night sky glimmered; the waning moon, clear and calm, cast its white glow over the silent, ruined city.

I must not have been the only one asking questions. A mute but profound uncertainty was pervading the ranks of the Wehrmacht. Cooperation with the SS was still excellent, but the Great Action had provoked anxious stirrings. A new order of the day by von Reichenau was beginning to circulate, a raw, harsh text, a brutal disclaimer of Rasch's conclusions. It described the men's doubts as *vague ideas about the Bolshevik system. The soldier in the territories of the East is not only a fighter according to the rules of the art of warfare,* he wrote, *but also the bearer of a pitiless* völkisch *ideology and the avenger of all the bestialities inflicted on the German and ethnically related nations. Therefore, the soldier must have a full understanding of the necessity for harsh but just countermeasures against Jewish subhumanity.* Human pity had to be banished: offering a traveling Slav, possibly a Bolshevik agent, something to eat was pure thoughtlessness, *a mistaken humanitarian act.* The cities would be destroyed, the partisans annihilated along with the uncommitted. These ideas, of course, didn't all come from von Reichenau; the Reichsführer must have suggested a few passages to him, but the main point was that this order *worked correctly toward the Führer, along his lines and toward his aims,* to use the fine expression of an obscure employee of the Prussian Ministry of Agriculture, and so it was hardly surprising that the Führer was delighted with it, that he caused it to be distributed as an example to all the armies in the East. But I doubted if it was enough to set people's minds at rest. National Socialism was a complete, total philosophy, a *Weltanschauung,* as we said; each person had to be able to find his place within it; there had to be room for all. But now, it was as if an opening had been forced into this whole, and all the destinies of National Socialism had been driven into it, on a one-way path of no return, which everyone had to follow until the end.

The fatality of things in Kiev only increased my unease. In the hallway of the palace of young virgins, I met an acquaintance from Berlin: "Sturmbannführer Eichmann! You've been promoted. Congratulations!"—"Ah! Dr. Aue. I've been looking for you. I have a package for you. It was given to me at the Prinz-Albrecht-Palais." I had known this officer back when he was setting up for Heydrich the Central Offices for Jewish Emigration; he would often come to my department to consult us on legal questions. He was an Obersturmführer then; now, he was sporting his four new diamonds on the neck of a black dress uniform that contrasted sharply with our campaign *feldgrau*. He strutted about like a little rooster; it was curious, he had left me with the impression of a hurried, plodding civil servant; I hardly recognized him now. "And what brings you here?" I asked him, inviting him into my office.—"Your package, and I have another one for one of your colleagues."—"No, I mean to Kiev." We had sat down and he leaned forward with a conspiratorial air: "I came to see the Reichsführer." He was obviously beaming with pride and seemed eager to talk: "With my Amtschef. On special invitation." He leaned over again: now he looked like a bird of prey, small and furtive. "I had to present a report. A statistical report. Prepared by my staff. You know that I head a whole *Referat* now?"—"No, I didn't know. My congratulations."—"The Four-B-four. Jewish affairs." He had put his cap on my desk and was holding a black leather briefcase tightly on his knees; he pulled a case out of his tunic pocket, took out some large glasses, put them on, and opened the briefcase to extract a large envelope, quite thick, which he gave me. "Here it is. Of course, I won't ask you what it is."—"Oh, I can tell you. They're scores."—"You're a musician? Me too, a little bit. I play the violin."—"Actually not. It was for someone else, but he's dead now." He took off his glasses: "Ah. I'm very sorry. This war is really terrible. Actually," he went on, "your friend Dr. Lulley also gave me a small bill, for the shipping costs."—"No problem. I'll send you some money this evening. Where are you staying?"—"With the Reichsführer's staff."— "Fine. Thank you very much for the favor. It was very kind of you."— "Oh, it was nothing. We SS men have to help each other out. I'm just sorry it arrived too late." I shrugged: "That's how it is. Can I pour you a drink?"—"Oh, I shouldn't. Work, you know. But . . ." He seemed sorry and I took the bait: "In the last war, they used to say *Krieg ist Krieg . . .*" He finished the sentence with me: ". . . *und Schnaps ist Schnaps*. Yes, I know. A very little one, then." I opened my safe and took out two glasses and the bottle I kept for my guests. Eichmann got up to offer the toast, ceremoniously: "To the health of our Führer!" We clinked glasses. I saw he still wanted to talk. "So what was in your report, then? . . . If it isn't a secret."—"Well, it's all very *hush-hush*, as the English say. But I can tell you. The Gruppenführer and myself were sent here by the Chief "—he meant Heydrich, now stationed in Prague as Assistant Reichsprotektor—"to discuss with the Reichsführer the plan for the evacuation of the Jews from the Reich."—"Evacuation?"—"Exactly. To the East. By the end of the year."—"All of them?"—"All of them."—"And where will they be sent?"—"Most of them to the Ostland, probably. And down South too, for the construction of the Durchgangstrasse Four. It hasn't yet been settled."—"I see. And your report?"—"A statistical summary. I presented it in person to the Reichsführer. On the global situation regarding Jewish emigration." He raised a finger. "Do you know how many there are?"—"Of what?"—"Of Jews. In Europe." I shook my head: "No idea."—"Eleven million! Eleven million, can you believe it? Of course, for the countries we don't control yet, like England, the numbers are approximate. Since they don't have any racial laws, we had to base our figures on religious criteria. But still that gives a rough estimate. Here in the Ukraine alone you have almost three million." He took on a more pedantic tone: "Two million nine hundred ninety-four thousand six hundred and eighty-four, to be exact."—"That *is* exact. But tell me, with one Einsatzgruppe we won't be able to do much."—"Precisely. Other methods are being studied." He looked at his watch and got up. "You'll have to excuse me now. I have to go back and find my Amtschef. Thank you for the drink."—"Thank you for the package! I'll send you the money for Lulley right away." Together, we raised our arms and bellowed, "Heil Hitler!"

After Eichmann had left, I sat down and contemplated the package left on my desk. It contained the Rameau and Couperin scores that I had ordered for the little Jew in Zhitomir. That had been a mistake, a sentimental naïveté; still it filled me with a great melancholy. I now thought I could understand better the reactions of the men and officers during the executions. If they suffered, as I had suffered during the Great Action, it wasn't just because of the smells and the sight of blood, but because of the terror and the moral suffering of the people they shot; in the same way, their victims often suffered more from the suffering and death, before their eyes, of those they loved, wives, parents, beloved children, than from their own deaths, which came to them in the end like a deliverance. In many cases, I said to myself, what I had taken for gratuitous sadism, the astonishing brutality with which some men treated the condemned before executing them, was nothing but a consequence of the monstrous pity they felt and which, incapable of expressing itself otherwise, turned into rage, but an impotent rage, without object, and which thus almost inevitably had to turn against those who had originally provoked it. If the terrible massacres of the East prove one thing, paradoxically, it is the awful, inalterable solidarity of humanity. As brutalized and habituated as they may have become, none of our men could kill a Jewish woman without thinking about his wife, his sister, or his mother, or kill a Jewish child without seeing his own children in front of him in the pit. Their reactions, their violence, their alcoholism, the nervous depressions, the suicides, my own sadness, all that demonstrated that the *other* exists, exists as an other, as a human, and that no will, no ideology, no amount of stupidity or alcohol can break this bond, tenuous but indestructible. This is a fact, not an opinion.

The hierarchy was beginning to perceive this fact and take it into consideration. As Eichmann had explained to me, new methods were being studied. A few days after his visit, a certain Dr. Widmann arrived in Kiev, come to deliver a new sort of truck to us. This truck, a Saurer, was driven by Findeisen, Heydrich's personal driver, a taciturn man who stubbornly refused, despite numerous requests, to explain to us why he had been chosen for this journey. Dr. Widmann, who headed the chemistry department at the Criminal-Technical Institute attached to the Kripo, gave the officers a long presentation: "Gas," he declared, "is a more elegant method." The truck, hermetically sealed, used its own exhaust gas to asphyxiate the people locked up inside; this solution, indeed, lacked neither elegance nor economy. As Widmann explained to us, other solutions had been tried out first; he himself had conducted experiments in Minsk, on the patients of an asylum, in the company of his Amtschef, Gruppenführer Nebe; one attempt, using explosives, had given disastrous results. "Indescribable. A catastrophe." Blobel looked enthusiastic: he liked this new toy and was eager to try it out for the first time. Häfner objected that the truck didn't hold many people—Dr. Widmann had told us fifty, sixty at most—and didn't work very quickly, and therefore seemed inefficient. But Blobel swept these reservations aside: "We'll keep it for the women and children, it will be good for morale." Dr. Widmann dined with us; afterward, around the billiard table, he told us how the thing had been invented: "Actually it's Gruppenführer Nebe who had the idea. One night, in Berlin, he had had a little too much to drink, and he fell asleep in his car, in his garage; the engine was still running and he almost died. We were already working on a truck model, but we were planning on using bottled carbon monoxide, which isn't at all practical in the conditions in the East. It's the Gruppenführer, after his accident, who thought of using the gas of the truck itself. A brilliant idea." He had heard the anecdote from his superior, Dr. Heess, who had told it to him on the U-Bahn. "Between Wittenbergplatz and Thielplatz, to be precise. I was very impressed."

★   ★   ★

For several days already, Blobel had been sending Teilkommandos outside Kiev to clean up the little towns, Pereyaslav, Yagotin, Kozelets, Chernigov, there were a lot of them. But the Teilkommandoführers were in despair: after an action, if they returned to the town, they found still more Jews there; the ones who had hidden kept coming back after they left. They complained that it upset all their statistics. According to Blobel's accrued totals, the Kommando had liquidated fifty-one thousand people, *including fourteen thousand without outside help* (meaning without Jeckeln's Orpo battalions). A Vorkommando was being formed to enter Kharkov, and I was supposed to be part of it; in the meantime, since I had nothing to do in Kiev (the Ek 5 had taken over all our tasks), Blobel asked me to go inspect the Teilkommandos. The rains had started, and as soon as you crossed the swollen Dnieper, you sank into the mud. The trucks, the cars were dripping with black, thick mud mixed with strands of the hay that the soldiers looted from the haystacks along the road to spread in front of their cars, uselessly. It took me two days to reach Häfner in Pereyaslav, towed most of the time by the Wehrmacht's tracked vehicles and covered in mud up to my eyes from wading around trying to push the Admiral. I spent the night in a little village with some officers from an infantry division that was moving up to the front from Zhitomir—exhausted men, who anxiously saw winter approaching and wondered what their ultimate objective was. I took care not to tell them about the Urals; we couldn't even advance up to Kharkov. They complained about the new recruits, sent from Germany to replace the casualties, but poorly trained and with a tendency to panic under fire, at least more readily than before. The equipment was falling to pieces: the modern German general-service wagons, with their rubber tires and ball bearings, were breaking apart on the tracks; they replaced them with almost indestructible *panje* carts, taken from the peasants. The beautiful German, Hungarian, or Irish horses with which they had started the campaign were dying in droves; only the scrubby Russian ponies were surviving, they could eat anything at all—birch shoots, the straw from the roofs of isbas—but they were too lightweight to pull the heavier carts, and the units had to abandon tons of provisions and equipment. "Every night, the men fight with each other to find a roof or a half-dry hole. Everyone's uniform is in rags, full of lice; we're not receiving anything, there's almost no more bread." Even the officers lacked the basics: no more razors, soap, toothpaste, no more leather to repair the boots, no more needles, no more thread. It rained day and night, and they were losing many more men from illness—dysentery, jaundice, diphtheria—than from gunfire. The sick had to walk up to thirty-five kilometers a day, since there was no way to transport them, and if they stayed alone in the villages, the partisans came and killed them. The partisans now were proliferating like lice; they seemed to be everywhere, and isolated couriers and dispatch bearers were vanishing in the woods. But I had also noticed among the soldiers a number of Russians in German uniforms, with the white armband of the *Hilf-swillige*. "The Hiwis?" replied an officer to whom I had mentioned this. "No, we're not really allowed to. But we take them anyway, we don't have a choice. The guys are volunteer civilians or prisoners. They do all the transport and B-echelon jobs; it works out pretty well, they're more used to these conditions than we are. And also Headquarters couldn't care less, they close their eyes. Anyway they must have forgotten us. By the time we reach Poltava they won't even know who we are."—"But aren't you afraid the partisans will take advantage of this to infiltrate your ranks and inform the Reds of your movements?" He shrugged his shoulders in a weary, disgusted way. "If it makes them happy. . . . In any case, there isn't a single Russian within a hundred kilometers. Nor a single German, either. No one. Rain and mud, that's all." This officer seemed completely discouraged; but he also showed me how to clean the mud off my uniform, it was useful and I didn't want to contradict him. "First you have to dry the mud by the stove, then you scrape it with a knife, see, then with a metal brush; and only then can you wash the uniform. For the underwear, you absolutely have to have it boiled." I watched the operation: it was disgusting, the lice came off in the boiling water in clusters, thick, swollen. I understood better Häfner's suppressed anger when I finally reached Pereyaslav. He had three Untersturmführers with him—Ott, Ries, and Dammann—who weren't getting much done, since they could hardly leave the town any longer, the roads were so impassable. "We would need tanks!" Häfner exclaimed when he saw me. "Soon we won't even be able to get back to Kiev. Here," he added before he abruptly turned away, "this is for you. All my congratulations." It was a teletype from Blobel, confirming my promotion; I had also received the War Merit Cross, Second Class. I followed Häfner into the school the Teilkommando was occupying and looked for a place to put my things. Everyone, soldiers and officers, was sleeping in the gymnasium; the classrooms served as offices. I changed and went to find Häfner, who gave me a report on the tribulations of his adjuncts: "You see this village, Zolotonosha? Apparently there are more than four hundred Jews there. Dammann tried three times to get there; three times he had to turn back, and even then, the last time, he nearly didn't make it here. The men are getting difficult." At night, there was soup and the awful black Wehrmacht *Kommissbrot*, and we went to bed early. I slept poorly. One of the Waffen-SS, a few meters away from my bedding, ground his teeth, an atrocious sound that raised my hackles; every time I began to doze off, he woke me up; it was driving me out of my mind. I wasn't the only one: some men shouted at him, I heard some blows and saw they were hitting him, but it didn't do any good, the infuriating sound went on, or else stopped only to start again a few moments later. "It's like that every night," grumbled Ries, who was sleeping next to me. "I'm going crazy. I'm going to strangle him one of these days." Finally I dozed off and had a strange, striking dream. Now I was a great Squid God, and I was ruling over a beautiful walled city of water and white stone. The center, especially, was all water, and tall buildings rose up all around. My city was peopled with humans who worshipped me. I had delegated part of my power and authority to one of them, my Servant. But one day I decided I wanted all these humans out of my city, at least for a while. The order went out, propagated by my Servant, and immediately droves of humans started fleeing out the gates of the city, to wait in hovels and shantytowns out in the desert beyond the walls. But they didn't leave fast enough to my liking, and I began to thrash violently, churning up the water of the center with my tentacles, then coiling them back and bearing down on swarms of terrified humans, lashing out and roaring with my terrible voice: "Out! Out! Out!" My Servant ran frantically about, commanded, guided, prompted the sluggish, and in this way the city emptied out. But in the buildings closest to the walls and farthest from the water where I was giving vent to my divine rage, some groups of humans were not heeding my commands. These were foreigners, not really aware of my existence, of my power over this city. They had heard the evacuation orders, but thought them ridiculous and were ignoring them. My Servant had to go see these groups one after another, to convince them diplomatically to leave: such as this conference of Finnish officers, who protested that they had rented the hotel and conference room and paid in advance, and wouldn't leave just like that. With them, my Servant had to lie skillfully, explaining for instance that there was an alert, a grave security problem, and that they had to evacuate for their own safety. I found this deeply humiliating, since the real reason was my Will; they were supposed to leave just because I wanted it, not because they were coaxed. My rage increased, I thrashed about and roared more violently than ever, sending great waves crashing through the city. When I woke up the rain was still streaming down the windows. At breakfast they served us some *Kommissbrot*, some coal-based margarine from the Ruhr, quite tasty, synthetic honey made from pine resin, and the frightful ersatz Schlüter tea, the identical packets of which never contained the same ingredients. The men ate in silence. Ries, glum,

pointed to a soldier leaning over his tea: "That's him."—"Who?" Ries
imitated a jaw grinding. I looked again: he was almost a teenager, he had
a hollow face spotted with acne, and eyes lost in dark bags. His comrades were rough on him, sending him off on chores and insulting him,
slapping him if he didn't go fast enough. The boy didn't say anything.
"Everyone is hoping he'll get himself killed by the partisans," Ries whispered to me. "We've tried everything, everything, we've even gagged
him. No use."

Häfner was a narrow but methodical man. He explained his plan of
action to me in front of a map, and wrote up a list of everything he
lacked, so that I could support his requests. I was supposed to inspect all
the Teilkommandos; that was obviously impossible, and I resigned myself to staying a few days in Pereyaslav while I waited to see what came
next. In any case, the Vorkommando was already in Poltava with Blobel: given the state of the roads, I had no hope of joining them before
the fall of Kharkov. Häfner was pessimistic: "The sector is swarming
with partisans. The Wehrmacht is conducting sweeps but isn't accom-
plishing much. They want us to back them up. But the men are exhausted, finished. You've seen the shit we're eating."—"It's regular army
food. And they're having a much harder time of it than we are."—
"Physically, yes, I agree. But our men are morally at the end of their
tether." Häfner was right and I would soon see so for myself. Ott went
out with a platoon of twenty men to search a nearby village where partisans had been reported; I decided to accompany him. We left at dawn,
with a truck and a *Kübelwagen*, an all-terrain vehicle, lent for the occasion by the division stationed in Pereyaslav. The rain slashed down,
thick, interminable, we were soaked even before we left. The smell of
wet wool filled the vehicle. Harpe, Ott's driver, maneuvered skillfully to
avoid the worst mudholes; the rear wheels kept slipping sideways in the
muck; sometimes he managed to control the skid, but often the vehicle
went completely sideways, and we had to climb out to set it right; then
we would sink up to our ankles in the sludge, some of us even lost our
boots in it. Everyone swore, shouted, cursed. Ott had loaded some
boards into the truck, which we wedged under the stuck wheels; sometimes that helped; but if the vehicle was off-kilter, one of the drive
wheels would start spinning on its own, projecting huge sprays of liquid
mud. My greatcoat and my pants were soon completely covered in
mud. Some of the men had their faces coated with it, you could just see
their exhausted eyes gleaming through; as soon as the vehicle was unstuck, they quickly washed their hands and faces in a puddle and
climbed back in. The village was seven kilometers from Pereyaslav; the
trip took us three hours. When we arrived, Ott sent a group into a

blocking position beyond the last houses while he deployed the others on both sides of the main street. The wretched isbas were lined up in the rain, their thatched roofs streaming into flooded gardens; a few soaked chickens were scattered here and there; we couldn't see anyone. Ott sent a noncom and the *Dolmetscher* to look for the Staroste. They returned after about ten minutes, accompanied by a little old man wrapped in a sheepskin coat and wearing a shabby rabbit fur hat. Ott interrogated him standing in the rain; the old man moaned, denied there were any partisans. Ott got angry. "He says there are only old men here, and women," the *Dolmetscher* translated. "All the men have died or left."—"Tell him that if we find anything we'll hang him first!" Ott shouted. Then he sent his men to search the houses. "Check the ground! Sometimes they dig bunkers." I followed one of the groups. The mud lay just as thick in the single little village lane as on the road; we entered the isbas with mud packed on our feet, and we tracked it everywhere. Inside we really did find only old men, filthy women, lice-ridden children lying on big whitewashed clay stoves. There wasn't much to search: the ground was of beaten earth, without any wood flooring; there was almost no furniture, and no attics, either, since the roofs rested directly on the walls. Everything stank of filth, mold, and urine. Behind the houses lined up to the left of the lane began a little birch wood, slightly higher up. I walked between two isbas to the edge of the forest. Water pattered on the branches, swelling the dead, rotting leaves that carpeted the ground; the slope was slippery and hard to climb. The wood seemed empty but with the rain you couldn't see very far. A strangely animated pile of branches drew my gaze: the brown leaves were swarming with hundreds of little black beetles; underneath, there were some decomposed human remains, still dressed in the rags of brown uniforms. I tried to cover them up, horrified by the creatures, but they kept overflowing and running everywhere. Exasperated, I aimed a kick at the mass. A skull detached itself and rolled to the bottom of the slope, scattering beetles in the mud. I walked back down. The skull was resting against a stone, quite clean, its empty sockets swarming with beetles, its gnawed lips baring yellow teeth, washed by the rain: and the skull had opened, revealing the intact flesh of the mouth, a thick, almost wriggling tongue, pink, obscene. I went back to join Ott, who was now in the center of the village with the Staroste and the *Dolmetscher*. "Ask him where the corpses in the wood come from," I said to the *Dolmetscher*. The old man's shapka was dripping into his beard; he muttered, half toothless, "They're soldiers from the Red Army. There were battles in the wood, last month. A lot of soldiers were killed. The villagers buried the ones they found, but they didn't look everywhere."—"What about their weapons?" Once again the *Dol-metscher* had to translate. "They gave them to the Germans, he says." A Scharführer approached and saluted Ott. "Untersturmführer, there's nothing here." Ott was in a foul mood. "Search again! I'm sure they're hiding something." Other soldiers and some Orpos drifted in. "Untersturmführer, we looked, and there's nothing."—"Search, I said!" At that moment we heard a sharp cry a little farther up. An indistinct form was running in the street. "There!" Ott shouted. The Scharführer took aim and shot through the curtain of rain. The form collapsed in the mud. The men deployed to advance, on the lookout. "It was a woman, idiot," a voice said. "You watch out who you call an idiot!" barked the Scharführer. A man turned the body over in the mud: it was a young peasant woman, with a colored scarf on her head, pregnant. "She just panicked," said one of the men. "You didn't have to shoot her like that."—"She isn't dead yet," said the man who was examining her. The orderly came over: "Take her into the house." Several men picked her up; her head fell back, her muddy dress stuck to her enormous belly, the rain pummeled her body. They carried her into the house and put her on a table. An old woman sat sobbing in a corner, otherwise the isba was empty. The girl was groaning. The orderly ripped open her dress and examined her. "She's finished. But she's at full term, we can still save the baby, with a little luck." He began to give directions to the two soldiers standing there. "Heat some water." I went out into the rain to find Ott, who had gone back to the vehicles. "What's happening, then?"—"The girl is going to die. Your orderly is trying to perform a caesarian section."—"A caesarian?! Christ, he's gone nuts!" He began to clamber up the street, squelching through the mud, to the house. I followed him. He burst in: "What is this mess, Greve?" The orderly was holding a little bloody bundle, swaddled in a sheet, and had just finished tying off the umbilical cord. The girl, dead, lay on the table with her eyes wide open, naked, covered in blood, sliced open from the navel to the sex. "It worked, Untersturmführer," Greve said. "He should live. But they'll have to find a wet nurse."—"You're crazy!" Ott shouted. "Give me that!"—"Why?"—"Give me that!" Ott was pale and trembling. He tore the newborn from Greve's hands and, holding it by its feet, smashed its skull against the corner of the stove. Then he threw it on the ground. Greve was foaming at the mouth: "Why did you do that?!" Ott was shouting too: "You should have let it croak in its mother's womb, you moron! You should have left it alone! Why did you take it out? Wasn't it cozy enough in there?" He turned on his heels and went out. Greve was sobbing: "You shouldn't have done that, you shouldn't have done that." I followed Ott, who stood raging in the mud and the rain in front

of the Scharführer and some men gathered round. "Ott . . . ," I called
out. Behind me a call resounded: "Untersturmführer!" I turned around:
Greve, his hands still red with blood, was coming out of the isba, his rifle shouldered. I stepped back and he headed straight for Ott. "Untersturmführer!" Ott turned around, saw the rifle and began yelling:
"What, you asshole, what do you want? You want to shoot, is that it?
Go ahead!" The Scharführer was also shouting: "Greve, in the name of
God, put that rifle down!"—"You shouldn't have done that," Greve was
yelling as he kept approaching Ott.—"Well, go on, you bastard,
shoot!"—"Greve, stop that right now!" the Scharführer roared. Greve
fired; Ott, hit in the head, flew back and collapsed in a puddle with a
great splash of water. Greve kept his rifle raised; everyone had fallen
silent. All that could be heard was the beating of the rain on the puddles, on the mud, on the men's helmets, on the roof thatch. Greve was
trembling like a leaf, his rifle at his shoulder. "He shouldn't have done
that," he repeated stupidly. "Greve," I said softly. A wild look in his eyes,
Greve aimed his rifle at me. I very slowly spread my hands apart without saying anything. Greve redirected his rifle at the Scharführer. Two
of the men were aiming their rifles at Greve. Greve kept his rifle
pointed at the Scharführer. The men could shoot him but he would
probably also kill the Scharführer. "Greve," the Scharführer said calmly,
"You've really fucked up. Ott was a scumbag, okay. But now you're
really in for it."—"Greve," I said. "Put down your weapon. Otherwise
we'll have to kill you. If you turn yourself in I'll testify in your favor."—
"I'm fucked anyway," Greve said. He was still aiming at the Scharführer.
"If you shoot I won't die alone." He aimed his rifle at me again, at
point-blank range. The rain was dripping from the muzzle, just in front
of my eyes, and was streaming on my face. "Hauptsturmführer!" the
Scharführer called. "Do you mind if I settle this my way? To avoid any
more trouble." I nodded. The Scharführer turned toward Greve.
"Greve. I'll give you a five minutes' head start. After that we'll come
looking for you." Greve hesitated. Then he lowered his rifle and bolted
toward the forest. We waited. I looked at Ott. His head floated in the
water, his face just above the surface, with a black hole in the center of
his forehead. The blood was forming blackish coils in the cloudy water.
The rain had washed his face, was drumming on his open, surprised
eyes, slowly filling his mouth, running out of the corners. "Andersen,"
the Scharführer said. "Take three men and go look for him."—"We
won't find him, Scharführer."—"Go find him." He turned toward me:
"Do you have any objections, Hauptsturmführer?" I shook my head:
"None." Other men had joined us. Four of them were heading for the
wood, their rifles shouldered. Four others picked up Ott's corpse and

carried it by the greatcoat to the truck. I followed them with the Scharführer. They loaded the body through a side panel; the Scharführer sent
some men to give the signal to regroup. I wanted to smoke but it was
impossible, even under the greatcoat. The men were drifting back to
the vehicles. We waited for the ones the Scharführer had sent in search
of Greve, listening for gunfire. I noticed that the Staroste had prudently
disappeared, but didn't say anything. Finally Andersen and the others
reappeared, gray shadows emerging through the rain. "We looked in
the wood, Scharführer. But we didn't find anything. He must be hiding."—"That's fine. Get in." The Scharführer looked at me: "The partisans will skin him alive anyway, the son of a bitch."—"I told you,
Scharführer, I have no objection to your decision. You avoided more
bloodshed, I congratulate you."—"Thank you, Hauptsturmführer." We
took to the road again, bearing Ott's body. Getting back to Pereyaslav
took even longer than the way out. When we arrived, without even
changing, I went to explain the incident to Häfner. He listened and then
kept silent for a long moment. "You think he'll go join the partisans?"
he finally asked.—"I think that if there are partisans there, and they find
him, they'll kill him. In any case he won't survive the winter."—"And
if he tries to live in the village?"—"They're much too afraid, they'll de-
nounce him. Either to us, or to the partisans."—"Fine." He thought
some more. "I'm going to declare him a deserter, armed and dangerous,
and that's it." He paused again. "Poor Ott. He was a good officer."—
"If you want my opinion," I said dryly, "he should have been sent on
leave a long time ago. That might have avoided this whole business."—
"You're probably right." A large puddle was forming under my chair.
Häfner stretched his neck, jutting out his wide square chin: "What a
mess, all the same. Do you want to deal with the report for the Stan-
dartenführer?"—"No, it's your Kommando after all. You do it and then
I'll countersign it, as a witness. And be sure to make me a copy, for Amt
Three."—"Understood." I finally went to change and smoke a cigarette.
Outside, the rain was still beating down, as if it would never end.

Once again, I slept poorly; that seemed to be the rule in Pereyaslav.
The men grunted and snored; as soon as I dozed off, the teeth-grinding of the little Waffen-SS cut into my sleep and pulled me out of it
abruptly. In this groggy drowsiness, Ott's face in the water and the skull
of the Russian soldier became confused: Ott, lying in the puddle,
opened his mouth wide and stuck his tongue out at me, a thick, pink,
fresh tongue, as if he were inviting me to kiss him. I awoke anxious,
tired. Over breakfast, once again I was overcome with coughing, then
with violent retching; I slipped out to an empty hallway, but nothing

came up. When I went back to the table, Häfner was waiting for me with a teletype: "Kharkov has just fallen, Hauptsturmführer. The Standartenführer is waiting for you in Poltava."—"In Poltava?" I pointed to the sodden windows. "He has to be kidding. How does he expect me to get there?"—"The trains are still running, from Kiev to Poltava. When the partisans don't derail them. There's a *Rollbahn* convoy that's leaving for Yagotin; I called the division, they said they'll take you. Yagotin is on the railroad, so from there you can get a train." Häfner was truly an efficient officer. "Fine, I'll go tell my driver."—"No, your driver will stay here. That Admiral will never get as far as Yagotin. You'll travel with the *Rollbahn* in one of their trucks. I'll send the driver with the car back to Kiev when it's possible."—"Fine."—"The convoy leaves at noon. I'll give you some dispatches for the Standartenführer, including the report about Ott's death."—"Fine." I went to get my kit ready. Then I sat down at a table and wrote a letter to Thomas, straightforwardly describing the previous day's incident: *You discuss this with the Brigadeführer, since I know Blobel won't do anything, aside from covering himself. We have to learn from this, otherwise it might happen again.* After I finished the letter, I sealed it in an envelope and put it aside. Then I went to find Ries. "Tell me, Ries, your little childsoldier, there, the one who grates his teeth. What's his name?"—"You mean Hanika? Franz Hanika. The one I showed you?"—"Yes, him. Can you give him to me?" He raised his eyebrows, taken aback. "Give him to you? Why?"—"I'm leaving my driver here; I left my orderly in Kiev, so I need another one. And in Kharkov I can have him put up in a separate room, that way he won't bother anyone anymore." Ries seemed delighted: "Listen, Hauptsturmführer, if you're serious . . . I'm all for it. I'll go ask the Obersturmführer; I don't think he'll have any objections."—"Fine. I'll go tell this Hanika." I found him in the mess, where he was scouring pots. "Hanika!" He stood at attention and I saw he had a bruise on one cheek. "Yes?"—"I'm leaving for Poltava and then Kharkov. I need an orderly. Do you want to come?" His strained face lit up: "With you?"—"Yes. Your work won't change much, but at least you won't have the others on your back." He looked radiant, like a child who has just received an unexpected present. "Go get your things ready," I said to him.

The journey by truck to Yagotin remains for me a long wandering, an endless foundering. The men spent more time outside the trucks pushing than in the cabs. But as terrible as the mud was, the idea of what would come later scared them even more. "We have nothing, Herr Hauptsturmführer, you understand? Nothing," a Feldwebel explained to me. "No warm underclothes, no sweaters, no winter coats, no anti-

freeze, nothing. The Reds are ready for winter, though."—"They're
men like us. They'll be cold too."—"It's not that. Cold can be dealt
with. But you have to be equipped, and they are. And even if they
aren't, they'll be able to improvise. They've lived with it all their lives."
He cited a striking example he had from one of his Hiwis: in the Red
Army, the men received boots two sizes bigger than their actual foot
size. "With the frost, the feet swell, and then it leaves more room to fill
them with straw and newspaper. We have boots that are just at the right
size. Half the men are going to end up in the infirmary with their toes
amputated."

When we reached Yagotin, I was so coated in mud that the noncom
in charge of the station didn't recognize my rank and greeted me with
a torrent of abuse because I was tracking mud into his waiting room. I
put my kit down on a bench and retorted harshly: "I am an officer and
you are not to speak to me like that." I went back out to join Hanika,
who helped me wash up a little at a hand pump. The noncom apologized profusely when he saw my insignia, which were still those of an
Obersturmführer; he invited me to take a bath and have dinner. I gave
him the letter for Thomas, which would leave with the mail. He put me
up in a small room for officers; Hanika slept on a bench in the waiting
room, with some men on leave waiting for the train to Kiev. The station chief woke me up in the middle of the night: "There's a train in
twenty minutes. Come." I quickly got dressed and went out. The rain
had stopped but everything was still dripping, the tracks were gleaming
under the bleak station lights. Hanika had joined me with our kit. Then
the train arrived, its brakes squealing for a long time, in spurts, before it
stopped. Like all the trains nearing the front, it was half empty; we had
our choice of compartments. I lay down and fell asleep. If Hanika
ground his teeth, I didn't hear him.

When I woke up we hadn't even passed Lubny. The train stopped
often, because of alerts or to let priority convoys pass. Near the toilets,
I met a Major from the Luftwaffe who was returning from leave to join
his squadron in Poltava. It had been five days since he left Germany. He
talked to me about the morale of the civilians of the Reich, who remained confident even though victory was slow in coming; very amiably he offered us a little bread and sausage. At the station stops too we
sometimes found something to snack on. The train kept its own time, I
didn't feel hurried. At the stops I lazily contemplated the sadness of the
Russian stations. The facilities, barely built, already took on a dilapidated look; brambles and weeds invaded the railways; here and there,
even in this season, one could see the burst of color of a stubborn
flower, lost among gravel soaked with black oil. The cows that placidly

wandered onto the tracks seemed surprised each time the roaring whistle of a train came to disturb their meditation. The dull gray of mud and
dust covered everything. On the paths alongside the tracks, a filthy kid
pushed a ramshackle bicycle, or else an old peasant hobbled along to the
station to try to sell us some of her moldy vegetables. Slowly I let this
endless ramification grow in me, this vast system of tracks, of switches
controlled by idiotic, alcoholic laborers. At the marshalling yards, I
watched interminable lines of dirty, oily, muddy freight cars waiting, full
of wheat, coal, iron, gasoline, livestock, all the wealth of occupied
Ukraine seized to be sent to Germany, all the things men need, moved
from one place to another according to a grandiose, mysterious plan of
circulation. Was that the reason why we were waging war, why men
were dying? But even in everyday life that's the way it is. Somewhere a
man wastes away his life, covered with coal dust, in the stifling depths
of a mine; elsewhere, another man rests warmly, clothed in alpaca,
buried in a good book in an armchair, without ever thinking whence
or how this armchair, this book, this alpaca, this warmth reach him. National Socialism wanted every German, in the future, to be able to have
his modest share of the good things of life; but within the limitations of
the Reich, that had turned out to be impossible; so now we were taking these things from others. Was that fair? So long as we had the
strength and the power, yes, since as far as justice is concerned, there is
no absolute authority, and each people defines its own truth and justice.
But if ever our strength weakened, if our power gave out, then we
would have to endure the justice of others, terrible as it might be. And
that too would be fair.

In Poltava, Blobel sent me to the delousing station as soon as he set
eyes on me. Then he filled me in on the situation. "The Vorkommando
finally entered Kharkov on the twenty-fourth, with the Fifty-fifth Army
Corps. They've set up offices already." But Callsen was sorely lacking in
men and urgently asking for reinforcements. For now, though, the roads
were blocked by the rains and the mud. The train didn't run any farther,
since the tracks had to be restored and widened, and that too could be
done only when travel became possible again. "As soon as it freezes
you'll go to Kharkov with some other officers and troops; the Kommandostab will join you a little later on. The entire Kommando will
take its winter quarters in Kharkov."

Hanika soon turned out to be a much better orderly than Popp.
Every morning, I found my boots polished and my uniform cleaned,
dried, and ironed; at breakfast, he often produced something to improve
the ordinary fare. He was very young; he had been drafted directly from
the Hitlerjugend to the Waffen-SS, and from there had been posted to

the Sonderkommando; but he wasn't lacking in qualities. I taught him
our file classification system, so he could sort or find documents for me.
Ries had overlooked a pearl: the boy was friendly and obliging; you just
had to know how to take him. At night, for a little, he would have slept
across my doorway, like a dog or a servant in a Russian novel. Better
nourished, and well rested, with his face rounded out, he was in fact a
handsome boy despite his teenage acne.

As for Blobel, he was growing more and more moody; he drank and
flew into hysterical rages, on the slightest pretext. He would pick out a
scapegoat from among the officers and pursue him for days on end,
without respite, harassing him on every aspect of his work. At the same
time he was a good organizer, he had a well-developed sense of priorities and practical constraints. Fortunately, he hadn't yet had an occasion
to test his new Saurer; the truck had stayed stuck in Kiev, and he was
impatiently waiting for it to be delivered. The very idea of the thing
made my blood run cold, and I hoped to be long gone by the time he
received it. I continued to suffer from sudden retchings, accompanied
sometimes by painful and exhausting upwellings of gas; but I kept that
to myself. Nor did I speak about my dreams to anyone. Almost every
night now, I rode in a metro, each time different but always skewed,
strange, unpredictable, haunting me with an endless circulation of trains
coming and going, escalators or elevators rising and falling from one
level to another, doors opening and closing at the wrong moment, signals changing from green to red without the trains stopping, lines crossing without any shunting, and terminus stops where the passengers
waited in vain, a broken-down, noisy, immense, interminable network
traveled by incessant and insane traffic. When I was young I loved the
Metro; I had discovered it when I was seventeen and went up to Paris,
and at the slightest occasion I took it simply for the pleasure of movement, of looking at people, at the stations going by. The CMP, the previous year, had taken over the north-south line, and for the price of a
single ticket I could cross the city from one end to the other. Soon I got
to know the underground geography of Paris better than its surface.
With other boarding students from my *prépa*, I slipped out at night,
thanks to a copy of a key the students passed on from one generation to
the next, and, armed with little flashlights, we waited on a platform for
the last train so we could then climb into the tunnels and walk on the
tracks from station to station. We had quickly discovered numerous tunnels and shafts closed to the public, which came in handy when railroad
men, disturbed in their nighttime work, tried to chase us. This underground activity still leaves a trace of strong emotion in my memory, a
friendly feeling of security and warmth, with probably a distant erotic

overtone too. Back then, metros already filled my dreams, but now they bore with them a translucent, nearly acid anguish; I could never arrive where I had to be, I missed my connections, the doors to the cars slammed in my face, I traveled without a ticket, in horror of the inspectors, and I often awoke filled with a cold, abrupt panic, that left me feeling utterly lost.

Finally the first frosts seized the roads, and I could leave. The cold had settled in suddenly, overnight; in the morning, the vapor of our breath, the windows white with frost, were a joyous sight. Before leaving, I put on all my sweaters; Hanika had managed to find an otterskin shapka for me for a few reichsmarks; in Kharkov, we would quickly have to find some warm clothes. On the road, the sky was pure and blue; clouds of sparrows whirled before the woods; near the villages, peasants were reaping frozen pond rushes to cover their isbas. The road itself was treacherous: the frost, in places, had seized the chaotic ridges of the mud, raised by the passage of tanks and trucks, and these hardened crests made the vehicles skid, tore the tires, sometimes even caused cars to flip over when a driver took a curve badly and lost control of his vehicle. Elsewhere, beneath a fine crust that crumbled under the wheels, the mud remained viscous, insidious. All around stretched the empty steppe, the harvested fields, some forests. It's about 120 kilometers from Poltava to Kharkov: the trip took a full day. We entered the city through devastated suburbs with charred, ruined, overturned walls, among which, hastily cleared away, lay piled in little stacks the twisted and burned wrecks of the fighting equipment wasted on the futile defense of the city. The Vorkommando had set itself up in the Hotel International, which sat at the side of an immense central square dominated, at the rear, by the constructivist pile of the *Dom Gosprom*, cubical buildings, arranged in a semicircle, with two tall square arches and a pair of skyscrapers—a surprising construction for this large lazy city with its wooden houses and old czarist churches. The House of the Plan, burned during the battles, raised its massive façades and columns of gutted windows nearby, over to the left; in the center of the square, an imposing bronze Lenin turned his back to the two blocks and, indifferent to the cars and German tanks lined up at his feet, welcomed the passersby with a large gesture. In the hotel, confusion reigned; most of the rooms had broken windows, and bitter cold swept in. I requisitioned a small suite that was more or less inhabitable, left Hanika to see to the windows and the heating, and went back down to find Callsen. "The battles for the city were very violent," he summarized for me, "there was a lot of destruction, as you saw; it will be hard to find quarters for the whole Sonderkommando." The Vorkommando had nonetheless started its SP work and was interrogating suspects; in addition, at the Sixth Army's request, they had taken a number of hostages to discourage sabotage, as in Kiev. Callsen had already formed his political analysis: "The population of the city is mostly Russian, so the delicate problems stemming from our relations with the Ukrainians will be less acute here. There's also a large Jewish population, although a lot of them fled with the Bolsheviks." Blobel had given him the order to summon the Jewish leaders and shoot them: "For the others, we'll see later on."

In the bedroom, Hanika had managed to plug the windows with some cardboard and canvas tarps, and he had found a few candles for light; but the rooms were still freezing. For a long while, sitting on the sofa while he made some tea, I let a pleasant fantasy come over me: I invited him to sleep with me, for mutual warmth, then slowly, during the night, I passed my hand under his tunic, kissed his young lips, and searched through his pants to take out his stiff penis. Seducing a subordinate, even a consenting one, was out of the question; but it had been a long time since I had even thought of such things, and I didn't try to resist the sweetness of these images. I looked at the nape of his neck and wondered if he had ever been with a girl. He was really very young, but even before his age, in the boarding school, we were already doing everything you can do among boys, and the older boys, who must then have been the age Hanika was now, knew how to find girls in the next village who were more than happy to go for a roll in the hay. Now my thoughts shifted: in place of his frail neck other powerful necks appeared, of men I had been with or even just looked at, and I considered these necks with a woman's eyes, suddenly understanding with a terrifying clarity that men control nothing, dominate nothing, that they are just children and even toys, put there for the pleasure of women, an insatiable pleasure all the more sovereign that the men think they are in charge, think they dominate women, whereas in reality women absorb them, wreck their dominion and dissolve their control, to take far more from them than they give. Men believe in all honesty that women are vulnerable, and that they must either take advantage of this vulnerability or protect it, whereas women laugh, with tolerance and love or else with scorn, at the childish, infinite vulnerability of men, at their fragility, this brittleness so close to a permanent loss of control, this perpetually threatening collapse, this vacuity embodied in such strong flesh. That is why, without a doubt, women so rarely kill. They suffer much more, but they will always have the last word. I drank my tea. Hanika had made my bed with all the blankets he could find; I took two of them and left them for him on the sofa in the first room, where he would sleep. I closed the door and rapidly masturbated, then fell asleep immediately, my hands and stomach still damp with sperm.

For one reason or another, maybe to stay close to von Reichenau, who had his HQ there, Blobel chose to remain in Poltava, and we waited for the Kommandostab for more than a month. The Vorkommando didn't remain inactive. As in Kiev, I set up networks of informers; it was all the more necessary given the motley population, full of immigrants from all over the USSR, among whom certainly lurked a number of spies and saboteurs; furthermore, we hadn't found a single NKVD list or file: before retreating, they had methodically cleaned out their archives, so there was nothing left for us that might make our job easier. Working in the hotel was becoming rather difficult: while I tried to type a report or talk with a local collaborator, the screams of some man being interrogated would ring out next door, overwhelming me. One night they served us red wine at dinner: my meal was scarcely over when everything started coming back up. This had never happened to me before with such violence, and I was beginning to worry: before the war, I never vomited, when I was little I had almost never thrown up, and I wondered what the reason for it could be. Hanika, who had heard my retching through the bathroom door, suggested maybe the food was bad, or else I was suffering from an intestinal flu: I shook my head, that wasn't it, I was sure of it, since it had started exactly like the retchings, with a cough and a feeling of heaviness or else of something blocked, except this had gone further and everything had come up all of a sudden, the scarcely digested food mixed with the wine, a frightening red mixture.

Finally Kuno Callsen obtained permission from the Ortskommandantur to set up the Sonderkommando in the premises of the NKVD, on Sovnarkomovskaya Street, the street of the Soviet People's Commissariats. This large L-shaped building dates from the beginning of the century, and the main entrance is off a little side street, lined with trees stripped bare by winter; a plaque in Russian at the corner states that during the civil war, in May and June 1920, the famous Dzerzhinsky had his headquarters here. The officers kept living at the hotel; Hanika had found a stove for us; unfortunately, he had installed it in the little living room where he slept, and if I left the door open, his atrocious teeth-grinding ruined my sleep. I asked him to warm the two rooms well during the day, so that I could close the door when I went to sleep; but at dawn the cold would wake me, and I ended up sleeping with my clothes on, with a wool cap, until Hanika found me some duvets that I piled up so I could sleep naked, as I was used to. I continued vomiting

almost every night or at least every other night, right away at the end
of meals, once even before finishing—I had just drunk a cold beer with
my pork chop and it came back up so quickly that the liquid was still
cool, a hideous sensation. I always managed to vomit neatly, in a bathroom or a washbasin, without drawing too much attention, but it was
exhausting: the huge retchings that preceded the upwelling of the food
left me emptied, drained of all energy for a long time. At least the food
returned so quickly that it wasn't yet acid, digestion had scarcely begun,
and it didn't have any taste; I just had to rinse my mouth out to feel
better.

The specialists from the Wehrmacht had meticulously searched all
the public buildings for explosives and mines, and had defused some
bombs; despite that, a few days after the first snowfall, the House of the
Red Army exploded, killing the commander of the Sixtieth Division,
its Chief of Staff, its Ia, and three clerks, who were found horribly mutilated. The same day there were four other explosions; the military was
furious. The chief engineer of the Sixth Army, Oberst Selle, gave the
order to place Jews in all the large buildings to discourage new bombings. As for von Reichenau, he wanted reprisals. The Vorkommando
was not involved in this: the Wehrmacht took care of it. The Ortskommandant had prisoners hanged from all the balconies in the city.
Behind our offices, two streets, Chernychevsky and Girchman, com-
bined to form an irregular expanse, like a vague square between small
buildings scattered about without any plan. Several of these buildings,
from different periods and in different colors, opened onto the street at
an abrupt angle, their elegant doorways topped by small balconies; soon,
at each railing, one or several men were hanging like sacks. On a town-
house built before the last war, pale green with three floors, two muscular Atlases, flanking the door, supported the balcony with their white
arms, bent back behind their heads: when I went by, a body was still
twitching between these impassive caryatids. Each hanged man had a
sign around his neck in Russian. To go to the office, I liked to walk, either under the bare linden and poplar trees of the long Karl-Liebknecht
Street, or cutting across the vast Trade Unions Park with its monument
to Shevchenko; it was just a few hundred meters, and during the day
the streets were safe. On Liebknecht Street they were also hanging people. Under a balcony, a crowd had gathered. Several Feldgendarmen had
come out the French door and were solidly attaching six ropes with
slipknots. Then they went back into the dark room. After a while they
reappeared, carrying a man with his arms and legs tied, his head covered with a hood. A Feldgendarm passed a slipknot around his neck,
then the sign, then pulled off his hood. For an instant, I saw the man's

bulging eyes, the eyes of a bolting horse; then, as if overcome with fatigue, he closed them. Two of the Feldgendarmen lifted him and slowly let him slide from the balcony. His bound muscles convulsed with great shudders, then calmed down; he swung quietly, his neck broken cleanly, while the Feldgendarmen hanged the next one. The people watched till the end; I watched too, full of an evil fascination. I eagerly examined the faces of the hanged men, of the condemned men before they were passed over the railing: these faces, these terrified or terrifyingly resigned eyes told me nothing. Several of the dead men had their tongues sticking out, grotesque; streams of saliva ran from their mouths to the sidewalk, some of the spectators laughed. Anguish filled me like a vast tide, the noise of the drops of saliva horrified me. When I was still young, I had seen someone hanged. It had taken place in the frightful boarding school where I had been locked up; I suffered there, but I wasn't the only one. One night, after dinner, there was a special prayer, I forget what for, and I had myself excused, because of my Lutheran origins (it was a Catholic school); that way I could return to my room. Each dormitory was organized by class and had about fifteen bunk beds. As I went up, I passed by the next room, where the *premières* slept (I was in *seconde*, I must have been fifteen); there were two boys there who had also been let off Mass: Albert, with whom I was more or less friendly, and Pierre R., a strange boy, not very well liked, who frightened the other students with his violent, frantic rages. I chatted with them for a few minutes before I went back to my room, where I lay down to read, a novel by E. R. Burroughs—such books of course were banned, like everything else in that prison. I was finishing another chapter when suddenly I heard Albert's voice, a wild scream: "Help! Help! Come help!" I leaped out of bed, my heart beating, then a thought held me back: What if Pierre R. were killing Albert? Albert was still yelling. So I forced myself to go see; terrified, ready to flee, I went toward the door and pushed it open. Pierre R. was hanging from a beam, a red ribbon around his neck, his face already blue; Albert, screaming, was holding him by his legs and trying to lift him up. I ran out of the room and down the stairs, yelling in turn, through the yard to the chapel. Some teachers came out, hesitated, then started running toward me, followed by a crowd of students. I led them to the room, everyone tried to go in; as soon as they grasped what was happening, two teachers blocked the doorway, forcing the students back into the hallway. But I had already entered, I saw everything. Two or three teachers supported Pierre R. while another furiously struggled to cut the big ribbon with a penknife or a key. Finally Pierre R. came crashing down like a felled tree, dragging the teachers to the ground with him. Albert, huddled in a corner, was sobbing, his hands clenched in front of his face. Father Labourie, my Greek teacher, was trying to pry open Pierre R.'s jaw; he was using both hands to force apart the teeth, with all his strength, but to no avail. I distinctly remember the deep, gleaming blue of Pierre R.'s face, and his purple lips, flecked with white foam. Then they made me go out. That night I spent in the infirmary; they wanted to isolate me from the other boys, I suppose; I don't know where they put Albert. A little later on, they sent Father Labourie to me, a gentle, patient man, rare qualities in that establishment. He wasn't like the other priests, and I enjoyed talking with him. The next morning, all the students were gathered together in the chapel for a long sermon on the abomination of suicide. Pierre R., we were told, had survived; and we had to pray for the salvation of his sinner's soul. We never saw him again. Since the students were quite shaken up, the good fathers decided to organize a long walk in the woods. "How stupid," I said to Albert when I met him in the courtyard. He seemed withdrawn, tense. Father Labourie came up to me and said gently, "Come, come with us. Even if it doesn't make a difference to you, it will do the others good." I shrugged and joined the group. They made us walk for several hours; and it's true, that night, everyone was calm. They let me return to my dormitory, where I was assailed by the other boys. During the walk, Albert had told me that Pierre R. had climbed onto his bed, and, after placing the slipknot around his neck, had called out, "Hey, Albert, look," then had jumped. Over the sidewalk in Kharkov, the hanged men swung slowly. There were, I knew, Jews, Russians, Gypsies there. All these dismal, bound men hanging made me think of sleeping chrysalises patiently waiting for metamorphosis. But there still was something I couldn't grasp. I was finally beginning to perceive that no matter how many dead people I might see, or people at the instant of their death, I would never manage to grasp death, that very moment, precisely in itself. It was one thing or the other: either you are dead, and then in any case there's nothing else to understand, or else you are not yet dead, and in that case, even with the rifle at the back of your head or the rope around your neck, death remains incomprehensible, a pure abstraction, this absurd idea that I, the only living person in the world, could disappear. Dying, we may already be dead, but we never die, that moment never comes, or rather it never stops coming, there it is, it's coming, and then it's still coming, and then it's already over, without ever having come. That's how I was reasoning in Kharkov, very poorly no doubt, but I wasn't doing very well.

It was the end of November; on the vast circular square, rebaptized Adolf-Hitler-Platz, a gray snow, pale as motes of light, was falling softly from the noon sky. A woman was hanging by a long rope from Lenin's outstretched hand; some children playing beneath raised their heads to look up her skirt. The hanged were increasingly numerous; the Ortskommandant had ordered that they remain strung up, *to set an example*. Russian passersby walked quickly in front of them, their heads lowered; German soldiers and children examined them curiously, and the soldiers often photographed them. For several days now I had stopped vomiting, I was beginning to hope I was getting better; but it was only a respite; and when it took me again, I vomited up my sausage, cabbage, and beer, an hour after the meal, in the street, half hidden in an alleyway. A little farther on, at the corner of the Trade Unions Park, they had raised a gallows, and that day they were leading two very young men and a woman there, their hands tied behind their backs, surrounded by a crowd made up mainly of German soldiers and officers. The woman had a large sign around her neck explaining that she was being punished in retaliation for a murder attempt on an officer. Then they hanged them. One of the young men looked dumbfounded, astonished at finding himself there; the other was simply sad; the woman grimaced terribly when they snatched the support out from under her feet, but that was all. God alone knows if they had in fact been involved in the attack; we were hanging almost anyone, Jews but also Russian soldiers, people without identity papers, peasants loitering in search of food. The idea was not to punish the guilty but to prevent new attacks by spreading terror. In Kharkov itself, it seemed to work; there had been no more explosions since the hangings. But outside the city the situation was getting worse. Oberst von Hornbogen, the Ic from the Ortskommandantur whom I often visited, had a large map on his wall of the area around Kharkov dotted with red push-pins, each representing a partisan attack or a bombing. "It's becoming a real problem," he explained to me. "We can only leave the city in force; isolated men get shot like rabbits. We raze all the villages where we find partisans, but that's not helping much. Food supplies are getting difficult, even for the troops; as for feeding the population this winter, it doesn't even bear thinking about." The city had about six hundred thousand inhabitants; there were no public food supplies, and already the elderly were dying of hunger. "Could you tell me about your discipline problems, if you don't mind," I asked the Oberst, with whom I had already developed fairly good relations.—"It's true, we're having difficulties. Especially cases of looting. Some soldiers emptied the apartment of the Russian mayor while he was visiting us. A lot of soldiers are taking coats or fur hats from the populace. There are also some cases of rape. A Russian woman was locked up in a basement and raped by six soldiers, one after the other."—"What do you attribute that to?"—"A question of morale, I guess. The troops are exhausted, dirty, covered with vermin, they're not even being provided with clean underwear, and also winter is coming, they sense it's going to get worse." He leaned forward with a faint smile: "Between you and me, I can tell you that they've even painted some inscriptions on the AOK buildings, in Poltava. Things like *We want to go back to Germany* or *We're dirty and we have lice and we want to go home.* The Generalfeldmarschall was mad with rage, he took it as a personal insult. Of course, he realizes there are tensions and privations, but he thinks the officers could do more for the political education of the men. But ultimately, the most worrisome thing is still the problem of the food supplies."

Outside, a thin layer of snow was covering the square, dusting the shoulders and the hair of the hanged. Next to me, a young Russian was rushing into the Ortskommandantur, keeping the heavy swinging door from banging back by catching it, with practiced delicacy, with his foot. My nose was running; a drop of water fell from my nose and crossed my lips with a cold streak. Von Hornbogen had made me feel extremely pessimistic. But life went on. Businesses, run by *Volksdeutschen*, were opening, along with Armenian restaurants, and even two nightclubs. The Wehrmacht had reopened the Shevshchenko Ukrainian Dramatic Theater, after repainting its elegant nineteenth-century façade, with its white columns and moldings mutilated by shrapnel, ochre yellow and a heavy burgundy. They had turned it into a cabaret called the *Panzer-sprenggranate*, the "Antitank Grenade," and a garish sign proclaimed its name above the ornate doors. I took Hanika there one night, to a satirical revue. It was pretty awful, but the men, delighted, laughed and applauded furiously; some numbers were nearly funny. In one parodic scene, a choir of rabbis wearing striped prayer shawls sang, more or less on key, an aria from the *St. John Passion*:

> *Wir haben ein Gesetz*
> *und nach dem Gesetz*
> *soll er sterben.*

Bach, I said to myself, a pious man, would not have appreciated such facetiousness. But I had to admit it was comical. Hanika's face glowed, he applauded every number; he seemed happy. That evening, I felt at ease, I hadn't vomited, and I appreciated the theater's warmth and the pleasant ambiance. At intermission, I went to the refreshment stand and offered Hanika a glass of ice-cold vodka; he turned red, he wasn't used to it. Adjusting my uniform in front of a mirror, I noticed a stain. "Hanika," I asked, "what is that?"—"What, Hauptsturmführer?"—

"The stain, there." He looked: "I don't see anything, Hauptsturm-führer."—"Yes, yes," I insisted, "there's a stain, there, it's a little dark. Rub better when you do the wash."—"Yes, Hauptsturmführer." This stain troubled me; I tried to forget it by having another drink, then returned to the hall for the second part of the program. Afterward, accompanied by Hanika, I walked up the former Liebknecht Street, now rebaptized Horst-Wesselstrasse or something like that. Farther up, near the park, some old women, supervised by soldiers, were unstringing a hanged man. At least, I thought when I saw this, these Russians we're hanging have mothers to wipe the sweat and dirt from their faces, close their eyes, cross their stiff arms, and tenderly bury them. I thought of all the Jews with their eyes still open under the earth in the ravine in Kiev: we had deprived them not only of life but also of that tenderness, for we had killed their mothers and wives and sisters with them, and hadn't left anyone to mourn them. Their fate was the bitterness of a mass grave, their only funeral feast the rich earth of the Ukraine filling their mouths, their only Kaddish the whistling of the wind over the steppe. And the same fate awaited their brethren in Kharkov. Blobel had finally arrived with the Hauptkommando, and discovered with fury that no measures had yet been taken, except the order to wear the yellow star. "But what the hell is the Wehrmacht doing?! Do they want to spend the winter with thirty thousand saboteurs and terrorists in their midst?" He had brought Dr. Kehrig's replacement, fresh from Germany; thus I found myself relegated to my old subordinate tasks, which, given my state of fatigue, didn't bother me much. Sturmbannführer Dr. Woytinek was a dry, glum little man, who nourished a keen resentment for having *missed the beginning of the campaign* and who hoped that *the opportunity to make up for it would soon present itself.* The opportunity indeed soon would present itself; but not right away. As soon as they arrived, Blobel and Vogt had begun negotiations with the representatives from the AOK about another *Grosse Aktion.* But in the meantime, von Rundstedt had been dismissed because of the retreat from Rostov, and the Führer had appointed von Reichenau to replace him as head of Army Group South. No replacement had yet been named to take command of the Sixth Army; for now, the AOK was headed by Oberst Heim, the Chief of Staff; and he, in terms of cooperation with the SP and the SD, turned out to be less complacent than his former boss. He never uttered any outright objection, but every day he raised new practical difficulties in his correspondence, and the discussions dragged on. Blobel was fuming, and taking out his anger on the officers in his Kommando. Dr. Woytinek was getting acquainted with the files and harassed me with questions throughout the day. When Dr. Sperath saw me, he remarked:

"You don't look very well."—"It's nothing. I'm just a little tired."—
"You should get some rest." I laughed: "Yes, after the war." But I was
also distracted by the traces of mud on my pants that Hanika, who
seemed to be growing a little negligent, hadn't cleaned well.

Blobel had come to Kharkov with the Saurer truck, and he was
counting on using it for the action being planned. He had finally been
able to try it out in Poltava. Häfner, who had been present—the
Teilkommandos had gathered in Poltava before marching together to
Kharkov—related the scene to me one night at the Kasino: "Actually it's
not an improvement at all. The Standartenführer loaded some women
and children in it, then started the engine. When the Jews understood
what was happening, they started beating on the sides, shouting 'Dear
Germans! Dear Germans! Let us get out!' I stayed in the car with the
Standartenführer, who was drinking schnapps. Afterward, during the
unloading, I can tell you he was not pleased. The bodies were covered
with shit and vomit, the men were disgusted. Findeisen, who was driving the truck, also inhaled some gas and was vomiting everywhere.
Horrible. If that's all they could come up with to simplify our lives, they
can try again. Only some damn bureaucrat could have thought that one
up."—"But the Standartenführer still wants to use it?"—"Oh yes! But
believe me, it will be without me."

Finally the negotiations with the AOK came to a conclusion.

Blobel, supported by the Ic Niemeyer, had asserted that the elimination of the Jewish population, as well as of other undesirables and political suspects, and even of non-residents, would contribute to easing
the problem of the food supplies, which was growing increasingly urgent. The Wehrmacht, in cooperation with the city's housing office,
agreed to place a site at the Sonderkommando's disposal for the evacuation: the KhTZ, a tractor factory, with barracks for the workers. It lay
outside of the city, twelve kilometers from the center, beyond the river
on the old road to Moscow. On December 14, an order was posted giving all Jews in the city two days to relocate there. As in Kiev, the Jews
went there on their own, without escort; and at first they actually were
housed in the barracks. On the day of the evacuation, it was snowing
and very cold; the children were crying. I took a car to go to the KhTZ.
The site hadn't been sealed off and a huge number of people were coming and going. Since in these barracks there was no water or food or
heat, the people left to find whatever they needed, and no one did anything to prevent them; informers simply pointed out those spreading
negative rumors and upsetting the others; they were discreetly arrested
and liquidated in the basements of the Sonderkommando's offices. In the
camp, utter chaos reigned; the barracks were going to ruin, children ran

around screaming, old people were already dying, and since their families couldn't bury them, they laid them out outside, where they remained, frozen by the frost. Finally the camp was closed and German guards were posted. But people kept flowing in, Jews who wanted to join their families, or else Russian or Ukrainian spouses, who were bringing food to their husbands, wives or children; we still let them come and go, since Blobel wanted to avoid panic and reduce the camp little by little, discreetly. The Wehrmacht had objected that a vast single action, as in Kiev, would create too much of a stir, and Blobel had accepted this argument. On Christmas Eve, the Ortskommandantur invited the officers from the Sonderkommando to a reception in the large conference hall of the Ukraine Communist Party, redecorated for the occasion; in front of a richly appointed buffet, we drank glass after glass of schnapps and brandies with the Wehrmacht officers, who raised their glasses to the Führer, to the *Endsieg*, and to our great common task. Blobel and the City Kommandant, General Reiner, traded gifts; then the officers who had a good voice sang some choruses. Beginning the next day—the Wehrmacht had insisted on delaying the date till after Christmas, to avoid spoiling the festivities—the Jews were invited to volunteer to go work in Poltava, in Lubny, in Romny. It was freezing cold, snow covered everything; the Jews, chilled to the bone, hurried to the selection point in the hope of leaving the camp as soon as possible. They were loaded onto trucks driven by Ukrainian drivers; their belongings were piled separately into other vehicles. Then they were brought in convoys to Rogan, a remote suburb of the city, and shot in *balki*, ravines chosen by our surveyors. Their belongings were brought to warehouses to be sorted and then distributed to *Volksdeutschen* by the NSV and the VoMi. In this way, the camp was emptied in small groups, a little each day. Just before the New Year, I went to attend an execution. The shooters were all young volunteers from the 314th Police Battalion; they weren't used to it yet, their shots missed and there were a lot of wounded. The officers bawled them out and had alcohol served to them, which didn't improve their performance. Fresh blood splattered the snow, flowed to the bottom of the ravine, spread in pools on the ground hardened by cold; it didn't freeze, but stagnated, viscous. All around, the gray, dead stems of sunflowers dotted the white fields. All sounds, even the shouts and the gunfire, were muted; underfoot, the snow crunched. I was vomiting often now and felt I was getting a little sick; I had a fever, not enough to keep me in bed, but rather long shivers and a sensation of fragility, as if my skin were turning to crystal. At the *balka*, between the volleys, bitter upsurges of this fever ran through my body. Everything was white, terrifyingly white, except the blood

staining everything, the snow, the men, my coat. In the sky, great formations of wild ducks calmly flew south.

The cold settled in and made itself at home, almost like a living organism stretching out over the earth and seeping in everywhere, in the
most unexpected places. Sperath informed me that frostbite was decimating the Wehrmacht, and often led to amputations: the hobnailed
soles of the regulation *Kommisstiefel* had turned out to be an effective
conductor of cold. Every morning dead sentinels were found, their
brains frozen by their helmets being placed directly on their heads,
without a wool cap underneath. The tank drivers had to burn tires under their engines to be able to start them up. Some of the troops had finally received warm civilian clothing, collected in Germany by the
Winterhilfe, but there was a little bit of everything there, and some soldiers strolled about in women's fur coats, feather boas, or fancy muffs.
The looting of civilians was getting worse: the soldiers took sheepskin
coats and shapkas by force, then threw their owners almost naked out
into the cold, where many died. In front of Moscow, reportedly, it was
even worse; ever since the Soviet counteroffensive at the beginning of
the month, our men, having moved to the defensive, were dying like
flies in their positions without even seeing the enemy. Politically too the
situation was becoming confused. In Kharkov, no one really understood
why we had declared war on the Americans: "We already have enough
to deal with as it is," Häfner grumbled, seconded by Kurt Hans, "the
Japanese can take care of them by themselves." Others, more farsighted,
saw danger for Germany in a Japanese victory. The purge of the army
high command also gave rise to questions. In the SS, most people
thought that the fact that the Führer had personally taken charge of
OKH was a good thing: now, they said, those old reactionary Prussians
won't be able to subtly hinder him anymore; in the spring the Russians
would be annihilated. The Wehrmacht officers, however, seemed more
skeptical. Von Hornbogen, the Ic, spoke of rumors of an offensive to
the south, with the oil fields of the Caucasus as objective. "I don't understand anymore," he confided to me after a drink or two at the
Kasino. "Are our objectives political or economic?" Both, probably, I
suggested; but for him the big question was that of our means. "The
Americans are going to take a while to increase their production and accumulate enough material. That gives us time. But if we haven't finished off the Reds by then, we're screwed." Despite everything, these
words shocked me; never had I heard a pessimistic opinion expressed so
crudely. I had already envisaged the possibility of a more limited victory
than planned, a compromise peace, for example, where we'd leave Russia proper to Stalin but would keep the Ostland and the Ukraine, along

with Crimea. But defeat? That seemed unthinkable to me. I would have liked to discuss it with Thomas, but he was far away, in Kiev, and I hadn't heard from him since his promotion to Sturmbannführer, which he had announced to me in reply to my letter from Pereyaslav. In Kharkov, there weren't many people to talk with. At night, Blobel drank and heaped abuse on the Jews, the Communists, even the Wehrmacht; the officers listened to him, played billiards, or withdrew to their rooms. I often did the same. At that time I was reading Stendhal's diaries, where I found cryptic passages that surprisingly echoed my feeling: *No to the Jews . . . The suffocation of these times is overwhelming me . . . Grief is making me a machine . . .* As an aftereffect, surely, of a feeling of filth produced by the vomiting, I was also beginning to pay almost obsessive attention to my hygiene; several times, already, Woytinek had surprised me scrutinizing my uniform, searching for traces of mud or other substances, and had ordered me to stop *gaping*. Right after my first inspection of the *Aktion* I had given my soiled uniform to Hanika to wash; but every time he brought it back to me I found new stains; finally I took him aside, reproached him brutally for his laziness and incompetence, and then flung my jacket in his face. Sperath had come to ask me if I was sleeping well; when I told him I was, he seemed satisfied, and it was true, at night I fell asleep like a stone as soon as I lay down, but my sleep was full of heavy, troubled dreams, not nightmares exactly, but like long underwater currents stirring up the mud in the depths while the surface remains smooth and calm. I should note that I went back regularly to witness the executions; no one required it, but I went of my own free will. I didn't shoot, but I studied the men who did, the officers especially, such as Häfner or Janssen, who had been there since the beginning and seemed now to have become perfectly hardened to their executioner's work. I must have been like them. By inflicting this piteous spectacle on myself, I felt, I wasn't trying to exhaust the scandal of it, the insurmountable feeling of a transgression, of a monstrous violation of the Good and the Beautiful, but rather this feeling of scandal came to wear out all by itself, one got used to it, and in the long run stopped feeling much; thus what I was trying, desperately but in vain, to regain was actually that initial shock, that sensation of a rupture, an infinite disturbance of my whole being; instead of that, I now felt only a dull, anxious kind of excitation, always briefer, more acrid, mixed with the fever and my physical symptoms, and thus, slowly, without truly realizing it, I was sinking into mud while searching for light. A minor incident threw a harsh light on these widening fissures. In the big snow-covered park behind the statue of Shevchenko, a young partisan was being led to the gallows. A crowd of Germans was gathering: Landsers from the Wehrmacht and some Orpos, but also men from the *Organisation Todt*, *Goldfasanen* from the *Ostministerium*, a few Luftwaffe pilots. The partisan was a rather thin young woman, her face, touched with hysteria, framed by heavy black hair cut short, very coarsely, as if with pruning shears. An officer bound her hands, placed her under the gallows, and put the rope around her neck. Then the soldiers and officers present filed in front of her and kissed her one after the other on the mouth. She remained silent and kept her eyes open. Some kissed her tenderly, almost chastely, like schoolboys; others took her head in both hands and forced open her lips. When my turn came, she looked at me, a clear, luminous look, washed of everything, and I saw that she understood everything, knew everything, and faced with this pure knowledge I burst into flames. My clothes crackled, the skin of my belly melted, the fat sizzled, fire roared in my eye sockets and my mouth, and cleaned out the inside of my skull. The blaze was so intense she had to turn her head away. I burned to a cinder, my remains were transformed into a salt statue; soon it cooled down, pieces broke off, first a shoulder, then a hand, then half the head. Finally I finished collapsing at her feet and the wind swept away the pile of salt and scattered it. Already the next officer was advancing, and when they had all gone by, they hanged her. For days on end I reflected on this strange scene; but my reflection stood before me like a mirror, and never returned anything to me but my own image, reversed of course, but true. The body of this girl was also a mirror for me. The rope had broken or they had cut it, and she lay in the snow in the Trade Unions Park, her neck broken, her lips swollen, one bare breast gnawed by dogs. Her rough hair formed a Medusa crest around her head and she seemed fabulously beautiful to me, inhabiting death like an idol, Our-Lady-of-the-Snows. Whatever path I took to go from the hotel to our offices, I always found her lying in my way, a stubborn, single-minded question that threw me into a labyrinth of vain speculations and made me lose my footing. This lasted for weeks.

Blobel put an end to the *Aktion* a few days after the New Year. They had kept several thousand Jews in the KhTZ for forced labor in the city; they would be shot later on. We had just learned that Blobel was going to be replaced. He had known it for weeks, but hadn't said anything. It was high time in any case for him to leave. Ever since he had arrived in Kharkov, he had become a nervous wreck, in just as bad a state, almost, as in Lutsk: one moment he'd gather us together and wax enthusiastic about the recent cumulative totals of the Sonderkommando, and the next he'd shout himself hoarse with incoherent rage over some trifle, a remark taken the wrong way. One day, in the beginning of January, I went into his office to bring him a report from Woytinek. Without returning my salute, he threw a sheet of paper at me: "Look at this piece of shit." He was drunk, white with anger. I took the paper: it was an order from General von Manstein, the commander of the Eleventh Army, in the Crimea. "Your boss Ohlendorf sent me that. Read it, read it. You see, there, on the bottom? *It is dishonorable for officers to be present at the executions of Jews.* Dishonorable! Those assholes. As if what *they* were doing was so honorable . . . as if they were treating their POWs with *honor!* . . . I was in the Great War. During the Great War we took care of our prisoners, we fed them, we didn't let them die of starvation like animals." A bottle of schnapps stood on the table; he poured himself a glassful, which he swallowed in one gulp. I was still standing facing his desk, not saying anything. "As if we all didn't take our orders from the same source. . . . The bastards. They want to keep their hands clean, those little Wehrmacht shits. They want to leave the dirty work to us." He raised his head, his face flushing bright red. "The dogs. They want to be able to say, afterward: 'Oh no, the atrocities, that wasn't us. That was them, those guys, those SS killers. We had nothing to do with all that. We fought like soldiers, with honor.' But who the hell captured all these cities we're cleansing? Whose ass are we protecting when we eliminate partisans and Jews and all the scum? You think they're complaining? They're begging us to do it!" He was shouting so much that he was spluttering. "That prick Manstein, that hypocrite, that half-yid who teaches his dog to raise its paw when it hears 'Heil Hitler,' and who hangs a sign behind his desk—Ohlendorf told me—that says *What would the Führer say about this?* Well, then, that's just it, what would he say, our Führer? What would he say, when AOK Eleven asks its Einsatzgruppe to liquidate all the Jews of Simferopol before Christmas, so the officers can have a *judenfrei* holiday? And then they spew this garbage about the honor of the Wehrmacht? The swine. Who signed the *Kommissarbefehl*? Who signed the Jurisdiction order? Who? The Reichsführer maybe?" He paused to catch his breath and down another glassful; he swallowed the wrong way, choked, coughed. "And if things go sour, they'll put all the blame on us. All of it. They'll come out all clean, all elegant, waving about this kind of toilet paper"—he had torn the sheet from my hands and was shaking it in the air—"and saying: 'No, we're not the ones who killed the Jews, the Commissars, the Gypsies, we can prove it, see, we never agreed, it's all the fault of the Führer and the SS . . .'" His voice turned into a whine. "Hell, even if we win they'll screw us. Because, listen to me, Aue, listen to me carefully"—he was almost whispering, now, his voice was hoarse—"someday all of this will come out. All of it. Too many people know, too many witnesses. And when it does come out, whether we've won or lost the war, there'll be hell to pay.

Scapegoats needed. Heads will have to roll. And it will be our heads they'll serve up to the crowd while all the Prusso-yids like von Manstein, all the von Rundstedts and von Brauchitsches and von Kluges, will return to their comfortable *von* estates and write their *von* memoirs, patting each other on the back for having been such decent and honorable *von* soldiers. And we'll end up in the trash. They'll pull another thirtieth of June on us, except this time the suckers will be the SS. The bastards." He was spluttering all over his papers. "The bastards, the bastards. Our heads on a platter, and them with their little white hands all clean and elegant, well manicured, not one drop of blood. As if not a single one of them had ever signed an execution order. As if not a single one of them had ever stretched out his arm shouting 'Heil Hitler!' when people talked to them about killing Jews." He leaped out of his chair and stood at attention, thrusting out his chest, his arm raised almost upright, and roared: "Heil Hitler! Heil Hitler! Sieg Heil!" He sat back down hard and began muttering. "The bastards. The honorable little bastards. If only we could shoot them too. Not Reichenau, he's a *muzhik*, but the others, all the others." He was growing more and more incoherent. Finally he fell silent. I took advantage of that quickly to hand him Woytinek's report and excuse myself. He started shouting again as soon as I got through the door but I didn't stop.

Finally his replacement arrived. Blobel didn't drag things out: he gave us a brief farewell speech and took the first train to Kiev. No one, I think, missed him, especially since our new commander, Standartenführer Dr. Erwin Weinmann, stood in positive contrast to his predecessor. He was a young man, just a few years older than I, restrained, with a worried, almost sad face, and genuine National Socialist convictions. Like Dr. Thomas, he was a medical doctor by profession, but he had been working for several years in the *Staatspolizei*. He immediately made a good impression. "I spent several days in Kiev with Brigadeführer Thomas," he informed us right away, "and he explained to me the immense difficulties the officers and men of this Kommando have had to face. You should know that it hasn't been in vain, and that Germany is proud of you. I'm going to spend the next few days familiarizing myself with the Kommando's work; to that end, I would like to have a frank, free discussion with each of you, individually."

Weinmann brought us some important news. Von Reichenau had finally been replaced at the head of AOK 6, in the beginning of the year, by a newcomer to the theater of operations, General der Panzertruppe Friedrich Paulus, one of his former chiefs of staff who, since 1940, had been in charge of planning at OKW, and whom he had recommended. But Paulus had already lost his protector. On the eve of Weinmann's arrival in Kharkov, after his morning run in twenty below, von Reichenau had collapsed, struck down by a heart attack according to some, a stroke according to others; Weinmann had learned about it on the train from an officer from the AOK. As Reichenau was still alive, the Führer had ordered him flown back to Germany; but his plane crashed near Lemberg, and they found him still strapped into his seat, his Feldmarschall baton in his hand, a sad end for a German hero. After some hesitation, Generalfeldmarschall von Bock was appointed in his place; on the very day of his nomination, the Soviets, trying to capitalize on their successes around Moscow, launched an offensive starting in Izyum, south of Kharkov, toward Poltava. It was now thirty degrees below zero; almost no vehicles were circulating, resupply had to be carried out in *panje* carts, and the *Rollbahn* was losing more men than the divisions at the front. The Russians had rolled out a formidable new tank, the T-34, invulnerable to the cold and terrifying for the Landsers; fortunately, it couldn't hold up to our .88s. Paulus transferred AOK 6 from Poltava to Kharkov, which brought some excitement to our city. The Reds were definitely aiming to surround Kharkov, but their northern pincer never budged; the southern branch pushed through our lines and was contained with difficulty near the end of the month, in front of Krasnograd and Paulograd, which left an enormous salient seventy kilometers long wedged into our front line, a dangerous bridgehead this side of the Donets. The partisans, at the rear of our lines, were intensifying their operations; even Kharkov was becoming unsafe: the attacks, despite fierce repression, were multiplying; no doubt the open famine now rampant in the city contributed to it. The Sonderkommando wasn't spared. One day toward the beginning of February, I had a meeting in an office of the Wehrmacht on the Tereleva Maidan in the center of town. Hanika accompanied me to try to find something to improve our rations, and I left him to his shopping. The discussion was short; I left quickly. At the top of the steps, I paused to breathe in the cold, sharp air, then lit a cigarette. I contemplated the square as I inhaled the first few drags. The sky was luminous, that pure blue of Russian winters that you don't see anywhere else. On the side, three old Kolkhozniks, sitting on crates, were waiting to sell some meager shriveled vegetables; on the square, at the foot of the Bolshevik monument to the liberation of Kharkov (the 1919 one), half a dozen children, despite the cold, were playing with a tattered rag ball. A few of our Orpos were shuffling about a little farther down. Hanika was standing at the corner, near the Opel, whose driver was letting the engine run. Hanika looked pale, withdrawn; my recent outbursts had shaken him; he was getting on my nerves too. Another child emerged suddenly from a little side street and ran toward the square. He was holding something in his hand. When he reached Hanika he exploded. The detonation blew out the windows of the Opel; I could distinctly hear the glass tinkling on the pavement. The Orpos, panicked, started firing volleys at the children playing. The old women screamed, the ball of rags came apart in the blood. I ran toward Hanika: he was kneeling in the snow and clutching his stomach. The skin of his face, speckled with acne, was terrifyingly pale; before I could reach him his head fell back and his eyes, I saw this, his blue eyes faded into the blue of the sky. The sky erased his eyes. Then he fell on his side. The boy was dead, his arm torn off; on the square, the policemen, shocked, approached the old women who, howling, craddled the limp bodies of the children in their arms. Weinmann seemed more concerned by the blunder of our Orpos than by Hanika's death: "It's unacceptable. We're trying to improve our relations with the local population and we kill their children. They should be court-martialed." I was skeptical: "That's going to be difficult, Standartenführer. Their reaction was unfortunate, but understandable. What's more, we've been making them shoot children for months; it would be hard to punish them for the same thing."—"It's not the same thing! The children we execute are condemned! These were innocent children."—"If you will allow me, Standartenführer, the basis on which the condemnations are decided makes such a distinction somewhat arbitrary." He opened his eyes wide and his nostrils quivered with rage; then he changed his mind and calmed down all of a sudden. "Let's move on to another matter, Hauptsturmführer. I've been wanting to talk with you anyway for several days now. I think you're very tired. Dr. Sperath thinks you're on the verge of nervous exhaustion."—"Excuse me, Standartenführer, but allow me to reject that opinion. I feel fine." He offered me a cigarette and lit one himself. "Hauptsturmführer, I'm a doctor by training. I too can recognize certain symptoms. You are, as the expression goes, completely fried. You're not the only one, either: almost all the officers of the Kommando are at the end of their tether. In any case, because of the winter we're already experiencing a strong decrease in activity and can permit ourselves to function for one or two months with reduced staff. A certain number of officers will be either relieved or sent on a prolonged medical leave. The ones with families will go back to Germany. The others, like you, will go to the Crimea, to one of the sanatoriums of the Wehrmacht. I hear it's very nice there. You might even be able to go swimming, in a few weeks' time." A little smile passed over his narrow face and he held out an envelope to me. "Here are your travel authorizations and your certificates. Everything is in order. You have two months; after that we'll see. Have a good rest."

* * *

Weinmann's decision had provoked an irrational surge of hatred and resentment in me; but when I arrived in the Crimea, I understood right away that he had been correct. During the long train journey, I had thought a little; I let my thoughts roam over the vast white expanses. I missed Hanika. The empty room, when I had returned to it to prepare my kit, had brought a lump to my throat; I felt as if I were covered from head to foot in Hanika's blood, and I changed furiously; all my uniforms seemed unclean to me, and that drove me out of my mind. Once again, I had a vomiting fit; but I didn't even think of crying. I left as soon as possible, via Dniepropetrovsk to Simferopol. Most of the men on the train were convalescents or men on leave, being sent to recover after the horrors of the front. A military doctor explained to me that in January alone, we had lost the equivalent of twelve divisions to frost and illness. Already the temperature was getting a little warmer, and we were starting to hope that the hardest part was over; but it had been one of the worst winters in memory, not just in Russia—so cold that everywhere in Europe they were burning books, furniture, pianos, even antique ones, just as from one end of the Continent to the other everything that had been the pride and joy of our civilization was burning. The Negroes in their jungle, I said to myself bitterly, must be having a good laugh at us if they're up on the news. Our mad ambitions, for now, were not bringing the anticipated result, and everywhere suffering was increasing, expanding. Even the Reich was no longer safe: the British were launching huge air raids, especially on the Ruhr and the Rhine; the officers who had their families in those regions were very much affected by them. In my compartment alone, a Hauptmann in the artillery, wounded in the leg in front of Izyum, had lost his two children during the bombing of Wuppertal; they had told him he could go back home, but he had asked to go to the Crimea instead, as he didn't want to face his wife. "I just couldn't," he let out laconically before relapsing into silence.

The military doctor, a rather chubby, almost bald Viennese named Hohenegg, turned out to be a very pleasant travel companion. He was a professor, holder of an important chair in Vienna, who had been named as the Sixth Army's chief pathologist. Even when he was expressing the most serious opinions, his soft, almost oiled voice seemed to betray a trace of irony. Medicine had given him his philosophical views: we discussed them at some length while the train crossed the steppe beyond Zaporozhie, as empty of life as the high seas. "The advantage of forensic pathology," he explained to me, "is that after you've opened up corpses of all ages and sexes, you have the impression that death loses its horror, is reduced to a physical phenomenon as ordinary and banal as the natural functions of the body. I can manage very calmly to imagine myself on a dissection table, under the hands of my successor, who would grimace slightly as he observed the state of my liver."—"Ah, but that's because you have the luck to get them when they're already dead. It's a very different thing when, as so often happens here, especially when you work in the SD, you're present at the *step beyond* itself."—"And are even contributing to it."—"Exactly. Whatever his attitude or his ideology, the spectator can never fully grasp the experience of the deceased." Hohenegg reflected: "I see what you mean. But this gap exists only for the person who watches. For he alone can see both sides. The man dying will only experience something confused, more or less brief, more or less brutal, but something in any case that will always escape his awareness. Do you know Bossuet?"—"In French, even," I replied, smiling, in that language. "Excellent. I see that your education was a little broader than that of the average lawyer." He declaimed the sentences in a rather thick, choppy French: *"This final instant, which in one single stroke will erase your whole life, will itself be lost, with all the rest, in that great abyss of nothingness. No trace of what we are will remain on earth: the flesh will change its nature; the body will take on another name; even that of corpse will not long remain. 'It will become,' said Tertullian, 'a strange something that no longer has a name in any language.'"*—"That," I said, "is fine for the dead man, I've often thought that way. The problem is only one for the living."—"Until their own death," he retorted, winking. I laughed gently and he did too; the other passengers in the compartment, who were discussing girls or sausages, looked at us with surprise.

In Simferopol, the terminus, they loaded us into trucks or ambulances for a convoy to Yalta. Hohenegg, who had come to visit the doctors of AOK 11, stayed in Simferopol; I parted from him regretfully. Our convoy took a mountain road, to the east, via Alushta, since Bakhchisaray was still in the zone of operations of the siege of Sebastopol. I was put up in a sanatorium west of Yalta, high over the road to Livadia, its back to the steep snow-covered mountains overlooking the city, a former royal palace converted into a *Kurort* for Soviet workers; it had been damaged a bit by the fighting but quickly patched up and repainted. I had a nice little bedroom on the third floor, with a bathroom and a small balcony: the furniture left something to be desired, but at my feet, beyond a few cypress trees, stretched the Black Sea, smooth, gray, calm. I couldn't get enough of looking at it. Though it was still a little cold, the air was much softer than in the Ukraine, and I could go out to smoke on the balcony; otherwise, lying on the sofa facing the French doors, I spent long tranquil hours reading. I didn't lack reading material: I had my own books, and the sanatorium too had a library, made up mostly of books abandoned by previous patients, very eclectic, even including, next to the unreadable *Myth of the Twentieth Century*, some German translations of Chekhov that I discovered with great pleasure. I didn't have any medical obligations. At my arrival a doctor had examined me and had me describe my symptoms. "It's nothing," he concluded after reading Dr. Sperath's note. "Nervous fatigue. Rest, baths, no excitement, as little alcohol as possible, and beware of Ukrainian girls. It will pass on its own. Have a nice stay."

A joyful atmosphere reigned in this sanatorium: most of the patients and convalescents were a mix of young subalterns from all branches, whose bawdy humor was sharpened, at night, by the Crimean wine served with the meals and by the scarcity of females. That might have contributed to the surprising freedom of tone during discussions: the most cutting jokes were circulating about the Wehrmacht, about Party dignitaries; one officer, showing me his medal for the winter campaign, asked me ironically, "And what about you in the SS—you haven't received the Order of the Frozen Meat yet?" The fact that they were in the presence of an officer from the SD didn't bother these young men at all; they seemed to think it went without saying that I shared their wildest ideas. The most critical of them were the officers from Army Group Center; whereas in the Ukraine, people thought that the transfer south of Guderian's Second Panzer Army, at the beginning of August, had been a stroke of genius that, by taking the Russians from the rear, had pried open the blocked Southern Front, and had led to the taking of Kiev and, in the end, the advance all the way to the Donets, the men from the Center thought it was a mad idea of the Führer's, a mistake that some even described as criminal. Without that, they argued vehemently, instead of loitering for two months around Smolensk, we could have taken Moscow in October, the war would have been over or almost over, and the men could have been spared a winter in snow holes, a detail that the gentlemen in OKH of course couldn't care less about, since who has ever seen a general get his feet frozen? History, since then, has certainly proven them right, as most experts would agree; yet the perspectives weren't the same then; words like that smacked of defeatism, even insubordination. But we were on vacation, it didn't matter, I wasn't offended. What's more, all this liveliness, so many handsome, cheerful young men made feelings and desires resurge that I hadn't experienced in many months. And it didn't seem impossible for me to satisfy them: it all depended on making the right choice. I often took my meals in the company of a young Leutnant of the Waffen-SS named Willi Partenau. Thin, with a fine bearing, his hair almost black, he was recovering from a chest wound received near Rostov. At night, while the others were playing cards or billiards, singing, or drinking at the bar, we sometimes stayed talking, sitting at a table in front of one of the bay windows of the dining room. Partenau came from a Catholic lower-middle-class family in the Rhineland. He had had a difficult childhood. Even before the 1929 crisis, his family was teetering on the brink of proletarianization; his father, an undersized but tyrannical military man, was obsessed with the question of his social status, and swallowed up their meager resources to keep up appearances: they would eat potatoes and cabbage every day, but at school the boys would wear suits with starched collars and polished shoes. Partenau had been raised in strict religiosity; for the slightest mistake, his father forced him to kneel on the cold tile floor and recite prayers; he had soon lost his faith, or rather had replaced it with National Socialism. The Hitlerjugend, then the SS, had finally allowed him to flee this stifling environment. He was still in training during the campaigns in Greece and Yugoslavia, and was disconsolate to have missed them; his joy knew no bounds when he was posted to the Leibstandarte Adolf Hitler for the invasion of Russia. One night, he confessed to me that he was horrified by his first experience of the radical methods used by the Wehrmacht and the SS to combat the partisans; but his profound conviction that only a barbarous, completely inhuman enemy could necessitate such extreme measures had in the end been reinforced. "In the SD, you must have seen some atrocious things," he added; I assured him I had, but preferred not to elaborate. Instead I told him a little about my life, especially my childhood. I had been a fragile child. My sister and I were just a year old when our father left for the war. Milk and food were rare; I grew up thin, pale, nervous. I loved playing in the forest near our house; we lived in Alsace, there were big forests there, I would go out to gaze at insects or wet my feet in the streams. One incident remained clearly in my memory: in a meadow or a field, I found an abandoned puppy, looking forlorn, and my heart was filled with pity for it, I wanted to bring it home; but when I approached to pick it up, the little dog, frightened, ran away. I tried to speak to it gently, to cajole it so it would follow me, but without success. It didn't run away, it always stayed a few meters away from me, but it didn't let me approach. Finally I sat down in the grass and burst out crying, broken with pity for this puppy that didn't want to let me help it. I begged it: "Please, puppy, come with me!" Finally it gave in. My mother was horrified when she saw it yapping in our garden, tied to the fence, and after a long argument convinced me to take it to the SPCA where, I've always thought, they must have killed it as soon as I turned my back. But maybe this incident took place after the war and my father's definitive return, maybe it took place in Kiel, where we had moved after the French reoccupied Alsace. My father, finally back among us, spoke little, and seemed somber, full of bitterness. Thanks to his diplomas, he soon landed a good job in a large company; at home, he often stayed by himself in his library, where, when he wasn't around, I would sneak in to play with his butterfly collection, some of them as big as a grown-up's hand; I took them out of their boxes and turned them around on their long needles like a pinwheel, until one day when he surprised me and punished me. Around that time, I began pinching things from our neighbor—no doubt, as I understood later, to attract his attention: I stole toy pistols, flashlights, other toys, which I buried in a hiding place in the back of our garden; even my sister didn't know; finally the whole thing came out. My mother thought I stole *for the pure pleasure of doing evil*; my father patiently explained the Law to me, then gave me a spanking. This happened not in Kiel but on the island of Sylt, where we spent our summer vacations. To get there, you took the train that runs along the Hindenburg Dam: at high tide, the tracks are surrounded by water, and from the train you have the impression of traveling on the sea, with the waves rising up to the wheels, beating against the hubs. At night, over my bed, electric trains burst through the starry sky of my dreams.

Very early, it seems to me, I greedily sought the love of everyone I met. This instinct, with adults at least, was generally repaid in kind, since I was both handsome and very intelligent as a boy. But at school, I found myself confronted with cruel, aggressive children, many of whom had lost their fathers in the war, or were beaten and neglected by fathers who had returned from the trenches brutalized and half mad. They avenged themselves, at school, for this lack of love at home by turning viciously against other children who were frailer and more sensitive. They hit me, and I had few friends; in sports, when teams were being formed, no one ever picked me. Then, instead of begging for their affection, I sought their attention. I also tried to impress the teachers, who were fairer than the boys my age; since I was intelligent, this was easy: but then the others called me a teacher's pet and beat me up even more. Of course, I never mentioned any of this to my father.

After the defeat, when we had settled in Kiel, he had had to leave again—we didn't really know where or why; from time to time he returned to see us, then he would disappear again; he didn't settle down with us for good till the end of 1919. In 1921, he fell seriously ill and had to stop working. His convalescence dragged on, and the atmosphere at home grew tense and gloomy. Around the beginning of the summer, still gray and cold as I remember it, his brother came to visit us. This younger brother, cheerful and funny, told wonderful stories about the war and about his travels that made me roar in admiration. My sister didn't like him so much. A few days later, my father left with him on a trip, to visit our grandfather, whom I had seen only once or twice and whom I scarcely remembered (my mother's parents, I think, were already dead). Even today I remember this departure: my mother, my sister, and I were lined up in front of the gate to the house, my father was loading his suitcase into the trunk of the car that would take him to the train station: "Goodbye, little ones," he said with a smile, "don't worry, I'll come back soon." I never saw him again. My twin sister and I were almost eight then. I learned much later that after some time my mother had gotten a letter from my uncle: after the visit to their father, it said, they had had a falling-out, and my father, apparently, had left in a train for Turkey and the Middle East; my uncle didn't know anything else about his disappearance; his employers, contacted by my mother, didn't know anything either. I never saw this letter from my uncle; it was my mother who explained it to me one day, and I could never confirm what she said, or locate this brother who nevertheless did exist. I did not tell all of this to Partenau: but I am telling it to you.

I spent a lot of time with Partenau now. Sexually, he left me with an uncertain impression. His rigor and his National Socialist and SS enthusiasm could turn out to be an obstacle; but deep down, I felt, his desire must not have been more oriented than anyone else's. In high school I had quickly learned that there was no homosexuality, as such; the boys made do with what there was, and in the army, as in prisons, it was certainly the same. Of course, since 1937, the date of my brief arrest for the Tiergarten affair, the official attitude had grown considerably harsher. The SS seemed particularly targeted. The previous autumn, when I arrived in Kharkov, the Führer had signed a decree, "On the Maintenance of Purity Within the SS and the Police," condemning to death any SS man or police employee who engaged in *indecent behavior* with another man or even *permitted himself to be abused*. This decree, *out of fear it might give rise to misinterpretation*, had not been published, but in the SD we had been informed of it. For my part, I thought it was mostly rhetorical posturing; in actual fact, if you stayed discreet, there were rarely any problems. It all depended on not compromising yourself with a personal enemy; but I didn't have any personal enemies. Partenau, however, must have been influenced by the hysterical rhetoric of the *Schwarzes Korps* and other SS publications. But my intuition told me that if one could provide him with the necessary ideological framework, the rest would come on its own.

It wasn't necessary to be subtle: it was just a question of being methodical. In the afternoons, occasionally, if there was some free time, we
would go out and walk about town, strolling through the little streets
or along the quays lined with palm trees; then we would go sit in a café
and drink a glass of Crimean muscatel, a little sweet to my taste, but
pleasant. On the esplanade, we met mostly Germans, sometimes accompanied by girls; as for the men of the region, aside from a few Tatars
or Ukrainians wearing the white armband of the Hiwis, we didn't see
any; in January, in fact, the Wehrmacht had evacuated the entire male
population, first to transit camps, then to the Nikolayev Generalkom-
missariat: a radical solution indeed to the problem of partisans, but it
must be acknowledged that with all those wounded or convalescent soldiers, they couldn't take any risks. Before springtime, there wasn't much
in the way of entertainment, aside from the theater, or some movies
arranged by the Wehrmacht. *Even bacilli fall asleep in Yalta*, wrote
Chekhov, but this slow boredom suited me. Sometimes several other
young officers joined us, and we would go sit on a café terrace overlooking the sea. If we found one—provisions from the requisitioned
supplies were ruled by mysterious laws—we'd order a bottle of wine;
along with the muscatel, there was a red *Portwein*, just as sweet but
suited to the climate. Talk centered on the local women sadly deprived
of husbands, and Partenau didn't seem indifferent to this. In the midst
of bursts of laughter, one of the bolder officers would accost some
young women and, talking gibberish, invite them to join us; sometimes
they blushed and went on their way, and sometimes they came and sat
down; Partenau, then, cheerfully joined in on a conversation made up
mainly of gestures, onomatopoeia, and isolated words. This had to be
cut short. "Meine Herren, I don't want to be a spoilsport," I began on
one of these occasions. "But I should warn you of the risks you're running." I rapped sharply a few times on the table. "In the SD, we receive
and synthesize all the reports on incidents in the rear zones of the
Wehrmacht. That gives us an overview of problems that you can't
have. I should tell you that having relations with Soviet, Ukrainian, or
Russian women is not only unworthy of a German soldier, but dangerous. I'm not exaggerating. Many of these females are Jews, whose Jewish origins can't be seen; that by itself is already risking *Rassenschande*,
racial soiling. But there's something else. Not only the Jewesses but also
Slav females are in league with the partisans; we know that they make
unscrupulous use of their physical advantages, and our soldiers' trust, for
espionage. You might think you can hold your tongue, but I can tell you
that there's no such thing as a harmless detail, and the work of an intelligence service consists of creating giant mosaics from minuscule ele-

ments that are insignificant if taken individually but, when connected to thousands of others, make sense. The Bolsheviks don't go about it any differently." My pronouncements seemed to be putting my comrades ill at ease. I continued. "In Kharkov, in Kiev, we had many cases of men and officers who slipped off to a rendezvous and were found horribly mutilated. And then of course there are the diseases. Our health services believe, based on Soviet statistics, that ninety percent of Russian females are afflicted with gonorrhea, and fifty percent with syphilis. Many of our soldiers are already infected; and these men, when they go home on leave, contaminate their wives or their girlfriends; the medical services of the Reich are horrified, and are talking of an epidemic. Such a profanation of the race, if it isn't violently combated, can lead in the end only to a form of *Entdeutschung*, a de-Germanizing of our race and our blood."

My speech had visibly affected Partenau. I didn't add anything else; it was enough to disturb him a little. The next day, when I was reading in the sanatorium's beautiful park of cypresses and fruit trees, he came to find me: "Tell me, do you really believe what you were saying yesterday?"—"Of course! It's nothing but the truth."—"But then how do you think we should manage? You understand . . ." He blushed, he was embarrassed but wanted to speak. "You understand," he went on, "soon we'll have been here for a year, without going back to Germany, it's really hard. A man has needs."—"I understand very well," I replied in a learned tone. "All the more so since masturbation, according to all the specialists, also involves grave risks. Of course, some people argue it is only a symptom of mental illness, and never the cause; others, however, like the great Sachs, are convinced it's a pernicious habit that leads to degeneracy."—"You know your medicine," Partenau said, impressed.— "I'm not a professional, of course. But I'm interested in it, I've read some books."—"And what are you reading now?" I showed him the cover: "*The Symposium*. Have you read it?"—"I must confess I haven't." I closed it and held it out to him: "Take it. I know it by heart."

The weather was getting warmer; soon we could go swimming, but the sea was still cold. You could sense spring in the air and everyone impatiently awaited its arrival. I brought Partenau to visit Nicholas II's summer palace in Livadia, burned out during the fighting, but still imposing with its regular and asymmetrical façades and its beautiful Florentine and Arabic-style courtyards. From there we climbed the Sunny Path that leads, between the trees, to a headland overhanging Oreanda; one has a magnificent view of the coast there, of the tall, still snow-covered mountains dominating the road to Sebastopol and, way down be-

low, of the elegant building made of white Crimean granite we had set
out from, still black from the smoke but luminous in the sunlight. The
day promised to be magnificent, the walk to the headland had us dripping with sweat and I took off my uniform jacket. Farther away, to the
west, you could make out a construction perched on the tall cliffs of a
promontory, the Swallow's Nest, a medieval fantasy thrown up there by
a German baron, an oil magnate, not long before the Revolution. I suggested to Partenau that we push on to this tower; he agreed. I started
out on a path that ran along the cliffs. Below, the sea calmly beat on the
rocks; above our heads, the sun sparkled on the snow of the jagged
peaks. A delicious odor of pine and heather scented the air. "You know,"
he said suddenly, "I finished the book you lent me." For some days now
we'd been addressing each other with the familiar *du*. "It was very interesting. Of course, I knew that the Greeks were inverts, but I didn't
realize how much they'd made an ideology of it."—"It's something they
thought a lot about, for centuries. It goes much further than simple sexual activity. For them, it was a complete way of life and organization,
which embraced friendship, education, philosophy, politics, even the
arts of war." I stopped talking; we continued in silence, our jackets
thrown over our shoulders. Then Partenau continued: "When I was little, in catechism, they taught me that it was an abomination, a horror.
My father talked about it too, he said homosexuals went to hell. I still
remember the text by St. Paul he quoted: *And likewise also the men, leaving the natural use of the woman, burned in their lust one toward another; men
with men working that which is unseemly, and receiving in themselves that rec-
ompence of their error which was meet.* I reread it the other night in the
Bible."—"Yes, but remember what Plato says: *On this subject nothing is
absolute; the thing is, in and of itself, neither beautiful nor ugly.* I'll tell you
what I think: the Christian prejudice, the Christian prohibition, is a
Jewish superstition. Paul, whose name was Saul, was a Jewish rabbi, and
he couldn't overcome this prohibition, as he did so many others. It has
a concrete origin: the Jews lived surrounded by pagan tribes, and in
many of them the priests practiced ritual homosexuality during certain
religious ceremonies. It was very common. Herodotus relates similar
things on the subject of the Scythians, who peopled this region and
later the whole Ukrainian steppe. He speaks of the Enarees, descendants
of the Scythians who supposedly pillaged the temple of Eskalon and
whom the goddess struck with a female sickness. According to him they
were soothsayers who behaved like women; thus he calls them *androgy-
noi*, men-women who had their periods every month. Obviously, he is
describing shamanic rituals that he misunderstood. I've heard it said that
you can still see such things in Naples, when during pagan ceremonies

a young man gives birth to a doll. Note too that the Scythians are the ancestors of the Goths, who lived here, in the Crimea, before they migrated west. Whatever the Reichsführer may say, there are strong reasons to think that they too were familiar with homosexual practices before they were corrupted by Judaicized priests."—"I didn't know that. But still, our *Weltanschauung* condemns homosexuality. In the Hitlerjugend they gave us a lot of speeches about it, and in the SS they teach us that it's a crime against the *Volksgemeinschaft*, the community of the people."—"I believe that what you're talking about is an example of poorly assimilated National Socialism, which serves to hide other interests. I know the Reichsführer's views on the subject very well; but the Reichsführer, like you, comes from a very repressive Catholic background; and despite all the force of his National Socialist ideology, he couldn't get rid of certain Catholic prejudices, so he confuses things that shouldn't be confused. And when I say 'Catholic' you understand very well that I mean 'Jewish,' Jewish ideology. There's nothing in our *Weltanschauung*, carefully considered, that could object to a masculine eros. Quite the contrary, and I can demonstrate it to you. You'll notice that the Führer himself has never really said anything about the question."—"Still, after the thirtieth of June, he violently condemned Röhm and the others for their perverse practices."—"For our nice German middle class frightened by everything, it was a strong argument, and the Führer knew it. But what you might not know is that before the thirtieth of June, the Führer had always defended Röhm's behavior; within the Party there were a lot of critics, but the Führer refused to listen to them; he told the malicious gossips that *the SA is not an institute for the moral education of genteel young ladies, but a formation of seasoned fighters.*" Partenau burst out laughing. "After the thirtieth of June," I went on, "when it turned out that many of Röhm's accomplices, like Heines, were also his lovers, the Führer was afraid that the homosexuals might form a State within a State, a secret organization, like the Jews, which would pursue its own interests and not the interests of the *Volk*, an 'Order of the Third Sex,' like our Black Order. That's what was behind the denunciations. But it's a political problem, not an ideological one. From a truly National Socialist point of view, you could on the contrary regard brotherly love as the real cement of a warlike, creative *Volksgemeinschaft*. Plato thought the same thing, in his way. You remember Pausanias's speech, where he criticizes the other nations, such as the Jews, that reject masculine eros: *Among the barbarians, that is deemed shameful, along with the love of knowledge and physical exercise. . . .* Thus, where it is deemed shameful to yield to a lover, custom is based on the moral defect of its authors: a wish for domination among masters, and cowardliness among sub*jects*. I have a French friend who regards Plato as the first authentically fascist author."—"Yes, but still! Homosexuals are effeminate, men–women as you said. How do you think a State could tolerate men that are unfit to be soldiers?"—"You're wrong. It's a false notion that contrasts the virile soldier with the effeminate invert. That type of man does exist, of course, but he's a modern product of the corruption and degeneration of our cities, Jews or Jewified men still caught in the clutches of priests or ministers. Historically, the best soldiers, the elite soldiers, have always loved other men. They kept women, to watch over their household and give them children, but reserved all their emotions for their comrades. Look at Alexander! And Frederick the Great, even if no one wants to acknowledge it, was the same. The Greeks even drew a military principle from it: in Thebes, they created the Sacred Band, an army of three hundred men that was the most famous of its time. The men fought as couples, each man with his lover; when the lover grew old and retired, his beloved became the lover of a younger man. Thus, mutually, they stimulated their courage to the point of becoming invincible; neither of them dared turn his back and flee in the presence of his lover; in battle, they pushed each other to excel. They were killed to the last man in Chaeronea, by Philip's Macedonians: a sublime example for our Waffen-SS. You can find a similar phenomenon in our Freikorps; any honest veteran will acknowledge it. You see, you have to consider it from an intellectual standpoint. It's obvious that only man is truly creative: woman gives life, she brings up children and nourishes them, but she doesn't *create* anything new. Blüher, a philosopher who was very close in his day to the men of the Freikorps, and who even fought alongside them, showed that intramasculine eros, by stimulating men to rival each other in courage, virtue, and morality, contributes both to war and to the formation of States, which are only an extended version of masculine societies like the army. Thus it's a question of a superior form of development, for intellectually evolved men. A woman's embrace is good for the masses, the herd, but not for leaders. You remember Phaedrus's speech: *As we see clearly, the beloved is most ashamed in front of his lovers, when he is surprised doing something shameful. If there were a way to form an army, or a city, with lovers and their beloveds, there could be no better government for them than rejecting everything that is ugly, and rivaling each other in the way of honor. And if such lovers fought elbow to elbow, even if they were only a handful, verily they could conquer the entire world.* That is certainly the text that inspired the Thebans."—"This Blüher you talked about, what became of him?"—"He's still alive, I think. During the *Kampfzeit*, the 'time of struggle,' he was very widely read in Germany and, despite his monarchist convictions, was much respected by certain rightist circles, including National Socialists. Afterward I think he was too closely identified with Röhm, and since 1934 he has been banned from publication. But someday they'll lift that ban. There's one other thing I'd like to tell you: even today, National Socialism makes too many concessions to the Churches. Everyone is aware of this, and the Führer is troubled by it, but in wartime he cannot allow himself to oppose them openly. The two Churches have too much sway over the minds of the middle class, and we're forced to tolerate them. That won't last forever: after the war, we'll be able once again to turn against the internal enemy and break this stranglehold, this moral asphyxia. When Germany is purified of its Jews, it will have to be purified of their pernicious ideas too. Then you'll see that many things will appear in a different light." I stopped speaking; Partenau didn't say anything. The path plunged along the rocks to the sea; then we walked in silence alongside a narrow empty beach. "Do you want to go swimming?" I suggested.—"It must be freezing."—"It's cold; but the Russians go swimming in winter. On the Baltic they do it too. It gets your blood flowing." We stripped naked and I ran into the sea; Partenau followed me, shouting; for a few instants the cold water bit into my skin, we shouted and laughed and wrestled with each other, staggering about in the waves, before running back out just as quickly. I lay down on my jacket, on my stomach; Partenau stretched out next to me. I was still wet but my body was warm, I felt the drops and the pale sun on my skin. For a long while I voluptuously resisted the desire to look at Partenau, then I turned to him: his white body was gleaming with seawater, but his face was red, speckled beneath the skin. He kept his eyes closed. As we were getting dressed, he looked at my penis: "You're circumcised?" he exclaimed with surprise, blushing. "I'm sorry."—"Oh, it's nothing. A teenage infection, it happens quite often." The Swallow's Nest was still two kilometers away, so we had to climb back up the cliffs; on top, on the terrace behind the crenellated tower, there was a little bar, empty of customers, perched over the sea; the building was closed, but they had some *Portwein* and an immense view of the coast and the mountains and Yalta nestled in back of the bay, white and vague. We had a few drinks, speaking little. Partenau was pale now; he was still winded from the climb and seemed withdrawn into himself. Then a truck from the Wehrmacht brought us back to Yalta. This little game lasted a few more days; but finally it ended as I wanted it to. It hadn't been so complicated in the end. Partenau's solid body concealed few surprises; he came with his mouth wide open, a black hole; and his skin had a sweetish, vaguely nauseating smell, which wildly excited me. How to describe these sensations to someone who has never experienced them? In the beginning, when it enters, it can be difficult, especially if it's a little dry. But once inside, oh how nice it is, you can't imagine. Your back arches and it's like a blue, luminous stream of molten lead filling your pelvis and rising slowly up your spine to seize your head and erase it. This remarkable effect might be due to the contact of the penetrating organ with the prostate, the poor man's clitoris, which, in the one penetrated, sits just against the rectum, whereas in the woman, if my notions of anatomy are correct, it's separated from it by a part of the reproductive apparatus, which would explain why women, in general, seem to have so little taste for sodomy, or else just as an intellectual pleasure. For men, it's different; and I've often told myself that the prostate and war are God's two gifts to man to compensate him for not being a woman.

I had not always liked boys, though. When I was young, still a child, as I had told Thomas, I had loved a girl. But I hadn't told Thomas everything. Like Tristan and Isolde, it had begun on a boat. A few months before, in Kiel, my mother had met a Frenchman named Moreau. My father must have been gone for three years, I think. This Moreau owned a small company in the South of France and was traveling in Germany on business. I don't know what went on between them, but some time afterward he returned and asked my mother to come live with him. She consented. When she spoke to us about it, she presented the thing to us skillfully, praising the fine weather, the sea, the plentiful food. This latter point was particularly attractive: Germany was just emerging from the great inflation, and even if we were too small to have understood much about it, we had suffered from it. So my sister and I replied: Fine, but what will we do when Papa comes back? "Well, he'll write to us and we'll return."—"Promise?"—"I promise."

Moreau lived in a large family house, a little old-fashioned and full of hiding places, in Antibes, near the sea. The rich food was soaked in olive oil, and the bright warm April sun, which in Kiel we saw only in July, delighted us right away. Moreau, who, despite his coarseness, was far from being a stupid man, made special efforts to win if not our affection then at least our acceptance. That same summer he rented a large sailboat from an acquaintance and took us on a cruise to the Îles des Lérins and even farther, up to Fréjus. At first I got seasick, but that passed quickly; she—the one I'm talking about—she didn't get seasick. We settled down together, in the bow of the boat, and we looked at the waves breaking into whitecaps, and then we looked at each other, and through this look, fired by the bitterness of our childhood and the all-consuming roar of the sea, something happened, something irremediable: love, bittersweet, until death. But at the time it was still just a look.

It didn't stay that way for long. It wasn't right away but maybe a year later that we discovered those things; then a boundless pleasure filled our childhood. And then one day, as I said, we were caught. There were endless scenes, my mother called me a *pig* and a *degenerate*, Moreau cried, and it was the end of all that is beautiful. A few weeks later, when school began, they sent us to Catholic boarding schools, hundreds of kilometers away from each other, and so, *vom Himmel durch die Welt zur Hölle*, began a nightmare that lasted many years and that, in a way, still continues. Frustrated, bitter priests, informed of my sins, forced me to spend hours on my knees on the ice-cold flagstones of the chapel, and let me take nothing but cold showers. Poor Partenau! I too have known the Church, and worse still. Yet my father was a Protestant, and I already despised the Catholics; under this treatment, the few remnants of my naïve child's faith disintegrated, and rather than repentance, I learned hatred.

Everything in that school was deformed and perverted. At night, the older boys came and sat down on the edge of my bed and put their hands between my legs until I slapped them; then they laughed, calmly got up, and left; but in the showers, after gym, they slipped up against me and quickly rubbed their things on my rear end. The priests also sometimes invited boys into their offices to hear their confessions, then, with promises of gifts or through intimidation, forced them to commit criminal acts. It was hardly surprising that the unhappy Pierre R. tried to kill himself. I was disgusted, I felt as if I were covered in mud. I didn't have anyone to appeal to: my father would never have allowed such things, but I had no idea where my father was.

Since I refused to submit to their hateful desires, the older boys treated me as viciously as the reverend fathers. They beat me up at the slightest pretext, forced me to serve them, to shine their shoes, to brush their suits. One night I opened my eyes: three of them were standing next to my bed, rubbing themselves over my face; before I could react, their horrible stuff blinded me. There was only one way to escape this kind of situation, the classic way—to choose a protector. For that the school had developed a precise ritual. The younger boy was called the *shot*; the older boy was supposed to make advances, which could be rejected right away; otherwise, he had the right to make his case. But I wasn't ready yet: I preferred to suffer, and dream of my lost love. Then an odd incident made me change my mind. The boy in the bunk next to mine, Pierre S., was my age. One night his voice woke me up. He wasn't moaning: on the contrary, he was speaking loudly and clearly, but to all appearances he was asleep. I myself was only half awake, but though I don't remember his words exactly, the horror they filled me

ALLEMANDES I AND II

with is still keen. It was something like: "No, no more, that's enough," or else: "Please, that's too far, just half." Thinking about it, the meaning of these words is ambiguous; but in the middle of the night my interpretation didn't seem doubtful at all. And I was frozen, overcome by this great fear; I curled up in the middle of my bed, trying not to hear. Even then, the violence of my terror, the quickness with which it had filled me, surprised me. These words, as I came to understand in the next few days, which said openly things that were hidden and unnamable, must have found their hidden counterparts deep down within me, and these, once awakened, raised their sinister heads and opened their shining eyes. Little by little, I came to tell myself this: If I can't have her, then what possible difference can any of this make? One day a boy confronted me on the staircase: "I saw you during gym," he said, "I was underneath you, on the hurdle, your shorts were wide open." He was an athletic boy about seventeen years old with disheveled hair, strong enough to intimidate the others. "All right," I replied, before running down the steps. After that I didn't have any more problems. This boy, whose name was André N., gave me little gifts and from time to time took me into the bathroom stalls. A poignant smell of fresh skin and sweat emanated from his body, sometimes mingled with slight hints of shit, as if he hadn't wiped himself properly. The stalls stank of urine and disinfectant, they were always dirty, and even today the smell of men and sperm reminds me of the odor of carbolic acid and urine, along with dirty porcelain, flaking paint, rust, and broken locks. In the beginning, he didn't do anything except touch me, or else I took him in my mouth. Then he wanted more. I was familiar with that already, I had already done it with her, after her periods had started; and it had given her pleasure, why couldn't it give me pleasure too? And also, I reasoned, it brought me even closer to her; in that way, I would feel almost everything she felt, when she touched me, kissed me, licked me, then offered me her thin, narrow buttocks. It hurt me, it must have hurt her too, and then I waited, and when I came, I imagined that it was she who was coming, a blinding, heartrending orgasm, I almost managed to forget how my coming was a poor, limited thing next to hers, her oceanic pleasure of a woman already.

Afterward it became a habit. When I looked at girls, trying to imagine myself taking their milk-white breasts in my mouth and then rubbing my penis in their mucous membrane, I said to myself: What's the point? It's not her and it never will be her. Better then for me to be her and all the others, me. I didn't love those others, I already explained that to you at the outset. My mouth, my hands, my penis, my ass desired them, intensely sometimes, breathlessly, but from them I only wanted their hands, their penises, and their mouths. That doesn't mean I didn't feel anything. When I contemplated Partenau's beautiful naked body, already so cruelly wounded, a secret anguish filled me. When I ran my fingers over his breast, grazing the nipple and then his scar, I imagined this breast once again crushed under metal; when I kissed his lips, I saw his jaw torn off by burning jagged shrapnel; and when I went down between his legs, plunging into the luxuriant forest of his genitals, I knew that somewhere a landmine was lurking, waiting to tear them to shreds. His powerful arms, his lean thighs were just as vulnerable, no part of his beloved body was safe from harm. Next month, in a week, tomorrow, an hour from now, all this beautiful, soft flesh could in an instant be transformed into pulp, into a bloody, charred mass of meat, and his green eyes be extinguished forever. Sometimes I almost cried thinking about it. But when he was healed, and had finally left, I didn't feel any sadness. He was killed in the end, the following year, at Kursk.

Alone, I read, took walks. In the sanatorium garden, the apple trees were in flower, the bougainvilleas, wisteria, lilacs, laburnum, were all in bloom and assailed the air with a riot of violent, heavy, contrasting odors. I also went every day to stroll about in the botanical gardens, east of Yalta. The different sections rose in tiers above the sea, with grand views over the blue and then the gray of the horizon, and always to the back the omnipresent snow-covered range of the Yaila Mountains. In the arboretum, signs guided the visitor to a pistachio tree over a thousand years old and a yew tree that might have been five hundred; higher up, in the Verkhniy Park, the rose garden displayed two thousand species that were just opening up but were already humming with bees, like the lavender of my childhood; in Primorsky Park there were subtropical plants in glass houses, hardly damaged at all, and I would sit facing the sea to read, at rest. One day, returning through town, I visited Chekhov's house, a comfortable little white dacha turned into a museum by the Soviets; the staff, judging from the signs on the walls, seemed especially proud of the living room piano, on which Rachmaninoff and Chaliapin had played; but for my part, I was stunned by the caretaker of the place, Masha, the actual sister, now an octogenarian, of Chekhov, who stayed seated on a simple wooden chair in the entryway, motionless, silent, her hands flat on her thighs. Her life, I knew, had been broken by the impossible, just like mine. Was she still dreaming, there in front of me, of the one who should have been standing at her side, Pharaoh, her dead brother and husband?

One evening near the end of my leave, I went to the Kasino in Yalta, set up in a sort of slightly outmoded, rather pleasant rococo palace. In the large stairway leading to the main hall, I ran into an SS-Oberführer

whom I knew well. I stepped aside and stood at attention to salute him,
and he returned my salute absentmindedly; but two steps farther down
he stopped, turned around suddenly, and his face lit up: "Dr. Aue! I
didn't recognize you." It was Otto Ohlendorf, my Amtschef in Berlin,
who now commanded Einsatzgruppe D. He nimbly climbed back up
the steps and shook my hand, congratulating me on my promotion.
"What a surprise! What are you doing here?" I briefly explained my
story. "Oh, you were with Blobel! I pity you. I don't understand how
they can keep mentally ill men like that in the SS, even less entrust them
with a command."—"Whatever the case," I replied, "Standartenführer
Weinmann seemed like a serious man."—"I don't know him much. He's
an employee of the *Staatspolizei*, isn't he?" He contemplated me for an
instant and then abruptly suggested: "Why don't you stay with me? I
need an adjunct for my Leiter III, in the Gruppenstab. My old one got
typhus and was sent home. I know Dr. Thomas well, he won't refuse
your transfer." The offer caught me by surprise: "Do I have to give you
an answer right away?"—"No. Actually, yes!"—"All right, then, if
Brigadeführer Thomas gives his consent, I accept." He smiled and
shook my hand again. "Excellent, excellent. Now I have to run. Come
see me tomorrow in Simferopol, we'll arrange everything and I'll explain the details to you. You won't have any trouble finding us, we're
next to the AOK, just ask. Good night!" He ran down the steps, waving, and disappeared. I headed for the bar and ordered a Cognac. I liked
Ohlendorf enormously, and always took keen pleasure in our conversations; a chance to work with him again was more than I could have
hoped for. He was a remarkably intelligent, penetrating man, definitely
one of the best minds of National Socialism, and one of the most un-
compromising; his attitude made him a lot of enemies, but for me he
was an inspiration. The lecture he had given in Kiel, the first time I met
him, had dazzled me. Speaking eloquently from a few scattered notes,
in a clear, well-modulated voice, which marked each point forcefully
and precisely, he had begun with a vigorous criticism of Italian fascism,
which, according to him, was guilty of deifying the State without recognizing human communities, whereas National Socialism was based on
community, the *Volksgemeinschaft*. Worse, Mussolini had systematically
suppressed all institutional constraints on the men in power. That led directly to a totalitarian version of State control, where neither power nor
its abuses knew the slightest limit. In principle, National Socialism was
based on the reality of the value of the life of the human individual and
of the *Volk* as a whole; thus, the State was subordinate to the requirements of the *Volk*. Under fascism, people had no value in themselves,
they were objects of the State, and the only dominant reality was the

State itself. Nevertheless, certain elements within the Party wanted to
introduce fascism into National Socialism. Since the Seizure of Power,
National Socialism, in certain sectors, had deviated, and was falling back
on old methods to overcome temporary problems. These foreign tendencies were especially strong in the agricultural economy, and also in
heavy industry, which was National Socialist in name only and which
was profiting from the uncontrolled overspending of the State to expand beyond all measure. The arrogance and megalomania that reigned
in certain sectors of the Party only aggravated the situation. The other
mortal danger for National Socialism was what Ohlendorf called its Bolshevist deviation, mainly the collectivist tendencies of the DAF, the Labor Front. Ley was constantly denigrating the middle classes; he wanted
to destroy small-and medium-size businesses, which formed the real social basis of the German economy. The fundamental and decisive measure of political economy should be Man; economics—and in this, one
could follow Marx's analyses completely—was the most important factor in the fate of mankind. It was true that a National Socialist economic
order did not yet exist. But National Socialist policies in all sectors—
economic, social, or constitutional—should always keep in mind that
their object was man and the *Volk*. The collectivist tendencies in economic and social policies, like the absolutist tendencies in constitutional
policies, deviated from this line. As the wellspring of National Socialism, we students, the future elite of the Party, should always remain
faithful to its essential spirit, and let this spirit guide each of our actions
and decisions.

It was the most incisive critique of the state of things in modern
Germany that I had ever heard. Ohlendorf, a man scarcely older than I,
had obviously meditated for a long time on these questions and had
based his conclusions on profound and rigorous analyses. What's more,
I later learned, when he was a student in Kiel, in 1934, he had been arrested and interrogated by the Gestapo for his virulent denunciations of
the prostitution of National Socialism; this experience had no doubt
contributed to inclining him toward the security services. He had a high
opinion of his work; he saw it as an essential part of the implementation
of National Socialism. After the lecture, when he had suggested that I
collaborate with him as a *V-mann*, I had the misfortune, when he described the tasks, of blurting out stupidly: "But that's a snitch's job!"
Ohlendorf had reacted dryly: "No, Herr Aue, it's not the job of an *in-
former*. We're not asking you to *squeal*, we couldn't care less if your
cleaning lady tells an anti-Party joke. But the joke interests us, since it
reveals the mood of the *Volk*. The Gestapo has perfectly competent services to take care of the enemies of the State, but that's not the jurisdic-

tion of the *Sicherheitsdienst*, which is essentially an organ of information." In Berlin, after I arrived, I had little by little attached myself to him, thanks especially to the intervention of my professor, Höhn, with whom he had stayed in touch after Höhn had left the SD. We saw each other from time to time over coffee; he invited me to his house to explain the Party's latest unhealthy tendencies, and his ideas for correcting and fighting them. At that time he wasn't working in the SD full time, he was also conducting research at the University of Kiel and later on became an important figure in the Reichsgruppe Handel, the Organization of German Commerce. When I finally entered the SD, he acted, as did Dr. Best, a little like my protector. But his ever-worsening conflict with Heydrich, and his difficult relations with the Reichsführer, had weakened his position, which didn't prevent him from being appointed Amtschef III—head of the *Sicherheitsdienst*—during the formation of the RSHA. In Pretzsch, there were a lot of rumors about the reasons for his departure for Russia; they said he had refused the position several times, until Heydrich, supported by the Reichsführer, forced him to accept it in order *to shove his nose in the mud.*

The next morning, I took a military shuttle and went up to Simferopol. Ohlendorf welcomed me with his usual politeness, which perhaps lacked warmth, but was suave and pleasant. "I forgot to ask you yesterday how Frau Ohlendorf is doing?"—"Käthe? Fine, thanks. Of course she misses me, but *Krieg ist Krieg.*" An orderly served us some excellent coffee and Ohlendorf launched into a quick presentation. "You'll find that the work will be very interesting to you. You won't have to worry about executive measures, I leave all that to the Kommandos; in any case, the Crimea is already nearly *judenrein*, and we've almost finished with the Gypsies too."—"All the Gypsies?" I interrupted, surprised. "In the Ukraine, we're not so systematic."—"For me," he replied, "they're just as dangerous as the Jews, if not more so. In every war, the Gypsies act as spies, or as agents to communicate through the lines. Just read the narratives by Ricarda Huch or Schiller on the Thirty Years' War." He paused. "At first, you'll mostly have to deal with research. We're going to advance into the Caucasus in the spring—that's a secret that I recommend you keep to yourself—and since it's still a mostly unknown region, I'd like to gather some information for the Gruppenstab and the Kommandos, especially about the different ethnic minorities and their relationships among themselves and with the Soviet government. In principle, the same system of occupation will be applied as in the Ukraine; we'll form a new Reichskommissariat, but of course the SP and the SD have to put their two cents in, and the better backed up those two cents are, the more chances they'll have of being listened to. Your immediate superior will be Sturmbannführer Dr. Seibert, who is also the Group's Chief of Staff. Come with me, I'll introduce you to him, and to Hauptsturmführer Ulrich, who will take care of your transfer."

I knew Seibert vaguely; in Berlin, he headed the SD Department D (Economics). He was a serious man, sincere, cordial, an excellent economist from the University of Göttingen, who seemed as out of place here as Ohlendorf. The premature loss of his hair had accelerated since his departure; but neither his broad bare forehead nor his preoccupied air nor the old dueling scar that gashed his chin managed to make him lose a kind of adolescent, perpetually dreamy look. He welcomed me kindly, introduced me to his other colleagues, and then, when Ohlendorf had left us, took me to the office of Ulrich, who seemed to me a fussy little bureaucrat. "The Oberführer has a somewhat loose vision of transfer procedures," he informed me sourly. "Normally, you have to send a request to Berlin, then wait for the reply. You can't just pick people off the street like that."—"The Oberführer didn't find me in the street, he found me in a Kasino," I pointed out. He took off his glasses and looked at me, squinting: "Tell me, Hauptsturmführer, are you trying to be funny?"—"Not at all. If you really think it isn't possible, I'll tell the Oberführer and return to my Kommando."—"No, no, no," he said, rubbing the bridge of his nose. "It's complicated, that's all. It will make more paperwork for me. However that may be, the Oberführer has already sent a letter about you to Brigadeführer Thomas. When he receives a reply, if it's positive, I'll refer to Berlin. It will take time. Go back to Yalta, then, and then come see me at the end of your leave."

Dr. Thomas quickly gave his assent. While we waited for Berlin to endorse the transfer, I was "temporarily detached" from Sonderkommando 4a to the Einsatzgruppe D. I didn't even have to return to Kharkov; Strehlke forwarded to me the few things I had left there. I was quartered in Simferopol in a pleasant pre-Revolutionary middle-class house, emptied of its occupants, on Chekhov Street, a few hundred meters from the Gruppenstab. I dove with pleasure into my Caucasian studies, beginning with a series of books, historical works, traveler's accounts, anthropological treatises, most of them unfortunately dating back to before the Revolution. This is not the place to expand on the peculiarities of that fascinating region: the interested reader should refer to the libraries or, if he likes, to the archives of the Federal Republic, where he might find, with persistence and a little luck, my original reports, signed by Ohlendorf or Seibert, but identifiable thanks to the dictation sign *M.A.* We knew very little about present conditions in the

Soviet Caucasus. A few Western travelers had still been able to go there in the twenties; since then, even the information provided by the *Auswärtiges Amt*, our Ministry of Foreign Affairs, was pretty scant. To find facts, you had to dig deep. The Gruppenstab had a few copies of a German scientific journal called *Caucasica*: most of the articles dealt with linguistics, in an extremely technical way, but you could also glean quite a few things from them; Amt VII, in Berlin, had ordered the complete collection. There was also copious Soviet scientific literature, but it had never been translated and was only partly available; I asked a *Dolmetscher* who wasn't a complete idiot to read the works available and provide me with extracts and synopses. In terms of intelligence, we had abundant information about the oil industry, the infrastructure, communications, and manufacturing; on the subject of ethnic or political relationships, on the other hand, our files were almost empty. A certain Sturmbannführer Kurreck, from Amt VI, had joined the Group to start up a Sonderkommando Zeppelin, a project of Schellenberg's: he was recruiting "anti-Bolshevist activists" from the Stalags and the Oflags, often from ethnic minorities, to send them behind the Russian lines for espionage or sabotage. But the program was just getting started and hadn't yielded anything yet. Ohlendorf sent me to consult the Abwehr. His relations with the AOK, very tense at the beginning of the campaign, had gotten noticeably better ever since the arrival of von Manstein as the replacement for General von Schobert, killed in September in a plane accident. Yet he still couldn't manage to get along with the Chief of Staff, Oberst Wöhler, who tended to want to treat the Kommandos as units of the Secret Military Police, and refused to call Ohlendorf by his rank, a serious insult. But working relations with the Ic/AO, Major Eisler, were good, and with the CI officer, Major Riesen, excellent, especially since the Einsatzgruppe began actively participating in the antipartisan struggle. So I went to see Eisler who directed me to one of his specialists, Leutnant Dr. Voss. Voss, an affable man about my age, wasn't a genuine officer but rather a university researcher seconded to the Abwehr for the duration of the campaign. He came from the University of Berlin, like me; he was neither an anthropologist nor an ethnologist, but a linguist, a profession that, as I would soon find out, could quickly go beyond the narrow problems of phonetics, morphology, or syntax to generate its own *Weltanschauung*. Voss received me in a little office where he was reading, his feet on a table covered with piled-up books and scattered sheets of paper. When he saw me knock on his open door, without even saluting me (I was his hierarchical superior and he should at least have stood up), he asked me: "Do you want some tea? I have real tea." Without waiting for a reply he called out: "Hans! Hans!" Then he grumbled: "Oh, where has he gone?" put down his book, got up, went past me and disappeared into the hallway. He reappeared an instant later: "It's fine. The water's heating." Then he said: "But don't stay standing there! Come in." Voss had a delicate, narrow face and animated eyes; with his rebellious blond hair, shaved on the sides, he looked like a teenager just out of high school. But his uniform was well tailored, and he wore it with elegance and assurance. "Hello! What brings you here?" I explained the object of my studies. "So the SD is interested in the Caucasus. Why? Are we planning on invading the Caucasus?" At my crestfallen demeanor, he burst out laughing. "Don't make such a face! Of course I know. In fact, I'm here only for that. I'm a specialist in Indo-Germanic and Indo-Iranian languages, with a subspecialization in Caucasian languages. So everything of interest to me is over there; here I'm just treading water. I learned Tatar, but it's not of great interest. Fortunately, I found some good scientific works in the library. As our advance progresses I have to gather a complete scientific collection and send it to Berlin." He burst out laughing. "If we'd remained at peace with Stalin, we could have just ordered them. It would have been pretty expensive, but certainly less than an invasion." An orderly brought some hot water and Voss took some tea out of a drawer. "Sugar? I can't offer you any milk, unfortunately."—"No, thanks." He prepared two cups, handed me one, and fell back into his chair, one leg raised against his chest. The pile of books partly masked his face and I shifted. "What should I tell you, then?"—"Everything."—"Everything! You have some time, then." I smiled: "Yes. I have time."—"Excellent. So let's begin with the languages, since I'm a linguist. You should know that the Arabs, in the tenth century, called the Caucasus *the Mountain of Languages*. It's just that. A unique phenomenon. No one really agrees on the exact number, since they're still arguing about certain dialects, especially in Dagestan, but it's around fifty. If you reason in terms of groups or families of languages, first you have the Indo-Iranian languages: Armenian, of course, a magnificent language; Ossetian, which particularly interests me, and Tat. Of course I'm not counting Russian. Then there are the Turkic languages, which are distributed around the perimeter of the mountains: Karachai, Balkar, Nogai, and Kumyk Turkish to the north, then Azeri and the Meskhetian dialect in the south. Azeri is the language that most resembles the one they speak in Turkey, but it has kept all the old Persian words that Kemal Atatürk purified out of so-called modern Turkish. All these peoples, of course, are leftovers from the Turco-Mongolian hordes that invaded the region in the thirteenth century, or else the remnants of subsequent migrations. And the Nogai Khans reigned for a very long time over the Crimea. You saw their palace in Bakhchisaray?"—"Unfortunately not. It's in the frontline zone."—"That's true. I have a permit, though. The troglodyte complexes are extraordinary too." He drank a little tea. "Where were we? Ah, yes. You then have by far the most interesting family, which is the Caucasian, or Ibero-Caucasian, family. I'll stop you right away: Kartvelian, that is Georgian, has no connection to Basque. That was an idea of Humboldt's, may his great soul rest in peace, and taken up since then, but wrongly. The term *Ibero* simply refers to the South Caucasian group. What's more, we're not even sure that these languages have any connection to each other. We think so—it's the basic postulate of Soviet linguists—but it's impossible to demonstrate genetically. At the very most we can outline subfamilies that form genetically related units. For the South Caucasian, that is, Kartvelian, Svan, Mingrelian, and Laz, it's almost certain. Likewise for Northwest Caucasian: despite the"—he emitted a sort of strange hissing whistle—"of the Abkhaz dialects that are a little perplexing, it's mainly a question, together with Abaza, Adyghe, and Kabardo-Cherkess, along with Ubykh, which is almost extinct and can still be found only among a few speakers in Anatolia, of a single language with strong dialectal variants. The same goes for Vainakh, which has several forms, of which the main ones are Chechen and Ingush. On the other hand, in Dagestan, it's still very confusing. We've distinguished a few major groups like Avar and the Andi, the Dido or Tsez, the Lak, and the Lesghian languages, but some researchers think that the Vainakh languages are related to them, and others not; and within the subgroups there are major controversies, for instance on the relationship between Kubachi and Dargva; or else on the genetic affiliation of Khynalug, which some prefer to regard as a language-isolate, along with Archi." I didn't understand much of this, but I marveled as I listened to him summarizing his material. And his tea was very good. Finally I asked: "Excuse me, but do you know all these languages?" He burst out laughing: "You've got to be joking! Can't you see how old I am? And also, without fieldwork, you can't do anything. No, I have an adequate theoretical knowledge of Kartvelian, and I've studied elements of the other languages, especially of the Northwest Caucasian family."—"And you know how many languages altogether?" He laughed again. "Speaking a language isn't the same thing as knowing how to read and write it; and having a precise knowledge of its phonology or its morphology is another thing entirely. To go back to the Northwest Caucasian or Adyghe languages, I've done some work on the consonantic systems—but much less on the vowels—and I have a general idea of the grammar. But I'd be incapable of talking with a native speaker. Now, if you consider that in everyday language you rarely use more than five hundred words and a pretty basic grammar, I can probably assimilate pretty much any language in ten or fifteen days. After that, each language has its own difficulties and problems that you have to work through if you want to master it. You could say, if you like, that language as a scientific subject is quite a different thing, in its approach, from language as a tool of communication. A four-year-old Abkhaz kid will be capable of phenomenally complex articulations that I could never reproduce correctly, but I, on the other hand, can then break down and describe, for instance, a plain or labialized alveolo-palatal series, which will mean absolutely nothing to the boy, who has his whole language in his head but can never analyze it." He thought for a minute. "For example, I once took a look at the consonantic system of a southern Chadian language, but it was just to compare it to that of Ubykh. Ubykh is a fascinating language. They were an Adyghe tribe, or Circassians, as they say in Europe, who were completely driven out of the Caucasus by the Russians, in 1864. The survivors settled in the Ottoman Empire, but mostly lost their language, which was replaced by Turkish or other Circassian dialects. The first partial description of it was made by a German, Adolf Dirr. He was a great pioneer in the description of Caucasian languages: he studied one a year, during his vacations. Unfortunately, during the Great War, he got stuck in Tiflis; he was finally able to escape, but only after losing most of his notes, including the ones on Ubykh that he had collected in 1913, in Turkey. He published what he had managed to keep in 1927, and it was still admirable. After that, a Frenchman, Dumézil, took it up and published a complete description of the language in 1931. Now, Ubykh has the peculiarity of having between eighty and eighty-three consonants, depending on how you count them. For several years people thought that was the world record. Then it was argued that some languages from southern Chad, like Margi, have more. But no conclusions have been reached yet."

I had set down my teacup: "All that is fascinating, Leutnant. But I have to stick to more concrete questions."—"Oh, sorry, of course! What you're interested in, basically, is the Soviet nationalities policies. But you'll see that my digressions weren't useless: those policies are based precisely on language. In czarist times, everything was much simpler: the conquered natives could do pretty much whatever they wanted, so long as they behaved and paid their taxes. The elite could be educated in Russian and even be Russianized—a number of Russian princely families were of Caucasian origin, especially after the marriage of Ivan the Fourth with a Kabardian princess, Maria Temrukovna. At the end of the last century, Russian researchers began studying these peoples, especially from an ethnological standpoint, and they came out with some remarkable studies, like those of Vsevolod Miller, who was also an excellent linguist. Most of these works are available in Germany and some have even been translated; but there's also a number of obscure or limited-edition monographs that I hope to locate in the libraries of the autonomous republics. After the Revolution and the civil war, the Bolshevik government, inspired in the beginning by a work of Lenin's, little by little outlined an absolutely original nationalities policy: Stalin, who at that time was the People's Commissar for Nationalities, played a major role. This policy is an astonishing synthesis of, on one hand, entirely objective scientific studies, like those of the great Caucasologists Yakovlev and Trubetskoy; on the other, of an internationalist communist ideology, incapable at the beginning of taking the fact of ethnicity into account; and, finally, of the reality of ethnic relationships and aspirations in the field. The Soviet solution can be summarized in this way: a people, or a nationality as they say, equals a language plus a territory. It's in order to obey this principle that they tried to provide the Jews, who had a language—Yiddish—but not a territory, with an autonomous region in the Far East, Birobidjan; but apparently the experiment failed, and the Jews didn't want to live there. Then, according to the demographic weight of each nationality, the Soviets created a complex scale of levels of administrative sovereignty, with precise rights and limitations for each level. The most important nationalities, such as the Armenians, the Georgians, and the so-called Azeris, just like the Ukrainians and the Byelorussians, are entitled to an SSR, a Soviet Socialist Republic. In Georgia, even university studies can be carried out, all the way through, in Kartvelian, and scientific works of great value are published in that language. The same is true for Armenian. It should be said that those are two very old literary languages, with a very rich tradition, that were written down long before Russian and even Slavonic, first transcribed by Cyril and Methodius. Also, if you'll allow me a digression, Mesrop, who at the beginning of the fifth century created the Georgian and Armenian alphabets—although those two languages don't have the slightest connection to each other—must have been a linguist of genius. His Georgian alphabet is entirely phonemic. Which is not something you can say about the Caucasian alphabets created by the Soviet linguists. It is also said that Mesrop invented a script for the Caucasian Albanians; but unfortunately no trace of that remains. To continue, you then have the autonomous republics, such as Kabardino-Balkaria, Chechnya-Ingushetia, or Daghestan. The Volga Germans had the same status, but as you know they were all deported and their republic was dissolved. And then it continues with the autonomous territories and so on. A key point is the notion of literary language. To have its own republic, a people must necessarily have a literary, that is to say, written, language. Now, aside from Kartvelian, as I've just explained, no Caucasian language fulfilled this condition at the time of the Revolution. There were some attempts made in the nineteenth century, but solely for scientific purposes, and there are some Avar inscriptions in Arabic characters that go back to the tenth or eleventh century, but that's all. This is where the Soviet linguists have carried out a formidable, colossal work: they created alphabets, based on Latin characters first and then on Cyrillic, for eleven Caucasian languages as well as for a large number of Turkic languages, including many Siberian tongues. These alphabets of course are far from perfect from a technical standpoint. Cyrillic is hardly adapted to these languages: modified Latin characters, as they attempted in the 1920s, or even the Arabic alphabet would have suited them much better. They did make a curious exception for Abkhaz, which is written now with a modified Georgian alphabet; but the reasons for this are certainly not technical. This obligatory use of Cyrillic has generated somewhat grotesque contortions, such as the use of diacritic signs and of digraphs, trigraphs, and even, in Kabardian, to represent the voiceless aspirated labialized uvular plosive, of a tetragraph." He snatched a piece of paper and scribbled some signs on the back, then held it out to show me the inscription КХЪУ. "That's one letter. It's as ridiculous as when we write, for Щ"— he scribbled again—"*shch*, or even worse, like the French, *chtch*. And then, also, some of the new spelling systems are extremely erratic. In Abkhaz, the marking of aspirates and ejectives is amazingly inconsistent. Mesrop would have been scandalized. Finally, and this is the worst, they insisted that each language have a different alphabet. Linguistically, that makes for some absurd situations, like Щ which in Kabard represents *sh* and in Adyghe *ch*, whereas it's the same language; in Adyghe, *sh* is written as ЩЪ, and in Kabardian *ch* is written as Ш. It's the same thing for the Turkic languages, where for instance the soft *g* is noted in a different way in almost every dialect. Of course, they did it on purpose: it was a political decision, not a linguistic one, which obviously aimed at separating the neighboring peoples as much as possible. Now here's a key for you: related peoples had to stop functioning as a network, horizontally, so that they would all refer vertically in parallel to each other, to the central government, which thus takes the position of the final arbiter of conflicts that it itself continually stirs up. But to return to these alphabets, despite all my criticisms, it's still an immense achievement, all the more so since it came with an entire educational program. In fifteen, sometimes ten years, entire illiterate peoples were provided, in their own language, with newspapers, books, magazines. Children are learning to read in their native language before they learn Russian. It's extraordinary."

Voss went on; I took notes as fast as I could. But what charmed me the most, more than the details, was his relation to his knowledge. The intellectuals I had known, like Ohlendorf or Höhn, were continually developing their knowledge and their theories; when they spoke, it was either to present their ideas or to drive them forward. Voss's knowledge, on the other hand, seemed to live inside him almost like an organism, and Voss enjoyed this knowledge as he would a mistress, sensually; he bathed in it, constantly discovered new aspects of it, already present in him but of which he had not yet been aware, and from it he took the pure pleasure of a child who has learned how to open and close a door or fill a pail with sand and empty it; and whoever listened to him shared this pleasure, since his talk was made up of capricious meanderings and perpetual surprises; you could laugh at it, but only with the laughter of pleasure of the father who watches his child open and close a door ten times in succession while laughing. I went back to see Voss many times, and each time he welcomed me with the same relaxed courtesy and the same enthusiasm. We soon struck up that frank, rapid friendship that war and exceptional situations favor. We would stroll through the noisy streets of Simferopol, enjoying the sun, in the midst of a motley crowd of German, Romanian, and Hungarian soldiers, of exhausted Hiwis, of tanned and turbaned Tatars, and of Ukrainian peasant women with rosy cheeks. Voss knew all the *chaikhonas* in the city and conversed familiarly, in various dialects, with the obsequious or jolly natives who served us, apologizing for the bad green tea. He took me one day to Bakhchisaray to visit the superb little palace of the Khans of Crimea, built in the six-teenth century by Italian, Persian, and Ottoman architects and by Rus-sian and Ukrainian slaves; and the Chufut-Kale, the Fort of the Jews, a city of caves first dug into the chalk cliffs in the sixth century and oc-cupied by various peoples, the last of whom, who had given the place its Persian name, were in fact Karaïtes, a dissident Jewish sect that, as I explained to Voss, had been exempted in 1937, based on a decision from the Ministry of the Interior, from the German racial laws, and had con-sequently, here in Crimea, also been spared by the special measures of the SP. "Apparently, the Karaïtes of Germany presented some czarist documents, including a ukase signed by Catherine the Great, that af-firmed that they were not of Jewish origin but had converted to Ju-daism at a later period. The specialists in the ministry accepted the authenticity of these documents."—"Yes, I heard talk of that," Voss said with a little smile. "They were clever." I would have liked to ask him what he meant by that, but he had already changed the subject. The day was radiant. It wasn't too hot yet, and the sky was pale and clear; in the distance, from the top of the cliffs, you could see the sea, a somewhat grayer expanse beneath the sky. From the southwest vaguely reached us the monotonous rumble of the artillery pounding Sebastopol, resounding gently along the mountains. Filthy little Tatars in rags were playing among the ruins or guarding their goats; many of them observed us curiously, but bolted when Voss hailed them in their language.

On Sundays, when I didn't have too much work, I'd take an Opel and we'd go to the beach, to Eupatoria. Often I'd drive myself. The heat was increasing by the day, we were in the heart of springtime, and I had to watch out for the clusters of naked boys who, lying on their stomachs on the burning asphalt of the road, scattered like sparrows before each vehicle, in a lively jumble of thin little tanned bodies. Eupatoria had a fine mosque, the largest one in the Crimea, designed in the sixteenth century by the famous Ottoman architect Sinan, and some curious ruins; but we couldn't find any *Portwein* there, or even really any tea; and the lake water was stagnant and muddy. So we would leave the city for the beaches, where we sometimes met groups of soldiers coming up from Sebastopol to rest from the fighting. Most of the time naked, almost always completely white, apart from their faces, necks, and forearms, they played around like children, rushing into the water, then sprawling on the sand still wet, breathing in its warmth like a prayer, to chase away the winter cold. Often the beaches were empty. I liked the old-fashioned look of these Soviet beaches: brightly colored parasols missing their canvas, benches stained with bird droppings, changing booths made of rusty metal with their paint flaking off, revealing your feet and head to the kids lazing by the fences. We had our favorite place, a beach south of the city. The day we discovered it, half a dozen cows, scattered around a brightly colored trawler lying on the sand, were grazing on the new grass of the steppe invading the dunes, indifferent to the blond child on a rickety bicycle weaving between them. Across the narrow bay, a sad little Russian tune drifted from a blue shack perched on a shaky dock, in front of which rocked, tied up with old ropes, three poor fishing boats. The place was bathed in calm forsakenness. We had brought some fresh bread and some red apples from the previous year that we snacked on while we drank some vodka; the water was cold, invigorating. To our right stood two old ramshackle refreshment stalls, padlocked, and a lifeguard's tower on the verge of collapse. The hours passed without our saying much. Voss read; I slowly finished the vodka and plunged back into the water; one of the cows, for no reason, galloped off down the beach. When we left, passing by a little fishing village to get our car, which was parked farther up, I saw a flock of geese slipping one after another beneath a wooden gate; the last one, with a little green apple wedged in her beak, was running to catch up with her sisters.

I often saw Ohlendorf too. At work, I mostly dealt with Seibert; but in the late afternoon, if Ohlendorf wasn't too busy, I would go to his office for a cup of coffee. He drank it constantly; gossips said it was his sole nourishment. He seemed always busy with a multitude of tasks that sometimes had little to do with the Group. Seibert, in fact, managed the daily work; he was the one who supervised the other officers from the Gruppenstab, and who led the regular meetings with the Chief of Staff or the Ic of the Eleventh Army. To submit an official question to Ohlendorf, you had to go through his adjutant, Obersturmführer Heinz Schubert, a descendent of the great composer and a conscientious man, although a little slow. So when Ohlendorf received me, a little like a professor meeting with a student outside of class, I never spoke to him about work; instead we discussed theoretical or ideological questions. One day I brought up the Jewish question. *"The Jews!"* he exclaimed. *"Damn them! They're worse than the Hegelians!"* He smiled one of his rare smiles before going on, in his precise, musical, slightly shrill voice. "You could say that Schopenhauer saw all the more correctly that Marxism, at bottom, is a Jewish perversion of Hegel. Isn't that so?"—"I wanted especially to ask your opinion about our work," I hazarded.—"You want to talk about the destruction of the Jewish people, I suppose?"— "Yes. I should confess to you that it poses some problems for me."—"It poses problems for everyone," he replied categorically. "To me too it poses problems."—"What is your opinion, then?"—"My opinion?" He stretched, and joined his fingertips in front of his lips; his eyes, usually piercing, had gone almost empty. I wasn't used to seeing him in uniform; Ohlendorf, for me, remained a civilian, and I had trouble imagining him other than in his discreet, perfectly cut suits. "It's a mistake," he finally said. "But a necessary mistake." He leaned forward and rested his elbows on his desk. "I should explain. Have some coffee. It's a mistake, because it's the result of our inability to manage the problem in a more rational way. But it's a necessary mistake because, in the present situation, the Jews present a phenomenal, urgent danger for us. If the Führer ended up imposing the most radical solution, it's because he was forced into it by the indecision and incompetence of the men put in charge of the problem."—"What do you mean by *our inability to solve the problem?*"—"I'm about to explain that. You must remember how, after the Seizure of Power, all the irresponsible idiots and psychopaths in the Party started bellowing for *radical measures*, and how all kinds of illegal or detrimental actions were launched, like Streicher's imbecilic initiatives. The Führer, very wisely, reined in those unrestrained actions and undertook a legal resolution of the problem, which ended with the racial laws of 1935, on the whole satisfactory. But even after that, between the fussy bureaucrats who drowned out every advance beneath a flood of paper, and the overexcited fools who encouraged *Einzelaktionen*, often for their own personal interests, a solution to the Jewish problem as a whole was still far from being found. The pogroms of 1938, which did so much harm to Germany, were a logical consequence of this lack of coordination. It was only when the SD began to concentrate seriously on the problem that an alternative to all these ad hoc initiatives could emerge. After lengthy studies and discussions we were able to elaborate and propose a coherent overall policy: accelerated emigration. I think even today that this solution could have satisfied everyone, and that it was perfectly realizable, even after the Anschluss. The structures that were created to promote emigration, especially the use of ill-gotten Jewish funds to finance the emigration of poor Jews, turned out to be very effective. You might remember that little obsequious half-Austrian, who worked under Knochen, then under Behrends . . . ?"— "You mean Sturmbannführer Eichmann? Indeed, I saw him again last year, in Kiev."—"Yes, that's right. Well, in Vienna, he put a remarkable organization into place. It worked very well."—"Yes, but afterward there was Poland. And no country in the world was ready to accept three million Jews."—"Exactly." He had straightened up and crossed one leg over the other. "But even then we could have resolved the difficulties step by step. Ghettoization, of course, was a catastrophe; but Frank's attitude contributed a lot to that, in my opinion. The real problem is that we wanted to do everything at the same time: repatriate the *Volksdeutschen* and resolve the Jewish problem as well as the Polish problem. So of course it was chaos."—"Yes, but really, the repatriation of the *Volksdeutschen* was urgent: no one could know how long Stalin would continue to cooperate. He could have slammed the door shut any day. And we never did manage to save the Volga Germans."—"We could have, I think. But they didn't want to come. They made the mistake of trusting Stalin. They felt protected because of their status, isn't that so? In any case, you're right: we absolutely had to begin with the *Volksdeutschen*. But that concerned only the Incorporated Territories, not the Generalgouvernement. If everyone had agreed to cooperate, there would have been a way to move the Jews and the Poles out of the Warthegau and Danzig-Westpreussen and into the Generalgouvernement, to make room for the repatriated *Volksdeutschen*. But here we're touching the limits of our National Socialist State as it now exists. It's a fact that the organization of the National Socialist administration is not yet equal to meeting the political and social requirements of our mode of society. The Party is eaten away by too many corrupt elements, who defend their private interests. So each dispute turns immediately into an exaggerated conflict. In the case of the repatriation, the Gauleiters of the Incorporated Territories behaved with phenomenal arrogance, and the Generalgouvernement reacted similarly. Everyone accused everyone else of treating his territory as a dumping ground. And the SS, which had been put in charge of the problem, didn't have enough power to impose a systematic regulation. At every stage, somebody would take an unauthorized initiative, or else challenge the Reichsführer's decisions by making use of his private access to the Führer. Our State is so far an absolute, national, and socialist *Führerstaat* only in theory; in practice, and it's only getting worse, it's a form of pluralist anarchy. The Führer can try to arbitrate, but he can't be everywhere, and our Gauleiters know very well how to interpret his orders, deform them, and then proclaim that they're following his *will* when actually they're doing whatever they want."

All this had brought us quite a way from the Jews. "Ah yes, the Chosen People. Even with all these obstacles, an equitable solution remained possible. For instance, after our victory over France, the SD, in conjunction with the *Auswärtiges Amt,* began to think seriously about a Madagascar option. Before that, we had envisaged parking all the Jews around Lublin, in a kind of large reservation where they could have lived quietly without posing any risks for Germany; but the Generalgouvernement categorically refused, and Frank, taking advantage of his connections, managed to have the project shelved. But Madagascar was serious. We carried out studies, there was room there for all the Jews within our sphere of control. We went very far in our planning, we even had employees of the *Staatspolizei* vaccinated against malaria, in preparation for their departure. It was mostly Amt IV that headed the project, but the SD provided information and ideas, and I read all the reports."—"Why didn't it come about?"—"Quite simply because the British, very unreasonably, refused to accept our crushing superiority and sign a peace treaty with us! Everything depended on that. First of all because France had to cede Madagascar to us, which would have figured in the treaty, and also because England would have had to contribute its fleet, isn't that so?"

Ohlendorf paused to go ask his orderly for another pot of coffee. "Here too, in Russia, the initial idea was much more limited. Everyone thought the campaign would be short and we planned to do what we did in Poland, that is, decapitate the leaders, the intelligentsia, the Bol-

shevist chiefs, all the dangerous men. A horrible task in itself, but vital
and logical, given the excessive character of Bolshevism, its absolute lack
of scruples. After the victory, we could have once again considered a
global, final solution, creating for instance a Jewish reservation in the
North or in Siberia, or sending them to Birobidjan, why not?"—"It's a
horrible task whatever the case," I said. "Can I ask you why you accepted? With your rank and your abilities, you could have been more
useful in Berlin."—"Of course," he replied briskly. "I'm neither a soldier nor a policeman, and this minion's work doesn't suit me. But it was
a direct order and I had to accept. And also, as I told you, we all thought
it would last a month or two, no more." I was surprised that he answered me so frankly; we had never had such an open conversation.
"And after the *Vernichtungsbefehl*?" I went on. Ohlendorf didn't reply
right away. The orderly brought the coffee; Ohlendorf offered me some
more: "I've had enough, thanks." He remained plunged in his thoughts.
Finally he replied, slowly, choosing his words carefully. "The *Vernichtungsbefehl* is a terrible thing. Paradoxically, it's almost like an order from
the God of the Jews' Bible, isn't it? *Now go and strike Amalek, and utterly
destroy all that they have, and spare them not; but slay both man and woman,
infant and suckling, ox and sheep, camel and ass.* You know that, it's in the
first Book of Samuel. When I received the order, that's what I thought
about. And as I told you, I believe that it's a mistake, that we should
have had the intelligence and ability to find a more . . . humane solution, let's say, one more in agreement with our conscience as Germans
and as National Socialists. In that sense, it's a failure. But you also have
to look at the realities of war. The war goes on, and every day that this
enemy force remains behind our lines reinforces our adversary and
weakens us. It's a total war, all the forces of the nation are involved in
it, and we can't afford to neglect any means to victory, any. That's what
the Führer understood clearly: he cut the Gordian knot of doubts, hesitations, divergent interests. He did it, as he does everything, to save
Germany, aware that if he can send hundreds of thousands of Germans
to their deaths, he can and must also send to theirs the Jews and all our
other enemies. The Jews are praying and striving for our defeat, and so
long as we haven't won we can't nourish such an enemy in our midst.
And for us, who have received the heavy burden of carrying out this
task to the end, our duty toward our people, our duty as true National
Socialists, is to obey. Even if *obedience is the knife that guts the will of man*,
as St. Joseph of Cupertino said. We have to accept our duty in the same
way that Abraham accepts the unimaginable sacrifice of his son Isaac demanded by God. You've read Kierkegaard? He calls Abraham *the knight
of faith*, who must sacrifice not only his son, but also and especially his

ethical principles. For us it's the same, isn't that so? We have to accomplish Abraham's sacrifice."

Ohlendorf, I could tell from what he said, would have preferred not to have been placed in this position; but who, these days, had the good fortune to do what he preferred? He had understood this and accepted it lucidly. As a Kommandant, he was strict and conscientious; unlike my old Einsatzgruppe, which had quickly abandoned this impractical method, he insisted that executions be conducted according to the military method, with a firing squad, and he often sent his officers, such as Seibert or Schubert, on inspection to make sure the Kommandos were respecting his orders. He also insisted on curbing as much as possible all acts of theft or misappropriations by the soldiers in charge of the executions. Finally, he had strictly forbidden anyone to strike or torment the condemned; according to Schubert, these orders were followed *as well as they could be*. Aside from that, he always sought to take positive initiatives. The previous autumn, in collaboration with the Wehrmacht, he had organized a brigade of Jewish artisans and farmers to bring in the harvest, near Nikolaev; he was forced to put an end to this experiment on direct orders from the Reichsführer, but I knew that he regretted that, and in private he regarded the order as a mistake. In the Crimea, he had invested himself in developing relations with the Tatar population, with considerable success. In January, when the Soviets' surprise offensive and the capture of Kerch had put our whole position in the Crimea in danger, the Tatars, spontaneously, placed a tenth of their male population at Ohlendorf 's disposal to help defend our lines; they also provided considerable help to the SP and the SD in the anti-partisan struggle, handing over to us those they captured, or liquidating them themselves. The army appreciated this assistance, and Ohlendorf 's efforts in this area had contributed a lot to improving his relations with the AOK, after the conflict with Wöhler. Still, he was hardly at ease in his role; and I wasn't unduly surprised when, immediately upon Heydrich's death, he began to negotiate his return to Germany. Heydrich was wounded in Prague on May 29 and died on June 4; the next day, Ohlendorf flew to Berlin to attend the funeral; he returned in the second half of the month promoted to SS-Brigadeführer and with a promise of a rapid replacement; as soon as he got back, he began making his farewell rounds. One evening, he briefly told me how it had happened: four days after Heydrich's death, the Reichsführer had called him to a meeting with most of the other Amtschefs, Müller, Streckenbach, and Schellenberg, to discuss the future of the RSHA, and the very ability of the RSHA to continue as an independent organization without Hey-

drich. The Reichsführer had chosen not to replace Heydrich right
away; he himself would be in charge during the interim, but from a distance; and this decision required the presence of all the Amtschefs in
Berlin, to supervise directly their Ämter in Himmler's name. Ohlendorf's relief was obvious; beneath his customary reserve, he seemed almost happy. But that was scarcely noticed amid the general excitement:
we were on the point of launching our big summer campaign in the
Caucasus. Operation Blue got under way on June 28 with Bock's offensive on Voronej; two days later, Ohlendorf 's replacement, Oberführer Dr. Walter Bierkamp, arrived in Simferopol. Ohlendorf wasn't
leaving alone: Bierkamp had brought his own adjutant with him,
Sturmbannführer Thielecke, and the plan was to replace most of the
veteran officers of the Gruppenstab, as well as the leaders of the Kommandos, during the summer, according to the availability of their replacements. At the beginning of July, in the enthusiasm generated by the
fall of Sebastopol, Ohlendorf gave us an eloquent departure speech, invoking, with his natural dignity, all the grandeur and difficulty of our
deadly fight against Bolshevism. Bierkamp, who came to us from Belgium and France, but who before had headed the Kripo in Hamburg,
his native city, then served as IdS in Düsseldorf, spoke a few words to
us. He seemed very satisfied with his new position: "The work in the
East, especially in wartime, is the most challenging possible for a man,"
he declared. By profession, he was a jurist and a lawyer; his statements,
during his speech and the reception that followed, revealed a policeman's mentality. He must have been about forty and was stocky, a little
short-legged, with a sly look; despite his doctorate, he was definitely not
an intellectual, and his language mixed Hamburg slang with SP jargon;
but he seemed determined and capable. I saw Ohlendorf again only one
more time after that evening, during the banquet offered by the AOK
to celebrate the fall of Sebastopol: he was busy with the army officers,
and spent a long time conversing with von Manstein; but he wished me
good luck, and invited me to come see him whenever I was in Berlin.

Voss had left too, suddenly transferred to the AOK of Generaloberst
von Kleist, whose Panzers had already passed the Ukrainian border and
were charging toward Millerovo. I felt a little lonely. Bierkamp was absorbed in the reorganization of the Kommandos, some of which were
to be dissolved in order to form the permanent structures of the SP and
the SD in the Crimea; Seibert was getting ready for his own departure.
With summer, the interior of the Crimea had become stifling, and I
continued to take advantage of the beaches as much as possible. I went
to visit Sebastopol, where one of our Kommandos had set to work:
around the long harbor of the southern bay stretched a field of still-

smoking ruins, haunted by exhausted and shocked civilians who were already being evacuated. Haggard, filthy kids ran between the soldier's legs begging for bread; the Romanians especially responded by cuffing them or kicking their backsides. I went down to visit the underground bunkers of the harbor, where the Red Army had set up weapons and ammunition factories; most of them had been looted, or burned out by flame-throwers; sometimes too, during the final battle, Commissars, entrenched there or in caves under the cliffs, had blown themselves up with their men and the civilians they were sheltering, along with German soldiers who had advanced too far. But all the Soviet officers and high-ranking functionaries had been evacuated by submarine before the city fell; we had captured only soldiers and underlings. The bare mountaintops overlooking the immense northern bay, around the city, were covered with ruined fortifications; the steel housings of their 30.5-centimeter artillery had been crushed by our 80-centimeter shells, fired from giant howitzers mounted on rails; and their long twisted gun barrels lay on their sides, or else stood aimed straight at the sky. In Simferopol, AOK 11 was packing up; von Manstein, promoted to Generalfeldmarschall, was leaving with his army to finish off Leningrad. Of Stalingrad, of course, no one spoke at that time: it was still a secondary objective.

In the beginning of August, the Einsatzgruppe went on the march. Our forces, reorganized into two Army Groups B and A, had just retaken Rostov after bitter street fighting, and the Panzers, having crossed the Don, were advancing into the Kuban Steppe. Bierkamp appointed me to the Vorkommando of the Gruppenstab and sent us, by Melitopol and then Rostov, to catch up with the First Panzer Army. Our little convoy quickly crossed the isthmus and the immense Trench of the Tatars, transformed by the Soviets into an antitank ditch, then veered off after Perekop to begin crossing the Nogai Steppe. The heat was terrible, I sweated profusely, the dust stuck to my face like a gray mask; but at dawn, soon after we left, subtle and magnificent colors altered the sky, slowly turning to blue, and I wasn't unhappy. Our guide, a Tatar, regularly made the vehicles stop so he could pray; I let the other officers grumble and got out to stretch my legs and smoke. On both sides of the road, the rivers and streams were dry, and traced a network of ravined *balki*, carved deep into the steppe. We could see neither trees nor hills around; only the regularly spaced poles of the Anglo-Iranian telegraph line, built at the beginning of the century by Siemens, punctuated this dismal expanse. The well water was salty, the coffee tasted salty, the soup seemed to be full of salt; several officers, who had gorged on unripe melons, suffered bouts of diarrhea, which slowed down our march even more. After Mariupol we followed a bad coastal road to Taganrog and then Rostov. Hauptsturmführer Remmer, an officer from the *Staatspolizei* who was in charge of the Vorkommando, twice gave the order to stop the convoy, near immense beaches of pebbles and yellowing grass, so the men could rush into the water; sprawled on the burning pebbles, we dried in a few minutes; already it was time to get dressed and leave. In Rostov, our column was welcomed by Sturmbannführer Dr. Christmann, who was replacing Seetzen as the head of Sonderkommando 10a. He had just finished executing the Jewish population, in a ravine known as the Snakes, on the other side of the Don; he had also sent a Vorkommando to Krasnodar, which had fallen two days before, and where the Fifth Army Corps had seized a mountain of Soviet documents. I asked him to have them analyzed as quickly as possible and to send me any information concerning the functionaries and members of the Party, to complete the little confidential handbook that Seibert, in Simferopol, had entrusted to me for his replacement; it contained, printed in tiny typeface on extra-thin paper, the names, addresses, and often the telephone numbers of active Communists or of non-Party intellectuals, of scholars, teachers, writers, and well-known journalists, of functionaries, directors of State companies and kolkhozes or sovkhozes, for the entire region of Kuban-Caucasus; there were even lists of friends and family relations, physical descriptions, and some photographs. Christmann also informed us of the advance of the Kommandos: Sk 11, still under the command of Dr. Braune, a close friend of Ohlendorf's, had just entered Maikop with the Thirteenth Panzer Division; Persterer, with his Sk 10b, was still waiting in Taman, but a Vorkommando from Ek 12 was already in Voroshilovsk, where the Gruppenstab was supposed to be based until Groznyi was taken; Christmann himself was getting ready, according to our preestablished plan, to move his Hauptkommando to Krasnodar. I saw almost nothing of Rostov; Remmer wanted to advance, and gave the order for departure as soon as the meal was over. After the Don, immense, spanned by one of the Engineer Corps' floating pontoons, stretched kilometers of fields of ripe corn, which little by little died out in the vast desert steppe of the Kuban; farther on, to the east, ran the long irregular line of lakes and swamps, interrupted by reservoirs maintained by colossal dams of the Manych River, which for some geographers marks the borderline between Europe and Asia. The leading columns of the First Panzer Army, which were advancing in motorized squares with the tanks surrounding the trucks and artillery, could be seen fifty kilometers away: immense pillars of dust in the blue sky, followed by the lazy curtain of black smoke coming from the burned villages. In their wake, we met only the odd *Rollbahn* convoy or some reinforcements. In Rostov, Christmann had shown us a copy of von Kleist's now-famous dispatch: *In front of me, no enemies; behind me, no reserves.* And the emptiness of this endless steppe was quite enough to terrify anyone. We progressed with difficulty: the tanks had transformed the roads into seas of fine sand; our vehicles often got stuck in it and, when we set foot outside, we sometimes sank up to our knees, as if it were mud. Finally, before Tikhoretsk, appeared the first fields of sunflowers, yellow expanses turned toward the sky, presaging water. Then began the paradise of the Kuban Cossacks. The road now passed through fields of corn, wheat, millet, barley, tobacco, and melons; there were also stretches of thistles tall as horses, crowned with pink and purple; and beyond all that a vast sky, pale and soft, cloudless. The Cossack villages were rich; each isba had its plum trees, its grape vines, a farmyard, a few pigs. When we stopped to eat we were warmly welcomed, we were brought fresh bread, omelettes, grilled pork chops, green onions, and cold water from the wells. Then came Krasnodar, where we found Lothar Heimbach, the Vorkommandoführer. Remmer ordered a three-day halt, to discuss and rapidly review the captured documents, which Christmann would have translated after he arrived. Dr. Braune also came up from Maikop for our meetings. After that our Vorkommando headed for Voroshilovsk.

The city rose up in the distance, spread out on a high plateau surrounded by fields and orchards. The road here was lined with overturned vehicles, wrecked heavy weaponry and tanks; on open stretches of track, in the distance, hundreds of freight cars were still burning brightly. In old times this city was called Stavropol, which in Greek means "the city of the Cross," or rather "the city of the Crossroads"; it had been established at the junction of the old roads to the north, and at one time, in the nineteenth century, during the campaign to pacify the mountain tribes, it had served as a military base for the Russian forces. Today it was a little provincial town, sleepy and peaceful, which hadn't grown fast enough to be disfigured, like so many others, by hideous Soviet suburbs. A long two-lane boulevard framing a mall of plane trees climbs up from the train station; toward the bottom, I noticed a fine Art Nouveau pharmacy, with an entryway and bay windows in the shape of circles, their panes blown out by the detonations. The Kommandostab from Ek 12 was also arriving, and they put us up temporarily at the Kavkaz Hotel. Sturmbannführer Dr. Müller, head of the Einsatzkommando, was supposed to have prepared for the Gruppenstab's arrival, but no arrangement had yet been decided on; everything was still in flux, since the general staff of Army Group A was also expected, and Oberst Hartung, from the Feldkommandantur, was taking his time in assigning quarters: the Einsatzkommando already had its offices in the House of the Red Army, opposite the NKVD, but there was talk about setting up the Gruppenstab with the OKHG. Yet the Vorkommando hadn't been idle. They had immediately gassed, in a Saurer truck, more than six hundred patients from a psychiatric hospital who might have caused difficulties; they had tried to shoot some of them, but that had caused an incident: one of the lunatics had started running in circles, and the Hauptscharführer who was trying to kill him had finally pulled the trigger when one of his colleagues was in the line of fire; the bullet, passing through the madman's head, had wounded the noncom in the arm. Some Jewish leaders, summoned to the old offices of the NKVD, had also been gassed. Finally, the Vorkommando had shot a number of Soviet prisoners outside of town, near a hidden storehouse of aircraft fuel; the bodies had been thrown into the underground storage tanks.

Einsatzkommando 12 wasn't supposed to stay in Voroshilovsk, since it had been assigned to the zone that the Russians call the KMV, the *Kavkazskie Mineralnye Vodi* or "Mineral Waters of the Caucasus," a string of little towns famous for their curative springs and their spas, scattered among volcanoes; the Kommando would move to Piatigorsk as soon as the region was occupied. Dr. Bierkamp and the Gruppenstab arrived a week after we did; the Wehrmacht had finally assigned us living quarters and offices, in a separate wing of the large complex of buildings housing the OKHG: they had built a wall to separate us from them, but we shared the same mess, which allowed us to celebrate together with the military the ascent, by a PK of the First Alpine Division, of the summit of Mount Elbruz, the highest mountain in the Caucasus. Dr. Müller and his Kommando had gone, leaving a Teilkommando under the command of Werner Kleber to finish cleaning up Voroshilovsk. Bierkamp was still awaiting the arrival of Brigadeführer Gerret Korsemann, the new HSSPF for the Kuban-Caucasus. As for Seibert's replacement, he still hadn't arrived, and Hauptsturmführer Prill was filling in for the interim. Prill sent me on a mission to Maikop.

A perpetual summer haze kept you from seeing the mountains of the Caucasus until you were at their feet. I crossed the foothills, passing the towns of Armavir and Labinskaya; as soon as you left Cossack territory, flags, green with a white crescent, burgeoned on the houses, raised by the Muslims to bid us welcome. The town of Maikop, one of the great oil centers of the Caucasus, was nestled right against the mountains, crossed by the Bielaya, a deep river above which rises the old city, perched atop tall chalk cliffs. Before the suburbs, the road ran alongside a railroad cluttered with thousands of cars, loaded with goods that the Soviets had not had time to evacuate. Then you crossed a bridge, still intact, and entered the city, a grid of long, straight streets, all identical, running alongside a Park of Culture where the plaster statues of heroes of labor slowly went on crumbling. Braune, a man with rather equine features, his large moon-face surmounted by a bulbous forehead, welcomed me eagerly: I sensed he was reassured to see again one of the last of "Ohlendorf 's men" still left in the Group, even though he himself was awaiting his replacement from one week to the next. Braune was worried about the oil installations in Neftegorsk: the Abwehr, just before taking the city, had managed to infiltrate a special unit, the Shamil, made up of mountain peoples from the Caucasus and disguised as a special battalion of the NKVD, to try to seize the oil wells intact; but the mission had failed and the Russians had dynamited the installations under the Panzers' noses. Already, though, our specialists were working to repair them, and the first vultures of Kontinental-Öl were making their appearance. These bureaucrats, all connected to Göring's Four-Year Plan, benefited from the support of Arno Schickedanz, the Reichskommissar-designate of the Kuban-Caucasus. "You know of course that Schickedanz owes his appointment to government minister Rosenberg, who was his high-school classmate in Riga. But then he had a falling out with his former schoolmate. I've heard that it's Herr Körner, Reichs marschall Göring's *Staatssekretär*, who brought the two together; and Schickedanz has been appointed to the board of directors of KontiÖl, the holding company set up by the Reichsmarschall to exploit the oil fields of the Caucasus and Baku." In Braune's opinion, when the Caucasus came under civilian control, we could expect an even more chaotic and unmanageable situation than in the Ukraine, where Gauleiter Koch did as he pleased, refusing to cooperate either with the Wehrmacht and the SS or with his own ministry. "The only positive point for the SS is that Schickedanz appointed SS officers as Generalkommissars for Vladikavkaz and Azerbaijan: in those districts, at least, it will make relations easier."

I spent three days working with Braune, helping him prepare documents and draw up reports. My only distraction consisted of going out to drink bad local wine in the courtyard of a canteen run by a wrinkled old mountain native. Still I made the acquaintance, not entirely by chance, of a Belgian officer, the Kommandeur of the Wallonia Legion, Lucien Lippert. I had in fact wanted to meet Léon Degrelle, the head of the Rexist movement, who was fighting in the area; Brasillach, in Paris, had spoken to me about him with wild lyricism. But the Hauptmann from the Abwehr whom I asked laughed in my face: "Degrelle?

Everyone wants to see him. He's probably the most famous noncom in
our army. But he's at the front, you know, and it's pretty hot up there.
General Rupp was almost killed last week in a surprise attack. The Belgians have lost a lot of people." Instead, he introduced me to Lippert, a
lanky, smiling young officer wearing worn, patched *feldgrau* a little too
big for him. I took him out to talk about Belgian politics under the apple tree at my canteen. Lippert was a career soldier, an artilleryman; he
had agreed to sign up for the Legion out of hostility to Bolshevism, but
he remained a true patriot, and complained that despite promises to the
contrary, the Legionnaires had been forced to wear a German uniform.
"The men were furious. Degrelle had trouble calming things down."
Degrelle, when he had signed up, had thought that his political role
would earn him officer's stripes, but the Wehrmacht had refused outright: no experience. Lippert still laughed about it. "Fine, so he left anyway, as an ordinary rifleman. To tell the truth, he didn't have much of
a choice, things weren't going so well for him in Belgium." Since then,
despite an initial muddle in Gromovo-Balka, he fought courageously
and had been promoted in combat. "The annoying thing is that he takes
himself for some sort of political officer, you know? He wants to go
himself to discuss the Legion's engagement, and that's not right. He's just
a noncom, after all." Now he was dreaming of transferring the Legion
to the Waffen-SS. "He met your General Steiner, last fall, and that completely turned his head. But I say no. If he does that, I'll ask to be replaced." His face had become very serious. "Don't get me wrong, I have
nothing against the SS. But I'm a soldier, and in Belgium soldiers don't
mix in politics. That's not our role. I'm a royalist, I'm a patriot, I'm an
anti-Communist, but I'm not a National Socialist. When I signed up, I
was assured, at the Palace, that this decision was compatible with my
oath of loyalty to the king, and I still don't consider myself absolved
from that oath, no matter what they say. The rest, all the political games
with the Flemish, that's not my problem. But the Waffen-SS is not a
regular branch, it's a Party formation. Degrelle says that only those who
have fought alongside Germany will have a right to speak, after the war,
and have a place in the new European order. I agree with that. But
there are limits." I smiled: despite his vehemence, I liked this Lippert, he
was an upright, honest man. I poured him some more wine and
changed the subject: "You must be the first Belgians ever to fight in the
Caucasus."—"Don't be so sure!" he laughed, and rapidly sketched out
the fantastic adventures of Don Juan van Halen, a hero of the Belgian
revolution of 1830, a half-Flemish, half-Spanish nobleman, and a former
Napoleonic officer, who because of his liberal convictions had landed in
the prisons of the Inquisition in Madrid, in the reign of Ferdinand VII.

He had escaped and ended up, God knows how, in Tiflis, where General Yermolov, the head of the Russian army in the Caucasus, had offered him a command. "He fought against the Chechens," Lippert laughed, "imagine that." I laughed with him, I found him very likeable. But he had to leave; AOK 17 was preparing the offensive on Tuapse, to take control of the pipeline terminals, and the Legion, attached to the Ninety-seventh Alpine Division, would have its role to play. As we parted I wished him good luck. But though Lippert, like his compatriot Van Halen, left the Caucasus alive, luck unfortunately deserted him a little farther on: near the end of the war, I learned that he had been killed in February 1944, during the Cherkasy breakthrough. The Wallonia Legion had been transferred to the Waffen-SS in June 1943, but Lippert hadn't wanted to leave his men without a Kommandeur, and was still waiting for a replacement eight months later. Degrelle, on the other hand, survived it all; during the final debacle, he abandoned his men on the road to Lübeck and fled to Spain in Speer's private plane; despite being sentenced to death in absentia, he was never really bothered. Poor Lippert would have been ashamed.

I returned to Voroshilovsk as our forces were taking Mozdok, an important Russian military center; the front now followed the Terek and Baksan rivers, and the 111th Infantry Division was getting ready to cross the Terek toward Groznyi. Our Kommandos were getting active: in Krasnodar, Sk 10a had liquidated the three hundred patients of the regional psychiatric hospital as well as those of a psychiatric clinic for children; in the KMV, Dr. Müller was preparing a large-scale *Aktion*, and had already formed Jewish Councils in every city; the Jews of Kislovodsk, headed by a dentist, had shown themselves to be so eager that they had come to hand over their carpets, jewelry, and warm clothes before they had even received the order. The HSSPF, Korsemann, had just arrived in Voroshilovsk with his staff and invited us, the night of my return, to his introductory speech. I had already heard about Korsemann, in the Ukraine: he had been a member of the Freikorps and the SA, had worked mostly with the Hauptamt Orpo and hadn't joined the SS until late, just before the war. Heydrich, they said, didn't want him and called him an *SA agitator*; but he was supported by Daluege and von dem Bach-Zelewski, and the Reichsführer had decided to make him an HSSPF, raising him up step-by-step. In the Ukraine, he was already serving as HSSPF z.b.V., that is, "for special tasks," but he had remained largely in the shadow of Prützmann, who had succeeded Jeckeln as HSSPF Russland-Süd in November 1941. So Korsemann still hadn't proven himself; the offensive in the Caucasus offered him the chance to demonstrate his capabilities. That seemed to have stimulated an enthusiasm in him that bubbled over in his speech. The SS, he hammered out, had to carry out not only negative tasks, of security and repression, but also positive tasks, to which the Einsatzgruppe could and should contribute: positive propaganda for the natives; fighting infectious diseases; renovating sanatoriums for the Waffen-SS wounded; and economic production, especially in the oil industry, but also in other mining assets still to be allocated, which the SS could assume control of for its businesses. He also urgently stressed the subject of relations with the Wehrmacht: "You're all certainly aware of the problems related to this that severely affected the work of the Einsatzgruppe at the beginning of the campaign. From now on, to avoid any incident, relations of the SS with the OKHG and the AOK will be centralized by my office. Beyond the usual liaisons and working relations, no SS officer under my command is authorized to negotiate questions of importance directly with the Wehrmacht. In case of any inopportune initiative in this domain, I will be ruthless, believe me." But despite this unusual stiffness, which seemed to stem from the lack of confidence of a newcomer still ill at ease in his functions, Korsemann spoke eloquently, and showed great personal charm; the general impression was mostly positive. Later that night, during a small informal meeting of subaltern officers, Remmer offered an explanation for Korsemann's pettifogging attitude: what worried him was still having almost no actual authority. According to the principle of double subordination, the Einsatzgruppe reported directly to the RSHA, and therefore Bierkamp could countermand any order from Korsemann that didn't suit him: the same was true for the SS economists from the WVHA, and of course for the Waffen-SS, which in any case was subordinated to the Wehrmacht. Ordinarily, to establish his authority and dispose of his own troops, an HSSPF had a few Orpo battalions; but Korsemann hadn't yet received such forces, and so in fact remained an HSSPF "without special tasks": he could make suggestions, but if Bierkamp didn't like them, he wasn't obliged to follow them.

At the KMV, Dr. Müller was launching his action and Prill asked me to go inspect it. I began to find this curious: I didn't have anything against inspections, but Prill seemed to be doing everything to keep me away from Voroshilovsk. We were expecting the imminent arrival of Seibert's replacement, Dr. Leetsch; perhaps Prill, whose rank was the same as mine, was worried that, playing on my relations with Ohlendorf, I could scheme with Leetsch to be named adjunct instead of him. If that was the case, it was idiotic: I had no ambition in that regard, and Prill had nothing to fear from me. But maybe I was imagining things for

no reason? It was hard to say. I had never mastered the baroque rituals
of precedence in the SS, and it was easy to err in either direction; instinct and Thomas's advice here would have been precious to me. But
Thomas was far away, and I didn't have any close friend in the Group.
To tell the truth, they weren't the kind of people with whom I could
easily strike up a bond. They had been picked out of the most obscure
offices of the RSHA, and most of them were very ambitious and saw
the work of the Einsatzgruppe only as a springboard; almost all of them,
as soon as they arrived, seemed to regard the work of extermination as
self-evident, and they didn't even ask themselves the questions that had
so worried the men in the first year. In the midst of these men, I was
seen as a somewhat complicated intellectual, and I remained isolated.
That didn't bother me: I have always been able to do without the
friendship of coarse loudmouths. But I had to stay on my guard.

I reached Pyatigorsk early in the morning. It was the beginning of
September and the blue-gray of the sky was still hazy and heavy with
summer dust. The road from Voroshilovsk crosses the railroad just before Mineralnye Vody, then, running alongside it, snakes between the
five volcanic peaks that give Pyatigorsk its name. You enter the city
from the north, skirting round the great hump of the Mashuk; the road
rises at this point, and the town appeared suddenly at my feet, with beyond it the undulating sweep of the foothills, dotted with volcanoes,
their collapsed domes scattered about. The Einsatzkommando was occupying one of the turn-of-the-century sanatoriums sprawled at the
foot of Mount Mashuk, in the eastern part of town; von Kleist's AOK
had requisitioned the immense Lermontov Sanatorium, but the SS had
been able to obtain the Voenaya Sanatoria, which would serve as a
lazaretto for the Waffen-SS. The Leibstandarte was fighting in the area,
and I thought with a vague twinge about Partenau; but it isn't good to
try to revive old affairs, and I knew I wouldn't make any effort to see
him again. Pyatigorsk was still mostly intact; after a brief skirmish with
a factory's self-defense militia, the town had been captured without
combat; the streets were swarming like those of an American mining
town during the Gold Rush. Wagons and even camels got in the way
of military vehicles pretty much everywhere to create traffic jams that
the Feldgendarmen broke up with a liberal sprinkling of insults and
blows. Opposite the large Tsvetnik Garden, in front of the Bristol Hotel, neatly parked cars and motorcycles marked the emplacement of the
Feldkommandantur; the offices of the Einsatzkommando were lower
down, on Kirov Boulevard, in a two-story former institute. The trees
on the boulevard hid its pretty façade; and I examined the ceramic flo-

ral motifs, set under stucco moldings representing, seated above two pi-
geons, a cherub with a basket of flowers on his head; at the top, you
could make out a parrot perched on a ring, and the head of a sad little
girl with pinched nostrils. On the right an archway led to an inner
courtyard. My driver parked there next to the Saurer truck while I
showed the guards my papers. Dr. Müller was busy, and I was received
by Obersturmführer Dr. Bolte, an officer from the *Staatspolizei*. The
staff occupied large rooms with high ceilings, well lit by tall wooden
casement windows; Dr. Bolte had his office in a pretty little circular
room, at the very top of one of the two towers set at the corners of the
building. He curtly explained the procedures of the action: each day, according to a timetable drawn up on the basis of the figures provided by
the Jewish Councils, a part or all of the Jews of one of the towns of the
KMV were evacuated by train; the posters inviting them to come "re-
settle in the Ukraine" had been printed by the Wehrmacht, which also
provided the train and the escort troops; they were sent to Mineralnye
Vody, where they were held in a glass factory before they were taken a
little farther off, to a Soviet antitank ditch. The figures had turned out
larger than expected: we had found a lot of Jews evacuated from the
Ukraine or from Byelorussia, as well as the teaching staff and students
from the University of Leningrad, sent to the KMV the previous year
for their safety, many of whom were either Jews or Party members, or
were regarded as dangerous because they were intellectuals. The Einsatzkommando was taking advantage of the occasion to liquidate arrested Communists, Komsomols, Gypsies, common law criminals found
in jail, and the staff and patients of several sanatoriums. "You understand," Bolte explained, "the infrastructure here is ideal for our administration. Envoys of the Reichskommissar, for example, asked us to free
up the sanatorium of the People's Commissariat for the oil industry, in
Kislovodsk." The *Aktion* was already well under way: on the first day
they had finished with the Jews of Minvody, then of Yessentuki and
Zheleznovodsk; the next day, they would start with the Jews of Pyatigorsk, then the action would end with the Jews of Kislovodsk. In each
case, the evacuation order was posted two days before the operation.
"Since they can't travel from one town to the other, they don't suspect
anything." He invited me to come with him to inspect the action under
way; I replied that I would rather visit the other towns of the KMV first.
"Then I won't be able to go with you: Sturmbannführer Müller is waiting for me." "That's all right. You can just lend me a man who knows
the offices of your Teilkommandos."
    The road left the town from the west, skirting round Beshtau, the
largest of the five volcanoes; below, one could glimpse now and then the

bends of the Podkumok, its waters gray and muddy. I didn't actually have much to do in these other towns, but I was curious to visit them, and I wasn't burning with desire to go see the *Aktion*. Yessentuki, under the Soviets, had been transformed into an industrial city of not much interest; I met the officers of the Teilkommando there, discussed their arrangements, and didn't linger. Kislovodsk, on the other hand, turned out to be very pleasant, an old spa town with a faded, outmoded charm, greener and prettier than Pyatigorsk. The main baths were housed in a curious imitation Indian temple, built around the turn of the century; I tasted the water they call Narzan, and found it pleasantly sparkling, but a little too bitter. After my discussions I took a stroll in the large park, then returned to Pyatigorsk.

The officers ate together in the sanatorium's dining room. Conversation dealt mostly with military events, and most of the diners showed proper optimism. "Now that Schweppenburg's Panzers have crossed the Terek," argued Wiens, Müller's adjunct, a bitter *Volksdeutscher* who hadn't set foot outside of the Ukraine until he was twenty-four, "our forces will soon be in Groznyi. After that, Baku is just a matter of time. Most of us will be able to celebrate Christmas at home."—"General Schweppenburg's Panzers are making no headway whatsoever, Hauptsturmführer," I politely remarked. "They've barely managed to establish a bridgehead. Soviet resistance in Chechnya-Ingushetia is much stiffer than they expected."—"Bah," exclaimed Pfeiffer, a fat red Untersturmführer, "it's their last gasp. Their divisions are bled dry. They're just leaving a thin screen in front of us to try to deceive us; but at the first serious thrust, they'll collapse or cut and run like rabbits."—"How do you know that?" I asked curiously.—"That's what they're saying at the AOK," Wiens answered for him. "Ever since the beginning of the summer, very few prisoners have been taken in the areas surrounded, like at Millerovo. From that they deduce that the Bolsheviks have exhausted their reserves, as our high command had foreseen."—"We talked a lot about this aspect of things at the Gruppenstab and with the OKHG," I said. "Not everyone shares your opinion. Some think that the Soviets learned a lesson from their terrible losses last year, and changed their strategy: they're withdrawing before us in an orderly way, so as to mount a sudden counteroffensive when our lines of communication are vulnerable and stretched too thin."—"I think you're too much of a pessimist, Hauptsturmführer," grumbled Müller, the head of the Kommando, his mouth full of chicken.—"I'm not a pessimist, Sturmbannführer," I replied. "I'm just saying that there are different opinions, that's all."—"Do you think our lines are stretched too thin?" Bolte asked curiously.—"That depends on what's actually facing them.

The front line of Army Group B follows the course of the Don, where there are still Soviet bridgeheads that we haven't been able to eliminate, all the way from Voronezh, which the Russians still hold despite all our efforts, down to Stalingrad."—"Stalingrad won't last much longer," said Wiens, who had just emptied his stein. "Our Luftwaffe crushed the defense last month; the Sixth Army will just have to clean up."—"Maybe. But since all our troops are concentrated on Stalingrad, the flanks of Army Group B are held only by our allies, on the Don and in the steppe. You know as well as I do that the quality of Romanian or Italian troops doesn't come close to that of the German forces; the Hungarians might be good soldiers, but they have no supplies. Here, in the Caucasus, it's the same, we don't have enough men to form a continuous front along the ridges. And between the two Army Groups, the front peters out in the Kalmuk Steppe; we only send patrols out there, and we're not safe from unpleasant surprises."—"On that point," interrupted Dr. Strohschneider, an immensely tall man, whose lips jutted out from under a bushy moustache and who commanded a Teilkommando on assignment in Budyonnovsk, "Hauptsturmführer Aue is not entirely wrong. The steppe is wide open. A bold attack could weaken our position."—"Oh," said Wiens as he drank some more beer, "they'll never be anything but mosquito bites. And if they take a shot at our allies, the German 'corsetting' will be more than enough to control the situation."—"I hope you're right," I said.—"In any case," Dr. Müller sententiously concluded, "the Führer will always be able to impose the right decisions on all those reactionary generals." That was certainly one way of seeing things. But the conversation had already shifted to the day's *Aktion*. I listened in silence. As always, there were the inevitable anecdotes about the way the condemned behaved, how they prayed, cried, sang the Internationale, or were silent, and then commentaries on the problems of organization and our men's responses. I put up with all this wearily; even the old-timers were only repeating what we'd been hearing for a year, there wasn't a single authentic reaction in all these boasts and platitudes. One officer, though, stood out because of his particularly prolonged, coarse invectives against the Jews. He was the Leiter IV of the Kommando, Hauptsturmführer Turek, a disagreeable man I'd already met in the Gruppenstab. This Turek was one of the few visceral, obscene anti-Semites, in the Streicher mode, whom I had met in the Einsatzgruppen; at the SP and the SD, traditionally, we cultivated an intellectual kind of anti-Semitism, and these kinds of emotional remarks were poorly viewed. But Turek was afflicted with a remarkably Jewish physique: he had dark curly hair, a prominent nose, sensual lips; behind his back, some people cruelly called him "Jew Süss," while others insinuated that he had Gypsy blood. He must have suffered from this since childhood; and at the slightest provocation he boasted about his Aryan ancestry: "I know it's hard to see," he would begin before explaining that for his recent wedding he had had to carry out exhaustive research and had been able to go back to the seventeenth century; he would go so far as to produce his RuSHA certificate attesting that he was *of pure race* and *fit to procreate German children*. I understood all that, and might have pitied him; but his outrageousness and obscenities surpassed all bounds: at the executions, I had heard, he taunted the condemned men for their circumcised penises, and forced women to strip naked so he could tell them that *their Jewish vaginas would never produce any more children*. Ohlendorf would not have tolerated such behavior, but Bierkamp closed his eyes to it; as for Müller, who should have called him to order, he said nothing. Turek was talking now with Pfeiffer, who directed the firing squads during the action; Pfeiffer was laughing at his jokes and egging him on. Sickened, I excused myself before dessert and went up to my room. My bouts of nausea had started up again; since Voroshilovsk, or earlier maybe, I was again suffering from the brutal retching that had so exhausted me in the Ukraine. I had vomited only once, in Voroshilovsk, after a rather heavy meal, but sometimes I had to make an effort to control the nausea: I coughed a lot, grew red, I found this unseemly and preferred to withdraw.

The next morning, I went to Minvody with the other officers to supervise the *Aktion*. I watched the arrival and unloading of the train: the Jews seemed surprised at getting out so soon, since they thought they were being transferred to the Ukraine, but they stayed calm. To avoid any agitation, the known Communists were kept under separate guard. In the cluttered, dusty main hall of the glass factory, the Jews had to hand over their clothes, luggage, personal effects, and the keys to their apartments. That provoked a commotion, especially since the factory floor was strewn with broken glass, and the people, in their bare socks, were cutting their feet. I pointed this out to Dr. Bolte, but he shrugged his shoulders. The Orpos were hitting people left and right; the Jews, terrified, would run and sit down in their underwear, the women trying to calm the children. Outside blew a cool breeze; but the sun was beating down on the glass roof, and the heat inside was stifling, as in a greenhouse. A man of a certain age, in distinguished clothes with glasses and a little moustache, approached me. He was holding a very young boy in his arms. He took off his hat and addressed me in perfect German: "Herr Offizier, can I have a few words with you?"—"You speak German very well," I replied.—"I studied in Germany," he said with a slightly stiff dignity. "It was once a great country." He must have been one of the professors from Leningrad. "What do you wish to say to me?" I asked curtly. The little boy, who was holding the man by the neck, was gazing at me with large blue eyes. He was about two. "I know what you are doing here," the man said coolly. "It is an abomination. I simply want to wish that you'll survive this war and wake up for twenty years, every night, screaming. I hope you'll be incapable of looking at your children without seeing ours, the ones you murdered." He turned his back on me and went away before I could reply. The boy kept staring at me over his shoulder. Bolte came up to me: "What insolence! How dare he? You should have reacted." I shrugged my shoulders. What did it matter? Bolte knew perfectly well what we were going to do to that man and his child. It was natural that he should want to insult us. I walked away and headed for the exit. Some Orpos were organizing a group of people in their underwear and herding them toward the antitank trench, half a mile away. I watched them move off. The ditch was too far away for the gunfire to be heard; but these people must have suspected what fate was awaiting them. Bolte hailed me: "Are you coming?" Our car passed the group that I had seen leaving; they were shivering from the cold, the women were clutching their children by the hand. Then in front of us was the ditch. Some soldiers and Orpos were standing at ease, jeering; I heard a commotion and shouts. I passed through the group of soldiers and saw Turek, holding a shovel, striking an almost naked man lying on the ground. Other bloody bodies were lying in front of him; farther on, some terrorized Jews were standing under guard. "Vermin!" Turek bellowed, his eyes bulging. "Grovel, Jew!" He hit the man's head with the sharp edge of the shovel; the man's skull cracked, spraying Turek's boots with blood and brains; I clearly saw an eye, knocked out by the blow, fly a few meters away. The men were laughing. I reached Turek in two strides and seized him roughly by the arm: "You're insane! Stop that at once!" I was trembling. Turek turned on me in a rage and made as if to raise his shovel; then he lowered it and shrugged his arm free. He was trembling too. "Mind your own business," he spat. His face was purple; he was sweating and rolling his eyes. He threw down the shovel and strode away. Bolte had joined me; with a few curt words, he ordered Pfeiffer, who was standing there breathing heavily, to have the bodies picked up and to continue the execution. "It wasn't your place to intervene," he reproached me.—"But that sort of thing is unacceptable!"—"Maybe, but Sturmbannführer Müller is in charge of this Kommando. You're here only as an observer."—"Well, where is Sturmbannführer Müller, then?" I was still trembling. I returned to the car and ordered the driver to take me back to Pyatigorsk. I wanted to light a cigarette; but my hands were still shaking, I couldn't control them and had trouble with my lighter. Finally I managed it and took a few drags before throwing the cigarette out the window. We were passing, from the other direction, the column that was advancing at a walk; from the corner of my eye I saw a teenager break rank and run to pick up my cigarette butt before going back to his place.

In Pyatigorsk, I couldn't find Müller. The soldier on guard thought he must have gone to the AOK, but he wasn't sure; I thought about waiting for him, then decided to leave: might as well report the incident directly to Bierkamp. I went to the sanatorium to get my things and sent my driver to scare up some gasoline at the AOK. It wasn't very polite to leave without saying goodbye; but I had no desire to say goodbye to these people. In Mineralnye Vody, the road passed close to the factory, which lay behind the railroad, at the foot of the mountain; I didn't stop. Back in Vorshilovsk, I wrote my report, confining myself mostly to the technical and organizational aspects of the action. But I also inserted a sentence about "certain deplorable excesses on the part of officers supposed to set an example." I knew that would be enough. The next day, in fact, Thielecke came to my office to let me know that Bierkamp wanted to see me. Prill, after reading my report, had already asked some questions: I had refused to answer him, telling him it concerned no one but the Kommandant. Bierkamp received me politely, had me sit down, and asked what had happened; Thielecke was also present at the discussion. I related the incident to them as neutrally as possible. "And what do you think should be done?" Thielecke asked when I had finished.—"I think, Sturmbannführer, that it's a case for the *SS-Gericht*, a court of the SS and the police," I replied. "Or at the very least for a psychiatrist."—"You exaggerate," Bierkamp said. "Hauptsturmführer Turek is an excellent officer, very capable. His indignation and legitimate anger at the Jews, bearers of the Stalin system, are understandable. And also you yourself acknowledge that you didn't get there till the end of the incident. No doubt there was provocation."—"Even if those Jews were insolent or tried to run away, his reaction was unworthy of an SS officer. Especially in front of the men."—"On that point you're probably right." He looked at Thielecke for an instant, then turned to me: "I'm planning on going to Pyatigorsk in a few days. I'll discuss the incident myself with Hauptsturmführer Turek. Thank you for letting me know about these facts."

Sturmbannführer Dr. Leetsch, Dr. Seibert's replacement, was arriving that same day, accompanied by an Obersturmbannführer, Paul Schultz, who was supposed to take over for Dr. Braune in Maikop; but before I could even meet him, Prill asked me to leave again for Moz-

dok, to inspect Sk 10b, which had just arrived there. "That way you'll
have seen all the Kommandos," he said. "You can report to the Sturmbannführer when you return." The road to Mozdok took about six
hours, going through Minvody and then Prokhladny; so I decided to
leave the next morning, but didn't see Leetsch. My driver woke me up
a little before dawn. We had already left the Voroshilovsk plateau when
the sun rose, softly illuminating the fields and orchards and outlining the
first volcanoes of the KMV in the distance. After Mineralnye Vody, the
road, lined with linden trees, followed the foothills of the Caucasus
Mountains, still barely visible; only the Elbruz, its rounded humped
peak covered with snow, showed in the gray of the sky. North of the
road began the fields, with here and there a poor little Muslim village.
We drove behind long convoys of trucks from the *Rollbahn*, difficult to
pass. Mozdok was crawling with men and vehicles, long columns clogging the dusty streets; I parked my Opel and left on foot to look for the
HQ of the Fifty-second Corps. I was met by an officer from the Abwehr, very excited: "You haven't heard? Generalfeldmarschall List was
dismissed this morning."—"But why?" I exclaimed. List, a newcomer
on the Eastern Front, had barely lasted two months. The AO shrugged
his shoulders: "We were forced to go on the defensive after the failure
of our breakthrough on the right bank of the Terek. That must not have
been appreciated in high places."—"Why couldn't you advance?" He
raised his arms: "We lack the forces, that's all! Dividing Army Group
South in half was a fatal error. Now we don't have enough forces for either objective. In Stalingrad they're still mired down on the outskirts."—"And who was appointed in place of the Feldmarschall?" He
guffawed bitterly: "You're not going to believe me: the Führer took the
command himself!" That was, in fact, unheard-of: "The Führer personally took command of Army Group A?"—"Exactly. I don't know
how he plans on doing it; the OKHG is staying in Voroshilovsk, and the
Führer is in Vinnitsa. But since he's a genius, he must have a solution."
His tone was becoming more and more acerbic. "He's already commanding the Reich, the Wehrmacht, and the land forces. Now Army
Group A. Do you think he'll go on this way? He could take command
of an army, then a corps, then a division. In the end, who knows, he
might end up as a corporal at the front, just like at the beginning."—
"I find you extremely insolent," I said coldly.—"And you, old man," he
replied, "can fuck off. You're in a sector of the front, here; the SS has
no jurisdiction." An orderly came in. "There's your guide," the officer
pointed. "Have a nice day." I went out without saying anything. I was
shocked, but worried too: if our offensive in the Caucasus, on which
we had staked everything, was getting bogged down, it was a bad sign.

Time wasn't working on our side. Winter was approaching, and the *Endsieg* kept drawing farther back, like the magic peaks of the Caucasus. At least, I reassured myself, Stalingrad will soon fall; that will free up forces to resume the advance here.

The Sonderkommando was set up in a partially ruined wing of a Russian base; some rooms were still usable, others had been sealed off with boards. I was received by the head of the Kommando, a slender Austrian with a well-trimmed moustache just like the Führer's, Sturmbannführer Alois Persterer. He was a man from the SD who had been a Leiter in Hamburg back when Bierkamp was heading the Kripo there; but the two didn't seem any closer for it. He gave me a concise outline of the situation: in Prokhladny, a Teilkommando had shot some Kabards and Balkars associated with the Bolshevik authorities, along with a number of Jews and partisans; in Mozdok, aside from a few suspicious cases handed over by the Fifty-second Corps, they hadn't really begun. Someone had mentioned a Jewish kolkhoz in the region; he would look into it and take care of it. In any case there weren't too many partisans, and in the frontline areas the natives seemed hostile to the Reds. I asked him what his relations were with the Wehrmacht. "I can't even say they're mediocre," he finally replied. "They seem just to be ignoring us."—"Yes, the failure of the offensive is worrying them." I spent the night in Mozdok, on a camp bed set up in one of the offices, and left the next morning; Persterer had suggested I attend an execution in Prokhladny, with their gas truck, but I had politely declined. In Voroshilovsk, I introduced myself to Dr. Leetsch, an older officer, with a narrow, rectangular face, graying hair, and glum lips. After reading my report, he wanted to discuss it. I told him my impressions about the morale of the Wehrmacht. "Yes," he said finally, "you're completely right. That's why I think it's important to reestablish good ties with them. I'll take care of relations with the OKHG myself, but I want to appoint a good liaison officer in Pyatigorsk, with the Ic of the AOK. I wanted to ask you to take this position." I hesitated for an instant; I wondered if the idea really came from him, or had been suggested to him by Prill during my absence. Finally I replied: "To tell the truth, my relations with Einsatzkommando 12 are not the best. I had an altercation with one of their officers, and I'm afraid it might create complications."—"Don't worry about that. You won't have much to do with them. You'll have your quarters at the AOK and you'll report directly to me."

So I returned to Pyatigorsk and they gave me a place to stay some ways from the center, in a sanatorium at the foot of the Mashuk (the

highest part of the town). I had a French window and a little balcony
that looked out on the long bare ridge of the Goriatchaya Gora, with
its Chinese pavilion and a few trees, and then the plain and the volcanoes behind it, ranged in tiers in the haze. If I turned around and leaned
backward, I could see a wedge of the Mashuk over the roof, crossed by
a cloud that seemed to be moving almost at my level. It had rained during the night and the air smelled good and fresh. After going to the
AOK to introduce myself to the Ic, Oberst von Gilsa, and his colleagues, I went out for a walk. A long paved lane rises from the center
and follows the side of the mountain; behind the monument to Lenin,
you have to climb some wide steep steps, then, past some basins, between lines of young oak and fragrant pine trees, the slope grows gen-
tler. I passed the Lermontov Sanatorium, where von Kleist and his staff
were staying; my quarters were set a little farther back, in a separate
wing, right up against the mountain, now almost completely hidden by
clouds. Farther up, the lane widened into a road that skirts round the
Mashuk to connect a string of sanatoriums; there I veered off toward
the little pavilion called the Aeolian Harp, from which one has a broad
view of the plain to the south, scattered with otherworldly mounds, one
volcano and then another and then another, extinct, peaceful. To the
right, the sun drew gleams from the metal roofs of the houses, scattered
in thick greenery; and farther on, in the distance, clouds were forming,
masking the peaks of the Caucasus. A cheerful voice rose up behind me:
"Aue! Have you been here a long time?" I turned around: Voss was approaching, smiling, beneath the trees. I shook his hand warmly. "I've
just arrived. I've been appointed liaison officer to the AOK."—"Oh,
excellent! I'm at the AOK too. Have you eaten yet?"—"Not yet."—
"Come with me, then. There's a good café just down below." He set off
on a narrow stone path cut into the rock and I followed him. Below,
framing the tip of the long ravine that separates the Mashuk from the
Goriatchaya Gora, lay a long columned gallery made of pink granite,
decorated in an Italian style both ponderous and frivolous. "That's the
Academic Gallery," Voss said.—"Oh!" I exclaimed, very excited, "but
that's the old Elisabeth Gallery! This is where Pechorin saw Princess
Mary for the first time." Voss burst out laughing: "So you know Lermontov? Everyone here is reading him."—"Of course! *A Hero of Our
Time* was my favorite book, at one time." The path had brought us to
the level of the gallery, built to shelter a sulfur spring. Some crippled soldiers, pale and slow, were strolling or sitting on benches, facing the long
hollow that opens up toward the city; a Russian gardener was weeding
the tulip and red carnation beds along the grand staircase that descends
toward Kirov Street, at the bottom of the depression. The copper roofs

of the spas nestled against the Goriatchaya Gora, rising above the trees, glittered in the sunlight. Beyond the ridge you could only make out one of the volcanoes. "Are you coming?" said Voss.—"Just a minute." I entered the gallery to look at the spring, but I was disappointed: the room was bare and empty, and the water was pouring from an ordinary faucet. "The café is in the back," said Voss. He passed under the arch that separates the left wing of the gallery from the central building; behind, the wall joined the rock to form a wide alcove, where they had placed a few tables and some stools. We sat down and a pretty young girl appeared through a door. Voss exchanged a few words with her in Russian. "There isn't any shashlik today. But they have Kiev cutlets."—"That's perfect."—"Do you want some water from the spring or a beer?"—"I think I'd rather have a beer. Is it cold?"—"Cold enough. But I warn you, it's not German beer." I lit a cigarette and leaned against the wall of the gallery. It was pleasantly cool; water streamed down the rock, two little brightly colored birds were pecking at the ground. "So you like Pyatigorsk, then?" Voss asked me. I smiled, I was happy to see him here. "I haven't seen much yet," I said.—"If you like Lermontov, the city is a veritable pilgrimage. The Soviets created a nice little museum in his house. When you have an afternoon free, we'll go see it."—"Gladly. Do you know where the location of the duel is?"—"Pechorin's or Lermontov's?"—"Lermontov's."—"Behind Mashuk. There's a hideous monument, of course. And just imagine: we've even found one of his descendants." I laughed: "Not possible."—"Yes, yes. A Frau Evgenia Akimovna Shan-Girei. She is very old. The general had a pension allocated to her, larger than the one she had under the Soviets."—"Did she know him?"—"You've got to be kidding. The Russians were just preparing to celebrate the centenary of his death the day of our invasion. Frau Shan-Girei was born ten or fifteen years later, in the fifties, I think." The waitress returned with two dishes and some silverware. The "cutlets" were in fact chicken rolls, stuffed with melted butter and breaded, and accompanied by a fricassee of wild mushrooms with garlic. "This is delicious. And even the beer isn't too bad."—"I told you, didn't I? I come here whenever I can. It's never crowded." I ate without talking, deeply content. "You have a lot of work?" I finally asked him.—"Let's say that I have some free time for my research. Last month I looted the Pushkin library in Krasnodar and found some very interesting things. They had a lot of books about the Cossacks, but I also unearthed some Caucasian grammar books and some pretty rare monographs by Troubetskoy. I still have to go to Cherkessk, I'm sure they'll have some books on the Circassians and the Karachai. My dream, though, is to find an Ubykh who still knows his language. But for now, not a chance. Otherwise, I write leaflets for the AOK."—"What kind of leaflets?"—"Propaganda leaflets. They scatter them over the mountains by plane. I did one in Karachai, Kabardian, and Balkar, consulting the locals, of course, that was very funny: *Mountain people—Before, you had everything, but Soviet power took it away from you! Welcome your German brothers who have flown like eagles over the mountains to free you! Et cetera."* I chuckled along with him. "I've also made some passes that we're sending to the partisans to encourage them to switch sides. I wrote that we'd welcome them as *soyuzniki* in the general fight against Judeo-Bolshevism. The Jews among them must be having a good laugh. These *propuska* are valid *until the end of the war.*" The girl cleared the dishes and brought us some Turkish coffee. "They have everything here!" I exclaimed.—"Oh, yes. The markets are open, there's even food for sale in the stores."—"It's not like in the Ukraine."—"No. And with a little luck, it won't be."—"What do you mean?"—"Oh, some things might be changing." We paid the bill and went back through the arch. The wounded soldiers were still strolling in front of the gallery, drinking their water in little sips. "Does that really help?" I asked Voss, pointing at a glass.—"The region has a reputation. You know that people came to take the waters here long before the Russians. Have you ever heard of Ibn Battuta?"—"The Arab traveler? I know the name."—"He came through here, around 1375. He was in the Crimea, with the Tatars, where he had gotten married on the way. The Tatars were still living in large nomadic camps, cities on wheels made of tents on enormous wagons, with mosques and shops. Every year in the summer, when it began to get too warm in the Crimea, the Nogai Khan, with his entire city on the march, crossed the isthmus of Perekop and came as far as here. Ibn Battuta describes the place quite precisely, and praises the medicinal virtues of the sulfur water. He calls the site *Bish* or *Besh Dagh*, which, like *Pyatigorsk* in Russian, means 'the five mountains.'" I laughed with surprise: "And what became of Ibn Battuta?"—"Afterward? He continued on, through Daghestan and Afghanistan, and ended up in India. He was a qadi in Delhi for a long time, and served Mohammed Tughluq, the paranoid sultan, for seven years before falling into disgrace. Then he was a qadi in the Maldives, and he even went as far as Ceylon, Indonesia, and China. And then he went home, to Morocco, to write his book before he died."

That night, in the mess, I realized that Pyatigorsk truly was a place of reunions: sitting at a table with some other officers, I saw Dr. Hohenegg, the good-natured, cynical pathologist I had met in the train between Kharkov and Simferopol. I went up to greet him: "I see, Herr Oberstarzt, that General von Kleist surrounds himself only with the best people." He got up to shake my hand: "Oh, but I'm not with Generaloberst von Kleist: I'm still attached to the Sixth Army, with General Paulus."—"What are you doing here, then?"—"The OKH decided to take advantage of the KMV infrastructures to organize an interarmy medical conference. A very useful exchange of information. Everyone competes to describe the most atrocious case."—"I'm sure that honor will fall to you."—"Listen, I'm dining with my colleagues; but if you like, come by afterward, have a brandy in my room." I went to dine with the officers from the Abwehr. They were realistic, sympathetic men, but almost as critical as the officer in Mozdok. Some stated openly that if we didn't take Stalingrad soon, the war was lost; von Gilsa was drinking French wine and didn't contradict them. Afterward I went out to walk by myself in Tsvetnik Park, behind the Lermontov gallery, a curious pavilion of pale blue wood, in a medieval style, with pointed turrets and Art Deco windows tinted pink, red, and white: an utterly disparate effect, but wholly in keeping here. I smoked, absent-mindedly contemplating the faded tulips, then climbed back up the hill to the sanatorium and went to knock on Hohenegg's door. He welcomed me lying on his sofa, his feet bare, his hands crossed on his large round belly. "Excuse me for not getting up." He made a sign with his head toward an end table. "The brandy is over there. Pour me one too, will you?" I poured two measures into the glasses and held one out to him; then I settled into a chair and crossed my legs. "So what's the most atrocious thing you've seen?" He waved his hand: "Man, of course!"—"I meant medically."—"Medically, atrocious things don't interest me in the least. On the other hand one does see extraordinary curiosities, which completely revise our notions of what our poor bodies can endure."—"What, for example?"—"Well, a man will catch a tiny piece of shrapnel in the calf that will slice through the peroneal artery and he'll die in two minutes, still standing, his blood emptied into his boot without his noticing. Yet another man might take a bullet through the head, from one temple to the other, and will get up on his own to walk to the first-aid post."—"What an insignificant thing we are," I commented.—"Precisely." I tasted Hohenegg's brandy: it was Armenian, a little sweet but drinkable. "You'll excuse my brandy," he said without turning his head, "but I couldn't find any Rémy-Martin in this town of barbarians. To go back to what I was saying, almost all of my colleagues have stories like that. And it's not new: I once read the memoirs of a military doctor in Napoleon's army, and he talked about the same things. Of course, we're still losing far too many men. Military medicine has come a long way since 1812, but so have the methods of butchery. We're still lagging behind. But, little by little, we're getting better, and it's true that Gatling has done more for modern surgery than Dupuytren."—"But still you perform real wonders." He sighed: "Maybe. The fact is I can no longer bear to see a pregnant woman. It depresses me too much to think about what's in store for her fetus."—"*Nothing ever dies except what is born,*" I recited. "*Birth is indebted to death.*" He let out a short cry, got up suddenly, and swallowed his brandy in one gulp. "That's what I like about you, Hauptsturmführer. A member of the *Sicherheitsdienst* who quotes Tertullian instead of Rosenberg or Hans Frank is always a pleasure. But I could criticize your translation: *Mutuum debitum est nativitati cum mortalitate,* I'd say rather: 'Birth has a mutual debt with death,' or 'Birth and death are mutually indebted to each other.'"—"You're probably right. I was always better in Greek. I have a linguist friend here, I'll ask him." He held out his glass for me to fill. "Speaking of mortality," he asked me pleasantly, "are you still murdering poor defenseless people?" I handed him his glass coolly. "Coming from you, Doktor, I won't take that the wrong way. But in any case, I'm nothing but a liaison officer, which suits me fine. I observe and do nothing, that's my favorite position."—"You would have made a very poor physician, then. Observation without practice isn't worth much."—"That's why I'm a jurist." I got up and went to open the French window. Outside, the air was sweet, but you couldn't see the stars and I could feel rain coming. A light wind was rustling through the trees. I went back to the sofa where Hohenegg had stretched out again after unfastening his tunic. "What I can tell you," I said, standing in front of him, "is that some of my dear colleagues here are absolute bastards."—"I don't doubt it for an instant. It's a common defect in people who practice without observing. It even occurs among doctors." I rolled my glass between my fingers. I suddenly felt hollow, heavy. I finished my glass and asked him: "Are you here for long?"— "There are two sessions: now we're going over the wounds, then we'll come back at the end of the month for diseases. One day for venereal diseases, and two whole days devoted to lice and scabies."—"We'll see each other again, then. Good night, Doktor." He held out his hand and I shook it. "You'll excuse me if I don't get up," he said.

Hohenegg's brandy turned out to be a poor choice of after-dinner drink: back in my room, I vomited up my dinner. The retchings caught me so quickly I barely had the time to reach the bathtub. Since I had already digested, it was easy to rinse out; but it had a bitter, acidic, revolting taste; I preferred to vomit my meals right away, it came up more painfully and with more difficulty, but at least it didn't have any taste, or else it tasted like food. I thought about returning to have another drink with Hohenegg, to ask his advice; but finally I just washed out my mouth with water, smoked a cigarette, and went to bed. The next day, I had to go to the Kommando to pay a courtesy visit; they were also expecting Oberführer Bierkamp. I went there around eleven o'clock. From the lower part of town, on the boulevard, you could clearly see, in the distance, the jagged peaks of the Beshtau, rising like a guardian idol; it hadn't rained, but the air was still fresh. At the Kommando, they told me that Müller was busy with Bierkamp. I waited on the steps of the little courtyard, watching one of the drivers wash the mud off the bumpers and wheels of the Saurer truck. The rear door was open: out of curiosity, I went over to it to look inside, since I hadn't yet seen what it looked like; I recoiled and immediately began coughing; it was foul, a stinking pool of vomit, excrement, urine. The driver noticed my reaction and said a few words to me in Russian: *"Griaznyi, kazhdi raz,"* but I didn't understand the words. An Orpo, probably a *Volksdeutscher,* came over and translated: "He says that it's always like that, Hauptsturmführer, very dirty, but they're going to modify the interior, have the floor slope down, and put a little trapdoor in the middle. That will make it easier to clean out."—"Is he a Russian?"—"Who, Zaitsev? He's a Cossack, Hauptsturmführer, we have several of them." I went back to the steps and lit a cigarette; just at that instant I was summoned, and had to throw it away. Müller received me together with Bierkamp. I saluted him and introduced my mission in Pyatigorsk. "Yes, yes," Müller said, "the Oberführer explained it to me." They asked me some questions and I talked about the feeling of pessimism that seemed to be reigning among the army officers. Bierkamp shrugged: "The soldiers have always been pessimists. Already, when it came to the Rhineland and the Sudetenland, they were wailing like sissies. They have never understood the strength of the Führer's will and of National Socialism.—Tell me something else, have you heard this story about a military government?"—"No, Oberführer. What is it?"—"A rumor is circulating to the effect that the Führer has approved of a military government for the Caucasus, instead of a civilian administration. But we can't manage to get any official confirmation. At the OKHG they're very evasive."—"I'll try to find out more at the AOK, Oberführer." We exchanged a few more remarks and I took my leave. In the hallway, I met Turek. He gave me a sardonic, angry look and said with incredible rudeness: "Ah, the *Papiersoldat.* Don't worry, your turn will come." Bierkamp must have talked to him. I answered him amiably, with a little smile: "Hauptsturmführer, I'm at your service." He stared at me for an instant with a furious look, then disappeared into an office. There, I said to myself, you've made yourself an enemy; that's not so hard.

At the AOK, I requested a meeting with von Gilsa and put

Bierkamp's question to him. "It's true," he replied, "they're talking about it. But the details aren't clear yet for me."—"And what will happen to the Reichskommissariat, then?"—"The establishment of the Reichskommissariat will be delayed for a while."—"And why haven't the representatives of the SP and the SD been informed?"—"I couldn't say. I'm still waiting for more information. But you know, this question concerns the OKHG. Oberführer Bierkamp should apply directly to them." I left von Gilsa's office with the impression that he knew more than he was saying. I wrote a brief report and addressed it to Leetsch and Bierkamp. In general, that was what my work consisted of now: the Abwehr sent me a copy of the reports they wanted, generally having to do with the evolution of the partisan problem; I threw in some information gleaned here and there, most of the time at meals, and sent the whole thing on to Voroshilovsk; in exchange, I received other reports that I communicated to von Gilsa or one of his colleagues. Thus, the activity reports of Ek 12, whose offices were half a mile away from the AOK, had to be sent first to Voroshilovsk, then, collated with those of Sk 10b (the other Kommandos were operating in the theater of operations or the rear areas of the Seventeenth Army), some of them came down to me, and I passed them on to the Ic; and the whole time, of course, the Einsatzkommando maintained its own direct relations with the AOK. I didn't have much work to do. I took advantage of this: Pyatigorsk was a pleasant town, there were lots of things to see. Accompanied by Voss, always curious, I went to visit the local museum, located a little below the Hotel Bristol, across from the post office and Tsvetnik Park. There were some fine collections there, accumulated in the course of decades by the *Kavkazskoe Gornoe Obshchestvo*, an association of amateur but enthusiastic naturalists: they had brought back from their expeditions heaps of stuffed animals, minerals, skulls, plants, dried flowers; old gravestones and pagan idols; moving photographs in black-and-white, representing mostly elegant gentlemen in cravats, celluloid collars, and straw boaters perched on the steep slope of a peak; and (I remembered my father's office with delight) a whole wall of large cases of butterflies containing hundreds of specimens, each one labeled with the date and place of its capture, the name of the collector, and the sex and scientific name of the butterfly. They came from Kislovodsk, from Adyghea, from Chechnya, as far as Daghestan and Adjaria; the dates were 1923, 1915, 1909. At night, we sometimes went to the Teatr Operetty, another eccentric building, decorated with red ceramic tiles embossed with books, musical instruments, and garlands, and recently reopened by the Wehrmacht; then we would dine at the mess or in a café or at the Kasino, which was none other than the old hotel-restaurant Restoratsiya where Pechorin met Mary and where, as a plaque in Russian that Voss translated for me indicated, Lev Tolstoy celebrated his twenty-fifth birthday. The Soviets had turned it into a Central Government Institute of Balneology; the Wehrmacht had left this impressive title on the pediment, in gold letters above the massive columns, but had returned the building to its original use, and you could drink dry wine from Kakhetia there and eat shashlik and sometimes even venison; there, too, I introduced Voss to Hohenegg and they spent the evening discussing the origins of the names of diseases, in five languages.

Around the middle of the month, a dispatch from the Group shed some light on the situation. The Führer had in fact approved the setting up, for the Kuban-Caucasus, of a military administration under OKHG A, headed by the General der Kavallerie Ernst Köstring. The *Ostministerium* was detaching a high functionary to serve with this administration, but the creation of the Reichskommissariat was delayed indefinitely. Even more surprising, the OKH had ordered the OKHG to form autonomous territorial entities for the Cossacks and the different mountain peoples; the kolkhozes would be dissolved and forced labor prohibited: the systematic opposite of our policy in the Ukraine. That seemed to me too intelligent to be true. I had to return urgently to Voroshilovsk to attend a meeting: the HSSPF wanted to discuss the new decrees. All the leaders of the Kommandos were present, with most of their adjuncts. Korsemann seemed worried. "The disturbing thing is that the Führer made this decision at the beginning of August; but I myself was only informed of it yesterday. It's incomprehensible."— "The OKH must be worried about SS interference," Bierkamp said.— "But why?" Korsemann plaintively asked. "Our collaboration is excellent."—"The SS spent a lot of time cultivating good relations with the Reichskommissar-designate. For the time being, all that work has gone up in smoke."—"In Maikop," interrupted Schultz, Braune's replacement who'd been nicknamed Eisbein-Paule because of his girth, "they say the Wehrmacht will keep control of the oil installations."— "I will also point out to you, Brigadeführer," Bierkamp added, addressing Korsemann, "that if these 'local self-governments' are established, they will control police functions in their district themselves. From our point of view, that is unacceptable." The discussion went on in this vein for a while; the consensus seemed to be that the SS had been well and truly taken in. Finally we were dismissed and instructed to gather as much information as possible.

In Pyatigorsk, I had begun to develop tolerable relations with some officers in the Kommando. Hohenegg had left, and aside from the officers of the Abwehr, I saw almost no one except Voss. At night, I sometimes met SS officers in the Kasino. Turek of course never spoke to me; as for Dr. Müller, ever since I'd heard him publicly explain why he didn't like the gas truck, but found execution by firing squad much more *gemütlich*, I had decided that we wouldn't have much to say to each other. But among the subordinate officers there were some decent men, even if they were often boring. One night, as I was having a brandy with Voss, Obersturmführer Dr. Kern came over and I invited him to join us. I introduced him to Voss: "Oh, so you're the linguist from the AOK," said Kern.—"Apparently so," Voss replied with amusement.—"That's good," said Kern, "I wanted to submit a case to you. They tell me you know the peoples of the Caucasus well."—"A little," Voss admitted.—"Professor Kern teaches in Munich," I interrupted. "He is a specialist in Muslim history."—"That's an extremely interesting subject," Voss approved.—"Yes, I spent seven years in Turkey and I know a little about it," Kern said.—"How did you end up here, then?"—"Like everyone else, I was mobilized. I was already a member of the SS and a correspondent of the SD, and I ended up in the Einsatz."—"I see. And your case?"—"A young woman they brought me. A redhead, very beautiful, charming. Her neighbors denounced her as Jewish. She showed me an internal Soviet passport, delivered in Derbent, where her nationality is inscribed as *Tatka*. I checked in our files: according to our experts, the Tats are assimilated with the *Bergjuden*, the Mountain Jews. But the girl told me I was mistaken and that the Tats were a Turkic people. I had her speak: she has a curious dialect, a little hard to understand, but it was indeed a Turkic language. So I let her go."—"Do you remember the terms or expressions she used?" An entire conversation in Turkish ensued: "That can't be it exactly," Voss said, "are you sure?" and they started up again. Finally Voss declared: "According to what you're describing, it does in fact more or less resemble the vernacular Turkic spoken in the Caucasus before the Bolsheviks imposed Russian. I read they still used it in Daghestan, especially in Derbent. But all the peoples there speak it. Did you take down her name?" Kern pulled a notebook out of his pocket and leafed through it: "Here it is. Tsokota, Nina Shaulovna."—"Tsokota?" said Voss, knitting his brows. "That's strange."—"It's her husband's name," Kern explained.— "Oh, I see. And tell me, if she is Jewish, what will you do with her?" Kern looked surprised: "Well, we . . . we . . ." He was visibly hesitating. I came to his aid: "She'll be transported elsewhere."—"I see," said Voss. He thought a moment and then said to Kern: "To my knowledge, the Tats have their own language, which is an Iranian dialect and has nothing to do with Caucasian languages or with Turkish. There are Muslim Tats; in Derbent, I don't know, but I'll look into it."—"Thank you," said

Kern. "You think I should have kept her?"—"Not at all. I'm sure you did the right thing." Kern looked reassured; he had obviously not grasped the irony in Voss's last words. We chatted a little longer and he took his leave. Voss watched him leave with a puzzled look. "Your colleagues are a little strange," he said finally.—"How do you mean?"— "They sometimes ask disconcerting questions." I shrugged my shoulders: "They're doing their work." Voss shook his head: "Your methods seem a little arbitrary to me. But it's not my business." He seemed displeased. "When will we go to the Lermontov Museum?" I asked to change the subject.—"Whenever you like. Sunday?"—"If the weather is nice, you can take me to see the place of the duel."

The most divergent information, and sometimes the most contradictory, flowed in concerning the new military administration. General Köstring was setting up his offices in Voroshilovsk. He was an already elderly officer, called back from retirement, but my informants at the Abwehr claimed that he was still vigorous, and called him the Wise Marabu. He had been born in Moscow, had led the German military mission to Hetman Skoropadsky in Kiev in 1918, and had served twice as military attaché to our embassy in Moscow: he was seen as one of the best German experts on Russia. Oberst von Gilsa arranged an interview for me with the new representative of the *Ostministerium* to Köstring's office, a former consul in Tiflis, Dr. Otto Bräutigam. With his round wire-rimmed glasses, his starched collar, and his light brown uniform displaying the Party's Gold Badge, I found him a bit stiff; he remained distant, almost cold, but gave me a better impression than most of the *Goldfasanen*. Gilsa had explained to me that he had an important position at the political department in the ministry. "I'm pleased to meet you," I said to him as I shook his hand. "Perhaps you can finally bring us some clarifications."—"I met Brigadeführer Korsemann in Voroshilovsk and I had a long conversation with him. Was the Einsatzgruppe not informed?"—"Oh, of course! But if you have a few minutes, I'd be delighted to speak with you, since these questions interest me greatly." I led Bräutigam to my office and offered him a drink; he politely refused. "The *Ostministerium* must have been disappointed by the Führer's decision to suspend the establishment of the Reichskommissariat, I imagine?" I began.—"Not at all. On the contrary, we think the Führer's decision is a unique opportunity to correct the disastrous policies we are carrying out in this country."—"How do you mean?"— "You must realize that the two Reichskommissars now in place were appointed without Minister Rosenberg's being consulted, and that the *Ostministerium* exercises almost no control over them. So it's not our fault if Gauleiters Koch and Lohse do exactly as they please; responsibility falls on those who support them. It's their thoughtless and aberrant policies that have earned the ministry its reputation as the *Chaostministerium*." I smiled; but he remained serious.—"In fact," I said, "I spent a year in the Ukraine, and Reichskommissar Koch's policies caused quite a few problems for us. You could say that he was a very good recruiter for the partisans."—"Just like Gauleiter Sauckel and his slave-hunters. That's what we want to avoid here. Don't you see, if we treat the Caucasian tribes as we treated the Ukrainians, they'll rise and take to the mountains. Then we'll never be finished with them. Last century, the Russians spent thirty years trying to make the imam Shamil submit. There were only a few thousand rebels; to crush them, the Russians had to deploy up to three hundred and fifty thousand soldiers!" He paused and went on: "Minister Rosenberg, along with the political department of the ministry, has since the beginning of the campaign argued in favor of a clear political stance: only an alliance with the peoples of the East oppressed by the Bolsheviks will allow Germany to crush the Stalin system once and for all. Until now, this strategy, this *Ostpolitik* if you like, hasn't been accepted; the Führer has always supported the people who think Germany can carry out this task all by itself, repressing the peoples it should be liberating. The Reichskommissar-designate Schickendanz, despite his old friendship with the minister, also seems to be going along with this. But there are cool heads in the Wehrmacht, especially Generalquartiermeister Wagner, who wanted to avoid a repetition in the Caucasus of the Ukrainian disaster. Their solution, to keep the region under military control, seems good to us, all the more so since General Wagner expressly insisted on involving the most clearsighted elements of the ministry, as my presence here proves. For us as for the Wehrmacht, it's a unique opportunity to demonstrate that the *Ostpolitik* is the only valid one; if we succeed here, we might have the possibility of repairing the harm done in the Ukraine and in Ostland."—"So the stakes are considerable," I noted.—"Yes."—"And hasn't the Reichskommissardesignate Schickedanz been upset at finding himself sidelined in this way? He too has some support." Bräutigam made a scornful gesture with his hand; his eyes were gleaming behind his glasses: "No one asked his opinion. In any case, the Reichskommissar-designate Schickedanz is much too busy studying the sketches of his future palace in Tiflis, and discussing the number of gates with his deputies, to worry about practical matters in the way we must."—"I see." I thought for an instant: "One more question. How do you see the role of the SS and the SP in this arrangement?"—"The *Sicherheitspolizei* of course has important tasks to carry out. But they should be coordinated with the Army Group and the military administration in order not to interfere with the positive initiatives. In plain language, as I suggested to Brigadeführer Korsemann, we'll have to show a certain delicacy in our relations with the mountain and Cossack minorities. There are elements among them, in fact, who collaborated with the Communists, but out of nationalism rather than out of Bolshevist conviction, to defend the interests of their people. It's not a question of automatically treating them like Commissars or Stalinist functionaries."—"And what do you think of the Jewish problem?" He raised his hand: "That's another thing entirely. It's clear that the Jewish population remains one of the main supports of the Bolshevist system." He got up to take his leave. "Thank you for taking the time to speak with me," I said as I shook his hand on the steps.—"Not at all. I think it's very important that we keep up good relations with the SS as well as with the Wehrmacht. The better you understand what we want to do here, the better things will go."—"You can be sure that I'll make that clear in my report to my superiors."—"Very good! Here's my card. Heil Hitler!"

Voss deemed this conversation quite comical when I reported it to him. "It was about time! Nothing like failure to sharpen the wits." We had met as agreed, on Sunday, toward noon, in front of the Feldkommandantur. A troop of kids was clustered around the barricades, fascinated by the motorcycles and an amphibious *Schwimmwagen* parked there. "Partisans!" bellowed a territorial who was vainly trying to scatter them with a stick; no sooner were they chased away from one side than they streamed in on the other, and the reservist was already out of breath. We climbed the steep slope of Karl Marx Street, toward the museum, and I finished summing up Bräutigam's remarks. "Better late than never," Voss commented, "but in my opinion it won't work. We've developed too many bad habits. This business with the military administration is just a grace period. In six or ten months they'll have to hand over the reins, and then all the jackals being kept on the leash will pour in, the Schickedanzes, the Körners, the Sauckel-Einsatzes, and all hell will break loose again. You see, the problem is that we don't have a colonial tradition. Even before the Great War, we were managing our African possessions very badly. And then afterward, we didn't have any more possessions at all, and the little bit of experience we had accumulated in colonial administration was lost. Just compare us to the English: look at the delicacy, the tact with which they govern and exploit their empire. They know very well how to wield the stick when they have to, but they always offer the carrot first, and go back to the carrot right after they hit with the stick. Even the Soviets, at bottom, have done better than us: despite their brutality, they were able to create a feeling of a shared identity, and their empire is holding. The troops that kept us in

check on the Terek were made up mostly of Georgians and Armenians.
I've spoken with some Armenian prisoners: they think of themselves as
Soviet, and fight for the USSR without hesitation. We haven't been able
to offer them anything better." We had arrived at the green door of the
museum and I knocked. After a few minutes the vehicle gate, a little
higher up, opened a little, giving us a glimpse of an old wrinkled peasant wearing a cap, his beard and callous fingers yellowed by *makhorka*.
He exchanged a few words with Voss, then pulled the gate open a little
more. "He says the museum is closed, but if we like, we can come in
and look. Some German officers live here, in the library." The gate
opened onto a little paved courtyard, surrounded by charming little
whitewashed buildings; on the right, a second floor had been built over
a shed, with a staircase outside; the library was there. In the background
rose the Mashuk, omnipresent, massive, tatters of clouds clinging to its
eastern slope. To the left, lower down, you could see a little garden,
with vines on a trellis, then some other buildings, their roofs covered
with thatch. Voss climbed the steps to the library. Inside, the varnished
wooden shelves took up so much space that you could barely slip past
them. The old man had followed us; I handed him three cigarettes; his
face lit up, but he remained near the door, watching us. Voss examined
the books through the glass but didn't touch anything. My gaze came to
rest on a little oil portrait of Lermontov, rather nicely done: he was represented in a red dolman decked with epaulettes and gilt braid, his lips
moist, his eyes surprisingly anxious, wavering between rage, fear, and
unbridled mockery. In another corner hung an engraved portrait, under
which I could just make out an inscription in Cyrillic: this was Martynov, Lermontov's killer. Voss was trying to open one of the cases, but
it was locked. The old man said something and they conversed a little.
"The curator has run away," Voss translated for me. "One of the employees has the keys, but she isn't in today. Too bad, they have some nice
things."—"You'll be back."—"Certainly. Come, he's going to open Lermontov's house for us." We crossed the courtyard and the little garden
to reach one of the low houses. The old man pushed open the door; inside, it was dark, but the light let in by the opening was enough to see
by. The walls had been whitewashed, and the furniture was simple;
there were some beautiful oriental carpets and Caucasian sabers hanging from nails. A narrow sofa looked very uncomfortable. Voss had
paused in front of a desk and was stroking it with his fingers. The old
man explained something to him. "He wrote *A Hero of Our Time* at this
table," Voss translated pensively.—"Right here?"—"No, in St. Peters-
burg. When the museum was created, the government had the table
sent here." There was nothing else to see. Outside, clouds were veiling

the sun. Voss thanked the old man, and I gave him a few more cigarettes. "We'll have to come back when there's someone who can explain everything," said Voss. "By the way," he added at the gate, "I
forgot to tell you: Professor Oberländer is here."—"Oberländer? But I
know him. I met him in Lemberg, at the beginning of the campaign."—
"All the better. I was going to suggest we have dinner with him." In the
street, Voss turned left, toward the wide flagstone-paved lane that
started at Lenin's statue. The path kept rising; I was short of breath already. Instead of leaving the lane to head for the Aeolian Harp and the
Academic Gallery, Voss kept going straight ahead, along the Mashuk, on
a paved road that I hadn't yet taken. The sky was darkening rapidly and
I was afraid it would rain. We passed a few sanatoriums, then the pavement ended and we continued on a wide dirt path. This place was not
much traveled: a peasant sitting on a wagon passed us, the jingling of the
harnesses mingled with the lowing of the ox and the grating squeal of
ill-sprung wheels; after that, the road was deserted. A little farther on,
to the left, a brick archway opened into the mountainside. We went up
to it and squinted to see into the darkness; an iron gate, padlocked,
barred access to the tunnel. "That's the Proval," Voss said. "At the end,
there's an open-air grotto, with a sulfur spring."—"Isn't this where
Pechorin meets Vera?"—"I'm not sure. Isn't that in the grotto beneath
the Aeolian Harp?"—"We'll have to check." The clouds were passing
just over our heads: I felt that if I lifted my arm I could stroke the swirls
of vapor. We couldn't see the sky at all and the atmosphere had become
muffled, silent. Our footsteps crunched on the sandy earth; the path rose
gently; and soon the clouds surrounded us. We could barely make out
the tall trees lining the path; the air seemed heavy; the world had disappeared. In the distance, a cuckoo's call echoed in the woods, an anxious,
sorrowful cry. We walked in silence. This lasted a long time. Here and
there, I caught a fleeting glimpse of large, dark, indistinct masses, buildings probably; then forest again. The clouds were dissipating, the gray
shone with a confused gleam and all of a sudden they unraveled and
scattered and we found ourselves in the sunlight. It hadn't rained. To
our right, beyond the trees, the jagged shapes of the Beshtau stood out;
another twenty minutes' walk brought us to the monument. "We've
taken the long way round," said Voss. "From the other side it's faster."—
"Yes, but it was worth it." The monument, a white obelisk erected in
the middle of a poorly maintained lawn, offered little of interest: faced
with this setting, carefully landscaped by bourgeois piety, it was hard to
imagine the gunshots, the blood, the hoarse cries, the rage of the murdered poet. A few German vehicles were lined up in the parking area;
below, in front of the forest, there were tables and benches where some

soldiers were eating. For the sake of thoroughness I went over to examine the bronze medallion and the inscription on the monument. "I
saw the photo of a temporary monument that they built in 1901," Voss
told me. "A kind of fanciful half-rotunda made of wood and plaster,
with a bust perched high up top. It was much funnier."—"They must
have had trouble funding it. Should we go eat?"—"Yes, they make
good shashlik here." We crossed the parking area and went down to the
tables. Two vehicles bore the tactical marks of the Einsatzkommando; I
recognized several officers at one of the tables. Kern waved at us and I
waved back, but I didn't go over to say hello. There were also Turek,
Bolte, Pfeiffer. I chose a table that was set somewhat back, near the
woods, with coarse stools. A local mountain man in a skullcap, his
cheeks badly shaved around his thick moustache, approached: "No
pork," Voss translated. "Just mutton. But there's vodka and *kompot*."—
"That's fine." Bursts of conversation reached us from the other tables.
There were also some junior officers from the Wehrmacht and a few
civilians. Turek was watching us, then I saw him talking animatedly
with Pfeiffer. Some Gypsy children were running between the tables.
One of them came up to us: *"Khleb, khleb,"* he chanted, holding out a
hand black with filth. The mountain man had brought us some slices of
bread and I held one out to the boy, which he immediately crammed
into his mouth. Then he pointed to the forest: *"Sestra, sestra, dyev. Kra-
sivaya."* He made an obscene gesture. Voss exploded in laughter and
flung some words at him that made him run away. He headed toward
the SS officers and repeated his gestures. "You think they'll follow
him?" Voss asked.—"Not in front of everyone," I said. Turek in fact
gave the boy a clout that sent him rolling onto the grass. I saw him make
as if to take out his gun; the kid bolted into the trees. The native, who
was officiating behind a long metal box on legs, came back to us with
two skewers that he laid on top of the bread; then he brought us the
drinks and glasses. The vodka went wonderfully well with the meat
dripping with juice, and we each drank several measures, washing it all
down with *kompot*, a juice of marinated berries. The sun was shining on
the grass, the slender pines, the monument, with the slope of the
Mashuk behind it all; the clouds had completely disappeared on the
other side of the mountain. I thought again about Lermontov dying on
the grass a few steps away, his chest shattered, for an empty remark
about Martynov's clothes. Unlike his hero Pechorin, Lermontov had
fired into the air; his adversary, not. What could Martynov have been
thinking as he looked at his enemy's corpse? He himself had wanted to
be a poet, and he had certainly read *A Hero of Our Time*; so he could savor the bitter echoes and slow ripples of the growing legend, he knew

too that his name would remain only as that of Lermontov's murderer, another d'Anthès encumbering Russian letters. But he must have had other ambitions when he started out in life; he too must have wanted to create, and create good things. Perhaps he was simply jealous of Lermontov's talent? Or perhaps he chose to be remembered for the harm he had done, rather than not at all? I tried to remember his portrait but already couldn't manage to. And Lermontov? His last thought, when he had emptied his pistol into the air and saw that Martynov was aiming at him, had it been bitter, desperate, furious, ironic? Or had he simply shrugged his shoulders and looked at the sunlight on the pine trees? As with Pushkin, they said that his death had been a setup, a contrived assassination; if that was the case, he had gone to it with his eyes wide open, obligingly, demonstrating his dissimilarity from Pechorin. What Blok wrote about Pushkin was no doubt even truer for him: *It wasn't Dantes's bullet that killed him, it was the lack of air.* I too lacked air, but the sun and the shashliks, and Voss's joyous kindness, helped me breathe for an instant. We settled our bill with the native using occupation *carbovanets* and started again toward the Mashuk. "I suggest we go to the old cemetery," Voss said. "There's a stele there where Lermontov was buried." After the duel, his friends had laid the poet to rest here; one year later, a hundred years before our arrival in Pyatigorsk, his maternal grandmother had come for his remains and had brought them home with her, to bury them next to his mother, near Penza. I readily agreed to this suggestion of Voss's. Two cars passed us in a whirl of dust: the officers of the Kommando returning. Turek was driving the first vehicle himself; his hateful look, which I glimpsed through the window, made him look truly Jewish. The little convoy continued straight on but we went to the left, following a long zigzagging path that climbed up the side of the Mashuk. With the meal, the vodka, and the sun, I felt heavy; then the hiccups started and I left the path for the woods. "Are you all right?" Voss asked when I returned. I made a vague gesture and lit a cigarette. "It's nothing. The tail end of something I caught in the Ukraine. It comes back from time to time."—"You should see a doctor."—"Maybe. Dr. Hohenegg must be coming back soon, I'll see." Voss waited for me to finish my cigarette, then followed close behind me. I was warm and I took off my cap and jacket. At the top of the knoll, the path formed a wide loop from which there was a fine view over the city and the plain beyond. "If you continue straight on, you return to the sanatoriums," Voss said. "For the cemetery, we can go by these orchards." The steep slope, with its faded grass, was planted with fruit trees; a tethered mule was nuzzling the ground in search of fallen apples. We descended the hill, sliding a little, then cut through a wood that

was dense enough for us soon to lose the path. I put my jacket back on
as the branches and brambles were scratching my arms. Finally, following Voss, I emerged onto a little muddy hollow that ran alongside a ce-
mented stone wall. "This must be it," said Voss. "We'll go around."
Since the cars had passed us we hadn't seen anyone, and I felt as if I were
walking in the open countryside; but a few steps farther on a young boy,
his feet bare, leading a donkey, passed us without a word. Following the
wall, we finally arrived at a little square, in front of an Orthodox
church. An old woman dressed in black, sitting on a crate, was selling
some flowers; others were coming out of the church. Beyond the gate,
the graves lay scattered under tall trees that plunged the sloping cemetery into shadow. We followed a rising path paved with coarse stones
buried in the ground, between old graves lost in dry grass, ferns, and
thorn bushes. Patches of light fell in places between the trees and in
these islands of sun, little black-and-white butterflies were dancing
around faded flowers. Then the path curved and the trees opened out a
little to reveal the plain to the southwest. In an enclosure, two little trees
had been planted to give shade to the stele that marks the place of Lermontov's first grave. The only sounds were the chirping of crickets and
the breeze rustling the leaves. Near the stele were the graves of Lermontov's relations, the Shan-Gireis. I turned around: in the distance, the
long green *balki* furrowed the plain to the first rocky foothills. The
mounds of the volcanoes looked like clumps of earth fallen from the sky;
in the distance, I could make out the snowy peaks of the Elbruz. I sat
down on the steps leading to the stele, while Voss went to nose about a
little farther on, thinking again about Lermontov: like all poets, first
they kill him, then they venerate him.

We went back down to the town by the *Verkhnyi rynok*, where the
peasants were finishing packing up their unsold chickens, fruits, and
vegetables onto carts or mules. Around them the crowd of sunflower
seed sellers and boot polishers was dispersing; boys sitting on little wagons improvised from boards and baby carriage wheels were still waiting
for a lingering soldier to ask them to cart his packages. At the foot of
the hill, on Kirov Boulevard, rows of fresh crosses were lined up on a
small knoll surrounded by a low wall: the pretty little park, with its
monument to Lermontov, had been transformed into a cemetery for
German soldiers. The boulevard heading toward Tsvetnik Park passed
in front of the ruins of what had been the Orthodox cathedral, dynamited in 1936 by the NKVD. "Have you noticed," Voss remarked as he
pointed to the collapsed stones, "they didn't touch the German church.
Our men still go there to pray."—"Yes, but they emptied the three surrounding villages of *Volksdeutschen*. The czar had invited them to settle

here in 1830. They were all sent to Siberia last year." But Voss was still thinking about his Lutheran church. "Did you know that it was built by a soldier? A man named Kempfer, who fought against the Cherkess under Yevdokimov, and settled here." In the park, just after the entrance gate, stood a two-level wooden gallery, sporting turrets with futuristic cupolas and a loggia that wrapped around the upper level. There were some tables there where they served, to those who could pay, Turkish coffee and sweets. Voss chose a place on the side of the park's main path, above the groups of grizzled, cantankerous, grouchy old men, who came in the evening to sit on the benches and play chess. I ordered coffee and brandy; they also brought us some little lemon cakes; the brandy came from Daghestan and seemed even sweeter than the Armenian, but it went well with the cakes and my good mood. "How are your studies going?" I asked Voss. He laughed: "I still haven't found an Ubykh speaker; but I'm making considerable progress in Kabard. What I'm really waiting for is for us to take Ordzhonikidze."—"Why is that?"— "Well, I've already told you that Caucasian languages are only my subspecialty. What really interests me are the so-called Indo-Germanic languages, especially the languages of Iranian origin. And Ossetic is a particularly fascinating Iranian language."—"How so?" "You can see the geographic situation of Ossetia: whereas all the other non-Caucasian speakers live on the rim or in the foothills of the Caucasus, they straddle the massif, just at the level of the most accessible pass, the Darial where the Russians built their *Voyennaya doroga* from Tiflis to Ordzhonikidze, the old Vladikavkaz. Although these people adopted the clothing and customs of their mountain neighbors, it's obviously a late invasion. It is believed that these Ossetes or Osses are descended from the Alans and hence the Scythians; if that is correct, their language would constitute a living archeological remnant of the Scythian language. And there's something else: in 1930 Dumézil published a collection of Ossetian legends having to do with a fabulous people, half-divine, whom they call the Narts. Now Dumézil also postulates a connection between these legends and the ancient Scythian religion as it is reported by Herodotus. Russian researchers have been working on this subject since the end of the last century; the library and institutes in Ordzhonikidze must be overflowing with extraordinary materials, inaccessible in Europe. I just hope we don't burn everything down during the attack."—"In short, if I've understood you correctly, these Ossetes are an *Urvolk*, one of the original Aryan peoples."—"*Original* is a word that is much used and misused. Let's say that their language has some very interesting archaic characteristics from a scientific standpoint."— "What do you mean about the notion of 'original'?" He shrugged his

shoulders: "Original is more a fantasy, a psychological or political pre-
tense, than a scientific concept. Take German, for instance: for centuries, even before Martin Luther, people claimed it was an original
language under the pretext that it had no recourse to roots of foreign
origin, unlike the Romance languages, to which it was compared. Some
theologians, in their delirium, even went so far as to claim that German
was the language of Adam and Eve, and that Hebrew later derived from
it. But that's a completely illusory claim, since even if the roots are
'native'—actually, all derived directly from the languages of Indo-
European nomads—our grammar is entirely structured by Latin. Our
cultural imagination, however, was very strongly marked by these ideas,
and by this peculiarity German has in contrast to other European languages: the way it can sort of self-generate its vocabulary. It's a fact that
any eight-year-old German child knows all the roots of our language
and can take apart and understand any word, even the most abstruse
compound, which is not the case for a French child, for instance, who
will take a very long time to learn the 'difficult' words derived from
Greek or Latin. That, moreover, has a lot to do with the idea we have
of ourselves: *Deutschland* is the only country in Europe that doesn't have
a geographic designation, that doesn't bear the name of a place or a people like the Angles or the Franks, it's the country of the 'people' per se;
deutsch being an adjectival form of the old German *Tuits*, 'people.' That's
why none of our neighbors call us by the same name: *Allemands, Germans, Duits, Tedeschi* in Italian which also stems from *Tuits*, or *Nyemtsi*
here in Russia, which means 'the Mutes,' those who don't know how
to speak, like *Barbaros* in Greek. And our whole present-day racial and
völkisch ideology, in a certain way, is built on these very ancient German
pretensions. Which, I will add, are not unique to us: Goropius Becanus,
a Flemish author, made the same argument in 1569 about Dutch, which
he compared to what he called *the original languages of the Caucasus, vagina
of peoples.*" He laughed gaily. I would have liked to continue the conversation, especially about racial theories, but he was already standing
up: "I have to go. Would you like to have dinner with Oberländer, if
he's free?"—"Of course."—"Shall we meet at the Kasino? Around eight
o'clock." He ran down the steps. I sat back down and contemplated the
old men playing chess. Fall was advancing: already the sun was passing
behind the Mashuk, tinting the crest with pink and, farther down on the
boulevard, casting orange-colored reflections through the trees, up to
the windows and the gray roughcast of the façades.

    Around seven thirty I went down to the Kasino. Voss hadn't yet ar-
rived and I ordered a brandy, which I carried into an alcove set a little
back. A few minutes later Kern came in, examined the room, and

headed toward me. "Herr Hauptsturmführer! I was looking for you."
He took off his cap and sat down, casting glances around him: he looked
embarrassed, nervous. "Hauptsturmführer. I wanted to let you know
about something that concerns you, I think."—"Yes?" He hesitated:
"They . . . You are often in the company of that Leutnant from the
Wehrmacht. That . . . how should I say it? That's giving rise to some rumors."—"What sort of rumors?"—"Rumors . . . let's say dangerous rumors. The kind of rumors that lead straight to the concentration
camp."—"I see." I remained impassive. "And might this kind of rumor
by chance be spread by a certain kind of person?" He turned pale: "I
don't want to say anything else about it. I think it's low, shameful. I just
wanted to warn you so that you could . . . could act in a way that would
prevent it from going any further." I got up and held out my hand:
"Thank you for this information, Obersturmführer. But I have nothing
but contempt for those who spread sordid rumors in a cowardly way instead of confronting someone face-to-face, and I ignore them." He
shook my hand: "I completely understand your reaction. But take care
all the same." I sat back down, overcome with rage: so that's the game
they wanted to play! What's more, they were completely mistaken. I've
said it already: I never form bonds with my lovers; friendship is something else entirely. I loved a single person in this world, and even if I
never saw her, that was enough for me. But narrow-minded scum like
Turek and his friends could never understand that. I resolved to get my
revenge; I didn't know how yet, but the opportunity would present itself. Kern was an honest man, he had done well to warn me: that would
give me time to think.

Voss arrived soon after, accompanied by Oberländer. I was still
plunged in my thoughts. "Hello, Professor," I said as I shook Oberländer's hand. "It's been a long time."—"Yes, yes, lots of things have happened since Lemberg. And that other young officer, who had come
with you?"—"Hauptsturmführer Hauser? He must still be with Group
C. I haven't heard from him for a while." I followed them to the restaurant and let Voss order. They brought us some Kakhetian wine. Oberländer seemed tired. "I heard you're commanding a new special unit?"
I asked him.—"Yes, the Bergmann Kommando. All my men are Caucasian mountain tribesmen."—"Of what nationality?" Voss asked curiously.—"Oh, a little of everything. There are Karachai and Circassians,
of course, but also some Ingush, some Avars, a few Laks whom we recruited in the Stalags. I even have a Svan."—"Magnificent! I'd very
much like to talk with him."—"You'll have to go to Mozdok, then.
They're engaged in anti-partisan operations there."—"You don't have
any Ubykhs, by any chance?" I asked him maliciously. Voss giggled.

"Ubykhs? No, I don't think so. Who are they?" Voss choked to hold in his laughter and Oberländer looked at him, perplexed. I made an effort to remain serious and replied: "It's an obsession of Dr. Voss's. He thinks the Wehrmacht should absolutely carry out a pro-Ubykh policy, to restore the natural balance of power between the peoples of the Caucasus." Voss, who was trying to drink some wine, almost spat out what he had just swallowed. I also had trouble restraining myself. Oberländer still didn't understand and was beginning to get annoyed: "I don't know what you're talking about," he said dryly. I tried to explain: "They're a Caucasian nationality deported by the Russians. To Turkey. Before, they dominated a whole part of this region."—"They were Muslims?"— "Yes, of course."—"In that case, support of these Ubykhs would be entirely in keeping with our *Ostpolitik*." Voss, red, got up, murmured an excuse, and made for the bathroom. Oberländer was startled: "What's wrong with him?" I tapped my stomach. "Oh, I see," he said. "That's common here. Where was I?"—"Our pro-Muslim policy."—"Yes. Of course, it's a traditional German policy. What we hope to accomplish out here is in a way only a continuation of the pan-Islamic policy of Ludendorff. By respecting the cultural and social achievements of Islam, we are making useful allies for ourselves. What's more, it's a gesture toward Turkey, which still remains important, especially if we want to go past the Caucasus to take the English from the rear in Syria and Egypt." Voss returned; he seemed calmer. "If I understand you correctly," I said, "the idea would be to unite the peoples of the Caucasus and especially the Turkic-speaking peoples into a giant Islamic anti-Bolshevist movement."—"That's an option, but it hasn't yet been accepted high up. Some people are worried about a pan-Turanian resurgence that could give too much power to Turkey, on a regional level, and encroach on our conquests. Minister Rosenberg favors a Berlin-Tiflis axis. But that's the influence of that Nikuradze."—"And you, what do you think?"—"At the moment, I'm writing an article on Germany and the Caucasus. You know perhaps that after the disbanding of the Nachtigall, I worked as the Abwehroffizier with Reichskommissar Koch, who is an old friend from Königsberg. But he's almost never in the Ukraine and his subordinates, especially Dargel, carried out an irresponsible policy. That's why I left. In my article, I try to demonstrate that in the conquered territories we need the cooperation of the local populations to avoid overly heavy losses during the invasion and occupation. Any pro-Muslim or pro-Turanian policy should fit within this framework. Of course, only one power, and one alone, should have the last word."— "I thought that one of the objectives of our advance into the Caucasus was to persuade Turkey to enter into war on our side?"—"Of course.

And if we reach Iraq or Iran, it certainly will. Saracoğlu is cautious, but he won't want to let this chance to recover ancient Ottoman territories slip by."—"But wouldn't that encroach on our *Grossraum?*" I asked.—"Not at all. We are aiming for a continental empire; we have neither the interest nor the means to burden ourselves with distant possessions. We'll keep the oil-rich regions in the Persian Gulf, of course, but we can give all the rest of the British Near East to Turkey."—"And what would Turkey do for us, in exchange?" Voss asked.—"It could be very useful to us. Strategically, it holds a key position. It can procure naval and land bases that would allow us to finish off the British presence in the Middle East. It could also provide troops for the anti-Bolshevist front."—"Yes," I said, "they could send us an Ubykh regiment, for example." Voss was overcome again with uncontrollable laughter. Oberländer got angry: "But what is it with these Ubykhs? I don't understand."—"I told you, it's an obsession of Dr. Voss's. He's desperate because he keeps writing report after report, but no one at HQ wants to believe in the strategic importance of the Ubykhs. Here, they stick to the Karachai, Kabards, and Balkars."—"But then why is he laughing?"—"Yes, Dr. Voss, why are you laughing?" I asked him very seriously. "I think he's nervous," I said to Oberländer. "Here, Dr. Voss, have some more wine." Voss drank a little and tried to regain control of himself. "For my part," said Oberländer, "I don't know enough about this question to judge it." He turned to Voss: "If you have reports about these Ubykhs, I'd be delighted to read them." Voss nervously shook his head: "Doktor Aue," he said, "I would be grateful if you changed the subject."—"As you like. In any case, the meal is arriving." They served us. Oberländer seemed annoyed; Voss was very red. To get the conversation going again, I asked Oberländer: "Are your *Bergmänner* effective in the struggle against the partisans?"—"In the mountains, they're formidable. Some of them bring us heads or ears back every day. In the plains, they're not much better than our own troops. They burned a lot of villages around Mozdok. I try to explain to them that it's a bad idea to do it systematically, but it's as if it's in their genes. And also we've had somewhat serious problems of discipline: desertion, especially. It seems that a lot of them got involved only to go home; ever since we've been in the Caucasus, they keep disappearing. But I've had all the ones we caught shot in front of the others: I think that calmed them down a little. And also I have a lot of Chechens and Daghestanis; their homes are still in the hands of the Bolsheviks. Speaking of that, have you heard of an uprising in Chechnya? In the mountains."—"There are rumors," I replied. "A special unit attached to the Einsatzgruppe is going to try to parachute in some agents to make contact with the rebels."—"Oh, that's very interesting," said Oberländer. "Apparently there is fighting going on and the repression is fierce. That could create some possibilities for our forces. How could I find out more?"—"You should go see Ober-führer Bierkamp, in Voroshilovsk."—"Very good. And here? Are you having a lot of problems, with the partisans?"—"Not too many. There's a unit roaming around Kislovodsk. The Lermontov detachment. It's rather fashionable, here, to call everything Lermontov." Voss laughed, this time heartily: "Are they active?"—"Not really. They stick to the mountains, they're afraid of coming down. They mostly provide information to the Red Army. They send kids to count the motorcycles and trucks in front of the Feldkommandantur, for example." We finished eating; Oberländer was still talking about the *Ostpolitik* of the new military administration: "General Köstring is a very good choice. I think that with him the experiment has a chance to succeed."—"You know Dr. Bräutigam?" I asked.—"Herr Bräutigam? Of course. We often exchange ideas. He's a very motivated man, very intelligent." Oberländer finished his coffee and took his leave. We saluted each other and Voss went with him. I waited for him while I smoked a cigarette. "You were odious," he said to me as he sat back down.—"Why?"—"You know very well why." I shrugged my shoulders: "It wasn't very mean."—"Oberländer must have thought we were making fun of him."—"But we were making fun of him. Except: he'll never dare admit it. You know professors as well as I do. If he acknowledged his ignorance of the Ubykh question, that could harm his reputation as 'The Lawrence of the Caucasus.' " We left the Kasino. A fine, light rain was falling. "There it is," I said as if to myself. "It's autumn." A horse tied in front of the Feldkommandantur neighed and snorted. The sentinels had put on their waxed cloaks. In Karl Marx Street, the water was flowing down the slope in little streams. The rain intensified. We parted in front of our quarters, wishing each other good night. In my room, I opened the French door and stayed for a long while listening to the water streaming on the leaves of the trees, on the windows of the balcony, on the metal roofs, on the grass and the wet earth.

It rained for three days straight. The sanatoriums were filling up with wounded, brought from Malgobek and Sagopchi, where our renewed offensive on Groznyi was being run into the ground by the fierce resistance. Korsemann came to distribute medals to the Finnish volunteers of the Wiking, handsome, somewhat distraught blond boys decimated by the gunfire encountered in the Zhuruk Valley, below Nizhni Kurp. The new military administration of the Caucasus was being set in place. At the beginning of October, by decree of Generalquartiermeister Wagner, six Cossack *raions*, with 160,000 inhabitants, were accorded the new status of "self-government"; the Karachai autonomy would officially be announced during a big celebration in Kislovodsk. With the other leading officers of the SS in the region I was again summoned to Voroshilovsk by Korsemann and Bierkamp. Korsemann was worried about the limitation of SS police power in the self-governed districts, but wanted to pursue a reinforced policy of cooperation with the Wehrmacht. Bierkamp was furious; he called the *Ostpolitiker* "czarists" and "Baltic barons": "This famous *Ostpolitik* is nothing but a resurrection of the spirit of Tauroggen," he protested. In private, Leetsch gave me to understand in veiled words that Bierkamp was worried stiff because of the number of executions carried out by the Kommandos, which didn't exceed a few dozen a week: the Jews in the occupied regions had all been liquidated, aside from a few artisans preserved by the Wehrmacht to serve as leatherworkers and tailors; we didn't catch many partisans or Communists; as for the national minorities and the Cossacks, the majority of the population, they were now almost untouchable. I found Bierkamp's state of mind quite narrow, but I could understand it: in Berlin, the effectiveness of an Einsatzgruppe was judged based on its tallies, and a lessening of activity could be interpreted as a lack of energy on the part of the Kommandant. But the Group wasn't remaining inactive. In Elista, at the confines of the Kalmuk Steppe, Sk Astrakhan was being formed ahead of the fall of that city; in the region of Krasnodar, having carried out all the other priority tasks, Sk 10a was liquidating the asylums for the retarded, the hydrocephalics, and the insane, mostly using a gas truck. In Maikop, the Seventeenth Army was relaunching its offensive toward Tuapse, and Sk 11 was taking part in the repression of an intense guerilla warfare in the mountains, in very rough terrain made even more difficult by the persistent rain. On October 10, I celebrated my birthday at the restaurant with Voss, but without telling him about it; the next day, we went with most of the AOK to Kislovodsk to celebrate the Uraza Bairam, the breaking of the fast that ends the month of Ramadan. This was a kind of triumph. In a large field outside the city, the imam of the Karachai, a wrinkled old man with a firm, clear voice, led a long collective prayer; facing the nearby hills, hundreds of caps, skullcaps, felt or fur hats, in dense rows, bowed to the ground and stood up in time to his threnody. Afterward, on a platform decorated with German and Muslim flags, Köstring and Bräutigam, their voices amplified by a PK loudspeaker, proclaimed the establishment of the Autonomous Karachai District. Cheers and gunshots punctuated each phrase. Voss, his hands behind his back, translated Bräutigam's speech; Köstring read his directly in

Russian, and was then thrown into the air, several times, by young enthusiasts. Bräutigam had presented the qadi Bairamukov, an anti-Soviet peasant, as the new head of the district: the old man, wearing a *cherkesska* and a *beshmet*, with an enormous white woollen *papakha* on his head, solemnly thanked Germany for having delivered the Karachai from the Russian yoke. A young child led a superb white Kabarda horse up to the platform, its back covered in a bright-colored Daghestani *sumak*. The horse snorted, the old man explained that it was a present from the Karachai people to the leader of the Germans, Adolf Hitler; Köstring thanked him and assured him the horse would be conveyed to the Führer, in Vinnitsa in the Ukraine. Then some young natives in traditional garb carried Köstring and Bräutigam on their shoulders to the cheers of the men, the ululations of the women, and the redoubled salvos of the rifles. Voss, red with pleasure, looked on all this with delight. We followed the crowd: at the end of the field, a small army of women were loading foodstuffs onto long tables beneath some awnings. Incredible quantities of lamb, which they served with broth, were simmering in large cast-iron pots; there was also boiled chicken, wild garlic, caviar, and *manti*, a kind of Caucasian ravioli; the Karachai women, many of them beautiful and laughing, kept pushing more dishes in front of the guests; the young men stayed packed together at the side, whispering busily, while their seated fathers ate. Köstring and Bräutigam were sitting beneath a canopy with the elders, in front of the Kabarda horse, which they seemed to have forgotten and which, dragging its leash, was sniffing at the dishes to the laughter of the spectators. Some mountain musicians were singing long laments accompanied by small high-pitched stringed instruments; later on, they were joined by percussionists and the music became frantic, frenzied; a large circle formed and the young men, led by a master of ceremonies, danced the *lesghinka*, noble, splendid, virile, then some other dances with knives, of an astounding virtuosity. No alcohol was served, but most of the German guests, heated up by the meats and the dances, seemed drunk, bright-red, sweating, overexcited. The Karachai saluted the best dance movements with gunshots and that contributed even more to the frenzy. My heart was beating wildly; along with Voss, I tapped with my feet and clapped my hands, shouted like a madman in the circle of spectators. At nightfall they brought torches and it went on; when you felt too tired, you went over to the tables to drink some tea and eat a little. "The *Ostpolitiker* have certainly pulled it off!" I shouted to Voss. "This would convince anyone."

But the news from the front wasn't good. In Stalingrad, despite the military bulletins that daily announced a decisive breakthrough, the

Sixth Army, according to the Abwehr, had gotten completely bogged down in the center of town. The officers who came back from Vinnitsa affirmed that a deplorable atmosphere reigned at GHQ, and that the Führer had almost stopped talking to Generals Keitel and Jodl, whom he had banished from his table. Sinister rumors were rampant in military circles, which Voss reported to me sometimes: the Führer was on the edge of a nervous breakdown, he regularly flew into mad rages and was making contradictory, incoherent decisions; the generals were starting to lose confidence. It was certainly exaggerated, but I found the fact that such rumors were spreading in the army worrisome, and I mentioned it in the section of my report on the *Morale of the Wehrmacht*. Hohenegg was back, but his conference was taking place in Kislovodsk, and I hadn't seen him yet; after a few days he sent me a note inviting me to dinner. Voss had gone to join the Third Panzer Corps in Prokhladny; von Kleist was preparing another offensive toward Nalchik and Ordzhonikidze, and he wanted to be right behind the first units to protect the libraries and institutes.

That same morning, Leutnant Reuter, an adjunct of Gilsa's, came to my office: "We have a strange case that you should see. An old man, who presented himself here on his own. He's talking about strange things and he says he's Jewish. The Oberst suggested you interrogate him."—"If he's a Jew, he should be sent to the Kommando."—"Maybe. But don't you want to see him? I can assure you he's surprising." An orderly led the man in. He was a tall old man with a long white beard, still visibly vigorous; he wore a black *cherkesska*, a Caucasian peasant's soft leather ankle boots tucked into rubber galoshes, and a handsome embroidered skullcap, purple, blue, and gold. I motioned to him to take a seat and, a little annoyed, asked the orderly: "He only speaks Russian, I suppose? Where is the *Dolmetscher*?" The old man looked at me with piercing eyes and said to me in strangely accented but understandable classical Greek: "You are an educated man, I see. You must know Greek." Taken aback, I dismissed the orderly and replied: "Yes, I know Greek. And you? How do you come to speak this language?" He ignored my question. "My name is Nahum ben Ibrahim, from Magaramkend in the *gubernatorya* of Derbent. For the Russians, I took the name of Shamilyev, in honor of the great Shamil with whom my father fought. And you, what is your name?"—"My name is Maximilien. I come from Germany."—"And who was your father?" I smiled: "Why does my father interest you, old man?"—"How am I supposed to know who I'm talking to if I don't know who your father is?" His Greek, I heard now, contained unusual turns of phrase, but I managed to understand it. I told him my father's name and he seemed satisfied. Then I questioned him: "If your father fought with Shamil, you must be very old."—"My father died gloriously in Dargo after killing dozens of Russians. He was a very pious man, and Shamil respected his religion. He said that we, the *Dagh Chufuti*, believe in God better than the Muslims do. I remember the day he declared that in front of his *murid*, at the mosque in Vedeno."—"That's impossible! You couldn't have known Shamil yourself. Show me your passport." He held out a document to me and I quickly leafed through it. "See for yourself! It's written here that you were born in 1866. Shamil was already a prisoner of the Russians then, in Kaluga." He took the passport calmly from my hands and slipped it into an inner pocket. His eyes seemed to be sparkling with humor and mischief. "How do you think a poor *chinovnik*"—he used the Russian term—"from Derbent, a man who never even finished elementary school, could know when I was born? He guessed I was seventy when he wrote up this paper, without asking me anything. But I am much older. I was born before Shamil roused the tribes. I was already a man when my father died in Dargo, killed by those Russian dogs. I could have taken his place by Shamil's side, but I was already studying the law, and Shamil told me that he had enough warriors, but that he needed scholars too." I had absolutely no idea what to think: he would have had to be at least 120 years old. "And Greek?" I asked again. "Where did you learn that?"—"Daghestan isn't Russia, young officer. Before the Russians killed them without mercy, the greatest scholars in the world lived in Daghestan, Muslims and Jews. People came from Arabia, from Turkestan, and even from China to consult them. And the *Dagh Chufuti* are not the filthy Jews from Russia. My mother's language is Farsi, and everyone speaks Turkish. I learned Russian to do business, for as Rabbi Eliezer said, the thought of God does not fill the belly. Arabic I studied with the imams of the madrasas of Daghestan, and Greek, as well as Hebrew, from books. I never learned the language of the Jews of Poland, which is nothing but German, a language of *Nyemtsi*."—"So you are truly a scholar."—"Don't make fun of me, *meirakion*. I too have read your Plato and your Aristotle. But I have read them along with Moses de Leon, which makes a big difference." For some time I had been staring at his beard, square-cut, and especially his bare top lip. Something fascinated me: beneath his nose, his lip was smooth, without the usual hollow in the center, the philtrum. "How is it that your lip is like that? I've never seen that." He rubbed his lip: "That? When I was born, the angel didn't seal my lips. So I remember everything that happened before."—"I don't understand."—"But you are well educated. It's all written in the Book of the Creation of the Child, in the Lesser Midrashim. In the beginning, the man's parents mate. That creates a drop into which God introduces the man's spirit. Then the angel takes the drop in the morning to Paradise and at night to Hell, then he shows it where it will live on Earth and where it will be buried when God recalls the spirit he has sent. Then this is what is written. Excuse me if I recite badly, but I have to translate from the Hebrew, which you don't know: *But the angel always brings the drop back into the body of its mother and The Holy One, blessed be his name, closes the doors and bolts behind it. And The Holy One, blessed be his name, says to it: You will go up to there, and no further. And the child remains in his mother's womb for nine months.* Then it is written: *The child eats everything the mother eats, drinks everything the mother drinks and does not eliminate any excrement, for if he did, it would make the mother die.* And then it is written: *And when the time comes when he must come into the world, the angel presents itself before him and says to him: Leave, for the time has come for your appearance in the world. And the spirit of the child replies: I have already said in front of the One who was there that I am satisfied with the world in which I have lived. And the angel replies: The world to which I am taking you is beautiful. And then: Despite yourself, you have been formed in the body of your mother, and despite yourself, you have been born to come into the world. Immediately the child begins to cry. And why does he cry? Because of the world in which he had lived and which he is forced to leave. And as soon as he has left, the angel gives him a blow on the nose and extinguishes the light above his head, he makes the child leave in spite of himself and the child forgets all he has seen. And as soon as he leaves, he begins to cry.* This blow on the nose the book talks about is this: the angel seals the lips of the child and this seal leaves a mark. But the child does not forget right away. When my son was three years old, a long time ago, I surprised him one night near his little sister's cradle: 'Tell me about God,' he was saying. 'I'm beginning to forget.' That is why man must relearn everything about God through study, and that is why men become mean and kill each other. But the angel had me come out without sealing my lips, as you see, and I remember everything."—"So you remember the place where you will be buried?" I asked. He smiled wide: "That is why I came here to see you."—"And is it far from here?"—"No. I can show you, if you like." I got up and took my cap: "Let's go."

Going out, I asked Reuter for a Feldgendarm; he sent me to his company chief, who pointed to a Rottwachtmeister: "Hanning! Go with the Hauptsturmführer and do what he says." Hanning took his helmet and shouldered his rifle; he must have been close on to forty; his large metal half-moon plate bounced on his narrow chest. "We'll need a shovel, too," I added. Outside, I turned to the old man: "Which way?" He raised his finger to the Mashuk, whose summit, caught in a cloud

bank, looked as if it were spitting out smoke: "That way." Followed by
Hanning, we climbed the streets to the last one, which encircles the
mountain; there the old man pointed to the right, toward the Proval.
Pine trees lined the road and at one place a little path headed into the
trees. "It's that way," said the old man.—"Are you sure you've never
come here before?" I asked him. He shrugged. The path climbed and
zigzagged and the slope was steep. The old man walked in front with a
nimble, sure step; behind, the shovel on his shoulder, Hanning was
panting heavily. When we emerged from the trees, I saw that the wind
had chased the clouds away from the summit. A little farther on I turned
around. The Caucasus barred the horizon. It had rained during the
night, and the rain had finally swept away the ever-present summer
haze, revealing the mountains, clear, majestic. "Stop daydreaming," the
old man said to me. I started walking again. We climbed for about half
an hour. My heart was pounding wildly, I was out of breath, Hanning
too; the old man seemed as fresh as a young tree. Finally we reached a
kind of grassy terrace, a scant hundred meters or so from the top. The
old man went forward and contemplated the view. This was the first
time I really saw the Caucasus. Sovereign, the mountain chain unfurled
like an immense sloping wall, to the very edge of the horizon; you felt
as though if you squinted you could see the last mountains plunging into
the Black Sea far to the right, and to the left into the Caspian. The hills
were blue, crowned with pale-yellow, whitish ridges; the white Elbruz,
an overturned bowl of milk, sat atop the peaks; a little farther away, the
Kazbek loomed over Ossetia. It was as beautiful as a phrase of Bach. I
looked and said nothing. The old man stretched out his hand to the east:
"There, beyond the Kazbek, that's Chechnya already, and afterward,
that's Daghestan."—"And your grave, where is that?" He examined the
flat terrace and took a few steps. "Here," he said finally, stamping the
ground with his foot. I looked at the mountains again: "This is a fine
place to be buried, don't you think?" I said. The old man had an immense, delighted smile: "Isn't it?" I began to wonder if he wasn't making fun of me. "You really saw it?"—"Of course!" he said indignantly.
But I had the impression that he was laughing in his beard. "Then dig,"
I said.—"What do you mean, 'dig'? Aren't you ashamed, *meirakiske*? Do
you know how old I am? I could be the grandfather of your grandfather! I'd curse you rather than dig." I shrugged and turned to Hanning,
who was still waiting with the shovel. "Hanning. Dig."—"Dig, Herr
Hauptsturmführer? Dig what?"—"A grave, Rottwachtmeister. There."
He gestured with his head: "And the old man there? Can't he dig?"—
"No. Go on, start digging." Hanning set his rifle and cap down in the
grass and headed to the place indicated. He spat onto his hands and be-

gan to dig. The old man was looking at the mountains. I listened to the
rustling of the wind, the vague rumor of the city at our feet; I could also
hear the sound of the shovel hitting earth, the fall of the clumps of earth
thrown out, Hanning's panting. I looked at the old man: he was standing facing the mountains and the sun, and was murmuring something.
I looked at the mountains again. The subtle and infinite variations of
blue tinting the slopes looked as if they could be read like a long line of
music, with the summits marking time. Hanning, who had taken off his
neck plate and jacket, was digging methodically and was now at knee
level. The old man turned to me with a gay look: "Is it coming along?"
Hanning had stopped digging and was blowing, leaning on his shovel.
"Isn't that enough, Herr Hauptsturmführer?" he asked. The hole
seemed a good length now but was only a few feet deep. I turned to the
old man: "Is that enough for you?"—"You're joking! You aren't going
to give me a poor man's grave, me, Nahum ben Ibrahim! Come on,
you're not a *nepios*."—"Sorry, Hanning. You have to keep digging."—
"Tell me, Herr Hauptsturmführer," he asked me before going back to
work, "what language are you speaking to him in? It's not Russian."—
"No, it's Greek."—"He's a Greek?! I thought he was a Jew?"—"Go on,
keep digging." He went back to work with a curse. After about twenty
minutes he stopped again, panting hard. "You know, Herr Hauptsturmführer, usually there are two men to do this. I'm no longer young."—
"Pass me the shovel and get out of there." I took off my cap and jacket
and took Hanning's place in the ditch. Digging wasn't something I had
much experience of. It took me some minutes to find my pace. The old
man leaned over me: "You're doing it very badly. It's obvious you've
spent your life in books. Where I come from, even the rabbis know
how to build a house. But you're a good boy. I did well to go to you."
I dug; the earth had to be thrown out quite high up now, a lot of it fell
back into the hole. "Now is it all right?" I finally asked. "A little more.
I want a grave that's as comfortable as my mother's womb."—"Hanning," I called, "come spell me." The pit was now chest level and he had
to help me climb out. I put my jacket and cap back on, and smoked
while Hanning started digging again. I kept looking at the mountains; I
couldn't get enough of the view. The old man was looking too. "You
know, I was disappointed I wasn't to be buried in my valley, near the
Samur," he said. "But now I understand that the angel is wise. This is a
beautiful place."—"Yes," I said. I glanced to the side: Hanning's rifle was
lying on the grass next to his cap, as if abandoned. When Hanning's head
had just cleared the ground, the old man declared he was satisfied. I
helped Hanning get out. "And now?" I asked.—"Now, you have to put
me inside. What? You think God is going to send me a thunderbolt?" I

turned to Hanning: "Rottwachtmeister. Put your uniform back on and shoot this man." Hanning turned red, spat on the ground, and swore. "What's wrong?"—"With respect, Herr Hauptsturmführer, for special tasks, I have to have an order from my superior."—"Leutnant Reuter put you at my disposal." He hesitated: "Well, all right," he finally said. He put his jacket, his big crescent neck plate, and his cap back on, brushed off his pants, and seized his rifle. The old man had positioned himself at the edge of the grave, facing the mountains, and was still smiling. Hanning shouldered his rifle and aimed it at the old man's neck. Suddenly I was overcome with anguish. "Wait!" Hanning lowered his rifle and the old man turned his head toward me. "And my grave," I asked him, "have you seen that too?" He smiled: "Yes." I sucked in my breath, I must have turned pale, a vain anguish filled me: "Where is it?" He kept smiling: "That, I won't tell you."—"Fire!" I shouted to Hanning. Hanning raised his rifle and fired. The old man fell like a marionette whose string has been cut all at once. I went up to the grave and leaned over: he was lying at the bottom like a sack, his head turned aside, still smiling a little into his blood-splattered beard; his open eyes, turned toward the wall of earth, were also laughing. I was trembling. "Close that up," I curtly ordered Hanning.

At the foot of the Mashuk, I sent Hanning back to the AOK and went by the Academic Gallery to the Pushkin baths, which the Wehrmacht had partially reopened for its convalescents. There I stripped naked and plunged my body into the scalding, brackish, sulfurous water. I stayed in it for a long time and then rinsed myself off in a cold shower. This treatment reinvigorated my body and soul: my skin was mottled red and white, and I felt more awake, almost light. I returned to my quarters and lay down for an hour, my feet crossed on the sofa, facing the open French window. Then I changed and went down to the AOK to find the car I had requested that morning. On the way, I smoked and contemplated the volcanoes and the soft blue mountains of the Caucasus. Night was already setting in; it was fall. Entering Kislovodsk, the road passed the Podkumok; below, peasants' carts were fording the river; the last one, just a board on wheels, was pulled by a camel with long hair and a thick neck. Hohenegg was waiting for me at the Kasino. "You look fit," he said when he saw me.—"I'm a new man. But I had a strange day."—"Tell me all about it." Two bottles of white wine from the Palatinate were waiting next to the table in ice buckets: "I had those sent to me by my wife."—"You're in a class by yourself, Doktor." He uncorked the first one: the wine was cool and bit the tongue, leaving behind it a fruity caress. "How is your conference going?" I asked him.—"Very well. We've gone over cholera, typhus, and

dysentery, and now we're coming to the painful subject of frostbite."—
"It's not the season for that yet."—"It will be soon enough. And you?"
I told him about the old *Bergjude*. "A wise man, this Nahum ben
Ibrahim," he commented when I had finished. "We can envy him."—
"You're probably right." Our table was placed right against a partition;
behind it was a private booth, from which laughter and bursts of indistinct voices were emanating. I drank a little wine. "Still," I added, "I
have to admit that I had trouble understanding him."—"Not me," Hohenegg asserted. "You see, in my view there are three possible attitudes
faced with this absurd life. First the attitude of the mass, hoi polloi,
which simply refuses to see that life is a joke. They don't laugh at it, but
work, accumulate, masticate, defecate, fornicate, reproduce, get old, and
die like oxen harnessed to the plow, as idiotic as they lived. That's the
large majority. Then there are those, such as me, who know that life is
a joke and who have the courage to laugh at it, like the Taoists or your
Jew. Finally there are those, and if my diagnosis is correct you are one
of them, who know that life is a joke, but who suffer from it. It's like
your Lermontov, whom I've finally read: *I zhizn takaya pustaya i glupaya
shutka*, he writes." I knew enough Russian now to understand and complete the phrase: "He should have added: *i grubaya*, 'an empty, stupid and
dirty joke.'"—"He certainly thought of it. But it wouldn't have scanned
right."—"Those who have that attitude do know, however, that the
other laughing one exists," I said.—"Yes, but they don't manage to
adopt it." The voices on the other side of the partition had become
clearer: a waitress had left the curtain of the booth open as she went out.
I recognized the coarse intonations of Turek and his lackey Pfeiffer.
"Women like that should be banned from the SS!" Turek was screeching.—"That's right. He should be in a concentration camp, not a uniform," Pfeiffer replied.—"Yes," said another voice, "but you need
evidence."—"We saw them," said Turek. "The other day, behind the
Mashuk. They left the road to go do their things in the woods."—"Are
you sure?"—"I give you my word as an officer."—"And you recognized him?"—"Aue? He was as close to me as you are now." The men
suddenly fell silent. Turek turned slowly around and saw me standing in
the entrance to the booth. His flushed face drained of blood. Pfeiffer, at
the head of the table, went yellow. "It is very regrettable that you should
use your word as an officer so lightly, Hauptsturmführer," I said clearly,
in a measured, neutral tone. "That devalues it. Yet there is still time to
withdraw your despicable words. I warn you: if you don't, we must
fight." Turek had gotten up, abruptly pushing back his chair. An absurd
tic was deforming his lips, giving him an even more spineless and lost
look than usual. His eyes sought out Pfeiffer, who encouraged him with

a sign of his head. "I have nothing to withdraw," he squeaked in a monotone. He still hesitated to go all the way. I was filled with a strong exaltation; but my voice remained calm, precise. "Are you quite sure?" I wanted to push him, to inflame him and slam all the doors shut behind him. "I won't be as easy to kill as an unarmed Jew, you can be sure of that." These words provoked a commotion. "You're insulting the SS!" Pfeiffer roared. Turek was pale; he looked at me like a mad bull, without saying anything. "Very well, then," I said. "I will send someone soon to the Teilkommando offices." I turned on my heel and left the restaurant. Hohenegg caught up with me on the steps: "That's not very smart, what you did there. Lermontov has decidedly gone to your head." I shrugged my shoulders. "Doktor, I believe you are a man of honor. Will you be my second?" Now it was his turn to shrug his shoulders. "If you like. But it's idiotic." I patted him amiably on the shoulder. "Don't worry! Everything will go well. But don't forget your wine, we'll need it." He brought me to his room and we finished the first bottle. I spoke to him a little about my life and my friendship with Voss: "I like him a lot. He's an astonishing man. But it has nothing to do with what those swine are imagining." Then I sent him to the Teilkommando offices and began the second bottle as I waited for him, smoking and watching the autumn sun play on the large park and the slopes of the Maloe Sedlo. He returned from his errand after an hour. "I should warn you," he said point-blank, "they're plotting something."—"How's that?"—"I went into the Kommando and heard them bellowing. I missed the beginning of the conversation, but I heard the fat one say: 'That way we won't run any risks. Anyway he doesn't deserve anything else.' Then your enemy, the one who looks like a Jew, right? replied: 'And what about his second?' The other one shouted: 'Too bad for him.' After that I came in and they shut up. In my opinion they're getting ready to simply massacre us. Talk about the honor of the SS!"—"Don't worry, Doktor. I'll take my precautions. Did you settle on the arrangements?"—"Yes. We'll meet them tomorrow night at six o'clock outside of Zheleznovodsk and we'll go find an isolated *balka*. The dead man will be chalked up to the partisans lurking around there." "Yes, Pustov's gang. That's a good idea. Shall we go eat?"

I returned to Pyatigorsk after eating and drinking heartily. Hohenegg, during the dinner, had been glum: I saw that he disapproved of my action and of the whole business. I was still strangely exalted; it was as if a great weight had been taken from my shoulders. I would kill Turek with pleasure; but I had to think about how to foil the trap that he and Pfeiffer wanted to set for me. An hour after I got back, someone knocked on my door. It was an orderly from the Kommando, who handed me a piece of paper. "Sorry to disturb you so late, Hauptsturm-führer. It's an urgent order from the Gruppenstab." I tore it open: Bierkamp was summoning me at eight o'clock the next day, along with Turek. Someone had given the game away. I dismissed the orderly and collapsed on the sofa. I felt as if I were being pursued by a curse: whatever I tried to do, any pure action would be denied me! I thought I saw the old Jew, in his grave on the Mashuk, laughing at me. Drained, I burst into tears and fell asleep crying, fully dressed.

The next morning I presented myself at the appointed time at Voroshilovsk. Turek had come separately. We stood at attention in front of Bierkamp's desk, side by side, without any other witness. Bierkamp came straight to the point: "Meine Herren. Word has reached me that you have spoken words unworthy of SS officers to each other in public, and that, to resolve your quarrel, you were planning on engaging in an action that is formally forbidden by regulations, an action that would moreover have deprived the Group of two valuable and difficult-to-replace officers; for you can be sure that the survivor would have been immediately brought before a court of the SS and the police, and would have been sentenced to capital punishment or to a concentration camp. I would like to remind you that you are here to serve your Führer and your *Volk*, and not to satisfy your personal passions: if you lay down your lives, you will do so for the Reich. Consequently I have called you both here so that you can apologize to each other and make peace. I will add that that's an order." Neither Turek nor I replied. Bierkamp looked at Turek: "Hauptsturmführer?" Turek remained silent. Bierkamp turned to me: "And you, Hauptsturmführer Aue?"—"With all due respect, Oberführer, the insulting words I said were in response to Hauptsturmführer Turek's. So I believe that it is up to him to apologize first; otherwise I will be forced to defend my honor, whatever the consequences." Bierkamp turned to Turek: "Hauptsturmführer, is it true that the first offensive words were uttered by you?" Turek was clenching his jaw so hard that his muscles were quivering: "Yes, Oberführer," he finally said, "that is correct."—"In that case, I order you to apologize to Hauptsturmführer Dr. Aue." Turek pivoted a quarter turn, clicking his heels, and faced me, still at attention; I imitated him. "Hauptsturmführer Aue," he said slowly, in a harsh voice, "please accept my apologies for the insulting statements I made about you. I was under the influence of drink, and let myself get carried away."—"Hauptsturmführer Turek," I replied, my heart pounding, "I accept your apology, and present you my own in the same spirit for my wounding reaction."—"Very good," Bierkamp said curtly. "Now shake hands." I took Turek's hand and found it clammy. Then we turned to face Bierkamp

again. "Meine Herren, I don't know what you said to each other and I
don't want to know. I am happy you are reconciled. If such an incident
were to occur again, I will have you both sent to a disciplinary battalion of the Waffen-SS. Is that clear? Dismissed."

Leaving his office, still very upset, I headed toward Dr. Leetsch's office. Von Gilsa had informed me that a reconnaissance plane from the
Wehrmacht had flown over the region of Shatoi and photographed a
number of bombed villages; but our Fourth Air Corps was insisting on
the fact that its aircraft had conducted no attack on Chechnya, and the
destruction was now being attributed to the Soviet air force, which
seemed to confirm the rumors of a rather extensive insurrection. "Kurreck has already parachuted a number of men into the mountains,"
Leetsch told me. "But since then we haven't had any contact with them.
Either they've deserted, or they've been killed or captured."—"The
Wehrmacht thinks that an uprising behind the Soviet lines could facilitate the offensive on Ordzhonikidze."—"Maybe. But in my opinion
they've already crushed it, if it ever even took place. Stalin wouldn't take
such a risk."—"No doubt. If Sturmbannführer Kurreck finds anything
out, can you let me know?" As I was going out, I ran into Turek, leaning against a door-frame talking with Prill. They stopped and stared at me
as I passed them. I politely saluted Prill, and went back to Pyatigorsk.

Hohenegg, whom I met again that night, didn't look too disappointed. "It's the reality principle, my dear friend," he declared. "That
will teach you to try to play the romantic hero. So let's go have a drink."
But the business was worrying me. Who could have denounced us to
Bierkamp? It was certainly one of Turek's comrades, who was afraid of
the scandal. Or maybe one of them, aware of the trap being prepared,
wanted to prevent it? It was hardly conceivable that Turek himself had
had second thoughts. I wondered what he was plotting with Prill: nothing good, certainly.

A new burst of activity made this affair fade into the background.
Von Mackensen's Third Panzer Corps, supported by the Luftwaffe, was
launching its offensive on Ordzhonikidze; the Soviet defenses around
Nalchik collapsed in two days, and at the end of October our forces
took the city while the tanks continued their push to the east.

I asked for a car and went first to Prokhladny, where I met Persterer,
then on to Nalchik. It was raining but that didn't hinder traffic too
much; after Prokhaldny, columns of the *Rollbahn* were bringing up food
supplies. Persterer was getting ready to transfer his Kommandostab to
Nalchik and had already dispatched a Vorkommando there to prepare
quarters. The city had fallen so quickly that they had been able to arrest
a lot of Bolshevik officials and other suspects; there were also many

Jews, both bureaucrats from Russia and a large native community. I reminded Persterer of the orders from the Wehrmacht concerning the attitude toward the local populations: they were planning on quickly forming an autonomous Kabardo-Balkar district, and it was imperative not to damage good relations in any way. In Nalchik, I found the Ortskommandantur, still being set up. The Luftwaffe had bombed the city, and many houses and gutted buildings were still smoking in the rain. I found Voss there, sorting through some books in an empty room; he seemed delighted at his finds. "Look at that," he said, holding out an old book in French. I examined the title page: *On the peoples of the Caucasus and the countries north of the Black Sea and the Caspian Sea in the Xth Century, or, The Journey of Abu-el-Cassim*, published in Paris in 1828 by a certain Constantin Mouradgea d'Ohsson. I handed it back to him with an approving look: "Did you find a lot of them?"—"Quite a few. A bomb hit the library, but there wasn't too much damage. On the other hand, your colleagues wanted to seize a part of the collections for the SS. I asked them what interested them, but since they don't have an expert, they didn't really know. I offered them the shelf on Marxist political economy. They told me they had to consult with Berlin. By then I'll be done." I laughed: "My duty should be to throw a spanner in your works."—"Maybe. But you won't do that." I told him about the quarrel with Turek, which he found highly comical: "You wanted to fight a duel because of me? Doktor Aue, you are incorrigible. That's absurd."—"I wasn't going to fight because of you: I was the one who was insulted."—"And you say that Dr. Hohenegg was ready to serve as your second?"—"Somewhat against his will."—"That surprises me. I thought he was an intelligent man." I found Voss's attitude rather annoying; he must have noticed my vexed air, since he burst out laughing: "Don't make that face! Remind yourself that coarse and ignorant men punish themselves."

I couldn't spend the night at Nalchik; I had to go back up to Pyatigorsk to file a report. The next day, I was summoned by von Gilsa. "Hauptsturmführer, we have a little problem in Nalchik that also concerns the *Sicherheitspolizei*." The Sonderkommando, he explained, had already begun to shoot some Jews, near the racecourse: Russian Jews, most of them Party members or officials, but also some local Jews, who seemed to be those famous "Mountain Jews," or Jews of the Caucasus. One of their elders had gone to find Selim Shadov, the Kabard lawyer chosen by the military administration to be the leader of the future autonomous district; he in turn had met in Kislovodsk with Generaloberst von Kleist, to whom he had explained that the *Gorski Yevrei* were not racially Jewish, but a mountain people converted to Judaism just as the

Kabards had been converted to Islam. "According to him, these *Bergju-den* eat like the other mountain people, dress like them, get married like them, and speak neither Hebrew nor Yiddish. They've been living for more than one hundred and fifty years in Nalchik and they all speak both Kabard and Balkar Turkish, along with their own language. Herr Shadov told the Generaloberst that the Kabards would not accept having their mountain brothers killed, and that they should be spared and even excused from wearing the yellow star."—"And what does the Generaloberst say about this?"—"As you know, the Wehrmacht is carrying out a policy here that aims to create good relations with the anti-Bolshevist minorities. These good relations should not be thoughtlessly imperiled. Of course, the security of the troops is also a vital consideration. But if these people are not racially Jewish, it may be that they present no danger. The question is a delicate one and should be studied carefully. So the Wehrmacht is going to form a commission of specialists and conduct an assessment. In the meantime, the Generaloberst is asking the *Sicherheitspolizei* not to take any measures against this Group. Of course, the *Sicherheitspolizei* is entirely free to submit its own opinion on the question, which the Army Group will take into consideration. I think the OKHG will delegate the affair to General Köstring. After all, it concerns a zone that is intended for self-government."—"Very good, Herr Oberst. I have made a note of it and will send a report."—"Thank you. I would also be grateful to you if you would ask Oberführer Bierkamp to confirm to us in writing that the *Sicherheit-spolizei* will not undertake any action without a decision from the Wehrmacht."—"*Zu Befehl*, Herr Oberst."

I called Obersturmbannführer Hermann, the replacement for Dr. Müller, who had left the week before, and explained the matter to him: Bierkamp was arriving within the hour, he told me, and invited me to come down to the Kommando. Bierkamp already knew: "That's absolutely inadmissible!" he shouted. "The Wehrmacht is really going too far. Protecting Jews is a direct violation of the will of the Führer."—"If you will allow me, Oberführer, I thought I understood that the Wehrmacht was not convinced that these people should be considered Jews. If it is demonstrated that they are, the OKHG should not have any objections to the SP proceeding with the necessary measures." Bierkamp shrugged his shoulders: "You are naïve, Hauptsturmführer. The Wehrmacht will demonstrate what it wants to demonstrate. This is nothing but one more pretext to oppose the work of the *Sicherheits-polizei*."—"Excuse me," interrupted Hermann, a man with delicate features and a severe but rather dreamy aspect, "have we already had similar cases?"—"To my knowledge," I replied, "only individual cases.

We'll have to check."—"That's not all," Bierkamp added. "The OKHG wrote to me that according to Shadov we have liquidated an entire village of these *Bergjuden* near Mozdok. They're asking me to send them a report justifying it." Hermann seemed to be having trouble following. "Is it true?" I asked.—"Listen, if you think I know the list of our actions by heart . . . I'll ask Sturmbannführer Persterer, that must be his sector."—"Anyway," Hermann said, "if they were Jews, he can't be reproached for anything."—"You don't know the Wehrmacht here yet, Obersturmbannführer. They'll take any chance they can get to pick a quarrel with us."—"What does Brigadeführer Korsemann think?" I hazarded. Bierkamp shrugged his shoulders again. "The Brigadeführer says we shouldn't stir up useless friction with the Wehrmacht. That's his obsession, now."—"We could launch a counterassessment," Hermann suggested.—"That's a good idea," Bierkamp said. "Hauptsturmführer, what do you think?"—"The SS has ample documentation on the subject," I replied. "And of course, if we have to, we can have our own experts come." Bierkamp shook his head. "If I am not mistaken, Hauptsturmführer, you carried out some research on the Caucasus for my predecessor?" "That is correct, Oberführer. But it didn't exactly concern these *Bergjuden*."—"Yes, but at least you already know the documentation. And it's obvious from your reports that you understand these nationality questions. Could you take charge of this question for us? Centralize all the information and prepare our replies to the Wehrmacht. I'll write you a mission order to show them. Of course, you will consult with me, or with Dr. Leetsch, at every stage."—"*Zu Befehl*, Oberführer. I'll do my best."—"Fine. And, Hauptsturmführer?"—"Yes, Oberführer?"—"In your research, not too much theory, all right? Try not to lose sight of the interests of the SP."—"*Zu Befehl*, Oberführer."

The Gruppenstab kept all our research materials in Voroshilovsk. I compiled a brief report for Bierkamp and Leetsch with what I found: the results were meager. According to a 1941 pamphlet from the Institute for the Study of Foreign Countries, entitled *List of Nationalities Living in the USSR*, the *Bergjuden* were in fact Jews. A more recent SS brochure gave a few additional precisions: *Mixed Oriental peoples, of Indian or other descent, but of Jewish origin, arrived in the Caucasus in the eighth century.* Finally, I found a more detailed evaluation, ordered by the SS from the Wannsee Institute: *The Jews of the Caucasus are not assimilated*, the text asserted, referring to the Russian Jews as well as to the *Bergjuden*. According to the author, the Mountain Jews or Daghestani Jews (*Dagh Chufuti*), like the Jews of Georgia (*Kartveli Ebraelebi*), arrived, around the time of the birth of Jesus, from Palestine, Babylon, and the lands of the Medes. Without citing any sources, it concluded: *Regardless of the accuracy of one opinion or another, the Jews as a whole, newcomers as well as* Bergjuden, *are* Fremdkörper, *foreign bodies in the region of the Caucasus.* A cover note from Amt IV specified that this evaluation was enough to give the Einsatzgruppe the necessary clarity to identify the *Weltanschauungsgegner,* the "ideological enemies," in its theater of operations. The next day, when Bierkamp returned, I presented my report to him, which he quickly skimmed through. "Very good, very good. Here is your mission order for the Wehrmacht."—"What does Sturmbannführer Persterer say about the village mentioned by Shadov?"—"He says they did liquidate a Jewish kolkhoz in that region, on September twentieth. But he doesn't know if they were *Bergjuden* or not. In the meantime, one of the elders of those Jews came to the Kommando, to Nalchik. I had an account of the discussion drawn up for you." I examined the document he held out to me: the elder, a certain Markel Shabaev, had presented himself wearing a *cherkesska* and a tall astrakhan hat; speaking Russian, he had explained that there lived in Nalchik several thousand Tats, an Iranian people whom the Russians mistakenly called *Gorski Evrei.* "According to Persterer," Bierkamp added, visibly annoyed, "it's this same Shabaev who asked Shadov to intercede. You'll have to see him, I guess."

When von Gilsa called me to his office two days later, he looked preoccupied. "What's going on, Herr Oberst?" I asked him. He showed me a line on his large wall map: "Generaloberst von Mackensen's Panzers have stopped advancing. The Soviet resistance has dug itself in in front of Ordzhonikidze, and it's already snowing down there. But we're just seven kilometers away from the city." His eyes followed the long blue line that snaked along and then rose up to vanish in the sands of the Kalmuk Steppe. "They're stuck in Stalingrad too. Our troops are worn out. If the OKH doesn't send reinforcements soon we'll spend the winter here." I didn't say anything and he changed the subject. "Were you able to look at the problem of those *Bergjuden?*" I explained to him that according to our documentation they had to be considered Jews. "Our experts seem to believe the opposite," he replied. "And Dr. Bräutigam too. General Köstring suggests we call a meeting about this tomorrow, in Voroshilovsk; he wants the SS and the SP to be represented."—"Fine. I will inform the Oberführer." I telephoned Bierkamp, who asked me to come; he too would attend the meeting. I went up to Voroshilovsk with von Gilsa. The sky was overcast, gray but dry; the peaks of the volcanoes disappeared into shifting, wild, capricious, nebulous whorls. Von Gilsa was in a glum mood and was brooding over his pessimism of the day before. An assault had just failed again. "The front won't move anymore, I think." He was also very worried about Stalingrad: "Our flanks are very vulnerable. Our allied troops are really second-rate, and the corsetting doesn't help much. If the Soviets try to pull off something big, they'll collapse. In that case, the position of the Sixth Army could be weakened fast."—"You don't really think, though, that the Russians still have the reserves necessary for an offensive? Their losses in Stalingrad are enormous, and they're throwing in everything they have just to hold the city."—"No one really knows what the state of the Soviet reserves is," he replied. "Since the beginning of the war, we've been underestimating them. Why wouldn't we have underestimated them again here?"

The meeting was held in a conference room of the OKHG. Köstring had come with his aide-de-camp, Hans von Bittenfeld, and two officers of Berück von Roques's staff. Also present were Bräutigam and an officer from the Abwehr attached to the OKHG. Bierkamp had brought Leetsch and an adjunct of Korsemann's. Köstring opened the meeting by recalling the principles of the regime of military administration in the Caucasus and of self-governance. "The peoples who have welcomed us as liberators and accept our benevolent supervision know their enemies well," he concluded in a slow, knowing tone. "Therefore, we should know how to listen to them."—"From the Abwehr's standpoint," von Gilsa explained, "it's a purely objective question of the security of the rear areas. If these *Bergjuden* cause disturbances, hide saboteurs, or help partisans, then we have to treat them like any enemy group. But if they keep quiet, there's no reason to provoke the other tribes by comprehensive repressive measures."—"For my part," Bräutigam said in his slightly nasal voice, "I think we have to consider the internal relations of the Caucasian peoples as a whole. Do the mountain tribes regard these *Bergjuden* as belonging to them, or do they reject them as *Fremdkörper*? The fact that Herr Shadov intervened so vigorously in itself pleads in their favor."—"Herr Shadov may have, let's say, political reasons that we don't understand," Bierkamp suggested. "I agree with Dr. Bräutigam's premises, even if I cannot accept the conclusion he draws from them." He read some extracts from my report, concentrating on the opinion of the Wannsee Institute. "This," he added, "seems confirmed by all the reports of our Kommandos in the theater of operations of Army Group A. These reports show us that dislike of the Jews is general. The *Aktions* against the Jews—such as dismissals from public offices, yellow star, forced labor—all meet with full understanding from the general population and are heartily welcomed. Significant voices within the population even find actions so far against the Jews insufficient and demand more determined actions."—"You are quite right when it comes to the recently settled Russian Jews,"

Bräutigam retorted. "But we don't have the impression that this attitude extends to the so-called *Bergjuden,* whose presence dates back several centuries at least." He turned to Köstring: "I have here a copy of a communication to the *Auswärtiges Amt* from Professor Eiler. According to him, the *Bergjuden* are of Caucasian, Iranian, and Afghan descent and are not Jews, even if they have adopted the Mosaic religion."—"Excuse me," said Noeth, the Abwehr officer from the OKHG, "but where did they receive the Jewish religion from, then?"—"That's not clear," Bräutigam replied, tapping on the table with the tip of his pencil. "Maybe from those famous Khazars who converted to Judaism in the eighth century."—"It isn't the *Bergjuden* who converted the Khazars, is it?" Eckhardt, Korsemann's man, hazarded. Bräutigam raised his hands: "That's what we have to look into." The lazy, intelligent, deep voice of Köstring rose again: "Excuse me, but didn't we have to deal with something like this already in the Crimea?"—"Affirmative, Herr General," Bierkamp replied in a dry tone. "That was during my predecessor's time. I think Hauptsturmführer Aue can explain the details to you."—"Certainly, Oberführer. Besides the case of the Karaïtes, recognized as racially non-Jewish in 1937 by the Ministry of the Interior, a controversy arose in the Crimea concerning the Krimchaks, who represented themselves as a Turkish people that converted to Judaism in recent times. Our specialists conducted an investigation and concluded that they were in fact Italian Jews, come to the Crimea around the fifteenth or sixteenth century and afterward Turkified."—"And what did we do about it?" Köstring asked.—"They were regarded as Jewish and treated as such, Herr General."—"I see," he said suavely.—"If you allow me," Bierkamp interrupted, "we also had to deal with *Bergjuden* in the Crimea. It was a Jewish kolkhoz, in the district of Freidorf near Eupatoria. It was inhabited by *Bergjuden* from Daghestan relocated there in the thirties with the assistance of the JOINT, the well-known international Jewish organization. After investigation, they were all shot in March of this year."—"That may have been a somewhat premature action," Bräutigam suggested. "Like the kolkhoz of *Bergjuden* you liquidated near Mozdok."—"Oh yes," Köstring said with the air of a man who has just remembered a minor detail, "were you able to find out about that matter, Oberführer?" Bierkamp replied to Köstring without paying attention to Bräutigam's remark: "Yes, Herr General. Unfortunately our files contain few clarifications, for in the heat of action during the offensive, when the Sonderkommando had just arrived in Mozdok, some of the actions weren't accounted for with all the precision we would have liked. According to Sturmbannführer Persterer, Professor Oberländer's Bergmann Kommando was also very active in that region. It might have been them."—"That battalion is under our control," Noeth, the AO, retorted. "We would know."—"What was the name of the village?" asked Köstring.—"Bogdanovka," Bräutigam replied, consulting his notes. "According to Herr Shadov, four hundred and twenty villagers were killed and thrown into some wells. They were all clan relations of the *Bergjuden* of Nalchik, with names like Michiev, Abramov, Shamilyev; their deaths caused a major stir in Nalchik, not just among the *Bergjuden* but also among the Kabards and the Balkars, who were very upset by it."—"Unfortunately," Köstring said coldly, "Oberländer has gone. So we can't ask him."—"Of course," Bierkamp went on, "it is also entirely possible that it was my Kommando. After all, their orders are clear. But I'm not certain."—"Fine," Köstring said. "In any case it's not important. What counts now is to make a decision about the *Bergjuden* of Nalchik, of whom there are . . ." He turned to Bräutigam, who said, "Between six and seven thousand."—"Exactly," Köstring continued. "A decision, then, that is fair, scientifically based, and finally that takes into account both the security of our rear area"— he inclined his head to Bierkamp—"and our desire to follow a policy of maximum collaboration with the local populations. The opinion of our scientific commission will thus be very important." Von Bittenfeld leafed through a bundle of papers: "We already have on-site Leutnant Dr. Voss, who despite his youth is a reputed authority in scientific circles in Germany. We are also having an anthropologist or an ethnologist come."—"For my part," Bräutigam interrupted, "I have already contacted my ministry. They are sending a specialist from Frankfurt, from the Institute for Jewish Questions. They will also try to have someone from Dr. Walter Frank's institute in Munich."—"I have already sought the opinion of the scientific department of the RSHA," Bierkamp said. "I think I will also ask for an expert. In the meantime, I have entrusted our investigations to Hauptsturmführer Dr. Aue present, who is our specialist in matters concerning the Caucasian peoples." I politely bowed my head. "Fine, fine," Köstring approved. "In that case, we'll meet again when the various investigations have come to some conclusions? That will allow us, I hope, to settle this affair. Meine Herren, thank you for coming." The assembly dispersed with a shuffling of chairs. Bräutigam had taken Köstring aside by the arm and was talking with him. The officers filed out one by one, but Bierkamp stayed there with Leetsch and Eckhardt, his cap in his hand: "They're pulling out all the stops. We have to find a good specialist too, otherwise we're going to be sidelined right away."—"I'll ask the Brigadeführer," Eckhardt said. "Maybe in the Reichsführer's entourage in Vinnitsa we'll be able to find someone. Otherwise, we'll have to get him to come from Germany."

Voss, according to von Gilsa, was still in Nalchik; I had to see him and went there at the first opportunity. In Malka, a thin layer of snow already covered the fields; by the time I reached Baksan, flurries were darkening the sky, great whirls of flakes projected into the light from the headlamps. The mountains, the fields, the trees, everything had disappeared; the vehicles coming from the opposite direction looked like roaring monsters, surging out of the wings hidden by the curtain of the storm. I had only a wool coat from the previous year; it was still sufficient, but wouldn't be for long. I would have to think about getting some warm clothing, I said to myself. In Nalchik, I found Voss surrounded by his books at the Ortskommandantur, where he had set up his office; he took me to have some ersatz coffee at the mess, at a little beaten-up Formica table with a vase of plastic flowers on it. The coffee was revolting and I tried to drown it in milk; Voss didn't seem to mind it. "You aren't too disappointed by the failure of the offensive?" I asked him. "For your research, I mean."—"A little, of course. But I have enough to keep me busy here." He seemed distant, a little lost. "So General Köstring has asked you to take part in the commission to investigate the *Bergjuden*?"—"Yes. And I heard that you were going to represent the SS." I laughed dryly: "More or less. Oberführer Bierkamp automatically promoted me to the rank of specialist in Caucasian affairs. That's your fault, I think." He laughed and drank some coffee. Soldiers and officers, some still coated with snow, were coming and going or talking in low voices at the other tables. "And what do you think about the problem?" I asked.—"What do I think? The way they've put it, it's absurd. The only thing you can say about these people is that they speak an Iranian language, practice the Mosaic religion, and live according to the customs of the Caucasian mountain people. That's it."—"Yes, but they do have an origin." He shrugged his shoulders: "Everyone has an origin, most of the time a dreamed one. We talked about that. For the Tats, it's lost in time and legend. Even if they really were Jews who came from Babylonia—let's even say one of the lost tribes—in the meantime they must have mingled with the peoples from here so much that it wouldn't mean anything anymore. In Azerbaidjan, there are Muslim Tats. Are they Jews who accepted Islam? Or did these hypothetical Jews from elsewhere trade women with an Iranian, pagan tribe whose descendants converted later on to one or the other religion of the Book? It's impossible to say."—"But," I insisted, "there must be scientific clues that would allow us to decide?"—"There are plenty, and you can make them say anything. Take their language. I've already talked with them and I can situate it pretty well. Especially since I found a book by Vsevolod Miller about it. It's basically a western Iranian dialect, with

Hebrew and Turkish contributions. The Hebrew contribution concerns mostly the religious vocabulary, but not systematically: they call the synagogue *nimaz*, Passover *Nisanu*, and Purim *Homonu*; those are all Persian names. Before Soviet power, they wrote their Persian language with Hebrew characters, but according to them, those books didn't survive the reforms. Nowadays, Tat is written in Latinic characters: in Daghestan, they publish newspapers and educate their children in that language. Now, if they really were Chaldeans or Jews who came from Babylon after the destruction of the First Temple, as some people would like us to think, they should by all logic speak some dialect derived from Middle Iranian, close to the Pahlavi language of the Sassanid era. But this Tat language is a new Iranian dialect, posterior to the tenth century and hence close to Dari, Baluch, or Kurdish. Without stretching the facts, we could conclude that there was a relatively recent immigration, followed by a conversion. But if you want to prove the opposite, you could do that too. What I don't understand is what connection any of this has with the security of our troops. Aren't we capable of judging their attitude toward us objectively, based on fact?"—"It's quite simply a racial problem," I replied. "We know that racially inferior groups exist, including the Jews, who present marked characteristics that in turn predispose them to Bolshevik corruption, theft, murder, and all kinds of other harmful manifestations. Obviously, that is not the case for all members of the group. But in wartime, in a context of occupation, and with our limited resources, it is impossible for us to carry out individual investigations. So we are forced to consider the risk-bearing groups as a whole, and to react globally. That creates great injustices, but that's because of the exceptional situation." Voss gazed at his coffee with a bitter, sad look. "Doktor Aue. I have always thought of you as an intelligent, sensible man. Even if everything you're telling me is true, explain to me, if you please, what you mean by 'race.' Because for me, that's a concept that is scientifically indefinable and hence without any theoretical value."—"But race exists, that's a fact, our best researchers are studying it and writing about it. You know that very well. Our racial anthropologists are the best in the world." Voss suddenly exploded: "They are clowns. They have no competition in serious countries because their discipline doesn't exist and isn't taught there. If it weren't for politics, none of them would have a job or be published!"—"Doktor Voss, I respect your opinions very much, but you're going a little far, aren't you?" I said gently. Voss struck the table with the flat of his hand, causing the cups and the vase of fake flowers to jump; the noise and his outburst made some heads turn: "This *philosophy of veterinarians*, as Herder called it, has stolen all its ideas from linguistics, the only social science to this day that has a scientifically valid theoretical basis. Do you understand"—he had lowered his voice and was speaking quickly and furiously—"do you even understand what a scientific theory is? A theory is not a fact: it is a tool that allows one to make predictions and generate new hypotheses. We say a theory is good, first of all, if it is relatively simple and then if it allows us to make verifiable predictions. Newtonian physics allows us to calculate orbits: if you observe the position of Earth or Mars at several months' intervals, they are always exactly where the theory predicts they should be. On the other hand, it has been noted that the orbit of Mercury has slight irregularities that deviate from the orbit predicted by Newtonian theory. Einstein's theory of relativity predicts these deviations with precision: so it is a better theory than Newton's. Now, in Germany, once the greatest scientific country in the world, Einstein's theory is denounced as *Jewish science* and rejected without any other explanation. That is quite simply absurd, that's what we reproach the Bolsheviks for, with their own pseudo-sciences in the service of the Party. It's the same thing for linguistics as against so-called racial anthropology. In linguistics, for example, Indo-Germanic comparative grammar has allowed us to draw up a theory of phonological mutations that has an excellent predictive value. As early as 1820, Bopp derived Greek and Latin from Sanskrit. By starting with Middle Iranian and following the same fixed rules, we can find words in Gaelic. It works and it's demonstrable. So it's a good theory, although it's constantly being elaborated, corrected, and perfected. Racial anthropology, by comparison, has no theory. It postulates races, without being able to define them, then posits hierarchies, without the slightest criteria. All the attempts to define races biologically have failed. Cranial anthropometry was a total flop: after decades of measurements and compilations of tables, based on the most farfetched indices or angles, we still can't tell a Jewish skull from a German skull with any degree of certainty. As for Mendelian genetics, it gives good results for simple organisms, but aside from the Habsburg chin, we're still far from being able to apply it to man. All this is so much the case that in order to write our famous racial laws, we were forced to use the grandparents' religion as a basis! It was postulated that the Jews of the last century were racially pure, but that's absolutely arbitrary. Even you have to see that. As for what constitutes a racially pure German, no one knows, whatever your Reichsführer-SS may say. So racial anthropology, incapable of defining anything, was simply built on the so much more demonstrable categories of linguistics. Schlegel, who was fascinated by the work of Humboldt and Bopp, deduced from the existence of a supposedly original Indo-Iranian language the idea of an equally original people, whom he

baptized Aryan, taking the term from Herodotus. The same for the
Jews: once the linguists had demonstrated the existence of a so-called
Semitic group of languages, the racialists jumped on the idea, which
they apply in a completely illogical way, since Germany wants to cultivate the Arabs and the Führer officially welcomes the Grand Mufti of
Jerusalem! Language, as a vehicle of culture, can have an influence on
thought and behavior. Humboldt had already understood that a long
time ago. But language can be transmitted and so can culture, although
much more slowly. In Chinese Turkestan, the Muslim Turkic speakers
in Ürümqi or Kashgar have an appearance we'll call Iranian: you might
take them for Sicilians. Of course they are descendants of peoples who
must have migrated from the West and who once spoke an Indo-Iranian
language. Then they were invaded and assimilated by a Turkic people,
the Uighurs, from whom they took their language and some of their
customs. They now form a cultural group that is distinct, for example,
from Turkic peoples like the Kazakhs or the Kirghiz, and also from the
Islamicized Chinese called the Hui, or from Indo-Iranian Muslims such
as the Tadjiks. But trying to define them other than by their language,
their religion, their customs, their habitat, their economic usages, or
their own sense of identity would make no sense. And all that is acquired, not innate. Blood transmits a propensity for heart diseases; if it
also transmits a propensity for treason, no one has ever been able to
prove it. In Germany, some idiots are studying cats with their tails cut
off to try to prove that their kittens will be born without a tail; and because they wear a gold button they're given a university chair! In the
USSR, on the other hand, despite all the political pressure, the linguistic studies of Marr and his colleagues, at least on a theoretical level, are
still excellent and objective, because"—he rapped sharply on the table
with his knuckles—"like this table, it exists. As for people like Hans
Günther or that Georges Montandon, in France, who's also made a
name for himself, I say they're full of shit. And if it's criteria like theirs
that you use to decide whether people live or die, you'd do better to go
shooting at random into a crowd, the result would be the same." I hadn't
said anything during Voss's whole long tirade. Finally I replied, rather
slowly: "Doktor Voss, I didn't know you were so passionate. Your theses are provocative, and I cannot agree with you on every point. I think
you underestimate some of the idealistic notions that form our *Weltanschauung* and that are far from a *philosophy of veterinarians*, as you say.
Nevertheless, this requires thought, and I wouldn't want to answer you
lightly. So I hope you will agree to resume this conversation in a few
days, when I've had time to think about it."—"Of course," Voss said,
suddenly calmer. "I'm sorry I got carried away. Only, when you hear so

many stupid and inept things around you, it becomes difficult at a certain point to keep quiet. I'm not talking about you, of course, but about some of my colleagues. My only wish and my only hope would be that German science, when passions have calmed down, can recover the position it had acquired with so much difficulty thanks to the work of so many fine men, subtle, attentive, and humble before the things of this world."

I was open to some of Voss's arguments: if the *Bergjuden* did in fact think of themselves as authentic Caucasian mountain people, and were regarded as such by their neighbors, their attitude toward us, in general, might indeed remain loyal, whatever the origin of their blood. Cultural and social factors could also count; one had to consider, for example, the relations this people had with the Bolshevik authorities. The words of the old Tat, in Pyatigorsk, had suggested to me that the *Bergjuden* were not particularly fond of the Jews of Russia, and perhaps the same was true for the whole Stalinist system. The attitude of the other tribes toward them was also important, you couldn't depend on the word of Shadov alone: here too, perhaps, the Jews were living as parasites. Going back to Pyatigorsk, I thought about Voss's other arguments. To deny racial anthropology as a whole in that way seemed to me to be overdoing it; of course the methods could be refined, and I didn't doubt that people of little talent were able to profit from their Party connections to construct an undeserved career for themselves: Germany was swarming with parasites like that (and fighting that was also one of the tasks of the SD, in the minds of some people at least). But Voss, despite all his talent, had the definitive opinions of youth. Things were certainly more complex than he thought. I didn't have the knowledge to criticize him, but it seemed to me that if you believed in a certain idea of Germany and the German *Volk*, the rest had to follow naturally. Some things could be demonstrated, but others simply had to be understood; it was also no doubt a question of faith.

In Pyatigorsk, the first reply from Berlin was waiting for me, sent by telex. Amt VII had sought the opinion of a certain Professor Kittel, who wrote: *Difficult question, to be studied locally*. That was not very encouraging. Department VII B 1, on the other hand, had prepared documentation that would arrive soon by air mail. The specialist from the Wehrmacht, von Gilsa told me, was on his way, and Rosenberg's expert would follow him soon after. Waiting for ours to arrive, I settled the problem of my winter clothing. Reuter kindly placed one of the Jewish artisans from the Wehrmacht at my service, an old man with a long beard, quite thin; he came to take my measurements, and I ordered a long gray coat from him with an Astrakhan collar, lined with shearling, which the Russians call a *shuba*, and a pair of fleece-lined boots; as for the shapka (the one from the year before had disappeared a long time ago), I went myself and found one at the market, the *Verkhnyi rynok*, in silver fox. A number of officers from the Waffen-SS had adopted the custom of having a death's head insignia sewn onto their non-regulation shapkas; I thought that a bit affected; but on the other hand, I removed the epaulettes and an SD insignia from one of my jackets and had them sewn onto the coat.

My bouts of nausea and vomiting caught me at irregular intervals; and harrowing dreams began to deepen my unease. Often they remained black and opaque; morning erased all images and left only the weight of them. But sometimes too this darkness was ripped apart all of a sudden, revealing visions blinding in their clarity and horror. Two or three nights after I returned from Nalchik, I ill-advisedly opened one of these doors: Voss, in a dark, empty room, was on all fours, his rear end bare, and liquid shit was streaming from his anus. Worried, I seized some paper, some pages from *Izvestia*, and tried to sponge up this brown liquid, which was becoming increasingly darker and thicker. I tried to keep my hands clean, but it was impossible, the almost black pitch covered the pages and my fingers, then my whole hand. Sick with disgust, I ran to wash my hands in a bathtub nearby; but during this time it was still streaming. Waking up, I tried to understand these frightful images; but I must not have been completely awake, since my thoughts, which seemed to me at the time perfectly lucid, remained as cloudy as the meaning of the image itself: it seemed to me in fact from certain signs that these people represented others, that the man on all fours must have been me, and the one who was wiping him, my father. And what could the articles from *Izvestia* have been about? Could there have been a piece there that might have settled the Tat question once and for all? The mail from VII B 1, sent by a certain Oberkriegsverwaltungsrat Dr. Füsslein, did nothing to resolve my pessimism; the zealous Oberkriegsverwaltungsrat, in fact, had simply contented himself with culling excerpts from *The Jewish Encyclopedia*. There were some very erudite things there, but their contradictory opinions, alas, led to no conclusion. Thus I learned that the Jews of the Caucasus were mentioned for the first time by Benjamin of Tudela, who had traveled to these lands around 1170, and Pethahiah of Ratisbon, who asserted that they were of Persian origin and had come to the Caucasus around the twelfth century. Willem van Ruysbroeck, in 1254, had found a large Jewish population east of the massif, in the region of Astrakhan. But a Georgian text of 314 mentioned Hebrew-speaking Jews who had adopted the old Iranian language ("Parsee" or "Tat") after the occupation of the Transcaucasus by the Persians, mixing it with Hebrew and local languages. The Jews of Georgia, however, called, according to Koch, *Huria* (perhaps derived from *Iberia*), speak not Tat but a Kartvelian dialect. As for Daghestan, according to the *Derbent-Nameh*, the Arabs had already found Jews there during their conquest, in the eighth century. Contemporary researchers only complicated the affair. There was reason to despair; I resolved to send all of it to Bierkamp and Leetsch without commentary, insisting that a specialist be summoned as soon as possible.

The snow stopped for a few days, then started up again. In the mess, the officers spoke in low, worried voices: Rommel had been beaten by the English at El-Alamein, then, a few days later, the English and Americans had landed in North Africa; our forces had just occupied the Free Zone in France, in retaliation; but that had pushed the Vichy troops in Africa to go over to the Allies. "If only things were going better here," was von Gilsa's comment. But before Ordzhonikidze our divisions had gone on the defensive; the line ran from south of Chegem and Nalchik to Chikola and Gizel, then followed the Terek to the north of Malgobek; and soon, a Soviet counterattack recaptured Gizel. Then came the real blow. I didn't learn about it right away, since the officers from the Abwehr blocked my access to the map room and refused to give me any details. "I'm sorry," Reuter said. "Your Kommandant will have to discuss it with the OKHG." At the end of the day I managed to learn that the Soviets had launched a counteroffensive on the Stalingrad front; but I couldn't find out where or how large it was: the officers from the AOK, their faces somber and tense, obstinately refused to talk to me. Leetsch, on the telephone, told me that the OKHG was reacting in the same way; the Gruppenstab didn't know any more than I did, and asked me to pass on any new information immediately. This attitude persisted the next day, and I got angry with Reuter, who retorted curtly that the AOK had no obligation to inform the SS about operations under way outside of its own area of responsibility. But already the rumors were spreading, the officers could no longer control the *Latrinenparolen*; I fell back on the drivers, dispatch riders, and noncoms and, in a few hours, by cross-checking the various tidbits, managed to form some idea of the extent of the danger. I called back Leetsch, who seemed to have the same information; but as to what the Wehrmacht's reaction would be, no one could say. The two Romanian fronts, west of Stalingrad on the Don and to the south in the Kalmuk Steppe, were collapsing, and the Reds were evidently aiming to take the Sixth Army from the rear. Where had they found the necessary troops? I couldn't manage to find out where they were, the situation was evolving too quickly even for

the cooks to follow, but it seemed urgent that the Sixth Army begin a
retreat to keep from being surrounded; yet the Sixth Army wasn't moving. On November 21, Generaloberst von Kleist was promoted to Generalfeldmarschall and named Commander in Chief of Army Group A:
the Führer must have been feeling overwhelmed. Generaloberst von
Mackensen took Kleist's place at the head of the First Panzer Army. Von
Gilsa passed me this news officially; he seemed desperate, and hinted to
me that the situation was becoming catastrophic. The next day, a Sunday, the two Soviet pincer movements met up at Kalach-on-the-Don,
and the Sixth Army as well as part of the Fourth Panzer Army were surrounded. Rumors spoke of a debacle, of massive losses, of chaos; but
every seemingly precise piece of information contradicted the previous
one. By the end of the day, finally, Reuter took me to von Gilsa, who
gave me a quick summary on the maps. "The decision not to try to
evacuate the Sixth Army was made by the Führer himself," he told me.
The surrounded divisions now formed a giant *Kessel*, a "cauldron" as
they said, cut off from our lines, but stretching from Stalingrad through
the steppe almost to the Don. The situation was worrisome, but the
rumors were exaggerating things terribly; the German forces had lost
few men or materiel and kept their cohesion; what's more, the experience of Demiansk, the previous year, showed that a *Kessel*, if supplied
by air, could hold out indefinitely. "A breakthrough operation will soon
be launched," he concluded. A meeting called the next day by Bierkamp confirmed this optimistic interpretation: Reichsmarschall Göring,
Korsemann announced, had given his word to the Führer that the Luftwaffe was able to supply the Sixth Army; General Paulus had joined
his staff in Gumrak to direct operations from within the *Kessel*; and
Generalfeldmarschall von Manstein was being recalled from Vitebsk to
form a new Army Group Don, tasked with relieving the surrounded
forces. This last piece of news especially created a great sense of relief:
ever since the taking of Sebastopol, von Manstein was regarded as the
best strategist in the Wehrmacht; if anyone could resolve the situation,
it was he.

In the meantime, the expert we needed arrived. Since the Reichsführer had left Vinnitsa with the Führer at the end of October to return
to East Prussia, Korsemann had applied directly to Berlin and the
RuSHA had agreed to send a woman, Dr. Weseloh, a specialist in Iranian languages. Bierkamp was extremely unhappy when he learned the
news: he wanted a racial expert from Amt IV, but no one was available.
I reassured him by explaining that a linguistic approach would turn out
to be fruitful. Dr. Weseloh had been able to take a mail plane to Rostov, via Kiev, but from there had been forced to continue by train. I

went to greet her at the Voroshilovsk station, where I found her in the company of the famous writer Ernst Jünger, with whom she was having an animated conversation. Jünger, a little tired but still spruce, wore a captain's field uniform from the Wehrmacht; Weseloh was in civilian clothes, with a jacket and a long skirt made of thick gray wool. She introduced me to Jünger, obviously proud of her new acquaintance: she had found herself by chance in his compartment at Krapotkin, and had recognized him immediately. I shook his hand and tried to say a few words to him about the importance that his books, especially *The Worker*, had had for me, but already some officers from the OKHG were surrounding him and taking him away. Weseloh, visibly moved, waved as she watched him leave. She was a rather thin woman, her breasts scarcely visible, but with exaggeratedly wide hips; she had a long horselike face, blond hair drawn back in a crisp bun, and glasses that revealed slightly bewildered but eager eyes. "I'm sorry I'm not in uniform," she said after we had exchanged a German salute. "They asked me to leave so quickly that I didn't have time to have one made."— "That's fine," I replied amiably. "But you'll be cold. I'll find a coat for you." It was raining, and the streets were full of mud; on the way, she enthused about Jünger, who had come from France on an inspection mission; they had spoken about Persian inscriptions, and Jünger had congratulated her on her erudition. At the Group, I introduced her to Dr. Leetsch, who explained the object of her mission; after lunch, he entrusted her to me and asked me to put her up in Pyatigorsk, to help her in her work, and to look after her. On the road, she spoke again about Jünger, then asked me about the situation in Stalingrad: "I've heard a lot of rumors. What exactly is happening?" I explained to her the little that I knew. She listened attentively and finally said with conviction: "I'm sure that it's a brilliant plan of our Führer's, to draw the enemy forces into a trap and destroy them once and for all."—"You must be right." In Pyatigorsk, I found her quarters in one of the sanatoriums, then showed her my documentation and reports. "We also have a lot of Russian sources," I explained.—"Unfortunately," she answered curtly, "I don't read Russian. But what you have there should be enough."—"Fine, then. When you've finished, we'll go to Nalchik together."

Dr. Weseloh wasn't wearing a wedding ring, but didn't seem to pay any attention to the handsome soldiers around her. Yet despite her unprepossessing physique and her sweeping, clumsy gestures, in the next few days I received many more visits than usual: officers not only from the Abwehr but even from Operations, who usually disdained speaking with me, suddenly found urgent reasons to come see me. Not one failed to salute our specialist, who had set herself up in an office and remained plunged in her papers, scarcely greeting them, with a distracted word or a sign of her head, unless it was a superior officer whom she had to salute. She only really reacted once, when the young Leutnant von Open came and clicked his heels in front of her table and spoke a few words to her: "Allow me, Fräulein Weseloh, to bid you welcome to our Caucasus . . ." She raised her head and interrupted: "Fräulein Doktor Weseloh, if you please." The Leutnant, disconcerted, blushed and mumbled his apologies; but the Fräulein Doktor had returned to her reading. I had trouble holding back my laughter before this stiff, puritanical old maid; but she wasn't unintelligent and had her human side. I in turn had an occasion to experience her sharpness when I wanted to discuss with her the result of her reading. "I don't see why they had me come here," she sniffed haughtily. "The question seems clear to me." I encouraged her to go on. "The question of language has no importance. The question of customs is a little more important, but not much. If they are Jewish, they'll have remained so despite all their attempts at assimilation, just like the Jews in Germany who spoke German and dressed like Western bourgeoisie, but remained Jews under their starched shirtfronts and didn't fool anyone. Open the pinstripe pants of a Jewish industrialist," she went on crudely, "and you'll find a circumcised penis. Here, it will be the same thing. I don't see why they're racking their brains about it." I ignored her coarse language, which gave me reason to suspect, in this seemingly icy doctor, the troubled and agitated eddies of murky waters, but I did allow myself to point out to her that given Muslim practices, that particular sign, at least, would lead to little here. She regarded me with even more scorn: "I was speaking metaphorically, Hauptsturmführer. What do you take me for? What I mean is that *Fremdkörper* remain such whatever the context. I will show you what I mean on-site."

The temperature was noticeably falling, and my greatcoat still wasn't ready. Weseloh had a rather bulky but well-lined coat that Reuter had found for her; at least for field trips I had my shapka. But even that displeased her: "That outfit isn't regulation, is it, Haupsturmführer?" she said when she saw me putting on my hat. "The regulations were written before we came to Russia," I politely explained. "They haven't yet been brought up to date. I should point out to you that your Wehrmacht coat is not regulation, either." She shrugged her shoulders. While she was studying the documentation, I had tried going back to Voroshilovsk, hoping to find an opportunity to meet Jünger there; but it hadn't been possible, and I had to be content with Weseloh's commentaries, at night in the mess hall. Now I had to drive her to Nalchik.

On the way, I mentioned Voss's presence and his involvement in the Wehrmacht's commission. "Dr. Voss?" she asked pensively. "He's quite a well-known specialist, in fact. His studies are widely criticized, though, in Germany. But it will be interesting to meet him." I too was very much looking forward to seeing Voss again, but alone, or at least not in the presence of this Nordic shrew; I wanted to continue our discussion of the other day; and my dream too, I had to admit, had troubled me, and I thought that a conversation with Voss, without of course mentioning those awful images, might help me clarify some things. In Nalchik, I went first to the offices of the Sonderkommando. Persterer was absent, but I introduced Weseloh to Wolfgang Reinholz, an officer from the Kommando who was also looking into the question of the *Bergjuden*. Reinholz explained that the experts from the Wehrmacht and the *Ostministerium* had already been by. "They met Shabaev, the old man who is more or less representing the *Bergjuden*; he gave them some long speeches and took them to visit the *kolonka*."—"The *kolonka*?" Weseloh asked. "What is that?"—"The Jewish neighborhood. It's a little south of the center of town, between the station and the river. We'll take you there. According to my informers," he added, turning to me, "Shabaev had all the carpets, beds, and armchairs taken out of the houses, to hide their wealth, and had shashliks served to the experts. They were completely taken in."—"Why didn't you intervene?" Weseloh asked.—"It's a little complicated, Fräulein Doktor," Reinholz replied. "There are questions of jurisdiction. For now, they've forbidden us to get involved in the affairs of these Jews."—"Whatever the case," she retorted stiffly, "I can assure you that I will not let myself be taken in by such manipulations."

Reinholz sent two Orpos to summon Shabaev, and served tea to Weseloh; I telephoned the Ortskommandantur to arrange something with Voss, but he had gone out; they promised me he'd call me back when he returned. Reinholz, who like everyone else had heard about Jünger's arrival, questioned Weseloh about the writer's National Socialist convictions; Weseloh, obviously, didn't know anything about it, but thought she had heard it said that he wasn't a member of the Party. A little later on, Shabaev made his appearance: "Markel Avgadulovich," he introduced himself. He wore traditional mountain garb and had an imposing beard and a firm, assured manner. He spoke Russian with a marked accent, but the *Dolmetscher* didn't seem to have any trouble translating. Weseloh had him sit down and started the discussion in a language that none of us understood. "I know some dialects that are more or less close to Tat," she said. "I'll talk to him this way and I'll explain it to you later." I left them and went to have tea with Reinholz in another room. He spoke to me about the local situation; the Soviet successes around Stalingrad had stirred up a great deal of unease among the Kabards and the Balkars, and the partisans' activities in the mountains were gathering strength again. The OKHG was planning soon to declare the district autonomous and, to put people's minds at rest, was counting on dissolving the kolkhozes and sovkhozes in the mountain zone (the ones in the plains of the Baksan and the Terek, regarded as Russian, would be maintained) and on distributing the land to the natives. After an hour and a half, Weseloh reappeared: "The old man wants to show us their neighborhood and his house. Are you coming?"—"Of course. And you?" I asked Reinholz.—"I've already been. But you always eat well there." He took an escort of three Orpos and drove us in a car to Shabaev's home. The house, made of brick with a wide inner courtyard, was comprised of large bare rooms, without hallways. After asking us to remove our boots, Shabaev invited us to sit down on some uncomfortable cushions and two women spread a large piece of waxed canvas on the ground in front of us. Several children had slipped into the room and were huddled in a corner, looking at us with wide eyes and whispering and laughing among themselves. Shabaev sat down on a cushion facing us while a woman his age, her head wrapped in a colored scarf, served us tea. It was cold in the room and I kept my coat on. Shabaev said some words in his language. "He apologizes for the poor welcome," Weseloh translated, "but they weren't expecting us. His wife will prepare some tea for us. He has also invited some neighbors over so that we can talk together."—"Tea," Reinholz explained, "means eating till your belly explodes. I hope you're hungry." A little boy came in and said a few rapid phrases to Shabaev before running out again. "I didn't understand that," Weseloh said, annoyed. She exchanged some words with Shabaev. "He says that's a neighbor's son; they spoke in Kabard." From the kitchen, a very pretty young woman in trousers and a scarf brought in some large round flatbread, which she set on the canvas. Then she and Shabaev's wife set out bowls of yogurt, dried fruit, and bonbons in silver wrappers. Shabaev tore one of the breads and handed us pieces of it: it was still warm, crispy, delicious. Another old man in *papakha* and soft ankle boots came in and sat down next to Shabaev, then another. Shabaev introduced them. "He says the one on his left is a Muslim Tat," Weseloh explained. "From the beginning, he's been trying to tell me that only some Tats are Jewish. I'm going to question him." She began a long exchange with the second old man. Vaguely bored, I nibbled at the bread and studied the room. The walls, bare of any decoration, seemed freshly whitewashed. The children were listening and examining us in silence. Shabaev's wife and the young woman brought us some dishes of boiled mutton, with a garlic sauce and dumplings boiled in water. I started eating; Weseloh kept talking. Then they served ground chicken shashlik, which they heaped on one of the breads; Shabaev tore the other breads and handed the slices out for us to use as dishes, then with a long Caucasian knife, a *kinzhal*, served each of us some chunks from the skewer. They also brought us grape leaves stuffed with rice and meat. I preferred those to the boiled meat, and began eating with gusto; Reinholz imitated me, while Shabaev seemed to be chiding Weseloh, who wasn't eating anything. Shabaev's wife also came and sat down next to us to criticize Weseloh's lack of appetite with large gestures. "Fräulein Doktor," I said between mouthfuls, "can you ask them where they sleep?" Weseloh talked with Shabaev's wife: "According to her," she finally replied, "right here, on the ground, on the wooden floor."—"In my opinion," said Reinholz, "she's lying."—"She says that they used to have mattresses, but the Bolsheviks came and took everything away from them before the retreat."—"That could be true," I said to Reinholz; he was biting into his shashlik and contented himself with shrugging his shoulders. The young woman kept serving us more hot tea as we drank, following a curious technique: first she poured a black brew from a little teapot, then added hot water into it. When we had finished eating, the women took away the leftovers and removed the cloth; then Shabaev went out and returned with some men carrying instruments, whom he had sit along the wall, facing the corner with the children. "He says that now we are going to listen to traditional Tat music, and see their dances, to see that they're the same as the other mountain peoples'," Weseloh explained. The instruments included kinds of banjos with very long necks, called *tar*, others with shorter necks called *saz*—a Turkish word, Weseloh explained, in order to set her professional mind at rest—a clay pot into which you blow through a reed, and some hand drums. They played several pieces, and the young woman who had served us danced in front of us, quite modestly, but with extreme grace and suppleness. The men who didn't play beat time with the percussionists. Other people came in and sat down or stood against the walls, women with long skirts with children between their legs, men in mountain garb, in old threadbare suits, or else in the smocks and caps of Soviet workers. One of the seated women was breastfeeding a baby, without concealing it at all; a young man took off his jacket and came to dance too. He was handsome, elegant, proud. The music and dances did resemble those of the Karachai, which I had seen in Kislovodsk; most of the pieces, with syncopated rhythms that fell strangely on my ears, were cheerful and exciting. One of the old musicians sang a long complaint, accompanied only by a banjo with two strings, which he struck with a plectrum. The food and the tea had plunged me into a peaceful, almost somnolent state; I let myself be carried away by the music and found this whole scene picturesque and these people very warm, very nice. When the music stopped, Shabaev gave a kind of speech that Weseloh didn't translate; then they presented us with some gifts: a large oriental rug woven by hand for Weseloh, which two men unfolded in front of us before folding it back up, and some handsome finely worked *kinzhali*, in scabbards of dark wood and silver, for Reinholz and me. Weseloh also received some silver earrings and a ring from Shabaev's wife. The whole crowd escorted us into the street, and Shabaev solemnly shook our hands: "He thanks us for having given him the chance to be able to show us Tat hospitality," Weseloh curtly translated. "He apologizes for the poverty of the welcome, but says we have to blame the Bolsheviks, who stole everything from them."

"What a circus!" she exclaimed in the car.—"That's nothing compared to what they did for the commission from the Wehrmacht," Reinholz commented.—"And those gifts!" she went on. "What are they thinking? That they can buy off SS officers? That's really a Jewish tactic." I didn't say anything: Weseloh annoyed me, she seemed to have started out with her mind already made up; I didn't think that was the right way to go about it. At the Sonderkommando offices, she explained that the old man with whom she had talked knew the Koran, the prayers, and Muslim customs well, but according to her, that didn't prove anything. An orderly came in and addressed Reinholz: "There's a phone call from the Ortskommandantur. They say that someone was asking for a Leutnant Voss."—"Oh, that's me," I said. I followed the orderly into the communication room and took the receiver. An unknown voice spoke: "Are you the one that left a message for Leutnant Voss?"—"Yes," I replied, perplexed.—"I'm sorry to tell you that he was wounded and won't be able to call you back," the man said. My throat suddenly tightened: "Is it serious?"—"Yes, pretty serious."—"Where is he?"—"Here, at the medical station."—"I'll come." I hung up and went back into the room where Weseloh and Reinholz were. "I have to go to the Ortskommandantur," I said as I reached for my coat.—"What's wrong?" Reinholz asked. My face must have been white; I quickly turned away. "I'll be back soon," I said as I went out.

Outside, night was falling, and it was very cold. I had gone by foot; in my haste I had forgotten my shapka; soon I began shivering. I walked quickly and almost slipped on a sheet of black ice; I managed to catch hold of a streetlight, but I hurt my arm. The cold gripped my bare head; my fingers, buried in my pockets, went numb. I felt long shudders pass

through my body. I had underestimated the distance to the Ortskommandantur: when I got there it was pitch-dark and I was trembling like
a leaf. I asked for an operations officer. "Are you the one I spoke to?"
he asked when he arrived at the entryway where I was vainly trying to
warm myself. "Yes. What's happened?"—"We're not really sure yet.
Some mountain men brought him back in an ox cart. He was in a
Kabard *aul*, in the south. According to the witnesses, he was going into
houses and questioning people about their language. One of the neighbors thinks he must have been alone with a young woman and the father surprised them. They heard some gunshots: when they came in,
they found the Leutnant wounded and the girl dead. The father had disappeared. So they brought him here. Of course, that's what they tell us.
We'll have to open an investigation."—"How is he?"—"Not well, I'm
afraid. He got shot in the stomach."—"Can I see him?" The officer hesitated, examined my face with undisguised curiosity. "This affair doesn't
concern the SS," he said finally.—"He's a friend." He wavered another
instant, then said abruptly: "In that case, come along. But I warn you,
he's in bad shape."

He brought me through some hallways freshly painted gray and pale
green to a large room where some sick and lightly wounded were lying
in a row of beds. I didn't see Voss. A doctor, a slightly stained white
smock over his uniform, came toward us: "Yes?"—"He wants to see
Leutnant Voss," explained the operations officer, pointing to me. "I'll
leave you here," he said. "I have work to do."—"Thank you," I said.—
"Come along," said the doctor. "We've isolated him." He took me to a
door in the back of the room. "Can I talk to him?" I asked.—"He won't
hear you," the doctor replied. He opened the door and had me go in
before him. Voss was lying under a sheet, his face damp, a little green.
His eyes were closed and he was groaning softly. I went up to him.
"Voss," I said. There was no reaction. Yet the sounds kept coming from
his mouth, not really groans, but rather articulate though incomprehensible sounds, like a child babbling—the translation, in a private and
mysterious language, of what was going on inside him. I turned to the
doctor: "Will he make it?" The doctor shook his head: "I don't even
understand how he made it this far. We couldn't operate, it wouldn't do
any good." I turned back to Voss. The sounds continued uninterrupt-
edly, a description beyond language of his agony. It chilled me, I had
trouble breathing, as in a dream where someone is talking and you don't
understand. But here there was nothing to understand. I pushed back a
lock of hair that had fallen onto his eyelid. He opened his eyes and
stared at me, but these eyes were empty of all recognition. He had
reached that private, closed space from which you never return to the

surface, but from which he hadn't sunk deeper yet. Like an animal, his body was struggling with what was happening to him, and these sounds—that's what they were, too, animal sounds. From time to time the sounds broke off so he could pant, sucking air through his teeth with an almost liquid noise. Then it began again. I looked at the doctor: "He's suffering. Can't you give him some morphine?" The doctor looked annoyed: "We've already given him some."—"Yes, but he needs more." I stared at him straight in the eyes; he hesitated, tapped his teeth with a fingernail. "I'm almost out of it," he said finally. "We had to send all our stock to Millerovo for the Sixth Army. I have to keep what I have for cases that are still operable. Anyway, he's going to die soon." I kept staring at him. "You have no authority to give me orders," he added.—"I'm not giving you an order, I'm asking you," I said coldly. He blanched. "All right, Hauptsturmführer. You're right. . . . I'll give him some." I didn't move, didn't smile. "Do it now. I'll watch." A brief tic twisted the doctor's lips. He went out. I watched Voss: the strange, terrifying sounds, forming almost by themselves, kept coming out of his mouth, which was working convulsively. An ancient voice, come from the beginning of time; but if it was a language, it wasn't saying anything, and expressed only its own disappearance. The doctor returned with a syringe, uncovered Voss's arm, tapped to make the vein appear, and gave him the injection. Little by little the sounds spaced out, his breathing calmed down. His eyes had closed. Now and then another block of sounds came, like a final buoy thrown overboard. The doctor had gone out. I gently touched Voss's cheek with the back of my fingers, and went out too. The doctor was bustling about with a manner that expressed both annoyance and resentment. I thanked him briefly, then clicked my heels and raised my arm. The doctor didn't return my salute and I went out without a word.

A car from the Wehrmacht took me back to the Sonderkommando. I found Weseloh and Reinholz there still in midconversation, Reinholz arguing in favor of a Turkish origin of the *Bergjuden*. He paused when he saw me: "Ah, Hauptsturmführer. We were wondering what you were doing. I've had some quarters prepared for you. It's too late for you to go back."—"In any case," Weseloh said, "I'll have to stay here a few days, to continue my investigations."—"I'm going back to Pyatigorsk tonight," I said in a flat voice. "I have work to do. There aren't any partisans around here and I can drive at night." Reinholz shrugged his shoulders: "That's against the Group's instructions, Hauptsturmführer, but do as you please."—"I'll entrust Dr. Weseloh to you. Call me if you need anything."

Weseloh, her legs crossed on her wooden chair, looked perfectly at ease and happy with her adventure; my departure left her indifferent. "Thank you for your help, Hauptsturmführer," she said. "By the way, could I see this Dr. Voss?" I was already on the threshold, shapka in hand. "No." I didn't wait for her reaction and went out. My driver seemed rather unhappy at the idea of driving at night, but he didn't insist when I repeated my order in a sharper tone. The trip took a long time: Lemper, the driver, drove very slowly because of the black ice. Outside the narrow halo from the headlights, half covered because of enemy aircraft, we couldn't see anything; from time to time, a military checkpoint rose up out of the darkness in front of us. I fiddled distractedly with the *kinzhal* that Shabaev had given me; I smoked cigarette after cigarette, and looked out at the vast empty night without thinking.

The investigation confirmed what the villagers had said about the death of Leutnant Dr. Voss. In the house where the tragedy occurred they found his notebook, bloodstained and filled with Kabard consonants and grammatical notations. The girl's mother, hysterical, swore she had not seen her husband again since the incident; according to her neighbors, he had probably fled into the mountains with the murder weapon, an old hunting rifle, to turn *abrek*, as they say in the Caucasus, or to join a band of partisans. A few days later, a delegation of elders from the village came to see General von Mackensen: they solemnly presented their apologies in the name of the *aul*, reaffirmed their profound friendship for the German army, and set down a pile of carpets, sheepskins, and jewelry, which they offered to the dead man's family. They swore they would find the murderer themselves and kill him or hand him over; the few able-bodied men remaining in the *aul*, they asserted, had left to search the mountains. They feared reprisals: von Mackensen reassured them, promising there would be no collective punishment. I knew that Shadov had talked about this with Köstring. The army burned down the guilty man's house, and promulgated a new general order reiterating the prohibitions of fraternizing with mountain women, then promptly closed the case.

The Wehrmacht commission had finished its study of the *Bergjuden*, and Köstring wanted to hold a conference in Nalchik about it. This was becoming all the more urgent since the Kabardo-Balkar National Council was being set up and the OKHG wanted to settle the affair before the formation of the autonomous district, planned for December 18, the day of Kurban Bairam. Weseloh had finished her work and was writing her report; Bierkamp summoned us to Voroshilovsk to examine our position. After a few relatively mild days, during which it had once again snowed, the temperature had plummeted to some twenty degrees below; I had finally received my *shuba* and my boots; they were cumbersome, but they kept me warm. I made the trip with Weseloh; from Voroshilovsk, she would leave directly for Berlin. At the Gruppenstab, I found Persterer and Reinholz, whom Bierkamp had also summoned; Leetsch, Prill, and Sturmbannführer Holste, the Leiter IV/V of the Group, also attended the meeting. "According to my information," Bierkamp began, "the Wehrmacht and this Dr. Bräutigam want to exempt the *Bergjuden* from anti-Jewish measures so as not to harm good relations with the Kabards and the Balkars. So they're going to try to claim that they're not really Jews, to protect themselves from criticism from Berlin. For us, that would be a serious mistake. As Jews and *Fremdkörper* among the surrounding peoples, this population will remain a permanent source of danger for our forces: a nest of spies and saboteurs and a breeding ground for partisans. There is no room for doubt about the necessity for radical measures. But we must have solid proof to face the Wehrmacht's hairsplitting."—"Oberführer, I think it won't be difficult to demonstrate the soundness of our position," Weseloh asserted in her reedy little voice. "I will be sorry not to be able to do it myself, but I'll leave a complete report before I go, with all the important points. That will allow you to respond to all the Wehrmacht's or the *Ostministerium*'s objections."—"Perfect. For the scientific arguments, you'll go over all that with Hauptsturmführer Aue, who will present that part. I myself will present the concrete position of the *Sicherheitspolizei* from the security standpoint." As he was speaking, I was quickly going over the list of citations drawn up by Weseloh aiming at establishing a purely Jewish and very ancient origin of the *Bergjuden*. "If you don't mind, Oberführer, I would like to make a remark about the report drawn up by Dr. Weseloh. It's excellent work, but she has simply left out all the citations that contradict our point of view. The Wehrmacht and *Ostministerium* experts will not fail to use these as objections against us. So I think the scientific basis of our position is rather weak."—"Hauptsturmführer Aue," Prill interrupted, "you must have spent too much time talking with your friend Leutnant Voss. It seems he has influenced your judgment." I shot him an exasperated look: so that's what he was plotting with Turek. "You are mistaken, Hauptsturmführer. I was simply trying to point out that the scientific documentation presented here is inconclusive, and that basing our position on it would be a mistake."—"This Voss was killed, is that right?" Leetsch asked.—"Yes," Bierkamp replied. "By some partisans, maybe even by these very Jews. It is of course a shame. But I have reason to believe that he was actively working against us. Hauptsturmführer Aue, I understand your doubts; but you should stick to the main point and not the petty details. Here the interests of the SP and the SS are clear, and that's what counts."—"In any case," said Weseloh, "their Jewish character is as plain as day. Their manners are insinuating, and they even tried to corrupt us."—"Absolutely," Persterer confirmed. "They've come many times to the Kommando to bring us fur coats, blankets, cooking utensils. They say it's to help our troops, but they have also given us carpets, fine knives, and jewelry."—"We shouldn't be taken in," threw in Holste, who looked bored.—"Yes," said Prill, "but remember they did the same thing with the Wehrmacht." The discussion lasted for some time. Bierkamp concluded: "Brigadeführer Korsemann will come in person to the conference in Nalchik. I don't think, if we present the thing well, that the Army Group will dare to contradict us openly. After all, it's their security too that's at stake. Sturmbannführer Persterer, I'm counting on you to manage all the preparations for a rapid and effective *Aktion*. Once we have the green light, we have to act quickly. I want everything to be finished by Christmas, so I can include the numbers in my year-end report."

After the meeting, I went to say goodbye to Weseloh. She shook my hand warmly. "Hauptsturmführer Aue, I can't begin to tell you how happy I was to be able to carry out this mission. For you, here in the East, the war is an everyday affair; but in Berlin, in the offices, you soon forget the mortal danger the *Heimat* is in, and the difficulties and sufferings of the front. Coming here has allowed me to understand all that in a profound way. I will carry back the memory of all of you as a precious thing. Good luck, good luck. Heil Hitler!" Her face was shining, she was in the grip of a surprising exaltation. I returned her salute and left her.

Jünger was still in Voroshilovsk, and I had heard that he was receiving admirers who sought him out; he had to leave soon to inspect Ruoff's divisions in front of Tuapse. But I had lost all desire to meet Jünger. I went back to Pyatigorsk thinking about Prill. Obviously he was trying to harm me; I didn't really understand why: I had never tried to pick a quarrel with him; but he had chosen to take Turek's side. He was in continual contact with Bierkamp and Leetsch, and it would not be hard, by dint of little insinuations, to set them against me. This matter of the *Bergjuden* risked putting me in a bad position: I had no bias, I just wanted to respect a certain intellectual honesty, and I had trouble understanding Bierkamp's insistence on wanting to liquidate them at all costs; was he sincerely convinced of their Jewish racial origins? For me, that didn't emerge clearly from the documentation; as to their appearance and behavior, they didn't at all resemble the Jews we knew; seeing them at home, they seemed in every point like the Kabards, the Balkars, or the Karachai. They too offered us sumptuous gifts, it was a tradition, you didn't have to see that as corruption. But I had to watch out: indecisiveness could be interpreted as weakness, and Prill and Turek would take advantage of the slightest misstep.

In Pyatigorsk, I again found the map room sealed: Hoth's army, formed from the reinforced remnants of the Fourth Panzer Army, was launching its breakthrough from Kotelnikovo toward the *Kessel*. But the officers were acting optimistic, and their comments served to fill out the official communiqués and rumors for me; everything led us to believe that once again, as before Moscow the previous year, the Führer had been right to hold out. In any case I had to prepare for the conference on the *Bergjuden* and didn't have much time for anything else. As I reread the reports and my notes, I thought about Voss's words, during our last conversation; and examining the different accumulated proofs, I wondered: What would he have thought of this, what would he have accepted or rejected? The case, all things considered, was very thin. It honestly seemed to me that the Khazar hypothesis was untenable, that only the Persian origin made sense; as to what that meant, I was less sure than ever. I regretted Voss's death enormously; he was truly the only person here with whom I could have talked about this seriously; the others, the ones in the Wehrmacht or the SS, couldn't care less, really, about truth or scientific rigor: it was just a political question for them.

The conference took place around the middle of the month, a few days before the Great Bairam. There were a lot of people; the Wehrmacht had hastily replastered a large meeting hall in the former Communist Party headquarters, which had an immense oval table still scarred by the shrapnel that had come through the roof. There was a brief but animated discussion about a question of precedence: Köstring wanted each of the different delegations to be grouped together—the military administration, the Abwehr, the AOK, the *Ostiministerium*, and the SS—and that seemed logical, but Korsemann insisted that everyone be seated according to his rank; Köstring ended up giving in, which had Korsemann sitting on his right, Bierkamp a little lower, and me almost at the end of the table, across from Bräutigam, who was only a Hauptmann of the reserve, and next to the civilian expert from Minister Rosenberg's institute. Köstring opened the meeting and then introduced Selim Shadov, the head of the Kabardo-Balkar National Council, who gave a long speech on the very ancient relations of hospitality, mutual aid, friendship, and sometimes even marriage between the Kabard, Balkar, and Tat peoples. He was a rather fat man, wearing a twill suit made of shiny cloth, his somewhat flabby face strengthened by a thick moustache, and he spoke a slow, emphatic Russian; Köstring translated his words himself. When Shadov had finished, Köstring got up and assured him, in Russian (this time a *Dolmetscher* translated for us), that the opinion of the National Council would be taken into account, and that he hoped that the question would be settled to everyone's satisfaction. I looked at Bierkamp, sitting on the other side of the table, four seats away from Korsemann: he had placed his cap on the table next to his papers, and was listening to Köstring while tapping his fingers; Korsemann was scraping at a shrapnel gouge with his pen. After Köstring's reply, they had Shadov leave, and the general sat down without commenting on the exchange. "I suggest we begin with the experts' reports," he said. "Doktor Bräutigam?" Bräutigam pointed to the man seated to my left, a civilian with yellowish skin, a drooping little moustache, and carefully combed greasy hair, sprinkled, as were his shoulders, with a cloud of dandruff, which he kept nervously brushing off. "Allow me to introduce Dr. Rehrl, a specialist in Eastern Judaism at the Institute for Jewish Questions in Frankfurt." Rehrl slightly raised his buttocks from his chair in a little bow and began in a monotonous, nasal voice: "I believe we are dealing here with a remnant of a Turkic tribe, which adopted the Mosaic religion during the conversion of the Khazar nobility, and which later on sought refuge in the eastern Caucasus, around the tenth or eleventh centuries, during the destruction of the Khazar Empire. There, they mixed by marriage with an Iranian-speaking mountain tribe, the Tats, and a part of the group converted or reconverted to Islam while the others maintained a Judaism that became slowly corrupted." He began to tick off the proofs: first of all, the words in Tat for food, people, and animals, that is, the fundamental substratum of language, were mainly of Turkish origin. Then he went over the little that was known of the history of the conversion of the Khazars. There were some interesting points there, but his summary tended to present things in a jumble, and was a little hard to follow. I was nonetheless impressed by his argument about proper names: one found, among the *Bergjuden*, names of Jewish holidays such as Hanukkah or Pessach used as proper names, for example in the Russianized name Khanukayev, a usage that exists neither among the Ashkenazy Jews nor among the Sepharad, but which is attested among the Khazars: the proper name Hanukkah, for instance, appears twice in the *Kiev Letter*, a letter of recommendation written in Hebrew by the Khazar community of this city at the beginning of the tenth century; once on a gravestone in the Crimea; and once in the list of Khazar kings. For Rehrl, therefore, the *Bergjuden*, despite their language, were comparable from a racial perspective to the Nogai, the Kumyk, and the Balkar rather than to the Jews. After that, the head of the investigatory commission from the Wehrmacht, a rubi-

cund officer named Weintrop, spoke: "My opinion can't be as unequivocal as that of my respected colleague. In my opinion, the traces of a
Caucasian Jewish influence on these famous Khazars—about which we
know in fact quite little—are as numerous as are the proofs of an opposite influence. For example, in the document known as the *Anonymous
Cambridge Letter*, which must also date from the tenth century, it is written that *some Jews from Armenia intermarried with the inhabitants of this
land*—this refers to the Khazars—*mingled with the Gentiles, learned their
practices, and continually fought alongside them; and they became a single people*. The author is speaking here of Middle Eastern Jews and of the
Khazars: when he mentions Armenia, it's not the modern Armenia that
we know, but the ancient Greater Armenia, that is, almost all of Trans-
caucasia and a large part of Anatolia. . . ." Weintrop went on in this
vein; each element of proof that he put forward seemed to contradict
the one before it. "If we come now to ethnological observation, we
note few differences from their neighbors who converted to Islam, or
who became Christian, like the Ossetes. Pagan influences remain very
strong: the *Bergjuden* practice demonology, wear talismans to protect
themselves from evil spirits, and so on. That resembles the so-called Sufi
practices of the Muslim mountain people, such as the worship of graves
or the ritual dances, which are also survivals of pagan rituals. The standard of living of the *Bergjuden* is identical to that of the other mountain
peoples, whether in the city or in the *auls* that we visited: it's impossible to maintain that the *Bergjuden* profited from Judeo-Bolshevism in
order to advance their position. On the contrary, they seem in general
almost poorer than the Kabards. At the Shabbat meal, the women and
children sit apart from the men: this is contrary to Jewish tradition, but
it's the mountain tradition. On the other hand, during marriages like the
one we were able to attend, with hundreds of Kabard and Balkar guests,
the men and women of the *Bergjuden* dance together, which is strictly
forbidden by Orthodox Judaism."—"Your conclusions, then?" asked
von Bittenfeld, Köstring's adjutant. Weintrop scratched his white hair,
cropped almost to the skull: "As for the origin, it's hard to say: the information is contradictory. But it seems obvious to us that they are completely assimilated and integrated and, if you like, *vermischlingt*,
'mischlingized.' The traces of Jewish blood that remain must be negligible."—"However," Bierkamp interrupted, "they cling obstinately to
their Jewish religion, which they've preserved intact for centuries."—
"Oh, not intact, Herr Oberführer, not intact," Weintrop said genially.
"Quite corrupted, on the contrary. They have completely lost all
Talmudic knowledge, if they ever had any. With their demonology,
this makes them almost heretics, like the Karaïtes. What's more, the

Ashkenazy Jews scorn them and call them *Byky*, 'Bulls,' a pejorative term."—"On this subject," Köstring said suavely, turning to Korsemann, "what is the opinion of the SS?"—"It's certainly an important question," Korsemann opined. "I'm going to hand it over to Oberführer Bierkamp." Bierkamp was already gathering his pages together: "Unfortunately, our own specialist, Dr. Weseloh, had to return to Germany. But she has prepared a complete report, which I forwarded to you, Herr General, and which strongly supports our opinion: these *Bergjuden* are extremely dangerous *Fremdkörper* who represent a threat to the security of our troops, a threat to which we must react with vigor and energy. This point of view, which, unlike that of the researchers, takes into account the vital question of security, is also based on a study of the scientific documentation carried out by Dr. Weseloh, whose conclusions differ from those of the other specialists present here. I will let Hauptsturmführer Dr. Aue present them to you." I bowed my head: "Thank you, Oberführer. I think that, to be clear, it is preferable to differentiate the levels of proofs. First of all there are the historical documents, then the living document that is language; then there are the results of physical and cultural anthropology; and finally the ethnological research in the field like that carried out by Dr. Weintrop or Dr. Weseloh. If one considers the historical documents, it seems established that Jews lived in the Caucasus long before the conversion of the Khazars." I quoted Benjamin of Tudela and a few other ancient sources, such as the *Derbent-Nameh*. "In the ninth century, Eldad ha-Dani visited the Caucasus and noted that the Mountain Jews had an excellent knowledge of the Talmud . . ."—"Well, they certainly lost it!" Weintrop interrupted.— "Absolutely, but the fact remains that at one time the Talmudists of Derbent and Chemakha, in Azerbaijan, were quite renowned. Which may moreover be a rather late phenomenon: in fact, a Jewish traveler from the eighties of the last century, a certain Judas Chorny, thought that Jews had arrived in the Caucasus not after but before the destruction of the First Temple, and lived cut off from everything, under Persian protection, until the fourth century. Only later on, when the Tatars invaded Persia, did the *Bergjuden* meet some Jews from Babylon who taught them the Talmud. It was only at that time that they adopted rabbinic tradition and teachings. But that is not proven. For proof of their antiquity, you would have to refer to archeological traces, like the deserted ruins in Azerbaijan known as *Chifut Tebe*, the 'Hill of the Jews,' or *Chifut Kabur*, the 'Tomb of the Jews.' They are very ancient. As to the language, Dr. Weseloh's observations corroborate those of the late Dr. Voss: it is a modern Western Iranian dialect—I mean no older than the eighth or ninth century, maybe even the tenth—which seems to contradict a direct Chaldean descent, as Pantyukov suggests, following Quatrefages. What's more, Quatrefages thought that the Lesghins, some Svans, and the Khevsurs also had Jewish origins; in Georgian, *Khevis Uria* means 'the Jew from the Valley.' Baron Peter Uslar, more reasonably, suggests a frequent, regular Jewish immigration to the Caucasus over two thousand years, each wave more or less mingling with the local tribes. One explanation of the problem of the language would be that the Jews traded women with an Iranian tribe, the Tat, who arrived later on; they themselves would have arrived in the time of the Achaemenids, as military colonists to defend the Derbent Pass against the nomads from the plains in the North."—"The Jews, military colonists?" an Oberst from the AOK laughed sarcastically. "That seems ridiculous to me."—"Not really," Bräutigam retorted. "The Jews before the Diaspora have a long tradition of waging war. Just look at the Bible. And remember how they stood up to the Romans."—"Oh yes, that's in Flavius Josephus," Korsemann added.—"True, Herr Brigadeführer," Bräutigam agreed.—"In short," I went on, "this collection of facts seems to contradict a Khazar origin. On the contrary, the hypothesis of Vsevolod Miller, which is that the *Bergjuden* brought Judaism to the Khazars, seems more plausible."—"That's just what I was saying," Weintrop broke in. "But you yourself, with your linguistic argument, don't deny the possibility of 'racial mixing.'"—"It's a shame that Dr. Voss is no longer with us," Köstring said. "He would certainly have clarified this point for us."—"Yes," said von Gilsa sadly. "We miss him very much. He's a great loss."—"Judeo-Bolshevism," Rehrl added sententiously, "is also making German science pay a heavy price."—"Yes, but really, in the case of poor Voss, it's more a question of a, so to speak, cultural misunderstanding," suggested Bräutigam.—"Meine Herren, meine Herren," Köstring cut in. "We are straying from the subject. Hauptsturmführer?"—"Thank you, Herr General. Unfortunately, physical anthropology makes it hard for us to decide between the various hypotheses. Allow me to cite for you the data gathered by the great scholar Erckert in *Der Kaukasus und seine Völker*, published in 1887. For the cephalic index, he gives 79.4 (mesocephalic) for the Tatars of Azerbaijan, 83.5 (brachycephalic) for the Georgians, 85.6 (hyperbrachycephalic) for the Armenians, and 86.7 (hyperbrachycephalic) for the *Bergjuden*."—"Ha!" Weintrop exclaimed. "Just like the Mecklenburgers!"—"Shh . . ." Köstring said. "Let the Hauptsturmführer speak." I continued: "Height of head: Kalmuks, 62; Georgians, 67.9; *Bergjuden*, 67.9; Armenians, 71.1. Facial index: Georgians, 86.5; Kalmuks, 87; Armenians, 87.7; and *Bergjuden*, 89. Finally, nasal index: the *Bergjuden* are at the bottom of the scale, with 62.4, and the Kalmuks at the top, with

75.3, a significant interval. The Georgians and Armenians fall between the two."—"What does all that mean?" asked the Oberst from the AOK. "I don't understand."—"That means," explained Bräutigam, who had jotted down the numbers and was hastily carrying out some mental calculations, "that if you regard the shape of the head as an indicator of a more or less elevated race, the *Bergjuden* form the most handsome type of Caucasian population."—"That's exactly what Erckert says," I went on. "But of course, this approach, although it has not been completely refuted, is little used these days. Science has made some progress." I briefly raised my eyes to Bierkamp: he was regarding me severely, tapping on the table with his pencil. With his fingertips he signaled to me to go on. I plunged back into my documents: "As for cultural anthropology, it provides a wealth of data. It would take me too long to go over all of it. In general, it tends to present the *Bergjuden* as having completely adopted the customs of the mountain people, including those concerning *kanly*, or *ichkil*, the blood feud. We know that several great Tat warriors fought alongside Imam Shamil against the Russians. Also, before Russian colonization, the *Bergjuden* occupied themselves mostly with agriculture, and cultivated grapes, rice, tobacco, and various grains."—"That is not Jewish behavior," Bräutigam noted. "The Jews hate difficult labor like agriculture."—"Indeed, Herr Doktor. Later on, under the Russian Empire, economic circumstances turned them into artisans, specializing in leather tanning and jewelry, weapon- and carpet-making; they also became merchants. But that is a recent evolution, and some *Bergjuden* remain farmers."—"Like the ones that were killed near Mozdok, right?" Köstring recalled. "We never cleared up that business." Bierkamp's face darkened. I went on: "On the other hand, a rather convincing fact is that aside from the few rebels who joined Shamil, most of the *Bergjuden* in Daghestan, perhaps because of Muslim persecutions, chose the Russian side during the Caucasian wars. After the victory, the czarist authorities rewarded them with equal rights with the other Caucasian tribes, and access to administrative positions. That, of course, is more like the parasitic Jewish methods that we are familiar with. But it should be noted that most of these rights were rescinded under the Bolshevik regime. In Nalchik, since this was a Kabardo-Balkar autonomous republic, all the positions that weren't given to Russians or to Soviet Jews were distributed to the two titular peoples; the *Bergjuden*, here, mostly did not participate in the administration, aside from a few archivists and minor functionaries. It would be interesting to observe the situation in Daghestan." I ended by citing Weseloh's ethnological observations. "They don't seem to contradict our own," Weintrop grumbled. "No, Herr Major. They are complementary."—"On the other hand," Rehrl murmured pensively, "the bulk of your information is not very compatible with the thesis of a Khazar or Turkish origin. Nonetheless, I believe it's solid. Even your Miller . . ." Köstring interrupted him, coughing: "We are all very impressed by the erudition shown by the specialists from the SS," he said unctuously, addressing Bierkamp, "but your conclusions don't seem very different to me from those of the Wehrmacht, wouldn't you say?" Bierkamp seemed furious and worried now; he was chewing his lip: "As we have pointed out, Herr General, purely scientific observations remain very abstract. You have to add them to the observations provided by the work of the *Sicherheitspolizei*. That's what makes us conclude that we are dealing here with a racially dangerous enemy."—"Excuse me, Herr Oberführer," Bräutigam intervened. "I am not convinced of that."— "That's because you're a civilian and have a civilian point of view, Herr Doktor," Bierkamp dryly retorted. "It is not by chance that the Führer thought fit to entrust matters of the Reich's security to the SS. There is also a question of *Weltanschauung* here."—"No one here is calling into question the competence of the *Sicherheitspolizei* or the SS, Oberführer," Köstring continued with his slow, paternal voice. "Your forces are precious auxiliaries for the Wehrmacht. Nevertheless, the military administration, which is also the result of a decision made by the Führer, must consider all aspects of the question. Politically, an action that is not completely justified against the *Bergjuden* would harm us. There would have to be urgent considerations to counterbalance that. Oberst von Gilsa, what is the opinion of the Abwehr as to the level of risk posed by this population?"—"The question was already brought up during our first conference on the subject, Herr General, in Voroshilovsk. Since then, the Abwehr has been attentively observing the *Bergjuden*. As of today, we haven't noticed the slightest trace of subversive activity. No contact with partisans, no sabotage, no espionage, nothing. If only all the other populations would stay so quiet, our task here would be made much easier."—"The SP believes you shouldn't wait for the crime, but prevent it," Bierkamp furiously objected.—"Indeed," said von Bittenfeld, "but in a preventive intervention, you have to weigh the benefits and the risks."—"In short," Köstring went on, "if there is a risk from the *Bergjuden*, it is not immediate?"—"No, Herr General," von Gilsa confirmed. "Not in the Abwehr's opinion."—"So there's still the racial question," said Köstring. "We have heard a lot of arguments. But I think you will all agree that none of them was fully conclusive either way." He paused and rubbed his cheek. "It seems to me that we lack data. It is true that Nalchik is not the natural habitat of these *Bergjuden*, which certainly deforms the perspective. So I suggest that we put off the ques-

tion until our occupation of Daghestan. On-site, in their original habitat, our researchers should be able to find more convincing elements.
We will organize another commission, then." He turned to Korsemann.
"What do you think, Brigadeführer?" Korsemann hesitated, glanced
sideways at Bierkamp, hesitated again and said, "I don't see any objection to that, Herr General. That seems to me to satisfy the interests of
all parties involved, including the SS. Isn't that right, Oberführer?"
Bierkamp took a moment to reply: "If you think so, Brigadeführer."—
"Of course," Köstring added in his friendly manner, "in the meantime,
we will watch them closely. Oberführer, I am also counting on the vig-
ilance of your Sonderkommando. If they become insolent or make contact with the partisans, that's it. Doktor Bräutigam?" Bräutigam's voice
was more nasal than ever: "The *Ostministerium* has no objection to your
entirely reasonable proposition, Herr General. I think we should also
thank the specialists, some of whom have come here all the way from
the Reich, for their remarkable work."—"Absolutely, absolutely,"
Köstring agreed. "Doktor Rehrl, Major Weintrop, Hauptsturmführer
Aue, our congratulations, as well as to your colleagues." Everyone applauded. People were standing up in a noise of chairs scraping and papers shuffling. Bräutigam skirted round the table and came to shake my
hand: "Very good work, Hauptsturmführer." He turned to Rehrl: "Of
course, the Khazar thesis can still be defended."—"Oh," said Rehrl,
"we'll see in Daghestan. I'm sure that we'll find more proofs there,
archeological remains." I looked at Bierkamp, who had gone off to join
Korsemann and who was speaking to him quickly in a low voice, gesturing with his hand. Köstring was standing and talking with von Gilsa
and the Oberst from the AOK. I exchanged a few more words with
Bräutigam and then gathered my files together and headed to the antechamber, where Bierkamp and Korsemann were already waiting.
Bierkamp eyed me angrily: "I thought you cared more about the interests of the SS, Hauptsturmführer." I didn't let myself get flustered:
"Oberführer, I did not omit one single proof of their Jewishness."—
"You could have presented your arguments more clearly. With less ambiguity." Korsemann intervened with his jerky voice: "I don't see what
you are reproaching him for, Oberführer. He did very well. What's more,
the General congratulated him, twice." Bierkamp shrugged his shoulders: "I wonder if Prill was right, after all." I didn't reply. Behind us, the
other attendees were coming out. "Do you have any other instructions
for me, Oberführer?" I finally asked. He gestured vaguely with his hand:
"No. Not now." I saluted him and went out behind von Gilsa.

Outside, the air was dry, sharp, biting. I breathed in deeply and felt
the cold burning the inside of my lungs. Everything looked frozen,

silent. Von Gilsa got into his car with the Oberst from the AOK, offering me the front seat. We exchanged a few more words and then little by little everyone fell silent. I thought about the conference: Bierkamp's anger was understandable. Köstring had played a dirty trick on us. Everyone in that room knew perfectly well that there was no chance the Wehrmacht would ever reach Daghestan. Some even suspected— but perhaps not Korsemann or Bierkamp—that Army Group A would, on the contrary, soon have to evacuate the Caucasus. Even if Hoth managed to link up with Paulus, it would only be to allow the Sixth Army to fall back to the Chir, or even the lower Don. One just had to look at a map to understand that the position of Army Group A was becoming untenable. Köstring must have had some certainty about that. Thus, it was out of the question to set the mountain people against us over an issue as unimportant as that of the *Bergjuden*: as it was, when they understood that the Red Army was returning, there would be troubles— even if only to prove, a little late of course, their loyalty and their patriotism—and we had, at all costs, to prevent things from going further. A retreat through a completely hostile environment, in terrain favorable to guerilla warfare, could become catastrophic. So some goodwill had to be shown to the friendly populations. I didn't think Bierkamp could understand that; his police mentality, exacerbated by his obsession with numbers and reports, made him shortsighted. Recently, one of the Einsatzkommandos had liquidated a sanatorium for tubercular children, in a remote zone in the Krasnodar region. Most of the children were natives; the National Councils had vigorously protested, there had been skirmishes that had cost the lives of several soldiers. Bairamukov, the Karachai leader, had threatened von Kleist with a general insurrection if it happened again; and von Kleist had sent a furious letter to Bierkamp, who, according to what I had heard, had received it with a strange indifference: he didn't see what the problem was. Korsemann, more sensitive to the influence of the military, had had to intervene and force him to send new instructions to the Kommandos. So Köstring hadn't had a choice. When he arrived at the conference, Bierkamp thought the game wasn't over yet; but Köstring, along with Bräutigam, no doubt, had already loaded the dice, and the exchange of opinions was only theater, a representation for the benefit of the uninitiated. Even if Weseloh had been present, or if I had stuck to a completely one-sided argumentation, it wouldn't have changed a thing. The Daghestan trick was brilliant, irrefutable: it flowed naturally from what had been said, and Bierkamp could make no reasonable objection to it; as to saying the truth, that there would be no occupation of Daghestan, that was quite simply unthinkable; Köstring would have had an easy

time, then, having Bierkamp dismissed for defeatism. It wasn't for nothing that the soldiers also called Köstring "the old fox": it had been, I said
to myself with bitter pleasure, a masterstroke. I knew it was going to
create enemies for me: Bierkamp would try to off load the blame for his
defeat on someone, and I was the most likely person. I had carried out
my work with energy and rigor, though; but as during my mission in
Paris, I hadn't understood the rules of the game, I had looked for the
truth when what was wanted was not the truth but political advantage.
Prill and Turek would now have an easy time of it to slander me. At
least Voss would not have disapproved of my presentation. Alas, Voss
was dead, and I was alone again.

Night was falling. A thick frost covered everything: the twisted
branches of the trees, the wires and poles of the fences, the dense grass,
the earth in the almost bare fields. It was like a world of horrible white
shapes, harrowing, ghostlike, a crystalline universe from which life
seemed banished. I looked at the mountains: the vast blue wall barred
the horizon, guardian of another world, a hidden one. The sun, over
toward Abkhazia probably, was setting behind the ridges, but its light
still touched the summits, casting on the snow sumptuous and soft pink,
yellow, orange, fuchsia glints, which ran delicately from one peak to the
other. It was a cruel beauty, enough to take your breath away, almost
human but at the same time very remote from any human concerns.
Little by little, behind, the sea was swallowing up the sun, and the colors were extinguished one by one, leaving the snow blue, then a gray-
white that gleamed calmly in the night. The frost-encrusted trees
appeared in the beams of our headlights like creatures in full movement.
It was almost as if I had gone over to the other side, to that country that
children know well, from which no one returns.

I hadn't been wrong about Bierkamp: the axe fell even faster than I
thought it would. Four days after the conference, he summoned me to
Voroshilovsk. Two days before, they had proclaimed the Autonomous
Kabardo-Balkar District during the celebration of Kurban Bairam, in
Nalchik, but I hadn't attended the ceremony; Bräutigam, apparently,
had made a long speech, and the mountain people had showered the officers with gifts, *kinzhali*, carpets, Korans copied by hand. As for the
Stalingrad front, according to rumors, Hoth's Panzers were struggling to
advance, and had run aground in the Myshkova, sixty kilometers from
the *Kessel*; in the meantime the Soviets, farther north up the Don, were
launching a new offensive against the Italian sector of the front, routing
them; and the Russian tanks were said to be within striking distance of
the aerodromes from which the Luftwaffe was trying to supply the

Kessel! The officers from the Abwehr still refused to give out any exact information, and it was hard to form a precise idea of the critical nature of the situation, even by tallying together the various rumors. I reported to the Gruppenstab what I managed to understand or corroborate, but I had the impression that they weren't taking my reports very seriously: recently I had received from Korsemann's staff a list of the SSPF and other SS officials appointed to the different districts of the Caucasus, including Groznyi, Azerbaidjan, and Georgia, and a study on the plant called *kok-sagyz*, which is found around Maikop, and which the Reichsführer wanted to start cultivating on a large scale to produce a substitute for rubber. I wondered if Bierkamp was thinking just as unrealistically; in any case, his summons worried me. On the way there I tried to muster all the arguments in my defense, to prepare a strategy, but since I didn't know what he was going to say to me, I kept going in circles.

The interview was short. Bierkamp didn't invite me to sit down and I remained standing at attention while he held out a piece of paper to me. I looked at it without really understanding: "What is it?" I asked.— "Your transfer. The officer in charge of all police structures in Stalingrad asked for an SD officer urgently. His previous one was killed two weeks ago. I informed Berlin that the Gruppenstab could bear a reduction in personnel, and they approved your transfer. Congratulations, Hauptsturmführer. It's an opportunity for you." I remained rigid: "Can I ask you why you suggested me, Oberführer?" Bierkamp still looked displeased but he smiled slightly: "In my staff, I want officers who understand what is expected of them without having to explain the details to them; otherwise, one might as well do the work oneself. I hope the SD work in Stalingrad will be a useful apprenticeship for you. Also, allow me to point out to you that your personal conduct has been questionable enough to give rise to unpleasant rumors within the Group. Some have even gone so far as to mention an intervention from the *SS-Gericht*. I refuse on principle to believe such rumors, especially about an officer as politically aware as you are, but I will not allow a scandal to tarnish the reputation of my Group. In the future, I advise you to be careful that your behavior doesn't expose you to such gossip. Dismissed." We exchanged a German salute and I withdrew. In the hallway, I walked by Prill's office; the door was open, and I saw that he was looking at me with a slight smile. I stopped on the threshold and stared at him, while a radiant smile, a child's smile, grew on my face. Little by little his smile vanished and he contemplated me with a puzzled, troubled look. I didn't say anything, just kept smiling. I was still holding my transfer. Finally I went out.

It was still just as cold, but my fleece-lined coat protected me and I walked a bit, aimlessly. The snow, poorly swept, was frozen and slippery. On the corner of a street, near the Kavkaz Hotel, I witnessed a strange spectacle: German soldiers were coming out of a building carrying mannequins wearing Napoleonic uniforms. There were hussars in orange, pistachio, or daffodil-yellow shakos and dolmans, dragoons in green with amaranthine piping, soldiers of the Old Guard in blue coats with gold buttons, Hanoverians in shrimp red, a Croat lancer all in white with a red cravat. The soldiers were loading these mannequins, upright, into canvas-covered trucks, while others were securing them with rope. I approached the Feldwebel who was supervising the operation: "What's going on?" He saluted me and replied: "It's the regional museum, Herr Hauptsturmführer. We're evacuating the collection to Germany. Orders from the OKHG." I looked at them for a while and then returned to my car, my travel orders still in my hand. *Finita la commedia.*

COURANTE

nd so I took a train in Minvody and slowly made my way up north. The traffic was constantly disrupted; I had to change convoys several times. In filthy waiting rooms, hundreds of soldiers milled around, standing up or sprawling on their kits, waiting to be served soup or a little ersatz coffee before heading off into the unknown. Someone would give up a space on a bench for me and I would remain there, motionless, until an exhausted stationmaster came and shook me. In Salsk, finally, they put me on a train coming up from Rostov with men and materiel for Hoth's army. These makeshift units had been hastily and haphazardly formed: men on leave intercepted on the way home, as far as Lublin and even Posen, and sent back to Russia, under-age conscripts whose training had been sped up and then curtailed, convalescents swept out of the lazarettos, individual soldiers from the Sixth Army found wandering outside of the *Kessel*, after the catastrophe. Hardly any of them seemed to have any idea of the gravity of the situation; and that wasn't surprising, the military communiqués remained obstinately silent on the subject, at most mentioning *activity in the Stalingrad sector*. I didn't speak with these men; I stowed my kit and wedged myself into the corner of a compartment, withdrawn into myself, absently studying the large vegetal shapes, branching out, intricate, deposited on the window by the frost. I didn't want to think, but thoughts flooded in, bitter, full of self-pity. Bierkamp, a little inner voice raged inside me, would have done better to put me directly in front of a firing squad, that would have been more human, rather than making hypocritical speeches about the educational value of a siege in the middle of a Russian winter. Thank God, another voice groaned, at least I have my *shuba* and my boots. It was frankly a little difficult for me to conceive of the educational value of pieces of burning metal tearing through my

flesh. When you shot a Jew or a Bolshevik, it had no educational value, it killed them, that's all, even though we had a lot of nice euphemisms for that too. When the Soviets wanted to punish someone, they sent them to a *shtrafbat*, where the life expectancy was a few weeks at most: a brutal method, but an honest one, just like everything they did, in general. One of their great advantages over us (aside from their seemingly countless divisions and tanks): at least with them you knew where you stood.

The tracks were congested; we spent hours waiting on sidings, following unfathomable rules of priority set by mysterious, distant authorities. Sometimes I forced myself to go out and breathe in the biting air and stretch my legs: beyond the train there was nothing, a vast white expanse, empty, swept by the wind, cleansed of all life. Under my feet, the snow, hard and dry, cracked like a crust; the wind, when I faced it, chapped my cheeks; so I turned my back to it and looked at the steppe, the train with its windows white with frost, the rare other men propelled outside like me by their boredom or their diarrhea. Insane desires seized hold of me: to lie down on the snow, rolled in a ball in my coat, and to stay there when the train left, hidden already under a fine white layer, a cocoon that I imagined as soft, warm, tender as the womb from which I had one day been so cruelly expelled. These surges of melancholia frightened me; when I managed to regain control of myself, I wondered where this could be coming from. It wasn't a habit of mine. Fear, maybe, I finally said to myself. Fine, fear, but fear of what, then? Death was something I thought I had tamed within me, and not just since the massacres of the Ukraine, but for a long time already. Yet perhaps that was just an illusion, a curtain drawn by my mind over the low animal instinct that was still there, lurking? That was possible, of course. But maybe it was also the idea of being surrounded: of heading alive into this vast open-air prison, as into an exile with no return. I had wanted to serve, I had carried out, for my nation and my people and in the name of this service, difficult and terrible things that went against my grain; and now I was to be exiled from myself and from the common life, sent to join those already dead, the abandoned ones. Hoth's offensive? Stalingrad wasn't Demyansk, and even before November 19 we were already at the end of our tether, out of breath and out of strength, we had reached the farthest limits; we, who had been so powerful, who thought we were just getting started. Stalin, that cunning Ossete, had used the tactics of his Scythian ancestors on us: the endless retreat, always farther into the interior, *the little game*, as Herodotus called it, *the infernal pursuit*; playing, using the emptiness. *When the Persians gave the first signs of exhaustion and dejection, the Scythians imagined a way to give them some more courage and thus to make them drink their cup of sorrow to the dregs. They willingly sacrificed some herds that they let wander about in full visibility and that the Persians eagerly fell upon. Thus they regained a little optimism. Darius fell several times into this trap, but finally found himself driven to famine.* It was then (writes Herodotus) that the Scythians sent Darius their mysterious message in the form of an offering: a bird, a rat, a frog, and five arrows. But, for us, no offering, no message: death, destruction, and the end of hope. Is it possible that I thought about all this at the time? Didn't such ideas come to me later on, when the end was approaching, or even later, when it was already all over? Possible, but it is also possible that I already was thinking like that between Salsk and Kotelnikovo, for the proofs were there, you just had to open your eyes to see them, and my sadness had perhaps already begun to open my eyes. It's hard to say, like a dream that leaves only vague, sour traces in the morning, like the cryptic drawings that, in the manner of a child, I traced with my fingernail in the frost on the train's windows.

In Kotelnikovo, the staging area for Hoth's offensive, they were unloading another train before ours, so we had to wait a long time to disembark. It was a little country station made of worn brick, with a few platforms of bad cement laid between the tracks; on either side, the cars, stamped with the German emblem, bore Czech, French, Belgian, Danish, Norwegian markings: to gather materiel as well as men, they were scouring the farthest reaches of Europe now. I stood leaning on the open door of my car, smoking and watching the confused commotion of the station. There were German soldiers of all kinds there, Russian Polizei or Ukrainians wearing armbands with swastikas and carrying old rifles, Hiwis with hollow features, peasants red with cold come to sell or exchange a few meager marinated vegetables or a scrawny chicken. The Germans wore coats or furs; the Russians, padded jackets, most of them in rags, from which tufts of straw or pieces of newspaper escaped; and this motley crowd was talking, heckling, jostling each other at the level of my boots, in huge jerky waves. Just beneath me, two big, sad soldiers were holding each other by the arm; a little farther down, a haggard, dirty Russian, trembling and wearing only a thin cloth jacket, was stumbling along the platform with an accordion in his hands: he approached some groups of soldiers or Polizei, who sent him away with a rough word or a shove, or at best turned their backs to him. When he came up to me I took a small bill out of my pocket and held it out to him. I thought he would go on his way, but he stayed there and asked me, in a mixture of Russian and bad German: "What would you like? Popular, traditional, or Cossack?" I didn't understand what he was talking about and shrugged my shoulders: "It's up to you." He looked at me for an instant and struck up a Cossack song that I knew from having heard it often in the Ukraine, the one whose refrain goes so gaily *Oy ty Galia, Galia molodaya . . .* and which relates the atrocious story of a girl carried off by the Cossacks, tied by her long blond tresses to a pine tree, and burned alive. And it was magnificent. The man sang, his face raised up to me: his eyes, a faded blue, shone gently through the alcohol and the filth; his cheeks, beneath a scruffy reddish beard, quivered; and his bass voice, hoarse from coarse tobacco and drink, rose clear and pure and firm and he sang verse after verse, as if he would never stop. Beneath his fingers the keys of his accordion clicked. On the platform, the agitation had stopped, the people were watching and listening, a little surprised, even the ones who a few minutes before had treated him harshly, overcome by the simple and incongruous beauty of the song. From the other side, three fat peasant women were coming in single file, like three plump geese on a village path, with a large white triangle raised in front of their faces, a knitted wool shawl. The accordionist was blocking their path and they flowed around him the way a sea eddy skirts round a rock, while he pivoted slightly in the other direction without interrupting his song, then they continued along the train and the crowd shuffled and listened to the musician; behind me, in the corridor, some soldiers had come out of their compartments to listen to him. It seemed never to end, after each verse he attacked another one, and no one wanted it to end. Finally it did end, and without even waiting to be offered more money he continued on his way to the next car, and below my boots the people dispersed or resumed their activities or their waiting.

Finally our turn came to get out. On the platform, Feldgendarmen were examining documents and steering the men to various assembly points. They sent me to an office in the station where an exhausted clerk looked at me vacantly: "Stalingrad? I have no idea. Here is for the Hoth army."—"They told me to come here and that I'd be transferred to one of the aerodromes."—"The aerodromes are on the other side of the Don. Go see at HQ." Another Feldgendarm got me into a truck headed for the AOK. There, I finally found a somewhat better informed operations officer: "Flights for Stalingrad leave from Tatsinskaya. But usually the officers who have to join the Sixth Army go there from Novocherkassk, where the HQ of Army Group Don is located. We have a liaison with Tatsinskaya every three days, maybe. I don't understand why they sent you here. But we'll try to find you something." He set me up in a barrack room with a number of double beds. He reappeared a few hours later. "It's all set. Tatsinskaya is sending you a Storch. Come along." A driver ferried me outside the village to a makeshift runway in the snow. I waited some more in a hut heated by a stove, drinking ersatz coffee with a few noncoms from the Luftwaffe. The idea of an airlift to Stalingrad depressed them profoundly: "We're losing five to ten planes a day, and in Stalingrad, apparently, they're dying of hunger. If General Hoth doesn't manage to break through, they're fucked."—"If I were you," another one genially added, "I wouldn't be in such a hurry to join them."—"Couldn't you get a little lost?" the first one joked. Then the little Fieseler Storch landed, skidding. The pilot didn't even bother to cut the engine; he did a U-turn at the end of the runway and got into position for departure. One of the men from the Luftwaffe helped me carry my kit. "At least you'll be dressed warmly," he shouted out over the throb of the propeller. I hoisted myself up and settled in behind the pilot. "Thank you for coming!" I shouted to him.—"It's nothing," he answered, shouting to be heard. "We're used to being taxi drivers." He took off before I had even managed to buckle myself in, and veered off to the north. Night was falling but the sky was clear and for the first time I saw the earth from the skies. A flat, white, uniform surface extended to the horizon; here and there a track pathetically cut across the expanse, perfectly straight. The *balki* looked like long grooves of shadow nestled beneath the dying light that skimmed across the steppe. Where the tracks joined, remains of villages appeared, already half swallowed up, the roofless houses full of snow. Then came the Don, an enormous white snake curved in the whiteness of the steppe, made visible by its blue-tinted shores and the shadow of the hills overlooking the right bank. The sun, in the distance, was setting on the horizon like a swollen red ball, but the red gave no color to anything; the snow remained white and blue. After taking off, the Storch flew straight ahead, quite low, calmly, like a peaceable bumblebee; suddenly it veered left and went into a dive and beneath me there were rows of big transport planes on all sides, then already the wheels were touching down and the Storch was bouncing over the hard snow and taxiing over to pull up at the rear of the aerodrome. The pilot cut the engine and showed me a long, low building: "It's over there. They're waiting for you." I thanked him and walked quickly with my kit to a door lit by a hanging light-bulb. On the runway, a Junker was coming in for a heavy landing. With nightfall the temperature was falling fast; the cold struck me in the face like a slap and burned my lungs. Inside, a noncom invited me to put down my kit; he led me to an operations room buzzing like a hive. An Oberleutnant from the Luftwaffe greeted me and checked my papers. "Unfortunately," he said finally, "the flights for tonight are already full.

I can put you on a morning flight. There's another passenger waiting too."—"You fly at night?" He looked surprised: "Of course. Why not?" I shook my head. He led me with my things to a dormitory set up in another building: "Try to sleep," he said as he left. The dormitory was empty, but another kit lay on a bed. "That's the officer who's flying with you," the Spiess who was accompanying me said. "He must be at the mess. Would you care to have something to eat, Herr Hauptsturmführer?" I followed him to another room, with some tables and benches lit by a yellowish lightbulb, where some pilots and ground personnel were eating and talking in low voices. Hohenegg was sitting alone at the end of a table; he let out a guffaw when he saw me: "My dear Hauptsturmführer! What kind of foolishness has brought you here?" I blushed with happiness, and went to get a dish of thick pea soup, some bread, and a cup of ersatz before sitting down opposite him. "It's not your failed duel to which I owe the pleasure of your company, is it?" he asked again with his cheerful, pleasant voice, "I wouldn't forgive myself."—"Why do you say that?" He looked at once embarrassed and amused: "I have to confess that I was the one who denounced your plan."—"You!" I didn't know if I should burst out in a fit of rage or laughter. Hohenegg looked like a kid caught in the act. "Yes. First of all, let me tell you that it really was an idiotic idea, misplaced German romanticism. And also, remember, they wanted to ambush us. I had no intention of going and getting myself massacred with you."—"Doctor, you are a man of little faith. Together, we could have foiled their stratagem." I briefly explained my problems with Bierkamp, Prill, and Turek. "You shouldn't complain," he concluded. "I'm sure it will be a very interesting experience."—"That's what my Oberführer pointed out to me. But I'm not convinced."—"That's because you still lack philosophy. I thought you were made of sterner stuff."—"Maybe I've changed. And you, Doctor? What brought you here?"—"A medical bureaucrat in Germany decided we should take advantage of the occasion to study the effects of malnutrition on our soldiers. AOK 6 thought it wasn't necessary, but the OKH insisted. So they asked me to conduct this fascinating study. I confess that despite the circumstances it does excite my curiosity." I pointed my spoon at his round belly: "Let's hope you won't become a subject of study yourself."—"Hauptsturmführer, you are becoming rude. Wait till you're my age to laugh. And how is our young linguist friend?" I looked at him calmly: "He is dead." His face darkened: "Ah. I'm very sorry."—"So am I." I finished my soup and drank the tea. It was vile and bitter, but it quenched one's thirst. I lit a cigarette. "I miss your Riesling, Doctor," I said, smiling.—"I still have a bottle of Cognac," he replied. "But let's keep it. We'll drink it together in the *Kessel*."—"Doctor, never say: Tomorrow I shall do this or that, without adding: God willing." He shook his head: "You missed your calling, Hauptsturmführer. Let's go to bed."

A noncom woke me from my bad sleep at around six o'clock. The mess was cold and almost empty; I didn't taste the bitterness of the tea, but concentrated on its warmth, with both my hands around the tin cup. Then they led us with our kit to a freezing hangar where they made us wait for a long time, stamping our feet in the midst of oily machinery and crates of spare parts. My breath formed heavy condensation in front of my face, suspended in the moist air. Finally the pilot came and introduced himself: "We'll fill up and get going," he said. "Unfortunately, I don't have any parachutes for you."—"Are they of any use?" I asked. He laughed: "Theoretically, if we get shot down by a Soviet fighter plane, we might have time to jump. In practice, you can forget it." He led us to a little truck that took us to a Junker-52 parked at the end of the runway. During the night the sky had become overcast; to the east, the cottony mass was clearing up. Some men were finishing loading small crates into the aircraft; the pilot had us climb in and showed us how to buckle down on a narrow seat. A thickset mechanic came and sat down opposite us; he flashed us a sardonic smile, then ignored us. Bursts of static and chatter came from the radio. The pilot slipped back out of the cockpit to check something in the rear, climbing over the pile of crates and bags tied down with cable mesh. "It is a good thing you're leaving today," he said as he returned. "The Reds are almost in Skassirskaya, just to the north. Soon we'll close up shop here."—"Are you going to evacuate the aerodrome?" I asked. He made a face and returned to his post. "You know our traditions, Hauptsturmführer," Hohenegg commented. "We'll only evacuate when everyone's gotten killed." One by one, the engines coughed and started up. A high throbbing sound filled the cabin; everything vibrated, the seat beneath me, the metal wall to my back; a monkey wrench left on the floor trembled. Slowly, the plane began to taxi to the runway, U-turned, picked up speed; the tail lifted; then the whole mass tore itself off the ground. Our bags, which hadn't been tied down, slipped to the back; Hohenegg fell against me. I looked out the window: we were lost in the fog and the clouds; I could barely see the engine. The vibrations penetrated my body in an unpleasant way. Then the plane climbed beyond the cloud cover and the sky was a metallic blue; the dawning sun stretched its cold light over the immense landscape of clouds, undulating with *balki* like the steppe. The air was biting, the cabin wall icy; I wrapped myself in my coat and huddled down. Hohenegg seemed to be sleeping, his hands in his pockets, his head leaning forward; the plane's vibrations and jolts disturbed me, I couldn't do the same. Finally the plane began its descent; skimming over the summit of clouds, it dove, and once again everything was gray and dark. Through the monotonous buzzing of the propellers

I thought I heard a muffled explosion, but I couldn't be sure. A few minutes later, the pilot shouted into the cabin: "Pitomnik!" I shook Hohenegg, who woke up without any surprise, and wiped the condensation off the window. We had just passed beneath the clouds and the white steppe, almost shapeless, stretched beneath the wing. In front, everything was drastically changed: brown craters spattered the snow in large dirty spots; heaps of scrapped metal lay in tangles, powdered with white. The plane was coming down quickly, but I still couldn't see the runway. Then it suddenly touched the ground, bounced, landed. The mechanic was already unbuckling his strap: "Quick, quick!" he shouted. I heard an explosion and a spray of snow struck the window and the wall of the cabin. I unbuckled frantically. The plane had slewed a little sideways and the mechanic opened the door and threw down the ladder. The pilot hadn't cut the engines. The mechanic took our bags, tossed them unceremoniously out the opening, then motioned to us energetically to get out. A howling wind, loaded with fine, hard snow, struck me in the face. Some bundled-up men were busy around the plane, setting blocks in place, opening the hold. I slid down the ladder and gathered up my kit. A Feldgendarm armed with a submachine gun saluted me and gestured for me to follow him; I shouted out, "Wait, wait!" Hohenegg was getting out. A shell burst in the snow a few dozen meters away, but no one seemed to pay any attention to it. At the end of the runway rose a mound of swept snow; a group of men was waiting there, guarded by several armed Feldgendarmen, their sinister metal plates hanging over the coats. Hohenegg and I, behind our escort, approached them; closer up, I saw that most of these men were bandaged or holding makeshift crutches; two of them were lying on stretchers; all of them had the tag of the wounded pinned visibly on their greatcoats. At a signal, they rushed toward the plane. Behind them was a melee: Feldgendarmen were blocking an opening in the barbed wire, beyond which a mass of haggard men were pushing each other; they were shouting, begging, waving bandaged limbs, pressing against the Feldgendarmen who were also shouting and brandishing their submachine guns. Another detonation, closer this time, made some snow rain down; several of the wounded had thrown themselves to the ground, but the Feldgendarmen remained unruffled; behind us there was shouting; some of the men who were unloading the plane seemed to have been hit, they lay on the ground and others were pulling them aside, the wounded who were being allowed to board were shoving each other to climb up the ladder, still other men were finishing unloading the plane and tossing bags and crates to the ground. The Feldgendarm accompanying us fired a brief volley into the air and then dove forward into the hysterical, imploring crowd, hitting out with his elbows; I followed him as well as I could, dragging Hohenegg behind me. Beyond were rows of tents covered with frost, the brown openings of bunkers; farther on, radio trucks were parked in a tight group, in the midst of a forest of poles, antennas, wires; at the end of the runway began a vast dumping ground of metal wrecks, planes that had been blown up or split in half, burned trucks, tanks, smashed vehicles piled on top of each other, half hidden beneath the snow. Some officers were coming toward us; we exchanged salutes. Two military doctors welcomed Hohenegg; my interlocutor was a young Leutnant from the Abwehr, who introduced himself and bade me welcome: "I have to look after you and find you a vehicle to take you into the city." Hohenegg was walking away: "Doktor!" I shook his hand. "We'll surely see each other again," he said kindly. "The *Kessel* isn't so big. When you're feeling sad, come find me and we'll drink my Cognac." I made a wide gesture with my hand: "In my opinion, Doktor, your Cognac won't last long." I followed the Leutnant. Near the tents I noticed a series of large heaps powdered with snow. From time to time, a muffled explosion would resound all through the aerodrome. Already the Junker that had brought us was slowly taxiing toward the end of the runway. I paused to watch it take off and the Leutnant watched with me. The wind was blowing quite hard, you had to blink your eyes so as not to be blinded by the fine snow raised from the surface of the ground. Having reached the far point, the plane swung round and, without pausing the slightest bit, accelerated. It swerved once, then again, dangerously close to the snowy embankment; then the wheels left the ground and it rose up groaning, swaying, with great juddering, before vanishing into the opaque cloud bank. I looked again at the snowy pile beside me and saw that it was made up of corpses, piled like logs to form long cords, their frozen faces the color of bronze gone slightly green, studded with dense beards, and with ice crystals at the corners of their mouths, in their nostrils, their eye sockets. There must have been hundreds of them. I asked the Leutnant: "You don't bury them?" He stamped his foot: "How are we supposed to bury them? The ground is hard as iron. We don't have any explosives to waste. We can't even dig trenches." We walked on; where traffic had made paths, the ground was slick, slippery; you had to walk to the side, through the snowdrifts. The Leutnant led me to a long low line covered with snow. I thought they were bunkers, but when I approached I saw that they were in fact half-buried train cars, their walls and roofs covered with sandbags, with steps dug into the ground leading to the doors. The Leutnant brought me in; inside, some officers were bustling about in the hallway; the train compartments had been transformed into offices; a few weak lightbulbs spread a dirty, yellowish light, and they must have had a stove going somewhere, it wasn't all that cold. The Leutnant invited me to sit down in a compartment, after clearing the seat of the papers piled on it. I noticed some Christmas decorations, coarsely cut out of colored paper, hanging in the window, behind which were piled up the earth and snow and the frozen sandbags. "Would you like some tea?" the Leutnant asked. "I can't offer you anything else." I accepted, and he went out. I took off my shapka and unfastened my coat, then collapsed into the seat. The Leutnant returned with two cups of ersatz and held one out to me; he drank his own standing in the entrance to the compartment. "Hard luck for you," he said timidly, "being sent here like this just before Christmas." I shrugged my shoulders and blew on my scalding tea: "Christmas doesn't mean that much to me, really."—"For us, here, it's very important." He gestured at the decorations. "The men are very attached to it. I hope the Reds will leave us in peace. But you can't count on it." I found this strange: Hoth, in principle, was advancing to make his junction; it seemed to me that the officers should have been in the process of preparing their retreat rather than getting ready for Christmas. The Leutnant looked at his watch: "Movements are strictly limited and we can't take you into the city right away. There will be a liaison this afternoon."—"Fine. Do you know where I have to go?" He looked surprised: "To the city Kommandantur, I guess. All the SP officers are there."—"I have to present myself to Feldpolizeikommissar Möritz."—"Yes, that's right." He hesitated: "Have some rest. I'll come and get you." He left. A little later, another officer came in, greeted me absently, and began vigorously working at a typewriter. I went into the hallway, but it was too crowded. I began to feel hungry; they hadn't offered me anything, and I didn't want to ask. I went to smoke a cigarette outside, you could hear the droning of the planes, some explosions from time to time, then I went back in to wait, in the monotonous clacking of the typewriter.

The Leutnant reappeared in midafternoon. I was famished. He pointed to my kit and said, "The liaison is about to leave." I followed him to an Opel equipped with chains and driven, strangely, by an officer. "Good luck," the Leutnant said, saluting me.—"Happy Christmas," I replied. Five of us had to pile into the car; with our coats, there was hardly any room and I felt as if I were suffocating. I leaned my head against the cold window and breathed onto it to defrost it. The car started up and left, jolting. The road, marked out by tactical signs nailed to posts, boards, and even to frozen horse legs, planted in the snow hoof-up, was slippery, and despite its chains, the Opel often skidded sideways; most of the time, the officer righted it adroitly, but sometimes

it got buried in the snowdrifts and then we had to get out and push to
free it. Pitomnik, I knew, was near the center of the *Kessel*, but the liaison wasn't going directly to Stalingrad; it followed a capricious route,
stopping off at various command posts; each time, officers got out of the
car and others took their places; the wind had risen and it was becoming a snowstorm: we advanced slowly, as if we were feeling our way
along. Finally the first ruins appeared, some brick chimneys, stumps of
walls standing along the road. Between two blasts of wind I glimpsed a
sign: ENTER STALINGRAD AT THE RISK OF DEATH. I turned to my neighbor: "Is that a joke?" He looked at me dully: "No. Why?" The road was
descending a kind of cliff, snaking back and forth; at the bottom, the ruins of the city began: huge shattered buildings, burned, with gaping,
blind windows. The roadway was strewn with debris, sometimes hastily
cleared away so vehicles could thread their way through. The bomb
craters hidden by the snow inflicted brutal jolts on the shock absorbers.
On all sides flowed a chaos of wrecked cars, trucks, tanks, German and
Russian intermingled, sometimes even embedded in each other. Here
and there we passed a patrol or, to my surprise, civilians in rags, women
especially, carrying buckets or bags. With a clanking of chains, the Opel
crossed a long bridge repaired with prefabricated sections, over a railroad: below, hundreds of motionless train cars stretched out, covered
with snow, intact or mangled by explosions. After the silence of the
steppe, pierced only by the noise of the engine, the chains, and the
wind, a constant racket reigned here, detonations more or less muffled,
the abrupt barking of the PAKs, the crackle of machine guns. After the
bridge, the car turned left, following the railroad and the abandoned
freight trains. To our right a long bare park, completely treeless,
emerged; beyond, more ruined buildings, dark, silent, their façades collapsed into the street, or else raised up against the sky like a stage set.
The road skirted round the train station, a large building from the
czarist era, once probably yellow and white; on the square, in front, a
confusion of burned vehicles, torn to pieces by direct impacts, lay piled
up, their twisted forms scarcely softened by the snow. The car set out on
a long diagonal avenue: the noise of the gunfire intensified; in front, I
could see puffs of black smoke but didn't have the slightest idea where
the front line could be. The avenue emerged onto an immense empty
square, full of debris, surrounding a kind of park marked out by street-
lights. The officer parked the car in front of a large building: at its corner, a peristyle in a half-circle with its columns riddled by gunfire,
surmounted by large bay windows, empty and black; at the top, a flag
with a swastika hung limply on a pole. "You're here," he said to me,
lighting a cigarette. I extracted myself from the car, opened the trunk,

and got out my kit. Some soldiers armed with submachine guns were standing under the peristyle but didn't come forward. As soon as I closed the trunk, the Opel started up again, executed a rapid U-turn, and headed back up the avenue toward the train station, in a noisy clang of chains. I looked at the desolate square: in the center, a circle of children made of stone or plaster, probably the remnants of a fountain, seemed to be mocking the ruins all around. When I went toward the peristyle, the soldiers saluted me but barred my way; I saw with surprise that they were all wearing the white armband of the Hiwis. One of them asked me in bad German for my papers, and I held out my paybook. He examined it, returned it to me with a salute, and gave a brief order, in Ukrainian, to one of his comrades. He signed for me to follow. I climbed the steps between the columns, broken glass and stucco crackling beneath my boots, and entered the dark building through a wide opening without any doors. Just beyond stood a row of pink plastic mannequins dressed in varied attire: women's dresses, blue work clothes, twill suits; the figures, some of their skulls smashed by bullets, were still smiling inanely, their hands raised or pointing in childish, unformed gestures. Behind them, in the darkness, stood shelves still full of household objects, shattered or overturned glass cases, counters covered with plaster and debris, display shelves of polka-dot dresses or bras. I followed the young Ukrainian through the aisles of this phantom store to a stairway guarded by two other Hiwis; on an order from my escort, they stood aside to let me pass. He led me down to a basement lit by the yellow, diffuse light of weak bulbs: hallways, rooms swarming with Wehrmacht officers and soldiers dressed in the most disparate uniforms, regulation coats, padded gray jackets, Russian greatcoats with German insignias. The farther in we went, the hotter, damper, heavier the air became; I was sweating profusely under my coat. We went down even more stairs, then crossed a large, high-ceilinged operations room lit by a chandelier overloaded with glass, with Louis XVI furniture and crystal glasses scattered among the maps and files; a crackling Mozart aria was emanating from a portable gramophone set on top of two crates of French wine. The officers were working in slippers, wearing casual slacks and even shorts; no one paid any attention to me. Beyond the room was another hallway, and I finally saw someone in an SS uniform: the Ukrainian left me there and the Untersturmführer led me to Möritz.

The Feldpolizeikommissar, a stocky bulldog with wire-rimmed glasses, wearing nothing more than a pair of pants with suspenders and a stained undershirt, welcomed me rather dryly: "It's about time. I've been requesting someone for three weeks now. Ah well, Heil Hitler." A heavy silver ring gleamed on his hand stretched almost to the level of the lightbulb hanging over his massive head. I recognized him vaguely: in Kiev, the Kommando worked closely with the Secret Feldpolizei; I must have crossed him in a hallway. "I received the assignment order just four days ago, Herr Kommissar. I couldn't come any faster."—"I'm not blaming you. It's those damn bureaucrats. Have a seat." I took off my *shuba* and my shapka, put them on my kit, and looked for a seat in the cluttered office. "As you know, I'm not an SS officer, and my group of the *Geheime Feldpolizei* is under the control of the AOK. But as a Kriminalrat of the Kripo, all branches of the police in the *Kessel* are under my command. It's a rather delicate arrangement, but we understand each other. The Feldgendarmen take care of the executive tasks, or else my Ukrainians do it. I used to have eight hundred in all, but there've been some losses. They're divided up between the two Kommandanturen, this one and another one south of the Tsaritsa. You are the only SD officer in the *Kessel*, so your jobs will be pretty varied. My Leiter IV will explain it all to you in detail. He'll also take care of your logistics problems. He's an SS-Sturmbannführer, so unless there's an emergency, you'll report to him and he'll summarize it for me. Good luck."

Coat and kit under my arm, I went back out into the hallway and found the Untersturmführer: "The Leiter IV, please?"—"This way." I followed him to a little room cluttered with desks, papers, crates, files, with candles stuck on every available surface. An officer raised his head: it was Thomas. "Well," he said happily, "it's about time." He got up, skirted round the table, and warmly shook my hand. I looked at him, speechless at first. Then I said: "But what are you doing here?" He spread his arms; as was his habit, he was impeccably turned out, freshly shaved, his hair combed with brilliantine, his tunic buttoned up to the neck, with all his decorations. "I volunteered, Max. What have you brought us to eat?" I opened my eyes wide: "To eat? Nothing, why?" His face took on a horrified expression: "You've just come from outside of Stalingrad and you haven't brought anything to eat? You should be ashamed. Didn't anyone explain to you the situation, here?" I bit my lip, I couldn't tell if he was joking: "Actually, it didn't occur to me. I told myself that the SS would have whatever they needed." He briskly sat back down and his voice took on a mocking tone: "Find yourself a free crate. You should know that the SS controls neither the planes nor what they bring. We receive everything from the AOK, and they distribute our rations to us at the standard rate, which is, right now"—he searched his desk and pulled out a piece of paper—"two hundred grams of meat, usually horse, per man per day, two hundred grams of bread, and twenty grams of margarine or fat. Needless to say," he went on as he put the paper down, "one could do with more."—"You don't look too badly off,"

I remarked. "Yes, well, fortunately, some people are more provident than you. And also our Ukrainian boys are pretty resourceful, especially if you don't ask them too many questions." I pulled some cigarettes out of my jacket pocket and lit one. "At least," I said, "I brought some smokes."—"Ah! You see, you're not such a simpleton. So, apparently you ran into some trouble with Bierkamp?"—"In a way, yes. A misunderstanding." Thomas leaned forward a little and shook a finger: "Max, I've been telling you for years now to tend to your relations. One day it'll end badly." I made a vague gesture toward the door: "You could say it's already ended badly. And also I should point out that you're here too."—"Here? It's fine here, aside from the grub. Afterward, there will be promotions, decorations, *e tutti quanti*. We'll be real heroes and we can parade our medals at the finest *soirées*. They'll even forget your little troubles."—"You seem to be omitting one detail: between you and your *soirées*, there are a few Soviet armies. *Der Manstein kommt*, but he hasn't arrived yet." Thomas made a scornful face: "You're a defeatist, as always. What's more, you're not well informed: *der Manstein* isn't coming anymore; he gave Hoth the order to retreat several hours ago. With the Italian front collapsing, they need him elsewhere. Otherwise we'll lose Rostov. In any case, even if he had reached us, there wouldn't have been an order to evacuate. And without orders, Paulus would never have budged. This whole business with Hoth, if you want my opinion, was just for show. So that Manstein could have a good conscience. And the Führer too, for that matter. All that's to say that I never counted on Hoth. Give me a cigarette." I handed him one and lit it for him. He exhaled for a long time and threw himself back on his chair: "The indispensable men, the specialists, will be evacuated just before the end. Möritz is on the list—me too, of course. Obviously, some will have to stay to the end to hold down the shop. That's called being out of luck. The same goes for our Ukrainians: they're screwed and they know it. It makes them mean, and they take their revenge in advance."—"You could get yourself killed first. Or even when you leave: I saw that quite a few planes weren't making it." He smiled widely: "That, my friend, is an occupational hazard. You can also get yourself run over by a car when you're crossing Prinz-Albrechtstrasse."—"I'm happy to see you've lost none of your cynicism."—"My dear Max, I've explained to you a hundred times that National Socialism is a jungle that functions according to strictly Darwinian principles. It's the survival of the fittest or the cleverest. But you never want to recognize that."—"Let's just say that I have a different vision of things."—"Yes, and look at the result: you're in Stalingrad."—"And you really asked to come here?"—"Before the encirclement, of course. Things didn't seem to be going so badly in the beginning. And at the Group, it was getting rather dull. I had no desire to wake up as a KdS in some godforsaken hole in the Ukraine. Stalingrad offered interesting possibilities. And if I get out, it will have been worth it. Otherwise . . ." he laughed out loud. *"C'est la vie."*—"Your optimism is admirable. And what about my own prospects?"—"You? That might be a little more complicated. If they sent you here, it's because they don't think you're indispensable: you'll agree with me on that. So for a place on the evacuation lists, I'll see what I can do, but I can't guarantee anything. Otherwise, you can always get yourself a *Heimatschuss*. Then we could manage to ship you out on priority. But be careful! Don't get wounded too seriously; they only repatriate the ones who can be patched up to serve again. Speaking of which, we're beginning to have quite a lot of experience with self-inflicted wounds. You should see what the guys invent, sometimes they're very ingenious. Since the end of November, we've been shooting more of our own men than Russians. *To encourage the others*, as Voltaire once said about Admiral Byng."—"But you're not suggesting . . ." Thomas waved his hands: "No, no! Don't be so gullible. I was just saying that because we were on the subject. Have you eaten?" I hadn't thought about it since I had arrived in the city; my stomach grumbled. Thomas laughed. "Actually, not since this morning. In Pitomnik, they didn't offer me anything."—"People are losing all sense of hospitality. Come, let's go put your things away. I had you bunk in my room, so I can keep an eye on you."

Once I had eaten, I felt better. While I was swallowing a kind of broth in which vague scraps of meat were floating, Thomas had explained the gist of my duties: collecting gossip, rumors, and *Latrinen-parolen* and reporting on the soldiers' morale; fighting Russian defeatist propaganda; and maintaining a few informers, civilians, often children, who slipped from one line to the other. "It's something of a double-edged sword," he said, "because they give the Russians as much information as they report to us. And also they often lie. But sometimes they're useful." In our quarters, a narrow room furnished with a metal bunk bed and an empty ammunition crate with an enamel basin and a cracked mirror to shave with, he had brought me a reversible winter uniform, a typical product of German ingenuity, white on one side, *feld-grau* on the other. "Take that for your sorties," he said. "Your coat is fine for the steppe; in town it's much too heavy."—"Can we go out?"—"You'll have to. But I'll give you a guide." He led me to a guard room where some Ukrainian auxiliaries were playing cards and drinking tea. "Ivan Vassilievitch!" Three men raised their heads; Thomas pointed to one, who came out and joined us in the hallway. "This is Ivan. He's one of my best. He'll take care of you." He turned to him and explained something to him in Russian. Ivan, a young, blond, rather slim youth with prominent cheekbones, listened to him attentively. Thomas turned back to me: "Ivan isn't an ace at discipline, but he knows every nook and cranny of this city and he's very trustworthy. Never go out without him, and outside, do anything he tells you, even if you don't see why. He speaks a little German, you'll be able to understand each other. *Capisce?* I told him that he was now your personal bodyguard and that he would have to answer for your life." Ivan saluted me and went back into the room. I felt exhausted. "Go on, go to sleep," Thomas said. "Tomorrow night, we're celebrating Christmas."

My first night in Stalingrad, I still remember, I had another metro dream. It was a station with many levels, but they communicated with each other, a huge labyrinth of steel beams, footbridges, steep metal ladders, spiral staircases. The trains arrived at the platforms and left them in a deafening racket. I didn't have a ticket and I was terrified of being checked by the station police. I went down a few levels and slipped into a train that was leaving the station and then dive-bombed almost vertically on its tracks; below, it slowed down, reversed its direction and, passing by the platform again without stopping, plunged in the other direction, into a vast abyss of light and harsh noise. When I awoke, I felt drained; I had to make an immense effort to wash my face and shave. My skin itched; I hoped I wasn't catching lice. I spent a few hours studying a map of the city and some files; Thomas helped me orient myself: "The Russians are still holding a thin strip along the river. They were surrounded, especially when the river was carrying ice floes and wasn't completely frozen; now it doesn't matter if they have their backs to the river; they're the ones surrounding us. Here, above, is Red Square; last month, we finally managed, a little farther down, there, to cut their front in half, and so we have a foot on the Volga, here at the level of their old landing area. If we had ammunition we could almost prevent them from getting supplies, but we can really only shoot in case of attack, and they come and go as they please, even in daytime, on ice roads. All their logistics, their hospitals, their artillery, is on the other bank. From time to time we send them a few Stukas, but that's just to tease them. Near here, they've hung on to a few blocks along the river, then they hold the whole big refinery, up to the foot of Hill 102, which is an old Tatar kurgan we've taken and lost dozens of times. The One Hundredth Jägerdivision holds this sector—Austrians, with a Croat regiment. Behind the refinery, there are some cliffs that lead to the river, and the Russians have a whole underground network inside them, untouchable since our shells pass right over them. We tried to liquidate it by blowing up the oil tanks, but they rebuilt everything as soon as the fires went out. Farther on, they also hold a large section of the Lazur chemical factory, with the whole zone we call the "Tennis Racket," because of the shape of the tracks. Farther north, most of the factories are ours, except a sector of the Red October foundry. From there on we're on the river, up to Spartakovka, the northern limit of the *Kessel*. The city itself is held by General Seydlitz's LIST Corps; but the factories sector belongs to the Eleventh Corps. To the south, it's the same thing: the Reds hold just a strip, about a hundred meters wide. It's those hundred meters we never managed to reduce. The city is more or less cut in half by the Tsaritsa ravine; we've inherited a fine underground complex dug into the cliffs, and that has become our main hospital. Behind the train station, there's a Stalag, administered by the Wehrmacht; we have a little KL in the Vertyashyi kolkhoz, for the civilians we arrest and don't execute right away. What else? There are brothels in the basements, but you'll find those on your own, if you're interested. Ivan knows them well. That said, the girls are mostly covered in lice."—"Speaking of lice . . ."—"Oh, you'll have to get used to them. Look." He unfastened his tunic, slipped his hand inside, searched, and pulled it out: it was full of little gray creatures, which he threw on the stove where they began to crackle. Thomas continued calmly: "We have huge fuel problems. Schmidt, the Chief of Staff—the one who replaced Heim, you remember?—Schmidt controls all the reserves, even our own, and he dispenses it in dribs and drabs. Anyway, you'll see: Schmidt controls everything here. Paulus is just a marionette. The result is that moving around by car is forbidden. Between Hill 102 and the south station, we do everything on foot; to go farther, you have to hitch a ride with the Wehrmacht. They have pretty regular liaisons between the sectors." There was still a lot to absorb, but Thomas was patient. Midmorning, we learned that Tatsinskaya had fallen at dawn; the Luftwaffe had waited till the Russian tanks were at the edge of the runway to evacuate, and had lost 72 aircraft, almost 10 percent of their transport fleet. Thomas had shown me the supply figures: they were catastrophic. The previous Saturday, December 19, 154 planes had been able to land with 289 tons; but there were also days with only 15 or 20 tons; AOK 6, at the beginning, had demanded 700 tons per day, at a minimum, and Göring had promised 500. "As for that one," Möritz commented dryly during the meeting when he announced to his officers the news of the loss of Tatsinskaya, "a few weeks' diet in the *Kessel* would do him good." The Luftwaffe planned to move to Salsk, 300 kilometers away from the *Kessel*, the maximum range of the Ju–52s. That promised a merry Christmas.

Near the end of the morning, after a soup and some dry biscuits, I said to myself, All right, time to start work. But where to start? With troop morale? Why not then, troop morale. I could well guess it wasn't going to be good, but it was my duty to verify my opinions. Studying the morale of the Wehrmacht soldiers meant going out; I didn't think Möritz wanted a report on the morale of our Ukrainian Askaris, the only soldiers I had within reach. The idea of leaving the entirely relative security of the bunker worried me, but I had to do it. And also, I did have to see this city. Maybe I would get used to it and things would go better. As I was putting on my new outfit, I hesitated; I decided on the gray side, but saw from Ivan's face that I had made a mistake. "It's snowing today. Wear the white side out." I ignored the inappropriate informality of the *du* form of address and went back to change. I also took a helmet; Thomas had insisted on it: "You'll see, it's very useful." Ivan handed me a submachine gun; I dubiously contemplated the mechanism, unsure if I knew how to use it, but slung it over my shoulder nonetheless. Outside, a violent wind was still blowing, carrying with it large swirls of snowflakes: from the entrance of the Univermag, you couldn't even see the fountain with the children. After the stifling dampness of the bunker, the cold, sharp air invigorated me. *"Kuda?"* Ivan asked. I had no idea. "To the Croats," I said at random; Thomas, that morning, had mentioned some Croats. "Is it far?" Ivan grunted and turned right, down a long street that seemed to head toward the train station. The city seemed relatively calm; from time to time, a muffled explosion resounded through the snow, and even that made me nervous; I unhesitatingly copied Ivan, who walked right next to the buildings, I clung to the walls. I felt terrifyingly naked, vulnerable, like a crab that's left its shell; I realized keenly that for all the eighteen months I had been in Russia, this was the first time I was actually *under fire*; and an unpleasant sense of dread made my limbs heavy and numbed my thoughts. I have spoken before about fear: what I felt then I won't call fear, or else not an honest, conscious fear, but rather an almost physical discomfort, like an itch that you can't scratch, concentrated on the blind parts of the body—the nape of the neck, the back, the buttocks. To try to distract myself, I looked at the buildings on the other side of the street. Many façades had collapsed, revealing the interior of the apartments, a series of dioramas of everyday life, powdered with snow and sometimes odd: on the third floor, a bicycle hanging on the wall; on the fourth, flowered wallpaper, an intact mirror, and a framed reproduction of Kramskoy's haughty *Unknown Woman*; on the fifth, a green sofa with a corpse lying on it, its feminine hand dangling in the void. A shell, hitting the roof of a building, broke this illusion of peacefulness: I hunched

over and understood why Thomas had insisted on the helmet: I was hit
by a rain of debris, fragments of roof tiles and bricks. When I raised my
head I saw that Ivan hadn't even leaned over, he had just covered his
eyes with his hand. "Come on," he said, "it's nothing." I calculated the
direction of the river and of the front and understood that the buildings
we were walking alongside were partly protecting us: for the shells to
fall in this street, they had to pass over the roofs; it wasn't very likely
they'd burst on the ground. But this thought didn't do much to reassure
me. The street led to some ruined outbuildings and railway warehouses;
Ivan, in front of me, crossed the long square at a trot, and slipped into
one of the warehouses through a metal door rolled up on itself like the
lid of a sardine can. I hesitated, then followed him. Inside, I threaded my
way through mountains of crates long ago plundered, skirted round a
section of collapsed roof, and emerged into the open through a hole in
a brick wall, where there were many traces of footprints in the snow.
The path ran alongside the walls of the warehouses; on the slope overhanging the path stretched the freight train cars that I had seen the day
before from the bridge, their sides riddled with bullet holes and shrapnel strikes and covered with Russian and German graffiti, ranging from
the comic to the obscene. An excellent color caricature showed Stalin
and Hitler fornicating while Roosevelt and Churchill jacked off around
them: but I couldn't decide who had painted it, one of ours or one of
theirs, and so it was not very useful for my report. A little farther on, a
patrol coming from the opposite direction passed us without a word,
without a salute. The men's faces were haggard, sallow, scraggly with
beards; they kept their fists shoved into their pockets, and dragged along
in boots wrapped with rags or enveloped in enormous cumbersome galoshes made of braided straw. They disappeared behind us into the snow.
Here and there, in a train car or on the rails, appeared a frozen corpse,
its uniform an indistinguishable color. We heard no more explosions
and everything seemed calm. Then in front of us it started up again: detonations, gunshots, or machine-gun volleys. We had passed the last
warehouses and crossed another residential zone: the landscape opened
up onto a snowy terrain dominated, on the left, by an enormous round
hillock like a little volcano, its summit periodically spitting out black
smoke from explosions. "Mamaev Kurgan," Ivan pointed, before turning left and entering a building.
    A few soldiers were sitting in empty rooms, leaning against the wall,
their knees pulled up to their chests. They looked at us with empty eyes.
Ivan led me through several buildings, passing through inner courtyards
or alleyways; then, since we were probably by now far enough from the
lines, he continued down a street. The buildings here were low, two

stories at most, perhaps workers' dormitories; then came smashed
houses, collapsed, ruined, but still more recognizable than the ones I had
seen entering the city. Occasionally a movement or a sound indicated
that some of these ruins were still inhabited. The wind continued blowing; now I could hear the roar of detonations on the kurgan, which was
outlined on our right, behind the houses. Ivan led me through some
small gardens, recognizable beneath the snow from the debris of fences
or railings. The place looked deserted, but the path we were following
was well used, footsteps had cleared away the snow. Then he dove into
a *balka*, sliding down the slope. The kurgan disappeared from sight; at
the far end, the wind blew less strongly, the snow fell gently, and suddenly things became animated; two Feldgendarmen barred our way; behind them soldiers were coming and going. I presented my papers to
the Feldgendarmen, who saluted me and stepped aside to let us pass; and
then I saw that the eastern side of the *balka*, its back to the kurgan and
the front, was riddled with bunkers, dark tunnels propped up by beams
or boards from which emerged little smoking chimneys made of tin cans
stuck to each other. The men entered and left this troglodyte city on
their knees, often backward. At the end of the ravine, on a wooden
block, two soldiers were cutting up a frozen horse with an axe; the
pieces, chopped at random, were thrown into a pot where some water
was heating. After about twenty minutes the path joined up with another *balka* that housed similar bunkers; in places rudimentary trenches
rose toward the kurgan we were skirting; here and there, a tank buried
up to its turret served as a fixed artillery piece. Russian shells occasionally fell around these ravines, sending up immense sprays of snow; I
could hear them whistling, a piercing, nerve-shattering, gut-wrenching
sound; each time I had to resist the impulse to throw myself to the
ground, and forced myself to follow the example of Ivan, who haughtily ignored them. After a while I managed to regain confidence: I let
myself be invaded by the feeling that everything here was a vast children's game, a huge adventure playground of the sort you dream about
when you're eight or nine, with sound effects, special effects, secret passages, and I was almost laughing with pleasure, caught up as I was in this
idea that brought me back to my earliest games, when Ivan dove onto
me without warning and pinned me to the ground. A deafening explosion tore the world apart, it was so close that I could feel the air slamming onto my eardrums, and a rain of mixed snow and earth fell onto
us. I tried to curl up, but already Ivan was pulling me by the shoulder
and lifting me up: thirty meters away, black smoke was lazily rising from
the ground of the *balka*, the raised dust slowly settled onto the snow, an
acrid smell of cordite filled the air. My heart was pounding wildly, I felt

such an intense heaviness in my thighs that it was painful, I wanted to
sit back down, like a mass. But Ivan didn't seem to be taking it seriously;
he was carefully brushing off his uniform. Then he had me turn my
back to him and he vigorously brushed it while I shook off my sleeves.
We continued on our way. I began to find this episode idiotic: What was
I doing there, after all? I seemed to have trouble grasping the fact that I
was no longer in Pyatigorsk. Our road emerged from the *balki*: then a
long empty unkempt plateau began, dominated by the rear side the kurgan. The frequency of the detonations at the summit, which I knew to
be occupied by our troops, fascinated me: How was it possible for men
to stay there, to undergo that rain of fire and metal? I was a kilometer
or two away from it, yet it scared me. Our path snaked between
mounds of snow that the wind, here and there, had eroded to reveal a
cannon pointing to the sky, the twisted door of a truck, the wheels of
an overturned car. In front of us we joined up again with the railroad
tracks, empty this time, disappearing in the distance into the steppe.
They led out from behind the kurgan, and I was seized by the irrational
terror of seeing a column of T-34s suddenly appear along the tracks.
Then another ravine cut through the plateau and I hurtled down its side
following Ivan, as if I were diving into the warm security of a childhood
house. Here too were bunkers, petrified and scared soldiers. I could
have stopped anywhere, talked to the men and then gone back, but I
docilely followed Ivan, as if he knew what I had to do. Finally we
emerged from this long *balka*: once again a residential zone stretched
out; but the houses were razed, burned to the ground, even the chimneys had collapsed. Ruined military gear cluttered up the narrow
streets, tanks, assault vehicles, Soviet artillery, German too. Carcasses of
horses lay in absurd positions, sometimes tangled in the harnesses of
carts volatilized like straw; under the snow, you could still make out
corpses, also often surprised in curious contortions, fixed in place by the
cold until the next thaw. From time to time a patrol passed us; there
were also checkpoints, where Feldgendarmen a little better off than the
soldiers went through our papers before letting us pass into the next sector. Ivan started up a wider street; a woman came toward us, hunched
into two coats and a scarf, a small nearly empty bag on her shoulder. I
looked at her face: impossible to say if she was twenty or fifty. Farther
on, a fallen bridge lay collapsed on the bed of a deep ravine; to the east,
near the river, another bridge, very high up, surprisingly intact, spanned
the mouth of this same ravine. We had to descend here by clinging to
debris and then, skirting round or scaling the pieces of smashed concrete, climb back up the other side. A Feldgendarm post stood in a shelter formed by a piece of broken roadway. *"Khorvati?"* Ivan asked them.

"The Croats?" The Feldgendarm directed us; it wasn't much farther away. We entered another residential neighborhood: everywhere, you could see former gun emplacements with red signs, ACHTUNG! MINEN, the remnants of barbed wire, trenches half filled with snow between buildings; this had once been a frontline sector. Ivan led me through a series of alleyways, sticking to the walls again; at a corner, he motioned with his hand: "Who do you want to see?" It was hard for me to get used to his use of the familiar *du*. "I don't know. An officer."—"Wait." He entered a building, a little farther on, from which he emerged with a soldier who pointed out to him something in the street. He gestured to me and I joined him. Ivan raised his arm toward the river, from which the punctual noise of mortars and machine guns came: "There, *Krasnyi Oktyabr. Russki.*" We had come a long way: now we were near one of the last factories held in part by the Soviets, beyond the kurgan and the "Tennis Racket." The buildings must have been collective workers' lodgings. Having reached one of these barracks, Ivan went up the three front steps and exchanged a few words with a soldier on guard. The soldier saluted me, and I went into the hallway. All the rooms were dark, their windows roughly blocked with boards, piled-up bricks, and blankets; each room sheltered a group of soldiers. Most of them were sleeping, close to each other, sometimes with several under one blanket. Their breaths formed little clouds of condensation. A horrible odor filled the place, a stench made of all the secretions of the human body, with urine and the sweetish smell of diarrhea dominating. In one long room, probably the former canteen, many men were crammed around a stove. Ivan pointed out an officer sitting on a little bench; like the others, he had the red-and-white checkerboard pattern on the arm of his German *feldgrau*. Several of these men knew Ivan: they conversed in a kind of lingua franca made up of Ukrainian and Croat, peppered with the crudest words (*pitchka, pizda, pizdets*, these are common to all Slavic languages, and one learns them very quickly). I headed toward the officer, who got up to salute me. "Do you speak German?" I asked him after clicking my heels and raising my arm.—"Yes, yes." He looked at me with curiosity; my new uniform didn't have any distinctive markings on it. I introduced myself. Behind him, on the wall, they had stuck some meager Christmas decorations: garlands made from newspaper around a tree sketched in coal on the wall, stars cut out of tin, and other products of the soldiers' ingenuity. There was also a large, handsome drawing of the Bethlehem crèche: but instead of a manger, the scene was represented in a destroyed house, in the midst of burned ruins. I sat down with the officer. He was a young Oberleutnant; he commanded one of the companies of this Croatian unit, the 369th Infantry Regiment: some of his men were standing guard at a sector on the front, before the Red October factory; others were resting here. The Russians had remained relatively calm for the past few days; from time to time they lobbed a few rounds of mortar fire, but the Croats thought it was mainly to annoy them. They had also set up loudspeakers opposite the trenches and played sad, or happy, music throughout the day, interrupted with propaganda encouraging the soldiers to desert or surrender. "The men don't pay too much attention to the propaganda, because they used a Serb to record it; but the music really depresses them." I asked him about attempts at desertion. He replied rather vaguely: "It happens . . . but we do everything to prevent them." He was much more talkative about the Christmas celebration they were preparing; the commander of the division, an Austrian, had promised them extra rations; he himself had managed to save a bottle of lozavitsa, distilled by his father, which he planned on sharing with his men. But more than anything he wanted news of von Manstein. "He's coming, then?" The failure of Hoth's offensive had of course not been announced to the troops, and it was my turn to be vague: "Be ready," I answered lamely. This young officer must once have been an elegant, agreeable man; now he seemed as pathetic as a beaten dog. He spoke slowly and chose his words carefully, as if he were thinking in slow motion. We discussed the food supply problems a little more, then I got up to leave. Once again, I wondered what I was doing there: What could this officer, cut off from everything, teach me that I hadn't already read in some report? True, I could see for myself the miserable condition of the men, their fatigue, their distress, but that, too, I already knew. I had vaguely thought, on my way there, about a discussion on the political involvement of the Croat soldiers with Germany, on Ustashi ideology: now I understood there was no sense in that; it was worse than futile, and this Oberleutnant would probably not have known how to respond; in his head there was room only for food, his home, his family, captivity, or his imminent death. All of a sudden I was tired and disgusted, I felt hypocritical, idiotic. "Merry Christmas," the officer said to me as he shook my hand, smiling. A few of his men looked at me, without the slightest glint of curiosity. "Merry Christmas to you too," I forced myself to reply. I collected Ivan and went out, greedily breathing in the cold air. "And now?" Ivan asked. I thought: if I had come as far as this, I said to myself, I should at least go see one of the outposts. "Can we go up to the front?" Ivan shrugged his shoulders: "If you want to, boss. But we have to ask the officer." I went back into the large room: the officer hadn't moved; he was still absently staring at the stove. "Oberleutnant? Could I inspect one of your advanced positions?"—"If you like." He called one of his men and gave him an order in Croatian. Then he said to me: "This is Oberfeldwebel Nišić. He'll be your guide." Suddenly it occurred to me to offer him a cigarette: his face lit up and he slowly stretched out his hand to take one. I shook the packet: "Take more."— "Thank you, thank you. Merry Christmas again." I also offered one to the Oberfeldwebel, who said, *"Hvala,"* and carefully stowed it away in a case. I looked once more at the young officer: he was still holding his three cigarettes, his face radiant as a child's. How long, I wondered, before I was like him? The thought made me want to cry. I went back out with the Oberfeldwebel, who led us first down the street, then through some courtyards and inside a warehouse. We must have been on the grounds of the factory; I hadn't seen a wall, but everything was in such a shambles you often couldn't recognize anything. The warehouse floor was furrowed by a trench into which the Oberfeldwebel made us climb. The wall, opposite, was pockmarked with holes; light and snow poured with murky brightness into this large empty space; smaller trenches branched off the central trench toward the corners of the warehouse; they weren't straight, and I couldn't see anyone there. We passed in single file under the warehouse wall: the trench crossed a courtyard and disappeared into the ruins of a red brick administrative building. Nišić and Ivan walked bent over, their backs beneath the rim of the trench, and I carefully copied them. In front of us, everything was strangely silent; farther on, to our right, we heard brief volleys, gunshots. Inside the administrative building it was dark, and it stank even more than the house where the soldiers were sleeping. "We're here," Nišić said calmly. We were in a basement, the only light coming from little slits or holes in the brick. A man appeared out of the darkness and spoke to Nišić in Croatian. "They had a skirmish. A few Russians tried to infiltrate. They killed some of them," Nišić translated into rough German. He coolly explained their setup: where the mortar was, where the MG was, where the little machine guns were, what range of fire was covered, where the blind spots were. I wasn't interested in any of that, but I let him talk; in any case I didn't really know what I was interested in. "What about their propaganda?" I asked. Nišić spoke to the soldier: "After the fight they stopped." We were silent for a bit. "Can I see their lines?" I finally asked, probably to give the impression I had come for something. "Follow me." I crossed the basement and climbed a staircase littered with plaster and brick fragments. Ivan, submachine gun under his arm, brought up the rear. On the landing, a corridor led us to a room, in the back. All the windows were blocked by bricks and boards, but the light filtered through thousands of holes. In the last room, two soldiers were leaning against the wall with an MG. Nišić pointed out a hole surrounded by sandbags held up by boards. "You can look from there. But not for too long. Their snipers are very good. They're women, apparently." I knelt near the hole and then slowly stretched up my head; the slit was narrow, I could just see a landscape of shapeless, almost abstract ruins. Then I heard the scream, on the left: a long hoarse cry, suddenly interrupted. Then the scream began again. There was no other noise and I heard it very clearly. It came from a young man, and they were long piercing cries, terrifyingly hollow; he must have been shot in the belly. I leaned forward and looked sideways: I could see his head and part of his torso. He screamed until he was breathless, stopped to breathe in, then began again. Without knowing Russian, I understood what he was shouting: *"Mama! Mama!"* I couldn't stand it. "What is it?" I stupidly asked Nišić.—"He's one of the guys from before."—"Couldn't you finish him off?" Nišić stared at me with a hard look, full of contempt: "We don't have ammunition to waste," he spat. I sat against the wall, like the soldiers. Ivan was leaning on the doorjamb. No one spoke. Out there, the boy was still screaming: *"Mama! Ya ne khachu! Ya ne khachu! Mama! Ya khachu domoi!"* and other words that I couldn't make out. I squatted down and wrapped my arms around my knees. Nišić, squatting, kept looking straight at me. I wanted to block my ears, but his leaden stare petrified me. The kid's shouts were boring into my brain, a trowel burrowing in thick, sticky mud, full of worms and messy life. I wondered, would I too beg for my mother, when the time came? The idea of that woman filled me with hatred and disgust. It had been years since I last saw her, and I didn't want to see her; the idea of invoking her name, her help, seemed inconceivable to me. Still, somehow I wondered if behind that mother there was not another one, the mother of the child I had been before something was irremediably broken. I too would probably writhe and cry out for that mother. And if not for her, it would be for her womb, the one from before the light, the diseased, sordid, sick light of day. "You shouldn't have come here," Nišić suddenly said. "There's no point. And it's dangerous. There are often accidents." He stared at me with an openly angry look. He was holding his submachine gun by the grip, finger on the trigger. I looked at Ivan: he was holding his weapon in the same way, pointed toward Nišić and the two soldiers. Nišić followed my gaze, examined Ivan's weapon, his face, and spat on the ground: "You'd better head back." An abrupt detonation made me jump, a little explosion, probably a grenade. The screams stopped for a bit, then began again, monotonous, nerve-shattering. I got up: "Yes. Anyway I have to go back to the center. It's getting late." Ivan stepped aside to let us pass and followed close behind, keeping an eye on the two soldiers until he was in the corridor. We left by the same trench, without a word; at the house where his company was staying, Nišić left me without saluting me. It had stopped snowing and the sky was clearing up, I could see the moon, white and swollen in the sky, which was quickly darkening. "Can we go back by night?" I asked Ivan. "Yes. It's actually faster. An hour and a half." We probably could take some shortcuts. I felt drained, old, out of place. The Oberfeldwebel had been right, in fact.

As we walked, the thought of my mother returned to me violently, rushing, barging about my head like a drunken woman. For a long time, I had not had such thoughts. When I spoke about it to Partenau, in the Crimea, I had stuck to the facts, the ones that counted least. Here it was another order of thoughts, bitter, full of hate, tinged with shame. When had that begun? When I was born? Was it possible that I had never forgiven her for the fact of my birth, that insanely arrogant right she had granted herself to bring me into the world? One strange fact: I had turned out to be acutely allergic to her breast milk; as she herself had told me much later on, off handedly, I was allowed only baby bottles, and I watched my twin sister breastfeed with a look full of bitterness. But in my early childhood I must have loved her, as all children love their mothers. I still remember the tender, female odor of her bathroom, which plunged me into numb delight, like a return to the lost womb: it must have been, if I thought about it, a mixture of the humid vapor of the bath, of perfumes, soaps, maybe too the smell of her sex and maybe too that of her shit; even when she didn't let me get into the bath with her, I never got enough of sitting on the edge of the tub, near her, blissfully. Then everything had changed. But when, exactly, and why? I hadn't blamed it right away on the disappearance of my father: that idea didn't come till later on, when she prostituted herself to that Moreau. But even before meeting him, she had begun to behave in ways that sent me into a wild rage. Was it my father's departure? It's hard to say, but the pain seemed sometimes to drive her mad. One night, in Kiel, she had gone all alone into a worker's café, near the docks, and had gotten drunk, surrounded by foreigners, dock workers, sailors. It's even possible that she sat down on a table and lifted her skirt, exposing her sex. Whatever the case, things got scandalously out of hand, till the *lady* got thrown out into the street, where she fell into a puddle. A policeman brought her home, soaking, disheveled, her dress filthy; I thought I would die of shame. Little as I was—I must have been about ten—I wanted to beat her, and she wouldn't even have been able to defend herself, but my sister intervened: "Have pity on her. She's sad. She doesn't deserve your anger." I took a long time to calm down. But even then I must not have hated her, not yet; I was just humiliated. The hatred must have come later, when she forgot her husband and sacrificed her children to give herself to a stranger. Of course that didn't happen in one day, there were several stages on the way. Moreau, as I've said, was not a bad man, and in the beginning he made great efforts to be accepted by us; but he was a narrow-minded fellow, a prisoner of his coarse bourgeois, capitalist concepts, slave to his desire for my mother, who soon turned out to be more masculine than he; thus, he willingly became an accomplice to her erring ways. Then there was that great catastrophe, after which I was sent away to boarding school; there were also more traditional conflicts, like the one that broke out when I was finishing high school. I was about to pass my baccalauréat, I had to make a decision about what to do afterward; I wanted to study philosophy and literature, but my mother firmly refused: "You have to have a profession. Do you think we'll always live on the kindness of others? Afterward, you can do what you like." And Moreau said mockingly: "What? Teacher in some godforsaken village for ten years? A two-cent, half-starved hack? You're no Rousseau, my boy, come back to earth." God how I hated them. "You have to have a career," Moreau said. "Afterward, if you want to write poems in your spare time, that's your business. But at least you'll earn enough to feed your family." That lasted for more than a week; running away wouldn't have done any good, I would have been caught, as when I had tried to run away before. I had to give in. Both of them decided on enrolling me in the *École libre des sciences politiques*, from which I could have entered one of the major government branches: *Conseil d'État*, the accounts court, the *Inspection générale des finances*. I would be a civil servant, a mandarin: a member, they hoped, of the elite. "It will not be easy," Moreau explained to me, "you'll have to work hard"; but he had connections in Paris, he would help me. Ah, things didn't happen as they wished and hoped: the mandarins of France now were serving my country; and I had ended up here, in the frozen ruins of Stalingrad, and probably for good. My sister had more luck: she was a girl, and what she wished didn't count as much; just finishing touches, to appeal to her future husband. They allowed her to go freely to Zurich to study psychology with a certain Dr. Carl Jung, who has become quite well-known since then.

The worst had already happened. Around the spring of 1929, I was still in boarding school when I received a letter from my mother. She announced that since there had never been any news from him, and since her repeated inquiries at various German consulates had yielded nothing, she had filed a request for my father to be declared legally dead. Seven years had gone by since his disappearance, and the court had issued the decision she had hoped for; now she was going to marry

Moreau, a good, generous man who was like a father to us. This odious letter threw me into a paroxysm of rage. I sent her a letter full of violent insults: My father, I wrote, was not dead, and the profound desire they both had of it would not be enough to kill him. If she wanted to sell herself to a despicable little French shopkeeper, that was entirely up to her; as for me, I would regard their marriage as illegitimate and bigamous. I hoped at least that they wouldn't try to inflict on me a bastard whom I could only detest. My mother, wisely, did not answer this philippic. That summer, I arranged to have myself invited by the parents of a rich friend, and so didn't set foot in Antibes. They got married in August; I tore up the invitation and flushed it down the toilet; the following school vacation, I still persisted in not going back; finally they managed to get me to return, but that's another story. In the meantime, my hatred was there, intact, full-fledged, something whole and almost succulent inside me, a pyre waiting for a match. But to avenge myself I only knew low, shameful means: I had kept a photo of my mother; I jacked off or sucked my lovers in front of it and made them ejaculate onto it. I did worse than that. In Moreau's large house, I gave myself over to baroque, fantastically elaborate erotic games. Inspired by the Martian novels of E. R. Burroughs (the author of the *Tarzan* of my childhood), which I devoured with the same passion as the Greek classics, I locked myself up in the large upstairs bathroom, running the water so as not to attract attention, and created extravagant scenes from my imaginary world. Captured by an army of four-armed green men from Barsoom, I was stripped naked, bound, and led before a superb copper-skinned Martian princess, haughty and impassive on her throne. There, using a belt for the leather bonds and with a broom or a bottle stuck in my anus, I writhed on the cold tiles while half a dozen of her massive, mute bodyguards took turns raping me in front of her. But brooms or bottles could hurt: I looked for something more suitable. Moreau loved thick German sausages; at night, I took one from the fridge, rolled it between my hands to warm it up, lubricated it with olive oil; afterward, I washed it carefully, dried it, and put it back where I had found it. The next day I watched Moreau and my mother slicing it up and eating it with great pleasure, and I refused my portion with a smile, offering a lack of appetite as my excuse, delighted at going hungry so I could watch them eat. It's true that this happened before their wedding, when I still regularly visited their house. So it wasn't their marriage in itself that bothered me. But these were just the miserable, pitiful acts of revenge of a powerless child. Later on, after I came of age, I turned away from them, left for Germany, and stopped answering my mother's letters. But the story went on, secretly, and it just needed a trifle, the cries of a dying man, for everything to come back all at once, since it had always existed, it came from elsewhere, from a world that was not the world of men and of everyday work, a world that was usually sealed but whose doors the war could suddenly throw open, freeing in a hoarse, inarticulate, brutal shout its gaping darkness, a pestilential swamp, overturning the established order of things, customs and laws, forcing men to kill each other, putting them back under the yoke from which they had with so much difficulty liberated themselves, the weight of all that came before. We were once again following the tracks along the abandoned train cars: lost in my thoughts, I had scarcely noticed the long walk around the kurgan. The hard snow, which crackled beneath my boots, was taking on bluish tints beneath the pallid moon that lit up our path. Another fifteen minutes and we were back at the Univermag; I felt quite fresh, reinvigorated by the walk. Ivan saluted me casually and left to join his compatriots, taking my submachine gun with him. In the large operations room, beneath the enormous chandelier salvaged from a theater, the officers of the Stadtkommandantur were drinking and singing in chorus "O Du fröhliche" and "Stille Nacht, heilige Nacht." One of them handed me a glass of red wine; I drained it in one swallow, even though it was good French wine. In the hallway, I passed Möritz, who looked at me, stunned: "You went out?"—"Yes, Herr Kommissar. I went to reconnoiter some of our positions, to get an idea of the city." His face darkened: "Don't go risking yourself uselessly. I had a hard job getting you; if you get yourself killed right away, I'll never be able to replace you."—"*Zu Befehl*, Herr Kommissar." I saluted him and went to change. A little later, Möritz offered his officers a drink, from two bottles of Cognac carefully held in reserve; he introduced me to my new colleagues, Leibbrandt, Dreyer, Vopel, the intelligence officer, Hauptsturmführer von Ahlfen, Herzog, Zumpe. Zumpe and Vopel, the Untersturmführer I had met the day before, worked with Thomas. There was also Weidner, the Gestapoleiter for the city (Thomas was Leiter IV for the whole *Kessel*, and thus Weidner's superior). We drank to the Führer and to the *Endsieg* and wished each other a merry Christmas; it all remained sober and cordial—I vastly preferred it to the sentimental or religious effusions of the soldiers. Thomas and I, out of curiosity, went to the midnight Mass that was celebrated in the main hall. The Catholic priest and Lutheran pastor of one of the divisions took turns officiating, in a perfect ecumenical spirit, and the faithful of both confessions prayed together. General von Seydlitz-Kurbach, who commanded the LIST Corps, was there with several division commanders and their chiefs of staff; Thomas pointed out Sanne, who commanded the One Hundredth Jägerdivision, Korfes, von Hartmann.

Some of our Ukrainians were also praying: they were, Thomas explained, Uniates from Galicia, who celebrate Christmas at the same time as we do, unlike their Orthodox cousins. I examined them, but didn't see Ivan among them. After the Mass, we went back to drink Cognac; then, suddenly exhausted, I went to bed. I dreamed of metros again: this time, two parallel tracks ran side by side between brilliantly lit platforms, then joined each other farther on down the tunnel, after a separation marked by large round cement pylons; but this switch didn't work and a team of women in orange uniforms, including a black woman, were working feverishly to repair it while the train, crowded with passengers, was already leaving the station.

I finally set myself to my task in a more structured and rigorous way. On Christmas morning, a violent blizzard put an end to hopes of a special supply delivery; at the same time, the Russians launched an attack on the northeast sector and also on the factories, taking a few kilometers of territory back from us and killing more than twelve hundred of our men. The Croats, I saw from a report, had been violently hit, and Oberfeldwebel Nišić was on the list of the killed. Carpe diem! I hoped he at least had had time to smoke his cigarette. I digested reports and wrote other ones. Christmas didn't seem to affect the men's morale too much: most of them, according to the reports or letters opened by the censors, had kept intact their faith in the Führer and in victory; nevertheless, every day we were executing deserters or men guilty of self-mutilation. Some of the divisions shot their condemned men themselves; others handed them over to us; the executions took place in a courtyard behind the Gestapostelle. They also handed over to us civilians caught looting by the Feldgendarmen, or suspected of passing messages to the Russians. A few days after Christmas, I passed two dirty, snot-nosed kids in a hallway; the Ukrainians were taking them away to shoot them after an interrogation: the kids had polished the boots of our officers at various HQ and mentally took down details; at night, they slipped through a sewer to go inform the Soviets. On one of them, they had found a Russian medal hidden: he claimed he had been decorated, but it may simply have been stolen or taken from a dead man. They must have been about twelve or thirteen, but they looked under ten, and while Zumpe, who was going to command the firing squad, was explaining the matter to me, they both stared at me with large eyes, as if I were going to save them. That made me enraged: What do you want from me? I wanted to shout at them. You're going to die, so what? I too am probably going to die here, everyone here is going to die. That's the deal. I took a few minutes to calm down; later on, Zumpe told me that they had wept but had also cried out: "Long live Stalin!" and *"Urra po-bieda!"* before they were shot. "Is that supposed to be an edifying story?" I rapped out at him; he left a little crestfallen.

I began to meet some of my own so-called informers, who were brought to me by Ivan or another Ukrainian, or who came on their own. These women and men were in a lamentable state, foul-smelling, covered with filth and lice; lice I had already, but the smell of these people made me nauseated. They seemed to me more like beggars than agents: the information they gave me was invariably useless or unverifiable; in exchange, I had to give them an onion or a frozen potato, which I kept for this purpose in a safe, a veritable *slush fund* in local currency. I had no idea how to treat the contradictory rumors they reported to me; if I had transmitted them to the Abwehr, they would have laughed at us; I ended up creating a file entitled *Miscellaneous information, unconfirmed*, which I passed on every other day to Möritz.

Information about the supply problems, which affected morale, particularly interested me. Everyone knew, without speaking about it, that the Soviet prisoners in our Stalag, whom we had virtually stopped feeding for some time, had sunk into cannibalism. "It's their true nature that's being revealed," Thomas had snapped at me when I tried to discuss it with him. It was understood, though, that the German Landser, when in distress, would keep his dignity. So the shock caused by a report on a case of cannibalism in a German company posted at the western edge of the *Kessel* was all the keener in high places. The circumstances made the affair particularly atrocious. When famine made them resolve on this course, the soldiers in the company, still concerned with the *Weltanschauung*, had debated the following point: Should they eat a Russian or a German? The ideological problem posed was about the legitimacy of eating a Slav, a Bolshevik *Untermensch*. Couldn't that sort of meat corrupt their German stomachs? But eating a dead comrade would be dishonorable; even if they couldn't bury them anymore, they still had respect for those who had fallen for the *Vaterland*. Finally they agreed to eat one of their Hiwis, an entirely reasonable compromise, given the terms of the debate. They killed him and an Obergefreiter, a former butcher from Mannheim, proceeded to dismember him. The surviving Hiwis panicked: three of them were killed trying to desert, but another managed to reach the regiment's HQ, where he had told the story to an officer. No one had believed him; after an investigation, they had been forced to face the facts, since the company hadn't been able to dispose of the victim's remains, and they had found his entire rib cage and some of the bits deemed unsuitable for consumption. The soldiers, when they were arrested, had confessed everything; the meat, according to them,

tasted like pork, and was every bit as good as horse. They had discreetly
shot the butcher and four ringleaders, then hushed up the affair, but it
had created a stir in the various headquarters. Möritz asked me to write
a general report on the nutritional situation of the troops since the *Kessel*
had been sealed off; he had the numbers from the AOK 6, but suspected
them of being mostly theoretical. I thought of going to see Hohenegg.

This time, I prepared my expedition a little better. I had already
gone out with Thomas, to visit some division Ic/AOs; after my Croatian escapade, Möritz had ordered me, if I wanted to go out alone, to
fill out an itinerary first. I made a phone call to Pitomnik, to the office
of Generalstabsarzt Dr. Renoldi, the chief medical officer of AOK 6,
where I was told that Hohenegg was based in the main campaign hospital in Gumrak; there I was told that he was traveling around within
the *Kessel*, to make observations; I finally located him in Rakotino, a
stanitsa in the southern part of the pocket, in the sector of the 376th Division. I then had to call the different HQs to organize liaisons. The trip
would take half a day, and I would definitely have to spend the night either in Rakotino itself, or in Gumrak; but Möritz agreed to the expedition. There were still a few days left before the New Year; it had been
twenty-five below zero since Christmas, and I decided to get out my
shuba, despite the risk that lice would nest in it. I was already covered
with them in any case—my vigilant hunt through the seams every night
didn't do any good: my belly, my armpits, the inside of my legs were red
with bites, and I couldn't stop myself from scratching till I drew blood.
I was also suffering from diarrhea, probably because of the bad water
and irregular food, a mixture, depending on the day, of tinned ham or
French pâté and *Wassersuppe* with horse. At HQ it was all right, the officers' latrines were revolting but at least accessible, but on the move it
could soon become problematic.

I went without Ivan: I didn't need him in the *Kessel*; anyway, seats
in the liaison vehicles were strictly limited. The first car brought me to
Gumrak, another to Pitomnik; there I had to wait several hours for a liaison to Rakotino. It wasn't snowing, but the sky remained a milky,
somber gray, and the planes, which were now taking off from Salsk, arrived irregularly. On the runway an even more horrible chaos reigned
than the week before; there was a stampede for each plane, wounded
men fell and were crushed by the others, the Feldgendarmen had to fire
volleys in the air to force the horde of desperate men to fall back. I exchanged a few words with a Heinkel 111 pilot who had gotten out of
his plane to smoke; he was livid, and watched the scene with a bewildered look, murmuring: "It's not possible, it's not possible. . . . You
know," he finally said to me before he walked off, "every night, when

I get back to Salsk alive, I cry like a child." This simple sentence made my head swim; turning my back on the pilot and the desperate mob, I started sobbing: the tears froze on my face, I wept for my childhood, for a time when snow was a pleasure that knew no end, when a city was a wonderful space to live in, and when a forest was not yet a convenient place to kill people. Behind me, the wounded howled like men possessed, mad dogs, almost drowning out the throb of the engines with their cries. At least this Heinkel took off smoothly; that wasn't the case for the next Junker. Some shells were beginning to fall again, they must have botched the refueling, or maybe one of the engines was defective, because of the cold: a few seconds after the wheels had left the ground, the left engine stalled; the aircraft, which hadn't worked up enough speed yet, lurched to the side; the pilot tried to straighten it, but the plane was already too unbalanced and suddenly it toppled onto one wing and crashed a few hundred meters beyond the runway, in a giant ball of fire that lit up the steppe for an instant. I had taken refuge in a bunker because of the shelling but still saw everything, again my eyes filled with tears, but I managed to control myself. Finally they came to get me for the liaison, but not before an artillery shell had fallen on one of the tents of wounded near the runway, sending limbs and scraps of flesh flying over the whole unloading area. Since I was nearby, I had to help clear away the bloody debris, to look for survivors; as I caught myself studying the entrails spilled out of the belly of a young soldier on the reddened snow, to find traces of my past or signs of my future in them, I told myself that everything here was indeed taking on the look of an agonizing farce. I remained shaken, I smoked cigarette after cigarette, despite my limited supply, and every fifteen minutes had to run to the latrines to let out a thin stream of liquid shit; ten minutes after the car started, I had to make it stop to rush behind a snowdrift; my coat got in my way and I soiled it. I tried to clean it with some snow, but managed only to freeze my fingers; back in the car, I huddled against the door and closed my eyes to try to forget it all. I shuffled through the images of my past as through a worn pack of cards, trying to find one that could come to life before me for a few minutes: but they fled, dissolved, or remained dead. Even the image of my sister, my last recourse, seemed like a wooden figure. Only the presence of the other officers kept me from weeping again.

By the time we got to our destination, the snow had started up again, and snowflakes danced in the gray air, joyful and light; and for a brief moment one might have thought that the immense, empty, white steppe actually was a country of crystalline fairies, joyful and light like the snowflakes, whose laughter burst gently in the murmuring wind; but

the knowledge that it was polluted by men and their unhappiness and
sordid fear ruined the illusion. In Rakotino, I finally found Hohenegg
in a wretched little isba half buried beneath the snow, banging away on
a portable typewriter in the light of a candle stuck into a PAK cartridge
casing. He raised his head but showed no surprise: "Look at that. The
Hauptsturmführer. What good wind brings you here?"—"You." He
passed his hand over his bald skull: "I didn't know I was so desirable. But
I warn you: if you're sick, you've come in vain. I only deal in those for
whom it's too late." I made an effort to get a grip on myself to come up
with a repartee: "Doctor, I suffer from only one disease, sexually trans-
missible and irremediably fatal: life." He made a face: "Not only do I
find you a little pale, but you're sinking into clichés. I've known you in
better form. The state of siege doesn't agree with you." I took off my
shuba, hung it on a nail, and then, without being invited, sat down on a
coarsely carved bench, my back to the wall. The room was barely
heated, just enough to cut the cold a little; Hohenegg's fingers looked
blue. "How is your work going, Doktor?" He shrugged his shoulders:
"All right. General Renoldi didn't welcome me very politely; apparently he thought this whole mission was useless. I didn't take offense, but
I would have preferred it if he had expressed his opinion when I was
still in Novocherkassk. That said, he's wrong: I'm not done yet, but my
preliminary results are already extraordinary."—"That's just what I came
to discuss with you."—"The SD is interested in nutrition, now?"—
"The SD is interested in everything, Doktor."—"So let me finish my
report. Then I'll go look for some so-called soup in the so-called mess,
and we can talk while we pretend to eat." He patted his round belly:
"For now, it's a health cure for me. But it better not last."—"You have
some reserves, at least."—"That doesn't mean anything. Nervous thin
men like you seem to last much longer than the fat and the strong. Let
me work. You're not in too much of a hurry?" I raised my hands: "You
know, Doktor, given the critical importance of what I'm doing for the
future of Germany and of the Sixth Army . . ."—"That's just what I was
thinking. In that case, you'll spend the night here and we'll go back together to Gumrak tomorrow morning."

  The village of Rakotino remained strangely silent. We were less than
a kilometer from the front, but since I arrived I had heard just a few
gunshots. The clacking of the typewriter resounded in this silence and
made it even more nerve-wracking. At least my runs had calmed down.
Finally, Hohenegg stowed his papers into a briefcase, got up, and stuck
a scruffy shapka onto his round skull. "Give me your paybook," he said,
"I'm going to look for some soup. You'll find a little wood next to the
stove: start it up again, but use as little as possible. We have to keep till

tomorrow with that." He went out; I busied myself next to the stove. The wood supply was indeed meager: a few wet fence pickets, with bits of barbed wire attached. I finally managed to light a piece after cutting it up. Hohenegg returned with a mess tin of soup and a thick slice of *Kommissbrot*. "I'm sorry," he said, "but they refuse to give you a ration without a written order from the HQ of the Panzer Corps. We'll share."—"Don't worry," I replied, "I anticipated that." I went over to my coat and took from the pockets a piece of bread, some dry biscuits, and some tinned meat. "Magnificent!" he exclaimed. "Keep the tin for tonight, I have an onion: it'll be a feast. For lunch, I have this." He took a piece of bacon wrapped in a Soviet newspaper out of his bag. With a pocket knife, he cut the bread into slices and also cut two thick slices of bacon; he placed all of it directly on the stove, with the mess tin of soup. "Sorry, but I don't have a saucepan." While the bacon sizzled, he stored his typewriter away and spread the newspaper out on the table. We ate the bacon on the warmed slices of black bread: the slightly melted fat seeped into the thick bread, and it was delicious. Hohenegg offered me his soup; I refused, pointing to my stomach. He raised his eyebrows: "The *Flux*?" I nodded. "Be careful with that. Normally one gets over it, but here, it can carry men away in a few days. They become dehydrated and die." He explained the hygienic procedures I should follow. "That can be a little complicated here," I pointed out.—"Yes, that's true," he acknowledged sadly. While we were finishing our bacon toast, he talked to me about lice and typhus. "We already have a few cases, which we isolate as well as we can," he explained. "But inevitably, an epidemic will break out. And then it will be catastrophic. The men will fall like flies."—"In my opinion, they're dying fast enough as is."—"Do you know what our *tovarishchi* are doing now on the front of the division? They're playing a recording with a clock going *tick, tock, tick, tock,* very loud, then a sepulchral voice announcing in German: 'Every seven seconds, a German dies in Russia!' Then the *tick, tock* again. They put that on for hours. It's quite striking." For men devoured by cold and hunger, gnawed by vermin, crouching at the bottom of their bunkers of snow and frozen earth, I could see how it must have been terrifying, even if the calculation (as we have seen at the beginning of this memoir) was a little excessive. I responded by telling Hohenegg the story of the Solomonic cannibals. His only commentary was: "Judging from the Hiwis I've examined, they must not have had a very satisfying feast." That brought us to the object of my mission. "I haven't finished the tour of all the divisions," he explained, "and there are differences for which I haven't yet found any explanation. But I've already conducted about thirty autopsies and the results are irrefutable: more than half present symptoms of acute malnutrition. To put it simply, almost no adipose tissue left under the skin or surrounding the internal organs; gelatinous fluid in the mesentery; congested liver; pale, anemic organs; red and yellow marrow replaced by a vitreous substance; cardiac muscle atrophied, but with an enlargement of the right ventricle and the right auricle. In ordinary language, their body, lacking anything to sustain its vital functions, devours itself to find the necessary calories; when there's nothing left, everything stops, like a car that's run out of gas. It's a well-known phenomenon: but the curious thing here is that despite the dramatic reduction in rations, it's still much too soon to have so many cases. All the officers assure me that the food supplies are centralized by the AOK and that the soldiers are indeed receiving the official ration. Which, for now, is just under a thousand calories per day. That's far too little, but it's still something; the men should be weak, more vulnerable to diseases and opportunistic infections, but they shouldn't be dying of hunger yet. That's why my colleagues are looking for another explanation: they talk of *exhaustion, stress, physical shock.* But that's all vague and not very convincing. My autopsies don't lie."—"What do you think, then?"—"I don't know. There must be a number of reasons, hard to separate in these conditions. I suspect that the capacity of certain organisms to break down food properly, to digest it, is altered by other factors such as tension or lack of sleep. There are of course quite obvious cases: men with diarrhea that's so severe that the little they absorb doesn't stay in their stomach long enough and comes out almost as is; that's especially the case for the ones eating almost exclusively this *Wassersuppe*. Some of the food they distribute to the troops is even harmful; for example, canned meat like yours, very rich, sometimes kills men who haven't eaten anything except bread and soup for weeks; their organism can't bear the shock, the heart pumps too quickly and suddenly gives out. There's also the butter, which keeps arriving: it's delivered in frozen blocks, and out in the steppe, the Landsers don't have anything to make fires with, so they break it up with an axe and suck on the pieces. That provokes horrible diarrhea that soon finishes them off. If you want to know the truth, many of the bodies I receive have their pants still full of shit, frozen fortunately: in the end, they're too weak to drop their pants. And note that these are bodies picked up at the front lines, not in the hospitals. In short, to return to my theory, it will be hard to demonstrate, but it seems plausible to me. The metabolism itself is affected by the cold and fatigue, and can no longer function properly."—"And fear?"—"Fear too, of course. We saw it during the Great War: under some particularly intense bombardments, the heart fails; we find young, healthy, well-fed men dead without the slightest wound. But here I'd say rather that it's

an aggravating factor, not a primary cause. Once again, I have to continue my investigations. It won't be much use for the Sixth Army, I'm
sure, but I flatter myself that it will serve science, and that's what helps
me get up in the morning; that, and the inevitable *salyut* of our friends
across the lines. This *Kessel*, in fact, is a giant laboratory. A genuine researcher's paradise. I have as many bodies at my disposal as I could wish
for, perfectly preserved, even if it's sometimes a little hard to defrost
them. I have to force my poor assistants to spend the night with them
near the stove, turning them over regularly. The other day, in Baburkin,
one of them fell asleep; the next morning, I found my subject frozen on
one side and roasted on the other. Come along now, it'll soon be
time."—"Time? Time for what?"—"You'll see." Hohenegg gathered up
his briefcase and his typewriter and put on his coat; before going out,
he snuffed the candle. Outside, it was dark. I followed him to a *balka* behind the village, where he slithered, feet first, into a bunker that was almost invisible beneath the snow. Three officers were sitting on little
stools around a candle. "Good evening, meine Herren," Hohenegg said.
"Let me introduce Hauptsturmführer Dr. Aue, who has very kindly
come to visit us." I shook hands with the officers and, since there was
no other stool, sat down on the frozen ground, pulling my coattails under me. Despite the fleece lining, I felt the cold. "The Soviet commander opposite us is a man of remarkable punctuality," Hohenegg
explained to me. "Every day, since the middle of the month, he has
sprayed this sector three times a day, at 05:30, 11:00, and 16:00 sharp.
In the meantime, nothing, aside from a few mortar shells. It's very practical for my work." Indeed, three minutes later, I heard the piercing
screech, followed by a close series of enormous explosions, of a volley
of "Stalin organs." The whole bunker shook, snow came down and half
filled the entryway, clumps of earth rained from the ceiling. The frail
light of the candle flickered, projecting monstrous shadows on the exhausted, badly shaved faces of the officers. Other volleys followed,
punctuated by the staccato detonations of tank or artillery shells. The
noise had become a mad, insane thing, living its own life, occupying the
air and pressing against the partly obstructed entrance of the bunker. I
was seized with terror at the idea of being buried alive; I would almost
have fled, but I got control of myself. After ten minutes the pounding
abruptly stopped. But the noise, its presence and pressure, took longer
to withdraw and dissipate. The acrid smell of cordite stung the nose and
eyes. One of the officers cleared away the bunker's entrance by hand.
We went crawling out. Above the *balka*, the village looked crushed,
swept as if by a storm; isbas were burning, but I soon saw that only a
few houses had been struck: the bulk of the shells must have been aimed

at the trenches. "The only problem," Hohenegg commented as he brushed earth and snow off his cloak, "is that they never aim at quite the same spot. That would be much more practical. Let's go see if our humble refuge has survived." The hut was still standing; the stove was even giving off a little warmth. "Would you like to come over for some tea?" offered one of the officers who had accompanied us. We followed him to another isba, divided in half by a partition; the first room, where the two others already sat, was also equipped with a stove. "Here, in the village, it's all right," the officer said. "We find some wood after each bombardment. But the men on the line don't have anything. At the slightest little wound, they die of shock and frostbite caused by the loss of blood. We rarely have time to evacuate them to a hospital." Another officer was preparing the "tea," some Schlüter ersatz. All three of them were Leutnants or Oberleutnants, very young; they moved and spoke slowly, almost apathetically. The one who was making the tea was wearing the Iron Cross. I offered them some cigarettes: this produced the same effect on them as it had with the Croatian officer. One of them took out a greasy pack of cards: "Do you play?" I made a sign that I didn't, but Hohenegg agreed, and he dealt the cards for a game of skat. "Cards, cigarettes, tea . . ." joked the third one, who hadn't said anything yet. "Just like home . . ."—"Before," the first one explained to me, "we played chess. But we don't have the strength for that anymore." The officer with the Iron Cross served the tea in dented cups. "I'm sorry, there's no milk. No sugar, either." We drank, and they started playing. A noncom came in and began talking in a low voice with the officer with the Iron Cross. "In the village," he announced angrily, "four dead, thirteen wounded. The Second and Third companies were hit too." He turned to me with a look that was both enraged and helpless: "You're in charge of intelligence, Herr Hauptsturmführer, can you explain something to me? Where do they get all these weapons, cannons, and shells from? We've been chasing and pursuing them for a year and a half now. We've hunted them from the Bug to the Volga, we've destroyed their cities, wrecked their factories. . . . So where are they getting all these fucking tanks and cannons from?" He was almost on the verge of tears. "I'm not in charge of that kind of intelligence," I explained calmly. "Enemy military potential is the business of the Abwehr and the *Fremde Heere Ost*. In my opinion, it was underestimated from the start. And also, they managed to evacuate a lot of factories. Their production capacity in the Urals seems considerable." The officer appeared to want to continue the conversation, but was obviously too tired. He went back to playing cards in silence. A little later, I asked them about the Russian defeatist propaganda. The one who had invited us got up, passed behind the partition, and returned with some pieces of paper. "They send us this." One of them was a simple poem written in German, entitled "Think About Your Child!" and signed by a certain Erich Weinert; the other ended with a quotation: *If German soldiers or officers surrender, the Red Army must take them prisoner and spare their lives (Order No. 55 of the People's Commissar for Defense J. Stalin).* The work was quite sophisticated; the language and typography were excellent. "And is it working?" I asked. The officers looked at each other. "Unfortunately, yes," the third finally said.—"Impossible to prevent the men from reading them," the one with the Iron Cross said.—"Recently," the third one went on, "during an attack, an entire platoon surrendered without firing a shot. Fortunately, another platoon was able to intervene and block the attack. Finally we pushed the Reds back, and they didn't take their prisoners with them. A lot of them had been killed during the fighting; we shot the others." The Leutnant with the Iron Cross gave him a black look and he fell silent. "Can I keep this?" I asked, pointing to the papers. "If you like. We keep them for another purpose." I folded them and put them away in my jacket pocket. Hohenegg was finishing the game and got up: "Shall we go?" We thanked the three officers and returned to Hohenegg's isba, where I prepared a small meal with my tinned meat and some slices of grilled onion. "I'm sorry, Hauptsturm-führer, but I left my Cognac in Gumrak."—"Oh, that can be for another time." We talked about the officers; Hohenegg told me about the strange obsessions that seized some of them, like the Oberstleutnant from the Forty-fourth Division who had demolished an entire isba where a dozen of his men were sheltering, to heat water for a bath, and then who, after soaking for a long time and shaving himself, had put his uniform back on and shot himself in the mouth. "But Doktor," I pointed out, "you must know that in Latin 'to besiege' is *obsidere.* Stalingrad is an obsessed city."—"Yes. Let's go to bed. The morning wake-up is a little brutal." Hohenegg had a mattress and a sleeping bag; he found two blankets for me and I rolled up in my fleece-lined coat. "You should see my quarters in Gumrak," he said as he lay down. "I have a bunker with wooden walls, heated, and clean sheets. Luxury." Clean sheets: that, I said to myself, was something to dream about. A hot bath and clean sheets. Was it possible that I would die without ever taking another bath? Yes, it was possible, and seen from Hohenegg's isba, it seemed even probable. Once again, an immense desire to weep overwhelmed me. That seized me often nowadays.

Back in Stalingrad, I used the figures Hohenegg had provided me to draft a report that, according to Thomas, stunned Möritz: he had read it at one go, he told me, then returned it without any comments. Thomas wanted to forward it directly to Berlin. "You can do that without Möritz's authorization?" I asked him, surprised. Thomas shrugged his shoulders: "I'm an officer of the *Staatspolizei*, not of the *Geheime Feldpolizei*. I can do what I like." In fact, I realized, we were all more or less autonomous. Möritz only rarely gave me precise instructions, and in general I was left to myself. I wondered why he had had me come. Thomas kept direct contacts with Berlin, I didn't really know through what channels, and he seemed always sure of the next step. In the first months of the occupation of the city, the SP, along with the Feldgendarmerie, had liquidated the Jews and the Communists; then they had evacuated most of the civilians and sent the ones of working age to Germany, almost sixty-five thousand in all, for the *Aktion Sauckel*. But they too found little to do now. Thomas, though, seemed busy; day after day, he cultivated his intelligence officers with cigarettes and canned preserves. I decided, for lack of anything better to do, to reorganize the network of civilian informers that I had inherited. I summarily cut off supplies to the ones who seemed useless, and told the others I expected more of them. On a suggestion from Ivan, I went with a *Dolmetscher* to visit the basements of the destroyed buildings in the center of town: there were old women there who knew a lot but never went out. Most of them hated us, and were waiting impatiently for the return of *nashi*, "our own"; but a few potatoes, and especially the pleasure of having someone to talk to, loosened their tongues. From the military standpoint they didn't contribute anything; but they had lived for months just behind the Soviet lines, and spoke eloquently about the morale of the soldiers, their courage, their faith in Russia, and also about the immense hopes that the war had given rise to among the people, which the men discussed openly, even with their officers: liberalization of the regime, abolition of the sovkhozes and kolkhozes, elimination of the work booklet that prevented free movement. One of these old women, Masha, animatedly described to me their General Shuikov, whom she already called "the hero of Stalingrad": he hadn't left the right bank since the fighting began; the day we burned the oil tanks, he had just barely managed to find refuge on a rocky outcrop, and had spent the night between the rivers of fire, without batting an eyelid; the men now swore only by him; as for me, it was the first time I had heard this name. With these women, I also learned a lot about our own Landsers: many of them came to shelter for a few hours with them, to eat a little, talk, sleep. This zone on the front was a senseless chaos of collapsed buildings, constantly under the fire of Russian artillery, whose outgoing booms could sometimes be heard from the other bank of the Volga;

guided by Ivan, who seemed to know the tiniest nooks and crannies of the city, I moved almost exclusively underground, from one basement to the other, sometimes even traveling through sewer pipes. Elsewhere, however, we went through upstairs floors, for mysterious reasons Ivan thought it was safer; we passed through apartments with the tatters of burned curtains, their ceilings caved in and blackened, the bare brick visible behind torn wallpaper and plaster, still cluttered with nickel-plated bed frames, gutted sofas, sideboards, and children's toys; then came beams placed over gaping holes, exposed hallways you had to crawl through, and everywhere brick riddled like lace. Ivan seemed indifferent to the artillery but had a superstitious fear of snipers; with me it was the opposite: explosions terrified me, I always had to make an effort not to hunch over; as for the snipers, I didn't pay any attention to them. This was out of ignorance, and Ivan often had to jerk me away from a place that must have been more exposed but that, to me, looked like any other place. He too claimed that most of these snipers were women, and that he had with his own eyes seen the corpse of the most famous of them, a champion of the 1936 Pan-Soviet Games; yet he had never heard of the Sarmatians of the Lower Volga, descended, according to Herodotus, from intermarriages between Scythians and Amazons, who sent their wives to fight alongside the men, and built immense kurgans like those of the Mamai. In these devastated, desolate landscapes, I also met soldiers; some spoke to me with hostility, others amiably, yet others with indifference. They told of the *Rattenkrieg*, the "rat war" for these ruins, where a hallway, a ceiling, a wall, served as a front line, where they bombarded each other blindly with grenades in the dust and smoke, where the living suffocated in the heat of the fires, where the dead cluttered the stairways, the landings, the doorways to apartments, where you lost any notion of time and space, and where the war almost became an abstract, three-dimensional chess game. This was how our forces had come sometimes to within three, two streets of the Volga, and no farther. Now it was the Russians' turn: every day, usually at dawn and at nightfall, they launched fierce assaults on our positions, especially in the sector of the factories, but also in the center of town; the companies' ammunition, strictly rationed, was giving out, and after each attack the survivors would collapse, overcome; during the day, the Russians walked around out in the open, knowing our men weren't allowed to shoot. In the basements, packed together, they lived under carpets of rats that, having lost all fear, ran over the living as well as the dead and, at night, came and nibbled at the ears, noses, or toes of the exhausted sleepers. One day I was on the second floor of a building when a small mortar shell exploded in the street; a few instants later, I heard a

wild burst of uncontrollable laughter. I looked out the window and saw
what looked like a human torso in the midst of the rubble: a German
soldier, both his legs torn off by the explosion, was laughing madly. I
watched, and he didn't stop laughing, in the midst of a pool of blood
that kept growing larger among the debris. This spectacle chilled me to
the bone and knotted my gut; I sent Ivan out and dropped my pants in
the middle of the living room. Out on expedition, when I was seized
with diarrhea, I shat anywhere, in hallways, in kitchens, in bedrooms,
even, at times, sitting on a genuine toilet, not always connected to a
pipe, however. These vast destroyed buildings where, the summer before, thousands of families were living the ordinary, everyday life of all
families, never suspecting that soon men would be sleeping six together
in their conjugal bed, would be wiping their asses with their curtains
and sheets, would be massacring each other with shovels in their
kitchens, and laying the corpses of slaughtered men in their bathtubs—
these buildings filled me with a pointless, bitter despair; and through this
despair images from my past rose like drowned men after a shipwreck,
one by one, more and more frequently. Often they were pathetic memories. Thus, two months after we arrived at Moreau's house, a little before I turned eleven, my mother had placed me, when school began, in
a boarding school in Nice, on the pretext that there was no good school
in Antibes. It wasn't a horrible establishment; the teachers were ordinary people. (Later, among the priests, how I would miss that place!) I
could come home every Thursday afternoon and on weekends; still, I
hated it. I was determined not to become once again the favorite target
of the envy and spite of the other children, as in Kiel; the fact that in
the beginning I still had a slight German accent made me even more
nervous; our mother had always spoken to us in French at home, but
before we arrived in Antibes, we hadn't had much practice. What's
more, I was frail and small for my age. To compensate, I cultivated without really realizing it a vicious and sarcastic attitude, certainly an artificial one, which I directed at my teachers. I became the class clown; I
interrupted the lessons with deadpan comments or questions that made
my comrades shout with evil joy; I orchestrated carefully planned and
sometimes cruel farces. One teacher in particular became my victim: a
nice, slightly effeminate man who taught English, wore a bow tie, and
who was rumored to engage in practices that, like everyone else, I regarded then as vile, without, however, having the slightest idea of what
they were. For these reasons, and because he was weak by nature, I
made him my scapegoat, and humiliated him regularly in front of the
class, until one day, overcome with a mad, impotent rage, he slapped
me. Many years later this memory still shames me, and I have long un-

derstood that I had treated this poor man the way the bullies treated me, shamelessly, for the odious pleasure of demonstrating an illusory superiority. That is surely the immense advantage over the weak that those called strong possess: both are consumed with anxiety, fear, and doubt, but the weak know it and suffer because of it, while the strong do not perceive it and, to shore up the wall that protects them from the bottomless void, turn against the weak, whose all-too-visible fragility threatens their own fragile confidence. Thus the weak are a threat to the strong, and invite the violence and murder that pitilessly strike them down. And it's only when blind and irresistible violence strikes the strongest in turn that the wall of their certainty cracks: only then do they glimpse what awaits them, and see that they are finished. This was what was happening to the men of the Sixth Army, so proud, so arrogant when they were crushing Russian divisions, stripping civilians of their rights, eliminating suspects as one crushes flies: now, just as much as the Soviet artillery and snipers, as the cold, disease, and hunger, it was the slow rising of the internal flood that was killing them. In me too it was rising, acrid and stinking like the sweet-smelling shit that streamed from my bowels. A curious interview Thomas arranged for me demonstrated this in a blatant way. "I'd like you to talk with someone," he said to me, sticking his head into the tiny cubbyhole that served as my office. This happened, I'm sure of it, on the last day of the year 1942. "Who?"—"A *politruk* we caught yesterday near the factories. We've already squeezed everything we could out of him, the Abwehr too, but I thought it would be interesting for you to talk with him, to discuss ideology, see a little of what's going on in their heads, these days, on the other side. You have a subtle mind, you'll do it better than me. He speaks good German."—"If you think it might be useful."—"Don't waste any time with military questions: we've already taken care of that."—"He talked?" Thomas shrugged his shoulders, smiling slightly: "Not really. He's past his prime, but he's tough. We'll continue afterward maybe."—"Ah, I understand: you want me to soften him up."—"Precisely. Lecture him, talk to him about his children's future."

One of the Ukrainians led in the handcuffed man. He wore a tank crewman's short yellow jacket, oily, its right sleeve torn at the seam; his face was completely flayed on one side, as if peeled open; on the other, a bluish bruise almost closed his eye; but he must have shaved right before he was captured. The Ukrainian brutally sent him flying into a little classroom chair in front of my desk. "Take off his handcuffs," I ordered. "And go wait in the hallway." The Ukrainian shrugged his shoulders, undid the handcuffs, and went out. The Commissar massaged his wrists. "Nice guys, our national traitors, aren't they?" he said pleasantly. Despite his accent, his German was clear. "You can keep them when you leave."—"We're not going to leave," I replied curtly.—"Ah, all the better. That will save us the task of running after them to shoot them."—"I am Hauptsturmführer Dr. Aue," I said. And you?" He made a slight bow on his chair: "Pravdin, Ilya Semionovich, at your service." I took out one of my last packs of cigarettes: "Do you smoke?" He smiled, revealing two missing teeth: "Why do cops always offer cigarettes? Every time I've been arrested, they've offered me cigarettes. This being said, I won't refuse." I handed him one, and he leaned over so I could light it. "And your rank?" I asked. He exhaled a long puff of smoke with a sigh of contentment: "Your soldiers are dying of hunger, but I see that the officers still have good cigarettes. I'm a Regimental Commissar. But recently they gave us military ranks and I was made a Lieutenant-Colonel."—"But you're a member of the Party, not an officer in the Red Army."—"That is correct. And you? You're also from the Gestapo?"—"From the SD. It's not quite the same thing."—"I know the difference. I've already interrogated enough of your own."—"And how could a Communist like you let himself be captured?" His face darkened: "During an assault, a shell exploded next to me and I was hit in the head by some rubble." He pointed to the scorched part of his face. "I was knocked out. I suppose my comrades left me for dead. When I regained consciousness, I was in the hands of your people. There was nothing I could do," he concluded sadly.—"A high-ranking *politruk* who goes up to the front line, that's pretty rare, isn't it?"—"The commanding officer had been killed and I had to rally the men. But in general, I agree with you: the men don't see enough Party leaders under fire. Some abuse their privileges. But these abuses will be corrected." With his fingertips, he delicately felt the purplish, wounded skin around his swollen eye. "Is that from the explosion too?" I asked. He gave a gap-toothed smile: "No, that's from your colleagues. You must be quite familiar with that sort of method."—"Your NKVD uses the same."— "Absolutely. I'm not complaining." I paused: "How old are you, if I may?" I finally asked. "Forty-two. I was born with the century, like your Himmler."—"So you witnessed the Revolution?" He laughed: "Of course! I was a Bolshevik activist when I was fifteen. I was a member of a workers' soviet in Petrograd. You can't imagine what a time that was! A great wind of freedom."—"It's changed a lot, then." He became pensive: "Yes. That's true. Probably the Russian people weren't ready for such an immense, immediate freedom. But that will come, little by little. They must be educated first."—"And your German, where did you learn that?" He smiled again: "On my own, when I was sixteen, with some prisoners of war. Afterward, Lenin himself sent me to the

German Communists. Can you believe that I knew Liebknecht, Luxemburg! Extraordinary people. And after the civil war, I returned to Germany many times, secretly, to keep up contacts with Thälmann and others. You don't know what my life has been like. In 1929, I acted as an interpreter for your officers who came to train in Soviet Russia, to test your new weapons and your new tactics. We learned a lot with you."—"Yes, but it didn't do you any good. Stalin liquidated all the officers who had adopted our concepts, beginning with Tukhachevsky."—"I miss Tukhachevsky. Personally, I mean. Politically, I can't judge Stalin. Maybe it was a mistake. The Bolsheviks make mistakes too. But the important thing is that we have the strength to purge our own ranks regularly, to eliminate those who deviate, who let themselves be corrupted. It's a strength that you lack: your Party is rotting from within."—"With us, too, there are problems. In the SD, we know it better than anyone, and we're working to make the Party and the *Volk* better." He smiled softly: "In the end, our two systems aren't so different. In principle at least."—"That's an odd statement, for a Communist."—"Not really, if you think about it. What difference, at bottom, is there between National Socialism and socialism in a single country?"—"In that case, why are we locked together in such a death struggle?"—"You're the ones who wanted it, not us. We were ready to make compromises. But it's as once before, with the Christians and the Jews: instead of joining forces with the People of God with whom they had everything in common, to form a united front against the pagans, the Christians preferred, no doubt out of jealousy, to let themselves be paganized and to turn against the witnesses of truth, to their own misfortune. That was a huge waste."—"I'm guessing that in your comparison, the Jews are you?"—"Of course. After all, you took everything from us, even if only to caricature it. And I'm not talking about symbols, like the red flag and the First of May. I'm talking about the concepts that are dearest to your *Weltanschauung*."—"In what sense?" He began to count on his fingers, in the Russian way, folding them down one by one, starting with the little finger: "Where communism aims for a classless society, you preach the *Volksgemeinschaft*, which is basically strictly the same thing, reduced to your borders. Where Marx saw the proletariat as the bearer of truth, you decided that the so-called German race is a proletarian race, incarnation of Good and morality; consequently, for class struggle, you substituted the German proletarian war against capitalist governments. In economy too your ideas are just deformations of our values. I know your political economy well, since before the war I translated articles from your specialized newspapers for the Party. Where Marx posited a theory of value based on labor, your Hitler declares: *Our*

German mark, which is not backed by gold, is worth more than gold. This
rather obscure phrase was glossed by Goebbels's right-hand man, Die-
trich, who explained that National Socialism had understood that the
best foundation for a currency is confidence in the productive forces of
the nation and in the leadership of the State. The result is that for you,
money becomes a fetish that represents the productive power of your
country, hence a total aberration. Your relations with your great capitalists are grossly hypocritical, especially since your minister Speer's reforms: your leaders continue to advocate free enterprise, but your
industries are all subject to a plan and their profits are limited to six percent, with the State appropriating the rest in addition to the production." He fell silent. "National Socialism also has its deviations," I finally
replied. I briefly explained Ohlendorf's theses to him. "Yes," he said, "I
know his articles. But he too is mistaken. Because you didn't imitate
Marxism; you perverted it. The substitution of race for class, which
leads to your proletarian racism, is absurd."—"No more than your notion of the continual war of classes. Classes are a historical given; they
appeared at a certain moment and will likewise disappear, harmoniously
dissolving into the *Volksgemeinschaft*, instead of tearing each other to
pieces. Whereas race is a biological given, natural, and thus undeniable."
He raised his hand: "Listen, I won't argue with you, since it's a question
of faith, and so logical demonstrations, reasoning, won't serve any purpose. But you can at least agree with me on one point: even if the analysis of the categories at stake is different, our ideologies have this basic
thing in common, which is that they are both essentially deterministic;
racial determinism for you, economic determinism for us, but determinism all the same. We both believe that man doesn't freely choose his
fate, but that it is imposed on him by nature or history. And we both
draw the conclusion that *objective enemies* exist, that certain categories of
human beings can and must legitimately be eliminated not for what
they've done or even thought, but for what they are. In that, we differ
only in the definition of the categories: for you, the Jews, Gypsies, the
Poles, and, even I believe, the mentally ill; for us, the Kulaks, the bourgeois, the Party deviationists. At bottom, it's the same thing; we both
reject the *homo economicus* of the capitalists, the egotistical, individualis-
tic man trapped in his illusion of freedom, in favor of a *homo faber. Not
a self-made man but a made man,* you might say in English, or a man yet
to be made, since communist man must still be constructed, educated,
just like your perfect National Socialist. And this man-to-be-made justifies the pitiless liquidation of everything that is uneducable, and thus
justifies the NKVD and the Gestapo, gardeners of the social body, who
tear out the weeds and force the good plants to follow their stakes." I

handed him another cigarette and lit one for myself: "You have broad ideas, for a Bolshevist *politruk*." He laughed, a little bitterly: "That's because my old relations, German and otherwise, fell into disfavor. When you are sidelined, it gives you time, and especially a perspective, to reflect."—"Is that what explains why a man with your past holds such a modest position?"—"No doubt. At one time, you know, I was close to Radek—but never to Trotsky, which is why I'm still here. But my lack of advancement doesn't bother me, you know. I have no personal ambition. I serve my Party and my country, and I'm happy to die for them. But that doesn't keep one from thinking." "But if you believe our two systems are identical, why are you fighting against us?"—"I never said they were identical! And you're much too intelligent to think so. I tried to show you that the ways our ideologies function are similar. The contents, of course, differ: class and race. For me, your National Socialism is a heresy of Marxism."—"How, in your opinion, is Bolshevik ideology superior to National Socialism?"—"In that it wants the good of all humanity, whereas yours is selfish, it just wants the good of the Germans. Not being German, it's impossible for me to adhere to it, even if I wanted to."—"Yes, but if you were born a bourgeois, like me, it would be impossible to become a Bolshevik: you would remain, whatever your innermost convictions, an *objective enemy*."—"That's true, but that's because of education. A child of bourgeois parents, a grandchild of bourgeois parents, educated from birth in a socialist country, will be a good, a true Communist, above suspicion. When classless society becomes a reality, all classes will be dissolved within communism. In theory, this can be extended to the whole world, which isn't the case of National Socialism."—"In theory, maybe. But you can't prove it, and in reality you commit atrocious crimes in the name of this utopia."—"I won't answer that your crimes are worse. I'll simply tell you that if we can't prove the validity of our hopes to someone who refuses to believe in the truth of Marxism, we can and we will concretely prove to you the inanity of your own. Your biological racism postulates that the races are unequal among themselves, that some are stronger and more valid than others, and that the strongest and the most valid of all is the German race. But when Berlin looks like this city"—he pointed his finger at the ceiling—"and when our brave soldiers are camping on your Unter den Linden, you'll at least be forced, if you want to save your racist faith, to acknowledge that the Slavic race is stronger than the German race." I didn't let myself be intimidated: "You sincerely believe, when you've just barely held Stalingrad, that you're going to take Berlin? You're joking."—"I don't believe it, I know it. You just have to look at the respective military potentials. Without counting the second front that our allies are going to open in Europe soon. You're finished."—"We'll fight to the last man."—"No doubt, but you'll perish all the same. And Stalingrad will remain as the symbol of your defeat. Wrongly, too. In my opinion, you already lost the war last year, when we stopped you in front of Moscow. We lost land, cities, men; all that can be replaced. But the Party didn't collapse, and that was your only hope. Without that, you could even have taken Stalingrad, it wouldn't have changed anything. And you *could* have taken Stalingrad, too, if you hadn't made so many mistakes, if you hadn't underestimated us so much. It wasn't inevitable that you'd lose here, that your Sixth Army would be completely destroyed. But if you had taken Stalingrad, then what? We would still have been in Ulianovsk, in Kuibyshev, in Moscow, in Sverdlovsk. And we would have ended up doing the same thing to you a little farther along. Of course, the symbolism wouldn't have been the same, it wouldn't have been Stalin's city. But who is Stalin, really? And what does his hubris and his glory mean to us Bolsheviks? We, here, who are dying every day, what do his daily telephone calls to Zhukov mean to us? It's not Stalin who gives the men the courage to rush in front of your machine guns. Of course, you need a leader, you need someone to coordinate everything, but that could have been any other man of ability. Stalin is no more irreplaceable than Lenin, or me. Our strategy here has been a strategy of common sense. And our soldiers, our Bolsheviks, would have shown as much courage in Kuibyshev. Despite all our military defeats, our Party and our people have remained unvanquished. Now things are going to go the other way. Your troops are already beginning to evacuate the Caucasus. There's no doubt whatsoever about our final victory."—"Maybe," I retorted. "But at what price for your communism? Ever since the beginning of the war, Stalin has appealed to national values, the only things that truly inspire men, not to communist values. He reintroduced the czarist orders of Suvorov and Kutuzov, as well as golden epaulettes for the officers, which your comrades in Petrograd used to nail to their shoulders in 'seventeen. In the pockets of your dead soldiers, and even of superior officers, we find hidden icons. Better yet, we know from our interrogations that racial values are appearing in broad daylight in the highest spheres of the Party and the Red Army, a Great Russian, anti-Semitic spirit that Stalin and the Party leaders cultivate. You too are beginning to mistrust your Jews; but they're not a class."—"What you say is certainly true," he acknowledged sadly. "Under the pressure of the war, atavisms are resurfacing. But you can't forget what the Russian people were before 1917, their state of ignorance, of backwardness. We haven't even had twenty years to educate and correct them; that's not very long. After the war we'll resume that task, and little by little all those mistakes will be corrected."—"I think you're wrong. The problem isn't the people: it's your leaders. Communism is a mask stuck onto the unchanged face of Russia. Your Stalin is a czar, your Politburo are boyars, or greedy and egotistical aristocrats, your Party cadres, the same *chinovniki* as the ones under Peter or Nicholas. It's the same Russian autocracy, the same permanent insecurity, the same paranoia of the foreign, the same fundamental inability to govern correctly, the same substitution of terror for the common consensus, and thus for real power, the same unbridled corruption, in other forms, the same incompetence, the same drunkenness. Read the correspondence between Kurbsky and Ivan, read Karamzin, read Custine. The crucial given of your history has never been changed: humiliation, from father to son. Ever since the beginning, but especially since the Mongols, everything humiliates you, and all the politics of your ruling class consists not of correcting this humiliation and its causes, but of hiding it from the rest of the world. Peter's city is nothing but another Potemkin village: it's not a window opening onto Europe, but a theater set put up to mask from the West all the poverty and endless filth stretching out behind it. But one can humiliate only those who can be humiliated; and in turn, only the humiliated humiliate. The humiliated of 1917, from Stalin down to the *muzhik*, have done nothing since then but inflict their fear and their humiliation on others. For in this country of the humiliated, the czar, whatever his strength may be, is powerless, his will is lost in the muddy swamp of his administration, and he is soon reduced, like Peter, to ordering his minions to obey his orders; in front of him people bow, but behind his back, they steal from him or conspire against him; everyone flatters his superiors and oppresses his subordinates, everyone has a slave mentality, *raby* as you say, and this slave spirit rises to the top; and the greatest slave of all is the czar, who can do nothing against the cowardliness and humiliation of his people of slaves, and who thus, in his powerlessness, kills them, terrorizes them, and humiliates them even more. And every time there's a real rupture in your history, a real chance to get out of this infernal cycle to begin a *new history*, you blow it: faced with freedom, the freedom of 1917 you were talking about, everyone, people and leaders alike, recoils and goes to the old tried-and-true methods. The end of the NEP, the declaration of socialism in a single country, is nothing but that. And since hope wasn't completely extinguished, there had to be purges. The present Great Russianism is only the logical outcome of this process. The Russian, the eternally humiliated man, can never escape from this humiliation except by identifying himself with the abstract glory of Russia. He may work fifteen hours a day in a freezing factory, eat nothing his entire life but black bread and cabbage, and serve a fat boss who calls himself a Marxist-Leninist but who rides around in a limousine with his high-class hookers and his French Champagne—none of that matters to him, so long as the Third Rome is at hand. And this Third Rome can call itself Christian or communist, it's not important. As for the factory boss, he will constantly tremble for his position, he will flatter his superior and offer him sumptuous gifts and, if he's demoted, another one identical to him will be appointed in his place, just as greedy, ignorant, and humiliated, and full of scorn for his workers, because after all he serves a proletarian State. One day, no doubt, the communist façade will disappear, with or without violence. Then we'll discover that same Russia, intact. If you ever do win this war, you'll emerge from it more National Socialist and more imperialistic than us, but your socialism, unlike ours, will be nothing but an empty name, and you'll have nothing but nationalism left to cling to. In Germany, and in the capitalist countries, everyone says communism ruined Russia; but I believe it's the opposite: it's Russia that ruined communism. It could have been a fine idea, and who can say what would have happened if the Revolution had taken place in Germany rather than Russia? If it had been led by self-assured Germans, like your friends Rosa Luxemburg and Karl Liebknecht? For my part, I think it would have been a disaster, since it would have exacerbated our specific conflicts, which National Socialism is trying to resolve. But who knows? What is certain is that having been attempted here, the communist experiment could be nothing but a failure. It's like a medical experiment conducted in a contaminated environment: the results can go straight in the trash."—"You are an excellent dialectician, and I congratulate you; you sound like a trained Communist. But I am tired and I am not going to argue with you. In any case, all this is nothing but words. Neither you nor I will see the future you describe."—"Who knows? You're a high-ranking Commissar. Maybe we'll send you to a camp to interrogate you."— "Don't play with me," he replied harshly. "Seats in your planes are much too limited for you to evacuate small fry. I know perfectly well I'll be shot, in a short while or tomorrow. It doesn't bother me." He went on in a cheerful voice: "Do you know the French writer Stendhal? Then you'll certainly have read this phrase *Only a death sentence truly distinguishes a man. It's the only thing that cannot be bought.*" I couldn't help laughing; he too laughed, but more quietly. "But where did you dig that up?" I finally got out. He shrugged his shoulders: "Oh. I've read more than just Marx, you know."—"It's too bad I have nothing to drink," I said. "I'd have gladly offered you a glass." I became serious again: "It's also too bad we're enemies. In other circumstances, we could have gotten along."—"Maybe," he said pensively, "but also maybe not." I got up, went to the door, and called the Ukrainian. Then I went back behind my desk. The Commissar had gotten up and was trying to straighten his torn sleeve. Still standing, I offered him the rest of my pack of cigarettes. "Oh, thanks," he said. "Do you have any matches?" I gave him the box of matches too. The Ukrainian was waiting in the doorway. "Allow me not to shake your hand," the Commissar said with a little ironic smile.— "Of course," I replied. The Ukrainian took him by the arm and he went out, putting the pack of cigarettes and the box of matches into his jacket pocket. I shouldn't have given him the whole pack, I said to myself; he won't have time to finish it, and the Ukrainians will smoke the rest.

I didn't file a report on this conversation; what would there have been to report? That night, the officers got together to wish each other a happy New Year and finish the last bottles that some of us still had. But the celebration was glum: after the usual toasts, my colleagues spoke little, each one standing apart, drinking and thinking; the gathering soon broke up. I had tried to describe to Thomas my discussion with Pravdin, but he cut me off: "I know all that interests you; but theoretical rantings aren't my main concern." Out of a curious sense of propriety I didn't ask him what had happened to the Commissar. The next morning I woke up, long before a dawn that was invisible here underground, racked with shudders of fever. As I shaved, I attentively examined my eyes, but didn't see any traces of pink; at the mess, I had to force myself to swallow my soup and tea; I couldn't touch my bread. Sitting, reading, writing reports soon became unbearable; I felt as if I were suffocating; I decided, without Möritz's authorization, to go out and get some air: Vopel, Thomas's deputy, had just been wounded, and I'd go visit him. Ivan, as usual, shouldered his weapon without a word. Outside, it was unusually warm and humid; the snow on the ground was turning to mud, and a thick layer of clouds hid the sun. Vopel must have been at the hospital set up in the municipal theater a little farther down. Shells had smashed the main steps and blown out the heavy wooden doors; inside the main foyer, among the fragments of marble and shattered pillars, lay dozens of corpses; some nurse's aides were carrying them up from the basements and stacking them until they could be burned. A horrible stench rose from the underground entrances, filling the lobby. "I'll wait here," Ivan declared, taking up position next to the main doors to roll a cigarette. I looked at him, and my surprise at his composure turned into a sudden, keen sadness: though I, in fact, had every chance of remaining here, he had none to get out. He was calmly smoking, indifferent. I headed for the basements. "Don't get too close to the bodies," a nurse said next to me. He pointed and I looked: a dark, indistinct swarming was streaming over the piled-up corpses, detaching from them, moving among the rubble. I looked closer and my stomach turned over: the lice were leaving the cold bodies, en masse, in search of new hosts. I carefully walked round them and went down; behind me, the nurse was sniggering. In the crypt, the smell enveloped me like a wet sheet, a living, polymorphous thing that curled up into your nostrils and throat, comprised of blood, gangrene, rotting wounds, the smoke from damp wood, wet or urine-soaked wool, almost cloying diarrhea, vomit. I breathed, hissing through my teeth, forcing myself to hold in my retching. The wounded and sick had been lined up, on blankets or sometimes right on the ground, throughout the vast, cold cement basements of the theater; moans and shouts resounded from the vaulted ceiling; a thick layer of mud covered the floor. Some doctors or nurses in dirty smocks were slowly moving between the rows of the dying, carefully looking before setting their feet down to avoid crushing a limb. I had no idea how to find Vopel in this chaos. Finally I located what seemed to be an operating room and went in without knocking. The tiled floor was splattered with mud and blood; on my left, a man with one arm was sitting on a bench, his eyes open and empty. On the table lay a blond woman—probably a civilian, since they had already evacuated all our female nurses—naked, with horrible burns on her stomach and the underside of her breasts, and both her legs cut off above the knees. This spectacle stunned me; I had to force myself to turn my eyes away, not to stare at her swollen sex exposed between the stumps. A doctor came in and I asked him to show me the wounded SS man. He made a sign for me to follow him and led me to a little room where Vopel, half dressed, was sitting on a folding cot. Some shrapnel had hit his arm; he seemed very happy, he knew that now he could leave. Pale, envious, I looked at his bandaged shoulder the way I must have looked at my sister suckling our mother's breast. Vopel smoked and chatted, he had his *Heimatschuss* and his luck made him euphoric as a child, he had trouble hiding it, it was unbearable. He kept fiddling with the verwundete tag attached to the lapel of the jacket thrown over his shoulders, as if it were a fetish. I left him, promising to discuss his evacuation with Thomas. He had incredible luck: given his rank, he had no hope of being on the evacuation lists of indispensable specialists; and we all knew that for us SS, there wouldn't even be a prisoner's camp, the Russians would treat the SS the way we treated Commissars and the men from the NKVD. As I left, I thought again about Pravdin and wondered if I would have as much composure as he did; suicide still seemed preferable to me to what awaited me with the Bolsheviks. But I didn't know if I'd have the courage. More than ever I felt cornered like a rat; and I couldn't accept the fact that it would end like this, in this filth and misery. The shivers of fever seized me again, I thought with horror that it wouldn't take much for me to be stretched out in that stinking basement, caught in the trap of my own body until I too in turn was carried to the entryway, finally rid of my lice. Having reached the lobby, I didn't go out to join Ivan but climbed the main staircase to the auditorium of the theater. It must have been a beautiful hall, with balconies and velvet seats; now the ceiling, torn open by shelling, had almost completely collapsed, the chandelier had crashed into the seats, a thick layer of rubble and snow covered everything. In the grip of curiosity, but also maybe out of a sudden fear of going out again, I went to explore the upper floors. Here, too, there had been fighting: the walls had been drilled through to set up gun emplacements, and the hallway was strewn with empty cartridge cases and ammunition boxes; on a balcony, two Russian corpses, whom no one had gone to the trouble of taking downstairs, lay sprawled in their seats, as if they were waiting for the beginning of an endlessly postponed play. Through a broken-down door at the end of a hallway, I reached a catwalk over the stage: most of the lights and set machinery had fallen, but some were still in place. I reached the attic: where the hall opened up down below there was just a gaping hole, but over the stage the floorboards were still intact, and the roof, pierced through all over, still rested on its tangled mass of beams. I risked a peek through one of the holes: I saw blackened ruins, smoke rising up in several places; a little to the north, a violent attack was under way, and behind, I could hear the characteristic wailing of invisible Sturmoviks. I looked for the Volga, which I'd have liked to see at least once, but it remained hidden behind the ruins; this theater wasn't tall enough. I turned back and contemplated the desolate attic: it reminded me of the one in Moreau's big house, in Antibes. Whenever I came back from the boarding school in Nice, my sister and I could never be separated, and together we would explore the farthest recesses of his ramshackle house, invariably ending up in the attic. There we would set up a hand-cranked gramophone taken from the living room, and unpack some marionettes belonging to my sister, representing different animals, a cat, a frog, a hedgehog; pinning up a sheet between two beams, we would stage, just for ourselves, plays and operas. Our favorite was Mozart's *Magic Flute*: the frog represented Papageno, the hedgehog Tamino, the cat Pamina, and a human-shaped doll, the Queen of the Night. Standing in this rubble, my eyes open wide, I thought I could hear the music, glimpse the enchanting play of the marionettes. A heavy cramp seized my stomach and I lowered my pants and crouched down, and already as the shit flowed, liquid, I was far away,

thinking of the waves, the sea under the boat's keel, two children sitting in the bow facing that sea, myself and my twin sister, Una, our gaze
locked and our hands touching without anyone noticing, and our love
even vaster and more endless than that blue sea or the bitterness and
pain of the wounded years, a solar splendor, a voluntary abyss. My
cramps, my diarrhea, my surges of white-hot fever, my fear too, all that
was erased, dissolved in this unhoped-for return. Without even bothering to pull my pants back up I lay down in the dust and rubble and
the past unfolded like a flower in the springtime. What we loved, in the
attic, was that unlike in basements, there was always light. Even when
the roof isn't riddled with shrapnel, either the daylight filters through
little windows or through cracks between the tiles, or it rises up
through the trapdoor leading to the house, it's never entirely dark. And
it was in that diffuse, uncertain, fragmented light that we played and
learned the things we had to learn. Who knows how it happens? Maybe
we found, hidden behind other books in Moreau's library, certain forbidden books, maybe it happened naturally, proceeding along with our
games and our discoveries. That summer, we remained in Antibes, but
on Saturdays and Sundays we would go to a house rented by Moreau,
near Saint-Jean-Cap-Ferrat, by the sea. There our games spilled into
the fields, the pine woods, and the nearby *maquis*, vibrating with the
chirping of the crickets and the buzzing of the bees in the lavender,
whose odor overlapped the scents of rosemary, thyme, and resin, mixed
too, near the end of the summer, with that of the figs we would devour
to the point of nausea, and then, farther away, the sea and the chaotic
rocks that formed this jagged coast, up to a little sloping island that
we reached by swimming or by rowboat. There, naked as savages, we
would dive with an iron spoon to detach the fat black sea urchins clinging to the rocks underwater; when we had gathered a pile of them, we
would open them with a pocketknife and swallow the bright orange
mass of little eggs gathered within the shell, then throw the scraps into
the sea and patiently extract the broken spines from our fingers, opening the skin up with the tip of the penknife and urinating into the
cut. Sometimes, especially when the mistral was blowing, the waves
grew, crashing against the rocks; reaching the shore became a perilous
game, all childlike skill and ardor: once, while I was hoisting myself
out of the water, having waited for an ebb to get hold of the rock,
an unexpected wave swept me onto the stone, my skin was scraped
on the rough edges, the blood flowed in multiple little trickles, diluted
by seawater; my sister rushed onto me and lay me down in the grass, to
kiss the scratches one by one, lapping up the blood and salt like a greedy
little cat. In our sovereign delirium, we had invented a code that al-

lowed us, in front of our mother and Moreau, openly to suggest precise gestures and actions. It was the age of pure innocence, superb, magnificent. Freedom possessed our narrow little bodies, thin and tanned; we swam like seals, dashed through the woods like foxes, rolled, twisted together in the dust, our naked bodies indissociable, neither one nor the other specifically girl or boy, but a couple of snakes intertwined.

At night, the fever rose; I shivered on my bed above Thomas's, hunched under the blankets, devoured by lice, dominated by these distant images. When school began again, after the summer, almost nothing changed. Separated, we dreamed of each other, waiting for the moment we'd be together again. We had our public lives, lived openly like those of all children, and our private lives, which belonged to us alone, a space vaster than the world, limited only by the possibilities of our united minds. As time went by, the settings changed, but the pavane of our love continued to mark its own rhythm, elegant or furious. For the winter vacation, Moreau took us to the mountains; at the time, that was much rarer than it is now. He rented a chalet that had belonged to a Russian nobleman: this Muscovite had transformed an annex into a sauna, something none of us had ever seen; but the owner showed us how to work it, and Moreau, especially, developed a passion for this invention. At the end of the afternoon, after we had returned from skiing or sledding or hiking, he spent a good hour there sweating; he didn't have the courage to go out and roll in the snow, though, as we did, clothed, alas, in swimming trunks, which our mother forced us to wear. She, for her part, did not like this sauna and avoided it. But when we were alone in the house, either during the day, when they went out for a walk in the town, or at night, when they were sleeping, we reoccupied the room after it had grown cold and finally shed our clothes, and our little bodies became a mirror for each other. We also nestled in the long empty closets built beneath the large sloping roof of the chalet, tall enough to stand up in, but where we stayed sitting or lying down, slithering, snuggled against each other, skin against skin, slaves of each other and masters of everything.

During the day, I tried to find my fragile bearings in that devastated city; but the fever and diarrhea wore me down, separating me from the nonetheless heavy and grief-filled reality surrounding me. My left ear also hurt, a numb, insistent pain, just beneath the skin inside the canal. I tried soothing it by rubbing the spot with my little finger, to no avail. Distracted, I spent many long, gray hours in my office wrapped in my soiled fleece-lined coat, humming a little mechanical, toneless tune, try-

ing to find my way back to the lost paths of old. The angel opened my
office door and came in, bearing the hot coal that burns away all sins;
but instead of touching my lips with it, he buried it whole in my mouth;
and if then I went out into the street, at the touch of the fresh air, I
burned alive. I stayed standing, I didn't smile, but my gaze, I knew, remained calm, yes, even as the flames were eating into my eyelids, hollowing out my nostrils, filling my jaw and veiling my eyes. Once these
conflagrations were extinguished, I saw astonishing, extraordinary
things. In a slightly sloping street, lined with destroyed cars and trucks,
I noticed a man on the sidewalk leaning with one hand on a streetlight.
He was a soldier, dirty, ill-shaven, dressed in rags held together by strings
and pins, his right leg cut off under the knee, a fresh, open wound from
which blood was gushing in streams; the man was holding a can or a tin
cup under the stump and trying to gather this blood and drink it quickly,
so as not to lose too much of it. He carried out these gestures methodically, with precision, and my throat tightened with horror. I'm not a
doctor, I said to myself, I cannot intervene. Fortunately we were near
the theater, and I rushed through the long, dark, cluttered basements,
scattering the rats running over the wounded: "A doctor! I need a doctor!" I shouted; the nurses looked at me dully, without interest, no one
answered. Finally I found a doctor sitting on a stool near a stove, slowly
drinking tea. He took some time to respond to my agitation; he seemed
tired, slightly annoyed by my insistence; but he ended up following me.
In the street, the man with his leg cut off had fallen down. He was still
calm and impassive, but he was obviously weakening. The stump was
now foaming with a whitish substance that mixed with the blood,
maybe it was pus; the other leg was also bleeding and looked as if it were
about to fall away. The doctor knelt down next to him and began to
look after his atrocious wounds with cold, professional gestures; his
composure amazed me, not just his ability to touch these sources of horror but to work on them without emotion or revulsion; as for me, it was
making me sick. While he was working, the doctor looked at me and I
understood his gaze: the man wasn't going to last long, there was nothing to do but seem to be helping him to make his anguish and the last
moments of his fleeting life a little easier to bear. All this is real, believe
me. Elsewhere, Ivan had taken me to a large building, not very far from
the front, on the Prospekt Respublikanskyi, where a Russian deserter
was supposed to be hidden. I didn't find him; I was going through some
rooms, wishing I hadn't come, when a child's high-pitched laughter
burst out down the hallway. I went out of the apartment and didn't see
anything, but a few instants later the stairway was invaded by a horde of
feral, shameless little girls, who brushed past me and dashed between my

legs before lifting their skirts to show me their dirty behinds and bounding upstairs; then they all came tumbling back down, giggling wildly. They looked like frantic little rats in the throes of a sexual frenzy: one of them sat down on a step at the level of my head and spread her legs, exhibiting her bare, smooth vulva; another bit my fingers; I grasped her by the hair and pulled her toward me to slap her, but a third girl slipped her hand between my legs from behind while the one I was holding twisted around, tore herself away, and disappeared into a hallway. I ran after her but the hallway was already empty. I looked for an instant at the closed doors of the apartments, leaped, opened one: I had to throw myself backward so as not to fall into the void, since there was nothing behind the door, and I slammed it shut, just before a Russian machine-gun volley riddled it with holes. I threw myself down to the ground: an antitank shell exploded against the wall, deafening me and showering me with plaster and fragments of wood and old newspapers. I crawled furiously and rolled into an apartment on the other side of the hallway, which had lost its door. In the living room, gasping to get my breath back, I distinctly heard a piano; submachine gun in hand, I opened the door to the bedroom: inside, a Soviet corpse was lying on the unmade bed, and a Hauptmann in a shapka, sitting with his legs crossed on a stool, was listening to a record on a gramophone placed on the floor. I didn't recognize the tune and asked him what it was. He waited for the end of the piece, a light tune with an obsessive little ritornello, and picked up the record to look at the label: "Daquin. *The Cuckoo.*" He wound the gramophone up, got out another disk from an orange sleeve, and set the needle down. "You'll recognize this one." In fact, it was Mozart's *Turkish Rondo*, in an interpretation that was at once fast and cheerful but also imbued with romantic gravity; a Slav pianist, certainly. "Who's playing?" I asked.—"Rachmaninov, the composer. You know him?"—"A little. I didn't know he played too." He handed me a pile of records. "He must have been some music lover, our friend," he said, pointing to the bed. "And he must have had good contacts in the Party, given the source of the records." I examined the labels: they were printed in English—these records came from the United States; Rachmaninov played Gluck, Scarlatti, Bach, Chopin, as well as one of his own pieces; the recordings dated back to the early 1920s, but seemed to have been recently issued. There were also some Russian records. Mozart's piece came to an end, and the officer put on the Gluck, a transcription of a melody from his *Orfeo ed Euridice*, delicate, haunting, terribly sad. I motioned with my chin toward the bed: "Why don't you get rid of him?"—"Why should I? He's fine where he is." I waited for the end of the piece to ask him: "Listen, you haven't seen a little girl around, have you?"—"No, why, do you need one? Music is better." I turned my back on him and went out of the apartment. I opened the next door: the little girl who had bitten me was peeing, squatting over a rug. When she saw me she looked at me with shining eyes, rubbed her crotch, and dove between my legs before I could react, running into the stairwell again, laughing. I went to sit down on the sofa and looked at the wet spot on the flowered carpet; I was still reeling from the bomb explosion, and the piano music was ringing in my infected ear, which throbbed with pain. I touched it delicately with my finger and brought it back covered with yellowish pus, which I wiped distractedly on the cloth of the sofa. Then I blew my nose in the curtains and went out; so much for the little girl, someone else would have to administer the punishment she deserved. In the basement of the Univermag, I went to consult a doctor: he confirmed the infection, cleaned it as well as he could, and put a bandage over my ear, but couldn't give me anything else, as he had nothing left to give. I couldn't say what day it was, I couldn't even say whether the great Russian offensive west of the *Kessel* had begun; I had lost all notion of time and of the technical details of our collective agony. When people spoke to me, the words reached me as if from far away, a voice underwater, and I understood nothing of what they were trying to tell me. Thomas must have noticed that I was rapidly losing my footing and he made efforts to guide me, to bring me back to less obviously rambling paths. But he too was having trouble maintaining a sense of the continuity and importance of things. To keep me busy, he took me out: some of the Ics he frequented still had a bottle of Armenian brandy or schnapps, and while he talked with them I would sip a glass and bury myself in the buzzing inside me. Coming back from such an expedition, I saw a metro entrance at a street corner: I didn't know that Stalingrad had a metro. Why hadn't they ever shown me a map of it? I took Thomas by the sleeve, pointing to the steps disappearing into the darkness, and said: "Come on, Thomas, let's go see this metro up closer." He answered very kindly but firmly: "No, Max, not now. Come along." I insisted: "Please. I want to see it." My voice took on a plaintive tone, I was filled with a mute anguish, this entrance drew me irresistibly, but Thomas still refused. I was about to begin sobbing like a child who's been denied a toy. At that moment an artillery shell exploded near us and the blast knocked me over. When the smoke cleared, I sat up and shook my head; Thomas, I saw, was still lying in the snow, his greatcoat splattered with blood mixed with pieces of earth; his intestines spilled out of his stomach in long, sticky, slippery, smoking coils. As I watched him, stupefied, he sat up with jerky, uncoordinated movements, like a baby who's just learned to walk, and buried his gloved hand in his stomach to draw out jagged pieces of shrapnel, which he tossed into the snow. These shards were still almost red-hot and, despite the glove, they burned his fingers, which he sucked sadly after each piece; when they touched the snow, they disappeared into it sizzling, letting off a little cloud of steam. The last few pieces must have been deeply lodged, since Thomas had to stick his whole fist in to pry them out. While he began to gather his intestines together, pulling them gently toward him and looping them around one hand, he gave me a lopsided smile: "There are still a few bits left, I think. But they're too small." He pushed the coils of intestines in and smoothed the fold of skin of his stomach back over them. "Could I borrow your scarf?" he asked me; always the dandy, he wore only a turtleneck sweater. Feeling faint, I handed him my scarf without a word. Passing it under the shreds of his uniform, he carefully wrapped it around his belly and made a tight knot in front. Then, firmly holding his work with one hand, he hoisted himself up, staggering, leaning on my shoulder. "Shit," he mumbled, swaying, "that hurts." He stood on tiptoe and bounced several times, then risked a hop. "Well, it looks like it'll hold." With all the dignity he could muster, he gathered the remnants of his uniform around him and drew them over his stomach. The sticky blood held them more or less in place. "That's the last thing I needed. And of course, you might as well forget about finding a needle and thread, in this place." His little rasping laugh turned into a grimace of pain. "What a mess," he sighed. "Lord," he added as he glimpsed my face, "you do look a little green."

I didn't insist on taking the metro anymore, but accompanied Thomas to the Univermag, to wait for the end. The Russian offensive, west of the *Kessel*, had completely smashed through our lines. A few days later, Pitomnik was evacuated in an indescribable chaos that left thousands of wounded scattered throughout the frozen steppe; troops and HQ flowed toward the city; even the AOK, in Gumrak, was preparing its retreat, and the Wehrmacht expelled us from the bunker of the Univermag, to rehouse us temporarily in the former premises of the NKVD, which had once been a handsome building, with a large glass cupola now shattered and a polished granite floor, but whose basements were already occupied by a medical unit, which left us only the demolished offices on the first floor, over which we still had to fight with Seydlitz's staff (as in a hotel with a sea view, everyone wanted to be on one side, not the other). But all these frenetic events left me indifferent, I barely noted the latest changes, since I had made a wonderful discovery, an edition of Sophocles. The book was torn in half, someone must have wanted to share it, and it was alas only in translation, but *Electra* was still there, my favorite. Forgetting the shivers of fever that shook my body, the pus that was oozing from my bandage, I lost myself blissfully in the verses. At the boarding school where my mother had had me locked up, to flee the surrounding brutality, I had taken refuge in my studies, and I especially liked Greek, thanks to our professor, the young priest I've already mentioned. I wasn't yet fifteen but I spent all my free time at the library, deciphering the *Iliad* line by line, with passion and limitless patience. At the end of the school year, our class organized a performance of a tragedy, *Electra*, in fact, in the school gym, rigged out for the occasion; and I was chosen for the title role. I wore a long white dress, sandals, and a wig whose black curls danced on my shoulders: when I looked at myself in the mirror, I thought I saw Una, and I almost fainted. We had been separated from each other for almost a year. When I walked onto the stage I was so possessed by hatred and love and the sensation of my young virgin's body that I saw nothing, heard nothing; and when I moaned *Oh my Orestes, your death is killing me*, tears streamed from my eyes. When Orestes reappeared, I screeched, possessed by the Erinyes, vociferated my injunctions in that beautiful, sovereign language, *Go on, then, one more blow, if you still feel the strength*, I cried, encouraging him, urging him to murder, *Kill him quickly, then expose his body: let his gravediggers be whatever creatures find him*. And when it was over, I didn't hear the applause, didn't hear the words of Father Labourie who was congratulating me, I was sobbing, and the butchery in the House of Atreus was the blood in my own house.

Thomas, who seemed to have completely recovered from his accident, scolded me amicably, but I didn't pay any attention to him. To tease him, when I emerged from my Sophocles, I quoted Joseph de Maistre at him: *What is a lost battle? It's a battle you think you have lost.* Thomas, delighted, had a sign painted with these words, which was posted in our hallway: this, apparently, earned him Möritz's congratulations, and the new slogan got as far as General Schmidt, who wanted to adopt it as the motto for the army; but Paulus, it was said, opposed it. Neither Thomas nor I, by mutual agreement, spoke any longer of evacuation; but everyone knew that it was only a question of days, and the fortunate chosen ones of the Wehrmacht were already leaving. I sank into a sordid indifference; only the obsessive fear of typhus shook me now and then, and not content with scrutinizing my eyes and lips, I undressed to look for black spots on my torso. I didn't even think about the diarrhea anymore; on the contrary, squatting in the stinking latrines, I found a certain tranquility, and would have liked, as when I was a child, to lock myself up in them for hours reading, but there was no light, and no door, either, so I had to make do with a cigarette, one of my last. My fever, almost permanent now, had become a warm cocoon in which I could curl up, and I took an insane enjoyment in my filth, my sweat, my dehydrated skin, my stinging eyes. I hadn't shaved for days and a fine reddish beard contributed to my voluptuous feeling of dirtiness and neglect. My sick ear was suppurating, resounding by turns like a bell or a muffled siren; sometimes I couldn't hear anything at all. The fall of Pitomnik had been followed by a few days' lull; then, around January 20, the methodical annihilation of the *Kessel* resumed (for these dates, I'm citing books, not my memory, since the calendar had become an abstract notion for me, a fleeting memory of a bygone world). The temperature, after the brief thaw at the beginning of the year, had plummeted catastrophically—it must have been twenty-five or thirty below. The meager fires lit in empty oil drums weren't enough to warm the wounded; even in town, the soldiers had to wrap their penises in cloth to piss, a stinking rag, preciously guarded in one's pocket; and others took advantage of these occasions to hold out their hands, swollen with frostbite, beneath the warm stream. All these details were reported to me by the somnambulistic mechanisms of the army; just as somnambulistically, I read and classified these reports, after having issued them a file number; but it had been some time already since I stopped writing reports myself. When Möritz wanted information, I grabbed some reports from the Abwehr at random and brought them to him; maybe Thomas had explained to him that I was sick, he looked at me strangely but didn't say anything. As for Thomas, he had never returned my scarf, and when I went out to take the air, my neck was cold: but I still went out, the dense stench of the buildings was becoming unbearable. Thomas's rapid recovery intrigued me: he seemed entirely well, and when I asked him, raising my eyebrows significantly and looking at his abdomen: "So, are you all right?" he looked surprised and answered: "Yes, I'm fine, why shouldn't I be?" As for me, however, my sores and my fevers weren't getting any better; I would have liked to know his secret. One of those days, probably around the twentieth or the twenty-first, I went out to smoke in the street, and soon after, Thomas joined me. The sky was clear, cloudless, the cold biting, the sun, streaming everywhere through the gaping openings of the façades, was reflected on the dry snow, brilliant, dazzling, and where it couldn't reach it projected steel shadows. "Do you hear?" Thomas asked, but my mad ear was ringing, I couldn't hear anything. "Come." He pulled me by the sleeve. We skirted round the building and discovered a strange sight: two or three Landsers, wrapped in greatcoats or blankets, were standing near an upright piano in the middle of the little street. A soldier, perched on a little chair, was playing, and the others seemed to be listening to him

attentively, but I couldn't hear anything—it was curious, and it saddened
me: I too would have liked to listen to this music, I thought I had as
much a right to it as anyone. A few Ukrainians were heading toward us;
I recognized Ivan, who made a little sign to me with his hand. My ear
was itching terribly, and I couldn't hear anything anymore: even the
words of Thomas, right next to me, reached me now only as an indistinct rumbling. I had the horrible and terrifying impression of living a
silent film. Exasperated, I tore off my bandage and buried my pinky into
the ear canal; something gave way, a flow of pus gushed out onto my
hand and ran onto the neck of my coat. That soothed me a little, but I
still could hear almost nothing; the piano, if I turned my ear toward it,
seemed to be emitting a watery gurgle; the other ear wasn't functioning
any better; disappointed, I turned aside and slowly walked away. The
sunlight was truly splendid, it chiseled each detail of the jagged façades.
Behind me, I thought I could make out some agitation: I turned
around, Thomas and Ivan were gesturing toward me, the others were
looking at me. I didn't know what they wanted, but I was embarrassed
at being such an object of attention; I made a friendly little sign to them
and went on walking. I glanced at them again: Ivan was running toward
me, but I was distracted by a slight tap on my forehead: a piece of gravel,
perhaps, or an insect, since when I felt it, a little drop of blood beaded
on my finger. I wiped it off and continued on toward the Volga, which
I knew lay somewhere that way. This was a sector where our forces held
the riverbank; and I still hadn't seen it, this famous Volga, and I resolutely headed in that direction, to contemplate it at least once before
leaving this city. The streets wound between a shambles of quiet, deserted ruins lit by the cold January sun; it was very calm and I found it
extraordinarily pleasant; if there were gunshots, I didn't hear them. The
icy air invigorated me. The pus had stopped flowing from my ear, which
let me hope that the source of infection was pierced once and for all; I
felt in good form and full of strength. After the last buildings, running
along cliffs that loomed over the great river, there was an abandoned
railway, the tracks already eaten by rust. Beyond stretched the white surface of the river caught in the ice, and then beyond that the other bank,
the one we had never reached, completely flat and also white and as if
emptied of all life. Around me, there was no one, I didn't see any
trenches or positions, the lines must have been farther up. Emboldened,
I climbed down the steep sandy bank and found myself at the river's
edge. First hesitatingly, then with more confidence, I set one foot on the
snow-dusted ice, then another: I was walking on the Volga, and it made
me as happy as a child. The snowflakes lifted from the ice by the light
wind danced in the sun, a little will-o'-the-wisp around my feet. In

front of me, a dark hole opened up in the ice, quite wide, probably pierced by a high-caliber shell that had fallen short; deep inside the hole, water was flowing quickly, almost green in the sun, fresh, alluring; I leaned over and dunked my hand in it—it didn't seem cold: gathering it in both hands, I rinsed my face, my ear, the back of my neck, then drank several mouthfuls. I took off my *shuba*, folded it carefully, put it together with my cap on the ice, then, breathing in deeply, I dove in. The water was clear and welcoming, a maternal kind of warmth. The swift current created whirlpools that soon carried me away under the ice. All kinds of things were passing by me, which I could clearly make out in this green water: horses whose feet the current was moving as if they were galloping, fat and almost flat fish, bottom-feeders, Russian corpses with swollen faces, entwined in their curious brown capes, pieces of clothing and uniforms, tattered flags floating on their poles, a wagon wheel that, probably soaked in oil, was still burning as it swirled beneath the water. A body bumped into me, then went on its way; this one was wearing a German uniform; as it drifted farther away I saw its face and its dancing blond curls, it was Voss, smiling. I tried to catch up with him but an eddy separated us, and by the time I reestablished my position, he had disappeared. Above me, the ice formed an opaque screen, but the air lasted in my lungs, I wasn't worried and kept swimming, passing sunken barges full of handsome young men sitting in rows, their weapons still in their hands, little fish threading through their hair agitated by the current. Then slowly in front of me the water grew lighter, columns of green light plunged down from holes in the ice, became a forest, then melded into each other as the blocks of ice drifted farther apart. I finally rose back to the surface to regain my breath. A little iceberg bumped into me, I dove back down, straightened out, rose up again. Here, the river carried almost no more blocks of ice. Upriver, to my left, a Russian ship was drifting in the current, lying on its side, gently burning. Despite the sun, a few large flakes of luminous snow were falling, which lay hidden as soon as they touched the water. Paddling with my hands, I turned around: the city, stretched all along the shore, lay hidden behind a thick curtain of black smoke. Above my head, seagulls were reeling and shrieking, looking at me curiously, or possibly calculatingly, then flying off to perch on a block of ice; the sea was still far away, though; had they come all the way up from Astrakhan? Swallows too were whirling around and skimming the water's surface. I began swimming calmly toward the left bank. Finally I touched bottom and emerged from the water. The shore, on this bank, was made of a fine sand that rose gently up, forming little dunes; beyond, everything was flat. Logically I should have found myself at the level of the Kras-

naya Sloboda, but I didn't see anything: no artillery pieces neatly lined
up, no trenches, no village, no soldiers, no one. A few scraggly trees
adorned the top of the dunes or leaned toward the Volga, which was
flowing swiftly behind me; somewhere, a linnet was calling; a grass
snake threaded between my feet and disappeared into the sand. I
climbed the dunes and looked around: in front of me stretched an almost bare steppe, a land the color of ash lightly powdered with snow,
with here and there a brown, short, dense, grass, and a few tufts of sage-
brush; to the south, a line of poplars barred the horizon, probably bor-
dering an irrigation canal; there was nothing else to be seen. I searched
through my jacket pocket and fished out my pack of cigarettes, but they
were soaking wet. My wet clothes clung to my skin, but I wasn't cold;
the air was gentle and mild. Then I felt a wave of fatigue, probably the
effects of swimming: I fell to my knees and dug my fingers into the dry
ground, still frozen by winter. I finally managed to pull up some clumps
of earth, which I greedily stuffed into my mouth. They had a somewhat
bitter, mineral taste, but when mixed with my saliva this earth gave off
almost vegetable sensations, a fibrous life, which was still disappointing;
I would have liked it to be soft, warm, and oily, for it to melt in my
mouth, and for me to be able to bury my whole body in it, slip into it
as into a grave. In the Caucasus, the mountain people have a curious
way of digging graves: first they cut a trench two meters deep; then, at
the bottom, on one side they dig out a niche with a slanting roof. The
dead man, without a coffin, wrapped in a white shroud, is placed on his
side in this recess, his face turned toward Mecca; then the alcove is
walled in with bricks, or wood if the family is poor; only then is the
ditch filled in, the excess earth forming an oblong hillock; yet the dead
man doesn't lie beneath this hillock, but right next to it. That, I said to
myself when this custom was described to me, is a grave that would suit
me, at least the cold horror of the thing is clear, and also it must be more
comfortable, more intimate perhaps. But here there was no one to help
me dig, and I didn't have a tool, not even a knife: so I began walking,
more or less in an easterly direction. It was a vast plain with no one on
it, neither living on the earth nor dead beneath it; and I walked a long
time beneath a colorless sky, which didn't let me judge the time (my
watch, set like all military watches to Berlin time, hadn't stood up to the
swim and showed an eternal thirteen minutes to noon). Here and there
a bright red poppy grew, the only patches of color in this gloomy landscape; but when I tried to pick one, it turned gray and crumbled in a
light puff of ash. Finally, in the distance, I made out some shapes. As I
approached, I saw that it was a long white dirigible, floating over a large
kurgan. Several figures were walking on the sides of the tumulus: three

of them detached from the group and came toward me. When they were close enough, I could see that they were wearing white lab coats over suits, with high, slightly old-fashioned detachable collars and black ties; one of them also wore a bowler hat. *"Guten Tag, meine Herren,"* I said politely when they were standing in front of me. "Bonjour, monsieur," said the one wearing a hat. He asked me in French what I was doing there and, answering in the same language, I explained to him as best I could. The two others nodded as they listened. When I had finished my narrative, the man with the hat said: "In that case, you'll have to come with us; the doctor will want to talk with you."—"If you like. Who is this doctor?"—"Dr. Sardine, the head of our expedition." They brought me to the foot of the kurgan; three thick cables were anchoring the dirigible, a zeppelin that swayed slowly in the breeze more than fifty meters above our heads, its long oval mass carrying a two-story metal gondola. Another, thinner cable seemed to provide a telephone connection: one of the men spoke briefly into a receiver set up on a folding table. On the kurgan, the other gentlemen were digging, probing, measuring. I raised my head again: a kind of basket was slowly descending from the gondola, swaying back and forth in the wind. When it got close to the ground two men grasped it and guided it. This large basket was made of saplings and woven wicker; the man with the bowler hat opened a door and motioned me to get into it; then he joined me and closed it. The cable began to rise and with a heavy leap the basket tore itself from the ground; with our bodies as ballast, it reeled less, but it still made for a sort of seasick effect, and I gripped the edge; my chaperone held onto his hat. I looked at the steppe: as far as I could see, not one tree, not one house, just, at the horizon, a kind of hump, probably another kurgan.

The basket entered through a trapdoor into a room in the gondola; from there, my guide had me climb a spiral staircase, then go down a long hallway. Everything here was aluminum, brass, well-polished hardwood: a beautiful machine, truly. Having reached a padded door, the man rang a little doorbell. The door opened, he gestured for me to go in, and didn't follow.

It was a large room lined with a banquette and a long bay window and furnished with shelves, with a long table in the center covered with an unlikely assortment of bric-a-brac: books, maps, globes, stuffed animals, models of fantastic vehicles, astronomical, optical, navigational instruments. A white cat with different-colored eyes was silently threading its way between these objects. A little man, also in a white lab coat, was hunched over on a chair at the end of the table; when I came in, he turned around, swiveling in his seat. His hair, streaked with gray and combed back, looked dirty and stringy; a pair of thick-rimmed glasses, set on top of his forehead, held it back. His slightly sunken face was badly shaved and wore a quarrelsome, disagreeable expression. "Come in! Come in," he squealed in a hoarse voice. He pointed to the long banquette: "Have a seat." I skirted round the table and sat down, crossing my legs. He spluttered as he spoke; the remnants of a meal stained his lab coat. "You are very young!" he exclaimed. I turned my head slightly and contemplated the bare steppe from the bay window, then looked at the man again. "I am Hauptsturmführer Dr. Maximilien Aue, at your service," I said finally, bowing my head.—"Ah!" he croaked, "a doctor! A doctor! A doctor of what?"—"Of law, Monsieur."—"A lawyer!" he leaped out of his chair. "A lawyer! Hideous . . . wretched scum! You're worse than Jews! Worse than banksters! Worse than royalists! . . ."—"I am not a lawyer, Monsieur. I am a jurist, expert in constitutional law, and an officer of the *Schutzstaffel.*" He suddenly calmed down and sat down again in one bound: his legs, too short for his chair, reached only a few centimeters above the ground. "That's hardly any better . . ." He pondered. "I too am a doctor. But . . . of useful things. Sardine, I'm Sardine, Dr. Sardine."—"Pleased to meet you, Doktor."— "I can't say the same yet. What are you doing here?"—"In your airship? Your colleagues invited me to come up."—"Invited . . . invited . . . a big word. I mean here, in this region."—"Well, I was walking."—"You were walking . . . fine! But why?"—"I was walking at random. To tell you the truth I got a little lost." He leaned forward with a mistrustful look, gripping the armrests of his chair with both hands: "Are you quite sure of that? . . . Didn't you have a specific purpose?!"—"I must confess I did not." But he was still muttering: "Confess, confess . . . aren't you looking for something . . . aren't you actually . . . on my trail! Sent by my jealous competitors! . . ." He was getting worked up on his own. "Then how did you find us?"—"Your aircraft can be seen quite far away, in this plain." But he stuck to his guns: "Aren't you an accomplice of Finkelstein! . . . Of Krasschild! Those envious Yids . . . swollen up with their own importance . . . Squids! Dwarves! Boot-polishers! Falsifiers of diplomas and of results . . ."—"Allow me to point out to you, Doctor, that you must not read the papers much. Otherwise you would know that a German, especially an SS officer, rarely places himself at the service of Jews. I do not know the gentlemen you speak of, but if I met them, it would be my duty to arrest them."—"Yes . . . yes . . ." he said, rubbing his lower lip, "that's possible, in fact . . ." He searched through the pocket of his lab coat and took out a little leather purse; with fingers yellowed by nicotine, he fished out a pinch of tobacco and began rolling a cigarette. Since he didn't seem inclined to offer me one, I took out my own pack: it had dried out, and by rolling and tamping one of my cigarettes a little, I could make something suitable out of it. My matches, however, were useless; I looked at the table, but didn't see any others in the midst of the mess. "Do you have a light, Doktor?" I asked.—"One instant, young man, one instant . . ." He finished rolling his cigarette, took a rather large pewter cube from the table, put his cigarette into a hole, and pressed a little button. Then he waited. After a few minutes that I found rather long, a little *ping* could be heard; he drew out the cigarette, whose end glowed red, and breathed in little puffs: "Ingenious, no?"—"Very. But a little slow, perhaps."—"It's the element that takes time to warm up. Give me your cigarette." I held it out to him and he repeated the operation while spitting smoke out in little puffs; this time, the *ping* sounded a little more quickly. "It's my only vice . . ." he murmured, "the only one! All the rest . . . finished! Alcohol . . . a poison . . . As for fornication . . . All those greedy females! Plastered with paint! Syphilitic! Ready to suck the genius out of a man . . . to circumcise his soul! . . . Not to speak of the danger of procreation . . . omnipresent . . . Whatever you do, you can't escape it, they always find a way . . . an abomination! Hideous big-titted monsters writhing! Seductive Jewesses, waiting to strike the death blow! Always in heat! The smells! All year long! A man of science must know how to turn his back on all that. Build himself a shell of indifference . . . of will . . . *Noli me tangere.*" As he smoked, he let his ashes fall on the floor; since I couldn't see an ashtray, I did the same. The white cat was rubbing its neck against a sextant. Suddenly, Sardine put his glasses on his eyes and leaned forward to examine me: "And are you looking for the end of the world too?"—"Sorry?"—"The end of the world! The end of the world! Don't act innocent. What else could have brought you out here?"—"I don't know what you're talking about, Doktor." He grimaced, bounded out of his chair, ran around the table, seized an object, and hurled it at my head. I caught it in the nick of time. It was a cone mounted on a base, painted like a globe with the continents spread out around it; the flat base was gray and bore the caption TERRA INCOGNITA. "Don't tell me you've never seen that?" Sardine had gone back to his seat and was rolling another cigarette. "Never, Doktor," I replied.—"What is it?"— "It's the Earth! Idiot! Hypocrite! Two-faced bastard!"—"I'm very sorry, Doktor. At school, we were taught that the Earth was round." He let out a fierce growl: "Balderdash! Nonsense! . . . Medieval theories . . . hackneyed . . . Superstition! There!" he shouted, pointing with his cigarette at the cone I was still holding, "There! That's the truth. And I'm going to prove it! At this instant, we're headed for the Edge." In fact, I noticed that the cabin was gently vibrating. I looked out the bay win-

dow: the dirigible had raised anchor and was slowly gaining altitude.
"And when we arrive," I asked carefully, "will your aircraft pass over
it?"—"Don't be an imbecile! What an ignoramus. You are an educated
man, you say . . . Think! It goes without saying that beyond the Edge,
there is no gravitational field. Otherwise, the evidence would have been
proven a long time ago!"—"But then how do you count on . . ."—
"That's my whole genius," he replied maliciously. "This aircraft is hiding another one." He got up and came over to sit next to me. "I'll tell
you. In any case, you're going to stay with us. You, the Incredulous, will
be the Witness. At the Edge of the world, we will land, deflate the balloon, there, above us, which will be folded and put away in a compartment designed for this purpose. Below, there are legs that can be
unfolded, and that are articulated, eight in all, ending in strong pincers."
As he spoke, he mimed pincers with his fingers. "These pincers can grip
any soil whatsoever. Thus, we will pass over the Great Edge like an insect, a spider. But we will pass over it! I'm rather proud of myself . . .
Can you believe it?! The difficulties . . . in wartime . . . to construct
such a machine? . . . The negotiations with the occupying power? With
those morons in Vichy, drunk on mineral water? With the factions . . .
That whole alphabet soup, crawling with retards, microcephalics, ca-
reerists? And with Jews! Yes, Mr. German Officer, Jews too! A man of
science cannot have scruples . . . He must be ready to strike a deal with
the devil if necessary." A siren sounded somewhere inside the vessel, interrupting him. He stood up: "I have to go. Wait for me here." At the
door, he turned around: "Don't touch anything!" Alone, I got up too
and took a few steps. I held out my fingers to pet the cat with the different-colored eyes, but it bristled and hissed, baring its teeth. I looked
again at the objects piled up on the long table, fiddled with one or two,
leafed through a book, then went to kneel down on the banquette and
look at the steppe. A river crossed it, snaking gently, shimmering in the
sun. I thought I could make out an object on the water. At the end of
the room, a telescope mounted on a tripod stood in front of the bay
window. I set my eye to it, turned the knob to focus, and looked for the
river; when I had located it, I followed its course to find the object. It
was a small boat with figures in it. I adjusted the focus. A naked young
woman was sitting in the center of the boat, flowers in her hair; in front
and behind her, two awful creatures, in human form and also naked,
were paddling. The woman had long black hair. My heart suddenly
beating hard, I tried to make out her face, but it was difficult to distinguish her features. Little by little, this certainty dawned in me: it was
Una, my sister. Where was she going? Other boats were following hers,
heaped with flowers, it looked like a marriage procession. I had to join

her. But how? I rushed out of the cabin, down the spiral staircase: in the room with the basket, there was a man. "The doctor?" I panted. "Where is he? I must see him." He signaled me to follow him and led me to the bow of the vessel, into the control cabin where, in front of a vast circular bay window, men in white lab coats were busy. Sardine sat enthroned on a raised armchair in front of a command panel. "What do you want?" he asked abruptly when he saw me.—"Doktor . . . I have to go down. It's a question of life or death."—"Impossible!" he shouted in a shrill voice. "Impossible! I understand everything. You are a spy! An accomplice!" He turned to the man who had brought me there. "Arrest him! Clap him in irons!" The man put his hand on my arm; without thinking, I landed an uppercut on his chin and bounded to the door. Several men rushed at me, but the door was too narrow for them all to pass through, and it delayed them. I ran back up the spiral staircase, taking the steps three at a time, and positioned myself at the top: when the first head appeared beneath me, crowned with a bowler hat, I delivered a kick that propelled him backward; he tumbled down the steps, dragging his colleagues down with a huge racket. I could hear Sardine howling. I opened doors at random: cabins, a map room, a canteen. At the end of the hallway I came across a storage room with a ladder going up; the trapdoor at the top must have opened onto the inside of the hull, for repairs; there were metal lockers there, which I opened; they contained parachutes. My pursuers were approaching; I slipped a parachute on and began to climb. The trapdoor opened easily: above, an immense cylindrical cage of waxed canvas stretched over metal circlets rose through the body of the dirigible. A diffuse light passed through the cloth, there were also lightbulbs set at intervals; through portholes made of transparent rubber, one could make out the soft outlines of the hydrogen gasbags. I began the ascent. The shaft, held in place by a solid framework, was a few dozen meters tall, and I soon ran out of breath. I risked a glance beneath me: the first bowler hat was appearing through the trapdoor, followed by the man's body. I saw that he was brandishing a pistol and I resumed my climb. He didn't shoot; no doubt he was afraid of puncturing the gasbags. Other men followed him; they were climbing as slowly as I was. Every four meters an open landing interrupted the shaft, to allow one to rest, but I couldn't stop, I kept climbing, rung after rung, panting. I didn't look up and it seemed to me that this interminable ladder would never end. Finally my head bumped against the trapdoor at the top. Beneath me resounded the metallic noises of the men climbing. I turned the handle of the hatchway, pushed it, and stuck my head outside: a cold wind hit me in the face. I was at the top of the dirigible's hull, a large curved surface, quite rigid, seemingly. I hoisted myself outside and stood up; alas, no way to close the trapdoor from without. What with the wind and the vibrations of the airship, my balance was unsteady. I headed, staggering, toward the tail, checking the parachute's fastenings. A head appeared at the trapdoor and I began to run; the surface of the cover was slightly elastic and bounced under my feet; a gunshot rang out and a bullet whistled past my ear; I stumbled, rolled over, but instead of trying to catch hold of something I let myself go. I heard another gunshot. The slope grew increasingly steep, I slid quickly, trying to twist my feet forward, then it became al-most vertical and I fell into the void like a puppet with its strings cut, waving my arms and legs in the wind. The brown-and-gray steppe rose toward me like a wall. I had never jumped in a parachute before but I knew you had to pull on a cord; with an effort, I brought my arms back close to my body, found the handle, and pulled; the shock was so abrupt that I hurt my neck. I was now descending much more slowly, feet first; I caught hold of the risers and raised my head; the white corolla of the parachute filled the sky, hiding the dirigible from view. I looked for the river: it seemed to be a few kilometers away. The procession of boats was gleaming in the sun and I mentally calculated the path to take to reach it. The ground approached and I held out my legs together, a lit-tle worried. Then I felt a violent shock that went through my whole body, tumbled over, let myself be dragged by the parachute as it was car-ried off by the wind; finally I managed to find my footing and get up. I undid the harness and left the parachute there, blown by the wind and rolling about on the dirt. I looked at the sky: the dirigible was impas-sively drifting away. I got my bearings and began trotting toward the river.

The dirigible disappeared. The steppe seemed to be rising imper-ceptibly: I began to tire, but forced myself to go on. My feet stumbled on clumps of dry grass. Panting, I reached the river; but I found myself, as I saw only then, at the top of a high steep cliff that overlooked it from about twenty meters up; down below, the water was flowing with a swift current; impossible to jump, impossible too to climb down this cliff. I should have landed on the other shore: there, the almost flat bank gently descended to the water. To my left, upriver, I saw the procession of boats arriving. Musicians wearing garlands, who were following the carved gondola carrying my sister, were playing shrill, solemn music on flutes, string instruments, and drums. I could clearly see my sister, haughty between the two creatures who were rowing; she sat cross-legged and her long black hair fell over her breasts. I cupped my hands over my mouth and shouted her name, many times. She raised her head and looked at me, but without changing her expression or saying any-

thing; her gaze was riveted on mine while the boat passed slowly by; I
shouted her name like a madman, but she didn't react; finally she turned
away. The procession slowly drew away downstream, while I remained
there, stunned. Then I tried to begin pursuing her; but at that moment
violent stomach cramps seized me; feverishly, I undid my pants and
squatted down; but instead of shit, living bees, spiders, and scorpions
gushed out of my anus. It burned horribly, but they had to be evacuated; I strained, the spiders and scorpions scattered, running, the bees
flew away, I had to clench my jaw not to shout with pain. I heard something and turned my head: two boys, identical twins, were looking at
me in silence. Where in God's name had they come from? I stood and
pulled up my pants; but already they had done an about-face and were
going away. I dashed after them, calling out to them. But I couldn't
catch up to them. I followed them for a long time.

In the steppe, there was another kurgan. The two boys climbed it
and then went down its other side. I ran around it, but they had disappeared. "Where are you, boys?" I shouted. I realized that even from the
top of the kurgan, I had lost sight of the river; the dull gray of the sky
hid the sun, I didn't know how to get my bearings; I had let myself get
distracted, like an idiot! I had to find those boys again. I went around
the kurgan again and discovered a depression: I felt around and a door
appeared. I knocked, it opened and I went in; a long hallway stretched
in front of me, with, at the end, another door. I knocked again and it
opened too. There was a vast, high-ceilinged room, lit by oil lamps:
from outside, though, the kurgan hadn't seemed so large. In the back of
the room stood a dais covered with rugs and cushions, with a potbellied
dwarf playing a game; standing next to him was a tall, thin man with a
black triangle over one eye; a wizened old woman in a scarf was stirring
an immense ornamented cauldron hanging from the ceiling in a corner.
Of the two children there wasn't a trace. "Hello," I said politely. "You
haven't seen two boys by any chance, have you? Twins," I specified.—
"Ah!" the dwarf shouted, "a visitor! Do you know how to play *nardi?*"
I went up to the dais and saw that he was playing a game of backgammon, making his right hand play against his left hand: each took turns
rolling the dice and then moved the pieces, red or white. "Actually," I
said, "I'm looking for my sister. A very beautiful young woman with
black hair. They're taking her away in a boat." The dwarf, without stopping his game, looked at the one-eyed man, then turned back to me:
"They're bringing that girl here. We are going to marry her, my brother
and I. I hope she is as beautiful as they say." He leered lecherously and
nimbly buried one hand in his pants. "If you are her brother, then we'll
be in-laws. Have a seat and drink some tea." I sat down on a cushion,

legs crossed, facing the game; the old woman brought me a bowl of
good hot tea, real tea and not ersatz, which I drank with pleasure. "I
would rather you didn't marry her," I said finally. The dwarf kept on
playing one hand against the other. "If you don't want us to marry her,
play with me. No one wants to play with me."—"Why not?"—"Because of my conditions."—"And what are your conditions?" I asked
amiably. "Tell me, I don't know them."—"If I win, I kill you, if I lose,
I kill you."—"Fine, that's no problem, let's play." I watched how he was
playing: it didn't resemble any game of backgammon that I knew. In the
beginning of the game, the pieces, instead of being arranged in columns
of two, three, and five, were all placed at the ends of the board; and during the game, they couldn't be removed, but blocked the place they occupied. "Those aren't the rules for backgammon," I pointed
out.—"Listen, boy, you're no longer in Munich, here."—"I'm not from
Munich."—"Berlin, then. We're playing *nardi*." I looked again: the principle didn't seem hard to grasp, but there must have been subtleties. "All
right, let's play, then." In fact, it was more complicated than it seemed,
but I learned quickly and won the game. The dwarf got up, took out a
long knife and said: "All right, I'm going to kill you."—"Calm down.
If I had lost, you could have killed me, but I've won, so why should you
kill me?" He thought a bit and sat back down: "You're right. Let's play
again." This time, it was the dwarf who won. "What do you say now?
I'm going to kill you."—"All right, I won't say anything else, I lost, kill
me. But don't you think we should play a third game first to settle it?"—
"You're right." We played one more time and I won. "Now," I said,
"you have to give me back my sister." The dwarf got up in one bound,
turned his back to me, leaned over, and let loose an enormous fart in
my face. "But that's disgusting!" I exclaimed. The dwarf was bounding
up and down and letting off a fart at each leap, chanting: "I am a God,
I do what I like, I am a God, I do what I like. Now," he added interrupting himself, "I'm going to kill you."—"Honestly, you're incorrigible, you're just too rude." I got up, made an about-face, and went out.
In the distance, I saw a large cloud of dust appearing. I climbed up onto
the kurgan to see better: they were horsemen. They approached, divided themselves into two rows, and lined up, face-to-face, on either
side of the kurgan to form a long walkway. I could see the closest ones
clearly; the horses looked as if they were mounted on wheels. Looking
more closely, I saw that they were impaled front to back on fat beams
that rested on a wheeled platform; their feet dangled freely; and the
horsemen too were impaled, I saw the points of the stakes coming out
of their heads or mouths: a rather sloppy job, to tell the truth. Each
chariot or framework was pushed by a few naked slaves who, when they

had placed them in position, went to sit down in a group a little farther off. I stared at the horsemen and thought I recognized Möritz's Ukrainians. Had they too gotten all the way here, and undergone the fate that was awaiting them? But maybe it was a wrong impression. The tall, thin one-eyed man had joined me. "It's not proper," I scolded him, "to say that whether you win or lose, you'll kill everyone who plays with you."—"You are right. The fact is that we don't have many guests. But I'll have my brother cease this practice." A light wind had risen again and swept the dust raised by the chariots. "What are they?" I asked, pointing to them.—"That's the honor guard. For our wedding."—"Yes, but I won two games out of three. So you are going to give me my sister back." The man stared at me sadly with his single eye: "You can never get your sister back." An uneasy dread rose in my throat. "Why?" I cried out.--"It's not proper," he replied. In the distance, I saw some figures approaching on foot, raising a lot of dust, which was soon carried off by the wind. My sister was walking in the middle, still naked, escorted by the two awful creatures and the musicians. "Is it proper for her to walk like that, naked, in front of everyone?" I asked, enraged. His single eye never left me: "Why not? She's no longer a virgin, after all. But we'll take her all the same." I wanted to run down the kurgan to join her but the two twins, who had reappeared, barred my path. I tried to go around them but they moved to prevent me. Overcome with anger, I raised my hand at them. "Don't hit them!" the one-eyed man barked. I turned toward him, beside myself: "What are they to me, then?" I shouted furiously. He said nothing. At the end of the walkway, between the rows of horsemen impaled on their mounts, my sister was moving forward with an even tread.

SARABANDE

hy was everything so white? The steppe hadn't been so white. I was lying in an expanse of white. Maybe it had snowed, maybe I was resting there like a fallen soldier, a battle flag lying in the snow. But I wasn't cold. Actually, it was hard to say, I felt completely detached from my body. From far away, I tried to identify a concrete sensation: in my mouth, a taste of mud. But that mouth was floating, without even a jaw to support it. And my chest, it seemed crushed beneath tons of stone; I looked for them, but perceiving them proved impossible. Well, I said to myself, here I am really scattered. Oh my poor body. I wanted to huddle over it, the way you huddle over a beloved child, at night, in the cold.

In these endless white landscapes, a ball of fire was spinning, stabbing my gaze. But strangely its flames gave no heat to the whiteness. Impossible to stare at it, impossible to turn away from it too, it followed me with its displeasing presence. Panic overwhelmed me; and if I never found my feet again, how would I master it? Oh, this was all so difficult. How much time did I spend like this? I couldn't say, a fetal lifetime at least. It gave me time to observe things, and that's how I slowly became aware that all this white wasn't uniform; there were gradations— none of them could have been labeled even pale gray, really, yet there were variations all the same; to describe them, one would need a new vocabulary, as subtle and precise as that of the Inuit to describe different kinds of ice. There must also have been a question of texture; but my sight seemed as unresponsive, on this point, as my inert fingers. Distant rumblings reached me. I resolved to cling to detail, a discontinuity of the white, until it revealed itself to me. I devoted at least another century or two to this immense effort, but finally I understood what it was all about: it was a right angle. Come, another effort. By extending this angle, I ended up discovering another one, then yet another one; so, eureka, it was a frame, now it went faster, I discovered other frames, but all these frames were white, and outside of the frames everything was white, and inside the frames too: faint hope, I despaired, of getting to the bottom of this anytime soon. Perhaps I should proceed by hypotheses? Might it be modern art? But these regular frames were sometimes confused with other forms, also white but fluid, soft. Lord, what a labor of interpretation, what endless work. But my obstinacy kept giving me new results: the white surface that extended to the distance was in fact streaked, undulating, the steppe perhaps seen from a plane (but not from a dirigible; that didn't have the same appearance). What a success! I was more than a little proud of myself. Another final effort, it seemed to me, and I'd come to the end of these mysteries. But an unforeseen catastrophe abruptly put an end to my research: the ball of fire died, and I was plunged into darkness, a thick, asphyxiating blackness. Fighting was pointless; I shouted, but no sound came out of my crushed lungs. I knew I wasn't dead, since death itself couldn't be so black; it was much worse than death, a cesspit, a turgid bog; and eternity seemed only an instant compared to the time I spent there.

Finally, my sentence was repealed: slowly, the endless blackness of the world lifted. And with the magical return of the light, I saw things more clearly; then, as to a new Adam, the ability to name things was given back to me (or maybe just given): the wall, the window, the milky sky behind the glass. I contemplated this extraordinary spectacle with wonder; then I itemized everything my gaze could find: the door, the doorknob, the weak lightbulb under its shade, the foot of the bed, the sheet, veined hands, mine no doubt. The door opened and a woman appeared, dressed in white; but with her a color burst into this world, a red shape, bright as blood on snow, and it distressed me beyond all proportion, and I burst into tears. "Why are you crying?" she said in a melodious voice, and her pale, cool fingers caressed my cheek. Little by little I grew calm. She said something else, which I didn't make out; I felt her handling my body; terrified, I closed my eyes, and that finally gave me some kind of power over this blinding white. Later on, an older man came in, with white hair: "Ah, so you've woken up!" he exclaimed cheerfully. Why was he saying that? I had lain awake for an eternity, I had forgotten the very name of sleep. But maybe we weren't thinking of the same thing. He sat down next to me, pulled up my eyelid without ceremony, stuck a light in my eye: "Very good, very good," he repeated, satisfied with his cruel trick. Finally he too left.

It took a little more time for me to connect these fragmentary impressions and to understand that I had fallen into the hands of representatives of the medical profession. I had to be patient and learn to let myself be manhandled: not only did women, the nurses, take unheard-of liberties with my body, but doctors, solemn, serious men with paternal voices, entered at any moment, surrounded by a horde of young people, all wearing lab coats; lifting me up shamelessly, they moved my head and discoursed about my case, as if I were a mannequin. I found it all extremely disagreeable, but I couldn't protest: the articulation of sounds, like my other faculties, still failed me. But the day when I was finally able distinctly to call one of these gentlemen a swine, he didn't get angry; on the contrary, he smiled and applauded: "Bravo, bravo." Encouraged, I grew bolder and went on during their next visits: "Piece of filth, bastard, stinker, Jew, asshole." The doctors gravely shook their heads, the young people took notes on clipboards; finally, a nurse scolded me: "You could be a little more polite, really."—"Yes, that's true, you're right. Should I call you meine Dame?" She waved a pretty ringless hand in front of my eyes: "Mein Fräulein," she replied lightly, and slipped away. For a young woman, this nurse had a firm, skillful grip: when I had to relieve myself, she turned me over, helped me, then wiped me clean with a thoughtful efficiency, her gestures sure and pleasant, free of all disgust, like those of a mother cleaning her child; as if she, still a virgin perhaps, had done this all her life. I probably took pleasure in it, and delighted in asking her for this service. She or others also fed me, slipping spoonfuls of broth into my lips; I would have preferred a rare steak, but didn't dare ask, it wasn't a hotel, after all, but, I had finally understood, a hospital: and to be a patient means precisely what it says.

Thus, clearly, I had had some sort of health problem, in circumstances that still escaped me; and judging from the freshness of the sheets and the calm and cleanliness of the premises, I must no longer be in Stalingrad; or else things had changed quite a bit. And indeed, I no longer was in Stalingrad but, as I finally learned, in Hohenlychen, north of Berlin, at the German Red Cross hospital. How I had gotten there, no one could tell me; I had been delivered in a van, they had been told to look after me, they didn't ask any questions, they looked after me, and as for me, I didn't have to ask any questions, either: I had to get back on my feet again.

One day, there was a commotion: the door opened, my little room filled with people, most of them, this time, not in white but in black. I recognized the shortest of them after some effort, my memory was slowly coming back to me: he was the Reichsführer-SS, Heinrich Himmler. He was surrounded by other SS officers; next to him stood a giant whom I didn't know, with a rough-hewn, horselike face slashed with scars. Himmler planted himself next to me and gave a brief speech with his nasal, professorial voice; on the other side of the bed, men were photographing and filming the scene. I didn't understand much of what the Reichsführer said: isolated phrases bubbled to the surface of his words, *heroic officer, honor of the SS, lucid reports, courageous,* but they certainly didn't form a narration in which I could recognize myself, I had trouble applying these words to myself; and yet the meaning of the scene was clear, I was indeed the person being discussed, it was because of me that all these officers and these gleaming dignitaries were gathered in this tiny room. In the crowd, in back, I recognized Thomas; he made a friendly gesture toward me, but alas I couldn't speak to him. His speech over, the Reichsführer turned to an officer in round, thick glasses with black rims, who eagerly handed him something; then he leaned toward me, and with an increasing panic I saw his pincenez, his grotesque moustache, his fat, short, dirty-nailed fingers approach; he wanted to put something on my chest, I saw a pin, I was terrified at the thought of it pricking me; then his face descended even lower, he was paying no attention whatsoever to my anguish, his verbena-smelling breath was stifling me, and he deposited a wet kiss on my face. He straightened himself and launched his arm into the air, bellowing; the entire audience imitated him, and my bed was surrounded with a forest of raised arms, black, white, brown; timidly, so as not to be singled out, I too raised my arm; that had its effect, since everyone turned around and hurried to the door; the crowd quickly flowed out, and I was left alone, exhausted, incapable of removing this curious cold thing that was weighing on my chest.

I could now take a few steps, if someone supported me; this was useful, since it allowed me to go to the bathroom. My body, if I concentrated, began again to obey my orders, fractious at first, then with more docility; only my left hand continued to hold itself apart from the general entente; I could move the fingers, but they would under no conditions agree to close, to form a fist. In a mirror, I looked for the first time at my face: to tell the truth, I didn't recognize anything in it, I didn't see how this mosaic of such diverse features held together, and the more I considered them, the more foreign they became. The white bands wrapped around my skull at least prevented it from bursting open, that was already something and even a considerable something, but it didn't help my speculations make any progress; this face looked like a collection of pieces that fit together well enough but came from different puzzles. Finally, a doctor came to tell me that I was going to leave: I was healed, he explained, they couldn't do anything more for me, I was going to be sent elsewhere to regain my strength. Healed! What a surprising word, I didn't even know I had been hurt. In fact, a bullet had gone through my head. By a chance less rare than people think, they patiently explained to me, I not only had survived, but I wouldn't suffer any after-effects; the stiffness of my left hand, a slight neurological difficulty, would persist a little while longer, but that too would go away. This precise scientific information filled me with astonishment: so, these unusual and mysterious sensations had a cause, an explainable and rational one; but even with an effort, I couldn't manage to connect the sensations to this explanation, it seemed hollow to me, contrived; if this was really Reason, then I too, like Luther, would have called it *Hure*, a whore; and in fact, obeying the calm, patient orders of the doctors, Reason raised its skirt for me, revealing that there was nothing beneath. I could have said the same thing about it as about my poor head: a hole is a hole is a hole. The idea that a hole could also be a whole would never have occurred to me. Once the bandages were removed, I could see for myself that there was almost nothing there: on my forehead, a tiny round scar, just above my right eye; in back of the skull, scarcely visible, they assured me, a swelling; between the two, my reemerging hair was already hiding the traces of the operation I had undergone. But if these doctors so sure of their science were to be believed, a hole went right through my head, a narrow circular corridor, a fabulous, closed shaft, inaccessible to thought, and if that were true, then nothing was the same again, how could it have been? My thinking about the world now had to reorganize itself around this hole. But the only concrete thing I could say was: I have awakened, and nothing will ever be the same again. As I was thinking about this impressive question, they came to fetch me and put me on a stretcher in a hospital vehicle; one of the nurses had kindly slipped into my pocket the case with my medal, the one the Reichsführer had given me. They took me to Pomerania, on the island of Usedom near Swinemünde; there, by the sea, was a rest home belonging to the SS, a beautiful, spacious house; my room, full of light, looked out onto the sea, and during the day, pushed in a wheelchair by a nurse, I could place myself in front of a large bay window and contemplate the heavy, gray waters of the Baltic, the shrill play of the seagulls, the cold, wet sand of the pebble-strewn beach. The hallways and common rooms were regularly cleaned with carbolic acid; I liked this bitter, ambiguous smell, which reminded me harshly of the demeaning joys of my adolescence; the long hands, so translucent they were nearly blue, of the nurses, blond, delicate Frisian girls, also smelled of carbolic acid, and the convalescents, among themselves, called them the Carbolic Babes. These smells and strong sensations gave me erections, astonishingly detached from myself; the nurse who washed me smiled at them and sponged them with the same indifference as the rest of my body; some-

times they lasted, with a resigned patience; I would have been quite incapable of relieving myself. The very fact of day had become a mad, unexpected, undecipherable thing to me; a body that was still far too
complex for me, I had to take things little by little.

I liked the well-regulated life on this beautiful, bare, cold island, all
grays, yellows, and pale blues; there were just enough sharp edges to
cling to there, to keep from being carried away by the wind, but not
too many, so you didn't risk getting scraped. Thomas came to see me;
he brought me gifts, a bottle of French Cognac and a fine leather-bound
edition of Nietzsche; but I wasn't allowed to drink, and I would have
been quite incapable of reading: all meaning fled, and the alphabet
mocked me. I thanked him and tucked away his gifts in a chest of drawers. The insignia on the collar of his handsome black uniform now bore,
over the four diamonds embroidered in silver thread, two bars, and a
chevron adorned the center of his epaulettes: he had been promoted to
SS-Obersturmbannführer, and I too, he informed me, had been promoted, the Reichsführer had explained it to me when I received my
medal, but I hadn't remembered this detail. I was now a German hero,
the *Schwarzes Korps* had published an article about me; my decoration,
which I had never looked at, was the Iron Cross, first class (at the same
time I had also received the second class, retroactively). I had no idea
what I could have done to deserve this, but Thomas, happy and voluble, was already bubbling over with information and gossip: Schellenberg had finally taken Jost's place at the head of Amt VI, Best had gotten
himself kicked out of France by the Wehrmacht, but the Führer had appointed him plenipotentiary to Denmark; and the Reichsführer had finally made up his mind to appoint a replacement for Heydrich,
Obergruppenführer Kaltenbrunner, the big scarred ogre I had seen
standing beside him in my room. The name meant almost nothing to
me, I knew he had been HSSPF-Danube and that he was generally
thought of as an insignificant man; Thomas seemed delighted with the
choice, Kaltenbrunner was almost "a neighbor," spoke the same dialect
as he did, and had already invited him to dinner. Thomas himself had
been appointed Deputy Gruppenleiter of IV A, under Panzinger,
Müller's deputy. These details to tell the truth did not arouse much interest in me, but I had learned to be polite, and I congratulated him,
since he seemed very pleased, both with his lot and with his person. He
humorously told me about the grandiose funeral of the Sixth Army; officially, everyone, from Paulus to the lowest Gefreiter, had *resisted to the
death*; in fact, only one general, Hartmann, had been killed under fire,
and only one (Stempel) had chosen suicide; the twenty-two others, including Paulus, had ended up in Soviet hands. "They're going to turn

them inside out like gloves," Thomas said lightly. "You'll see." For three days, all the radios of the Reich had suspended their broadcasts to play funeral music. "The worst was Bruckner. The Seventh. Nonstop. Impossible to escape it. I thought I'd go mad." He also told me, but almost in passing, how I had gotten there: I listened to his story attentively, and so I can report it, but even less than the rest, I could connect it with nothing; it remained a story, a truthful one no doubt, but a story all the same, scarcely more than a series of phrases that fit together according to a mysterious and arbitrary order, ruled by a logic that had little to do with the one that allowed me, here and now, to breathe the salty air of the Baltic, to feel the wind on my face when they took me out, to bring spoonfuls of soup from the bowl to my mouth, then to open my anus when the time came to evacuate the waste. According to this story, which I am not altering in any way, I had walked away from Thomas and the others, toward the Russian lines and an exposed zone, without paying the slightest attention to their shouts; before they could catch up to me, there was a gunshot, just one, that had knocked me to the ground. Ivan had courageously broken cover to pull my body to safety, he too had been shot at, but the bullet had gone through his sleeve without touching him. As for me—and here Thomas's version confirmed the explanations of the doctor in Hohenlychen—the shot had hit me in the head; but, to the surprise of those pressed around me, I was still breathing. They had carried me to a first-aid station; there, the doctor declared he couldn't do anything, but since I persisted in breathing, he sent me to Gumrak, where they had the best surgical unit in the *Kessel*. Thomas had requisitioned a vehicle and transported me there himself, then, thinking he had done everything he could, he left me. That same night he had received his departure orders. But the next day, Gumrak, the main runway since the fall of Pitomnik, also had to evacuate in front of the Russian advance. So he went up to Stalingradsky, from which a few planes were still leaving; while he waited, for lack of anything better to do, he visited the field hospital set up in some tents and found me there, unconscious, my head bandaged, but still breathing like a pair of bellows. A nurse, in exchange for a cigarette, told him that they had operated on me in Gumrak, he didn't know much about it, there had been some kind of altercation, and then a little later the surgeon had been killed by a mortar shell that fell on the unit, but I was still alive, and as an officer, I was entitled to consideration; during the evacuation, they had put me in a vehicle and brought me here. Thomas had wanted to have me put on a plane, but the Feldgendarmen refused, since the red characters of my VERWUNDETE label meant "Untransportable." "I couldn't wait, because my plane was leaving. And also the shelling was starting up again. So I found a guy who was really smashed up but who had an ordinary label, and I switched it with yours. He wouldn't have made it anyway. Then I had you put with the wounded by the runway, and I left. They loaded you onto the next plane, one of the last. You should have seen their faces, in Melitopol, when I arrived. No one wanted to shake my hand, they were too afraid of the lice. Except for Manstein, he shook everyone's hand. Aside from me there was almost no one except Panzer officers. Not surprising, given that Hube wrote up the lists for Milch. You can't trust anyone." I let myself fall back onto the cushions and closed my eyes. "Aside from us, who else got out?"—"Aside from us? Only Weidner, you remember? From the Gestapostelle. Möritz also received orders, but we never found a trace of him. We're not even sure he was able to leave."—"And the little guy, there? Your colleague, the one who got hit by shrapnel and was so happy?"—"Vopel? He was evacuated before you were even wounded, but his Heinkel was shot down at takeoff by a Sturmovik."—"And Ivan?" He produced a silver cigarette holder: "Mind if I smoke? No?— Ivan? Well, he stayed, of course. You don't really think they'd have given a German's place to a Ukrainian?"—"I don't know. He was fighting for us too." He dragged on his cigarette and said, smiling: "You're indulging in misplaced idealism. I see that your shot in the head hasn't set you right. You should be happy to be alive." Happy to be alive? That seemed as incongruous to me as rejoicing at being born.

Every day, more wounded arrived: they came from Kursk, from Rostov, from Kharkov, recaptured one after the other by the Soviets, from Kasserine too; and a few words with the newcomers said much more about the current situation than the military communiqués. These communiqués, which were delivered to us in the common rooms over little loudspeakers, were introduced by the overture to Bach's cantata *Ein Feste Burg ist unser Gott*; but the Wehrmacht used the arrangement by Wilhelm Friedmann Bach, Johann Sebastian's dissolute son, who had added three trumpets and a kettledrum to his father's austere orchestration, an ample enough pretext, by my lights, to flee the room each time, thus avoiding being drugged by the flood of lulling euphemisms, which sometimes lasted a good twenty minutes. I wasn't the only one to show a certain aversion to these communiqués; a nurse whom I often found at those times ostensibly busy out on a terrace explained to me one day that most Germans had first heard of the encirclement of the Sixth Army at the same time as its destruction, and that this had done little to temper the shock on morale. It had had an effect on the life of the *Volks-gemeinschaft*; people were openly talking and criticizing; a semblance of a student rebellion had even broken out in Munich. That, of course, I had not learned from the radio or from the nurses or from the patients, but from Thomas, who was now well placed to be informed about this sort of event. Subversive pamphlets had been distributed, defeatist slogans painted on the walls; the Gestapo had to intervene vigorously, and they had already condemned and executed the ringleaders, most of them idealistic youth gone astray. Among the minor consequences of this catastrophe would have to be counted, alas, the sensational return to the forefront of the political scene of Dr. Goebbels: his renewed declaration of *total war*, in the Sportpalast, had been broadcast to us on the radio, no possibility of escaping it; in a rest house belonging to the SS, they unfortunately took this sort of thing very seriously.

The handsome Waffen-SS who filled the rooms were for the most part in a piteous state: often they were missing pieces of arms or legs, or even a jaw; the atmosphere wasn't always very cheerful. But I noticed with interest that despite what the most casual reflection on the facts or the studying of a map could suggest, their faith in the *Endsieg* and their veneration of the Führer remained for the most part intact. This wasn't the case for everyone; some people, in Germany, were clearly beginning to draw objective conclusions from the facts and from the maps; I had discussed this with Thomas, and he had even led me to understand that there were some, like Schellenberg, who thought through the logical consequences of their conclusions, and who were considering acting on that basis. I didn't discuss any of this, of course, with my comrades in misfortune: to demoralize them even more, thoughtlessly to take away from them the foundation of their wounded lives, would have made no sense to me. I was regaining my strength: I could now get dressed by myself, walk on the beach on my own, in the wind under the harsh calls of the seagulls; my left hand was finally beginning to obey me. Around the end of the month (all this happened in February 1943), the chief doctor of the establishment, after examining me, asked me if I felt able to leave: with everything that was happening, they were short on space, and I could just as easily finish my convalescence with my family. I amiably explained to him that returning to my family wasn't an option, but that if he liked, I would leave; I'd go to the city, to a hotel. The papers he handed me gave me three months' leave. So I took the train and went to Berlin. There I rented a room in a good hotel, the Eden, on the Budapesterstrasse: a spacious suite with a sitting room, a bedroom, and a beautiful tiled bathroom; hot water, here, wasn't rationed, and every day I slipped into the bathtub and emerged an hour later with my skin bright red, and collapsed naked onto my bed, my heart pounding wildly. There were also French windows and a narrow balcony looking out onto the zoo: in the morning, as I got up and drank my tea, I would watch the keepers make their rounds and feed the animals; I took great pleasure in this. Of course, all this was on the expensive side; but I had received all at once my back wages accumulated over twenty-one months; with the bonuses, that made a tidy little sum, I could easily indulge myself and spend a little. I ordered a magnificent black uniform from Thomas's tailor, onto which I had my new Sturmbannführer stripes sewn and to which I pinned my medals (along with the Iron Cross and my War Service Cross, I had received some minor medals: for my wound, for the '41-'42 winter campaign, a little late, and a medal from the NSDAP, which they gave out to pretty much anyone); although I don't like uniforms much, I had to admit that I cut a dashing figure, and it was a joy to stroll about town like this, my cap a little askew, my gloves held negligently in my hand; seeing me, who would have thought that I was actually nothing but a bureaucrat? The city, since I had left, had changed its appearance quite a bit. Everywhere the measures taken against the English air raids had disfigured it: a huge oversize circus tent, made of netting camouflaged with strips of cloth and fir tree tops, covered the Ost-West-Achse from the Brandenburg Gate to the end of the Tiergarten, darkening the avenue even in the middle of the day; the Victory Column, draped in netting, had had its gold leaf replaced by an awful brown paint; on Adolf-Hitler-Platz and elsewhere, they had set up dummy buildings, vast theater sets beneath which the cars and trams circulated; and a fantastic construction overlooked the zoo near my hotel, as if risen out of a nightmare—an immense medieval fort made of concrete, bristling with cannons that were supposed to protect humans and animals from the British *Luftmörder*; I was curious to see this monstrosity at work. But it should be said that the attacks, which already at that time were terrifying the population, were still nothing compared with what would come later on. Almost all the good restaurants had been closed in the name of *total mobilization*; Göring had tried his best to protect Horcher, his favorite place, and had posted a guard in front of it, but Goebbels, acting in his capacity as Gauleiter of Berlin, had organized a *spontaneous demonstration of the anger of the people*, during which they had broken all its windows; and Göring had had to cave in. Thomas and I weren't the only ones to laugh at this incident: failing a real "Stalingrad" diet, a little abstinence wouldn't harm the Reichsmarschall. Thomas, fortunately, knew several private clubs, exempt from the new regulations: there you could stuff yourself on lobster or oysters, which were expensive but not rationed, and drink Champagne, which was strictly limited in France itself but not in Germany; fish, alas, was still nowhere to be found, as well as beer. These places sometimes displayed a curious spirit, given the general mood: at

the Golden Horseshoe they had a black hostess, and the female customers could ride horseback on a little circus ring, to show off their legs;
at the Jockey Club the orchestra played American music; you couldn't
dance, but the bar was decorated with photographs of Hollywood stars,
and even of Leslie Howard.

I soon realized that the gaiety that had taken hold of me when I arrived in Berlin was but a thin veneer; beneath it, everything was terribly fragile, I felt made of a sandy substance that could break up at the
slightest gust. Wherever I looked, the sight of ordinary life, the crowd
in the trolleys or the S-Bahn, the laughter of an elegant woman, the satisfied creasing of a newspaper, struck me like contact with a sharp sliver
of glass. I had the feeling that the hole in my forehead had opened up a
third eye, a pineal eye, one not turned to the sun, not capable of contemplating the blinding light of the sun, but directed at the darkness,
gifted with the power of looking at the bare face of death, and of grasping this face behind each face of flesh and blood, beneath the smiles,
through the palest, healthiest skin, the most laughing eyes. The disaster
was already there and they didn't realize it, since the disaster is the very
idea of the disaster to come, which ruins everything long before term.
At bottom, I repeated to myself with a hollow bitterness, it's only the
first nine months that you're peaceful, and after that the archangel with
the flaming sword chases you forever out through the door marked *Las-
ciate ogni speranza*, and you want only one single thing, to go back, then
time keeps pushing you pitilessly forward, and in the end there is nothing, nothing at all. There was nothing original about these thoughts,
they could have come to the lowliest soldier lost in the frozen waters of
the East, who knows, when he listens to the silence, that death is near,
and who perceives the infinite value of each intake of breath, of each
heartbeat, of the cold, brittle sensation of the air, of the miracle of daylight. But the distance from the front is like a thick layer of moral fat,
and looking at these satisfied people, I sometimes felt short of breath, I
wanted to cry out. I went to the barber: there, suddenly, in front of the
mirror, incongruous, fear. It was a white, clean, sterile, modern room,
a discreetly expensive salon; one or two clients were occupying the
other chairs. The barber had put a long black smock on me, and beneath
this garment my heart was pounding, my intestines sank into a wet cold,
panic drowned my whole body, the tips of my fingers prickled. I looked
at my face: it was calm, but behind this calm, fear had erased everything.
I closed my eyes: *snip, snip,* went the barber's patient little scissors in my
ear. On my way home, I had this thought: Yes, go on repeating to yourself that everything will be fine, you never know, you might end up
convincing yourself. But I did not manage to convince myself, I was

vacillating. I had no physical symptoms such as those I had experienced in the Ukraine or in Stalingrad: I wasn't overcome with nausea, I didn't vomit, my digestion was perfectly normal. Only, in the street, I felt as if I were walking on glass that was ready at any instant to shatter beneath my feet. Living required a sustained attention to things, which exhausted me. In the calm little streets near the Landwehrkanal, I found, on a windowsill on the ground floor, a woman's long glove in blue satin. Without thinking, I took it and went on walking. I wanted to try it on; of course it was too small, but the texture of the satin excited me. I imagined the hand that must have worn this glove: this thought disturbed me. I wasn't going to keep it; but to get rid of it I needed another window, with a little wrought-iron railing around the sill, preferably in an old building; yet in this street there were only shops, with silent, closed storefronts. Finally, just before my hotel, I found the right window. The shutters were closed; I gently deposited the glove in the middle of the ledge, like an offering. Two days later the shutters were still closed, and the glove was still there, an opaque, discreet sign, which was certainly trying to tell me something, but what?

Thomas must have begun to guess my state of mind, since after the first few days, I stopped calling him and going out to dinner with him; to tell the truth, I preferred to wander around the city, or contemplate the lions, giraffes, and elephants in the zoo from my balcony, or else float in my luxurious bathtub, wasting hot water without the slightest shame. In his commendable anxiety to entertain me, Thomas asked me to go out with a young woman, a secretary of the Führer's who was spending her leave in Berlin and didn't know many people there; out of politeness, I didn't want to refuse. I took her to dinner at the Hotel Kempinsky: even though the dishes had been given idiotic patriotic names, the cuisine was still excellent, and at the sight of my medals, they didn't bother me much with rationing issues. The young woman, whose name was Grete V., greedily fell upon the oysters, sliding them one after the other between her rows of teeth: in Rastenburg, apparently, they didn't eat very well. "And it could be worse!" she exclaimed. "At least we don't have to eat the same thing as the Führer." While I poured her more wine, she told me that Zeitzler, the new Chief of Staff of the OKH, scandalized by Göring's brazen lies about the *Kessel* airlift, had openly started in December to have himself served the same ration, in the Kasino, as the soldiers of the Sixth Army. He had quickly lost weight, and the Führer had had to force him to stop *these unhealthy demonstrations*; on the other hand, Champagne and Cognac had been banned. As she spoke, I observed her: her appearance was far from ordinary. She had a strong, very wide jaw; her face tried to look normal but seemed to mask a heavy, secret desire, which welled up through the bloody stroke of her lipstick. Her hands were very animated, her fingers reddened from bad circulation; she had fine, birdlike joints, bony, sharp; and peculiar marks on her left wrist, like the traces of a bracelet or cord. I found her elegant and animated, but veiled by a faint insincerity. Since wine made her voluble, I had her talk about the Führer's private life, which she described with a surprising lack of restraint: every night, he discoursed for hours, and his monologues were so repetitive, so boring, so sterile, that the secretaries, assistants, and adjutants had set up a system of rotation to listen to him; the ones whose turn it was didn't go to bed till dawn. "Of course," she added, "he is a genius, the savior of Germany. But this war is exhausting him." In the evening, around five o'clock, after the meetings but before the dinner, the movies, and the nighttime tea, he held a coffee break with the secretaries; there, surrounded solely by women, he was much more cordial—before Stalingrad at least; he joked, teased the girls, and almost never discussed politics. "Does he flirt with you?" I asked with amusement. She looked serious: "Oh no, never!" She asked me about Stalingrad; I gave her a fierce, sardonic description, which at first made her laugh till tears came, but then made her so uneasy that she cut me off. I accompanied her back to her hotel, near the Anhalter Bahnhof; she invited me to come up for a drink, but I politely refused; my courtesy had its limits. As soon as I left her, I was filled with a feverish, uneasy feeling: What use was it to me to waste my time this way? What good were gossip and office rumors about our Führer to me? What interest did I have in strutting about this way in front of some painted-up doll who expected only one thing from me? It was better to be quiet. But even in my hotel, first-class though it was, quiet eluded me: the floor beneath mine was having a noisy party, and the music, shouts, and laughter rose up through the floorboards and seized me by the throat. Lying on my bed in the darkness, I thought about the men of the Sixth Army: the evening took place at the beginning of March, the last units had surrendered more than a month before; the survivors, rotting with vermin and fever, must have been on the way to Siberia or Kazakhstan, at the very same moment that I was so laboriously breathing the night air in Berlin, and for them, no music, no laughter—shouts of an entirely different kind. And it wasn't just them, it was everywhere, the whole world was twisted in pain, and people should not be having fun, not right away in any case, they should wait a little while, a decent amount of time should go by. A mean, fetid anguish rose and suffocated me. I got up, searched through my desk drawer, took out my service pistol, checked it was loaded, put it back. I looked at my watch: 2:00 a.m. I put on my uniform jacket (I hadn't undressed) and went down without buttoning it. At reception, I asked for the telephone and called Thomas at the apartment he was renting: "Sorry to bother you so late."—"No, it's fine. What's up?" I explained my homicidal urges to him. To my surprise, he didn't react ironically, but said very seriously: "That's normal. These people are bastards, profiteers. But if you shoot some of them, you'll still have problems."—"What do you suggest, then?"—"Go talk to them. If they don't calm down, we'll see. I'll call some friends."—"All right, I'll go." I hung up and went up to the floor below mine; I easily found the right door and knocked. A tall, beautiful woman in somewhat casual evening dress opened the door, her eyes shining. "Yes?" Behind her, the music roared, I could hear glasses clinking, mad laughter. "Is this your room?" I asked, my heart beating. "No. Wait." She turned around: "Dicky! Dicky! An officer is asking for you." A man in a vest, slightly drunk, came to the door; the woman watched us without hiding her curiosity. "Yes, Herr Sturmbannführer?" he asked. "What can I do for you?" His affected, cordial, almost slurred voice conveyed an aristocrat of old stock. I bowed slightly and said in the most neutral tone possible: "I live in the room over yours. I've just come back from Stalingrad, where I was seriously wounded and where almost all my comrades died. Your festivities are disturbing me. I wanted to come down and kill you, but I called a friend, who advised me to come talk with you first. So I've come to talk with you. It would be better for us all if I don't have to come down again." The man had turned pale: "No, no . . ." He turned around: "Gofi! Stop the music! Stop!" He looked at me: "Excuse us. We'll stop right away."—"Thank you." As I was climbing back up, vaguely satisfied, I heard him shout: "Everyone out! It's over. Out!" I had touched a nerve, and it wasn't a question of fear: he too, suddenly, had understood, and he was ashamed. In my room, everything was quiet now; the only noises were from the occasional passing of a car, the trumpeting of an insomniac elephant. But I didn't calm down: my action appeared to me like playacting, prompted by a genuine, obscure feeling, but then distorted, diverted into an outward show of rage, conventional. But that was precisely where my problem lay: seeing myself this way, constantly, with this external gaze, this critical camera, how could I utter the slightest authentic word, make the slightest authentic gesture? Everything I did became a spectacle for myself; my thinking itself was just a reflection, and I a poor Narcissus showing off for himself, but who wasn't fooled by it. This was the dead-end I had run into since the close of my childhood: only Una, before, could pull me out of myself, make me forget myself a little, and after I lost her, I kept looking at myself with a gaze that was confused with hers in thought but that remained, without any way out, my own. Without you, I am not me: and that was pure, deadly terror, unrelated to the delicious terrors of childhood, a sentence with no hope of appeal, with no judgment, either.

It was also during those first days of March 1943 that Dr. Mandelbrod invited me over for tea.

I had known Mandelbrod and his partner, Herr Leland, for some time. Many years before, after the Great War—and maybe even before it, but I have no way of checking—my father had worked for them (apparently my uncle had also served as an agent for them on occasion). Their relations, from what I had gleaned little by little, went beyond a simple employer-employee relationship: after my father's disappearance, Dr. Mandelbrod and Herr Leland had helped my mother in her searches, and may also have supported her financially, but that's not so certain. And they had continued to play a role in my life; in 1934, when I was preparing to break with my mother, to come to Germany, I got in touch with Mandelbrod, who had long been a respected figure within the Movement; he supported me and offered me his help; it was he too who encouraged me to pursue my studies—for the sake of Germany now, though, and not for France—and who organized my enrollment in Kiel as well as my enlisting in the SS. Despite his Jewish-sounding name, he was, like Minister Rosenberg, a pure German of old Prussian stock, with perhaps a drop of Slavic blood; as for Herr Leland, he was of British origin, but his Germanophile convictions had impelled him to turn his back on his native country long before my birth. They were industrialists, but their exact position would be hard to define. They sat on numerous boards, especially that of IG Farben, and held shares in other companies, without their names being linked to any one in particular; they were said to be very influential in the chemical sector (they were both members of the *Reichsgruppe* for the chemical industry) and also in the metals sector. Moreover, they had been close to the Party ever since the *Kampfzeit*, and had contributed to financing it when it was starting up; according to Thomas, with whom I had discussed them once before the war, they held positions in the Führer's chancellery, but were not entirely subordinate to Philipp Bouhler; and they had access to the highest spheres of the Party chancellery. Finally, the Reichsführer-SS had made them honorary SS-Gruppenführers, and members of the *Freundeskreis Himmler*; but Thomas, mysteriously, stated that this gave the SS no influence over them, and that any influence there might be worked the other way. He had been very impressed when I told him about my relationship with them, and obviously even envied me a little for having such protectors. Their interest in my career, however, had varied over time: when I had been in effect side-

lined, after my 1939 report, I had tried to see them; but that was a busy
period, it had taken me several months to get a reply, and it wasn't until the invasion of France that they invited me to dinner: Herr Leland,
as was his custom, remained for the most part taciturn, and Dr. Mandelbrod was mainly concerned with the political situation; my work
hadn't been mentioned, and I hadn't dared broach the subject myself. I
hadn't seen them again since then. So Mandelbrod's invitation caught
me off guard: What could he want from me? For the occasion, I put on
my new uniform and all my decorations. Their private offices occupied
the top two floors of a handsome building on Unter den Linden, next
to the Academy of Sciences and the headquarters of the *Reichsvereinigung
Kohle*, the Coal Board, where they also played a role. There was no
plaque on the entrance. In the lobby, my papers were checked by a
young woman with long light brown hair pulled back, who wore char-
coal-gray clothes without any insignia, but cut like a uniform, with
men's pants and boots instead of a skirt. Satisfied, she escorted me to a
private elevator, which she started up with a key hanging around her
neck on a long chain, and accompanied me to the top floor, without a
word. I had never come here: in the 1930s, they had another address,
and in any case I usually met them in a restaurant or in one of the big
hotels. The elevator opened onto a wide reception room furnished in
wood and dark leather inset with polished brass and frosted glass decorative elements, elegant and discreet. The woman who escorted me left
me there; another woman, in identical costume, took my coat and hung
it in a wardrobe. Then she asked me to hand her my service revolver,
and holding it with a surprising naturalness in her beautiful carefully
manicured fingers, she put it away in a drawer, which she locked shut.
I wasn't made to wait any longer; she led me in through a padded double door. Dr. Mandelbrod was waiting for me at the rear of an immense
room, behind a large reddish mahogany desk, his back to a long bay
window, also of frosted glass, that let a pale, milky light filter through.
He looked even fatter than at our last meeting. Several cats were
strolling about the carpets or sleeping on the leather furniture and on
his desk. He pointed with his pudgy fingers to a sofa on the left, in front
of a low table: "Hello, hello. Have a seat, I'll be right there." I had never
been able to understand how such a beautiful and melodious voice
could emanate from so many layers of fat; it still surprised me. With my
cap under my arm, I crossed the room and took a seat, displacing a sleek
tabby cat with white paws, who didn't seem to hold it against me, but
gently slipped under the table to settle down elsewhere. I examined the
room: all the walls were padded with leather, and aside from the stylish
ornaments such as those in the antechamber, there were no decorations,

no paintings or photographs, not even a portrait of the Führer. The surface of the low table, on the other hand, was made of superb marquetry, a complex labyrinth in precious wood, protected by a thick glass plate. Only the cat hair clinging to furniture and rugs disfigured this discreet, hushed décor. A vaguely unpleasant smell pervaded the room. One of the cats rubbed against my boots, purring, its tail up; I tried to get rid of it with the tip of my foot, but it didn't pay any attention. Mandelbrod, in the meantime, must have pressed a hidden button: an almost invisible door opened in the wall to the right of his desk and another woman came in, dressed like the first two, but with completely blond hair. She walked behind Mandelbrod, pulled him back, swiveled him around, and pushed him alongside his desk toward me. I got up. Mandelbrod had in fact gotten fatter; whereas before he got around in an ordinary wheelchair, he was now settled in a vast round armchair mounted on a little platform, like an enormous Oriental idol, placid, bovine, colossal. The woman pushed this massive apparatus without any visible effort, probably by starting up and controlling an electrical system. She set him in front of the low table; I walked round to shake his hand and he scarcely brushed me with the tips of his fingers while the woman left through the door by which she had come in. "Please, do sit down," he murmured in his beautiful voice. He was dressed in a thick brown wool suit; his tie disappeared beneath a breastplate of flesh hanging from his neck. A rude noise came from beneath him and a horrible smell reached me; I made an effort to remain impassive. At the same time a cat jumped onto his knees and he sneezed, then began caressing it, then sneezed again: each sneeze came like a little explosion that made the cat jump. "I am allergic to these poor creatures," he sniffled, "but I love them too much." The woman reappeared with a tray: she came up to us with a measured, assured step, placed a tea service on the low table, attached a tray to Mandelbrod's armrest, poured us two cups, and again disappeared—all as discreetly and silently as the cats. "There's milk and sugar," said Mandelbrod. "Help yourself. I don't take any." He examined me for a few minutes: an impish gleam glinted in his little eyes almost drowned beneath folds of fat. "You have changed," he declared. "The East did you good. You have matured. Your father would have been proud." These words touched me to the quick: "You think?"—"Certainly. You've done some remarkable work: the Reichsführer himself took note of your reports. He showed us the album you prepared in Kiev: your chief wanted to take all the credit for himself, but we knew the idea came from you. In any case that was a trifle. But the reports you wrote, especially these past few months, were excellent. In my opinion, you have a brilliant future before you." He fell silent and con-

templated me: "How is your wound?" he asked finally.—"Fine, Herr
Doktor. It's healed, I just have to rest a little more."—"And then?"—
"I'll resume my service, of course."—"And what do you plan on doing?"—"I'm not sure, actually. It will depend on what they offer
me."—"It's really up to you to receive the offer you like. If you choose
wisely, doors will open, I assure you."—"What are you thinking of,
Herr Doktor?" Slowly, he raised his teacup, blew on it, and drank noisily. I also drank a little. "In Russia, I believe you concerned yourself
mostly with the Jewish question, isn't that right?"—"Yes, Herr Doktor," I said, slightly annoyed. "But not just that." Mandelbrod was already going on in his measured, melodious voice: "From the position
you were in, you no doubt could not appreciate the full extent either
of the problem or of the solution being applied to it. You have probably heard rumors: they are true. Since the end of 1941, this solution has
been extended to all the countries in Europe, insofar as possible. The
program has been operational since the spring of last year. We have already recorded considerable successes, but it is far from over. There is
room there for energetic, devoted men like you." I felt myself blush:
"Thank you for your trust, Herr Doktor. But I should tell you: I found
that aspect of my work extremely difficult, beyond my strength. I'd
rather concentrate now on something that corresponds better to my talents and knowledge, like constitutional law or even legal relations with
the other European countries. The construction of the new Europe is a
field that attracts me very much." During my little speech, Mandelbrod
had finished his tea; the blond Amazon had reappeared and crossed the
room, poured him another cup, and left again. Mandelbrod drank some
more. "I understand your hesitations," he said finally. "Why take on difficult tasks if there are others to do them? That's the spirit of the time.
During the other war, it was different. The more difficult or dangerous
a task was, the more men strove to carry it out. Your father, for example, thought that difficulty in itself was reason enough to do a thing, and
to do it to perfection. Your grandfather was a man of the same mold.
These days, despite all the Führer's efforts, the Germans are sinking into
laziness, indecision, compromise." I felt the indirect insult like a slap; but
something else in what he had said was more important to me: "Excuse
me, Herr Doktor. I thought I understood you to say that you knew my
grandfather?" Mandelbrod put down his cup: "Of course. He too
worked with us, in our early years. An amazing man." He stretched his
swollen hand out to the desk. "Go look, there." I obeyed. "You see that
morocco portfolio? Bring it to me." I went over and handed it to him.
He put it on his knees, opened it, and took out a photograph, which he
held out to me. "Look." It was an old sepia photo, slightly yellowed:

three figures side by side, in front of a background of tropical trees. The woman, in the middle, had a chubby little face, still marked by the plumpness of adolescence; the two men wore light summer suits: the one on the left, with narrow somewhat fluid features and a forehead streaked with a lock of hair, also wore a tie; the shirt of the man on the right was open, beneath an angular face, as if engraved in precious stone; even a pair of tinted glasses didn't manage to hide the joyful, cruel intensity of his eyes. "Which one is my grandfather?" I asked, fascinated, full of anxiety too. Mandelbrod pointed to the man in the tie. I examined him again: unlike the other man, he had secretive, almost transparent eyes. "And the woman?" I asked again, guessing already.—"Your grandmother. Her name was Eva. A superb, magnificent woman." I actually hadn't really known either one: my grandmother had died long before my birth, and the rare visits of my grandfather, when I was very little, hadn't left me any memories. He had died not long after my father's disappearance. "And who is the other man?" Mandelbrod looked at me with a seraphic smile. "You can't guess?" I looked at him: "It's not possible!" I exclaimed. He didn't stop smiling: "Why? You don't think I've always looked like this, do you?" Confused, I stammered: "No, no, that's not what I meant, Herr Doktor! But your age . . . In the photo, you look the same age as my grandfather." Another cat, who was walking on the carpet, leaped nimbly onto the back of the armchair and climbed onto his shoulder, rubbing against his enormous head. Mandelbrod sneezed again. "In fact," he said between two sneezes, "I was older than he. But I've aged well." I was still greedily scrutinizing the photo: how many things it could teach me! Timidly, I asked: "Can I keep it, Herr Doktor?"—"No." Disappointed, I gave it back; he put it away in the portfolio and sent me to replace it on his desk. I came back and sat down. "Your father was an authentic National Socialist," Mandelbrod declared, "even before the Party existed. People then were living under the sway of wrong ideas: for them, nationalism meant a blind, narrow-minded patriotism, a parochial patriotism, coupled with an immense domestic injustice; socialism, for their adversaries, signified a false international equality of the classes, and a class struggle within each nation. In Germany, your father was among the first to understand that there had to be an equal role, with mutual respect, for all members of the nation, but only within the nation. In their own way, all great societies in history have been national and socialist. Look at Temujin, the excluded one: it was only when he could impose this idea, and unify the tribes on that basis, that the Mongols were able to conquer the world, in the name of this man from nowhere who became the Oceanic Emperor, Genghis Khan. I had the Reichsführer read a book about him, he was very impressed. With immense, fierce wisdom, the Mongols razed everything in their path, to rebuild it all afterward on healthy foundations. The entire infrastructure of the Russian Empire, all the foundations on which the Germans later built, under czars who were in fact also German—it was the Mongols who brought them: the roads, the money, the postal system, customs, the administration. It was only when the Mongols compromised their purity, by taking foreign women generation after generation, and often from among the Nestorians—the most Jewish of Christians—that their empire broke apart and collapsed. The Chinese present an opposite but equally instructive example: they never leave their Middle Kingdom, but absorb and irremediably sinicize any population that enters it, however powerful it may be; they drown the invader in a limitless ocean of Chinese blood. They are very strong. And we shouldn't forget that when we've finished with the Russians, we'll still have the Chinese to contend with. The Japanese will never resist them, even if they look as if they're on top today. If not right away, we'll have to confront them someday in any case, in a hundred, two hundred years. So we might as well keep them weak, prevent them if possible from understanding National Socialism and applying it to their own situation. Do you know, by the way, that the very term *National Socialism* was coined by a Jew, a precursor of Zionism, Moses Hess? Read his book someday, *Rome and Jerusalem*, you'll see. It's very instructive. And that's not by chance: what's more *völkisch* than Zionism? Like us, they realized that there can be no *Volk* or *Blut* without *Boden*, without land, and so the Jews must be brought back to the land, *Eretz Israël*, purified of any other race. Of course, those are ancient Jewish ideas. The Jews were the first genuine National Socialists, for almost three thousand five hundred years they've been so, ever since Moses gave them a Law to separate them forever from the other peoples. All our great ideas come from the Jews, and we must have the lucidity to recognize it: the Land as promise and as accomplishment, the notion of the Chosen People, the concept of the purity of blood. That's why the Greeks, degenerate, democrats, travelers, cosmopolitans, hated them so much, and that's why they tried first to destroy them, then, through Paul, to corrupt their religion from within, by detaching it from the soil and from the blood, by making it *catholic*, that is, universal, by suppressing all the laws that served as a barrier to maintaining the purity of Jewish blood: food prohibitions, circumcision. And that's also why the Jews, of all our enemies, are the worst, the most dangerous; the only ones who truly deserve being hated. They are our only real competitors, in fact. Our only serious rivals. The Russians are weak, a horde deprived of a center despite the attempts of that arrogant Georgian to impose a

'National Communism' on them. And the islanders, British or American, are rotten, corrupt, polluted. But the Jews! Who was it who, in the scientific era, discovered the truth of race by drawing on the age-old intuition of his people, humiliated but unconquered? Disraeli, a Jew. Gobineau learned everything from him. You don't believe me? Go look." He pointed to the shelves next to his desk: "There, go look." I got up again and went over to the shelves: several books by Disraeli stood next to books by Gobineau, Vacher de Lapouge, Drumont, Chamberlain, Herzl, and others. "Which one, Herr Doktor? There are many."—"It doesn't matter, it doesn't matter. They all say the same thing. Take *Coningsby*. You read English, don't you? Page two hundred and three. Begin with *But Sidonia and his brethren* . . . Read it out loud." I found the passage and read: *"But Sidonia and his brethren could claim a distinction which the Saxon and the Greek, and the rest of the Caucasian nations, have forfeited. The Hebrew is an unmixed race. . . . An unmixed race of a first-rate organisation are the aristocracy of Nature."*—"Very good! Page two-thirty-one, now. *The fact is, you cannot destroy* . . . He's talking about the Jews, of course."—"Yes. *The fact is, you cannot destroy a pure race of the Caucasian organisation. It is a physiological fact; a simple law of nature, which has baffled Egyptian and Assyrian Kings, Roman Emperors, and Christian Inquisitors. No penal laws, no physical tortures, can effect that a superior race should be absorbed in an inferior, or be destroyed by it. The mixed persecuting races disappear; the pure persecuted race remains."*—"There you have it! Just think that this man, this Jew, was Queen Victoria's Prime Minister! That he founded the British Empire! A man who, when still unknown, advanced such arguments in front of a Christian Parliament! Come back here. Serve me some more tea, please." I went back to him and poured him another cup. "Out of love and respect for your father, Max, I have helped you, I have followed your career, I've supported you when I could. You owe it to yourself to make him proud, both for his race and for your own. There's room on this earth for only one chosen people, called on to dominate the others: either it will be them, as the Jew Disraeli and the Jew Herzl wanted, or it will be us. And so we must kill them down to the last one, extirpate their stock. Because even if only ten remain, an intact quorum, or if only two remain, a man and a woman, in a hundred years we'll have the same problem, and we'll have to do everything over again."—"May I ask you a question, Herr Doktor?"—"Ask away, my boy."—"What is your role in all this, precisely?"—"Leland's and mine, you mean? It's a little hard to explain. We don't have a bureaucratic position. We . . . we stand by the Führer's side. You see, the Führer had the courage and the lucidity to make this historic, fatal decision; but, of course, the practical side of things doesn't concern him.

Between that decision and its realization, which has been entrusted to
the Reichsführer-SS, there is, however, an immense space. Our task
consists of reducing this space. In this sense, we don't even answer to the
Führer, but rather to that space."—"I'm not sure I entirely understand.
But what do you expect from me?"—"Nothing, except that you follow
the path that you yourself have traced, to the end."—"I'm not really
sure what my path is, Herr Doktor. I have to think about it."—"Oh,
think! Think. And then call me. We'll discuss it again." Another cat was
trying to climb up onto my lap, leaving white hairs on the black fabric
before I could chase it away. Mandelbrod, without even batting an eyelid, still just as impassive, almost sleeping, emitted another huge fart. The
odor made my throat seize up and I breathed in tiny breaths through
my mouth. The main door opened and the young woman who manned
the reception desk came in, seemingly oblivious to the smell. I got up:
"Thank you, Herr Doktor. Please pass on my respects to Herr Leland.
Soon, then." But Mandelbrod seemed already almost asleep; only one of
his enormous hands, which was slowly caressing a cat, showed the contrary. I waited for an instant, but he didn't seem to want to say anything
else, so I went out, followed by the girl, who closed the doors without
a sound.

When I had spoken with Dr. Mandelbrod about my interest in issues of European relations, I wasn't lying, but I hadn't said everything,
either: in fact, I had an idea in mind, a precise idea of what I wanted. I
don't really know how it came to me: during a night of semi-insomnia
at the Eden Hotel, probably. It was time, I thought, for me to do something for myself, to think of myself. And what Mandelbrod was suggesting didn't correspond to the idea that had come to me. But I wasn't
sure I knew how to go about putting it in play. Two or three days after
my interview in the offices on Unter den Linden, I called Thomas, who
invited me to come see him. Instead of meeting me at his office, on
Prinz-Albrechtstrasse, he gave me an appointment at the headquarters
of the SP and the SD, on the neighboring Wilhelmstrasse. Situated a
block down from Göring's Ministry of Aviation—an immense angular
cement structure, in a sterile and pompous neoclassical style—the Prinz-
Albrecht-Palais was quite the opposite: an elegant little eighteenth-century classical palazzo, renovated in the nineteenth by Schinkel, but with
taste and delicacy, and rented to the SS by the government since 1934.
I knew it well; before I left for Russia, my department was housed
there, and I had spent many hours strolling through the gardens, a little
masterpiece of asymmetry and calm variety designed by Lenné. From
the street, a large colonnade and some trees hid the façade; guards, in
their red-and-white kiosks, saluted me as I went by, but another, more

discreet team checked my papers in a little office next to the driveway, then escorted me to reception. Thomas was waiting for me: "Shall we go to the park? It's nice out." The garden, which one reached by a few steps lined with stoneware flowerpots, stretched from the palace to the Europahaus, a plump modernist cube set down on the Askanischer Platz and contrasting oddly with the calm, sinuous volutes of the lanes laid out between the mulched flower-beds, the little round fountains, and the still-bare trees on which the first buds were forming. No one was there. "Kaltenbrunner never comes here," Thomas remarked, "so it's quiet." Heydrich liked to walk there; but then no one else could have access to it, except the people he invited. We strolled through the trees and I told Thomas the gist of my conversation with Mandelbrod. "He exaggerates," he said when I had finished. "The Jews are indeed a problem and we have to take care of them, but that's not an end in itself. The objective isn't to kill people, it's to manage a population; physical elimination is part of the management tools. We can't make it into an obsession, there are other problems that are just as serious. You really think he believes everything he told you?"—"That's the impression I got. Why?" Thomas thought for a minute; the gravel crunched under our boots. "Look," he finally went on, "for a lot of people, anti-Semitism is an instrument. Since it's a subject that means a lot to the Führer, it has become one of the best ways to get close to him: if you manage to play a role in the solution to the Jewish question, your career will advance much more quickly than if you concern yourself, say, with Jehovah's Witnesses or homosexuals. In that sense, you can say that anti-Semitism has become the currency of power of the National Socialist State. You remember what I said to you in November 'thirty-eight, after the *Reichskristallnacht?*" Yes, I remembered. I had found Thomas the day after the SA's rampage, seized by a cold rage. "The morons!" he had barked as he slipped into the booth in the bar where I was waiting for him. "The bloody fools."—"Who, the SA?"—"Don't be an idiot. The SA didn't do that all on their own."—"Who gave the orders, then?"— "Goebbels, that horrid little cripple. He's been frantic for years to get his grubby hands on the Jewish question. But he's screwed it up good now."—"But don't you think it was time to do something concrete? After all . . ." He had given a brief, bitter laugh: "Of course we have to do something. The Jews will drink their cup, to the dregs. But not like that. That's just *idiotic*. Do you have the slightest idea what it's going to cost us?" My empty look must have encouraged him, since he went on almost without a pause. "In your opinion, all those broken windows belong to whom? To the Jews? The Jews rent their shops. And it's always the owner who's responsible in case of damage. And also there are the insurance companies. German companies, who will have to reimburse the owners of German buildings, and even Jewish owners. Otherwise, it's the end of the German insurance business. And then there's the glass. Plate glass like that, you know, isn't manufactured in Germany. It all comes from Belgium. We're still estimating the damage, but it's already more than half of their total annual production. And it will have to be paid for in hard currency. Just when the nation was directing all its energy at autarky and rearmament. Oh yes, there are truly complete idiots in this country." His eyes glittered while he spat the words out: "But let me tell you something. All that is *finished* now. The Führer has just officially entrusted the question to the Reichsmarschall. But actually the fat man will delegate everything to us, to Heydrich and us. And none of those Party cretins will be allowed to get involved again, ever. From now on, things will be done correctly. We've been pushing for a global solution for years. Now we can put it to work. Properly, efficiently. Rationally. Finally we'll be able to do things as they should be done."

Thomas had sat down on a bench and, with his legs crossed, held out his silver case to offer me a luxury cigarette, with a gold tip. I took one and lit his too, but remained standing. "The *global solution* you were talking about, then, was emigration. Things have changed quite a bit since then." Thomas let out a long puff of smoke before replying: "That's true. And it's also true that we have to change with the times. That doesn't mean we have to become stupid. The rhetoric is mostly for those playing second, even third, fiddle."—"That's not what I'm talking about. What I mean is that we're not necessarily forced to get mixed up in it."—"You'd rather do something else?"—"Yes. I'm tired of it." It was my turn to take a long pull on my cigarette. It was delicious, a rich, fine tobacco. "I've always been impressed by your formidable lack of ambition," Thomas finally said. "I know ten men who'd kill their father and mother to get a private interview with a man like Mandelbrod. Just think that he lunches with the Führer! And you play hard-to-get. Do you know what you want, at least?"—"Yes. I'd like to go back to France."—"To France!" He thought. "It's true, with your contacts, your knowledge of the language, that's not so dumb. But it won't be easy. Knochen is BdS now, I know him well, but he doesn't have a lot of openings, and a lot of people are after them."—"I know Knochen too. But I don't want to be with the BdS. I want a job where I can get involved in political relations."—"That means a job at the embassy or with the *Militärbefehlshaber*. But I heard that since Best left, the Wehrmacht there doesn't think much of the SS—and same goes for Abetz. We might be able to find something that would suit you with Oberg, the HSSPF. But for that, the Amt I can't do much: you have to go directly through the *SS-Personal Hauptamt*, and I don't know anyone there."—"If a suggestion came from the Amt I, would that work?"—"Possibly." He drew a last puff and negligently threw the butt into the flowerbed. "If it had still been Streckenbach, no problem. But he's like you, he thinks too much and he got sick of it all."—"Where is he now?"—"At the Waffen-SS. He's commanding a Lithuanian division at the front, the Fifteenth."—"And who replaced him? I haven't even asked."—"Schulz."—"Schulz? Which one?"—"Don't you remember? The Schulz who headed a Kommando, in Group C, and who asked to leave, way back in the beginning. The weasel, with that ridiculous little moustache."—"Oh, him! But I never met him. I've heard he's a decent sort."—"No doubt, but I don't know him personally, and things didn't go well between the Gruppenstab and him. He was a banker before, you know the type. Whereas I served with Streckenbach, in Poland. And also Schulz has just been appointed, so he'll overdo things. Especially since he has a lot to make up for. Conclusion: if you make an official request, they'll send you anywhere but France."—"What would you suggest, then?" Thomas had gotten up and we had resumed our walk. "Listen, I'll see. But it's not going to be simple. On your side, can't you try too? You used to know Best well: he comes to Berlin often, go ask him his opinion. You can easily contact him through the *Auswärtiges Amt*. But if I were you, I'd try to think of other options. And it's wartime. You don't always have a choice."

Before leaving me, Thomas had asked me for a favor: "I'd like you to see someone. A statistician."—"From the SS?"—"Officially, he's the statistics inspector for the Reichsführer-SS. But he's a civil servant, he's not even a member of the *Allgemeine-SS*."—"That's odd, isn't it?"—"Not really. The Reichsführer clearly wanted someone from outside."—"And what would you like me to tell your statistician?"—"He's in the process of preparing a new report for the Reichsführer. An overview of the diminution of the Jewish population. But he's questioning the numbers in the reports from the Einsatzgruppen. I've already seen him, but it would be good for you to talk with him. You were closer to the field than I was." He scribbled an address and phone number in a notebook and tore the page out: "His office is right near here, at the SS-Haus, but he's always closeted at the IV B 4, with Eichmann, you know who that is? That's where they archive everything on this question. They have an entire building, now." I looked at the address; it was on the Kurfürstenstrasse: "Oh, that's near my hotel. Fine." The conversation with Thomas had depressed me, I felt as if I were sinking into a marsh. But I didn't want to let myself go, I had to take myself in hand. I made the effort to call this statistician, Dr. Korherr. His assistant set up an appointment. The headquarters of IV B 4 were housed in a handsome building made of stone with four floors, from the end of the last century: no other section of the *Staatspolizei*, to my knowledge, had such offices; their activities must have been colossal. A large marble staircase led up to the main lobby, a cavernous, dimly lit space; Hofmann, the assistant, was waiting for me to lead me to Korherr. "This is huge here," I remarked as I climbed another staircase with him.—"Yes. It's a former Judeo-Masonic lodge, confiscated of course." He led me into Korherr's office, a tiny room cluttered with boxes and files: "Excuse the disorder, Sturmbannführer. It's a temporary office." Dr. Korherr, a glum little man, was wearing civilian clothes and shook my hand instead of saluting. "Please, have a seat," he said as Hofmann withdrew. He tried to clear some papers from a desk, then gave up and left things as they were. "The Obersturmbannführer has been very generous with his documentation," he murmured, "but there's really no order." He stopped rummaging, took off his glasses and rubbed his eyes. "Is Obersturmbannführer Eichmann here?" I asked.—"No, he's on assignment. He'll be back in a few days. Did Obersturmbannführer Hauser explain to you what I do?"—"In general terms."—"In any case, you've come a little late. I've almost finished my report, which I have to hand in in a few days."—"What can I do for you, then?" I retorted with a touch of annoyance.—"You were in the Einsatz, weren't you?"—"Yes. In a Kommando first . . ."—"Which one?" he interrupted.—"Four-A."—"Ah yes. Blobel. Good show." I couldn't tell if he meant that seriously or ironically. "Then, I served in the Gruppenstab D, in the Caucasus." He made a face: "Yes, I'm not so interested in that one. The numbers are negligible. Tell me about Four-A."—"What do you want to know?" He bent down behind his desk and came back up with a cardboard box, which he put in front of me. "These are the reports from Group C. I went through them in minute detail, with my deputy, Dr. Plate. And we noticed some curious things: sometimes, there are extremely precise numbers—two hundred eighty-one, one thousand four hundred seventy-two, or thirty-three thousand seven hundred seventy-one, as in Kiev; other times, they're round numbers. Including for a single Kommando. We also found contradictory numbers. For example, a city where twelve hundred Jews were supposed to live, but where the reports mentioned two thousand people convoyed to the special measures. And so on. What interests me, then, are the counting methods. I mean the practical methods, on-site."—"You should have talked directly to Standartenführer Blobel. I think he'd have been better able to inform you than me."—"Unfortunately Standartenführer Blobel is in the East again and can't be reached. But, you know,

I have my own idea anyway. Your testimony will only confirm it, I think. Tell me about Kiev, for instance. Such an enormous but precise number is curious."—"Not at all. On the contrary, the bigger the *Aktion*, the more means we had, the easier it was to get a precise calculation. In Kiev, there were very tight cordons. Just before the operation site, the . . . the patients, or rather the condemned, were divided into equal groups, always a round number, twenty or thirty, I don't remember. A noncom counted the number of groups that passed by his table and noted it down. The first day, they stopped at twenty thousand exactly."—"And everyone who walked by the table was submitted to the special treatment?"—"In principle, yes. Of course, a few could, let's say, pretend, then run away under cover of night. But that would be at most a handful of individuals."—"And the smaller actions?"—"They were under the responsibility of a Teilkommandoführer who was in charge of counting and passing on the numbers to the Kommandostab. Standartenführer Blobel always insisted on exact counts. For the case you mentioned, I mean the one where they took away more Jews than there were in the beginning, I think I can give you an explanation: when we arrived, a lot of Jews fled into the woods or the steppe. The Teilkommando treated those who were found on-site in an appropriate manner, then left. But the Jews couldn't remain hidden: the Ukrainians chased them out of the villages, sometimes the partisans killed them. So little by little, impelled by hunger, they returned to their towns or villages, often with other refugees. When we found out, we conducted a second operation that liquidated a certain number again. But again others returned. Some villages were declared *judenfrei* three, four, five times, but each time, more appeared."—"I see. That's an interesting explanation."—"If I understand correctly," I said, a little annoyed, "you think the Groups inflated the figures?"—"To be frank with you, yes. For several reasons, no doubt, advancement being only one. There are also bureaucratic habits. In statistics, we're used to seeing agencies get fixated on some number, no one really knows how, and then this number is taken up and repeated as fact, without any criticism or modification in time. We call that a *house number*. But it also differs from Group to Group and from Kommando to Kommando. The worst case is clearly that of Einsatzgruppe B. There are also gross irregularities among certain Kommandos in Group D."—"In 'forty-one or 'forty-two?"—"In 1941 especially. At the beginning, then in the Crimea too."—"I was in the Crimea briefly, but I didn't have anything to do with the actions then."—"And in your experience of Four-A?" I thought for a minute before replying: "I think the officers were honest. But in the beginning, things were badly organized, and some figures might be a little arbi-

trary."—"In any case it's not very serious," Korherr said sententiously.
"The Einsatzgruppen represent only a fraction of the overall numbers.
Even a deviation of ten percent would scarcely affect the overall results."
I felt something tighten around my diaphragm. "Do you have the fig-
ures for all of Europe, Herr Doktor?"—"Yes, of course. Up to Decem-
ber thirty-first, 1942."—"Can you tell me what they add up to?" He
looked at me through his little glasses: "Of course not. That's a secret,
Herr Sturmbannführer." We talked some more about the work of the
Kommando; Korherr asked precise, meticulous questions. In the end,
he thanked me. "My report will go directly to the Reichsführer," he explained. "If your responsibilities require it, you'll have access to it then."
He accompanied me back to the main entrance. "Good luck! And Heil
Hitler."

Why had I asked him that idiotic, useless question? How did that
concern me? It had been nothing but morbid curiosity, and I regretted
it. I wanted to take an interest in nothing but positive things now: National Socialism still had a lot to build; that's where I wanted to direct
my energies. But the Jews, *unser Unglück*, kept pursuing me like a bad
dream in early morning, stuck in the back of my head. In Berlin,
though, not many were left: all the so-called protected Jewish workers
in the arms factories had just been rounded up. Yet fate decreed that I
would meet up with them in the most incongruous places.

On March 21, Heroes' Memorial Day, the Führer gave a speech. It
was his first public appearance since the defeat at Stalingrad, and like
everyone else, I awaited his words with impatience and anxiety: What
was he going to say, how would he seem? The wave of shock from the
catastrophe was still vividly felt; the most varied rumors were running
rampant. I wanted to be present at this speech. I had seen the Führer in
person only once, a dozen years before (I had since then heard him often on the radio and seen him in newsreels); that had been during my
first trip back to Germany, in the summer of 1930, before the Seizure
of Power. I had extorted that trip from my mother and Moreau, in exchange for my consent to continue the course of study they demanded.
Once I had passed my baccalauréat (without honors, which meant I had
to take a preparatory class to pass the ELSP entrance exam), they let me
go. It was a wonderful trip, from which I came back dazzled, bewitched.
I had gone accompanied by two high-school friends, Pierre and Fab-
rice; and we, who didn't even know what the *Wandervögel* were, followed their traces as if instinctively, heading for the forests, walking
during the day, talking at night around little campfires, sleeping on hard
earth and pine needles. Then we went south to visit the cities of the
Rhine and ended up in Munich, where I spent many hours in the

Pinakotek or wandering through the streets. Germany, that summer, was growing turbulent again: the aftereffect of the previous year's American stock market crash was making itself harshly felt; elections in the Reichstag, planned for September, would decide the future of the nation. All the political parties were agitating, using speeches, parades, sometimes violence and brawls. In Munich, one party clearly set itself apart from the others: the NSDAP, which I heard about then for the first time. I had already seen Italian Fascists on the news, and these National Socialists seemed to draw inspiration from their style; but their message was specifically German, and their leader, a frontline soldier who was a veteran of the Great War, spoke of a German renewal, of German glory, of a rich, vibrant German future. This, I said to myself as I watched them march by, was what my father had fought for during four long years, until he was finally betrayed, he and all his comrades, and lost his land, his house, our house. This was also everything that Moreau, that good French patriot and radical, who drank to the health of Clemenceau, Foch, and Pétain every year on their birthdays, detested. The leader of the NSDAP was going to give a speech in a *Braukeller.* I left my French friends in our little hotel. I found myself at the back, behind the crowd, and could scarcely hear the speakers; as for the Führer, I just remember his gestures, made frenetic by emotion, and the way his hair kept falling over his forehead. But he was saying, as I knew with absolute certainty, the things that my father would have said, if he had been present; if he had still been there, he would certainly have been on the platform, one of the men close to that man, one of his foremost companions; he might even, if such had been his fate, who knows, have been there in his place. What's more, the Führer looked like him, when he stood still. I returned from that trip now for the first time with the idea that something was possible besides the narrow and stifling path outlined for me by my mother and her husband, and that my future was there, with this unfortunate people, my father's people, my people too.

Since then, many things had changed. The Führer still had all the confidence of the *Volk,* but the certainty of final victory was beginning to ebb away among the masses. The people blamed the High Command, the Prussian aristocrats, Göring and his Luftwaffe; but I knew too that within the Wehrmacht some were blaming the interference of the Führer. Within the SS, it was being whispered that he had had a nervous breakdown after Stalingrad, that he wasn't talking to anyone anymore; that at the beginning of the month, when Rommel had tried to convince him to evacuate North Africa, he had listened to him without comprehension. As for the public rumors, in the trains, the tramways, the lines, they were becoming downright ludicrous: according to the

SD reports that Thomas received, people were saying that the Wehrmacht had put the Führer under house arrest in Berchtesgaden, that he had lost his reason and was kept under guard, drugged, in an SS hospital, that the Führer we saw was just a double. The speech was going to be given in the Zeughaus, the former arsenal at the end of Unter den Linden, right next to the Spree Canal. As a Stalingrad veteran, wounded and decorated, I didn't have any trouble getting an invitation; I suggested to Thomas that he come with me, but he replied, laughing: "I'm not on leave, I have work to do." So I went alone. They had taken considerable security precautions; the invitation said that service weapons would be forbidden. The possibility of a British raid frightened some: in January, the English had reveled at launching a Mosquito attack on the anniversary of the Seizure of Power, producing many victims; yet now the chairs had been set up in the Zeughaus courtyard, under the large glass cupola. I found myself seated in the center, between an Oberstleutnant covered with decorations and a civilian wearing the Gold Badge of the Party on his lapel. After the introductory speeches, the Führer made his appearance. I opened my eyes wide: on his head and shoulders, over his simple feldgrau uniform, I seemed to see a large blue-and-white striped rabbi's shawl. The Führer had started speaking right away in his rapid, monotone voice. I examined the glass roof: Could it be a play of the light? I could clearly see his cap; but underneath it, I thought I made out long side curls, unrolling along his temples down over his lapel, and on his forehead, the *tefillin*, the little leather box containing verses of the Torah. When he raised his arm, I thought I could make out other leather straps bound around his wrist; and under his jacket, weren't those the white fringes of what the Jews call the *little tallith* showing through? I didn't know what to think. I scrutinized my neighbors: they were listening to the speech with solemn attention, the civil servant was studiously nodding his head. Didn't they notice anything? Was I the only one to see this unprecedented spectacle? I looked at the dignitaries' stand: behind the Führer, I recognized Göring, Goebbels, Ley, the Reichsführer, Kaltenbrunner, other well-known leaders, high-ranking Wehrmacht officers; they were all contemplating the Führer's back or the audience, impassive. Maybe, I said to myself, panic-stricken, it's the story of the Emperor's New Clothes: everyone sees how it really is, but hides it, counting on his neighbor to do the same. No, I reasoned, I must be hallucinating, with a wound like mine, that's entirely possible. Yet I felt perfectly sound of mind. I was far from the platform, though, and the Führer was lit from the side; maybe it was simply an optical illusion? But I still saw it. Maybe my "pineal eye" was playing a trick on me? But there was nothing dreamlike about it. It was also possible that I had gone mad. The speech was short, and I found myself standing in the midst of the crowd trying to head for the exit, unable to make any headway in my thoughts. The Führer would now go to the galleries in the Zeughaus to visit an exhibition of war trophies captured from the Bolsheviks, before going on to inspect an honor guard, and place a wreath at the Neue Wache; I could have followed him, since this was included in my invitation, but I was too rattled and disoriented; I extricated myself from the crowd as quickly as possible and headed back up the avenue toward the S-Bahn station. I crossed the avenue and went to sit in a café, under the arcades of the Kaiser Gallerie, where I ordered a schnapps, drained it in one swallow, then ordered another. I had to think, but the meaning of my thinking escaped me, I was having trouble breathing, I undid my collar and drank some more. There was one way to discover the truth of the matter: in the evening, at the movies, the newsreels would show excerpts from his speech; that would set me straight. I ordered a paper with a list of showings: at seven o'clock, not far away, they were showing *Uncle Krüger*. I ordered a sandwich and then went for a walk in the Tiergarten. It was still cold, and not many people were strolling under the bare trees. Different interpretations were whirling around in my head, I was impatient for the film to start, even if the prospect of seeing nothing there wasn't any more reassuring than the opposite. At six o'clock, I headed for the movie theater and took my place in the line to buy my ticket. In front of me, a group of people were discussing the speech, which they must have heard on the radio; I listened to them eagerly. "He blamed the Jews for everything again," said a skinny man wearing a hat. "What I don't understand is that there aren't any more Jews in Germany, so how can it be their fault?"—"But no, *Dummkopf*," replied a rather vulgar woman with bleached hair stacked in an elaborate permanent, "it's the international Jews."—"Yes," the man retorted, "but if these international Jews are so powerful, why couldn't they save their Jewish brothers here?"—"They're punishing us by bombing us," another grayish, stringy woman said. "Did you see what they did in Münster, the other day? It's just to make us suffer. As if we weren't suffering enough already with all our men at the front."—"What I found scandalous," said a ruddy, paunchy man dressed in a gray pinstripe suit, "is that he didn't even mention Stalingrad. It's shameful."—"Oh, don't talk to me about Stalingrad," said the fake blonde. "My poor sister had her son Hans over there, in the Seventy-sixth Division. She's almost mad with grief, she doesn't even know if he's alive or dead."—"On the radio," said the grayish woman, "they said they were all dead. They fought to the last bullet, they said."—"And you believe everything they say on the radio, you poor thing?" the man with the hat said. "My cousin, who is an Oberst, says there were a lot of prisoners. Thousands. Maybe even a hundred thousand."—"So Hansi might be a prisoner?" asked the blonde.—"It's possible."—"Why don't they write, then?" asked the fat bourgeois. "Our prisoners in England or America write; it even comes through the Red Cross."—"That's true," said the mouse-faced woman.—"And how could they write when they're all officially dead? They write, but our people don't pass on the letters."—"Excuse me," another person interrupted, "but that is true. My sister-in-law, my wife's sister, she got a letter from the front, it was just signed: *A German patriot*, which said that her husband, who is a Leutnant in the Panzers, is still alive. The Russians dropped leaflets on our lines, near Smolensk, with lists of names and addresses, printed in tiny letters, and messages to the families. Soldiers collect them and they write anonymous letters, or send the leaflet as is." A man with a military haircut joined the conversation: "Anyway, even if there are prisoners, they won't survive for long. The Bolsheviks will send them to Siberia and make them dig canals until they die. Not one of them will come back. And after what we did to them, that will be only fair."—"What do you mean, after what we did to them?" the fat man asked sharply. The fake blonde had noticed me and was staring at my uniform. The man with the hat spoke before the soldier did: "The Führer said we have lost five hundred and forty-two thousand men since the beginning of the war. Do you believe that? I think he's just lying." The blonde elbowed him and glanced in my direction. The man followed her gaze, reddened and stammered: "Or, well, maybe they don't give him all the figures . . ." The others were also looking at me and fell silent. I tried to look neutral and absent. Then the fat man tried to restart the conversation on another subject, but the line had begun to move toward the ticket counter. I bought a ticket and found my seat. Soon the lights went out and they played the news, which opened with the Führer's speech. The film was grainy, it jumped and went blurry at times, they must have rushed to develop it and print the copies. I still seemed to see the large striped shawl over the Führer's head and shoulders; I couldn't make out anything else, aside from his moustache; impossible to be sure of anything. My thoughts fled in all directions, like a school of fish in front of a diver; I scarcely noticed the main film, a flimsy Anglophobic thing, I was still thinking about what I had seen, it didn't make any sense. That it was real seemed impossible to me, but I couldn't believe that I was hallucinating. What had that bullet done to my head? Had it irremediably blurred the world for me, or had it truly opened a third eye, the one that sees through the opacity of things? Outside, when I exited, it was night, time for dinner, but I didn't want to eat. I went back to my hotel and locked myself up in my room. For three days I didn't go out again.

Someone knocked and I opened the door: a bellboy was there to tell me that Obersturmbannführer Hauser had left a message. I had him cart away the leftovers of the meal I had had sent up the day before, and took the time to shower and comb my hair before going down to reception to call Thomas. Werner Best was in Berlin, he told me; he was willing to see me, that very evening, in the bar at the Hotel Adlon. "You'll be there?" I went back up to run a bath, as hot as possible, and plunged into it until my lungs felt as if they would crush. Then I sent for a barber to come shave me. At the appointed time I was at the Adlon, toying nervously with the stem of a martini glass, gazing at the Gauleiters, diplomats, high-ranking SS officers, wealthy aristocrats who stayed there while they were passing through Berlin, or were just dining there. I thought about Werner Best. How would a man like Best react if I told him I thought I'd seen the Führer draped in a rabbi's shawl? No doubt he'd give me the address of a good doctor. But maybe he'd also coldly explain to me why it *had* to be that way. An odd man. I had met him in the summer of 1937, after he had helped me, through Thomas, during my arrest in the Tiergarten; he had never again alluded to it. After my recruitment, although I was at least ten years younger than he, he seemed to take an interest in me and invited me several times to dinner, usually along with Thomas and one or two other officials from the SD, once with Ohlendorf, who drank a lot of coffee and spoke little, and sometimes also one-on-one. He was an extraordinarily precise, cold, and objective man, and at the same time passionately devoted to his ideals. When I still barely knew him, it seemed obvious to me that Thomas Hauser imitated his style, and I saw later on that this was the case for most of the young SD officers, who definitely admired him more than they did Heydrich. Best, at that time, still liked to preach what he called *heroic realism*: "What counts," he asserted, quoting Jünger, whom he read avidly, "is not what you fight for, but how you fight for it." For this man, National Socialism was not a political opinion, but rather a way of life, a hard, radical one that blended a capacity for objective analysis with the ability to act. The highest morality, he explained to us, consists in surmounting traditional inhibitions in the search for the good of the *Volk*. In that, the *Kriegsjugendgeneration*, the "war youth generation," to which he belonged along with Ohlendorf, Six, Knochen, and also Heydrich, was clearly distinct from the previous generation, the *junge Frontgeneration*, the "youth of the front," who had been in the war. Most of the Gauleiters and Party leaders, like Himmler and Hans Frank and also Goebbels and Darré, belonged to that generation, but Best thought them too idealistic, too sentimental, naïve, and unrealistic. The *Kriegsjungen*, too young to have been in the war or even fought with the Freikorps, had grown up during the troubled Weimar years, and against this chaos they had forged a *völkisch*, radical approach to the problems of the nation. They had joined the NSDAP not because its ideology was different from that of the other *völkisch* parties of the 1920s, but because instead of getting bogged down in ideas, in leaders' quarrels, in endless, unproductive debates, it had concentrated on organization, mass propaganda, and activism, and had thus naturally emerged in a guiding position. The SD embodied this hard, objective, realistic approach. As for our generation—by that, Best, in these discussions, meant the generation of Thomas and me—it hadn't yet fully defined itself: it had reached adulthood under National Socialism, but hadn't yet been confronted with its real challenges. That was why we had to prepare ourselves, cultivate a severe discipline, learn to fight for our *Volk* and if necessary destroy our enemies, without hatred and without animosity, not like those Teutonic big shots who behaved as if they were still wearing animal pelts, but in a systematic, efficient, carefully thought-out way. That was the mood of the SD then—and, for example, of Professor Dr. Alfred Six, my first department head, who was also at the same time the head of the foreign economics faculty at the university: a bitter, somewhat disagreeable man who spoke more often of bioracial politics than of economics; but he advocated the same methods that Best did, and the same held true for all the young men recruited through the years by Höhn, the *young wolves* of the SD, Schellenberg, Knochen, Behrends, d'Alquen, Ohlendorf of course, but also less well known men now, such as Melhorn, Gürke who was killed in combat in 1943, Lemmel, Taubert. It was a race apart, not much appreciated within the Party, but lucid, active, disciplined, and after I entered the SD, I had aspired only to become one of them. Now I wasn't so sure. I had the impression, after my experiences in the East, that the idealists in the SD had been overwhelmed by the policemen, the bureaucrats of violence. I wondered what Best thought of the *Endlösung*. But I had no intention of asking him, or even of broaching the subject, not to mention that of my strange vision.

Best arrived half an hour late, wearing an extraordinary black uniform with two rows of gold buttons and immense lapels lined in white velvet. After a formal exchange of salutes, he vigorously shook my hand, apologizing for his lateness: "I was with the Führer. I didn't even have time to change." While we congratulated each other on our respective promotions, a maître d'hôtel appeared, greeted Best, and led us to a reserved booth. I ordered another martini and Best a glass of red wine. Then he questioned me about my career in Russia: I replied without going into details; in any case, Best knew better than anyone what an Einsatzgruppe was. "And now?" So I explained my idea to him. He listened to me patiently, nodding his head; his high-domed forehead, gleaming beneath the chandeliers, still bore the red mark of his cap, which he had placed on the banquette. "Yes, I remember," he said finally. "You were beginning to be interested in international law. Why haven't you published anything?"—"I've never really had a chance. At the RSHA, after you left, they entrusted me only with questions of constitutional and penal law, and afterward, in the field, it was impossible. I have acquired a solid practical experience of our methods of occupation, though."—"I'm not sure that the Ukraine is the best example."—"Of course not," I said. "No one in the RSHA can understand how we let Koch go on like that. It's a catastrophe."—"That's one of the dysfunctions of National Socialism. On this point, Stalin is much more rigorous than we are. But men like Koch, I hope, have no future. You read the *Festgabe* that we arranged to have published for the Reichsführer's fortieth birthday?" I shook my head: "Unfortunately not."—"I'll have a copy sent to you. My contribution to it developed a theory of the *Grossraum* founded on a *völkisch* basis; your old professor Höhn wrote an article on the same subject, as did Stuckart, from the Ministry of the Interior. Lemmel, you remember him, has also published work on these concepts, but elsewhere. It was a question both of completing our critical reading of Carl Schmitt and at the same time of putting forward the SS as the driving force behind the construction of the New European Order. The Reichsführer, surrounded by men like us, could have been its main architect. But he let the chance slip by."—"What happened, then?"—"It's hard to say. I don't know if the Reichsführer was obsessed by his plans for the reconstruction of the German East, or if he was overwhelmed with too many tasks. Certainly the involvement of the SS in the processes of demographic planning in the East played a role. That's part of the reason I decided to quit the RSHA." This last assertion, I knew, lacked sincerity. Around the time I was finishing my thesis (it had to do with the reconciliation of positive State law with the notion of *Volksgemeinschaft*) and was entering the SD full-time, to help write legal opinions, Best was already beginning to have problems, especially with Schellenberg. Schellenberg, in private but also in writing, accused Best of being too bureaucratic, too narrow-minded, an *academic lawyer*, a *hair-splitter*. That, according to rumor, was also Heydrich's opinion; at least Heydrich had given Schellenberg free rein. Best, for his part, criticized the "de-officialization" of the police: concretely, he ar-

gued that all employees of the SD assigned to the SP, like Thomas and
me, had to be subject to the ordinary rules and procedures of the State
administration; department heads should all have legal training. But
Heydrich made fun of this *kindergarten for ticket punchers*, and Schellenberg launched attack after attack. Best, on this subject, had made a striking remark to me one day: "You know, despite all my hatred for 1793,
I sometimes feel close to Saint-Just, who said: *I fear less the austerity or the
delirium of some than the flexibility of others.*" All that occurred during the
last spring before the war; I have already spoken about what ensued in
the fall, Best's departure, my own troubles; but I understood why Best
preferred to see the positive side of these developments. "In France and
now in Denmark," he said, "I tried working on the practical aspects of
these theories."—"And how is that going?"—"In France, the idea of a
supervised administration was good. But there was too much interference from the Wehrmacht, which continued its own policy, and from
Berlin, which spoiled things a little with that business of hostages. And
also, of course, the Eleventh of November put an end to all that. In my
opinion it was a gross mistake. But well! I have every hope, on the other
hand, of turning Denmark into a model Protektorat."—"People have
only good things to say about your work."—"Oh, I have my critics too!
And also, you know, I've only just begun. But beyond these precise issues, what counts is to get down to developing a global postwar vision.
For now, all our measures are ad hoc and incoherent. And the Führer is
giving contradictory signals about his intentions. So it's very hard to
make concrete promises."—"I see perfectly what you mean." I spoke to
him briefly about Lippert, about the hopes he had raised during our
conversation in Maikop. "Yes, that's a good example," said Best. "But
you see, other people are promising the same things to the Flemish. And
also now the Reichsführer, encouraged by Obergruppenführer Berger,
is launching his own policy, with the creation of foreign legions of the
Waffen-SS, and this is incompatible with, or in any case not coordinated
with, the policies of the *Auswärtiges Amt*. That's the whole problem: so
long as the Führer doesn't intervene in person, everyone pursues his
own personal policies. There's no overall vision, and so no truly *völkisch*
policies. The real National Socialists are incapable of doing their work,
which is to direct and guide the *Volk*; instead, it's the *Parteigenossen*, the
Party men, who carve out fiefs for themselves and then govern them as
they please."—"You don't think the members of the Party are authentic National Socialists?" Best raised a finger: "Watch out. Don't confuse
a member of the Party with a man of the Party. All members of the
Party, like you and me, are not necessarily 'PGs.' A National Socialist
must believe in his vision. And necessarily, since the vision is unique, all

real National Socialists can work only in a single direction, which is that of the *Volk*. But do you think that all these people"—he made a wide gesture encompassing the room—"are authentic National Socialists? A Party man is someone who owes his career to the Party, who has a position to defend within the Party, and who thus defends the interests of the Party in controversies with other hierarchies, whatever the real interests of the *Volk* may be. The Party, in the beginning, was conceived as a movement, an agent of mobilization for the *Volk*; now it has become a bureaucracy like all the others. For a long time, some of us hoped the SS could take up that role. And it's not too late yet. But the SS is also succumbing to dangerous temptations." We drank a little; I wanted to return to the subject that concerned me. "What do you think of my idea?" I finally asked. "It seems to me that with my past, my knowledge of the country and of the various trends in French thinking, it's in France that I could be most useful."—"You might be right. The problem, as you know, is that aside from strictly police functions, the SS is a little out of the picture in France. And I don't think my name would be very useful to you with the *Militärbefehlshaber*. With Abetz I can't do anything either, he's very jealous of his shop. But if you're really interested, contact Knochen. He should remember you."—"Yes, that's an idea," I said half heartedly. That wasn't what I wanted. Best went on: "You could tell him that I recommended you. What about Denmark? Wouldn't that interest you? I could probably find a good job for you there." I tried not to show my increasing embarrassment too much: "Thank you very much for the suggestion. But I have very concrete ideas about France, and I'd like to follow them up if that's possible."— "I understand. But if you change your mind, contact me."—"Of course." He looked at his watch. "I'm dining with my minister and I really have to change. If I think of something else, for France, or if I hear of an interesting position opening up, I'll let you know."—"I would be very grateful to you. Thank you again for taking the time to see me." He finished his glass and replied: "It was a pleasure. That's what I miss the most, since I left the RSHA: the possibility of openly discussing ideas with men of convictions. In Denmark, I have to be on my guard all the time. Good night, then!" I walked him out and left him in the street, in front of the former British embassy. I watched his car head off down Wilhelmstrasse and then I made for the Brandenburg Gate and the Tiergarten, troubled by his last words. A man of convictions? Before, probably, I had been one, but now, where was the clarity of my convictions hidden away? I could glimpse these convictions, they were dancing gently around me: but if I tried to grasp one, it slipped between my fingers, like a nervous, powerful eel.

Thomas was certainly a man of convictions; convictions, obviously, that were entirely compatible with the pursuit of his ambitions and of pleasure. Back at my hotel, I found a note from him inviting me to the ballet. I called him with my excuses; without giving me time to present them, he said abruptly, "So how did it go?," then began to explain why he wasn't having any success on his side. I listened patiently and at the first opportunity tried to turn down his invitation. But he would hear nothing of it: "You're turning into a caveman. It will do you good to get out." To tell the truth the idea bored me profoundly, but I ended up giving in. All the Russian ballets were of course forbidden; so they put on little pieces by Mozart, ballets from *Idomeneo*, followed by a *Gavotte* and his *Petits Riens*. The orchestra was conducted by von Karajan, then a rising young star whose fame hadn't yet eclipsed Furtwängler's. I found Thomas near the artists' entrance: one of his friends had procured a private box for him. Everything was superbly organized. Bustling usherettes took our coats and caps and led us to a buffet, where we were served drinks in the company of musicians and starlets from Goebbels's studios, who were immediately charmed by Thomas's wit and good looks. When they led us to our box, which was right at the edge of the stage, above the orchestra, I whispered: "Aren't you going to try to invite one of the girls?" Thomas shrugged his shoulders: "You're joking! To get in behind the good Doktor, you have to be at least a Gruppenführer." I had teased him mechanically, without conviction; I remained withdrawn into myself, closed, hostile to everything; but as soon as the ballet began I was delighted. The dancers were just a few yards away from me, and as I watched them I felt poor and haggard and miserable, as if I hadn't yet shaken the cold and fear of the front from my body. The dancers leaped in their brilliant costumes, splendid, as if to mark an insuperable distance, and their shining, sumptuous bodies petrified me and drove me mad with excitement (but it was a vain, aimless, distraught excitement). The gold, the crystal in the chandeliers, the tulle, the silk, the opulent jewelry, the artists' sparkling teeth, their gleaming muscles, overwhelmed me. During the first intermission, sweating in my uniform, I rushed to the bar and had several drinks, then brought the bottle back with me to the box. Thomas looked at me amusedly and drank too, more slowly. On the other side of the theater, sitting in a raised box, a woman was eying me through some opera glasses. She was too far away, I couldn't make out her features and I didn't have any opera glasses, but she was obviously staring at me, and this little game began to annoy me enormously; during the second intermission, I made no attempt to look for her, I took refuge in the private buffet and kept drinking with Thomas; but as soon as the ballet began again, I was like a child. I applauded and even considered sending flowers to one of the dancers, but I didn't know which one to choose, and also I didn't know their names, and I didn't know how to go about it, and I was afraid of making a mistake. The woman kept peering at me, but I couldn't care less. I drank some more, laughed. "You were right," I said to Thomas, "this was a good idea." Everything dazzled me and frightened me. I couldn't begin to understand the beauty of the dancers' bodies, an almost abstract, asexual beauty, with no distinction between the men and the women: this beauty almost scandalized me. After the ballet, Thomas took me to a little street in Charlottenburg; when we went in, I realized to my horror that it was a brothel, but it was too late to retreat. I drank some more and ate some sandwiches while Thomas danced with the unclothed girls, who obviously knew him well. There were some other officers there and some civilians. A gramophone played American records, a frenzied, irritating jazz mingled with the brittle, lost laughter of the whores. Most of them wore nothing but colored silk negligees, and their soft, insipid, dormant skin, which Thomas grasped with both hands, filled me with disgust. A girl tried to sit on my lap; I gently pushed her away, my hand on her naked belly, but she insisted, and so I brutally shoved her off and upset her. I was pale, distraught; everything was shiny and jangling and making me ill. Thomas came over to pour me another drink, laughing: "If you don't like her, you don't have to make a scene, there are others." He waved his hand, his face flushed. "Choose, choose, it's on me." I had no desire whatsoever, but he insisted; finally, so that he would leave me alone, I seized the bottle I was drinking by the neck and went up with one of the girls, picked out at random. In her room, it was calmer. She helped me take off my tunic; but when she wanted to unbutton my shirt, I stopped her and made her sit down. "What's your name?" I asked her.—"Émilie," she answered, using the French form of the name.—"Tell me a story, Émilie."— "What kind of story, Herr Offizier?"—"Tell me about your childhood." Her first words froze me: "I had a twin sister. She died when she was ten. We both had the same illness, rheumatic fever, and then she died of uremia, the water kept rising, rising. . . . She suffocated to death." She rummaged through a drawer and took out two framed photographs. The first one showed the two twins, side by side, with large eyes and ribbons in their hair, about ten years old; the other, the dead girl in her coffin, surrounded by tulips. "At home, they hung this photo up. From that day on my mother couldn't bear tulips anymore, the smell of tulips. She said: *I have lost the angel and kept the devil.* After that, whenever I caught a glimpse of myself in a mirror, I thought I was seeing my dead sister. And if I came running back from school, my mother would get hysterical, she thought she was seeing my sister, so I forced myself always to walk back from school slowly."—"And how did you end up here?" I asked. But the girl, overcome with fatigue, had fallen asleep on the sofa. I leaned on the table and watched her, sipping my drink from time to time. She woke up: "Oh, I'm sorry, I'll get undressed right away." I smiled and replied: "Don't bother." I sat down on the sofa, took her head on my lap and stroked her hair. "Go on, sleep a little more."

Another message was waiting for me at the Hotel Eden: "Frau von Üxküll," the porter explained. "Here is the number where you can reach her." I went up to my room and sat down on the sofa without even unbuttoning my tunic, overwhelmed. Why contact me like this, after all these years? Why now? I would have been incapable of saying if I did or didn't want to see her again; but I knew that if she wanted to, not seeing her again would be as impossible for me as not breathing anymore. That night I didn't sleep at all, or only a little. The memories came brutally rushing back; unlike the ones that had welled up in great waves in Stalingrad, these were not solar, dazzling memories of the force of happiness, but memories already tinged with the cold light of the full moon, white and bitter. In the springtime, back from our winter sports, we continued our games in the attic, naked, shining in the dust-filled light, among the dolls and piles of trunks and suitcases overloaded with old clothes behind which we nestled together. After the winter, I was pale, and still hairless; as for her, the shadow of a tuft was appearing between her legs, and minuscule breasts were beginning to deform her chest, which I loved so flat and smooth. But there was no way back. It was still cold, our skin was taut and bristling. She climbed on top of me, but already a trickle of blood was running down the inside of her thighs. She cried: "It's beginning, the end is beginning." I took her in my thin arms and cried with her. We weren't yet thirteen. It wasn't right, I wanted to be like her; why couldn't I bleed too, share that with her? Why couldn't we be the same? I didn't have ejaculations yet, our games continued; but maybe now we were observing each other, we were observing ourselves a little more, and that already introduced a distance, an infinitesimal one still, but one that may have made us push things sometimes. Then came the inevitable: one day, the whitish cream on my hand, my thighs. I told Una and showed her. It fascinated her, but she was afraid, she had learned the mechanics of the thing. And for the first time the attic seemed gloomy to us, dusty, full of spiderwebs. I wanted to kiss her breasts, round now, but that didn't interest her, and she knelt down, presenting her narrow adolescent buttocks to me. She had brought some cold cream taken from our mother's bathroom: "Take it," she said. "There nothing can happen." More than the sensation, I remember the acrid, heady smell of the cold cream. We were between the Golden Age and the Fall.

When I called her, in the late morning, her voice was perfectly calm. "We're at the Kaiserhof."—"Are you free?"—"Yes. Can we see each other?"—"I'll come by and pick you up." She was waiting for me in the lobby and got up when she saw me. I took off my cap and she kissed me delicately on the cheek. Then she stepped back and contemplated me. She held out a finger and tapped one of the silver buttons on my tunic with the tip of her fingernail: "It suits you nicely, this uniform." I looked at her without saying anything: she hadn't changed, a little older of course, but she was still just as beautiful. "What are you doing here?" I asked.—"Berndt had some business with his lawyer. I thought you might be in Berlin, and I wanted to see you."—"How did you find me?"—"A friend of Berndt's at the OKW called the Prinz-Albrecht-strasse and they told him where you were staying. What would you like to do?"—"You have some time?"—"The whole day."—"Let's go to Potsdam, then. We can eat and walk in the park."

It was one of the very first fine days of the year. The air was getting warmer, the trees were budding beneath a pale sun. In the train we didn't say much; she seemed distant, and to tell the truth, I was terrified. Her face turned to the window, she watched the still-bare trees of the Grunewald go by; and I watched that face. Beneath her heavy, jet black hair, it looked almost translucent; the long blue veins were clearly outlined beneath her milk white skin. One of them started at the temple, touched the corner of her eye, then, in a long curve, crossed her cheek like a scar. I imagined the blood pulsing slowly beneath this surface as thick and deep as the opalescent oils of a Flemish master. At the base of her neck, another network of veins began, unfurled over the delicate clavicle, and passed beneath her sweater, I knew, like two large open hands to irrigate her breasts. As for her eyes, I could see them reflected in the window, on the dense brown background of the trees, colorless, distant, absent. In Potsdam I knew a little restaurant near the Garnisonskirche. The pealing bells were ringing out their little melancholic tune, to a melody by Mozart. The restaurant was open: "Goebbels's obsessions don't hold sway in Potsdam," I commented; but even in Berlin most of the restaurants were already reopening. I ordered some wine and asked my sister about her husband's health. "He's fine," she replied laconically. They were just in Berlin for a few days; after that, they would go to a sanatorium in Switzerland, where von Üxküll would get his treatment. Hesitant, I wanted her to talk about her life in Pomerania. "I have nothing to complain about," she said, looking at me with her large clear eyes. "Berndt's farmers bring us food to eat, we have everything we need. Sometimes we even have fish. I read a lot, take walks. The war seems very far away."—"It's getting closer," I said harshly.—"You don't think they'll get as far as Germany?" I shrugged my shoulders: "Anything is possible." Our words remained cold, awkward, I could see, but I didn't know how to break this coldness to which she seemed indifferent. We drank and ate a little. Finally, more gently, she ventured: "I heard you were wounded. From some of Berndt's army friends. We live a somewhat retired life, but he keeps his contacts. I didn't get any details and I was worried. But seeing you, it must not have been very serious." So, calmly, I told her what had happened and showed her the hole. She put down her silverware and turned pale; she raised her hand, then put it down. "I'm sorry. I didn't know." I held out my fingers and touched the back of her hand; she slowly withdrew it. I didn't say anything. In any case I didn't know what to say: everything I wanted to say, everything I should have said, I couldn't say. There was no coffee; we finished our meal and I paid. The streets of Potsdam were quiet: some soldiers, some women with strollers, not many vehicles. We headed for the park, without speaking. The Marlygarten, where you enter, prolonged the calm of the streets and deepened it; from time to time we saw a couple, or some convalescent soldiers, on crutches or in wheelchairs. "It's terrible," murmured Una. "What a waste."—"It's necessary," I said. She didn't reply: we were still talking past each other. Some tame squirrels were scampering in the grass; to our right, one of them ran up to snatch some pieces of bread from a little girl's hand, withdrew, returned to nibble, and the girl broke out in peals of laughter. On the ornamental ponds, some mallards and other ducks were swimming or had just landed: just before impact, they quickly beat their wings, leaning backward to slow down, and pointing their webbed feet at the water; as soon as they touched the surface, they folded back their feet and ended up skidding on their rounded bellies, in a little spray of water. The sun was shining through the pines and bare oak branches; where the paths joined, little cherubs or nymphs stood on gray stone pedestals, superfluous and laughable. At the Mohrenrondell, a circle of busts set in topiary hedges, beneath terraced vines and greenhouse plants, Una gathered her skirt around her and sat down on a bench, casually, like a teenager. I lit a cigarette; she borrowed it from me and took a few drags before giving it back. "Tell me about Russia." I explained to her, in short, dry sentences, what security work in the rear areas consisted of. She listened without saying anything. In the end she asked: "And you, did you kill people?"—"Once, I had to give the coups de grâce. Most of the time I gathered information, wrote reports."—"And when you shot at people, what did you feel?" I answered without hesitating: "The same thing as when I watched other people shoot. As long as it has to be done, it doesn't matter who does it. And also, I consider that watching involves my responsibility as much as doing."—"But do you have to do it?"—"If we want to win this war, yes, certainly." She thought about this and then said: "I'm happy I'm not a man."—"And I've often wished I had your luck." She held out her arm and brushed her hand over my cheek, pensive: I thought happiness would suffocate me, that I would huddle in her arms, like a child. But she stood up and I followed her. She calmly climbed the terraces toward the little yellow palace. "Have you heard from Mother?" she asked over her shoulder.— "No. We stopped writing years ago. What's happened with her?"— "She's still in Antibes, with Moreau. He was doing business with the German army. Now they're under Italian control: apparently they're very well behaved, but Moreau is furious because he's convinced Mussolini wants to annex the Côte d'Azur." We had reached the last terrace, an expanse of gravel reaching to the façade of the palace. From there, we looked out over the park; the roofs and steeples of Potsdam were silhouetted behind the trees. "Papa liked this place very much," Una said calmly. The blood rose to my face and I grasped her arm: "How do you know that?" She shrugged her shoulders: "I know it, that's all."—"You never . . ." She looked at me sadly: "Max, he's dead. You should get that into your head."—"You too, even you say that," I spat out angrily. But she remained calm: "Yes, I too say that." And she recited these lines in English:

> Full fathom five thy father lies;
> Of his bones are coral made;
> Those are pearls that were his eyes;
> Nothing of him that doth fade,
> But doth suffer a sea-change
> Into something rich and strange.

Disgusted, I turned and walked away. She caught up with me and took my arm. "Come. Let's visit the palace." The gravel crunching under our steps, we went round the building and under the rotunda. Inside, I looked vaguely at the gilt finish, the small, precious furniture, the voluptuous eighteenth-century paintings; I was moved only in the music room, when I saw the fortepiano and wondered if it was the same one on which old Bach had improvised for the king what would become the *Musical Offering*, the day he had come there: if it weren't for the guard, I would have stretched out my hand and struck the keys that might have felt Bach's fingers. The famous painting by von Menzel that shows Frederick II, illumined by cathedrals of candles, playing his flute just as on the day he received Bach, had been taken down, likely from fear of bombs. A little farther on, the tour went through the guest room known as Voltaire's Room, with a tiny bed where the great man supposedly had slept during the years he taught Frederick the Enlightenment and hatred of the Jews; actually he stayed at the Potsdam town castle. Una studied the frivolous decorations with amusement: "For a king who couldn't even take off his own boots, let alone his pants, he certainly appreciated naked women. The whole palace seems eroticized."—"That's to remind himself of what he had forgotten." At the exit, she pointed to the hill where some artificial ruins stood out, products of this rather capricious prince's whim: "Would you like to climb up there?"—"No. Let's go toward the orangery." We strolled lazily along, without looking much at the things around us. We sat down for a bit on the terrace of the orangery, then went down the steps framing the large ponds and flowerbeds in a regular, classical, perfectly symmetrical order. Afterward the park began again and we walked on at random, down one of the long footpaths. "Are you happy?" she asked me.—"Happy? Me? No. But I've known happiness. Now I'm content with what there is, I can't complain. Why do you ask me that?"—"Just like that. No reason." A little farther, she went on: "Can you tell me why we haven't spoken in more than eight years?"—"You got married," I answered, holding back a burst of rage.—"Yes, but that was later. And also, that's not a reason."—"For me it is. Why did you get married?" She stopped and looked at me closely: "I don't owe you any explanations. But if you want to know, I love him." I looked at her now: "You have changed."—"Everyone changes. You've changed too." We continued walking. "And you, you've never loved anyone?" she asked.—"No. I keep my promises."—"I never made you any."—"That's true," I acknowledged.—"Anyway," she went on, "obstinate attachment to old promises is no virtue. The world changes, you have to be able to change with it. You're still a prisoner of the past."—"I'd rather call it loyalty, fidelity."—"The past is over, Max."—"The past is never over."

We had reached the Chinese pavilion. A mandarin under his parasol sat enthroned at the top of the cupola, which was trimmed with a blue-and-gold canopy supported by gilt columns in the shape of palm trees. I glanced inside: a round room, Oriental paintings. Outside, at the foot of each palm tree, sat exotic figures, also gilded. "A real *folie*," I commented. "That's what the great used to dream of. It's a little ridiculous."—"No more than the mad fantasies of the powerful today," she replied calmly. "I like this century a lot. It's the only one of which you

can at least say it wasn't a century of faith."—"From Watteau to Robespierre," I retorted ironically. She made a face: "Robespierre is already
the nineteenth. He's almost a German romantic. Do you still like that
French music as much as you used to—Rameau, Forqueray, Couperin?"
I felt my face darken: her question had suddenly reminded me of Yakov,
the little Jewish pianist from Zhitomir. "Yes," I answered finally. "But I
haven't had a chance to listen to them for a long time now."—"Berndt
plays them now and then. Especially Rameau. He says it's not bad, that
there are some things that are almost as good as Bach, for the keyboard."—"That's what I think too." I had had almost the same conversation with Yakov. I didn't say anything more. We had come to the edge
of the park; we turned around and then, by common consent, headed
off toward the Friedenskirche and the exit. "And you?" I asked. "Are
you happy, in your Pomeranian hideout?"—"Yes. I'm happy."—"You
don't get bored? You must feel a little lonely sometimes." She looked at
me again, for a long time, before replying: "I don't need anything." This
statement chilled me. We took a bus to the train station. Waiting for the
train, I went and bought the *Völkische Beobachter*; Una laughed when she
saw me come back with it. "Why are you laughing?"—"I was thinking
about one of Berndt's jokes. He calls the *VB* the *Verblödungsblatt*, the
Mindless Rag." I scowled: "He should be careful about what he says."—
"Don't worry. He's not an idiot, and his friends are intelligent men."—
"I wasn't worried. I was warning you, that's all." I looked at the front
page: the English had bombed Cologne again, causing many civilian
deaths. I showed her the article: "Those *Luftmörder* really have no
shame," I said. "They say they're defending freedom and they kill
women and children."—"We're killing women and children too," she
replied gently. Her words made me ashamed, but immediately my
shame turned into anger: "We're killing our enemies, to defend our
country."—"They're defending their country too."—"They're killing
innocent civilians!" I was turning red, but she remained calm. "The
people you were executing—you didn't catch them all with weapons in
their hands. You too have killed children." Rage was suffocating me, I
didn't know how to explain to her; the difference seemed obvious to
me, but she was acting stubborn and pretending not to see it. "You're
calling me a murderer!" I shouted. She took my hand: "No, I'm not.
Calm down." I calmed down and went out to smoke; then we got on
the train. As on the way down, she watched the Grunewald go by, and
as I watched her I shifted, slowly at first, then vertiginously, into the
memory of our last meeting. It was in 1934, just after our twenty-first
birthday. I had finally won my freedom, I had announced to my mother
that I was leaving France; on my way back to Germany, I made a de-

tour through Zurich; I rented a room in a little hotel and went to find
Una, who was studying there. She seemed surprised to see me: but she
already knew about the scene in Paris, with Moreau and our mother,
and about my decision. I took her out to dinner at a modest, quiet
restaurant. She was happy in Zurich, she told me, she had friends, Jung
was a magnificent man. These last words made my hackles rise, it must
have been something in her tone, but I didn't say anything. "And you?"
she asked me. I revealed my hopes to her then, my enrollment in Kiel,
my joining the NSDAP too (I had done so during my second trip to
Germany, in 1932). She listened to me as she drank her wine; I drank
too, but more slowly. "I'm not sure I share your enthusiasm for this
Hitler," she commented. "He seems a neurotic to me, full of unresolved
complexes, frustrations, and dangerous resentments."—"How can you
say that!" I launched into a long tirade. But she frowned, withdrew into
herself. I stopped as she poured herself another glass, and I took her
hand on the checkered tablecloth. "Una. It's what I *want* to do, it's what
I *have* to do. Our father was German. My future is in Germany, not with
the corrupt bourgeoisie of France."—"You may be right. But I'm afraid
you'll lose your soul with those men." I flushed with anger and struck
the table. "Una!" It was the first time I had raised my voice with her.
Her glass tipped over from the blow, rolled, and smashed at her feet,
bursting into a puddle of red wine. A waiter hurried over with a broom
and Una, who until then had kept her eyes lowered, raised them to me.
Her gaze was clear, almost transparent. "You know," I said, "I've finally
read Proust. You remember this passage?" I recited, my throat tight:
"This glass will be, as in the Temple, the symbol of our indestructible union."
She waved her hand. "No, no. Max, you don't understand anything,
you've never understood anything." She was red, she must have drunk
a lot. "You've always taken things too seriously. They were games, children's games. We were children." My eyes, my throat swelled up. I
made an effort to control my voice. "You're wrong, Una. You're the
one who never understood anything." She drank some more. "You have
to grow up, Max." It had been seven years then since we were apart.
"Never," I said, "never." And I kept that promise, even if she never
thanked me for it.

In the train from Potsdam, I watched her, dominated by a feeling of
loss, as if I had sunk and had never come back to the surface. And what
was she thinking about? Her face hadn't changed since that night in
Zurich, it had simply filled out a little; but it remained closed to me, inaccessible; behind it, there was another life. We passed between the elegant residences in Charlottenburg; then came the zoo and the
Tiergarten. "You know," I said, "since I got to Berlin I haven't even

been to the zoo yet."—"But you used to like zoos."—"Yes. I should go for a walk there." We got out at the Lehrter Hauptbahnhof and I took a taxi to accompany her to the Wilhelmplatz. "Do you want to have dinner with me?" I asked her in front of the entrance to the Kaiserhof. "Yes," she replied, "but now I have to go see Berndt." We agreed to meet in two hours, and I went back to my hotel to bathe and change. I felt exhausted. Her words were confused with my memories, my memories with my dreams, and my dreams with my most insane thoughts. I remembered her cruel Shakespeare quotation: so had she too joined our mother's camp? It was undoubtedly the influence of her husband, the Baltic baron. I said to myself with rage: She should have remained a virgin, like me. The incoherence of this thought made me burst out laughing, a long crazy laughter; at the same time I wanted to cry. At the appointed time, I was at the Kaiserhof. Una joined me in the lobby, among the comfortable square armchairs and little potted palm trees; she wore the same clothes as in the afternoon. "Berndt is resting," she said. She too felt tired and we decided to stay and eat at the hotel. Ever since the restaurants had reopened, a new directive from Goebbels enjoined them to offer customers *Feldküchengerichte*, field rations, in solidarity with the troops at the front; the maître d'hôtel's gaze, while he explained that to us, remained fixed on my medals, and my expression made him stutter; Una's cheerful laughter cut his embarrassment short: "I think my brother has already eaten enough of that."—"Yes, of course," he hastened to say. "We also have some venison from the Black Forest. With a prune sauce. It's excellent."—"Fine," I said. "And some French wine."—"Burgundy, with the venison?" During the meal we chatted about this and that, skirting around what concerned us most. I talked to her again about Russia, not the horrors, but my more human experiences: Hanika's death, and especially about Voss: "You liked him a lot."—"Yes. He was a decent fellow." She spoke to me about the matrons who had been pestering her since she arrived in Berlin. With her husband, she had gone to parties and society dinners, where wives of high-ranking Party dignitaries decried *deserters from the reproduction front*, the childless women guilty of *treason against nature* for their *childbearing strike*. She laughed: "Of course, no one had the gall to attack me directly, everyone can see the state Berndt is in. Luckily, because otherwise I would have slapped them. But they were dying of curiosity, they came prowling around me without daring to ask me right out if he can *function*." She laughed again and drank a little wine. I kept quiet; I too had asked myself the same question. "There's even one, just picture this, a fat Gauleiter's wife dripping with diamonds, with a bluish permanent, who had the nerve to suggest, *if someday it should become necessary*, that I go find a handsome SS man to impregnate me. How did she phrase it? A *decent, dolichocephalic,* völkisch *will-bearing, physically and psychically healthy man.* She explained to me that there was an SS office that was in charge of *eugenic assistance* and that I could apply to it for help. Is that true?"—"So they say. It's a project of the Reichsführer's called *Lebensborn.* But I don't know how it works."—"They've really gone mad. Are you sure it's not just a brothel for SS officers and socialites?"—"No, no, it's something else." She shook her head. "Anyway, you'll love the punchline: *You won't receive your child from the Holy Ghost,* she said to me. I had to keep myself from replying that in any case I didn't know any SS officer patriotic enough to impregnate her." She laughed again and kept drinking. She had scarcely touched her food but had already drunk almost an entire bottle of wine on her own; still, her gaze remained clear, she wasn't drunk. For dessert, the maître d'hôtel suggested grapefruit: I hadn't tasted any since the beginning of the war. "They come from Spain," he said. Una didn't want any; she watched me prepare mine and eat it; I gave her a few pieces to try, lightly sprinkled with sugar. Then I accompanied her back to the lobby. I looked at her, with the taste of sweet grapefruit still in my mouth: "Do you share his bedroom?"—"No," she replied, "that would be too complicated." She hesitated, then touched the back of my hand with her oval nails: "If you like, come up and have a drink. But behave. Afterward, you have to leave." In the bedroom, I put my cap on a table and sat down in an armchair. Una took her shoes off and, crossing the carpet in silk stockings, poured me some Cognac; then she sat on the bed with her feet crossed and lit a cigarette. "I didn't know you smoked."—"From time to time," she replied. "When I drink." I thought she was more beautiful than anything in the world. I talked to her about my plans for a position in France, and the difficulties I was encountering. "You should ask Berndt," she said. "He has a lot of friends in high places in the Wehrmacht, comrades from the other war. Maybe he could do something for you." These words unleashed my suppressed anger: "Berndt! He's all you talk about."—"Calm down, Max. He's my husband." I got up and began pacing up and down the room. "I don't give a damn! He's an intruder, he has no business getting between us."—"Max." She was still talking softly; her eyes remained serene. "He is not between us. The us you're talking about does not exist, it no longer exists, it's come undone. Berndt is my everyday life, you have to understand that." My rage was so mixed with my desire that I no longer knew where one began and the other ended. I went up to her and took both her arms: "Kiss me." She shook her head; for the first time, I saw a harsh look in her eyes. "You're not going to start that again." I felt sick, I was suffocating; overcome, I fell down next to the bed, my head against her knees as on a chopping block. "In Zurich, you kissed me," I sobbed.—"In Zurich I was drunk." She moved over and put her hand on the bedspread. "Come here. Lie down next to me." Still with my boots on, I climbed onto the bed and lay curled up against her legs. I thought I could smell her odor through the stockings. She caressed my hair. "My poor little brother," she murmured. Laughing through my tears, I managed to say: "You call me that because you were born fifteen minutes before me, because it was your wrist they tied the red thread to."—"Yes, but there's another difference: now I'm a woman, and you're still a little boy." In Zurich, things had gone differently. She had drunk a lot, as had I. After the meal we had gone out. Outside, it was cold and she shivered; she was staggering a little, so I put my arm around her and she clung to me. "Come with me," I had said. "To my hotel." She protested in a thickish voice: "Don't be stupid, Max. We're not children anymore."— "Come," I insisted. "To talk a little." But we were in Switzerland and even in that kind of hotel the concierges made difficulties: "I'm sorry, mein Herr. Only guests of the establishment are allowed into the rooms. You can go to the bar, if you like." Una turned toward it, but I held her back. "No. I don't want to see people. Let's go to your place." She didn't resist and brought me back to her little student's room, cluttered with books, freezing. "Why don't you heat it more?" I asked, clearing away the inside of the stove to prepare a fire. She shrugged her shoulders and showed me a bottle of white wine from the Valais. "That's all I have. Is it all right with you?"—"Anything is all right with me." I opened the bottle and filled to the brim two glasses she held out, laughing. She drank, then sat down on the bed. I felt tense, strained; I went to the table and examined the spines of the piled-up books. Most of the names were unknown to me. I took one at random. Una saw it and laughed again, a sharp laughter that set my nerves on edge. "Oh, Rank! Rank is good."—"Who is he?"—"A former disciple of Freud, a friend of Ferenczi. He wrote a fine book on incest." I turned toward her and stared at her. She stopped laughing. "Why do you say that word?" I said finally. She shrugged her shoulders and held out her glass. "Stop with your nonsense," she said. "Pour me some more wine instead." I put the book down and took the bottle: "It's not nonsense." She shrugged her shoulders again. I poured wine into her glass and she drank. I went up to her, my hand outstretched to touch her hair, her beautiful thick black hair. "Una . . ." She brushed my hand away. "Stop, Max." She was swaying slightly and I put my hand under her hair, stroked her cheek, her neck. She stiffened but didn't push my hand away; she drank some more. "What do you want, Max?"—"I want everything to be like before," I said gently, my heart pounding.—"That's impossible." She clicked her teeth a little and drank again. "Even before wasn't like before. Before never existed." She was rambling, her eyes were closed. "Pour me some more wine."—"No." I took her glass and leaned over to kiss her lips. She pushed me harshly away, but the gesture made her lose her balance and she fell back onto the bed. I put her glass down and lay down next to her. She had stopped moving, her stockinged legs hung off the bed, her skirt had risen up over her knees. The blood was beating in my temples, I was overwhelmed, at that moment I loved her more than ever, more even than I had loved her in our mother's womb, and she had to love me too, now and forevermore. I leaned over her, and she didn't resist.

I must have fallen asleep; when I woke up, the room was dark. I didn't know where I was anymore, Zurich or Berlin. No light filtered through the blackout curtains. I could vaguely make out a shape next to me: Una had slipped under the sheets and was sleeping. I spent a long while listening to her gentle, even breathing. Then, with infinite slowness, I brushed back a lock of hair from her ear and leaned over her face. I stayed there without touching her, breathing in her skin and her breath still tinged with the smell of cigarette. Finally I got up and, tiptoeing on the rug, went out. In the street I realized I had forgotten my cap, but I didn't go back up; I asked the porter to call a taxi for me. In my room at the hotel, the memories kept flowing in, feeding my insomnia, but now they were brutal, confused, hideous memories. As adults, we visited a kind of Torture Museum; there were all kinds of whips there, tongs, an "iron maiden of Nuremberg," and a guillotine in the back room. At the sight of that instrument my sister flushed bright crimson: "I want to lie down on it." The room was empty; I went to see the guard and slipped him a bill: "That's to leave us alone for twenty minutes."—"Fine," he agreed with a slight smile. I closed the door and heard him turn the key. Una had stretched out on the bed of the guillotine; I lifted the lunette, made her put her head through it, and closed it on her long neck, after carefully lifting her heavy hair. She was panting. I tied her hands behind her back with my belt, then raised her skirt. I didn't even bother to lower her panties, just pushed the lace to one side and spread her buttocks with both hands: in the slit, nestling in hair, her anus gently contracted. I spit on it. "No," she protested. I took out my penis, lay on top of her, and thrust it in. She gave a long stifled cry. I was crushing her with all my weight; because of the awkward position—my pants were hindering my legs—I could only move in little jerks. Leaning over the lunette, my own neck beneath the blade, I whispered to her: "I'm going to pull the lever, I'm going to let the blade drop." She begged me: "Please, fuck my pussy."—"No." I came suddenly, a jolt that emptied my head like a spoon scraping the inside of a soft-boiled egg. But this memory is dubious, after our childhood we had seen each other only once, that time in Zurich, and in Zurich there was no guillotine, I don't know, it was probably a dream, an old dream perhaps that, in my confusion, alone in my dark room at the Eden Hotel, I had remembered, or even a dream dreamt that night, during a brief moment of sleep, almost unnoticed. I was angry, for the day, despite all my distress, had remained shot through with purity for me, and now these foul images were coming and soiling it. It repelled me but at the same time troubled me, since I knew that, memory or image or fantasy or dream, this also lived inside me, and that my love must have been made of this too.

In the morning, around ten o'clock, a bellboy knocked on my door: "Herr Sturmbannführer, a phone call for you." I went down to reception and took the receiver; Una's joyful voice resounded at the other end: "Max! Can you come have lunch with us? Say yes. Berndt wants to meet you."—"All right. Where?"—"At Borchardt's. You know it? On Französischestrasse. At one o'clock. If you get there before us, give our name, I've reserved a table." I went back up to shave and shower. Since I didn't have my cap anymore I dressed in civilian clothes, with my Iron Cross on my jacket pocket. I arrived early and asked for Freiherr von Üxküll: they led me to a table set a little back and I ordered a glass of wine. Pensive, still saddened by the images from the night before, I thought about my sister's strange marriage, her strange husband. It had taken place in 1938, when I was finishing my studies. After the night in Zurich, my sister wrote to me only rarely; that year, in the spring, I had received a long letter from her. She told me that in the fall of 1935, she had become very ill. She had gone into analysis, but her depression had only gotten worse, and they had sent her to a sanatorium near Davos to rest and regain her strength. She had stayed there for several months and, in the beginning of 1936, had met a man there, a composer. They had seen each other regularly since then and were going to get married. *I hope you will be happy for me*, she wrote.

This letter had left me prostrate for many days. I stopped going to the university and didn't leave my room anymore; I stayed on the bed, facing the wall. So, I said to myself, that's what it all comes to. They talk to you about love, but at the first opportunity, at the prospect of a nice happy bourgeois marriage, upsy-daisy, they roll onto their backs and spread their legs. Oh, my bitterness was immense. It seemed to me the inevitable end of an old story that pursued me relentlessly: the story of my family, which had almost always persisted in destroying any trace of love in my life. I had never felt so alone. When I recovered a little, I wrote her a stiff, conventional letter, congratulating her and wishing her all happiness.

At that time, I was beginning to form a friendship with Thomas, we were already calling each other by the familiar *du*, and I asked him to find out about the fiancé, Karl Berndt Egon Wilhelm, Freiherr von Üxküll. He was much older than she; and this aristocrat, a German Balt, was a paralytic. I didn't understand. Thomas gave me some details: he had distinguished himself during the Great War, which he had finished as an Oberst with the *Pour le Mérite*; then he had led a Landeswehr regiment into Courland against the Red Latvians. There, on his own property, he had been hit with a bullet in the spinal column, and from his stretcher, before being forced to retreat, he had set fire to his ancestral home, *so the Bolsheviks wouldn't soil it with their debauchery and their shit*. His SD file was quite thick: without being regarded exactly as an opponent, he was seen in an unfavorable light, apparently, by certain authorities. During the Weimar years, he had acquired European renown as a composer of modern music; he was known to be a friend and supporter of Schönberg, and he had corresponded with musicians and writers in the Soviet Union. After the Seizure of Power, moreover, he had rejected Strauss's invitation to enroll in the *Reichsmusikkammer*, which had in fact put an end to his public career, and he had also refused to become a member of the Party. He lived in seclusion on the estate of his mother's family, a manor house in Pomerania where he had moved after the defeat of Bermondt's army and the evacuation from Courland. He left it only for treatment in Switzerland; the Party and local SD reports said that he received few guests and went out even less, avoiding mingling with the society of the *Kreis*. "An odd sort," Thomas summed up. "A bitter, uptight aristo, a dinosaur. And why is your sister marrying a cripple? Does she have a nursing complex?" Why, indeed? When I received an invitation for the wedding, which was going to be held in Pomerania, I replied that my studies prevented me from coming. We were twenty-five then, and it seemed to me that everything that had been truly ours was dying.

The restaurant was filling up: a waiter pushed von Üxküll's wheelchair, and Una was holding my cap under her arm. "Here!" she said cheerfully as she kissed me on the cheek. "You forgot this."—"Yes, thanks," I said, blushing. I shook von Üxküll's hand while the waiter removed a chair, and I declared somewhat solemnly: "Freiherr, delighted to meet you."—"Likewise, Sturmbannführer. Likewise." Una pushed him into place and I sat down opposite him; Una came and sat down between us. Von Üxküll had a severe face, very thin lips, gray hair in a crew cut: but his brown eyes seemed sometimes curiously laughing, with crow's feet. He was simply dressed, in a gray woollen suit with a knit tie, no medals, and his only piece of jewelry was a gold signet ring, which I noticed when he placed his hand on Una's: "What will you have to drink, darling?"—"Some wine." Una seemed very cheerful, happy; I wondered if she was forcing it. Von Üxküll's stiffness was obviously entirely natural. They brought the wine, and von Üxküll asked me some questions about my wound and my convalescence. He drank as he listened to my answer, but very slowly, in little sips. Then, since I didn't really know what to say, I asked him if he had been to a concert since he arrived in Berlin. "There's nothing that interests me," he answered. "I don't like that young Karajan much. He's much too full of himself, too arrogant."—"So you prefer Furtwängler, then?"—"There are rarely any surprises with Furtwängler. But he is very solid. Unfortunately, they don't let him conduct Mozart's operas anymore, and that's what he does best. Apparently Lorenzo da Ponte was half Jewish, and *The Magic Flute* is a Masonic opera."—"You don't think it is?"—"It may be, but I challenge you to show me a German spectator who would realize it on his own. My wife told me you like old French music?"— "Yes, especially the instrumental works."—"You have good taste. Rameau and the great Couperin are still far too neglected. There is also a whole treasure trove of music for viola da gamba from the seventeenth century, still unexplored—but I've been able to consult some manuscripts. It's superb. But the early French eighteenth century is truly a high point. No one can write like that anymore. The Romantics spoiled everything, we're still struggling to emerge from it."—"You know that Furtwängler did conduct, this week," Una interrupted. "At the Admiralpalast. That Tiana Lemnitz sang there, she isn't half bad. But we didn't go. It was Wagner, and Berndt doesn't like Wagner."—"That's an understatement," he went on. "I detest him. Technically, there are some extraordinary discoveries, some truly new, objective things, but that's all lost in bombast, gigantism, and also the coarse manipulation of emotions, like the vast majority of German music since 1815. It's written for people whose main musical reference is still basically the military fanfare. Reading Wagner's scores fascinates me, but I could never listen to them."—"Is there any German composer who finds favor with you?"— "After Mozart and Beethoven? A few pieces by Schubert, some passages from Mahler. And even there, I'm being indulgent. At bottom, there's almost no one but Bach . . . and now, of course, Schönberg."—"Excuse me, Freiherr, but it would seem to me that it would be difficult to describe Schönberg's music as German music."—"Young man," von Üxküll retorted dryly, "don't you try to give me lessons in anti-Semi-

tism. I was an anti-Semite before you were born, even if I remain old-
school enough to believe that the sacrament of baptism is powerful
enough to wash away the strain of Judaism. Schönberg is a genius, the
greatest since Bach. If the Germans don't want him, that's their problem." Una let out a ringing burst of laughter: "Even the *VB* still talks
about Berndt as one of the great representatives of German culture. But
if he were a writer, he would be either in the United States with Schönberg and the Manns, or in Sachsenhausen."—"Is that why you haven't
produced anything in ten years?" I asked. Von Üxküll shook his fork as
he answered: "First of all, since I'm not a member of the *Musikkammer*,
I can't. And I refuse to have my music played abroad if I can't present it
in my own country."—"So why don't you enroll, then?"—"Out of
principle. Because of Schönberg. When they threw him out of the
Academy and he had to leave Germany, they offered me his place: I told
them to go screw themselves. Strauss came to see me in person. He had
just taken the place of Bruno Walter, a great conductor. I told him he
should be ashamed, that it was a government of gangsters and bitter pro-
letarians and that it wouldn't last. Anyway, they kicked Strauss out two
years later, because of his Jewish daughter-in-law." I forced myself to
smile: "I'm not going to get into a political discussion. But it's hard for
me, listening to your opinions, to understand how you can think of
yourself as an anti-Semite."—"But it's simple," replied von Üxküll
haughtily. "I fought against the Jews and the Reds in Courland and in
Memel. I advocated the exclusion of the Jews from German universities, from German political and economic life. I drank to the health of
the men who killed Rathenau. But music is different. You just have to
close your eyes and listen to know right away if it's good or not. It has
nothing to do with blood, and all great music is equal, whether it's German, French, English, Italian, Russian, or Jewish. Meyerbeer isn't worth
anything, not because he was Jewish, but because he's not worth anything. And Wagner, who hated Meyerbeer because he was Jewish and
because he had helped him, is scarcely any better, in my opinion."—
"If Max repeats what you're saying to his colleagues," Una said, laughing, "you're going to have problems."—"You told me he was an
intelligent man," he replied, looking at her. "I'm doing you the honor
of taking you at your word."—"I'm not a musician," I said, "so it's hard
for me to answer you. What I've heard of Schönberg I've found inaudible. But one thing is certain: you are definitely not in tune with the
mood of your country."—"Young man," he retorted, shaking his head,
"I'm not trying to be. I stopped meddling in politics a long time ago,
and I'm counting on politics not to meddle with me." We don't always
have a choice, I wanted to reply; but I held my tongue.

At the end of the meal, urged by Una, I had spoken with von Üxküll about my wish to land a position in France. Una had added: "Can't you help him?" Von Üxküll reflected: "I'll see. But my friends in the Wehrmacht don't hold the SS close to their hearts." That I was beginning to understand; and sometimes I told myself that at bottom it was Blobel, losing his mind in Kharkov, who had been right. All my paths seemed to be leading to dead ends: Best had sent me his *Festgabe*, but without mentioning France; Thomas was trying to be reassuring, but couldn't seem to do anything for me. And I, completely absorbed by the presence and thought of my sister, I wasn't attempting anything anymore, I was sinking into my despondency, stiff, petrified, a sad salt statue on the shores of the Dead Sea. That night, my sister and her husband were invited to a reception, and Una suggested I come with them; I refused: I didn't want to see her like that, in the midst of thoughtless, arrogant, drunk aristocrats drinking Champagne and joking about everything I held sacred. In the midst of those people, it was certain, I would feel powerless, ashamed, an idiotic kid; their sarcasm would wound me, and my anguish would prevent me from responding; their world remained closed to people like me, and they knew just how to get that across. I shut myself up in my room; I tried to leaf through the *Festgabe*, but the words made no sense to me. So I abandoned myself to the gentle sway of mad fantasies: Una, overcome with remorse, left her party, came to my hotel, the door opened, she smiled at me, and the entire past, at that instant, was redeemed. All that was perfectly idiotic, and I knew it, but the more time passed, the more I managed to convince myself it would happen, here, now. I remained in the dark, sitting on the sofa, my heart leaping at every noise in the hallway, every clank of the elevator, waiting. But it was always another door that opened and closed, and the despair rose like black water, like that cold, pitiless water that engulfs the drowned and steals their breath away, the precious air of life. The next day, Una and von Üxküll were leaving for Switzerland.

She called me in the morning, just before taking the train. Her voice was soft, tender, warm. The conversation was short, I wasn't really paying attention to what she was saying, I was listening to that voice, clinging to the receiver, lost in my distress. "We can see each other again," she said. "You can come visit us."—"We'll see," replied the other person who was speaking through my mouth. I was overcome with nausea again, I thought I would throw up, I convulsively swallowed my saliva by breathing through my nose and managed to control myself. Then she hung up and I was alone again.

★ ★ ★

Thomas, in the end, had managed to arrange an interview for me with Schulz. "Since things aren't really getting anywhere, I think it's worth the trouble. Try to handle him tactfully." I didn't have to make much of an effort: Schulz, a scrawny little man who mumbled into his moustache, his mouth streaked with a bad dueling scar, spoke in long circumlocutions that were sometimes hard to follow and, while he stubbornly leafed through my file, didn't leave me many openings to speak. I managed to get two words in about my interest in the Reich's foreign policy, but he seemed not to notice. The upshot of this interview was that *people were taking an interest in me in high places* and that *we'd see at the end of my convalescence.* It wasn't very encouraging, and Thomas confirmed my interpretation: "They have to ask for you over there, for a specific job. Otherwise, if they send you anywhere, it will be Bulgaria. True, it's quiet there, but the wine isn't so great." Best had suggested I contact Knochen, but Thomas's words gave me a better idea: after all, I was on leave, nothing was forcing me to stay in Berlin.

I took the night express and arrived in Paris a little after dawn. The controls didn't pose any problems. In front of the station I happily contemplated the pale gray stone of the buildings, the bustle in the streets; because of the restrictions, there weren't many vehicles, but the streets were congested with bicycles and carts, through which the German cars made their way with difficulty. Suddenly joyous, I went into the first café and drank a Cognac, standing at the bar. I was in civilian clothes, and no one had any reason to take me for anything but a Frenchman; I found a curious pleasure in this. I walked calmly up to Montmartre and checked into a discreet little hotel, on the side of the hill, above Pigalle; I knew this place: the rooms were simple and clean, and the owner devoid of curiosity, which suited me. For this first day, I didn't want to see anyone. I went out for a walk. It was April, spring was starting to show through everywhere, in the pale blue of the sky, the buds and flowers coming out on the branches, a certain liveliness or at least a lightness in people's steps. Life, I knew, was hard here, the sallow tint of many faces betrayed the difficulties of finding food. But nothing seemed to have changed since my last visit, aside from the traffic and the graffiti: on the walls now you could see STALINGRAD or "1918," usually erased and sometimes replaced by "1763," no doubt a brilliant initiative of our services. I headed downhill toward the Seine, then went slowly rummaging through the booksellers along the quays: to my surprise, next to Céline, Drieu, Mauriac, Bernanos and Montherlant, they were openly selling Kafka, Proust, and even Thomas Mann; permissiveness seemed to be the rule. Almost all the sellers had a copy of Rebatet's book, *Les Décombres*, which had been published the previous year: I leafed through it with curiosity, but put off buying it till later. I finally decided on a collection of essays by Maurice Blanchot, a critic from the *Journal des débats*, some of whose articles I had read with interest before the war; it was an advance copy, probably resold by a reviewer, bearing the title *Faux Pas*; the bookseller explained to me that the publication of the book had been delayed because of the paper shortage, while assuring me that it was still the best thing written recently, unless I liked Sartre, but he didn't like Sartre (I hadn't even heard of Sartre then). At the Place Saint-Michel, near the fountain, I sat down at a table on a terrace and ordered a sandwich and a glass of wine. The previous owner of the book had cut open only the first pages; I asked for a knife and, while I waited for the sandwich, cut the remaining pages, a slow, placid ritual that I always savored. The paper was of very poor quality; I had to be careful not to tear the pages by going too fast. After eating, I walked up to the Luxembourg. I had always loved this cold, geometric, luminous park, traversed with a calm agitation. Around the great circle of the central fountain, along the lanes curving out among trees and flowerbeds still bare, people walked, hummed, conversed, read, or, their eyes closed, sunbathed in the pale sun, a long and peaceful murmuring. I sat down on a metal chair with chipped green paint and read a few essays at random, the one on Orestes first, which actually had more to do with Sartre; this latter had apparently written a play where he used the figure of the unfortunate matricide to develop his ideas on man's freedom in crime; Blanchot judged it harshly, and I could only approve. But I was especially charmed by an article on Melville's *Moby-Dick*, where Blanchot speaks of this *impossible book*, which had marked a moment of my own youth, of this *written equivalent of the universe*, mysteriously, as a work that *presents the ironic quality of an enigma and reveals itself only by the questions it raises*. To tell the truth, I didn't understand much of what he was writing there. But it awoke in me a nostalgia for a life that I could have had: the pleasure of the free play of thought and language, rather than the ponderous rigor of the Law; I let myself be carried along happily by the meanderings of this heavy, patient thinking, which dug a way for itself through ideas the way an underground river slowly carves itself a path through the rock. Finally I closed the book and continued my walk, first toward the Odéon, where more writing covered the walls, then up the Boulevard Saint-Germain, almost empty, toward the Assemblée Nationale. Every place awoke precise memories in me, of my preparatory years and afterward, when I had entered the ELSP; I must have been rather tormented in those days, and I remembered the quick surge of my hatred for France, but these memories, given the distance, reached me as if appeased, almost happy, wreathed in a serene, probably distorted light. I continued toward the Invalides esplanade, where passersby were congregating to watch some workers who, with draught horses, were plowing up the lawns so as to plant vegetables; farther on, near a light tank of Czech manufacture stamped with the swastika, indifferent children were playing with a ball. Then I crossed the Alexandre III Bridge. At the Grand Palais, the posters announced two exhibitions: one entitled *Why Did the Jew Want War?*, the other a collection of Greek and Roman art. I felt no need to broaden my anti-Semitic education, but antiquity attracted me; I paid for my ticket and went in. There were some superb pieces there, most of them probably borrowed from the Louvre. For a long time I admired the cold, calm, inhuman beauty of a large *Apollo with Cithara* from Pompeii, a life-size bronze now turned greenish. He had a slender, not entirely formed body, with a child's sex and narrow, well-rounded buttocks. I walked from one end of the exhibition to the other, but I kept coming back to him: his beauty fascinated me. He might have been nothing but an exquisite, ordinary adolescent, but the verdigris that was eating away at his skin in large patches conferred a stupefying profundity upon him. One detail struck me: regardless of the angle from which I looked at his eyes, painted realistically directly on the bronze, he never looked me in the eye; it was impossible to capture his gaze, drowned, lost in the void of his eternity. The metallic leprosy was blistering his face, his chest, his buttocks, almost devouring his left hand, which must have held the vanished cithara. His face seemed vain, almost smug. Looking at him, I felt overcome with desire, with a wish to lick him; and he was decomposing in front of me with a calm, infinite slowness. After that, avoiding the Champs-Élysées, I walked through the silent little streets of the eighth arrondissement, then slowly climbed back up to Montmartre. Night was falling, the air smelled good. At the hotel, the owner showed me a little black-market restaurant where I could eat without ration cards: "It's full of lowlife, but the food is good." The clientele in fact seemed made up of collaborators and black-market dealers; I was served a top cut of sirloin with shallots and green beans, and some decent Bordeaux in a carafe; for dessert, a tarte Tatin with crème fraîche, and, supreme luxury, real coffee. But the Apollo from the Grand Palais had awakened other desires. I went down to Pigalle and found a little bar that I knew well: sitting at the counter, I ordered a Cognac and waited. It didn't take long, and I brought the boy back to my hotel. Under his cap, he had curly, unruly hair; a light down covered his stomach and darkened in curls on his chest; his olive skin awoke in me a furious desire of mouth and of ass. He was as I liked them, taciturn and available. For him, my ass opened like a flower, and when he finally slipped it in, a ball of white light began to grow at the base of my spine, slowly rose up my back, and annihilated my head. And that night, more than ever, it seemed to me that in this way I was responding directly to my sister, incorporating her into me, whether she accepted it or not. What happened in my body, under the hands and sex of this unknown boy, overwhelmed me. When it was over, I sent him away but didn't fall asleep; I lay there on the creased sheets, naked and spread out like a child crushed with happiness.

The next day, I went to the editorial office of *Je Suis Partout*. Almost all my Parisian friends worked there or gravitated around it. This went back quite a long way. When I had gone to Paris to take my preparatory classes, at seventeen, I didn't know anyone. I was attending Janson-de-Sailly as a boarder; Moreau had allocated a small monthly allowance for me, as long as I got good grades, and I was relatively free; after the carceral nightmare of the three preceding years, it would have taken a lot less to turn my head. But I behaved, I didn't do anything stupid. After classes, I would dash over to the Seine to hunt through the booksellers' stalls, or else join my friends in a little bar in the Latin Quarter, to drink cheap red wine and set the world to rights. But I found my classmates a little dull. Almost all of them were from the upper middle class and were getting ready to follow blindly in their fathers' footsteps. They had money, and they had been taught very early on how the world was made and what their place in it would be: the dominant one. Toward workers, they felt only scorn, or fear; the ideas that I had brought back from my first trip to Germany—that workers were just as much a part of the nation as the middle class, that the social order had to be arranged organically for the advantage of all, not just a few of the well-off, that workers should not be oppressed but rather offered a life of dignity and a place in this order so as to counter the seductions of Bolshevism—all that was foreign to them. Their political opinions were as narrow as their feeling of bourgeois propriety, and it seemed to me even more pointless to try to discuss with them fascism or German National Socialism (which had just, in September of that year, won a crushing electoral victory, thus becoming the second largest party in the country and sending shockwaves across the victors' Europe) than to talk about the youth movement ideals preached by Hans Blüher. Freud, for them (if they had even heard of him), was a sexual maniac, Spengler a mad, monomaniacal Prussian, Jünger a warmonger flirting dangerously with Bolshevism; even Péguy they found suspect. Only a few students on scholarship from the provinces seemed a little different, and it was mostly toward them that I gravitated. One of these boys, Antoine F., had

an older brother at the École normale supérieure, which I had dreamed
of attending, and it was he who took me there for the first time, to
drink rum toddies with his brother and his dorm mates and discuss
Nietzsche and Schopenhauer, whom I was just discovering. This
Bertrand F. was a *carré*, or "squared"—a second-year student; the best
study rooms, with sofas, engravings on the walls, and stoves, were mostly
occupied by *cubes*, or the "cubed," third-year students. One day, passing
by one of these rooms, I noticed a Greek inscription painted on the lintel: in this carrel work six fine and good men (*hex kaloi kagathoi*)—and
a certain other one (*kai tis allos*). The door was open, so I pushed it and
asked in Greek: "So who is this other one?" A young man with a round
face raised his thick glasses from his book and answered in the same language: "A Hebrew, who doesn't know Greek. And you, who are
you?"—"Another too, but made of finer stuff than your Hebrew: a German."—"A German who knows Greek?"—"What better language to
speak with a Frenchman?" He burst out laughing and introduced himself: he was Robert Brasillach. I explained to him that I was in fact half
French, and had lived in France since 1924; he asked me if I had gone
back to Germany since, and I told him about my summer trip; soon we
were chatting about National Socialism. He listened attentively to my
descriptions and explanations. "Come back whenever you like," he said
at the end. "I have some friends who will be happy to meet you."
Through him, I discovered another world, which had nothing to do
with that of the civil servants in training. These young people cultivated
visions of the future of their country and of Europe that they argued
about bitterly, while also drawing on a rich study of the past. Their ideas
and interests burst out in all directions. Brasillach, together with his future brother-in-law Maurice Bardèche, was a passionate student of the
cinema and had me discover not only Chaplin and René Clair but also
Eisenstein, Lang, Pabst, Dreyer. He brought me to the offices of *L'Action française*, in their printing house on the Rue Montmartre, a fine narrow building with a Renaissance staircase, full of the din of the rotary
presses. I saw Maurras a few times; he would arrive late, around eleven
at night, half deaf, bitter, but always ready to open his heart and vent his
spleen against the Marxists, the bourgeois, the republicans, the Jews.
Brasillach, at that time, was still completely under his spell, but Maurras's stubborn hatred for Germany formed an obstacle that I couldn't
overlook, and Robert and I often quarreled about it. If Hitler reached
power, I asserted, and united the German worker with the middle class,
once and for all countering the Red Peril, and if France did the same,
and if the two together managed to eliminate the pernicious influence
of the Jews, then the heart of Europe, both nationalist and socialist,

would form, along with Italy, an invincible bloc of common interests. But the French were still bogged down, floundering in their petty shop-keepers' interests and their backward-looking spirit of revenge. Of course, Hitler would sweep aside the unjust Versailles clauses, that was a pure historical necessity; but if the healthy forces of France could on their side liquidate the corrupt republic and its Jewish puppets, then a Franco-German alliance would not only be a possibility, but would become an inevitable reality, a new European entente that would clip the wings of the British plutocrats and imperialists, and would soon be ready to confront the Bolsheviks and bring Russia back into the bosom of civilized nations. (As you can see, my German trip had served my intellectual education well; Moreau would have been horrified if he had known the use I put his money to.) Brasillach, in general, agreed with me: "Yes," he said, "the postwar is already over. We have to act quickly if we want to avoid another war. That would be a disaster, the end of European civilization, the triumph of the barbarians." Most of Maurras's young disciples thought likewise. One of the most brilliant and caustic of them was Lucien Rebatet, who wrote the literary and film criticism in *L'Action française* under the name of François Vinneuil. He was ten years older than I, but we quickly formed a friendship, drawn to each other by his attraction to Germany. There were also Maxence, Blond, Jacques Talagrand who became Thierry Maulnier, Jules Supervielle, and many others. We met at the Brasserie Lipp, when someone had money in his pocket, or else at a restaurant for students in the Latin Quarter. We feverishly discussed literature and tried to define a "fascist" literature: Rebatet put forward the names of Plutarch, Corneille, Stendhal. "Fascism," Brasillach said one day, "is the very poetry of the twentieth century," and we could only agree with him: *fascist, fascio, fascination* (but later on, having become wiser or more prudent, he would confer the same title on communism).

In the spring of 1932, when I passed my entrance exam, most of my friends from the ENS were finishing their studies; when the summer was over, they scattered throughout France, either to do their military service or to take up the teaching positions offered them. I once again spent my vacation in Germany, which was then in the midst of upheaval: German production had fallen to half the level of 1929, and Brüning, with Hindenburg's support, was governing by means of emergency decrees. Such a situation couldn't last. Elsewhere, too, the established order was faltering. In Spain, the monarchy had been overturned by a cabal of Freemasons, revolutionaries, and priests. America was almost on its knees. In France, the direct effects of the crisis were less felt, but the situation wasn't rosy, and the Communists were quietly and me-

thodically undermining things. Without telling anyone, I sent in my ap-
plication for the NSDAP, *Ausland* section (for *Reichsdeutschen* living
abroad), and was quickly accepted. When I entered the ELSP, in the fall,
I continued to see my friends from the École normale and from *L'Action française*, who came up regularly to spend weekends in Paris. My
classmates remained pretty much the same as at Janson, but to my surprise I found the classes interesting. It was also around this period, probably under the influence of Rebatet and his new friend Louis
Destouches, who hadn't yet become famous (his *Journey to the End of the
Night* had just come out, but enthusiasm hadn't yet spread beyond the
circle of initiates, and Céline still liked to spend time with young people), that I formed a passion for French keyboard music, which was just
being rediscovered and played; with Céline, I went to hear Marcelle
Meyer; and more bitterly than ever I regretted my laziness and casual-
ness that had made me abandon the piano so quickly. After the New
Year, President Hindenburg invited Hitler to form a government. My
classmates trembled, my friends waited with bated breath, I exulted. But
while the Party was crushing the Reds, sweeping aside the garbage of
plutodemocracy, and dissolving the bourgeois parties, I remained stuck
in France. A real national revolution was taking place in front of our
eyes and in our own time, and I could only follow it from afar, in the
newspapers and the newsreels in the movie theaters. France too was
seething. Many people went to Germany to see things firsthand; everyone wrote about and dreamed of a similar recovery for their country.
People made contact with the Germans, official Germans now, who
called for a Franco-German rapprochement; Brasillach introduced me
to Otto Abetz, von Ribbentrop's man (at that time still the Foreign Affairs Advisor of the Party): his ideas were no different from the ones I
had aired since my first trip to Germany. But for many, Maurras remained an obstacle; only the best acknowledged that it was time to
move on beyond his hypochondriac vaticinations, but even they hesitated, his charisma and the fascination he exercised held them under his
sway. At the same time the Stavisky affair exposed the police connections of corruption in government and gave Action Française a moral
authority it hadn't known since 1918. All that came to an end on February 6, 1934. Actually it was a confused business: I too was in the
streets, along with Antoine F. (who had entered the ELSP at the same
time as I), Blond, Brasillach, a few others. From the Champs-Élysées,
we vaguely heard some gunshots; farther down, near the Place de la
Concorde, people were running. We spent the rest of the night walking through the streets, chanting slogans when we met other young
people. We didn't learn till the next day that there had been several

deaths. Maurras, to whom everyone had instinctively turned, had stood down. The whole affair had just been a damp squib. "French inaction!" foamed Rebatet, who never forgave Maurras. It was all the same to me: my decision was taking shape, and I no longer saw a future for me in France.

It was actually Rebatet I ran into at *Je Suis Partout*. "Will you look at that! A revenant."—"As you see," I retorted. "Apparently you're famous, now." He spread his arms and made a face: "I don't understand it at all. I even racked my brains to be sure I wasn't forgetting anyone in my invectives. And in the beginning it worked: Grasset rejected my book because *I insulted too many friends of the house*, as they said, and Gallimard wanted to make some major cuts. Finally it was that Belgian who took me on, you remember him, the one who printed Céline? Result: he's raking it in and I am too. At the Rive Gauche,' when I went there to sign books, you'd have thought I was a movie star. In fact, the only ones who didn't like it were the Germans." He looked at me suspiciously: "Have you read it?"—"Not yet, I'm waiting for you to give me a copy. Why? Do you insult me too?" He laughed: "Not as much as you deserve, you filthy Kraut. Anyway, everyone thought you had died on the field of honor. Shall we go out for a drink?" Rebatet had an appointment a little later on, near Saint-Germain, and he took me to the Café Flore. "I always like to go stare at the dirty mugs of our official *antifascists*, especially the faces they make when they see me." When he went in, in fact, people shot him black looks; but several persons also got up to greet him. Lucien, obviously, was enjoying his success. He wore a pale, well-cut suit and a slightly skewed polka-dot bow tie; a crest of disheveled hair crowned his narrow, mobile face. He chose a table to the right, under the windows, a little apart, and I ordered some white wine. When he began to roll a cigarette, I offered him a Dutch one, which he gladly accepted. But even when he smiled, his eyes remained worried. "So, tell me everything," he said. We hadn't seen each other since 1939, he just knew I was in the SS: I told him rapidly about the Russian campaign, without going into details. He opened his eyes wide: "You were in Stalingrad, then? Well, damn." He had a strange look, a mixture of fear and desire perhaps. "You were wounded? Show me." I showed him the hole, and he let out a long whistle: "You've got some luck, don't you." I didn't say anything. "Robert's going to Russia soon," he went on. "With Jeantet. But it's not the same thing."—"What are they going to do there?"—"It's an official trip. They're accompanying Doriot and Brinon, they're going to inspect the Legion of French Volunteers, near Smolensk I think."—"And how is Robert doing?"— "Actually, we've sort of fallen out, these days. He's become an out-and-out Pétainist. If he goes on like that, we'll kick him out of JSP."—"Has it come to that?" He ordered two more drinks; I gave him another cigarette. "Listen," he spat out aggressively, "it's been a while since you were in France: believe me, things have changed. They're all like starving dogs, fighting over the scraps of the corpse of the republic. Pétain is senile, Laval is behaving worse than a Jew, Déat wants Social Fascism, Doriot National Bolshevism. A bitch wouldn't be able to find her pups among them all. What we've lacked is a Hitler. That's the tragedy."— "And Maurras?" Rebatet made a disgusted face: "Maurras? *Action marrane*, they should call it. I gave him a rough time, in my book; apparently he was livid. And I'll tell you something else: ever since Stalingrad, everyone's bolting. The rats are jumping ship. You've seen the graffiti? Not one Vichyist who doesn't keep a Resistant or a Jew in his house, as life insurance."—"It's not over yet, though."—"Oh, I know. But what do you expect? It's a world of cowards. I made my choice, and I won't go back on it. If the boat sinks, I'll sink with it."—"In Stalingrad, I interrogated a Commissar who quoted Mathilde de la Mole, you remember, in *The Red and the Black*, near the end?" I repeated the sentence to him and he let out a guffaw: "Oh, that's unbelievable. He got that out in French?"—"No, German. He was an old Bolshevik, a militant, a real tough guy. You'd have liked him."—"What did you do with him?" I shrugged my shoulders. "Sorry," he said. "Stupid question. But he was right. I admire the Bolsheviks, you know. None of this trained cockroach show with them. It's a system of order. You submit or you croak. Stalin is an extraordinary man. If there were no Hitler, I might have been a Communist, who knows?" We drank a little and I watched the people coming and going. At a table near the back of the room some people were staring at Rebatet and whispering, but I didn't recognize them. "Are you still into cinema?" I asked him.—"Not anymore, no. I'm interested in music, now."—"Really? You know Berndt von Üxküll?"—"Of course. Why?"—"He's my brother-in-law. I met him the other day, for the first time."—"No kidding! You have some relatives! What's become of him?"—"Not much, from what I could make out. He's sulking at home, in Pomerania."—"Too bad. He did some good stuff."—"I don't know his music. We had a long discussion about Schönberg, whom he defends."—"That doesn't surprise me. No serious composer could think otherwise."—"Oh, you're on his side too?" He shrugged his shoulders: "Schönberg never got involved in politics. And also his greatest disciples, like Webern or Üxküll, are real Aryans, aren't they? What Schönberg discovered, serial composition, is a sonic potentiality that was always there, a rigor that was so to speak hidden by the deliberate vagueness of the tempered scales, and after him, anyone can use it to do what he wants with it. It's the first genuine advance in music since Wagner."—"Actually, von Üxküll hates Wagner."—"That's impossible!" he cried in a horrified tone. "Impossible!"—"But it's true." And I quoted von Üxküll's statements to him. "That's absurd," Rebatet retorted. "Bach, of course . . . nothing comes close to Bach. He is untouchable, immense. What he achieved is the definitive synthesis of the horizontal and the vertical, harmonic architecture with melodic thrust. With that, he put an end to everything that came before him, and created a framework from which everyone who followed him tried in one way or another to escape, until finally Wagner blew it apart. How can a German, a German composer, not be on his knees before Wagner?"—"What about French music?" He made a face: "Your Rameau? He's *amusing*."—"You didn't always say that."—"One grows up, doesn't one?" He finished his drink, pensive. I considered for an instant telling him about Yakov, then decided against it. "And in modern music, aside from Schönberg, what do you like?" I asked.—"A lot of things. For thirty years now, music has been waking up, it's becoming really interesting. Stravinsky, Debussy, it's great."—"And Milhaud, Satie?"—"Don't be an idiot." At that moment, Brasillach came in. Rebatet called out to him: "Hey, Robert! Look who's here!" Brasillach examined us through his thick round glasses, made a little sign to us with his hand, and went to another table to sit down. "He's really becoming unbearable," Rebatet muttered. "He doesn't even want to be seen with a Kraut anymore. You're not even in uniform, so far as I can tell." But that wasn't quite the reason, and I knew it. "We got into an argument, the last time I was in Paris," I said to placate Rebatet. One night, after a small party where he had drunk a little more than usual, Brasillach had found the courage to invite me back to his place, and I had followed him. But he was the kind of shameful invert who doesn't like anything so much as jacking off listlessly while languorously gazing at his *eromenos*; I found that boring and even slightly repugnant, and had curtly cut his excitement short. That said, I thought we had remained friends. Probably I had wounded him without realizing it, and in one of his most vulnerable spots: Robert had never been able to face the sordid, bitter reality of desire; and he had remained, in his way, the great boy scout of fascism. Poor Brasillach! So casually and summarily shot, once it was all over, just so that so many good folk, their conscience at peace, could return to the fold. I have often wondered, too, if his leanings had worked against him: collaboration, after all, remained within the family, whereas pederasty was something else entirely, for De Gaulle as well as for the good workers on the jury. Whatever the case, Brasillach would certainly rather have died for his ideas than for his tastes. But wasn't he the one who described collaboration with this memorable phrase *We have slept with Germany, and the memory will remain sweet to us?* Rebatet, on the other hand, despite his admiration for Julien Sorel, was cleverer: he got his death sentence, and his pardon with it; he did not become a Communist; and he found time after all that to write a fine *History of Music*, and to let himself be forgotten.

He left, suggesting we meet up that evening with Cousteau, near Pigalle. As I headed out, I went over to greet Brasillach, who was sitting with a woman I didn't know; he acted as if he hadn't recognized me and welcomed me with a smile, but did not introduce me to his companion. I asked him for news of his sister and his brother-in-law; he politely enquired about the conditions of life in Germany; we vaguely agreed to see each other again, without fixing a date. I went back to my hotel room, changed into my uniform, wrote a note to Knochen, and left to drop it off at Avenue Foch. Then I returned to put my civilian clothes back on and went out walking until the time we'd agreed on. I found Rebatet and Cousteau at the Liberty, a drag bar at the Place Blanche. Cousteau, not that he was into that sort of thing, knew the owner, Tonton, and obviously at least half the queens, whom he called by their first names; several of them, proud and absurd with their wigs, makeup, and glass jewelry, exchanged taunts with him and Rebatet while we drank martinis. "That one, you see," Cousteau pointed, "I nicknamed her 'Pompe-Funèbre.' Because she sucks you to death."—"You stole that from Maxime Du Camp, you creep," Rebatet retorted with a face, before diving into his vast literary knowledge to try to surpass him. "And you, darling, what do you do?" one of the queens asked me, pointing an impressively long cigarette holder at me. "He's with the Gestapo," Cousteau said ironically. The fairy placed her lace-gloved fingers on her lips and let out a long "Ooooh." But Cousteau had already launched into a long anecdote about Doriot's boys giving blow jobs to German soldiers in the Palais Royal urinals; the Parisian cops who regularly raided them or those toward the bottom of the Champs-Élysées sometimes ran into bad surprises; but while the Préfecture bitched, the Majestic seemed not to care. These ambiguous stories put me ill at ease: What were they playing at, these two? Other comrades, I knew, showed off less and practiced more. But neither of them had the slightest scruple about publishing anonymous denunciations in the columns of *Je Suis Partout*; and if someone didn't have the misfortune of being a Jew, he could just as easily be made into a homosexual; more than one career, or even life, had been ruined that way. Cousteau and Rebatet, I thought, were trying to show that their revolutionary radicalism surmounted all prejudices (except those that were *scientific and racialist*, as

French thinking had to be); basically, they too were just trying to *shock the bourgeois*, like the surrealists and André Gide, whom they so execrated. "Did you know, Max," Rebatet asked me, "that the sacred phallus the Romans paraded during the *Liberalia*, in the spring and at harvest time, was called a *fascinus*? Mussolini may have remembered that." I shrugged my shoulders: all this seemed false to me, bad theater, a stage production, while everywhere people were dying for real. I, for one, really did want a boy—not just for show, but for the warmth of his skin, the sharpness of his sweat, the sweetness of his sex nestled between his legs like a little animal. As for Rebatet, he was afraid of his shadow, of men and of women, of the presence of his own flesh, of everything except abstract ideas that could offer him no resistance. More than ever I wanted to be left alone, but it seemed this was impossible: I was scraping my skin on the world as on broken glass; I kept deliberately swallowing fishhooks, then being surprised when I tore my guts out of my mouth.

My interview with Helmut Knochen, the next day, only reinforced this feeling. He received me with a curious mixture of ostentatious camaraderie and condescending haughtiness. When he was working at the SD, I never saw him outside the office; of course, he must have known that I spent a lot of time with Best then (but maybe now that was no longer a recommendation). Whatever the case, I told him that I had seen Best in Berlin and he asked me how he was doing. I also mentioned that I had served under the command of Dr. Thomas, as he had; he then asked me about my experiences in Russia, while still making me subtly feel the distance between us: he, the Standartenführer in charge of an entire country; I, a convalescent with an uncertain future. He had received me in his office, around a low table decorated with a vase of dried flowers; he had settled into the sofa, crossing his long legs sheathed in riding breeches, leaving me to cram into the depths of a small and too low armchair: from where I sat, his knee almost hid his face and the vagueness of his eyes. I didn't know how to broach the subject that concerned me. Finally, I told him somewhat at random that I was preparing a book about the future of Germany's international relations, embroidering on the ideas I had picked up from Best's *Festgabe* (and as I spoke, I picked up steam and began convincing myself that I really did intend to write such a book, which would make an impression and ensure my future). Knochen listened politely, nodding his head. Finally I slipped in that I was thinking of taking up a position in France to gather concrete experiences there, which would complete those of Russia. "Have you been offered something?" he asked with a gleam of curiosity. "I hadn't heard."—"Not yet, Standartenführer, it's under discussion.

It doesn't pose any problems in principle, but the appropriate position would have to open up or be created."—"With me, you know, there's nothing for now. It's a pity, the position of Specialist for Jewish Affairs was vacant in December, but it has already been filled." I forced myself to smile: "That's not what I'm looking for."—"But you've acquired some good experience in that field, it seems to me. And the Jewish question, in France, touches very closely on our diplomatic relations with Vichy. But in any case your rank is too high: it's at most a position for a Hauptsturmführer. What about with Abetz? Have you been to see him? If I remember correctly, you had personal contacts with the Parisian protofascists. That should interest the ambassador."

I found myself on the wide, almost deserted sidewalk of Avenue Foch in a state of profound discouragement: I felt as if I were confronted with a wall—a soft, elusive, blurry one, but still just as insurmountable as a high stone wall. At the top of the avenue, the Arc de Triomphe still hid the morning sun and cast long shadows on the pavement. Go to Abetz? True, I could probably mention our brief meeting in 1933 as a reference, or have myself introduced by someone from *Je Suis Partout*. But I didn't feel up to it. I thought of my sister, in Switzerland: perhaps a posting in Switzerland would suit me? I could see her from time to time, when she accompanied her husband to the sanatorium. But there were almost no SD positions in Switzerland, and everyone fought for them. Dr. Mandelbrod could probably have swept aside all obstacles, for France as well as for Switzerland; but Dr. Mandelbrod, I knew, had his own ideas in mind for me.

I went back to change into civilian clothes and then went to the Louvre: there, at least, surrounded by these immobile, serene figures, I felt calmer. I sat for a long time in front of Philippe de Champaigne's dead Christ; but it was especially a little painting by Watteau that held my attention, *L'indifférent*: a character dressed for a party stepping forward in a dance, almost with an entrechat, his arms poised as if waiting for the first note of an overture, feminine, but with an obvious erection under his pistachio-green silk breeches, and with an indefinably sad, almost lost face, having already forgotten everything and perhaps not even trying to remember why or for whom he was posing this way. It struck me as a rather pertinent commentary on my situation, and even the title brought its counterpoint: indifferent? no, I wasn't indifferent, I had only to pass in front of a painting of a woman with heavy black hair to feel an axe blow of the imagination; and even when the faces didn't look at all like hers, under the rich Renaissance or Regency trappings, under those dazzling fabrics, loaded with colors and gemstones, as thick as the dripping oil of the painters, it was her body I could make out, her breasts, her belly, her hips, pure, flowing smoothly over the bones or slightly curved, enclosing the only source of life I knew where to find. Angry, I left the museum, but that wasn't enough, for every woman I met or saw laughing behind a window had the same effect on me. I downed drink after drink whenever I passed a café, but the more I drank, the more lucid I seemed to become, my eyes opened and the world rushed into them, roaring, bleeding, voracious, spattering the inside of my head with fluids and excrement. My pineal eye, gaping vagina in the middle of my forehead, projected a crude, gloomy, implacable light on this world, and allowed me to read each drop of sweat, each pimple, each poorly shaven hair on the garish faces that assailed me as an emotion, the infinite cry of anguish of the child forever prisoner in the atrocious body of a clumsy adult incapable, even by killing, of avenging himself for the fact of living. Finally, it was already late in the night, a boy accosted me in a bistro to ask me for a cigarette: there, maybe, I could drown myself for a few instants. He agreed to come up to my room. Another one, I said to myself as I climbed the stairs, another one, but it will never be enough. We each got undressed on opposite sides of the bed; ridiculously, he kept on his shoes and watch. I asked him to have me standing up, leaning on the chest of drawers, facing the narrow mirror that dominated the room. When the pleasure seized me, I kept my eyes open, I scrutinized my crimson, hideously swollen face, trying to see in it, my true face filling my features from behind, the features of my sister's face. But then this surprising thing happened: between these two faces and their perfect fusion there slid, smooth, transparent as a glass leaf, another face, the bitter, placid face of our mother, infinitely fine but more opaque, denser than the thickest of walls. Seized with an enormous rage, I roared and smashed the mirror with my fist; the boy, frightened, jumped and fell back onto the bed as he came in long spurts. I came too, but reflexively, without feeling it, already going limp. Blood dripped from my fingers onto the floor. I went into the bathroom, washed my hand, pulled a piece of glass out of it, wrapped it in a towel. When I came out, the boy was getting dressed, obviously worried. I searched through my pants pocket and threw a few bills on the bed: "Get out." He seized the money and fled without a word. I wanted to go to bed but first I carefully collected the pieces of broken glass, throwing them into the wastepaper basket and examining the floor to be sure I hadn't overlooked any, then I wiped up the drops of blood and went to wash. Finally I could lie down; but the bed was a crucifix to me, a torture rack. What was she doing here, the *odious bitch*? Hadn't I suffered enough because of her? Did she have to persecute me again this way? I sat cross-legged on the sheets and smoked cigarette af-

ter cigarette as I thought. The wan gleam of a streetlight filtered through
the closed shutters. My thinking—carried away, panic-stricken—had
turned into a sly old assassin; a new Macbeth, it murdered my sleep. I
kept feeling as if I were on the point of understanding something, but
this comprehension remained at the tip of my lacerated fingers, mocking me, imperceptibly withdrawing as I approached it. Finally a thought
allowed itself to be grasped: I contemplated it with disgust, but since
none other wanted to come take its place, I had to grant it its due. I
placed it on the night table like a heavy old coin: if I tapped it with my
fingernail, it sounded true, no matter how often I flipped it, it always
presented me with the same impassive face.

In the morning, very early, I paid my bill and took the first train
south. The French had to reserve their seats days or even weeks in advance, but the compartments for Germans were always half empty. I
went down to Marseille, at the limit of the German zone. The train
made frequent stops; in the stations, just as in Russia, farmers crowded
round to sell the passengers food—hard-boiled eggs, chicken drum-
sticks, salted boiled potatoes—and when I was hungry, I took something
at random, through the window. I didn't read, I just idly watched the
landscape flow by and toyed with my torn fingers; my thoughts wandered, detached from both the past and the present. In Marseille, I went
to the Gestapostelle to inquire about access to the Italian zone. A young
Obersturmführer received me: "Relations are a little delicate, right
now. The Italians show no understanding for our efforts to resolve the
Jewish question. Their zone has become a veritable paradise for Jews.
When we asked them at least to intern them, they put them up in the
best ski resorts in the Alps." But I didn't care about this Obersturmführer's problems. I explained what I wanted: he looked worried, but I
assured him that I relieved him of all responsibility. Finally he agreed to
write a letter for me asking the Italian authorities to *facilitate my movements for personal reasons*. It was getting late and I took a room for the
night, on the Vieux Port. The next morning, I got on a bus headed for
Toulon; at the boundary line, the *bersaglieri*, with their ridiculous feathered hats, let us pass without any inspections. In Toulon, I changed
buses, then again in Cannes; finally in the afternoon I reached Antibes.
The bus dropped me off at the main square; my bag on my shoulder, I
walked round the Port Vauban, passed the squat mass of the Fort Carré,
and began to follow the road by the sea. A light, salty breeze was coming in from the bay; little waves licked the strip of sand, the cry of the
seagulls resounded over the surf and the sounds of the occasional vehicle; aside from a few Italian soldiers, the beach was deserted. With my

civilian clothes, no one paid any attention to me: an Italian policeman hailed me, but only to ask me for a light. The house was a few kilometers away from the center of town. I walked calmly, I didn't feel in a hurry; the sight and smell of the Mediterranean left me indifferent, but I no longer felt any anguish, I remained calm. Finally I reached the dirt path that led to the property. A faint breeze rustled the branches of the umbrella pines along the path, and their fragrance mixed with that of the sea. The gate, its paint chipped, stood half open. A long lane cut across a handsome park planted with black pines; I didn't follow it, but glided along the inside of the wall to the end of the park; there I got undressed and put on my uniform. It was a little wrinkled from having been folded in my traveling bag; I smoothed it out with my hand, it would do. The sandy ground, between the spaced-out trees, was covered with pine needles; beyond the long, slender trunks, you could see the ochre wall of the house, with its terrace; the sun, behind the wall surrounding the property, shone through the undulating tops of the trees, confusingly. I went back to the gate and up the path; at the front door, I rang the bell. I heard something like a stifled laugh on my right, among the trees: I looked, but didn't see anything. Then a man's voice called out from the other side of the house: "Hello! Over here." Right away I recognized Moreau's voice. He was waiting in front of the entrance to the living room, below the terrace, an extinguished pipe in his hand; he wore an old knitted sweater and a bow tie, and looked to me lamentably old. He frowned when he saw my uniform: "What do you want? Who are you looking for?" I came forward and took off my cap: "You don't recognize me?" He stared, and his mouth opened; then he took a step forward and shook my hand vigorously, patting me on the shoulder. "Of course, of course!" He stepped back and contemplated me, embarrassed: "But what's this uniform?"—"The one I serve under." He turned around and called into the house: "Héloïse! Come see who's here!" The living room was deep in shadow; I saw a form move forward, slim, gray; then an old woman appeared behind Moreau and contemplated me in silence. So this was my mother? "Your sister wrote us that you had been wounded," she said finally. "You could have written to us too. You could at least have told us you were coming." Her voice, compared to her yellowed face and her gray hair pulled back in a severe bun, seemed still young; but for me, it was as if the most ancient times were speaking, in an immense voice that made me shrink, reduced me almost to nothing, despite the protection of my uniform, laughable talisman that it was. Moreau must have seen my confusion: "Of course," he said quickly, "we're happy to see you. You're always at home, here." My mother was still staring at me enigmatically. "Well, come in," she said finally. "Come kiss your mother." I put down my bag, went up to her, and, leaning over, kissed her on the cheek. Then I took her in my arms and hugged her to me. I felt her stiffen; she was like a branch in my arms, a bird I could easily have suffocated. Her hands came up and rested on my back. "You must be tired. Come, we'll settle you in." I let her go and straightened up. Again, behind me, I heard soft laughter. I turned around and saw two little identical twins, dressed in matching shorts and jackets, who, standing next to each other, were staring at me with big, curious, amused eyes. They must have been seven or eight. "Who are you?" I asked them.—"The children of a friend," my mother replied. "We're keeping them for now." One of them raised his hand and pointed at me: "And him, who is he?"—"He's a German," said the other one. "Can't you see?"—"He's my son," my mother declared. "His name is Max. Come say hello."—"Your son is a German soldier, Aunt?" the first one asked.—"Yes. Shake his hand." They hesitated, then came forward together and held out their little hands to me. "What are your names?" I asked. They didn't answer. "These are Tristan and Orlando," my mother said. "But I always mix them up. They love passing for each other. You're never really sure."—"That's because there is no difference between us, Aunt," said one of the little ones. "One name would be enough for both of us."—"I warn you," I said, "I'm a policeman. For us, identities are very important." Their eyes widened: "Oh, super," said one.—"Have you come to arrest someone?" asked the other.— "Maybe," I said.—"Stop being silly," said my mother.

She put me in my old room: but there was nothing there that could help me recognize it as mine. My posters, the few things I'd left there, had all disappeared; they had changed the bed, the chest of drawers, the wallpaper. "Where are my things?" I asked.—"In the attic," she replied. "I kept everything. You can go see later." She looked at me, both hands in front of her on her dress. "And Una's room?" I continued.—"For now, we've put the twins there." She left and I went into the main bathroom to wash my face and neck. Then I went back into the room and changed again, putting my uniform away in the closet. As I came out, I hesitated for an instant in front of Una's door, then kept going. I went out onto the terrace. The sun was shining behind the tall pines, projecting long shadows through the park, pouring a beautiful, rich saffron color on the stone walls of the house. I saw the twins go by: they ran onto the lawn, then disappeared into the trees. Once, from this terrace, angry over a trifle, I had shot an arrow (a blunt-tipped one, though) at my sister, aiming for her face; it had struck right above her eye, and just missed blinding her. Thinking about it, it seemed to me that I had then been severely punished by my father: if he was still there, the incident must have taken place in Kiel, and not here. But in Kiel there was no terrace at our house, and I thought I clearly remembered, in connection with this gesture, the large clay flowerpots scattered around the graveled area where Moreau and my mother had just welcomed me. I couldn't make any sense of it and, frustrated by this uncertainty, I turned around and reentered the house. I walked through the hallways, breathing in the smell of furniture polish, opening doors at random. Few things, aside from my room, seemed to have changed. I reached the foot of the stairs that led to the attic; there too, I hesitated, then turned back. I went down the main entryway staircase and out through the front door. Leaving the lane swiftly, I walked again under the trees, brushing past their gray, rough trunks, the streaks of sap hardened but still thick and sticky, kicking at pinecones fallen to the ground. The sharp, heady smell of pine filled the air; I wanted to smoke but didn't, so I could go on smelling it. There the ground was bare, without any grass, without bushes, without ferns: but it brought powerfully back to memory the forest near Kiel where I played my curious child's games. I tried leaning against a tree, but the trunk was sticky, so I stayed standing there, my arms dangling, spinning crazily around in my thoughts.

Dinner passed in brief, constrained phrases, almost lost in the clicking of silverware and plates. Moreau complained about his business and about the Italians, and insisted pathetically on his good relations with the German economic administration in Paris. He tried to make conversation and I, on my side, politely, baited him with little aggressive jabs. "What is your rank there, on your uniform?" he asked me.—"SS-Sturmbannführer. It's the same as a major, in your army."—"Oh, a major, you've been promoted, that's great—congratulations." In return, I asked him where he had served, before June '40; blind to the ridicule, he threw his arms up: "Oh, my boy! I would have liked to serve. But they didn't take me, they said I was too old. Of course," he hurried to add, "the Germans beat us fairly. And I completely approve of the Maréchal's policy of collaboration." My mother didn't say anything; she followed this little game with alert eyes. The twins ate cheerfully; but from time to time their expression changed completely, as if a veil of gravity descended on them. "What about your Jewish friends? What's their name? The Benahums, I think. What happened to them?" Moreau reddened. "They went away," my mother replied curtly. "To Switzerland."—"That must have been hard for your business," I went on to Moreau. "You were partners, weren't you?"—"I bought him out," Moreau said.—"Oh, very good. At a Jewish price, or an Aryan price? I hope you didn't let yourself be cheated."—"That's enough," my mother said. "Aristide's business has nothing to do with you. Tell us about your experiences. You were in Russia, weren't you?"—"Yes," I said, suddenly humiliated. "I went to fight Bolshevism."—"Ah! Now that is praiseworthy," Moreau remarked sententiously.—"Yes, but the Reds are advancing now," my mother said.—"Oh, don't worry!" Moreau exclaimed. "They won't reach here."—"We've had some set-backs," I said. "But that's temporary. We're preparing new weapons. And we'll crush them."—"Excellent, excellent," Moreau breathed, nodding his head. "I hope you'll take care of the Italians, afterward."—"The Italians have been our brothers in arms from the beginning," I re-torted. "When the new Europe is formed, they will be the first to have their share." Moreau took this very seriously and got angry: "They're cowards! They declared war on us when we were already beaten, so they could plunder us. But I'm sure Hitler will respect France's integrity. They say he admires the Maréchal." I shrugged my shoulders: "The Führer will treat France as it deserves." Moreau grew red. "Max, that's enough," my mother said again. "Have some dessert."

After dinner, my mother had me go up to her dressing room. It was a room that adjoined her bedroom, which she had decorated tastefully; no one entered it without her authorization. She didn't beat around the bush. "What did you come here for? I warn you, if it's just to annoy us, you shouldn't have bothered." Once again, I felt as if I were shrinking; before this imperious voice, these cold eyes, I was going to pieces, I was becoming a fearful child, smaller than the twins. I tried to get control of myself, but it was a lost cause. "No," I managed to articulate, "I wanted to see you, that's all. I was in France for my work, and I thought of you. And also, I was almost killed, you know, Mother. I might not survive this war. And we have so many things to make up." She softened a lit-tle and touched the back of my hand, with the same gesture as my sis-ter: gently, I removed my hand, but she didn't seem to notice. "You're right," she said. "You could have written, you know; that wouldn't have cost you anything. I know you disapprove of the choices I've made. But for you to disappear like that, when you're someone's child, that's just not right. It's as if you were dead. Can't you understand that?" She thought, then went on, speaking quickly, as if she would run out of time. "I know you're angry at me because of your father's disappearance. But it's him you should be angry with, not me. He abandoned me with you, he left me alone; for more than a year I didn't sleep, your sister woke me up every night, she was crying in her nightmares. You never cried, but it was almost worse. I had to take care of you both alone, feed you, dress you, educate you. You can't imagine how hard that was. Then, when I met Aristide, why should I have said no? He's a good man, he helped me. What should I have done, according to you? Where was your father? Even when he was still there he was never there. I was the one who had to do everything, change your diapers, wash you, feed you. Your father came to see you fifteen minutes a day, he played with you a little, then he went back to his books or his work. But it's me you hate." Emotion knotted my throat: "No, Mother. I don't hate you."— "Yes, you hate me, I know it, I can see it. You came in that uniform to tell me how much you hate me."—"Why did my father leave?" She took a long breath: "No one knows that except him. Maybe just out of boredom."—"I don't believe it! What did you do to him?"—"I didn't do anything to him, Max. I didn't chase him away. He left, that's all. Maybe he was tired of me. Maybe he was tired of you." Anguish swelled my face: "No! That's impossible. He loved us!"—"I don't know if he ever knew what loving means," she replied very gently. "If he loved us, if he loved you, he would at least have written. If only to say he wouldn't be coming back. He wouldn't have left us in doubt, in anguish."—"You had him declared dead."—"I did that mostly for you both. To protect your interests. He never gave a sign of life, he never touched his bank account, he left all his affairs in the lurch, I had to settle everything, the accounts were blocked, I had a lot of problems. And I didn't want you to be dependent on Aristide. The money you left for Germany with, where do you think that came from? It was his money, you know that very well, and you took it and used it. He probably really is dead, somewhere."—"It's as if you killed him." My words were making her suffer, I could see it, but she remained calm. "He killed himself, Max. It was his choice. You have to understand that."

But I didn't want to understand it. That night, I fell into sleep as into dark, thick, agitated waters, but dreamless. The twins' laughter, rising up from the park, woke me. It was day, the sun was shining through the slits in the shutters. As I washed and got dressed, I thought about my mother's words. One of them had struck me painfully: my departure from France, my break with my mother, all that had in fact been made possible by the inheritance from my father, the meager capital that Una and I had to share when we came of age. But I had never, at that time, made the link between my mother's odious actions and this money that had allowed me to free myself of her. I had prepared that departure for a long time. In the months following the February 1934 riot, I had contacted Dr. Mandelbrod to ask him for help and support; and as I said earlier, he had provided them generously; by my birthday, everything was organized. My mother and Moreau came up to Paris for the formalities concerning my inheritance: at dinner, the notary's papers in my pocket, I announced to them my decision to leave the ELSP for Ger-

many. Moreau had swallowed his anger and remained silent while my
mother tried to reason with me. In the street, Moreau had turned to my
mother: "Don't you see that your son has become a little Fascist? Let
him go goose-step with them, if he wants to." I was too happy to get
angry, and I left them on the Boulevard Montparnasse. Nine years and
a war had to pass before I saw them again.

Downstairs, I found Moreau sitting in a garden chair in a square of
sunlight, in front of the French windows to the living room. It was
rather cool out. "Hello," he said in his sly way. "Sleep well?"—"Yes,
thanks. Has my mother gotten up?"—"She's awake, but she's still resting. There's some coffee and toast on the table."—"Thanks." I went to
serve myself and then came back to him, cup of coffee in hand. I looked
at the grounds. I didn't hear the twins anymore. "Where are boys?" I
asked Moreau.—"At school. They come back in the afternoon." I drank
a little coffee. "You know," he continued, "your mother is happy you've
come."—"Yes, that's possible," I said. But he placidly went on with his
thought: "You should write more often. Times are going to be hard.
Everyone is going to need their family. Family is the only thing you can
count on." I didn't say anything, just watched him absently; he was contemplating the garden. "Listen, Mother's Day is next month. You could
send her your best wishes."—"What is this holiday?" He looked surprised: "The Maréchal instituted it, two years ago. To honor maternity.
It's in May, this year it falls on the thirtieth." He was still looking at me:
"You could send a card."—"Yes, I'll try." He fell silent and turned back
to the garden. "If you have time," he said after a while, "could you go
cut some wood in the shed, for the stove? I'm getting old." I looked at
him again, huddled in his chair: in fact, he had aged. "If you like," I
replied. I went back into the house, put the empty cup on the table, nibbled on a cracker, and went upstairs; this time I went straight to the attic. I closed the trapdoor behind me and walked carefully between the
furniture and boxes, making the floorboards creak under my feet. My
memories rose around me, tactile now with the air, the smell, the light,
the dust: and I dove into these sensations as I had plunged into the
Volga, with complete abandon. It seemed to me I could see the shadow
of our bodies in the recesses, the brightness of our white skins. Then I
shook myself and found the boxes containing my things. I dragged them
into a large empty space near a pillar, crouched down, and began sorting through them. There were tin cars, report cards, and school notebooks, youth novels, photographs in thick envelopes, more envelopes,
sealed, containing letters from my sister—a whole past, strange and
sudden. I didn't dare look at the photos or open the envelopes; I felt an
animal terror growing in me; even the most commonplace, innocent

details bore the imprint of the past, of that past, and the very fact of this past chilled me to the bone; each new but so familiar object inspired in me a mixture of repulsion and fascination, as if I were holding a live bomb in my hands. To calm down, I examined the books: it was the collection of any adolescent of my generation—Jules Verne, Paul de Kock, Victor Hugo, Eugène Sue, the Americans E. R. Burroughs and Mark Twain, the adventures of Fantômas and Rouletabille, travel books, some biographies of famous men. I was seized with the desire to reread some of them and, after reflection, I put aside the first three volumes of Burroughs's Martian series, the ones that had so excited my fantasies in the upstairs bathroom, curious to see if they would still correspond to the intensity of my memories. Then I returned to the sealed envelopes. I weighed them in my hands, turned them over between my fingers. In the beginning, after the scandal, when we were sent to boarding school, my sister and I were still allowed to write to each other; when I received one of her letters, I had to open it in front of a priest and give it to him to read before I could myself; and she, on her side, probably had to do the same thing. Her letters, curiously written on a typewriter, were long, edifying, and solemn: *My dear brother: Everything is fine here, they're treating me nicely. I am awakening to a renewed sense of spirituality*, etc. But at night, I locked myself up in the bathroom with a candle stub, trembling with anxiety and excitement, and held the letter over the flame until a second message appeared, scribbled between the lines with milk: HELP! GET ME OUT OF HERE! I BEG YOU! We had gotten that idea by reading, secretly of course, a life of Lenin, found at a bookseller's near the mairie. These desperate messages threw me into panic, and I decided to run away and save her. But my attempt was poorly prepared, and I was soon caught. They punished me severely, I was given the cane and a week of stale bread, and the abuse of the older boys only got worse, but it was all the same to me; only, they had forbidden me from receiving any letters, and that plunged me into rage and despair. I didn't even know if I had saved those last letters, if they too were in these envelopes; and I didn't want to open them to check. I put everything away in the boxes, took the three books, and went back downstairs.

Compelled by a silent force, I went into Una's old room. There was now a double bed there, a wooden one painted red and blue, and toys carefully lined up, among which I angrily recognized some of my own. All the clothes were folded and put away in drawers and in the wardrobe. I quickly searched through the room looking for clues, letters, but found nothing. The family name written on the report cards was unknown to me, and seemed Aryan. These report cards went back

a few years: so they had been living here for quite some time. I heard
my mother behind me: "What are you doing?"—"I'm looking," I said
without turning round.—"You'd do better to go downstairs and cut
wood as Aristide asked you. I'm going to get lunch ready." I turned
around: she was standing in the doorway, severe, impassive. "Who are
these children?"—"I told you: the children of a close friend. We took
them in when she couldn't look after them anymore. They didn't have
a father."—"How long have they been here?"—"A while. You left a
long time ago too, my boy." I looked around me, then stared at her
again: "They're little Jews, aren't they? Admit it. They're Jews, right?"
She didn't let herself be intimidated: "Stop talking nonsense. They're
not Jews. If you don't believe me, just look at them when they're taking their bath. That's how you do it, isn't it?"—"Yes. Sometimes that's
how we do it."—"Anyway, even if they were Jews, what difference
would that make? What would you to do them?"—"I wouldn't do anything to them."—"What do you do, with the Jews?" she went on. "We
hear all kinds of horrors. Even the Italians say it's not acceptable, what
you're doing." I felt suddenly old, tired: "We send them to work, in the
East. They build roads, houses, they work in factories." She stuck to her
guns: "And the children? You send them away to build roads? You take
the children too, don't you?"—"The children go to special camps. They
stay with the mothers who can't work."—"Why do you do that?" I
shrugged: "Someone had to do it. The Jews are parasites, exploiters:
now they're serving the people they used to exploit. And I should point
out that the French help us a lot: in France, it's the French police who
arrest them and hand them over to us. It's French law that decides.
Someday, history will judge that we were right."—"You are completely
mad. Go cut the wood." She turned around and headed to the side
stairs. I went to put the three Burroughs books in my bag, then went
out to the shed. I took off my jacket, picked up the axe, put a log on
the block, and split it. It was difficult, I wasn't used to this kind of work;
I had to start over several times. As I raised the axe, I thought about my
mother's words; it wasn't her lack of political comprehension that bothered me, it was the way she looked at me: What did she see, when she
looked at me? I could feel the extent to which I labored under the
weight of the past, of wounds received or imagined, of irreparable mistakes, of the unredeemability of time. Struggling against it did no good.
When I got some logs finished, I loaded them up in my arms and carried them to the kitchen. My mother was peeling potatoes. I put the
wood on the woodpile near the stove and went out again without a
word, to split some more. I made several trips this way. As I worked, I
thought: in the end, the collective problem of the Germans was the

same as my own; they too were struggling to extract themselves from a painful past, to wipe the slate clean so they'd be able to begin new things. That was how they arrived at the most radical solution of them all: murder, the painful horror of murder. But was murder a solution? I thought of the many conversations I had had about this: in Germany, I wasn't the only one to have my doubts. What if murder weren't a definitive solution, what if on the contrary this new fact, even less reparable than the ones before it, opened in turn onto new abysses? Then, what way out was left? In the kitchen, I noticed I still had the axe with me. The room was empty: my mother must have been in the living room. I looked at the pile of wood; there seemed to be enough there. I was dripping with sweat; I put the axe in the corner next to the wood and went up to wash and change my shirt.

The meal passed in a dull silence. The twins were having lunch at school, there were just the three of us. Moreau tried to comment on the latest news—the Anglo-Americans were rapidly advancing toward Tunis; in Warsaw, some disturbances had broken out—but I obstinately kept silent. Looking at him, I said to myself: He's a clever man, he must also keep in contact with the terrorists, and help them a little; if things get worse, he'll say he was always on their side, that he worked with the Germans only as a cover. Whatever happens, he'll be able to make his nest, that cowardly, toothless old lion. Even if the twins weren't Jewish, I was sure he had hidden Jews: too good an opportunity, at so little cost (with the Italians, he wasn't risking anything), to give himself an alibi for whatever comes later. But then a raging thought occurred to me: we'll show him, him and everyone like him, what Germany is made of; we're not finished yet. My mother too was silent. After the meal I told them I was going out for a walk. I crossed the grounds, passed the still-half-open gate and went down to the beach. On the path the salt smell of the sea blended strongly with that of the pines, and once again the past rose up in me, the happy past that had bathed in these fragrances, the unhappy past too. At the beach, I turned right, toward the harbor and the town. At the base of Fort Carré, on a strip of earth overlooking the sea and surrounded by stone pines, stretched a playground where some children were playing with a ball. When I was little I was a puny child, I didn't like sports, I preferred reading; but Moreau, who thought I was sickly, had advised my mother to sign me up for a soccer club; so I too had played on this field. It wasn't much of a success. Since I didn't like to run, they made me the goalkeeper; one day, another child kicked the ball so hard into my chest that I was hurled to the back of the cage. I remember lying there on the ground, looking through the net at the tops of the pine trees waving in the breeze, until the coach finally came over to see if I had passed out. A little later we played our first game against another club. The team captain didn't want me to play; finally, after the halftime, he let me go out onto the field. I found myself, I'm not sure how, with the ball at my feet and began running toward the goal. In front of me, the empty field opened wide, the spectators were shouting, whistling, I didn't see anything except this goal, the powerless goalkeeper trying to stop me and waving his arms, I was triumphing over everything and I scored, but it was an "own goal," my own team's goal. In the locker room, I was beaten by the other boys, and I gave up soccer. Beyond the fort, Port Vauban curves inward, a large natural cirque converted to a harbor, where fishing craft and patrol boats from the Italian navy were rocking. I sat down on a bench and lit a cigarette, watching the seagulls wheel around the fishing boats. Here, too, I had often come. There had been one walk in 1930, just before my baccalauréat, during Easter vacation. I had been avoiding Antibes for almost a year, since my mother's marriage to Moreau, but for this vacation, she used a clever trick: she wrote to me, without any allusion to what had happened or to my letter full of insults, to tell me that Una was coming back for the vacation and would be delighted to see me. They had kept us apart for three years by then: those bastards, I said to myself, but I couldn't refuse, and they knew it. Our reunion was awkward, we didn't say much; of course my mother and Moreau practically never left us alone. When I arrived, Moreau had taken me by the arm: "No dirty business, okay? I'm keeping my eye on you." To him, dense bourgeois that he was, it was obvious that I had seduced her. I didn't say anything, but when she finally was there, I knew that I loved her more than ever. When, in the middle of the living room, she brushed me as she went by, the back of her hand touching mine for a fraction of a second, it was as if an electric shock riveted me to the floor; I had to bite my lip so as not to cry out. And then we went for a stroll around the harbor. Our mother and Moreau were walking in front of us, there, a few steps away from where I was sitting and remembering that moment; I spoke to my sister about my school, the priests, the corruption and the depraved habits of my classmates. I also told her I had been with boys. She smiled gently and gave me a quick kiss on the cheek. Her own experiences hadn't been much different, although the violence was more moral than physical. The nuns, she told me, were all *neurotic, inhibited and frigid.* I laughed and asked where she had learned these words; boarding school girls, she replied with a light, joyful laugh, now bribed the concierges so they would secretly smuggle them books not by Voltaire or Rousseau, but by Freud, Spengler, and Proust, and if I hadn't read them yet, it was high time I started. Moreau stopped to buy us some ice-cream cones.

But when he had rejoined our mother, we continued the conversation: this time, I talked about our father. "He's not dead," I whispered passionately.—"I know," she said. "And even if he is, it's not up to them to bury him."—"It's not a question of burial. It's as if they had murdered him. Murdered him with paper. What a disgrace! For their shameful desires."—"You know," she said then, "I think she loves him."—"I don't give a damn!" I whispered. "She married our father and she's his wife. That's the truth. A judge can't change any of that." She stopped and looked at me: "You're probably right." But already our mother was calling us, and we walked toward her, licking our vanilla ice-cream cones.

In town, I had a glass of white wine at a counter, still thinking back on those things, and told myself that I had seen what I had come to see, even if I still didn't know what that was; already I was thinking about leaving. I went to the ticket office near the bus station and bought a ticket for the next day, for Marseille; at the train station next door, they sold me a ticket for Paris; the transfer was short, I'd be there by nightfall. Then I returned to my mother's house. The grounds around the house stretched out calm and still, permeated by the gentle murmuring of pine needles caressed by the sea breeze. The French door to the living room was still open: I approached and called out, but no one answered. Maybe they're taking a nap, I said to myself. I too felt tired, it was probably the wine and the sun; I walked around the house and climbed the main staircase, without meeting anyone. My room was dark, cool. I lay down and fell asleep. When I woke up the light had changed, it was quite dark: on my doorstep, I saw the two twins, standing side by side, looking at me fixedly with their large round eyes. "What do you want?" I asked. At these words, they stepped back together, and fled. I could hear their little footsteps echoing on the floorboards and then rushing down the main staircase. The front door slammed and it was silent again. I sat up on the edge of the bed and realized I was naked; but I had no memory of getting undressed. My injured fingers hurt and I sucked them distractedly. Then I turned on the lamp switch and, blinking, looked for the time: my watch, on the night table, had stopped. I looked around me but didn't see my clothes. Where could they have gone? I took some fresh underwear out of my bag and got my uniform out of the closet. My beard rasped a little, but I decided to shave later on, and got dressed. I went down the side stairs. The kitchen was empty, the stove cold. I went out the service entrance: outside, on the sea side, dawn was breaking and was just starting to turn the bottom of the sky pink. Strange that the twins have gotten up so early, I said to myself. Had I slept through dinner, then? I must have been more tired than I thought. My bus left early, I had to get ready. I turned back and closed the door, went up the three steps that led to the living room and came in, groping my way to the French door. In the half-light I stumbled against something soft lying on the rug. This contact froze me. I stepped back to the light switch, put my hand behind me without looking, and turned it on. The light sprang from several lamps, bright, harsh, almost bleak. I looked at the shape I had bumped into: it was a body, as I had instinctively felt, and now I saw that the rug was soaked with blood, that I was walking in a pool of blood that overflowed the rug and spread out on the stone tiles, under the table, up to the French door. Horror and terror threw me into a panicked urge to flee, to hide in some dark place; I made an effort to control myself and drew my sidearm from my holster. I felt around with my finger to unfasten the safety catch. Then I approached the body. I wanted to avoid walking in the blood, but it was impossible. When I was closer I saw— but I knew it already—that it was Moreau, his chest smashed in, his neck nearly cut through, his eyes still open. The axe that I had left in the kitchen was lying in the blood next to the body; this almost black blood soaked his clothes, splattered his slightly tilted face, his graying moustache. I looked around but didn't see anything. The French door seemed closed. I returned to the kitchen and opened the storage room, but there was no one there. My boots left long trails of blood on the tiled floor: I opened the service door, went out, and wiped them on the grass, while still scrutinizing the back of the park, on the lookout. But there was nothing there. The sky was growing paler, the stars were beginning to disappear. I walked around the house, opened the main door, and went upstairs. My room was empty; the twins' room also. Still gripping my pistol, I found myself in front of the door to my mother's room. I stretched my left hand out to the doorknob: my fingers were trembling. I seized it and opened the door. The shutters were closed, it was dark; on the bed I could make out a gray shape. "Mother?" I murmured. Groping my way, aiming my gun, I found the light switch and turned it on. My mother, in a nightgown with a lace collar, was lying across the bed; her feet hung a little off it, one of them still wearing a pink slipper, the other, dangling, was bare. Petrified with horror, I didn't forget to look behind the door and quickly bend down to check under the bed: aside from the fallen slipper, there was nothing there. Trembling, I went up to her. Her arms were resting on the bedspread, her nightgown, properly pulled down to her feet, wasn't wrinkled, she didn't seem to have defended herself. I leaned over and put my ear close to her open mouth: there was no breath. I didn't dare touch her. Her eyes were bulging and there were red marks on her bare throat. Oh my God, I said to myself, she's been strangled, someone has strangled my mother. I examined the room. Nothing was overturned, the dresser drawers were all closed, the closets too. I went into the dressing room, it was empty, everything seemed in place; I returned to the bedroom. On the bedspread, on the rug, on her nightgown, I saw then, there were bloodstains: the murderer must first have killed Moreau, then come upstairs. Anguish was suffocating me, I didn't know what to do. Search the house? Find the twins and interrogate them? Call the police? I didn't have time, I had to catch my bus. Gently, very gently, I took the foot that was dangling and replaced it on the bed. I should have put the fallen slipper back on, but I didn't have the courage to touch my mother again. I went out of the room, almost backing out. In my room, I shoved my few things into my bag and left the house, closing the front door. My boots still bore traces of blood, I rinsed them off with a little rainwater in an abandoned basin. I didn't see any sign of the twins: they must have run away. Anyhow those children were no concern of mine.

The trip unfurled like a film, I didn't think; the methods of transportation followed one another, I held out my tickets when I was asked, the authorities didn't make any problems for me. When I left the house, on the path to town, the sun now fully risen over the gently booming sea, I met an Italian patrol that glanced curiously at my uniform, but didn't say anything; just before getting into the bus, a French policeman accompanied by two *bersaglieri* accosted me to ask for my papers: when I showed him the letter from the Einsatzkommando in Marseille and translated it for him, he saluted and let me go. It was better that way, I would have been incapable of talking, I was petrified with anguish, my thoughts were frozen in place. In the bus, I realized I had forgotten my suit and all my clothes from the day before. At the train station in Marseille I had to wait for an hour, so I ordered a coffee and drank it at the bar, in the hubbub of the main concourse. I had to try to reason things out a little. There must have been cries, noise; how could I not have been awakened? I had only drunk a glass of wine. And also the man hadn't killed the twins, they must have yelled. Why hadn't they come looking for me? What were they doing there, silent, when I had woken up? The murderer must not have searched the house, in any case he hadn't come into my room. And who was he? A bandit, a thief? But nothing seemed to have been touched, moved, overturned. Maybe the twins had surprised him and he had run away. But that didn't make any sense, they hadn't cried out, they hadn't come looking for me. Was the killer alone? My train was leaving, I got in and sat down, still reasoning. If he wasn't a thief, or thieves, then what? A settling of accounts? One

of Moreau's business deals gone sour? Terrorists from the Maquis, come
to set an example? But the terrorists didn't massacre people with axes
like savages, they took them into a forest for a show trial, then shot
them. And, again, I hadn't woken up, I who sleep so lightly, I didn't understand, anguish was racking my body, I sucked my half-healed fingers,
my thoughts flew round and round, set off on insane tangents, caught
in the jerking rhythm of the train, I wasn't sure of anything, nothing
made sense. In Paris, I easily caught the midnight express to Berlin;
when I arrived, I took a room in the same hotel. Everything was calm,
silent, a few cars went by; the elephants, which I still hadn't gone to see,
were trumpeting in the early morning light. I had slept a few hours in
the train, a black, dreamless sleep; I was still exhausted, but it was impossible to go back to sleep. My sister, I said to myself finally, I have to
let Una know. I went to the Kaiserhof: Had Freiherr von Üxküll left an
address? "We cannot give out the addresses of our clients, Herr Sturmbannführer" was the reply. But could they at least send a telegram? It
was a family emergency. Yes, that was possible. I asked for a form
and wrote it on the reception counter: MOTHER DEAD MURDERED STOP
MOREAU TOO STOP AM IN BERLIN CALL ME STOP, followed by the number
of the Eden Hotel. I handed it to the receptionist with a ten-reichsmark
bill; he read it gravely and said, bowing his head slightly: "My condolences, Herr Sturmbannführer."—"You'll send it right away?"—"I'm
calling the post office this instant, Herr Sturmbannführer." He gave me
the change and I went back to the Eden, leaving instructions for someone to come get me immediately in case of a phone call, whatever the
time. I had to wait till nightfall. I took the call in a booth next to the
reception, fortunately isolated. Una's voice was panicked: "What happened?" I could hear that she had been crying. I began as calmly as possible: "I was in Antibes, I went to visit them. Yesterday morning . . ."
My voice faltered. I cleared my throat and went on: "Yesterday morning I woke up . . ." My voice broke and I couldn't go on. I heard my
sister calling: "What is it? What happened?"—"Wait," I said harshly and
lowered the receiver to my thigh while I tried to get control of myself.
This had never happened to me, losing control of my voice like this;
even at the worst moments, I had always been able to explain things in
an orderly, precise way. I coughed, coughed again, then brought the receiver back to face level and explained to her in a few words what had
happened. She had only one question, frantic, panic-stricken: "And the
twins? Where are the twins?" And then I went mad, started thrashing
about in the phonebooth, hitting the walls with my back, my fist, my
foot, shouting into the receiver: "Who are those twins?! Those fucking
brats, whose are they?" A bellboy, alerted by the racket, had stopped in

front of the booth and was looking at me through the glass. I calmed down with an effort. My sister, at the other end, remained silent. I took a breath and said into the receiver: "They're alive. I don't know where they went." She didn't say anything, I thought I could hear her breathing through the crackle of the international line. "Are you there?" No answer. "Whose are they?" I asked again, gently. She still didn't speak. "Fuck!" I shouted, and hung up abruptly. I burst out of the booth and stood in front of the reception desk. I took out my address book, found a number, scribbled it on a piece of paper and handed it to the concierge. After a few minutes the telephone rang in the booth. I picked up the receiver and heard a woman's voice. "Good evening," I said. "I would like to speak with Dr. Mandelbrod. It's Sturmbannführer Aue."—"I'm sorry, Herr Sturmbannführer. Dr. Mandelbrod is not available. Can I take a message?"—"I would like to see him." I left the hotel's number and went back up to my room. An hour later a bellboy came with a note for me: Dr. Mandelbrod would receive me the next day, at 10:00 a.m. The same women, or ones who looked just like them, led me in. In the large light-filled office, with cats everywhere, Mandelbrod was waiting in front of the low table; Herr Leland, upright and thin in a pinstriped suit, was sitting next to him. I shook their hands and sat down. This time they didn't serve me tea. Mandelbrod spoke first: "I'm delighted to see you. Have you had a good leave?" He seemed to be smiling into his folds of fat. "Have you had time to think about my proposal?"—"Yes, Herr Doktor. But I would like something else. I would like to be transferred to the Waffen-SS to go to the front." Mandelbrod made a slight movement, as if he were shrugging his shoulders. Leland was staring at me with a harsh, cold, lucid gaze. I knew he had a glass eye, but could never tell which. It was he who answered, in a gravely voice with a minute trace of an accent: "That is impossible. We have seen your medical file: your wound is regarded as a serious disability, and you have been classified for office work." I looked at him and stammered: "But they need men. They're recruiting everywhere."—"Yes," Mandelbrod said, "but they're not taking just anyone. Rules are rules."—"They'll never take you back for active service," Leland hammered out.—"Yes," Mandelbrod went on, "and for France there's not much hope, either. No, you should put your trust in us." I got up: "Meine Herren, thank you for having me. I'm sorry I disturbed you."—"But there's no problem, my boy," Mandelbrod whispered. "Take your time, think some more."—"But remember," Leland added severely: "a soldier at the front cannot choose his place. He must do his duty, whatever his post."

From the hotel, I sent a telegram to Werner Best in Denmark, telling him I was ready to accept a position in his administration. Then I waited. My sister didn't call back, and I didn't try to contact her, either. Three days later they brought me a letter from the *Auswärtiges Amt*; it was Best's reply: the situation in Denmark had changed, and he had nothing to offer me for the moment. I crumpled the letter up and threw it out. Bitterness and fear were welling up; I had to do something to avoid collapsing. I called back Mandelbrod's office and left a message.

MENUET
(EN RONDEAUX)

It was Thomas, as you might have guessed, who brought me the letter. I had gone down to listen to the news at the hotel bar, along with some officers from the Wehrmacht. It must have been around the middle of May: in Tunis, our troops had carried out a *voluntary contraction of the front in accordance with the preestablished plan*; in Warsaw, the liquidation of the terrorist bands *was proceeding without obstacles*. The officers around me listened glumly, in silence; only a one-armed Hauptmann laughed loudly at the terms *freiwillige Frontverkürzung* and *planmässig*, but stopped when he met my anguished gaze; like him and the others too, I knew enough to interpret these euphemisms: the Jews who had revolted in the ghetto had been resisting our best troops for several weeks now, and Tunisia was lost. I looked around for the waiter to order another Cognac. Thomas came in. He crossed the room with a martial stride, ceremoniously gave me a German salute while clicking his heels, then took me by the arm and drew me toward a booth; there, he slipped into the banquette, negligently throwing his cap on the table, and brandished an envelope that he held delicately between two gloved fingers. "Do you know what's inside?" he asked, frowning. I made a sign that I didn't. The envelope, I saw, bore the header of the *Persönlicher Stab des Reichsführer-SS*. "I know what's inside," he went on in the same tone. His face cleared up: "Congratulations, dear friend. You play your cards close to your chest. I always knew you were smarter than you let on." He was still holding the letter. "Take it, take it." I took it, broke it open, and pulled out a sheet of paper, an order to present myself at the earliest opportunity to Obersturmbannführer Dr. Rudolf Brandt, personal adjutant to the Reichsführer-SS. "It's a summons," I said somewhat stupidly.—"Yes, it's a summons."—"And what does it mean?"—"It means that your friend Mandelbrod has a very long arm.

You've been assigned to the Reichsführer's personal staff, my friend. Shall we celebrate?"

I didn't feel much like celebrating, but I let myself be carried along. Thomas spent the night buying me American whiskies and excitedly holding forth on the stubbornness of the Jews in Warsaw. "Can you imagine? *Jews!*" As to my new assignment, he seemed to think I had brought off a masterstroke; I had no idea what it was all about. The next morning, I presented myself at the SS-Haus, located on Prinz-Albrechtstrasse right next to the *Staatspolizei*, in a former grand hotel converted into offices. Obersturmbannführer Brandt, a stooped little man with a wan, timid look, his face hidden behind large, round, black horn-rimmed glasses, received me right away: it seemed to me I had seen him already, in Hohenlychen, when the Reichsführer had decorated me on my hospital bed. In a few terse, precise sentences, he filled me in about what was expected of me. "The transition of concentration camps from a purely corrective finality to a function as a reservoir of labor force, which was begun more than a year ago now, has not been accomplished without conflicts." The problem involved both relations between the SS and outside participants, and internal relations within the SS itself. The Reichsführer wanted to get a better understanding of the source of the tensions in order to reduce them and also to maximize the productive capacity of this considerable human labor pool. He had consequently decided to appoint an already experienced officer as his personal representative for the *Arbeitseinsatz* ("labor operation" or "labor organization"). "After examination of the files and receipt of a number of recommendations, you were selected. The Reichsführer has complete confidence in your ability to carry out this task successfully—it will require a strong capacity for analysis, a sense of diplomacy, and an SS spirit of initiative, the kind you've already demonstrated in Russia." The SS offices concerned would receive an order to cooperate with me; but it would be up to me to ensure that this cooperation would be effective. "All your questions, as well as your reports," Brandt finished, "should be addressed to me. The Reichsführer will see you only when he deems it necessary. He will receive you today to explain what he expects of you." I had listened without batting an eye; I didn't understand what he was talking about, but thought it more politic to keep my questions to myself for the moment. Brandt asked me to wait in a lounge on the ground floor; I found some magazines there, along with tea and cakes. I soon tired of leafing through old issues of *Schwarzes Korps* in the subdued lighting of this room; unfortunately, there was no smoking allowed in the building—the Reichsführer had forbidden it because of the smell—and you couldn't go out to the street to smoke, either, in case you were summoned. They came looking for me around the end of the afternoon. In the antechamber, Brandt gave me his final recommendations: "Don't make any comments, don't ask any questions, only talk if you're asked to." Then he led me in. Heinrich Himmler was sitting behind his desk; I came forward with a military stride, followed by Brandt who introduced me; I saluted, and Brandt, after handing the Reichsführer a file, withdrew. Himmler motioned to me to sit down and consulted the file. His face seemed strangely vague, colorless; his little moustache and his pince-nez only emphasized the elusive quality of his features. He looked at me with a small, friendly smile; when he raised his head, the light, reflected in the glass of his pince-nez, made them opaque, hiding his eyes behind two round mirrors: "You look in better form than the last time I saw you, Sturmbannführer." I was quite surprised that he remembered me; perhaps there was a note in the file. He went on: "You have fully recovered from your wound? That's good." He leafed through a few pages. "Your mother is French, I see?" That seemed to be a question and I attempted an answer: "Born in Germany, my Reichsführer. In Alsace."—"Yes, but French all the same." He raised his head and this time the pince-nez did not reflect the light, revealing little eyes too close together, with a surprisingly gentle look. "You know, in principle I never accept men with foreign blood into my staff. It's like Russian roulette: too dangerous. You never know what will manifest, even in very good officers. But Dr. Mandelbrod convinced me to make an exception. He is a very wise man, whose judgment I respect." He paused. "I had considered another candidate for the position. Sturmbannführer Gerlach. Unfortunately he was killed a month ago. In Hamburg, during an English air raid. He didn't take shelter in time and a flowerpot fell on his skull. Begonias, I think. Or maybe tulips. He died on the spot. These English are monsters. Bombing civilians like that, without discrimination. After the victory we should organize war crimes trials. The people responsible for these atrocities have to answer for them." He fell silent and plunged into my file again. "You'll be thirty soon and you're not married," he said, raising his head. "Why?" His tone was severe, professorial. I blushed: "I haven't had an opportunity yet, my Reichsführer. I finished my studies just before the war."—"You should seriously consider it, Sturmbannführer. Your blood is valuable. If you are killed during this war, it shouldn't be lost for Germany." My words came to my lips of their own accord: "My Reichsführer, please excuse me, but my spiritual approach to my National Socialist commitment and to my service in the SS does not allow me to consider marriage so long as my *Volk* has not mastered the dangers threatening it. Affection for a woman can only weaken a man. I have to give myself

wholly and I couldn't share my devotion before the ultimate victory."
Himmler listened, scrutinizing my face; his eyes had opened slightly.
"Sturmbannführer, despite your foreign blood, your Germanic and National Socialist qualities are impressive. I don't know if I can accept your
reasoning: I continue to think that the duty of every SS-Mann is to
continue the race. But I will reflect on your words."—"Thank you, my
Reichsführer."—"Did Obersturmbannführer Brandt explain your work
to you?"—"In broad terms, my Reichsführer."—"I don't have much to
add. Above all, use delicacy. I don't want to provoke useless conflicts."—
"Yes, my Reichsführer."—"Your reports are very good. You have an
excellent ability to seize the overall picture based on a proven *Weltanschauung*. That's what made up my mind to choose you. But watch out!
I want practical solutions, not whining."—"Yes, my Reichsführer."—
"Dr. Mandelbrod will no doubt ask you to send him copies of your reports. I don't object. Good luck, Sturmbannführer. You may go." I got
up, saluted, and prepared to leave. Suddenly Himmler called out to me
in his dry little voice: "Sturmbannführer!"—"Yes, my Reichsführer?"
He hesitated: "No false sentimentality, yes?" I remained rigid, at attention: "Of course not, my Reichsführer." I saluted again and left. Brandt,
in the antechamber, gave me an inquisitive look: "Did it go well?"—"I
think so, Obersturmbannführer."—"The Reichsführer read your report
on the nutritional problems of our soldiers in Stalingrad with great interest."—"I'm surprised that report reached him."—"The Reichsführer
is interested in a lot of things. Gruppenführer Ohlendorf and the other
Amtschefs often send him interesting reports." Brandt gave me a book
from the Reichsführer entitled *Jewish Ritual Murders*, by Helmut
Schramm. "The Reichsführer had copies printed for all SS officers with
at least the rank of Standartenführer. But he also asked that it be distributed to subaltern officers concerned with the Jewish question. You'll
see, it's very interesting." I thanked him: one more book to read, when
I hardly read anymore. Brandt advised me to take a few days to get organized: "You won't achieve anything worthwhile if your personal affairs aren't in order. Then come see me."

It quickly became apparent to me that the most delicate question
would be that of lodging: I couldn't stay indefinitely at the hotel. The
Obersturmbannführer from the *SS-Personal Hauptamt* proposed two
options: SS housing for single officers, very inexpensive, with meals included; or a room with a lodge, for which I would have to pay rent.
Thomas stayed in a three-room apartment, spacious and very comfortable, with high ceilings and valuable old furniture. Given the grave
housing crisis in Berlin—people who had a room empty were in prin-

ciple forced to take on a tenant—it was a luxurious apartment, especially
for a single Obersturmbannführer; a married Gruppenführer with children wouldn't have turned it down. He laughingly told me how he had
gotten it: "It's not at all complicated. If you like, I can help you find one,
maybe not as large, but with two rooms at least." Thanks to an acquaintance working at the Berlin *Generalbauinspektion*, he had had a
Jewish apartment, liberated in view of the reconstruction of the city, assigned to him by special dispensation. "The only problem is that it was
only granted to me provided I pay for the renovation, about five hundred reichsmarks. I didn't have the money, but I managed to get it allocated to me by Berger as a one-time aid." Leaning back on the sofa, he
ran a satisfied eye around him: "Not bad, don't you agree?"—"And the
car?" I asked, laughing. Thomas also had a little convertible, which he
loved to go out in and in which he sometimes came to pick me up in
the evening. "That, my friend, is another story that I'll tell you someday. I did tell you, in Stalingrad, that if we got out of it, life would be
good. There's no reason to deprive ourselves." I thought about his offer, but finally decided on a furnished room with a family. I wasn't keen
on living in a building for the SS, I wanted to be able to choose whom
I met with outside of work; and the idea of staying alone, of living in
my own company, made me a little afraid, to tell the truth. Lodgers
would at least be a human presence, I would have my meals prepared,
there would be noise in the hallways. So I filed my request, specifying
that I would like two rooms and that there had to be a woman for cooking and housekeeping. They offered me something in Mitte, with a
widow, six stations on a direct U–Bahn line from Prinz-Albrechtstrasse,
at a reasonable price; I accepted without even visiting it and they gave
me a letter. Frau Gutknecht, a fat, ruddy-cheeked woman past sixty,
with voluminous breasts and dyed hair, examined me with a long, wily
look when she opened the door to me: "So you're the officer?" she said
with a thick Berlin accent. I stepped across the threshold and shook her
hand: she stank of cheap perfume. She retreated into the long hallway
and showed me the doors: "This is my place; that's yours. Here's the key.
I have one too, of course." She opened the door and showed me
around: mass-market furniture laden with curios, yellowing, wrinkled
wallpaper, a musty smell. After the living room was the bedroom, isolated from the rest of the apartment. "The kitchen and toilets are in the
back. Hot water is rationed, so no baths." Two black-framed portraits
hung on the wall: a man about thirty, with a little civil servant's moustache, and a young, solid, blond boy in a Wehrmacht uniform. "Is that
your husband?" I asked respectfully. A grimace deformed her face: "Yes.
And my son, Franz, my little Franzi. He fell the first day of the French

campaign. His Feldwebel wrote me that he died a hero, to save a comrade, but he didn't get a medal. He wanted to avenge his dad, my Bubi,
there, who died gassed in Verdun."—"My condolences."—"Oh, for
Bubi, I'm used to it, you know. But I still miss my little Franzi." She cast
me a calculating look. "Too bad I don't have a daughter. You could have
married her. I would have liked that, an officer son-in-law. My Bubi
was Unterfeldwebel and my Franzi was still a Gefreiter."—"Yes," I
replied politely, "it's too bad." I pointed to the curios: "Could I ask you
to take all those away? I'll need some room for my things." She looked
indignant: "And where do you suggest I put them? In my place there's
even less room. Plus they're pretty. You just have to push them over a
little. But watch out! If you break it you pay for it." She pointed to the
portraits: "If you like, I can take those away. I wouldn't want to inflict
my mourning on you."—"That's not important," I said.—"Fine, then
I'll leave them. This was Bubi's favorite room." We came to an agreement on the meals, and I gave her a section of my ration book.

I settled in as well as I could; in any case I didn't have a lot of things.
By piling up the curios and the cheap prewar novels, I managed to free
up a few shelves where I put my own books, delivered from the basement where I had stored them before I left for Russia. It made me
happy to unpack them and leaf through them, even though many of
them had been damaged by humidity. Next to them I put the edition of
Nietzsche that Thomas had given me and that I had never opened, the
three Burroughs books brought back from France, and the Blanchot,
which I had given up reading; the Stendhal books I had taken to Russia had remained there, just like Stendhal's own 1812 diaries and somewhat in the same way, really. I regretted not having thought to replace
them during my Paris trip, but there would always be another opportunity, if I were still alive. The booklet on ritual murder puzzled me a
little: whereas I could easily arrange the *Festgabe* next to my economics
and political science books, it was a little harder to find a place for this
book. I finally slipped it in with the history books, between von
Treitschke and Gustav Kossinna. These books and my clothes were all
that I owned, aside from a gramophone and a few records; the *kinzhal*
from Nalchik, alas, had also stayed in Stalingrad. After I had put everything away, I put on some Mozart arias, dropped into an armchair and
lit a cigarette. Frau Gutknecht came in without knocking and was immediately upset: "You're not going to smoke here! It'll make the curtains stink." I got up and pulled down the tails of my tunic: "Frau
Gutknecht. Please be so kind as to knock, and to wait for my reply before you come in." She turned crimson: "Excuse me, Herr Offizier! But
I'm in my own home, aren't I? And also, with all due respect, I could

be your mother. What does it matter to you, if I come in? You don't intend to have girls up here, do you? This is a respectable house, the house
of a good family." I decided it was urgent to make things clear: "Frau
Gutknecht, I am renting your two rooms; so it's no longer your home
but my home. I have no intention of having girls up, as you say, but I
am attached to my private life. If this arrangement doesn't suit you, I'll
take my things and my rent back and leave. Do you understand?" She
calmed down: "Don't take it like that, Herr Offizier . . . I'm not used to
it, that's all. You can even smoke if you like. Only you might open the
windows . . ." She looked at my books: "I see you're cultivated . . ." I
interrupted her: "Frau Gutknecht. If you have nothing else to ask me,
I would be grateful if you left me alone."—"Oh yes, sorry, yes." She
went out and closed the door behind her, leaving the key in the lock.

I put my papers in order with the personnel office and returned to
see Brandt. He had freed up one of the small, light-filled offices fitted
out in the attic of the old hotel. I had an antechamber with a telephone
and a work room with a sofa; a young secretary, Fräulein Praxa; the services of an orderly who assisted three offices; and of a pool of typists
available for the whole floor. My driver was named Piontek, a *Volksdeutscher* from Upper Silesia who would also serve as my orderly whenever I went anywhere; the vehicle was at my disposal, but the
Reichsführer insisted that any trip of a personal nature be itemized separately, and the cost of the gas taken from my salary. I found all this almost extravagant. "It's nothing. You have to have the means to work
correctly," Brandt assured me with a little smile. I couldn't meet the
head of the *Persönlicher Stab*, Obergruppenführer Wolff; he was recovering from a serious illness, and Brandt had in effect taken over all his
duties for months. He gave me a few additional instructions on what
was expected of me: "First of all, it's important that you familiarize
yourself with the system and its problems. All reports addressed to the
Reichsführer about this are archived here: have them brought up to
you and look them over. Here is a list of the SS officers who head the
various departments covered by your mandate. Make appointments and
go talk with them, they're expecting you and will talk frankly to you.
When you've gotten a suitable overall impression, you can go on an inspection tour." I consulted the list: they were mostly officers from the
Wirtschafts-Verwaltungs-hauptamt (the SS Main Office for Economics and
Administration) and from the RSHA. "The Inspectorate for Concentration Camps has been incorporated in the WVHA, isn't that right?" I
asked.—"Yes," replied Brandt, "a little over a year ago. Look at your list,
that's the Amtsgruppe D now. You've been referred to Brigadeführer

Glücks, who heads the directorate, and his deputy Obersturmbannführer Liebehenschel—who between you and me will probably be
more useful to you than his superior—along with some department
heads. But the camps are only one facet of the problem; there are also
the SS enterprises. Obergruppenführer Pohl, who heads the WVHA,
will receive you to talk to you about that. Of course, if you want to
meet other officers to go more deeply into certain points, please do: but
see these people first. At the RSHA, Obersturmbannführer Eichmann
will explain the system of special transports to you, and he'll also present you with the current progress of the resolution of the Jewish
question, and its future perspectives.—"May I ask you a question,
Obersturmbannführer?"—"Of course."—"If I understand correctly, I
can have access to all documents concerning the definitive solution to
the Jewish question?"—"Insofar as the resolution of the Jewish problem
directly affects the maximum deployment of manual labor, yes. But I
should point out that this will make you a *Geheimnisträger*, a bearer of
secrets, to a far greater degree than your duties in Russia did. You are
strictly forbidden to discuss this with anyone outside of the service, including the civil servants in the ministries or the Party functionaries
with whom you will be in contact. The Reichsführer allows only one
sentence for any violation of this rule: the death penalty." He again
pointed to the sheet he had given me: "You can talk freely with all the
officers on this list; for their subordinates, check first."—"Understood."—"For your reports, the Reichsführer has issued *Sprachregelungen*, language regulations. Any report that doesn't conform to them will
be returned to you."—"*Zu Befehl*, Obersturmbannführer."

I plunged into my work as into an invigorating bath in one of
Piatigorsk's sulfurous springs. For days on end, sitting on the little sofa
in my office, I devoured reports, correspondence, orders, and organizational tables, smoking a discreet cigarette from time to time at my window. Fräulein Praxa, a somewhat scatterbrained Sudetenlander who
would obviously have preferred spending her days chattering on the
telephone, had to keep going up and down to the archives, and complained that her ankles were swelling. "Thank you," I said without
looking at her when she came into my room with a new bundle. "Put
it down there and take these; I'm done with them, you can take them
back." She sighed and left, trying to make as much noise as possible.
Frau Gutknecht quickly revealed herself to be an execrable cook,
knowing three dishes at most, all with cabbage, which she often spoiled;
so at night I got into the habit of dismissing Fräulein Praxa and going
down to the mess for a bite, and then to keep working in my office till
late at night, returning home only to sleep. So as not to keep Piontek

waiting, I took the U-Bahn; at those late hours the C line was almost empty, and I liked observing the rare passengers, their faces worn out, exhausted; it took me out of my work a little. Many times I found myself in a car with the same man, a civil servant who like me must have been working late; he never noticed me, since he was always immersed in a book. This man, otherwise so unremarkable, read in a remarkable way: while his eyes ran over the lines, his lips moved as if he were saying the words, but without any sound that I could hear, not even a whisper; and I felt then something like Augustine's surprise when he saw for the first time Ambrose of Milan reading silently, with his eyes only—a thing the provincial Augustine didn't know was possible, since he could only read out loud, listening to himself.

In the course of my own reading, I came upon the report turned in to the Reichsführer at the end of March by Dr. Korherr, the glum statistician who had questioned our figures: his, I have to admit, horrified me. At the end of a statistical argument difficult to follow for a non-specialist, he concluded that by December 31, 1942, 1,873,549 Jews, not including Russia and Serbia, had died, been "transported to the East," or had been "sluiced through the camps" (*durchgeschleust*, a curious term imposed, I imagine, by the Reichsführer's *Sprachregelungen*). In all, he estimated in conclusion, German influence, since the Seizure of Power, had reduced the Jewish population of Europe by four million—a number including, if I understood correctly, prewar emigration. Even after what I had seen in Russia, this was impressive: we had long since moved beyond the primitive methods of the Einsatzgruppen. Through a whole series of orders and instructions, I was also able to form an idea of the difficult adaptation of the Inspectorate for Concentration Camps to the requirements of total war. Whereas the very formation of the WVHA and its absorption of the IKL, which were supposed to signal and implement a passage to maximal war production, dated back to March 1942, serious measures to reduce the mortality of the inmates and improve their output had not been promulgated until October; in December still, Glücks, the head of the IKL, was ordering doctors in the *Konzentrationslager* to improve sanitary conditions, lower mortality, and increase productivity, but once again without specifying any concrete measures. According to the statistics of the D II that I consulted, mortality, expressed in monthly percentages, had gone down considerably: the overall rate for all of the KLs had gone from losses of 10 percent in December to 2.8 percent in April. But this reduction was entirely relative, since the population of the camps continued to increase; the net losses hadn't changed. A semiannual report of the D II indicated that from July to December 1942, 57,503 inmates out of 96,770, or 60 per-

cent of the total, had died; since January, the losses continued to hover
at around 6,000 or 7,000 a month. None of the measures taken seemed
able to reduce them. What's more, certain camps appeared clearly worse
than others; the mortality rate in March at Auschwitz, a KL in Upper
Silesia that I was hearing about for the first time, had been 15.4 percent.
I began to see what the Reichsführer was driving at.

Nevertheless I felt rather unsure of myself. Was that because of recent events, or simply my innate lack of bureaucratic instinct? Whatever
the case, after I had managed to gather an overall idea of the problem
from the documents, I decided, before going up to Oranienburg where
the IKL people had their headquarters, to consult Thomas. I liked
Thomas, but I would never have spoken to him about my personal
problems; for my professional doubts, though, he was the best confidant
I knew. He had once demonstrated to me in luminous terms the principle of how the system functioned (this must have been in 1939, or
maybe even the end of 1938, during the internal conflicts that had
shaken the movement after the *Kristallnacht*): "It's normal that orders are
always vague; it's even deliberate, and it stems from the very logic of the
Führerprinzip. It's up to the recipient to recognize the intentions of the
one who gives the command, and to act accordingly. The ones who insist on having clear orders or who want legislative measures haven't understood that it's the will of the leader, and not his orders, that counts,
and that it's up to the receiver of the orders to know how to decipher
and even anticipate that will. Whoever knows how to act this way is an
excellent National Socialist, and he'll never be reproached for his excess
of zeal, even if he makes mistakes; the others are the ones who, as the
Führer says, *are afraid of jumping over their own shadows*." I had understood
that; but I also understood that I lacked the skill to go beyond the sur-
faces of things, to guess at the hidden stakes; and Thomas had precisely
this talent to the highest degree, and that's why he was driving in a
sports convertible while I was going home on the U-Bahn. I found him
at the Neva Grill, one of the good restaurants he liked to frequent. He
talked to me with cynical amusement about the population's morale, as
it was revealed in Ohlendorf 's confidential reports, copies of which he
received: "It's remarkable how well informed people are of the so-called
secrets—the euthanasia program, the destruction of the Jews, the camps
in Poland, the gas, everything. You, in Russia, had never heard of the
KLs in Lublin or Silesia, but the lowliest tramcar driver in Berlin or
Düsseldorf knows they're burning prisoners there. And despite
Goebbels's propaganda, people are still capable of forming opinions for
themselves. The foreign radio broadcasts aren't the only explanation,
since a lot of people are still afraid of listening to them. No, all of Ger-

many today is a vast tissue of rumors, a spider's web that extends to all the territories under our control—the Russian front, the Balkans, France. Information circulates at an incredible speed. And the cleverest are able to match up these pieces of information so as sometimes to arrive at surprisingly precise conclusions. You know what we did, recently? We deliberately started a rumor in Berlin, a real false rumor, based on authentic but distorted information, to study how quickly and by what means it was transmitted. We picked it up in Munich, Vienna, Königsberg, and Hamburg in twenty-four hours, and in Linz, Breslau, Lübeck, and Jena in forty-eight. I'm tempted to try the same thing starting in the Ukraine, just to see. But the encouraging thing is that despite everything, people continue to support the Party and the authorities; they still have faith in our Führer and believe in the *Endsieg*. Which demonstrates what? That barely ten years after the Seizure of Power, the National Socialist spirit has become *the* truth of the daily life of the *Volk*. It has penetrated into the most obscure recesses. And so even if we lose the war, it will survive."—"Let's talk instead about how the war can be won, all right?" While eating, I told him about the instructions I had received and the general state of the situation as I understood it. He listened to me while drinking wine and cutting his steak, perfectly grilled, pink and juicy inside. He finished his meal and poured some more wine before he replied. "You've landed yourself a very interesting job, but I don't envy you. I have the impression they're sending you into a lion's den, and even if you don't make any blunders you're going to be eaten alive. What do you know about the political situation? The internal one, I mean." I too finished eating: "I don't know much about the internal political situation."—"Well you should. It has radically changed since the beginning of the war. Firstly, the Reichsmarschall is *out*, for good, in my opinion. What with the failure of the Luftwaffe against the bombings, his Homeric corruption, and his immoderate use of drugs, no one pays any attention to him anymore: he serves as an extra, they take him out of the closet when they need someone to talk in the Führer's place. Our dear Dr. Goebbels, despite his valiant efforts after Stalingrad, is on the sidelines. The rising star today is Speer. When the Führer appointed him, no one gave him more than six months; since then, he's tripled our weapons production, and the Führer grants him anything he asks for. What's more, this little architect whom everyone used to make fun of has turned out a remarkable politician, and he's now got several heavy-weights on his side: Milch, who oversees the Aviation Ministry for Göring, and Fromm, the head of the *Ersatzheer*. What is Fromm's interest? Fromm has to provide men for the Wehrmacht; so every German worker replaced by a foreign worker or an inmate is one more soldier for Fromm. Speer thinks only about how to increase production, and Milch does the same for the Luftwaffe. They all demand just one thing: men, men, men. And that's where the Reichsführer has a problem. Of course, no one can criticize the *Endlösung* program in itself: it's a direct order from the Führer, so the ministries can just quibble at the margins, playing on the diversion of some of the Jews for work. But after Thierack agreed to empty his prisons into the KLs, they have come to represent a considerable pool of manual labor. It's nothing, of course, next to the foreign workers, but it's still something. Now the Reichsführer is very jealous about his SS's autonomy, and Speer is encroaching on it. When the Reichsführer demanded that the factories be built inside his camps, Speer went to see the Führer and, presto! The inmates left for the factories. You see the problem: the Reichsführer feels he's in a weak position and has to give guarantees to Speer, to demonstrate that he's showing goodwill. Of course, if he actually manages to inject more labor into industry, everyone's happy. But that, in my opinion, is where the internal problem comes in: the SS, you see, is like the Reich in miniature, people tug it every which way. Take the example of the RSHA: Heydrich was a genius, a force of nature and an admirable National Socialist; but I'm convinced that the Reichsführer was secretly relieved by his death. Sending him to Prague was a brilliant move: Heydrich took it as a promotion, but he also saw that he was forced to let go a little of the RSHA, simply because he was no longer in Berlin. His tendancy toward autonomy was very strong, that's why the Reichsführer didn't want to replace him. And then each of the Amtschefs began to go his own way. So the Reichsführer appointed Kaltenbrunner to control them, hoping that Kaltenbrunner, who is a complete idiot, would himself remain controllable. But you'll see, it'll start all over again: the job requires it, more than the man. And it's the same thing for all the other departments and divisions. The IKL is particularly rich in *alte Kämpfer*: there, even the Reichsführer has to tread softly."—"If I understand correctly, the Reichsführer wants to promote reforms without upsetting the IKL too much?"—"Or else he doesn't care about reforms, but wants to use them as an instrument to tighten the screws on the stubborn ones. And at the same time, he has to demonstrate to Speer that he's cooperating with him, but without giving him the possibility of interfering with the SS or cutting back its privileges."—"It certainly is delicate."—"Ah! Brandt said it well: analysis and diplomacy."—"He also said 'initiative.'"—"Of course! If you find answers, even to problems that weren't directly submitted to you but that play to the vital interests of the Reichsführer, your career is made. But if you start indulging in bureaucratic romanticism and try to change everything all

at once, you'll very quickly end up as a deputy Leiter in some shabby
SD-Stelle in the hinterlands of Galicia. So beware: if you pull off the
same kind of trick you did in France, I'll regret having gotten you out
of Stalingrad. Staying alive has to be earned."

This mocking and at the same time formidable warning was
painfully emphasized by a brief letter I got from my sister. As I suspected, she had left for Antibes just after our phone conversation:

> *Max, the police were talking about a psychopath or a thief or even*
> *a gangland killing. In fact they don't know anything. They told me they*
> *were looking into Aristide's business affairs. It was odious. They asked*
> *me all kinds of questions about the family: I told them about you, but I*
> *don't know why, I took care not to tell them you were there. I don't know*
> *what I was thinking of but I was afraid of making trouble for you. And*
> *what would be the use, anyway? I left immediately after the funeral. I*
> *wanted you to be there and at the same time I would have hated you to*
> *be there. It was sad and poor and awful. They were buried together at*
> *the town cemetery. Aside from me and a policeman who had come to see*
> *who would be at the funeral there were just a few old friends of Aris-*
> *tide's and a priest. I left immediately afterward. I don't know what else*
> *to write you. I'm terribly sad. Take care of yourself.*

Of the twins, she didn't breathe a word: after her violent reaction on
the telephone, I found that surprising. What was even more surprising,
for me, was my own lack of reaction: this frightened and mournful letter had the same effect on me as a yellow fall leaf, detached and dead before it had even touched the ground. A few minutes after reading it, I
was thinking again about work problems. The questions that just a
handful of weeks before had been eating away at me and keeping me
awake at night now seemed to me like a row of closed, silent doors; the
thought of my sister, a stove that had gone out and smelled of cold ashes,
and the thought of my mother, a quiet, long-neglected gravestone. This
strange apathy extended to all other aspects of my life: my landlady's
petty annoyances left me indifferent, sexual desire seemed like an abstract old memory, anxiety about the future a frivolous, vain luxury.
That is somewhat the state in which I find myself today, and I feel fine
this way. Only work occupied my thoughts. I meditated on Thomas's
advice: he seemed to me to be even righter than he knew. Toward the
end of the month, with the Tiergarten flowering and the trees covering the still-gray city with their insolent greenery, I went to visit the offices of the Amtsgruppe D, the former IKL, in Oranienburg, near KL

Sachsenhausen: long, white, clean buildings, perfectly straight lanes, flower-beds meticulously mulched and weeded by well-fed inmates in clean uniforms, energetic, busy, motivated officers. I was courteously received by Brigadeführer Glücks. Glücks talked quickly and volubly, and this flow of confused words presented a marked contrast with the aura of efficiency that characterized his kingdom. He completely lacked an overall picture, and lingered at length and stubbornly over unimportant administrative details, quoting statistics—often wrong—to me at random, which I noted down out of politeness. To every somewhat specific question, he invariably replied: "Oh, you'd do better to see about that over at Liebehenschel's," all the while cordially pouring me French Cognac and offering me cookies. "Made by my wife. Despite the restrictions, she knows how to get by, she's a wonder." He clearly wanted to get rid of me as quickly as possible, without, however, taking the risk of offending the Reichsführer, so as to return to his torpor and his cookies. I decided to cut things short; as soon as I paused, he called his adjutant and poured me a last Cognac: "To the health of our dear Reichsführer." I took a sip, put down the glass, saluted him, and followed my guide. "You'll see," Glücks called to me as I was going out the door, "Liebehenschel can answer all your questions." He was right, and his deputy, a small man with a sad, tired face who also ran the Central Office of Amtsgruppe D, gave me a concise, lucid, realistic summary of the situation and the state of progress of the reforms that had been undertaken. I already knew that most of the orders given out under Glücks's signature were in fact prepared by Liebehenschel: that wasn't very surprising. For Liebehenschel, a large share of the problems came from the Kommandanten: "They have no imagination, and they don't know how to apply our orders. As soon as we get anything like a motivated Kommandant, the situation changes completely. But we sorely lack personnel, and there's no prospect of replacing these cadres."— "And the medical departments can't make up for the deficiencies?"— "You'll see Dr. Lolling after me, you'll understand." In fact, although the hour I spent with Standartenführer Dr. Lolling didn't teach me much about the problems of the medical departments of the KLs, it at least allowed me, despite my irritation, to understand why these departments had no choice but to try to function autonomously. Elderly, his eyes watery, his mind confused and muddled, Lolling, whose department supervised all the sanitary structures of the camps, not only was an alcoholic but, according to widespread rumor, helped himself daily from his stock of morphine. I didn't understand how such a man could remain in the SS, even less occupy a position of responsibility in it. No doubt he benefited from protection within the Party. Nevertheless I extracted a pile of highly useful reports from him: Lolling, for lack of anything better to do and to mask his own incompetence, spent his time ordering reports from his subordinates; they weren't all men like him, there was some substantial material there.

That left Maurer, the creator and head of the *Arbeitseinsatz*, now department D II in the WVHA organizational table. Actually, I could have done without the other visits, even the one to Liebehenschel. Standartenführer Gerhard Maurer, a man still young, without any diplomas but endowed with a solid professional experience in accounting and management, had been pulled out of obscurity from an office in the old SS administration by Oswald Pohl and had quickly distinguished himself by his administrative abilities, his spirit of initiative, and his keen understanding of bureaucratic realities. When Pohl had taken the IKL under his wing, he had asked Maurer to set up the D II in order to centralize and rationalize the exploitation of camp labor. I was to see him again several times afterward and to correspond with him regularly, always with the same satisfaction. Maurer represented for me a certain ideal National Socialist who, though he must be a man with a *Weltanschauung*, still has to be a man who gets results. And concrete, measurable results formed Maurer's very life. Although he himself hadn't invented all the measures set in place by the *Arbeitseinsatz*, he had out of whole cloth created the impressive statistical data collection system that now covered all the WVHA camps. This system he patiently explained to me, itemizing the standardized, pre-printed forms that each camp had to fill out and send in, pointing out the most important figures and the right way to interpret them: considered thus, these numbers became fungible, more legible than a narrative report; capable of being compared and thus conveying an enormous amount of information, they allowed Maurer to follow precisely, without leaving his office, to what extent his orders were implemented, and with what success. These data allowed him to confirm Liebehenschel's diagnosis for me. He gave me a severe speech on the reactionary attitude of the corps of Kommandanten, "trained in the Eicke method," competent enough when it came to the old repressive, police functions, but in the main, limited and inept, unable to integrate modern management techniques adapted to new requirements: "These men aren't bad, but they're just not up to what's being asked of them now." Maurer himself had only one aim in mind: to extract the maximum amount of work from the KLs. He didn't serve me any Cognac but when I took my leave he warmly shook my hand: "I'm delighted that the Reichsführer is finally looking more carefully into these problems. My office is at your service, Sturmbannführer, you can always count on me."

I returned to Berlin and made an appointment with my old acquaintance Adolf Eichmann. He came to welcome me in person in the
vast main lobby of his department on the Kurfürstenstrasse, walking in
short strides in his heavy rider's boots on the polished marble slabs and
warmly congratulating me on my promotion. "You too," I congratulated him in turn, "you were promoted. In Kiev, you were still a Sturmbannführer."—"Yes," he said with satisfaction, "that's true, but you, in
the meantime, got two stripes . . . Come in, come in." Despite his superior rank, I found him curiously attentive, affable; perhaps the fact
that I had come on behalf of the Reichsführer impressed him. In his office, he dropped into his chair and crossed his legs, negligently dropped
his cap on a pile of files, took off his large glasses, and began to clean
them with a handkerchief while calling out to his secretary: "Frau Werl-
mann! Some coffee, please." I observed this little game with amusement:
Eichmann had gained self-confidence, since Kiev. He raised his glasses
to the window, inspected them meticulously, rubbed them some more,
put them back on. He took a box out from under a folder and offered
me a Dutch cigarette. Lighter in hand, he gesticulated at my chest:
"You've received a lot of decorations, I congratulate you again. That's
the advantage of being at the front. Here, in the rear, we have no opportunity to win decorations. My Amtschef managed to get me the Iron
Cross, but that was really just so I'd have something. I volunteered for
the Einsatzgruppen, did you know that? But C (that was how Heydrich,
wanting to give himself an English touch, had himself called by his co-
terie) ordered me to stay. *You're indispensable to me*, he said. *Zu Befehl*, I
said, but in any case I didn't have a choice."—"You have a good position, though. Your Referat is one of the most important in the *Staatspolizei*."—"Yes, but as far as advancement goes, I'm completely blocked.
A Referat is headed by a Regierungsrat or an Oberregierungsrat or an
equivalent SS rank. So in principle, in this position, I can't go beyond
Obersturmbannführer. I complained to my Amtschef: he told me I deserved to be promoted, but that he didn't want to stir up problems with
his other department heads." He made a pinched face that deformed his
lips. His balding head gleamed under the overhead lamp, turned on despite the daylight. A no-longer-young secretary came in with a tray and
two steaming cups, which she placed in front of us. "Milk? Sugar?"
Eichmann asked. I shook my head and smelled the cup: it was real coffee. While I was blowing on it Eichmann asked me out of the blue:
"Were you decorated for the *Einsatzaktion*?" His complaining was beginning to annoy me; I wanted to get to the point of my visit. "No," I
replied. "I was posted in Stalingrad, afterward." Eichmann's face darkened and he took off his glasses in an abrupt gesture. *"Ach so,"* he said,

straightening. "You were in Stalingrad. My brother Helmut was killed there."—"I'm sorry. All my condolences. Was he your older brother?"—"No, the younger one. He was thirty-three. Our mother still hasn't gotten over it. He fell as a hero, doing his duty for Germany. I'm sorry," he added ceremoniously, "that I haven't had that chance myself." I seized the opening: "Yes, but Germany is asking you for other sacrifices." He put his glasses back on and drank a little coffee. Then he put out his cigarette in an ashtray: "You're right. A soldier doesn't choose his post. What can I do for you, then? If I understood the letter from Obersturmbannführer Brandt correctly, you're in charge of studying the *Arbeitseinsatz*, is that right? I don't quite see what that has to do with my departments." I pulled a few sheets of paper from my imitation-leather briefcase. (I felt a disagreeable sensation every time I used this briefcase, but I hadn't been able to find anything else, because of the restrictions. I had asked Thomas's advice, but he had laughed in my face: "I wanted a leather office set, you know, with a writing pad and a penholder. I wrote to a friend in Kiev, a guy who was in the Group and who stayed on with the BdS, to ask him if he could have one made for me. He answered that ever since we had killed all the Jews, you couldn't even get a pair of boots resoled in the Ukraine.") Eichmann was observing me, knitting his brows. "The Jews you are in charge of are today one of the main pools the *Arbeitseinsatz* can draw on to renew its workforce," I explained. "Aside from them, there's really nothing else but foreign workers sentenced for petty crimes, and political deportees from the countries under our control. All the other possible sources, the war prisoners or the criminals transferred by the Ministry of Justice, are mostly exhausted. What I would like is to have an overall view of how your operations function, and especially of your prospects for the future." While he was listening to me, a curious tic deformed the left corner of his mouth; I had the impression that he was chewing his tongue. He leaned back again in his chair, his long veined hands joined in a triangle, index fingers taut: "Fine, fine. I'll explain things to you. As you know, in every country subject to the *Endlösung*, there is a representative from my Referat, subordinate either to the BdS, if it's an occupied country, or to the embassy's police attaché, if it's an allied country. I should point out right away that the USSR doesn't come into my domain; as for my representative in the Generalgouvernement, he has an entirely minor role."—"How is that?"—"The Jewish question, in the GG, is the responsibility of the SSPF in Lublin, Gruppenführer Globocnik, who reports directly to the Reichsführer. So the *Staatspolizei* isn't concerned, in general." He pinched his lips: "Except for a few exceptions that still have to be settled, the Reich itself can be considered

judenrein. As to the other countries, everything depends on the degree
of understanding about the resolution of the Jewish question shown by
the national authorities. Because of that, in a way every country poses
a special case that I can explain to you." As soon as he began to talk
about his work, I noticed, his already curious mixture of Austrian accent and Berlin slang was complicated by a particularly muddled bureaucratic syntax. He spoke calmly and clearly, choosing his words, but
it was sometimes hard for me to follow his phrases. He himself seemed
to get a little lost in them. "Take the example of France, where we have
so to speak only begun to work last summer once the French authorities, guided by our specialist and also by the advice and wishes of the
Auswärtiges Amt, um, if you like, had agreed to cooperate and especially
when the Reichsbahn agreed to provide us with the necessary transportation. We were thus able to begin, and in the beginning it even had
some success, since the French showed a lot of understanding, and also
thanks to the assistance of the French police, without which we could
have done nothing, of course, since we don't have the resources, and
the *Militärbefehlshaber* certainly wasn't going to provide them, so the aid
of the French police was a vital element, since they're the ones who arrested the Jews and transferred them to us, and they even overdid it,
since we had only officially asked for Jews over sixteen—to begin with
of course—but they didn't want to keep the children without their parents, which is understandable, so they gave them all to us, even the orphans—in short we soon understood that in fact they were only giving
us their foreign Jews, I even had to cancel a transport from Bordeaux
because they couldn't find enough to fill it, of those foreign Jews, a real
scandal, since when it comes to their own Jews, the ones who were
French citizens, I mean, for a long time, well then, you see, it was nothing doing. They didn't want to and there was nothing to be done. According to the *Auswärtiges Amt* it was Maréchal Pétain himself who
made problems, and it was useless for us to explain to him, it didn't do
any good. So after November, of course, the situation changed completely, because we were no longer necessarily bound by all those agreements or by the French laws, but even then, this is what I told you,
there was the problem of the French police, which didn't want to cooperate anymore, I don't want to complain about Herr Bousquet, but
he too had his orders, and of course it wasn't possible to send the German police knocking on doors, so, in fact, in France, we're not making
much progress anymore. What's more, a lot of Jews have gone to the
Italian sector, and that's really a problem, since the Italians have no understanding at all, and we're having the same problem everywhere, in
Greece and in Croatia, where they're in charge, there they protect the

Jews, and not only their own Jews but all of them. And this is a real problem and it's completely beyond my competence, and also I think I know for a fact that it was discussed at the highest level, the highest there is, and that Mussolini replied that he would take care of it, but obviously it's not a priority, is it, and at the lower levels, the ones we're dealing with, there it's downright bureaucratic obstruction, delaying tactics and that's something I know a lot about, they never say no but it's like quicksand, and nothing happens. That's where we are with the Italians."—"And the other countries?" I asked. Eichmann got up, put on his cap, and motioned for me to follow: "Come. I'll show you." I followed him to another office. He was, I noticed for the first time, bowlegged, like a rider. "Do you ride horses, Obersturmbannführer?" He made another face: "In my youth. Now I don't get much of a chance." He knocked at a door and went in. Some officers got up and saluted; he returned their salute, crossed the room, knocked at another door, and entered. In the back of the room, behind a desk, was a Sturmbannführer; there was also a secretary there and a subaltern. They all got up when we came in; the Sturmbannführer, a handsome blond animal, tall and muscular, buttoned up tight in his tailored uniform, raised his arm and shouted a martial "Heil!" We returned his salute before walking over to him. Eichmann introduced me and then turned to me: "Sturmbannführer Günther is my permanent deputy." Günther contemplated me with a taciturn look and asked Eichmann: "What can I do for you, Obersturmbannführer?"—"I'm sorry to disturb you, Günther. I wanted to show him your board." Günther moved away from his desk without a word. Behind him on the wall was a large multicolored chart. "You see," Eichmann explained, "it's organized by country and brought up to date every month. On the left, you have the objectives, and then the totals accrued to realize the objective. You can see at a glance that we're approaching the goal in Holland, fifty percent in Belgium, but that in Hungary, Romania, and Bulgaria we're still close to zero. In Bulgaria, we've had a few thousand, but that's deceptive: they let us evacuate the territories they occupied in 1941, in Thrace and Macedonia, but we can't touch the ones in Old Bulgaria. We officially asked them again a few months ago, in March I think, there was an approach from the AA, but they refused again. Since it's a question of sovereignty, everyone wants guarantees that his neighbor will do the same thing, that's to say that the Bulgarians want the Romanians to start, and the Romanians the Hungarians, and the Hungarians the Bulgarians or something like that. Note that since Warsaw we've at least been able to explain to them the danger it represents, having so many Jews in one's country, it's a hotbed of partisans, and well, I think that impressed them. But we haven't reached the end of our efforts yet. In Greece, we began in March, I have a Sonderkommando over there, in Thessalonica right now, and you see that it's going quite rapidly, it's already almost over. After that we'll still have Crete and Rhodes, no problem, but for the Italian zone, Athens and the rest, I've already explained to you. Then, of course, there are all the associated technical problems, they're not just diplomatic problems, that would be too easy, no, and so especially the problem of transport, that's to say rolling stock and thus the allocation of freight cars and also, how should I say, of time on the tracks even if we have the cars. For example, sometimes, we're negotiating an agreement with a government, we have the Jews in hand, bam, *Transportsperre*, everything's blocked because there's an offensive in the East or something and they can't let anything else go through Poland. So of course when it's quiet we work twice as hard. In Holland or in France, we centralize everything in transit camps, and we're emptying them out little by little, when there's transport and also according to the admission capacity, which is also limited. For Thessalonica, on the other hand, it was decided to do everything all at once, one two three four and that's it. In fact, since February, we've really had a lot of work, transport is available and I received an order to speed things up. The Reichsführer wants it to be over this year and then we won't talk about it anymore."—"And can that be realized?"—"Where it depends on us, yes. I mean transport is always a problem, finances too, since we have to pay the Reichsbahn, you know, for each passenger, and I don't have any budget for that, I have to make do. We ask the Jews to help out, that's fine, but the Reichsbahn only accepts payment in reichsmarks or at a pinch in zlotys, if we send them within the GG, but in Thessalonica they have drachmas and of course it's impossible to exchange currency there. So we have to make do, but we know how to do that. After that of course there are the diplomatic questions, if the Hungarians say no, I can't do anything about it, it doesn't depend on me and it's up to Herr Minister von Ribbentrop to see to that with the Reichsführer, not me."—"I see." I studied the chart for a bit: "If I understand correctly, the difference between the numbers there in the 'April' column and the numbers on the left represents the potential pool, subject to the various complications you've explained to me."—"Exactly. But note that those are overall figures, that is to say that a large part, in any case, doesn't interest the *Arbeitseinsatz*, because you see they're old people or children or I don't know what, so from that total you can deduct a large number."—"How big, in your opinion?"—"I don't know. You should check that with the WVHA—admission and selection is their problem. My responsibility stops when the train leaves—the rest I can't talk about. What I can tell you is that in the opinion of the RSHA, the number of Jews temporarily kept for work should be as limited as possible: creating large concentrations of Jews, you see, is inviting a repetition of Warsaw, it's dangerous. I think I can tell you that that's the opinion of Gruppenführer Müller, my Amtschef, and of Obergruppenführer Kaltenbrunner."—"I see. Could you give me a copy of these figures?"—"Of course, of course. I'll send them to you tomorrow. But for the USSR and the GG, I don't have those, as I told you." Günther, who hadn't said a word, let out another resounding "Heil Hitler!" while we got ready to leave. I returned with Eichmann to his office so that he could explain a few more points to me. When I was ready to go, he accompanied me. In the lobby he made a low bow: "Sturmbannführer, I would like to invite you to my place one night this week. We sometimes give chamber music performances. My Hauptscharführer Boll plays first violin."—"Oh. That's very nice. And you, what do you play?"—"Me?" He stretched out his neck and head, like a bird. "Violin too, second violin. I don't play as well as Boll, unfortunately, so I gave way to him. C . . . Obergruppenführer Heydrich, I mean, not Obergruppenführer Kaltenbrunner whom I know well, we're from the same province and he's the one who had me enter the SS and he still remembers—no, the Chief played the violin magnificently. Yes, really very fine, he had a huge amount of talent. He was a fine man, whom I respected very much. Very . . . considerate, a man who suffered in his heart. I miss him."—"I hardly knew him. And what are you playing?"—"At the moment? Mostly Brahms. A little Beethoven."—"No Bach?" He pinched his lips again: "Bach? I don't like him very much. I find him dry, too . . . calculated. Sterile, so to speak, very beautiful, of course, but soulless. I prefer Romantic music, it sometimes overwhelms me, yes, it takes me far beyond myself."—"I'm not sure I share your opinion of Bach. But I'll happily accept your invitation." The idea in fact bored me profoundly, but I didn't want to offend him. "Good, good," he said, shaking my hand. "I'll check with my wife and I'll call you. And don't worry about your documents. You'll have them tomorrow, you have my word as an SS officer."

I still had to see Oswald Pohl, the big boss of the WVHA. He received me, in his offices on Unter den Eichen, with expansive cordiality and chatted with me about Kiel, where he had spent many years in the Kriegsmarine. It was there, in the Kasino, that the Reichsführer had noticed and recruited him, in the summer of 1933. Pohl had begun by centralizing the administration and finances of the SS, then little by little had built up his network of companies. "Like any multinational, we're very diversified. We're in construction materials, wood, ceramics,

furniture, publishing, even mineral water."—"Mineral water?"—"Oh!
That's very important. It allows us to provide our Waffen-SS with
drinkable water throughout all the territories in the East." He said he
was particularly proud of one of his recent creations: Osti, the East Industries, a corporation set up in the district of Lublin in order to put the
remaining Jews to work for the SS. But despite his geniality, he quickly
grew vague as soon as I wanted to talk to him about the *Arbeitseinsatz*
in general; according to him, most of the effective measures were in
place, it was simply a matter of giving them time to take effect. I questioned him about the criteria of selection, but he referred me to the
functionaries in Oranienburg: "They know the details better. But I can
guarantee you that ever since the selection has been medicalized, it's going very well." He assured me that the Reichsführer was fully informed
of all these problems. "I don't doubt it, Obergruppenführer," I replied.
"But the Reichsführer has put me in charge of seeing what the points
of blockage are and what possible improvements there might be. The
fact of having been integrated into the WVHA, under your orders, has
entailed considerable modifications in our system of National Socialist
camps, and the measures that you ordered or encouraged, as well as
your choice of subordinates, have had a massively positive impact. The
Reichsführer, I think, simply wants now to obtain an overall picture.
Your suggestions for the future will count enormously, I don't doubt
that for an instant." Did Pohl feel threatened by my mission? After this
soothing little speech, he changed the subject; but a little later, he became animated again and even went out with me to introduce me to
some of his co-workers. He invited me to come back and see him when
I returned from my inspection (I was to leave for Poland soon, and also
to visit some camps in the Reich); he followed me into the hallway, putting his hand on my shoulder in a familiar way; outside, I turned around,
he was still waving his hand, smiling: "Bon voyage!"

Eichmann had kept his word: when I returned from Lichtenfelde at
the end of the afternoon, I found on my desk a large sealed envelope
marked GEHEIME REICHSSACHE! It contained a bundle of documents accompanied by a typed letter; there was also a handwritten note from
Eichmann inviting me to his place the next evening. Driven by Piontek,
I went to buy some flowers first—an uneven number, as I had learned
to do in Russia—and some chocolate. Then I had him drop me off at
the Kurfürstenstrasse. Eichmann had his apartment in a wing of his office building, intended too for single officers passing through. He
opened the door himself, dressed in civilian clothes: "*Ach!* Sturmbannführer Aue. I should have told you not to come in uniform. It's a very
simple soirée. But that's fine. Come in, come in." He introduced me to

his wife, Vera, a small Austrian with a discreet personality, but who blushed with pleasure and gave a charming smile when I handed her the flowers with a low bow. Eichmann had two of his children line up, Dieter, who must have been six, and Klaus. "Little Horst is already asleep," Frau Eichmann said.—"He's our latest one," her husband added. "He's not yet a year old. Come, I'll introduce you." He led me into the living room where there were already several men and women, standing or sitting on sofas. There were, if I remember correctly, Hauptsturmführer Novak, an Austrian of Croatian origin with firm, angular features, quite handsome but curiously arrogant; Boll, the violinist; and some others whose names I have unfortunately forgotten, all colleagues of Eichmann's, with their wives. "Günther will come by too, but just for a cup of tea. He rarely joins us."—"I see you cultivate the spirit of camaraderie in your section."—"Yes, yes. I like having friendly relations with my subordinates. What would you like to drink? A little schnapps? *Krieg ist Krieg* . . ." I laughed and he joined in with me: "You have a good memory, Obersturmbannführer." I took the glass and raised it: "This time, I drink to the health of your charming family." He clicked his heels and bowed his head: "Thank you." We conversed a little, then Eichmann led me to the sideboard to show me a photograph framed in black, showing a man, still young, in uniform. "Your brother?" I asked.—"Yes." He looked at me with his curious birdlike air, particularly accentuated in this light by his hooked nose and protruding ears. "I don't suppose you ran into him, over there?" He mentioned a division and I shook my head: "No. I arrived rather late, after the encirclement. And I didn't meet many people."—"Oh, I see. Helmut fell during one of the fall offensives. We don't know the exact circumstances, but we received an official notification."—"All that was a hard sacrifice," I said. He rubbed his lips: "Yes. Let's hope it wasn't in vain. But I believe in the Führer's genius."

Frau Eichmann served cakes and tea; Günther arrived, took a cup, and stationed himself in a corner to drink it, without talking with anyone. I secretly observed him while the others were talking. He was obviously a very proud man, jealous of his impenetrable, closed bearing, which he exhibited to his more talkative colleagues as a silent reproach. He was said to be the son of Hans F. K. Günther, the doyen of German racial anthropology, whose work had an immense influence at that time; if this was true, the elder Günther could be proud of his offspring, who had gone from theory to practice. He slipped away, saying goodbye distantly after a scant half hour. We proceeded to the music: "Always before dinner," Eichmann said to me. "Afterward, we're too busy digesting to play well." Vera Eichmann picked up the viola and another officer

brought out a cello. They played two of the three Brahms string quar-
tets, pleasant, but of little interest, in my opinion; the execution was adequate, without any great surprises: only the cellist had any special
talent. Eichmann played calmly, methodically, his eyes riveted to the
score; he didn't make any mistakes, but didn't seem to understand that
that wasn't enough. I remembered then his comment two days before:
"Boll plays better than I, and Heydrich played even better." Maybe after all he understood this, and accepted his limits, taking pleasure in the
little he could manage.

I applauded vigorously; Frau Eichmann seemed especially flattered.
"I'll go put the children to bed," she said. "Then we'll have dinner." We
had another drink while we waited: the women spoke about rationing
or rumors, the men about the latest news, which wasn't very interesting, since the front remained stable and nothing had happened since the
fall of Tunis. The atmosphere was informal, *gemütlich* in the Austrian
style, an exaggerated offhandedness. Then Eichmann had us pass into
the dining room. He himself assigned the seats, placing me at his right,
at the head of the table. He uncorked some bottles of Rhine wine, and
Vera Eichmann brought in a roast with a bay leaf sauce and some green
beans. This was a change for me from Frau Gutknecht's inedible cooking and even from the usual canteen at the SS-Haus. "Delicious," I
complimented Frau Eichmann. "You are an outstanding cook."—"Oh,
I am lucky. Dolfi often manages to find scarce foods. The stores are almost empty." Inspired, I gave vent to a character sketch of my landlady,
beginning with her cooking and then going on to other peculiarities.
"Stalingrad?" I said, imitating her dialect and voice. "But what on earth
were you messing around there for? Aren't we fine as we are, here? And
also where is it, exactly?" Eichmann laughed and choked on his wine. I
went on: "One day, in the morning, I went out at the same time as she
did. We see someone wearing the star, probably a privileged *Mischling*.
She exclaims: *Oh! Look, Herr Offizier, a Jew! You haven't gassed that one
yet?*" Everyone laughed; Eichmann was laughing so hard he cried, and
hid his face in his napkin. Only Frau Eichmann kept a straight face:
when I noticed, I interrupted myself. She seemed to want to ask a question, but held back. To regain my composure, I poured Eichmann some
wine: "Go on, drink." He laughed again. The conversation shifted
again, and I ate; one of the guests told a joke about Göring. Eichmann
looked serious and turned to me: "Sturmbannführer Aue, you're a cultivated man. I would like to ask you a question, a serious question." I
gestured with my fork for him to continue. "You have read Kant, I
imagine? Right now," he went on, rubbing his lips, "I'm reading his
Critique of Practical Reason. Of course, a man like me, without any uni-

versity education I mean, can't understand everything. But still one can understand some things. And I've thought a lot about the question of the Kantian Categorical Imperative, especially. You agree with me, I'm sure, in saying that every honest man must live according to this imperative." I drank a mouthful of wine and agreed. Eichmann continued: "The Imperative, as I understand it, says: The principle of my individual will must always be such that it can become the principle of moral law. By acting, man legislates." I wiped my mouth: "I think I see where you're heading. You're wondering if our work is in agreement with the Kantian Imperative."—"That's not quite it. But one of my friends, who is also interested in these kinds of questions, maintains that in wartime, by virtue if you like of the state of exception caused by danger, the Kantian Imperative is suspended, since of course what one wants to do to the enemy, one doesn't want the enemy to do to us, and so what one does cannot become the basis for a general law. That's his opinion, you see. I sense that he's wrong, though, and that in fact it is by our fidelity to duty, in a way, by our obedience to superior orders . . . that precisely we have to bend our will on following orders better. To live them in a positive way. But I haven't yet found the irrefutable argument to prove that he's wrong."—"But it's quite simple, I think. We all agree that in a National Socialist State the ultimate foundation of positive law is the will of the Führer. That's the well-known principle *Führerworte haben Gesetzeskraft*. Of course, we realize that in practice the Führer cannot take care of every single thing, and so others must also act and legislate in his name. In principle, this idea should be extended to the entire *Volk*. Thus Dr. Frank, in his treatise on constitutional law, extended the definition of the *Führerprinzip* in the following way: *Act in such a way that the Führer, if he knew of your action, would approve of it*. There is no contradiction between that principle and Kant's Imperative."—"I see, I see. *Frei sein ist Knecht sein*, To be free is to be a vassal, as the old German proverb says."—"Precisely. This principle is applicable to every member of the *Volksgemeinschaft*. You have to live out your National Socialism by living your own will as if it were the Führer's, and so, to use Kant's terms, as a foundation of the *Volksrecht*. Whoever only obeys orders like an automaton, without examining them critically to penetrate their inner necessity, does not work closer to the Führer; most of the time, he distances himself from him. Of course, the very foundation of *völkisch* constitutional law is the *Volk*: it cannot be applied outside of the *Volk*. Your friend's mistake is to appeal to an entirely mythical supranational law, an aberrant invention of the French Revolution. All law must rest on a foundation. Historically, this has always been a fiction or an abstraction—God, the King, or the People. Our great advance has been to

base the legal concept of the Nation on something concrete and in-
alienable: the *Volk*, whose collective will is expressed by the Führer who
represents it. When you say *Frei sein ist Knecht sein*, you have to understand that the foremost vassal of all is precisely the Führer, since he is
nothing but pure service. We are not serving the Führer as such, but as
the representative of the *Volk*, we serve the *Volk* and must serve it as the
Führer serves it, with total abnegation. That's why, confronted with
painful tasks, we have to bow down, master our feelings, and carry them
out with firmness." Eichmann listened attentively, his neck stretched
out, his eyes staring behind his large glasses. "Yes, yes," he said warmly,
"I completely understand you. Our duty, our accomplishment of duty,
is the highest expression of our human freedom."—"Absolutely. If our
will is to serve our Führer and our *Volk*, then, by definition, we are also
bearers of the principle of the law of the *Volk*, as it is expressed by the
Führer or derived from his will."—"Excuse me," one of the guests interrupted, "but wasn't Kant anti-Semitic, in any case?"—"Indeed," I
replied. "But his anti-Semitism remained purely religious, dependent
on his belief in a life to come. Those are concepts that we have for the
most part moved beyond." Frau Eichmann, helped by one of the guests,
cleared the table. Eichmann served schnapps and lit a cigarette. For some
minutes ordinary talk resumed. I drank my schnapps and smoked too.
Frau Eichmann served coffee. Eichmann signed to me: "Come with me.
I want to show you something." I followed him into his bedroom. He
turned on the light, pointed me to a chair, pulled a key out of his
pocket, and, as I sat down, he opened a drawer of his desk and took out
a rather thick album bound in black pebble-grained leather. Eyes shining, he handed it to me and sat down on the bed. I leafed through it: it
was a series of reports, some of them on Bristol board, others on ordinary paper, and photographs, all bound into an album like the one I had
put together in Kiev after the *Grosse Aktion*. The title page, written in
calligraphic Fraktur, announced: WARSAW'S JEWISH QUARTER NO LONGER
EXISTS! "What is this?" I asked.—"Those are Brigadeführer Stroop's reports on the suppression of the Jewish uprising. He offered this album
to the Reichsführer, who gave it to me so I could study it." He was radiant with pride. "Look, look, it's astonishing." I examined the photos,
some were impressive: fortified bunkers, burned buildings, Jews jumping from rooftops to escape the flames; and the ruins of the neighborhood after the battle. The Waffen-SS and the auxiliary forces had had to
reduce the pockets of resistance with artillery, at point-blank range. "It
lasted almost a month," Eichmann whispered, biting a cuticle. "A
month! With more than six battalions. Look at the beginning, at the list
of losses." The first page listed sixteen dead, including a Polish police-

man. A long list of wounded followed. "What kind of weapons did they have?" I asked.—"Not much, fortunately. A few machine guns, some grenades and pistols, some Molotov cocktails."—"How did they get them?"—"Probably from the Polish partisans. They fought like wolves, did you see? Jews who had been starving for three years. The Waffen-SS was shocked." This was almost the same as Thomas's reaction, but Eichmann seemed more frightened than admiring. "Brigadeführer Stroop says even the women hid grenades under their skirts to blow themselves up with a German when they surrendered."—"That's understandable," I said. "They knew what was waiting for them. Was the district completely emptied?"—"Yes. All the Jews who were taken alive were sent to Treblinka. That's one of the centers led by Gruppenführer Globocnik."—"Without any selection."—"Of course! Much too dangerous. You know, once again, Obergruppenführer Heydrich was right. He compared it to a disease: it's always the final residue that's the most difficult to destroy. The weak, the old, die right away; in the end, only the young, the strong, the clever, remain. It's very worrisome, because it's the result of natural selection, the strongest biological pool: if they survive, in fifty years everything will start all over again. I've already explained to you that this uprising worried us a lot. If it happens again, it could be a catastrophe. No opportunity must be left. Imagine a similar revolt in a concentration camp! Unthinkable."—"But we need workers, as you know very well."—"Of course, I'm not the one who decides. I just wanted to stress the risks to you. The question of labor, I've already told you, isn't at all my field, and everyone has his own ideas. But still: as the Amtschef often says, *you can't plane a board without chips flying.* That's all I mean." I returned the album. "Thank you for showing me this, it was very interesting." We rejoined the others; the first guests were already taking their leave. Eichmann held me back for one last drink, then I excused myself, thanking Frau Eichmann and kissing her hand. In the front hallway, Eichmann gave me a friendly slap on the back: "Allow me, Sturmbannführer, you're a regular guy. Not one of those kid-gloved boys over at the SD. No, you're on the level." He must have had a little too much to drink, and it was making him sentimental. I thanked him and shook his hand, leaving him on his doorstep, hands in his pockets, smiling from one side of his mouth.

If I have described these meetings with Eichmann at such length, it's not because I remember them better than the others: but this little Obersturmbannführer, in the meantime, has become a kind of celebrity, and I thought that my memories, shedding light on his character, might interest the public. A lot of stupid things have been written about him: he was certainly not *the enemy of mankind* described at Nuremberg (since he wasn't there, it was easy to blame everything on him, especially since the judges didn't understand much about how our services functioned); nor was he an incarnation of *banal evil*, a soulless, faceless robot, as some sought to present him after his trial. He was a very talented bureaucrat, extremely competent at his functions, with a certain stature and a considerable sense of personal initiative, but solely within the framework of clearly circumscribed tasks: in a position of responsibility, where he would have had to make decisions, in the place of his Amtschef Müller, for example, he would have been lost; but as a middle manager, he would have been the pride of any European firm. I never perceived that he nourished a particular hatred of the Jews: he had simply built his career on them, they had become not just his specialty but, in a way, his stock in trade; later on, when they tried to take it away from him, he defended it jealously, which is understandable. But he could just as easily have done something else, and when he told his judges that he thought the extermination of the Jews was a mistake, we can believe him; many people, in the RSHA and especially in the SD, thought similarly—I've already shown this—but once the decision was made, it had to be seen through to the end, he was very aware of that; what's more, his career depended on it. Of course he wasn't the kind of person I liked to see frequently, his ability to think on his own was extremely limited, and when I returned to my place, that night, I wondered why I had been so expansive, why I had fallen so easily into that familial, sentimental atmosphere that is usually so repugnant to me. Maybe I too had some need to feel I belonged to something. His interest was clear; I was a potential ally in a higher sphere to which he would normally have had no access. But despite all his friendliness I knew that for him I remained an outsider to his department, and thus a potential threat to his domain. And I sensed that he would cunningly and stubbornly confront any obstacle to what he regarded as his objective, that he wasn't a man to let himself be easily checked. I understood his apprehensions, faced with the danger posed by concentrations of Jews: but for me this danger, if needed, could be minimized, one simply had to be aware of it and take the necessary measures. For the moment, I kept an open mind, I hadn't reached any conclusions, I reserved my judgment till my analysis was complete.

And the Kantian Imperative? To tell the truth, I didn't have much of an idea, I had told poor Eichmann pretty much whatever came into my head. In the Ukraine or in the Caucasus, questions of this kind still concerned me, difficulties distressed me and I discussed them seriously, with the feeling that they were a vital issue. But that feeling seemed to have gotten lost. Where, when did that happen? In Stalingrad? Or afterward? For a while I thought I had drowned, submerged by the things resurfaced from the depths of my past. And then, with the stupid, incomprehensible death of my mother, this anguish too had disappeared: the feeling that dominated me now was a vast indifference—not dull, but light and precise. Only my work engaged me; I felt I had been offered a stimulating challenge that would call on all my abilities, and I wanted to succeed—not for a promotion or for any ulterior ambitions, I had none, but simply to enjoy the satisfaction of a thing well done. It was in this state of mind that I left for Poland, accompanied by Piontek, leaving Fräulein Praxa in Berlin to see to my mail, my rent, and her nails. I had chosen a good time to begin my trip: my former superior in the Caucasus, Walter Bierkamp, was replacing Oberführer Schöngarth as BdS of the Generalgouvernement, and, having learned this from Brandt, I had gotten myself invited to the presentation ceremony. This took place in mid-June 1943, in Cracow, in the inner courtyard of the Wawel Castle, a magnificent building, even with its tall, thin columns hidden beneath banners. Hans Frank, the Generalgouverneur, gave a long speech from a platform set up in the rear of the courtyard, surrounded by dignitaries and by an honor guard. He looked a little ridiculous in his brown SA uniform with his tall stovepipe cap, the strap of which cut into his jowls. The crude frankness of the speech surprised me, I still remember, since there was a considerable audience there, not just representatives from the SP and the SD, but also from the Waffen-SS, civil servants in the GG, and officers from the Wehrmacht. Frank congratulated Schöngarth, who stood behind him, stiff and a head taller than Bierkamp, on his *successes in the implementation of difficult aspects of National Socialist ideology*. This speech has survived in the archives; here's an extract that gives a good idea of the tone: *In a state of war, where victory is at stake, where we are looking eternity in the face, this is an extremely difficult problem. How, it is often asked, can the need to cooperate with an alien culture be reconciled with the ideological aim of, say, wiping out the Polish* Volkstum? *How is the need to maintain industrial output compatible with the need, for example, to annihilate the Jews?* These were good questions, yet I found it surprising that they were so openly aired. A GG civil servant assured me later on that Frank always spoke this way, and that in any case in Poland the extermination of the Jews wasn't a secret for anyone. Frank, who must have been a handsome man before his face drowned in fat, spoke with a powerful but squeaky, almost hysterical voice; he kept rising on his toes, stretching his paunch over the podium, and waving his hand. Schöngarth, a man with a tall, square forehead, who spoke in a calm, somewhat pedantic voice, also gave a

speech, followed by Bierkamp, whose National Socialist proclamations
of faith I couldn't help myself from finding a little hypocritical (but I
probably found it hard to forgive the dirty trick he'd played on me).
When I came up to congratulate him during the reception, he acted
as if he were delighted to see me: "Sturmbannführer Aue! I heard you
behaved heroically, in Stalingrad. My congratulations! I never doubted
you." His smile, in his little otter face, looked like a grimace; but it was
entirely possible that he had in fact forgotten his last words in
Voroshilovsk, which were hardly compatible with my new situation.
He asked me some questions about my duties and assured me of the
complete cooperation of his departments, promising me a letter of
recommendation to his subordinates in Lublin, where I counted on beginning my inspection; he also told me, over a few drinks, how he had
brought Group D back through Byelorussia, where, renamed Kampfgruppe Bierkamp, it had been assigned to the anti-partisan fight, especially north of the Pripet Marshes, taking part in the major cleansing
operations, like the one code-named "Cottbus" that had just ended at
the time of his transfer to Poland. About Korsemann, he whispered to
me in a confidential tone that he had acted poorly and was on the point
of losing his position; there was talk of putting him on trial for cowardice in the face of the enemy, he would at the very least be stripped
of his rank and sent to redeem himself at the front. "He should have
followed the example of a man like you. But his indulgence toward
the Wehrmacht has cost him dearly." These words made me smile: for
a man like Bierkamp, obviously, success was everything. He himself
hadn't done too badly; BdS was an important position, especially in
the Generalgouvernement. I didn't mention the past, either. What
counted was the present, and if Bierkamp could help me, so much the
better.

I spent a few days in Cracow, to go to meetings and also to enjoy this
beautiful city a little. I visited the old Jewish quarter, the Kasimierz, now
occupied by haggard, sickly, and unkempt Poles, displaced by the Germanization of the Incorporated Territories. The synagogues hadn't been
destroyed: Frank, they said, wanted some material traces of Polish Judaism to survive, for the edification of future generations. Some served
as warehouses, others remained closed; I had the two oldest ones
opened for me, around the long Szeroka Square. The so-called Old
Synagogue, which dated back to the fifteenth century, with its long
crenellated-roof annex added for women in the sixteenth or early seventeenth century, served the Wehrmacht to store food supplies and
spare parts; the brick façade, many times remodeled, the blocked windows, white limestone arches, and somewhat randomly set sandstone

blocks had an almost Venetian charm, and owed much to the Italian architects working in Poland and Galicia. The Remuh Synagogue, at the other end of the square, was a small, narrow, sooty building of no architectural interest. But of the large Jewish cemetery surrounding it, which would certainly have been worth the trouble of visiting, nothing more remained but a vacant, desolate lot; the old gravestones had been taken away as construction material. The young officer from the Gestapostelle who accompanied me knew the history of Polish Judaism very well, and showed me where the grave of Rabbi Moses Isserles, a famous Talmudist, had been. "As soon as Prince Mieszko began to impose the Catholic faith on Poland, in the tenth century," he explained, "the Jews appeared to sell salt, wheat, furs, wine. Since they made the kings richer, they obtained franchise after franchise. The people, at that time, were still pagan, healthy and unspoiled, apart from a few Orthodox Christians to the East. So the Jews helped Catholicism implant itself on Polish soil, and in exchange, Catholicism protected the Jews. Long after the conversion of the people, the Jews kept this position of agents of the powerful, helping the *pan* bleed the peasants by every means possible, serving them as bailiffs, usurers, holding all commerce firmly in their hands. Hence the persistence and strength of Polish anti-Semitism: for the Polish people, the Jew has always been an exploiter, and even if the Poles hate us profoundly, they still approve of our solution to the Jewish problem from the bottom of their hearts. That's also true for the supporters of the Armia Krajowa, who are all Catholics and bigots, even if it's a little less true for the Communist partisans, who are forced, sometimes against their will, to follow the Moscow Party line."—"But the AK sold weapons to the Jews in Warsaw."—"Their worst weapons, in ridiculous quantities, at exorbitant prices. According to our information, they agreed to sell them only on direct orders from London, where the Jews are manipulating their so-called government in exile."—"And how many Jews are left now?"—"I don't know the exact number. But I can assure you that before the end of the year all the ghettos will be liquidated. Aside from our camps and a handful of partisans, there won't be any more Jews left in Poland. Then it will finally be time to look seriously into the Polish question. They too will have to submit to a major demographic diminution."—"Total?"—"I don't know about total. The economics departments are in the process of studying it and making calculations. But it will be sizeable: the overpopulation is far too important. Without that, this region can never prosper or flourish."

★   ★   ★

Poland will never be a beautiful country, but some of its landscapes have a melancholy charm. It took me about half a day to get from Cracow to Lublin. Along the road, large, gloomy potato fields, interspersed with irrigation canals, alternated with Scotch pine and birch woods, the ground bare, without undergrowth, dark and silent, seemingly sealed off from the beautiful June light. Piontek drove capably, at a steady speed. This taciturn family man was an excellent travel companion: he spoke only when addressed, and carried out his tasks calmly and methodically. Every morning, I found my boots polished and my uniform brushed and ironed; when I went out, the Opel was waiting, cleaned of any dust or mud from the day before. At meals, Piontek ate with gusto and drank little, and between meals, he never asked for anything. I had immediately given him our travel budget folder, and he kept the expenses meticulously up to date, noting down, with a pencil stub wetted between his lips, every pfennig spent. He spoke a rasping German, with a strong accent but correctly, and also got by in Polish. He had been born near Tarnowitz; in 1919, after the Partition, he and his family had found themselves Polish citizens, but had chosen to stay there, so as not to lose their plot of land; then his father had been killed in a riot, during the days of unrest before the war: Piontek assured me that it was an accident, and didn't blame his old Polish neighbors, most of them expelled or arrested during the reincorporation of that part of Upper Silesia. Having become a citizen of the Reich again, he had been mobilized and had ended up in the police, and from there, he didn't really know how, he had been assigned to the service of the *Persönlicher Stab* in Berlin. His wife, his two little girls, and his old mother still lived on their farm, and he didn't see them often, but sent them most of his salary; in return they sent him things to supplement the usual fare—a chicken, half a goose, enough to treat a few comrades. Once I had asked him if he missed his family: Especially the little girls, he had replied, he missed not seeing them grow up; but he didn't complain; he knew he was lucky, and that it was much better than freezing his ass off in Russia. "Begging your pardon, Sturmbannführer."

In Lublin, as in Cracow, I put up at the Deutsches Haus. The taproom, when we arrived, was already animated; I had called ahead, and my room was reserved; Piontek would sleep in a dormitory for enlisted men. I took my things up and asked for some hot water to wash with. Twenty minutes later there was a knock on my door, and a young Polish servant came in with two steaming buckets. I pointed to the bathroom, and she went in to put them down. Since she didn't come back out, I went in to see what she was doing: I found her half naked, undressed to the waist. Stunned, I looked at her red cheeks, her little breasts, tiny but charming; fists on her hips, she was staring at me with a bold smile. "What are you doing?" I asked severely.—"Me . . . wash . . . you," she answered in broken German. I picked up her blouse from the stool where she had put it and handed it to her: "Get dressed and leave." She obeyed with the same naturalness. That was the first time such a thing had happened to me: the Deutsches Häuser I knew were strictly run, but obviously this must have been a common practice here, and I didn't think for an instant that it was restricted to the bath. After the girl had gone, I got undressed, washed, and, having changed into a dress uniform (for long journeys, because of the dust, I wore a gray field uniform), I went downstairs. A noisy crowd was now filling the bar and the restaurant. I went out into the backyard to smoke and found Piontek standing, cigarette dangling from his mouth, watching two teenagers wash our car. "Where did you find them?" I asked.—"Not me, Sturmbannführer. The Haus. The garage owner complains about it, actually— he says he could have Jews for free, but that the officers made scenes if a Jew touched their car. So he pays Poles like them, one reichsmark a day." (Even in Poland, that was a ridiculous amount. A night at the Deutsches Haus, although subsidized, with three meals, came to about 12 RM; a coffee in Cracow cost 1.50 RM.) I watched the young Poles wash the car with him. Then I invited him to have dinner with me. We had to clear our way through the throng to find a free spot at a table. The men were drinking, shouting as if for the pleasure of hearing their own voices. There were SS there, Orpos, men from the Wehrmacht and from the *Organisation Todt*; almost everyone was in uniform, including many women, probably typists or secretaries. Polish waitresses threaded their way with difficulty with trayfuls of beer and food. The meal was plentiful: sliced roast beef, beets, seasoned potatoes. As I ate I observed the crowd. A lot of people were just drinking. The waitresses were having trouble: the men, already drunk, groped the girls' breasts or buttocks as they went by, and since they had their hands full, they couldn't defend themselves. Near the long bar was a group in SS-Totenkopf uniforms, probably personnel from the Lublin camp, with two women among them, *Aufseherinnen*, I imagine. One of them, who was drinking brandy, had a masculine face and laughed a lot; she held a riding crop with which she tapped her tall boots. At one point, one of the waitresses was blocked near them: the *Aufseherin* held out her whip and slowly, to the laughter of her comrades, lifted the girl's skirt from behind, up to her buttocks. "You like that, Erich!" she exclaimed. "But her ass is filthy, like all Poles." The others laughed louder: she let the skirt fall and whipped the backside of the girl, who let out a cry and had to make an effort not to spill her glasses of beer. "Go on, move, sow!"

the *Aufseherin* shouted. "You stink." The other woman chuckled and rubbed shamelessly against one of the noncoms. In the back of the room, under an arch, some Orpos were playing billiards, shouting loudly; near them, I noticed the young servant who had brought me hot water; she was sitting on the lap of an OT engineer, who had his hand slipped under her blouse and was feeling her up while she laughed and stroked his balding forehead. "Well," I said to Piontek, "it's definitely lively here, in Lublin."—"Yeah. It's known for that." After the meal, I had a Cognac and a little Dutch cigar; the Haus had a full shelf at the bar; you could choose from many quality brands. Piontek had gone to bed. They had put music on, and couples were dancing; the second *Aufseherin*, obviously drunk, was holding her partner by the buttocks; an SS secretary was letting her neck be kissed by a Supply Corps Leutnant. This stifling, cloying, lewd, noise-filled atmosphere got on my nerves and ruined the pleasure I took from traveling, the joyful feeling of freedom I had felt during the day on the long, almost deserted roads. And it was impossible to escape this grating, sordid atmosphere; it followed you even into the john. The large room, though, was remarkably clean, tiled in white up to the ceiling, with thick oak doors, mirrors, fine porcelain sinks, and brass taps for running water; the stalls too were white and clean, they must have scrubbed the seatless Turkish-style toilets regularly. I undid my trousers and squatted down; when I had finished, I looked for paper, but there didn't seem to be any; then I felt something touch my backside; I jumped and turned around, trembling, already reaching for my service revolver, my underpants ridiculously lowered: a man's hand was stretched out through a hole in the wall and was waiting, palm up. A little fresh shit was already staining the tips of his fingers, where they had touched me. "Go away!" I screamed. "Go away!" Slowly, the hand withdrew from the hole. I burst into nervous laughter: it was vile, they had really gone mad, in Lublin. Fortunately I still had some squares of newspaper in my tunic, a good precaution when traveling. I quickly wiped myself and fled, without pulling the chain to flush. When I went back into the main room I had the impression that everyone would look at me, but no one was paying any attention, they were drinking and shrieking, with brutal or hysterical, crude laughter, like a medieval court. Shaken, I leaned on the bar and ordered another Cognac; as I drank, I looked at the fat Spiess from the KL, with the *Aufseherin*, and, repulsive thought, imagined him squatting down, having his ass wiped with delight by a Polish hand. I also wondered if the women's bathroom benefited from a similar arrangement: looking at them, I thought the answer was yes. I finished my Cognac in one gulp and went up to go to bed; I slept poorly, because of the noise, but still better than poor Piontek: some Orpos had brought Polish girls back to the dormitory, and spent the night fornicating in the beds next to his, without any qualms, trading girls and making fun of him because he didn't want one. "They pay them in canned food," he explained to me laconically over breakfast.

From Cracow, I had already phoned to make an appointment with Gruppenführer Globocnik, the SSPF of the Lublin district. Globocnik in fact had two offices: one for his SSPF staff, and another, on Pieradzky Street, from which the Einsatz Reinhard was run and where he had invited me to meet him. Globocnik was a powerful man, much more than his rank indicated; his superior in the hierarchy, the HSSPF of the Generalgouvernement (Obergruppenführer Krüger), had almost no right of supervision over the Einsatz, which covered all the Jews in the GG and thus extended quite a bit beyond Lublin; for that, Globocnik reported directly to the Reichsführer. He also held important functions within the Reichskommissariat for the Strengthening of Germandom. The HQ of the Einsatz was set up in a former medical school, a squat, yellow ocher building with a red pitched roof, characteristic of this region where German influence had always been strong, and where you entered through a wide double door under a half-moon archway, still surmounted by the inscription COLLEGIUM ANATOMICUM. An orderly welcomed me and led me to Globocnik. The Gruppenführer, buttoned into a uniform so tight it seemed a size too small for his imposing build, received my salute perfunctorily and waved a mission order in front of me: "So, just like that, the Reichsführer sends me a spy!" He let out a loud laugh. Odilo Globocnik was a Carinthian, born in Trieste, and was probably of Croat origin; an *Altkämpfer* from the Austrian NSDAP, he had briefly been Gauleiter in Vienna, after the Anschluss, before being sacked over some currency trafficking. He had served prison time under Dollfuss, for the murder of a Jewish jeweler: officially, that made him a martyr of the *Kampfzeit*, but malicious tongues argued that the Jew's diamonds had played a larger role in the affair than ideology. He was still waving my paper: "Admit it, Sturmbannführer! The Reichsführer doesn't trust me anymore, is that it?" Still standing at attention, I tried to justify myself: "Gruppenführer, my mission . . ." He let out another Homeric burst of laughter: "I'm joking, Sturmbannführer! I know better than anyone that I have the Reichsführer's full confidence. Doesn't he call me his *old Globus*? And not just the Reichsführer! The Führer in person has come to congratulate me on our great work. Have a seat. Those are his own words, *a great work*. 'Globocnik,' he said to me, 'you are one of the forgotten heroes of Germany. I would like every newspaper to be able to publish your name and your exploits! In a hundred years, when we can talk about all this, your great deeds will be taught to children right in elementary school! You are a valiant knight, and I admire the fact that you have been able to remain so modest, so discreet, having accomplished such things.' And I said—the Reichsführer was there too—'My Führer, I've only done my duty.' Have a seat, have a seat." I took the armchair he indicated; he flopped down next to me, slapping me on my thigh, then reached behind himself for a box of cigars and offered me one. When I refused, he insisted: "In that case, keep it for later." He lit one himself. His moonlike face beamed with satisfaction. On the hand that held the lighter, his thick, gold SS ring looked as if it were encrusted in a pudgy finger. He exhaled the smoke with a grimace of pleasure. "If I understand the Reichsführer's letter right, you're one of those bores who want to save the Jews under the pretext that we need labor?"—"Not at all, Gruppenführer," I replied courteously. "The Reichsführer gave me the order to analyze the problems of the *Arbeitseinsatz* as a whole, in view of future evolutions."—"I imagine you want to see our installations?"—"If you mean the gassing stations, Gruppenführer, that doesn't concern me. It's more the question of the selections, and the use of the *Arbeitsjuden* that preoccupies me. So I would like to begin with Osti and the DAW."—"Osti! Another of Pohl's grand ideas! We're gathering millions, here, for the Reich, millions, and Pohl wants me to look after secondhand clothes, like a Jew. Ostindustrie, give me a break! Another fine piece of crap they've inflicted on me."—"Perhaps, Gruppenführer, but . . ."—"No 'but'! The Jews are going to have to disappear in any case, all of them, industry or no industry. Of course, we can keep a few, long enough to train Poles to replace them. The Poles are dogs, but they can look after secondhand clothes, if that's useful for the *Heimat*. So long as it's profitable, I'm not against it. But you'll see that. I'll fix you up with my deputy, Sturmbannführer Höfle. He'll explain to you how it all works and you'll sort things out with him." He got up, the cigar wedged between two fingers, and shook my hand. "You can see anything you want, of course. If the Reichsführer sent you, that's because you know how to hold your tongue. Here I shoot blabbermouths. That happens every week. But for you, I'm not worried. If you have a problem, come see me. Goodbye."

Höfle, his deputy for the Einsatz Reinhard, was also an Austrian, but much more staid than his superior. He received me with a dispirited, weary air: "Not too shaken up? Don't worry about him, he's like that with everyone." He chewed his lip and pushed a piece of paper toward me: "I have to ask you to sign this." I skimmed over the text: it was a declaration of secrecy, in five points. "But it seems to me," I said, "that

I'm already compelled to secrecy by my very position."—"I know. But it's a rule imposed by the Gruppenführer. Everyone has to sign." I shrugged my shoulders: "If it makes him happy." I signed. Höfle put the paper away in a folder and crossed his hands on his desk. "Where do you want to start?"—"I don't know. Explain your system to me."—"It's quite simple, really. We have three installations: two on the Bug and one on the Galician border, in Belzec, which we're in the process of closing because Galicia, aside from the labor camps, is mostly *judenrein*. Treblinka, which mainly served Warsaw, is also going to be closed. But the Reichsführer has just given the order to transform Sobibor into a KL, which will be done toward the end of the year."—"And all the Jews pass through these three centers?"—"No. For logistical reasons, it wasn't possible or practical to evacuate all the little towns in the region. For that, the Gruppenführer received some Orpo battalions that dealt with those Jews on-site, little by little. I'm the one who directs the Einsatz on a day-to-day basis, together, with my inspector of the camps, Sturm-bannführer Wirth, who's been there since the beginning. We also have a training camp for Hiwis, mostly Ukrainians and Latvians, in Travniki."—"And aside from them, all your personnel are SS?"—"Actually, no. Out of about four hundred and fifty men, not counting the Hiwis, almost a hundred were assigned to us by the Führer's Chancellery. Almost all our camp commanders are from there. Tactically, they're under control of the Einsatz, but administratively, they depend on the Chancellery. They supervise everything having to do with salaries, leaves, promotions, and so on. Apparently it's a special agreement between the Reichsführer and Reichsleiter Bouhler. Some of those men aren't even members of the *Allgemeine-SS* or of the Party. But they're all veterans of the Reich's euthanasia centers; when most of those centers were closed, some of the personnel, with Wirth at their head, were transferred here so that the Einsatz could profit from their experience."—"I see. And Osti?"—"Osti is a recent creation, the result of a partnership between the Gruppenführer and the WVHA. Since the beginning of the Einsatz, we've had to set up centers to deal with the confiscated goods; little by little, they've expanded into various kinds of workshops, for the war effort. Ostindustrie is a limited liability corporation created last November to regroup and rationalize all those workshops. The board of directors named an administrator from the WVHA, Dr. Horn, to run it, along with the Gruppenführer. Horn is a rather nitpicking bureaucrat, but I suppose he's competent."—"And the KL?" Höfle waved his hand: "The KL has nothing to do with us. It's an ordinary WVHA camp; of course, the Gruppenführer is responsible for it as SS- und Polizeiführer, but it's completely separate from the Einsatz.

They also manage companies, especially a workshop of the DAW, but that's the responsibility of the SS economist attached to the SSPF. Of course, we cooperate closely; some of our Jews have been handed over to them, either to work, or for *Sonderbehandlung*; and not long ago, since we were overflowing, they set up their own installations for the 'special treatment.' Then you have all the armament enterprises of the Wehrmacht, which also use the Jews we've provided them; but that's the responsibility of the Armaments Inspectorate of the GG, headed by Generalleutnant Schindler, in Cracow. Finally, you have the civilian economic network, under the control of the new district governor, Gruppenführer Wendler. You might be able to see him, but be careful, he doesn't get along at all with Gruppenführer Globocnik."—"The local economy doesn't interest me; what concern me are the channels for assigning prisoners, in terms of the economy as a whole."—"I think I understand. Go see Horn, then. His head's a little in the clouds, but you can probably get something out of him."

I found this Horn to be nervous, agitated, overflowing with zeal but also with frustration. He was an accountant, educated at the Stuttgart polytechnic university; when the war started, he had been called up by the Waffen-SS, but instead of sending him to the front, they assigned him to the WVHA. Pohl had chosen him to set up Osti, a subsidiary of the German Economic Enterprises, the holding company created by the WVHA to consolidate the SS companies. He was strongly motivated, but faced with a man like Globocnik, he couldn't hold his own, and he knew it. "When I arrived, it was unimaginable . . . chaos," he told me. "There were all kinds of things: a basket factory and carpentry workshops in Radom, a brush factory here in Lublin, a glass factory. Already, right away, the Gruppenführer insisted on keeping a work camp for himself, for self-provisioning as he said. All right, in any case there was plenty to do. All this was managed any which way. The accounts weren't kept up to date. And production was close to zero. Which is completely understandable, given the state of the workforce. So I set to work: but then they did everything they could to complicate my existence. I train specialists; they take them away from me and they disappear God knows where. I ask for better food for the workers; they tell me there is no extra food for Jews. I ask them at least to stop beating them all the time; they give me to understand that I shouldn't interfere in what isn't my business. How is anyone supposed to work properly in such conditions?" I understood why Höfle didn't much like Horn: with complaints, one rarely succeeded at anything. But Horn had a good analysis of the dilemmas: "The problem too is that the WVHA doesn't support me. I sent report after report to Obergruppenführer Pohl. I keep asking him: What is the priority factor? The political-police factor? In that case, yes, the concentration of Jews is the main objective, and economic factors recede to the background. Or the economic factor? If that's it, production has to be rationalized, the camps have to be organized in a flexible manner so that a range of orders can be dealt with as they come in, and above all the workers have to be guaranteed a vital minimum subsistence. And Obergruppenführer Pohl answers: both. It's enough to make you tear your hair out."—"And you think that if they provided you with the means, you could create modern, profitable businesses with Jewish forced labor?"—"Of course. The Jews, it goes without saying, are inferior people, and their work methods are completely archaic. I studied the organization of labor in the Litzmannstadt ghetto; it's a catastrophe. All supervision, from the reception of the raw materials to the delivery of the finished product, is carried out by Jews. Of course there's no quality control. But with well-trained Aryan supervisors, and a rational, modern division and organization of labor, we could have very good results. A decision has to be made about this. Here, I encounter nothing but obstacles, and I know I have no support."

Obviously he was looking for some. He had me visit several of his enterprises, frankly showing me the state of undernourishment and poor hygiene of the prisoners placed in his charge, but also the improvements he had been able to introduce, the increase in quality of the products, which mainly served to supply the Wehrmacht, and the quantitative increase too. I had to acknowledge that his presentation was convincing: he did seem to have found a way here to reconcile the requirements of war with increased productivity. Horn, of course, was not informed of the Einsatz, at least not of its extent, and I took care not to speak of it to him; so it was difficult to explain to him the causes of the obstructions from Globocnik, who must have found it difficult to reconcile Horn's requests with what he regarded as his main mission. But at bottom Horn was right: by choosing the strongest or most specialized Jews, by concentrating them and adequately supervising them, one could certainly provide a considerable contribution to the war economy.

I visited the KL. It was spread out along a rolling hill just outside the city, west of the road to Zamosc. It was an immense establishment, with rows of long wooden barracks stretching all the way back inside barbed-wire fences, surrounded by watchtowers. The Kommandantur was outside the camp near the road, at the foot of the hill. I was received there by Florstedt, the Kommandant, a Sturmbannführer with an abnormally narrow, elongated face, who looked through my mission orders with obvious mistrust: "It is not stated that you have access to the camp."—"My orders give me access to all structures controlled by the WVHA.

If you don't believe me, get in touch with the Gruppenführer, he'll confirm it for you." He went on leafing through the papers. "What do you want to see?"—"Everything," I said with a friendly smile. Finally, he handed me over to an Untersturmführer. It was the first time I had visited a concentration camp, and I had everything shown to me. Among the inmates, or *Häftlinge*, there were all kinds of nationalities: Russians, Poles of course, as well as Jews, but also German political prisoners and criminals, Frenchmen, Dutchmen, and who knows what else. The barracks, long field stables of the Wehrmacht modified by SS architects, were dark, stinking, crowded; the inmates, most of them in rags, were piled up, three or four to a bunk, on several levels. I discussed the sanitary and hygienic problems with the head doctor: it was he, still with the Untersturmführer trailing behind, who showed me the Bath and Disinfection barrack, where on one side newcomers were given a shower, and on the other those unfit for work were gassed. "Up until spring," the Untersturmführer said, "it was only *dusting out*. But since the Einsatz transferred some of its load to us, we've been overflowing." The camp didn't know what to do with the corpses and had ordered a crematorium, equipped with five single-muffle furnaces designed by Kori, a specialized company in Berlin. "They're competing for the business with Topf und Söhne, of Erfurt," he added. "In Auschwitz, they work only with Topf, but we thought Kori's conditions were more competitive." The gassing, curiously, was not carried out with carbon monoxide, as in the vans we used in Russia or, according to what I had read, in the fixed installations of the Einsatz Reinhard; here, they used hydrocyanic acid, in the form of tablets that released the gas when in contact with air. "It's much more effective than carbon monoxide," the head doctor assured me. "It's quick, the patients suffer less, there are never any failures."—"Where does the product come from?"—"It's actually an industrial disinfectant, which they use for fumigation, against lice and other vermin. Apparently it was Auschwitz that had the idea to test it for the 'special treatment.' It works very well." I also inspected the kitchen and the supply warehouses; despite the assurances of the SS-Führers and even of the prisoner employees who distributed the soup, the rations looked insufficient to me, an impression that was confirmed for me in veiled terms by the head doctor. I came back several days running to study the files of the *Arbeitseinsatz*; each *Häftling* had his individual index card, filed with what was called the *Arbeitstatistik*, and was assigned, if he wasn't sick, to a work Kommando, some inside the camp, for maintenance, others outside; prisoners in the largest Kommandos lived at their worksite, like that of the DAW, the German Armament Works, in Lipowa. On paper, the system seemed solid; but the losses in manpower remained considerable; and Horn's criticisms helped me see that most of the prisoners employed—poorly fed, dirty, regularly beaten—were incapable of any consistent, productive work.

I spent several weeks in Lublin and also visited the region around it. I went to Himmlerstadt, formerly Zamosc, an excentric Renaissance gem built *ex nihilo* at the end of the sixteenth century by a rather megalomaniac Polish chancellor. The city had flourished thanks to its advantageous position on the commercial routes between Lublin and Lemberg and between Cracow and Kiev. It was now the heart of the most ambitious project of the RKF, the SS organization in charge, since 1939, of ensuring the repatriation of the *Volksdeutschen* from the USSR and the Banat, thus bringing about the Germanization of the East: the creation of a Germanic buffer region on the threshold of the Slavic regions, confronting eastern Galicia and Volhynia. I discussed the details of this with Globocnik's delegate, a bureaucrat from the RKF who had his headquarters in the town hall, a tall baroque tower by the side of the square, its entrance on the upper story reached by a majestic, crescent-moon-shaped double staircase. From November to March, he explained to me, more than a hundred thousand people had been expelled—the able-bodied Poles sent to German factories via the *Aktion Sauckel*, the others to Auschwitz, and all the Jews to Belzec. The RKF aimed to replace them with *Volksdeutschen*; but despite all the incentives and the natural wealth of the region, they were having trouble attracting enough settlers. When I asked him if our setbacks in the East discouraged them—this conversation took place in the beginning of July; the great battle of Kursk had just begun—this conscientious administrator looked at me with surprise and assured me that not even the *Volksdeutschen* were defeatist, and that, in any case, our brilliant offensive would soon reestablish the situation and bring Stalin to his knees. This optimistic man did, though, allow himself to talk about the local economy with some discouragement: despite the subsidies, the region was still far from self-sufficient, and depended entirely on money and food inputs from the RKF; most of the settlers, even the ones who had taken immediate possession of entire working farms, weren't managing to feed their families; and as for the ones who wanted to set up enterprises, it would take them years to stay afloat. After this visit, I was driven by Piontek south of Himmlerstadt: it was a beautiful region, made of gentle hills with meadows and copses, dotted with fruit trees; it already looked more Galician than Polish, with rich fields spread out beneath a light blue, unvarying sky, broken only here and there by little puffs of white clouds. Out of curiosity, I went on to Belzec, one of the last towns before the district's border. I stopped near the train station, where there was some bustle: cars and wagons moved up and down the main street, officers from various branches, as well as settlers in threadbare suits, were waiting for a train, farmers who looked more Romanian than German were selling apples on upturned crates by the side of the road. Beyond the track stood brick warehouses, a kind of small factory; and just behind, a few hundred meters farther on, thick black smoke rose up from a birch wood. I showed my papers to an SS noncom standing there and asked him where the camp was: he pointed to the wood. I got back into the car and traveled about three hundred meters on the main road alongside the railway toward Rawa Ruska and Lemberg; the camp stood on the other side of the tracks, surrounded by a forest of pine and birch. They had put tree branches in the barbed-wire fence, to hide the interior; but some of them had already been removed, and one could see through these gaps teams of prisoners, busy as ants, tearing down barracks and, in places, the fence itself; the smoke came from a hidden zone, a little higher up in the back of the camp; despite the lack of wind, a sweetish, nauseating smell made the air reek, and spread even into the car. After everything I had been told and shown, I had thought that the camps of the Einsatz were set up in uninhabited areas, difficult to access; but this one was right next to a little town swarming with German settlers and their families; the main railroad linking Galicia to the rest of the GG, on which civilians and soldiers traveled daily, passed right by the barbed wire, through the horrible smell and the smoke: and all these people, trading, traveling, scurrying in one direction or another, chatted, argued, wrote letters, spread rumors, told jokes.

But in any case, despite the interdictions, the promises of secrecy and Globocnik's threats, the men of the Einsatz remained talkative. You just had to wear an SS uniform and frequent the bar in the Deutsches Haus, occasionally buying someone a drink, to be quickly informed of everything. The obvious discouragement caused by the military news, clearly decipherable through the optimism radiating from the communiqués, contributed to loosening people's tongues. When they proclaimed that in Sicily *our courageous Italian allies, backed by our forces, are holding firm*, everyone understood that the enemy had not been driven back into the sea, and had finally opened a second front in Europe; as for Kursk, anxiety increased as the days passed, for the Wehrmacht, after its initial successes, remained obstinately, unusually silent: and when finally they began to mention *the planned implementation of elastic tactics* around Orel, even the most obtuse must have understood something was wrong. There were many who ruminated over these developments; and among the loudmouths who ranted every night, it was never hard to find a man drinking alone and in silence, and to engage him in conversation. That's how one day I began talking with a man in an Untersturmführer's uniform, leaning on the bar in front of a tankard of beer. Döll—that was his name—seemed flattered that a superior officer would treat him so familiarly; yet he must have been ten years older than me. He pointed to my "Order of the Frozen Meat" and asked me where I had spent that winter; when I answered Kharkov, he relaxed even further. "Me too, I was there, between Kharkov and Kursk. Special Operations."—"You weren't with the Einsatzgruppe, though?"—"No, it was something else. Actually, I'm not in the SS." He was one of those famous functionaries from the Führer's Chancellery. "Between us, we say T-four. That's how it's called."—"And what were you doing around Kharkov?"—"You know, I was in Sonnenstein, one of the centers for the sick there . . ." I motioned with my head to show I knew what he meant, and he went on. "In the summer of 'forty-one, they closed it. And some of us, we were considered specialists, they wanted to keep us, so they sent us to Russia. There was a whole delegation of us, it was Oberdienstleiter Brack himself who led us, there were the doctors from the hospital, everything, and we carried out special actions. With gas trucks. We each had a special notice in our pay book, a red piece of paper signed by the OKW, that forbade us from being sent too close to the front: they were afraid we'd fall into the hands of the Russians."—"I don't really understand. The special measures, in that region, all the SP measures, those were the responsibility of my Kommando. You say that you had gas trucks, but how could you be carrying out the same tasks as us without our knowing it?" His face took on a belligerent, almost cynical look: "We weren't carrying out the same tasks. The Jews or the Bolsheviks, over there, we didn't touch them."—"So?" He hesitated and drank some more, in long draughts, then wiped the foam from his lips with the back of his fingers. "We took care of the wounded."—"Russian wounded?"—"You don't understand. Our own wounded. The ones who were too messed up to have a useful life were sent to us." I understood and he smiled when he saw: he had produced his effect. I turned to the bar and ordered another round. "You're talking about German wounded," I finally said, softly. "As I told you. A real shit pile. Guys like me and you, who had given everything for the *Heimat*, and bang! That's how they were thanked. I can tell you, I was happy when they sent me here. It's not very cheerful here, either, but at least it's not that." Our drinks arrived. He told me about his youth: he had gone to a technical school; he wanted to be a farmer, but with the crisis he had joined the police: "My children were hungry, it was the only way to be sure I could put food on the table every day." At the end of 1939, he

had been assigned to Sonnenstein for the Euthanasia Einsatz. He didn't
know how he had been chosen. "On one hand, it wasn't very pleasant.
But on the other, it wasn't the front, and the pay was good, my wife was
happy. So I didn't say anything."—"And Sobibor?" He had already told
me that's where he worked now. He shrugged his shoulders: "Sobibor?
It's like everything, you get used to it." He made a strange gesture,
which made a strong impression on me: with the tip of his boot, he
scraped the floor, as if he were crushing something. "Little men and little women, it's all the same. It's like stepping on a cockroach."

There was a lot of talk, after the war, in trying to explain what had
happened, about inhumanity. But I am sorry, there is no such thing as
inhumanity. There is only humanity and more humanity: and that Döll
is a good example. What else was he, Döll, but a good family man who
wanted to feed his children, and who obeyed his government, even
though in his innermost being he didn't entirely agree? If he had been
born in France or America, he'd have been called a pillar of society and
a patriot; but he was born in Germany, and so he is a criminal. Necessity, as the Greeks knew already, is not only a blind goddess, but a cruel
one too. Not that there was any lack of criminals, at the time. All of
Lublin, as I've tried to show, was steeped in a sleazy atmosphere of corruption and excess; the Einsatz, but also colonization and exploitation of
that isolated region, made more than one person lose his head. Since my
friend Voss's remarks about this, I have thought about the difference between German colonialism, as it was practiced in the East during those
years, and the colonialism of the British and the French, in principle
more civilized. There are, as Voss stressed, objective facts: after the loss
of its colonies in 1919, Germany had to recall its cadres and close its
colonial administration offices; the training institutes remained open in
principle, but didn't attract anyone, because of the lack of prospects;
twenty years later, a whole specialized field of knowledge had been lost.
That being the case, National Socialism had given impetus to an entire
generation, full of new ideas and greedy for new experiences, which, as
regards colonization, were perhaps just as valid as the old ones. As for
the excesses—the aberrant outbursts like those you could see in the
Deutsches Haus or, more systematically, the seeming incapability of our
administrators to treat the colonized peoples, some of whom would
have been ready to serve us willingly if we had left the door open, other
than with violence and contempt—one shouldn't forget, either, that our
colonialism, even in Africa, was a young phenomenon, and that the
others, in the beginning, scarcely did any better: just consider the Belgian exterminations in the Congo, and their policy of systematic muti-

lation, or else the American policy, precursor of and model for our own, of the creation of living space through murder and forced displacement—America, we tend to forget, was anything but a "virgin territory," but the Americans succeeded where we failed, which makes all the difference. Even the British, so often cited as an example, and whom Voss so admired, needed the trauma of 1858 to begin to develop more sophisticated tools of control; and if, little by little, they learned to play a virtuoso game of carrot-and-stick, we shouldn't forget that the stick was far from neglected, as one can see from the Amritsar Massacre, the bombing of Kabul, and other examples, many and forgotten.

But now I've strayed from my first reflections. What I wanted to say is that if man is certainly not, as some poets and philosophers have made him out to be, naturally good, he is not naturally evil, either: good and evil are categories that can serve to qualify the effect of the actions of one man on another; but they are, in my opinion, fundamentally unsuitable, even unusable, to judge what goes on in the heart of that man. Döll killed people or had them killed, so he's Evil; but within himself, he was a good man to those close to him, indifferent to all others, and, what's more, one who respected the law. What more do we ask of the individual in our civilized, democratic cities? And how many philanthropists, throughout the world, made famous by their extravagant generosity are, on the contrary, monsters of egotism and harshness, greedy for public glory, full of vanity, tyrannical toward those close to them? Every man wants to satisfy his own needs and remains indifferent to the needs of others. And in order for men to be able to live together, avoiding the Hobbesian state of "all against all," and, on the contrary, to be able, thanks to mutual aid and the increased productivity that stems from it, to satisfy a greater portion of their desires, you need a regulatory authority, which prescribes limits to these desires and arbitrates conflicts: this mechanism is the Law. But it is also necessary for men, egotistical and weak, to accept the constraint of the Law, and so this Law must refer to an authority outside of man, must be founded on a power that man feels is superior to himself. As I had suggested to Eichmann during our dinner, this supreme and imaginary reference point was for a long time the idea of God; from that invisible, omnipotent God, it shifted to the physical presence of the king, sovereign by divine right; and when that king lost his head, sovereignty passed to the People or to the Nation, and was based on a fictive "contract," without any historical or biological foundation, and thus just as abstract as the idea of God. German National Socialism sought to anchor it in the *Volk*, a historical reality: the *Volk* is sovereign, and the Führer expresses or represents or embodies this sovereignty. From this sovereignty the Law is derived, and for most men, in all countries, morality is nothing but Law: in this sense, Kantian moral law, with which Eichmann was so preoccupied, stemming from reason and identical for all men, is a fiction like all laws (but perhaps a useful fiction). Biblical Law says, Thou shalt not kill, and doesn't brook any exception; but every Jew or Christian accepts that in wartime that law is suspended, that it is just to kill the enemy of one's people, that there is no sin in that; once the war is over and the weapons stored away, the old law resumes its peaceful course, as if the interruption had never taken place. So for a German, to be a good German means to obey the laws and thus the Führer: there can be no other morality, since there would be nothing to support it. (And it's not by chance that the rare opponents of our power were for the most part believers: they preserved another moral reference point, they could judge Good and Evil on another basis than the will of the Führer, and God served them as a fulcrum to betray their leader and their country: without God, that would have been impossible for them, since where could they have found a justification? What man alone, of his own free will, can come to a decision and say, This is good, that is evil? How outrageous that would be, and how chaotic too, if everyone dared to act that way: if every man lived according to his private Law, Kantian as it might be, we'd be back with Hobbes again.) So if you wish to judge German actions during this war as criminal, it's all of Germany you have to call to account, not just the Dölls. If Döll and not his neighbor ended up in Sobibor, that's chance, and Döll is no more responsible for Sobibor than his luckier neighbor; at the same time, his neighbor is just as responsible as he is for Sobibor, since both served the same country with integrity and devotion, the country that created Sobibor. When a soldier is sent to the front, he doesn't protest; not only is he risking his life, but he is forced to kill, even if he doesn't want to kill; his free will abdicates; if he remains at his post, he's a virtuous man, if he runs away, he's a deserter, a traitor. The man posted to a concentration camp, like the man assigned to an Einsatzkommando or a police battalion, most of the time doesn't reason any differently: he knows that his free will has nothing to do with it, and that chance alone makes him a killer rather than a hero, or a dead man. Otherwise, you would have to consider these things from a moral standpoint not Judeo-Christian (or secular and democratic, which amounts to exactly the same thing) but rather Greek: for the Greeks, chance played a part in the doings of men (chance, it should be said, often disguised as an intervention of the gods), but they did not consider that this chance diminished one's responsibility in any way. Crime has to do with the deed, not the will. When Oedipus kills his father, he doesn't know he is committing parricide; killing a stranger who has insulted you on the open road, for Greek conscience and law, is a legitimate action, there's no sin in it; but that man was Laius, and ignorance doesn't alter the crime in the least: and Oedipus himself recognizes this, and when he finally learns the truth, he chooses his own punishment, and inflicts it on himself. The link between will and crime is a Christian notion, which persists in modern law; the penal code, for example, regards involuntary or negligent homicide as a crime, but a lesser one than premeditated homicide; the same is true for the legal concept of diminished responsibility in case of insanity; and the nineteenth century ended by linking the notion of crime to that of the abnormal. For the Greeks, it doesn't matter whether Heracles kills his children in a fit of madness, or if Oedipus kills his father by accident: that changes nothing, it's a crime, they are guilty; you can pity them, but you can't absolve them—and that is true even if often their punishment is left to the gods, and not to men. From this perspective, the principle of the postwar trials, which tried men for their concrete actions, without taking chance into account, was just; but they went about it clumsily; tried by foreigners whose values they denied (while still acknowledging their rights as the victors), the Germans could feel they had been relieved of this burden, and were hence innocent: since the person who wasn't tried regarded the one who was as a victim of bad luck, he absolved him, and at the same time absolved himself; and the man rotting in a British jail, or a Russian gulag, did the same. But could it have been otherwise? How, for an ordinary man, can something be righteous one day and a crime the next? Men need to be guided, it's not their fault. These are complex questions and there are no simple answers. Who knows where the Law is? Everyone must look for it, but it's difficult, and it's normal to bow to the common consensus. Everybody can't be a legislator. It's no doubt my meeting with a judge that made me think about all that.

For those who didn't enjoy the binges at the Deutsches Haus, distractions were rare in Lublin. In my spare time, I visited the old town and the castle; at night, I had my meal served to me in my room and I read. I had left Best's *Festgabe* and the volume on ritual murder in Berlin, on my bookshelf, but I had brought along the collection by Maurice Blanchot that I had purchased in Paris, which I had started again at the beginning, and after days of difficult discussions, I took great pleasure in plunging into this other world, all made of light and thought. Minor incidents continued to eat away at my tranquility; in this Deutsches Haus, it didn't seem it could be otherwise. One night, somewhat agitated, too distracted to read, I had gone down to the bar for a schnapps and some talk (I knew most of the regulars now). Going back upstairs, it was dark, and I mistook the room; the door was open and I went in: on the bed, two men were copulating simultaneously with a girl, one lying on his back, the other kneeling, the girl, also kneeling, between them. I took a minute to understand what I was seeing, and when, as in a dream, things finally fell into place, I muttered an apology and tried to go out. But the kneeling man, naked except for a pair of boots, withdrew and stood up. Holding his erect penis in one hand and stroking it gently, he pointed, as if to invite me to take his place, to the girl's buttocks, where the anus, surrounded by a pink halo, gaped open like a sea anemone between two white globes. Of the other man I saw only his hairy legs, testicles and penis disappearing into the tufted vagina. The girl was moaning feebly. Without a word, smiling, I shook my head, and went out, gently closing the door. After that, I was even less inclined to leave my room. But when Höfle invited me to an outdoor reception Globocnik was giving for the birthday of the commanding officer of the district garrison, I unhesitatingly accepted. The party took place at the Julius Schreck Kaserne, the HQ of the SS: behind the mass of an old building a rather beautiful park spread out, with a very green lawn, tall trees at the rear, and flowerbeds at the sides; in the distance, you could see some houses, then countryside. Wooden tables had been set up on trestles, and the guests were drinking in clusters on the grass; in front of the trees, over some pits that had been dug for the purpose, a whole stag and two pigs were roasting on spits, supervised by a few enlisted men. The Spiess who had escorted me from the gate led me straight to Globocnik, who was standing with his guest of honor, Generalleutnant Moser, and some civilian officials. It was barely noon, Globocnik was drinking Cognac and smoking a fat cigar, his red face sweating over his buttoned collar. I clicked my heels in front of the group and saluted, and then Globocnik shook my hand and introduced me to the others; I congratulated the General on his birthday. "So, Sturmbannführer, your investigations are going forward? What have you found?"—"It's a little too early yet to draw conclusions, Gruppenführer. And also the problems are rather technical. What is definite is that in terms of exploitation of labor, we could conduct some improvements."—"We can always improve! In any case, a real National Socialist knows nothing but movement and progress. You should speak to the Generalleutnant here: he was complaining just now that we took some Jews away from the factories of the Wehrmacht. Explain to him that he just needs to replace them with Poles." The General interrupted: "My dear Gruppenführer, I wasn't complaining; I understand these measures as well as the next person. I was simply saying that the interests of the Wehrmacht should be taken into consideration. Many Poles have been sent to work in the Reich, and it takes time to train the remaining ones; by acting unilaterally, you are disturbing the war production." Globocnik let out a burst of crude laughter: "What you mean, my dear Generalleutnant, is that the Polacks are too stupid to learn how to work correctly, and that the Wehrmacht prefers Jews. That's true, the Jews are cleverer than the Poles. That's why they're more dangerous too." He stopped and turned to me: "But, Sturmbannführer, I don't want to detain you. The drinks are on the tables, help yourself, have fun!"—"Thank you, Gruppenführer." I saluted and headed to one of the tables, which was groaning beneath the bottles of wine, beer, schnapps, Cognac. I poured myself a glass of beer and looked around. More guests were flowing in, but I didn't recognize many people. There were some women, a few employees of the SSPF in uniform, but mostly officers' wives, in civilian clothes. Florstedt was talking with his camp colleagues; Höfle was smoking alone on a bench, elbows on the table, a bottle of beer open in front of him, with a pensive air, lost in the void. In the spring, I had recently learned, he had lost both his children, twins, carried off by diphtheria; at the Deutsches Haus, they said that at the funeral he had collapsed, raving, seeing divine punishment in his misfortune, and that since then he was no longer the same man (he would in fact commit suicide twenty years later, at the remand center in Vienna, without even waiting for the verdict of the Austrian court, certainly more clement than God's, though). I decided to leave him alone and joined the little group surrounding the Lublin KdS, Johannes Müller. I knew the KdO Kintrup by sight; Müller introduced me to his other interlocutor: "This is Sturmbannführer Dr. Morgen. Like you, he works directly under the Reichsführer's orders."—"Excellent. In what capacity?"—"Dr. Morgen is an SS judge, attached to the Kripo." Morgen continued the explanation: "For now, I head a special commission appointed by the Reichsführer to investigate the concentration camps. And you?" I explained my mission to him in a few words. "Ah, so you're also concerned with the camps," he commented. Kintrup had wandered off. Müller patted my shoulder: "Meine Herren, if you want to talk shop, I'll leave you. It's Sunday." I saluted him and turned to Morgen. He examined me with his keen, intelligent eyes, slightly veiled behind thin-rimmed glasses. "What exactly does your commission consist of?" I asked him.—"It's essentially an SS and police court 'for special tasks.' I have direct authority from the Reichsführer to investigate corruption in the KLs."—"That's very interesting. Are there a lot of problems?"—"That's an understatement. The corruption is massive." He signed with his head to someone behind me and smiled slightly: "If Sturmbannführer Florstedt sees you with me, your own work won't be made any easier."—"You're investigating Florstedt?"—"Among others."—"And he knows it?"—"Of course. It's an official investigation, I've already questioned him several times." He was holding a glass of white wine in his hand; he drank a little, and I drank too, emptying my glass. "What you're talking about interests me enormously," I continued. I explained my impressions to him about the gaps between the official dietary norms and what the prisoners actually received. He listened, nodding his head: "Yes, definitely, the food is looted too."—"By whom?"—"By everyone. From the lowest to the highest. The cooks, the kapos, the SS-Führers, the warehouse managers, and the top of the hierarchy too."—"If that's true, it's a scandal."—"Absolutely. The Reichsführer is very troubled by it personally. An SS-Mann should be an idealist: he cannot do his work and at the same time fornicate with the prisoners and fill up his pockets. But that happens."—"And are your investigations succeeding?"—"It's very difficult. These people stick together, and resistance is enormous."—"But if you have the Reichsführer's full support . . ."—"That's quite recent. This special court was created scarcely a month ago. My investigations have been going on for two years and I have encountered considerable obstacles. We began—at the time I was a member of the SS and Police Court Twelve, in Kassel—with KL Buchenwald, near Weimar. More precisely with the Kommandant of that camp, a certain Koch. The investigations were blocked: Obergruppenführer Pohl wrote a letter of congratulations then to Koch, where he said among other things that he would step in as a shield *whenever an unemployed lawyer should stretch out his hangman's hands again to grasp the white body of Koch.* I know this because Koch circulated this letter widely. But I didn't let him go. Koch was transferred here, to command the KL, and I followed him. I discovered a network of corruption that covered all the camps. Finally, last summer, Koch was suspended. But he had also had most of the witnesses assassinated, including a Hauptscharführer in Buchenwald, one of his accomplices. Here, he had all the Jewish witnesses killed; we opened an investigation into that too, but then all the Jews in the KL were executed; when we tried to react, they pleaded *superior orders* to us."—"But such orders exist, you must know that."—"I learned it then. And it's clear that in that case we have no jurisdiction. But, still, there is a distinction: if a member of the SS has a Jew killed in the context of superior orders, that's one thing; but if he has a Jew killed to cover his embezzlements, or for his own perverted pleasure, as also happens, that's another thing, that's a crime. Even if the Jew is to die anyway."—"I entirely agree with you. But the distinction must be hard to make."—"Legally, yes: you can have doubts, but to charge someone, you need evidence, and as I've told you, these men help each other out, they make witnesses disappear. Sometimes, of course, there's no ambiguity: for instance, I'm also investigating Koch's wife, a sexual deviant who had tattooed prisoners killed in order to remove their skin; she used the tanned skins for lampshades or other things like that. Once all the evidence is gathered, she'll be arrested, and I don't doubt she'll be condemned to death."—"And how did your investigations into Koch end?"—"They're still under way; when I've finished my work here and have all the evidence in hand, I plan on arresting him again. He too deserves the death penalty."—"So he was let go? I'm not following you very well."—"He was acquitted in February. But I wasn't in charge of the case anymore. I had problems with another man, not a camp officer but a Waffen-SS officer, a certain Dirlewanger. A raving lunatic, at the head of a unit of reprieved criminals and poachers. In 1941, I received information that he was conducting so-called scientific experiments, here in the GG, with his friends: he was killing girls with strychnine and watching them die while he smoked cigarettes. But when I wanted to prosecute him, he and his unit were transferred to Byelorussia. I can tell you that he benefits from protection at a very high level of the SS. Finally I was demoted, relieved of my functions, reduced to the rank of SS-Sturmmann, and sent to a field battalion, then to the SS-'Wiking,' in Russia. It was during that time that the proceedings against Koch collapsed. But in May the Reichsführer had me recalled, appointed me Sturmbannführer of the Reserve, and assigned me to the Kripo. After another complaint from the authorities in the district of Lublin, about thefts of property belonging to prisoners, he ordered me to form this commission." I nodded admiringly: "You're not afraid of trouble." Morgen laughed dryly: "Not really. Already, before the war, when I was a judge in the *Landgericht* in Stettin, I was demoted because I disagreed with a ruling. That's how I ended up in the *SS-Gericht*."—"Can I ask you where you studied?"—"Oh, I moved around a lot. I studied in Frankfurt, Berlin, and Kiel, then also in Rome and in The Hague."—"Kiel! At the Institute for World Economics? I did some of my studies there too. With Professor Jessen."—"I know him well. I studied international law with Professor Ritterbusch." We chatted for a while, exchanging memories of Kiel; Morgen, I discovered, spoke very good French, and four other languages besides. I returned to the initial subject: "Why did you begin with Lublin?"—"First of all to corner Koch. I'm almost there. And also the complaint about theft in the district gave me a good pretext. But all kinds of bizarre things go on here. Before I came, I received a report from the KdS on a Jewish wedding in a work camp. There were more than a thousand guests."—"I don't under-

stand."—"A Jew, an important kapo, got married in this *Judenlager*.
There were astronomical quantities of food and alcohol. SS guards took
part. Clearly, there must have been criminal infractions there."—
"Where did that take place?"—"I don't know. When I arrived in
Lublin, I asked Müller; he was very vague. He sent me to the camp of
the DAW, but there they didn't know anything. Then they advised me
to go see Wirth, a Kriminalkommissar, you know who he is? And Wirth
told me it was true, and that it was his method for the extermination of
the Jews: he gave privileges to some, who helped him kill the others;
then he killed them too. I wanted to learn more, but the Gruppenführer
forbade me from going into the camps of the Einsatz, and the Reichsführer confirmed this prohibition."—"So you have no jurisdiction over
the Einsatz?"—"Not on the question of extermination, no. But no one
forbade me from looking into what's happening with the confiscated
property. The Einsatz is generating colossal sums, in gold, currency, and
goods. All that belongs to the Reich. I've already gone to see the warehouses here, on Chopin Street, and I count on investigating further."—
"Everything you say," I said warmly, "is hugely interesting to me. I hope
we can discuss it more in detail. In a certain sense, our missions are complementary."—"Yes, I see what you mean: the Reichsführer wants to
put his house in order. And maybe, since they don't mistrust you as
much, you'll be able to dig up some things that are kept hidden from
me. We'll see each other again."

For some minutes, Globocnik had been calling the guests to sit down
to lunch. I found myself opposite Kurt Claasen, a colleague of Höfle's,
and next to a very talkative SS secretary. She immediately wanted to tell
me about her tribulations, but fortunately Globocnik began a speech in
honor of General Moser, which forced her to wait. He ended quickly
and everyone there got up to drink to Moser's health; then the General
said a few words of thanks. The food was brought over: the roasted animals had been expertly carved, the pieces piled on wooden trays spread
out on the tables, everyone could serve himself as he pleased. There
were also salads and fresh vegetables, it was delicious. The girl nibbled
on a carrot and straight away wanted to go on with her story: I listened
to her with half an ear while I ate. She talked about her fiancé, a
Hauptscharführer stationed in Galicia, in Drohobycz. It was a tragic
story: she had broken off her engagement to a Viennese soldier for him,
and as for him, he was married, but to a woman who didn't love him.
"He wanted to get a divorce, but I did a stupid thing, I saw that soldier
I broke up with again, he's the one who asked to see me but I said yes,
and Lexi"—the fiancé—"knew it, and it discouraged him because he
wasn't sure about my love anymore and he went back to Galicia. But

fortunately he still loves me."—"And what is he doing, in Drohobycz?"—
"He's in the SP, he's playing general with the Jews on the Durchgangstrasse."—"I see. And you see each other often?"—"When we have
leave. He wants me to come live with him, but I don't know. Apparently it's very dirty there. But he says I won't have to see his Jews, he
can find a good house. But if we're not married, I don't know, he'd have
to get a divorce. What do you think?" My mouth was full of venison
and I merely shrugged. Then I talked a little with Claasen. Around the
end of the meal an orchestra appeared, set up on the steps that led to the
garden, and began a waltz. Several couples got up to dance on the lawn.
The young secretary, disappointed no doubt by my lack of interest in
her sentimental misfortunes, went to dance with Claasen. At another
table I noticed Horn, who had arrived late, and got up to exchange a
few words with him. One day, noticing my leatherette satchel, he had
offered, as a way of showing me the quality of his Jews' work, to have
one made for me in leather; I had just received it, a beautiful morocco
portfolio with a brass zipper. I thanked him warmly, but insisted also on
paying for the leather and the labor, in order to avoid any misunderstanding. "No problem," Horn agreed. "We'll send you a bill." Morgen
seemed to have disappeared. I drank another beer, smoked, watched the
dancers. It was warm out, and with the heavy meats and the alcohol I
was sweating in my uniform. I looked around: many people had unfastened or even unbuttoned their tunics; I opened the collar on mine.
Globocnik didn't miss one dance, each time inviting one of the women
in civilian dress or a secretary; my lunch companion also ended up in
his arms. But not many people had his spirit: after several waltzes and
other dances, they had the orchestra change its music, and a choir of
Wehrmacht and SS officers gathered to sing "Drei Lilien, kommt ein
Reiter, bringt die Lilien" and other songs. Claasen had joined me with
a glass of Cognac; he was in shirtsleeves, his face red and swollen; he was
laughing mechanically and while the orchestra played "Es geht alles
vorüber" he intoned a cynical variation:

> *Es geht alles vorüber*
> *Es geht alles vorbei*
> *Zwei Jahre in Russland*
> *Und nix ponimai.*

"If the Gruppenführer hears you, Kurt, you'll end up a Sturmmann
in Orel and no more *nix ponimai*." Wippern, another department head
in the Einsatz, had come over and was scolding Claasen. "Listen, we're
going swimming, are you coming?" Claasen looked at me: "Will you

come? There's a pool in the back of the park." I took another beer from an ice bucket and followed them through the trees: in front of us, I heard laughter, splashing. On the left, barbed wire ran behind the pines: "What's that?" I asked Claasen. "A little camp of *Arbeitsjuden*. The Gruppenführer keeps them there for maintenance work, the garden, the vehicles, things like that." The pool was separated from the camp by a narrow rise; several people, including two women in bathing suits, were swimming or sunbathing on the grass. Claasen stripped down to his boxer shorts and dove in. "Are you coming?" he shouted as he resurfaced. I drank a little more, then, folding my uniform next to my boots, got undressed and went into the water. It was cool, somewhat the color of tea; I did a few laps and then stayed in the middle, floating on my back and contemplating the sky and the trembling treetops. Behind me, I heard the two girls chatting, sitting by the edge of the pool, paddling their feet in the water. A quarrel broke out: some officers had pushed Wippern, who didn't want to get undressed, into the water; he was swearing and raging as he extracted himself from the pool in his soaking uniform. While I watched the others laughing, maintaining my position in the middle of the pool with little hand movements, two helmeted Orpos appeared behind the rise, rifles on their shoulders, pushing in front of them two very thin men in striped uniforms. Claasen, standing by the edge of the pool, still dripping in his boxer shorts, called out: "Franz! What the hell are you up to?" The two Orpos saluted; the prisoners, who were walking with their eyes to the ground, caps in hand, stopped. "These Yids were caught stealing potato peelings, Sturmbannführer," explained one of the Orpos in a thick *Volksdeutschen* dialect. "Our Scharführer told us to shoot them." Claasen's face darkened: "Well, you're not going to do that here, I hope. The Gruppenführer has guests."—"No, no, Sturmbannführer, we'll go farther away, to the trench over there." A vivid anguish seized me without any warning: the Orpos were going to shoot the Jews right here and throw them into the pool, and we would swim in the blood, between the bodies bobbing on their stomachs. I looked at the Jews; one of them, who must have been about forty, was furtively examining the girls; the other, younger, his skin yellowish, kept his eyes riveted to the ground. Far from being reassured by the Orpo's last words, I felt an intense tension, my distress only increased. When the Orpos started moving again I remained in the middle of the pool, forcing myself to breathe deeply and to float. But the water now weighed on me like a wet woollen cloak, suffocating me. This strange state lasted until I heard the two gunshots, a little farther away, scarcely audible, like the *pop! pop!* of Champagne bottles being opened. Slowly, my anguish ebbed away and then disappeared altogether when I saw the Orpos return, still walking with their heavy, steady steps. They saluted us again as they went by and continued on to the camp. Claasen was talking with one of the girls, Wippern was trying to dry out his uniform. I let myself go and floated.

I saw Morgen again. He was on the verge of indicting Koch and his wife, as well as several other officers and noncoms in Buchenwald and Lublin; under seal of secrecy, he told me that Florstedt too would be charged. He showed me in detail the tricks used by these corrupt men to hide their embezzlements, and the means he used to catch them in the act. He compared the records of the *Abteilungen* of the camp: even when the culprits forged something, they didn't go to the trouble of reconciling their forgeries with the documents and reports from other departments. Thus, in Buchenwald, he had gathered his first serious evidence of the murders committed by Koch when he had noticed that the same inmate was registered at the same time in two different places: at a given date, the prison register of the *Politische Abteilung* bore, next to the name of the inmate, the comment "Released, noon," while the register of the Revier indicated: "Patient deceased at 9:15." The inmate had in fact been killed at the Gestapo prison, but his killers had tried to make it look as if he had died of illness. Similarly, Morgen explained to me how one could compare the different administration or Revier records with those of the blocks to try to find evidence of diversions of food, medicine, or property. He was quite interested in the fact that I planned on going to Auschwitz: several leads he was following up on seemed to lead to that camp. "It's probably the richest Lager, because that's where most of the special transports of the RSHA go now. Just like here, with the Einsatz, they have immense warehouses to sort and package all the confiscated goods. I suspect that must give rise to colossal misappropriations and thefts. We were alerted by a package sent from the KL by military post: because of its unusual weight, it was opened; inside, they found three chunks of dental gold, big as fists, sent by a camp nurse to his wife. I calculated that such a quantity of gold represents more than a hundred thousand dead." I let out an exclamation. "And imagine!" he went on. "That's what a single man could divert. When we've finished here, I'll go set up a commission in Auschwitz."

I myself had almost finished with Lublin. I made a brief round to say goodbye. I went to settle with Horn, for the portfolio, and found him just as depressed and agitated, struggling with his management difficulties, his financial losses, his contradictory instructions. Globocnik received me much more calmly than the first time: we had a brief but serious discussion about the work camps, which Globocnik wanted to develop further: it was just a matter, he explained to me, of liquidating the last ghettos, so that not a single Jew would remain in the General-gouvernement outside of the camps under SS control; that, he asserted, was the Reichsführer's inflexible desire. In all of the GG, 130,000 Jews remained, mostly in Lublin, Radom, and Galicia, with Warsaw and Cracow being entirely *judenrein*, apart from a handful of clandestines. That was still a lot. But the problems would be solved with determination.

I had thought of going to Galicia to inspect a work camp, such as the one run by the unfortunate Lexi; but my time was limited, I had to make choices, and I knew that aside from minor differences due to local conditions or personalities, the problems would be the same. I wanted to concentrate now on the camps in Upper Silesia, the "Ruhr of the East": the KL Auschwitz and its many annexes. From Lublin, the quickest way was to drive through Kielce and then the industrial region of Kattowitz, a flat, gloomy landscape dotted with pine or birch copses, and disfigured by the tall chimneys of factories and blast furnaces that, standing out against the sky, vomited bitter, sinister smoke. Thirty kilometers before Auschwitz, already, SS checkpoints carefully verified our papers. Then we reached the Vistula, broad and murky. In the distance we could see the white line of the Beskids, pale, shimmering in the summer mist, less spectacular than the Caucasus, but wreathed in a gentle beauty. Chimneys were smoking here too, on the plain, at the foot of the mountains: there was no wind and the smoke rose straight up before bending under its own weight, scarcely disturbing the sky. The road ended at the train station and the Haus der Waffen-SS, where we waited for our quarters. The lobby was almost empty; they showed me to a simple, clean room; I put away my things, washed, and changed my uniform, then went out to present myself at the Kommandantur. The road to the camp ran along the Sola, a tributary of the Vistula; half hidden by dense trees, greener than the broad river into which it ran, it flowed in peaceful twists and meanderings, at the foot of a steep, grassy bank; on the water, pretty ducks with green heads let themselves be carried along by the current, then took off with a tension of their whole bodies, necks stretched out, feet folded in, their wings projecting this mass upward, before lazily dropping down again a little farther on, near the shore. A checkpoint barred the entrance to the Kasernestrasse; beyond, behind a wooden watchtower, stood the long gray cement wall of the camp, topped with barbed wire, behind which the red roofs of the barracks were silhouetted. The Kommandantur occupied the first of three buildings between the street and the wall, a squat stucco building with an entrance reached by a flight of steps, flanked by wrought iron lamps. I was taken immediately to the camp's Kommandant, Obersturmbannführer Höss. This officer, after the war, acquired a certain notoriety because of the colossal number of people put to death under his command and also because of the frank, lucid memoirs he wrote in prison, during his trial. Yet he was an absolutely typical officer of the IKL, hardworking, stubborn, and of limited abilities, without any whims or imagination, but with just, in his movements and conversation, a little of the virility, already diluted by time, left by a youth rich in Freikorps brawls and cavalry charges. He welcomed me with a German salute and then shook my hand; he didn't smile, but didn't seem unhappy to see me. He wore leather riding breeches, which, on him, didn't seem an officer's affectation: he kept a stable in the camp and rode often; he could be found, they said in Oranienburg, much more often on horseback than behind his desk. While he spoke, he kept his surprisingly pale, vague eyes—I found them disconcerting, as if he were constantly on the point of grasping something that had just evaded him—fixed on my face. He had gotten a telex about me from the WVHA: "The camp is at your disposal." The camps, rather, for Höss managed an entire network of KLs: the *Stammlager*, the main camp behind the Kommandantur, but also Auschwitz II, a camp for war prisoners transformed into a concentration camp and situated a few kilometers past the station in the plain, near the old Polish village of Birkenau; a large work camp beyond the Sola and the town, created to serve the synthetic rubber factory of IG Farben in Dwory; and about a dozen scattered auxiliary camps, or *Nebenlager*, set up for agricultural projects or for mining or metallurgical enterprises. Höss, as he spoke, showed me all this on a large map pinned to his office wall: and with his finger he traced the camp's zone of interest, which covered the entire region between the Vistula and the Sola, more than a dozen kilometers to the south, except for some plots of land around the train station, which were controlled by the municipality. "About that," he explained, "we had a disagreement, last year. The town wanted to build a new neighborhood there, to house the railway workers, whereas we wanted to acquire part of that land in order to create a village for our married SS officers and their families. Finally nothing came of it. But the camp is constantly expanding."

Höss, when he took a car rather than a horse, liked to drive himself, and he came by to pick me up the next morning, at the door to the Haus. Piontek, seeing I wouldn't need him, had asked for a day off; he wanted to take the train to go see his family in Tarnowitz; I gave him the night off too. Höss suggested we begin with Auschwitz II: an RSHA convoy was arriving from France, and he wanted to show me the selection process. It took place on the ramp of the freight station, midway between the two camps, under the direction of a garrison doctor, Dr. Thilo. When we arrived, he was waiting at the head of the platform, with Waffen-SS guards and dogs and teams of inmates in striped uniforms, who when they saw us snatched their caps off their shaved heads. The weather was even finer than the previous day, the mountains in the south gleamed in the sun; the train, after passing through the Protektorat and through Slovakia, had arrived from that direction. While we waited, Höss explained the procedure to me. Then the train was brought up and the doors of the cattle cars were opened. I expected a chaotic outburst: despite the shouts and the barking of the dogs, things happened in a relatively orderly way. The newcomers, obviously disoriented and exhausted, poured out of the cars in the midst of an abominable stink of excrement; the *Häftlinge* of the work Kommando, shouting in a mixture of Polish, Yiddish, and German, made them abandon their luggage and line up in rows, the men to one side, the women and children to the other; and while these lines shuffled toward Thilo, and Thilo separated the men fit for work from the unfit, sending mothers to the same side as their children, toward trucks waiting a little farther away—"I know they could work," Höss had explained to me, "but trying to separate them from their kids would be exposing ourselves to all kinds of disorder."—I walked slowly between the rows. Most of the people were talking, in low voices, in French; others, no doubt naturalized Jews or foreigners, in various languages: I listened to the sentences I understood, the questions, the comments; these people had no idea where they were or what was awaiting them. The Kommando *Häftlinge*, obeying orders, reassured them: "Don't worry, you'll see each other afterward, they'll return your suitcases, tea and soup are waiting for you after the shower." The columns inched forward. A woman, seeing me, asked me, in bad German, pointing to her child: "Herr Offizier! Can we stay together?"—"Don't worry, Madame," I replied politely in French, "you won't be separated." Immediately questions rained down from all sides: "Are we going to work? Can families stay together? What will you do with the old people?" Before I could reply, a noncom had rushed forward, flogging people. "That's enough, Rottenführer!" I shouted. He looked sheepish: "It's just that we're not supposed to let them get excited, Sturmbannführer." Some people were bleeding, children were crying. The smell of filth that emanated from the cars and even from the clothes of the Jews was suffocating me, I felt the old, familiar nausea rise up again and I breathed deeply through my mouth to master it. In the cars, teams of inmates were hurling the abandoned suitcases down onto the ramp; the corpses of people who had died on the way were treated the same way. Some children were playing hide-and-seek: the Waffen-SS let them, but shouted if they got close to the train, for fear they'd slip under the cars. Behind Thilo and Höss, the first trucks were already setting off. I went toward them and watched Thilo at work: for some, a glance was enough; for others, he asked a few questions, made them unbutton their shirts. "In Birkenau, you'll see," Höss commented, "we have just two ridiculous delousing stations. On full days, that considerably limits the capacity for admission. But for a single convoy, it's enough."—"What do you do if there are several?"—"That depends. We can send some to the admission center in the *Stammlager*. Otherwise, we have to reduce the quota. We plan on building a new central sauna to remedy this problem. The plans are ready, I'm just waiting for the approval of Amtsgruppe C for the budget. But we constantly have financial problems. They want me to enlarge the camp, accept more inmates, select more, but they make a fuss when money is at stake. I often have to improvise." I frowned: "What do you mean, 'improvise'?" He looked at me with his drowned eyes: "All sorts of things. I make agreements with the companies we provide workers to: sometimes they pay me in kind, with construction materials or such things. I've even gotten trucks, like that. One company sent me some to transport its workers, but never asked me to return them. You have to know how to get by." The selection was coming to an end: the whole thing had lasted less than an hour. When the last trucks were loaded, Thilo quickly added up the numbers and showed them to us: out of 1,000 newcomers, he had kept 369 men and 191 women. "Fifty-five percent," he commented. "With the convoys from the West, we get good averages. But the Polish convoys are a disaster. It never goes beyond twenty-five percent, and sometimes, aside from two or three percent, there's really nothing to keep."—"What do you think is the reason for that?"—"Their condition on arrival is deplorable. The Jews in the GG have been living for years in ghettos, they're malnourished, they have all kinds of diseases. Even among the ones we select, we try to be careful, a lot of them die in quarantine." I turned to Höss: "Do you get many convoys from the West?"—"From France, this one was the fifty-seventh. We've had twenty from Belgium. From Holland, I don't remember. But these last few months especially we've had convoys from Greece. They're not very good. Come, I'll show you the process for reception." I saluted Thilo and got back into the car. Höss drove fast. On the way, he went on explaining his difficulties to me: "Ever since the Reichsführer decided to allocate Auschwitz for the destruction of the Jews, we've had nothing but problems. All last year, we were forced to work with improvised installations. A real mess. I was able to begin building permanent installations, with an adequate reception capacity, only in January of this year. But everything still isn't in perfect running order. There have been delays, especially in the transport of construction materials. And also, because of the haste, there have been manufacturing defects: the oven of Crematorium III cracked two weeks after it was put into service, it overheated. I had to close it down so it could be repaired. But we can't get worked up about it, we have to remain patient. We've been so overwhelmed that we've had to divert a large number of convoys to Gruppenführer Globocnik's camps, where of course no selection is carried out. Now it's much calmer, but it will start up again in ten days: the GG wants to empty its last ghettos." In front of us, at the end of the road, stretched a long red brick building, pierced at one end by an arch, and topped with a peaked guard tower; from its sides stretched out cement poles with barbed wire and a series of watchtowers, regularly spaced; and behind, as far as the eye could see, were lined rows of identical wooden barracks. The camp was immense. Groups of inmates in striped uniforms were walking down the lanes, tiny, insects in a colony. Beneath the tower, in front of the gate to the arch, Höss turned right. "The trucks keep going straight ahead. The Kremas and the delousing stations are in the back. But we'll go to the Kommandantur first." The car ran alongside the whitewashed poles and watchtowers; the barracks streamed past, and their perfect alignment made long brown perspectives unfurl, fleeting diagonals that opened up and then intersected with the next one. "Are the fences electrified?"— "Recently, yes. That was another problem, but we solved it." At the end of the camp, Höss was developing another sector. "It will be the *Häftlingskrankenbau*, an enormous hospital that will serve all the camps in the region." He had just stopped in front of the Kommandantur and pointed to a vast empty field, surrounded by barbed wire. "Do you mind waiting five minutes for me? I have to have a quick word with the Lagerführer." I got out of the car and smoked a cigarette. The building that Höss had just entered was also made of red brick, with a steep roof and a three-story tower in the center; beyond, a long road passed in front of the new sector and disappeared toward a birch wood, visible behind the barracks. There was very little noise; just, from time to time, a brief order or a harsh cry. A Waffen-SS on a bicycle came out of one of the sections of the central sector and headed toward me; when he reached me, he saluted without pausing and turned toward the entrance of the camp, pedaling calmly, without hurrying, alongside the barbed wire. The watchtowers were empty: during the day, the guards positioned themselves on a "large chain" around the two camps. I looked distractedly at Höss's dusty car: didn't he have anything better to do than to show a visitor around? A subaltern, as in the Lublin KL, could have done the job just as well. But Höss knew that my report would go to the Reichsführer; perhaps he was anxious to make me understand the extent of his accomplishments. When he reappeared, I threw away my cigarette butt and got in next to him; he took the road toward the birch trees, pointing out the "fields," or subcamps, of the central section as we went along: "We're in the process of reorganizing everything for the maximum deployment of labor. When it's done, this whole camp will serve only to supply workers to the industries of the region and even of the Altreich. The only permanent inmates will be the ones who provide for the upkeep and management of the camp. All political inmates, especially the Poles, will stay in the *Stammlager*. Since February, I also have a family camp for the Gypsies."—"A family camp?"—"Yes. It's a directive from the Reichsführer. When he decided to deport the Gypsies from the Reich, he wanted them not to be selected, to remain together, in families, and not to work. But a lot of them are dying of illness. They have no resistance." We had reached a barrier. Beyond, a long line of trees and bushes hid a barbed-wire fence, isolating two buildings, long, identical, each one with two tall chimneys. Höss parked near the building on the right, in the middle of a sparse pine grove. In front, on a well-kept lawn, Jewish women and children were finishing undressing, supervised by guards and by inmates in striped uniforms. The clothes were piled up pretty much everywhere, properly sorted, with a piece of wood stamped with a number on each pile. One of the inmates shouted: "Go on, quick, quick, to the shower!" The last Jews entered the building; two mischievous kids were playing at switching the numbers on the piles; they ran away when a Waffen-SS raised his club. "It's like in Treblinka or Sobibor," Höss commented. "Until the last minute, we make them think they're going to be deloused. Most of the time, it happens very calmly." He began explaining the arrangements: "Over there, we have two other crematoriums, but much bigger: the gas chambers are underground and can accommodate up to two thousand people. Here the chambers are smaller and there are two per Krema: it's much more practical for small convoys."—"What is the maximum capacity?"—"In terms of gassing, practically unlimited; the major constraint is the capacity of the ovens. They were conceived especially for us by the Topf firm. These officially have a capacity of seven hundred and sixty-eight bodies per installation per twenty-four-hour period. But you can cram in up to a thousand or even fifteen hundred, if you have to." An ambulance with a red cross on it arrived and parked next to Höss's car; an SS doctor with a white smock over his uniform came over and saluted us. "This is Hauptsturmführer Dr. Mengele," Höss said. "He joined us two months ago. He's the head doctor of the Gypsy camp." I shook his hand. "Are you supervising, today?" Höss asked him. Mengele nodded. Höss turned to me: "Do you want to observe?"—"That's all right," I said. "I know what it's like."—"But it's much more efficient than Wirth's method."—"Yes, I know. They explained it to me in the Lublin KL. They adopted your method." Höss seemed displeased; I asked, to be polite: "How long does it take, in all?" Mengele replied with his melodious, suave voice: "The Sonderkommando opens the doors after half an hour. But we let some time pass so the gas can disperse. In principle, death occurs in less than ten minutes. Fifteen if it's damp out."

We had already moved on to the *Kanada*, where the confiscated goods were sorted and warehoused before being distributed, when the chimneys of the crematorium that we had just left began to smoke, spreading that same sweetish, hideous smell I had experienced in Belzec. Höss, noticing my discomfort, commented: "I've been used to this smell ever since I was a boy. It's the smell of cheap church candles. My father was very religious and took me to church often. He wanted me to be a priest. Since there wasn't enough money for wax, they made the candles from animal tallow, and they gave off the same smell. It's due to a chemical compound, but I've forgotten the name; it was Wirths, our head doctor, who explained it to me." He also insisted on showing me the other two crematoria, colossal structures, inactive at that time; the *Frauenlager*, or women's camp; and the sewage treatment station, built after repeated complaints from the district, which alleged that the camp was contaminating the Vistula and the surrounding aquifer. Then he took me to the *Stammlager*, which he also had me visit from top to bottom; finally he drove me to the other side of town to show me rapidly the Auschwitz III camp, where the inmates working for IG Farben lived: he introduced me to Max Faust, one of the factory engineers, with whom I agreed to return another day. I won't describe all these installations: they are very well known and are described in many other books, I have nothing to add. Back at the camp, Höss sought to invite me horseback riding; but I could barely stand up and wanted a bath more than anything, and I managed to convince him to drop me off at my quarters.

Höss had assigned me an empty office in the *Stammlager* Kommandantur. I had a view of the Sola and of a pretty square house surrounded by trees on the other side of the Kasernestrasse, which was in fact the home of the Kommandant and his family. The Haus where I was staying turned out to be much quieter than the one in Lublin: the men who slept there were sober professionals, passing through for various reasons; at night, the camp officers came to drink and play billiards, but always behaved correctly. We ate very well there, copious helpings washed down with Bulgarian wine, with Croatian slivovitz as an after-dinner drink, and sometimes even vanilla ice cream. My main interlocutor, aside from Höss, was the chief physician of the garrison, Sturmbann-führer Dr. Eduard Wirths. He had his offices in the SS hospital in the *Stammlager* at the end of the Kasernestrasse, opposite the premises of the *Politische Abteilung* and a crematorium due to go out of service any day now. Alert, intelligent, with fine features, pale eyes, and sparse hair, Wirths seemed exhausted by his tasks, but motivated to overcome all difficulties. His obsession was the struggle against typhus: the camp was already going through its second epidemic of the year, which had dec-imated the Gypsy camp and also struck, sometimes fatally, SS guards and their families. I spent long hours in discussion with him. He reported, in Oranienburg, to Dr. Lolling, and complained about the lack of sup-port; when I let on that I shared his opinion, he opened up to me and confessed his inability to work constructively with a man so incompe-tent and furthermore addled by drugs. He himself was not an IKL pro-fessional. He had served at the front with the Waffen-SS since 1939, and had won the Iron Cross, second class, but he had been discharged be-cause of a serious illness and assigned to camp service. He had found Auschwitz in a catastrophic state: for almost a year, the desire to im-prove matters consumed him.

Wirths showed me the reports he sent monthly to Lolling: the con-ditions in the different sections of the camp, the incompetence of many doctors and officers, the brutality of the subalterns and kapos, the daily obstacles blocking his work, everything was described in plain, straight-forward language. He promised to have copies of his last six reports typed out for me. He was particularly up in arms about the use of crim-inals in positions of responsibility in the camp: "I've talked about it dozens of times with Obersturmbannführer Höss. Those 'greens' are brutes, sometimes psychopaths, they're corrupt, they reign with terror over the other inmates, and all with the connivance of the SS. It's inad-missible, not to speak of the fact that the results are lamentable."— "What would you prefer? Political prisoners, Communists?"—"Of course!" He began to count on his fingers: "One: they are by definition men who have a social conscience. Even if they can be corrupted, they'll never commit the same atrocities as the common-law prisoners. Do you realize that in the women's camp the *Blockältesten* are prosti-tutes, degenerates! And most of the male block elders keep what they call here a *Pipel*, a young boy who serves as their sex slave. That's what we have to rely on here! Whereas the 'reds,' to a man, refuse to use the brothel reserved for inmate functionaries, even though some of them

have been in the camp for ten years. Two: the priority now is organization of labor. Now, what better organizer than a Communist or an SD
activist? The 'greens' just know how to hit and hit again. Three: they
object to me that the 'reds' will deliberately sabotage production. To
which I reply that, first of all, it couldn't be worse than the present production, and then that there are ways to control this: political prisoners
aren't idiots, they'll understand very quickly that at the slightest problem they'll be sacked and that the common-law criminals will return. It
will thus be wholly in their own interest, for themselves and for all of
the *Häftlinge*, if they guarantee good production. I can even give you an
example, that of Dachau, where I worked briefly: there, the 'reds' control everything and I can assure you that the conditions are incompara-
bly better than in Auschwitz.

Here, in my own department, I use only political prisoners. I have
no complaints. My private secretary is an Austrian Communist, a serious, self-possessed, efficient young man. We sometimes have very frank
conversations, and it's very useful for me, since he learns from other inmates things that are hidden from me, and he reports them to me. I trust
him much more than some of my SS colleagues." We also discussed the
selection. "I think the principle is odious," he frankly confessed to me.
"But if it has to be done, then it might as well be done by doctors. Before, it was the Lagerführer and his men who ran it. They did it any
which way, and with unimaginable brutality. At least now it takes place
in an orderly fashion, according to reasonable criteria." Wirths had ordered all the camp doctors to take their turn at the ramp. "I myself go
there too, even if I find it horrifying. I have to set an example." He
looked a little lost as he said that. It wasn't the first time someone had
opened up to me this way: since the beginning of my mission, certain
individuals, either because they instinctively understood that I was interested in their problems or because they hoped to use me as a channel to air their grievances, confided far beyond the requirements of the
service. It's true that, here, Wirths must not often have found a friendly
ear: Höss was a good professional, but devoid of any sensitivity, and the
same must have been true for most of his subordinates.

I inspected the different parts of the camp in detail. I went back several times to Birkenau, and had them show me the systems for invento-
rying the confiscated property at the *Kanada*. It was chaos: crates of
uncounted currency lay in heaps, one walked on banknotes, torn and
pressed into the mud of the alleys. In principle, the inmates were
searched at the zone's exit; but I imagined that with a watch or a few
reichsmarks, it must not have been difficult to bribe a guard. The
"green" kapo who kept the accounts confirmed this to me indirectly:

after showing me around his piles of clutter—the shifting mountains of used clothing, from which teams unstitched the yellow stars before repairing the clothes, sorting them, re-piling them; the crates of glasses, watches, pens, jumbled together; the orderly rows of strollers and baby carriages; the clumps of women's hair, consigned in bales to German firms that transformed it into socks for our submariners, mattress stuffing, and insulating material; and the disparate piles of religious paraphernalia, which no one really knew what to do with—this inmate functionary, as he was about to leave me, said to me carelessly, in his cheeky Hamburg dialect: "If you need anything, let me know, I'll take care of it."—"What do you mean?" "Oh, sometimes it's pretty easy. Anything to be of service, y'know—we like to oblige." That was what Morgen was talking about: the camp SS, with the complicity of the inmates, had come to consider this *Kanada* as their private reserve. Morgen had advised me to visit the guards' barrack rooms: I found SS officers lounging on expensively upholstered sofas, half drunk, staring off into emptiness; a few female Jewish inmates, dressed not in regulation striped uniforms but in light dresses, were cooking sausages and potato pancakes on a large cast-iron stove; they were all real beauties, and they had kept their hair; and when they served the guards, bringing them food or pouring them alcohol from crystal carafes, they addressed them familiarly, using the *du* form, and calling them by their nicknames. Not one of the guards had gotten up to salute me. I gave the Spiess who accompanied me on my visits a shocked look; he shrugged: "They're tired, Sturmbannführer. They've had a hard day, you know. Two transports already." I'd have liked to have them open their lockers, but my position didn't authorize me to: I was sure I'd have found all kinds of objects and money. What's more, this generalized corruption appeared to rise to the highest level, as remarks I'd overheard suggested. At the bar of the Haus der Waffen-SS, I had surprised a conversation between a camp Oberscharführer and a civilian; the noncom, sniggering, was explaining that he had delivered to Frau Höss "a basket full of panties, the best quality, in silk and lace. She wanted to replace her old ones, you see." He didn't say where they came from, but I guessed readily enough. I myself received propositions; I was offered bottles of Cognac or victuals, *to improve my usual fare*. I refused, but politely: I didn't want these officers to mistrust me; that would have harmed my work.

As agreed, I went to visit the great IG Farben factory, known as Buna, the name of the synthetic rubber it was eventually supposed to produce. Construction, apparently, was going forward slowly. Since Faust was busy, he assigned one of his assistants to my visit, an engineer named Schenke, a man about thirty years old, in a gray suit with the

Party insignia. This Schenke seemed fascinated by my Iron Cross; while he spoke to me, his eyes kept shifting over to it; finally he asked me, timidly, how I had gotten it. "I was in Stalingrad."—"Oh! You were lucky."—"To have gotten out?" I asked, laughing. "Yes, I think so too." Schenke looked confused: "No, that's not what I meant. To have been over there, to have been able to fight like that, for the *Heimat*, against the Bolsheviks." I looked at him curiously and he blushed. "I have a childhood deformity, in my leg. A bone that broke and didn't heal well. That prevented me from going to the front. But I would have liked to serve the Reich too."—"You're serving it here," I pointed out.—"Of course. But it's not the same. All my childhood friends are at the front. One feels . . . excluded." Schenke did limp, but it didn't prevent him from striding along with a nervous, quick step, so that I had to hurry to follow him. As he walked, he explained the factory's history to me: the leadership of the Reich had insisted that Farben build a factory for Buna—a vital product for armaments—in the East, because of the bombardments that were already ravaging the Ruhr. The site had been chosen by one of the directors of the IG, Dr. Ambros, because of a large number of favorable criteria: the confluence of three rivers providing the considerable quantities of water required by the production of Buna; the existence of a broad plateau that was almost empty (aside from a Polish village that had been razed), geologically ideal since it was elevated; the intersection of several railway lines; and the proximity of many coal mines. The presence of the camp had also been a positive factor: the SS had declared it was delighted to support the project and had promised to provide inmates. But the factory's construction was dragging, partly because of the difficulties of getting supplies, and partly because the output of the *Häftlinge* had turned out poor, and management was furious. However often the factory returned to the camp the inmates unable to work and demanded replacements, as the contract allowed, the new ones would arrive in a scarcely better state. "What happens to the ones you send back?" I asked in a neutral tone. Schenke looked at me with surprise: "I have no idea. That's not my business. I guess they fix them up in the hospital. Don't you know?" I pensively contemplated this young, motivated engineer: Was it really possible that he didn't know? The chimneys in Birkenau were smoking daily eight kilometers away, and I knew as well as anyone else how gossip spread. But after all, if he didn't want to know, it was possible for him not to know. The rules of secrecy and concealment could serve that purpose too.

However, judging from the treatment of the inmates employed, it didn't seem that their ultimate fate was a major preoccupation for

Schenke or his colleagues. In the midst of the immense, muddy construction site that was to become the factory, columns of scrawny *Häftlinge* in rags carried at a run, under the shouts and cudgel blows of the kapos, beams or bags of cement far too heavy for them. If a worker, in his big wooden clogs, stumbled and let his load fall, or collapsed himself, the blows redoubled, and blood, fresh and red, gushed onto the oily mud. Some never got up again. The din was infernal, everyone was yelling, the SS noncoms, the kapos; the beaten inmates screamed pitifully. Schenke guided me through this Gehenna without paying the slightest attention to it. Here and there, he paused and conversed with other engineers in well-pressed suits, holding yellow folding rulers and little fake-leather notebooks in which they jotted down figures. They commented on the progress of the construction of a wall, then one of them muttered a few words to a Rottenführer, who began to yell and viciously hit the kapo with his boot or rifle butt; the kapo, in turn, dove into the mass of inmates, distributing savage blows with full force, bellowing; and then the *Häftlinge* attempted a surge of activity, which died down on its own, since they could scarcely stand up. This system seemed to me extremely inefficient, and I said as much to Schenke; he shrugged his shoulders and looked around him as if he were seeing the scene for the first time: "In any case they don't understand anything but blows. What else can you do with such a workforce?" I looked again at the undernourished *Häftlinge*, their rags coated in mud, black grease, diarrhea. A Polish 'red' stopped for an instant in front of me and I saw a brown stain appear on the back of his pants and the rear of his leg; then he resumed his frenetic run before a kapo could approach. Pointing him out, I said to Schenke: "Don't you think it's important to oversee their hygiene better? I'm not just talking about the stench, but it's dangerous, that's how epidemics break out." Schenke replied somewhat haughtily: "All that is the responsibility of the SS. We pay the camp to have inmates fit for work. But it's up to the camp to wash them, feed them, and take care of them. That's included in the package." Another engineer, a thickset Swabian sweating in his twill jacket, let out a coarse guffaw: "Anyway, Jews are like venison, they're better when they're a little gamy." Schenke smiled thinly; I retorted curtly: "Your workers aren't all Jews."—"Oh! the others are hardly any better." Schenke was beginning to grow annoyed: "Herr Sturmbannführer, if you think the condition of the *Häftlinge* is unsatisfactory, you should complain to the camp, not to us. The camp is responsible for their upkeep, I told you. All that is specified in our contract."—"I understand very well, believe me." Schenke was right; even the blows were administered by SS guards and their kapos. "But it seems to me that you could obtain better output by treating them a little better. Don't you think so?" Schenke shrugged: "Ideally, maybe. And we often complain to the camp about the workers' condition. But we have other priorities besides constantly splitting hairs." Behind him, knocked down by a cudgel, an inmate was dying; his bloody head was buried in the thick mud; only the mechanical trembling of his legs showed that he was still alive. Schenke, as we left, stepped over him without looking at him. He was still thinking about my words with irritation: "We can't have a sentimental attitude, Herr Sturmbannführer. We are at war. Production counts above all else."— "I'm not saying otherwise. My objective is just to suggest ways to increase production. That should concern you. After all, it's been, what? Two years now that you've been constructing, and you still haven't produced a kilo of Buna."—"Yes. But I should point out to you that the methanol factory has been functioning for a month."

Despite his retort, my last remark must have annoyed Schenke; for the rest of the visit, he confined himself to dry, brief comments. I had myself shown around the KL attached to the factory, a rectangle surrounded by barbed wire, set up south of the complex in fallow fields, on the site of the razed village. I thought the conditions there were deplorable; the Lagerführer seemed to find it normal. "In any case, we send the ones the IG rejects to Birkenau, and they send us fresh ones." On my way back to the *Stammlager*, I noticed on a wall in town this surprising inscription: KATYN = AUSCHWITZ. Ever since March, in fact, Goebbels's press had kept harping about the discovery in Byelorussia of Polish corpses, thousands of officers assassinated by Bolsheviks after 1939. But who, here, could have written that? There weren't any more Poles in Auschwitz, and no Jews, either, for a long time now. The town itself looked gray, glum, affluent, like all the old German towns in the East, with its market square, its Dominican church with sloping roofs, and, just at the entrance, dominating the bridge over the Sola, the old castle of the duke of the region. For many years, the Reichsführer had promoted plans to enlarge the town and make it a model community of the German East, but with the intensification of the war, these ambitious projects had been put aside, and it remained a sad, dull town, almost forgotten between the camp and the factory, a superfluous appendage.

As for the life of the camp, it was turning out to be full of unusual phenomena. Piontek had dropped me off in front of the Kommandantur and backed up to park the Opel; I was about to go in when my attention was drawn by some noise in the garden of the Hösses' house. I lit a cigarette and discreetly approached: through the gate, I saw children playing *Häftlinge*. The biggest one, who had his back to me, wore an armband marked kapo and was shrilly shouting the standardized commands: *"Ach . . . tung! Mützen . . . auf! Mützen . . . ab! Zu fünf!"* The other four, three little girls, one of them very young, and a boy, were standing in a row facing me and were clumsily trying to obey; each one wore a triangle, sewn on their chests, of a different color: green, red, black, purple. Höss's voice resounded behind me: "Hello, Sturmbannführer! What are you watching?" I turned around: Höss was coming toward me, his hand outstretched; near the barrier, an orderly was holding his horse's lead. I saluted him, shook his hand, and without a word pointed to the garden. Höss blushed suddenly, passed through the gate, and hurried toward the children. Without saying anything, without slapping them, he tore the triangles and the armband off and sent them inside. Then he came back to me, still red, holding the pieces of cloth. He looked at me, looked at the badges, looked at me again, and then, still silent, walked past me and into the Kommandantur, tossing the badges into a metal trash can near the door. I picked up my cigarette, which I had dropped to salute him and which was still smoking. An inmate gardener, in a clean, well-pressed striped uniform, holding a rake, came out, removing his cap as he passed me, went to get the trashcan, and emptied it into the basket he was carrying; then he went back into the garden.

During the day, I felt fresh, alert; at the Haus, I ate well, and in the evenings I thought with pleasure about my bed, with its clean sheets; but at night, ever since I had arrived, the dreams came in vast gusts, sometimes short and abrupt and soon forgotten, other times like a long worm uncoiling inside my head. One sequence in particular repeated itself and expanded nightly, an obscure, difficult-to-describe dream, without any narrative meaning, but that unfurled according to a spatial logic. In this dream I was traveling, at different altitudes, but always as if in the air, I was more like a pure gaze or even a camera than a living being, traveling through an immense city, without any visible end, its topography monotonous and repetitive, divided into geometric sectors, its way animated with an incessant flow. Thousands of beings came and went, entered and exited identical buildings, walked along long, straight avenues, plunged underground through subway entrances to emerge at some other place, constantly and without any apparent aim. If I, or rather the gaze I had become, went down toward these avenues to examine them close up, I noticed that these men and women weren't distinguished from one another by any special characteristic; they all had white skin, light-colored hair, blue, pale, lost eyes, Höss's eyes, the eyes of my old orderly Hanika, too, when he died in Kharkov, eyes the color of the sky. Railroad tracks crisscrossed the city, little trains came forward and made regular stops to spew out an instantly replaced wave of passengers, as far as the eye could see. During subsequent nights, I entered some of the buildings: lines of people moved between long communal tables and latrines, eating and defecating in a row; on bunk beds, others were fornicating, then children were born, played between the bedsteads, and, when they had grown big enough, went out to take their place in the human waves of this city of perfect happiness. Little by little, by dint of looking from different points of view, a tendency became apparent in the seemingly arbitrary swarm: imperceptibly, a certain number of people always ended up on the same side, and finally went into windowless buildings, where they lay down to die without a word. Specialists came and collected from them whatever could still contribute to the city's economy; then their bodies were burned in ovens that served simultaneously to warm the water distributed by pipes throughout the sectors; the bones were ground up; the smoke, coming from the chimneys, rejoined, like tributaries, the smoke of neighboring chimneys to form one long, calm, solemn river. And when the dream's point of view took on altitude again, I could make out an equilibrium in all this: the quantity of births, in the dormitories, equaled the number of deaths, and the society self-reproduced in perfect equilibrium, always in movement, producing no excess and suffering no diminution. When I woke up, it seemed obvious to me that these serene dreams, void of all anguish, represented the camp, but a perfect camp, having reached an impossible point of stasis, without violence, self-regulated, functioning perfectly and also perfectly useless since, despite all this movement, it produced nothing. But upon thinking more about it, as I tried to do while drinking my ersatz in the dining room of the Haus der Waffen-SS, wasn't it a representation of social life as a whole? Stripped of its tawdry rags and its pointless agitation, human life was reduced to scarcely more than that; once one had reproduced, one had fulfilled the purpose of mankind; and as for one's own purpose, that was just an illusion, a stimulus to encourage oneself to get up in the morning; but if you examined the thing objectively, as I thought I could do, the uselessness of all these efforts was obvious, as was the uselessness of reproduction itself, since it served only to produce more uselessness. So I came to think: Wasn't the camp itself, with all the rigidity of its organization, its absurd violence, its meticulous hierarchy, just a metaphor, a *reductio ad absurdum* of everyday life?

But I hadn't come to Auschwitz to philosophize. I inspected the *Nebenlager*: the experimental agricultural station in Rajsko, so dear to the Reichsführer, where Dr. Caesar explained to me how they were still trying to resolve the problem of large-scale cultivation of the kok-sagyz plant, discovered, you'll remember, near Maikop and capable of producing rubber; and also the cement factory in Golleschau, the steelworks in Eintrachthütte, the mines in Jawizowitz and Neu-Dachs. Aside from Rajsko, which was something of a special case, the conditions in these installations seemed if possible worse than at Buna: the absence of any security measures led to countless accidents, the lack of hygiene constantly assailed the senses, the savage and deadly violence of the kapos and civilian foremen broke out on the slightest excuse. I went down to the bottom of the mine shaft via shaky wire-caged elevators; at every level, perspectives of tunnels, weakly illuminated by yellowish lamps, pierced the darkness; any inmate who went down here must have lost all hope of ever seeing daylight again. At the bottom, water trickled from the walls, metallic sounds and shouts resounded through the low, stinking tunnels. Oil drums cut in half with a board across the top served as latrines: some *Häftlinge* were so weak that they fell inside. Others, skeleton-like, their legs swollen with edema, expended immense effort pushing overloaded carts on badly adjusted tracks, or cutting into the wall with picks or pneumatic drills that they could barely hold. At the exit, lines of exhausted workers, supporting half-fainting comrades and carrying their dead on improvised stretchers, were waiting to go back to the surface, to be sent back to Birkenau: they, at least, would see the sky again, even if only for a few hours. Learning that almost everywhere the work progressed less quickly than the engineers had foreseen didn't surprise me: usually they blamed *the bad quality of the goods supplied by the camp*. A young engineer from the Hermann-Göring Werke had tried, he told me with a resigned air, to obtain an extra ration for the inmates in Jawizowitz, but management had refused the additional expenditure. As for hitting them less, even this man with progressive ideas sadly acknowledged that it was difficult: if you hit them, the inmates advanced slowly, but if you didn't hit them, they didn't advance at all.

With Dr. Wirths, I had an interesting discussion about precisely this question of physical violence, since to me it evoked problems I had already encountered in the Einsatzgruppen. Wirths agreed with me in saying that even men who, in the beginning, hit only out of obligation ended up developing a taste for it. "Far from correcting hardened criminals," he passionately affirmed, "we confirm them in their perversity by giving them full rights over the other prisoners. And we're even creating new ones among our SS. These camps, with the present methods, are a breeding ground for mental illnesses and sadistic deviations; after

the war, when these men go back to civilian life, we'll find ourselves
with a considerable problem on our hands." I explained to him that, according to what I had heard, the decision to transfer the work of extermination to the camps was made partly because of the psychological
problems it caused among troops assigned to mass executions. "True,"
Wirths replied, "but we're only shifting the problem, especially by mixing extermination functions with the correctional and economic functions of ordinary camps. The mentality engendered by extermination
overpowers and affects all the rest. Even here, in my Reviers, I discovered that some doctors were killing patients, exceeding their instructions. I had a lot of trouble putting a stop to such practices. As for the
sadistic tendencies, they are very frequent, especially with the guards,
and they're often connected to sexual troubles."—"Do you have concrete examples?"—"They rarely come to consult me. But it happens. A
month ago, I saw a guard who's been here for a year. A man from
Breslau, thirty-seven years old, married, three children. He confessed to
me that he had beaten inmates until he ejaculated, without even touching himself. He no longer had any normal sexual relations; when he had
leave, he didn't go back home, he was so ashamed. But before he came
to Auschwitz, he told me, he was perfectly normal."—"And what did
you do for him?"—"In the conditions we have here, there's not much
I can do. He would need extensive psychiatric treatment. I'm trying to
have him transferred outside the camp system, but it's hard: I can't tell
the whole story, or he'd be arrested. But he's a sick man, he needs to be
taken care of."—"And how do you think this sadism develops?" I asked.
"I mean with normal men, without any predisposition that would be
revealed under these conditions?" Wirths looked out the window, pensive. He took a long while to reply: "That's a question I've thought a lot
about, and it's difficult to answer. An easy solution would be to blame
our propaganda, the way for instance it's taught here to the troops by
Oberscharführer Knittel, who heads the *Kulturabteilung*: the *Häftling* is
subhuman, he's not even human, so it's entirely legitimate to hit him.
But that's not the whole of it—after all, animals aren't human, either, but
none of our guards would treat an animal the way they treat the
Häftlinge. Propaganda does play a role, but in a more complex way. I
came to the conclusion that the SS guard doesn't become violent or
sadistic because he thinks the inmate is not a human being; on the contrary, his rage increases and turns into sadism when he sees that the inmate, far from being a subhuman as he was taught, is actually at bottom
a man, like him, after all, and it's this resistance, you see, that the guard
finds unbearable, this silent persistence of the other, and so the guard
beats him to try to make their shared humanity disappear. Of course,

that doesn't work: the more the guard strikes, the more he's forced to see that the inmate refuses to recognize himself as a non-human. In the end, no other solution remains for him than to kill him, which is an acknowledgment of complete failure." Wirths fell silent. He was still looking out the window. I broke the silence: "Can I ask you a personal question, Doktor?" Wirths answered without looking at me; his long, thin fingers tapped the table: "You can ask it."—"Are you a believer?" He took a while to reply. He was still looking outside, toward the street and the crematorium. "I used to be, yes," he said finally.

I had left Wirths and was walking up the Kasernestrasse toward the Kommandantur. Just before the checkpoint with its red-and-white barrier, I noticed one of Höss's children, the oldest one, squatting in the street in front of the gate to their house. I went over and greeted him. The boy raised frank, intelligent eyes to me and stood up: "Hello, Sturmbannführer."—"What's your name?"—"Klaus."—"What are you looking at, Klaus?" Klaus pointed toward the gate: "Look." The ground in front of the threshold was black with ants, an amazingly dense swarm. Klaus crouched down again to observe them and I bent over beside him. At first sight, these thousands of ants seemed to be running around in the most frenzied, utterly aimless disorder. But then I looked more closely, trying to follow one of them in particular, then another. I noticed then that the disrupted aspect of this swarm came from the fact that each insect kept pausing to touch antennas with every other one it met. Little by little I saw that some of the ants were leaving toward the left while others were arriving, carrying debris or food: an exhausting, vast labor. The ones that were coming must have been using their antennae to inform the others about where the food had come from. The gate to the house opened and a *Häftling*, the gardener I had seen before, came out. Seeing me, he stiffened and removed his cap. He was a man a little older than me, a Polish political prisoner, according to his triangle. He noticed the anthill and said: "I'll destroy that, Herr Offizier."—"Absolutely not! Don't touch it."—"Oh yes, Stani," Klaus gushed, "leave them alone. They haven't done anything to you." Klaus turned to me: "Where are they going?"—"I don't know. We'll have to look." The ants were following the garden wall, then hurrying along the curb, passing behind the cars and motorcycles parked opposite the Kommandantur; then they continued straight ahead, a long wavering line, beyond the camp's administration building. We followed them step-by-step, admiring their indefatigable determination. When we neared the *Politische Abteilung*, Klaus looked at me nervously: "I'm sorry, Sturmbannführer, but my father doesn't want me to come this way."—"Wait

for me, then. I'll tell you." Behind the barracks of the political department stood the squat mass of the crematorium, a former ammunition
bunker covered with earth and vaguely resembling, apart from the
chimney, a flattened kurgan. The ants continued toward its somber
mass; they climbed up the sloping side, weaving their way through the
grass; then they turned and went down a cement section of wall, where
the entrance to the bunker formed a recess between the dirt slopes. I
kept following them and saw that they went through the half-open door
and into the crematorium. I looked around: aside from a guard who was
staring at me curiously and a column of inmates pushing wheelbarrows
a little farther away, near the extension of the camp, there was no one.
I went up to the door, which was bracketed by two frames, like windows; inside, everything was black and silent. The ants were marching
over the angle of the doorstep. I turned around and rejoined Klaus.
"They're going that way," I said vaguely. "They found something to
eat." Followed by the little boy, I returned to the Kommandantur. We
separated in front of the entrance. "Are you coming tonight, Sturmbannführer?" Klaus asked. Höss was giving a little reception and had invited me. "Yes."—"Till tonight, then!" Stepping over the anthill, he
went into the garden.

At the end of the day, after stopping by the Haus der Waffen-SS to
wash and change, I went back to the Hösses. In front of the gate, there
were now only a few dozen ants left, rapidly crisscrossing the surface.
The thousands of others must have been underground now, digging,
clearing away, shoring up, invisible but continuing their mad labor without respite. Höss welcomed me on the steps, glass of Cognac in hand.
He introduced me to his wife, Hedwig, a blond woman with a fixed
smile and hard eyes, wearing a becoming evening gown with a lace collar and sleeves, and his two eldest daughters, Kindi and Püppi, also prettily dressed. Klaus shook my hand in a friendly way; he was wearing a
tweed jacket of English cut, with suede patches on the elbows and large
horn buttons. "That's a handsome jacket," I remarked. "Where did you
find that?"—"My dad brought it back for me from the camp," he
replied, beaming with pleasure. "The shoes too." They were polished
brown leather ankle boots, with buttons up the side. "Very elegant," I
said. Wirths was there and he introduced me to his wife; the other
guests were all camp officers: there were Hartjenstein, the garrison
commander; Grabner, the head of the political department; Lagerführer
Aumeier, Dr. Caesar, and a few others. The ambiance was somewhat
formal, more than at Eichmann's, in any case, but cordial. Caesar's wife,
a woman still young, laughed a lot; Wirths explained that she had been
one of Caesar's assistants, and he had proposed to her soon after his sec-

ond wife died of typhus. Conversation turned on Mussolini's recent fall and arrest, which had made a strong impression on everybody; the protestations of loyalty from Badoglio, the new Prime Minister, didn't inspire much confidence. Then we discussed the Reichsführer's plans for developing the German East. All sorts of contradictory ideas flew among the guests; Grabner tried to draw me into a discussion on the Himmlerstadt colonization project, but I replied evasively. One thing remained clear: whatever people's views were on the future of the region, the camp was an integral part of it. Höss thought it would last at least ten or twenty years. "The extension of the *Stammlager* has been planned with that in mind," he explained. "Once we've finished with the Jews and the war, Birkenau will disappear, and the land will be given back to agriculture. But the industry of Upper Silesia, especially with the German losses in the East, won't be able to do without Polish labor; the camp will remain vital for control of these populations, for a long time." Two inmates, wearing simple but clean dresses made of good material, circulated among the guests with trays; they wore the purple triangle of the IBVs, also known as "Jehovah's Witnesses." The rooms were nicely furnished, with rugs, leather sofas and armchairs, furniture in rich, well-tooled wood, vases with fresh flowers on lace doilies. The lamps gave off a yellow, discreet, almost subdued light. Signed enlargements of photographs of the Reichsführer visiting the camp with Höss or holding his children on his knees decorated the walls. The brandies and wines were of good quality; Höss also offered his guests fine Yugoslavian cigarettes, Ibars. I contemplated with curiosity this rigid, conscientious man, who dressed his children in the clothes of Jewish children killed under his direction. Did Höss think of that as he looked at them? Probably the idea didn't even enter his mind. His wife held his elbow and emitted curt, sharp bursts of laughter. I looked at her and thought about her cunt, under her dress, nesting in the lace panties of a pretty young Jewish girl gassed by her husband. The Jewess had long ago been burned along with her own cunt and had gone up in smoke to join the clouds; her expensive panties, which she might have put on especially for her deportation, now adorned and protected the cunt of Hedwig Höss. Did Höss think about that Jewess, when he took off her panties to honor his wife? But maybe he wasn't much interested anymore in Frau Höss's cunt, however delicately it was covered: work in the camps, when it didn't make men insane, often made them impotent. Maybe he kept his own Jewess somewhere in the camp, clean, well fed, a lucky one, the Kommandant's whore? No, not him: if Höss took a mistress from among the inmates, it would be a German, not a Jew.

It is never good to have such thoughts, I know that. That night my recurrent dream had a final intensification. I was approaching that immense city by way of a derelict railroad track; in the distance, the line of chimneys was peacefully smoking; and I felt lost, isolated, an abandoned whelp, and the need for men's companionship tormented me. I mixed with the crowd and wandered for a long time, irresistibly drawn by the crematoriums vomiting spirals of smoke and clouds of sparks into the sky, *like a dog, both attracted and repell'd / By the stench of his own kind / Burning.* But I couldn't reach it, and entered instead one of the vast building-barracks, where I occupied a bunk, shoving away an unknown woman who wanted to join me. I fell asleep promptly. When I woke up, I noticed a little blood on my pillow. I looked closer and saw there was also some on the sheets. I removed them; beneath, they were soaking in blood mixed with sperm, big gobs of sperm too thick to seep through the cloth. I was sleeping in a room in Höss's house, upstairs, next to the children's room; and I had no idea how I could bring these soiled sheets to the bathroom, to wash them, without Höss noticing. This problem was causing me a horrible, agonizing discomfort. Then Höss came into my room with another officer. They took off their underpants, sat down cross-legged next to my bed, and began to masturbate vigorously, each crimson glans disappearing and reappearing from the foreskin, until they had sent huge jets of sperm onto my bed and onto the rug. They wanted me to imitate them, but I refused; the ceremony apparently had a precise significance, but I didn't know what it was.

This brutal, obscene dream marked the end of my first stay in the KL Auschwitz: I had finished my work. I returned to Berlin and from there went to visit some camps in the Altreich, the KLs Sachsenhausen, Buchenwald, and Neuengamme, as well as many of their satellite camps. I won't expand any further on these visits: all these camps have been amply described in the historical literature, better than I could do; and it's also quite true that when you've seen one camp, you've seen them all: all camps look alike, it's a well-known fact. Nothing of what I saw, despite local variations, perceptibly changed my opinion or my conclusions. I returned to Berlin for good around mid-August, in the period between the recapture of Orel by the Soviets and the final conquest of Sicily by the Anglo-Americans. I wrote my report quickly; I had already gathered my notes together along the way, I just needed to organize the sections and type it all out, a matter of a few days. I was careful with both my prose and the logic of my argumentation: the report was addressed to the Reichsführer, and Brandt had warned me that I would probably have to give a verbal report. When the final version was corrected and typed up, I sent it off and waited.

I had gone back, without much pleasure I have to confess, to my landlady Frau Gutknecht. She went into raptures, and was determined to make me tea; but she didn't understand how, since I was coming home from the East, *where one can find everything to eat*, I hadn't thought to bring back a pair of geese, for the household of course. (Actually, she wasn't the only one with this in mind: Piontek had returned from his stay in Tarnowitz with a trunkful of food, and had offered to sell me some without coupons.) What's more, I got the impression that she had taken advantage of my absence to search through my belongings. My indifference to her whining and her childish behavior was beginning, unfortunately, to wear thin. As for Fräulein Praxa, she had changed her hairdo, but not the color of her nails. Thomas was happy to see me again: great changes were under way, he affirmed, it was good I was in Berlin, I had to be prepared.

What a curious sensation, suddenly finding myself, after such a journey, with nothing to do! I had finished the Blanchot a long time ago; I opened the treatise on ritual murder only to shut it again right away, surprised that the Reichsführer could take an interest in such drivel; I had no private affairs to attend to; all my files were in order. With my office window open onto the park of the Prinz-Albrecht-Palais, sunny but already a little dried out by the August heat, my feet up on my sofa, or else leaning out the window to smoke a cigarette, I reflected; and when immobility began to weigh on me, I went down to take a walk in the garden, strolling through the dusty gravel lanes, greatly tempted by the pockets of shady grass. I thought about what I had seen in Poland, but for some reason I couldn't explain, my thinking skimmed over the images and came to rest on the words. The words preoccupied me. I had been wondering how much the differences between German and Russian reactions to mass killings (differences that caused us finally to change our method to make the thing somehow easier, while the Russians seemed, even after a quarter century, to remain unmoved by it) had to do with differences of vocabulary. The word *Tod*, after all, has the stiffness of a clean, already cold, almost abstract corpse, the finality in any case of the after-death, whereas *smiert'*, the Russian word, is as heavy and greasy as the thing itself. What about French, in that case? That language, for me, remained dependent on the feminization of death by Latin: What a difference finally between *la Mort* and all the almost warm, tender images it gives rise to, and the terrible *Thanatos* of the Greeks! The Germans had at least preserved the masculine (*smiert'*, it should be said in passing, is also feminine). There, in the brightness of summer, I thought about that decision we had made, the extraordinary idea of killing all the Jews, whoever they might be, young or old, good or bad, of destroying Judaism in the person of its bearers, a decision that had received the name, now well known, of *Endlösung*: the "Final Solution." But what a beautiful word! It had not always been a synonym for extermination, though: since the beginning, people had called for, when it came to the Jews, an *Endlösung*, or else a *völlige Lösung* (a complete solution) or also an *allgemeine Lösung* (a general solution), and according to the period, this meant exclusion from public life or exclusion from economic life or, finally, emigration. Then, little by little, the signification had slid toward the abyss, but without the signifier changing, and it seemed almost as if this final meaning had always lived in the heart of the word, and that the thing had been attracted, drawn in by it, by its weight, its fabulous gravity, into that black hole of the mind, toward the point of singularity: and then we had passed the event horizon, beyond which there is no return. We still believe in ideas, in concepts, we believe that words designate ideas, but that's not necessarily true, maybe there aren't really any ideas, maybe there's really nothing but words, and the weight peculiar to words. And maybe thus we had let ourselves be led along by a word and its inevitability. Within us, then, there would have been no ideas, no logic, no coherence? There would have been only words, in our oh so peculiar language, only that word, *Endlösung*, its streaming beauty? For, really, how could one resist the seduction of such a word? It would have been as inconceivable as resisting the word *obey*, the word *serve*, the word *law*. And perhaps that, at bottom, was the reason for our *Sprachregelungen*, quite transparent finally in terms of camouflage (*Tarnjargon*), but useful for keeping those who used these words and expressions—*Sonderbehandlung* (special treatment), *abtransportiert* (transported onward), *entsprechend behandelt* (treated appropriately), *Wohnsitzverlegung* (change of domicile), or *Executivmassnahmen* (executive measures)—between the sharp points of their abstraction. This tendency spread to all our bureaucratic language, our *bürokratisches Amtsdeutsch*, as my colleague Eichmann would say: in correspondance, in speeches too, passive constructions dominated: "it has been decided that . . . ," "the Jews have been conveyed to the special treatment," "this difficult task has been carried out," and so things were done all by themselves, no one ever did anything, no one acted, they were actions without actors, which is always reassuring, and in a way they weren't even actions, since by the special usage that our National Socialist language made of certain nouns, one managed, if not completely to eliminate verbs, at least to reduce them to the state of useless (but nonetheless decorative) appendages, and that way, you did without even action, there were only facts, brute realities, either already present or waiting for their inevitable accomplishment, like the *Einsatz*, or the *Einbruch* (the breakthrough), the *Verwertung* (the utilization), the *Entpolonisierung* (the de-Polonization), the *Ausrottung* (the extermination), but also, in a contrary sense, the *Versteppung*, the "steppification" of Europe by the Bolshevik hordes who, contrary to Attila, razed civilization in order to let the grass grow for their horses. *Man lebt in seiner Sprache*, wrote Hanns Johst, one of our best National Socialist poets: "You live in your language." Voss, I was sure, would not have denied it.

I was still waiting for my summons from the Reichsführer when the English resumed their massive strikes on Berlin, with considerable vigor. It was August 23, a Monday, I remember, late at night: I was at home, in bed, but I probably wasn't asleep yet, when the sirens went off. I was tempted to remain lying, but already Frau Gutknecht was banging my door. She was bellowing so loudly you could scarcely hear the sirens: "Herr Offizier! Herr Offizier! . . . Doktor Aue! Get up! The *Luftmörder!* Help!" I pulled on a pair of trousers and unlocked the door: "Well, yes, Frau Gutknecht. It's the RAF. What do you want me to do?" Her jowls were trembling, her cheeks were pale, and she was crossing herself convulsively, muttering: "Jesus-Mary-Joseph, Jesus-Mary-Joseph, what are we going to do?"—"We are going to go down into the shelter, like everyone else." I shut the door and got dressed, then calmly went downstairs, locking my door against looters. We could hear the flak thundering, especially to the south and near the Tiergarten. The building's basement had been turned into an air-raid shelter: it would never have survived a direct hit, but it was better than nothing. I threaded my way through the suitcases and legs and settled into a corner, as far as possible from Frau Gutknecht, who was sharing her terrors with some neighbors. Children were crying anxiously, others were running between the adults, some wearing suits, others still in their bathrobes. Just two candles lit the basement, little quivering, trembling flames that registered the nearby explosions like seismographs. The alert lasted for several hours; unfortunately, it was forbidden to smoke in these shelters. I must have dozed, I think no bombs hit our neighborhood. When it was over I went upstairs to go back to bed, without even going to look in the street. The next day, instead of taking the U-Bahn, I called the SS-Haus and sent for Piontek. He reported that the bombers had come from the south, from Sicily, probably, and that it was mostly Steglitz, Lichterfelde, and Marienfelde that had been hit, although some buildings had been destroyed at Tempelhof and all the way to the zoo. "Our boys used a new tactic, *Wilde Sau*, they called it on the radio, but they didn't really explain what it was, Sturmbannführer. Heard it works, and we shot down more than sixty of their planes, the bastards. Poor Herr Jeschonnek, he should have waited a little." General Jeschonnek, the Chief of Staff of the Luftwaffe, had just committed suicide, because of his service's repeated failures to prevent the Anglo-American raids. Even before crossing the Spree, Piontek had to make a detour to avoid a street blocked by rubble, the ruins of a building rammed by a bomber, a Lancaster, I think: its tail was sticking out of the ruins, desolate, like a ship's stern after a shipwreck. Thick black smoke hid the sun. I ordered Piontek to drive me to the southern part of the city: the farther we got, the more buildings were still burning, and the streets were full of debris. People were trying to pull their furniture out of gutted homes to pile it in the middle of streets flooded by fire hoses; mobile field kitchens were serving soup to lines of shocked, exhausted, soot-covered survivors; near the fire trucks, shapes were lined up on the sidewalks, sometimes with a foot, bare or still wearing a pathetic shoe, sticking out from under a dirty sheet. Some streets were barred by streetcars toppled onto to their sides by the force of the explosions or blackened by fire; power lines trailed on the pavement, trees lay crushed or remained standing but bare, stripped of all their leaves. The neighborhoods most affected were impassable; I had Piontek turn around and return to the SS-Haus. The building itself hadn't been hit, but nearby impacts had blown out the windows, and broken glass on the steps crunched beneath my feet. Inside, I met Brandt in the lobby, looking terribly excited, animated by a glee that was rather surprising in the circumstances. "What is happening?" He paused for an instant: "Ah, Sturmbannführer, you don't know the news yet. Great news! The Reichsführer was appointed Minister of the Interior." So that was it, the changes Thomas was talking about, I thought while Brandt rushed into the elevator. I walked up the stairs: Fräulein Praxa was at her place, made up, fresh as a rose. "Sleep well?"— "Oh, you know, Sturmbannführer, I live in Weissensee, I didn't hear anything."—"All the better for you." The window in my office was intact: I had gotten into the habit of leaving it open at night. I thought about the repercussions of the news announced by Brandt, but I lacked information to analyze it in detail. A priori, it seemed to me, it wouldn't change much for us: although Himmler, as chief of the German police, was technically subordinate to the Minister of the Interior, he was actually completely autonomous, and had been since 1936 at least; neither Frick, the outgoing minister, nor his Staatssekretär Stuckart had ever had the slightest influence over the RSHA or even the Hauptamt Orpo. The only thing over which they had kept control was the civilian administration, the civil servants; now that would also revert to the Reichsführer; but I couldn't believe it was a major issue. Obviously, to have the rank of minister could only reinforce the Reichsführer's hand against his rivals: but I didn't know enough about the struggles at the top to gauge this fact to its full extent.

I had imagined that this appointment would postpone the presentation of my report indefinitely: that showed I didn't really know much about the Reichsführer. I was summoned to his office two days later. The night before, the English had returned, fewer than the first time, but I still didn't get much sleep. I splashed cold water on my face before going downstairs, to try to muster some kind of human appearance. Brandt, staring at me with his owl-like look, made a few preliminary comments to me, as was his wont: "As you can imagine, the Reichsführer is extremely busy right now. Nonetheless, he was anxious to see you, since this concerns an issue he wants to make progress on. Your report was deemed excellent, a little too direct perhaps, but conclusive. The Reichsführer will certainly ask you to summarize it for him. Be concise. He doesn't have a lot of time." This time, the Reichsführer welcomed me with an almost friendly tone: "My dear Sturmbannführer Aue! Forgive me for making you wait, these past few days." He waved his soft, vein-covered hand toward a chair: "Have a seat." Brandt, as on the first time, had given him a file, which he consulted. "You saw the good Globus, then. How is he doing?"—"Gruppenführer Globocnik seemed in excellent form, my Reichsführer. Very enthusiastic."—"And what do you think of his management of the yield of the Einsatz? You can speak freely." His cold little eyes shone behind his pince-nez. I suddenly remembered Globocnik's first words; he certainly knew his Reichsführer better than I. I chose my words carefully: "The Gruppenführer is a fervent National Socialist, my Reichsführer, there's no doubt about that. But such wealth can give rise to formidable temptations in his entourage. I got the impression that the Gruppenführer could have been stricter on that level, that he might trust some of his subordinates too much."—"You talk a lot about corruption in your report. Do you think it's a real problem?"—"I'm convinced of it, my Reichsführer. To a certain extent, it's affecting the work of the camps and also of the *Arbeitseinsatz*. An SS man who steals is an SS man the inmate can buy." Himmler took off his pince-nez, took a handkerchief out of his pocket, and began polishing his glasses: "Summarize your conclusions. Be brief." I took a sheet of notes out of my briefcase and began. "In the KL system as it presently functions, my Reichsführer, I see three obstacles to a maximum, rational use of available labor. We've just discussed the first obstacle, corruption among the SS in the camps. It is not only a moral question; it also poses practical problems on many different levels. But for that, the remedy already exists—it's the special com-

mission you appointed, which should intensify its work. Second obstacle: a persistent bureaucratic incoherence, which Obergruppenführer
Pohl's efforts have not yet resolved. Allow me, my Reichsführer, to give
you an example, drawn from those cited in my report: Brigadeführer
Glücks's order of December twenty-eighth, 1942, addressed to all head
doctors in the KLs, giving them, among other things, the responsibility
of improving the nourishment of the *Häftlinge* so as to reduce the mortality rate. Yet in the camps, the kitchens report to the administrative
department, which is subordinated to Department D-Four of the
WVHA; as for the rations, they are decided centrally by the D-Four-
two, in conjunction with the SS-Hauptamt. Neither the doctors on-site
nor Department D-Three have any right of oversight in regard to this
process. So that part of the order was quite simply not implemented; the
rations remain identical to what they were last year." I paused; Himmler, watching me in a friendly way, nodded: "But the death rate has
fallen, it seems to me."—"Indeed, my Reichsführer, but for other reasons. There has been progress in the field of medical care and hygiene,
which the doctors control directly. But it could be lowered even more.
In the present state of things, if you allow me the remark, my Reichsführer, every *Häftling* who dies prematurely represents a net loss for the
war production of the Reich."—"I know that better than you, Sturmbannführer," he barked in a displeased, pedantic-schoolmaster tone of
voice. "Continue."—"Very good, my Reichsführer. Third obstacle: the
mentality of the superior officers who are IKL veterans. These remarks
do not at all concern their considerable qualities as men, SS officers, or
National Socialists. But most of them, and this is a fact, were trained at
a time when the functioning of the camps was completely different, according to the directives of the late Obergruppenführer Eicke."—"Did
you know Eicke?" Himmler cut in.—"No, my Reichsführer. I did not
have that honor."—"That's too bad. He was a great man. We miss him
a lot. But excuse me, I interrupted you. Go on."—"Thank you, my
Reichsführer. What I meant was that these officers have acquired a perspective that is directed toward the political and police functions of the
camps, as was predominant then. That is a problem both of state of
mind and of training: few of them have the slightest experience in economic management, and they work poorly with the administrators of
the WVHA enterprises. I should stress that this is an overall problem, a
generational problem, if I may put it that way, and not one of individual personalities, even if I have cited some as an example." Himmler had
brought his hands together to a point under his receding chin. "Fine,
Sturmbannführer. Your report will be distributed to the WVHA, and I
think it will give ammunition to my friend Pohl. But so as not to of-

fend anyone, you will first make a few corrections. Brandt will show you the list. Above all, you will not mention anyone by name. You understand why."—"Of course, my Reichsführer."—"On the other hand, I authorize you, in confidence, to send an uncorrected copy of your report to Dr. Mandelbrod."—"*Zu Befehl*, my Reichsführer." Himmler coughed, hesitated, took out a handkerchief, and coughed again, covering his mouth. "Excuse me," he said as he put the handkerchief away. "I have another task for you, Sturmbannführer. The question of feeding in the camps, which you mention, is a recurrent problem. It seems to me that it's a question you are beginning to be familiar with."—"My Reichsführer . . ." He made a sign with his hand: "Yes, yes. I remember your report from Stalingrad. This is what I want: While Department D-Three covers all medical and sanitary problems, we do not have, as you stressed, any centralized authority for the inmates' diet. So I have decided to create an interdepartmental study group to solve this problem. You will coordinate it. You will involve all the competent departments of the IKL; Pohl will also assign you a representative from the SS enterprises who will give their point of view. I also want the RSHA to have its say. Finally, I want you to consult the other ministries concerned, especially Speer's, which keeps showering us with complaints from private enterprises. Pohl will put all the necessary experts at your disposal. I want a consensual solution, Sturmbannführer. When you have prepared some concrete suggestions, you will submit them to me; if they are valid and realistic, they will be adopted. Brandt will help you with the means necessary. Any questions?" I straightened up: "My Reichsführer, your trust is an honor to me, and I thank you for it. I would like to make sure about one point."—"Which is?"—"That increased production remains the main objective." Himmler had leaned back in his armchair, his hands dangling from the armrests; his face had resumed its sly expression: "Insofar as that does not harm the other interests of the SS, and does not interfere with the programs under way, the answer is yes." He paused. "The requirements of the other ministries are important, but you know that there are constraints beyond their purview. Take that into account too. If you have any doubts, check with Pohl. He knows what I want. Good day, Sturmbannführer."

As I left Himmler's office, I have to confess, I felt as if I were floating in my boots. Finally I was being given a responsibility, an authentic responsibility! So they had recognized my true worth. And it was a positive job, a way to contribute to the war effort and to the victory of Germany by other means than murder and destruction. Even before talking

with Rudolf Brandt, I gave in to glorious, ridiculous fantasies, like a
teenager: convinced by my flawless argumentation, the departments fell
in behind me; the inept and the criminal were overthrown, sent back
to their lairs; in a few months, considerable progress had been made, inmates recovered their strength, their health; many of them, their hearts
swept away by the force of unchained National Socialism, began working joyously to help Germany in its struggle; production soared from
month to month; I got a more important position, real influence, al-
lowing me to improve things in accord with the principles of the true
Weltanschauung, and the Reichsführer himself listened to my advice, the
advice of one of the best National Socialists there was. Ridiculous,
puerile, I am well aware, but intoxicating. Of course, things wouldn't
turn out quite like that. But in the beginning I was truly bursting with
enthusiasm. Even Thomas seemed impressed: "You see what happens,
when you follow my advice instead of doing whatever you please," he
said to me with his sardonic smile. But when I thought about it, I hadn't
acted very differently than during our shared mission in 1939: once
again, I had written the strict truth, without thinking too much about
the consequences; but it just happened that I had more luck, and that
the truth, this time, corresponded to what they wanted to hear.
   I threw myself into the job with dedication. Since there wasn't
enough room in the SS-Haus, Brandt had a suite of offices assigned to
me in the Minister of the Interior's *Zentralabteilung*, on the Königsplatz
in a bend of the Spree, on the top floor; from my windows, the Reichstag remained hidden, but I could see to one side, behind the Kroll
Opera, the entire green, serene expanse of the Tiergarten, and to the
other, beyond the river and the Moltke Bridge, the Lehrter customs rail
station, with its vast network of sidings, constantly alive with a slow,
juddering, soothing traffic, a perpetual childlike pleasure. Even better,
the Reichsführer never came here: I could finally smoke in peace in my
office. Fräulein Praxa, whom after all I didn't really mind, and who
knew at least how to answer the telephone and take messages, moved
with me; I also managed to keep Piontek. Brandt also assigned me a
Hauptscharführer, Walser, to take care of the filing, and two stenogra-
phers, and he authorized me to take on an administrative assistant with
the rank of Untersturmführer; I had Thomas recommend one for me,
a young man named Asbach, who had just entered the *Staatspolizei* after studying law and passing a training course at the Junkerschule in Bad
Tölz.
   The British planes had come back several nights running, but each
time there were fewer: the *Wilde Sau*, which allowed our fighter planes
to shoot down enemy aircraft from above while themselves remaining

above the level of the flak, did a lot of damage, and the Luftwaffe had also begun to use flares to light up their targets as if in broad daylight; after September 3, the raids stopped completely: our new tactics had discouraged them. I went to see Pohl at his headquarters in Lichterfelde to discuss the composition of my research group. Pohl seemed very happy that this problem was finally being looked into in a systematic way; he told me frankly he was sick of sending his Kommandanten orders that weren't followed through. We agreed that the Amtsgruppe D would appoint three representatives, one for each department; Pohl also suggested an administrator from the main office of the DWB, the German Economic Enterprises, to advise us about the economic aspects and constraints of companies using inmate labor; finally, he seconded to me his Nutrition Inspector, Professor Weinrowski, a man with moist eyes and hair already white, with a deep cleft in his chin, in which nested rough stubble that had escaped the razor. For almost a year already, Weinrowski had been trying to improve the nourishment of the *Häftlinge*, without any success; but he had a good experience with the obstacles, and Pohl wanted him to participate in our work. After an exchange of correspondence with the departments concerned, I summoned a preliminary meeting to take stock of the situation. At my request, Professor Weinrowski, along with his assistant, Hauptsturmführer Dr. Isenbeck, had prepared a brief memo for us that was distributed to all the participants; he also gave us an oral presentation. It was a beautiful September day, the end of the Indian summer; the sun shone on the trees of the Tiergarten and cast great patches of light into our conference room, illuminating the professor's hair like a halo. The nutritional situation of the *Häftlinge*, Weinrowski explained to us in his jerky, didactic voice, was quite confused. Central regulations set norms and budgets, but the camps got their supplies locally, of course, which gave rise to sometimes considerable variation. As a typical ration, he gave the example of KL Auschwitz, where a *Häftling* assigned to heavy labor was supposed to receive, per day, 350 grams of bread, half a liter of ersatz, and a liter of potato or turnip soup, with the addition, four times a week, of 20 grams of meat in the soup. The inmates assigned to light work or to the infirmary obviously received less; there were also all kinds of special rations, such as those for children in the family camp or for inmates selected for medical experiments. To summarize the situation, roughly: an inmate assigned to heavy labor officially received about 2,150 calories per day and, for light work, 1,700. Now, without even knowing if these norms were applied, they could already be seen to be insufficient: a man at rest needs, depending on his size and weight, and taking environment into account, a minimum of 2,100 calories per

day to stay in good health, and a man who works, 3,000. So the inmates
could only waste away, all the more so since the balance between fats,
carbohydrates, and proteins was far from being respected: 6.4 percent of
the ration, at most, consisted of proteins, whereas the requirement
ought to be 10 percent, or even 15 percent. His presentation over,
Weinrowski sat down with a satisfied air, and I read extracts from the
series of orders from the Reichsführer to Pohl for the improvement of
nutrition in the camps, which I had had my new assistant, Asbach, analyze. The first of these orders, which dated back to March 1942, remained somewhat vague: the Reichsführer simply asked Pohl, a few
days after the incorporation of the IKL into the WVHA, to *gradually develop a diet, like that of the Roman soldiers or Egyptian slaves, that would contain all the vitamins and would remain simple and inexpensive.* The ensuing
letters were a little more precise: *more vitamins, large quantities of raw vegetables and onions, carrots, kohlrabi, turnips,* and also *garlic,* a lot of garlic, especially *in winter, to improve the state of health.* "I know these orders,"
Professor Weinrowski declared when I had finished. "But in my opinion that's not the main point." For a man working, the important thing
is calories and proteins; vitamins and micronutrients remain secondary
when all is said and done. Hauptsturmführer Dr. Alicke, who represented the D III, agreed with this point of view; the young Isenbeck,
on the other hand, had his doubts: classical nutrition, he seemed to
think, underestimates the importance of vitamins, and he put forward in
favor of this opinion, as if it settled everything, an article taken from a
1938 British medical journal, a reference that seemed not to impress
Weinrowski much. Then Hauptsturmführer Gorter, the representative
of the *Arbeitseinsatz,* spoke in turn: As regards the overall statistics of registered inmates, the situation was continuing to show progressive improvement; from 2.8 percent in April, the average rate of mortality had
fallen to 2.23 percent in July, then to 2.09 percent in August. Even in
Auschwitz, it hovered around 3.6 percent, a remarkable drop since
March. "At the moment, the system of KLs includes about one hundred
and sixty thousand inmates: of this number, only thirty-five thousand
are classified by the *Arbeitseinsatz* as unfit for work, and a hundred thousand, which is not inconsiderable, work outside, in factories or enterprises." Thanks to the construction program undertaken by Amtsgruppe
C, overcrowding, a source of epidemics, was diminishing; although
clothing remained problematic, despite the use of goods taken from the
Jews; the medical aspect had made great progress. In short, the situation
seemed to be stabilizing. Obersturmführer Jedermann, from the administration, stated that he mostly agreed with this; but he reminded us
too that control of costs remained a vital problem: the budgets allocated

were restrictive. "That's entirely true," said Sturmbannführer Rizzi, the economic specialist chosen by Pohl, "but there are still a number of factors to take into account." He was an officer about my age, with sparse hair and an upturned, almost Slavic nose; when he spoke, his thin, bloodless lips scarcely moved, yet his statements were lucid and precise. The productivity of an inmate could in general be expressed in terms of a percentage of the productivity of a German worker or a foreign worker; but those two categories entailed much greater expense than the *Häftling*, not to speak of the fact that their availability was growing more and more limited. Indeed, ever since the major corporations and the Armaments Ministry had complained about unfair competition, the SS could no longer provide inmates for its own enterprises at cost, but had to bill for them at the same price as for outside companies, four to six reichsmarks a day, while the cost for an inmate's upkeep obviously remained less than that sum. Now, a slight increase of the actual cost of upkeep, carefully managed, could lead to a considerable increase in the ratio of productivity, from which everyone would gain. "I will explain: the WVHA presently spends, let's say, one point five reichsmarks per day for an inmate capable of carrying out ten percent of the daily work of a German worker. So we need ten inmates, or fifteen reichsmarks per day, to replace a German. But what if, by spending two reichsmarks per day for an inmate, we could give him back his strength, increase the period during which he's fit for work, and thus train him correctly? In that case, it would be conceivable that an inmate could, after a few months, provide fifty percent of the work of his German counterpart: thus, we would need no more than two inmates, or four reichsmarks per day, to carry out the job of one German. You follow me? Of course, these figures are approximate. A study would have to be carried out."—"Could you take charge of that?" I asked with interest.—"Wait, wait," Jedermann cut in. "If I have to provide for one hundred thousand inmates at two reichsmarks instead of one point five, that is an overcost of fifty thousand reichsmarks per day, every day. The fact that they're producing more or less doesn't change anything. My budget doesn't change."— "That's true," I replied. "But I see what Sturmbannführer Rizzi is getting at. If his idea is valid, the overall profits of the SS will increase, since the inmates will produce more without any increase in cost for the companies that employ them. It would be enough, if that can be demonstrated, to convince Obergruppenführer Pohl to transfer part of these increased profits to the maintenance budget of Amtsgruppe D."— "Yes, that's a good point," agreed Gorter, Maurer's man. "And if the inmates don't get worn out so quickly, in the end, the labor pool will grow more quickly, in fact. Hence the importance of lowering the death rate, in the end."

The meeting concluded on this note, and I suggested a division of tasks to prepare for the next meeting. Rizzi would try to study the validity of his idea; Jedermann would explain his budgetary constraints to us in detail; as for Isenbeck, I directed him, with Weinrowski's consent (he himself obviously didn't want to move around much), to conduct a quick inspection of four camps: the KLs Ravensbrück, Sachsenhausen, Gross-Rosen, and Auschwitz, with the aim of collecting all their ration lists, the menus that were actually prepared for the main categories of inmates in the past month, and especially samples of the rations that we would have analyzed: I wanted to be able to compare the theoretical menus with the food actually served.

At this last remark, Rizzi had thrown me a curious glance; after the meeting was adjourned, I brought him into my office. "Do you have reasons to believe that the *Häftlinge* don't receive what they are supposed to?" he asked in his dry, abrupt manner. He seemed to me an intelligent man, and his query led me to imagine that our ideas and objectives should be able to intersect: I decided to make him my ally; in any case, I didn't see any risk in opening up to him. "Yes, I do," I said. "Corruption is a major problem in the camps. A large part of the food bought by the D-Four is diverted. It's hard to estimate, but the *Häftlinge* at the end of the chain—I'm not talking about the kapos or the *Prominenten*—must be deprived of twenty to thirty percent of their ration. Since it's inadequate to begin with, only the inmates who manage to obtain extra, legally or illegally, have any chance of staying alive more than a few months."—"I see." He thought, rubbing the bridge of his nose under his glasses. "We should try to calculate life expectancy precisely and adjust it according to the degree of specialization." He paused again and concluded: "Very well, I'll see."

I swiftly understood, alas, that my initial enthusiasm would be damped. The ensuing meetings got bogged down in a mass of technical details as voluminous as they were contradictory. Isenbeck had made a good analysis of the menus, but seemed incapable of demonstrating their relationship to the rations actually distributed; Rizzi seemed to be focused on the idea of emphasizing the division between skilled and nonskilled workers, and of concentrating our efforts on the former; Weinrowski couldn't manage to come to an agreement with Isenbeck and Alicke on the question of vitamins. To try to stimulate the debate, I invited a representative from Speer's ministry. Schmelter, who headed their department for the allocation of labor, told me it was high time for the SS to take this problem into account, and sent me as his representative an Oberregierungsrat with a long list of grievances. Speer's ministry had just absorbed some of the responsibilities of the Ministry of Finance and had been rebaptized Ministry for Armaments and War Production, or RMf RuK according to the barbaric acronym, in order to reflect his expanded authority in this domain; and this reorganization seemed to be reflected in the unwavering self-confidence of Dr. Kühne, Schmelter's envoy. "I don't speak just for the ministry," he began when I introduced him to my colleagues, "but also for the companies that use the labor the SS provides, whose repeated complaints reach us daily." This Oberregierungsrat wore a brown suit with a bow tie, and had a Prussian toothbrush moustache; his few strands of stringy hair were carefully combed to the side, to cover the oblong dome of his skull. But the firmness of his speech contradicted his rather ludicrous appearance. As we surely knew, the inmates generally arrived in the factories in a feeble condition, and often, exhausted after only a few weeks, they had to be sent back to the camp. Their training required a minimum of several weeks; there was a shortage of instructors, and they didn't have the means to train new groups every month. What's more, for the slightest job requiring even a minimum level of qualification, at least six months had to go by before output reached a satisfactory level: and few inmates lasted that long. Reichsminister Speer was very disappointed by this state of things and thought that the contribution of the SS to the war effort, on this level, would benefit from being improved. He concluded by handing out a memo containing extracts of letters from various firms. After he left, as I looked through the memo, Rizzi shrugged his shoulders and licked his thin lips: "That's what I've been saying since the beginning. Skilled workers." I had also asked the office of Sauckel, the General Plenipotentiary for the *Arbeitseinsatz* or GBA, to send someone to express their views: one of Sauckel's assistants had replied somewhat acidly that so long as the SP saw fit to find any pretext whatsoever to arrest foreign workers and send them off to increase the manpower of the camps, it was up to the SS to take care of their upkeep, and the GBA, for its part, no longer felt involved. Brandt had called me to remind me that the Reichsführer attached a lot of importance to the RSHA's opinion, so I had also written to Kaltenbrunner, who referred me to Müller, who in turn told me to get in touch with Obersturmbannführer Eichmann. In vain I protested that the problem didn't only concern Jews, Eichmann's sole area of responsibility, Müller had insisted; so I placed a call to the Kurfürstenstrasse and asked Eichmann to send a colleague; he told me he preferred to come in person. "My deputy Günther is in Denmark," he explained to me when he came over. "Anyway, I prefer to deal with questions of this importance my-

self." At our roundtable, he launched into a pitiless indictment of the
Jewish inmates, who, according to him, represented an ever greater
threat; after Warsaw, revolts were increasing; an uprising in a special
camp in the East (this was Treblinka, but Eichmann didn't mention it by
name) had caused many deaths among the SS, and hundreds of inmates
had escaped; not all of them had been recaptured. The RSHA, as well
as the Reichsführer himself, was afraid that such incidents would mul-
tiply. This, given the tense situation on the front, we could not allow.
He also reminded us that the Jews conveyed to the camps in RSHA
convoys were all under a death sentence: "We can't change anything
about that, even if we wanted to. At the most we have the right to extract from them, as it were, their work capacity, for the Reich, before
they die." In other words, even if certain political objectives were de-
ferred for economic reasons, they remained no less in force; thus it
wasn't a question of distinguishing between skilled inmates and nonskilled ones—I had briefly summarized the state of our discussions for
him—but between the different political-police categories. The Russian
or Polish workers arrested for theft, for example, were sent to a camp,
but their punishment didn't extend further than that; so the WVHA
could use them as it liked. As for those condemned for "defiling the
race," that was more delicate. But for the Jews and the asocials transferred by the Ministry of Justice, everyone had to be clear: they were,
in a way, only on loan to the WVHA, since the RSHA preserved jurisdiction over them until their death; for these prisoners, the policy of
Vernichtung durch Arbeit, annihilation through work, had to be strictly
applied: so it was useless to waste food on them. These statements made
a strong impression on my colleagues, and, once Eichmann had left,
some began to propose that rations for Jewish inmates be differentiated
from the others; I even went so far as to see Oberregierungsrat Kühne
again to tell him about this suggestion; he answered me in writing that,
in that case, the enterprises would certainly refuse the Jewish inmates,
which went against the agreement between Reichsminister Speer and
the Führer, as well as the decree of January 1943 on the mobilization of
manpower. Nevertheless my colleagues did not entirely abandon the
idea. Rizzi asked Weinrowski if it was technically possible to calculate
rations that were liable to make a man die within a given period of time;
one ration, for example, that would give three months to an unskilled
Jew, another ration that would give nine months to an asocial specialized worker. Weinrowski had to explain to him that, no, it wasn't possible; not even mentioning the other factors such as cold and disease,
everything depended on the weight and resistance of the subject; with
a given ration, one individual could die in three weeks, another might

last indefinitely; all the more so since the clever inmate would always find something extra, whereas the one who was already weakened and apathetic would only let himself go more quickly. This reasoning gave a brilliant idea to Hauptsturmführer Dr. Alicke: "What you are saying," he said, as if thinking out loud, "is that the strongest inmates will always find a way to steal some of the rations of the weaker inmates, and so to survive. But in a way, isn't it in our own interest for the weakest inmates not to get their complete ration? Once they've passed a certain level of weakness, automatically so to speak, their rations get stolen, so they eat even less and die faster, and so we save on their food. As to what is stolen from them, that strengthens the inmates who are already stronger, so that they work better. It's simply the natural mechanism of survival of the fittest; in the same way, a sick animal succumbs quickly to predators." That was going a little far, I thought, and I reacted sharply: "Hauptsturmführer, the Reichsführer did not set up the concentration camp system to conduct experiments on the theories of social Darwinism. Your reasoning does not seem very pertinent to me." I turned to the others: "The real problem is what we want to prioritize: The political imperatives? Or the economic needs?"—"It's certainly not at our level that a decision like that can be made," Weinrowski said calmly.— "True," Gorter interrupted, "but still, for the *Arbeitseinsatz*, the instructions are clear: Everything must be implemented to increase the productivity of the *Häftlinge*."—"From the standpoint of our SS enterprises," Rizzi confirmed, "that's true too. But we still cannot ignore certain ideological imperatives."—"In any case, meine Herren," I concluded, "we don't have to settle this question. The Reichsführer asked me to make recommendations that would satisfy the interests of your different departments. In the worst case we can prepare several options and leave the choice to him; whatever the case, the final decision is up to him."

I began to see that these fruitless discussions could go on indefinitely, and this prospect alarmed me; so I decided to change tactics: prepare a concrete suggestion, and have it endorsed by the others, or else modify it a little, if necessary. For that, I decided to come to an agreement first with the specialists Weinrowski and Isenbeck. When I approached Weinrowski, he quickly understood my intentions and promised me his support; as for Isenbeck, he would do whatever he was told to do. But we still lacked concrete data. Weinrowski believed the IKL had already carried out research on this subject; I sent Isenbeck to Oranienburg with a mission order; triumphant, he brought back a pile of files: at the end of the 1930s, the medical department of the IKL had in fact carried out a set of experiments, at the KL Buchenwald, on minimal feeding for inmates subjected to forced labor; with punishment or the threat of punishment as the sole incentive, they had tested a large number of formulas, frequently changing the rations and weighing the subjects regularly; a whole array of statistics had been generated from this. While Isenbeck analyzed these reports, I talked with Weinrowski about what we called the "secondary factors," such as hygiene, cold, illness, beatings. I had a copy of my Stalingrad report sent to me by the SD, which dealt with precisely these subjects; skimming through it, Weinrowski exclaimed: "Oh, but you quote Hohenegg!" At these words, the memory of that man, buried inside me like a glass bubble, detached from the depths and rose up, gathering speed by the second, before bursting at the surface: how curious that is, I said to myself, I hadn't thought of him in a long time. "Do you know him?" I asked Weinrowski, overcome with intense emotion.—"Of course! He's one of my colleagues from the faculty of medicine in Vienna."—"So he's still alive?"—"Yes, of course, why not?"

I immediately set out looking for him: he was well and truly alive, and I had no difficulty finding him; he too was working in Berlin, at the medical department of the Bendlerstrasse. Happy, I called him on the telephone without giving my name; his throaty, musical voice sounded a little annoyed when he answered: "Yes?"—"Professor Hohenegg?"—"Speaking. What's this about?"—"I'm calling from the SS. It's about an old debt." His voice became a shade more irritated. "What are you talking about? Who are you?"—"I'm talking about a bottle of Cognac you promised me nine months ago." Hohenegg let out a long burst of laughter: "Alas, alas, I have to confess something to you: I thought you were dead, and I drank it to your health."—"Man of little faith."—"So you are alive."—"And promoted: Sturmbannführer."—"Bravo! Well, I'll just have to unearth another bottle."—"I give you twenty-four hours: we'll drink it tomorrow night. In exchange, dinner will be on me. At Borchardt's, eight o'clock, does that suit you?" Hohenegg gave a long whistle: "They must have given you a raise too. But allow me to point out that it's not quite oyster season yet."—"That's all right; we'll eat wild boar pâté. Till tomorrow."

Hohenegg, as soon as he saw me, wanted at all cost to feel my scars; I graciously permitted him, under the surprised eye of the maître d'hôtel, who had come to proffer the wine list. "Good work," Hohenegg said, "good work. If you had had that before Kislovodsk, I would have cited you in my seminar. All in all, I did well to insist."—"What do you mean?"—"The surgeon in Gumrak didn't want to operate on you, which is understandable. He had pulled a sheet over your face and had told the nurses to put you out in the snow, as they did then, to get it over with. I happened to be walking by, I noticed this sheet moving at mouth level, and of course I thought that was curious, a dead man breathing like an ox under his shroud. I turned down the sheet: imagine my surprise. So I told myself that ordering someone else to take care of you was the least I could do. The surgeon didn't want to; we had a few words, but I was his hierarchical superior, and he had to give in. He kept complaining that it was a waste of time. I was in something of a hurry, I let him get on with it; I imagine he made do with a hemostasis. But I'm happy it was of some use." I remained motionless, riveted to his words; at the same time I felt immensely remote from all that, as if it concerned another man, whom I scarcely knew. The maître d'hôtel brought the wine. Hohenegg interrupted him before he could pour: "Just a minute, please. Could you bring us two Cognac glasses?"—"Of course, Herr Oberst." With a smile, Hohenegg took a bottle of Hennessy out of his briefcase and placed it on the table: "There. A promise is a promise." The maître d'hôtel returned with the glasses, uncorked the bottle, and poured us each a measure. Hohenegg took his glass and got up; I did the same. Suddenly he looked serious and I noticed that he had aged perceptibly from what I remembered of him: his yellow, soft skin drooped under his eyes and on his round cheeks; his whole body, still fat, seemed to have shrunk somehow on his frame. "I suggest," he said, "that we drink to all our comrades in misfortune who didn't have as much luck as we did. And especially to those who are still alive, somewhere." We toasted, and sat back down. Hohenegg remained silent for a little bit, playing with his knife, then resumed his cheerful air. I told him how I had gotten out, or at least what Thomas had told me, and asked him for his story. "With me it's simpler. I had finished my work, turned in my report to General Renoldi, who was already packing his bags for Siberia and couldn't have cared less about anything else, and I realized they had forgotten me. Fortunately, I knew an obliging young man at the AOK; thanks to him, I was able to send a signal to the OKHG with a copy for my faculty, stating simply that I was ready to submit my report. Then they remembered me and the next day I received orders to leave the *Kessel*. And it was when I was waiting for a plane in Gumrak that I came across you. I wanted to take you with me, but in that state, you were unfit for travel, and I couldn't wait for your operation, since flights were becoming rare. I think I actually got one of the last flights leaving Gumrak. The plane just before mine crashed right in front of my eyes; I was still a bit dazed by the noise of the explosion when I got to Novorossisk. We took off straight through the smoke and the flames rising up from the wreck, it was very impressive. Afterward I got leave, and instead of reassigning me to the new Sixth Army, they

gave me a job at the OKW. And you, what's become of you?" While
we ate I described my work group's problems to him. "Indeed," he
commented, "it sounds tricky. I know Weinrowski well; he's an honest
man and a scholar of integrity, but he has no political sense and often
makes blunders." I remained pensive: "You couldn't meet him with me?
To help us get our bearings."—"My dear Sturmbannführer, I would remind you that I am an officer of the Wehrmacht. I don't think your superiors—or mine—would appreciate your mixing me up in this dark
business."—"Not officially, of course. A simple private discussion, with
your old faculty friend?"—"I never said he was my friend." Hohenegg
ran his hand pensively over the dome of his bald skull; his wrinkled neck
stuck out of his buttoned collar. "Of course, as a clinical pathologist, I
am always delighted to be of help to the human species; after all, I never
lack customers. If you like, the three of us can just finish off this bottle
of Cognac together."

Weinrowski invited us to his place. He lived with his wife in a three-
room apartment in Kreuzberg. He showed us two photos on the piano
of young men, one framed in black with a ribbon: his eldest son, Egon,
killed in Demiansk; the younger one was serving in France and had
been quiet till then, but his division had just been rushed to Italy to reinforce the new front. While Frau Weinrowski served us tea and cakes,
we talked about the Italian situation: as pretty much everyone expected,
Badoglio was just waiting for the occasion to switch sides, and as soon
as the Anglo-Americans had set foot on Italian soil, he had seized it.
"Fortunately, fortunately, the Führer was cleverer than he!" Weinrowski
exclaimed.—"You say that," Frau Weinrowski murmured sadly as she
offered us sugar, "but it's your Karl who is there, not the Führer." She
was a rather heavy woman, with puffy, tired features; but the outline of
her mouth and especially the light in her eyes hinted at past beauty.
"Oh, be quiet," Weinrowski grumbled, "the Führer knows what he's
doing. Look at that Skorzeny! Tell me that wasn't a master stroke." The
raid on the Gran Sasso, to liberate Mussolini, had made headlines for
days in Goebbels's press. Since then, our forces had occupied northern
Italy, interned six hundred and fifty thousand Italian soldiers, and set up
a Fascist republic in Salò; and all that was presented as a significant victory, a brilliant maneuver of the Führer's. But the resumption of raids
on Berlin was also a direct consequence; the new front was draining our
divisions, and in August the Americans had managed to bomb Ploesti,
our last source of oil. Germany was truly caught in the crossfire.

Hohenegg got out his Cognac and Weinrowski went to look for
glasses; his wife had disappeared into the kitchen. The apartment was
dark, with the musty, stale smell of old people's apartments. I had always

wondered where this smell came from. Would I smell that way too, if I ever lived long enough? Strange idea. Today, in any case, I don't think I smell; but one can never smell one's own odor, they say. When Weinrowski returned, Hohenegg poured three measures and we drank to the memory of his dead son. Weinrowski seemed a little moved. Then I took out the documents I had prepared and showed them to Hohenegg, after asking Weinrowski for a little more light. Weinrowski was sitting next to his old colleague and commenting on the papers and the charts as Hohenegg examined them; unconsciously, they had slipped into a Viennese dialect that I had trouble following. I settled into my armchair and drank Hohenegg's Cognac. Both had a rather odd attitude: in fact, as Hohenegg had explained to me, Weinrowski, at the faculty, had seniority; but as Oberst, Hohenegg was superior in rank to Weinrowski, who in the SS had the rank of Sturmbannführer of the Reserve, the equivalent of a Major. They didn't seem to be sure which of them had precedence over the other, so they had adopted a diffident attitude, with much "If you please," "No, no, of course you're right," "Your experience . . ." "Your practice . . . ," which was starting to get rather comical. Hohenegg raised his head and looked at me: "If I understand correctly, according to you, the inmates don't even receive the complete rations described here?"—"Aside from a few privileged ones, no. They lose at least twenty percent." Hohenegg resumed his conversation with Weinrowski. "That's bad."—"It certainly is. That gives them between thirteen hundred and seventeen hundred calories a day."—"It's still more than our men in Stalingrad." He looked at me again: "What are you aiming for, in the end?"—"The ideal thing would be a normal minimum ration." Hohenegg tapped the papers: "Yes, but if I understood correctly, that's impossible. Lack of resources."—"In a way, yes. But we could suggest improvements." Hohenegg thought: "In fact, your real problem is the argumentation. The inmate who should receive seventeen hundred calories only receives thirteen hundred; in order for him actually to receive seventeen hundred . . ."—"Which is insufficient in any case," Weinrowski interjected.—". . . the ration would have to be twenty-one hundred. But if you ask for twenty-one hundred, you have to justify twenty-one hundred. You can't say you're asking for twenty-one hundred in order to get seventeen hundred."—"Doktor, as always, it's a pleasure talking with you," I said, smiling. "As is your wont, you go straight to the heart of the matter." Hohenegg went on without letting himself be interrupted: "Wait. To ask for twenty-one hundred, you would have to demonstrate that seventeen hundred wasn't enough, which you can't do, since they don't actually receive seventeen hundred. And of course, you can't take the diversion factor into account in your arguments."—"Not really. Management knows the problem exists, but we can't get mixed up in it. There are other authorities for that."—"I see."—"In fact, the problem is to obtain an increase of the overall budget. But the people who manage that budget think that it *should be* enough, and it's hard to prove the contrary. Even if we demonstrate that the inmates continue to die too quickly, they tell us that throwing money at the problem won't solve it."—"In which they aren't necessarily wrong." Hohenegg rubbed the top of his skull; Weinrowski was silent and listened. "Couldn't we modify the distributions?"—"Meaning?"—"Well, without increasing the overall budget, favor the working inmates a little more, and the ones who don't work a little less."—"In principle, dear Doktor, there are no inmates who don't work. There are only sick inmates: but if they are fed even less than they are now, they would have no chance to recover and become fit for work again. In that case, might as well not feed them at all; but then the death rate would increase again."—"Yes, but what I mean is that you must keep the women and the children somewhere? So they must be fed too?" I stared at him without replying. Weinrowski too remained silent. Finally I said: "No, Doktor. We don't keep the women, the elderly, or the children." Hohenegg opened his eyes wide and looked at me without replying, as if he wanted me to confirm that I had indeed said what I had said. I nodded. Finally he understood. He gave a long sigh and rubbed the back of his neck: "Well . . ." Weinrowski and I still remained silent. "Ah yes . . . yes. That's rough." He breathed heavily: "Well. I see how it is. I imagine that, after all, especially after Stalingrad, we don't have much of a choice."—"No, Doktor, not really."—"Still, that's hard. All of them?"—"All those who can't work."—"Well . . ." He pulled himself together: "At bottom, it's normal. There's no reason for us to treat our enemies better than our own soldiers. After what I saw in Stalingrad. . . . Even these rations are luxurious. Our men survived with much less. And also, the ones who survived, what are they getting to eat now? What are our comrades in Siberia getting? No, no, you're right." He stared at me pensively: "Still, it's a *Schweinerei*, a filthy business. But still, you're right."

I had been right, too, to ask his opinion: Hohenegg had understood right away what Weinrowski couldn't see, that it was a political problem, not a technical one. The technical aspect had to serve to justify a political decision, but couldn't dictate it. Our discussion that day reached no conclusions; but it made me think, and in the end I found the solution. Since Weinrowski seemed incapable of grasping it, to keep him busy I asked him to develop another report, and turned to Isenbeck for the necessary technical support. I had underestimated this boy: he was very keen and turned out to be fully capable of understanding my thinking, and even of anticipating it. In one night of work, alone in our big office at the Ministry of the Interior, drinking coffee brought to us by a drowsy orderly, we sketched the rough outlines of the project together. I started with Rizzi's concept, setting up a distinction between skilled and unskilled workers: all rations would be increased, but just a little for the unskilled workers, while skilled workers could receive a whole series of new advantages. The project didn't deal with the different categories of inmates, but allowed, if the RSHA insisted, for the categories meant to be disadvantaged, such as the Jews, to be assigned solely to unskilled jobs: in any case, the options remained open. Starting from this central distinction, Isenbeck helped me define others: heavy labor, light labor, hospitalization; in the end, it formed a scale to which we merely had to index the rations. Instead of struggling with fixed rations, which in any case could not be guaranteed because of restrictions and difficulties in obtaining provisions, I asked Isenbeck to calculate—based on standard menus—a daily budget corresponding to each category, then, in addition, to suggest various menus that would correspond to these budgets. Isenbeck insisted that these suggestions also include qualitative options, such as distributing raw onions rather than cooked ones, because of the vitamins; I agreed. At the bottom line, there was nothing revolutionary about this project: it took the current practices and modified them slightly to try to produce a net increase; in order to justify it, I went to find Rizzi, explained the concept to him, and asked him to write an economic argument for me in terms of output; he immediately agreed, all the more so since I readily attributed authorship of the key ideas to him. For myself I reserved the drafting of the project, once I had all the technical elements in hand.

The important thing, I saw clearly, was for the RSHA not to have too many objections; if the project was acceptable to them, Department D IV of the WVHA couldn't oppose it. So I called Eichmann to sound him out: "Ah, my dear Sturmbannführer Aue! Meet with me? It's just that I'm absolutely snowed under at the moment. Yes, Italy, and something else too. Tonight, then? For a drink. There's a little café not too far from my office, at the corner of Potsdamerstrasse. Yes, next to the U-Bahn entrance. Till tonight, then." When he arrived, he flopped onto the banquette with a sigh and threw his cap on the table, massaging the bridge of his nose. I had already ordered two glasses of schnapps and I offered him a cigarette, which he took with pleasure, leaning back in the banquette with his legs crossed, one arm thrown over the back. Between puffs he chewed his lower lip; his broad bare forehead reflected the lights of the café. "So, Italy?" I asked.—"The problem isn't so much Italy—well, we'll get eight or ten thousand of them there, of course—it's mostly the zones that they occupied: with their imbecilic policies they've become paradise for Jews. They're everywhere! In the South of France, the Dalmatian coast, the Italian zone in Greece. I sent teams right away pretty much everywhere, but it's going to be a big job; with the transport problems on top of that, it won't get done in a day. In Nice, with the benefit of surprise, we managed to arrest a few thousand; but the French police are becoming less and less cooperative, and that complicates matters. We lack resources terribly. And also Denmark is worrying us a lot."—"Denmark?"—"Yes. It should have been quite simple, but it's become a real mess. Günther is furious. Did I tell you I sent him there?"—"Yes. What happened?"—"I don't know exactly. According to Günther, it's Dr. Best, the ambassador, who's playing a weird game. You know him, don't you?" Eichmann emptied his schnapps in one gulp and ordered another. "He was my superior," I replied. "Before the war."—"Yes, well, I don't know what's on his mind now. For months and months, he's been doing everything he can to get in our way, under the pretext that it's going to . . ."—he made a repeated gesture from top to bottom—"interfere with his policy of cooperation. And then in August, after the riots, when we imposed a state of emergency, we said, fine, let's do it. Onsite, there's a new BdS, Dr. Mildner, but he's already overwhelmed; what's more the Wehrmacht immediately refused to cooperate, that's why I sent Günther, to get things going. So we prepared everything, a boat for the four thousand who are in Copenhagen, trains for the others, and then Best keeps creating difficulties. He always has an objection, the Danish, the Wehrmacht, *e tutti quanti*. What's more, this was supposed to stay a secret, so we could round them all up at once, without their expecting it, but Günther says they already know everything. It looks like it's off to a pretty bad start."—"So where are you at now?"—"It's planned for a few days from now. We'll do it all at once, there aren't all that many of them anyway. I called Günther and said to him, Günther, my friend, if that's the way it is, tell Mildner to move the date up, but Best refused. Too sensitive, he had to talk some more with the Danes. Günther thinks he's doing it on purpose so it'll fail."—"But I know Dr. Best well: he's anything but a friend of the Jews. You'd have a hard time finding a better National Socialist than him." Eichmann made a face: "Mmmh. You know, politics change people. Well, we'll see. Me, I'm covered, we prepared everything, planned everything, if it goes wrong, it won't fall on my shoulders, I'm telling you that right now. But how about your project, how's that going?"

I ordered another round: I had already had a chance to notice that drinking tended to relax Eichmann, to arouse his sentimental, friendly side. I wasn't trying to con him, far from it, but I wanted him to trust me and see that my ideas weren't incompatible with his vision of things. I gave him a rough outline of the project; as I had foreseen, he scarcely listened. One single thing interested him: "How do you reconcile all that with the principle of *Vernichtung durch Arbeit*?"—"It's very simple: the improvements relate only to the skilled workers. It will be enough to make sure that the Jews and the asocials are assigned to heavy but un-skilled labor." Eichmann scratched his cheek. Of course I knew that in actual fact the assignments of each individual worker were decided by the *Arbeitseinsatz* of each camp, but if they wanted to keep skilled Jews, that would be their problem. Eichmann, in any case, seemed to have other concerns. After a minute of thought, he said abruptly: "Fine, that's okay," and began talking about the South of France again. I listened to him as I drank and smoked. After a while, at an opportune moment, I asked him politely: "To come back to my project, Obersturmbann-führer, it's almost ready, and I'd like to send it to you so you can study it." Eichmann waved his hand: "If you like. I already get so much pa-per."—"I don't want to bother you. It's just to be sure you don't have any objections."—"If it's as you say . . ."—"Listen, if you have the time, look at it, and then send me a little letter. That way I can show that I took your opinion into account." Eichmann gave an ironic little smile and waved a finger at me: "Ah, you're a clever one, Sturmbannführer Aue. You have to cover your tracks too." I kept my face impassive: "The Reichsführer wants the opinions of all departments involved to be taken into account. Obergruppenführer Kaltenbrunner told me that for the RSHA, I would have to see you. I find it normal." Eichmann scowled: "Of course, I'm not the one who decides: I'll have to submit it to my Amtschef. But if I give a positive recommendation, there's no reason he'll refuse to sign it. In principle, of course." I raised my glass: "To the success of your Danish Einsatz, then?" He smiled; when he smiled that way, his ears seemed to stick out, and he looked more than ever like a bird; at the same time, a nervous tic deformed his smile, making it al-most into a grimace. "Yes, thank you, to the Einsatz. To your project too."

I drafted the text in two days; Isenbeck had meticulously prepared handsome detailed charts for the annexes, and I used Rizzi's arguments without altering them too much. I hadn't quite finished when Brandt summoned me. The Reichsführer was going to the Warthegau to de-liver important speeches there; on October 6, a conference of the Reichsleiters and Gauleiters was taking place, at which Dr. Mandelbrod would be present; and the latter had asked that I be invited. How far was

I with my project? I assured him that I had almost finished. I just had to present it to my colleagues before sending it to the relevant offices for approval. I had already discussed it with Weinrowski, presenting Isen-beck's scales to him as a simple technical elaboration of his ideas: he seemed to think it was fine. The general meeting went off without any hitches; I let Rizzi do most of the talking, and contented myself with stressing that I had secured the verbal agreement of the RSHA. Gorter seemed satisfied, and just wondered if we had gone far enough; Alicke seemed unable to follow Rizzi's economic arguments; Jedermann grumbled that it was still going to be expensive, and where would we find the money? But he was reassured when I guaranteed that if the project were approved, it would be financed through additional alloca-tion. I asked each person for a written reply from his Amtschef for the tenth, counting on being back in Berlin by then; I also forwarded a copy to Eichmann. Brandt had let me know that I could probably present the project to the Reichsführer in person, once the departments had given their agreement.

The day of our departure, at the end of the afternoon, I went to the Prinz-Albrecht-Palais. Brandt had invited me to attend a speech of Speer's before joining Dr. Mandelbrod in the special train for the big-wigs. In the lobby, I was welcomed by Ohlendorf, whom I hadn't seen since he left the Crimea. "Dr. Aue! How nice to see you again.

I hear you've been in Berlin for months. Why didn't you call me? I would have been happy to see you."—"I'm sorry, Brigadeführer. I was terribly busy. You too, I imagine." He seemed to be radiating intensity, a dark, concentrated energy. "Brandt sent you for our conference, isn't that right? As I understood it, you're looking into questions of produc-tivity."—"Yes, but only in matters concerning concentration camp in-mates."—"I see. Tonight we're going to introduce a new cooperation agreement between the SD and the Armaments Ministry. But the sub-ject is much vaster; it will also cover the treatment of foreign workers, among other things."—"You're in the Ministry of Economics now, Brigadeführer, isn't that so?"—"That's right. I'm wearing several hats these days. It's too bad you're not an economist: with these agreements, a whole new field will open up for the SD, I hope. Well then, let's go up, it's going to start soon."

The conference took place in one of the great oak-paneled halls of the palace, where National Socialist decorations clashed somewhat with the eighteenth-century woodwork and gilt candelabra. More than a hundred SD officers were present, among them a number of my former colleagues or superiors: Siebert, with whom I had served in the Crimea,

Regierungsrat Neifend, who had worked in Amt II but had since been appointed Gruppenleiter in Amt III, and others. Ohlendorf had his seat near the rostrum, next to a man in an SS-Obergruppenführer's uniform, with a broad, bare forehead and firm, set features: Karl Hanke, the Gauleiter from Lower Silesia, who was representing the Reichsführer at this ceremony. Reichsminister Speer arrived a little late. He struck me as surprisingly young, even though his hair was starting to recede, slim, vigorous; he wore a simple twill suit, with the Gold Badge of the Party as sole decoration. Some civilians accompanied him, and took their seats on chairs lined up behind Ohlendorf and Hanke, while he stepped up to the podium and began his speech. He spoke, in the beginning, in an almost gentle voice, precise and polished, which emphasized rather than masked an authority that Speer seemed to draw more from himself than from his position. His dark, keen eyes remained fixed on us and left our faces only occasionally, to look at his notes; when they were lowered, they almost disappeared under his thick, bushy eyebrows. The notes were just there to serve as pointers for his speech; he hardly consulted them at all, and seemed to take all the figures he ticked off directly from his head, as he needed them, as if they were constantly stored there, ready for use. His statements were brutally and, to my way of thinking, refreshingly frank: if total military production was not rapidly implemented, the war was lost. These weren't Cassandra warnings; Speer compared our present production with the estimates we had of Soviet and especially American production; at this pace, he demonstrated, we wouldn't hold out for a year. But our industrial resources were far from being fully exploited; and one of the major obstacles, aside from the problems of manual labor, was the obstruction, at a regional level, by private interests: it was especially for that reason that he counted on the support of the SD, and that was one of the main subjects of the agreements he was going to conclude with the SS. He had just signed an important agreement with the French Economics Minister, Bichelonne, to transfer the majority of our production of consumer goods to France. That would certainly give a considerable commercial advantage to postwar France, but we didn't have a choice: if we wanted victory, it was up to us to make sacrifices. This measure would allow us to transfer an additional million and a half workers to armaments. But we could expect a number of Gauleiters to oppose the necessary closures of firms; and this was one particular area where the SD could intervene. After this speech, Ohlendorf got up, thanked Speer, and swiftly presented the terms of the agreement: the SD would be authorized to examine the conditions of recruitment and the treatment of foreign workers; similarly, any refusal by the Gauleiters to follow the minister's instructions

would be subject to an SD investigation. On a table set up for this purpose the agreement was ceremoniously signed, by Hanke, Ohlendorf,
and Speer; then everyone exchanged a German salute, Speer shook
their hands, and left. I looked at my watch: I had less than forty-five
minutes, but I had brought my travel bag. In all the milling around, I
slipped next to Ohlendorf, who was talking to Hanke: "Brigadeführer,
excuse me. I'm taking the same train as the Reichsminister; I have to
go." Ohlendorf, a little surprised, raised his eyebrows: "Call me when
you get back," he said.

The special train left not from one of the main stations but from the
S-Bahn station on Friedrichstrasse. The platform, cordoned off by police and Waffen-SS forces, was swarming with senior officials and
Gauleiters, in SA or SS uniforms, greeting one another noisily. While a
Leutnant from the Schupo checked his list and my orders, I examined
the crowd: I didn't see Dr. Mandelbrod, whom I was supposed to meet
there. I asked the Leutnant to show me his compartment; he consulted
his list: "Herr Doktor Mandelbrod, Mandelbrod . . . here it is, the special car, at the end of the train." This car was specially built: instead of
an ordinary door, there was a double door, as in a cattle car, comprising
about a third of its length; and steel blinds hid all the windows. One of
Mandelbrod's amazons was standing in front of the door, in an SS uniform with an Obersturmführer's stripes; she was wearing not the regulation skirt but masculine riding breeches, and was at least an inch taller
than I. I wondered where Mandelbrod recruited his aides: he must have
had a special arrangement with the Reichsführer. The woman saluted
me: "Sturmbannführer, Dr. Mandelbrod is waiting for you." She
seemed to have recognized me, but I didn't recognize her; they all
looked pretty much alike. She took my bag and led me into a carpeted
antechamber, from which a hallway branched out to the left. "Your
cabin will be the second on the right," she said. "I'll put your things
there. Dr. Mandelbrod is this way." A double sliding door, opposite the
hallway, opened automatically. I went in. Mandelbrod, bathed in his
usual frightful odor, was sitting in his enormous platform-armchair,
which could be hoisted on board thanks to the arrangement of the
doors; next to him, in a little rococo armchair, his legs casually crossed,
sat Minister Speer. "Ah, Max, there you are!" Mandelbrod exclaimed in
his musical voice. "Come in, come in." A cat slipped between my boots
when I wanted to step forward and I almost tripped; I caught myself and
saluted Speer, then Mandelbrod. He turned his head to the Minister:
"My dear Speer, let me introduce you to one of my young protégés, Dr.
Aue." Speer examined me under his voluminous eyebrows and unfolded
himself from his chair; to my surprise, he came forward to shake my

hand: "Pleased to meet you, Sturmbannführer."—"Dr. Aue is working for the Reichsführer," Mandelbrod explained. "He is trying to improve the productivity of our concentration camps."—"Ah," Speer said, "that's very good. Will you succeed?"—"I've been looking into this question for several months now, Herr Reichsminister, and my role is a minor one. But on the whole a lot of things have been accomplished. I think you've been able to see the results."—"Yes, of course. It's a subject I recently discussed with the Reichsführer. He agreed with me that it could be even better."—"Without a doubt, Herr Reichsminister. We're working hard on it." There was a pause; Speer was obviously looking for something to say. His eyes fell on my medals: "You were at the front, Sturmbannführer?"—"Yes, Herr Reichsminister. In Stalingrad." His gaze darkened, and he lowered his eyes; his jaw twitched. Then he looked at me again with his precise, searching eyes, circled, I noticed for the first time, by heavy shadows of fatigue. "My brother Ernst disappeared in Stalingrad," he said in a calm, slightly tense voice. I bowed my head: "I'm sorry, Herr Reichsminister. My condolences. Do you know how he fell?"—"No. I don't even know if he's dead." His voice seemed distant, almost detached. "Our parents received letters, he was sick, in one of the hospitals. The conditions were . . . horrible. In his penultimate letter, he said he couldn't bear it anymore and he was going to rejoin his comrades at his artillery post. But he was almost an invalid."—"Dr. Aue was seriously wounded in Stalingrad," Mandelbrod interrupted. "But he was lucky, he was able to be evacuated."— "Yes . . . ," Speer said. He looked dreamy now, almost lost. "Yes . . . you were lucky. His entire unit disappeared during the January Russian offensive. He is certainly dead. Without a doubt. My parents still can't quite get over it." His eyes met mine again. "He was my father's favorite son." Embarrassed, I muttered another polite phrase. Behind Speer, Mandelbrod said: "Our race is suffering, my dear friend. We must ensure its future." Speer nodded and looked at his watch. "We're about to leave. I'll go back to my compartment." He held out his hand to me again: "Goodbye, Sturmbannführer." I clicked my heels and saluted him, but he was already shaking hands with Mandelbrod, who pulled him toward him and said something softly that I didn't hear. Speer listened attentively, nodded, and went out. Mandelbrod pointed to the armchair he had left: "Have a seat, have a seat. Have you eaten? Are you hungry?" A second double door, in the back of the sitting room, opened silently, and in came a young woman in an SS uniform who looked just like the first one, but must have been a different one—unless the one who had welcomed me had gone round the car from the outside. "Would you like anything, Sturmbannführer?" she asked. The train had slowly started off and was leaving the station. Curtains hid the windows, the room was lit by the warm, golden light of many little lamps; on a curve, one of the curtains gaped open, and I could see the metal shutters beyond the glass and thought the whole car must have been armored. The young woman reappeared and set down a tray of sandwiches and beer on a folding table that she unfolded adroitly next to me with one hand. As I ate, Mandelbrod asked me about my work; he had much appreciated my August report, and was waiting with pleasure for the project I was about to finish; he seemed already to know about most of the details. Herr Leland in particular, he added, was interested in questions of individual output. "Is Herr Leland traveling with us, Herr Doktor?" I asked.—"He will join us in Posen," Mandelbrod replied. He was already in the East, in Silesia, in some places I had visited and where they both had considerable interests. "It's very good that you've met Reichsminister Speer," he said almost off handedly. "He is a man with whom it is important to get along. The SS and he should grow even closer." We talked a little more as I finished eating and drank my beer; Mandelbrod stroked a cat that had slipped onto his knees. Then he allowed me to withdraw. I went back through the antechamber and found my cabin. It was roomy, with a comfortable couchette already made up, a little work table, and a sink with a mirror over it. I opened the curtain: there too, steel shutters closed the window, and there seemed no way to open them. I abandoned the idea of smoking and took off my tunic and shirt to wash. I had scarcely washed my face, with a pretty little cake of perfumed soap placed next to the faucet— there was even hot water—when someone knocked on my door. "Just a minute!" I toweled off, put my shirt back on, put on my tunic without buttoning it, and then opened the door. One of the assistants was standing in the hallway and staring at me with her light-colored eyes, with the shadow of a smile on her lips, delicate as her perfume, which I could just make out. "Good evening, Sturmbannführer," she said. "Do you find your cabin satisfactory?"—"Yes, very." She looked at me, barely blinking. "If you like," she went on, "I could keep you company for the night." This unexpected offer, uttered in the same indifferent tone with which they had asked me if I wanted anything to eat, caught me a little unawares, I have to admit: I felt myself blush and searched hesitatingly for a reply. "I don't think Dr. Mandelbrod would approve," I said finally.—"On the contrary," she answered in the same friendly, calm tone, "Dr. Mandelbrod would be very happy. He is firmly convinced that all occasions to perpetuate our race must be taken advantage of. Of course, if I happened to become pregnant, your work wouldn't be disturbed: the SS has institutions for this purpose."—"Yes, I know,"

I said. I wondered what she would do if I accepted: I had the impression she would come in, get undressed without comment, and would wait, naked, on the bed, until I finished washing up. "That's a very tempting proposition," I said finally, "and I'm truly sorry I have to refuse. But I'm very tired and tomorrow will be a busy day. Another time, with a little luck." Her expression didn't show any change; perhaps she barely blinked. "As you like, Sturmbannführer," she replied. "If you need anything at all, you can ring. I'll be next door. Good night."— "Good night," I said, forcing myself to smile. I closed the door. Once I had finished washing, I put the light out and went to bed. The train sailed into the invisible night, swaying slightly when it passed over the switches. It took me a long time to fall asleep.

About the hour-and-a-half-long speech the Reichsführer gave on the night of October 6 to the assembled Reichsleiters and Gauleiters, I don't have much to say. This speech is less well known than the one, almost twice as long, he read on October 4 to his Obergruppenführers and HSSPFs; but aside from a few differences due to the nature of the respective audiences, and the less informal, less sardonic, less colloquial tone of the second speech, the Reichsführer said essentially the same thing. Thanks to the chance survival of archives, and the victors' justice, these speeches have become famous far beyond the closed circles for which they were intended; you won't find a book on the SS, the Reichsführer, or the destruction of the Jews in which they aren't cited; if their content interests you, you can easily consult them, in several languages; the October 4 speech was entered as evidence in the Nuremberg trials, under document number 1919-PS (it was obviously in this form that I was finally able to study it in detail, after the war, although I learned its general import in Posen itself); moreover, it was recorded, either on a wax disk or on a red oxide magnetic tape—the historians aren't in agreement, and on this point I cannot enlighten them, not having been present at that speech, but whatever the case the recording has survived and, if you feel so inclined, you can listen to it, and thus hear for yourself the Reichsführer's monotone, pedantic, didactic, precise voice, a little more urgent when he waxes ironic; there are even, though rarely, moments of anger, especially obvious, in hindsight, when he comes to subjects over which he must have felt he had little control— the widespread corruption, for instance, which he also spoke about on the sixth to the regime's dignitaries, but on which he insisted especially, as I heard at the time from Brandt, during his speech to the Gruppenführers given on the fourth. If these speeches have entered history, it's not of course because of all that, but because in this speech the Reichsführer, with a frankness he has never to my knowledge equaled either before or since, with frankness thus and in a manner that could even be called crude, outlined the program of the destruction of the Jews. Even I, when I heard it on October 6, didn't at first believe my ears, the hall was full, the sumptuous Golden Hall in the castle at Posen, I was in the very back, behind about fifty Gauleiters and leaders of the Party, not to mention a few industrialists, two service chiefs, and three (or maybe two) ministers of the Reich; and I found it, considering the secrecy rules we were bound to, truly shocking, almost indecent, and at the beginning, it made me very ill at ease, and I was certainly not the only one, I could see Gauleiters sigh and mop their foreheads or necks, it wasn't that they were learning something new, no, everyone, in that great hall with its subdued lighting must have been in the know, even though some of them, until then, probably hadn't had to think the thing through to the end, to discern its full extent, to think, for instance, about the women and children, and that's probably why the Reichs-führer insisted on this point, far more, moreover, to the Reichsleiters and Gauleiters than to his Gruppenführers, who couldn't in any case have had any illusions, which is probably why he insisted that, yes, we were indeed killing the women and the children too, so as not to let any ambiguity linger, and that's precisely what was so uncomfortable, that total absence, for once, of ambiguity, and it was as if he were violating an unwritten rule, even stronger than his own rules he decreed for his subordinates, his *Sprachregelungen* already absolutely strict, the rule of tact perhaps, that tact he spoke of in his first speech, evoking it in the context of the execution of Röhm and his SA comrades, *a kind of natural tact that is alive in us, thank God*, he said, *a consequence of this tact due to which we have never spoken about it among ourselves*, but perhaps it was also a matter of something other than the question of that tact and of those rules, and that's when I began to understand, I think, the profound reason for these declarations, and also why the dignitaries sighed and sweated so much, for they too, like me, were beginning to understand, to understand that it wasn't by chance that the Reichsführer, in the beginning of the fifth year of the war, was thus openly referring to the destruction of the Jews before them, without euphemisms, without winks, with simple and brutal words like *kill—exterminate*, he said, *meaning kill or order to have killed*—that, *for once*, the Reichsführer spoke to them *quite openly about this question . . . to tell you how it was*, no, that certainly wasn't by chance, and if he allowed himself to do it, then the Führer knew about it, and worse, the Führer had wanted it, hence their anguish, the Reichsführer was speaking necessarily here in the name of the Führer, and he was saying this, these words that you weren't supposed to say, and he was recording them, on a disk or a tape, it doesn't matter, and he was carefully taking note of those present and those absent—among the SS leaders, the only ones who didn't attend the October 4 speech were Kaltenbrunner, who was sick with phlebitis, Daluege, who had a serious heart disease and was on leave for a year or two, Wolff, just recently appointed HSSPF for Italy and plenipotentiary to Mussolini, and Globocnik, who had just, although I didn't know it yet and heard about it only after Posen, suddenly been transferred from his little Lublin kingdom to his native town of Trieste, as SSPF for Istria and Dalmatia, under Wolff's orders in fact, accompanied—but this I wouldn't know till even later on—by almost the entire personnel of Einsatz Reinhard, T-4 included, everything was being shut down, Auschwitz would henceforth be enough, and the beautiful Adriatic coast would make a fine dumping ground for all these people we had no further use for, even Blobel would come join them a little later on, let them go get killed by Tito's partisans, that would spare us some housekeeping; and as to the Party dignitaries, note was also taken of the missing heads, but I never saw the list—all that, then, the Reichsführer was doing deliberately, on instructions, and for that there could only have been one reason, hence the perceptible emotion of the listeners, who grasped this reason very well: it was so that none of them could, later on, say that he didn't know, couldn't try to make people think, in case of defeat, that he was innocent of the worst, couldn't think he might someday be able to get off scot-free; it was in order to *drag them in*, and they understood it very well, hence their distress. The Moscow Conference, at the end of which the Allies swore to pursue the "war criminals" *to the furthest corners of the earth*, hadn't yet taken place, that would come a few weeks later, before the end of that month of October 1943, but already, especially since summer, the BBC was conducting an intensive propaganda campaign on this theme, naming names, and with a certain precision, for it sometimes quoted officers and even noncoms from specific KLs, it was very well informed, and the *Staatspolizei* certainly wondered how, and this, it is entirely correct to note, provoked a certain nervousness among the interested parties, all the more so since the news from the front wasn't good, to hold on to Italy we had had to strip the Eastern Front, and there wasn't much chance we could remain on the Donets, we had already lost Briansk, Smolensk, Poltava, and Kremenchug, the Crimea was threatened, in short, anyone could see that things were going badly, and certainly there must have been many who were asking themselves questions about the future, the future of Germany in general of course but their own in particular too, hence a certain effectiveness of this English propaganda, which demoralized not only some who were named, but also others not yet named, by encouraging them to think that the end of the Reich might not automatically mean their own end, and thus rendering the specter of defeat a tiny bit less inconceivable, hence, one can well understand this, when it came to the cadres of the Party, the SS, and the Wehrmacht, the necessity to make them understand that a potential defeat would concern them too, personally, so as to remotivate them a little, that the so-called crimes of some would in the eyes of the Allies be the crimes of all, in the upper echelons at least, that all the boats, or bridges, if you like, were burning, that no return to the past was possible, and that the only salvation was victory. And indeed victory would have settled everything, for if we had won, imagine it for an instant, if Germany had crushed the Reds and destroyed the Soviet Union, there would have been no more question of crimes, or rather, yes, but of Bolshevik crimes, duly documented thanks to the archives seized (the archives of the NKVD in Smolensk, evacuated to Germany and recovered at the end of the war by the Americans, played precisely this role, when the time finally came when they had to explain almost overnight to the good democratic voters why the evil monsters of the day before now had to serve as a bulwark against the heroic allies of the day before, now revealed as even worse monsters), we might even perhaps have conducted full-blown trials, why not, have prosecuted the Bolshevik leaders, imagine that, doing things seriously as the Anglo-Americans later sought to (Stalin, we know, couldn't have cared less about these trials, he took them for what they were, a hypocrisy, and pointless to boot), and then everyone, with the British and the Americans leading the way, would have made do with us, the diplomats would have adjusted to the new realities, and despite the inevitable squalling of the New York Jews, the European Jews, whom in any case no one would have missed, would have been written off as a loss, like all the other dead, the Gypsies, the Poles, what do I know, the grass grows thick on the graves of the defeated, and no one holds the victor to account, I'm not saying this to try to justify us, no, it's the simple, frightening truth, look at Roosevelt, that good man, with his dear friend Uncle Joe, how many millions had Stalin already killed, in 1941, or even before 1939, many more than we did, that's certain, and even if you drew up a full balance sheet he might well remain ahead of us, between collectivization, de-kulakization, the great purges and the deportations of peoples in 1943 and 1944, and all that, everyone knew it at the time, everyone knew more or less what was happening in Russia during the 1930s, Roosevelt knew it too, that friend of mankind, but that never prevented him from praising Stalin's loyalty and humanity, despite the repeated warnings of

Churchill, who was a little less naïve from a certain point of view, a little less realistic, from another, and so if we Germans had in fact won this war, it would certainly have been the same, little by little, the stubborn ones who kept calling us the enemies of mankind would have fallen silent one by one, for lack of an audience, and the diplomats would have smoothed things out, since after all, *Krieg ist Krieg und Schnaps ist Schnaps*, isn't that right, and that's the way of the world. And maybe even in the end our efforts would have been applauded, as the Führer often predicted, or maybe not, in any case many would have applauded, who in the meantime have fallen silent, for we lost, harsh reality. And even if a certain tension had persisted on this subject, for ten or fifteen years, it would have dissipated sooner or later, when for example our diplomats would have firmly condemned, while still reserving the possibility of showing a certain degree of comprehension, the harsh measures, liable to impinge on human rights, that someday or other Great Britain or France would have had to apply in order to restore order in their restive colonies, or, in the case of the United States, to ensure the stability of world commerce and fight the communist hotbeds of revolt, as they indeed ended up doing, with the results we all remember. For it would be a mistake, a serious one, in my opinion, to think that the moral sense of the Western powers differs so fundamentally from our own: after all, a great power is a great power, it doesn't become one by chance, and doesn't remain one by chance, either. The people of Monaco, or the inhabitants of Luxembourg, can afford the luxury of a certain political uprightness; it's a little different for the English. Wasn't it a British administrator, educated at Oxford or Cambridge, who in 1922 advocated *administrative massacres* to ensure the security of the colonies, and bitterly regretted that the political situation *in the Home Islands* rendered these salutary measures impossible? Or, if like some people, you want to charge all our sins to the account of anti-Semitism alone—a gross mistake, in my opinion, but a seductive one for many— wouldn't you have to acknowledge that France, on the eve of the Great War, went much further in this domain than us (not to mention the Russia of the pogroms!)? I hope, by the way, that you won't be too surprised that I thus discount anti-Semitism as a fundamental cause of the massacre of the Jews: that would be forgetting that our extermination policies went much further. By the time of our defeat—and far from wanting to rewrite History, I would be the first to acknowledge it—we had already, aside from the Jews, completed the destruction of all the German incurable physically and mentally handicapped, of most of the Gypsies, and of millions of Russians and Poles. And the projects, as you know, were even more ambitious: for the Russians, the necessary *natu-*

ral diminution, according to the experts of the Four-Year Plan and the RSHA, was to reach thirty million, or even forty-six to fifty-one million, according to the dissident opinion of a somewhat zealous Dezernent in the *Ostministerium*. If the war had lasted a few more years, we would certainly have begun a massive reduction of the Poles. The idea had already been in the air for some time: *viz* the voluminous correspondence between Gauleiter Greiser in Warthegau and the Reichsführer, where Greiser asks, in May 1942, for permission to use the Kulmhof gassing installations to destroy thirty-five thousand tubercular Poles, who constituted, he said, a grave health menace for his *Gau*; after seven months, the Reichsführer finally let him understand that his proposition was interesting, but premature. You must think I'm explaining all this to you rather coldly: that's simply in order to demonstrate to you that the destruction by our deeds of the people of Moses did not stem solely from an irrational hatred of the Jews—I think I've already shown how poorly the emotional type of anti-Semite was regarded by the SD and the SS in general—but above all from a firm, well-reasoned acceptance of the recourse to violence to resolve the most varied social problems, in which, moreover, we differed from the Bolsheviks only by our respective evaluations of the categories of problems to be resolved: their approach being based on a horizontal reading of social identity (class), ours on a vertical one (race), but both equally deterministic (as I think I've already stressed) and reaching similar conclusions in terms of the remedy to be employed. And if you think carefully about it, you could deduce from this that this will, or at least this capacity, to accept the necessity of a much more radical approach to the problems afflicting all societies, can have been born only from our defeats during the Great War. Every country (except perhaps the United States) suffered; but victory, and the arrogance and moral smugness born of victory, probably allowed the English and the French and even the Italians more readily to forget their sufferings and their losses, and to settle down again, sometimes even to wallow in their self-satisfaction, and thus to grow frightened again more easily, from fear of seeing this oh so fragile compromise fall apart. As for us, we had nothing more to lose. We had fought just as honorably as our enemies; we had been treated like criminals, humiliated and dismembered, and our dead were scorned. The fate of the Russians, objectively, was scarcely any better. What could be more logical, then, than to say: Well, then, if that's the way it is, if it's just to sacrifice the best of the nation, to send to their deaths the most patriotic, the most intelligent, the most devoted men, those most loyal to our race, and all in the name of the salvation of the nation—and if that was all for naught—and if their sacrifice is spat upon—then, what right to life should the worst elements have, the criminals, the insane, the retarded, the asocials, the Jews, not to mention our external enemies? The Bolsheviks, I am convinced, reasoned in the same way. Since respecting the rules of so-called humanity was useless to us, why stubbornly persist in a respect for which no one was even grateful? Hence, inevitably, a much harsher, stiffer, more radical approach to our problems. In every society, in every age, social problems have been subject to arbitration between the needs of the group and the rights of the individual, and thus have given rise to a number of responses that are ultimately quite limited: roughly, death, charity, or exclusion (especially, historically, in the form of exile). The Greeks exposed their deformed children; the Arabs, acknowledging that they constituted, economically speaking, a burden that was too heavy for their families, but not wanting to kill them, put them in the care of the community, thanks to the *zakat*, that obligatory religious charity (a tax for good works); even in our days, in our countries, there exist specialized establishments for such cases, so that their misfortune need not spoil the view of those in good health. Now, if you adopt such an overall vision, you can see that in Europe at least, from the eighteenth century onward, all the distinct solutions to the various problems—public torture for criminals, exile for the contagiously ill (leprosariums), Christian charity for imbeciles—converged, under the influence of the Enlightenment, toward a single type of solution, applicable to all cases and infinitely variable: institutionalized imprisonment, financed by the State, a form of inner exile, if you like, sometimes with pedagogical pretensions, but above all with a practical finality: the criminals to prison, the sick to the hospital, the crazy to the asylum. And who cannot see that these humane solutions, too, resulted from compromise, were made possible by wealth, and remained, in the end, contingent? After the Great War many understood that they were no longer adapted, that they no longer sufficed to address the new amplitude of the problems, because of restricted economic means and also because of the hitherto unthinkable level of the stakes (the millions of dead of the war). New solutions were necessary, and they were found, as man always finds the solutions he needs, as the so-called democratic countries too would have found them, if they had needed them. But then why, you might ask today, the Jews? What do the Jews have in common with your lunatics, your criminals, your contagious? Yet it's not hard to see that, historically, the Jews constituted themselves as a "problem," by wanting to remain apart at all costs. Didn't the first writings against the Jews, those of the Greeks of Alexandria, long before Christ and theological anti-Semitism, accuse them of being an asocial people, of violating the laws of hospitality, the main foundation and political principle of the ancient world, in the name of their food prohibitions, which prevented them from eating at other people's houses or from receiving them as guests, from being hosts? Then, of course, there was the religious question. I am not seeking here, as some might think, to make the Jews responsible for their catastrophe; I'm simply trying to say that a certain aspect of European history, unfortunate according to some, inevitable according to others, has made it so that even in our days, in times of crisis, it is natural to turn against the Jews, and that if you become involved in a reshaping of society through violence, sooner or later the Jews will end up on the receiving end—sooner, in our case, later, in the Soviets'—and that this is not entirely by chance. Some Jews too, with the threat of anti-Semitism averted, succumb to hubris.

You must find these reflections extremely interesting, I don't doubt it for an instant; but I have wandered off the subject a little, I still haven't spoken of that famous day of October 6, which I wanted to describe briefly. A few quick knocks on the door of my compartment had tugged me from my sleep; with the blinds fastened, it was impossible to know the time, I was probably in the midst of a dream, I remember being completely disoriented by them. Then I heard the voice of Mandelbrod's assistant, gentle but firm: "Sturmbannführer. We're arriving in half an hour." I washed, got dressed, and went to stretch my legs in the antechamber. The young woman was standing there: "Hello, Sturmbannführer. Did you sleep well?"—"Yes, thanks. Is Dr. Mandelbrod awake?"—"I don't know, Sturmbannführer. Would you like some coffee? A full breakfast will be served when we arrive." She returned with a small tray. I drank the coffee standing up, my legs slightly apart because of the train's swaying; she sat down on a little armchair, her legs discreetly crossed—she was wearing now, I noticed, a long skirt instead of the black breeches of the day before. Her hair was pulled back in a severe chignon. "You aren't having any?" I asked.—"No, thanks." We stayed thus in silence until the squeal of brakes sounded. I gave her back the cup and took my travel bag. The train was slowing down. "Have a good day," she said. "Dr. Mandelbrod will find you later on." On the platform, there was a certain amount of confusion; the tired Gauleiters were exiting the train one by one, yawning, welcomed by a squad of civil servants in civilian clothes or in SA uniform. One of them saw my SS uniform and frowned. I pointed to Mandelbrod's car, and his face lit up: "I'm sorry," he said as he came forward. I gave him my name, and he consulted a list: "Yes, I see. You are with the members of the Reichsführung, at the Posen Hotel. There's a room for you. I'll go find you a car. Here's the program." At the hotel, a fancy but rather staid building dating back to the Prussian period, I showered, shaved, changed, and downed a few pieces of toast with jam. Around eight o'clock, I went down to the lobby. People were beginning to come and go. I finally found one of Brandt's assistants, a Hauptsturmführer, and showed him the program I had been given. "Listen, you can go right now. The Reichsführer won't come until the afternoon, but there will be some officers there." The car lent me by the *Gau* was still waiting, and I had myself driven to the Schloss Posen, admiring on the way the blue belfry and the arcaded loggia of the city hall, then the many-colored façades of the narrow houses of burghers crowded onto the Old Square, reflections of many centuries of subtly fanciful architecture, until this fugitive morning pleasure collided with the castle itself, a vast pile of blocks abutting a large empty square, crude and bristling with pointed roofs and a tall buttressed tower propped against it, massive, proud, severe, dreary, in front of which the penant-bearing Mercedes of the dignitaries were lining up one by one. The program began with a series of lectures given by experts from Speer's entourage, including Walter Rohland, the steel magnate, who exposed one after the other, with distressing precision, the state of war production. In the first row, listening gravely to this somber news, could be seen most of the government elite: Dr. Goebbels, Minister Rosenberg, Axmann, the Reich Youth Führer, Grand Admiral Dönitz, Feldmarschall Milch from the Luftwaffe, and a beefy man with a bull's neck, his thick hair combed back, whose name I asked during one of the breaks: Reichsleiter Bormann, the personal secretary of the Führer and the head of the NSDAP chancellery. His name was known to me, of course, but I didn't know much about him; the newspapers and newsreels at the cinema never mentioned him, and I didn't remember seeing his photo. After Rohland, it was Speer's turn: his presentation, which lasted less than half an hour, reiterated the same themes as those dealt with the day before at the Prinz-Albrecht-Palais, but in a surprisingly direct, almost brusque language. Only then did I notice Mandelbrod: a special place had been arranged on the side for his cumbersome platform-chair, and he listened, his eyes creased, with Buddhist detachment, flanked by two of his assistants—so there really were two of them—and by the tall rugged figure of Herr Leland. Speer's last words provoked a tumult: returning to the theme of obstruction by individual *Gaus*, he mentioned his agreement with the Reichsführer, threatening to deal ruthlessly with the recalcitrant. As soon as he had come down from the podium, several Gauleiters surrounded him, expostulating; I was too far away, at the back of the hall, to hear what they said, but I could imagine it. Leland had leaned over and was murmuring something into Mandelbrod's ear.

Then we were invited to return to town, to the Ostland Hotel, where the dignitaries were staying, for a buffet reception. Mandelbrod's assistants led him out a side exit, but I found him in the courtyard and went to greet him and Herr Leland. I could see then how he was traveling: his special Mercedes, with its immense interior, was equipped with a mechanism by which his armchair, detached from its platform, slid into the car; a second vehicle carried the platform, along with the two assistants. Mandelbrod had me get in with him, and I sat down on a jump seat; Leland sat in front, next to the chauffeur. I regretted not traveling with the young women: Mandelbrod didn't seem to notice the stinking gases his body emitted; fortunately the journey was a short one. Mandelbrod didn't speak; he seemed to be drowsing. I wondered if he ever got up out of his armchair, and if not, how did he get dressed, how did he attend to his bodily functions? His assistants, in any case, must have been able to bear anything. During the reception, I talked with two officers from the *Persönlicher Stab*, Werner Grothmann, who still hadn't gotten over being appointed to Brandt's position (Brandt, promoted to Standartenführer, was taking Wolff's), and an adjutant in charge of the police. It was they, I think, who first told me about the strong impression caused among the Gruppenführers by the Reichsführer's speech two days before. We also talked about Globocnik's departure, a real surprise for everyone; but we didn't know each other well enough to speculate on the motives for this transfer. One of the two amazons—it was indeed hard for me to tell them apart, I couldn't even say which one had offered herself to me the night before—appeared beside me. "Excuse me, meine Herren," she said with a smile. I excused myself in turn and followed her through the crowd. Mandelbrod and Leland were talking with Speer and Rohland. I saluted them and congratulated Speer on his speech; he assumed a melancholy air: "Obviously it wasn't to everyone's taste."—"It doesn't matter," Leland retorted. "If you manage to get on with the Reichsführer, none of these drunken idiots can stand in your way." I was surprised: I had never heard Herr Leland speak so brutally. Speer was nodding. "Try to stay in regular contact with the Reichsführer," Mandelbrod whispered. "Don't let this new momentum lapse. For minor questions, if you don't want to bother the Reichsführer himself, just contact my young friend here. I can guarantee his reliability." Speer contemplated me absentmindedly: "I already have a liaison officer at the ministry."—"Of course," Mandelbrod said. "But Sturmbannführer Aue will, I'm sure, have more direct access to the Reichsführer. Don't worry about bothering him."—"Fine, fine," Speer said. Rohland had turned to Leland: "We agree, then, about Mannheim . . ." With a brief pressure on my elbow, Mandelbrod's assistant let me understand that I was no longer required. I saluted and withdrew discreetly to the buffet. The young woman had followed me and ordered a tea while I nibbled on a hors d'oeuvre. "I think Dr. Mandelbrod is very pleased with you," she said in her beautiful, flat voice.—"I don't see why, but if you say so, I must believe you. Have you been working for him for a long time?—"For several years."—"And before?"—"I studied for my doctorate in Latin and German philology, in Frankfurt." I raised my eyebrows: "I'd never have guessed. It isn't too difficult, working full-time for Dr. Mandelbrod? He seems pretty demanding."—"Everyone serves where he has to," she replied without hesitating. "I am extremely honored by Dr. Mandelbrod's trust. It's thanks to men like him and Herr Leland that Germany will be saved." I examined her smooth, oval, barely made-up face. She must have been very beautiful, but no detail, no particularity allowed one to grab hold of this entirely abstract beauty. "May I ask you a question?"—I asked her.—"Of course."—"The hallway outside my compartment wasn't very well lit. Are you the one who came and knocked on my door?" She gave a pearly little laugh: "The hallway wasn't all that badly lit. But the answer is no: that was my colleague Hilde. Why? Would you rather it had been me?"—"No, I was just wondering," I said stupidly.—"If the opportunity comes up again," she said, looking me straight in the eye, "it will be my pleasure. I hope you'll be less tired." I blushed: "What is your name, then? So I'll know." She held out her little hand with its shimmering nails; her palm was dry and soft and her handshake as firm as a man's. "Hedwig. Have a good afternoon, Sturmbannführer."

The Reichsführer, surrounded by a silent horde of officers and flanked by Rudolf Brandt, made his appearance around three o'clock in the afternoon, soon after we returned to the Schloss. Brandt noticed me and motioned to me with his head; he was already wearing his new stripes, but didn't give me time to congratulate him when I came over: "After the Reichsführer's speech, we're leaving for Cracow. You will come with us."—"Fine, Standartenführer." Himmler had sat down in the first row, next to Bormann. First we were fed a speech by Dönitz, who justified the temporary cessation of submarine warfare, while hoping it would soon resume; by Milch, who hoped the Luftwaffe's new tactics would soon put an end to the terrorist raids on our cities; and by Schepmann, the new Chief of Staff of the SA, who hoped for nothing that I could remember. Around five thirty, the Reichsführer mounted the podium. Blood-red flags and the black helmets of the honor guard framed his small silhouette on the high platform; the tall microphone stands almost hid his face; the light from the hall played on his glasses. The amplification gave his voice a metallic tone. Of the reactions of the audience, I have already spoken; I was sorry, finding myself in the rear of the hall, to have to contemplate the backs of people's necks rather than their faces. Despite my alarm and surprise, I might add that some of his words touched me personally, especially those that had to do with the effect of this decision on those in charge of carrying it out, of the danger they ran in their minds *of becoming cruel and heartless and no longer respecting human life, or of going soft and succumbing to weakness and nervous depression*—yes, I knew this *appallingly narrow way between Scylla and Charybdis* well, these words could have been addressed to me, and to a certain extent, in all modesty, they were, to me and to those who like me were afflicted with this horrific responsibility, by our Reichsführer who understood well what we were enduring. Not that he let himself give in to the slightest sentimentality; as he said so brutally, toward the end of the speech: *Many will weep, but that doesn't matter; there is a lot of weeping already*, words, to my ear, almost Shakespearean in breath, but maybe that was in the other speech, the one I read later on, I'm not sure, it matters little. After the speech—it must have been seven o'clock—Reichsleiter Bormann invited us to a buffet in a neighboring room. The dignitaries, especially the older Gauleiters, stormed the bar; since I had to travel with the Reichsführer, I abstained from drinking. I saw him in a corner, standing in front of Mandelbrod, with Bormann, Goebbels, and Leland; his back was turned to the room and he wasn't paying the slightest attention to the effect his words had produced. The Gauleiters downed drink after drink and talked in low voices; from time to time one of them barked out a platitude; his colleagues solemnly nodded and drank some more. I must confess that I, for my part, was, despite the effect of the speech, more preoccupied by the little scene of that afternoon: I felt clearly that Mandelbrod was seeking to position me, but how and in relation to whom, I didn't yet see; I knew too little about his relations with the Reichsführer, or with Speer, for that matter, to come to any conclusion, and that worried me, I felt that these issues went beyond me. I wondered if Hilde or Hedwig could have enlightened me; at the same time I knew very well that, even in bed, they would have told me nothing that Mandelbrod didn't want me to know. And Speer? For a long time I thought I remembered, but without thinking about it, that he too was talking with the Reichsführer during this reception. Then one day, some time ago, in a book, I learned that for years Speer has energetically denied having been there, that he claims he left at lunchtime with Rohland, and that he wasn't present at the Reichsführer's speech. All I can say about it is that it's possible: for my part, after the words we exchanged at the noon reception, I didn't pay any special attention to him, I was more concentrated on Dr. Mandelbrod and the Reichsführer, and also, there were really a lot of people; nonetheless, I thought I had seen him that evening, and he himself has described the frantic drinking bout of the Gauleiters, at the end of which, according to his own book, many of them had to be carried to the special train; at that moment, I had already left with the Reichsführer, so I didn't see that myself, but he describes it as if he had been there, so it's hard to say, and in any case it's a rather pointless quibble: whether or not he heard the Reichsführer's words that day, Reichsminister Speer knew, like everyone else; at the very least, by that point, *he knew enough to know that it was better not to know any more*, to quote a historian, and I can affirm that a little later on, when I knew him better, he knew everything, including about the women and children who, after all, couldn't have been warehoused without his knowing it, even if he never spoke about it, that's true, and even if he wasn't up to date on all the technical details, which didn't concern his specific field of responsibility, after all. I won't deny that he would no doubt have preferred not to know; Gauleiter von Schirach, whom I saw that night sprawled on a chair, his tie undone and his collar open, drinking one Cognac after another, would certainly have preferred not to know, either, and many others along with him, either because the courage of their convictions failed them or because they were already afraid of the Allied reprisals, but it should be added that those men, the Gauleiters, did little for the war effort, and even hampered it in some cases, whereas Speer, as all the specialists now affirm, gave at least two extra years to National Socialist Germany, more than anyone he contributed to prolonging the business, and he would have prolonged it even more if he could have, and certainly he wanted victory, he struggled vehemently for victory, the victory of this National Socialist Germany that was destroying the Jews, women and children included, and the Gypsies too and many others besides, and that's why I permit myself, despite the immense respect I have for his accomplishments as Minister, to find his oh so very public postwar regrets somewhat indecent, regrets that saved his skin, indeed, whereas he deserved life neither more nor less than the others, Sauckel, for instance, or Jodl, and which then forced him, in order to maintain the pose, into ever more intricately baroque contortions, whereas it would have been so simple, especially after he had served his sentence, to come out and say: Yes, I knew, and so what? As my comrade Eichmann stated so well, in Jerusalem, with all the direct simplicity of simple men: "Regrets, that's for children."

I left the reception around eight o'clock, on Brandt's orders, without managing to say a proper goodbye to Dr. Mandelbrod, deep in discussion. With several other officers, I was driven to the Posen Hotel so I could pick up my things, then to the train station, where the Reichsführer's special train was waiting for us. Once again, I had a private cabin, but of much more modest dimensions than in Dr. Mandelbrod's car, with a tiny couchette. This train, called *Heinrich*, was extraordinarily well designed: in front, along with the Reichsführer's personal armored cars, were cars made into offices and into a mobile communications center, all of them protected by flatcars equipped with antiaircraft weaponry; the entire Reichsführung-SS, if necessary, could keep working on the move. I didn't see the Reichsführer get in; a little while after we arrived, the train started off; this time there was a window in my cabin, so I could put out the light and, sitting in the dark, contemplate the night, a beautiful, clear fall night, lit by stars and a crescent moon that shed a fine metallic gleam over Poland's poor landscape. From Posen to Cracow it's about four hundred kilometers; with the many stops required by alerts or blockages, we arrived long after dawn; awake already and sitting on my couchette, I watched the gray plains and potato fields slowly turn pink. At the Cracow train station, an honor guard was waiting for us, led by the Generalgouverneur, with a red carpet and a brass band; from a distance I saw Frank, surrounded by young Polish women in national dress carrying baskets of hothouse flowers, give the Reichsführer a German salute that almost made the seams of his uniform burst, then exchange a few animated words with him before they were swallowed up by an enormous sedan. We were given rooms in a hotel at the foot of the Wawel; I bathed, shaved carefully, and sent one of my uniforms to the cleaners. Then, strolling through the sunny, beautiful old streets of Cracow, I headed toward the HSSPF's offices, where I sent a telex to Berlin to ask for news of my project's progress. At midday, I attended the official lunch as a member of the Reichsführer's delegation; I was seated at a table with several SS and Wehrmacht officers, as well as minor civil servants of the Generalgouvernement; at the main table, Bierkamp sat next to the Reichsführer and the Generalgouverneur, but I had no opportunity to go over and greet him. The conversation centered on Lublin, with Frank's men confirming the rumor, in the GG, that Globocnik had been fired because of the epic scale of his embezzlements: according to one version, the Reichsführer even wanted to have him arrested and tried, as an example, but Globocnik had prudently accumulated a large number of compromising documents, and had used them to negotiate an almost golden retreat for himself to his native coast. After the banquet there were speeches, but I didn't wait and went back to town to make my report to Brandt, who had established himself at the HSSPF's. There wasn't much to say: aside from the D III, which had immediately said yes, we were still waiting for the opinions of the other departments as well as the RSHA. Brandt told me to speed things up as soon as I returned: the Reichsführer wanted the project to be ready by midmonth.

For the evening reception, Frank had not skimped. An honor guard, swords in hand, uniforms streaming with gold stripes, formed a diagonal line across the main courtyard of the Wawel; on the stairway, other soldiers presented arms at every third step; at the entrance to the ballroom, Frank himself, in an SA uniform and flanked by his wife, a stout woman with her white flesh bursting out of a monstrous green velvet concoction, was welcoming his guests. The Wawel gleamed with all its lights: from the town you could see it sparkling atop its cliff; garlands of electric lightbulbs decorated the tall columns surrounding the courtyard, and soldiers, posted behind the guard of honor, held torches; and if you left the ballroom to stroll in the loggias, the courtyard looked as if it were circled by flaming rings, a well of light at the bottom of which the parallel rows of torches gently roared; on the other side of the palace, from the immense balcony jutting out of its flank, the city, below the guests' feet, stretched out dark and silent. On a stage at the back of the main hall, an orchestra was playing Viennese waltzes; the GG officials had brought their wives; some couples were dancing, others were drinking, laughing, digging into the hors d'oeuvres on the overloaded tables, or, like me, studying the crowd. Aside from some colleagues from the Reichsführer's delegation, I didn't recognize many people. I examined the coffered, multicolored ceiling made of precious wood, with a polychrome head in relief set into each square—bearded soldiers, hat-wearing burghers, feathered courtiers, coquettish ladies—all contemplating vertically, impassive, the strange invaders below them. Beyond the main staircase, Frank had had other rooms opened, each one with a buffet, armchairs, sofas, for those who wanted to rest or be quiet. Large, handsome ancient carpets broke the harmonious perspectives of the black-and-white tiled floor, muting the footsteps that resounded elsewhere on marble. Two helmeted guards, swords drawn and held in front of their noses like English Horse Guards, framed each door leading from one room to the other. Glass of wine in hand, I wandered through these rooms, admiring the friezes, the ceilings, the paintings; the Poles, alas, had at the beginning of the war taken away Sigismond Augustus's famous Flemish tapestries: they were said to be in England, or even Canada, and Frank had often denounced what he regarded as the looting of the Polish cultural heritage. Bored, I finally joined a group of SS officers talking about the fall of Naples and Skorzeny's exploits. I listened to them absentmindedly, for a curious noise had come to capture my attention, a kind of rhythmic scraping noise. It grew closer and I looked around; I felt a bump against my boot and lowered my eyes: a multicolored pedal car, driven by a handsome blond child, had just rammed into me. The child was looking at me severely without saying anything, his chubby little hands gripping the steering wheel; he must have been four or five, and wore a pretty little houndstooth suit. I smiled, but he still didn't say anything. Then I understood and stepped aside with a little bow; still silent, he began again to pedal furiously, heading toward a neighboring room and disappearing between the caryatid guards. A few minutes later I heard him come back: he was charging straight ahead without paying attention to people, who had to step out of his way. Having reached a buffet, he paused and extricated himself from his vehicle to get a piece of cake; but his little arm was too short; even standing on tiptoe he couldn't reach anything. I went over and asked: "Which do you want?" Still silent, he pointed to a Sacher torte. "Do you speak German?" I asked him. He looked indignant: "Of course I speak German!"—"So you should have learned to say *bitte*." He shook his head: "I don't need to say *bitte*!"—"And why is that?"—"Because my papa is the King of Poland, and everyone here has to obey him!" I nodded: "That's very good. But you should learn to recognize uniforms. I don't serve your father, I serve the Reichsführer-SS. So if you want some cake, you have to say *bitte* to me." The child, his lips pinched, hesitated; he must not have been used to such resistance. Finally he gave in: "Can I have the cake, *bitte*?" I took a piece of torte and handed it to him. As he ate, smearing his mouth with chocolate, he examined my uniform. Then he pointed at my Iron Cross: "Are you a hero?"—"In a way, yes."—"Have you been to war?"—"Yes."—"My papa commands, but he doesn't go to war."—"I know. Do you live here all the time?" He nodded. "And do you like living in a castle?" He shrugged: "It's all right. But there aren't any other children."—"You have brothers and sisters, though?" He nodded: "Yes. But I don't play with them."—"Why not?"—"Dunno. That's how it is." I wanted to ask his name, but a big commotion was taking place at the entrance to the room: a crowd was headed toward us, Frank and the Reichsführer in the lead. "Ah, there you are!" Frank exclaimed to the little boy. "Come, come with us. You too, Sturmbannführer." Frank took his son in his arms and pointed to the car: "Could you carry that?" I picked the car up and followed them. The crowd crossed all the rooms and massed in front of a door that Frank had opened. Then he stood aside to let Himmler pass: "After you, my dear Reichsführer. Come in, come in." He put his son down and pushed him in front of him, hesitated, searched me out with his eyes, then whispered to me: "Just leave that in a corner. We'll get it later." I followed them into the room and went to put the car down. In the center of the room there was a large table with something on top of it beneath a black sheet. Frank, with the Reichsführer at his side, waited for the other guests and arranged them around the table, which was at least three-by-four meters. The little boy, again, stood against the table on tiptoe, but barely reached the top. Frank looked around, saw me standing a little apart, and called to me: "Excuse me, Sturmbannführer. You're already friends, I see. Would you mind carrying him so he can see?" I bent down and took the child in my arms; Frank made room for me next to him, and while the last guests came in, he ran his pointed fingers through his hair and fiddled with one of his medals; he seemed scarcely able to contain his impatience. When everyone was there, Frank turned to Himmler and declared in a solemn voice: "My dear Reichsführer, what you are now about to see is an idea that has occupied my spare time for a while now. It's a project that, I hope, will make the city of Cracow, capital of the Generalgouvernement of Poland, famous, and will be an attraction for all of Germany. When it is finished, I plan on dedicating it to the Führer for his birthday. But since you are giving us the pleasure of visiting us, I don't want to keep it secret any longer." His puffy face, with its weak, sensual features, gleamed with pleasure; the Reichsführer, his hands crossed behind his back, contemplated him through his pince-nez with a half-sarcastic, half-bored look. I hoped more than anything that he would hurry up: the child was beginning to get heavy. Frank gave a signal, and some soldiers pulled the sheet, revealing a large architectural model, a kind of park, with trees and curving paths, outlined between houses of different styles, surrounded by a wall. While Frank puffed himself up, Himmler scrutinized the model. "What is it?" he finally asked. "It looks like a zoo."—"Almost, my dear Reichsführer," Frank chuckled, his thumbs in the pockets of his tunic. "It is, in the words of the Viennese, a *Menschengarten*, an anthropological garden that I hope to establish here, in Cracow." He made a wide gesture over the model. "You remember, my dear Reichsführer, in our youth, before the war, those Hagenbeck *Völkerschauen*? With families of Samoans, Laplanders, Sudanese? One of them came to Munich, my father took me to see it; you must have seen it too. And there were some in Hamburg, Frankfurt, Basel, it was a huge success." The Reichsführer rubbed his chin: "Yes, yes, I remember. They were traveling exhibitions, right?"—"Yes. But this one will be permanent, like a zoo. And it won't be a public amusement, my dear Reichsführer, but a pedagogical, scientific tool. We will gather together specimens of all the peoples who have disappeared or are about to disappear in Europe, to preserve a living trace of them this way. German

schoolchildren will come in buses to learn here! Look, look." He
pointed to one of the houses: it was half open, sectioned; inside, one
could see little figurines sitting around a table, with a seven-branched
candelabrum. "For the Jew, for example, I chose the Jew from Galicia
as the best representative of the *Ostjuden*. The house is typical of their
filthy habitat; of course, it will have to be disinfected regularly, and the
specimens subjected to medical supervision, to avoid contaminating the
visitors. For these Jews, I want pious ones, very pious, we'll give them
a Talmud, and the visitors can see them muttering their prayers, or
watch the wife prepare kosher food. Over here are Polish peasants from
Masuria; over there, Bolshevized Kolkhozniks; and there, Ruthenians,
and over there, Ukrainians, see, with the embroidered shirts. This big
building here will house an institute for anthropological research; I will
endow it with a chair myself; scholars can come and study on-site these
peoples who were once so numerous. It will be a unique opportunity
for them."—"Fascinating," the Reichsführer murmured. "And ordinary
visitors?"—"They can walk freely around the fences, watch the specimens working in their gardens, beating rugs, hanging out the wash.
Then there will be guided tours of the houses, which will allow them
to observe the habitat and customs."—"And how would you maintain
the institution in the long run? After all, your specimens will grow old,
and some will die."—"That is precisely, my dear Reichsführer, where I
would need your support. They will marry among themselves and reproduce. One single family will be exhibited at a time; the others will
serve to replace them if they fall ill, to procreate, to teach the children
the customs, the prayers and the rest. I picture them being guarded
nearby in a camp, under SS surveillance."—"If the Führer authorized it,
it would be possible. But we'll have to discuss it. It's not certain that it's
desirable to preserve certain races from extinction, even this way. It
could be dangerous."—"Of course, every precaution will be taken. In
my opinion, such an institution will be found to be precious and irreplaceable for science. How do you think future generations will be able
to understand the amplitude of our work, if they have no idea of the
conditions that prevailed before?"—"You are certainly right, my dear
Frank. It's a fine idea. And how do you plan to finance this . . . *Völker-
schauplatz*?"—"On a commercial basis. Only the research institute will
receive government subsidies. For the park itself, we will create a public corporation to raise capital by subscription. Once the initial invest-
ment is amortized, the entry fees will cover the cost of upkeep. I looked
into the Hagenbeck exhibitions: they made considerable profits. The
Paris Jardin d'Acclimatation regularly lost money until its director organized ethnological exhibits of Nubians and Eskimos, in 1877. The first

year, they drew a million paying visitors. That continued until the Great War." The Reichsführer was nodding: "A fine idea." He examined the model up close; Frank pointed out a detail to him from time to time. The little boy had begun to squirm, so I put him down: he got into his pedal car and fled out the door. The guests were also leaving. In one of the rooms, I found Bierkamp, as unctuous as always, with whom I talked a little. Then I went out to smoke under the colonnade, admiring the baroque splendor of the illuminations, of the martial, barbaric guard who seemed specially designed to bring out the gracious forms of the palace. "Good evening," a voice next to me said. "It's impressive, isn't it?" I turned around and recognized Osnabrugge, the friendly civil engineer I had met in Kiev. "Hello! What a nice surprise."—"Ah, there's been a lot of water under the destroyed bridges of the Dnieper." He was holding a glass of red wine and we toasted our meeting. "So," he asked, "what brings you to the *Frankreich*?"—"I'm with the Reichsführer. And you?" His nice oval face took on a look that was both mischievous and knowing: "State secret!" He creased his eyes and smiled: "But to you, I can say it: I'm on a mission for the OKH. I'm preparing demolition programs for the bridges in the districts of Lublin and Galicia." I looked at him, stunned: "For what earthly reason?"—"In the event of a Soviet advance, you know."—"But the Bolsheviks are on the Dnieper!" He rubbed his pug nose; his pate, I noticed, had grown much balder. "They crossed it today," he finally said. "They also took Nevel."—"But that's still far away. We'll stop them first. Don't you think your preparations are a little defeatist?"—"Not at all: it's foresight. A quality still prized by the military, I assure you. But in any case I'm just doing what I'm told. I did the same thing in Smolensk in the spring and in Byelorussia during the summer."—"And what does a bridge demolition program consist of, can you explain it to me?" He looked mournful: "Oh, it's not very complicated. Local engineers write up studies of each bridge to be demolished; I look them over, approve them, and afterward we calculate the necessary amount of explosives for the whole area, the number of detonators, et cetera, then we decide where and how to store them, on-site; finally we outline the different stages that will allow local commanders to know exactly when and where they should set the explosives, when they should set up the detonators, and under what conditions they should press the button. A plan, you know. So in case anything crops up, we wouldn't have to leave the bridges for the enemy because we didn't have anything on hand to blow them up."—"And you still haven't built any?"—"Unfortunately not! My mission in the Ukraine was my downfall: the chief engineer of the OKHG South liked my report on Soviet demolitions so much that he forwarded it to the OKH. I was recalled to Berlin and promoted to the Demolitions Department—just for bridges, there are other sections that take care of factories, railroads, roads; airfields are the Luftwaffe's responsibility, but occasionally we hold conferences together. So since then, that's all I've been doing. All the bridges on the Manych and the lower Don, that's me. The Donets, the Desna, the Oka, that's me too. I've already had hundreds blown up. It's enough to make you cry. My wife is happy, because I've gone up in rank"—he tapped his epaulettes: in fact, he had been promoted several times since Kiev—"but it breaks my heart. Every time I feel as if I'm killing a child."—"You shouldn't take it that way, Herr Oberst. After all, they're just Soviet bridges."—"Yes, but if it keeps up, someday they'll be German bridges." I smiled: "That's really defeatism."—"I'm sorry. Sometimes I'm filled with discouragement. Even when I was little, I liked to build things, when all my classmates just wanted to break them."—"There's no justice. Come, let's go in and fill our glasses." In the main hall, the orchestra was playing Liszt and some couples were still dancing. Frank was sitting around a table with Himmler and his Staatssekretär Bühler, talking animatedly and drinking coffee and Cognac; even the Reichsführer, who was smoking a fat cigar, had, contrary to his custom, a full glass in front of him. Frank was leaning forward, his moist gaze already misted over by alcohol; Himmler was frowning stiffly: he must have disapproved of the music. I clinked glasses again with Osnabrugge while the piece came to an end. When the orchestra stopped, Frank, his glass of Cognac in hand, got up. Looking at Himmler, he declared in a voice that was strong but too shrill: "My dear Reichsführer, you must know the popular old quatrain: *Clarum regnum Polonorum / Est coelum Nobiliorum / Paradisum Judeorum / Et infernum Rusticorum.* The nobles disappeared a long time ago, and now, thanks to our efforts, the Jews too; the peasantry, in the future, will only grow richer and will bless us; and Poland will be the Heaven and Paradise of the German people, *Coelum et Paradisum Germanorium.*" His shaky Latin made a woman standing nearby titter; Frau Frank, sprawling not far from her husband like a Hindu idol, glared at her. Impassive, his eyes cold and inscrutable behind his little pince-nez, the Reichsführer raised his glass and wet his lips with it. Frank walked around the table, crossed the hall, and leaped nimbly onto the stage. The pianist jumped up and disappeared; Frank slid into his place and, with a deep breath, shook his long, chubby white hands over the keyboard, then began to play a Chopin *Nocturne.* The Reichsführer sighed; he blinked rapidly and puffed vigorously on his cigar, which was threatening to go out. Osnabrugge leaned toward me: "In my opinion, the Generalgouverneur is teasing your Reichsführer on purpose. Don't you think?"—

"That would be a little childish, wouldn't it?"—"He's annoyed. They say he tried to resign last month, and that the Führer refused again."— "If I understood right, he doesn't control much here."—"According to my Wehrmacht colleagues, nothing at all. Poland is a *Frankreich ohne Reich*. Or rather *ohne Frank*."—"In short, a little prince rather than a king." That said, aside from the choice of music—even if you have to play Chopin, there are surely better things than the *Nocturnes*—Frank played pretty well, but used too much pedal. I looked at his wife, whose shoulders and chest, fat and flushed, were gleaming with sweat in her low-cut dress: her little eyes, set deep into her face, shone with pride. The boy seemed to have disappeared, I hadn't heard the obsessive rolling of his pedal car for some time. It was getting late, some guests were taking their leave; Brandt had gone over to the Reichsführer and, calmly contemplating the scene with his birdlike attentive face, was standing at the ready. I scribbled my telephone numbers into a notebook, tore out the sheet, and gave it to Osnabrugge. "Here. If you're in Berlin, call me, we'll go out for a drink."—"Are you leaving?" I pointed to Himmler with my chin, and Osnabrugge raised his eyebrows: "Ah. Good night, then. It was a pleasure seeing you again." Onstage, Frank was concluding his piece, nodding to the beat. I made a face: even for Chopin, it wouldn't do, the Generalgouverneur was really overdoing the legato.

The Reichsführer was leaving the next morning. In the Warthegau, a fall rain had soaked the plowed fields, leaving puddles the size of small ponds, dull, as if they'd absorbed all the light from the unchanging sky. The pine woods, which always seemed to be hiding horrifying and obscure deeds, darkened this muddy, receding landscape; here and there, rare in these parts, birch trees crowned with flames still raised a last protest against the coming of winter. In Berlin it was raining, and people scurried by in their wet clothes; on the bomb-damaged sidewalks, water sometimes formed impassable areas, pedestrians had to turn back and take another street. The day after my return, I went up to Oranienburg to spur my project along. I was convinced it would be Sturmbannführer Burger, the new Amtschef of D IV, who would give me the most trouble; but Burger, after listening to me for a few minutes, said simply: "If it's financed, it's fine with me," and ordered his adjutant to write me a letter of support. Maurer, on the other hand, made a lot of difficulties for me. Far from being happy with the progress my project represented for the *Arbeitseinsatz*, he thought it didn't go far enough, and told me frankly that he was afraid if he approved it he'd close the door to any future improvements. For over an hour I exhausted all my arguments on him, explaining to him that without the agreement of the RSHA, we couldn't do anything, and that the RSHA wouldn't support a project that was overgenerous, for fear of favoring the Jews and other dangerous enemies. But on this subject it was especially difficult to come to an understanding with him: he got muddled up, he kept repeating that precisely, for the Jews, in Auschwitz, the numbers didn't match up, that, according to the statistics, scarcely 10 percent of them worked, where did the others go, then? It wasn't possible that so many of them were unfit for work. He sent letter after letter about this to Höss, who replied vaguely or not at all. He was obviously looking for an explanation, but I decided that it wasn't my role to give him one; I confined myself to suggesting that an on-site inspection might clear some things up. But Maurer didn't have time to carry out inspections. I ended up wresting a limited agreement from him: he wouldn't oppose the system of categories, but would request on his side that the scales be increased. Back in Berlin, I reported to Brandt. I told him that, according to my information, the RSHA would approve the project, even if I didn't yet have any written confirmation. He ordered me to send him the report, with a copy for Pohl; the Reichsführer would eventually come to a final decision, but it would serve in the meantime as a working basis. As for me, he asked me to start going through the SD reports on foreign workers, and to begin thinking about this question as well.

It was my birthday: my thirtieth. As in Kiev, I had invited Thomas to dinner, I didn't want to see anyone else. In truth, I had a lot of acquaintances in Berlin, old friends from university or the SD, but no one aside from Thomas whom I regarded as a friend. Ever since my convalescence I had resolutely cut myself off; plunged into my work, I had almost no social life, aside from professional relationships, and no emotional or sexual life. Nor did I feel any need for that; and when I thought about my excesses in Paris, it made me feel ill at ease, I didn't want to lapse into those murky pursuits anytime soon. I didn't think about my sister, or about my dead mother; at least, I don't remember thinking about them much. Maybe after the horrible shock of my wound (although it was completely cured, it terrified me every time I thought about it, it stripped away all my abilities, as if I were made of glass, of crystal, and might shatter into pieces at the slightest jolt) and the nightmarish events of the spring, my soul aspired to a monotonous calm, and rejected anything that might trouble it. That evening, though—I had arrived early, to have time to think a little, and I was drinking Cognac at the bar—I thought again about my sister: it was after all her thirtieth birthday too. Where could she be celebrating it: In Switzerland, in a sanatorium full of strangers? In her remote home in Pomerania? It had been a long time since we'd celebrated our birthday together. I tried to remember the last time: it must have been when we were children in Antibes, but to my utter confusion, no matter how hard I concentrated, I was incapable of remembering, of visualizing the scene. I could calculate the date: logically, it was in 1926, since in 1927 we were already in boarding school; so we were thirteen, I should have been able to remember, but it was impossible, I saw nothing. Maybe there were photographs of this party in the crates or boxes in the attic in Antibes? I was sorry I hadn't looked through them more thoroughly. The more I thought about this rather idiotic detail, the more the defects of my memory upset me. Fortunately Thomas arrived to draw me out of my funk. I've probably said this already, but it bears repeating: What I liked about Thomas was his spontaneous optimism, his vitality, his intelligence, his calm cynicism; his gossip, his chatter sprinkled with innuendos always delighted me, for with him one seemed to penetrate the underside of life, hidden from the profane gazes that see only people's obvious actions, but as if flipped over into the light of day by his knowledge of the hidden connections, secret liaisons, closed-door discussions. He could deduce a realignment of political forces from the simple fact of a meeting, even if he didn't know what had been said; and if he was sometimes mistaken, his avidity in gathering new information allowed him constantly to correct the chancy constructions he devised in that manner. At the same time he had no imagination, and I had always thought, despite his ability to paint a complex scene in a few strokes, that he would have made a poor novelist: in his reasoning and intuitions, his polestar always remained personal interest; and although, sticking to that, he was rarely wrong, he was incapable of imagining any different motivation for people's actions and words. His passion—and in this he was Voss's opposite (and I thought back to my previous birthday, and missed that brief friendship)—his passion was not a passion for pure knowledge, for knowledge for its own sake, but solely for practical knowledge, providing tools for action. That night, he told me a lot about Schellenberg, but in a curiously allusive way, as if I were supposed to understand on my own: Schellenberg had doubts, Schellenberg was thinking over alternatives, but what these doubts were about, and what these alternatives consisted of, he didn't want to say. I knew Schellenberg a little, but I can't say I liked him. At the RSHA, he had a position that was somewhat apart, thanks, above all, I think, to his special relationship with the Reichsführer. By my lights, I didn't regard him as a real National Socialist, but rather as a technician of power, seduced by power in itself and not by its object. Reading over what I've written, I realize that, judging from my own statements, you might think the same about Thomas; but Thomas was different; even if he had a holy terror of theoretical and ideological discussions—which explained, for example, his aversion to Ohlendorf—and even if he always took great care to look out for his own future, his slightest actions were as if guided by an instinctive National Socialism. Schellenberg was constantly changing his mind, and I had no trouble imagining him working for the British Secret Service or the OSS, which in Thomas's case was unthinkable. Schellenberg had the habit of calling people he didn't like *whores*, and this term suited him well—and when I think about it, it's true that the insults people prefer, the ones that come most spontaneously to their lips, often in the end reveal their own hidden faults, since they naturally hate what they most resemble. This idea stayed with me all evening, and when I was back home, late at night, a little drunk perhaps, I took down from a shelf an anthology of the Führer's speeches that belonged to Frau Gutknecht and began leafing through it, looking for the most virulent passages, especially on the Jews, and as I read them I wondered if, when he said, *The Jews lack ability and creativity in every walk of life but one: lying and cheating,* or else *The Jew's entire building will collapse if he's refused a following,* or *They are liars, forgers, deceivers. They only got anywhere through the simplemindedness of those around them,* or *We can live without the Jew. But he cannot live without us,* the Führer, without knowing it, was really describing himself. Yet this man never spoke in his own name, so the accidents of his personality counted for little: his role was almost that of a lens, he captured and concentrated the will of the *Volk* to bring it into focus always at the right point. Thus, even if in those passages he was speaking about himself, wasn't he speaking about us all? But it is only now that I can say that.

During dinner, Thomas had once again reproached me for my unsociability and impossible hours: "I know everyone has to give his utmost, but you're going to ruin your health if you go on like that. And I shouldn't have to tell you that Germany isn't going to lose the war if you take your evenings and Sundays off. This is going to last a while, you should pace yourself, otherwise you'll collapse. And look, you're even getting a belly." It was true: I wasn't getting fat, but my abdominal muscles were sagging. "At least come and get some exercise," Thomas insisted. "Twice a week I fence, and on Sunday I go to the pool. You'll see, it will do you good." As always, he was right. I soon regained my taste for fencing, which I had practiced a little at university; I took up the saber, I liked the keen, nervous aspect of this weapon. What I liked in this sport was that, despite its aggressiveness, it's not a brute's sport: as much as the good reflexes and agility required to handle the weapon, it's the mental work before the pass that counts, the intuitive anticipa-

tion of the other's movements, the swift calculation of possible responses, a physical chess game where you have to foresee several moves,
for once a decision has been made, there's no more time to think, and
one can often say that the pass is won or lost even before it began, according to whether one saw rightly or not, the thrusts themselves only
confirming or refuting the calculation. We practiced in the arms room
of the RSHA, at the Prinz-Albrecht-Palais; but for swimming we went
to a public pool in Kreuzberg, instead of the Gestapo's: first of all, an essential point for Thomas, there were women there (and not just the unavoidable secretaries); it was bigger too, so that after swimming one
could go in a bathrobe and sit down at wooden tables, on a wide balcony upstairs, to drink cold beer while watching the swimmers, whose
happy shouts and splashes resounded throughout the vast dome. The
first time I went there, I had a violent shock that left me for the rest of
the day with a distressing anguish. We were getting undressed in the
changing room: I looked at Thomas and saw that a wide forked scar ran
across his belly. "Where did you get that?" I exclaimed. Thomas looked
at me, surprised: "In Stalingrad of course. Don't you remember? You
were there." A memory, yes, I had one, and I wrote it down with the
others, but I had filed it away in the back of my head, in the attic of hallucinations and dreams; now this scar came to turn everything upside
down, I suddenly felt as if I couldn't be sure of anything anymore. I kept
staring at Thomas's belly; he slapped his abdominal muscles with the flat
of his hand, smiling widely: "It's all right, don't get upset, it's all better.
And also it drives the girls wild, it must excite them." He closed one eye
and pointed at my head, his thumb up, like a child playing cowboy:
"Pow!" I almost felt the shot in my forehead, my anguish grew like a
gray, flaccid, endless thing, a monstrous body that occupied the limited
space of the changing room and prevented me from moving, a terrified
Gulliver stuck in a Lilliputian house. "Don't look like that," Thomas
shouted cheerfully, "come swim!" The water, heated but still a little
cool, did me good; tired after just a few laps—I had definitely let myself get out of shape—I stretched out on a deck chair while Thomas
frolicked, bellowing and letting his head be dunked underwater by spirited young women. I watched these people letting off steam, having
fun, taking pleasure in their own strength; I felt far away. Bodies, even
the handsomest ones, no longer threw me into a panic, as the ballet
dancers' had a few months before; they left me indifferent, boys' as well
as girls'. I could admire with detachment the play of muscles under the
white skin, the curve of a hip, water streaming down a neck: the crumbling bronze Apollo in Paris had excited me much more than all this insolent young musculature, which was deployed casually, as if jeering at

the flabby, yellowing flesh of the few old people who came there. My attention was drawn to a young woman who stood out from the others by her serenity; as her girlfriends ran or splashed around Thomas, she remained motionless, her arms folded on the edge of the pool, her body floating in the water, and her head, oval beneath an elegant black rubber cap, resting on her forearms, her large somber eyes calmly directed at me. I couldn't tell if she was really looking at me; without moving, she seemed to be contemplating with pleasure everything that was in her field of vision; after a long while, she raised her arms and let herself slowly sink down. I waited for her to come back to the surface, but the seconds passed; finally she reappeared at the other end of the pool, which she had crossed underwater, as calmly as I had once crossed the Volga. I leaned back on my chaise and closed my eyes, concentrating on the sensation of the chlorinated water slowly evaporating on my skin. My anguish, that day, was slow to relax its asphyxiating embrace. The next Sunday, though, I went back to the pool with Thomas.

In the meantime, I had once again been summoned by the Reichsführer. He asked me to explain how we had arrived at our results; I launched into a detailed explanation, since there were technical points that were difficult to summarize; he let me talk, looking cold and unforthcoming, and when I had finished he asked me curtly: "And the *Reichssicherheitshauptamt?*"—"Their specialist agrees in principle, my Reichsführer. He is still waiting for Gruppenführer Müller's confirmation."—"We have to be careful, Sturmbannführer, very careful," he rapped out in his most pedantic voice. Another Jewish rebellion, I knew, had just taken place in the GG, at Sobibor this time; again, some SS had been killed, and despite a vast manhunt, some of the fugitives hadn't been recaptured; and these were *Geheimnisträger*, witnesses of the extermination operations: if they managed to join the partisans in the Pripet Marshes, chances were good that the Bolsheviks would then pick them up. I understood the Reichsführer's anxiety, but he had to make up his mind. "You have met Reichsminister Speer, I think?" he said suddenly.—"Yes, my Reichsführer. I was introduced by Dr. Mandelbrod."—"Did you talk to him about your project?"—"I didn't go into details, my Reichsführer. But he knows that we are working to improve the state of health of the *Häftlinge.*"—"And what does he say about it?"—"He seemed satisfied, my Reichsführer." He leafed through some papers on his desk: "Dr. Mandelbrod wrote me a letter. He tells me that Reichsminister Speer seemed to like you. Is that true?"—"I don't know, my Reichsführer."—"Dr. Mandelbrod and Herr Leland very much want me to move closer to Speer. In principle, that's not a bad idea, since we have interests in common. Everyone always thinks Speer and

I are in conflict. But that's not true at all. Why, as long ago as 1937, I created the DESt and set up camps especially for Speer, to provide him with construction materials, bricks, and granite for the new capital he was going to build for the Führer. At the time, the whole of Germany could provide him with only four percent of his needs in granite. He was very grateful for my help and delighted to cooperate. But of course you can't trust him. He's not an idealist, and he doesn't understand the SS. I wanted to make him one of my Gruppenführers, and he refused. Last year, he took the liberty of criticizing our labor organization to the Führer: he wanted to obtain jurisdiction over our camps. Even today he dreams of having the right to look into our internal functioning. But still, it's important to cooperate with him. Did you consult his ministry, as you prepared your project?"—"Yes, my Reichsführer. One of their people came and gave us a presentation." The Reichsführer slowly nodded: "Fine, fine . . ." Then he seemed to come to a decision: "We don't have much time to lose. I'll tell Pohl that I approve the project. You'll send a copy to Reichsminister Speer, directly, with a personal note signed by you reminding him of your meeting and indicating to him that the project will be implemented. And of course send a copy to Dr. Mandelbrod."—"*Zu Befehl*, my Reichsführer. And what would you like me to do regarding the foreign workers?"—"For now, nothing. Study the question, from the angle of nutrition and productivity, but confine yourself to that. We'll see how things turn out. And if Speer or one of his associates makes contact with you, inform Brandt and react favorably."

I followed the Reichsführer's instructions to the letter. I don't know what Pohl did with our project, so lovingly conceived: a few days later, around the end of the month, he sent another order to all the KLs, instructing them to diminish the mortality and morbidity rate by ten percent, but without giving the slightest concrete suggestion; to my knowledge, Isenbeck's rations were never applied. Nevertheless I received a very flattering letter from Speer, who was pleased with the project's adoption, *concrete proof of our new, recently inaugurated cooperation*. He ended: *I hope to have the opportunity to see you again soon to discuss these problems. Yours, Speer.* I forwarded this letter to Brandt. In the beginning of November, I received a second letter: the Gauleiter of the Westmark had written to Speer to demand that the five hundred Jewish workers delivered by the SS to a weapons factory in Lorraine be withdrawn immediately: *Thanks to my care, Lorraine is Judenfrei and will remain so*, wrote the Gauleiter. Speer asked me to forward this letter to the relevant authority to settle the problem. I consulted Brandt; a few days later, he sent me an internal memo, asking me to answer the Gauleiter myself in

the Reichsführer's name, negatively. *Tone: abrupt*, wrote Brandt. I pulled
out all the stops:

> *Dear Party Comrade Bürckel!*
>
> *Your request is inopportune and cannot be accepted. In this difficult*
> *hour for Germany, the Reichsführer is aware of the need to use the labor*
> *of the enemies of our Nation to the utmost. Decisions about assignment*
> *of workers are made in consultation with the RMfRuK, the only*
> *authority competent today to deal with this question. Since the*
> *prohibition presently in force not to employ Jewish inmate workers*
> *concerns only the Altreich and Austria, I cannot avoid the impression*
> *that your request stems chiefly from your desire to avoid being ignored in*
> *the overall handling of the Jewish question.*
>
> *Heil Hitler! Yours, etc.*

I sent a copy to Speer, who thanked me. Little by little, this began to
be repeated: Speer had irritating demands and requests sent to me, and
I replied to them in the Reichsführer's name; for more complicated
cases, I referred to the SD, going through acquaintances rather than the
official route, to speed things up. In this way I again saw Ohlendorf,
who invited me to dinner, and inflicted on me a long tirade against the
industry self-management system set in place by Speer, which he regarded as a simple usurpation of the powers of the State by capitalists
without the slightest responsibility toward the community. If the Reichsführer approved of it, according to him, that was because he didn't understand anything about economics, and moreover he was under the
influence of Pohl, himself a pure capitalist obsessed with the expansion
of his industrial SS empire. To tell the truth, I didn't understand much
about economics, either, or about Ohlendorf's violent arguments on the
subject, for that matter. But it was always a pleasure just to listen to him:
his frankness and intellectual honesty were as refreshing as a glass of cold
water, and he was right to stress that the war had caused or accentuated
a number of abuses; afterward, we would have to reform the structures
of the State in depth.

I began to regain a taste for life outside work: whether this was
thanks to the beneficial effects of exercise or to something else, I don't
know. One day I realized that I hadn't been able to bear Frau Gutknecht
for a long time now; the next day, I set to work looking for another
apartment. This was a little complicated, but finally Thomas helped me
find something: a small furnished bachelor apartment on the top floor
of a fairly new building. It belonged to a Hauptsturmführer who had

just gotten married and was leaving for a post in Norway. I quickly settled with him on a reasonable rent, and in one afternoon, with Piontek's
help, and under salvos of Frau Gutknecht's squeals and entreaties, I
transferred my few belongings. My new apartment wasn't very big: two
square rooms separated by a double door, a little kitchen, and a bathroom; but it had a balcony, and since the living room was at the corner
of the building, the windows opened onto two sides; the balcony looked
out over a little park, where I could watch children playing. It was quiet
too, and I wasn't disturbed by car noises; from my windows, I had a fine
view over a landscape of roofs, a comforting tangle of shapes, constantly
changing with the weather and the light. On days when it was nice out,
the apartment was bright from morning to night: on Sunday, I could
watch the sun rise from my bedroom and set from the living room. To
make it even brighter, I had the faded old wallpaper stripped, with the
owner's permission, and the walls painted white; in Berlin, this wasn't
very common, but I had known apartments like that in Paris, and I liked
it, with the wooden floor it was almost ascetic, it corresponded to my
state of mind: quietly smoking on my sofa, I wondered why I hadn't
thought of moving sooner. In the morning, I got up early, before sun-
rise, in that season, ate a few pieces of toast and drank some genuine
black coffee; Thomas had it sent to him from Holland by an acquaintance, and he sold me some of it. To get to work I took the trolley. I
liked watching the streets go by, contemplating the faces of my neighbors in the light of day, sad, closed, indifferent, tired, but also sometimes
surprisingly happy, and if you pay attention to such things, you know
that it's rare to see a happy face in the street or on the trolley, but when
it happened, I was happy too, I felt I was rejoining the community of
men, these people for whom I was working but from whom I had been
living so far apart. For several days in a row, on the trolley, I noticed a
beautiful blond woman who took the same line that I did. She had a
quiet and grave face; I noticed her mouth first, especially her upper lip,
two muscular, aggressive wings. Sensing my gaze, she had looked at me:
under high-arched, thin eyebrows, she had dark, almost black eyes,
asymmetrical and Assyrian (but perhaps this last likeness only came to
my mind through assonance). Standing, she held on to a strap and stared
at me with a calm, serious look. I had the impression that I had already
seen her somewhere, at least her gaze, but I couldn't remember where.
The next day she spoke to me: "Hello. You don't remember me," she
added, "but we've already seen each other. At the swimming pool." She
was the young woman leaning on the edge of the pool. I didn't see her
every day; when I saw her, I greeted her amiably, and she smiled, gently. At night, I went out more often: I went to dinner with Hohenegg,

whom I introduced to Thomas, I saw old university friends again, I let myself be invited out to suppers and little parties where I drank and chatted happily, without horror, without anguish. This was normal life, everyday life, after all, this too was worth living.

Not long after my supper with Ohlendorf, I had received an invitation from Dr. Mandelbrod to come spend the weekend at a country estate belonging to one of the directors of IG Farben, in the north of Brandenburg. The letter made it clear that there would be a hunting party and an informal dinner. Massacring fowl didn't tempt me much, but I didn't have to shoot, I could just walk in the woods. The weather was rainy: Berlin was sinking into fall, the beautiful October days had come to an end, the trees were all stripped bare now; sometimes, though, the sky cleared and you could go out and enjoy the already cool air. On November 18, at dinnertime, the sirens wailed and the flak began to thunder, for the first time since the end of August. I was at a restaurant with some friends, including Thomas—we had just left our fencing session. We had to go down into the basement without even eating; the alert lasted for two hours, but they had wine served to us, and the time passed in pleasantries. The raid caused serious damage to the center of town; the English had sent more than four hundred aircraft: they had decided to brave our new tactics. That took place on the Thursday evening; on the Saturday morning, I had Piontek drive me toward Prenzlau, to the village mentioned by Mandelbrod. The house was a few kilometers outside of town, at the end of a long lane bordered with ancient oaks, many of which were missing, however, decimated by disease or storms; it was an old manor house, bought by the director, next to a forest dominated by pine trees mixed in with beech and maple trees, and surrounded by a handsome, open park, and then, farther away, big, empty, muddy fields. It had drizzled during the journey, but the sky, whipped by a bracing little north wind, had cleared up. On the gravel in front of the steps, several sedans had parked side by side, and a uniformed chauffeur was washing the mud from the bumpers. I was welcomed on the steps by Herr Leland; that day he looked very soldierly, despite his brown woollen knit cardigan: the owner was away, he explained, but he had lent them the house; Mandelbrod wouldn't arrive till evening, after the hunting party. On his advice, I sent Piontek back to Berlin: the guests would return together, there would certainly be room for me in one of the cars. A black-uniformed servant girl wearing a lace apron showed me my room. A fire was roaring in the chimney; outside it had begun to rain again gently. As the invitation had suggested, I wasn't wearing my uniform but a country outfit, woollen trousers with boots and a collarless Austrian jacket with bone buttons, made to be water-resistant; for the evening, I had brought a suit that I unfolded, brushed, and hung in the closet before going downstairs. In the living room, several guests were drinking tea or talking with Leland; Speer, sitting in front of a casement window, recognized me right away and got up with a friendly smile to come shake my hand. "Sturmbannführer, what a pleasure to see you again. Herr Leland told me you'd be coming. Come, I'll introduce you to my wife." Margret Speer was sitting near the fireplace with another woman, a certain Frau von Wrede, the wife of a general who was going to join us; standing in front of them, I clicked my heels and gave a German salute that Frau von Wrede returned; Frau Speer just held out an elegant little gloved hand to me: "Pleased to meet you, Sturmbannführer. I've heard about you: my husband tells me you've been a great help to him, in the SS."—"I do what I can, meine Dame." She was a thin, blond woman of a decidedly Nordic beauty, with a strong, square jaw and very light blue eyes under blond eyebrows; but she seemed tired and that gave her skin a slightly sallow cast. I was served tea, and chatted a little with her while her husband joined Leland. "Your children didn't come?" I asked politely.— "Oh! If I had brought them, it wouldn't have been a vacation. They stayed in Berlin. It's already so hard for me to tear Albert away from his ministry, once he accepts, I don't want him to be disturbed. He so needs rest." The conversation turned to Stalingrad, for Frau Speer knew I had been there; Frau von Wrede had lost a cousin there, a Generalmajor who was commanding a division and was probably in the hands of the Russians: "It must have been terrible!" Yes, I confirmed, it had been terrible, but I didn't add, out of courtesy, that it had surely been less so for a divisional general than for an ordinary trooper like Speer's brother, who, if by some miracle he was still alive, would not be benefiting from the preferential treatment that the Bolsheviks, hardly egalitarian for once, gave superior officers, according to our information. "Albert was very affected by the loss of his brother," Margret Speer said dreamily. "He doesn't show it, but I know. He gave his name to our last-born child."

Little by little, I was introduced to the other guests: industrialists, superior officers from the Wehrmacht or the Luftwaffe, a colleague of Speer's, other senior officials. I was the only member of the SS and also the lowest-ranking of the gathering, but no one seemed to pay that any heed, and Herr Leland introduced me as "Dr. Aue," sometimes adding that I carried out "important functions for the Reichsführer-SS"; so I was treated quite cordially, and my nervousness, which at the outset had been rather strong, slowly diminished. Around noon we were served sandwiches, pâté, and beer. "A light snack," Leland declared, "so we won't get too tired." The hunting began afterward; we were poured coffee, then everyone was given a game bag, some Swiss chocolate, and a flask of brandy. The rain had stopped and weak sunlight seemed to want to pierce the grayness; according to one general who said he knew hunting, it was perfect weather. We were going to hunt black grouse, a privilege that was apparently very rare in Germany. "This house was bought after the war by a Jew," Leland explained to his guests. "He wanted to give himself lordly airs, and he had the grouse imported from Sweden. The woods suited them well, and the present owner puts strict limits on hunting." I knew nothing about it, and had no intention of learning; out of politeness, I had nonetheless made up my mind to accompany the hunters rather than set off on my own. Leland gathered us on the front steps, and some servants distributed the shotguns, ammunition, and dogs. Since black grouse is hunted either singly or in pairs, we would be divided into little groups; to avoid accidents, everyone was assigned a section of the forest, and was not to stray from it; what's more, our departures would be staggered. The hunt-loving general set off first, alone with a dog, then after him a few pairs. Margret Speer, to my surprise, had joined the group and had also taken a shotgun; she set out with her husband's colleague, Hettlage. Leland turned to me: "Max, why don't you accompany the Reichsminister? Go that way. I'll go with Herr Ströhlein." I spread out my hands: "As you wish." Speer, his shotgun already under his arm, smiled at me: "Good idea! Come." We went through the park toward the woods. Speer was wearing a leather Bavarian jacket with rounded lapels, and a hat; I had also borrowed a hat. At the entrance to the wood, Speer loaded his weapon, a double-barreled shotgun. I kept mine on my shoulder, unloaded. The dog they had given us fidgeted, stationed at the edge of the wood, its tongue lolling out, pointing. "Have you hunted grouse before?" Speer asked.— "Never, Herr Reichsminister. In fact, I don't hunt at all. If it's all right with you, I'll just walk with you." He looked surprised: "As you like." He pointed to the forest: "If I understood correctly, we should walk a kilometer till we reach a stream, then cross it. Everything beyond it, to the edge of the forest, is ours. Herr Leland will stay on this side." He set out into the undergrowth. It was quite dense; we had to go around the bushes, it was impossible to walk straight; drops of water streamed from the leaves and splattered onto our hats and hands; on the ground, the dead, wet leaves gave off a strong odor of earth and humus—beautiful, rich, and invigorating, but it brought unhappy memories to my mind. A sudden burst of bitterness invaded me: so this is what they've turned me into, I said to myself, a man who can't see a forest without thinking about a mass grave. A dead branch snapped under my boot. "It's surprising that you don't like hunting," Speer commented. Absorbed in my thoughts, I answered without thinking: "I don't like killing, Herr Reichsminister." He gave me a curious look, and I explained: "It's sometimes necessary to kill out of duty, Herr Reichsminister. Killing for pleasure is a choice." He smiled: "As for me, thank God, I've done nothing but kill for pleasure. I've never been to war." We walked a little more in silence, amid the crackling of branches and the noise of water, soft and discreet. "What were you doing in Russia, Sturmbannführer?" Speer asked. "You served in the Waffen-SS?"—"No, Herr Reichsminister. I was with the SD. In charge of security matters."—"I see." He hesitated. Then he said in a calm, detached voice: "We hear a lot of rumors about the fate of the Jews, in the East. You must know something about it?"—"I know the rumors, Herr Reichsminister. The SD collects them and I've read the reports. They have many different sources."—"You must have some idea of the truth, in your position." Curiously, he made no allusion to the Reichsführer's Posen speech (I was convinced at the time that he had been there, but maybe he had in fact left early). I answered courteously: "Herr Reichsminister, for a large part of my functions, I'm compelled to secrecy. I think you can understand. If you really want some explanations, might I suggest that you address the Reichsführer or Standartenführer Brandt? I'm sure they'll be happy to send you a detailed report." We had reached the stream: the dog, happy, capered about in the shallow water. "Here it is," Speer said. He pointed to a zone a little farther off: "You see, there, in the hollow, the forest changes. There are evergreens, and fewer alder trees, and some bay shrubs. That's the best place to flush grouse. If you're not shooting, stay behind me." We crossed the stream in long strides; over the hollow, Speer closed his shotgun, which he had been carrying open under his arm, and shouldered it. Then he began walking forward, on the lookout. The dog stayed near him, its tail pointing. After a few minutes I heard a loud noise and saw a large brown shape fly up through the trees; at the same instant, Speer pulled the trigger, but he must have missed the mark, since I could still hear the sound of wings through the echo. Thick smoke and the acrid smell of cordite filled the undergrowth. Speer hadn't lowered his shotgun, but everything was quiet now. Once again, there was the noise of wings among the wet branches, but Speer didn't shoot; I hadn't seen anything, either. The third bird took off right under our noses, I saw it very clearly, it had rather broad wings and a collar of feathers, and twisted through the trees with an agility surprising for its mass, accelerating as it turned; Speer pulled the trigger but the bird was too quick, he hadn't had time to traverse and the shot went wide. He opened the gun, ejected the casings, blew on it to get rid of the smoke, and pulled two cartridges out of his jacket pocket. "Grouse

are very difficult to hunt," he commented. "That's why it's interesting.
You have to choose your weapon well. This one is balanced, but a little too long for my taste." He looked at me, smiling: "In the spring, it's
very beautiful, during the mating season. The cocks clack their beaks,
they gather together in clearings to strut and sing, displaying their colors. The females are very dull, as is often the case." He finished loading
his shotgun, then raised it before starting off again. In dense places, he
cleared a path for himself between the branches with the barrel of the
gun, without ever lowering it. When he flushed another bird, he pulled
the trigger right away, a little in front of him; I heard the bird falling and
at the same time the dog leaping and disappearing into the brush. It
reappeared a few seconds later, the bird in its mouth, the head hanging
down. It set it down at Speer's feet, and he put it away in his bag. A little farther on, we came out into a clearing in the wood covered with
yellowing tufts of grass and opening out onto the fields. Speer took out
his chocolate bar: "Would you like some?"—"No, thanks. Do you
mind if I take the time to smoke a cigarette?"—"Not at all. It's a good
place to rest." He opened his gun, put it down, and sat down at the foot
of a tree, nibbling on his chocolate. I drank a swig of brandy, handed
him the flask, and lit a cigarette. The grass I was sitting on was wetting
my pants, but I didn't mind: hat on my knees, I rested my head against
the rough bark of the pine tree I was leaning against and contemplated
the calm stretch of grass and the silent woods. "You know," Speer said,
"I entirely understand the requirements of security. But more and more
they are in conflict with the needs of the war industry. Too many potential workers are not deployed." I exhaled the smoke before replying:
"That's possible, Herr Reichsminister. But in this situation, with our
difficulties, I think priority conflicts are inevitable."—"But they should
be resolved."—"Indeed. But in the end, Herr Reichsminister, it's up to
the Führer to decide, isn't it? The Reichsführer is only obeying his orders." He bit into his chocolate bar again: "You don't think that the priority, for the Führer, as well as for us, is to win the war?"—"Certainly,
Herr Reichsminister."—"Then why deprive us of precious resources?
Every week, the Wehrmacht comes and complains to me that Jewish
workers are being taken away from them. And they're not being rede-
ployed elsewhere, otherwise I'd know it. It's ridiculous! In Germany, the
Jewish question is resolved, and elsewhere, what importance does it
have for now? Let's win the war first; afterward there will always be
time to resolve the other problems." I chose my words carefully: "Perhaps, Herr Reichsminister, some people believe that since the war is
taking so long to be won, some problems ought to be resolved right
away . . ." He turned his head to me and stared at me with his keen eyes:

"You think so?"—"I don't know. It's a possibility. Can I ask you what the Führer says about it when you talk to him?" He bit his lip pensively: "The Führer never talks about these things. Not with me, at least." He got up and brushed off his pants. "Shall we go on?" I threw away my cigarette, then drank a little more brandy and put the flask away: "Which way?"—"That's a good question. I'm afraid, if we cross to the other side, we might come across one of our friends." He looked toward the back of the opening, at the right: "If we go that way, we should come back toward the stream. Then we can go back the way we came." We started off, walking alongside the edge of the wood; the dog followed us a few steps away, in the wet grass of the meadow. "Actually," Speer said, "I haven't thanked you yet for your help. I appreciate it a lot."—"It's a pleasure, Herr Reichsminister. I hope it's useful. Are you satisfied with your new cooperation with the Reichsführer?"—"To tell the truth, Sturmbannführer, I expected more from him. I have already sent him several reports on Gauleiters who refuse to close down useless companies for the sake of war production. But from what I can see, the Reichsführer is content to forward these reports to Reichsleiter Bormann. And Bormann of course always sides with the Gauleiters. The Reichsführer seems to accept it quite passively." We had reached the end of the clearing and were entering the wood. It began to rain again, a fine, light rain that soaked through our clothes. Speer had fallen silent and was walking with his gun raised, concentrating on the bushes in front of him. We walked along this way for half an hour, to the stream, then retraced our steps diagonally, before returning again to the stream. From time to time I would hear an isolated gunshot farther away, a dull sound in the rain. Speer pulled the trigger four more times and shot a black grouse that had a beautiful ruff of feathers with metallic glints. Soaked to the bone, we crossed the stream again, heading toward the house. A little before the park, Speer spoke to me again: "Sturmbann-führer, I have a request. Brigadeführer Kammler is in the process of building an underground installation, in the Harz, for the production of rockets. I would like to visit these installations, to see how the work is coming along. Could you arrange that for me?" Taken by surprise, I replied: "I don't know, Herr Reichsminister. I haven't heard about it. But I'll make the request." He laughed: "A few months ago, Obergrup-penführer Pohl sent me a letter to complain that I'd visited only one single concentration camp and that I had formed my opinion about prisoner labor employment with too little information. I'll send you a copy. If they make difficulties for you, just show them that."

I was tired, but with the long, pleasant tiredness after exercise. We had walked for a long time. In the entry of the manor house, I returned

my shotgun and game bag, scraped the mud off my boots, and went up
to my room. Someone had put more logs on the fire, it was warm; I
took off my wet clothes and went to inspect the adjoining bathroom:
not only was there running water, but it was hot; that seemed a miracle
to me, in Berlin hot water was a rarity; the owner must have had a boiler
installed. I ran an almost scalding bath and slipped in: I had to clench my
teeth, but once I got used to it, stretched out full length, it was soft and
gentle like amniotic fluid. I stayed in as long as possible; when I got out,
I opened the windows wide and stood naked in front of them, as they
do in Russia, until my skin was marbled red and white; then I drank a
glass of cold water and stretched out on my stomach on the bed.

In the early evening I put on my suit, without a tie, and went downstairs. Not many people were in the living room, but Dr. Mandelbrod
was ensconced in his big armchair in front of the fireplace, sitting cater-
corner, as if he wanted to warm one side but not the other. His eyes
were closed and I didn't disturb him. One of his assistants, in a severe
country outfit, came over to shake my hand: "Good evening, Dr. Aue.
It's a pleasure to see you again." I examined her face: it wasn't my imagination, they all really did look alike. "Forgive me, but are you Hilde or
Hedwig?" She gave a crystalline little smile: "Neither! You're a very
poor physiognomist. My name is Heide. We saw each other at Dr. Mandelbrod's offices." I bowed with a smile and apologized. "You weren't
at the hunt?"—"No. We've just arrived."—"That's too bad. I can easily
picture you with a shotgun under your arm. A German Artemis." She
eyed me with a little smile: "I hope you're not going to push the comparison too far, Dr. Aue." I felt myself blush: Mandelbrod definitely recruited odd assistants. No doubt about it, this one too would ask me to
get her pregnant. Fortunately, Speer arrived with his wife. "Ha! Sturmbannführer," he exclaimed cheerfully. "We're very poor hunters. Margret brought back five birds, Hettlage three." Frau Speer laughed
lightly: "Oh! You must have been talking about work." Speer went over
to pour himself some tea from a large, finely wrought ornate urn like a
Russian samovar; I took a glass of Cognac. Dr. Mandelbrod opened his
eyes and called to Speer, who went over to greet him. Leland came in
and joined them. I went to talk with Heide; she had a solid philosophical background and spoke to me almost clearly about Heidegger's theories, which at the time I was not at all familiar with. The other guests
arrived one by one. A little later on, Leland invited us all into another
room, where the dead birds had been set out on a long table, grouped
together like a Flemish still life. Frau Speer held the record; the hunt-
loving general had killed only one, and complained with bad grace
about the section of wood he had been assigned. I thought we were at

least going to eat the victims of this slaughter, but no: the birds had to be left to hang, and Leland undertook to have them delivered when they were ready. Nonetheless the dinner was varied and succulent—venison with berry sauce, potatoes roasted in goose fat, asparagus and zucchini, all washed down with a Burgundy of excellent vintage. I was seated opposite Speer, next to Leland; Mandelbrod sat at the head of the table. For the first time since I had met him, Herr Leland was extremely talkative: while drinking glass after glass, he talked about his past as a colonial administrator in Southwest Africa. He had known Rhodes, for whom he professed a boundless admiration, but remained vague about his move to the German colonies. "Rhodes said once: *The colonizer can do no wrong; whatever he does becomes right. It is his duty to do what he wants.* It is this principle, strictly applied, that won Europe its colonies, its domination over inferior peoples. It's only when the corrupt democracies wanted to mix in, to give themselves a good conscience, hypocritical principles of morality, that the decline began. You'll see: whatever the outcome of this war, France and Great Britain will lose their colonies. Their grip has slackened, they won't be able to close their fists anymore. It's Germany now that has picked up the torch. In 1907, I worked with General von Trotha. The Herero and the Nama had rebelled, but Trotha was a man who had understood Rhodes's idea in all its strength. He said it openly: *I wipe out rebel tribes with rivers of blood and rivers of money. Only following this cleansing can something new emerge.* But Germany at the time was already weakening, and Trotha was recalled. I have always thought that was a sign foreshadowing 1918. Fortunately, the course of things has now been reversed. Today, Germany dominates the world. Our youth isn't afraid of anything. Our expansion is an irresistible process."—"Still," broke in General von Wrede, who had arrived a little before Mandelbrod, "the Russians . . ." Leland tapped the table with the tip of his finger: "Precisely, the Russians. They are the only people today who are our equals. That's why our war with them is so terrible, so pitiless. Only one of us will survive. The others don't count. Can you imagine the Yankees, with their corned beef and their chewing gum, enduring a tenth of the Russian losses? A hundredth? They'd pack their bags and go home, and let Europe go to hell. No, what we have to do is show the Westerners that a Bolshevik victory is not in their interest, that Stalin will take half of Europe as his spoils, if not all of it. If the Anglo-Saxons help us finish off the Russians, we could leave them the scraps, or else, when we've regained our strength, crush them in turn, calmly. Look at what our *Parteigenosse* Speer has accomplished in less than two years! And that's just a beginning. Imagine

if our hands were unchained, if all the resources of the East were at our
disposal. Then the world could be remade as it should be."

After dinner I played chess with Hettlage, Speer's associate. Heide
came over and watched us play, in silence; Hettlage won easily. I had
one last Cognac and chatted a little with Heide. The guests went up to
bed. Finally she got up and, as directly as her colleagues, said: "I have to
go help Dr. Mandelbrod now. If you don't want to be alone, my room
is two doors down from yours, on the left. You can come have a drink,
a little later on."—"Thank you," I replied. "I'll see." I went up to my
room, pensive, got undressed, and lay down. The remnants of the fire
were glowing in the hearth. Lying there in the dark, I said to myself:
After all, why not? She was a beautiful woman, she had a superb body,
what was preventing me from taking advantage of it? There was no
question of an ongoing relationship, it was a simple, clear-cut proposition. And even if my experience of them was limited, women's bodies
didn't repel me, they must be pleasant too, soft and pliable, you must be
able to forget yourself in them as in a pillow. But there was that promise, and if I was nothing else, I was a man who kept his promises. Things
weren't settled yet.

Sunday was a quiet day. I slept late, until about nine o'clock—usually I got up at 5:30—and went down to breakfast. I sat down in front
of one of the big casement windows and leafed through an old edition
of Pascal, in French, which I had found in the library. At the end of the
morning, I accompanied Frau Speer and Frau von Wrede on a walk in
the park; the latter's husband was playing cards with an industrialist
known for having built his empire through clever Aryanizations, the
hunter general, and Hettlage. The grass, still wet, glistened, and puddles
punctuated the gravel and dirt paths; the humid air was cool, invigorating, and our breaths formed little clouds in front of our faces. The sky
remained uniformly gray. At noon I had coffee with Speer, who had just
made his appearance. He spoke to me in detail about the question of
foreign workers and his problems with Gauleiter Sauckel; then the conversation turned to the case of Ohlendorf, whom Speer seemed to regard as a romantic. My notions of economics were too rudimentary for
me to be able to support Ohlendorf's theories; Speer vigorously defended his principle of industrial self-responsibility. "In the end, there's
only one argument: it works. After the war, Dr. Ohlendorf can reform
as he likes, if anyone wants to listen to him; but in the meantime, as I
said to you yesterday, let's win the war."

Leland or Mandelbrod, whenever I found myself near them, chatted
to me about various things, but neither one seemed to have anything
special to say to me. I began to wonder why they had invited me: cer-

tainly not so I could enjoy Fräulein Heide's charms. But when I thought about the question again, at the end of the afternoon, in the von Wredes' car, which was taking me back to Berlin, the answer seemed obvious: it was to put me in contact with Speer, so I could get closer to him. And that seemed to have had its effect; when it was time to go, Speer had taken leave of me very cordially, and had promised me that we would see each other again. But one question troubled me: What was the point? In whose interest were Herr Leland and Dr. Mandelbrod *bringing me up* in this way? For there was no doubt it was a question of planned ascent: ministers, usually, don't spend their time chatting thus with simple majors. That worried me, for I didn't have the means to gauge the exact relations between Speer, the Reichsführer, and my two protectors; they were obviously maneuvering, but in what direction, and for whose benefit? I was willing to play the game, but which one? If it wasn't that of the SS, it could be very dangerous. I had to remain discreet and be very careful; I was no doubt part of a plan; if it failed, there would have to be a scapegoat.

I knew Thomas well enough to know without asking him what he would have advised: cover yourself. On the Monday morning, I requested a meeting with Brandt, which he granted me that afternoon. I described to him my weekend and told him about my conversations with Speer, the main points of which I had already jotted down in an aide-mémoire that I gave him. Brandt didn't seem to disapprove. "So he asked you to bring him to visit Dora?" That was the code name for the installation Speer had mentioned to me, officially called Mittelbau, "Central Construction."—"His ministry has filed a request. We haven't replied yet."—"And what do you think of it, Standartenführer?"—"I don't know. It's up to the Reichsführer to decide. That said, you did well to report to me." He briefly discussed my work too, and I told him about the initial impressions that emerged from the documents I had studied. When I got up to go, he said: "I think the Reichsführer is satisfied with the course things are taking. Continue on as you are."

After this meeting I went back to my offices to work. It was pouring outside, I could barely see the trees of the Tiergarten through the downpour whipping the leaf-stripped branches. Around five o'clock, I let Fräulein Praxa go; Walser and Obersturmführer Elias, another specialist sent by Brandt, left at around six o'clock, with Isenbeck. An hour later I went to find Asbach, who was still working. "Are you coming, Untersturmführer? I'll buy you a drink." He looked at his watch: "Don't you think they're coming back? It's almost their time." I looked out the window: it was dark out and still raining a little. "You think— with this weather?" But in the lobby the porter stopped us: "*Luftgefahr*

Fifteen, meine Herren," a serious raid on its way. They must have detected the planes ahead of time. I turned to Asbach and said cheerfully:
"You were right, after all. What should we do? Take our chances outside or wait in here?" Asbach looked a little worried: "It's just that I
have my wife . . ."—"In my opinion, you don't have time to go home.
I would have given you Piontek, but he left already." I thought. "We'd
do better to wait here till it passes, you can go home afterward. Your
wife will go to a shelter, she'll be fine." He hesitated: "Listen, Sturmbannführer, I'll go call her. She's pregnant, I don't want her to worry."—
"Right. I'll wait for you." I went out onto the steps and lit a cigarette.
The sirens began to wail, and the passersbys on the Königsplatz hurried
along, anxious to find a shelter. I wasn't worried: this annex of the ministry had an excellent bunker. I finished my cigarette as the flak opened
up and returned to the lobby. Asbach was running down the stairs: "It's
fine, she's going to her mother's. It's just next door."—"Did you open
the windows?" I asked him. We went down into the shelter, a block of
solid concrete, well lit, with chairs, folding cots, and large casksful of
water. Not many people were there: most of the civil servants went
home early, because of the lines for shopping and the air raids. In the
distance, it was beginning to thunder. Then I heard well-spaced, massive explosions: one by one they came closer, like the mammoth footsteps of a giant. At each impact the pressure of the air increased, pressing
painfully on our ears. There was an immense roar, very close, I could
feel the bunker's walls tremble. The lights flickered and then went out
all at once, plunging the shelter into darkness. A girl yelped in terror.
Someone turned on a flashlight; others scraped matches. "Isn't there an
emergency generator?" another voice began, but was interrupted by a
deafening explosion; rubble rained down from the ceiling, people cried
out. I smelled smoke, the smell of explosives bit into my nose: the building must have been hit. The explosions drew off; through the ringing
in my ears, I could dimly hear the throbbing of the squadrons. A woman
was crying; a man's voice grunted out curses; I lit my lighter and headed
for the armored door. With the porter, I tried to open it: it was blocked,
the stairway must have been obstructed by debris. Three of us rammed
it with our shoulders and managed to open it enough to slip outside.
Bricks were piled on the stairs; I climbed up to the ground floor, followed by a civil servant: the main entrance door had been blown off its
hinges and hurled into the lobby; flames were licking the paneling and
the porter's lodge. I ran up the staircase, down a hallway cluttered with
window frames and ripped-off doors, then up another floor, to my offices: I wanted to try to save the most important files. The iron
balustrade on the staircase was bent: the pocket of my tunic caught on

a piece of twisted metal and ripped open. Upstairs, the offices were burning and I had to turn back. In the hallway, an employee was carrying a pile of files; another joined us, his face pale beneath the black traces of smoke and dust: "Leave that! The west wing is burning. A bomb came through the roof." I had thought the attack was over, but again squadrons were rumbling in the sky; a series of explosions approached at a frightening speed, we ran for the basement, a massive explosion lifted me up and threw me into the stairway. I must have stayed there for a bit, stunned; I came to, blinded by a glaring white light that turned out to be a little flashlight; I heard Asbach shouting, "Sturmbannführer! Sturmbannführer!"—"I'm all right," I muttered, getting up. In the glow from the fire in the entryway, I examined my tunic: the metal point had cut through the cloth, it was ruined. "The ministry is burning," another voice said. "We have to get out." With some other men we cleared the entrance to the bunker as well as we could, so everyone could climb out. The sirens were still wailing but the flak had fallen silent, the last planes were flying away. It was 8:30, the raid had lasted an hour. Someone pointed to some buckets and we formed a chain to fight the fire: it was laughable, in twenty minutes we had used up the water stored in the basement. The faucets didn't work, the bombs must have burst the pipes; the porter tried to call the firemen, but the telephone was cut off. I recovered my overcoat from the shelter and went out into the square to examine the damage. The east wing looked intact, aside from the gaping windows, but part of the west wing had collapsed, and the neighboring windows vomited thick black smoke. Our offices must have been burning too. Asbach joined me, his face covered in blood. "Are you hurt?" I asked.—"It's nothing. A brick." I was still deafened, my ears were ringing painfully. I looked at the Tiergarten: the trees, lit up by several fires, had been smashed, broken, toppled—it looked like a wood in Flanders after an attack, in the books I read as a child. "I'm going home," Asbach said. Anguish twisted his bloodstained face. "I want to find my wife."—"Go on. Be careful of falling walls." Two fire trucks arrived and maneuvered into position, but there seemed to be a problem with the water. The ministry employees were leaving, many carrying files that they put down a little farther away, on the sidewalks: for half an hour I helped them carry binders and papers; my own offices were unreachable in any case. A strong wind had arisen, and to the north, the east, and farther to the south, beyond the Tiergarten, the nighttime sky glowed red. An officer came over to tell us that the fires were spreading, but the ministry and the neighboring buildings seemed to me to be protected by the bend in the Spree on one side and the Tiergarten and Königsplatz on the other. The Reichstag, dark and closed, didn't seem damaged.

I hesitated. I was hungry, but I couldn't count on finding anything to eat. At home I had some food, but I didn't know if my apartment still existed. I finally decided to go to the SS-Haus and report for duty. I set off down the Freidensallee at a run: in front of me, the Brandenburg Gate stood under its camouflage nets, intact. But behind it, almost all of Unter den Linden seemed to be in flames. The air was dense with smoke and dust, thick and hot, I was beginning to have trouble breathing. Clouds of sparks burst forth, crackling, from the buildings on fire. The wind was blowing ever more strongly. On the other side of the Pariser Platz, the Armaments Ministry was burning, partially crushed under the impacts. Secretaries wearing civil defense metal helmets were bustling about in the rubble, recovering files there too. A Mercedes with a fanion stood parked to the side; among the crowd of employees, I recognized Speer, bare-headed, his face black with soot. I went over to greet him and offered him my help; when he saw me, he shouted something to me that I didn't understand. "You're burning!" he repeated.—"What?" He came toward me, took me by the arm, turned me around, and beat my back with his open hand. Sparks must have set fire to my overcoat, but I hadn't felt anything. Confused, I thanked him and asked him what I could do. "Nothing, really. I think we've gotten out what we could. My own office took a direct hit. There's nothing left." I looked around: the French embassy, the former British embassy, the Bristol Hotel, the offices of IG Farben—everything was heavily damaged or burning. The elegant façades of the Schinkel town houses, next to the Gate, stood out against a background of fire. "How awful," I muttered.—"It's terrible to say," Speer said pensively, "but it's better that they're concentrating on the cities."—"What do you mean, Herr Reichsminister?"—"During the summer, when they attacked the Ruhr, I was terrified. In August, they attacked Schweinfurt, where our entire production of ball bearings is concentrated. Then again in October. Our production fell by sixty-seven percent. You may not realize it, Sturmbannführer, but no ball bearings, no war. If they concentrate on Schweinfurt, we capitulate in two months, three at the most. Here"— he waved his hand at the fires—"they're killing people, wasting all their resources on our cultural monuments." He gave a dry, harsh laugh: "We were going to rebuild everything anyway. Ha!" I saluted him: "If you don't need me, Herr Reichsminister, I'll keep going. But I wanted to tell you that your request is being considered. I'll contact you soon to tell you where things stand." He shook my hand: "Fine, fine. Good night, Sturmbannführer."

I had soaked my handkerchief in a bucket and was holding it over my mouth to go forward; I had also soaked my shoulders and cap. In the

Wilhelmstrasse, the wind roared between the ministries and whipped the flames licking the empty windows. Soldiers and firemen were running everywhere, with little result. The *Auswärtiges Amt* looked severely hit, but the chancellery, a little farther on, had fared better. I was walking on a carpet of broken glass: in the entire street there wasn't one window left unbroken. On the Wilhelmplatz some bodies had been stretched out near an overturned Luftwaffe truck; frightened civilians were still coming out of the U-Bahn station and looking around, horrified and lost; from time to time a blast could be heard, a delayed-action bomb, or else the muffled roar of a building collapsing. I looked at the bodies: a man without pants, his bloody buttocks grotesquely exposed; a woman with her stockings intact, but without a head. I thought it especially obscene that they were left there like that, but no one seemed to care. A little farther on, guards had been posted in front of the Aviation Ministry: passersbys shouted insults at them or sarcastic remarks about Göring, but didn't linger, no crowd was forming; I showed my SD card and went through the cordon. I finally arrived at the corner of Prinz-Albrechtstrasse: the SS-Haus had no windows left, but otherwise didn't seem damaged. In the lobby, troops were sweeping away the debris; officers were hoisting boards or mattresses to cover the gaping windows. In a hallway, I found Brandt giving instructions in a calm, flat voice: he was especially concerned with getting the telephone restored. I saluted him and informed him of the destruction of my offices. He nodded: "Well, we'll take care of that tomorrow." Since there didn't seem to be much to do, I went next door, to the *Staatspolizei*; they were busy nailing up the doors that had been torn off, as well as they could; some bombs had struck nearby, an enormous crater disfigured the street a little farther on, and water was escaping from a burst pipe. I found Thomas in his office drinking schnapps with three other officers, unbuttoned, black with filth, laughing. "Look at you!" he exclaimed. "You're a sorry sight. Have a drink. Where were you?" I briefly told him about my experiences at the ministry. "Ha! I was home already, I went down to the basement with the neighbors. A bomb came through the roof and the building caught fire. We had to break down the walls of the neighboring basements, several in a row, to come out at the end of the street. The whole street burned down and half of my building, including my apartment, collapsed. To top it all off, I found my poor convertible under a bus. In short, I'm ruined." He poured me another glass. "Since misfortune is upon us, let us drink, as my grandmother Ivona used to say."

In the end I spent the night at the *Staatspolizei*. Thomas had sandwiches, tea, and soup delivered. He lent me one of his spare uniforms, a little too big for me, but more presentable than my rags; a smiling typist took charge of switching the stripes and insignia. They had set up folding cots in the gymnasium for about fifteen homeless officers; I ran into Eduard Holste there, whom I had briefly known as Leiter IV/V of Group D, at the end of 1942; he had lost everything and was almost crying with bitterness. Unfortunately the showers still didn't work, and I could wash only my hands and face. My throat hurt, I coughed, but Thomas's schnapps had cut the taste of ash a little. Outside, we still heard explosions. The wind roared, raging and relentless.

Very early in the morning, without waiting for Piontek, I took the car from the garage and went home. The streets, obstructed by burned or overturned trolleys, fallen trees, rubble, were hard to navigate. A cloud of black, acrid smoke veiled the sky and many passersby were holding wet towels or handkerchiefs over their mouths. It was still drizzling. I passed lines of people pushing strollers or little wagonsful of belongings, or else lugging or dragging suitcases. Everywhere water was escaping from pipes, I had to drive through pools hiding debris that could shred my tires at any moment. Still, many cars were still circulating, most of them without windows and some even missing doors, but full of people: those who had space picked up bombing victims, and I did the same for an exhausted mother with two young children who wanted to go see her parents. I cut through the devastated Tiergarten; the Victory Column, still standing as if out of defiance, rose in the midst of a large lake formed by the water from shattered mains, and I had to make a big detour to skirt round it. I dropped the woman off in the rubble of the Händelallee and went on to my apartment. Everywhere, teams were at work repairing the damage; in front of destroyed buildings, sappers were pumping air into collapsed basements and digging to free survivors, assisted by Italian prisoners—everyone nowadays just called them the *Badoglios*—with the letters *KGF* painted in red on their backs. The S-Bahn station in the Brückenallee lay in ruins; I lived a little farther, on Flensburgerstrasse; my building looked miraculously intact: a hundred and fifty meters farther, there was nothing but rubble and gaping façades. The elevator, of course, didn't work, so I climbed the eight flights, passing my neighbors sweeping the stairway or nailing up their doors as best they could. I found mine torn from its hinges and lying sideways; inside, a thick layer of broken glass and plaster covered everything; there were traces of footsteps and my gramophone had disappeared, but nothing else seemed to have been taken. A cold, biting wind blew through the windows. I quickly filled a suitcase, then went downstairs to arrange with my neighbor, who came from time to time to do housework for me, to come and clean up; I gave her money to have the door repaired that day, and the windows as soon as possible; she promised to contact me at the SS-Haus when the apartment was more or less livable. I went out in search of a hotel: above all, I dreamed of a bath. The closest was the Eden Hotel, where I had already stayed for a time. I had luck, the entire Budapesterstrasse seemed razed, but the Eden was still open. The front desk was being taken by storm, rich people who had been left homeless, officers arguing over rooms. When I had mentioned my rank, my medals, my disability, and lied by exaggerating the state of my apartment, the manager, who had recognized me, agreed to give me a bed, provided I share the room. I held out a banknote to the floor waiter so he would bring hot water to my room: finally, around ten o'clock, I was able to run a bath, lukewarm but delectable. The water immediately turned black, but I didn't care. I was still soaking when they let my roommate in. He excused himself politely through the closed bathroom door and told me he'd wait below until I was ready. As soon as I was dressed I went down to look for him: he was a Georgian aristocrat, very elegant, who had fled his burning hotel with his things and had ended up here.

My colleagues all had the idea to meet at the SS-Haus. I found Piontek there, imperturbable; Fräulein Praxa, prettily dressed, although her wardrobe had gone up in smoke; all cheerful because his neighborhood had been spared, Walser; and, a little shaken up, Isenbeck, whose old neighbor had died of a heart attack right next to him, during the alert, in the dark, without his noticing. Weinrowski had returned some time ago to Oranienburg. As for Asbach, he had sent word: his wife was wounded, he would come as soon as he could. I sent Piontek to tell him to take a few days if he needed to: there wasn't much chance we could get back to work right away anyway. I sent Fräulein Praxa home, and in the company of Walser and Isenbeck went to the ministry to see what could still be saved. The fire had been contained, but the west wing was still closed; a fireman escorted us through the rubble. Most of the top floor had burned down, as well as the attic: in our offices, only one room, with a file cabinet that had survived the fire, remained, but it had been flooded by the firemen's hoses. Through a section of collapsed wall you could see part of the ravaged Tiergarten; leaning out, I saw that the Lehrter Bahnhof had also suffered, but the thick smoke that weighed over the city prevented me from seeing farther; in the distance, though, the lines of burned avenues could still be made out. I undertook to move the surviving files with my colleagues, along with a typewriter and a telephone. It was a delicate task, since the fire had burned holes in the floor in places, and the hallways were obstructed with rubble that had to be cleared. When Piontek joined us, we filled the car and I sent

him to take everything to the SS-Haus. There I was assigned a temporary storage closet, but nothing more; Brandt was still too overwhelmed
to worry about me. Since I had nothing else to do, I dismissed Walser
and Isenbeck and had Piontek drop me off at the Eden Hotel, after ar-
ranging with him to come pick me up the next morning: without a
family, he could just as well sleep in the garage. I went down to the bar
and ordered a Cognac. My roommate, the Georgian, wearing a fedora
and a white scarf, was playing Mozart on the piano, with a remarkably
precise touch. When he stopped, I offered him a drink and chatted a little with him. He was vaguely affiliated with one of those groups of émi-
grés who were always bustling about the dens of the *Auswärtiges Amt*
and the SS; the name Misha Kedia, when he mentioned it, sounded
vaguely familiar. When he learned that I had been in the Caucasus, he
leapt up enthusiastically, ordered another round, gave a solemn and interminable toast (although I had never set foot on his side of the mountains), forced me to empty my glass in one swallow, and invited me on
the spot to come stay in Tiflis after our forces had freed it, in his ancestral home. Little by little the bar filled up. Around seven o'clock, conversations trailed off, people began to eye the clock over the bar: ten
minutes later the sirens started up, then the flak, violent and close. The
manager had come to assure us that the bar also served as a shelter; all
the hotel clients came downstairs, and soon there was no more room.
The ambiance became cheerful and animated: as the first bombs got
closer, the Georgian went back to the piano and dove into a jazz tune;
women in evening gowns got up to dance, the walls and chandeliers
trembled, glasses fell from the bar and shattered, you could scarcely hear
the music beneath the explosions, the air pressure became unbearable, I
drank, several women, hysterical, laughed, another tried to kiss me, then
burst out sobbing. When it was over, the manager handed out a round
on the house. I went out: the zoo had been hit, pavilions were burning,
again you could see fires pretty much everywhere; I smoked a cigarette,
regretting I hadn't gone to see the animals while there was still time. A
section of wall had collapsed; I walked over to it, men were running in
every direction, some were carrying shotguns, there was talk of lions
and tigers roaming free. Several firebombs had fallen, and beyond the
avalanche of bricks, I saw the galleries burning; the large Indian temple
had been gutted; inside, a man who was walking next to me explained,
they had found the elephants' corpses torn to pieces by the bombs, as
well as a rhinoceros seemingly intact but also dead, maybe from fear.
Behind me, most of the buildings on Budapesterstrasse were burning
too. I went to lend a hand to the firemen; for hours I helped clear away
the rubble; every five minutes a whistle blew, and work stopped so the

rescuers could listen for the muffled sounds of trapped people; and we got some of them out alive, wounded or even unhurt. Around midnight I went back to the Eden; the façade was damaged, but the structure had escaped a direct hit; at the bar, the party was still going on. My new Georgian friend forced me to drink several glasses in a row; the uniform Thomas had lent me was covered in filth and soot, but that didn't prevent women of the highest society from flirting with me; few of them, it seemed, wanted to spend the night alone. The Georgian did so well that I got completely drunk: the next morning, I woke up on my bed, without any memory of climbing up to my room, with my tunic and shirt removed, but not my boots. The Georgian was snoring in the next bed. I cleaned up as well as I could, put on one of my clean uniforms, and gave Thomas's over to be washed; leaving my sleeping neighbor there, I downed a bad coffee, took an aspirin for my headache, and returned to the Prinz-Albrechtstrasse.

The officers of the Reichsführung all looked a little wild: a number of them hadn't slept all night; many had ended up homeless, and several had lost someone in their family. In the lobby and the stairways, inmates in striped uniforms, guarded by some Totenkopf-SS, were sweeping the floor, nailing up boards, repainting the walls. Brandt asked me to help some officers draw up an estimation of the damage for the Reichsführer, by contacting the municipal authorities. The work was simple enough: each of us chose a sector—victims, housing, government buildings, infrastructure, industry—and contacted the proper authorities to note down their figures. I was set up with an office that had a telephone and a directory; a few lines still worked, and I put Fräulein Praxa there—she had unearthed a new outfit somewhere—so she could call the hospitals. To get him out from underfoot, I decided to send Isenbeck, with the salvaged files, to join his boss Weinrowski in Oranienburg, and asked Piontek to drive him there. Walser hadn't come. When Fräulein Praxa managed to reach a hospital, I asked for the number of dead and wounded they had received; when she had made a list of three or four institutions we couldn't reach by phone, I sent a driver and an orderly to collect the data. Asbach arrived around noon, his features drawn, making a visible effort to look composed. I took him to the mess for sandwiches and tea. Slowly, between mouthfuls, he told me what had happened: The first night, the building where his wife had joined her mother had taken a direct hit and had collapsed onto the shelter, which had only partly held up. Asbach's mother-in-law had apparently been killed immediately or had at least died quickly; his wife had been buried alive and they hadn't been able to free her till the next morning, unhurt aside from a broken arm, but incoherent; she had had a miscarriage during the night, and still hadn't recovered her wits; she went from a child-like babbling to hysterical tears. "I'm going to have to bury her mother without her," Asbach said sadly as he sipped his tea. "I'd have liked to wait a little, for her to recover, but the morgues are overflowing and the medical authorities are afraid of epidemics. Apparently all the bodies that haven't been reclaimed in twenty-four hours will be buried in mass graves. It's terrible." I tried my best to console him, but, I have to admit, I'm not very good at that sort of thing: my words about his future conjugal happiness must have sounded pretty hollow. Still it seemed to comfort him. I sent him home with a driver from the Reichsführung, promising I'd find him a van for the funeral the next day.

The Tuesday raid, even though it had involved only half as many aircraft as Monday's, promised to turn out to be even more disastrous. The working-class neighborhoods, especially Wedding, had been hit hard. By the end of the afternoon we had gathered enough information to form a brief report: we counted about 2,000 dead, with hundreds more beneath the rubble; 3,000 buildings burned or destroyed; and 175,000 people homeless, of whom 100,000 had already been able to leave the city, either for surrounding villages or other cities in Germany. Around six o'clock we dismissed all the people who weren't doing essential work; I stayed a little longer, and was still on the road, with a driver from the garage, when the sirens began to wail again. I decided not to continue on to the Eden: the bar-shelter didn't inspire much confidence in me, and I preferred to avoid a repetition of the drinking bout of the night before. I ordered the driver to go around the zoo to reach the large bunker. A crowd was pressed at the doors, which were too narrow and too few; cars came and parked at the foot of the concrete façade; in front of them, in a reserved area, dozens of baby carriages stretched out in concentric circles. Inside, soldiers and policemen barked out orders for people to move upstairs; at each floor a crowd formed, no one wanted to go higher up, women were screaming, while their children ran through the crowd playing war games. We were directed to the third floor, but the benches, lined up as in a church, were already crowded, and I went to lean against the concrete wall. My driver had disappeared in the crowd. Soon afterward the .88s on the roof opened fire: the entire immense structure vibrated, pitching like a ship on the high seas. People, thrown against their neighbors, shouted or groaned. The lights dimmed but didn't go out. In recesses and in the darkness of the spiral staircases leading from floor to floor, teenage couples clung to each other, intertwined; some even seemed to be making love—you could hear through the explosions moans of a different tone from those of panic-stricken housewives; old people protested indignantly, the Schupos bellowed, ordering people to remain seated. I wanted to smoke but it was forbidden. I looked at the woman sitting on the bench in front of me: she kept her head lowered, I could just see her blond, exceptionally thick, shoulder-length hair. A bomb exploded nearby, making the bunker tremble and throwing up a cloud of concrete dust. The young woman raised her head and I recognized her right away: she was the one I met sometimes in the morning, on the trolley. She too recognized me and a gentle smile lit up her face while she held out her white hand to me: "Hello! I was worried about you."—"Why?" With the flak and the explosions we could barely hear each other, I crouched down and bent toward her. "You weren't at the pool Sunday," she said into my ear. "I was afraid something had happened to you." Sunday was already another life, it seemed to me; but it was only three days ago. "I was in the country. Does the pool still exist?" She smiled again: "I don't know." Another powerful explosion shook the structure and she seized my hand and grasped it strongly; when it was over she let it go, excusing herself. Despite the yellowish light and the dust, I had the impression she was blushing slightly. "Forgive me," I asked her, "what is your name?"—"Helene," she replied. "Helene Anders." I introduced myself. She worked at the press agency of the *Auswärtiges Amt*; her office, like most of the ministry, had been destroyed Monday night, but her parents' house, in Alt Moabit, where she lived, was still standing. "Before this raid, in any case. And you?" I laughed: "I had offices at the Ministry of the Interior, but they burned down. For now, I'm at the SS-Haus." We continued chatting till the end of the alert. She had gone on foot to Charlottenburg to comfort a homeless girlfriend; the sirens had caught her on the way back, and she had taken refuge there, in the bunker. "I didn't think they'd come back a third night in a row," she said softly.—"To tell the truth, I didn't either," I replied, "but I'm happy it's given us the chance to see each other again." I said that to be polite; but I realized it wasn't just to be polite. This time, she blushed visibly; her tone still remained frank and clear: "Me too. Our trolley will probably be out of service for a while." When the lights came back on, she got up and brushed off her coat. "If you like," I said, "I can take you home. If I still have a car," I added, laughing. "Don't say no. It's not very far away."

I found my driver next to his vehicle, looking very upset: it no longer had any windows, and the whole side had been crushed in by the car next to it, propelled by the blast of an explosion. Of the baby carriages, only scattered debris remained on the square. The zoo was burning again, you could hear atrocious sounds, the bellowing, trumpeting, lowing of dying animals. "The poor beasts," Helene murmured, "they

don't know what's happening to them." The driver was only thinking
about his car. I went to find some Schupos so they could help us free it.
The passenger door was jammed; I had Helene get in the back, then
slipped in over the driver's seat. The ride turned out to be a little complicated, we had to take a detour through the Tiergarten, because of the
blocked streets, but I was happy to see, passing by Flensburgerstrasse,
that my building had survived. Alt Moabit, aside from a few stray
bombs, had been more or less spared, and I dropped Helene off in front
of her small building. "Now," I said as I left her, "I know where you
live. If you don't mind, I'll come visit when things have calmed down
a little."—"I'd be delighted," she replied with again that very beautiful,
calm smile she had. Then I went back to the Eden Hotel, where I found
nothing but a gaping shell in flames. Three bombs had gone through the
roof and nothing was left. Fortunately the bar had held up, the hotel residents had escaped with their lives and had been evacuated. My Georgian neighbor was drinking Cognac straight from the bottle with some
other now-homeless people; as soon as he saw me, he made me take a
swig. "I've lost everything! Everything! What I miss most are the shoes.
Four new pairs!"—"Do you have a place to go?" He shrugged: "I've
got some friends not too far away. On Rauchstrasse."—"Come on, I'll
drive you there." The house that the Georgian pointed out had no more
windows but seemed still inhabited. I waited for a few minutes while he
went in to see what he could find out. He returned looking cheerful:
"Perfect! They're going to Marienbad, I'll leave with them. Will you
come in and have a drink?" I refused politely, but he insisted: "Come
on! For the *pososhok.*" I felt drained, exhausted. I wished him good luck
and left without further ado. At the *Staatspolizei*, an Untersturmführer
told me that Thomas had found refuge at Schellenberg's place. I had a
bite to eat, had a bed set up for me in the improvised dormitory, and
fell asleep.

The next day, Thursday, I continued collecting statistics for Brandt.
Walser still hadn't reappeared but I wasn't too worried. To make up for
the lack of telephone lines, we now had a squad of Hitlerjugend on loan
from Goebbels. We sent them all over, on bikes or on foot, to send or
get messages and mail. In town, the hard work of the municipal services
was already yielding results: in some neighborhoods, water had come
back, electricity too, sections of the trolley lines were put back in service, along with the U-Bahn and S-Bahn, where it was possible. We also
knew that Goebbels was contemplating a partial evacuation of the city.
Everywhere, on the ruins, chalk messages were proliferating, people
trying to find their parents, their friends, their neighbors. Around noon,
I requisitioned a small van from the police and went to help Asbach

bury his mother-in-law in the Plötzensee cemetery, alongside her husband who had died of cancer four years earlier. Asbach seemed a little better: his wife was recovering her senses, she had recognized him; but he hadn't told her anything yet, either about her mother or about the baby. Fräulein Praxa accompanied us and even managed to find flowers; Asbach was visibly touched. Aside from us there were only three of his friends, including a couple, and a minister. The coffin was made of coarse, badly planed boards; Asbach kept saying that as soon as possible he would ask for a permit to exhume the body to give his mother-in-law a proper funeral: they had never gotten along well, he added, she hadn't hidden her scorn for his SS uniform, but still, she was his wife's mother, and Asbach loved his wife. I didn't envy his situation: to be alone in the world is sometimes a great advantage, especially in wartime. I dropped him off at the military hospital where his wife was, and went back to the SS-Haus. That night, there was no raid; an alert went off in the early evening, provoking an outburst of panic, but they were just reconnaissance planes, come to photograph the damage. After the alert, which I spent in the *Staatspolizei* bunker, Thomas took me to a little restaurant that had already reopened its doors. He was in a cheerful mood: Schellenberg had arranged to have a small house in Dahlem lent to him, in a fashionable neighborhood near the Grunewald, and he was going to buy a small Mercedes convertible from a widow who needed money; her husband, a Hauptsturmführer, had been killed during the first raid. "Fortunately, my bank is intact. That's what counts." I made a face: "Still, there are other things that count."—"Like what, for example?"—"Our sacrifices. The suffering of the people, here, around us, on the front." In Russia things were going very badly: after losing Kiev, we had managed to retake Zhitomir, only to lose Cherkassy the day I was hunting grouse with Speer; in Rovno, the Ukrainian insurgents of the UPA, as anti-German as they were anti-Bolshevik, were picking off isolated German soldiers like rabbits. "I've always said, Max," Thomas said, "you take things too seriously."—"It's a question of *Weltanschauung*," I said, raising my glass. Thomas gave a brief, mocking laugh. "*Weltanschauung here, Weltanschauung there,* as Schnitzler said. Everyone has a *Weltanschauung* these days, the lowliest baker or plumber has his *Weltanschauung*, my mechanic overcharges me thirty percent for repairs, but he too has his *Weltanschauung*. I have one too . . ." He fell silent and drank; I drank too. It was a Bulgarian wine, a little rough, but given the circumstances there was nothing to complain about. "I'm going to tell you what counts," Thomas said urgently. "Serve your country, die if you have to, but take advantage of life as much as possible in the meantime. Your posthumous *Ritterkreuz* might console your old mother, but it'll be cold comfort for you."—"My mother is dead," I said softly.—"I know. I'm sorry." One night, after many drinks, I had told him about my mother's death, without going into too much detail; since then we hadn't talked about it again. Thomas drank some more, then burst out: "Do you know why we hate the Jews? I'll tell you. We hate the Jews because they're a thrifty, prudent people, greedy not just for money and security but also for their traditions, their knowledge, and their books, incapable of giving and spending, a people that doesn't know war. A people that just knows how to accumulate, never to waste. In Kiev you said the murder of the Jews was a waste. Well, precisely, by wasting their lives the way you throw rice at a wedding, we've taught them expense, we've taught them war. And the proof that it's working, that the Jews are beginning to learn the lesson, is Warsaw, Treblinka, Sobibor, Bialystok, it's the Jews who are becoming warriors again, who are becoming cruel, who also are becoming killers. I find that very beautiful. We've made them into an enemy worthy of us. The *Pour la Semite*"— he struck his chest at the heart, where the Jews sew the star—"is picking up value again. And if the Germans don't pull themselves together like the Jews, instead of moaning, they'll just get what they deserve. *Vae victis.*" He emptied his glass in one swallow, his gaze distant. I realized he was drunk. "I'm going home," he said. I offered to drive him back, but he refused: he had taken a car from the garage. In the still-half-cleared street, he absentmindedly shook my hand, slammed the door, and shot off. I went back to sleep at the *Staatspolizei*; it was heated, and the showers, at least, had been fixed.

The next night there was another raid, the fifth and last in that series. The damage was terrible: the center of the city lay in ruins along with a large part of Wedding; they counted more than four thousand dead and four hundred thousand homeless, many factories and several ministries had been destroyed, communications and public transport would take weeks to be restored. People were living in apartments without any windows or heat: a large portion of the coal reserves, stored in gardens for the winter, had burned. Finding bread had become impossible, the stores remained empty, and the NSV had set up field kitchens in the ravaged streets to serve cabbage soup. In the Reichsführung and RSHA complex, we fared a little better: it was possible to eat and sleep, clothes and uniforms were provided to those who had lost everything. When Brandt received me, I suggested I transfer part of my team to Oranienburg, to the IKL premises, and keep a little office in Berlin for liaison purposes. The idea seemed good to him but he wanted to consult the Reichsführer. The latter, Brandt informed me, had agreed to let Speer visit Mittelbau: I was to take charge of organizing everything. "Arrange things so that the Reichsminister is . . . satisfied," he said. He had another surprise for me: I was promoted to the rank of Obersturmbannführer. I was happy, but surprised: "Why?"—"It was the Reichsführer's decision. Your functions have already taken on a certain importance and will continue to do so. Speaking of that, what do you think of the reorganization of Auschwitz?" In the beginning of the month, Obersturmbannführer Liebehenschel, Glücks's deputy at the IKL, had traded places with Höss; since then, Auschwitz had been divided into three distinct camps: the *Stammlager*, the Birkenau complex, and Monowitz with all the *Nebenlager*. Liebehenschel remained as Kommandant of Auschwitz I and also Standortälteste for all three camps, which gave him a right of oversight over the work of the other two new Kommandanten, Hartjenstein and Hauptsturmführer Schwarz, who till then had been Arbeitskommandoführer and then Lagerführer under Höss. "Standartenführer, I think the administrative restructuring is an excellent initiative: the camp was much too large and was becoming unmanageable. As for Obersturmbannführer Liebehenschel, judging from what I could see of him, it's a good choice, he understands the new priorities very well. But I must confess that when I think about Obersturmbannführer Höss's appointment to the IKL, I have a hard time grasping this organization's personnel policy. I have the greatest respect for Obersturmbannführer Höss; I regard him as an excellent soldier; but if you ask my opinion, he should be out there leading a Waffen-SS regiment at the front. He is not an administrator. Liebehenschel dealt with most of the daily work at the IKL. Höss is certainly not the man to take an interest in administrative details." Brandt scrutinized me through his owl glasses. "Thank you for the frankness of your opinion. But I don't think the Reichsführer is in agreement with you. In any case, even if Obersturmbannführer Höss has other talents than Liebehenschel, there's still Standartenführer Maurer." I nodded; Brandt shared the common opinion of Glücks. When I saw Isenbeck the following week, he told me what was being said in Oranienburg: everyone understood that Höss had done his time in Auschwitz, except Höss himself; apparently the Reichsführer in person had informed him of his transfer, during a camp visit, using as a pretext—this is what Höss was saying at Oranienburg— the BBC broadcasts on the exterminations; his promotion to the head of DI made that plausible. But why were they treating him so carefully? For Thomas, to whom I posed the question, there was only one explanation: Höss had done time in prison with Bormann, in the 1920s, for a *Vehmgericht* murder; they must have remained in touch, and Bormann was protecting Höss.

As soon as the Reichsführer had approved of my suggestion, I proceeded to reorganize my office. The entire unit in charge of research, with Asbach as chief, was transferred to Oranienburg. Asbach seemed relieved to be leaving Berlin. With Fräulein Praxa and two other assistants I set myself up again in my old premises at the SS-Haus. Walser had never come back: Piontek, whom I finally sent to find out about him, reported that the shelter in his building had been struck, on the Tuesday night. The number of dead was estimated at twenty-three, the entire population of the building; there were no survivors, but most of the corpses unearthed were unrecognizable. To set my mind at rest, I reported him missing: that way, the police would look for him in the hospitals; but I had little hope of finding him alive. Piontek seemed very upset about it. Thomas, already over his bout of spleen, was overflowing with energy; now that we were office neighbors again, I saw him more often. Instead of telling him about my promotion, I waited, to surprise him, until I had received my official notification and had had my new stripes and collar tabs sewn on. When I presented myself at his office, he burst out laughing, searched through his desk, pulled out a sheet of paper, waved it in the air, and cried out: "Ah! You scoundrel. You thought you could catch up with me!" He made the document into a paper plane and launched it at me; its nose hit my Iron Cross and I unfolded it to read that Müller was proposing Thomas as Standartenführer. "And you can be sure it won't be refused. But," he added with good grace, "until it's official, dinners are on me."

My promotion had just as little effect on the imperturbable Fräulein Praxa, but she couldn't hide her surprise when she received a direct phone call from Speer: "The Reichsminister wants to speak to you," she informed me in a breathless voice, handing me the receiver. After the last raid, I had sent him a message giving him my new coordinates. "Sturmbannführer?" his firm, pleasant voice said. "How are you? Not too much damage?"—"My archivist has probably been killed, Herr Reichsminister. Otherwise, everything's fine. And you?"—"I moved into temporary offices and sent my family to the country. So?"—"Your visit to Mittelbau has just been approved, Herr Reichsminister. I've been appointed to organize it. As soon as possible, I'll contact your secretary to set up a date." For important questions, Speer had asked me to call his personal secretary, rather than an assistant. "Very good," he said. "See you soon." I had already written to Mittelbau to warn them to prepare for the visit. I called Obersturmbannführer Förschner, the Kommandant of Dora, to confirm the arrangements. "Listen," his tired voice grumbled at the other end, "we'll do our best."—"I'm not asking you to do your best, Obersturmbannführer. I'm asking that the installations be presentable for the Reichsminister's visit. The Reichsführer personally insisted on that. Do you understand?"—"Fine, fine. I'll give some more orders."

My apartment had been more or less fixed up. I had finally managed to find some glass for two windows; the others remained covered with a waxed canvas tarp. My neighbor had not only had my door repaired but had also unearthed some oil lamps to use until electricity was restored. I had some coal delivered, and once the big ceramic stove was started, it wasn't cold at all. I told myself that taking an apartment on the top floor hadn't been very smart: I had had incredible luck escaping the raids of that week, but if they returned, and they certainly would, it wouldn't last. Yet, I refused to worry: the apartment didn't belong to me, and I didn't have many personal possessions; you had to keep Thomas's serene attitude about these things. I simply bought myself a new gramophone, with records of Bach's Partitas for piano, as well as some opera arias by Monteverdi. In the evening, in the soft, archaic light of an oil lamp, a glass of Cognac and some cigarettes within arm's reach, I would lie back on my sofa to listen to them and forget everything else.

A new thought, though, came more and more often to occupy my mind. The Sunday after the air raids, around noon, I had taken the car from the garage and had gone to visit Helene Anders. The day was cold and wet, the sky overcast, but it wasn't raining. On the way, I had managed to find a bouquet of flowers, sold in the street by an old woman near an S-Bahn station. Having reached Helene's building, I realized I didn't know what apartment she lived in. Her name wasn't on the letter boxes. A rather hefty woman who was leaving at that moment stopped and eyed me from head to foot before barking at me, in strong Berlin slang: "Who are you looking for?"—"Fräulein Anders."—"Anders? There's no Anders here." I described her. "You mean the Winnefeld daughter. But she's not a *Fräulein*." She directed me to the apartment and I went up to ring. A lady with white hair opened the door and frowned. "Frau Winnefeld?"—"Yes." I clicked my heels and bowed my head. "My respects, meine Dame. I came to see your daughter." I held out the flowers and introduced myself. Helene appeared in the hallway, a sweater over her shoulders, and her face colored slightly: "Oh!" she smiled. "It's you."—"I came to ask you if you were planning to swim today."—"Is the pool still working?" she said.—"Unfortunately not." I had passed it on my way: a firebomb had gone through the dome, and the concierge who was watching over the ruins had assured me that, given the priorities, it certainly wouldn't reopen before the end of the war. "But I know of another one."—"Then I'd be happy to. I'll go get my things." Downstairs, I helped her into the car and set off. "I didn't know you were a *Frau*," I said after a few minutes. She looked at me pensively: "I'm a widow. My husband was killed in Yugoslavia last year, by the partisans. We'd been married for less than a year."—"I'm sorry." She looked out the window. "Me too," she said. She turned to me: "But life goes on, doesn't it?" I didn't say anything. "Hans, my husband," she went on, "liked the Dalmatian coast a lot. In his letters, he talked about settling there after the war. Do you know Dalmatia?"—"No. I served in the Ukraine and in Russia. But I wouldn't want to settle there."—"Where would you like to live?"—"I don't know, actually. Not Berlin, I think. I don't know." I told her briefly about my childhood in France. She herself was of old Berlin stock: already her grandparents lived in Moabit. We arrived at the Prinz-Albrechtstrasse and I parked in front of number eight. "But that's the Gestapo!" she cried out, terrified. I laughed: "That's right. They have a small heated pool in the basement." She stared at me: "Are you a policeman?"—"Not at all." Through the window, I pointed to the former Prinz-Albrecht Hotel next door: "I work there, in the Reichsführer's offices. I'm a legal advisor, I'm in charge of economic questions." That seemed to reassure her. "Don't worry. The pool is used more by typists and secretaries than by policemen, who have other things to do." In fact, the pool was so small you had to sign up in advance. We found Thomas there, already in a bathing suit. "Oh, I know you!" he exclaimed, gallantly kissing Helene's white hand. "You're the friend of Liselotte and Mina Wehde." I showed her where the women's changing rooms were and went to change also, while Thomas smiled at me mockingly. When I emerged, Thomas, in the water, was talking with a girl, but Helene hadn't reappeared yet. I dove in and did a few laps. Helene came out of the changing room. Her fashionable swimsuit molded to her contours, rounded but slim; beneath the curves the muscles were clearly apparent. Her face, whose beauty wasn't altered by the swimming cap, was joyful: "Hot showers! What luxury!" She dove in, crossed half the pool underwater, and began doing laps. I was already tired; I got out, put on a bathrobe, and sat down on one of the chairs placed around the pool, to smoke and watch her swim. Thomas, dripping, came to sit next to me: "It was high time you pulled yourself together."—"Do you like her?" The lapping of the water resounded on the room's vaulted ceiling. Helene did forty laps without stopping, a thousand meters. Then she came over to lean on the edge, like the first time I'd seen her, and smiled at me: "You don't swim much."—"It's the cigarettes. I get out of breath."—"That's too bad." Again, she raised her arms and let herself sink down; but this time she came back up in the same place and hoisted herself out of the pool in one supple movement. She took a towel, dried her face and came to sit down next to us, taking off her cap and shaking her damp hair. "And you," she said to Thomas, "do you also deal with economic questions?"—"No," he replied. "I leave that to Max. He's much more intelligent than me."—"He's a policeman," I added. Thomas made a face: "Let's say I'm in security."—"Brrr . . ." Helene said. "That must be sinister."—"Oh, not really." I finished my cigarette and went back in to swim a little. Helene did twenty more laps; Thomas was flirting with one of the typists. Afterward, I washed under the shower and changed; leaving Thomas there, I suggested to Helene that we go out for some tea. "Where?"—"Good question. On Unter den Linden there's nothing left. But we'll find something." Finally I took her to the Esplanade Hotel, on Bellevuestrasse: it was a little damaged, but had survived the worst; inside the tea room, aside from the boards on the windows, masked by brocade curtains, you might have thought it was before the war. "What a beautiful place," Helene murmured. "I've never been here."—"The cakes are excellent, I hear. And they don't serve ersatz." I ordered a coffee for me and a tea for her; we also ordered a little assortment of cakes. They were in fact delicious. When I lit a cigarette, she asked for one. "You smoke?"—"Sometimes." Later on, she said pensively: "It's too bad there's this war. Things could have been so nice."—"Maybe. I have to admit I don't think about it." She looked at me: "Tell me frankly: we're going to lose, aren't we?"—"No!" I said, shocked. "Of course not." Again, she looked into emptiness and drew a last puff from her cigarette. "We're going to lose," she said. I took her home. In front of the entrance, she shook my hand, looking serious. "Thank you," she said. "I enjoyed that very much."—"I hope it won't be the last time."—"Me too. See you soon." I watched her cross the sidewalk and disappear into the building. Then I went back to my place to listen to Monteverdi.

I didn't understand what I was seeking with this young woman; but I didn't try to understand it. What I liked about her was her gentleness, a gentleness I thought existed only in the paintings of Vermeer of Delft, through which could clearly be felt the supple force of a steel blade. I had enjoyed that afternoon very much, and for now I didn't look any further, I didn't want to think. I felt that thinking would immediately have led to painful questions and demands: for once, I didn't feel the need, I was happy to let myself be carried by the course of events, as I was by Monteverdi's music, at once utterly lucid and emotional, and then we'd see. During the week that followed, in the slack moments during work, or at night, at home, the thought of her grave face or of the calmness of her smile came back to me, almost warm, a friendly, affectionate thought, which didn't alarm me.

*   *   *

But the past is a thing that, once it has sunk its teeth into your flesh, doesn't let go. Around the middle of the week after the air raids, Fräulein Praxa knocked on my office door. "Obersturmbannführer? There are two gentlemen from the Kripo who would like to see you." I was immersed in a particularly complex report; annoyed, I replied, "Well, let them do what everyone else does: make an appointment."— "Very well, Obersturmbannführer." She closed the door. A minute later she knocked again: "Excuse me, Obersturmbannführer. They insist. They said to tell you that it's about a personal matter. They say it concerns your mother." I breathed in deeply and closed my file: "Show them in, then."

The two men who pushed their way into my office were genuine policemen, not honorary ones like Thomas. They wore long gray overcoats made of coarse, stiff wool, probably woven with wood pulp, and held their hats in their hands. They hesitated and then raised their arms, saying, "Heil Hitler!" I returned their salute and motioned them to the sofa. They introduced themselves: Kriminalkommissar Clemens and Kriminalkommissar Weser, from Referat V B 1, "Einsatz/Capital Crimes." "In fact," said one of them, possibly Clemens, by way of introduction, "we're acting at the request of the Five A One, which is in charge of international cooperation. They received a request for legal assistance from the French police . . ."—"Excuse me," I interrupted curtly, "can I see your papers?" They handed me their ID cards along with a mission order signed by a Regierungsrat Galzow, assigning them the task of replying to questions sent to the German police by the Prefect of the Alpes-Maritimes in the context of an investigation into the murders of Moreau, Aristide, and his wife, Moreau, Héloïse, formerly Frau. Aue, née C. "So you're investigating my mother's death," I said, returning their documents. "How does that concern the German police? They were killed in France."—"True, true," said the second one, probably Weser. The first one pulled a notebook out of his pocket and leafed through it. "It was a very violent murder, apparently," he said. "A madman, possibly, a sadist. You must have been very upset." My voice remained dry and hard: "Kriminalkommissar, I am aware of what happened. My personal reactions are my business. Why are you coming to see me?"—"We'd like to ask you a few questions," said Weser.—"As a potential witness," Clemens added.—"A witness of what?" I asked. He looked me straight in the eyes: "You saw them at the time, didn't you?" I too continued staring at him: "That's right. You're well informed. I went to visit them. I don't know exactly when they were killed, but it was soon afterward." Clemens examined his notebook, then showed it to Weser. Weser went on: "According to the Gestapo in Marseille, a travel pass was issued to you for the Italian zone on April twenty-sixth. How long did you stay at your mother's house?"—"Just a day."—"Are you sure?" Clemens asked.—"I think so. Why?" Weser again consulted Clemens's notebook: "According to the French police, a gendarme saw an SS officer leaving Antibes in a bus on the morning of the twenty-ninth. There weren't many SS officers in the sector, and they certainly weren't traveling by bus."—"I may have stayed two nights. I traveled a lot, at the time. Is it important?"—"It could be. The bodies were discovered on May first, by a milkman. They weren't very fresh. The coroner estimated the time of death at sixty to eighty-four hours prior, that is sometime between the night of the twenty-eighth and the night of the twenty-ninth."—"Well, I can tell you that when I left them they were very much alive."—"So," said Clemens, "if you left on the morning of the twenty-ninth, they would have been killed during the day."—"That's possible. I never asked myself the question."—"How did you learn of their deaths?"—"I was informed by my sister." "In fact," said Weser, still leaning over to look at Clemens's notebook, "she arrived almost right away. On May second, to be precise. Do you know how she learned the news?"—"No."—"Have you seen her again since?" asked Clemens.—"No."—"Where is she now?" asked Weser.—"She lives with her husband in Pomerania. I can give you the address, but I don't know if they're there. They often go to Switzerland." Weser took the notebook from Clemens and jotted something down. Clemens asked me: "You're not in touch with her?"—"Not very often," I replied.— "And your mother, did you see her often?" asked Weser. They seemed systematically to take turns talking, and this little game was grating on my nerves. "Not much, either," I replied as dryly as possible.—"So," said Clemens, "you're not very close to your family."—"Meine Herren, I've already told you, I'm not about to talk to you about my inner feelings. I don't see how my relations with my family can concern you."— "When there's murder, Herr Obersturmbannführer," Weser said sententiously, "anything can concern the police." They really did look like a pair of cops from an American movie. But they probably acted that way on purpose. "This Herr Moreau was your stepfather by marriage, isn't that right?" Weser continued.—"Yes. He married my mother in . . . 1929, I think. Or maybe 'twenty-eight."—"1929, that's right," Weser said, studying his notebook.—"Are you aware of his last will?" Clemens abruptly asked. I shook my head: "Not at all. Why?"— "Herr Moreau wasn't poor," said Weser. "You'll probably inherit a tidy little sum."—"That would surprise me. My stepfather and I didn't get along at all."—"That's possible," Clemens continued, "but he had no children, and no brothers or sisters. If he died intestate, you and your sister will share everything."—"I hadn't even thought about it," I said sincerely. "But instead of pointlessly speculating, tell me: did they find a will?" Weser leafed through the notebook: "Actually, we don't know that yet."—"Well," I declared, "no one has contacted me about it." Weser scribbled a note in the notebook. "Another question, Herr Obersturmbannführer: there were two children at Herr Moreau's house. Twins. Alive."—"I saw those children. My mother told me they were a friend's. Do you know who they are?"—"No," Clemens grumbled. "Apparently the French don't know, either."—"Did they witness the murder?"—"They never opened their mouths," said Weser.— "They might have seen something," added Clemens.—"But they didn't want to talk," repeated Weser.—"Maybe they were shocked," Clemens explained.—"And what's become of them?" I asked.—"Actually," Weser replied, "that's the curious thing. Your sister took them with her."—"We don't really understand why," said Clemens.—"Or how." "What's more, it seems highly irregular," Weser commented.—"Highly," Clemens repeated. "But at the time, the Italians were running things there. With them anything is possible."—"Yes, absolutely anything," Weser added. "Except an investigation by the rules."—"It's the same thing with the French, too," Clemens went on.—"Yes, they're the same," Weser confirmed. "It's no pleasure working with them."— "Meine Herren," I interrupted. "That's all very well, but how does it concern me?" Clemens and Weser looked at each other. "You see, I'm very busy right now. Unless you have other specific questions, I think we can leave things there?" Clemens nodded; Weser leafed through the notebook and returned it to him. Then he got up: "Excuse us, Herr Obersturmbannführer."—"Yes," said Clemens, getting up in turn. "Excuse us. For now, that's all."—"Yes," Weser went on, "that's all. Thank you for your cooperation." I held out my hand: "Not at all. If you have other questions, don't hesitate to contact me." I took some business cards from my stand and gave one to each. "Thank you," Weser said, pocketing the card. Clemens examined his own: *"Special representative of the Reichsführer-SS for the Arbeitseinsatz,"* he read. "What is that?"— "That's a State secret, Kriminalkommissar," I replied.—"Oh. I'm sorry." They both saluted and headed for the door. Clemens, who was a good head taller than Weser, opened it and went out; Weser paused on the threshold and turned around: "Excuse me, Herr Obersturmbannführer. I forgot one detail." He turned around: "Clemens! The notebook." He leafed through it again. "Oh yes, here it is: When you went to visit your mother, were you in uniform or in civilian clothes?"—"I don't remember. Why? Is it important?"—"Probably not. The Obersturmführer in

Marseille who issued the travel pass thought you were in civilian clothes."—"That's possible. I was on leave." He nodded: "Thank you. If there's anything else, we'll call you. Forgive us for coming like this. Next time we'll make an appointment."

This visit left me with a bad taste in my mouth. What did these two characters want with me? They had struck me as very aggressive, insinuating. Of course I had lied to them: but if I had told them I had seen the bodies, that would have created all kinds of complications. I didn't have the impression that they suspected me on this point; their suspicion seemed systematic, an occupational trait, probably. I had found their questions about the Moreau legacy unpleasant: they seemed to be suggesting that I might have had a motive, a pecuniary interest, it was ridiculous. Could they possibly suspect me of murder? I tried to remember the conversation, and had to acknowledge that it was possible. I found that frightening, but the mind of a career policeman must be made that way. Another question worried me even more: Why had my sister taken the twins away? What relationship was there between them and her? All that, I must say, troubled me deeply. I found it almost unfair: just at the moment when my life seemed finally to be headed for a kind of equilibrium, a feeling of normality, almost like anyone else's life, those idiotic cops came to stir up questions, give rise to anxieties, questions without answers. The most logical thing, actually, would have been to call or write to my sister, to ask her what the story was with those twins, and also to be sure, if ever those policemen came to question her, that her story didn't contradict my own, on the point where I had deemed it necessary to dissimulate part of the truth. Yet, I didn't really know why, I didn't do so right away; it's not that something held me back, but rather that I didn't want to hurry. Telephoning wasn't a difficult thing, I could do it when I wanted, no need to rush.

What's more, I was very busy. My team in Oranienburg, which, under Asbach's direction, continued to grow, regularly sent me summaries of its research on the foreign workers, what was called the *Ausländereinsatz*. These workers were divided into a number of categories, based on racial criteria, with different levels of treatment; they also included prisoners of war from Western countries (but not the Soviet KGF, a separate category, completely under control of the OKW). The day after the visit of the two inspectors, I was summoned to the Reichsführer's office; he was interested in the subject. I gave a rather long, but complete, presentation, for the problem was complex: the Reichsführer listened almost wordlessly, inscrutable beneath his little steel-rimmed glasses. At the same time, I had to prepare Speer's visit to Mittelbau, and I went to Lichterfelde—after the raids, cruel Berlin tongues called the neighborhood *Trichterfelde*, the "crater meadow"—to have the project explained to me by Brigadeführer Kammler, the head of Amtsgruppe C ("Construction") of the WVHA. Kammler, an abrupt, nervous, precise man whose rapid-fire speech and quick gestures masked an inflexible will, spoke to me—and this was the first time I heard something other than rumors about this subject—about the A-4 rocket, a miraculous weapon that according to him would irreversibly change the course of the war as soon as it could be mass-produced. The English had caught wind of its existence and, in August, had bombed the secret installations where it was being developed, on the north of the island of Usedom, where my convalescence had been spent. Three weeks later, the Reichsführer suggested to the Führer and to Speer that the installations be transferred underground and their secrecy guaranteed by using solely concentration camp inmates for their construction. Kammler himself had picked the site, underground galleries in the Harz Mountains, used by the Wehrmacht to store fuel reserves. A company had been formed to manage the project, Mittelwerke GmbH, under the control of Speer's ministry; the SS, however, maintained complete responsibility for designing the premises as well as for on-site security. "The assembly of rockets has already begun, even though the installations aren't finished; the Reichsminister should be satisfied."—"I just hope that the working conditions for the inmates are adequate, Brigadeführer," I replied. "I know that's a constant concern of the Reichsminister's."—"The conditions are what they are, Obersturmbannführer. It's war, after all. But I can assure you that the Reichsminister won't have any reason to complain about the level of productivity. The factory is under my personal control, I myself chose the Kommandant, an efficient man. The RSHA doesn't give me any problems, either: I sent one of my own men, Dr. Bischoff, to supervise production security and prevent sabotage. Up to now, there haven't been any problems. Anyway," he added, "I inspected several KLs with subordinates of Reichsminister Speer's, in April and May; they didn't have too many complaints, and Mittelbau is no worse than Auschwitz."

The visit took place on a Friday in December. It was bitterly cold. Speer was accompanied by specialists from his ministry. His special plane, a Heinkel, took us as far as Nordhausen; there, a delegation from the camp led by Kommandant Förschner welcomed us and escorted us to the site. The road, barred by numerous SS checkpoints, ran alongside the south side of the Harz; Förschner explained to us that the entire mountain chain had been declared a no-entry zone; other underground projects had been launched a little farther north, in Mittelbau satellite camps; in Dora itself, the northern sections of the two tunnels had been allocated for the manufacture of Junker airplane engines. Speer listened to his explanations without saying anything. The road led to a large dirt plaza; on one side were lined up the barracks of the SS guards and of the Kommandantur; opposite, cluttered with piles of construction materials and covered with camouflage nets, recessed beneath a ridge planted with pine trees, gaped the entrance to the first tunnel. We entered it behind Förschner and some engineers from Mittelwerke. Gypsum dust and the acrid smoke of industrial explosives caught my throat; mixed in with them were other indefinable odors, sweet and nauseating, which reminded me of my first camp visits. As we advanced, the *Häftlinge*, alerted by the Spiess who preceded the delegation, lined up at attention and removed their caps. Most were horribly thin; their heads, balanced precariously on scrawny necks, looked like hideous balls decorated with enormous noses and ears cut out of cardboard; they were set with immense, empty eyes that refused to rest on you. Close to them, the smells I had noticed upon entering became a rank stench that emanated from their dirty clothes, their wounds, their very bodies. Many of Speer's men, green, were holding handkerchiefs to their faces; Speer kept his hands behind his back and examined everything with a closed, tense look. Connecting the two main tunnels, A and B, transverse galleries were spaced out every twenty-five meters: the first of them revealed rows of bunk beds made of coarse wood, four levels high, from which, under cudgel blows of an SS noncom, there tumbled down to come stand at attention a swarming horde of ragged inmates, most of them naked or almost naked, some with their legs stained with shit. The bare concrete ceilings were sweating with humidity. In front of the bunks, at the intersection of the main tunnel, large metal barrels, cut in half lengthwise and placed on their sides, served as latrines; they were almost overflowing with a yellow, green, brown, stinking liquid. One of Speer's assistants exclaimed: "But it's Dante's Inferno!" Another, standing a little back, was vomiting against the wall. I too felt the old nausea returning, but I held myself in and breathed in long hisses, between my teeth. Speer turned to Förschner: "Do the inmates live here?"— "Yes, Herr Reichsminister."—"They never go outside?"—"No, Herr Reichsminister." As we continued advancing, Förschner explained to Speer that he lacked everything and that he was incapable of ensuring the requisite sanitary conditions; epidemics were decimating the inmates. He even showed us a few corpses piled in front of the perpendicular galleries, naked or covered with a loose canvas tarp, human skeletons with ravaged skin. In one of the dormitory-galleries, soup was being served: Speer asked to taste it. He swallowed his spoonful, then had me taste it in turn; I had to force myself not to spit it out; it was a bitter, revolting gruel; it tasted like boiled weeds; even at the bottom of the pot, there was almost nothing solid. We visited the entire length of the tunnel this way, up to the Junker factory, wading through the mud and the refuse, breathing with difficulty, in the midst of thousands of *Häftlinge* who mechanically presented themselves one after the other, their faces stripped of the slightest expression. I examined their badges: aside from Germans, mostly "greens," there were "reds" there from every country in Europe, Frenchmen, Belgians, Italians, Dutchmen, Czechs, Poles, Russians, and even Spaniards, republicans interned in France after their defeat (but of course there were no Jews: at that time, Jewish workers were still forbidden in Germany). In the transverse galleries, after the dormitories, inmates supervised by civil engineers worked on the components and assembly of the rockets; farther on, in a deafening din and in a thick cloud of dust, a veritable ant battalion was digging new galleries and emptying the stones into dump carts pushed by other inmates on hastily installed tracks. As we left, Speer asked to see the Revier; it was an extremely makeshift installation, with room for about forty men at the most. The chief physician showed him the mortality and morbidity statistics: dysentery, typhus, and tuberculosis especially wrought havoc. Outside, in the face of the whole delegation, Speer exploded with a contained but virulent rage: "Obersturmbannführer Förschner! This factory is a scandal! I've never seen anything like it. How can you hope to work properly with men in that condition?" Förschner, under the invective, had instinctively stood at attention. "Herr Reichsminister," he replied, "I'm ready to improve the conditions, but I'm not given the means. I can't be held responsible." Speer was white as a sheet. "Very well," he barked. "I order you to have a camp built immediately, here, outside, with showers and toilets. Have the papers for the allocation of materials drawn up for me immediately and I will sign them before I leave." Förschner led us to the barracks of the Kommandantur and gave the necessary orders. While Speer talked with his aides and the engineers, I, furious, took Förschner aside: "I asked you expressly in the Reichsführer's name to make sure the camp was presentable. This is a *Schweinerei*." Förschner didn't let himself get flustered: "Obersturmbannführer, you know as well as I do that an order without the means to carry it out isn't worth much. I'm sorry, but I have no magic wand. I had the galleries washed this morning, but I couldn't do anything else. If the Reichsminister provides us with construction materials, so much the better." Speer had joined us: "I'll see to it that the camp receives additional rations." He turned to a civil engineer who was standing next to him: "Sawatsky, it goes without saying that the inmates under your orders will have priority. We cannot demand complex assembly labor from the sick and dying." The civilian nodded: "Of course, Herr Reichsminister. It's especially the turnover that's becoming unmanageable. We have to replace them so often that it's impossible to train them correctly." Speer turned to Förschner: "That doesn't mean that you should neglect the ones who are assigned to the construction of the galleries. You will also increase their rations, insofar as possible. I'll talk about it to Brigadeführer Kammler."—"*Zu Befehl*, Herr Reichsminister," said Förschner. His expression remained opaque, closed; Sawatsky looked happy. Outside, some of Speer's men were waiting for us, scribbling in notebooks and greedily breathing in the cold air. I shivered: winter had set in.

In Berlin, I again found myself overwhelmed by the Reichsführer's requests. I had reported Speer's visit to him, and he made only one comment: "Reichsminister Speer should know what he wants." I saw him regularly now to discuss labor questions: he wanted at all costs to increase the quantity of workers available in the camps to supply the SS industries, private enterprises, and especially the new underground construction projects that Kammler wanted to develop. The Gestapo was making more and more arrests, but on the other hand, with the coming of fall and then winter, the mortality rate, which had dropped markedly during the summer, was increasing again, and the Reichsführer wasn't pleased. Still, when I suggested a series of measures I thought were realistic, that I was planning with my team, he didn't respond, and the actual measures implemented by Pohl and the IKL seemed random and unpredictable, not corresponding to any plan. Once I seized the occasion of a remark of the Reichsführer's to criticize what I regarded as arbitrary, unconnected initiatives: "Pohl knows what he's doing," he retorted curtly. Soon after, Brandt summoned me and scolded me in a courteous but firm tone: "Listen, Obersturmbann-führer, you're doing very good work, but I'm going to tell you what I've already said a hundred times to Brigadeführer Ohlendorf: instead of annoying the Reichsführer with negative, pointless criticisms and complicated questions that he doesn't even understand, you'd do better to cultivate your relationship with him. Bring him, I don't know, a medieval treatise on medicinal plants, nicely bound, and talk with him a little about it. He'll be delighted, and it will allow you to form a bond with him, to make yourself better understood. That will make things a lot easier for you. And also, I'm sorry, but when you present your reports, you're so cold and haughty it only annoys him even more. That's not how you're going to settle things." He went on a little more in the same vein; I didn't say anything, I was thinking: he was probably right.

"One more piece of advice: you'd do well to get married. Your attitude on the subject is deeply annoying to the Reichsführer." I stiffened: "Standartenführer, I've already explained my reasons to the Reichsführer. If he doesn't approve of them, he should tell me so himself." An incongruous thought made me repress a smile. Brandt wasn't smiling and was staring at me like an owl through his large round glasses. Their lenses reflected my own doubled image; the reflection prevented me from discerning his gaze. "You're wrong, Obersturmbannführer, you're wrong. But it's your choice."

I resented Brandt's attitude, it was completely unjustified, in my opinion: he had no business getting involved in my private life that way. My private life, actually, was taking a pleasant turn; and it had been a long time since I had enjoyed myself so much. On Sundays I went to the pool with Helene, sometimes also with Thomas and one of his girlfriends; we'd go out for tea or hot chocolate, then I'd take Helene to the movies, if there was something worth seeing, or else to the concert to hear Karajan or Furtwängler; and we'd have dinner before I took her home. I also saw her from time to time during the week: a few days after my visit to Mittelbau, I had invited her to our fencing hall, at the Prinz-Albrecht-Palais, where she watched us fence and applauded the thrusts, then, in the company of Thomas, who flirted outrageously with her friend Liselotte, to an Italian restaurant. On December 19, we were together during the great English attack; in the public shelter where we had taken refuge, she sat next to me without saying anything, her shoulder against mine, flinching slightly at the closest explosions. After the raid, I took her to the Esplanade, the only restaurant I found open: sitting opposite me, her long white hands resting on the table, she stared at me silently with her beautiful, deep, dark eyes, a searching, curious, serene gaze. In such moments, I said to myself that if things had been different, I could have married this woman, I could have had children with her as I did much later with another woman who wasn't her equal. It would certainly not have been done to please Brandt or the Reichsführer, to fulfill a duty or satisfy conventions: it would have been a part of everyday, ordinary life, simple and natural. But my life had taken another path, and it was too late. She too, when she looked at me, must have had similar thoughts, or rather women's thoughts, different from men's, in their tonality and color probably more than in their content, difficult to imagine for a man, even me. I pictured them this way: Is it possible I will enter this man's bed someday, give myself to him? *To give oneself*, a strange phrase in our language; but the man who doesn't grasp its full extent should try in turn to let himself be penetrated, it will open his eyes. These thoughts, in general, didn't cause me any regrets, but rather a bitter feeling that was almost sweet. But sometimes, in the street, without thinking, with a natural gesture, she took my arm, and then, yes, I surprised myself by missing that other life that could have been, if something hadn't been broken so early. It wasn't just the question of my sister; it was vaster than that, it was the entire course of events, the wretchedness of the body and of desire, the decisions you make and on which you can't go back, the very meaning you choose to give this thing that's called, perhaps wrongly, your life.

It had begun to snow, a warm snow that didn't stick. Then finally it lasted for a night or two, and gave a brief, strange beauty to the ruins of the city, before it melted and thickened the muck disfiguring the broken streets. With my tall riding boots, I walked through it without paying any attention—an orderly would clean them for me the next day—but Helene wore simple shoes, and when we reached a gray stretch thick with melted snow, I would look for a board I could throw over it, then hold her delicate hand so she could cross; and if even that was impossible, I carried her, light in my arms. On Christmas Eve, Thomas organized a small party in his new house in Dahlem, a luxurious little villa: as usual, he knew how to get by. Schellenberg was there with his wife, along with several other officers; I had invited Hohenegg, but hadn't been able to locate Osnabrugge, who must have been in Poland still. Thomas seemed to have had his way with Liselotte, Helene's friend: when she arrived, she kissed him passionately. Helene had put on a new dress, God knows where she had found the cloth, the restrictions were becoming more and more severe, she smiled charmingly and seemed happy. All the men, for once, were in civilian clothes. We had scarcely arrived when the sirens began wailing. Thomas reassured us by explaining that the planes coming from Italy almost never dropped their first bombs before Schöneberg and Tempelhof, and the ones from England passed north of Dahlem. Still, we dimmed the lights; thick black curtains masked the windows. The flak began to boom, Thomas put on a record, furious American jazz, and led Liselotte in a dance. Helene drank white wine and watched them dance; afterward, Thomas put on some slow music and she asked me to dance with her. Above we could hear the squadrons roaring; the flak barked without stopping, the windows trembled, we could scarcely hear the record; but Helene danced as if we were alone in a ballroom, leaning lightly on me, her hand firm in mine. Then she danced with Thomas while I exchanged a toast with Hohenegg. Thomas was right: to the north, we could sense more than hear an immense muffled vibration, but around us nothing fell. I looked at Schellenberg; he had gained weight, his successes didn't encourage moderation. He was talking pleasantly with his specialists on our setbacks in Italy. Schellenberg, I had finally gathered from the few remarks Thomas sometimes let escape, thought he held the key to Germany's future; he was convinced that if people listened to him, to him and his indisputable analyses, there would still be time to salvage something from the situation. The mere fact that he talked about *salvaging something* was enough to make my hackles rise: but apparently he had the Reichsführer's ear, and I wondered where he might have gotten with his schemes. Once the alert was over, Thomas tried to call the RSHA, but the lines were cut off. "Those bastards did it on purpose to ruin our Christmas," he said to me. "But we won't let them." I looked at Helene: she was sitting next to Liselotte and talking animatedly. "She's very nice, that girl," declared Thomas, who had followed my gaze. "Why don't you marry her?" I smiled: "Thomas, mind your own business." He shrugged: "At least spread the rumor that you're engaged. That way Brandt will get off your back." I had told him about Brandt's comments. "And you?" I retorted. "You're a year older than I am. Don't they bother you?" He laughed: "Me? It's not the same thing. First of all, my congenital inability to stay more than a month with the same girl is well known. But above all"—he lowered his voice—"keep it to yourself, but I've already sent two of them to the *Lebensborn*. I hear the Reichsführer was delighted." He went to put another jazz record on; I figured he must help himself from the Gestapo's stocks of confiscated records. I followed him and asked Helene to dance again. At midnight, Thomas put out all the lights. I heard a girl's joyful shout, a muffled laugh. Helene was next to me: for a brief instant, I felt her sweet, warm breath on my face, and her lips grazed mine. My heart was pounding. When the light returned, she said to me in a composed, calm way: "I have to go home. I didn't tell my parents, with the alert they must be worried." I had taken Piontek's car. We drove up toward the center of town by the Kurfürstendamm; on our right, fires lit by the bombing were roaring. It had started to snow. Some bombs had fallen on the Tiergarten and on Moabit, but the damage seemed minor compared to the big raids of the previous month. In front of her building, she took my hand and briefly kissed my cheek: "Merry Christmas! See you soon." I went back to get drunk in Dahlem, and ended the night on the carpet, having ceded the sofa to a secretary upset at having been ousted from the host's bedroom by Liselotte.

Clemens and Weser came back to see me a few days later, this time having duly made an appointment with Fräulein Praxa, who showed them into my office, rolling her eyes. "We tried to contact your sister," said Clemens, the tall one, by way of introduction. "But she's not home."—"That's quite possible," I said. "Her husband is an invalid. She often accompanies him to Switzerland for treatment."—"We asked the embassy in Berne to try to find her," Weser said aggressively, swaying his narrow shoulders. "We'd very much like to talk with her."—"Is it that important?" I asked.—"It's still that damn business of the little twins," Clemens ejected with his coarse Berliner's voice.—"We don't really understand it," Weser added in his weaselly way. Clemens took out his notebook and read: "The French police investigated."—"A little late," Weser interrupted.—"Yes, but better late than never. Apparently, those twins have been living with your mother since at least 1938, when they began going to school. Your mother introduced them as orphaned great-nephews. And some of her neighbors seem to think they may have arrived earlier, as babies, in 1936 or 1937."—"It's quite curious," Weser said acidly. "You never saw them before?"—"No," I said curtly. "But there's nothing odd about that. I never went to my mother's house."—"Never?" snorted Clemens. "Never?"—"Never."—"Except exactly at that time," Weser spat. "A few hours before her violent death. You see that it's odd."—"Meine Herren," I retorted, "your insinuations are completely inappropriate. I don't know where you learned your profession, but I find your attitude grotesque. What's more, you have no authority to investigate me without an order from the SS-Gericht."—"That's true," acknowledged Clemens, "but we're not investigating you. For now, we're interviewing you as a witness."—"Yes," repeated Weser, "as a witness, that's all."—"That's just to say," continued Clemens, "that there are a lot of things we don't understand and that we'd like to understand."—"For instance, this business with the twins," added Weser. "Let's say they are actually great-nephews of your mother's . . ."—"We didn't find any trace of brothers or sisters, but let's say so," interrupted Clemens.—"Hey, you don't know, do you?" asked Weser.—"What?"—"If your mother had a brother or a sister?"—"I heard talk of a brother, but I never saw him. We left Alsace in 1918, and after that, to my knowledge, my mother had no more contact with her family in France."—"So let's say," Weser went on, "that they are in fact great-nephews. We haven't found any paper that proves it, no birth certificates, nothing."—"And your sister," rapped out Clemens, "showed no papers when she took them with her."—Weser smiled cunningly: "For us, these are very important potential witnesses who have disappeared."—"We don't know where," grumbled Clemens. "It's unacceptable that the French police let them slip away like that."—"Yes," said Weser, looking at him, "but what's done is done. No use going back over it."—Clemens went on without stopping: "Still, afterward, we're the ones who get stuck with all the problems."—"In short," Weser said to me, "if you talk to her, ask her to contact us. Your sister, I mean." I nodded. They seemed to have nothing more to say, and I ended the interview. I had never tried to reach my sister; it was beginning to become important, for if they found her and her story contradicted mine, their suspicions would be exacerbated; they would even be, I thought with horror, capable of accusing me. But where could I find her? Thomas, I said to myself, must have contacts in Switzerland, he could ask Schellenberg. I had to do something, this situation was becoming ridiculous. And the question of the twins was worrisome.

Three days before New Year's Day there was a heavy snow, and this time the snow stuck. Inspired by his Christmas party success, Thomas decided to re-invite everyone: "Might as well take advantage of this shack before it burns down too." I asked Helene to tell her parents she'd come home late, and it was a really wonderful party. A little before midnight, the whole gang armed itself with Champagne and baskets of Dutch oysters and set out on foot for the Grunewald. Beneath the trees, the snow lay virgin and pure; the sky was clear, lit by an almost full moon, which shed a bluish light on the white expanses. In a clearing, Thomas cracked open the Champagne—he had supplied himself with a real cavalry saber, taken down from the wall of our weapons hall—and the less clumsy ones struggled to open the oysters, a delicate and dangerous art for those who don't have the knack. At midnight, instead of fireworks, the Luftwaffe artillerymen lit their searchlights, launched flares, and shot off some .88-millimeter rounds. This time, Helene kissed me outright, not for long, but a strong, happy kiss that sent a rush of fear and pleasure through my limbs. Surprising, I said to myself as I drank to hide my confusion, I who thought no sensation was foreign to me, now a woman's kiss overwhelms me. The others were laughing, throwing snowballs at each other and swallowing oysters from the shell. Hohenegg, who kept a moth-eaten shapka planted on his bald, oval head, had turned out to be the most skillful of the shuckers: "That or a thorax, they're pretty much the same thing," he laughed. Schellenberg had gashed the entire base of his thumb, and was bleeding quietly onto the snow, drinking Champagne, without anyone thinking to bandage it. Seized with happiness, I began running around and throwing snowballs too; the more we drank, the more frenzied the game became—we tackled one another by the legs, as in rugby, rammed fistfuls of snow down each other's necks, our coats were soaking, but we didn't feel the cold. I pushed Helene into the powdery snow, stumbled, and collapsed next to her; lying on her back, her arms stretched out in the snow, she laughed; when she fell, her long skirt had ridden up, and without thinking, I rested my hand on her bare knee, protected only by a stocking. She turned her head to me and looked at me, still laughing. Then I removed my hand and helped her get up. We didn't go back until after we'd emptied the last bottle; we had to hold back Schellenberg, who wanted to shoot at the empties; walking in the snow, Helene held my arm. In the house, Thomas gallantly gave up his bedroom as well as the guest room to the tired girls, who fell asleep still dressed, three to a bed. I ended the night playing chess and discussing Augustine's *Trinity* with Hohenegg, who had dunked his head in cold water and was drinking tea. So began the year 1944.

Speer hadn't gotten back in touch with me since the visit to Mittelbau; in the beginning of January, he called to wish me a happy New Year and to ask me a favor. His ministry had submitted a request to the RSHA to forego deportation of a few Jews from Amsterdam, specialists in metals purchasing with precious contacts in neutral countries; the RSHA had refused the request, pleading the deterioration of the situation in Holland and the need to appear *especially severe* there. "It's ridiculous," Speer said to me in a voice heavy with fatigue. "What risk can three Jews dealing in metals pose to Germany? Their services are precious to us right now." I asked him to send me a copy of the correspondence, promising to do my best. The refusal letter from the RSHA was signed by Müller but bore the dictation mark IV B 4a. I telephoned Eichmann and began by wishing him a happy New Year. "Thank you, Obersturmbannführer," he said with his curious blend of Austrian and Berlin accents. "Congratulations on your promotion, by the way." Then I explained Speer's problem to him. "I didn't have anything to do with it myself," said Eichmann. "It must have been Hauptsturmführer Moes, he's in charge of individual cases. But of course he's right. Do you know how many requests we receive like that? If we said yes every time, we might as well just close up shop, we couldn't touch a single Jew."—"I understand, Obersturmbannführer. But this is a request from the Minister of Armaments and War Production in person."—"Yeah. It must be their guy in Holland who's a little overeager, and then little by little it reached the Minister. But it's all just about interdepartmental rivalry. No, you know, we can't agree. What's more, the situation in Holland is rotten. There are all sorts of groups wandering around free, it just won't do." I insisted some more, but Eichmann was obstinate. "No. If we agree, you know, people will just say again that besides the Führer there isn't a single anti-Semite of conviction left among the Germans. It's impossible."

What could he have meant by that? In any case, Eichmann couldn't decide on his own, and he knew it. "Listen, send it to us in writing," he ended up saying grudgingly. I decided to write directly to Müller, but

Müller told me the same thing: they couldn't make any exceptions. I was hesitant to ask the Reichsführer; I decided to contact Speer again, to see how much he really needed these Jews. But at the ministry they told me he was on sick leave. I made inquiries: he had been hospitalized in Hohenlychen, the SS hospital where I had been treated after Stalingrad. I found a bouquet of flowers and went to see him. He had requisitioned an entire suite in the private wing and had installed his personal secretary and some assistants there. The secretary told me that an old inflammation of the knee had flared up after a Christmas trip to Lapland; his condition was worsening, Dr. Gebhardt, the famous knee specialist, thought it was a rheumatoid inflammation. I found Speer in a wretched mood: "Obersturmbannführer, it's you. Happy New Year. So?" I explained to him that the RSHA was maintaining its position; possibly, I suggested, if he saw the Reichsführer, he could have a word with him about it. "I think the Reichsführer has other fish to fry," he replied abruptly. "So do I. I have to run my ministry from here, as you can see. If you can't resolve the matter yourself, drop it." I stayed a few more minutes, then withdrew: I could feel I was in the way.

His condition did in fact deteriorate rapidly; when I called back a few days later to ask after him, his secretary informed me that he wasn't taking any phone calls. I made a few calls: apparently he was in a coma, close to death. I found it strange that an inflammation of the knee, even a rheumatoid one, could reach that point. Hohenegg, to whom I talked about it, had no opinion. "But if he passes away," he added, "and if they let me do an autopsy, I'll tell you what he had." I too had other fish to fry. The night of January 30, the English inflicted on us their worst air raid since November; I lost my windows again, and part of my balcony collapsed. The next day, Brandt summoned me and informed me, amiably, that the SS-Gericht had asked the Reichsführer for permission to investigate me in connection with my mother's murder. I reddened and leaped out of my seat: "Standartenführer! That business is a disgrace born from the sick minds of careerist policemen. I'm willing to accept an investigation to clear my name of all suspicion. But in that case, I ask to be put on leave until I'm found innocent. It would be inappropriate for the Reichsführer to keep a man suspected of such a horror in his personal staff."—"Calm down, Obersturmbannführer. No decision has been made yet. Tell me what happened instead." I sat down and recounted the events, sticking to the version I had given the policemen. "It's my visit to Antibes that's made them crazy. It's true that my mother and I had been on bad terms for a long time. But you know what kind of wound I received in Stalingrad. Being so close to death makes you think: I said to myself that we had to settle things between us once and for all. Unfortunately she's the one who died, in a horrible, unexpected way."—"And how do you think it happened?"—"I have no idea, Standartenführer. I began working for the Reichsführer soon afterward, and I haven't returned there. My sister, who went to the funeral, mentioned terrorists, a settling of accounts; my stepfather supplied a number of items to the Wehrmacht."—"That's unfortunately entirely possible. This sort of thing is happening more and more often, in France." He pinched his lips and tilted his head, making the light play on his glasses. "Listen, I think the Reichsführer will want to talk with you before he makes a decision. In the meantime, allow me to suggest that you visit the judge who wrote the request. It's Judge Baumann, of the Berlin SS and Police Court. He's a perfectly honorable man: if you really are the victim of special malice, maybe you can convince him of that yourself."

I immediately made an appointment with Judge Baumann. He received me in his office at court: a jurist in a Standartenführer's uniform, getting on in years, with a square face and a crooked nose, and a fighter's look. I had put on my best uniform and all my medals. After I had saluted him, he asked me to sit down. "Thank you for receiving me, Herr Richter," I said, using the customary address instead of his SS rank. "Not at all, Obersturmbannführer. It's the least I could do." He opened a folder on his desk. "I asked for your personal file. I hope you don't mind."—"Not at all, Herr Richter. Allow me to tell you what I plan on telling the Reichsführer: I regard these accusations, which touch me in such a personal question, hateful. I am ready to cooperate with you in every way possible so they can be completely refuted." Baumann gave a discreet cough: "You understand that I haven't yet ordered an investigation. I can't do so without the Reichsführer's agreement. The case file I have is very meager. I made the request based on an appeal from the Kripo, which states they have convincing information that their investigators would like to look into."—"Herr Richter, I spoke twice with those investigators. All they gave me by way of information was groundless insinuations without proof, some—excuse me—delirious fabrication of their own fantasy."—"That is possible," he said pleasantly. "I see here that you attended the best universities. If you had gone on with law, we might have ended up colleagues. I know Dr. Jessen very well, your old professor. A very good jurist." He went on leafing through the file. "Excuse me, but did your father fight with the Freikorps Rossbach, in Courland? I remember an officer named Aue." He said the Christian name. My heart began beating violently. "That is my father's name, Herr Richter. But I don't know anything about what you ask. My father disappeared in 1921, and I haven't heard anything about him since. It's possible it's the same man. Do you know what became of him?"—"Unfortunately not. I lost sight of him during the retreat, in December of 'nineteen. He was still alive, at the time. I also heard that he had taken part in the Kapp putsch. Many *Baltikumer* were there." He thought. "You could do some research. There are still Freikorps veterans' associations."—"Yes, Herr Richter. That's an excellent idea." He coughed again and settled into his armchair. "Good. Let's return, if you don't mind, to your affair. What can you tell me about it?" I gave him the same narrative I had given Brandt. "It's a horrible business," he said at the end. "You must have been extremely upset."—"Of course, Herr Richter. And I was even more so by the accusations of those two defenders of the public order who have never, I am sure, spent a day at the front and who allow themselves to slander the name of an SS officer." Baumann scratched his chin: "I can understand how wounding that is for you, Obersturmbannführer. But perhaps the best solution would be to shed the full light of day on the affair."—"I have nothing to fear, Herr Richter. I will accept the decision of the Reichsführer."—"You are right." He got up and accompanied me to the door. "I still have some old photographs from Courland. If you like, I can take a look and see if there's one of that Aue."—"Herr Richter, I'd be delighted." In the hallway he shook my hand. "Don't worry about all this, Obersturmbannführer. Heil Hitler!" My interview with the Reichsführer took place the next day and was brief and conclusive. "What is this ridiculous story, Obersturmbannführer?"—"They're accusing me of being a murderer, my Reichsführer. It would be comical if it weren't so tragic." I briefly explained the circumstances to him. Himmler quickly made up his mind: "Obersturmbannführer, I'm beginning to know you. You have your faults: you are, excuse me for saying so, stubborn and sometimes pedantic. But I don't see the slightest trace of a moral defect in you. Racially, you are a perfect Nordic specimen, with perhaps just a touch of alpine blood. Only the racially degenerate nations, Poles, Gypsies, can commit matricide. Or else a hot-blooded Italian, during a quarrel, not in cold blood. No, it's ridiculous. The Kripo is completely lacking in discernment. I'll have to give instructions to Gruppenführer Nebe to have his men trained in racial analysis, they'll waste much less time that way. Of course I won't authorize the investigation. That's all we need."

Baumann called me a few days later. It must have been around mid-February, since I remember it was right after the massive bombing in which the Bristol Hotel was hit during an official banquet: some sixty people died, crushed under the rubble, including a number of well-known generals. Baumann seemed in a good mood and congratulated me warmly. "Personally," his voice said at the other end of the line, "I thought the whole business was ridiculous. I'm happy for you that the

Reichsführer settled it. It will avoid problems." As for the photographs, he had found one showing Aue, but blurred and barely visible; he wasn't even sure it was he, but he promised to have a copy of it made and to send it to me.

The only people who were unhappy with the Reichsführer's decision were Clemens and Weser. I found them one night in the street in front of the SS-Haus, hands in the pockets of their long coats, their shoulders and hats covered with fine snow. "Well," I said mockingly, "Laurel and Hardy. What brings you here?" This time, they didn't salute me. Weser replied: "We wanted to say hello to you, Obersturmbann-führer. But your secretary didn't want to give us an appointment." I didn't react to the omission of the *Herr*. "She was entirely right," I said haughtily. "I think we have nothing more to say to each other."—"Well, see, Obersturmbannführer," Clemens grumbled, "we think we do, actually."—"In that case, meine Herren, I suggest you go ask for an authorization from Judge Baumann." Weser shook his head: "We realize, Obersturmbannführer, that Judge Baumann will say no. We realize that you are, so to speak, an untouchable."—"But still," Clemens went on, the steam from his breath masking his fat pug-nosed face, "it's not normal, Obersturmbannführer, you can see that. There should be some justice, all the same."—"I agree with you completely. But still, your insane calumnies have nothing to do with justice."—"Calumnies, Obersturmbannführer?" Weser rapped out, raising his eyebrows. "Calumnies? Are you so sure? In my opinion, if Judge Baumann had really read the file, he'd be less certain than you."—"Yeah," said Clemens. "For instance, he could have wondered about the clothes."—"The clothes? What clothes are you talking about?" Weser replied in his place: "Clothes the French police found in the bathtub, on the second floor. Civilian clothes . . ." He turned to Clemens: "Notebook." Clemens pulled the notebook out of an inner pocket and handed it to him. Weser leafed through it: "Oh yes, here it is: *clothing splattered with blood. Splattered.* That's the word I was looking for."—"It means 'soaked,'" Clemens explained.—"The Obersturmbannführer knows what it means, Clemens," Weser grunted. "The Obersturmbannführer is an educated man. He has a good vocabulary." He dove back into the notebook. "Civilian clothing, then, splattered, thrown into the bathtub. There was also blood on the tile floor, on the walls, in the sink, on the towels. And downstairs, in the living room and the entrance, there were traces of footsteps pretty much everywhere, because of the blood. There were prints of shoes, we found the shoes with the clothes, but there were also prints of boots. Heavy boots."—"Well," I said, shrugging, "the murderer changed before he left, to avoid attracting attention."—"You see, Clemens, when I tell you that the Obersturmbannführer is an intelligent man. You should listen to me." He turned to me and looked at me under his hat. "Those clothes were all of German make, Obersturmbannführer." He leafed again through the notebook: "*A brown two-piece suit, wool, good quality, label of a German tailor. A white shirt, German make. A silk tie, German make, a pair of cotton socks, German make, a pair of underwear, German make. A pair of brown leather town shoes, size forty-two, German make.*" He raised his eyes to me: "What's your shoe size, Obersturmbannführer? If you allow me the question. What's your suit size?" I smiled; "Gentlemen, I don't know what godforsaken hole you crawled out of, but I advise you to go back to it on the double. Vermin aren't allowed to remain in Germany anymore." Clemens frowned: "Say, Weser, he's insulting us, isn't he?"—"Yes. He's insulting us. He's threatening us too. Actually, you might be right. He might be less intelligent than he seems, this Obersturmbannführer." Weser put a finger on his hat: "Good night, Obersturmbannführer. See you soon, maybe."

I watched them walk away under the snow toward the Zimmerstrasse. Thomas, whom I had come to meet, had joined me. "Who's that?" he said, motioning with his head at the two silhouettes.—"Pains in the ass. Lunatics. Couldn't you have them put into a concentration camp, to calm them down?" He shrugged: "If you have a valid reason, it's possible. Shall we go eat?" Thomas, in fact, took hardly any interest in my problems; but he was very interested in Speer's. "Things are hopping over there," he said to me at the restaurant. "At the OT too. It's very hard to follow. But obviously some people see his hospitalization as an opportunity."—"An opportunity?"—"To replace him. Speer has made himself a lot of enemies. Bormann is against him, Sauckel too, all the Gauleiters, except Kaufmann and maybe Hanke."—"And the Reichsführer?"—"The Reichsführer more or less supported him up to now. But that could change."—"I have to confess that I don't really understand the sense of all these intrigues," I said slowly. "You just have to look at the numbers: without Speer, we'd probably already have lost the war. Now the situation is clearly critical. All of Germany should be united to confront this peril." Thomas smiled: "You really still are an idealist. That's fine! But most of the Gauleiters don't see further than their own personal interests, or those of their *Gau*."—"Well, instead of opposing Speer's efforts to increase production, they'd do better to remember that if we lose, they too will all end up at the end of a rope. I'd call that their personal interest, wouldn't you?"—"Certainly. But you must see that there's something else in all that. There's also a question of political vision. Schellenberg's diagnosis isn't accepted by everyone, nor are the solutions he recommends." Now we've reached the crucial point, I said to myself. I lit a cigarette. "And what is your friend Schellenberg's diagnosis? And the solutions?" Thomas looked around him. For the first time I could remember, he looked vaguely worried. "Schellenberg thinks that if we continue on like this, the war is lost, whatever Speer's industrial prowess may be. He thinks the only viable solution is a separate peace with the West."—"And you? What do you think?" He thought: "He isn't wrong. I'm beginning to get into trouble at the *Staatspolizei*, among certain circles, because of this business. Schellenberg has the Reichsführer's ear, but he hasn't convinced him yet. And a lot of other people don't agree, such as Müller and Kaltenbrunner. Kaltenbrunner is trying to move closer to Bormann. If he succeeds, he could pose problems for the Reichsführer. At that level, Speer is a secondary problem."—"I'm not saying Schellenberg is right. But what sort of solution do the others envisage? Given the industrial potential of the Americans, no matter what Speer does, time is against us."—"I don't know," Thomas said dreamily. "I imagine they believe in the miracle weapons. You saw them. What do you think of them?" I shrugged: "I don't know. I don't know what they're worth." The food arrived and conversation turned to other things. During dessert, though, Thomas reverted to Bormann, with a mischievous smile. "You know, Kaltenbrunner is putting together a file on Bormann. I'm handling part of it for him."—"On Bormann? You just told me he wanted to move closer to him."—"That's not a reason. Bormann has files on everyone, on the Reichsführer, on Speer, on Kaltenbrunner, even on you possibly." He had put a toothpick in his mouth and was rolling it around on his tongue. "So, what I wanted to tell you . . . It's between us, all right? Seriously . . . so Kaltenbrunner, then, has intercepted quite a few letters between Bormann and his wife. And we found some real gems there. Worthy of an anthology." He leaned forward, looking cheeky. "Bormann was after some little actress. You know how hot-blooded he is, the top secretary-stud of the Reich. Schellenberg calls him *The Typist Fucker*. Well, he got her. But the great thing is that he wrote about it to his wife, who is Buch's daughter, you know, the head of the Party Court? She's already given him nine or ten kids, I've lost count. And she answers, basically: That's fine, I'm not angry, I'm not jealous. And she suggests he bring the girl home. And then she writes: *Given the terrible decline in child production caused by this war, we will work out a system of motherhood by shifts, so that you will always have a wife who is usable.*" Thomas paused, smiling, while I burst out laughing: "No kidding! She really wrote that?"—"I swear it. *A wife who is usable.* Can you believe it?" He was laughing too. "And Bormann, do you know what he answered?" I asked.—"Oh, he congratulated her, of course. Then he fed her some ideological platitudes. I think he called her a *pure child of National Socialism*. But it's obvious that he was saying that to make her happy. Bormann doesn't believe in anything. Aside from the absolute elimination of anything that could come between him and the Führer." I looked at him, mocking: "And you, what do you believe in?" I wasn't disappointed by his answer. Straightening up on his banquette, he declared: "To quote a passage written by our illustrious Minister of Propaganda in his youth: *The important thing is not so much what one believes; the important thing is to believe.*" I smiled; Thomas sometimes impressed me. I said so to him: "Thomas, you impress me."—"What do you expect? I'm not satisfied with stagnating in back offices. I'm a real National Socialist, I am. And Bormann too, in his own way. Your Speer, I'm not so sure. He has talent, but I don't think he's very devoted to the regime he's serving." I smiled again, thinking about Schellenberg. Thomas went on: "The more difficult things become, the more we'll be able to count only on the real National Socialists. The rats are all going to start to jump ship. You'll see."

In fact, deep in the hold of the Reich, the rats were getting agitated, squealing, swarming, bristling with a formidable anxiety. Ever since Italy's defection, tensions with our other allies let networks of fine cracks appear on the surface of our relations. Each, in his own way, was beginning to look for a way out, and that way was not German. Schellenberg, according to Thomas, believed the Romanians were negotiating with the Soviets in Stockholm. But mostly people talked about the Hungarians. Russian forces had taken Lutsk and Rovno; if Galicia fell into their hands, they would find themselves at Hungary's gates. For more than a year, in diplomatic circles, Prime Minister Kállay had conscientiously been forging for himself a reputation as the worst friend of Germany. The Hungarian attitude on the Jewish question also posed problems: not only did they not want to go beyond a discriminatory legislation that was, given the circumstances, particularly inadequate— the Jews of Hungary maintained important positions in industry; and half-Jews, or men married to Jews, in government—but, still having a considerable supply of Jewish labor, much of it highly skilled, they refused all German requests to make part of this force available for the war effort. Already in the beginning of February, during conferences involving experts from different departments, these questions were beginning to be discussed: I sometimes attended them myself or sent one of my specialists. The RSHA advocated a change of regime; my participation was limited to studies on the possible employment of Hungarian Jewish workers in case the situation evolved favorably. Within that framework, I held a series of consultations with Speer's collaborators. But their positions were often strangely contradictory and hard to reconcile. Speer himself remained inaccessible; he was said to be in critical condition. It was rather disconcerting: I felt as if I were making plans in the void, accumulating studies that were worth scarcely more than pieces of fiction. Yet my office was filling out: I now had three specialist officers, and Brandt had promised me a fourth; but the awkwardness of my position made itself felt; to drive my suggestions forward, I had little support, neither from the RSHA, despite my connections at the SD, nor from the WVHA, aside from Maurer sometimes, when it suited him.

In the beginning of March, things began to speed up, but not to get any clearer. Speer, I had learned from a phone call from Thomas at the end of February, had pulled through and, even though he was still in Hohenlychen for now, was slowly resuming control of his ministry. Together, with Field Marshall Milch, he had decided to set up a Jägerstab, a special staff to coordinate the production of fighter planes; from a certain point of view, it was a great step forward toward the consolidation of the last sector of war production that still escaped his ministry; on the other hand, intrigues were proliferating, it was said that Göring had opposed the creation of the Jägerstab, that Saur, Speer's deputy appointed to head it, was not the person he would have chosen, and other things besides. What's more, the men in Speer's ministry were now openly discussing a fabulous, outlandish idea: burying the entire production of planes underground to shelter it from the Anglo-American bombers. That would involve the construction of hundreds of thousands of square meters of underground workshops. Kammler, they said, passionately supported this project, and his offices had already almost completed the necessary studies: it was clear to everyone that in the present state of affairs, only the SS could carry out such a mad concept successfully. But it greatly exceeded the capacities of the labor available: new sources had to be found, and in the present situation—especially since the agreement between Speer and Minister Bichelonne forbade any more siphoning off of French labor—only Hungary was left. The resolution of the Hungarian problem, then, was taking on new urgency. Speer's and Kammler's engineers, gradually, were already integrating the Hungarian Jews into their calculations and plans, although no agreement with the Kállay government had been achieved yet. At the RSHA, they were studying alternative solutions now: the details I had were sketchy, but Thomas sometimes informed me of the evolution of the plans, so that I could adjust my own. Schellenberg was closely involved in these projects. In February, a shady currency traffic affair with Switzerland had led

to the fall of Admiral Canaris; the entire Abwehr had then been incorporated into the RSHA, fusing with the Amt VI to form an Amt Mil
under the control of Schellenberg, who now thus headed all the foreign
intelligence services of the Reich. He didn't have much time to exploit
this position: the career officers of the Abwehr weren't particularly fond
of the SS, and his control over them was far from being assured. Hungary, from this perspective, would allow him to test the limits of his new
tool. As for labor, a change of policy would open up considerable
prospects: the optimists spoke of four hundred thousand workers available and easy to mobilize, most of whom were already skilled workers
or specialists. Given our needs, that would represent a considerable contribution. But their allocation, I saw already, would be the object of
fierce controversy: against Kammler and Saur, I heard a number of experts, sober, clear-headed men, tell me that the concept of underground
factories, tempting as it might sound, was illusory, for they would never
be ready soon enough to change the course of events; and in the meantime, it would represent an inadmissible waste of labor, workers who
would be much more useful, trained in brigades, to repair the factories
that had been hit, to construct housing for our workers or the homeless, or to help decentralize certain vital industries. Speer, according to
these men, was also of that opinion; but I no longer had access to Speer
at the time. For my own part, these arguments seemed sensible to me,
yet to the tell the truth, it didn't really concern me.

At bottom, the more I managed to observe clearly the maelstrom of
intrigues in the high spheres of government, the less interested I was in
taking part in them. Before reaching my present position, I had, naïvely
no doubt, thought that major decisions were made on the basis of ideological correctness and rationality. I now saw that, even if that remained partially true, many other factors were involved, conflicts of
bureaucratic precedence, special interests, or the personal ambition of
some. The Führer, of course, couldn't settle all questions himself; and his
intervention aside, a large part of the mechanisms to achieve consensus
seemed distorted, even warped. Thomas, in these situations, was like a
fish in water; but I felt ill at ease, and not only because I lacked talent
for intrigue. It had always seemed to me that these lines of Coventry
Patmore would be borne out: *The truth is great, and shall prevail, / When
none cares whether it prevail or not*; and that National Socialism could be
nothing but the common search for this truth, in good faith. For me it
was all the more necessary since the circumstances of my troubled life,
divided between two countries, placed me apart from other men: I too
wanted to bear my stone to the common edifice, I too wanted to be able
to feel a part of the whole. Alas, in our National Socialist State, and es-

pecially outside the circles of the SD, few people thought as I did. In this sense, I could admire the brutal frankness of an Eichmann: he had his own idea—about National Socialism, about his own place, and about what was to be done—and he stood by this idea, he put all his talent and stubbornness at its service, and so long as his superiors confirmed him in this idea, it was the right one, and Eichmann remained a happy man, sure of himself, leading his office with a firm hand. That was far from being my case. My misfortune, perhaps, came from the fact that they had assigned me to tasks that did not correspond to my natural inclination. Ever since Russia, already, I felt out of place, capable of doing what was asked of me, but as if I were limited in terms of initiative, for I had indeed studied these tasks—first police-related and then economic—and mastered them, but I hadn't yet succeeded in convincing myself of their rightness, I couldn't manage fully to grasp the profound necessity that guided them, and so find my path *with the precision and sureness of a sleepwalker,* as did the Führer and so many of my colleagues and comrades who were more gifted than I. Could there have been another realm of activity that might have agreed with me better, where I would have felt more at home? There might have been, but it's hard to say, for it didn't happen, and in the end, the only thing that counts is what was, and not what could have been. From the very beginning, things weren't as I would have liked them: I had resigned myself to that a long time ago (yet at the same time, it seems to me, I never accepted things as they are, so wrong and so bad; at the most, I finally came to acknowledge my powerlessness to change them). It is also true that I have changed. When I was young, I felt transparent with lucidity, I had precise ideas about the world, about what it should be and what it actually was, and about my own place in that world; and with all the madness and the arrogance of that youth, I had thought it would always be so; that the attitude induced by my analysis would never change; but I had forgotten, or rather I did not yet know, the force of time, of time and fatigue. And even more than my indecision, my ideological confusion, my inability to take a clear position on the questions I was dealing with, and to hold to it, it was this that was wearing me down, taking the ground away from under my feet. Such a fatigue has no end, only death can put an end to it, it still lasts today, and for me it will always last.

I never spoke of these things with Helene. When I saw her, in the evenings or on Sundays, we chatted about current events, the hardships of life, the bombings, or else about art, literature, cinema. At times I spoke to her about my childhood, my life; but I didn't talk about everything—I avoided the distressing, difficult things. Sometimes I was tempted to talk to her more openly: but something stopped me. Why?

I don't know. You might say I was afraid of shocking her, of offending her. But it wasn't that. I still didn't know very much about this woman, at bottom, just enough to understand that she must have known how to listen, to listen without judging (writing that now, I am thinking of the personal failings of my life; what her reaction might have been in learning the whole extent and implications of my work, I had no way at the time of telling, but in any case, talking about that was out of question, because of the rule of secrecy first of all, but also by a tacit agreement between us, I think, a kind of "tact" also). So what blocked the words in my throat when, at night after dinner, in a fit of fatigue and sadness, they began to rise up? Fear, not of her reaction but simply of laying myself bare? Or else simply fear of letting her come even closer to me than she already had and than I had let her, without even wanting to? For it was becoming clear that if our relationship remained that of good but new friends, in her, slowly, something was happening, the thought of the bed and maybe something else besides. Sometimes that made me sad; I felt overwhelmed by my powerlessness to offer her anything, or even to accept what she had to offer me: she looked at me with that long, patient gaze that so impressed me, and I said to myself, with a violence that increased with each thought, At night, when you go to bed, you think of me, maybe you touch your body, your breasts, thinking about me, you place your hand between your legs thinking about me, maybe you sink into the thought of me, and I, I love only one person, the very one I cannot have, the thought of whom never releases me and leaves my head only to seep into my bones, the one who will always be there between the world and me and thus between you and me, the one whose kisses will always mock yours, the one whose very marriage makes it so that I can never marry you except to try to feel what she feels in marriage, the one whose simple existence makes it so that you will never completely exist for me, and for the rest—for the rest exists too—I still prefer having my ass drilled by unknown boys, paid if necessary, it brings me closer to her, in my own way, and I still prefer fear and emptiness and the sterility of my thinking, than to give way to weakness.

The plans for Hungary were taking shape; in the beginning of March, the Reichsführer summoned me. The day before, the Americans had launched their first daytime raid on Berlin; it was a very small raid, there were just thirty or so bombers, and Goebbels's press had crowed about the minimal damage, but these bombers, for the first time, came accompanied by long-range fighter planes, a new weapon that was terrifying in its implications, since our own fighter planes had been driven back with losses, and you had to be a fool not to understand that this raid was just a test, a successful test, and that from then on there would be no more respite, neither by day nor on nights with a full moon, and that the front was everywhere now, all the time. The failure of our Luftwaffe, incapable of mounting an effective counterattack, was complete. This analysis was confirmed for me by the Reichsführer's dry, precise statements: "The situation in Hungary," he informed me without any further details, "will soon rapidly evolve. The Führer has decided to intervene, if necessary. New opportunities will arise, which we must seize vigorously. One of these opportunities concerns the Jewish question. At the right time, Obergruppenführer Kaltenbrunner will send his men. They'll know what they have to do and you are not to get involved in that. But I want you to go with them to assert the interests of the *Arbeitseinsatz*. Gruppenführer Kammler"—Kammler had just been promoted at the end of January—"will need men, a great many men. The Anglo-Americans are innovating"—he pointed at the sky—"and we have to react quickly. The RSHA must take this into account. I have given instructions concerning this to Obergruppenführer Kaltenbrunner, but I want you to make sure they're rigorously applied by his specialists. More than ever, the Jews owe us their labor force. Is that clear?" Yes, it was. Brandt, after this meeting, filled me in on the details: the special intervention group would be headed by Eichmann, who would more or less have carte blanche as regards the settlement of this question; as soon as the Hungarians had accepted the principle and their collaboration was assured, the Jews would be directed to Auschwitz, which would serve as a sorting center; from there, all those who were fit for work would be allocated as needed. At each stage, the number of potential workers had to be maximized.

A new round of preparatory conferences took place at the RSHA, much more focused than those of the month before; soon only the date had yet to be decided. Excitement became palpable; for the first time in a long time, the officials concerned had the clear feeling of regaining initiative. I saw Eichmann again several times, at these conferences and in private. He assured me that the Reichsführer's instructions had been perfectly understood. "I'm happy you're the one who's taking care of this aspect of the question," he said to me, chewing the inside of his left cheek. "With you, we can work, if you permit me to say so. Which isn't the case with everyone." The question of the air war dominated everyone's thoughts. Two days after the first raid, the Americans sent more than 800 bombers, protected by nearly 650 of their new fighter planes, to strike Berlin at lunchtime. Thanks to bad weather, the bombing lacked precision and the damage was limited; what's more, our fighter planes and flak shot down 80 enemy aircraft, a record; but these fighter planes were heavy and ill-adapted against the new Mustangs, and our own losses came to 66 aircraft, a catastrophe, with the dead pilots being even harder to replace than the planes. Not discouraged in the least, the Americans returned for several days running; each time, the population spent hours in shelters, all work was interrupted; at night, the English sent their Mosquitos, which didn't do much damage but again forced the people down into the shelters, ruining their sleep, sapping their strength. Human losses fortunately remained lower than in November: Goebbels had decided to evacuate a large part of the city center, and most of the office employees, now, came in to work every day from the suburbs; but that involved hours of exhausting commutes. The quality of work suffered: when preparing correspondence, our Berlin specialists, insomniac now, made more and more mistakes, I had to have the letters retyped three, five times before I could send them.

One evening, I was invited to Gruppenführer Müller's place. The invitation was passed on to me, after an air-raid alert, by Eichmann, in whose offices an important planning meeting was taking place that day. "Every Thursday," he came over to tell me, "the Amtschef likes to gather some of his specialists together at his place, to talk things over. He would be delighted if you could come." I would have to cancel my fencing session, but I agreed: I scarcely knew Müller, and it would be interesting to see him close up. Müller lived in an SS apartment a little ways out of town, spared by the bombs. A rather self-effacing woman with a bun and eyes set close together opened the door to me; I thought she might be a maid, but she was in fact Frau Müller. She was the only woman present. Müller himself was in civilian clothes; and instead of returning my salute, he shook my hand with his massive grip, with thick, square-tipped fingers; apart from this demonstration of familiarity, though, the ambiance was much less *gemütlich* than at Eichmann's. Eichmann had also donned civilian clothes, but most of the officers were in uniform, like me. Müller, a rather short-legged, thickset man with the square skull of a farmer, yet nicely, almost elegantly dressed, wore a knitted cardigan over a silk open-collared shirt. He poured me some Cognac and introduced me to the other guests, almost of them Gruppenleiter or Referenten from Amt IV: I remember two men from IV D, who were in charge of Gestapo services in occupied countries, and a certain Regierungsrat Berndorff, who headed the *Schutzhaftreferat*. There was also an officer from the Kripo, and Litzenberg, a colleague of Thomas's. Thomas himself, casually sporting his new Standartenführer stripes, arrived a little late and was cordially welcomed by Müller. The conversation dealt mostly with the Hungarian problem: the RSHA had already identified Magyars ready to cooperate with Germany; the main question was to find out how the Führer would bring about Kállay's fall. When Müller wasn't taking part in the conversation, he surveyed his guests with his restless, mobile, penetrating little eyes. Then he spoke in curt, simple sentences, drawled in a coarse Bavarian accent with a show of cordiality that did little to mask his innate coldness. From time to time, though, he let down his guard. With Thomas and Dr. Frey, a former member of the SD who, like Thomas, had gone on to the *Staatspolizei*, I had started discussing the intellectual origins of National Socialism. Frey remarked that he thought the name itself was ill-chosen, since the term *national* for him referred to the tradition of 1789, which National Socialism rejected. "What would you suggest in its place?" I asked him.—"In my opinion, it should have been *Völkisch* Socialism. That's much more precise." The man from the Kripo had joined us: "If you follow Möller van der Bruck," he declared, "it could be Imperial Socialism."—"Yes, actually that's closer to Strasser's deviation, isn't it?" Frey retorted stiffly. That's when I noticed Müller: he was standing behind us, a glass clutched in his big paw, and listening to us, blinking rapidly. "We should really push all the intellectuals into a coal mine and blow it up . . ." he blurted out in a grating, harsh voice.—"The Gruppenführer is absolutely right," Thomas said. "Meine Herren, you're even worse than Jews. Follow his example: action, not words." His eyes were sparkling with laughter. Müller nodded; Frey seemed confused: "It's clear that with us the sense of initiative has always taken precedence over theoretical elaboration . . ." the man from the Kripo mumbled. I moved off and went to the buffet to fill my plate with salad and sausages. Müller followed me. "And how is Reichsminister Speer doing?" he asked me.—"Actually, Gruppenführer, I don't know. I haven't been in touch with him since his illness began. I hear he's doing better."—"Apparently he'll get out soon."—"That's likely. It would be a good thing. If we manage to get workers from Hungary, it will very quickly open new possibilities for our armaments industries."—"Maybe," Müller grunted. "But it will mostly be Jews, and Jews are forbidden in Altreich territory." I swallowed a little sausage and said: "Then that rule will have to change. We are now at our maximum capacity. Without those Jews, we can't go any further." Eichmann had drawn closer and listened to my last words as he drank his Cognac. He interrupted without even giving Müller time to respond: "Do you truly believe that between victory and defeat, the balance depends on the work of a few thousand Jews? And if that were the case, would you want Germany's victory to be due to Jews?" Eichmann had drunk a lot, his face was red and his eyes moist; he was proud of uttering such words in front of his superior. I listened to him as I picked sausage slices off the plate I was holding. I remained calm, but his nonsense irritated me. "You know, Obersturmbannführer," I replied evenly, "in 1941, we had the most modern army in the world. Now we've gone almost half a century back. All our transports, at the front, are driven by horses. The Russians are advancing in American Studebakers. And in the United States, millions of men and women are building those trucks day and night. And they're also building ships to transport them. Our experts confirm that they're producing a cargo ship a day. That's many more than our submarines could sink, if our submarines still dared to go out. Now we're in a war of attrition. But our enemies aren't suffering from attrition. Everything we destroy is replaced, right away, the hundred aircraft we shot down this week are already being replaced. Whereas with us, our losses in materiel aren't made good, except maybe for the tanks, if that." Eichmann puffed himself out: "You're in a defeatist mood tonight!" Müller observed us in silence, unsmiling; his mobile eyes flew from one of us to the other. "I'm not a defeatist," I retorted. "I'm a realist. You have to see where our interests lie." But Eichmann, a little drunk, refused to be logical: "You reason like a capitalist, a materialist . . . This war isn't a question of interests. If it were just a question of interests, we'd never have attacked Russia." I wasn't following him anymore, he seemed to be on a completely different tack, but he didn't stop, he pursued the leaps of his thinking. "We're not waging war so that every German can have a refrigerator and a radio. We're waging war to purify Germany, to create a Germany in which you'd want to live. You think my brother Helmut was killed for a refrigerator? Did you fight at Stalingrad for a refrigerator?" I shrugged, smiling: in this state, there wasn't any point in talking with him. Müller put his hand on his shoulder: "Eichmann, my friend, you're right." He turned to me: "That's why our dear Eichmann is so gifted for his work: he sees only what is essential. That's what makes him such a good specialist. And that's why I'm sending him to Hungary: for Jewish affairs, he's our *Meister.*" Eichmann, presented with these compliments, blushed with pleasure; for my part, I found him rather narrow-minded, at that moment. But that didn't prevent Müller from being right: he truly was quite effective, and in the end, it's often the narrow-minded ones who are the most effective. Müller went on: "The only thing, Eichmann, is that you shouldn't think just about the Jews. The Jews are among our great enemies, that's true. But the Jewish question is already almost settled in Europe. After Hungary there won't be many left. We have to think of the future. And we have a lot of enemies." He spoke softly, his monotonous voice, cradled by his rustic accent, seemed to flow through his thin, nervous lips. "You have to think about what we're going to do with the Poles. Eliminating the Jews but leaving the Poles makes no sense. And here too, in Germany. We've already begun, but we have to follow it through to the end. We also need an *Endlösung der Sozialfrage*, a "Final Solution to the Social Question." There are still far too many criminals, asocials, vagabonds, Gypsies, alcoholics, prostitutes, homosexuals. We have to think about people with tuberculosis, who contaminate healthy people. About the heart patients, who pass on defective blood and cost a fortune in medical care: them at least we can sterilize. We have to take care of all of them, category by category. All our good Germans oppose it, they always have good reasons. That's why Stalin is so strong: he knows how to make himself obeyed, and he knows how to go all the way." He looked at me: "I know the Bolsheviks very well. Since the executions of hostages in Munich, during the Revolution. After that, I fought them for fourteen years, until the Seizure of Power, and I'm still fighting them. But you know, I respect them. They are people who have an innate sense of organization, of discipline, and who don't shrink back from anything. We could learn lessons from them. Don't you think so?" Müller didn't wait for the reply to his question. He took Eichmann by the arm and led him to a low table, where he set up a chess game. I watched them play from afar while I finished my plate. Eichmann played well, but he couldn't hold his own against Müller: Müller, I said to myself, plays as he works, methodically, with stubbornness and a cold, thought-out brutality. They played several games, I had time to observe them. Eichmann tried cunning, calculated combinations, but Müller never let himself be trapped, and his defenses always remained just as strong as his attacks, systematically planned, irresistible. And Müller always won.

The following week, I put together a small team for the Einsatz in Hungary. I appointed a specialist, Obersturmführer Elias; a few clerks, orderlies, and administrative assistants; and of course Piontek. I left my office under Asbach's responsibility, with precise instructions. On Brandt's orders, on March 17, I set out for the KL Mauthausen, where a Sondereinsatzgruppe of the SP and the SD was assembling, under the command of Oberführer Dr. Achamer-Pifrader, the former BdS of the Ostland. Eichmann was already there, at the head of his own Sondereinsatzkommando. I presented myself to Oberführer Dr. Geschke, the officer in charge, who set me up with my team in a barracks. I already knew when I left Berlin that the Hungarian leader, Horthy, was meeting the Führer at Klessheim Palace, near Salzburg. Since the war, the events at Klessheim are well known: confronted with Hitler and von Ribbentrop, who bluntly gave him the choice between the formation of

a new pro-German government or the invasion of his country, Horthy—
admiral in a country without a navy, regent of a kingdom without a king—
decided, after a brief heart attack, to avoid the worst. At the time,
though, we knew nothing of that: Geschke and Achamer-Pifrader contented themselves with summoning the superior officers on the night of
the eighteenth, to inform us that we were leaving the next day for Budapest. Rumors, of course, were flying; many people expected Hungarian resistance at the border, they had us put on our field uniforms
and they handed out submachine guns. The camp was simmering with
excitement: for many of these functionaries of the *Staatspolizei* or the
SD, it was their first experience of the field; and even I, after almost a
year in Berlin, and the dullness of bureaucratic routine, the permanent
tension of underhand intrigues, the fatigue of bombings you had to undergo without reacting, I let myself be caught up in the general exhila-
ration. That evening, I went to have a few drinks with Eichmann,
whom I found surrounded by his officers, beaming and strutting about
in a new field gray uniform, tailored as elegantly as a parade uniform. I
knew only a few of his colleagues; he explained to me that for this operation he had sent for his best specialists from all over Europe, from
Italy, Croatia, Litzmannstadt, Theresienstadt. He introduced me to his
friend Hauptsturmführer Wisliceny (the godfather of his son Dieter), a
frightfully fat, placid, serene man, who had come from Slovakia. The
mood was cheerful, there wasn't much drinking; everyone was champ-
ing at the bit. I went back to my barracks to sleep a little, since we were
leaving around midnight, but I had trouble getting to sleep. I thought
about Helene: I had left her two days earlier, telling her I didn't know
when I'd return to Berlin; I had been somewhat abrupt, giving few explanations and not making any promises; she had accepted it gently,
gravely, without any obvious anxiety, and yet, it was clear I think to
both of us, a connection had been formed, tenuous perhaps, but solid,
which wouldn't dissolve by itself; it was already a relation, in some way.

I must have dozed off a little: Piontek shook me awake around midnight. I had lain down fully dressed, with my kit ready; I went out to
take the air while they checked the vehicles. I ate a sandwich and drank
some coffee that Fischer, an orderly, had brewed for me. It was late winter, bitter cold out, and I gladly inhaled the pure mountain air. A little
farther on, I heard the sound of engines: the Vorkommando, led by a
deputy of Eichmann's, was starting out. I had decided to join the convoy of the Sondereinsatzkommando, which included, aside from Eichmann and his officers, more than 150 men, most of them Orpos and
representatives of the SD and the SP, as well as some Waffen-SS.
Geschke's and Achamer-Pifrader's convoy brought up the rear. When

our two cars were ready, I sent them to join the staging area and went on foot to find Eichmann. He was wearing a tank soldier's goggles on his cap and was holding a Steyr machine pistol under his arm: with his riding breeches, it made him look a little ridiculous, almost as if he were wearing a disguise. "Obersturmbannführer," he cried out when he saw me. "Your men are ready?" I signed yes and went to join them. At the assembly area, it was still that last-minute confusion, the shouts and commands before a mass of vehicles can get under way in good order. Eichmann finally made his appearance, surrounded by many of his officers, including Regierungsrat Hunsche, whom I knew from Berlin; after having given some more contradictory orders, he got into his *Schwimmwagen*, a kind of amphibious all-terrain vehicle, driven by a Waffen-SS; I wondered amusedly if he was afraid the bridges would be dynamited, if he planned on crossing the Danube in his tub, with his Steyr and his chauffeur, to sweep away the Magyar hordes on his own. Piontek, at the steering wheel of my car, exuded sobriety and seriousness. Finally, under the harsh light of the camp searchlights, in a thunder of engines and a cloud of dust, the column set off. I had put Elias and Fischer in the back, with the weapons they had distributed to us; I sat in front, next to Piontek, and he started up. The sky was clear, the stars shining, but there was no moon; going down the winding road toward the Danube, I clearly saw the gleaming expanse of the river at my feet. The convoy crossed over to the right bank and headed toward Vienna. We drove in single file, our headlights kept low because of enemy fighter planes. I soon fell asleep. From time to time an alert woke me up, forced the vehicles to stop and douse the headlights, but no one left the car, we waited in the dark. There was no attack. In my interrupted half-sleep I had strange dreams, vivid and evanescent, which disappeared like a soap bubble as soon as a jolt or a siren woke me up. Around three o'clock, as we were skirting Vienna from the south, I shook myself awake and drank some coffee from a thermos readied by Fischer. The moon had risen, a thin crescent that made the wide water of the Danube gleam whenever we glimpsed it on our left. The alerts forced us to pause again, a long line of disparate vehicles that we could now distinguish in the moonlight. To the east, the sky was turning pink, outlining, higher up, the summits of the Little Carpathians. One of these pauses found us above the Neusiedler See, just a few kilometers from the Hungarian border. The fat Wisliceny passed by my car and rapped on my window: "Take your rum and come with us." They had delivered a few measures of rum to us for the march, but I hadn't touched it. I followed Wisliceny, who was going from car to car, getting other officers to come out. In front of us, the red ball of the sun weighed on the summits, the sky was pale, a luminous blue tinged with yellow, without a cloud. When our group reached Eichmann's *Schwimmwagen*, near the head of the column, we surrounded it and Wisliceny asked him to get out. He had brought along the officers from IV B 4, as well as the commanders of the seconded companies. Wisliceny raised his flask, congratulated Eichmann, and drank his health: Eichmann was celebrating his thirty-eighth birthday that day. He hiccupped with pleasure: "Meine Herren, I am touched, very touched. Today is my seventh birthday as an SS officer. I can't imagine a better gift than your company." He was beaming, all red, smiling at everyone, drinking in little sips to the cheers.

Crossing the border took place without incident: by the roadside, customs officials or soldiers of the Honvéd, glum or indifferent, watched us pass, showing nothing. The morning turned into a luminous one. The column paused in a village to breakfast on coffee, rum, white bread, and Hungarian wine bought on the spot. Then it started up again. We now drove much more slowly, the road was congested with German vehicles, troop trucks and tanks, which we had to follow at a crawl for kilometers before we could pass them. But it didn't look like an invasion, everything happened in a calm, orderly way; the civilians by the side of the road lined up to watch us pass, some even made friendly gestures at us.

We arrived in Budapest around the middle of the afternoon and settled in quarters on the right bank, behind the castle, on the Schwabenberg where the SS had requisitioned the big hotels. I was temporarily assigned a suite at the Astoria, with two beds and three sofas for eight men. The next morning I went to find out what I could. The city was swarming with German personnel, officers from the Wehrmacht and from the Waffen-SS, diplomats from the *Auswärtiges Amt*, police functionaries, engineers from the OT, economists from the WVHA, agents from the Abwehr whose names were always changing. In all this confusion I didn't even know to whom I was subordinate, and I went to see Geschke, who told me he had been named BdS, but that the Reichsführer had also appointed an HSSPF, Obergruppenführer Winkelmann, and that Winkelmann would explain everything to me. But Winkelmann, a plump career policeman with a crew cut and a jutting jaw, hadn't even been informed of my existence. He explained to me that, despite appearances, we hadn't occupied Hungary, but had come at Horthy's invitation to advise and support the Hungarian services: despite the presence of an HSSPF, a BdS, a BdO, and all the related structures, we had no executive function, and the Hungarian authorities preserved the full prerogatives of their sovereignty. Any serious dispute should be submitted to our new ambassador, Dr. Veesenmayer, an honorary SS-Brigadeführer, or to his colleagues at the *Auswärtiges Amt*. Kaltenbrunner, according to Winkelmann, was also in Budapest; he had come in Veesenmayer's special train car, which had been linked up to Horthy's train on his return from Klessheim, and he was negotiating with Lieutenant General Döme Sztójay, the former Hungarian ambassador to Berlin, about the formation of a new government (Kállay, the fallen prime minister, had sought refuge in the Turkish legation). I had no reason to go see Kaltenbrunner, so instead I went over to introduce myself at the German legation: Veesenmayer was busy, and I was received by his chargé d'affaires, Legationsrat Feine, who took note of my mission, suggested I wait for the situation to become clearer, and advised that I stay in contact with them. It was a fine mess.

At the Astoria, I saw Obersturmbannführer Krumey, Eichmann's deputy. He had already held a meeting with the leaders of the Jewish community and had emerged from it very satisfied. "They came with suitcases," he explained to me with a big laugh. "But I reassured them and told them no one was going to be arrested. They were terrified of *far right hysteria*. We promised them that if they cooperated, nothing would happen, that calmed them down." He laughed again. "They must think we're going to protect them from the Hungarians." The Jews were to form a council; so as not to frighten them—the term *Judenrat*, used in Poland, was known here well enough to provoke a certain anxiety—it would be called the *Zentralrat*. In the days that followed, as members of this new council brought mattresses and blankets to the Sondereinsatzkommando—I requisitioned several for our suite—then, in response to various requests, typewriters, mirrors, cologne, lingerie, and some very pretty little paintings by Watteau, or at least his school, I held meetings with them, especially with the president of the Jewish community, Dr. Samuel Stern, and had a series of consultations so that I could form an idea of the resources available. There were Jews, men and women, employed in Hungarian armaments factories, and Stern could provide me with approximate figures. But a major problem arose immediately: all the able-bodied Jewish men, who were without essential jobs and of working age, had for several years already been drafted into the Honvéd, to serve in labor battalions behind the lines. And it was true, I remembered, when we had entered Zhitomir, which was still held by the Hungarians, I had heard talk of these Jewish battalions; they infuriated my colleagues in Sk 4a. "Those battalions have nothing to do with us," Stern explained. "You'll have to see about that with the government."

A few days after the formation of Sztójay's government, the new cabinet, in a single eleven-hour legislative session, promulgated a series of anti-Jewish laws that the Hungarian police began to apply immediately. I saw little of Eichmann: he was always hidden away with officials, or else visiting the Jews, taking an interest, according to Krumey, in their culture, taking tours of their library, their museum, their synagogues. At the end of the month he addressed the *Zentralrat* himself. His whole SEk had just moved to the Majestic Hotel; I had remained at the Astoria, where I had been able to obtain two more rooms to set up offices. I wasn't invited to the meeting, but I saw him afterward: he looked very pleased with himself, and assured me that the Jews would cooperate and submit to German demands. We discussed the question of workers; the new laws would allow the Hungarians to augment the civilian labor battalions—all Jewish civil servants, journalists, notaries, lawyers, accountants who were going to lose their jobs could be drafted, and that made Eichmann snigger: "Imagine, my dear Obersturmbannführer, Jewish lawyers digging antitank ditches!"—but we had no idea about what they would agree to give us; Eichmann feared as I did that they would try to keep the best for themselves. But Eichmann had found himself an ally, a functionary of the county of Budapest, Dr. Lászlo Endre, a fanatical anti-Semite whom he hoped to have appointed to the Ministry of the Interior. "We have to avoid repeating the mistake of Denmark, you know," he explained to me, his head resting on his large veined hand as he chewed on his pinky. "The Hungarians must do everything themselves, they have to offer us their Jews on a plate." Already, the SEk, along with the Hungarian police and the forces of the BdS, were arresting Jews who violated the new rules; a transit camp, guarded by the Hungarian police, had been set up in Kistarcsa, near the city; more than three thousand Jews had been interned there. On my side, I didn't remain inactive: via the legation, I had made contact with the ministries of Industry and Agriculture to sound out their views; and I studied the new legislation in the company of Herr von Adamovic, the legation expert, an affable, intelligent man almost paralyzed by sciatica and arthritis. In the meantime I stayed in contact with my Berlin office. Speer, who by coincidence celebrated his birthday on the same day as Eichmann, had left Hohenlychen to spend his convalescence in Meran, in Italy; I had sent a congratulatory telegram and some flowers to him, but hadn't received a reply. I had also been invited to attend a conference in Silesia, on the Jewish question, headed by Dr. Franz Six, my very first department head in the SD. He now worked at the *Auswärtiges Amt*, but from time to time still lent a hand to the RSHA. Thomas had also been invited, along with Eichmann and some of his specialists. I arranged to travel with them. Our group left by train, passing through Pressburg, then changing in Breslau for Hirschberg; the conference was being held in Krummhübel, a well-known ski resort in the Silesian Sudeten Mountains, now largely occupied by the foreign ministry's offices, including Six's, evacuated from Berlin because of the bombings. We were put up in a crowded Gasthaus; their new barracks weren't yet ready. I was glad to find Thomas there; he had arrived a little before us and was taking advantage of the occasion to ski in the company of beautiful young secretaries or assistants, including one of Russian origin whom he introduced to me, and who all seemed to have very little work to do. Eichmann had gathered colleagues from all over Europe and was strutting about. The conference began the day after we arrived. Six opened the discussions with a speech on "the tasks and aims of anti-Jewish operations abroad." He spoke to us about the political structure of world Jewry, asserting that *Jewry in Europe has finished playing its political and biological role*. He also made an interesting digression on Zionism, which was still not well known at the time in our circles; for Six, the question of the return of the remaining Jews to Palestine should be subordinate to the Arab question, which would take on importance after the war, especially if the British withdrew from part of their empire. His speech was followed by that of the specialist from the *Auswärtiges Amt*, a certain von Thadden, who explained the standpoint of his ministry on "the political situation of Jews in Europe and the situation in relation to anti-Jewish executive measures." Thomas spoke about the security problems raised by the Jewish rebellions of the previous year. Other specialists or advisors explained the present situation in the countries where they were posted. But the high point of the day was Eichmann's speech. The Hungarian Einsatz seemed to have inspired him, and he painted us a nearly complete picture of anti-Jewish operations as they had unfolded from the beginning. He quickly passed over the failure of ghettoization and criticized the inefficiency and confusion of the mobile operations: "Whatever the successes racked up, they remain sporadic, they allow too many Jews to escape, to reach the woods to swell the ranks of the partisans, and they sap the morale of our men." Success, in foreign countries, depended on two factors: mobilizing local authorities and securing the cooperation, even the collaboration, of the Jewish community leaders. "As to what happens, when we try to arrest the Jews ourselves, in countries where we have insufficient resources, it's enough to look at the example of Denmark, a complete failure, or the South of France, where we got very mixed results, even after our occupation of the former Italian zone, or Italy, where the population and the Church hide thousands of Jews that we can't find. . . . As for the *Judenräte*, they permit a considerable savings in personnel, and they harness the Jews themselves to the task of their destruction. Of course, these Jews have their own aims, their own dreams. But the dreams of Jews serve us too. They dream of grandiose corruptions, they offer us their money, their property. We take this money and this property and we pursue our own task. They dream of the economic needs of the Wehrmacht, of the protection provided by work certificates, and we, we use these dreams to feed our armaments factories, so that we are offered the labor we need to build our underground complexes, and also to get the weak and the old, the useless mouths, handed over to us. But understand this too: the elimination of the first one hundred thousand Jews is much easier than getting rid of the last five thousand. Look at what happened in Warsaw, or during the other rebellions that Standartenführer Hauser told us about. When the Reichsführer sent me the report on the fighting in Warsaw, he noted that he couldn't bring himself to believe that Jews in a ghetto could fight like that. Yet our late lamented Chief, Obergruppenführer Heydrich, had understood this long before. He knew that the strongest Jews, the toughest, the cleverest, the wiliest, would escape all selections and would be the hardest to destroy. And it is precisely those who form the vital reservoir from which Jewry could spring back, *the germ cell for Jewish regeneration*, as the late Obergruppenführer said. Our struggle prolongs that of Koch and Pasteur—we have to follow it through to the end . . ." A thunder of applause welcomed these words. Did Eichmann really believe in them? It was the first time I heard him talk this way, and I had the impression that he had gotten carried away, let himself be swept along by his new role, that he liked the game so much that he ended up becoming one with it. But his practical comments were far from idiotic; it was obvious that he had attentively analyzed all the past experiences to draw the essential lessons from them. At dinner—Six, out of politeness and for old time's sake, had invited me along with Thomas to a little private supper—I remarked favorably on Eichmann's speech. But Six, who never abandoned his glum, depressed air, thought much more negatively of it: "Intellectually uninteresting. He's a relatively simple man, not particularly gifted. Of course, he is snappish, and he's good at what he does, within the limits of his specialization."—"Precisely," I said, "he's a good officer, motivated and talented in his way. In my opinion, he could go far."—"That would surprise me," Thomas dryly interrupted. "He's too stubborn. He's a bulldog, a gifted executor. But he has no imagination. He is incapable of reacting to events outside his field, of evolving. He built his career on Jews, on the destruction of Jews, and for that he's very efficient. But once we've done with the Jews—or else if the wind shifts, if the time comes no longer to destroy Jews—then he'll be unable to adapt, he'll be lost."

The next day, the conference continued with minor speakers. Eichmann didn't stay, he had work to do: "I have to go inspect Auschwitz and then go back to Budapest. Things are on the move over there." I left in turn on April 5. In Hungary, I learned that the Führer had just consented to the use of Jewish workers in Reich territory: now that the ambiguity had been settled, Speer's men and the men from the Jägerstab came to see me constantly to ask when we could send them the first consignments. I told them to be patient, the operation wasn't finalized yet. Eichmann returned furious from Auschwitz, railing against the Kommandanten: "Idiots, incompetents. Nothing is ready for reception." On April 9 . . . ah, but what's the point of relating all these details day by day? It's exhausting me, and also it's boring me, and you too no doubt. How many pages have I already stacked up on these uninteresting bureaucratic episodes? No, I can't go on like this anymore: the quill falls from my fingers, the pen, rather. I might return to it some other day; but what's the point of going over that sordid Hungarian business again? It is amply documented in the books, by historians who have a much more coherent overall view than my own. I played only a minor role in it, after all. Although I was able to meet some of the participants, I don't have much to add to their own memories. The great intrigues that ensued, especially those negotiations between Eichmann, Becher, and the Jews, that whole business of ransoming Jews in exchange for money, trucks, all that, yes, I was more or less aware of them, I discussed it, I even met some of the Jews involved, and Becher too, a disturbing man, who had come to Hungary to buy horses for the Waffen-SS and who had quickly taken over, for the Reichsführer, the largest armaments factory in the country, the Manfred-Weiss Werke, without informing anyone, neither Veesenmayer, nor Winkelmann, nor me, and to whom the Reichsführer had then entrusted tasks that either duplicated or contradicted my own and Eichmann's too—which, I ended up realizing, was a typical method of the Reichsführer's, but on the ground it served only to spread discord and confusion, no one coordinated anything, Winkelmann had no influence over Eichmann or over Becher, who never told him about anything, and I must confess that I hardly behaved any better than they, I negotiated with the Hungarians without Winkelmann's knowing, with the Ministry of Defense especially, where I had made contacts via General Greiffenberg, Veesenmayer's military attaché, to see if the Honvéd couldn't also second its Jewish labor battalions to us, even with specific guarantees of a special treatment, which of course the Honvéd refused categorically, leaving us, for potential workers, only civilians who had been pressed into service in the beginning of the month, the ones they could remove from the factories, and

their families, in short, a human potential of little value, which is one of
the reasons why I had to end up regarding this mission as a total failure,
but not the only reason, I'll talk some more about that, and I might even
talk a little about the negotiations with the Jews, for that too in the end
fell somewhat within my jurisdiction, or, to be more precise, I used, no,
I tried to use these negotiations to push my own objectives forward,
with little success, I will readily admit, for a whole jumble of reasons,
not just those already mentioned, there was also the attitude of Eichmann, who was becoming more and more difficult, Becher too, the
WVHA, the Hungarian police, everyone joined in, you see—whatever
the case, what I would like to say more precisely is that if you want to
analyze the reasons for which the Hungarian operation yielded such
poor results for the *Arbeitseinsatz*, my main concern after all, you have
to take into account all these people and all these institutions, who each
played their role, but also kept blaming all the others, and they blamed
me too, no one refrained from that, you can believe me, in short, it was
a mess, genuine havoc, due to which in the end most of the deported
Jews died, right away I mean, gassed even before they could be put to
work, for very few of those who reached Auschwitz were fit, considerable losses, 70 percent perhaps, no one is really sure, and because of
which people after the war believed, and this is understandable, that it
was the true aim of the operation, to kill all those Jews, those women,
those old people, those chubby healthy children, and thus people
couldn't understand why the Germans, when they were losing the war
(though the specter of defeat may not have been so clear, at the time,
from the German standpoint at least), still persisted in massacring Jews,
in mobilizing considerable resources, men and trains, especially, to exterminate women and children, and thus since people couldn't understand, they attributed it to the anti-Semitic madness of the Germans, to
a delirium of murder that was very remote from the thinking of most
of the participants, for in fact, for me as well as for so many other functionaries and specialists, the stakes were essential, crucial, to find labor
for our factories, a few hundred thousand workers who might have let
us reverse the course of things, we wanted Jews who were not dead but
very much alive, able-bodied, preferably male, but the Hungarians
wanted to keep the males or at least a large part of them, and so it was
already off to a bad start, and then there were the transport conditions,
deplorable, and God knows how much I argued about this with Eichmann, who countered with the same thing every time, "It's not my responsibility, it's the Hungarian gendarmerie who load and supply the
trains, not us," and then there was also Höss's stubbornness, in
Auschwitz, because in the meantime, possibly following Eichmann's re-

port, Höss had returned as Standortälteste in place of Liebehenschel, who had been sent to cool his heels in Lublin, there was thus this obstinate inability of Höss to change his methods, but this I might discuss later on and in more detail, in short, few of us deliberately wanted what happened, and yet, you'll say, it happened, it's true, and it's also true that we sent all those Jews to Auschwitz, not just the ones who could work, but all of them, knowing perfectly well that the old people and the children would be gassed, and so we return to the initial question, why this obstinacy to empty Hungary of its Jews, given the conditions of war and all that, and there, of course, I can only put forward hypotheses, for it wasn't my personal objective, or rather, I'm not being precise here, I know why we wanted to deport (at the time we said *evacuate*) all the Jews from Hungary and kill those unfit for work immediately, that was because our authorities, the Führer, the Reichsführer, had decided to kill all the Jews in Europe, that is clear, we knew that, just as we knew that even those who would be put to work would die sooner or later, and the *why* of all that is a question I've talked a lot about and to which I still don't have an answer, people, in those days, believed all sorts of things about the Jews, the bacillus theory like the Reichsführer and Heydrich, cited at the Krummhübel conference by Eichmann, but for whom in my opinion it must have been a purely theoretical construct, the argument of Jewish uprisings, espionage or fifth column for our enemies who were getting closer, an argument that obsessed a large part of the RSHA and even preoccupied my friend Thomas, the fear too of Jewish omnipotence, in which some still firmly believed, which incidentally gave rise to some comical misunderstandings, as in the beginning of April in Budapest, when we had to move a number of Jews to free up their apartments, and the SP called for the creation of a ghetto, which the Hungarians refused because they were afraid the Allies would bomb around this ghetto and spare it (the Americans had already struck Budapest when I was in Krummhübel), and so the Hungarians scattered the Jews near strategic military and industrial targets, which greatly worried some of our officials, for then if the Americans went ahead and bombed these targets anyway, that would prove that global Judaism was not as powerful as was thought, and I have to add, to be fair, that the Americans did in fact bomb these targets, killing in passing many Jewish civilians, but for me it had been a long time since I believed in the omnipotence of global Judaism, otherwise why would all those countries have refused to take in the Jews, in 1937, '38, '39, when we wanted just one thing, for them to leave Germany, the only reasonable solution at bottom? What I mean, returning to the question I asked, for I've strayed a little from it, is that even if, objectively, there was no

doubt about the final aim, it wasn't with this aim in mind that most of
the participants were working, it wasn't that which motivated them and
drove them to work so energetically and single-mindedly, it was a whole
gamut of motivations, and even Eichmann, I'm convinced, he had a
very harsh attitude but at bottom it was the same to him whether or not
the Jews were killed, the only thing that counted, for him, was to show
what he could do, to prove his worth, and also to use the abilities he
had developed, for the rest of it, he didn't give a fuck, either about industry or about the gas chambers for that matter, the only thing he did
give a fuck about was that no one fucked with him, and that's why he
was so reluctant in the negotiations with the Jews, but I'll come back to
that, it's interesting all the same, and for the others it's the same, everyone had his reasons, the Hungarian bureaucracy that helped us just
wanted to see the Jews leave Hungary but didn't give a fuck about what
would happen to them, and Speer and Kammler and the Jägerstab
wanted workers and relentlessly pushed the SS to deliver Jews to them,
but didn't give a fuck about what happened to the ones who couldn't
work, and then there were also all sorts of pragmatic motivations, for
example, I was concentrating only on the *Arbeitseinsatz*, but that was far
from being the only economic stake, as I learned when I met an expert
from our Ministry of Food and Agriculture, a very intelligent young
man, passionate about his work, who explained to me one evening, in
an old café in Budapest, the alimentary aspect of the question, which
was that because of the loss of the Ukraine Germany had to face a grave
deficit in food supplies, especially in wheat, and so had turned to Hungary, a major producer, according to him that was even the main reason
for our pseudo-invasion, to secure this source of wheat, and so in 1944
we asked the Hungarians for 450,000 tons of wheat, 360,000 tons more
than in 1942, or an increase of 400 percent, but the Hungarians had to
take this wheat from somewhere, after all they had to feed their own
population, but precisely, these 360,000 tons corresponded to rations for
about one million people, a little more than the total number of Hungarian Jews, and so the specialists in the Ministry of Food saw the evacuation of the Jews by the RSHA as a measure that would allow
Hungary to free up a surplus of wheat for Germany, corresponding to
our needs, and as for the fate of the evacuated Jews, who in principle
would have to be fed elsewhere if they weren't killed, that didn't concern this young and all in all pleasant expert, a little obsessed with his
figures though, for there were other departments in the Ministry of
Food to take care of that, feeding the inmates and other foreign workers in Germany, that wasn't his business, and for him the evacuation of
the Jews was the solution to his problem, even if it became someone

else's problem in turn. And he wasn't the only one, this man, everyone was like him, I too was like him, and you too, in his place, you would have been like him.

But perhaps you really don't care about any of this. Maybe, instead of my unwholesome, abstruse reflections, you would rather have anecdotes, spicy little stories. For my part I don't know anymore. I'm quite willing to tell you a few stories: but then let me just dig at random among my memories and my notes; I've told you, I'm getting tired, I have to start bringing this to an end. And also if I still had to recount the rest of 1944 in detail, a little like I've done up to now, I'll never be done. You see, I'm thinking of you too, not just of me, a little bit in any case, there are limits of course, if I'm putting myself to so much trouble, it's not to make you happy, I will willingly admit, it's above all for my own mental hygiene, like when you've eaten too much, at some point you have to evacuate the waste, whether or not it smells nice, you don't always have a choice; but here, you have an irrevocable power, that of closing this book and throwing it in the trash, a final recourse against which I am powerless, so I don't see why I should wear kid gloves. And that is why, I'll admit it, if I change my method a little, it's mostly for me, whether you like it or not, another mark of my boundless selfishness, certainly a fruit of my bad education. Maybe I should have done something else, you'll tell me, that's true, maybe I should have done something else, I would have been delighted to play music, if I had known how to put two notes together and recognize a treble clef, but there it is, I've already explained my limits in that field, or else painting, why not, that seems a pleasant occupation to me, painting, a quiet occupation, losing yourself that way in forms and colors, but what can I do, in another life maybe, for in this one I never had a choice, maybe a little, of course, a narrow margin for maneuvering, but limited, because of the weight of fate, and lo, we're back just where we started from. But let us return to Hungary.

About the officers around Eichmann, there's not much to say. They were, for the most part, peaceable men, good citizens doing their duty, proud and happy bearers of the SS uniform, but timorous, with little initiative, always going "Yes . . . but," and admiring their leader as a great genius. The only one who stood out a little was Wisliceny, a Prussian my age, who spoke very good English and had an excellent grasp of history, and with whom I liked to spend my evenings discussing the Thirty Years' War, the turning point of 1848, or else the moral bankruptcy of the Wilhelmine era. His views weren't always original, but they were solidly documented and he could work them into a coherent narrative, which is the foremost quality of the historical imagination. He had once been Eichmann's superior, in 1936 I think, in any case during the time of the SD-Hauptamt, when the Department of Jewish Affairs was still called Abteilung II 112; but his laziness and indolence had quickly led to his being surpassed by his disciple, which he didn't hold against him, they had remained good friends, Wisliceny was a close family friend, they even publicly called each other by their first names (later on they had a falling-out, for reasons I am unaware of). Wisliceny, a witness at Nuremberg, painted a negative portrait of his old comrade that for a long time helped to distort the image that historians and writers had of Eichmann, some even going so far as to argue in good faith that the poor Obersturmbannführer gave orders to Adolf Hitler. You can't blame Wisliceny: he was trying to save his neck, and Eichmann had disappeared, at the time it was customary to incriminate the absent, though it didn't get poor Wisliceny very far; he ended up at the end of a rope in Pressburg, the Bratislava of the Slovaks (and it must have been solid, that rope, to support his corpulence). Another reason that made me appreciate Wisliceny was that he kept a level head, unlike some others, especially the Berlin bureaucrats, who, having been sent to the field for the first time in their lives and seeing themselves suddenly so powerful compared to these Jewish dignitaries, educated men sometimes twice their age, lost all sense of moderation. Some of them insulted the Jews in the coarsest and most unseemly way; others succumbed to the temptation of abusing their position; all of them demonstrated an arrogance that was unbearable and, in my opinion, utterly inappropriate. I remember Hunsche, for example, a Regierungsrat, that is, a career civil servant, a jurist with an accountant's mentality, the little gray man you never notice behind the desk of a bank where he patiently shuffles paper as he waits till he can draw his pension and go out in a cardigan knitted by his wife and grow Dutch tulips, or else paint Napoleonic lead soldiers, which he will arrange lovingly, in perfect rows, nostalgic for the lost order of his youth, in front of a plaster model of the Brandenburg Gate, what do I know of the dreams that haunt this sort of man? And there, in Budapest, ridiculous in a uniform with an extra-baggy pair of riding breeches, he smoked expensive cigarettes, received Jewish leaders with his dirty boots resting on a velvet armchair, and shamelessly indulged his slightest whims. In the very first few days after our arrival, he had asked the Jews to provide him with a piano, saying negligently to them, "I've always dreamed of having a piano"; the Jews, terrified, brought him eight; and Hunsche, right in front of me, planted in his tall boots, reprimanded them in a voice that was trying to sound ironic: "But meine Herren! I don't want to open a store, I just want to play the piano." A piano! Germany is groaning under the bombs, our soldiers at the front are fighting with frozen limbs and missing fingers, but Hauptsturmführer Regierungsrat Dr. Hunsche, who has never left his Berlin office, needs a piano, no doubt to calm his frayed nerves. When I watched him prepare orders for the men in the transit camps—the evacuations had begun—I wondered if, as he appended his signature, he didn't get hard under the table. He was, I'm the first to acknowledge it, a truly poor specimen of the *Herrenvolk*: and if you are to judge Germany from this kind of man, alas only too common, then, yes, I can't deny it, we have deserved our fate, the judgment of history, our *dikè*.

And what, then, is there to say about Obersturmbannführer Eichmann? For as long as I had known him, he had never taken so readily to his role. When he received the Jews, he was the *Übermensch* from head to foot, he took off his glasses, spoke to them in a brittle, choppy, but polite voice, he had them sit down and called them "meine Herren," he called Dr. Stern "Herr Hofrat," and then he would burst into obscenities, deliberately, to shock them, before returning to that icy politeness that seemed to hypnotize them. He was also extremely gifted with the Hungarian authorities, at once friendly and polite, he impressed them and also he had formed solid friendships with some of them, especially Lászlo Endre, who showed him in Budapest a social life till then unknown to him and which ended up dazzling him, inviting him to castles, introducing him to countesses. All this, the fact that everybody merrily let themselves get caught up in the game, Jews and Hungarians, might explain why Eichmann too lapsed into hubris (but never with the stupidity of a Hunsche) and ended up believing he really was *der Meister*, the Master. He took himself in fact for a condottiere, a von dem Bach-Zelewski, he forgot his deepest nature, that of a bureaucrat of talent, even of great talent in his limited field. Yet as soon as you saw him one-on-one, in his office, or in the evening, if he had had a little to drink, he became the old Eichmann again, the one who scuttled about the offices of the *Staatspolizei*, respectful, busy, impressed by the slightest stripe superior to his own and at the same time devoured by envy and ambition, the Eichmann who had himself covered, in writing, for each action and each decision, by Müller or Heydrich or Kaltenbrunner, and who kept all these orders in a safe, carefully arranged, the Eichmann who would have been just as happy—and no less efficient—buying and transporting horses or trucks, if that had been his task, as concentrating and evacuating tens of thousands of human beings destined to die. When I came to talk with him about the *Arbeitseinsatz*, in private, he listened to me, sitting behind his fine desk, in his luxurious room in the Majestic Hotel, with a bored, irritated look, playing with his glasses or with a mechanical pencil he kept pressing, going *click-clack, click-clack,* compulsively, and before replying, he would rearrange his documents covered with notes and little doodles, blow the dust off his desk, then, scratching his already balding skull, launch into one of his long replies, so muddled that he himself would soon get lost in it. In the beginning, when the Einsatz was finally truly under way, after the Hungarians, around the end of April, had given their consent for the evacuations, he was almost euphoric, seething with energy; at the same time, and even more when the problems piled up, he became more and more difficult, intransigent, even with me, whom he rather liked, he began to see enemies everywhere. Winkelmann, who was his superior only on paper, didn't like him at all, but in my opinion it was still this severe, gruff policeman, with the innate common sense of an Austrian peasant, who judged him the best. Eichmann's haughty demeanor, verging on impertinence, drove him into a fury, but he saw right through him: "He has the mentality of a subaltern," he explained to me when I came to see him once, to ask if he could intervene or at least use his influence to improve the very bad transport conditions of the Jews. "He uses his authority unreservedly, he doesn't know any moral or mental restraints on the exercise of his power. Nor does he have the slightest scruple about exceeding the limits of his authority, if he believes he's acting in the spirit of the person giving him his orders and protecting him, as Gruppenführer Müller and Obergruppenführer Kaltenbrunner do." That is probably quite right, all the more so since Winkelmann didn't deny Eichmann's abilities. Eichmann, at the time, was no longer living at the hotel, but was occupying the beautiful villa of a Jew on Apostol Street, on the Rosenberg, a house with two stories and a tower overlooking the Danube, surrounded by a superb orchard unfortunately disfigured by the trenches dug for the air-raid shelter. He was living it up and spending most of his time with his new Hungarian friends. The evacuations were already well under way, zone by zone according to a very strict plan, and complaints were flowing in from everywhere, from the Jägerstab, from Speer's offices, from Saur himself, they were flying every which way, at Himmler, Pohl, Kaltenbrunner, but in the end everything came back to me, and indeed, it was a catastrophe, a real scandal, the work-sites were receiving only skinny young girls or men already half dead, whereas they were hoping for an influx of healthy, solid, strapping fellows well used to work, they were outraged, no one understood what was happening. Part of the fault, I've already explained, was the Honvéd's, which despite all our remonstrances jealously kept its labor battalions. But among those who remained there were still some men, who not long before had been living a normal life, eating their fill, they must have been in good health. But it turned out that the conditions of the concentration points, where the Jews some- times had to wait for days or weeks, barely fed, before being trans- ported, crammed into overloaded cattle cars, without water, without food, with one slop pail per car, these conditions were exhausting their strength, illnesses were spreading, many people died on the way, and those who arrived looked awful, few passed selection, and even these were turned down or else rapidly returned by the factories and work sites, especially the ones run by the Jägerstab, who howled that they were being sent girls incapable of lifting a pickaxe. When I transmitted these complaints to Eichmann, as I've said, he rejected them curtly, stat- ing that it wasn't his responsibility, that only the Hungarians could change anything in these conditions. So I went to see Major Baky, the Secretary of State in charge of the Gendarmerie; Baky swept aside my complaints with a single sentence, "Just take them more quickly," and sent me to Lieutenant-Colonel Ferenczy, the officer in charge of the technical management of the evacuations, a bitter, closed man, who talked to me for more than an hour to explain that he would be de lighted to feed the Jews better, if he were provided with food, and to pack the cars less, if he were sent more trains, but that his main mission consisted of evacuating them, not coddling them. With Wisliceny, I went to one of these "collection points," I forget where, in the region of Kaschau maybe: it was a depressing sight, the Jews were parked by whole families into an open-air brickworks, under the spring rain, chil- dren in shorts were playing in the puddles of water, the adults, apathetic, sat on their suitcases or paced up and down. I was struck by the contrast between these Jews and the ones, the only ones I had really known till then, from Galicia and the Ukraine; these were well-educated people, often middle-class, and even the craftsmen and the farmers, quite nu- merous, had a proper and dignified bearing, the children were washed, combed, well dressed in spite of the conditions, sometimes wearing the green national costume, with black frogging and little caps. All that made the scene even more oppressive, despite their yellow stars, they could have been German or at least Czech villagers, and it gave me sin- ister thoughts, I imagined those neat, tidy boys or those young women with their discreet charm being gassed—thoughts that turned my stom- ach, but there was nothing to be done, I looked at the pregnant women and imagined them in the gas chambers, their hands on their rounded bellies, I wondered with horror what happened to the fetus of a gassed woman, if it died right away with its mother or else survived a little, im- prisoned in its dead cocoon, its suffocating paradise, and from that

thought memories of the Ukraine flowed in, and for the first time in a
long time I wanted to vomit, vomit my powerlessness, my sadness, my
useless life. By chance I ran into Dr. Grell there, a Legationsrat appointed by Feine to identify foreign Jews arrested by mistake by the
Hungarian police, especially those from allied or neutral countries, and
to remove them from the transit centers so that they could eventually
be sent back to their own countries. This poor Grell, a wounded veteran of the Great War disfigured by a head wound and horrible burns
that terrified the children, who ran away screaming when they saw him,
waded through the mud from one group to the other, his hat dripping
water, politely asking if there were any holders of foreign passports, examining their papers, ordering the Hungarian gendarmes to take some
of them aside. Eichmann and his colleagues hated him, accused him of
indulgence, of lack of discernment, and it was true, too, that many Hungarian Jews, for a few thousand pengö, bought foreign passports, Romanian ones especially, the easiest to get, but Grell was just doing his
job, it wasn't up to him to judge whether or not these passports had
been obtained legally, and after all, if the Romanian attachés were corrupt, that was the problem of the authorities in Bucharest, not our own,
if they wanted to accept or tolerate all these Jews, so much the worse
for them. I knew Grell a little, for in Budapest, from time to time, I had
a drink or went out to dinner with him; among the German officials,
almost everyone avoided him or fled him, even his own colleagues,
probably because of his atrocious appearance, but also because of his severe and extremely disconcerting fits of depression; as for me, that didn't
bother me so much, maybe because his wound was in the end rather
similar to my own, he too had received a bullet in the head, but with
much worse consequences than me, we didn't talk, by tacit agreement,
about the circumstances, but when he had had a little to drink he said I
was lucky, and he was right, I was insanely lucky, to have an intact face
and a pretty much intact head too, whereas he, if he drank too much,
and he often drank too much, exploded into extraordinary fits of rage,
almost epileptic attacks, he changed color, began screaming, once, with
a café waiter, I even had to restrain him forcibly from breaking all the
dishes, he came to apologize the next day, contrite, depressed, and I
tried to reassure him, I understood him well. There, in that transit center, he came to see me, looked at Wisliceny, whom he also knew, and
just said: "Filthy business, isn't it?" He was right, but there was worse.
To try to understand what happened during the selections, I went to
Auschwitz. I arrived at night, by the Vienna-Cracow train; well before
the station, to the left of the train, you could see a line of points of white
light, the barbed-wire spotlights perched on whitewashed poles, and be-

hind that line, more darkness, an abyss giving off that abominable stench of burned flesh, which wafted through the car. The passengers, mainly soldiers or functionaries returning to their posts, crowded around the windows, often with their wives. Comments flew: "It's burning nicely," a civilian said to his wife. At the station, I was welcomed by an Untersturmführer who quartered me in a room at the Haus der Waffen-SS. The next morning I saw Höss again. In the beginning of May, after Eichmann's inspection, as I said, the WVHA had again drastically modified the organization of the Auschwitz complex. Liebehenschel, certainly the best Kommandant the camp had known, had been replaced by a useless idiot, Sturmbannführer Bär, a former pastry cook who had for a time been Pohl's adjutant; Hartjenstein, in Birkenau, had swapped places with the Kommandant of Natzweiler, Hauptsturmführer Kramer; and Höss, finally, for the duration of the Hungarian Einsatz, supervised the others. It seemed obvious to me, speaking to him, that he thought his appointment concerned only extermination: while the Jews were arriving at the rate of sometimes four trains of three thousand units each every day, he hadn't had any new barracks built to receive them, but on the contrary had put all his considerable energy into repairing the crematoriums and extending the tracks into the very midst of Birkenau, of which he was especially proud, so they were able to unload the cars at the foot of the gas chambers. With the first convoy of the day, he took me to watch the selection and the rest of the operations. The new ramp passed under the guard tower of the entrance building to Birkenau and went on, with three branches, to the crematoriums at the rear. A huge crowd was swarming on the dirt platform—noisy, poorer and more colorful than the people I had seen in the transit center, these Jews must have come from Transylvania, the women and girls wore multicolor scarves, the men, still in coats, had big, bushy moustaches and unshaven cheeks. There wasn't too much disorder; for a long time I observed the doctors who carried out the selection (Wirths wasn't there), they spent one or two seconds on each case, at the slightest doubt it was *no*, they seemed also to refuse many women who looked perfectly able-bodied to me; when I pointed this out to him, Höss told me they were following his instructions, the barracks were overcrowded, there wasn't any more room to put people in, the factories were making a fuss, weren't taking these Jews fast enough, and the Jews were piling up, epidemics were beginning again, and since Hungary kept sending them every day, he was forced to make room, he had already carried out several selections among the inmates, he had also tried to liquidate the Gypsy camp, but there had been problems and it had been put off till later, he had asked for permission to empty the Theresienstadt "family camp" and hadn't yet received it, so in the meantime he could really only select the best, in any case if he took any more they would soon die of disease. He explained all this to me calmly, his empty blue eyes aimed at the crowd and the ramp, absent. I felt hopeless, it was even more difficult to talk sense to this man than to Eichmann. He insisted on showing me the killing installations and explaining everything to me: he had increased the Sonderkommandos from 220 to 860 men, but they had overestimated the capacity of the Kremas; it wasn't so much the gassing that posed a problem, but the ovens were overloaded, and to remedy that he had had to have incineration trenches dug, and by driving the Sonderkommandos on, that did the trick, he had reached an average of six thousand units per day, which meant that some had to wait sometimes till the next day, if they were especially overwhelmed. It was appalling, the smoke and the flames in the trenches, fed by gasoline and the fat from the bodies, must have been visible for miles all around, I asked him if he didn't think it might make trouble: "Oh, the authorities of the Kreis are worried, but that's not my problem." To listen to him, nothing of what should have been was his problem. Exasperated, I asked to see the barracks. The new sector, planned originally as a transit camp for Hungarian Jews, was still incomplete; thousands of women, already haggard and thin although they hadn't been there long, were herded into long, stinking stables; many couldn't find a place and slept outside, in the mud; even though they didn't have enough striped uniforms to clothe them, they still didn't let them keep their own clothes, but dressed them in rags taken from the *Kanada*; and I saw some women completely naked, or dressed just in a shirt from which two yellow, flabby legs stuck out, sometimes covered in excrement. Hardly surprising that the Jägerstab was complaining! Höss vaguely shifted the blame to the other camps, which according to him were refusing to accept the transports, out of lack of room. All day I surveyed the camp, section by section, barrack after barrack; the men were hardly in better shape than the women. I inspected the registers: no one, of course, had thought to respect the basic rule of warehousing, *first in, first out*; whereas some arrivals didn't even spend twenty-four hours in the camp before being sent on, others stagnated there for three weeks, broke down, and often died, which increased the losses even more. But for each problem I pointed out to him, Höss unfailingly found someone else to blame. His mentality, formed by the prewar years, was completely unsuited to the job, that was plain as day; but he wasn't the only one to blame, it was also the fault of the people who had sent him to replace Liebehenschel, who, from the little I knew of him, would have gone about it completely differently. I continued on till evening. It rained several times during the day, brief and refreshing spring rains, which made the dust die down but also increased the misery of the inmates who stayed out in the open, even if most of them thought above all of collecting a few drops to drink. The entire rear of the camp was dominated by fire and smoke, even beyond the quiet expanse of the Birkenwald. At night, endless columns of women, children, and old people kept coming up from the ramp along a long barbed-wire corridor, toward Kremas III and IV, where they would wait their turn patiently under the birch trees, and the beautiful light of the setting sun skimmed the treetops of the Birkenwald, stretched to infinity the shadows of the rows of barracks, made the dark gray of the smoke gleam with the opalescent yellow of Dutch paintings, cast gentle reflections on the puddles and pools of water, tinted the bricks of the Kommandantur a bright, cheerful orange, and suddenly I had had enough and I ditched Höss there and went back to the Haus, where I spent the night writing a virulent report on the deficiencies of the camp. While I was at it, I wrote another one on the Hungarian part of the operation and, in my anger, didn't hesitate to describe Eichmann's attitude as *obstructionism*. (The negotiations with the Hungarian Jews had already been under way for two months, the offer for the trucks must have taken place a month earlier, for my visit to Auschwitz happened a few days before the Normandy landings; Becher had been complaining for a long time about the uncooperative attitude of Eichmann, who seemed to both of us to be conducting the negotiations only for the sake of form.) *Eichmann is clouded by his logistician's mentality*, I wrote. *He is incapable of understanding or integrating complex aims into his approach.* And I know on good authority that after these reports, which I sent to Brandt for the Reichsführer and directly to Pohl, Pohl summoned Eichmann to the WVHA and reprimanded him in direct and blunt terms about the condition of the consignments and the unacceptable number of dead and sick people; but Eichmann, in his stubbornness, contented himself with replying that that was the jurisdiction of the Hungarians. Against such inertia, there was nothing to be done. I was sinking into depression, and my body felt its effect: I slept badly, a sleep troubled by unpleasant dreams and interrupted three or four times a night by thirst, or else a desire to urinate that turned into insomnia; in the morning, I woke up with splitting headaches, which ruined my concentration for the day, sometimes forcing me to interrupt work and stretch out on a sofa for an hour with a cold compress on my forehead. But no matter how tired I was, I feared the return of night: periods of insomnia during which I vainly went over my problems, or my increasingly anguished dreams, I don't know what tormented me the most. Here is one of these dreams, which struck me especially: the

Rabbi of Bremen had emigrated to Palestine. But when he heard that the Germans were killing the Jews, he refused to believe it. He went to the German consulate and asked for a visa for the Reich, to see for himself if the rumors were justified. Of course, he came to a bad end. In the meantime, the scene changed: I found myself, a specialist in Jewish affairs, waiting for an audience with the Reichsführer, who wants to learn certain things from me. I am quite nervous, for it is obvious that if he is not satisfied with my replies, I am a dead man. This scene takes place in a large, dark castle. I meet Himmler in one room; he shakes my hand, a small, unremarkable, calm man, dressed in a long coat, with his eternal pince-nez with its round lenses. Then I lead him down a long hallway whose walls are covered with books. These books must belong to me, for the Reichsführer seems very impressed by the library and congratulates me on it. Then we find ourselves in another room in the process of discussing things he wants to know. Later on, it seems to me that we are outside, in the midst of a city in flames. My fear of Heinrich Himmler is gone, I feel entirely safe with him, but now I'm afraid of the bombs, of the fire. We have to sprint through the burning courtyard of a building. The Reichsführer takes my hand: "Trust me. Whatever happens, I won't let you go. We'll cross together or we'll fail together." I don't understand why he wants to protect the *Judelein*, the little Jew I am, but I trust him, I know he's sincere, I could even feel love for this strange man.

But I really should tell you about those famous negotiations. I didn't participate in them directly: only once did I meet Kastner, with Becher, when Becher was negotiating one of those private agreements that made Eichmann so upset. But I took a keen interest in them because one of the propositions consisted in putting a certain number of Jews "on ice," that is, sending them to work without going through Auschwitz, which would have suited me perfectly. This Becher was the son of a high-society businessman in Hamburg, a cavalryman who had ended up as an officer in the *Reiter-SS* and had distinguished himself several times in the East, especially in the beginning of 1943, on the Don front, where he had gotten the German Cross in gold; since then, he occupied important logistical functions at the *SS-Führungshauptamt*, the FHA that supervised the entire Waffen-SS. After he had gotten his hands on the Manfred-Weiss Werke—he never spoke to me about it, and I know how it happened just from books, but apparently it began entirely by chance—the Reichsführer ordered him to continue negotiations with the Jews, while giving similar instructions to Eichmann, no doubt on purpose, so that they would compete with each other. And Becher could promise a lot, he had the Reichsführer's ear, but wasn't in principle responsible for Jewish affairs and had no direct authority over the matter, even less than I did. All sorts of other people were mixed up in this business: a team of Schellenberg's guys, noisy, undisciplined, some from the former Amt VI, such as Höttl, who went by the name of Klages and later on published a book under yet another name, others from Canaris's Abwehr, Gefrorener (alias Dr. Schmidt), Durst (alias Winniger), Laufer (alias Schröder), but maybe I'm mixing up the names and the pseudonyms, there was also that odious Paul Carl Schmidt, the future Paul Carrell whom I've already mentioned, and who I don't think I'm confusing with Gefrorener alias Dr. Schmidt, but I'm not so sure about that. And the Jews gave money and jewelry to all these people, and they all took it, in the name of their respective services or else for themselves, impossible to know; Gefrorener and his colleagues, who in March had placed Joel Brandt under arrest to "protect" him from Eichmann, had asked him for several thousand dollars to introduce him to Wisliceny, and then Wisliceny, Krumey, and Hunsche had received a lot of money from him, before the matter of the trucks came up. But I never met Brandt, it was Eichmann who dealt with him, then he left quite quickly for Istanbul and never came back. I saw his wife, once, at the Majestic, with Kastner; she was a girl of a pronounced Jewish type, not really beautiful, but with a lot of character, it was Kastner who introduced her to me as Brandt's wife. The idea of the trucks, no one really knows who had it first, Becher said it was he, but I'm convinced it was Schellenberg who whispered the idea to the Reichsführer, or else if it really was an idea of Becher's then Schellenberg developed it, whatever the case at the beginning of April the Reichsführer summoned Becher and Eichmann to Berlin (it was Becher who told me this, not Eichmann) and gave Eichmann the order to motorize the Eighth and Twenty-second SS Cavalry Divisions, with trucks, about ten thousand, that he was to get from the Jews. And so this is the famous story of the proposition known as "goods for blood," ten thousand trucks equipped for winter in exchange for a million Jews, which has made a lot of ink flow and will continue to do so. I don't have a lot to add to what has already been said: the main participants, Becher, Eichmann, the Brandt-Kastner pair, all survived the war and testified about this affair (though the unfortunate Kastner was killed three years before Eichmann's arrest, in 1957, by Jewish extremists in Tel Aviv—for his "collaboration" with us, which is sadly ironic). One of the clauses of the proposition made to the Jews stipulated that the trucks would be used solely on the Eastern Front, against the Soviets, but not against the Western powers; and these trucks, of course, could only have come from the American Jews. Eichmann, I'm convinced, took this proposition literally, all the more so

since the commander of the Twenty-second Division, SS-Brigadeführer
August Zehender, was one of his good friends: he really thought that
motorizing these divisions was the objective, and even if he grumbled
at "letting go" of so many Jews, he wanted to help his friend Zehender.
As if some trucks could have changed the course of the war. How many
trucks or tanks or planes could a million Jews have built, if we had ever
had a million Jews in the camps? The Zionists, I suspect, and Kastner in
the lead, must have understood right away that it was a lure, but a lure
that could also serve their own interests, let them gain time. They were
lucid, realistic men, they must have known as well as the Reichsführer
that not only would no enemy country ever agree to deliver ten thousand trucks to Germany, but also that no country, even at that time, was
ready to welcome a million Jews, either. For my part, it was in the stip-
ulation according to which the trucks would not be used in the West
that I see Schellenberg's hand. For him, as Thomas had led me to understand, there was only one solution left, breaking the unnatural alliance between the capitalist democracies and the Stalinists, and playing
the "bulwark of Europe against Bolshevism" card to the end. Postwar
history has since proven that he was entirely right, and that he was only
ahead of his time. The proposition of the trucks could have had several
meanings. Of course, you never knew, a miracle could happen, the Jews
and Allies could agree to the deal, and then it would have been easy to
use those trucks to create dissension between the Russians and the Anglo-Americans, even incite them to turn against each other. Himmler
possibly dreamed about that; but Schellenberg was much too realistic to
place his hopes in that scenario. For him, the whole affair must have
been much simpler, it was a question of sending a diplomatic signal, via
the Jews who still had a certain influence, that Germany was ready to
discuss anything, a separate peace, a cessation of the extermination program, and then to watch how the English and the Americans reacted so
as to pursue other approaches: a trial balloon, in other words. And
what's more the Anglo-Americans interpreted it that way at once, as
their reaction proves: information about the proposition was published
in their newspapers and denounced. It is also possible that Himmler
thought that if the Allies refused the offer, that would demonstrate that
they didn't care about the lives of the Jews, or even that they secretly
approved of our measures; at the very least, that would throw part of
the responsibility onto them, it would *drag them in* as Himmler had already dragged in the Gauleiters and the other dignitaries of the regime.
Whatever the case, Schellenberg and Himmler didn't give up, and negotiations continued until the end of the war, as we know, always with
the Jews as stake; Becher even managed, thanks to intervention of the

Jews, to meet McClellan, Roosevelt's man, in Switzerland, a violation by the Americans of the Tehran agreements, which led to nothing for us. For a long time already I had had nothing to do with this: from time to time, rumors reached me, via Thomas or Eichmann, but that was all. Even in Hungary, as I've explained, my role remained peripheral. I got especially interested in these negotiations after my visit to Auschwitz, at the time of the Anglo-American Normandy landings, around the beginning of June. The mayor of Vienna, the (honorary) SS-Brigade-führer Blaschke, had asked Kaltenbrunner to send him some *Arbeitsjuden* for his factories, which desperately lacked workers; and I saw this as an occasion both to advance Eichmann's negotiations—these Jews, delivered to Vienna, could have been considered as "on ice"—and to obtain labor. So I set about pushing the negotiations in that direction. It was at that time that Becher introduced me to Kastner, an impressive man, always perfectly elegant, who dealt with us as equals, with a complete disregard for his own life, which gave him a certain strength when confronted with us: no one could make him afraid (there were attempts, he was arrested many times, by the SP or by the Hungarians). He sat down without being invited to do so by Becher, took an aromatic cigarette out of a silver case, and lit it without asking us for permission, and without offering us one, either. Eichmann claimed he was very impressed by his coldness and his ideological rigor and thought that if Kastner had been a German, he would have made a very good officer in the *Staatspolizei*, which for him was probably the highest compliment possible. "He thinks like us, that Kastner," he said to me one day. "He thinks only about the biological potential of his race, he is ready to sacrifice all the old to save the young, the strong, the fertile women. He thinks about the future of his race. I said to him: 'Me, if I were Jewish, I'd have been a Zionist, a fanatical Zionist, like you.'" The Viennese offer interested Kastner: he was ready to put down money, if the security of the Jews being sent could be guaranteed. I transmitted this offer to Eichmann, who was worried sick because Joel Brandt had disappeared and there was no reply about the trucks. Becher, during this time, was negotiating his own arrangements, evacuating Jews in small groups, especially via Romania, for money of course, gold, merchandise, Eichmann was mad with rage, he even ordered Kastner to stop talking to Becher; Kastner, of course, didn't pay any attention to him, and Becher arranged for his family to get out. Eichmann, seething with indignation, told me that Becher had shown him a gold necklace he was planning on offering the Reichsführer for his mistress, a secretary with whom he had a child: "Becher has a hold on the Reichsführer, I don't know what to do anymore," he groaned. In the end, my maneuverings had some success: Eichmann got sixty-five thousand reichsmarks and some rather rancid coffee, which he regarded as an advance on the five million Swiss francs he had asked for, and eighteen thousand young Jews left to work in Vienna. I proudly reported this to the Reichsführer, but received no reply. In any case, the Einsatz was already reaching its end, even though we didn't know that yet. Horthy, apparently terrified by BBC broadcasts and American diplomatic cables intercepted by his services, had summoned Winkelmann to ask him what was happening to the evacuated Jews, who were still, after all, Hungarian citizens; Winkelmann, not knowing what to reply, had in turn summoned Eichmann. Eichmann told us about this episode, which he found hilarious, one night at the bar in the Majestic; Wisliceny and Krumey were there, along with Trenker, the KdS for Budapest, an affable Austrian, a friend of Höttl's. "I told him: we're sending them to work," Eichmann said, laughing. "He didn't ask me anything else." Horthy wasn't satisfied with this rather evasive response: on June 30, he put off the evacuation of Budapest, which was supposed to begin the next day; a few days later, he completely forbade it. Eichmann still managed, despite the prohibition, to empty Kistarcsa and Szarva: but that was only a gesture *to save face*. The evacuations were over. There were a few more episodes: Horthy dismissed Endre and Baky, but was forced under German pressure to take them back; later on, at the end of August, he removed Sztójay and replaced him with Lakatos, a conservative general. But by then I had been gone for some time: sick, exhausted, I had returned to Berlin, where I ended up collapsing. Eichmann and his colleagues had managed to evacuate four hundred thousand Jews; out of those, barely fifty thousand had been retained for industry (plus the eighteen thousand in Vienna). I was shattered, horrified by so much incompetence, obstruction, ill will. Eichmann was doing hardly any better than I. I had seen him one last time before I left, in his office at the beginning of July: he was both elated and gnawed by doubts. "Hungary, Obersturmbannführer, is my masterpiece. Even if we have to stop here. You know how many countries I've already emptied of their Jews? France, Holland, Belgium, Greece, part of Italy, Croatia. Germany too of course, but that was easy, it was simply a technical question of transport. My only failure is Denmark. But here I gave Kastner more Jews than I let go in Denmark. What's a thousand Jews? Dust. Now, I'm sure, the Jews will never get over it. Here it's been magnificent, the Hungarians offered them to us like sour beer, we just couldn't work fast enough. Too bad we had to stop, maybe we'll be able to continue later." I listened to him without saying anything. Tics were distorting his face even more than usual, he rubbed his nose, twisted his neck. Despite these proud words, he seemed very despondent. Suddenly he asked me: "And what about me, in all this? What's going to become of me? What's going to become of my family?" A few days before, the RSHA had intercepted a radio broadcast from New York that gave the numbers of Jews killed in Auschwitz, numbers that were quite close to the truth. Eichmann must have known, as he must have known that his name figured on all our enemies' lists. "You want my honest opinion?" I said gently.—"Yes," replied Eichmann. "You know that despite our differences, I've always respected your opinion."—"Well, if we lose the war, you're finished." He raised his head: "I know that. I don't plan on surviving. If we're vanquished, I'll put a bullet in my head, proud of having done my duty as an SS officer. But if we don't lose?"—"If we don't lose," I said even more softly, "you'll have to evolve. You can't always go one like this. Postwar Germany will be different, a lot of things will change, there will be new tasks. You'll have to adapt." Eichmann remained silent, and I took my leave to return to the Astoria. Along with the insomnia and the migraines, I was beginning to have strong spikes of fever, which vanished as abruptly as they had come. But what ended up completely depressing me was the visit of the two bulldogs, Clemens and Weser, who presented themselves at my hotel without prior notice. "But what are you doing here?" I exclaimed.—"Well, Obersturmbannführer," said Weser, or maybe Clemens, I forget which, "we came to talk with you."—"But what do you want to talk about?" I said, exasperated. "The case is closed."—"Ah, but actually, it isn't," said Clemens, I think. Both of them had taken off their hats and sat down without asking leave, Clemens on a rococo chair too small for his bulk, Weser perching on a long sofa. "You're not implicated, fine. We completely accept that. But the investigation into these murders is continuing. We're still looking for your sister and those twins, for example."—"Can you believe, Obersturmbannführer, that the French sent us the make of the clothes they found, you remember? In the bathroom. Thanks to that, we worked our way back to a well-known tailor, a certain Pfab. You've ordered some suits from Herr Pfab before, Obersturmbannführer?" I smiled: "Of course. He's one of the best tailors in Berlin. But I warn you: if you continue to investigate me, I'll ask the Reichsführer to have you dismissed for insubordination."—"Oh!" Weser exclaimed. "No need to threaten us, Obersturmbannführer. We have nothing against you. We just want to continue to interview you as a witness."—"Precisely," Clemens said in his coarse voice. "As a witness." He handed his notebook to Weser, who leafed through it, then returned it to him, indicating a page. Clemens read, then passed the notebook back to Weser. "The French police," whispered the latter, "found the late Herr

Moreau's last will. I can assure you right now, you're not named. Nor is your sister. Herr Moreau leaves everything, his fortune, his companies, his house, to the two twins."—"We," grumbled Clemens, "find that strange."—"Quite," continued Weser. "After all, from what we understand, they're just children who were taken in, maybe from your mother's family, maybe not, but not in any case from his own family." I shrugged: "I've already told you that Moreau and I didn't get along. I'm not surprised that he didn't leave me anything. But he didn't have any children, or any family. He must have ended up feeling close to those twins."—"Let's suppose so," said Clemens. "Let's suppose so. But still: they may have been witnesses to the crime, they inherit, and they disappear, thanks to your sister who has apparently not returned to Germany. And you, couldn't you enlighten us a little about it? Even if you have nothing to do with any of that."—"Meine Herren," I replied, clearing my throat, "I've already told you everything I know. If you came to Budapest to ask me that, you've wasted your time."—"Oh, you know," said Weser venomously, "we never completely waste our time. We always find something useful. And also, we like talking with you."— "Yeah," ejected Clemens. "It's very pleasant. What's more, we'll keep at it."—"Because, you see," said Weser, "once we begin something, we have to follow it through to the end."—"Yes," approved Clemens, "otherwise it wouldn't make any sense." I didn't say anything, just looked at them coldly, and at the same time I was full of fear, for I saw that these lunatics were convinced I was guilty, they wouldn't stop persecuting me, something had to be done. But what? I was too depressed to react. They asked me some more questions about my sister and her husband, to which I replied absentmindedly. Then they got up to leave. "Obersturmbannführer," said Clemens, his hat already on his head, "it's a real pleasure chatting with you. You're a reasonable man."—"We hope very much it won't be the last time," said Weser. "Do you plan on returning to Berlin soon? You're going to have a shock: the city isn't what it used to be."

Weser wasn't wrong. I returned to Berlin in the second week of July to report on my activities and await new instructions. I found the Reichsführer's and the RSHA's offices hard hit by the March and April bombings. The Prinz-Albrecht-Palais had been completely destroyed by high-explosive bombs; the SS-Haus was still standing, but only partly, and my office had had to move again, to another annex of the Ministry of the Interior. An entire wing of the *Staatspolizei* headquarters had burned down, giant cracks zigzagged through the walls, boards blocked up the gaping windows; most of the departments and sections had moved to the suburbs or even distant villages. *Häftlinge* were still working to repaint the hallways and stairways and clear away the rubble of the destroyed offices; several of them had been killed during a raid in the beginning of May. In town, for the people who stayed, life was hard. There was almost no running water, soldiers delivered two buckets a day to destitute families, no electricity, no gas. The functionaries who still laboriously came to work wrapped scarves around their faces to protect themselves from the perpetual smoke of the fires. Obeying Goebbels's patriotic propaganda, women no longer wore hats, nor elegant clothing; those who ventured out into the streets wearing makeup were scolded. The big raids with several hundred aircraft had stopped sometime ago; but the little Mosquito attacks continued, unpredictable, exhausting. We had finally launched our first rockets against London, not Speer's and Kammler's, but little ones from the Luftwaffe that Goebbels had baptized V-1, for *Vergeltungswaffen*, "retribution weapons"; they had little effect on English morale, even less on that of our own civilians, much too downcast by the bombings in central Germany and the disastrous news from the front, the successful landings in Normandy, the surrender of Cherbourg, the loss of Monte Cassino, and the debacle at Sebastopol at the end of May. The Wehrmacht was still keeping quiet about the terrible Soviet breakthrough in Byelorussia, few people knew about it, even though rumors were already flying, still short of the truth, but I knew everything, especially that in three weeks the Russians had reached the sea, that the Army Group North was cut off on the Baltic, and that the Army Group Center no longer existed at all. In this glum atmosphere, Grothmann, Brandt's deputy, gave me a cold, almost scornful welcome, he seemed to want to blame me personally for the poor results of the Hungarian Einsatz, and I let him talk, I was too demoralized to protest. Brandt himself was in Rastenburg with the Reichsführer. My colleagues seemed in utter confusion, no one really knew where he was supposed to go or what he was supposed to be doing. Speer, after his illness, had never tried to contact me again, but I still received copies of his furious letters to the Reichsführer: since the beginning of the year, the Gestapo had arrested more than three hundred thousand people for various offences, including two hundred thousand foreign workers, who had gone to increase the workforce in the camps; Speer was accusing Himmler of poaching his labor and was threatening to go to the Führer. Our other interlocutors were piling up complaints and criticisms, especially the Jägerstab, which believed itself deliberately wronged. Our own letters or requests received only indifferent replies. But that was all the same to me, I read through this correspondence without understanding half of it. Among the pile of mail awaiting me, I found a letter from Judge Baumann: I hastily tore open the envelope, took out a brief note and a photograph. It was a reproduction of an old picture, grainy, slightly blurry, with strongly contrasting tones; one could make out men on horseback in the snow, with disparate uniforms, metal helmets, navy caps, astrakhan hats; Baumann had drawn a cross in ink over one of these men, who was wearing a long coat with an officer's stripes; his oval, minuscule face was completely indistinct, unrecognizable. On the back, Baumann had written COURLAND, NEAR WOLMAR, 1919. His polite note told me nothing more.

Luck had been with me: my apartment had survived. Once again not a window remained, my neighbor had blocked the openings as well as she could with boards and canvas tarps; in the living room, the windows of the sideboard had been blown out, the ceiling had cracked, and the chandelier fallen; a burned smell stubbornly suffused my bedroom, for the apartment next to mine had caught fire when a firebomb had gone through the window; but it was livable and even tidy: my neighbor, Frau Zempke, had cleaned everything and re-whitewashed the walls to mask the traces of smoke; oil lamps, polished and filled, were lined up on the sideboard; a barrel and several cans of water cluttered up the bathroom. I opened the French windows and all the windows whose frames hadn't been nailed shut, to take advantage of the late afternoon light, then went downstairs to thank Frau Zempke, to whom I gave some money for her trouble—she would probably have preferred Hungarian sausages, but once again I hadn't even thought of that—and also coupons, so she could prepare food for me: these, she explained, wouldn't be of much use, the store where most of them were registered no longer existed, but if I gave her a little more money, she would make do. I went back upstairs. I pulled an armchair in front of the open balcony, it was a calm, beautiful summer evening; of half of the surrounding buildings, only empty, silent façades remained, or piles of rubble, and I contemplated this end-of-the-world landscape for a long time; the park at the foot of the building remained silent, all the children must have been sent out to the country. I didn't even put on any music, so I could take advantage of this quietness and calm a little. Frau Zempke brought me some sausage, bread, and a little soup, apologizing for not being able to do any better, but that suited me very well, I had gotten some beer at the *Staatspolizei* bar and I ate and drank with pleasure, caught in the curious illusion of floating on an island, a peaceful haven in the midst of the disaster. After clearing the table, I poured myself a large glass of cheap schnapps, lit a cigarette, and sat down, feeling in my pocket for Baumann's envelope. But I didn't take it out right away; I looked at the evening light playing on the ruins, a long, slanting light that turned the limestone façades yellow and passed through the gaping windows to illumine the chaos of charred beams and collapsed walls. In some apartments, you could see traces of the life that had gone on there: a frame with a photograph or a reproduction still hanging on the wall, torn wallpaper, a table half suspended in the void with its red-and-white-checked tablecloth, a column of tile stoves still recessed in the wall on each floor, while all the floors had disappeared. Here and there, people went on living: one could see laundry hanging from a window or a balcony, flowerpots, smoke from a stovepipe. The sun set quickly behind the ravaged buildings, projecting huge, monstrously deformed shadows. This, I said to myself, is what the capital of our eternal Reich is reduced to; whatever happens, we won't have enough of the rest of our lives to rebuild. Then I set up a few oil lamps next to me and finally took the photograph out of my pocket. This image, I must confess, frightened me: no matter how much I gazed at it, I didn't recognize this man whose face, under his helmet, was reduced to a white spot, not completely shapeless, you could make out a nose, a mouth, two eyes, but featureless, without distinctive markings, it could have been anyone's face, and I didn't understand, as I drank my schnapps, how that could be possible, how, looking at this poorly reproduced, bad photograph, I couldn't say to myself, instantly, without hesitation, Yes, that is my father, or else, No, that is not my father, such doubt was unbearable to me, I had finished my drink and poured myself another, I still examined the photo, wracked my memory to collect scraps about my father, about his appearance, but it was as if the details were fleeing each other and escaping me, the white spot on the photograph drove them away like two magnet tips with the same polarity, scattered them, corroded them. I didn't have a single picture of my father: sometime after his departure, my mother had destroyed them all. And now this ambiguous, elusive photograph was ruining whatever memories remained in me, was replacing his living presence with a blurry face and a uniform. Overcome with rage, I tore the photograph into pieces and threw them off the balcony. Then I emptied my glass and immediately poured another. I was sweating, I wanted to jump out of my skin, which felt too tight for my anger and my anguish. I got undressed and sat down naked in front of the open balcony, without even bothering to put out the lamps. Holding my sex and my scrotum in one hand, like a little wounded sparrow picked up in a field, I emptied glass after glass and smoked furiously; when the bottle was empty, I took it by the neck and hurled it far away, toward the park, without worrying about possible passersby. I wanted to keep throwing things, to empty the apartment, toss out the furniture. I went to splash a little water on my face and, raising an oil lamp, looked at myself in the mirror: my features were pale, distraught, I had the impression that my face was melting like wax deformed by the heat of my ugliness and hatred, my eyes were gleaming like two black pebbles stuck in the middle of these hideous, insane shapes, nothing held together anymore. I flung my arm back and hurled the lamp against the mirror, which shattered, a little hot oil gushed out and burned my shoulder and neck. I returned to the living room and lay down in a ball on the sofa. I was trembling, my teeth were chattering. I don't know where I found the strength to go over to my bed, it was certainly because I was dying of cold, I rolled up under the blankets, but that didn't change much. My skin was crawling, shivers shook my spine, cramps streaked through my neck and made me moan with discomfort, and all these sensations rose up in great waves, carried me away into murky, agitated water, and at each movement I thought it couldn't get any worse, then I was carried off again and found myself in a place where the previous pains and sensations seemed almost pleasant, a child's exaggeration. My mouth was dry, I couldn't unstick my tongue from the pasty coating surrounding it, but I couldn't even dream of standing up to get some water. I wandered this way for a long time through the dense woods of fever, my body haunted by old obsessions: with the shivers and cramps, a kind of erotic furor traversed my paralyzed body, my anus tingled, I had a painful hard-on, but I couldn't make the slightest gesture to relieve myself, it was as if I were jerking off with my hand full of ground glass, I let myself be carried by that as by the rest. At certain times, these violent and contradictory currents made me slide into sleep, for anguishing images filled my mind, I was a little naked child crouching and shitting in the snow, and I raised my head to see myself surrounded by riders with stony faces, in coats from the Great War but carrying long spears rather than rifles, and silently judging me for my inadmissible behavior, I wanted to flee, but it was impossible, they formed a circle around me, and in my terror I floundered in my shit, I soiled myself as one of the riders, with blurry features, detached from the group and advanced toward me. But that image disappeared, I must have drifted in and out of sleep and these oppressive dreams the way a swimmer, on the sea's surface, rises above and sinks below the limit between air and water, sometimes I rediscovered my useless body, which I would have liked to get rid of the way you shed a wet coat, then I set off into another muddled, confused narrative, where foreign policemen were pursuing me, bundling me into a patrol wagon that went over a cliff, I'm not sure, there was a village, stone houses stacked in tiers on a slope, and around them pine trees and maquis, a village perhaps in the Provençal backcountry, and I wanted that, a house in this village and the peace it could have brought me, and at the end of long adventures my situation found its resolution, the threatening policemen disappeared, I had bought the lowest house in the village, with a garden and a terrace and then the pine forest around it, oh sweet cliché country postcard image, and then it was night, there was a shower of shooting stars in the sky, meteorites burned with a pink or red gleam and fell slowly, vertically, like the dying sparks of fireworks, a large shimmering curtain, and I watched that, and the first of these cosmic projectiles touched the earth and at that place strange plants began to grow, multicolor organisms, red, white, spotted, thick and fat like certain kinds of seaweed, they grew larger and rose to the sky at a crazed speed, till they were several hundred meters high, scattering clouds of seeds that in turn gave birth to similar plants that grew upward but crushed everything around them by the force of their irresistible growth, trees, houses, cars, and terrified, I watched a giant wall of these plants filling the horizon of my sight and stretching in all directions, and I understood that this event that had seemed so harmless to me was in fact the final catastrophe, these organisms, come from outer space, had found our earth and our atmosphere to be an environment that was infinitely favorable to them and they were multiplying at an insane rate, occupying all the free space and crushing everything beneath them, blindly, without animosity, simply by the force of their urge to live and grow, nothing could check them, and in a few days the earth would disappear beneath them, everything that had made our life and our history and our civilization was going to be wiped away by these greedy vegetables, it was idiotic, an unfortunate accident, but there would never be time to find a way to counterattack, humanity was going to be erased. The meteorites continued falling and shimmering, the plants, moved by the mad, out-of-control life within them, rose to the sky, strove to fill the entire atmosphere, so intoxicating to them. And I understood then, but perhaps it was later on, when I came up from this dream, that this was right, that it was the law of every living thing, every organism just wants to live and reproduce, without malice, Koch's bacilli, which had eaten away the lungs of Pergolesi and of Purcell, of Kafka and of Chekhov, had no animosity for us, they didn't wish their hosts harm, but it was the law of their survival and their development, just as we fight those bacilli with medicines that we invent every day, without hatred, for our own survival, and our whole life is thus built on the murder of other creatures who also want to live, the animals we eat, the plants too, the insects we exterminate, whether they're actually dangerous, like scorpions or fleas, or simply annoying, like flies, that scourge of mankind, which one of us hasn't killed a fly whose irritating buzzing was disturbing his reading, that's not cruelty, it's the law of our life, we are stronger than other living beings and we do as we please with their lives and their deaths, cows, chickens, ears of wheat are on earth to serve us, and it's normal that among ourselves we act the same way, that each human group wants to exterminate those who challenge it over land, water, air, why, indeed, treat a Jew better than a cow or a Koch's bacillus, if we could, and if the Jew could he'd do the same with us, or with others, to guarantee his own life, that's the law of all things, the permanent war of all against all, and I know there's nothing original about this thought, that it's almost a commonplace of biological or social Darwinism, but that night in my fever its force of truth struck me as never before or since, stimulated by that dream where humanity succumbed to another organism whose life power was greater than our own, and I understood of course that this rule was true for everyone, that if others turned out to be stronger than we, they would do to us in turn what we had done to others, and that faced with these drives, the frail barriers that men erect to try to regulate common life, laws, justice, morality, ethics count for little, that the slightest fear or the slightest strong surge bursts them like straw fences, but that then too those who took the first step should not expect that the others, when their time comes, will respect justice or the laws, and I was afraid, for we were losing the war.

I had left my windows open and little by little dawn spilled into the apartment. Slowly, the fluctuations of my fever brought me back to an awareness of my body, of the soaking sheets wrapped around it. A violent urge finally finished waking me up. I don't really know how, but I managed to drag myself to the bathroom and sit on the toilet and empty myself, a long diarrhea that seemed never to end. When it finally stopped I wiped myself as well as I could, took the slightly dirty glass where I kept my toothbrush, and drew some water from the bucket to drink greedily the bad water that seemed to come from the purest spring to me; but pouring the rest of the bucket into the toilet bowl full of waste (the flush had stopped working a long time ago) was beyond me. I went back to roll myself up in the blankets and shivered violently, for a long time, overwhelmed by the effort. Later on I heard someone knocking on the door: it must have been Piontek, whom I usually met in the street, but I didn't have the strength to get up. The fever came and went, at times dry and almost gentle, at other times a blaze raging through my body. The telephone rang several times, each ring pierced my eardrums like a knife, but I couldn't do anything, could neither answer it nor disconnect it. The thirst had returned immediately and absorbed most of my attention, which, now almost detached from everything, coldly studied my symptoms, as if from without. I knew that if I didn't do something, if no one came, I would die here, on this bed, in pools of excrement and urine, for, incapable of getting up, I was soon going to have to go in my bed. But that idea didn't bother me, didn't arouse any pity or fear in me, I felt nothing but scorn for what I had become and wished neither that it stop nor that it continue. In the midst of the wanderings of my sick mind, daylight now lit up the apartment, the door opened and Piontek came in. I took him for another hallucination and just smiled foolishly when he spoke to me. He came over to my bed, touched my forehead, distinctly uttered the word "Shit," and called Frau Zempke, who must have opened the door for him. "Go get something to drink," he said to her. Then I heard him telephoning. He came back to see me: "Can you hear me, Obersturmbannführer?" I signed yes. "I called the office. A doctor is coming. Unless you'd rather I take you to the hospital?" I signed no. Frau Zempke returned with a jug of water; Piontek poured some into a glass, raised my head, and had me drink a little. Half of the glass spilled onto my chest and the sheets. "More," I said. Frau Zempke closed the windows. "Leave them open," I ordered.—"Do you want to eat something?" asked Piontek.—"No," I replied, and let myself fall back onto my soaking pillow. Piontek opened the wardrobe, took out some clean sheets, and began changing the bed. The dry sheets were cool, but too rough for my skin which had become hypersensitive, I couldn't find a comfortable position. A little later, an SS doctor arrived, a Hauptsturmführer I didn't know. He examined me from head to foot, palpated me, listened to my chest—the cold metal of the stethoscope burned my skin—took my temperature, tapped my chest. "You should be in the hospital," he finally declared.—"I don't want to," I said. He made a face: "Do you have someone who can take care of you? I'll give you a shot, but you will have to take some pills, drink some fruit juice, some broth." Piontek went to talk with Frau Zempke, who had gone back downstairs, then returned to say she could take care of that. The doctor explained to me what I had but either I didn't understand any of his words or I forgot them immediately, I retained nothing of his diagnosis. He gave me a shot, abominably painful. "I'll come back tomorrow," he said. "If the fever hasn't gone down, I'll have you hospitalized."—"I don't want to be hospitalized," I mumbled.—"I assure you it's all the same to me," he said sternly. Then he left. Piontek looked upset. "All right, Obersturmbannführer, I'm going to see if I can find some things for Frau Zempke." I nodded, and he left too. A little later, Frau Zempke appeared with a bowl of broth and forced me to swallow a few spoonfuls. The lukewarm liquid overflowed from my mouth and dribbled onto my chin, which had been invaded by a rough beard; Frau Zempke patiently wiped me and began again. Then she had me drink some water. The doctor had helped me urinate, but my diarrhea was coming back; after my stay in Hohenlychen, I had lost all shyness about this, I asked Frau Zempke to help me, apologizing, and this already elderly woman did it without disgust, as if I were a little child. Finally she left me and I floated on my bed. I felt light now, calm, the shot must have relieved me a little, but I was drained of all energy, conquering the weight of the sheet to raise my arm would have been beyond my strength. It was all the same to me, I let myself go, I calmly sank into my fever and the gentle summer light, the blue sky that filled the frames of the open windows, empty and serene. In thought, I drew around me not just my sheets and my blankets but also the entire apartment, I surrounded my body with it, it was warm and reassuring, like a uterus from which I never wanted to emerge, a dark, silent, elastic paradise, agitated only by the rhythm of my heartbeats and my blood flowing, an immense organic symphony, it wasn't Frau Zempke I needed, but a placenta, I bathed in my sweat as in amniotic fluid, and I would have liked birth not to exist. The sword of fire that chased me out of this Eden was Thomas's voice: "Well! You don't look so great." He too lifted me up, made me drink a little. "You should be in the hospital," he said like the others.—"I don't want to go to the hospital," I repeated stupidly, obstinately. He looked around, went out onto the balcony, came back. "What'll you do in case of an alert? You could never go down into the basement."—"I don't care."—"At least come to my place, then. I'm in Wannsee now, you'll be quiet. My housekeeper will take care of you."—"No." He shrugged: "As you like." I wanted to piss again, I took advantage of his presence to ask him to help. He wanted to talk some more to me, but I didn't reply. Finally he left. A little later, Frau Zempke returned to fuss around me: I gave in with gloomy indifference. Toward evening, Helene appeared in my room. She was carrying a little suitcase that she put near the door; then, slowly, she took the pin out of her hat and shook her thick, slightly wavy blond hair, without taking her eyes off me. "What the hell are you doing here?" I asked coarsely.—"Thomas told me. I came to take care of you."—"I don't want anyone to take care of me," I said cantankerously. "Frau Zempke is good enough."—"Frau Zempke has a family and can't come here all the time. I'm going to stay with you until you're better." I stared at her coldly: "Go away!" She came to sit down by the bed and took my hand; I wanted to remove it but didn't have the strength. "You're burning up." She rose, took off her jacket, hung it on the back of a chair, and then went to wet a towel and returned to put it on my forehead. I let her do it in silence. "Anyhow," she said, "I don't have much to do at work. I can take the time off. Someone has to stay with you." I said nothing. Daylight was fading. She had me drink some water, tried to give me a little cold broth, then sat down next to the window and opened a book. The summer sky was turning pale, it was evening. I looked at her: she was like a stranger. Since my departure for Hungary more than three months ago, I hadn't had any contact with her, hadn't written her one letter, and it seemed to me I had almost forgotten her. I examined her gentle, serious profile and told myself it was beautiful; but this beauty had neither sense nor usefulness to me. I turned my eyes to the ceiling and let myself go for a while, I was very tired. Finally, an hour later maybe, I said without looking at her: "Go get me Frau Zempke."—"Why?" she asked, closing her book.—"I need something," I said.—"What? I'm here to help you." I looked at her: the calmness of her brown eyes irritated me like an insult. "I need to shit," I said brutally. But provoking her seemed impossible: "Explain to me what I have to do," she said calmly. "I'll help you." I explained it to her, without coarse words but without euphemisms, and she did what needed to be done. I told myself bitterly that it was the first time she saw me naked, I had no pajamas, and that she must never have imagined she would see me naked in these conditions. I wasn't ashamed of it, but I was disgusted with myself and this disgust extended to her, to her patience and her gentleness. I wanted to offend her, to masturbate in front of her, ask her for obscene favors, but it was just an idea, I would have been incapable of getting an erection, incapable of making a gesture requiring a little strength. In any case the fever was rising again, I began trembling again, sweating. "You're cold," she said when she had finished cleaning me. "Wait." She left the apartment and returned after a few minutes with a blanket which she spread over me. I was rolled up in a ball, my teeth were chattering, I felt as if my bones were banging against each other like a handful of jacks. Night still didn't come, the interminable summer day prolonged itself, it threw me into a panic, but at the same time I knew that night would bring no respite, no appeasement. Again, with great gentleness, she forced me to drink. But this gentleness made me mad with rage: What did this girl want with me? What was she thinking about, with her kindness and her goodness? Was she hoping to convince me of something this way? She was treating me as if I were her brother, her lover, or her husband. But she was neither my sister nor my wife. I shivered, waves of fever shook me, and she wiped my forehead. When her hand approached my mouth, I didn't know if I should bite it or kiss it. Then everything became completely muddled. Images came to me, I couldn't say if they were dreams or thoughts, they were the same as the ones that had so preoccupied me in the first months of the year, I saw myself living with this woman, settling my life this way, I left the SS and all the horrors that had surrounded me for so many years, my own failings fell away from me like a snakeskin during molt, my obsessions dissolved like a summer cloud, I joined the common stream. But these thoughts, far from pacifying me, revolted me: What! Bleed my dreams dry to bury my penis in her blond vagina, kiss her belly that would swell up, bearing handsome, healthy children? I saw the young pregnant women again, sitting on their suitcases in the mud of Kachau or Munkacs, I thought about their sexes discreetly nestled between their legs, beneath their round bellies, those female sexes and bellies that they would carry to the gas like a badge of honor. It's always in a woman's belly that children are made, that's what's so terrible. Why this atrocious privilege? Why must relations between men and women always come down, in the end, to impregnation? A semen bag, an incubator, a milk cow, there you have her, woman in the sacrament of marriage. As unattractive as my habits might be, they at least remained pure of such corruption. A paradox maybe, I see now as I write it, but one that at that time, in the vast spirals drawn by my overheated mind, seemed perfectly logical and coherent to me. I wanted to get up, to shake Helene, to explain all that to her, but maybe I also dreamed of that desire, for I would have been quite incapable of making a gesture. With the morning, the fever went down a little. I don't know where Helene slept, probably on the sofa, but I know she came to see me every hour, to wipe my face and make me drink a little. With the sickness all energy had withdrawn from my body, I lay there, *my limbs broken and without strength*, oh what a fine old school memory. My panic-stricken thoughts had finally dissipated, leaving behind them only a profound bitterness, a sharp desire to die quickly, to put an end to it. In the morning, Piontek arrived with a full basket of oranges, an unheard-of treasure in Germany at the time. "Herr Mandelbrod sent them to the office," he explained. Helene took two and went downstairs to Frau Zempke's to squeeze them; then, aided by Piontek, she sat me up on some pillows and had me drink the juice in small sips; it left a strange, almost metallic taste in my mouth. Piontek had a brief consultation with her that I couldn't hear, then he left. Frau Zempke came up; she had washed and dried my sheets from the day before, and she helped Helene change my bed, again soaked with the night's sweat. "It's very good you're sweating," she said, "that chases the fever away." It was all the same to me, I just wanted to rest, but I didn't have a moment of peace, the Hauptsturmführer from the day before returned and examined me glumly: "You still don't want to go to the hospital?"—"No, no, no." He went into the living room to talk with

Helene, then reappeared: "Your fever has gone down a little," he said.
"I told your friend to take your temperature frequently: if you go back
over forty-one degrees, we'll have to send you to the hospital. Is that
understood?" He gave me a shot in the buttocks, as painful as the one
the day before. "I'm leaving another one here, your friend will give it
to you tonight—that will reduce the fever during the night. Try to eat
a little." After he left, Helene brought me some broth: she took a piece
of bread, crumbled it up, soaked it in the liquid, and tried to make me
swallow it, but I shook my head, it was impossible. I still managed to
drink a little broth. As after the first shot, my head was clearer, but I felt
drained, empty. I didn't even resist when Helene patiently washed my
body with a sponge and some warm water, then dressed me in pajamas
borrowed from Herr Zempke. It wasn't until she tucked me in and
wanted to sit down to read that I exploded. "Why are you doing all
this?" I said meanly. "What do you want from me?" She closed her
book and stared at me with her large, calm eyes: "I don't want anything
from you. I just want to help you."—"Why? What are you hoping
for?"—"Nothing whatsoever." She gave a slight shrug of her shoulders.
"I came to help you out of friendship, that's all." Her back was to the
window, so her face was in the shadow; I examined it greedily, but
couldn't read anything in it. "Out of friendship?" I barked. "What
friendship? What do you know about me? We went out together a few
times, that's all, and now you've settled here as if you lived here." She
smiled: "Don't get excited like that. You're going to tire yourself out."
This smile enraged me: "But what do you know about fatigue? What!
What do you know about it?" I had sat up; I fell back, exhausted, my
head against the wall. "You have no idea, you don't know anything
about fatigue, you live your nice German girl's life, with your eyes
closed, you don't see anything, you go to work, you look for a new husband, you don't see anything that's happening around you." Her face remained calm, she didn't notice the brutality of the *du* form I was using,
I went on, spluttering through my shouts: "You know nothing about
me, nothing about what I do, nothing about my fatigue, for the three
years we've been killing people, yes, that's what we do, we kill, we kill
the Jews, we kill the Gypsies, the Russians, the Ukrainians, the Poles,
the sick, the old, the women, young women like you, the children!"
She was clenching her teeth now, and still she didn't say anything, but I
couldn't stop: "And the people we don't kill, we send them to work in
our factories, like slaves, don't you see, that's what an economic question is. Don't act all innocent! Where do you think your clothes come
from? And the flak shells that protect you from enemy planes, where do
they come from? The tanks that are holding the Bolsheviks back, in the

East? How many slaves died to make them? You've never asked yourself that kind of question?" She still wasn't reacting, and the more she remained calm and silent, the more I got carried away: "Or maybe you didn't know? Is that it? Like all the other good Germans. No one knows anything, except the ones doing the dirty work. Where did they go, your Jewish neighbors in Moabit? You've never asked yourself? To the East? We sent them to work in the East? Where? If there were six or seven million Jews working in the East, we'd have built entire cities! You don't listen to the BBC? They know! Everyone knows, everyone except the good Germans who don't want to know anything." I was raging, I must have been ashen-faced, she seemed to be listening attentively, she didn't move. "And your husband, in Yugoslavia, what was he doing, in your opinion? In the Waffen-SS? Fighting the partisans? You know what that is, fighting the partisans? We hardly ever see any partisans, so we destroy the environment where they survive. You understand what that means? Can you imagine your Hans killing women, killing their children in front of them, burning their houses with their corpses inside?" For the first time she reacted: "Be quiet! You don't have the right!"—"And why don't I have the right?" I jeered. "You think maybe I'm better? You come to take care of me, you think I'm a nice man, with a law degree, a perfect gentleman, a good catch? We're murdering people, you understand, that's what we do, all of us, your husband was a murderer, I'm a murderer, and you, you're a murderer's accomplice, you wear and you eat the fruit of our labor." She was livid, but her face showed only infinite sadness: "You are an unhappy man."— "And why's that? I like what I am. I'm rising in the ranks. Of course, it won't last. It's no use killing everybody, there are too many of them, we're going to lose the war. Instead of wasting your time playing the nurse and the nice patient, you'd do better to start thinking about getting out of here. And if I were you, I'd head west. The Yankees won't be so quick to pull out their cocks as the Ivans. At least they'll wear rubbers: those brave boys are afraid of diseases. Unless you'd prefer a stinking Mongol? Maybe that's what you dream of at night?" She was still white, but she smiled at these words: "You're delirious. It's the fever, you should hear yourself."—"I hear myself very well." I was panting, the effort had exhausted me. She went to wet a compress and returned to wipe my forehead. "What if I asked you to strip naked, would you do that? For me? Masturbate in front of me? Suck my cock? Would you do that?"—"Calm down," she said. "You're going to make the fever rise." There was nothing for it, this girl was too stubborn. I closed my eyes and abandoned myself to the sensation of the cold water on my forehead. She readjusted the pillows, pulled up the blanket. My breath came in wheezes, once again I wanted to beat her, to kick her in the belly, for her obscene, her inadmissible kindness.

In the evening, she came to give me a shot. I turned over onto my stomach with difficulty; when I pushed down my pants, the memory of certain vigorous adolescents shot briefly through my head, then crumpled, I was too tired. She hesitated, she had never given a shot before, but when she stuck the needle in, it was with a firm, sure hand. She had a little cotton soaked in alcohol and she wiped my buttocks after the injection, I found that touching, she must have remembered nurses doing that. Lying on my side, I planted the thermometer into my rectum myself to take my temperature, without paying attention to her but without trying especially to provoke her either. I must have had a little over forty degrees. Then the night began again, the third of that stone eternity, I wandered again through the underbrush and the collapsed cliffs of my thoughts. In the middle of the night, I began sweating profusely, the soaking pajamas stuck to my skin, I was barely conscious, I remember Helene's hand on my forehead and cheek, pushing back my soaking hair, brushing against my beard, she told me later that I had begun talking out loud, it drew her out of her sleep and brought her to my side, scraps of phrases, mostly incoherent, she said, but she never wanted to tell me what she had understood. I didn't insist, I felt it was better that way. The next morning, the fever had fallen below thirty-nine. When Piontek came to ask about me, I sent him to the office to get some real coffee, which I kept in reserve, for Helene. The doctor, when he came to examine me, congratulated me: "You've come through the worst, I think. But it's not over yet and you should regain your strength." I felt like the victim of a shipwreck who, after a fierce, exhausting battle with the sea, finally lets himself roll onto the sand of a beach: maybe I wasn't going to die after all. But that's a bad comparison, for a shipwrecked person swims, fights to survive, and I hadn't done anything, I had let myself be carried along and it was only death that hadn't wanted me. I greedily drank the orange juice Helene brought me. Around noon, I sat up a little: Helene was standing in the open doorway between my bedroom and the living room, leaning on the doorframe, a summer pullover on her shoulders; she was looking at me absentmindedly, a steaming cup of coffee in her hand. "I envy you, being able to drink coffee," I said.—"Oh! Wait, I'll help you."—"That's all right." I was more or less sitting up, I had managed to pull a pillow behind my back. "Please forgive me for what I said yesterday. I was despicable." She made a little sign with her head, drank some coffee, and turned her face aside, toward the French window to the balcony. After a little while, she looked at me again: "What you said . . . about the dead. Was that true?"—"You really want to know?"—"Yes." Her beautiful eyes were examining me, I seemed to glimpse a worried glint in them, but she remained calm, in control of herself. "Everything I said is true."—"The women, the children too?"—"Yes." She turned her head away, bit her upper lip; when she looked at me again, her eyes were full of tears: "It's sad," she said.—"Yes. It's horribly sad." She thought before she spoke again: "You know we are going to pay for that."—"Yes. If we lose the war, our enemies' revenge will be pitiless."—"I wasn't talking about that. Even if we don't lose the war, we are going to pay. We will have to pay." She hesitated again. "I pity you," she concluded. She didn't speak of it again, she continued her ministrations, even the most humiliating ones. But her gestures seemed to have another quality—colder, more functional. As soon as I could walk, I asked her to go home. She protested a little, but I insisted: "You must be exhausted. Go get some rest. Frau Zempke can take care of what I need." Finally she agreed and put her things into her little suitcase. I called Piontek to take her home. "I'll phone you," I said to her. When Piontek arrived, I accompanied her to the apartment door. "Thank you for taking care of me," I said, shaking her hand. She nodded but didn't say anything. "See you later," I added coldly.

I spent the following days sleeping. I still had a fever, around thirty-eight, sometimes thirty-nine; but I drank orange juice and meat broth, I ate bread, a little chicken. At night, there were frequent alerts and I ignored them (there may have been alerts during my three nights of delirium, but I don't know). These were little raids, a handful of Mosquitos that dropped a few bombs haphazardly, mostly on the administrative center. But one night Frau Zempke and her husband forced me to go down to the basement, after putting me into my bathrobe; the effort exhausted me so much that I had to be carried back up. A few days after Helene's departure, Frau Zempke burst in in the early evening, red, in curlers and a dressing gown: "Herr Obersturmbannführer! Herr Obersturmbannführer!" She had woken me up and I was annoyed: "What is it, Frau Zempke?"—"They tried to kill the Führer!" She clumsily explained to me what she had heard on the radio: there had been an assassination attempt, at the Führer's HQ, in eastern Prussia, he was unhurt, had received Mussolini in the afternoon and had already returned to work. "And so?" I asked.—"Well, it's horrible!"—"Indeed," I retorted dryly. "But the Führer is alive, you say, that's the main thing. Thank you." I went back to bed; she waited a bit, a little at a loss, then beat a retreat. I must confess that I didn't even think about this piece of news: I no longer thought about anything. A few days later, Thomas came to see me. "You look like you're getting better."—"A little," I replied. I had finally shaved, I must have vaguely resumed a human appearance; but I had trouble formulating coherent thoughts, they broke up with the effort, only scraps remained, without any link between them, Helene, the Führer, my work, Mandelbrod, Clemens and Weser, an inextricable jumble. "You heard the news," said Thomas, who had sat down by the window and was smoking. "Yes. How is the Führer doing?"—"The Führer is doing fine. But it was more than a failed assassination. The Wehrmacht, or at least part of it, wanted to pull a coup d'état." I grunted in surprise, and Thomas gave me the details of the affair. "In the beginning we thought it was limited to an officers' plot. Actually it branched out in every direction: there were cliques in the Abwehr, at the *Auswärtiges Amt*, among the old aristocrats. Even Nebe, apparently, was in on it. He disappeared yesterday after trying to cover himself by arresting some conspirators. Like Fromm. In short, it's a bloody mess. The Reichsführer was appointed head of the *Ersatzheer*, in place of Fromm. It's clear that now the SS is going to have a crucial role to play." His voice was tense, but sure and determined. "What happened at the *Auswärtiges Amt*?" I asked.—"You're thinking of your girlfriend? We've already arrested quite a few people, including some of her superiors; we should be arresting von Trott zu Solz any day now. But I don't think you have to worry about her."—"I wasn't worrying. I was asking, that's all. Are you looking into all that?" Thomas nodded yes. "Kaltenbrunner has created a special commission to investigate the ramifications of the affair. Huppenkothen is in charge, I'll be his deputy. Panzinger is probably going to replace Nebe at the Kripo. We'd already begun reorganizing everything at the *Staatspolizei* anyway; this will just speed things up."—"And what were your conspirators aiming for?"— "They're not my conspirators," he hissed. "And it varies. Most of them apparently thought that without the Führer and the Reichsführer, the West would accept a separate peace. They wanted to dismantle the SS. They didn't seem to realize that it was just another *Dolchstoss*, a stab in the back like in 'eighteen. As if Germany would have followed them, the traitors. I have the impression that a lot of them were a little in the clouds: some of them even thought they'd be allowed to keep Alsace and Lorraine, once they'd dropped their pants. And the Incorporated Territories, of course. You know, dreamers. But we'll see all that—they were so stupid, the civilians especially, that they put almost everything down in writing. We found masses of projects, lists of ministers for their new government. They had even put your friend Speer on one of the lists: I can tell you he's feeling the heat a little right now."—"And who was supposed to take the lead?"—"Beck. But he's dead. He killed himself. Fromm also had quite a few guys shot right away, to try to cover

himself." He explained the details of the attempt and the failed putsch
to me. "It could have gone either way. We've never had such a close
shave before. You have to get better: there's going to be work to do."

But I didn't want to get better right away, I was happy to vegetate a
little. I began listening to music again. Slowly, I regained my strength,
relearned gestures. The SS doctor had granted me a month's leave for
my convalescence, and I intended to take full advantage of it, whatever
happened. In the beginning of August, Helene came back to see me. I
was still weak but I could walk; I received her in pajamas and a bathrobe
and made her some tea. It was extraordinarily hot out, not a breath of
air circulated through the open windows. Helene was very pale and had
a lost look I had never seen on her before. She asked about my health;
I saw then that she was crying: "It's horrible," she said, "horrible." I was
embarrassed, I didn't know what to say. Many of her colleagues had
been arrested, people with whom she had been working for years. "It's
not possible, they must have made a mistake . . . I heard that your friend
Thomas was in charge of the investigations, couldn't you talk to
him?"—"That wouldn't do any good," I said gently. "Thomas is doing
his duty. But don't worry too much about your friends. They might just
want to ask them some questions. If they're innocent, they'll let them
go." She had stopped crying and was wiping her eyes, but her face was
still tense. "I'm sorry," she said. "But still," she went on, "we should try
to help them, don't you think?" Despite my fatigue, I remained patient:
"Helene, you have to understand what is going on right now. The
Führer was nearly assassinated, those men wanted to betray Germany. If
you try to intervene, you'll just attract suspicion. There's nothing you
can do. It's in the hands of God."—"Of the Gestapo, you mean," she
replied with an angry movement. She got hold of herself: "I'm sorry,
I'm . . . I'm . . ." I touched her hand: "It will be all right." She drank
some tea as I contemplated her. "And you?" she asked. "Are you going
to go back to your . . . work?" I looked out the window, the silent ruins, the pale blue sky clouded by the omnipresent smoke. "Not right
away. I have to get my strength back." She held her cup up, with both
hands. "What's going to happen?" I shrugged: "In general? We'll keep
on fighting, people will keep on dying, and then someday it will end,
and the ones who are still alive will try to forget all this." She lowered
her head: "I miss the days we went swimming at the pool," she murmured.—"If you like," I offered, "when I'm better, we can go back."
She looked out the window in turn: "There aren't any more pools in
Berlin," she said quietly.

Leaving, she had paused on the threshold and looked at me again. I
was going to speak, but she put a finger on my lips: "Don't say any-

thing." She left that finger on an instant too long. Then she turned heel and quickly went downstairs. I didn't understand what she wanted, she seemed to be revolving around something without daring either to approach it or leave it. This ambiguity troubled me, I would have liked her to declare herself openly; then I could have chosen, said yes or no, and it would have been settled. But she herself must not have known what it was. And what I had told her during my fit must not have made things any easier; no bath, no swimming pool would be enough to wash away such words.

I had also begun reading again. But I would have been quite incapable of reading serious books, literature; I went over the same sentence ten times before realizing I hadn't understood it. That's how I found on my shelves the Martian adventures of E. R. Burroughs, which I had brought back from the attic of Moreau's house and carefully put away without ever opening them. I read these three books at one go; but to my regret I found none of the emotion that had gripped me when I read them as a teenager, when, locked in the bathroom or buried in my bed, I forgot the external world for hours to lose myself voluptuously in the meanderings of this barbaric universe with its confused eroticism, peopled with warriors and princesses wearing nothing but weapons and jewelry, a whole weird jumble of monsters and machines. I made some surprising discoveries, though, in them, unsuspected by the dazzled boy I had been: certain passages in these science fiction novels, in fact, revealed this American prose writer as one of the unknown precursors of *völkisch* thinking. His ideas, in my idleness, led me to others; remembering Brandt's advice, which I had till then been much too busy to follow, I sent for a typewriter and wrote a brief memo for the Reichsführer, quoting Burroughs as a model for *the profound social reforms that the SS should envisage after the war*. Thus, to increase the birthrate after the war and force men to marry young, I took as an example the red Martians, who recruited their forced labor not just from criminals and prisoners of war, but also from *confirmed bachelors who were too poor to pay the high celibacy tax which all red-Martian governments impose*; and I devoted an entire chapter to this *celibacy tax* that, if it were ever imposed, would put a heavy strain on my own finances. But I reserved even more radical suggestions for the SS elite, which should follow the example of the green Martians, those three-meter-tall monsters with four arms and fangs: *All property among the green Martians is owned in common by the community, except the personal weapons, ornaments, and sleeping silks and furs of the individuals. . . . The women and children of a man's retinue may be likened to a military unit for which he is responsible in various*

*ways, as in matters of instruction, discipline, sustenance, etc. . . . His women
are in no sense wives. . . . Their mating is a matter of community interest solely,
and is directed without reference to natural selection. The council of chieftains
of each community control the matter as surely as the owner of a Kentucky racing stud directs the scientific breeding of his stock for the improvement of the
whole.* I drew inspiration from this to suggest progressive reforms of the
Lebensborn. I was actually digging my own grave, and part of me almost
laughed as I wrote it, but it also seemed to me to stem logically from
our *Weltanschauung*; what's more I knew that it would please the Reichsführer; the passages from Burroughs reminded me obscurely of the
prophetic utopia he had revealed to us in Kiev, in 1941. In fact, ten days
after I sent my memorandum, I received a reply signed by his hand (his
instructions, most of the time, were signed by Brandt or even Grothmann):

Very Dear Doktor Aue!

*I read your memorandum with keen interest. I'm happy to know
that you are recovering and that you are devoting your convalescence to
useful research; I didn't know you were interested in these questions, so
vital for the future of our race. I wonder if Germany, even after the war,
will be ready to accept such profound and necessary ideas. A lot of work
still has to be done on ways of thinking. Whatever the case, when you're
all better, I'll be happy to discuss these projects and this visionary author
with you in more detail.*

Heil Hitler!
Yours,
Heinrich Himmler

Flattered, I waited for Thomas to visit me to show him this letter, as
well as my memorandum; but to my surprise, he reacted angrily to it:
"You really think this is the right time for such childishness?" He
seemed to have lost all his sense of humor; when he started to describe
the latest arrests to me, I began to understand why. Even in my own circle some men were implicated: two of my university friends and my
former professor in Kiel, Jessen, who had apparently grown closer to
Goerdeler in recent years. "We also found evidence against Nebe, but
he's disappeared. Vanished into thin air. Well, if anyone knows how to
do that, it's he. He must have been a little twisted: at his place, there was
a movie of a gassing in the East, can you imagine him putting that on at
night?" I had rarely seen Thomas so nervous. I made him drink, offered

him cigarettes, but he didn't let much drop; I was just able to divine that Schellenberg had had contact with certain opposition circles, before the attempt. At the same time, Thomas ranted angrily against the conspirators: "Killing the Führer! How could they think that would be a solution? That he be removed from command of the Wehrmacht, all right, he's ill anyway. One could even have imagined, I don't know, forcing him into retirement, if it was really necessary, letting him remain President but handing over power to the Reichsführer . . . According to Schellenberg, the British would agree to negotiate with the Reichsführer. But killing the Führer? It's insane, they didn't realize . . . They swore an oath to him, then they try to kill him!" It seemed really to bother him; as for me, the very idea that Schellenberg or the Reichsführer had thought of putting the Führer aside shocked me. I didn't see much difference between that or killing him, but I didn't say so to Thomas; he was already too depressed.

Ohlendorf, whom I saw toward the end of the month, when I finally began to go out again, seemed to think as I did. I found him—he who had already been so glum to begin with—even more despondent than Thomas. He confessed to me that the night before the execution of Jessen, to whom he had remained close in spite of everything, he hadn't been able to sleep a wink. "I kept thinking about his wife and children. I'll try to help them, I'm going to give them part of my salary." He still thought, though, that Jessen deserved the death sentence. For years, he explained to me, our professor had broken his ties to National Socialism. They had continued to see each other, to talk, and Jessen had even tried to recruit his former student. Ohlendorf agreed with him on a number of points: "It's obvious—the widespread corruption within the Party, the erosion of the rule of law, the pluralist anarchy that's replaced the *Führerstaat*, all that's unacceptable. And the measures against the Jews, the *Endlösung*, were a mistake. But overthrowing the Führer and the NSDAP, that's unthinkable. We have to purge the Party, bring up the veterans of the front, who have a realistic vision of things, the leaders of the Hitlerjugend, maybe the only idealists we have left. It's those young people who will have to spur the Party on after the war. But we can't dream of going backward, to the middle-class conservatism of the career soldiers and the Prussian aristocrats. This deed discredits them forever. What's more, the people understand this." It was true: all the SD reports showed that ordinary people and soldiers, despite their concerns, their fatigue, their anxieties, their demoralization, even their defeatism, were scandalized by the conspirators' treason. The war effort and the campaign for austerity had re-

ceived a jolt of energy; Goebbels, finally authorized to truly declare the
"total war" he held so dear, went to great lengths to whip it up, without it really being necessary. The situation, though, was only getting
worse: the Russians had retaken Galicia and gone beyond their 1939
border, Lublin was falling, and the wave had finally died down on the
outskirts of Warsaw, where the Bolshevik command was obviously just
waiting for us to crush for them the Polish insurrection, launched at the
beginning of the month. "We're playing Stalin's game there," Ohlendorf commented. "It would be better to explain to the AK that the Bolsheviks represent a much greater danger than we do. If the Poles fought
at our side, we could still hold the Russians back. But the Führer
doesn't want to hear about it. And the Balkans are going to fall like a
house of cards." In Bessarabia, in fact, the Sixth Army, reconstituted
from scratch under Fretter-Pico, was getting itself cut into pieces a second time around: the gates to Romania gaped wide open. France was
obviously lost; after having opened another front in Provence and taken
Paris, the Anglo-Americans were getting ready to clear the rest of the
country, while our bruised troops ebbed back to the Rhine. Ohlendorf
was very pessimistic: "The new rockets are almost ready, according to
Kammler. He's convinced they will change the course of the war.
But I don't see how. A rocket carries fewer explosives than an American B-17, and can be used only once." Unlike Schellenberg, about
whom he refused to speak, he didn't have any plans or concrete solutions: he could only talk about a "final National Socialist leap forward,
a giant surge," which to me resembled Goebbels's rhetoric a little too
much. I had the impression that he was secretly resigned to defeat. But
I don't think he had yet admitted that to himself.

   The events of July 20 had another consequence—minor, but unfortunate for me: in mid-August, the Gestapo arrested Judge Baumann, of
the Berlin SS court. I learned of it fairly rapidly from Thomas, but didn't
immediately realize all the consequences. At the beginning of September, I was summoned by Brandt, who was accompanying the Reichsführer on an inspection in Schleswig-Holstein. I joined the special train
near Lübeck. Brandt began by announcing that the Reichsführer
wanted to confer the first-class distinction on my War Service Cross:
"Whatever you may have thought of it, your action in Hungary was
very positive. The Reichsführer is pleased with it. He was also favorably impressed by your recent initiative." Then he informed me that the
Kripo had asked Baumann's replacement to reopen the case against me;
the latter had written to the Reichsführer: in his opinion, the accusations deserved an investigation. "The Reichsführer hasn't changed his
mind, and you have all his confidence. But he thinks it would be detri-

mental to you to prevent an investigation again. Rumors are beginning to circulate, you must know that. The best thing would be for you to defend yourself and prove your innocence: that way, we can close the case once and for all." I didn't like this idea at all, I was beginning to know the manic stubbornness of Clemens and Weser too well, but I didn't have a choice. Back in Berlin, I went on my own initiative to introduce myself to Judge von Rabingen, a fanatical National Socialist, and explained my version of the facts to him. He retorted that the case put together by the Kripo contained disturbing elements, he kept going back to the bloodstained German clothes, made to my size, and he was also intrigued by the business with the twins, which he wanted to clear up at all costs. The Kripo had finally questioned my sister, who was back in Pomerania: she had placed the twins in a private institution, in Switzerland; she affirmed they were our orphaned second cousins, born in France, whose birth certificates had disappeared in the French rout in 1940. "That could be true," von Rabingen superciliously declared. "But for now it's unverifiable."

This permanent suspicion haunted me. For many days running, I almost succumbed to a relapse of my illness; I remained locked up at home in a black prostration, even going so far as to refuse to answer the door to Helene, who came to visit me. At night, Clemens and Weser, animated marionettes, poorly made and badly painted, jumped on my sleep, creaked through my dreams, buzzed around me like dirty little mocking creatures. My mother herself sometimes joined this chorus, and in my anguish I came to believe these two clowns were right, that I had gone mad and had in fact killed her. But I wasn't insane, I felt it, and the whole business came down to a monstrous misunderstanding. When I got hold of myself a little, I had the idea of contacting Morgen, the upright judge I had met in Lublin. He worked in Oranienburg: he immediately invited me to come see him, and received me affably. He talked to me first about his activities: after Lublin, he had set up a commission in Auschwitz, and charged Grabner, the head of the *Politische Abteilung*, for two thousand illegal murders; Kaltenbrunner had had Grabner released; Morgen had re-arrested him and the investigation was following its course, along with that of numerous accomplices and other corrupt subalterns; but in January a fire of criminal origin had destroyed the barracks where the commission stored all the evidence and some of the files, which complicated things quite a bit. Now, he confessed to me in confidence, he was aiming for Höss himself: "I'm convinced he's guilty of diversion of State property and of murder, but it will be hard for me to prove it; Höss has powerful protections. What about you? I heard you were having some problems." I explained my case to him.

"Accusing you isn't enough," he said thoughtfully, "they have to prove it. Personally, I trust your sincerity: I know the worst elements of the SS only too well, and I know you're not like them. Whatever the case, to charge you, they have to prove concrete things, that you were there at the time of the murder, that those famous clothes were yours. Where are those clothes? If they stayed in France, it seems to me that the prosecution doesn't have much to go on. And also, the French authorities who sent the request for legal assistance are now under the control of an enemy power: you should ask an expert in international law to study that aspect of things." I left this interview a little reassured: the obsessive stubbornness of the two investigators was making me paranoid, I could no longer see what was true and what was false, but Morgen's good legal sense was helping me find terra firma again.

In the end, and as always with the course of justice, this business lasted for many more months. I won't go into it in detail. I had several more confrontations with von Rabingen and the two investigators; my sister, in Pomerania, had to testify: she was on her guard, she never revealed that I had informed her of the murders; she just claimed that she had received a telegram from Antibes, from an associate of Moreau's. Clemens and Weser were forced to acknowledge that they had never seen the famous clothes: all their information came from letters from the French criminal police, which had little legal value, especially now. What's more, since the murders had been committed in France, an indictment could only have led to my extradition, which had obviously become impossible—although one lawyer did suggest to me, not at all unpleasantly, that before an SS court I could risk being sentenced to death for breach of honor, without any reference to the civil criminal code. These considerations did not seem to shake the favor the Reichsführer was showing me. During one of his lightning visits to Berlin, he had me come on board his train, and after a ceremony where I received my new decoration in the company of a dozen other officers, most of them from the Waffen-SS, he invited me into his private office to discuss my memorandum, whose ideas, according to him, were sound but required a more thorough examination. "For example, there's the Catholic Church. If we impose a celibacy tax, they'll certainly require an exemption for the clergy. And if we grant it to them, that will be another victory for them, another demonstration of their strength. Therefore, I think that a precondition for any positive development, after the war, will be to settle the *Kirchenfrage*, the question of the two Churches. Radically, if necessary: those *Pfaffen*, those little monks, are almost worse than the Jews. Don't you think so? I'm in complete agreement with the Führer about this: the Christian religion is a Jewish religion, founded by a Jewish rabbi, Saul, as a vehicle to bear Judaism to another level, the most dangerous of all, together with Bolshevism. Eliminating the Jews and keeping the Christians would be like stopping halfway." I listened gravely to all this, taking notes. Only at the end of the interview did the Reichsführer mention my case: "They haven't produced any evidence, isn't that right?"—"No, my Reichsführer. There is none."—"That's very good. I saw right away it was all nonsense. But it's better that they convince themselves of that on their own, isn't that right?" He accompanied me to the door and shook my hand after I had saluted him: "I'm very happy with your work, Obersturmbannführer. You are an officer with a bright future ahead."

A bright future? The future seemed to me rather to be growing narrower every day, mine as well as Germany's. When I turned around, I contemplated with horror the long dark corridor, the tunnel leading from the depths of the past to the present moment. What had become of the infinite plains that opened up before us when, just out of childhood, we approached the future with energy and confidence? All that energy seemed to have served only to build ourselves a prison, a gallows, even. Ever since my illness, I had stopped seeing people; sports I had left to others. Most of the time I ate alone at my place, the French windows wide open, taking advantage of the gentle end-of-summer air, of the last green leaves that, slowly, in the midst of the ruins of the city, were preparing their final blaze of color. From time to time, I went out with Helene, but a painful embarrassment tinged these meetings; we both must have been seeking the gentleness, the intense sweetness of those first months, but it had disappeared and we didn't know how to find it again, while at the same time we tried to pretend nothing had changed, it was strange. I didn't understand why she persisted in staying in Berlin: her parents had gone to a cousin's house near Baden, but when—with sincerity and not with that inexplicable cruelty I had shown while sick—I urged her to join them, she gave laughable excuses, her work, looking after the apartment. In my moments of lucidity I told myself that she was staying because of me, and I wondered if, precisely, the horror my words must have aroused in her didn't actually encourage her, if she weren't hoping, perhaps, to *save* me from myself, a ridiculous idea if ever there was one, but who knows what goes on in a woman's head? There must have been something else besides, and I glimpsed it sometimes. One day, we were walking in the street when a car drove through a puddle next to us: the stream of water gushed under Helene's skirt, spattering her up to her thigh. She let out an incongruous, almost harsh burst of laughter. "Why are you laughing so hard, what's so funny?"—"You, it's you," she let out through her laughter. "You've never touched me so far up." I didn't say anything, what could I have said? I could have had her read the memo I had sent to the Reichsführer, to put her in her place; but I felt that neither that nor even a frank explanation of my tastes would have discouraged her, she was like that, stubborn, she had made her choice almost at random and now she was obstinately sticking to it, as if the choice itself counted more than the person who had been the object of it. Why didn't I send her packing? I don't know. I didn't have many people to talk to. Thomas was working fourteen, sixteen hours a day, I hardly ever saw him. Most of my colleagues had been *relocated*. Hohenegg, I learned when I called the OKW, had been sent to the front in July, and was still in Königsberg with part of the OKHG Center. Professionally, and despite the Reichsführer's encouragements, I had reached a dead end: Speer had nothing more to do with me, I had contact only with subalterns, and my office, which was no longer asked to do anything, served almost solely as a mailbox for the complaints of numerous enterprises, agencies, or ministries. Every now and then, Asbach and the other members of the team would churn out some report that I sent out right and left; I would receive polite responses, or none at all. But I hadn't fully understood the extent to which I was on the wrong track until the day Herr Leland invited me to tea. It was at the bar of the Adlon, one of the only good restaurants still open, a veritable Tower of Babel, where a dozen languages were spoken; all the members of the foreign diplomatic corps seemed to meet there. I found Herr Leland at a table set a little apart. A maître d'hôtel came over and served me tea with precise gestures, and Leland waited until he had moved away to talk to me. "How is your health?" he enquired.—"Fine, mein Herr. I'm all better."—"And your work?"—"It's going well, mein Herr. The Reichsführer seems satisfied. I was recently decorated." He didn't say anything, but drank a little tea. "But it's been several months since I last saw Reichsminister Speer," I went on. He made an abrupt sign with his hand: "That's not important. Speer has disappointed us very much. We have to move on now."— "Toward what, mein Herr?"—"It's still being worked out," he said slowly, with his slight, somewhat peculiar accent. "And how is Dr. Mandelbrod, mein Herr?" He stared at me with his cold, severe gaze. As always I was incapable of distinguishing his glass eye from the other one. "Mandelbrod is doing fine. But I should tell you that you disappointed him a little." I didn't say anything. Leland drank a little more tea before continuing: "I must say that you haven't satisfied all our expectations. You haven't shown much initiative, these past few months. Your performance in Hungary was disappointing."—"Mein Herr . . . I did my best. And the Reichsführer congratulated me on my work. But there's so much interdepartmental rivalry, everyone makes obstructions . . ." Leland didn't seem to be paying any attention to my words. "We have the impression," he said finally, "that you haven't understood what we expect of you."—"What do you expect of me, mein Herr?"—"More energy. More creativity. You should produce solutions, not create obstacles. And also, allow me to say, you're letting yourself go. The Reichsführer forwarded your recent memorandum to us: instead of wasting your time with childish pranks, you should think about Germany's salvation." I felt my cheeks burning and made an effort to control my voice. "I am thinking of nothing else, mein Herr. But, as you know, I was very sick. I also had . . . other problems." Two days before I had had a difficult interview with von Rabingen. Leland didn't say anything; he made a sign, and the maître d'hôtel reappeared to serve him. At the bar, a young man with wavy hair, in a plaid suit with a bow tie, was laughing too loudly. A brief look was enough for me to size him up: it had been a long time since I had thought about that. Leland spoke: "We are aware of your problems. It is inadmissible that things have gone this far. If you needed to kill that woman, fine, but you should have done it properly." The blood had drained from my face: "Mein Herr . . . ," I managed to articulate in a strangled voice. "I didn't kill her. It wasn't me." He contemplated me calmly: "Very well," he said. "You should know that it's all the same to us. If you did it, it was your right, your sovereign right. As old friends of your father, we completely understand it. But what you didn't have a right to do was compromise yourself. That greatly reduces your usefulness to us." I was going to protest again, but he cut me off with a gesture. "Let's wait and see how things develop. We hope you'll get hold of yourself." I didn't say anything and he raised a finger. The maître d'hôtel reappeared; Leland whispered a few words to him and got up. I got up too. "See you soon," he said in his monotone voice. "If you need something, get in touch with us." He left without shaking my hand, followed by the maître d'hôtel. I hadn't touched my tea. I went to the bar and ordered a Cognac, which I drained in one swallow. A pleasant, drawling, strongly accented voice spoke next to me: "It's a little early in the day to drink like that. You want another one?" It was the young man with the bow tie. I accepted; he ordered two and introduced himself: Mihaï I., third secretary in the Romanian legation. "How are things going, at the SS?" he asked after clinking glasses. "At the SS? All right. And the diplomatic corps?" He shrugged: "Glum. Now there are only"—he made a wide gesture at the room—"the last of the Mohicans left. We can't really or-

ganize cocktail parties, because of the restrictions, so we meet each other
here at least once a day. Anyway I don't even have a government to represent anymore." Romania, after having declared war on Germany at
the end of August, had just capitulated to the Soviets. "That's true. What
does your legation represent, then?"—"In principle, Horia Sima. But
that's a fiction, Herr Sima can represent himself very well on his own.
Whatever the case"—he pointed again at several people—"we're all
pretty much in the same bag. Especially my French and Bulgarian colleagues. The Finns have almost all gone. The Swiss and the Swedes are
the only real diplomats left." He looked at me, smiling: "Come have
dinner with us, I'll introduce you to some other ghosts of my friends."

In my relations, as I may have said, I always took care to avoid intellectuals or men of my social class: they always wanted to talk, and had
an annoying tendency to fall in love. With Mihaï, I made an exception,
but there weren't too many risks; he was a cynic, frivolous and amoral.
He had a little house west of Charlottenburg; I let him invite me over
there the first night, after dinner, under the pretext of having a last
drink, and I spent the night there. Beneath his eccentric mannerisms, he
had the hard, taut body of an athlete, no doubt inherited from his peasant origins, brown, curly, luxuriant body hair, a rough, male odor. It
greatly amused him to have seduced an SS officer: "The Wehrmacht or
the *Auswärtiges Amt*, they're too easy." I saw him again from time to
time. Sometimes I went to see him after dining with Helene; I used him
brutally, as if to wash her silent desires out of my head, or my own ambiguity.

In October, just after my birthday, I was sent back to Hungary. Horthy had been overthrown by a coup organized by von dem Bach-
Zelewski and Skorzeny; now Szálasi's Arrow Cross Party was in power.
Kammler was clamoring for labor for his underground factories and his
V-2s, the first models of which had just been launched in September.
Soviet troops were already penetrating Hungary, from the south, as well
as the Reich's own territory, in eastern Prussia. In Budapest, the SEk
had been dissolved in September, but Wisliceny was still there and Eichmann quickly made another appearance. Once more, it was a disaster.
The Hungarians agreed to give us fifty thousand Jews from Budapest (in
November, Szálasi was already insisting on the fact that they were only
"on loan"), but they had to be conveyed to Vienna, for Kammler and
for the construction of an *Ostwall*, and there was no more transport
available: Eichmann, probably with Veesenmayer's agreement, decided
to send them there on foot. The story is well known: many died on the
road, and the officer in charge of reception, Obersturmbannführer

Höse, refused most of the ones who arrived, for once again he could not employ women for excavation work. I could do absolutely nothing, no one listened to my suggestions, not Eichmann, not Winkelmann, not Veesenmayer, not the Hungarians. When Obergruppenführer Jüttner, the head of the SS-FHA, arrived in Budapest with Becher, I tried to intercede with him; Jüttner had passed the marchers, who were falling like flies in the mud, the rain, and the snow; this spectacle had scandalized him and he did in fact go and protest to Winkelmann; but Winkelmann sent him to Eichmann, over whom he had no control, and Eichmann bluntly refused to see Jüttner—he sent one of his subordinates, who haughtily brushed aside the complaints. Eichmann, obviously, was so full of himself that he no longer listened to anyone, except maybe Müller and Kaltenbrunner, and Kaltenbrunner no longer seemed to listen even to the Reichsführer anymore. I spoke about it with Becher, who was to see Himmler; I asked him to intervene, and he promised to do what he could. As for Szálasi, he soon took fright: the Russians were advancing; in mid-November he put an end to the marches, they hadn't even sent thirty thousand, one more senseless waste, on top of the others. No one seemed to know what he was doing anymore, or rather everyone did just as he pleased, alone and separately; it was becoming impossible to work in such conditions. I made one final attempt to approach Speer, who had taken over complete control of the *Arbeitseinsatz* in October, including the use of the WVHA inmates; he finally agreed to see me, but he rushed through the interview, in which he hadn't the slightest interest. It's true that I didn't have anything concrete to offer him. As for the Reichsführer, I no longer understood his position at all. At the end of October, he gave Auschwitz the order to stop gassing the Jews, and at the end of November, declaring the Jewish question resolved, he ordered the destruction of the camp's extermination installations; at the same time, at the RSHA and at the *Persönlicher Stab*, they were actively discussing the creation of a new extermination camp in Alteist-Hartel, near Mauthausen. It was also said that the Reichsführer was conducting negotiations with the Jews, in Switzerland and Sweden; Becher seemed to know all about it, but eluded my questions when I asked him for clarification. I also learned that he finally got the Reichsführer to agree to summon Eichmann (that was later on, in December); but I didn't find out what was said on that occasion until seventeen years later, during the good Obersturmbannführer's trial in Jerusalem: Becher, having become a businessman and a millionaire in Bremen, stated in his deposition that the meeting had taken place in the Reichsführer's special train, in the Black Forest, near Triberg, and that the Reichsführer had spoken to Eichmann with *both kindness and anger*. One sentence in particular, that the Reichsführer, according to Becher, supposedly threw at his stubborn subordinate has often been quoted since in books: "Though you have been exterminating Jews up to now, from now on, if I give you the order, as I do now, you will be a nursemaid to the Jews. I should remind you that in 1933 it was I who set up the RSHA, and not Gruppenführer Müller or you. If you cannot obey me, tell me so!" This could be true. But Becher's testimony should certainly be treated with caution; he takes credit himself, for example, thanks to his influence over Himmler, for the cessation of the forced marches from Budapest— whereas the order actually came from the panicking Hungarians—and also, an even more outrageous claim, the initiative for the order to interrupt the *Endlösung*: yet if anyone could have slipped that idea to the Reichsführer, it was certainly not that clever wheeler-dealer (Schellenberg, maybe).

My legal case continued its course; Judge von Rabingen regularly summoned me to clear up one point or another. From time to time I saw Mihaï; as for Helene, she seemed to be growing increasingly transparent, not from fear, but from pent-up emotion. When, back from Hungary, I told her about the atrocities of Nyíregyháza (the Third Armored Corps had retaken the city from the Russians at the end of October, and had found women of all ages raped, parents nailed alive to doors in front of their mutilated children; and these had been Hungarians, not Germans), she looked at me for a long time, then said gently: "And in Russia, was it very different?" I didn't say anything. I looked at the extraordinarily thin wrists her sleeves revealed; I could easily have looped my thumb and index finger around them. "I know their revenge will be terrible," she said then. "But we'll have deserved it." In the beginning of November, my apartment, miraculously preserved till then, disappeared in a bombing: a bomb came through the roof and took the top two floors with it; poor Herr Zempke succumbed to a heart attack as he left the half-collapsed cellar. Fortunately, I had gotten into the habit of keeping some of my clothes and my underwear at the office. Mihaï suggested I move to his apartment; I preferred to go to Wannsee, to Thomas's place, where he had moved after his Dahlem house burned down in May. He led a wild life there, there were always a few firebrands from the Amt VI around, one or two of Thomas's colleagues, Schellenberg, and of course girls. Schellenberg often talked in private with Thomas but obviously mistrusted me. One day I came home a little early and heard an animated discussion in the living room, loud voices, Schellenberg's mocking, insistent intonation: "If that Bernadotte agrees . . ." He interrupted himself as soon as he saw me on the doorstep and greeted me in a pleasant tone: "Aue, nice to see you." But he didn't continue his conversation with Thomas. When I wearied of my friend's parties, I sometimes let myself be taken around by Mihaï. He often attended the daily farewell parties of Dr. Kosak, the Croatian ambassador, which took place either at the legation or in his villa in Dahlem; the upper crust of the diplomatic corps and the *Auswärtiges Amt* went there to stuff themselves, get drunk, and meet the prettiest UFA starlets, Maria Milde, Ilse Werner, Marikka Rökk. Around midnight, a choir sang traditional Dalmatian songs; after the usual Mosquito raid, the artillerymen from the Croatian flak battery stationed next door came to drink and play jazz till dawn; among them was an officer who had escaped from Stalingrad, but I took care not to tell him I had been there too, he would never have left me alone. These bacchanales sometimes degenerated into orgies, couples intertwined in the alcoves of the legation and frustrated idiots went out to empty their pistols in the garden: one night, drunk, I made love with Mihaï in the bedroom of the ambassador, who was snoring downstairs on a sofa; then, overexcited, Mihaï came back up with a little actress and took her in front of me as I finished a bottle of slivovitz and meditated on the servitudes of the flesh. This vain, frenetic gaiety couldn't last. At the end of December, as the Russians were attacking Budapest and our last offensive was getting bogged down in the Ardennes, the Reichsführer sent me to inspect the evacuation of Auschwitz.

In the summer, the hurried, belated evacuation of KL Lublin had caused us a lot of concern: the Soviets had taken the installations intact, with the warehouses full, grist for the mill of their atrocity propaganda. Since the end of August, their forces had been camping on the Vistula, but it was obvious they wouldn't linger there. Measures had to be taken. The evacuation of the camps and the subcamps of the Auschwitz complex, should the need arise, fell under the responsibility of Obergruppenführer Ernst Schmauser, the HSSPF for Military District VIII, which included Upper Silesia; the operations, Brandt explained to me, would be conducted by the camp personnel. My task would be to ensure that priority was given to the evacuation of the utilizable workforce, in good condition, to be put back to use within the Reich. After my Hungarian tribulations, I was on my guard: "What will my authority be?" I asked Brandt. "Can I give the necessary orders?" He eluded the question: "Obergruppenführer Schmauser has full authority. If you see that the camp personnel aren't cooperating in the right spirit, refer to him and he'll give the necessary orders."—"What if I have problems with the Obergruppenführer?"—"You won't have any problems with the Obergruppenführer. He's an excellent National Socialist. Anyway, you'll be in contact with the Reichsführer or me." I knew from experience that this was a feeble guarantee. But I had no choice.

The possibility of an enemy advance threatening a concentration camp had been raised by the Reichsführer on June 17, 1944, in a directive titled *Fall-A*, "Plan A," which granted the HSSPF of the region, in case of crisis, extensive powers over camp personnel. So if Schmauser understood the importance of preserving the maximum quantity of labor, things might just possibly unfold correctly. I went to see him at his HQ in Breslau. He was a man of the older generation, he must have been about fifty or fifty-five, severe, stiff, but professional. The evacuation plan for the camps, he explained, fell within the general framework of the ARLZ retreat strategy: *Auflockerung-Raümung-Lähmung-Zerstörung* ("Dismantling-Evacuation-Immobilization-Destruction"), formulated at the end of 1943 "and applied with so much success in the Ukraine and in Byelorussia, where the Bolsheviks not only found no housing or food, but couldn't even, in certain districts like Novgorod, recover even a single potentially useful human being." District VIII had promulgated the order to carry out ARLZ on September 19. With this in view, sixty-five thousand *Häftlinge* had already been evacuated to the Altreich, including all the Polish and Russian inmates, who were liable to present a danger in the rear in case of enemy approach. Sixty-seven thousand inmates remained, of whom thirty-five thousand were still working in the factories of Upper Silesia and neighboring regions. Already in October, Schmauser had entrusted the plans for the final evacuation as well as the last two phases of ARLZ to his liaison officer, Major der Polizei Boesenberg; I would see to the details with him, while keeping in mind that only Gauleiter Bracht, in his capacity as Reichskommissar for Defense of the *Gau*, could make the decision to implement the plans. "You understand," Schmauser declared in conclusion, "we all know how important the preservation of the labor potential is. But for us, and for the Reichsführer too, questions of security are still top priority. Such an enemy human mass, within our lines, represents a formidable risk, even if they're not armed. Sixty-seven thousand inmates is almost seven divisions: imagine seven enemy divisions roaming free behind our troops during an offensive! In October, as you may know, we had an uprising in Birkenau, among the Jews of the Sonderkommando. Fortunately it was brought under control, but we lost some men and one of the crematoriums was dynamited. Imagine that: if they had been able to link up with the Polish partisans constantly prowling around the camp, they could have caused incalculable damage, allowed thousands of inmates to escape! And since August, the Americans come to bomb the IG Farben factory, and each time, inmates take advantage of it to try to escape. For the final evacuation, if it takes place, we must do everything we can to prevent such a situation from occurring again. We'll have to keep our eyes open." I understood this point of view very well, but I was afraid of the practical consequences that might result from it. Boesenberg's briefing didn't do much to reassure me. On paper, his plan had been meticulously prepared, with precise maps for all the evacuation routes; but Boesenberg harshly criticized Sturmbannführer Bär, who had refused to participate in consultations about the development of this plan (a final administrative reorganization, at the end of November, had left the former baker as Kommandant of the recombined camps I and II, as well as Standortältester of the three camps and of all the *Nebenlager*); Bär had given as pretext that the HSSPF had no authority over the camp, which was technically true until *Fall-A* was declared, and he would only accept to report to Amtsgruppe D. A close, flexible cooperation of the authorities in charge, during an evacuation, didn't look very likely. Furthermore—and this worried me even more after my experiences in October and November—Boesenberg's plan anticipated an evacuation of the camps on foot, with the inmates having to walk between fifty-five and sixty-three kilometers before being put on trains in Gleiwitz and Loslau. This plan was logical: the war situation anticipated by the plan wouldn't allow full use of the railroads close to the front; in any case the rolling stock was desperately scarce (in all of Germany, only some two hundred thousand cars were left, a loss of more than 70 percent of the railway equipment in two months). The evacuation of German civilians, who had priority, also had to be considered, along with foreign workers and war prisoners. On December 21, Gauleiter Bracht had promulgated a complete *U-Plan/Treckplan* for the province, incorporating into it Boesenberg's plan, according to which the inmates of the KL, for security reasons, would have priority for crossing the Oder, the main bottleneck on the evacuation routes. Once again, on paper it looked fine, but I knew what could result from a forced march in the middle of winter, without any preparation; what's more, the Jews of Budapest had left in good health, whereas here we would have exhausted, weakened, undernourished, and poorly dressed *Häftlinge*, in a panic situation that, even if it were well planned, could easily degenerate into a rout. I questioned Boesenberg at length on the key points: he assured me that before departure, warm clothing and additional blankets would be distributed, and that stores of provisions would be prepositioned on the routes. One couldn't do any better, he asserted. I had to agree he was probably right.

At Auschwitz, at the Kommandantur, I met Sturmbannführer Kraus, a liaison officer sent by Schmauser with an SD Sonderkommando, and set up in the camp as the head of a "Liaison and Transition Office." This Kraus, a pleasant, competent young officer, whose neck and left ear bore traces of severe burns, explained to me that he was mainly responsible for the "Immobilization" and "Destruction" phases: he especially had to ensure that the extermination installations and the warehouses didn't fall intact into the hands of the Russians. The responsibility for the implementation of the evacuation order, when it was given, fell to Bär. Bär received me somewhat unpleasantly; obviously to him I was yet another bureaucrat from the outside who was coming to hinder his work. He struck me with his piercing, anxious eyes, a fleshy nose, a thin but curiously sensual mouth; his thick, wavy hair was carefully combed back with brilliantine, like a Berlin dandy's. I thought him astonishingly dull and narrow-minded, even more than Höss who at least kept the flair of a former Freikorps soldier. Taking advantage of my rank, I reprimanded him severely for his lack of open cooperation with the services of the HSSPF. He retorted with an ill-concealed arrogance that Pohl fully supported his position. "When *Fall-A* is declared, I will obey the orders of Obergruppenführer Schmauser. Until then, I report to Oranienberg alone. You have no authority to give me orders."—"When *Fall-A* is declared," I replied angrily, "it will be too late to make up for your incompetence. I warn you that in my report to the Reichsführer I will hold you personally responsible for all excessive losses." My threats seemed to have no effect on him; he listened to me in silence, with barely hidden contempt.

Bär assigned me an office in the Kommandantur in Birkenau, and I had Obersturmführer Elias and one of my new subordinates, Untersturmführer Darius, come from Oranienburg. I took my quarters at the Haus der Waffen-SS; they gave me the same room as during my first visit, a year and a half before. The weather was horrible—cold, damp, fickle. The whole region lay beneath snow, a thick layer of it, often dusted with the soot from the mines and factory chimneys, a dirty gray lace. In the camp it was almost black, packed down by the footsteps of thousands of inmates, and mixed with mud frozen by frost. Violent snow squalls came down without warning from the Beskids and for twenty minutes or so smothered the camp under a white, swirling veil, before disappearing with the same swiftness, leaving everything immaculate for a few moments. In Birkenau only one chimney was still smoking, in fits and starts, the Krema IV, which was being kept active to dispose of the inmates who died in the camp; Krema III was in ruins since the October uprising, and the other two, following Himmler's instructions, were partially dismantled. The new construction zone had been abandoned and most of the barracks removed, and the vast, empty terrain left to the snow; the problems of overpopulation had been solved by the preliminary evacuations. When the clouds lifted on rare occasions, the blue-tinted line of the Beskids appeared behind the geometric rows of the barracks: and the camp, beneath the snow, seemed as if peaceful and tranquil. I went almost every day to inspect the different satellite camps, Günthergrube, Fürstergrube, Tschechowitz, Neu Dachs, the little camps of Gleiwitz, to check the state of the preparations. The long, flat roads were almost deserted, scarcely disturbed by Wehrmacht trucks; I would come home at night under a dark sky, a heavy, gray mass; beyond it, snow fell sometimes like a sheet on the distant villages, and beyond that a delicate sky, blue and pale yellow, with just a few clouds of muted purple, rimmed by the light of the setting sun, colored the snow and the ice of the marshes that soak the Polish earth. The night of December 31, the Haus organized a quiet celebration for the officers passing through and some camp officers: people sang melancholy carols, the men drank slowly and spoke in low voices; everyone understood it was the last New Year's Eve of the war, and that it wasn't very likely the Reich would survive till the next one. I found Dr. Wirths there, profoundly depressed, he had sent his family back to Germany; and I met Untersturmführer Schurz, the new head of the *Politische Abteilung*, who treated me with much more deference than his Kommandant. I talked for a long time with Kraus; he had served several years in Russia, until he was seriously wounded in Kursk, where he had just barely managed to drag himself out of his burning tank; after his convalescence, he had been assigned to the Southeast SS District, in Breslau, and he had ended up on Schmauser's staff. This officer, who bore the same first names, Franz Xaver, as another Kraus, a well-known Catholic theologian from the previous century, gave me the impression of being a serious man, open to others' opinions, but fanatically determined to see his mission through; although he said he understood my aims, he maintained that no inmate should, naturally, fall alive into the hands of the Russians, and thought that these two constraints were not incompatible. He was probably right in principle, but for my part I was worried—rightly so, as we will see—that overly severe orders would rouse the brutality of the camp guards, made up in this sixth year of the war from the dregs of the SS, men too old or too sick to serve at the front, *Volksdeutschen* who barely spoke German, veterans suffering from psychiatric disorders but deemed fit for service, alcoholics, drug addicts, degenerates clever enough to have avoided the punitive battalion or the firing squad. Many officers were hardly any better than their men: with the enormous expansion, this last year, of the system of KLs, the

WVHA had been forced to recruit just about anyone, to promote no-
toriously incompetent subalterns, to reappoint officers who had been
cashiered for serious offenses, or to appoint people no one else wanted.
Hauptsturmführer Drescher, an officer I also met that night, confirmed
me in my pessimistic outlook. Drescher directed the branch of the Morgen commission still operating in the camp, and had seen me once with
his superior in Lublin; that night, in an alcove set a little back from the
restaurant dining room, he opened up to me quite frankly about the investigations under way. The case against Höss, which was nearly
wrapped up in October, had suddenly collapsed in November, despite
the testimony of a female inmate, an Austrian prostitute Höss had seduced and then tried to kill by locking her up in a disciplinary cell of
the PA. After his transfer to Oranienburg at the end of 1943, Höss had
left his family in the Kommandant's house, forcing his successive replacements to take quarters elsewhere; he had only finally moved them
the previous month, probably because of the Russian threat, and it was
common knowledge, in the camp, that Frau Höss had required four
whole trucks to carry their belongings. Drescher was appalled, but
Morgen had come up against Höss's protectors. The investigations were
continuing, but concerned only small fry. Wirths had joined us, and
Drescher went on talking without being bothered by the doctor's presence; obviously, he wasn't telling him anything new. Wirths was worried about the evacuation: despite Boesenberg's plan, no measures had
been taken in the *Stammlager* or in Birkenau to prepare rations or warm
clothing for the journey. I too was worried.

Yet the Russians still weren't moving. In the West, our forces were
still struggling to break through (the Americans were clinging to Bas-
togne), and we also had gone over to the offensive in Budapest, which
gave us a little hope again. But the famous V-2 rockets had turned out,
if you knew how to read between the lines, to be ineffective, our secondary offensive in Northern Alsace had immediately been contained,
and it was obvious that it was just a question of time now. At the beginning of January, I gave Piontek a day off so he could evacuate his
family from Tarnowitz, at least as far as Breslau; I didn't want him worrying himself sick about them when the time came. Snow fell steadily,
and when the sky did clear, the heavy, dirty smoke from the foundries
dominated the Silesian landscape, bearing witness to a production of
tanks, cannons, and munitions that would continue till the last minute.
A dozen days went by like this in anxious tranquility, punctuated by bureaucratic quarrels. I finally managed to persuade Bär to prepare special
rations, to be distributed to the inmates at the time of departure; as for

warm clothing, he told me they would take them from the *Kanada*, whose warehouses, for lack of transport, were still full. A good piece of news briefly came to lighten this tension. One night, at the Haus, Drescher presented himself at my table with two glasses of Cognac, smiling into his goatee: "Congratulations, Obersturmbannführer," he declared, handing me a glass and raising the other.—"That's fine with me, but why?"—"I spoke to Sturmbannführer Morgen today. He asked me to tell you that your affair is closed." That Drescher knew about it scarcely bothered me, I was so relieved by the news. Drescher went on: "In the absence of any material evidence, Judge von Rabingen decided to dismiss the case against you. Von Rabingen told the Sturmbannführer that he'd never seen such a shoddy case with so little to back it up, and that the Kripo had done an abominable job. He was close to thinking it all stemmed from some plot against you." I breathed in: "That's what I always said. Fortunately, the Reichsführer kept his confidence in me. If what you say is true, then my honor is cleared."—"That's right," said Drescher, nodding. "Sturmbannführer Morgen even told me that Judge von Rabingen was thinking of taking disciplinary measures against the inspectors who were working against you."—"I'd be delighted." The news was confirmed to me three days later by a letter from Brandt, which included a copy of a letter to the Reichsführer in which von Rabingen stated he was *fully convinced of my innocence*. Neither of the two letters mentioned Clemens or Weser, but that was enough for me.

Finally, after this brief respite, the Soviets launched the long-dreaded offensive from their bridgeheads over the Vistula. Our meager covering forces were swept aside. The Russians, during their pause, had accumulated incredible firepower; their T-34s rushed in columns across the Polish plains, smashing our divisions, imitating our 1941 tactics with brio; in many places, our troops were surprised by enemy tanks when they thought the lines were a hundred kilometers away. On January 17, Generalgouverneur Frank and his administration evacuated Cracow, and our last units withdrew from the ruins of Warsaw. The first Soviet tanks were already penetrating Silesia when Schmauser launched *Fall-A*. For my part, I had done everything I thought possible: stored cans of gasoline, sandwiches, and rum in our two vehicles, and destroyed all the copies of my reports. On the night of the seventeenth, I was summoned by Bär along with all the other officers; he announced that according to Schmauser's instructions, all fit inmates would be evacuated, by foot, starting the following morning: the roll call under way that night would be the last one. The evacuations would take place according to the plan. Each column commander was to make sure no inmate escaped or stayed behind on the road; any attempt would be pitilessly punished; Bär urged them, though, to avoid shooting inmates as they passed through villages, so as not to shock the populace. One of the column commanders, an Obersturmführer, spoke: "Sturmbannführer, isn't that order too severe? If a *Häftling* tries to escape, it's normal to shoot him. But what if he's simply too weak to walk?"—"All the *Häftlinge* who are leaving are classified as fit for work and must be able to do fifty kilometers without any problems," Bär retorted. "The sick and the unfit will remain in the camps. If there are sick prisoners in the columns, they must be eliminated. These orders must be applied."

That night, the camp SS men slept little. From the Haus, near the train station, I watched pass by the long columns of German civilians fleeing the Russians; after crossing the city and the bridge over the Sola, they poured into the station, or else laboriously continued westward on foot. SS men were guarding a special train reserved for the families of the camp personnel; it was already packed, husbands were trying to heap bundles in next to their wives and children. After dinner, I went to inspect the *Stammlager* and Birkenau. I visited some of the barracks: the inmates were trying to sleep, the kapos told me that no additional clothes had been handed out, but I still hoped it would happen the next day, before they left. In the lanes, piles of documents were burning: the incinerators were overflowing. In Birkenau, I noticed a big commotion near the *Kanada*: under the glare of spotlights, inmates were loading all sorts of merchandise onto trucks; an Untersturmführer supervising the operation assured me they were being directed toward the KL Gross-Rosen. But I could see that the SS guards were also helping themselves, sometimes openly. Everyone was shouting, running about frantically, uselessly, and I felt that panic was overtaking these men, that all sense of moderation and discipline was escaping them. As always, they had waited till the last minute to do everything, for acting earlier would have been showing defeatism; now, the Russians were upon us, the Auschwitz guards remembered the fate of the SS captured in the Lublin camp, they were losing all notion of priorities and sought only one thing, to escape. Depressed, I went to see Drescher in his office at the *Stammlager*. He too was burning his documents. "Have you seen how they're looting?" he said to me, laughing into his goatee. From a drawer, he took out a bottle of expensive Armagnac: "What do you think of this? An Untersturmführer I've been investigating for four months but haven't managed to nab offered this to me as a goodbye present, the bastard. He stole it, of course. Will you have a drink with me?" He poured two measures into water glasses: "Sorry, I don't have anything better." He raised his glass and I imitated him. "Go on," he said, "make a toast." But nothing came to mind. He shrugged: "Me neither. Let's drink, then." The Armagnac was exquisite, a light, sweet, burned sensation. "Where are you going?" I asked him.—"To Oranienburg, to make my report. I have enough already to prosecute eleven more men. Afterward, they can send me wherever they like." As I was getting ready to leave, he handed me the bottle: "Here, keep it. You'll need it more than I." I put it into my coat pocket, shook his hand, and left. I went to the HKB, where Wirths was supervising the evacuation of the medical material. I spoke to him about the problem of warm clothes. "The warehouses are full," he assured me. "It shouldn't be too difficult to have blankets, boots, coats distributed." But Bär, whom I found around 2:00 a.m. at the Kommandantur in Birkenau in the process of planning the order of departure for the columns, didn't seem to be of that opinion. "The goods stored are the property of the Reich. I have no orders to distribute them to the inmates. They'll be evacuated by truck or by train, when possible." Outside, it must have been ten degrees below zero, the lanes were frozen over, slippery. "Dressed like that, your inmates won't survive. Many of them are almost barefoot."—"The ones who are fit will survive," he asserted. "The others, we don't need." More and more furious, I went down to the communications center and got in contact with Breslau; but Schmauser wasn't reachable, nor was Boesenberg. An operator showed me a telegram from the Wehrmacht: Tschenstochau had just fallen, the Russian troops were at the gates of Cracow. "It's getting hot," he said laconically. I thought of sending a telex to the Reichsführer, but that wouldn't do any good; better to find Schmauser the next day, with the hope he'd have more common sense than that fool Bär. Suddenly tired, I went back to the Haus to go to bed. The columns of civilians, mixed with soldiers from the Wehrmacht, were still flowing in, exhausted peasants all bundled up, their things piled up on a cart with their children, pushing their livestock in front of them.

Piontek didn't wake me, and I slept until eight o'clock. The kitchen was still working and I had an omelette with sausage. Then I went out. At the *Stammlager* and in Birkenau, the columns were pouring out of the camp. The *Häftlinge*, their feet wrapped in whatever they'd been able to find, were walking slowly, at a shuffling pace, surrounded by SS guards and led by well-fed, warmly dressed kapos. All those who had one had taken their blanket, which they generally wore draped over their heads, a little like Bedouins; but that was all. When I asked, I was told they had received a piece of sausage and bread for three days; no one had received any orders about clothes.

The first day, though, despite the ice and the wet snow, it still seemed to be going all right. I studied the columns leaving the camp,

talked with Kraus, walked up the roads to observe a little farther on.
Everywhere, I noticed abuses: the guards had prisoners pushing carts
loaded with their things, or else forced them to carry their suitcases.
Here and there by the side of the road I noticed a corpse lying in the
snow, the head frequently bloody; the guards were applying Bär's stern
orders. Yet the columns were advancing without confusion and without any attempt at revolt. At midday I managed to make contact with
Schmauser to discuss the problem of the clothes. He listened to me
briefly and then swept aside my objections: "We can't give them civilian clothing, they could escape."—"Then shoes at least." He hesitated.
"Arrange things with Bär," he said finally. He must have had other preoccupations, I could tell, but I would still have preferred a clear order.
I went to find Bär at the *Stammlager*. "Obergruppenführer Schmauser
has given the order to have shoes distributed to the inmates who don't
have any." Bär shrugged: "Here, I don't have any more, everything has
already been loaded for shipment. Just see about it in Birkenau with
Schwarzhuber." I spent two hours finding this officer, the Lagerführer
of Birkenau, who had left to inspect one of the columns. "Very well, I'll
take care of it," he promised me when I gave him the order. Around
nightfall, I found Elias and Darius, whom I had sent to inspect the evacuation of Monowitz and several *Nebenlager*. Everything was happening
in a more or less orderly way, but already, by late afternoon, more and
more inmates, exhausted, were stopping and letting themselves be shot
by the guards. I left again with Piontek to inspect the nighttime stopover
points. Despite Schmauser's formal orders—there was a fear that inmates
would take advantage of the darkness to escape—some columns were
still advancing. I criticized the officers, but they replied that they hadn't
yet reached their designated stopping point, and that they couldn't let
their columns sleep outside, in the snow or on the ice. The points I visited turned out to be insufficient in any case: a barn or a school, for two
thousand inmates, sometimes; many of them slept outside, huddled next
to each other. I asked that fires be lit, but there was no wood, the trees
were too damp and no one had tools to cut them down; where boards
or old crates could be found, they made little campfires, but these didn't
last till dawn. No soup had been planned, the inmates were supposed to
survive on what had been distributed in the camp; farther on, they assured me, there would be rations. Most of the columns hadn't gone five
kilometers; many were still in the almost deserted camp zone; at this
pace, the marches would last ten to twelve days.

I went back to the Haus muddy, wet, and tired. Kraus was there,
having a drink with some of his colleagues from the SD. He came and
sat down with me: "How are things?" he asked.—"Not so good. There

are going to be needless losses. Bär could have done a lot more."—"Bär couldn't care less. You know he has been named Kommandant at Mittelbau?" I raised my eyebrows: "No, I didn't know. Who will supervise the closing of the camp?"—"Me. I've already received the order to set up an office, after the evacuation, to manage the administrative dissolution."—"Congratulations," I said.—"Oh," he replied, "don't think I'm happy about it. Frankly, I'd have preferred something else."—"And your immediate tasks?"—"We're waiting for the camps to be emptied. Afterward, we'll start."—"What will you do with the inmates who are left?" He shrugged and gave an ironic little smile: "What do you think? The Obergruppenführer gave the order to liquidate them. No one must fall alive into the hands of the Bolsheviks."—"I see." I finished my drink. "Well, good luck. I don't envy you."

Things got gradually worse. The next morning, the columns kept on leaving the camps through the main gates, the guards were still manning the line of watchtowers, order reigned; but a few kilometers farther on, the columns began to grow longer and unravel as the weaker inmates slowed down. More and more corpses could be seen. It was snowing heavily, but it wasn't too cold, for me in any case, I had seen much worse in Russia, but I was warmly dressed, I was traveling in a heated car, and the guards who had to walk had pullovers, good coats, and boots; as for the *Häftlinge*, they must have felt pierced through to the bone. The guards were getting more and more frightened, they shouted at the inmates and beat them. I saw one guard beating an inmate who had stopped to defecate; I reprimanded him, then asked the Untersturmführer who was in command of the column to place him under arrest; he replied that he didn't have enough men to do that. In the villages, the Polish peasants, who were waiting for the Russians, watched the inmates pass by in silence, or shouted something at them in their language; the guards treated harshly those who tried to hand out bread or food; they were nervous, the villages were swarming with partisans, as everyone knew, they were afraid of being attacked. But at night, at the stopping points I visited, there still was no soup or bread, and many inmates had already finished their ration. I figured that at this rate half or two-thirds of the columns would drop off before reaching their destination. I ordered Piontek to drive me to Breslau. Because of the bad weather and the columns of refugees, I didn't arrive until after midnight. Schmauser was already asleep and Boesenberg, they told me at HQ, had gone to Kattowitz, near the front. A poorly shaven officer showed me an operations map: the Russian positions, he explained, were mostly theoretical, since they were advancing so quickly they couldn't keep the markings up to date; as for our divisions still shown on the map, some

no longer existed at all, while others, according to fragmentary information, must have been moving as roving *Kessels* behind the Russian
lines, trying to meet up with our retreating forces. Tarnowitz and Cracow had fallen in the afternoon. The Soviets were also entering eastern
Prussia in force, and there was talk of worse atrocities than in Hungary.
It was a catastrophe. But Schmauser, when he received me in midmorning, seemed calm and sure of himself. I described the situation to
him and set out my demands: rations and wood for fires at the stopover
points, and carts to transport the inmates who were too exhausted, so
they could be cared for and put back to work instead of liquidated: "I'm
not talking about people sick with typhus or tuberculosis, Obergruppenführer, but just the ones who aren't up to the cold and hunger."—
"Our soldiers too are cold and hungry," he retorted sharply. "The
civilians too are cold and hungry. You don't seem to realize the situation, Obersturmbannführer. We have a million and a half refugees on
the roads. That's much more important than your inmates."—"Obergruppenführer, these inmates, as a labor force, are a vital resource for
the Reich. We cannot allow ourselves, in the present situation, to lose
twenty or thirty thousand of them."—"I have no resources to allocate
to you."—"Then at least give me an order so I will be obeyed by the
column leaders." I typed out an order, in several copies for Elias and
Darius, and Schmauser signed them in the afternoon; I left again immediately. The roads were horribly congested, endless columns of
refugees on foot or in wagons, isolated trucks from the Wehrmacht, lost
soldiers. In the villages, mobile canteens from the NSV distributed soup.
I reached Auschwitz late; my colleagues had returned earlier and were
already asleep. Bär, I was told, had left the camp, probably for good. I
went to see Kraus and found him with Schurz, the head of the PA. I
had brought along Drescher's Armagnac, and we drank some together.
Kraus explained that he had had Kremas I and II dynamited that morning, leaving IV till the last minute; he had also begun the liquidations
that had been ordered, shooting two hundred Jewesses who had stayed
in the *Frauenlager* in Birkenau; but Springorum, the President of the
Kattowitz province, had taken away his Sonderkommando for urgent
tasks and he didn't have enough men to continue. All the fit inmates had
left the camps, but there remained, according to him, within the entire
complex, more than eight thousand inmates who were sick or too weak
to walk. Massacring these people seemed to me, in the present state of
things, perfectly idiotic and pointless, but Kraus had his orders, and it
didn't fall within my jurisdiction; and I had enough problems as it was
with the columns of evacuees.

I spent the next four days running after the columns. I felt as if I were struggling against a mudslide: I spent hours advancing, and when I finally found an officer in charge and showed him my orders, he would apply my instructions as grudgingly as possible. Here and there I managed to organize distributions of rations (elsewhere, too, they were being distributed without my intervention); I had the blankets of the dead collected to give to the living; I was able to confiscate carts from Polish peasants and pile exhausted inmates on them. But the next day, when I found these same columns again, the officers had had shot all those who could no longer get up, and the carts were almost empty. I hardly looked at the *Häftlinge*, it wasn't their individual fate that concerned me, but their collective fate, and in any case they all looked alike, they were a gray, dirty mass, stinking despite the cold, undifferentiated, you could only grasp isolated details, the colored badges, a bare head or bare feet, a jacket different from the others; men and women could be distinguished only with difficulty. Sometimes I glimpsed their eyes, under the folds of the blanket, but they never returned a gaze, they were empty, completely eaten away by the need to walk and keep moving forward. The farther away we got from the Vistula, the colder it was and the more inmates we lost. Sometimes, to make room for the Wehrmacht, columns had to wait for hours by the side of the road, or else cut across frozen fields, struggle to cross the innumerable canals and embankments, before finding the road again. As soon as a column paused, the inmates, dying of thirst, fell to their knees to lick the snow. Each column, even the ones where I had put carts, was followed by a team of guards who, with a bullet or a blow from a rifle butt, finished off the inmates who had fallen or simply stopped; the officers left up to the municipalities the job of burying the bodies. As always in this kind of situation, the natural brutality of some was aroused, and their murderous zeal went beyond orders; their young officers, as frightened as they, controlled them with difficulty. It wasn't just the simple soldiers who were losing all sense of limits. On the third or fourth day, I went to find Elias and Darius on the roads; they were inspecting a column from Laurahütte whose itinerary had changed because of the swiftness of the advance of the Russians, who were coming not just from the east but also from the north, almost reaching Gross Strehlitz, according to my information, a little before Blechhammer. Elias was with the column's commander, a young, very nervous and agitated Oberscharführer; when I asked him where Darius was, he told me he had gone to the rear and was looking after the sick. I joined him to see what he was doing and found him in the process of finishing off inmates with gunshots. "What the hell are you doing?" He saluted me and replied without losing countenance: "I'm following your orders, Obersturmbannführer. I carefully picked out the sick or weak *Häftlinge* and had the ones who can still get better loaded onto carts. We've just liquidated the ones who are completely unfit."—"Untersturmführer," I spat out in an icy voice, "liquidations are not your job. Your orders are to limit them as much as possible, and certainly not to participate in them. Understood?" I also reprimanded Elias; Darius, after all, was under his responsibility.

Sometimes I found more understanding column leaders, who accepted the logic and necessity of what I explained to them. But the resources they were given were limited, and they were commanding narrow-minded, frightened men, hardened by years in the camps, incapable of changing their methods, and, with the relaxation of discipline that resulted from the chaos of the evacuation, returning to all their old failings and habits. Everyone, I imagined, had his reasons for his violent behavior; Darius had no doubt wanted to demonstrate his firmness and resolution in front of these men, most of whom were much older than he. But I had other things to do than analyze motivations, I was just seeking, with the greatest difficulty, to have my orders carried out. Most of the column leaders were simply indifferent—they just had one idea in their heads, getting away from the Russians as quickly as possible with the livestock that had been entrusted to them, without complicating their lives.

During these four days, I slept where I could, in inns, at the village town halls, in local houses. On January 25, a light wind had cleared the clouds, the sky was clean and pure, brilliant, I went back to Auschwitz to see what was going on. At the station, I found an antiaircraft battery unit, most of them Hitlerjugend assigned to the Luftwaffe, children, getting ready to evacuate; their Feldwebel, rolling his eyes, informed me in a monotone that the Russians were on the other side of the Vistula and that there was fighting in the IG Farben factory. I took the road that led to Birkenau and came across a long column of inmates climbing the slope, surrounded by SS men who were firing at them pretty much randomly; behind them, all the way to the camp, the road was strewn with bodies. I stopped and hailed their leader, one of Kraus's men. "What are you doing?"—"The Sturmbannführer ordered us to empty Sectors IIe and IIf and to transfer the inmates to the *Stammlager*."—"And why are you shooting at them like that?" He made a face: "Otherwise they won't move."—"Where is Sturmbannführer Kraus?"—"At the *Stammlager*." I thought for a minute: "You might as well drop it. The Russians will be here in a few hours." He hesitated, then made up his mind; he gave a signal to his men and the group left at a trot for Auschwitz I, leaving the *Häftlinge* there. I looked at them: they weren't moving, some were looking at me too, others were sitting down. I contemplated Birkenau, whose whole extent I could see from the top of this hill: the *Kanada* sector, in the back, was burning, sending a thick column of black smoke to the sky, next to which the little plume emerging from the chimney of Krema IV, still in operation, could scarcely be noticed. The snow on the barracks roofs sparkled in the sun; the camp looked deserted, I couldn't make out a human form, aside from spots scattered in the lanes that must have been bodies; the watchtowers stood empty, nothing moved. I got back into my car and made a U-turn, abandoning the inmates to their fate. At the *Stammlager*, where I arrived before the Kommando I had encountered, other members of the Kattowitz SD or Gestapo were running all over the place, agitated and worried. The camp's lanes were full of corpses already covered with snow, garbage, piles of dirty clothing; here and there I glimpsed a *Häftling* searching the bodies or slipping furtively from one building to another; when he saw me he promptly bolted. I found Kraus at the Kommandantur, its empty hallways strewn with papers and files; he was finishing off a bottle of schnapps and smoking a cigarette. I sat down and imitated him. "You hear it?" he said calmly. In the north, in the east, the hollow, monotonous booming of the Russian artillery resounded dully. "Your men don't know what they're doing anymore," I declared as I poured myself some schnapps.— "It doesn't matter," he said. "I'm leaving soon. And you?"—"Me too, probably. Is the Haus still open?"—"No. They left yesterday."—"And your men?"—"I'll leave a few to finish the dynamiting tonight or tomorrow. Our troops will hold till then. I'm taking the others to Kattowitz. Did you know the Reichsführer was appointed commander of an Army Group?"—"No," I said, surprised, "I didn't know."—"Yesterday. It was named Army Group Vistula, even though the front is already almost on the Oder, or even past it. The Reds also reached the Baltic. East Prussia is cut off from the Reich."—"Yes," I said, "that's not good news. Maybe the Reichsführer can do something."—"That would surprise me. In my opinion, we're done for. But we'll fight to the end." He emptied the bottle into his glass. "I'm sorry," I said, "I finished the Armagnac."—"That's all right." He drank a little and then looked at me: "Why are you so determined? For your workers, I mean. Do you really think a few *Häftlinge* are going to change anything in our situation?" I shrugged and finished my drink. "I have orders," I said. "And you? Why are you so determined to liquidate these people?"—"I also have my orders. They are enemies of the Reich, there's no reason they should get away while our nation is perishing. That said, I'm dropping it. We've run out of time."—"Anyway," I commented, looking at my empty glass, "most of them will only hold out for a few days. You saw the state they're in." He emptied his glass in turn and got up: "Let's go." Outside, he gave a few more orders to his men, then turned to me and saluted: "Goodbye, Obersturmbannführer. Good luck."—"You too." I got into my car and ordered Piontek to drive me to Gleiwitz.

Trains had been leaving Gleiwitz every day since January 19, taking inmates as they arrived from the closest camps. The first trains, I knew, had been sent to Gross-Rosen, where Bär had gone to prepare for reception, but Gross-Rosen, soon overwhelmed, had refused to take any more; the convoys were now passing through the Protektorat, then shunted either to Vienna (for the KL Mauthausen) or to Prague to then be scattered among the KLs of the Altreich. They were loading another train when I arrived at the Gleiwitz station. To my great horror, I saw that all the cars were open, already full of snow and ice before the exhausted inmates were driven into them with rifle butts; inside, no water, no provisions, no sanitary bucket. I questioned the inmates: they came from Neu Dachs and hadn't received anything since their departure from the camp; some hadn't eaten in four days. Alarmed, I looked at these skeletal phantoms, wrapped in soaking, frozen blankets, standing up, squeezed against each other in the car full of snow. I shouted at one of the guards: "Who's in charge here?" He shrugged angrily: "I don't know, Obersturmbannführer. We were just told to load them in." I went into the main building and asked for the station chief, a tall, thin man with a toothbrush moustache and a teacher's round glasses: "Who is responsible for these trains?" He pointed at my stripes with his red flag, which he was holding rolled up in one hand: "It isn't you, Herr Offizier? In any case, I think it's the SS"—"Who, exactly? Who's organizing the convoys? Who's allocating the cars?"—"In principle," he replied, slipping his flag under his arm, "for the cars, it's the Kattowitz *Reichsbahndirektion*. But for these *Sonderzüge*, they sent an Amtsrat down here." He led me out of the station and pointed to a barracks a little lower down, alongside the tracks. "He set himself up in there." I went over and entered without knocking. A man in civilian clothes, fat, poorly shaved, was sprawled behind a desk covered with papers. Two railroad men were warming themselves by a stove. "Are you the Amtsrat from Kattowitz?" I barked. He raised his head: "That's me, the Amtsrat from Kattowitz. Kehrling, at your service." An unbearable reek of schnapps emanated from his mouth. I pointed at the tracks: "Are you the one responsible for this *Schweinerei*?"—"Which *Schweinerei* are you talking about, precisely? Because at the moment there are quite a few." I controlled myself: "The trains, the open cars for the *Häftlinge* from the KLs."—"Ah, that *Schweinerei*. No, that's your colleagues. I coordinate the assembling of the trains, that's all."—"So you're the one who allocates the cars." He leafed through his papers. "I'll explain to you. Have a seat, old man. Here. These *Sonderzüge* are allocated by the *General-betriebsleitung Ost*, in Berlin. We have to find the cars on-site, among the available rolling stock. Now, you may have noticed"—he waved his hand at the outside—"that it's something of a mess these days. The open cars are the only ones left. The Gauleiter requisitioned all the closed cars for the evacuation of civilians or for the Wehrmacht. If you don't like it, just have them covered." I had remained standing during his explanation: "And where am I supposed to find tarpaulins?"—"Not my problem."—"You could at least have the cars cleaned out!" He sighed: "Listen, old man, at the moment, I have to organize twenty, twenty-five special trains per day. My men scarcely have the time to couple the cars together."—"And the supplies?"—"Not my job. But if you're interested in that, there's an Obersturmführer somewhere who's supposed to take care of all that." I went out, slamming the door. Near the trains, I found an Oberwachtmeister from the Schupo: "Ah, yes, I saw an Obersturmführer who was giving orders. He's probably at the SP." In the offices, I was told there was in fact an Obersturmführer from Auschwitz who was coordinating the evacuation of inmates, but that he had gone out to eat. I sent for him. When he arrived, scowling, I showed him Schmauser's orders and began assailing him with reprimands about the state of the convoys. He listened to me, standing at attention, red as a poppy; when I had finished, he answered, stammering: "Obersturmbannführer, Obersturmbannführer, it's not my fault. I have nothing, no provisions at all. The *Reichsbahn* refuses to give me closed cars, there are no supplies, nothing. I keep getting phone calls asking me why the trains aren't leaving faster. I'm doing what I can."—"You mean that in all of Gleiwitz there's no food stock you can requisition? Tarps? Shovels to clean out the cars? These *Häftlinge* are a resource of the Reich, Obersturmführer! Aren't SS officers taught to show initiative anymore?"—"Obersturmbannführer, I don't know. I can find out." I raised my eyebrows: "Then go find out. I want suitable convoys for tomorrow. Understood?"—"*Zu Befehl*, Obersturmbannführer." He saluted me and went out. I sat down and had some tea brought to me by an orderly. As I was blowing on it, a Spiess came to find me: "Excuse me, Obersturmbannführer. Are you from the Reichsführer's staff?"—"Yes."—"There are two gentlemen from the Kripo who are looking for an Obersturmbannführer from the *Persönlicher Stab*. That must be you?" I followed him and he showed me into an office: Clemens was resting both his elbows on a table; Weser was perched on a chair, hands in his pockets, leaning back against the wall. I smiled and leaned on the doorframe, my cup of tea still steaming in my hand. "Look at this," I said, "old friends. What fair wind brings you here?" Clemens aimed a thick finger at me: "You, Aue. We're looking for you." Still smiling, I tapped my epaulettes: "Are you forgetting I have a rank, Kriminalkommissar?"—"We couldn't care less about your rank," Clemens muttered. "You don't deserve it." Weser spoke for the first time: "You must have said to yourself, when you got Judge von Rabingen's decision: That's it, it's over, right?"—"Indeed, I took it that way. If I'm not mistaken, your case was deemed extremely open to criticism." Clemens shrugged: "No one knows what judges want. But that doesn't mean they're right."—"Unfortunately for you," I said pleasantly, "you're in the service of the law."—"Precisely," Clemens grunted, "we serve the law. We sure are the only ones."—"And you came all the way here just to tell me that? I'm flattered."—"Not entirely," said Weser, bringing his chair back to the ground. "You see, we had an idea."—"That's novel," I said, bringing the teacup to my lips.— "I'm going to tell you about it, Aue. Your sister told us she had gone to Berlin, not long before the murder, and that she had seen you. That she had stayed at the Kaiserhof. So we went to the Kaiserhof. They know Freiherr von Üxküll very well at the Kaiserhof, he's an old customer who has his habits. At the front desk, one of the employees remembered that a few days after his departure, an SS officer had come by to send a telegram to Frau von Üxküll. And you see, when you send a telegram from a hotel, it's noted down in a register. There's a number for every telegram. And at the post office, they keep a copy of telegrams. Three years, that's the law." He pulled a piece of paper from the inside pocket of his coat and unfolded it. "You recognize this, Aue?" I was still smiling. "The investigation is closed, meine Herren."—"You lied to us, Aue!" Clemens thundered.—"Yes, it's not good to lie to the police," Weser said. I calmly finished my tea, motioned politely to them with my head, wished them a good afternoon, and closed the door on them.

Outside, it was snowing again, harder than ever. I returned to the station. A mass of inmates was waiting in an empty lot, sitting in the snow and the mud under the gusts of wind. I tried to have them come into the station, but the waiting rooms were occupied by soldiers from the Wehrmacht. I slept with Piontek in the car, overcome with fatigue. The next morning, the lot was deserted, aside from a few dozen snow-covered corpses. I tried to find the Obersturmführer from the day before, to see if he was following my instructions, but the immense futility of it all oppressed me and paralyzed my movements. At noon, I had made my decision. I ordered Piontek to find some gas, then, through the SP, I contacted Elias and Darius. By early afternoon I was on my way to Berlin.

★ ★ ★

The fighting forced us to make a considerable detour, via Ostrau and then through Prague and Dresden. Piontek and I took turns driving; it took us two days. Dozens of kilometers before Berlin, we had to clear a way for ourselves through floods of refugees from the East, whom Goebbels was forcing to skirt round the city. In the center, all that was left of the annex of the Ministry of the Interior where my office had been was a gutted shell. It was raining, a cold, evil rain that soaked into the patches of snow still clinging to the rubble. The streets were dirty and muddy. I finally found Grothmann, who told me that Brandt was at Deutsch Krone, in Pomerania, with the Reichsführer. I then went to Oranienburg, where my office was still functioning, as if detached from the rest of the world. Asbach explained to me that Fräulein Praxa had been wounded during a bombing, with burns to her arm and breast, and that he had had her evacuated to a hospital in Franconia. Elias and Darius had retreated to Breslau during the fall of Kattowitz and were awaiting instructions: I ordered them to return. I started going through my mail, which no one had touched since Fräulein Praxa's accident. Among the official letters was a private letter: I recognized Helene's writing. *Dear Max,* she wrote, *my house was bombed and I have to leave Berlin. I am in despair, I don't know where you are, your colleagues won't tell me anything. I'm leaving to join my parents in Baden. Write to me. If you want, I'll come back to Berlin. All is not lost. Yours, Helene.* It was almost a declaration, but I didn't understand what she meant by *All is not lost.* I quickly wrote to her at the address indicated to tell her I'd returned, but that it was better for now that she stay in Baden.

I devoted two days to writing a very critical report on the evacuation. I also spoke about it in person to Pohl, who swept aside my arguments: "Anyway," he declared, "we have no more room to put them, all the camps are full." In Berlin, I had run into Thomas; Schellenberg had left, he had stopped throwing parties and seemed in a glum mood. According to him, the Reichsführer's performance as commander of an Army Group was turning out rather pathetic; he wasn't far from thinking that Himmler's appointment was a maneuver of Bormann's to discredit him. But these imbecilic games of the eleventh hour no longer interested me. I was feeling sick again, my vomiting had resumed, I got nauseated as I sat at my typewriter. When I found out that Morgen was also in Oranienburg, I went to see him and told him about the incomprehensible stubbornness of the two Kripo agents. "It's true," he said thoughtfully, "it's odd. They seem to have something against you personally. But I saw the file, there's nothing substantial in it. If it had been one of those shiftless types, a man without any education, you could imagine anything, but I know you, it seems ridiculous to me."—

"Maybe it's some form of class resentment," I suggested. "They want to bring me down at any cost, it seems."—"Yes, that's possible. You're a cultivated man, there are a lot of prejudices against intellectuals among the dregs of the Party. Listen, I'll mention it to von Rabingen. I'll ask him to send them an official reprimand. They shouldn't be pursuing an investigation against a judge's decision."

Around noon, a speech of the Führer's was broadcast on the occasion of the twelfth (and, as it turned out, last) anniversary of the Seizure of Power. I listened without paying it much heed in the mess hall in Oranienburg, I don't even remember what he said, he must still have been talking about *the Asiatic flood of Bolshevism* or something of the sort; what struck me above all was the reaction of the SS officers present: only some of them stood up to raise their arms when the national anthem was played at the end, a nonchalance that, a few months before, would have been deemed inadmissible, unpardonable. The same day, a Soviet submarine torpedoed the *Wilhelm-Gustloff* off the coast of Danzig, the jewel of Ley's "Kraft durch Freude" fleet, which was transporting more than ten thousand evacuees, half of them children. There were almost no survivors. In the time it took me to return to Berlin the next day, the Russians had reached the Oder and had crossed it almost casually to occupy a wide bridgehead between Küstrin and Frankfurt. I was vomiting up almost every meal, I was afraid the fever might return.

At the beginning of February, the Americans reappeared in full daylight above Berlin. Despite the prohibitions, the city was full of sour, aggressive refugees, who settled into the ruins and looted warehouses and stores without any interference from the police. I was passing by the *Staatspolizei*, it must have been around 11:00 a.m.; with the few officers who were still working there, I was directed to the antiaircraft shelter built in the garden, at the edge of the devastated park of the Prinz-Albrecht-Palais, itself an empty, roofless shell. This shelter, which wasn't even underground, was basically a long cement hallway; it didn't seem very reassuring to me, but I didn't have a choice. Along with the officers from the Gestapo, they brought in some prisoners, scruffy men with chains on their feet, who must have been pulled out of the neighboring cells: I recognized some of them, July conspirators, whose photograph I had seen in the papers or on the news. The raid was incredibly violent; the squat bunker, whose walls were more than a meter thick, swayed from side to side like a linden tree in the wind. I felt as if I were in the heart of a hurricane, a storm not of the elements but of pure, wild noise, all the noise in the world unleashed. The pressure from the explosions pressed painfully on my eardrums, I couldn't hear anything anymore; it hurt so much I was afraid they'd burst. I wanted to be swept away, crushed, I couldn't bear it anymore. The prisoners, who had been forbidden to sit down, were lying on the ground, most of them rolled up in a ball. Then I was lifted from my seat as if by a giant hand and hurled in the air. When I opened my eyes, several faces were floating above me. They seemed to be shouting, I didn't understand what they wanted. I shook my head but felt hands holding it firmly and forcing me to keep still. After the alert, they took me out. Thomas was supporting me. The sky, at high noon, was black with smoke; flames were licking the windows of the *Staatspolizei* building; in the park, trees were burning like torches, an entire section of the rear façade of the palace had collapsed. Thomas had me sit down on the remains of a pulverized bench. I touched my face: blood was flowing down my cheek. My ears were ringing, but I could distinguish sounds. Thomas turned to me: "Can you hear me?" I signaled that I could; despite the horrible pain in my ears, I understood what he was saying. "Don't move. You took a bad crack." A little later they loaded me into an Opel. On the Askanischer Platz, cars and twisted trucks were burning, the Anhalter Bahnhof seemed to have crumpled in on itself and was disgorging a black, acrid smoke, the Europa Haus and the buildings around it were also burning. Soldiers and auxiliaries, their faces black with soot, were vainly fighting the fires. I was driven to the Kurfürstenstrasse, to Eichmann's offices, which were still standing. There I was laid down on a table, among other wounded. A Hauptsturmführer arrived, the doctor whom I knew but whose name I had again forgotten: "You again," he said amiably. Thomas told him that my head had hit the wall of the bunker and that I had lost consciousness for about twenty minutes. The doctor had me stick out my tongue and then aimed a dazzling light into my eyes. "You have a concussion," he said. He turned to Thomas: "Have him get an X-ray of his skull. If there's no fracture, three weeks' rest." He scribbled a note on a piece of paper, gave it to Thomas, and disappeared. Thomas said to me: "I'm going to find you a hospital for the X-ray. If they don't keep you there, come back to my place to rest. I'll take care of Grothmann." I laughed: "What if there is no more 'your place'?" He shrugged: "Then come back here."

I didn't have a fracture of the skull, Thomas still had his place. He returned around evening and handed me a signed, stamped piece of paper: "Your leave of absence. You'd better leave Berlin." My head was hurting; I was sipping Cognac diluted with mineral water. "To go where?"—"I don't know. What if you went to see your girlfriend, in Baden?"—"The Americans could get there before me."—"Precisely. Take her to Bavaria, or Austria. Find yourself a little hotel, you can have a nice little romantic vacation. If I were you, I'd take advantage of it.

You might not have any more for a while." He described the results of
the raid: the offices of the *Staatspolizei* were unusable, the old chancellery was destroyed, the new one, Speer's, had been severely damaged,
even the Führer's private apartments had burned down. A bomb had
struck the People's Court in midtrial, they were trying Oberleutnant
von Schlabrendorff, one of the conspirators from the OKHG Center;
after the raid, they had found Judge Freisler stone dead, von Schlabrendorff's file in his hand, his head crushed, they said, by the bronze bust
of the Führer, which sat enthroned behind him during his ranting
speeches for the prosecution.

Leaving seemed like a good idea to me, but where? Baden, the romantic vacation: they were out of the question. Thomas wanted to have
his parents evacuated from the outskirts of Vienna, and suggested I go
in his place to take them to a cousin's farm. "You have parents?" He
looked at me, puzzled: "Of course. Everyone has parents. Why?" But
the Viennese option seemed terribly complicated to me for a convalescence, and Thomas readily agreed. "Don't worry. I'll make other
arrangements, it's no problem. Go rest somewhere." I still had no idea
where, yet I asked Piontek to come the next morning, with several cans
of gasoline. That night I didn't sleep much; my head and ears hurt,
shooting pains woke me up, I vomited twice, but there was something
else besides. When Piontek presented himself, I took my letter of
leave—essential to get me through the checkpoints—the bottle of Cognac and four packs of cigarettes that Thomas had given me, my bag
with a few things and a change of clothes, and without even offering
him a coffee, I gave him the order to start off. "Where are we going,
Obersturmbannführer?"—"Take the road to Stettin."

I had said it without thinking, I'm sure of it; but when I had spoken,
it seemed obvious to me that it couldn't have been otherwise. We had
to take complicated detours to reach the autobahn; Piontek, who had
spent the night in the garage, explained that Moabit and Wedding had
been leveled and that hordes of Berliners had come to swell the ranks
of refugees from the East. On the autobahn, the line of carts, most of
them surmounted by white tents that people had improvised to protect
themselves from the snow and the bitter cold, stretched out endlessly,
the nose of each horse on the back of the cart in front, kept to the right
by Schupos and Feldgendarmen, to let the military convoys going up to
the front pass. From time to time, a Russian Sturmovik made its appearance, and then there was panic, people jumped from the carts and
fled into the snow-covered fields while the fighter plane went up the
column, letting loose bursts of shells that struck down stragglers, blew
open the heads and bellies of panicking horses, burned mattresses and

carts. During one of these attacks, my car took several hits, its doors were riddled with holes and the rear window broken; the engine, fortunately, was unharmed, and the Cognac too. I handed the bottle to Piontek, then drank a swig myself as we started up again in the midst of the screams of the wounded and the cries of terrified civilians. At Stettin, we passed the Oder, whose early thaw had been accelerated by the Kriegsmarine with dynamite and icebreakers; then, skirting round the Manü-See from the north, we crossed Stargard, occupied by Waffen-SS with black-gold-red badges, Degrelle's men. We continued on the main road to the East; I guided Piontek with a map, for I had never been in these parts. Alongside the congested roadway stretched undulating fields, covered with clean, soft, crystalline snow, and then dark, lugubrious birch or pine woods. Here and there, one could see an isolated farm, long, squat buildings, nestled under their thatched, snow-covered roofs. The little redbrick villages, with their gray, steep-sloping roofs and austere Lutheran churches, seemed surprisingly calm, the inhabitants going about their business. After Wangerin, the road rose above wide, cold, gray lakes, only the rims of which had frozen. We crossed Dramburg and Falkenburg; in Tempelburg, a little town on the southern bank of the Dratzig-See, I told Piontek to leave the autobahn and head north, by the road to Bad Polzin. After a long, straight line through wide fields stretching between the fir woods that hid the lake, the road ran atop a steep isthmus crowned with trees, which separates the Dratzig-See from the smaller Sareben-See like a knife blade. Below, forming a long curve between the two lakes, a little village was spread out, Alt Draheim, terraced around a block of square, massive stone, the ruins of an old castle. Beyond the village, a pine forest covered the north bank of the Sareben-See. I stopped and asked my way from a farmer, who showed us almost without a gesture: we had to drive two more kilometers, then turn right. "You can't miss the turn," he said. "There's a big lane of birch trees." But Piontek almost passed it without seeing it. The lane crossed a little wood and then cut straight through lovely open countryside, a long, clear track between two tall curtains of bare, pale birch trees, serene in the midst of the white, virgin expanse. At the far end was the house.

AIR

The house was closed up. I had Piontek stop at the entrance to the courtyard and I walked up to it through virgin, compact snow. The weather was strangely gentle. Along the front, all the shutters were drawn. I walked around the house; the back faced a wide terrace with a balustrade and a curved stairway leading to a snow-covered garden, level at first and then sloping away. Beyond rose the forest, slim pines in the midst of which stood out a few beech trees. Here too everything was shuttered down, silent. I went back to Piontek and had him take me to the village, where I was shown the house of a woman named Käthe, who worked on the estate as a cook and looked after the property when the owners were away. Impressed by my uniform, this Käthe, a sturdy peasant in her early fifties, still very blond and pale, made no difficulty about giving me the keys; my sister and her husband, she explained, had left before Christmas, and since then hadn't sent any word. I went back to the house with Piontek. Von Üxküll's home was a fine little eighteenth-century manor, with a façade the color of rust and ochre, very bright in the midst of all this snow, in a baroque style that was curiously light, subtly asymmetrical, almost fanciful, unusual in these cold, severe regions. Grotesques, each one different from the other, decorated the front door and the lintels of the windows on the ground floor; from the front, the characters seemed to be smiling with all their teeth, but if you looked at them from the side, you saw that they were pulling their mouths open with both hands. Above the heavy wooden door, a cartouche decorated with flowers, muskets, and musical instruments bore a date: 1713. In Berlin, von Üxküll had told me the story of this almost French house, which had belonged to his mother, a von Recknagel. The ancestor who had built it was a Huguenot who had gone to Germany after the revocation of the Edict

of Nantes. He was a rich man and had managed to preserve a good
amount of his wealth. In his old age, he married the daughter of a minor Prussian nobleman, an orphan who had inherited this estate. But
he didn't like his wife's house and had it torn down to build this one.
The wife, however, was devout, and thought such luxury scandalous:
she had a chapel built, along with an annex behind the house, where she
ended her days and which her husband promptly razed after her death.
The chapel itself was still there, set a little apart under old oak trees, stiff,
austere, with a bare façade of red brick and a gray, steeply sloping slate
roof. I slowly walked around it, but didn't try to open it. Piontek was
still standing near the car, waiting without saying anything. I went over
to him, opened the rear door, took out my bag, and said: "I'll stay for a
few days. Go back to Berlin. I'll call or send a telegram for you to come
get me. Will you be able to find this place again? If anyone asks, say you
don't know where I am." He maneuvered to make a U-turn and started
off again, bumping down the long lane of birch trees. I went to put my
bag in front of the door. I contemplated the snow-covered courtyard,
Piontek's car going back down the lane. Besides the tracks the tires had
just left, there were no others in the snow, no one came here. I waited
till he reached the end of the lane and started off on the road to Tempelburg; then I opened the door.

The iron key that Käthe had given me was large and heavy, but the
lock, well oiled, opened easily. The hinges must also have been well
oiled, for the door didn't creak. I pushed open a few shutters to light the
entry hall, then examined the handsome, intricately carved wooden
staircase, the long bookcases, the parquet floor polished by time, the little sculptures and moldings where one could still make out traces of
chipped gold leaf. I turned the switch: a chandelier in the middle of the
room lit up. I turned it off and went upstairs, without bothering to close
the door or take off my cap, coat, or gloves. Upstairs, a long hallway
lined with windows traversed the house. I opened the windows one by
one, threw open the shutters, and closed the windows. Then I opened
the doors: next to the stairway there was a storeroom, a maid's room,
another hallway that led to a service staircase; opposite the windows, a
bathroom and two cold little bedrooms. At the end of the hallway, a
cloth-covered door opened onto a vast master bedroom that took up
the entire rear of the floor. I turned on the light. There was a large four-
poster bed with twirling posts, but no curtains or canopy, a cracked, polished old leather sofa, a wardrobe and a writing desk, a vanity with a tall
mirror, another full-length mirror, facing the bed. Next to the
wardrobe another door must have led to the bathroom. It was obviously
my sister's bedroom, cold and odorless. I contemplated it a while and

then went out and closed the door, without opening the shutters. Downstairs, the hall led to a vast living room, with a piano and a long dining table made of old wood; then came the pantries and kitchen. There I opened everything, going out for a moment to gaze at the terrace, the woods. It was almost warm out, the sky was gray, the snow was melting, dripping from the roof with a pleasant little sound on the flagstones of the terrace and, farther away, hollowing out little wells in the snowy layer at the foot of the walls. In a few days, I thought, if the weather doesn't get cold again, there will be mud, that will slow the Russians down. A crow took off heavily from the pines, cawed, then settled a little farther on. I closed the French windows and returned to the entry hall. The front door was still open: I brought in my bag and closed it. Behind the stairway was another double door, of varnished wood with round ornaments. That must have led to von Üxküll's apartments. I hesitated, then went back to the living room, where I looked at the furniture, the rare, carefully chosen bibelots, the large stone fireplace, the grand piano. A full-length portrait hung behind the piano, in a corner: von Üxküll, still young, in three-quarter profile, with his gaze turned to the spectator, his head bare, in a uniform from the Great War. I examined it, noting the medals, the signet ring, the suede gloves held negligently in his hand. This portrait frightened me a little, I felt my stomach tighten, but I had to admit that he must have been a handsome man, once. I went over to the grand piano and raised the cover. My gaze went from the painting to the long line of ivory keys, then back to the painting. With a finger that was still gloved, I hit a key. I didn't even know what the note was, I knew nothing, and in front of von Üxküll's handsome portrait I was again filled with the old regret. I said to myself: I would so have liked to know how to play the piano, I would so like to hear Bach one more time, before I die. But such regrets were pointless, I replaced the cover and left the living room through the terrace. In a storage room by the side of the house I found the wood supply, and in several trips I carried some large logs to the fireplace, along with smaller pieces of wood, already cut, which I piled into a log holder made of thick leather. I also carried some wood upstairs and lit the stove in one of the small spare bedrooms, fuelling the fire with old issues of the *VB* piled up in the bathroom. In the entry hall, I finally removed my outer clothes, trading my boots for some big slippers I found there; then I went back upstairs with my bag, which I unpacked on the narrow brass bed, putting my clothes away in the closet. The room was simple, with functional furniture, a ewer and a sink, discreet wallpaper. The ceramic stove heated up quickly. I went back downstairs with the bottle of Cognac and began making a fire in the fireplace. It was more trouble than the stove but it finally caught. I poured myself a glass of Cognac, found an ashtray, and settled into a comfortable armchair near the hearth, with my tunic unfastened. The daylight outside was gently waning, and I thought about nothing.

About what happened in that beautiful empty house, I don't know if I can say much. I have already written an account of these events, and when I wrote it, it seemed true to me, equal to the reality, but apparently it doesn't actually correspond to the truth. Why is that the case? Hard to say. It's not that my memories are confused, on the contrary, I have many of them and very precise ones, but many of them overlap and even contradict one another, and their status is uncertain. For a long time I thought that my sister must have been there when I arrived, that she was waiting for me near the entrance to the house in a dark dress, her long, heavy black hair mixing with the mesh of a thick black shawl wrapped round her shoulders. We had spoken, standing in the snow, I wanted her to leave with me, but she didn't want to, even when I explained to her that the Reds were coming, that it was just a question of weeks, or even of days, she refused, her husband was working, she said, he was writing music, it was the first time in a long time and they couldn't leave now, so I decided to stay and sent Piontek away. In the afternoon, we had had tea and talked, I had told her about my work and also about Helene; she had asked me if I had slept with her, if I loved her, and I hadn't known what to say; she had asked me why I didn't marry her and I still hadn't known what to say, finally she had asked me: "Is it because of me that you didn't sleep with her, that you won't marry her?"; and I, ashamed, had kept my eyes lowered, lost in the geometric patterns in the carpet. That is what I remembered, yet it seems that things didn't happen that way, and now I have to acknowledge that my sister and her husband were probably not there, and that is why I am starting this story over from the beginning, trying to hold as close as I can to what can be affirmed. Käthe arrived in the evening with some provisions, in a little cart drawn by a donkey, and prepared a meal for me. As she cooked, I went down to look for wine in the long, vaulted, dusty cellar full of the pleasant smell of damp earth. There were hundreds of bottles there, some of them very old, I had to blow the dust off to read the labels, many of which were completely mildewed. I chose the best bottles without the slightest hesitation, there was no point leaving such treasures to Ivan, anyway he just liked vodka, I found a Château-Margaux 1900 and also took an Ausone from the same year, along with, somewhat at random, a Graves, an Haut-Brion from 1923. Much later, I understood that this was a mistake, 1923 wasn't really a great year, I should have chosen the 1921, better by far. I opened the

Margaux while Käthe served the meal, and arranged with her, before
she left, that she come by every day to make me dinner, but would leave
me alone the rest of the time. The dishes were simple and copious: soup,
meat, potatoes roasted in fat, all the better to savor the wine. I had sat
down at the end of the long table, not in the host's seat but on the side,
with my back to the fireplace, where the fire was crackling, with a tall
candelabrum beside me; I had turned off the electric light and ate in the
golden light of the candles, methodically devouring the rare meat and
the potatoes and drinking the wine in long draughts, and it was as if my
sister were sitting opposite me, also eating calmly with her beautiful
floating smile, we were sitting opposite each other and her husband was
at the head of the table between us, in his wheelchair, and we were
chatting amicably, my sister spoke in a gentle, clear voice, von Üxküll
cordially, with that stiffness and severity that never seemed to leave him,
but without ever relinquishing all the thoughtfulness of a born aristocrat, never putting me ill at ease, and in this warm, shifting light I saw
and heard our conversation perfectly, it occupied my mind as I ate and
finished the bottle of unctuous, opulent, fabulous Bordeaux. I was describing the destruction of Berlin for von Üxküll. "It doesn't seem to
shock you," I finally remarked.—"It's a catastrophe," he retorted, "but
not a surprise. Our enemies are imitating our methods, what's more
normal than that? Germany will drink her cup of sorrow to the dregs
before it's all over." From there, the conversation moved to July 20. I
knew from Thomas that several friends of von Üxküll's were directly
involved. "A large part of the Pomeranian aristocracy has been decimated by your Gestapo since then," he commented coldly. "I knew von
Tresckow's father very well, a man of great moral rigor, like his son.
And of course von Stauffenberg, a family relation."—"How is that?"—
"His mother is a von Üxküll-Gyllenband, Karoline, my second cousin."
Una listened in silence. "You seem to approve of their action," I said.
His answer came to my mind on its own: "I have a great deal of personal respect for some of them, but I disapprove of their attempt for two
reasons. First of all, it's much too late. They should have done it in 1938,
during the Sudeten crisis. They considered it, and Beck wanted to do
it, but when the English and French turned yellow in front of that
ridiculous corporal, it took the wind out of their sails. And also Hitler's
successes demoralized them and finally swept them along, even Halder,
a very intelligent man, but too cerebral. Beck had the intelligence of
honor, he must have understood that now it was too late, but he didn't
back down, to support the others. The real reason, though, is that Germany chose to follow this man. He wants his *Götterdämmerung* at all
costs, and now Germany has to follow him to the end. Killing him now

to save what's left would be cheating, rigging the game. I told you, we have to drink the cup of sorrow to the dregs. That's the only way for something new to begin."—"Jünger thinks the same thing," said Una. "He wrote to Berndt."—"Yes, that's what he let on between the lines. There's also an essay of his about this that's going round."—"I saw Jünger in the Caucasus," I said, "but I didn't have an opportunity to talk with him. In any case, wanting to kill the Führer is an insane crime. There might be no way out, but I think treason is unacceptable, both today and in 1938. It's the reflex of your class, condemned to disappear. It won't survive any better under the Bolsheviks."—"No doubt," von Üxküll calmly said. "I told you: everyone followed Hitler, even the Junkers. Halder thought we could beat the Russians. Ludendorff was the only one who understood, but too late, and he cursed Hindenburg for having brought Hitler to power. I have always detested the man, but I don't take that as a warrant that exempts me from Germany's fate."— "You and your kind, excuse me for saying so, have had your day."— "And you will soon have had yours. It will have been much shorter." He contemplated me fixedly, the way one contemplates a cockroach or a spider, not with disgust, but with the cold passion of an entomologist. I could imagine it very clearly. I had finished the Margaux, I was slightly tipsy, I uncorked the Saint-Émilion, changed our glasses, and had von Üxküll taste the wine. He looked at the label. "I remember this bottle. It was a Roman cardinal who sent it to me. We had had a long discussion about the role of the Jews. He maintained the very Catholic proposition that the Jews must be oppressed, but kept as witnesses to the truth of Christ, a position I've always found absurd. Actually, I think he defended it more for the pleasure of the argument, he was a Jesuit, after all." He was smiling and he asked me a question, no doubt to annoy me: "Apparently the Church caused you some problems when you wanted to evacuate the Jews of Rome?"—"Apparently. I wasn't there."—"Not just the Church," said Una. "You remember, your friend Karl-Friedrich told us that the Italians didn't understand anything about the Jewish question?"—"Yes, that's true," von Üxküll replied. "He said the Italians weren't even applying their own racial laws, that they were protecting foreign Jews from Germany."—"That's true," I said, ill at ease. "We had some difficulties with them about it." And this is what my sister answered: "That's the proof that they are healthy people. They appreciate life at its full value. I understand them: they have a beautiful country, a lot of sun, they eat well, and their women are beautiful."— "Not like Germany," von Üxküll said laconically. I finally tasted the wine: it had the fragrance of roasted clove and a little of coffee, I found it broader than the Margaux, sweet and round and exquisite. Von

Üxküll was looking at me: "Do you know why you're killing the Jews? Do you know?" Throughout this strange conversation he kept provoking me, I didn't reply, I savored the wine. "Why have the Germans shown so much determination to kill the Jews?"—"You're wrong if you think it's only the Jews," I said calmly. "The Jews are only one category of enemy. We are destroying all our enemies, whoever and wherever they are."—"Yes, but admit it, for the Jews you've shown a special determination."—"I don't think so. The Führer, in fact, may have personal reasons to hate the Jews. But at the SD, we don't hate anyone, we objectively pursue our enemies. The choices we make are rational ones."—"Not as rational as all that. Why did you have to eliminate the mentally ill, the handicapped in hospitals? What danger did they pose, those poor wretches?"—"Useless mouths. Do you know how many millions of reichsmarks we saved that way? Not to speak of the hospital beds freed for the wounded from the front."—"I know," said Una, who had been listening to us in silence in this warm golden light, "I know why we killed the Jews." She spoke in a clear, firm voice, I heard her clearly and listened to her as I drank, having finished my meal. "By killing the Jews," she said, "we wanted to kill ourselves, kill the Jew within us, kill that which in us resembles the idea we have of the Jew. Kill in us the potbellied bourgeois counting his pennies, hungry for recognition and dreaming of power, but a power he pictures in the form of a Napoleon III or a banker, kill the petty, reassuring morality of the bourgeoisie, kill thriftiness, kill obedience, kill the servitude of the *Knecht*, kill all those fine German virtues. For we've never understood that these qualities that we attribute to the Jews, calling them baseness, spinelessness, avarice, greed, thirst for domination, and facile malice are fundamentally German qualities, and that if the Jews show these qualities, it's because they've dreamed of resembling the Germans, of *being* Germans, it's because they imitate us obsequiously like the very image of all that is fine and good in High Bourgeoisie, the Golden Calf of those who flee the harshness of the desert and the Law. Or else maybe they were pretending, maybe they ended up adopting these qualities almost out of courtesy, out of a kind of sympathy, so as not to seem so distant. And we, on the other hand, our German dream, was to be Jews, pure, indestructible, faithful to a Law, different from everyone else and under the hand of God. But actually they're all mistaken, the Germans as well as the Jews. For if *Jew*, these days, still means anything, it means Other, an Other and an Otherwise that might be impossible, but that are necessary." She drained her glass in one long swallow. "Berndt's friends didn't understand any of that, either. They said that in the end the massacre of the Jews wasn't really important, and that by killing

Hitler they could lay the crime on him, on Himmler, on the SS, on a few sick assassins, on you. But they're just as responsible for it as you are, for they too are Germans and they too waged war for the victory of this Germany, and not any other. And the worst thing is that if the Jews pull through, if Germany collapses and the Jews survive, they'll forget what the name *Jew* means, they'll want to be more German than ever before." I kept drinking as she spoke in her clear, rapid voice, the wine going to my head. And all of a sudden my vision of the Zeughaus came back to me, the Führer as a Jew with the prayer shawl of the rabbis and the leather ritual objects, in front of a vast audience where no one noticed it, *except me*, and all of that suddenly disappeared, Una and her husband and our conversation, and I was left alone with the remains of my meal and the extraordinary wines, drunk, full, a little bitter, a guest no one had invited.

That night, I slept poorly in my little bed. I had drunk too much, my head was spinning, I was still suffering from the aftereffects of the shock from the day before. I hadn't closed the shutters and the moonlight fell softly into the room, I pictured it penetrating the bedroom at the end of the hallway too, sliding over my sister's sleeping body, naked under the sheet, and I would have liked to be this light, this intangible gentleness, but at the same time my mind was raging, the febrile arguments at dinner echoed in my head like the mad ringing of Orthodox bells at Easter and ruined the calm in which I'd have liked to bathe. Finally I sank into sleep, but the unease continued, stained my dreams in horrible colors. In a dark bedroom, I could see a tall, beautiful woman in a long white dress, maybe a wedding dress, I couldn't make out her features but it was obviously my sister, she was lying on the ground, on the carpet, prey to uncontrollable convulsions and diarrhea. Black shit oozed through her dress, the inner folds must have been full of it. Von Üxküll, having found her this way, went back into the hallway (he was walking) to call in a peremptory tone a bellboy or a floor waiter (thus it must have been a hotel, I imagine it was their wedding night). Returning to the room, von Üxküll ordered the attendant to pick her up by her arms as he took her feet to carry her into the bathroom so she could be undressed and washed. He did this coldly, efficiently, he seemed indifferent to the foul smells emanating from her and choking me, I had to force myself to control my disgust, my rising nausea (but where was I, then, in this dream?).

I got up early and crossed the empty, silent house. In the kitchen I found some bread, some butter, honey, and coffee, and I ate. Then I went into the living room and examined the books in the library. There were a lot of volumes in German but also in English, Italian, Russian; I ended up choosing, with a rush of pleasure, *L'Éducation sentimentale*, which I found in French. I sat down near a window and read for a few hours, raising my head from time to time to look at the woods and the gray sky. Around noon, I fixed an omelette with bacon for myself, and ate at the old wooden table that took up the corner of the kitchen, pouring myself some beer, which I drank in long draughts. I made some coffee and smoked a cigarette, then decided to take a walk. I put on my officer's coat without buttoning it: it was still warm out, the snow wasn't melting but was hardening and forming a crust. I set out across the garden and entered the forest. The pines were well spaced out, very tall, they rose and at the very top came together like a vast vault set on columns. There were still patches of snow in places, the bare ground was hard, red, carpeted with dry needles that crackled under my steps. I came to a sandy path, a straight line between the pines. Tracks of wagon wheels were imprinted in the ground; by the edge of the path, here and there, logs were carefully piled up. The path led to a gray river, a dozen meters wide; on the far shore rose a plowed field whose black furrows streaked the snow, running up to a beech wood. I turned right and entered the forest, following the course of the gently murmuring river. As I walked, I imagined Una walking with me. She was wearing a wool skirt and boots, a man's leather jacket, and her large knit shawl. I saw her walking in front of me, with a sure, calm step, I watched her, aware of the play of her muscles and thighs, her buttocks, her proud, straight back. I couldn't imagine anything nobler or truer or more beautiful. Farther on, oak and beech trees mixed with the pines, the ground became swampy, covered with waterlogged dead leaves through which my feet sank into a mud that was still hard from the cold. But a little farther along, the ground rose slightly and became dry and pleasant underfoot again. Here there were almost nothing but pines, thin and arrow-straight, young stock replanted after clear-cutting. Then finally the forest opened onto a brushy, cold, almost snowless meadow, looking down on the still water of the lake. To the right I saw a few houses, the road, the crest of the isthmus crowned with firs and birches. I knew that the river was called the Drage, and that it went from this lake to the Dratzig-See and then continued on to the Krössin-See, where there was an SS school, near Falkenburg. I looked at the gray expanse of the lake: around it lay the same ordered landscape of black earth and woods. I followed its bank to the village. A farmer in his garden hailed me, and I exchanged a few words with him; he was worried, he was afraid of the Russians, I couldn't give him any definite news but I knew he was right to be afraid. At the road, I headed left and slowly climbed the long hill between the two lakes. The slopes were steep and hid the water from

me. At the top of the isthmus, I climbed the hillock and went between
the trees, pushing the branches aside, to a place overlooking, from high
up, a bay that opened up into wide, irregular planes of water. The immobility of the water, of the black forests on the other bank, gave this
landscape a solemn, mysterious look, like a kingdom beyond life, yet still
on this side of death, a land between the two. I lit a cigarette and looked
at the lake. A childhood conversation came to my mind, my sister, one
day, had told me an old Pomeranian myth, the legend of Vineta, a beautiful, arrogant city swallowed up in the Baltic, whose bells fishermen still
heard ringing on the water at noon, somewhere near Kolberg, it was
said. This rich, great city, she had explained to me with her childlike seriousness, was lost because of the limitless desire of a woman, the king's
daughter. Many sailors and knights came to drink and amuse themselves
there, handsome, strong men, full of life. Every night, the king's daughter went out disguised into the town, she went down to the inns, the
most sordid dens, and there she chose a man. She brought him back to
her palace and made love to him all night; in the morning, the man was
dead of exhaustion. Not one, even the strongest, resisted her insatiable
desire. She had their corpses thrown into the sea, into a storm-tossed
bay. But being unable to satisfy the immensity of her desire only excited
that desire more. She could be seen walking on the beach, singing for
the Ocean, to whom she wanted to make love. Only the Ocean, she
sang, would be vast enough, powerful enough to fulfill her desire. Finally one night, unable to stand it any longer, she went out of her palace
naked, leaving the corpse of her last lover in her bed. There was a storm
that night, the Ocean was lashing the sea wall protecting the city. She
went out onto the dyke and opened the great bronze door placed there
by her father. The Ocean entered the city, took the princess and made
her his wife, and kept the drowned city as her dowry. When Una had
finished her story, I had pointed out that it was the same as the French
legend of the city of Ys. "Indeed," she had retorted haughtily, "but this
one is more beautiful."—"If I understand it correctly, it explains that the
order of the city is incompatible with the insatiable pleasure of
women."—"I would say, rather, the excessive pleasure of women. But
what you are proposing is a man's morality. I believe that all these
ideas—moderation, morality—were invented by men to compensate for
the limits of their pleasure. For men have known for a long time that
their pleasure can never be compared to the pleasure we endure, which
is of a different order."

On the way back, I felt like an empty shell, an automaton. I thought
about the terrible dream of the night before, I tried to imagine my sister with her legs covered in liquid, sticky diarrhea, with its abominably

sweet smell. The emaciated evacuees of Auschwitz, huddled under their blankets, also had their legs covered in shit, their legs like sticks; the ones who stopped to defecate were executed, they were forced to shit as they walked, like horses. Una covered in shit would have been even more beautiful, solar and pure under the mire that would not have touched her, that would have been incapable of soiling her. Between her stained legs I would have nestled like a newborn starving for milk and love, lost. These thoughts ravaged my head, impossible to chase away, I was having trouble breathing and didn't understand what was invading me so brutally. Back at the house, I wandered aimlessly through the hallways and rooms, opening and closing doors at random. I wanted to open the ones to von Üxküll's rooms, but stopped at the last instant, my hand on the doorknob, held back by a wordless confusion, like when as a child I entered my father's office to stroke his books and play with his butterflies. I went upstairs and into Una's bedroom. I rapidly opened the shutters, throwing them back with a clatter of wood. The windows overlooked the courtyard on one side, and on the other, the terrace, the garden, and the forest, beyond which one could glimpse a tip of the lake. I sat down on the chest at the foot of the bed, opposite the large mirror. I contemplated the man in front of me in the mirror, a slumping, tired, glum man, his face swollen with resentment. I didn't recognize him, that couldn't be me, but it was. I straightened up and lifted my head, but that didn't change much. I imagined Una standing in front of this mirror, naked or wearing a gown, she must have found herself fabulously beautiful, and how fortunate she was to be able to look at herself this way, to be able to gaze at her beautiful body, but maybe not, maybe she didn't see the beauty, invisible to her own eyes, maybe she didn't perceive the frightening strangeness, the scandal of those breasts and that sex, that thing between her legs that can't be seen but that jealously hides all its splendor, maybe she felt only its heaviness and slow aging, with a light sadness or at most a gentle feeling of familiar complicity, never the acridness of panicking desire: Look, there's *nothing* to be seen there. Breathing with difficulty, I got up, went over to the window to look out, toward the forest. The warmth I'd worked up from my long walk had dissipated, the room seemed icy to me, I was cold. I turned to the writing desk standing against the wall between the two windows that looked out onto the garden, and tried absentmindedly to open it. It was locked. I went downstairs, found a big knife in the kitchen, piled some kindling into the log holder, took also the bottle of Cognac and a tumbler, and went back upstairs. In the bedroom, I poured myself a measure of alcohol, drank a little, and started making a fire in the heavy stove built into the corner. When it had caught, I straightened up and snapped the lock of the writing desk with the knife. It gave way easily. I sat down, the glass of Cognac next to me, and went through the drawers. There were all sorts of trinkets and papers, jewelry, some exotic shells, fossils, business correspondence, which I skimmed over absentmindedly, letters addressed to Una from Switzerland dealing mostly with questions of psychology mixed with ordinary gossip, other things besides. In one drawer, crammed into a little leather portfolio, I found a sheaf of papers written in her handwriting: drafts of letters addressed to me, which she had never sent. With my heart beating, I cleared the desk, stuffing the rest of the things into the drawers, and fanned the letters out like a deck of playing cards. I let my fingers play over them and chose one, at random I thought, but it was probably not entirely at random, since the letter was dated April 28, 1944, and began: *Dear Max, it was a year ago today that Mother died. You never wrote to me, you never told me anything about what happened, you never explained anything to me . . .* The letter broke off there, I quickly skimmed over a few others, but they all looked unfinished. Then I drank a little Cognac and began telling my sister everything, exactly as I've written it here, without omitting anything. That took some time; when I finished, the room was growing dark. I took another letter and rose to hold it up near the window. This one talked about our father, and I read it at one go, my mouth dry, tense with anguish. Una wrote that my resentment toward our mother, on our father's account, had been unfair, that our mother had had a hard life because of him, his coldness, his absences, his final, unexplained departure. She asked me if I even remembered him. In fact I didn't remember many things, I recalled his smell, his sweat, how we rushed at him to attack him, when he was reading on the sofa, and how he took us then in his arms, roaring with laughter. Once when I was coughing he had me swallow some medicine that I had immediately vomited onto the carpet; I was dying of shame, I was afraid he would get angry, but he had been very kind, he had comforted me and then cleaned the carpet. The letter went on, Una explained to me that her husband had known our father in Courland, that our father, as Judge Baumann had indicated, commanded a Freikorps. Von Üxküll commanded another unit, but he knew him well. *Berndt says he was a mad animal,* she wrote. *A man without faith, without limits. He had raped women crucified to trees, he himself threw living children into burning barns, he handed captured enemies over to his men, a pack of insane beasts, and laughed and drank as he watched them tortured. In command, he was stubborn and narrow, he wouldn't listen to anyone. The entire flank he was supposed to defend at Mitau collapsed because of his arrogance, precipitating the army's retreat. I know you're not going to believe me,* she added, *but that is the truth, you can think what you like about it.* Horrified, overcome with rage, I crumpled the letter up, made as if to tear it up, but restrained myself. I threw it on the secretary and walked across the room, I wanted to go out, but came back, hesitated, blocked by a flood of contradictory impulses, finally I drank some Cognac, that calmed me down a little, I took the bottle and went downstairs to drink some more in the living room.

Käthe had arrived and was preparing dinner, going in and out of the kitchen; I didn't want to be around her. I went back to the entry hall and opened the door to von Üxküll's apartments. There were two handsome rooms there, a study and a bedroom, tastefully furnished with old pieces in heavy, dark wood, oriental carpets, simple metal objects, a bathroom with special equipment, probably adapted to his paralysis. Looking at all this, I again felt a vivid sense of confusion, but at the same time I didn't care. I walked around the study: no objects cluttered the massive, chairless desk; on the shelves there were only music scores, by all sorts of composers, arranged by country and period, and, set aside, a small pile of bound scores, his own works. I opened one and contemplated the series of notes, an abstraction for me, I didn't know how to read music. In Berlin, von Üxküll had spoken to me about a work he was planning, a fugue or, as he had said, a suite of serial variations in the form of a fugue. "I don't know yet if what I envisage is actually possible," he had said. When I had asked him what the theme would be, he had made a face: "It's not romantic music. There is no theme. It's just an étude."—"Whom are you writing it for?" I had then asked.—"For no one. You know quite well they never play my works in Germany. I'll probably never hear it played."—"Why are you writing it, then?" And he had smiled, a big, happy smile: "To have done it before I die."

Among the scores there were of course some Rameau, some Couperin, Forqueray, Balbastre. I took a few from the shelf and leafed through them, looking at the titles I knew well. There was Rameau's *Gavotte à six doubles*, and by looking at the page the music immediately unfurled in my head, clear, joyous, crystalline, like the galloping of a purebred horse raced across the Russian steppe in winter, so light that its hooves just brushed the snow, leaving only the slightest of traces. But no matter how much I stared at the page I couldn't connect those bewitching trills to the signs drawn on it. At the end of the meal in Berlin, von Üxküll had mentioned Rameau again. "You're right to like that music," he had said. "It's a lucid, sovereign music. It never foresakes its elegance but remains bristling with surprises and even traps, it is playful, joyful with a gay knowledge that neglects neither mathematics, nor life." He had also defended Mozart in curious terms: "For a long time I had little regard for him. When I was young, he seemed to me a gifted hedonist, without any depth. But that might have been the judgment of my own Puritanism. As I get older, I'm beginning to think he may have had a sense of life as strong as Nietzsche's, and that his music seems simple only because life, in fact, is rather simple. But I haven't entirely decided yet, I have to listen some more."

Käthe was leaving and I went to eat, ceremoniously emptying another one of von Üxküll's marvelous bottles. The house was beginning to seem familiar and warm to me, Käthe had made a fire in the fireplace, the room was pleasantly heated, I felt assuaged, akin to all this, this fire and this good wine and even the portrait of my sister's husband, hanging over the piano I couldn't play. But this feeling didn't last. After the meal, I had cleared the table and poured myself a measure of Cognac, I settled in front of the fireplace and tried to read Flaubert, but couldn't concentrate. Too many mute things worried me. I had an erection, the idea came to me to strip naked, to go explore this big and dark and cold and silent house naked, a vast, free space that was also private and full of secrets, just like Moreau's house when we were children. And this thought brought along another one, its obscure twin, that of the controlled, disciplined space of the camps: the overcrowding of the barracks, the swarming in the collective latrines, no place possible to have, alone or with someone else, a human moment. I had talked about this once with Höss, who had told me that despite all the prohibitions and precautions, the inmates continued to have a sexual activity, not just the kapos with their *Pipel* or the lesbians among themselves, but men and women, the men bribed the guards so they'd bring them their mistresses, or slipped into the *Frauenlager* with a work Kommando, and risked death for a quick jolt, a rubbing together of two emaciated pelvises, a brief contact of shaved, lice-ridden bodies. I had been strongly impressed by this impossible eroticism, doomed to end crushed beneath the guards' hobnail boots, the very opposite in its despair of the free, solar, transgressive eroticism of the rich, but maybe also its hidden truth, slyly and obstinately signifying that all real love is inevitably turned toward death and, in its desire, doesn't take the body's wretchedness into account. For man has taken the coarse, limited facts given to every sexed creature and has built from them a limitless fantasy, murky and profound, an eroticism that, more than anything, distinguishes him from the animals, and he has done the same thing with the idea of death, but this imagination, curiously, has no name (you could call it *thanatism*, perhaps): and it is these imaginations, these forever rehearsed obsessions, and not the thing itself, that are the frantic driving forces behind our thirst for life, for knowledge, for the agonizing struggle of self. I was still holding *L'Éducation sentimentale*, set down on my lap almost touching my sex, forgotten, I let these idiot's thoughts dig into my head, my ears full of the anguished beating of my heart.

In the morning I was calmer. In the living room, I tried to resume reading after having some bread and coffee, and then my thoughts drifted away again, detached from the torments of Frédéric and Madame Arnoux. I wondered: What did you come here for? What do you want, exactly? To wait till Una returns? To wait till a Russian comes and slits your throat? To commit suicide? I thought about Helene. She and my sister, I said to myself, were the only two women, aside from a few nurses, to have seen my body naked. What had she seen, what had she thought when she saw that? What did she see in me that I didn't see, and that my sister, for a long time now, didn't want to see anymore? I thought about Helene's body, I had often seen her in a bathing suit, her curves were finer and lither than my sister's, her breasts smaller. Both had the same white skin, but this whiteness stood in stark contrast to the thick black hair of my sister, whereas with Helene, it continued in the soft blondness of her hair. Her sex too must have been blond and soft, but I didn't want to think about that. I was seized by a sudden disgust. I said to myself: love is dead, the only love is dead. I shouldn't have come, I should leave, go back to Berlin. But I didn't want to go back to Berlin, I wanted to stay. A little later I got up and went out. I set off again through the forest, I found an old wooden bridge over the Drage and crossed it. The thickets became increasingly dense, dark, one could only continue on the foresters' and loggers' paths, across which branches stretched and scratched my clothes. Farther on stood an isolated hill from which one could probably see the whole region, but I didn't push on as far as that, I walked aimlessly, in a circle perhaps, finally I found the river again and came back to the house. Käthe was waiting for me and came out of the kitchen to meet me: "Herr Busse is here, with Herr Gast and some other people. They're waiting for you in the courtyard. I gave them some schnapps." Busse was von Üxküll's farmer. "What do they want with me?" I asked.—"They want to talk with you." I crossed the house and went out into the courtyard. The farmers were sitting on an open wagon drawn by a scrawny draught horse, which was grazing on the tufts of grass emerging from the snow. When they saw me they bared their heads and jumped to the ground. One of them, a red-faced man, his hair gray but his moustache still black, came forward and bowed slightly in front of me. "Good day, Herr Obersturmbannführer. Käthe told us that you are the Baronness's brother?" His tone was polite, but he was hesitating, searching for his words. "That's right," I said.—"Do you know where the Freiherr and the Freifrau are? Do you know what their plans are?"—"No. I thought

I'd find them here. I don't know where they are. In Switzerland, prob-
ably."—"It's just that we'll soon have to leave, Herr Obersturmbann-
führer. We shouldn't wait much longer. The Reds are attacking
Stargard, they've surrounded Arnswalde. People are worried. The
Kreisleiter says they'll never reach this far, but we don't believe him."
He was embarrassed, he kept turning his hat around in his hands. "Herr
Busse," I said, "I understand your concern. You have to think of your
families. If you feel you should leave, leave. No one's holding you back."
His face cleared a little. "Thank you, Herr Obersturmbannführer. It's
just that we were concerned, seeing as how the house was empty." He
hesitated. "If you like, I can give you a cart and a horse. We'll help you,
if you want to load some furniture. We can take it with us, put it somewhere safe."—"Thank you, Herr Busse. I'll think about it. I'll send
Käthe to get you, if I decide on something."

The men climbed back up, and the wagon moved slowly away down
the birch lane. Busse's words had no effect on me, I couldn't manage to
think about the Russians' arrival as a concrete, imminent thing. I stayed
there, leaning on the frame of the large door, and smoked a cigarette as
I watched the wagon disappear down the end of the lane. Later on in
the afternoon, two other men presented themselves. They wore blue
jackets made of coarse cloth, big hobnail boots, and held caps in their
hands; I understood right away that they were the two Frenchmen from
the STO that Käthe had told me about, who carried out maintenance
or farm work for von Üxküll. They were the only personnel, along
with Käthe, who still remained: all the men had been drafted, the gardener was with the *Volkssturm*, the maid had left to join her parents,
who had been evacuated to Mecklenburg. I didn't know where these
two men were staying, maybe with Busse. I talked to them directly in
French. The older one, Henri, was a stocky, broad-backed farmer in his
forties from the Lubéron, he knew Antibes; the other probably came
from a provincial city, and seemed still young. They too were worried,
they had come to say they wanted to leave, if everyone else was leaving. "You understand, Monsieur l'Officier, we don't like the Bolsheviks
any more than you do. They're savages, we don't know what to expect
from them."—"If Herr Busse leaves," I said, "you can leave with him.
I won't hold you back." Their relief was palpable. "Thank you, Monsieur l'Officier. Please give our respects to Monsieur le Baron and to
Madame, when you see them."

When I see them? This idea seemed almost comical to me; at the
same time, I was entirely incapable of accepting the thought that I might
never see my sister again: it was literally *unthinkable*. That evening, I had
dismissed Käthe early and served myself, I dined for the third time alone

in this large candlelit room, solemnly, and as I ate and drank I was overcome with startling fantasies, the demented vision of a perfect co-
prophagic autarky. I pictured myself confined alone in this manor house
with Una, isolated from the world, forever. Every evening, we put on
our finest clothing, suit and a silk shirt for me, a beautiful, close-fitting,
barebacked evening gown for her, enhanced by heavy, almost barbaric
silver jewelry, and we sat down to an elegant dinner, at this table covered with a lace tablecloth and set with crystal tumblers, silverware
stamped with our crest, Sèvres porcelain plates, massive silver candelabra
bristling with long white tapers; in the glasses, our own urine, on the
plates well-formed pieces of excrement, pale and firm, which we calmly
ate with little silver spoons. We wiped our lips with monogrammed
cambric napkins, we drank, and when we had finished, we went into
the kitchen ourselves to wash the dishes. This way, we were self-sufficient, without loss and without trace, neatly. This aberrant vision filled
me for the rest of the meal with a sordid anguish. Afterward I went up
to Una's room to drink Cognac and smoke. The bottle was almost
empty. I looked at the secretary, now closed again, my evil feeling
wouldn't let me go, I didn't know what to do, but above all I didn't want
to open the secretary. I opened the wardrobe and inspected my sister's
dresses, breathing in deeply to immerse myself in the smell they gave
off. I chose one, a beautiful evening gown made of delicate material,
black and gray with silver threads; standing in front of the tall mirror, I
held the dress draped over my body, and with great seriousness made a
few feminine gestures. But immediately I was afraid and put the dress
away, full of disgust and shame: What was I playing at here? My body
wasn't hers and never would be. At the same time, I couldn't contain
myself, I should have left the house right away, but I couldn't leave the
house. Then I sat down on the sofa and finished the bottle of Cognac,
forcing myself to think about the scraps of letters I had read, about these
endless, answerless enigmas, my father's departure, my mother's death. I
got up, went to get the letters, and sat down again to read a few more
of them. My sister was trying to ask me questions, she asked me how I
could have slept while our mother was being killed, what I had felt
when I saw her body, what we had talked about the day before. I could
answer almost none of these questions. In one letter, she told me about
the visit from Clemens and Weser: intuitively, she had lied to them, she
hadn't said I had seen the bodies, but she wanted to know why I had
lied, and what exactly I remembered. What I remembered? I didn't
even know what a memory was anymore. When I was little, one day, I
climbed, and even today, as I write, I can see myself very clearly climbing the gray steps of a great mausoleum or a monument lost in a forest.

The leaves were red, it must have been the end of autumn, I couldn't
see the sky through the trees. A thick layer of dead leaves, red, orange,
brown, gold, covered the steps, I sank into them up to my thighs, and
the steps were so high that I was forced to use my hands to hoist myself
up to the next one. In my memory, this whole scene is thick with an
overwhelming feeling, the burned colors of the leaves weighed on me,
and I cleared a path for myself on these steps for giants through this dry,
crumbling mass, I was afraid, I thought I would sink into it and disappear. For years, I believed this image was the memory of a dream, an
image from a childhood dream that had stayed with me. But one day, in
Kiel, when I returned there for university, I chanced upon this ziggu-
rat, a little granite war monument, I walked around it, the steps weren't
higher than other steps, this was the place, this place existed. Of course,
I must have been very small when I had gone there, that's why the steps
seemed so tall to me, but that's not what overwhelmed me, it was seeing, after so many years, something that I had always located in the
world of dreams present itself this way as reality, as a concrete, material
thing. And the same was true with everything Una had tried to talk to
me about in these unfinished letters that she had never sent me. All these
endless thoughts were bristling with sharp angles, I gashed myself on
them viciously, the hallways of this cold, oppressive house were streaming with the bloody shreds of my feelings; a young, healthy maid should
have come and washed everything clean, but there was no more maid.
I put the letters away in the secretary and, leaving the empty bottle and
glass there, went into the bedroom next to hers to go to bed. But as
soon as I lay down, obscene, perverse thoughts began to flood in again.
I got up again and in the trembling light of a candle contemplated my
naked body in the wardrobe mirror. I touched my flat belly, my stiff penis, my buttocks. With the tip of my fingers I caressed the hairs on the
back of my neck. Then I blew the candle out and lay down again. But
these thoughts refused to go away, they emerged from the corners of the
room like mad dogs and rushed at me to tear into me and inflame my
body, Una and I were exchanging our clothes, naked except for stockings, I pulled on her long dress as she buttoned herself up in my uniform and put up her hair and fastened it under my cap, then she sat me
down in front of her dressing table and carefully made up my face,
combing my hair back, applying lipstick to my mouth, mascara on my
eyelashes, powder on my cheeks, she dabbed drops of perfume on my
neck and painted my nails, and when it was over we just as brutally exchanged our roles, she equipped herself with a sculpted ebony phallus
and took me like a man, in front of her tall mirror that impassively reflected our bodies intertwined like snakes, she had coated the phallus

with cold cream, and the acrid smell bit into my nose as she used me as
if I were a woman, until all distinctions were erased and I could say to
her: "I am your sister and you are my brother," and she: "You are my
sister and I am your brother."

These appalling images kept gnawing at me for days on end like
overexcited puppies. My relation to these thoughts was that of two
magnets whose polarities were constantly reversed by a mysterious
force: if we attracted each other, they changed so that we repelled each
other; but scarcely had this happened than they changed again, we attracted each other again, and all this took place very rapidly, so that we
oscillated before each other, these thoughts and I, at an almost constant
distance, as incapable of approaching each other as we were of drawing
away from each other. Outside the snow was melting, the ground was
turning muddy. Käthe came one day to tell me that she was leaving; officially, it was still forbidden to evacuate, but she had a cousin in Lower
Saxony, she was going to live with her. Busse returned also to renew his
offer: he had just been recruited into the *Volkssturm* but wanted to send
his family away, before it was too late. He asked me to go over his accounts with him, in von Üxküll's name, but I refused and dismissed him,
asking him to take the two Frenchmen along with his family. When I
went walking by the road, I didn't see much traffic; but in Alt Draheim,
the prudent ones were discreetly getting ready to leave; they were emptying their stores of supplies and sold me provisions cheaply. The countryside was calm, from time to time you could just make out the sound
of an airplane, high in the sky. One day, while I was upstairs, a car came
down the lane. Hiding behind a curtain, I watched it from a window;
when it had come closer, I recognized a Kripo license plate. I ran to my
bedroom, took out my service weapon from the holster in my bag, and,
without thinking, ran down the servants' stairway and through the
kitchen door to take refuge in the woods beyond the terrace. Clutching
my pistol nervously, I skirted a little around the garden, well back behind the line of trees, then drew closer under cover of a thicket to observe the house. I saw a figure come out through the French windows
of the living room and cross the terrace to position himself at the
balustrade and observe the garden, hands in his coat pockets. "Aue!" he
called twice, "Aue!" It was Weser, I recognized him easily. The tall figure of Clemens stood outlined in the doorway. Weser barked my name
out a third time, in a definitive tone, then turned around and went into
the house, preceded by Clemens. I waited. After a long while, I saw
their shadows busy behind the windows of my sister's bedroom. A mad
rage seized me and brought blood to my face as I cocked the pistol,
ready to run into the house and kill these two evil bloodhounds piti-

lessly. I restrained myself with difficulty and stayed there, my fingers white from clutching the pistol, trembling. Finally I heard the sound of an engine. I waited a little more and then went in, on the lookout in case they had set a trap for me. The car had left, the house was empty. In my bedroom, nothing seemed to have been touched; in Una's bedroom, the secretary was still closed, but inside, the drafts of her letters had disappeared. Stunned, I sat down on a chair, the pistol on my knee, forgotten. What were they after, these rabid, obstinate animals, deaf to all reason? I tried to think about what the letters contained, but I couldn't manage to put my thoughts in order. I knew they provided a proof of my presence in Antibes at the time of the murder. But that had no importance anymore. What about the twins? Did these letters talk about the twins? I made an effort to remember, it seemed that no, they said nothing about the twins, whereas obviously that was the only thing that mattered to my sister, much more than our mother's fate. What were they to her, these two kids? I got up, put the pistol on the end table, and set about searching through the secretary again, slowly and methodically this time, as Clemens and Weser must have done. And then I found, in a little drawer that I hadn't noticed, a photograph of the two boys, showing them naked and smiling, in front of the sea, probably near Antibes. Yes, I said to myself as I examined this image, in fact it's possible, they must be hers. But who then was the father? Certainly not von Üxküll. I tried to imagine my sister pregnant, holding her swollen belly in her hands, my sister giving birth, torn apart, screaming, it was impossible. No, if that was indeed the case they must have cut her open, taken them out through the belly, it wasn't possible otherwise. I thought about her fear while faced with this thing swelling inside her. "I've always been afraid," she had said to me one day, a long time ago. Where was that? I don't know anymore. She had spoken to me about the permanent fear women have, that old friend that lives with them, all the time. Fear when you bleed every month, fear of taking something inside yourself, of being penetrated by the parts of men who are so often selfish and brutal, fear of gravity dragging the flesh, the breasts, downward. It must have been the same for the fear of being pregnant. Something's growing, something's growing in your belly, a strange body inside you, which moves and sucks up all your body's strength, and you know it has to come out, even if it kills you, it has to come out, how horrible. Even with all the men I had known I couldn't approach that, I could understand nothing of women's overwhelming fear. And once the children are born, it must be even worse, since then begins the constant fear, the terror that haunts you day and night, and that ends only with you, or with them. I saw the image of those mothers clutching their children as they were shot, I saw those Hungarian Jewesses sitting on their suitcases, pregnant women and girls waiting for the train and the gas at the end of the trip, it must have been that which I had seen in them, that which I had never been able to get rid of and had never been able to express, that fear, not their open and explicit fear of the gendarmes or the Germans, of us, but the mute fear that lived inside them, in the fragility of their bodies and their sexes nestling between their legs, that fragility we were going to destroy without ever seeing it.

It was almost warm out. I had taken a chair out onto the terrace, I stayed there for hours, reading or listening to the snow melting in the sloping garden, watching the topiary reappear, reimposing their presence. I read Flaubert and also, when I tired momentarily of the *great moving walkway* of his prose, verses translated from Occitan that sometimes made me laugh out loud in surprise: *I have a lady, don't know who she is, / Never saw her, by my faith.* I had the joyous feeling of being on a deserted island, cut off from the world; if, as in fairy tales, I could have surrounded the estate with a barrier of invisibility, I would have stayed there forever, waiting for my sister's return, almost happy, as Bolsheviks and trolls overran the surrounding lands. For like the poet-princes of the Lower Middle Ages, the thought of the love of a woman cloistered in a distant castle (or a Helvetian sanatorium) fully contented me. With a serene gaiety, I pictured her sitting like me on a terrace, facing high mountains instead of a forest, also alone (let her husband deal with his treatment), and reading books like the ones I was reading, taken from her library. The keen mountain air must have bitten at her mouth, perhaps she had wrapped herself in a blanket to read, but beneath it her body remained, with its heaviness and its presence. As children, our spindly bodies rushed at each other, clashed together furiously, but they were like two cages of skin and bone, which prevented our naked feelings from touching each other. We hadn't yet grasped the extent to which love lives in bodies, nests in their most secret folds, in their wearinesses and their weight too. I imagined with precision Una's body reading, adjusting itself to the chair, I guessed the curve of her backbone, of the back of her neck, the weight of one leg crossed over the other, the almost inaudible sound of her breathing, and the very idea of her sweat, under her armpits, delighted me, lifted me into a transport that abolished my own flesh and turned me into pure perception, strained to the breaking point. But such moments couldn't last: water was slowly dripping from the trees and there, in Switzerland, she got up, pushing off her blanket, and went back into the common rooms, leaving me with my chimeras, my dark chimeras that, as I in turn went back into the house, blended into its architecture, spread out according to the layout of the rooms I lived in, avoided, or, like her bedroom, wanted to avoid but couldn't. I had finally pushed open the door to her bathroom. It was a large woman's room, with a long porcelain bathtub, a bidet, a toilet in the back. I fingered the perfume flasks, contemplating myself bitterly in the mirror over the sink. As in her bedroom, there was almost no odor in this bathroom; no matter how deeply I breathed in, it was in vain, she had left too long ago, and Käthe had cleaned well. If I put my nose over the perfumed soaps, or else opened the flasks of eau de toilette, then I smelled magnificent, profoundly feminine scents, but they weren't hers, even her sheets had no smell, I had gone out of the bathroom and returned to the bed to sniff it in vain, Käthe had put on clean, white, stiff, cool sheets, even her underwear had no smell, the few black lace panties left in her drawers, carefully washed, and it was only with my head buried in the dresses in the closet that I noticed something, a distant, indefinable odor, which made my temples pulsate and the blood beat dully in my ears. At night, in the light from a candle (the electricity had been cut off for some days), I heated two large buckets of water on the stove and went up to pour them into my sister's bathtub. The water was boiling, I had to wear gloves to hold the burning handles; I added a few buckets of cold water, dipping my hand in to check the temperature, and added some flakes of scented bubbles. I was now drinking a local plum brandy, a large demijohn of which I had found in the kitchen, and I had also brought up a flask of it, with a glass and an ashtray, which I placed on a little silver tray across the bidet. Before entering the water I lowered my eyes to my body, my pale skin that took on a softly golden tint in the light of the candles stuck in a candelabrum at the foot of the bath. I didn't like this body very much, and yet, how could I not adore it? I got into the water thinking about the creaminess of my sister's skin, alone and naked in a tiled bathroom in Switzerland, with the thick blue veins snaking beneath that skin. I hadn't seen her body naked since we were children; in Zurich, overcome with fear, I had turned off the lights, but I could picture it down to the smallest details, the heavy, ripe, firm breasts, the solid hips, the beautiful round belly that was lost in a dense black triangle of curls, creased possibly now by a thick vertical scar, from the navel to the pubis. I drank a little brandy and relaxed into the embrace of the hot water, my head resting on the shelf near the candlestick, my chin scarcely rising above the thick layer of soap bubbles, as the serene face of my sister must have floated, her long hair put up in a heavy bun stabbed by a silver needle. The thought of that body stretched in the water, its legs slightly apart, reminded me of the conception of Rhesos. His mother, one of the Muses, I forget which, Calliope perhaps, was still a virgin and she was going to a musical contest to answer the challenge of Thamyris; to get there, she had to cross the River Strymon, which slipped its cool ripples into her, between her thighs, and that's how she conceived. Was that how my sister conceived her twins, I said to myself sourly, in the soapy water of her bath? She must have known men, after me, many men; and since she had betrayed me in this way, I hoped it was with many men, an army, and that she deceived her impotent husband every day with anything that came her way. I imagined her having a man come up to this bathroom, a farm boy, the gardener, a milkman, one of the Frenchmen from the STO. Everyone in the neighborhood must have known, but no one said anything, out of respect for von Üxküll. And von Üxküll couldn't care less, he stayed hunched like a spider in his apartments, dreaming about his abstract music, which carried him far from his broken body. And my sister too couldn't care less about what her neighbors thought or said, as long as they kept coming up. She asked them to carry the water, to help her unfasten her dress; and they were clumsy, they blushed, their stubby fingers, hardened by work, got tangled up, she had to help them. Most of them were already hard when they came in, that was obvious through their pants; they didn't know what to do, she had to tell them everything. They rubbed her back, her breasts, and afterward, she fucked them in her bedroom. They smelled of earth, of filth, of sweat, of cheap tobacco, she must have liked that, madly. Their cocks, when she pulled back the foreskin to suck them, stank of urine. And when it was over she dismissed them, amicably but without smiling. She didn't wash, she slept in their smell, like a child. Thus her life, when I wasn't there, was no better than mine, both of us, without the other, knew only how to wallow in our bodies, their infinite, yet at the same time so limited possibilities. The bath was slowly growing colder, but I didn't get out, I warmed myself in the evil fire of these thoughts, I found an insane comfort in these daydreams, even the most sordid ones, I sought a refuge in my dreams like a kid under his blanket, for however cruel and corrupt they might have been, it was always better than the unbearable bitterness of the outside. Finally I got out of the bath. Without even drying myself I swallowed a glass of brandy, then rolled myself up in one of the large bath towels hanging there. I lit a cigarette and, without troubling to get dressed, went to smoke at one of the windows looking out onto the courtyard: in the farthest distance, a pale line rimmed the sky, shifting slowly from pink to white to gray then to a dark blue that melted into the nighttime sky. The cigarette finished, I went to drink another glass and then lay down on the large four-poster bed, pulling the starched sheets and heavy blankets over me. I stretched out my limbs, turned onto my stomach, my head buried in the soft pillow, lying as she had lain there, after her bath, for so many years. I saw it clearly, all these agitated and contradictory things were rising up in me like a black water, or like a loud noise that threatened to drown out all other sounds, reason, prudence, even conscious desire. I slipped my hand between my thighs, and said to myself: If I slipped my hand there, on her, she wouldn't be able to stand it anymore, but at the same time this thought revolted me, I didn't want her to take me as she would have taken a farm boy, just to satisfy herself, I wanted her to desire me, freely as I desired her, I wanted her to love me as I loved her. Finally I sank into sleep and into ferocious, dislocated dreams, of which only the dark trace of this phrase, uttered by Una's serene voice, remains in my mind: "You are a very heavy man for women to bear."

I was gradually reaching the limit of my abilities to contain the disconcerting rushes, the incompatible surges that were sweeping over me. I roamed aimlessly through the house, I spent a whole hour caressing with my fingertips the polished wooden ornaments decorating the doors to von Üxküll's apartments, I went down to the basement with a candle to lie down on the hard dirt floor, damp and cold, I inhaled with delight the dark, stale, archaic smells of this underground chamber, I went to inspect with an almost forensic meticulousness the two ascetic bedrooms of the house servants and their bathrooms, Turkish-style toilets with carefully polished corrugated foot rests, set far apart to leave ample room for the intestinal discharge of these women whom I pictured as strong, white, and well built, like Käthe. I no longer thought about the past, I was no longer at all tempted to turn back to look at Eurydice, I kept my eyes firmly in front of me on this unacceptable present, which was swelling endlessly, on the innumerable objects cluttering it, and I knew, with an unwavering confidence, that she, she was following me step by step, like my shadow. And when I opened up drawers to go through her lingerie, her hands passed delicately beneath my own, unfolded, caressed these sumptuous underclothes made of very delicate black lace, and I didn't need to turn around to see her sitting on the sofa unrolling a silk stocking, adorned at midthigh with a wide band of lace, on that smooth and carnal expanse of white skin, slightly hollowed out between the tendons, or else putting her hands behind her back to hook her bra, in which she adjusted her breasts, one by one, with a quick movement. She would have carried out these gestures in front of me, these everyday gestures, shamelessly, without false modesty, without exhibitionism, exactly as she must have carried them out alone, not mechanically but with attention, taking great pleasure in them, and if she wore lace underwear, it wasn't for her husband, or for her lovers of a night, or for me, but for herself, for her own pleasure, the pleasure of feeling this lace and this silk on her skin, of contemplating her beauty thus adorned in her tall mirror, of looking at herself exactly as I looked at myself or wanted to be able to look at myself: not with a narcissistic gaze, or with a critical gaze that searches for defects, but with a gaze that is desperately trying to grasp the elusive reality of what it sees—a painter's gaze, if you like, but I am not a painter, any more than I am a musician. And if she had stood thus in front of me in reality, almost naked, I would have looked at her with a similar gaze, whose desire would only have sharpened its lucidity, I would have looked at the texture of her skin, the weft of her pores, the little brown flecks of beauty spots strewn by chance, constellations yet to be named, the thick strokes of veins that surrounded her elbow, climbed her forearm in long branches, then came to swell the back of her wrist and hand before ending up, channeled between the joints, disappearing into her fingers, exactly as in my own man's arms. Our bodies are identical, I wanted to explain to her: aren't men the vestiges of woman? For every fetus starts out female before it differentiates itself, and men's bodies forever keep the trace of this, the useless tips of breasts that never grew, the line that divides the scrotum and climbs the perineum to the anus, tracing the place where the vulva closed to contain ovaries that, having descended, evolved into testicles, as the clitoris grew unrestrainedly. Only one thing was actually lacking to be a woman like her, a real woman, the mute *e*, in French, of feminine word endings, the extraordinary possibility in that language we shared of saying and writing: "Je suis nu*e*, je suis aimé*e*, je suis désiré*e*." It's this *e* that makes women so terribly female, and I suffered inordinately from being stripped of it, it was a flat loss for me, even harder to compensate for than the loss of that vagina I had left at the gates of existence.

From time to time, when these inner tempests calmed down a little, I took up my book again, I let myself be carried peacefully away by Flaubert's pages, facing the forest and the low, gray sky. But, inevitably, I came to forget the book on my lap, as the blood rose to my face. Then to gain time I again took up one of the old French poets, whose condition must not have differed much from my own: *I know not when I am asleep / Or when I wake, unless I'm told.* My sister had an old edition of Thomas's *Tristan*, which I also lazily leafed through until I saw, with a terror almost as keen as that of a nightmare, that she had marked the following lines in pencil:

> *Quant fait que faire ne desire*
> *Pur sun buen qu'il ne puet aveir*
> *Encontre desir fait voleir.*

> When he does what he does not desire to do
> Because he can't have what he wants
> He turns his will against desire.

And once again it was as if her long ghostlike hand had come and slipped under my arm, all the way from her Helvetian exile or else right behind me, to place a finger gently in front of my eyes under these words, this irrevocable sentence that I couldn't accept, that I rejected with all the miserable determination I could still muster.

And thus I fell into a long, endless *stretto*, where every response came before the question was over, but in retrograde, like a *cancrizans*. Of the last days spent in that house, only scraps of images, disconnected and senseless, remain, confused but animated too by the implacable logic of dream, the very speech or rather the clumsy croaking of desire. I slept every night now in her odorless bed, stretching myself out on my stomach with all my limbs extended, or else curling into a ball on my side, my head empty of all thought. Nothing remained in this bed that recalled her, not even a strand of hair, I had taken off the sheets to examine the mattress, hoping to find at least a bloodstain, but the mattress was as clean as the sheets. So I set about soiling it myself, squatting with my legs wide apart, the ghostly body of my sister open beneath me, her head turned slightly aside and her hair pulled back to reveal her small, delicate, round ear that I loved so, then I collapsed in my slime and abruptly fell asleep, my belly still sticky. I wanted to possess this bed, but it was the bed that possessed me, no longer let me go. All kinds of phantoms came to coil up in my sleep, I tried to chase them away, for I wanted only my sister there, but they were stubborn, they returned by the ways I least expected them, like the shameless little feral girls in Stalingrad, I opened my eyes and one of them had slid right up against me, she was turning her back to me and pushing her buttocks against my belly, my penis entered her from that end and she stayed like that, moving very slowly, and then afterward she kept me in her ass, we fell asleep that way, embedded in each other. And when we woke up she slipped her hand between her thighs and raked my scrotum, almost painfully, and again I became hard inside her, one hand on the bone of her taut hip, and I turned her over onto her stomach and began again, as she clenched her little fists in the sheets and moved without a sound. She never left me free. But then another, unexpected feeling came over me, a gentle and forlorn feeling. Yes, that's exactly it, it's coming back to me now, she was blond, gentle and forlorn. I don't know how far things went between us. The other image, the one of the girl sleeping with her lover's cock in her ass, doesn't involve her. It wasn't Helene, that's certain, for I have a confused idea that her father was a policeman, a high official who didn't approve of his daughter's choice and regarded me with hostility, and then also with Helene my hand had never gone farther than her knee, which here was perhaps not the case. This blond girl too took up room in the big bed, room that wasn't hers. All this caused me a great deal of concern. But finally I succeeded in driving them all away, by brute force, at least up against the torsaded posts of the canopy, and in leading my sister back by the hand and laying her down in the middle of the bed, I spread out on top of her with all my weight, my belly naked right against the scar slicing across hers, I thrust against her, vainly and with increasing rage, and finally there was a great opening, as if my body in turn were split open by the surgeon's blade, my bowels poured onto her, the children's door opened on its own beneath me and everything flowed in that way, I was lying on her as one lies in the snow, but I was still clothed, I took off my skin, abandoned my naked bones to the embrace of this cold white snow that was her body, and it closed in over me.

A gleam of light from the setting sun passed under the clouds and struck the wall of the bedroom, the secretary, the side of the wardrobe, the foot of the bed. I got up and went to piss, then went downstairs to the kitchen. Everything was quiet. I cut some slices of good coarse peasant bread, buttered them, put some thick slices of ham on top. I also found some pickles, a terrine of pâté, some hard-boiled eggs, and put it all onto a tray with silverware, two glasses, and a bottle of good Burgundy, a Vosne-Romanée, I think it was. I returned to the bedroom and placed the tray on the bed. I sat down cross-legged and contemplated the empty sheets before me, across the tray. Slowly my sister took shape there, with a surprising solidity. She was sleeping on her side, folded in on herself; gravity drew down her breasts and even, a little, her belly, her skin was stretched over her raised, angular hip. It wasn't her body that was sleeping but she who, sated, was sleeping nestled inside her body. A little bright red blood was seeping between her legs, without staining the bed, and all this heavy humanity was like a stake driven into my eyes; it didn't blind me, though, but on the contrary opened up my third eye, the pineal eye grafted into my head by a Russian sniper. I uncorked the bottle, breathed in the heady odor deeply, then poured two glasses. I drank and began to eat. I was immensely hungry, I devoured everything that was there and emptied the bottle of wine. Outside, the day was drawing to a close, the room was growing dark. I cleared the tray, lit some candles, and brought over some cigarettes that I smoked lying on my back, the ashtray on my stomach. Above me, I could hear a frantic buzzing. I looked around, without moving, and saw a fly on the ceiling. A spider was leaving it and slipping into a crack in the molding. The fly was trapped in the spiderweb, struggling with this buzzing to free itself, in vain. At that instant a breath passed over my penis, a phantom finger, the tip of a tongue; immediately it began to swell up, to unfold. I put the ashtray aside and imagined her body slipping over me, rearing up to bury me inside her while her breasts sat heavy in my hands, her thick black hair forming a curtain round my head, framing a face lit up by an immense, radiant smile, which said to me: "You have been placed in this world for one single thing, to fuck me." The fly kept buzzing, but ever less frequently, it would start suddenly and then stop. I felt the base of her spine beneath my hands, the small of her back, her mouth, above me, murmured: "Oh, God, oh, God." Afterward, I looked at the fly again. It was silent and still, the poison had finally overcome it. I waited for the spider to reemerge. Then I must have fallen asleep. A furious outbreak of buzzing woke me up, I opened my eyes and watched. The spider was hovering near the struggling fly. The spider hesitated, came forward and withdrew, returned finally to its crack. Again the fly stopped moving. I tried to imagine its silent terror, its fear fractured in its faceted eyes. From time to time the spider reemerged, tested its prey with a leg, added a few spins to the cocoon, returned; and I observed this interminable agony, until the moment the spider, hours later, finally dragged the dead or overcome fly into the molding to consume it in peace.

When day came, still naked, I put on some shoes so as not to get my feet dirty and went to explore this large, cold, dark house. It unfurled around my charged body, my skin white and bristling from the cold, as sensitive over its entire surface as my stiff penis or my tingling anus. It was an invitation to the worst excesses, to the most insane, transgressive games, and since the tender, warm body I desired was denied to me, I used her house as I would have used her, I made love to her house. I went everywhere, lay down in the beds, stretched out on the tables or the carpets, rubbed my backside against the corners of furniture, jerked off in armchairs or closed wardrobes, in the midst of clothes smelling of dust and mothballs. I even thus entered von Üxküll's apartments, with a feeling of childlike triumph at first, then of humiliation. And humiliation in one form or another never let go of me, a sense of the mad vanity of my gestures, but this humiliation and this vanity too placed themselves at my service, and I profited from them with an evil, limitless joy.

These disjointed thoughts, this frantic exhaustion of all possibilities, had replaced my sense of time. Sunrises, sunsets, only marked out the rhythm, like hunger or thirst or natural needs, like sleep that rose up at any time to engulf me, restore my strength, and return me to the wretchedness of my body. Sometimes I put on some clothes and went out walking. It was almost hot out, the abandoned fields beyond the Drage had become heavy, slippery, their crumbling soil stuck to my feet and forced me to walk around them. During these walks I saw no one. In the forest, a breath of wind was enough to drive me into a frenzy, I lowered my pants and pulled up my shirt and lay down on the hard, cold ground covered with pine needles that pricked my rear end. In the dense woods beyond the bridge over the Drage, I stripped completely naked, except for my shoes, which I kept on, and began running, as when I was a kid, through branches that scratched my skin. Finally I stopped against a tree and turned around, both hands behind me clutching the trunk, to rub my anus slowly against the bark. But that didn't satisfy me. One day I found a tree lying down, overturned by a storm, with a broken branch on the top of the trunk, and with a pocket knife I shortened this branch some more, removed its bark and smoothed the wood, carefully rounding out the tip. Then, soaking it copiously in saliva, I straddled the trunk and, leaning on my hands, slowly buried this branch inside me, all the way. It gave me an immense pleasure, and all this time, my eyes closed, my penis forgotten, I imagined my sister doing the same thing, making love in front of me like a lustful dryad with the trees of her forest, using her vagina as well as her anus to take an infinitely more terrifying pleasure than my own. I came in huge disordered spasms, tearing myself away from the stained branch, falling to the side and backward onto a dead branch that made a deep gash in my back, a raw, adorable pain on which I remained for several minutes leaning with the weight of my almost fainting body. Finally I rolled over onto my side, blood flowing freely from my wound, dead leaves and needles sticking to my fingers; I got up, my legs trembling with pleasure, and began running between the trees. Farther on, the woods grew wet, a fine mud dampened the earth, patches of moss covered the driest places, I slipped in the mud and fell onto my side, panting. The cry of a buzzard echoed through the undergrowth. I got up and went down to the Drage, took off my shoes and dove into icy water that shocked my lungs, to wash off the mud and the still-flowing blood, mixed, when I got out, with the cold water streaming down my back. Once dry, I felt revived, the air on my skin was warm and gentle. I would have liked to cut down some branches, build a hut that I'd have carpeted with moss, and spend the night there, naked; but it was still too cold out, and also there was no Iseult to share it with me, no King Mark either to chase us from the castle. Instead I tried to lose myself in the woods, first with a childlike joy, then almost with despair, for it was impossible, I always stumbled onto a path or else a field, all ways led me to known landmarks, whatever direction I chose.

Of the outside world I no longer had the slightest idea, I didn't know what was happening in it. There was no radio, no one came. Abstractedly, I understood that to the south, while I was losing myself here in the mad bitterness of my impotence, many human lives were coming to an end, as so many other lives already had, but it all was the same to me. I couldn't have said if the Russians were twenty kilometers away or a hundred, and I couldn't have cared less, worse, I didn't even think about it, for me all that was occuring in a time—not to mention a space— completely different from my own, and if that time came to meet my time, well, then, we'd see which one would give way. But despite my abandon, a naked anguish welled up from my body, trickled out of it, the way droplets of melted snow fall from a branch to strike the branches and needles below it. This anguish was mutely corroding me. Like an animal digging through its fur to find the source of a pain, like a child, obstinate and furious at his fractious toys, I sought to put a name on my sorrow. I drank, I emptied several bottles of wine or else glasses of brandy and then I abandoned my body to the bed, thrown open to the winds. A cold, wet breeze circulated through it. I looked at myself sadly in the mirror, contemplating my red, tired sex hanging in the middle of the pubic hair, I said to myself it had changed quite a bit, and that even if she had been there it would no longer be as it was before. When we were eleven or twelve our sexes were minuscule, it was almost our skeletons that collided with each other in the twilight; now, there was all this thickness of flesh, and also the terrible wounds it had undergone, a slit belly no doubt for her, and for me the long hole through my skull, a scar wrapped around itself, a tunnel of dead flesh. A vagina, a rectum, is also a hole in the body, but inside the flesh is alive, it forms a surface, for it, there is no hole. What is a hole, a void, then? It's what is inside the head when thought dares to try to flee from itself, to separate itself from the body, to act as if the body didn't exist, as if you could think without a body, as if the most abstract thought, the thought of the starry sky above and the moral law within, for example, were not wedded to the rhythm of the breath, the pulsing of blood in the veins, the grating of cartilage. And it's true, when I played with Una when we were children, and later on, when I learned to use for my own purposes the bodies of the boys who desired me, I was young, I hadn't yet understood the specific weight of bodies, and what the commerce of love involves, destines and condemns us to. Age meant nothing to me, even in Zurich. Now, I had begun the preliminary work, I sensed what living in a body could signify, and even in a woman's body, with its heavy breasts, a body forced to sit on the toilet or crouch down to urinate, whose belly has to be cut open with a knife to take the children out. I would have loved to set that body down in front of me, on the sofa, its thighs open like the pages of a book, a narrow band of white lace hiding the bulge of the sex, the beginnings of the thick scar above it and, to the sides, the ridges of the tendons, hollows where I longed to set my lips, and to stare at it as two fingers slowly came to push the fabric aside: "Look, look how white it is. Think, think how black it is beneath." I desired madly to see this sex lying between those two coombs of white flesh, swollen, as if offered on the serving tray of its thighs, and to slip my tongue through the almost dry cleft, from bottom to top, delicately, just once. I also wanted to watch this beautiful body pissing, leaning forward on the toilet seat, elbows resting on the knees, and to hear the urine gushing into the water; and I then wanted her mouth to lean forward as she finished, take my still-limp penis in her lips, I wanted her nose to sniff at my pubic hair, the hollow between my scrotum and my thigh, the line of my hips, to grow intoxicated with my rough, sour smell, that male smell I know so well. I was burning to lay this body down on the bed and spread its legs, to bury my nose in that moist vulva like a sow nuzzling for a nest of black truffles, then to turn the body over on its stomach, spread its buttocks with both hands to contemplate the purplish rosette of the anus blinking gently like an eye, put my nose to it, and breathe in. And I dreamed of pushing my face as I slept into the curly hair of her armpit and of letting her breast weigh on my cheek, my two legs wrapped around one of hers, my hand resting lightly on her shoulder. And when, upon waking, this body beneath me had completely absorbed me, she would have looked at me with a floating smile, would have spread her legs once again and rocked me inside her to the slow, subterranean rhythm of one of Josquin's old Masses, and we would have slowly moved away from the shore, carried by our bodies as by a warm, becalmed sea rich in salt, and her voice would have come whispering next to my ear, clearly and distinctly: "The gods created me for love."

It was beginning to grow cold again, it snowed a little, the terrace, the courtyard, the garden were dusted with snow. There wasn't much left to eat, I had finished the bread, I tried to make some myself with Käthe's flour, I didn't really know how to go about it, but I found a recipe in a cookbook and made several loaves, from which I tore pieces that I swallowed hot as soon as they came out of the oven, crunching at the same time on raw onions that gave me an awful breath. There were no more eggs or ham, but in the basement I found some crates of little green apples from the previous summer, a little mealy but sweet, which

I ate throughout the day, drinking sips of brandy. The wine cellar, however, was inexhaustible. There were also some pâtés, so I dined on pâté, on bacon grilled on the stove with onions, and on the greatest wines of France. At night, it snowed again, in heavy gusts; the wind, coming from the north, struck the house mournfully, banging the poorly fastened shutters as the snow beat against the windows. But there was no lack of wood, the stove in the bedroom roared, it was pleasant in this bedroom, where I stretched out naked in a darkness illumined by snow, as if the storm were whipping my skin. The next day it was still snowing, the wind had fallen and the snow was coming down, thick and heavy, covering the trees and the ground. A shape in the garden made me think of the bodies lying in the snow at Stalingrad, I could see them clearly, their blue lips, their bronze-colored skin pricked with stubble, surprised, stunned, dumbstruck in death but calm, almost peaceful, the very opposite of Moreau's body bathing in its blood on the carpet, of my mother's body with its twisted neck, spread out on the bed, atrocious, unbearable images, I couldn't stay with them despite all my efforts, and to chase them away I climbed in my mind the steps leading to the attic of Moreau's house, I took refuge there and huddled in a corner, to wait for my sister to come find me and console me, her doleful knight with the broken head.

That night, I took a long, hot bath. I placed one foot and then the other on the ledge and, rinsing the razor in the bathwater, I shaved both my legs, carefully. Then I shaved my armpits. The blade slid over the thick hair, coated with shaving cream, which fell in curly bundles into the soapy bathwater. I got up, changed the blade, placed one foot on the edge of the bathtub and shaved my sex. I proceeded attentively, especially for the hard-to-reach parts between the legs and the buttocks, but I slipped and cut myself just behind the scrotum, where the skin is most sensitive. Three drops of blood fell one after the other into the white foam of the bath. I patted some eau de Cologne on, it burned a little but also soothed my skin. Everywhere hair and shaving cream floated on the water, I took a bucket of cold water to rinse myself off, my skin was bristling, my scrotum shriveled. Leaving the bath, I looked at myself in the mirror, and this frighteningly naked body seemed foreign to me, it looked more like the body of the green Apollo in Paris than my own. I leaned against the mirror with my whole body, I closed my eyes and imagined myself shaving my sister's sex, slowly, delicately, pulling the folds of flesh between two fingers so as not to wound her, then turning her over and making her lean forward so I could shave the curly hairs around her anus. Afterward, she came to rub her cheek against my skin, naked and withered by the cold, she tickled my little boy's shrunken testicles and licked the tip of my circumcised penis, with short, exciting tongue strokes: "I almost liked it better when it was as big as *that*," she said laughing, holding her thumb and forefinger a few centimeters apart, and I stood her up and looked at her naked sex protruding from her legs, prominent, the long scar I always imagined there not quite reaching it but stretching toward it, it was the sex of my little twin sister and I burst into tears in front of it.

I lay down on the bed, I touched my child's parts, so strange under my fingers, I turned over onto my stomach, caressed my buttocks, gently touched my anus. I put all my effort into imagining that these buttocks were my sister's, I kneaded them, slapped them. She laughed. I kept spanking her, with the flat of my hand, the elastic behind rang beneath my palms, and she, her breasts, her face lying like mine on the sheet, was overcome with uncontrollable laughter. When I stopped, the buttocks were red, I don't know if mine actually were, for in this posture I couldn't hit hard, but on the sort of invisible stage in my head they were, I could see the shaved vulva overflowing between them, still white and pink, and I turned her body around, buttocks toward the great full-length mirror and I said to her: "Look," and she, still laughing, turned her head to see, and what she saw cut off her laughter and her breath, just as it cut off my own. Held by my thought, floating in this dark and empty space inhabited only by our bodies, I slowly reached my hand out toward her, with my forefinger out, and I ran my finger in the slit that parted like a poorly healed wound. Then I slipped behind her and, rather than remaining on my knees, I squatted so that I could see between my legs and she could see too. Leaning with one hand on her bared neck—her head was resting on the bed and she was looking between her legs—I took my penis in my other hand and pushed it between the lips of her sex; in the mirror, when I turned my head, I could clearly see my penis enter her childlike vulva, and, beneath, her upended face, flushed with blood and hideous. "Stop, stop," she moaned, "that's not how it should be done," and then I pushed her forward so her body was again flat on the bed, crushed by my own, and I took her that way, both hands on her long neck, she panted as I came, my breath rattling. Then I tore myself from her and rolled on the bed, as she cried like a little girl: "That's not how it should be done," then I too began crying and touched her cheek: "How should it be done?" and she slid onto me, kissed my face, my eyes, my hair, "Don't cry, don't cry, I'll show you," she was calming down, I too was calming down, she was sitting astride me, her belly and smooth vulva rubbing against my stomach, she straightened up, crouched down so as to be sitting on my hips, her knees up and her sex swollen, like a strange, decorative thing attached to her body, placed on my abdomen, she began rubbing it and it opened up, sperm mixed with her own secretions flowed from it which she smeared on my belly, facing me, kissing my belly with her vulva as if it were a mouth, I drew up, took her by the neck and, leaning against her, kissed her in the mouth, her buttocks were pushing now against my hardening penis, she pushed me back down and, one hand leaning on my chest, still crouching, she guided my penis with her other hand and impaled herself on it. "Like that," she repeated, "like that." She rocked back and forth, starting and stopping, her eyes closed, and I, I looked at her body, I sought out her little flat body from before beneath the breasts and curves of her hips, dazed, almost stunned. The dry and nervous orgasm, almost spermless, tore me open as a fish knife would, she kept plunging on me, her vulva like an open shell, prolonged by the long straight scar that cut across her belly, and all that now formed one long slit, which my sex opened up to the navel.

It was snowing in the night, but I continued wandering in this limitless space where my thought reigned sovereign, making and unmaking forms with an absolute freedom that nevertheless kept running into the limits of bodies, mine real, material, and hers imagined and thus inexhaustible, in an erratic to-and-fro that left me each time emptier, more febrile, more desperate. Sitting naked on the bed, drained, I drank brandy and smoked and my gaze went from the outside, from my reddened knees, my long veined hands, my sex shriveled up at the bottom of my slightly bulging belly, to the inside, where it traveled over her sleeping body, sprawled out on her stomach, her head turned toward me, her legs stretched out, like a little girl. I gently parted her hair and bared her neck, her beautiful, powerful neck, and then my thoughts returned, as in the afternoon, to the strangled neck of our mother, she who had borne us together in her womb, I caressed my sister's neck and tried seriously and attentively to imagine myself twisting my mother's neck, but it was impossible, the image didn't come, there was no trace of such an image inside me, it stubbornly refused to form in the mirror that I contemplated within myself, this mirror reflected nothing, remained empty, even when I placed both my hands under my sister's hair and said to myself: Oh my hands on my sister's nape. Oh my hands on my mother's neck. No, nothing, there was nothing. Suddenly shivering, I curled up in a fetal ball at the end of the bed. After a long while I opened my eyes. She lay fully stretched out, one hand on her belly, her legs apart. Her vulva was opposite my face. The small lips protruded slightly from the pale, domed flesh. This sex was watching at me, spying on me, like a Gorgon's head, like a motionless Cyclops whose single eye never blinks. Little by little this silent gaze penetrated me to the marrow. My breath sped up and I stretched out my hand to hide it: I no longer saw it, but it still saw me and stripped me bare (whereas I was already naked). If only I could still get hard, I thought, I could use my prick like a stake hardened in the fire, and blind this Polyphemus who made me Nobody. But my cock remained inert, I seemed turned to stone. I stretched out my arm and buried my middle finger into this boundless eye. The hips moved slightly, but that was all. Far from piercing it, I had on the contrary opened it wide, freeing the gaze of the eye still hiding behind it. Then I had an idea: I took out my finger and, dragging myself forward on my forearms, I pushed my forehead against this vulva, pressing my scar against the hole. Now I was the one looking inside, searching the depths of this body with my radiant third eye, as her own single eye irradiated me and we blinded each other mutually: without moving, I came in an immense splash of white light, as she cried out: "What are you doing, what are you doing?" and I laughed out loud, sperm still gushing in huge spurts from my penis, jubilant, I bit deep into her vulva to swallow it whole, and my eyes finally opened, cleared, and saw everything.

In the morning, a thick fog had come and covered everything: from the bedroom, I couldn't see the birch lane, or the forest, or even the end of the terrace. I opened the window, again I could hear the drops falling from the roof, the screech of a buzzard far off in the forest. Barefoot, I went downstairs and out onto the terrace. The snow on the flagstones was cold beneath my feet, the cool air made my skin bristle, I went over and leaned against the stone railing. When I turned around, I couldn't even see the house anymore, the railing disappeared into the mist, I felt as if I were floating, isolated from everything. A shape under the snow in the garden, possibly the one I had glimpsed the day before, attracted my attention. I leaned over to see it better, the fog half veiled it, again it made me think of a body, but this time of the body of the young hanged woman in Kharkov, lying in the snow in the Trade Unions Park, her breast gnawed by dogs. I shivered, my skin tingled, the cold made it extraordinarily sensitive, my naked, shaved sex, the cold air, the fog enveloping me all gave me a wonderful feeling of nudity, an absolute, almost raw nudity. The shape had disappeared now, it must have been a dip in the land, I forgot it and leaned my body against the railing, letting my fingers wander over my skin. When my hand began rubbing my penis I scarcely noticed it, so little did it alter the sensations that were slowly peeling back my flesh, then thinning out my muscles, then removing my very bones, leaving only something nameless that, reflecting itself, gave itself pleasure as if to something identical yet slightly shifted, not opposite to it but merging with it in its oppositions. The orgasm thrust me backward like a discharge and sent me sprawling onto the snow-covered flagstones of the terrace where I remained in a stupor, all my limbs trembling. I thought I could see a shape lurking in the fog near me, a feminine form, I heard cries, they seemed far away but they must have been my own, and at the same time I knew that all this was happening in silence, and that not a sound came from my mouth to trouble this gray morning. The form detached itself from the fog and came to lie down on me. The cold of the snow bit into my bones. "It's us," I whispered into the labyrinth of its little round ear. "It's us." But the form remained mute and I knew it was still me, only me. I got up and went back into the house, I was trembling, I rolled on the carpets to dry myself out, breathing heavily. Then I went down into the basement. I pulled out bottles at random and blew on them to clear the labels, the clouds of dust made me sneeze. The cold and dank smell of this basement penetrated my nostrils, the soles of my feet enjoyed the cold, damp, almost slippery feeling of the hard earthen floor. I settled on a bottle and opened it with a corkscrew hanging from a string, I drank straight from the bottle, the wine ran from my lips onto my chin and my chest, I was getting hard again, now the shape was standing behind the shelves and swaying gently, I offered it wine but it didn't move, then I lay down on the hard earth and it came to crouch over me, I kept drinking from the bottle as it used me, I spat some wine at it, but it didn't take notice, it continued its disjointed movement. Each time, now, my orgasm came harsher, more acrid, even slightly acidic, the tiny stubble that was reappearing irritated my flesh and my penis, and when, immediately afterward, it went limp, the red, crumpled skin showed the thick jutting green veins, the network of purple venules. And yet I couldn't rest, I ran heavily throughout the big house, into the bedrooms, the bathrooms, arousing myself every possible way but without coming, for I no longer could. I played at hide-and-seek, knowing there was no one to find me, I didn't really know what I was doing anymore, I followed the impulses of my bewildered body, my mind remained clear and transparent but my body took refuge in its opacity and its weakness, the more I worked it, the less it served me as a passageway and the more it turned into an obstacle, I cursed it and also tried to outsmart this thickness, irritating and exciting it to the point of madness, but a cold excitation, almost sexless. I committed all sorts of infantile obscenities: in a maid's room, I knelt on the narrow bed and stuck a candle into my anus, I lit it with difficulty and maneuvered it, letting big drops of hot wax fall onto my buttocks and the back of my testicles, I roared, my head crushed against the iron bedstead; afterward, I shat crouching on the Turkish-style toilets in the servants' dark cubbyhole; I didn't wipe myself, but jerked off standing in the service staircase, rubbing my shit-stained buttocks against the railing, the smell assaulting my nose and going to my head; and as I came, I almost fell down the stairs, I caught myself just in time, laughing, and looked at the traces of shit on the wood, which I carefully wiped off with a little lace tablecloth taken from the guest room. I grated my teeth, I could hardly bear to touch myself, I laughed like a madman, finally I fell asleep stretched out on the floor in the hallway. When I woke up I was famished, I devoured everything I could find and drank another bottle of wine. Outside, the fog veiled everything, it must still have been daytime, but it was impossible to guess the hour. I opened up the attic: it was dark, dusty, full of a musty odor, my feet left great tracks in the dust. I had taken some leather belts, which I threw over a beam, and I began showing the shape, which had discreetly followed me, how I hanged myself in the forest when I was little. The pressure on my neck made me hard again, it panicked me, to avoid suffocating I had to stand on tiptoe. I jerked off very quickly this way, just rubbing the glans coated with saliva, until the sperm spurted across the attic, a few drops only but projected with incredible force, I yielded to the orgasm with all my weight, if the shape hadn't supported me I would really have hanged myself. Finally I unfastened myself and collapsed into the dust. The shape, on all fours, sniffed at my limp member like an avid little animal, raised its leg to expose its vulva to me, but avoided my hands when I reached out to it. I didn't get hard quickly enough for it, and it strangled me with one of the belts; when my penis was finally erect, it freed my neck, tied my feet together, and impaled itself on me. "Your turn," it said. "Squeeze my neck." I took its neck in my hands and pressed with both thumbs as it raised its legs and, its feet on the floor, moved back and forth on my aching penis. Its breathing gushed from its lips in a high-pitched whistle, I pressed harder, its face swelled, flushed crimson, horrible to see, its body remained white, but its face was red as raw meat, its tongue stuck out from its teeth, it couldn't even rattle, and when it came, burying its nails into my wrists, it emptied itself, and I began howling, bellowing and bashing my head against the floor, I was past all restraint, I bashed my head and sobbed, not out of horror, because this female form that would never remain my sister had pissed on me, it wasn't that, but when I saw it come and piss, strangled, I saw the hanged women in Kharkov who as they suffocated emptied themselves over the passersby, I had seen that girl we had hanged one winter day in the park behind the statue of Shevchenko, a young and healthy girl bursting with life, had she too come when we hanged her and soiled her panties, when she fought and shuddered, strangled, was she coming, had she ever even come before, she was very young, had she ex-perienced that before we hanged her, what right did we have to hang her, how could we hang this girl, and I sobbed endlessly, ravaged by her memory, my very own Our-Lady-of-the-Snows, it wasn't remorse, I didn't have remorse, I didn't feel guilty, I didn't think things could or should have been otherwise, yet I understood what it meant to hang a girl, we had hanged her the way a butcher slaughters a steer, without passion, because it had to be done, because she had done something stu-pid and had to pay for it with her life, that was the rule of the game, of our game, but the girl we had hanged wasn't a pig or a steer that you kill without thinking about it because you want to eat its flesh, she was a young girl who had been a little girl who may have been happy and who was then just entering life, a life full of murderers whom she hadn't been able to avoid, a girl like my sister in a way, someone's sister, per-haps, as I too was someone's brother, and such cruelty had no name, no matter how objectively necessary, it ruined everything, if one could do that, hang a girl like that, then one could do anything, nothing could be assured, my sister could be happily pissing in a toilet one day and the next day be emptying herself as she suffocated on the end of a rope, there was absolutely no sense to it, and that is why I wept, I didn't un-derstand anything anymore and I wanted to be alone to no longer understand anything.

I woke up in Una's bed. I was still naked but my body was clean and my legs free. How had I gotten there? I had no memory of it. The stove had gone out and I was cold. I uttered my sister's name softly, stupidly: "Una, Una." The silence froze me and made me shiver, but maybe it was the cold. I got up: it was daytime outside, the sky was cloudy but there was a beautiful light, the fog had dissipated and I looked at the for-est, the trees with their branches still loaded with snow. A few absurd lines came to mind, an old song of Guillem IX, that slightly crazed duke of Aquitaine:

> *Farai un vers de dreyt nien:*
> *non er de mi ni d'autra gen,*
> *non er d'amor ni de joven,*
> *ni de ren au.*

> I'll make a song about nothing at all:
> not about me, or anybody else,
> not about love not about youth,
> or anything else.

I rose and headed for the corner where some of my clothes were piled up, to pull on a pair of pants, drawing the suspenders over my bare shoulders. Passing in front of the bedroom mirror I looked at myself: a thick red mark cut across my throat. I went downstairs; in the kitchen I bit into an apple, drank a little wine from an open bottle. There was no more bread. I went out onto the terrace: the weather was still cold, I rubbed my arms. My irritated penis hurt, the wool pants made it worse. I looked at my fingers, my forearms, I idly played at emptying the thick blue veins in my wrist with the tip of my fingernail. My nails were dirty, the thumbnail on my left hand was broken. On the other side of the house, in the courtyard, birds were cawing. The air was sharp, biting, the snow on the ground had melted a little then hardened on the surface, the traces left by my footsteps and my body on the terrace were still visible. I went to the railing and leaned over. A woman's body was lying in the snow of the garden, half naked in her gaping bathrobe, motionless, her head tilted, her eyes open to the sky. The tip of her tongue rested delicately on the corner of her blue lips; between her legs, a shadow of hair was reappearing on her sex, it must still have been continuing to grow, stubbornly. I couldn't breathe: this body in the snow was the mirror of the girl's body in Kharkov. And I knew then that the body of that girl, that her twisted neck, her prominent chin, her frozen, gnawed breasts, were the blind reflection not, as I had thought then, of one image but of two, intermingled and separate, one standing on the terrace and the other down below, lying in the snow. You must be thinking: Ah, finally this story is over. But no, it still goes on.

GIGUE

Thomas found me sitting on a chair at the edge of the terrace. I was looking at the woods and the sky and drinking brandy out of the bottle, in little sips. The raised balustrade hid the garden from me, but the thought of what I had seen was softly eating away at my spirit. One or two days must have gone by, don't ask me how I spent them. Thomas had come walking around the side of the house: I hadn't heard anything, neither the sound of an engine nor a call. I handed him the bottle: "Hail, comrade! Drink." I was probably a little drunk. Thomas looked around him, drank a little, but didn't hand the bottle back. "What the hell are you up to?" he finally asked. I smiled inanely at him. He looked at the house. "You're alone?"—"I think so, yes." He walked up to me, looked at me, repeated: "What the hell are you doing? Your leave ended a week ago. Grothmann is furious, he's talking about court-martialing you for desertion. These days, courts-martial last five minutes." I shrugged and reached for the bottle, which he was still holding. He moved it away. "And you?" I asked. "What are you doing here?"—"Piontek told me where you were. He brought me. I came to get you."—"We have to go, then?" I said sadly.—"Yes. Go get dressed." I got up, went upstairs. In Una's bedroom, instead of getting dressed, I sat down on her leather sofa and lit a cigarette. I thought about her, with difficulty, strangely empty, hollow thoughts. Thomas's voice, in the stairway, drew me out of my reverie: "Hurry up! Shit!" I got dressed, pulling on my clothes somewhat at random, but with some good sense, since it was cold out—long underwear, wool socks, a turtleneck sweater under my office uniform. *L'Éducation sentimentale* was lying on the secretary: I slipped the book into my tunic pocket. Then I began opening the windows to pull the shutters closed. Thomas appeared in the doorway: "What are you doing?"—"Well, I'm closing up. We can't leave the house wide open." His bad mood burst out then: "You don't seem to realize what's happening. The Russians have been attacking along the whole front for a week. They could be here any minute now." He took me unceremoniously by the arm: "Come on." In the entryway, I briskly freed myself from his grip and went to find the big key to the front door. I put on my coat and cap. As we left I carefully locked the door. In the courtyard in front of the house, Piontek was wiping the headlight of an Opel. He straightened to salute me, and we got into the car, Thomas next to Piontek, me in the back. In the long lane, between jolts, Thomas asked Piontek: "Do you think we can pass through Tempelburg again?"—"I don't know, Standartenführer. It looked calm, we can try." On the main road Piontek turned left. In Alt Draheim, a few families were still loading some wagons, harnessed to little Pomeranian horses. The car passed around the old fort and began climbing the long slope of the isthmus. A tank appeared on top, low and squat. "Shit!" Thomas exclaimed. "A T-thirty-four!" But Piontek had already slammed on the brakes and started going in reverse. The tank lowered its cannon and fired at us, but it couldn't traverse low enough and the shell went over us and exploded by the side of the road, at the entrance to the village. The tank advanced in a rattle of treads to fire lower; Piontek quickly backed the car across the road and started off at top speed toward the village; the second shell hit quite close, shattering one of the left side windows, then we were around the fort and hidden from the tank. In the village, people had heard the explosions and were running in all directions. We drove through without stopping and headed north. "They couldn't have taken Tempelburg!" Thomas was raging. "We went through there two hours ago!"—"Maybe they came round by the fields," Piontek suggested. Thomas was examining a map: "All right, go to Bad Polzin. We'll get information there. Even if Stargard has fallen, we can take the Schivelbein-Naugard road and then reach Stettin." I wasn't paying much attention to what he said, I was looking at the landscape out of the smashed window, after having cleared away the debris. Tall, widely spaced poplar trees lined the long straight road, and beyond them stretched snowy, silent fields, a gray sky where some birds were flitting, isolated, shuttered, silent farms. In Klaushagen, a neat little village, sad and dignified, a few kilometers farther on, a checkpoint of *Volkssturm* in civilian clothes with armbands blocked the road, between a little lake and a wood. Anxiously, the farmers asked us for news: Thomas advised them to head with their families toward Polzin, but they hesitated, twisted their moustaches and fiddled with their old rifles and the two *Panzerfäuste* they had been allocated. Some had pinned their medals from the Great War onto their jackets. The Schupos in bottle-green uniforms sent to supervise them seemed just as uneasy, the men talked with the slow deliberation of a town council meeting, almost solemn with anxiety.

At the entrance to Bad Polzin, the defenses seemed more solidly organized. Waffen-SS were guarding the road, and a PAK gun, positioned on a hill, covered the approach. Thomas got out of the car to confer with the Untersturmführer commanding the platoon, but he didn't know anything and referred us to his superior in town, at the command post set up in the old castle. Vehicles and wagons were clogging the streets, the atmosphere was tense, mothers shouted after their children, men brutally pulled the reins of their horses, scolded the French farm workers who were loading the mattresses and the bags of provisions. I followed Thomas into the command post and stayed behind him, listening. The Obersturmführer didn't know much, either; his unit was attached to the SS Tenth Corps, they had sent him here at the head of a company to hold the main roads; and he thought the Russians would come from the south or from the east—the Second Army, around Danzig and Gotenhafen, was already cut off from the Reich, the Russians had broken through to the Baltic along the Neustettin-Köslin axis, he was almost sure of it—but he guessed the ways leading west were still free. We took the road to Schivelbein. It was a paved highway, long wagons of refugees occupied one full lane, a continuous flow, the same sad spectacle as a month before on the autobahn from Stettin to Berlin. Slowly, at a horse's pace, the German East was emptying out. There wasn't much military traffic, but many soldiers, armed or not, walked alone among the civilians, *Rückkämpfer* who were trying to rejoin their units or find another one. It was cold out, a fierce wind blew through the car's broken window, bringing wet snow with it. Piontek honked as he passed the wagons; men on foot, horses, livestock congested the road, giving way slowly. We drove alongside fields, then again the road passed through a fir forest. In front of us, wagons were stopping, there was commotion, I heard an enormous, incomprehensible noise, people were yelling and running toward the forest. "The Russians!" Piontek roared.—"Get out, get out!" Thomas ordered. I got out on the left with Piontek: two hundred meters in front of us, a tank was moving swiftly toward us, crushing wagons, horses, straggling fugitives. Terrified, I ran as fast as I could with Piontek and some civilians to hide in the forest; Thomas had crossed through the column to the other side. Beneath the treads of the tank, the carts shattered like matches; the horses died with horrible neighing, cut short by the metallic grinding. Our car was caught from the front, driven back, swept aside, and, in a great racket of crushed sheet metal, thrown into the ditch, on its side. I could make

out the soldier perched on the tank, just in front of me, an Asiatic with
a pug-nosed face black with engine oil; under his leather tanker's helmet, he wore little women's sunglasses, hexagonal with pink rims, and
he held in one hand a big machine gun with a round magazine, in the
other, perched on his shoulder, a summer parasol, trimmed with lace;
his legs apart, leaning against the turret, he straddled the cannon like a
horse, absorbing the impacts of the tank with the ease of a Scythian rider
guiding a nervy little horse with his heels. Two other tanks with mattresses or mesh springs attached to their sides followed the first one, finishing off under their treads the crippled screaming and wriggling
among the debris. The whole passage took a dozen seconds at most;
they continued on toward Bad Polzin, leaving in their wake a wide band
of wood shards mixed with blood and crushed flesh in pools of horse
intestines. Long trails left by the wounded who had tried to crawl to
shelter reddened the snow on both sides of the road; here and there, a
man writhed, without any legs, howling; on the road there were head-
less torsos, arms emerging from a red, vile pulp. I was trembling un-
controllably, Piontek had to help me get back to the road. Around me
people were screeching, gesticulating, others stayed motionless and in a
state of shock, the children let out endless, piercing cries. Thomas
quickly rejoined me and searched through the wreckage of the car to
retrieve the map and a little bag. "We'll have to continue on foot," he
said. I made a dazed gesture: "And the people . . . ?"—"They'll have to
manage," he cut in. "We can't do anything. Come on." He made me
cross the road again, Piontek following. I was careful not to step on human remains, but it was impossible to avoid the blood, my boots left big
red tracks in the snow. Beneath the trees, Thomas unfolded the map.
"Piontek," he ordered, "go search through those carts, find us something to eat." Then he studied the map. When Piontek returned with
some provisions tied up in a pillowcase, Thomas showed the map to us.
It was a large-scale map of Pomerania, it indicated the main roads and
the villages, but not much more. "If the Russians came from there, then
they've taken Schivelbein. They must also be heading up toward Kolberg. We'll go north, try to reach Belgarde. If our people are still there,
fine; if not we'll see. By avoiding the roads we should be all right: if
they're moving so fast, it means their infantry is still far behind." He
pointed to a village on the map, Gross Rambin: "The railroad passes
here. If the Russians haven't reached it yet, we might find something."
    We quickly crossed the forest and took to the fields. The snow was
melting on the plowed earth, we sank into it up to our calves; between
each plot of land ran rivulets full of water bordered with barbed-wire
fences, not tall but hard to pass. Then we traveled on little dirt paths,

also muddy, but easier, which we had to leave whenever we approached villages. It was tiring, but the air was brisk and the countryside deserted and quiet; on the roads, we walked at a good pace, Thomas and I a little ridiculous in our dress uniforms with our legs all smeared with mud. Piontek carried the supplies; our only weapons were our two service pistols, Lüger automatics. Near the end of the afternoon, we reached Rambin and paused in a small grove of beech and ash trees. It was snowing again, a wet, sticky snow that the wind blew into our faces. A little river flowed on our right; to our left, a little farther on, we could make out the railroad and the first houses. "We'll wait for nightfall," Thomas said. I leaned back against a tree, pulling the folds of my coat under me, and Piontek handed us hard-boiled eggs and sausages. "I couldn't find any bread," he said sadly. Thomas pulled out of his bag the little bottle of brandy he had taken from me and offered us each a swig. The sky was darkening, the snow flurries were beginning again. I was tired and fell asleep against the tree. When Thomas woke me my coat was dusted with snow and I was stiff from the cold. There was no moon, no light came from the village. We followed the edge of the wood up to the railroad, then walked in the dark in single file along the embankment. Thomas had taken out his pistol and I imitated him, without really knowing what I'd do with it if we were surprised. Our footsteps crunched on the snowy gravel between the tracks. The first houses, dark and silent, appeared to the right of the rails, near a large pond; the little train station at the entrance to the village was locked; we stayed on the tracks to pass through the hamlet. Finally we could put our pistols away and walk more easily. The track bed was slippery and crumbled beneath our feet, and the spacing of the ties kept us from walking at a normal pace along the tracks; at last, one by one, we left the embankment and walked alongside it in the virgin snow. A little farther on, the tracks once again went through a large pine forest. I felt tired, we'd been walking for hours, I wasn't thinking about anything, my head remained void of any idea or any image, all my effort went into my footsteps. I was breathing heavily, and along with the crunching of our boots on the wet snow it was one of the only sounds I heard, a haunting sound. A few hours later, the moon rose behind the pines, not quite full; it cast patches of white light on the snow through the trees. Later still, we reached the edge of the forest. Beyond a large plain, a few kilometers in front of us, a yellow light danced in the sky and we could make out the crackle of guns, hollow, muffled explosions. The moon illuminated the snow on the plain and I could make out the black line of the railroad, the bushes, the little scattered woods. "They must be fighting around Belgarde," Thomas said. "Let's sleep a little. If we approach now, we'll get shot by our own men." Sleeping in the snow wasn't very appealing to me; with Piontek, I gathered some dead branches together to form a nest, rolled myself up in a ball, and fell asleep.

A rude blow on my boot woke me up. It was still dark. Several forms were standing around us, I could see the steel of machine guns glinting. A voice whispered abruptly: *"Deutsche? Deutsche?"* I sat up and the shape moved back: "Excuse me, Herr Offizier," a voice said in a strong accent. I stood up; Thomas was already standing. "You are German soldiers?" he asked then, also in a low voice. *"Jawohl, Herr Offizier."* My eyes were growing used to the darkness: I could make out SS insignia and blue-white-red badges on the men's coats. "I'm an SS-Obersturmbannführer," I said in French. A voice exclaimed: "You see that, Roger, he speaks French!" The first soldier replied: "Our apologies, Obersturmbannführer. We couldn't see you well in the dark. We thought you were deserters."—"We're from the SD," Thomas said, also in French, with his Austrian accent. "We were cut off by the Russians and we're trying to rejoin our lines. And you?"—"Oberschütze Lanquenoy, Third Company, First Platoon, *zu Befehl*, Standartenführer. We're with the Charlemagne Division. We were separated from our regiment." There were a dozen of them. Lanquenoy, who seemed to be leading them, explained the situation in a few words: they had been given the order to leave their position several hours ago and to retreat to the south. Most of the regiment, which they were trying to rejoin, must have been a little farther to the east, near the Persante River. "Oberführer Puaud is in charge. There are still some guys from the Wehrmacht in Belgarde, but it's bloody hot over there."—"Why aren't you heading north?" Thomas asked curtly. "Toward Kolberg?"—"We don't know, Standartenführer," Lanquenoy said. "We don't know anything. There are Russkoffs everywhere."—"The road must be cut off," another voice said.—"Are our troops still holding Körlin?" Thomas asked.—"We don't know," Lanquenoy said.—"Do we still hold Kolberg?"—"We don't know, Standartenführer. We don't know anything." Thomas asked for a flashlight and had Lanquenoy and another soldier show us the terrain on the map. "We're going to try to head north and reach Körlin or, if not that, Kolberg," Thomas said finally. "Do you want to come with us? In a little group, we could pass the Russian lines, if we have to. They must just be holding the roads, maybe a few villages."—"It's not that we don't want to, Standartenführer. We'd like to, I think. But we have to rejoin our buddies."—"As you like." Thomas had them give him a weapon and some ammunition, which he handed to Piontek. The sky was growing gradually paler, a thick layer of fog filled the hollows of the plain near the river. The French soldiers saluted us and moved off into the forest. Thomas said to me: "We'll take advantage of the fog to get round Belgarde, fast. On the other side of the Persante, between the bend in the river and the road, there's a forest. We'll go that way up to Körlin. Afterward, we'll see." I didn't say anything, I felt as if I had no will of my own. We went back along the railroad. The explosions, in front of us and on our right, resounded in the fog, keeping pace with our advance. When the tracks crossed a road, we lurked, waited a few minutes, then crossed it running. Sometimes too we heard the clanking of gear, boxes, canteens: armed men were passing us in the fog; and we stayed down, on the lookout, waiting for them to move away, without ever knowing if they were our own men or not. To the south, behind us, heavy gunfire was starting up; in front of us, the noises were getting more distinct, but they were isolated gunshots and volleys, just a few explosions, the fighting must have been winding down. In the time it took us to reach the Persante, a wind rose up and began to scatter the fog. We moved away from the railroad and hid in the reeds to observe. The metal railroad bridge had been dynamited and lay, twisted, in the gray, turbid water of the river. We waited for about fifteen minutes observing it; the fog had almost lifted now, a cold sun glowed in the gray sky. Behind us, to the right, Belgarde was burning. The ruined bridge didn't seem to be guarded. "If we're careful, we could cross on the beams," Thomas murmured. He stood up, and Piontek followed him, the Frenchmen's submachine gun raised. From the shore, the crossing looked easy, but once we were on the bridge, the girders turned out to be treacherous, wet and slippery. We had to hang on the outside of the deck, just above the water. Thomas and Piontek crossed safely. A few meters from the shore, my reflection drew my gaze; it was blurred, deformed by the movements of the surface; I leaned over to see it more clearly, my foot slipped and I fell to meet it. Tangled in my heavy coat, I sank for a second into the cold water. My hand found a metal bar, I caught hold, hoisted myself back to the surface; Piontek, who had turned back, pulled me out onto the bank, and I lay there, dripping, coughing, furious. Thomas was laughing and his laughter added to my anger. My cap, which I had slipped into my belt before crossing, was safe; I had to take off my boots to empty the water, and Piontek helped me wring out my coat as best we could. "Hurry up," Thomas whispered, still laughing. "We can't stay here." I felt my pockets, my hand encountered the book I had brought and then forgotten. The sight of the soaking, curling pages made my stomach turn. But there was nothing for it, Thomas was hurrying me,

I put it back in my pocket, slung my wet coat over my shoulders and started off again.

The cold cut through my drenched clothes and I shivered, but we walked fast and that warmed me a little. Behind us, the fires in the city were crackling, thick smoke blackened the gray sky and veiled the sun. For a while, a dozen starving, panic-stricken dogs harassed us, rushing at our heels and barking furiously; Piontek had to cut a stick and lay into them to make them go away. Near the river, the ground was swampy; the snow had already melted, a few isolated patches showed the dry places. Our boots sank in up to our ankles. A long grassy dyke dusted with snow took shape, running alongside the Persante; to our right, at the foot of the embankment, the marsh thickened, then the woods began, also swampy; and soon we were stuck on this dyke, but couldn't see anyone, neither Germans nor Russians. Others had come this way before us, though: here and there, slumped in the wood, with a foot or an arm caught in the branches, or else lying head-down on the side of the dyke, we saw a corpse, a soldier or civilian who had dragged himself there to die. The sky was clearing, the pale late-winter sun gradually scattered the grayness. Walking on the dyke was easy, we moved quickly, Belgarde had already disappeared. On the brown water of the Persante, ducks were floating, some with green heads, others black-and-white; they took off suddenly when we approached, quacking plaintively, then settling a little farther off. Across, beyond the river, stretched a large forest of tall, dark pines trees; to our right, after the little stream that separated the dyke from land, we saw mostly birch trees, with some oaks. I heard a distant buzzing: above us, very high in the light-green sky, a solitary plane was circling. The sight of this aircraft worried Thomas and he pulled us over to the little canal; we crossed it on a fallen trunk to reach the trees; but there, firm ground disappeared under water. We made our way through a little meadow covered with tall, thick grass, sodden and bent; beyond stretched out more sheets of water; there was a little padlocked hunter's cabin, also standing in water. The snow had completely disappeared. There was no use sticking to the trees, our boots sank into the water and the mud, the wet ground was covered with rotten leaves that hid quagmires. Here and there a little island of firm land gave us courage. But farther on it became completely impossible again; the trees grew on isolated clumps or in the water itself, the strips of earth between the puddles were also flooded, wading was difficult, we had to give up and go back to the dyke. Finally it opened up onto fields, wet and covered with damp snow, but at least we could walk on them. Then we entered a woodlot of pine trees ready for cutting, thin, straight and tall with ruddy trunks. The sun filtered through the trees, scattering spots of light on the black, almost bare ground dotted with patches of snow or cold green moss. Trunks, abandoned where they fell, and broken branches blocked the way between the trees; but it was even harder to walk in the black mud, churned up by wagon wheels, on the logger's paths that snaked through the pine grove. I was out of breath, hungry too, Thomas finally agreed to pause. Thanks to the heat given off from walking, my underwear was almost dry; I took off my tunic, boots, and pants, and stretched them out with my coat in the sun, on a cord of pine logs, carefully piled up in a square by the side of the road. I also put the Flaubert there, open, to dry out the curled paper. Then I perched on a neighboring cord, ridiculous in my long underwear; after a few minutes I was cold again, and Thomas passed me his coat, laughing. Piontek handed out some food and I ate. I was exhausted, I wanted to lie down on my coat in the weak sunlight and fall asleep. But Thomas was adamant that we reach Körlin, he still hoped to get to Kolberg the same day. I put my wet clothes back on, pocketed the Flaubert, and followed him. Soon after the wood a little hamlet appeared, nestled in the bend of the river. We watched it for a while—we'd have to make a long detour if we had to go around it; I could hear dogs barking, horses neighing, cows mooing, with that long painful sound they have when they're not milked and their udders are swelling. But that was all. Thomas decided to move forward. There were large old farm buildings made of brick, crumbling, the broad roofs covering generous haylofts; the doors were smashed, the path strewn with overturned carts, broken furniture, torn sheets; here and there, we stepped over the corpse of a farmer or an old woman, shot point-blank; a strange little snowstorm blew through the little streets, flurries of down raised from ripped-open quilts and mattresses and carried by the wind. Thomas sent Piontek to look for food in the houses and, as we waited, translated a sign hastily painted in Russian, placed around the neck of a farmer tied high up on an oak tree, his intestines dripping from his split stomach, half torn out by dogs: YOU HAD A HOUSE, COWS, TINNED FOOD. WHAT THE FUCK DID YOU WANT WITH US, PRIDUROK? The smell of the intestines made me nauseous, I was thirsty and I drank from the pump of a well that still worked. Piontek joined us: he had found bacon, onions, apples, some preserves, which we shared between us and put in our pockets; but he was pale and his jaw was trembling, he didn't want to tell us what he'd seen in the house, and his anguished gaze shifted from the disemboweled man to the growling dogs that were drawing close through the whirlwinds of down. We left this hamlet as fast as we could. Beyond stretched large undulating fields, pale yellow and beige under the still-dry snow. The path skirted round a little stream, climbed a hill, went past a deserted prosperous farm adjacent to a wood. Then it led down to the Persante. We followed the bank, which was high above the river; on the other side of the water there were more woods. Another tributary barred our way, we had to take off our boots and socks and ford it, the water was freezing, I drank some and sprinkled my neck with it before continuing. Then more snow-covered fields and, far off on a hill to the right, the edge of a forest; right in the middle, empty, stood a gray wooden tower, for duck-hunting or maybe to shoot at crows during harvest time. Thomas wanted to cut through the fields, in front of us the forest descended to join the river, but leaving the paths wasn't easy, the ground got treacherous, we had to pass over barbed-wire fences, so we went back to following the river when we found it again a little farther on. Two swans were drifting on the water, not at all alarmed by our presence; they paused near a little island, raised and stretched their huge necks in one long gesture, then started preening themselves. Farther, the woods began again. Here the trees were mostly pine, young ones, a forest carefully managed for cutting, open and airy. The paths made walking easier. Twice, the noise of our footsteps caused small deer to run from us, we could see them leaping through the trees. Thomas led us along various paths under the calm high vault of branches and regularly found the Persante again, our Ariadne's thread. A path cut through a little grove of oak trees, not very tall, a dense, gray tracery of shoots and bare branches. The ground under the snow was carpeted with dead leaves, dry and brown. When I was thirsty, I went down to the Persante, but often, at the shore, the water was stagnant. We were getting close to Körlin; my legs were heavy, my back ached, but here now the paths were easy.

In Körlin, battle was raging. Crouching by the edge of the wood, we watched the Russian tanks scattered along a slightly raised road relentlessly shelling the German positions. Infantrymen were running around the tanks, lying in trenches. There were lots of dead bodies, brown spots dotting the snow or the blackish ground. We cautiously retreated into the forest. A little farther back we had spotted a little stone bridge over the Persante, intact; we returned to it and crossed it, then, hiding in a beech grove, we slipped toward the main road to Plathe. In these woods too there were bodies everywhere, Russians and Germans both, they must have fought furiously; most of the German soldiers were wearing the French badge; now, though, everything was quiet. Searching through their pockets we found a few useful things, pocketknives, a compass, some dried fish in a Russian's haversack. On the road, above us, Soviet tanks were headed at top speed toward Körlin. Thomas had decided that we would wait for night, then try to cross to see farther ahead who held the roadway to Kolberg, the Russians or our own men. I sat down behind a bush, with my back to the road, and ate an onion, which I washed down with some brandy, then I pulled *L'Éducation sentimentale* out of my pocket, its leather binding swollen and deformed, delicately unstuck a few pages, and began to read. The long, steady flow of the prose soon carried me away, I didn't hear the rattle of treads or the rumble of engines, the absurd shouts in Russian, *"Davaï! Davaï!"* or the explosions, a little farther away; only the curling, sticking pages got in the way of my reading. The fading light forced me to close the book and put it away. I slept a little. Piontek was sleeping too; Thomas remained seated, watching the woods. When I woke up, I was covered in a thick, powdery snow; it was falling heavily, in big flakes that whirled between the trees before settling. On the road a tank passed by from time to time, its headlights on, the light piercing whirlwinds of snow; everything else was silent. We went close to the road and waited. Over toward Körlin, they were still shooting. Two tanks came along, followed by a truck, a Studebaker painted with the red star: as soon as they had passed, we crossed the road at a run to bolt into a wood on the other side. A few kilometers farther on, we had to repeat the process to cross the little road leading to Gross-Jestin, a neighboring village; there too tanks and vehicles clogged the road. The thick snow hid us as we crossed the fields, there was no wind and the snow fell vertically, muting sounds, explosions, motors, shouts. From time to time, we heard metallic clicking or bursts of Russian voices; we quickly hid, flat on our stomachs in a ditch or behind a bush; once, a patrol passed right by without noticing us. Again the Persante barred our way. The road to Kolberg was on the other side; we followed the bank northward and Thomas finally unearthed a boat hidden in the reeds. There were no oars, so Piontek cut some long branches to maneuver it, and the crossing was easy enough. On the road there was heavy traffic in both directions: Russian tanks and trucks were driving with all lights on, as if on an autobahn. A long column of tanks flowed toward Kolberg, a fairytale spectacle, each vehicle draped with lace, large white lengths attached to the cannons and to the gun turrets and dancing on the sides, and in the whirlwinds of snow illumined by their headlights, these dark and thundering machines took on a light, almost airy quality; they seemed to float over the road, through the snow that blended with their delicate sails. We slowly retreated to hide in the woods. "We'll cross the Persante again," Thomas's tense voice whispered, disembodied in the dark and the snow. "We can forget about Kolberg. We'll have to go all the way to the Oder, probably." But the boat had disappeared, and we had to walk for a while before we could find a fordable stretch, indicated by posts and a kind of footbridge stretched beneath the water, to which the corpse of a French Waffen-SS was caught by the foot, floating on its stomach. The cold water rose up to our thighs, I held my book in my hand to spare it another dip; thick snowflakes were falling onto the water and disappeared instantly. We had taken off our boots but our pants stayed wet and cold all night and into the morning, when we fell asleep, all three of us, without posting a guard, in a little forester's cabin deep in the woods. We had been walking for almost thirty-six hours, we were worn out; now we had to walk some more.

We advanced at night; during the day, we hid in the woods; then I slept or read Flaubert, I didn't talk much with my companions. An impotent rage was welling up in me, I didn't understand why I had left the house near Alt Draheim, I was furious at myself for letting myself be led along to wander like a savage in the woods, instead of staying there quietly alone. Beards covered our faces, dried mud stiffened our uniforms, and under the rough cloth, cramps racked our legs. We ate poorly, there was only what we could find in abandoned farms or the debris of refugees' convoys; I didn't complain, but I found the raw bacon vile, the fat stayed stuck inside your mouth for a long time, there was no bread to help it down. We were always cold and couldn't make a fire. Still, I liked this grave, quiet countryside, the serene, airy quiet of the birch woods or pine groves, the gray sky scarcely agitated by wind, the hushed rustle of the last snowfalls of the year. But it was a dead, deserted countryside: empty fields, empty farms. Everywhere the disasters of war had left their traces. Every sizeable hamlet, which we skirted around from afar, at night, was occupied by Russians; from the outskirts, in the dark, we could hear drunken soldiers singing and firing off volleys in the air. There were still some Germans, though, in these villages, we could make out their frightened but patient voices between the Russian exclamations and curses; screams were common too, especially women's screams. But that was still better than the burned villages to which hunger drove us: dead livestock made the streets stink; the houses gave off a stench of carrion, mixed with the smell of cold ashes, and since we had to go inside to find food, we couldn't avoid seeing the twisted corpses of women, often stripped naked, even old women or ten-year-old girls, with blood between their legs. But staying in the woods didn't mean we could escape the dead: at crossroads, immense, ancient oak branches bore clusters of hanged men, usually *Volkssturm*, dismal bundles, victims of zealous Feldgendarmen; bodies dotted the clearings, like that of a naked young man, lying in the snow with one leg folded, as serene as the hanged man on the Twelfth Tarot Trump, frightening in his strangeness; and further on, in the forests, cadavers polluted the pale ponds we walked alongside, fighting our thirst. In these woods and forests, we also found living people, terrorized civilians, incapable of giving us the slightest bit of information, isolated soldiers or little groups who were trying like us to thread their way through the Russian lines. Waffen-SS or Wehrmacht, they never wanted to stay with us; they must have been afraid, if we were captured, of being found with high-ranking SS officers. That made Thomas think, and he had me destroy my pay book and my papers and tear off my insignia, as he did, in case we fell into Russian hands; but out of fear of the Feldgendarmen, he decided, somewhat irrationally, that we should keep our handsome black uniforms, a little incongruous for this walk in the countryside. All these decisions were made by him; I agreed without thinking and followed, closed to everything except to what fell under my eyes, in the slow unfurling of the march.

When something did arouse a reaction in me, it was even worse. The second night after Körlin, around dawn, we entered a hamlet, a few farms surrounding a manor house. A little to the side stood a brick church, set against a pointed bell tower and topped with a gray slate roof; the door was open, and organ music was coming out; Piontek had already left to search the kitchens; followed by Thomas, I went into the church. An old man, near the altar, was playing Bach's *Art of the Fugue*, the third contrapunctus, I think, with that beautiful rolling of the bass that on an organ is played with the pedals. I approached, sat down on a pew, and listened. The old man finished the piece and turned to me: he wore a monocle and a neatly trimmed little white moustache, and an Oberstleutnant's uniform from the other war, with a cross at his neck. "They can destroy everything," he said to me calmly, "but not this. It is impossible, this will remain forever: it will go on even when I stop playing." I didn't say anything and he attacked the next contrapunctus. Thomas was still standing. I got up too. I listened. The music was magnificent, the organ wasn't very powerful but it echoed in this little family church, the lines of counterpoint met each other, played, danced with each other. But instead of pacifying me, this music only fueled my anger, I found it unbearable. I wasn't thinking about anything, my head was empty of everything except this music and the black pressure of my rage. I wanted to shout at him to stop, but I let the end of the piece go by, and the old man immediately started the next one, the fifth. His long aristocratic fingers fluttered over the keys, pulled or pushed the stops. When he slapped them shut at the end of the fugue, I took out my pistol and shot him in the head. He collapsed forward onto the keys, opening half the pipes in a desolate, discordant bleat. I put my pistol away, went over, and pulled him back by the collar; the sound stopped, leaving only the sound of blood dripping from his head onto the flagstones. "You've gone completely mad!" Thomas snarled. "What's the matter with you?!" I looked at him coldly, I was livid but my cracked voice didn't tremble: "It's because of these corrupt Junkers that Germany is losing the war. National Socialism is collapsing and they're playing Bach. It should be forbidden." Thomas stared at me, he didn't know what to say. Then he shrugged: "You know, you might be right. But don't do that again. Let's go." Piontek, in the main courtyard, had taken fright at the shot and was brandishing his submachine gun. I suggested we sleep in the manor house, in a real bed, with sheets; but Thomas, I think, was furious at me, he decided we'd sleep in the woods again, to annoy me, probably. But I didn't want to get angry again, and also, he was my friend; I obeyed, I followed him without protesting.

The weather was fickle, it suddenly got warmer; as soon as the cold disappeared, it got hot, and I sweated copiously in my coat, the slippery earth of the fields stuck to my feet. We remained north of the road to Plathe; imperceptibly, to avoid spaces that were too open, and to stay close to the forests, we were drifting even farther north. Whereas we thought we would cross the Rega around Greifenberg, we reached it near Treptow, less than ten kilometers from the sea. Between Treptow and the river's mouth, according to Thomas's map, the entire left bank was swampy; but at the sea's edge lay a large forest, where we could walk safely to Horst or Rewahl; if these seaside resorts were still in German hands, we could pass through the lines; if not, we would head back inland. That night, we crossed the railroad that links Treptow to Kolberg, then the road to Deep, waiting for an hour for a Soviet column to pass by. After the road, we were almost out in the open, but there were no villages there; we followed little isolated paths in the bend of the Rega, approaching the river. The forest, opposite, was growing visible in the darkness, a large black wall in front of the clear wall of the night. We could already smell the sea. But we couldn't see any way of crossing the river, which kept getting wider as it neared its mouth. Instead of turning back, we continued on toward Deep. Skirting around the town where the Russians were sleeping, drinking, and singing, we went down to the beach and the bathhouses. A Soviet guard was sleeping on a chaise longue, and Thomas bashed his head in with the metal shaft of a beach umbrella; the noise of the waves drowned out all sounds. Piontek broke the chain fastening the pedal-boats. An icy wind was blowing over the Baltic, from west to east; along the coast, the black water was rough; we dragged the pedal-boat onto the sand to the mouth of the river; there it was calmer, and I launched onto the waves with a swell of joy; as I pedaled, I remembered the summers on the beaches in Antibes or Juan-les-Pins, where my sister and I begged Moreau to rent us a pedal-boat and then set off on our own on the sea, as far as our little legs could push us, before drifting happily in the sun. We crossed quickly, Thomas and I pedaling with all our strength, Piontek, lying between us with his gun, watching the shore; on the far bank, I abandoned our craft almost with regret. The forest began immediately, stocky low trees of all kinds bent by the wind that swept this long, gloomy coast unceasingly. Walking in these woods is not easy: there are few paths, and young saplings, birch trees especially, invade the ground between the trees, you have to clear a path for yourself among them. The forest came up to the sand on the beach and overlooked the sea, right up against the large dunes that, shifting under the wind, poured their sand between the trees and buried them up to midtrunk. Behind this barrier the backwash of the invisible sea thundered endlessly. We walked until dawn; farther on, it was mostly pine trees; we made better time. When the sky cleared, Thomas climbed a dune to look at the beach. I followed him. An uninterrupted line of debris and corpses cluttered the cold, pale sand, wrecks of vehicles, abandoned artillery guns, overturned, shattered carts. Bodies lay where they had fallen, on the sand or with their heads in the water, half covered by white foam, others floated farther away, tossed by the waves. The seawater looked heavy, almost dirty on this beige, pale beach, the gray-green of lead, hard and sad. Fat seagulls flew level with the sand or soared above the rumbling swell, facing the wind, as if suspended, before heading off away with a precise movement of wing. We ran down the dune to rapidly search some corpses for provisions. There were all kinds of people among the dead, soldiers, women, little children. But we didn't find much to eat and soon hurried back to the forest. As soon as I moved away from the beach, the calm of the woods enveloped me, letting the roar of the surf and the wind resound in my head. I wanted to sleep on the flank of the dune, the cold, hard sand drew me, but Thomas was afraid of patrols, and led me farther into the forest. I slept a few hours on pine needles and then read my misshapen book until nightfall, forgetting my hunger in the sumptuous descriptions of the banquets of the bourgeois monarchy. Then Thomas gave the signal for departure. After two hours of walking, we reached the end of the forest, a curve overlooking a little lake separated from the Baltic by a dyke of gray sand, surmounted by a line of pretty beach cottages, abandoned, built down to the sea on a long, gentle strand scattered with debris. We threaded our way from house to house, keeping an eye out on the paths and the beach. Horst was a little farther on: a former seaside resort, popular in its day, but for some years past given over to invalids and the convalescent. On the beach, the jumble of wrecks and bodies grew thicker, a big battle had taken place here. Farther on, we could see lights and hear engine noises, it must have been the Russians. We had already passed the little lake; according to the map, we were no more than twenty or twenty-two kilometers from the island of Wollin. In one of the houses we found a wounded man, a German soldier hit in the stomach by a piece of shrapnel. He was crouching under a stairway but called to us when he heard us whispering. Thomas and Piontek carried him onto a gutted sofa, holding his mouth so he wouldn't cry out; he wanted something to drink, Thomas wet a cloth and wiped his lips with it several times. He had been lying there for days, and his words, between the panting, were scarcely audible. The remains of several divisions, herding tens of thousands of civilians, had formed a pocket in Horst, Rewahl, Hoff; he had arrived there with what was left of his regiment, from Dramburg. Then they had tried to break through to Wollin. The Russians held the cliffs above the beach and fired methodically at the desperate mass that passed beneath them. "It was like a pigeon shoot." He had been wounded almost immediately, and his comrades had abandoned him. During the day, the beach was swarming with Russians, who came to strip the dead. He knew they had taken Kammin and probably controlled the whole shore of the Haff. "The region must be swarming with patrols," Thomas commented. "The Reds are going to look for survivors of the breakthrough." The man kept muttering and moaning, he was sweating; he asked for water, but we didn't give him any, it would have made him shout; and we didn't have any cigarettes to offer him, either. Before letting us go, he asked us for a pistol; I gave him mine, with the rest of the bottle of brandy. He promised to wait till we were far away before shooting. Then we started off south again: after Gross Justin and Zitzmar there were woods. On the roads the traffic was incessant, American Jeeps or Studebakers with the red star, motorcycles, more tanks; on the paths there were now foot patrols of five or six men, and it took all our alertness to avoid them. Ten kilometers from the coast, we found snow again in the fields and woods. We headed toward Gülzow, west of Greifenberg; then, Thomas explained, we could continue on and try to cross the Oder near Gollnow. Before dawn we found a forest and a hut, but there were traces of footsteps and we left the path to sleep farther off, in the pine trees near a clearing, rolled up in our coats on the snow.

I awoke surrounded by children. They formed a wide circle around us, dozens of them, looking at us in silence. They were in rags, dirty, their hair disheveled; many of them wore scraps of German uniforms, a jacket, a helmet, a coarsely cut coat; some were clutching farm tools, hoes, rakes, shovels; others, rifles and submachine guns made of wire or cut from wood or cardboard. Their gazes were sullen and threatening. Most of them looked between ten and thirteen years old; some of them weren't yet six; and behind them stood a few girls. We rose, and Thomas greeted them politely. The tallest of them, a blond, lanky boy wearing a staff officer's coat with red velvet lapels over a tank-driver's black jacket, stepped forward and barked: "Who are you?" He spoke German with a thick *Volksdeutscher* accent, from Ruthenia or maybe even the Banat. "We are German officers," Thomas calmly replied. "And you?"—"Kampfgruppe Adam. I'm Adam, Generalmajor Adam, and this is my command." Piontek burst out laughing. "We are from the SS," Thomas said.—"Where are your insignia?" the boy spat out. "You're deserters!" Piontek stopped laughing. Thomas didn't lose his calm, he kept his hands behind his back and said: "We are not deserters. We were forced to remove our insignia for fear of falling into Bolshevik hands."—"Standartenführer!" Piontek shouted, "why are you talking to these brats? Can't you see they're nuts? We should give them a thrashing!"—"Shut up, Piontek," Thomas said. I didn't say anything, I was beginning to be horrified at the fixed, insane gaze of these children. "Well, I'll show them, I will!" Piontek bellowed, reaching for the submachine gun on his back. The boy in an officer's coat made a sign and a half-dozen children rushed Piontek, hitting him with their tools and dragging him to the ground. A boy lifted a hoe and split his face open, crushing his teeth and flinging an eye out of its socket. Piontek was still screaming; a blow from a metal pipe caved in his forehead, and he fell silent. The children kept hitting until his head was nothing but red pulp in the snow. I was petrified, seized with uncontrollable terror. Thomas wasn't moving a muscle, either. When the children abandoned the corpse, the tallest one shouted again: "You are deserters and we are going to hang you like traitors!"—"We are not deserters," Thomas coldly repeated. "We are on a special mission for the Führer behind Russian lines, and you have just killed our driver."—"Where are your papers to prove it?" the boy insisted.—"We destroyed them. If the Reds captured us, if they guessed who we were, they would torture us and make us speak."—"Prove it!"—"Escort us to the German lines and you'll see."—"We have other things to do besides escorting deserters," the child hissed. "I'm going to call my superiors."—"As you like," Thomas said calmly. A little boy about eight years old came through the group, a box on his shoulder. It was a wooden ammunition crate with Russian markings, on the bottom of which were fixed a number of screws and nailed several colored cardboard circles. A tin can, tied to the crate by a wire, hung from the side; clamps held a long metal rod in the air; around his neck, the boy wore real operator's earphones. He adjusted them on his ears, put the crate on his lap, turned the cardboard circles, played with the screws, brought the tin can to his mouth and called: "Kampfgruppe Adam to HQ! Kampfgruppe Adam to HQ! Answer!" He repeated this several times and then freed one ear from the earpieces, much too big for him. "I have them on line, Herr Generalmajor," he said to the tall blond boy. "What should I say?" The blond boy turned to Thomas: "Your name and rank!"—"SS-Standartenführer Hauser, attached to the *Sicherheitspolizei*." The boy turned back to the little one with the radio: "Ask them if they confirm the mission of Standartenführer Hauser of the Sipo." The little boy repeated the message into his tin can and waited. Then he declared: "They don't know anything, Herr Generalmajor."—"That's not surprising," Thomas said with his incredible calm. "We report directly to the Führer. Let me call Berlin and he'll confirm it to you in person."—"In person?" the boy in charge asked, a strange glint in his eyes.—"In person," repeated Thomas. I was still petrified; Thomas's boldness froze me. The blond youth made a sign and the little boy took off the helmet and passed it with the tin can to Thomas. "Speak. Say 'Over' at the end of each sentence." Thomas brought the earpieces to one ear and took the can. Then he called into the can: "Berlin, Berlin. Hauser to Berlin, answer." He repeated this several times, then said: "Standartenführer Hauser, on special assignment, reporting. I have to talk to the Führer. Over . . . Yes, I'll wait. Over." The children surrounding us kept their eyes riveted on him; the jaw of the boy who went by the name of Adam was quivering slightly. Then Thomas stiffened, clicked his heels, and shouted into the can; "Heil Hitler! Standartenführer Hauser from the *Geheime Staatspolizei*, reporting, mein Führer! We have met Kampfgruppe Adam and request confirmation of our mission and our identity. Over." He paused again and then said: "*Jawohl*, mein Führer. Sieg Heil!" He handed the earpieces and the can to the boy in the officer's coat. "He wants to speak to you, Herr Generalmajor."—"It's the Führer?" the boy said in a muted voice.—"Yes. Don't be afraid. He's a kind man." The boy slowly took the earpieces, put them to his ears, stiffened, threw an arm into the air, and shouted into the can: "Heil Hitler! Generalmajor Adam, *zu Befehl*, mein Führer! Over!" Then: "*Jawohl*, mein Führer! *Jawohl! Jawohl!* Sieg Heil!" When he took off the earpieces to return them to the little boy, his eyes were moist. "That was the Führer," he said solemnly. "He confirms your identity and your mission. I'm sorry for your driver, but he had an unfortunate reaction and we couldn't know. My Kampfgruppe is at your disposal. What do you need?"—"We need to rejoin our lines safe and sound to transmit secret information of vital importance for the Reich. Can you help us?" The boy withdrew with some others and conferred with them. Then he returned: "We came here to destroy a concentration of Bolshevik forces. But we can accompany you as far as the Oder. To the south there's a forest, we'll pass under the nose of those brutes. We'll help you."

So we started off with this horde of children in rags, leaving poor Piontek's body lying there. Thomas took his submachine gun, and I picked up the bag of provisions. The group included almost seventy kids in all, including a dozen girls. Most of them, as we gradually learned, were orphan *Volksdeutschen*; some came from the region of Zamosc and even from Galicia and as far as Odessa. They had been roaming like this for months behind Russians lines, living on what they could find, picking up other children, pitilessly killing Russians and isolated Germans, whom they regarded as deserters. Like us, they marched at night and rested during the day, hidden in the forests. On the march they advanced in military order, with scouts out front, then the rest of the troupe, girls in the middle. Twice, we saw them massacre little groups of sleeping Russians: the first time it was easy, the soldiers, drunk, were sleeping off their vodka on a farm and had their throats cut or were hacked to pieces in their sleep; the second time, a kid shattered a guard's skull with a rock, then the others rushed the ones snoring around a fire, near their broken-down truck. Curiously, they never took their weapons: "Our own Germans weapons are better," the boy who commanded them and who claimed his name was Adam explained. We also saw them attack a patrol with amazing guile and savagery. The little unit had been spotted by the scouts; most of the group withdrew into the woods, and twenty or so boys advanced onto the path toward the Russians, shouting, *"Russki! Davaï! Khleb, khleb!"* The Russians weren't suspicious and let them approach, some even laughed and took some bread out of their bags. When the children had surrounded them, they attacked them with their tools and their knives, it was an insane butchery, I saw a little seven-year-old boy jump onto a soldier's back and plant a big nail in his eye. Two of the soldiers still managed to fire off a few volleys before they collapsed: three children were killed on the spot and five were wounded. After the fight, the survivors, covered in blood, brought back the wounded, who were crying and howling in pain. Adam saluted them and himself finished off, with his knife, the ones who were hit in the legs or stomach; the two others were handed over to the girls, and Thomas and I tried as well as we could to clean their wounds and bandage them with rags from shirts. Among themselves they behaved almost as brutally as with the adults. During the breaks, we had time to observe them: Adam had himself waited on by one of the older girls, then led her off into the woods; the others fought for pieces of bread or sausage, the smallest had to run to pilfer from the bags while the big ones clouted them or even hit them with shovels; then two or three boys would grab a girl by the hair, throw her on the ground, and rape her in front of the others, biting her neck like cats; some boys openly jerked off as they watched; others would hit the one on top of the little girl and shove him aside to take his place; when the girl tried to run away, they caught her and knocked her down with a kick in the stomach, all this in a racket of shouts and piercing screams; several of these barely pubescent girls looked pregnant. These scenes shattered my nerves profoundly; I found it very hard to bear this demented company. Some of the children, especially the older ones, scarcely spoke German; whereas, at least until the previous year, they all must have gone to school, no trace of their education seemed to remain, aside from the unshakeable conviction that they belonged to a superior race. They lived like a primitive tribe or a pack, cleverly cooperating to kill or find food, then viciously fighting over the booty. The authority of Adam, who was physically the tallest, seemed uncontested; I saw him strike against a tree, till it bled, the head of a boy who had been slow to obey him. Maybe, I said to myself, he has all the adults he meets killed so he can remain the oldest.

This march with the children lasted for several nights. I felt as if I were gradually losing control of myself, I had to make an immense effort not to hit them in turn. Thomas still kept his Olympian calm; he followed our progression on the map and with a compass, conferring with Adam about what direction to take. Before Gollnow, we had to cross the Kammin railroad, then, in several compact groups, the road. Beyond was nothing but an immense, dense forest, deserted but dangerous because of the patrols, which, fortunately, kept to the paths. We also began again meeting, alone or in groups, German soldiers, who like us were headed toward the Oder. Thomas stopped Adam from killing the isolated ones; two of them joined us, including a Belgian SS man, the others went their own way, preferring to try their luck alone. After another road, the forest became a marsh, we weren't far from the Oder; to the south, according to the map, these swamps led to a tributary, the Ihna. Moving became difficult, we sank up to our knees, sometimes our waists, the children almost drowned in the bogs. It was very warm now, even in the forest the snow had disappeared; I finally got rid of my coat, still wet and heavy. Adam decided to escort us to the Oder with a smaller troupe and left part of his group, the girls and the smallest ones, under the guard of the two wounded children, on a strip of dry land. Crossing these desolate marshes took most of the night; sometimes we had to make considerable detours, but Thomas's compass helped guide us. Finally we reached the Oder, black and gleaming beneath the moon. A line of long islands seemed to stretch between us and the German shore. We couldn't find a boat. "No matter," Thomas said, "we'll swim across."—"I don't know how to swim," the Belgian said. He was a Walloon, he had known Lippert well in the Caucasus and had told me about his death in Novo Buda. "I'll help you," I said. Thomas turned to Adam: "You don't want to cross with us? Go back to Germany?"—"No," the boy said. "We have our own mission." We took off our boots to tuck them into our belts and I shoved my cap inside my tunic; Thomas and the German soldier, whose name was Fritz, kept their submachine guns in case the island wasn't deserted. At this spot the river must normally have been about three hundred meters wide, but with the thaw, it had risen and the current was strong; the Belgian, whom I held under the chin as I swam on my back, slowed me down, I was soon carried away and almost missed the island; as soon as I managed to get my footing, I let the soldier go and pulled him by the collar, until he could walk on his own in the water. On the bank, I was overcome with fatigue and had to sit down for a while. Opposite, the marshes barely rustled, the children had already disappeared; the island on which we found ourselves was wooded, and I didn't hear anything here, either, except the murmuring of the water. The Belgian went to find Thomas and the German soldier, who had landed farther up, then came back to tell me that the island seemed deserted. When I could get up I went through the wood with him. On the other side, the shore was also silent and dark. But on the beach, a pole painted red and white indicated the location of a field telephone, protected beneath a tarp, whose wire vanished into the water. Thomas took the receiver and made the call. "Hello," he said. "Yes, we're German soldiers." He gave our names and ranks. Then: "Good." He hung up, straightened, looked at me with a big smile. "They say we should stand in a row with our arms out." We scarcely had time to get in place: a powerful spotlight on the German shore came on and aimed at us. We stayed that way for several minutes. "Good idea, their system," Thomas commented. An engine noise started up in the night. A rubber dinghy approached and landed near us; three soldiers examined us in silence, holding their weapons until they were sure we were indeed German; still without a word, they herded us into the boat and the dinghy set off, bouncing through the black water.

On the bank, in the darkness, Feldgendarmen were waiting. Their big curved neck plates shone in the moonlight. They led us into a bunker to face a police Hauptmann, who asked for our papers; none of us had any. "In that case," the officer said, "I have to send you under escort to Stettin. I'm sorry, but all kinds of people are trying to infiltrate." As we waited, they handed out cigarettes and Thomas talked amiably with him: "You have a lot of crossings?"—"Ten or fifteen a night. In our entire sector, dozens. The other day, more than two hundred men arrived all at once, still armed. Most of them end up here because of the swamps, where the Russians don't patrol much, as you saw."—"The idea of the telephone is ingenious."—"Thank you. The water has risen, and a lot of men drowned when they tried to swim across. The telephone spares us bad surprises . . . at least, so we hope," he added, smiling. "It seems the Russians have traitors with them." Around dawn, they had us get into a truck with three other *Rückkämpfer* and an armed escort of Feldgendarmen. We had crossed the river just above Pölitz; but the city was under Russian artillery fire and our truck made a long detour before we reached Stettin. There too shells were falling, buildings were cheerfully burning; in the streets, from the truck sides, I saw almost no one but soldiers. They took us to a Wehrmacht HQ, where we were immediately separated from the soldiers, then a severe Major interrogated us, soon joined by a representative of the Gestapo in civilian clothes. I let Thomas talk, he told our story in detail; I spoke only when questioned directly. On Thomas's suggestion, the man from the Gestapo finally agreed to call Berlin. Huppenkothen, Thomas's superior, wasn't there, but we were able to reach one of his deputies, who immediately identified us. Right away the attitude of the Major and the Gestapo man changed; they began calling us by our rank and offering us schnapps. The Gestapo functionary left, promising to find us transportation to Berlin; in the meantime, the Major gave us some cigarettes and had us sit on a bench in the hallway. We smoked without talking: since the beginning of the march, we'd hardly smoked at all, and it was intoxicating. A calendar on the Major's desk bore the date March 21, our adventure had lasted for seventeen days, and it must have been obvious from our appearance: we stank, our faces were bearded, our torn uniforms were coated in mud. But we weren't the first to arrive in this state, and it didn't seem to shock anyone. Thomas sat upright, one leg crossed over the other, he seemed very happy with our escapade; I was slumped, my legs spread straight in front of me in a rather unmilitary fashion; a bustling Oberst, passing by with a briefcase under his arm, threw me a look of disdain. I recognized him immediately, leapt up, and greeted him warmly: it was Osnabrugge, the demolisher of bridges. He took a few moments to recognize me, then his eyes opened wide: "Obersturmbannführer! What a state you're in." I briefly described our adventure to him. "And you? Are you dynamiting German bridges now?" His face fell: "Yes, unfortunately. I blew up the Stettin bridge two days ago, when we evacuated Altdamm and Finkenwalde. It was horrible, the bridge was covered with hanged men, runaways caught by the Feldgendarmen. Three of them were still hanging after the explosion, right at the entrance to the bridge, all green. But," he went on, pulling himself together, "we didn't destroy everything. The Oder in front of Stettin has five branches, and we decided to demolish only the last bridge. That leaves some chance for rebuilding."—"That's good," I remarked, "you're thinking about the future, you're keeping up your morale." We separated at these words: a few bridgeheads, farther south, hadn't yet fallen back, Osnabrugge had to go inspect the preparations for demolitions. Soon afterward, the man from the local Gestapo returned and had us get into a car with an SS officer who also had to go to Berlin and didn't seem the least bit bothered by our smell. On the autobahn, the spectacle was even more horrible than in February: a continuous flow of haggard refugees and exhausted, ragged soldiers, trucks loaded with wounded, the debris of the debacle. I fell asleep almost immediately, they had to wake me up during a Sturmovik attack; as soon as I could get back in the car I fell asleep again.

In Berlin, we had some trouble justifying ourselves, but less than I expected; not like ordinary soldiers, who were unceremoniously hanged or shot on suspicion alone. Even before shaving or washing, Thomas went to present himself to Kaltenbrunner, whose headquarters were now in the Kurfürstenstrasse, in Eichmann's old premises, one of the last RSHA buildings still pretty much standing. Since I didn't know where to report to—even Grothmann had left Berlin—I accompanied him. We had agreed on a story that was for the most part plausible: I was taking advantage of my leave to try to evacuate my sister and her husband, and the Russian offensive had caught me short with Thomas, who had come to help me; Thomas had had the foresight to provide himself with a mission order from Huppenkothen before leaving. Kaltenbrunner listened to us in silence and then dismissed us without any comment, informing me that the Reichsführer, who had resigned the day before from his command of Army Group Vistula, was in Hohenlychen. The report on Piontek's death took me no time at all, but I had to fill out a number of forms to justify the loss of the vehicle. In the evening, we went to Thomas's place, in Wannsee: the house was intact, but there was neither electricity nor running water, and we could only have a quick wash with cold water, and shave with difficulty before going to bed. The next morning, wearing a clean uniform, I went to Hohenlychen to present myself to Brandt. As soon as he saw me, he ordered me to shower, have my hair cut, and come back when I looked presentable. The hospital had hot showers, I spent almost an hour under the stream of water, voluptuously; then I went to the barber and, while I was at it, had myself shaved with hot water and sprinkled with eau de Cologne. Almost cheerful, I went back to see Brandt. He listened to my story severely, berated me curtly for having cost the Reich, through my imprudence, several weeks of my work, then informed me that in the meantime I had been reported missing; my office was dissolved, my colleagues reassigned, and my files archived. For now, the Reichsführer had no more need of my services; and Brandt ordered me to return to Berlin to put myself at Kaltenbrunner's disposal. After the interview, his secretary led me into his office and handed me my personal mail, transmitted by Asbach when the Oranienburg office was closed: mostly bills, a note from Ohlendorf about my wound in February, and a letter from Helene, which I pocketed without opening. Then I went back to Berlin. A chaotic atmosphere reigned at the Kurfürstenstrasse: the building now housed the headquarters of the RSHA and of the Staatspolizei, as well as numerous representatives of the SD; everyone needed more room, hardly anyone knew what he was supposed to be doing, all wandered aimlessly through the hallways, trying to look busy. Since Kaltenbrunner couldn't receive me before nightfall, I settled into a chair in a corner and resumed my reading of *L'Éducation sentimentale*, which had suffered again from the crossing of the Oder, but which I was determined to finish. Kaltenbrunner had me summoned just as Frédéric meets Madame Arnoux for the last time; it was frustrating. He could have waited a little, especially since he had no idea what to do with me. He ended up, almost at random, appointing me liaison officer with the OKW. My work consisted of this: three times a day, I had to go to the Bendlerstrasse and bring back dispatches about the situation on the front; the rest of the time, I could calmly daydream. The Flaubert was soon finished, but I found other books. I could also have gone out walking, but that wasn't recommended. The city was in a bad state. Everywhere, windows were gaping; one regularly heard part of some building collapse with a huge roar. In the streets, teams of people tirelessly cleared away the rubble and piled it up in neatly spaced heaps so that the rare cars could pass, slaloming their way through, but often these piles too toppled over, and they had to start again. The spring air was acrid, full of black smoke and brick dust gritty in the teeth. The last major raid had occurred three days before our return: on that occasion, the Luftwaffe had introduced its new weapon, surprisingly rapid jet aircraft, which had inflicted some losses on the enemy; since then, there had been only harassing Mosquito raids. The Sunday after our arrival was the first fine spring day of 1945: in the Tiergarten, the trees were budding, grass was appearing on the heaps of debris and turning the gardens green. But we had few occasions to take advantage of the nice weather. Food rations, ever since the loss of the eastern territories, were reduced to a strict minimum; even the best restaurants didn't have much. The ministries were being emptied of their personnel to fill out the Wehrmacht, but with the destruction of most of the index files and the general disorganization, most of the men thus freed waited for weeks to be called up. At the Kurfürstenstrasse, they had set up an office that delivered false papers from the Wehrmacht or from other organizations to senior RSHA officials who were regarded as *compromised.* Thomas had several cards made up for himself, all different, and showed them to me, laughing: engineer at Krupp's, Hauptmann of the Wehrmacht, civil servant in the Ministry of Agriculture. He wanted me to do the same, but I kept putting it off; instead I had another pay book and SD card made up, to replace the ones I had destroyed in Pomerania. From time to time, I saw Eichmann, who was still hanging around there, completely dejected. He was very nervous, he knew that if our enemies got their hands on him, he was finished, he wondered what was going to happen to him. He had sent his family away and wanted to join them; I saw him one day in a hallway arguing bitterly, probably about this, with Blobel, who was also wandering about without knowing what to do, almost constantly drunk, hateful, enraged. A few days before, Eichmann had met the Reichsführer in Hohenlychen, and had returned from this interview extremely depressed; he invited me to his office to drink some schnapps and to listen to him talk, he seemed to have a certain regard for me and treated me almost as his confidant, though I had no idea why. I drank in silence and let him vent. "I don't understand," he said plaintively, pushing his glasses back up on his nose. "The Reichsführer said to me: 'Eichmann, if I had to start over again, I'd organize the concentration camps as the British do.' That's what he said to me. He added: 'I made a mistake there.' What could he have meant? I don't understand. Do you understand? Maybe he meant the camps should have been, I don't know, more elegant, more artful, more polite." I didn't understand what the Reichsführer had meant, either, but it was all the same to me, really. I knew from Thomas, who had immediately plunged back into his intrigues, that Himmler, prompted by his Finnish masseur, Kersten, and by Schellenberg, kept making gestures— mostly incoherent ones, to tell the truth—toward the Anglo-Americans: "Schellenberg managed to get him to say: 'I protect the throne. That doesn't necessarily mean the one who is sitting on it.' That's real progress," Thomas explained to me.—"Truly. Tell me, Thomas, why are you still in Berlin?" The Russians had stopped on the Oder, but everyone knew it was just a question of time. Thomas smiled: "Schellenberg asked me to stay. To keep an eye on Kaltenbrunner and especially Müller. They're running a bit wild." Everyone, in fact, was running a bit wild, Himmler first and foremost, Schellenberg, Kammler who now had his own direct access to the Führer and no longer listened to the Reichsführer; Speer, it was said, was racing around the Ruhr trying, in the face of the American advance, to countermand the Führer's destruction orders. The population was losing all hope, and Goebbels's propaganda wasn't helping things: by way of consolation, he promised that in case of defeat the Führer, *in his great wisdom*, was preparing an easy death, by gas, for the German people. That was very encouraging and it led the malicious to suggest: "What is a coward? It's a guy who's in Berlin and who signs up for the front." The second week of April, the Philharmonic gave a final concert. The program, execrable, was entirely in the taste of that period—Brünnhilde's last aria, the *Götterdämmerung* of course, and to end it all Bruckner's *Romantic Symphony*—but I went all the same. The icy auditorium was intact, the chandeliers shone with all their lights; I could see Speer, from a distance, with Admiral Dönitz in the box of honor; at the exit, uniformed Hitlerjugend holding baskets offered members of the audience cyanide capsules: I was almost tempted to swallow one on the spot, in a fit of pique. Flaubert, I was sure, would have had a fit in front of such a display of inanity. These ostentatious demonstrations of pessimism alternated with ecstatic effusions of optimistic joy: the same day as this famous concert, Roosevelt died, and Goebbels, confusing Truman with Peter III, immediately launched a new slogan, "The Czarina is dead." Soldiers claimed they had seen the face of "Uncle Fritz" in the clouds, and were promised a decisive counteroffensive and victory for the Führer's birthday, on April 20. Thomas, at least, even though he didn't give up his maneuvering, still kept his wits about him; he had managed to send his parents through to the Tyrol, near Innsbruck, to a zone that would certainly be occupied by the Americans: "Kaltenbrunner took care of it. Through the Gestapo in Vienna." And when I showed a little surprise: "He's an understanding man, is Kaltenbrunner. He has a family too, he knows what it means." Thomas had immediately resumed his frantic social life and took me from party to party, where I drank myself into a stupor as he exaggeratedly narrated our Pomeranian wanderings to titillated ladies. There were parties every night, pretty much everywhere, people no longer paid any attention to the Mosquito raids or to the propaganda orders. Beneath the Wilhelmplatz, a bunker had been transformed into a nightclub, very cheerful, where they served wine, hard liquor, brand-name cigars, fancy hors d'oeuvres; the place was frequented by high-ranking officers from the OKW, the SS, and the RSHA, wealthy civilians and aristocrats, as well as actresses and flirtatious young ladies, superbly decked out. We dined almost every evening at the Adlon, where the maître d'hôtel, solemn and impassive, welcomed us in a tail-coat, led us into the well-lit restaurant, and had us served, by waiters wearing tails, purple slices of cabbage in silver dishes. The basement bar was always crowded, packed with the last diplomats, Italian, Japanese, Hungarian, or French. I met Mihaï there one night, dressed in white, with a canary yellow silk shirt. "Still in Berlin?" he asked me with a smile. "It's been a long time since I saw you last." He began openly flirting with me, in front of several people. I took him by the arm and, squeezing him tightly, drew him aside: "Stop," I ordered.—"Stop what?" he said, smiling. This smug, calculating smile drove me out of my mind. "Come on," I said, and pushed him discreetly into the bathroom. It was a large white tiled room, with massive sinks and urinals, brightly lit. I checked the stalls: they were empty. Then I shot the bolt on the door. Mihaï was looking at me, smiling, one hand in the pocket of his white jacket, next to the sinks with their big brass faucets. He came toward me, still with his eager smile; when he raised his head to kiss me, I took off my cap and hit him hard in the face with my forehead. His nose, under the violence of the blow, burst, blood gushed out, he screamed and fell to the ground. I stepped over him, still holding my cap, and went to look at myself in the mirror: I had blood on my forehead, but my collar and uniform weren't stained. I carefully washed my face and put my cap back on. On the ground, Mihaï was writhing in pain and holding his nose, groaning pitifully: "Why'd you do that?" His hand found the hem of my pants; I removed my foot and looked around the room. A mop was leaning in a corner, in a galvanized metal bucket. I took this mop, placed the handle across Mihaï's neck, and stood on it; with one foot to each side of his neck, I rocked slowly on the handle. Mihaï's face beneath me became red, scarlet, then purplish-blue; his jaw quivered convulsively, his bulging eyes stared at me with terror, his nails scratched my boots; behind me, his feet beat the tiled floor. He wanted to speak, but no sound came out of his mouth from which a swollen, obscene tongue stuck out. He emptied himself with a soft noise and the stench of shit filled the room; his legs struck the ground one last time, then fell limp. I got down off the mop, set it aside, tapped Mihaï's cheek with the tip of my boot. His inert head rolled a bit, then slowly came back. I took him by the armpits, dragged him into one of the stalls, and sat him down on the toilet, making sure the feet were straight. These stalls had latches that pivoted on a screw: by holding the raised latch with the tip of my pocketknife, I could shut the door and make it fall so as to lock the stall from inside. A little blood had run on the tiled floor; I used the mop to clean it, then rinsed it off, wiped the handle with my handkerchief, and put it back in the bucket where I had found it. Finally I went out. I went to the bar to get a drink; people were going in and out of the bathroom, no one seemed to notice anything. An acquaintance came over to ask me: "Have you seen Mihaï?" I looked around: "No, he must be somewhere around." I finished my drink and went to chat with Thomas. Around one in the morning, there was a disturbance: someone had found the body. Diplomats uttered horrified exclamations, the police came, they questioned us, like everyone else I said I hadn't seen a thing. I never heard anything more about this business. The Russian offensive was finally under way: on April 16, at night, they attacked the Seelow Heights, our last defensive position before the city. The sky was overcast, it was drizzling; I spent the day and then part of the night carrying dispatches from the Bendlerstrasse to the Kurfürstenstrasse, a short trip complicated by the incessant Sturmovik raids. Around midnight, I ran into Osnabrugge at the Bendlerstrasse: he looked lost, exhausted. "They want to blow up all the bridges in the city." He was almost weeping. "Well," I said, "if the enemy's advancing, that's normal, isn't it?"—"You don't realize what that means! There are nine hundred and fifty bridges in Berlin. If we blow them up, the city dies! Forever. No more food supplies, no more industry. Even worse, all the electric cables, all the water pipes pass through these bridges. Can you picture it? The epidemics, the people dying of hunger in the ruins?" I shrugged: "We can't just hand the city over to the Russians."—"But that's no reason to demolish everything! We can choose, we can just destroy the bridges on the main routes." He was wiping his forehead. "In any case, I'll say this to you, have me shot if you want, but for me it's the last time. When this madness is over, I don't care who I have to work for, I'm going to build. They'll have to rebuild, won't they?"—"No doubt. Would you still know how to build a bridge?"—"Probably, probably," he said as he moved off, nodding gently. Later on, that same night, I found Thomas in the Wannsee house. He wasn't sleeping, he was sitting alone in the living room, in shirtsleeves, drinking. "So?" he asked me.—"We still hold the Seelow redoubt. But farther south, their tanks are crossing the Neisse." He made a grimace: "Yes. Well. In any case it's *kaput*." I took off my wet cap and coat and poured myself a drink. "It's really over, then?"—"It's over," Thomas confirmed.—"Defeat, again?"—"Yes, once again, defeat."—"And afterward?"—"Afterward? We'll see. Germany won't be wiped off the map, whatever Herr Morgenthau may say. The unnatural alliance of our enemies will hold up until their victory, but not much longer. The Western powers will need a bastion against Bolshevism. I give them three years, at most." I drank and listened. "I wasn't talking about that," I said finally.—"Ah. Us, you mean?"—"Yes, us. Accounts will have to be settled."—"Why didn't you have some ID papers made up?"—"I don't know. I don't really believe in them. What will we do, with these papers? Sooner or later, they'll find us. Then it'll be the rope or Siberia." Thomas swirled the liquid around in his glass: "It's obvious that we'll have to leave for a while. Lie low a bit, long enough for people to calm down. Then we can come back. The new Germany, whatever it might be, will need brains."—"Go? Where? And how?" He looked at me, smiling: "You think we haven't thought of that? There are networks, in Holland, in Switzerland, people ready to help us, out of conviction or self-interest. The best networks are in Italy. In Rome. The Church will not let down its flock in its time of distress." He raised his glass as if for a toast, and drank. "Schellenberg, Wolfie too, have received good guarantees. Of course, it won't be easy. Endgames are always delicate."—"And afterward?"—"We'll see. South America, the sun, the pampas, the horses, doesn't that tempt you? Or, if you like, the pyramids. The British are going to pull out, they'll need good specialists, over there." I poured myself some more and drank: "What if Berlin is surrounded? How do you plan on getting out? Are you staying?"—"Yes, I'm staying. Kaltenbrunner and Müller are still giving us a hard time. They're really not reasonable. But I've thought it over. Come and see." He led me into his bedroom, opened his wardrobe, took out some clothes, which he spread out on the bed: "Look." They were coarse work clothes made of blue canvas, stained with oil and grease. "Look at the labels." I looked: they were French clothes. "I also have shoes, the beret, the armband, everything. And the papers. Here." He showed me the papers: they were those of a French worker from the STO. "Of course, in France, I'll have trouble passing, but it will be enough for the Russians. Even if I come across an officer who speaks French, it's not very likely he'll balk at my accent. I can always tell him I'm Alsatian."—"That's not a bad idea," I said. "Where did you find all that?" He tapped the rim of his glass and smiled: "You think they count foreign workers these days, in Berlin? One more, one less . . ." He drank. "You should think about it. With your French, you could get as far as Paris." We went back downstairs to the living room. He poured me another glass and clinked glasses with me. "It won't be without risks," he said laughing. "But what is? We got out of Stalingrad. You have to be clever, that's all. You know that there are guys in the Gestapo who are trying to get themselves stars and Jewish papers?" He laughed again. "They're having a hard time of it. There aren't a lot left on the market."

I slept little and returned early to the Bendlerstrasse. The sky had cleared and there were Sturmoviks everywhere. The next day it was even nicer out, the gardens, in the ruins, were flowering. I didn't see Thomas, he had gotten caught up in some business between Wolff and Kaltenbrunner, I don't know too much about it, Wolff had come up from Italy to discuss the possibility of a surrender, Kaltenbrunner had gotten angry and wanted to arrest him or have him hanged, as usual it ended up in front of the Führer, who let Wolff go. When I finally saw Thomas again, the day the Seelow Heights fell, he was furious, raging against Kaltenbrunner, his stupidity, his narrow-mindedness. I myself didn't understand at all what Kaltenbrunner was playing at, what use it could be to him to turn against the Reichsführer, to intrigue with Bormann, to maneuver to become the Führer's new favorite. Kaltenbrunner wasn't an idiot, he must have known, better than anyone, that the game was coming to an end; but instead of positioning himself for what would come after, he was wasting his energy in pointless, futile quarrels, affecting a hard-line attitude that he would never, as was obvious to anyone who knew him, have the courage to bring to its logical conclusion. Yet Kaltenbrunner was far from being the only one to lose all sense of moderation. Everywhere, in Berlin, Sperrkommandos were appearing, blocking units made up of men from the SD, the police, various Party organizations, Feldgendarmen, who administered an extremely summary justice to those who, more reasonable than they, just wanted to live, and sometimes even to some who had nothing to do with anything, but who just had the misfortune to be there. The little fanatics of the Leibstandarte hauled wounded soldiers out of basements to execute them. Everywhere, exhausted veterans from the Wehrmacht, recently called-up civilians, sixteen-year-old kids, their faces purplish-blue, decorated lampposts, trees, bridges, S-Bahn elevated tracks, anyplace from which a man can be hanged, and always with the invariable sign around their necks: I AM HERE BECAUSE I ABANDONED MY POST WITHOUT ORDERS. Berliners had a resigned attitude: "Instead of getting hanged, I'd rather believe in victory." I myself had problems with these maniacs; since I moved around a lot, they were constantly checking my papers, I thought of asking for an armed escort to defend myself. At the same time, I almost pitied these men, drunk with fury and bitterness, devoured by an impotent hatred that, as it could no longer be directed at the enemy, they turned against their own, like rabid wolves devouring one another. At the Kurfürstenstrasse, a young Obersturmführer from the *Staatspolizei*, Gersbach, hadn't shown up one morning; he didn't have any work to do, true, but it had been noticed; some policemen finally found him at his home, dead drunk; Müller waited for him to sober up, then had him shot with a bullet in the neck in front of the officers gathered in the building's courtyard. Afterward, his corpse was thrown out onto the asphalt, while a young SS recruit, almost hysterical, emptied the magazine of his submachine gun into the poor man's body.

The news I was bearing several times a day was rarely good. Day after day, the Soviets were advancing, entering Lichtenberg and Pankow, taking Weissensee. Refugees crossed the city in large columns, many of them were hanged, at random, as deserters. The Russian artillery bombardments caused more victims: on the Führer's birthday, they had arrived within cannon's range of the city. It had been a beautiful day, a warm, sunny Friday, the smell of lilacs filled the air of the abandoned gardens with their fragrance. Here and there flags with swastikas had been hung on the ruins, as well as large signs whose irony I hoped was unconscious, like the one that dominated the rubble on the Lützowplatz: WE THANK OUR FÜHRER FOR EVERYTHING. But people's hearts weren't really in it. In midmorning, the Anglo-Americans had launched one of their massive raids, more than a thousand aircraft in two hours, followed by Mosquitos; after they left, the Russian artillery had taken over. It was certainly a beautiful fireworks display, but few appreciated it, on our side at least. Goebbels did try to have extra rations distributed in the Führer's honor, but even that turned sour: the artillery caused many victims among the civilians standing in line; the next day, in spite of the heavy rain, it was even worse, a shell struck a line of people waiting in front of the Karstadt department store, the Hermannplatz was full of bloody corpses, scattered pieces of limbs, children screaming and shaking the inert bodies of their mothers, I saw it myself. On Sunday there was a brilliant spring sun, then showers, then sun again that shone on the rubble and the soaking ruins. Birds sang; everywhere tulips and lilacs were blooming, apple trees, plum and cherry trees, and in the Tiergarten, rhododendrons. But these gorgeous flower aromas couldn't mask the stench of rotting and burned brick floating over the streets. A heavy, stagnant smoke veiled the sky; when it rained, this smoke grew even thicker, filling people's throats. The streets, despite the artillery strikes, were full of life: at the antitank barricades, children with paper helmets, perched on top of the obstacles, were waving wooden swords; I passed old women pushing strollers full of bricks, and even, crossing the Tiergarten toward the zoo bunker, soldiers chasing a herd of mooing cows before them. At night it rained again; and the Reds, in turn, celebrated Lenin's birthday with a brutal riot of artillery.

The public services were shutting down one by one, their personnel evacuating. A day before being dismissed, General Reynmann, the city Kommandant, had distributed to NSDAP officials two thousand passes to leave Berlin. Whoever hadn't been lucky enough to get one could still buy his way out: at the Kurfürstenstrasse, a Gestapo officer explained to me that a complete set of valid papers fetched around eighty thousand reichsmarks. The U-Bahn ran until April 23, the S-Bahn until the twenty-fifth, the interurban telephone worked until the twenty-sixth (they say a Russian managed to reach Goebbels at his office, from Siemensstadt). Kaltenbrunner had left for Austria immediately after the Führer's birthday, but Müller stayed on, and I continued my liaisons for him. I usually went by the Tiergarten, because the streets south of the Bendlerstrasse, by the Landwehrkanal, were blocked; in the Neue Siegesallee, repeated explosions had smashed the statues of the sovereigns of Prussia and Brandenburg, the street was strewn with Hohenzollern heads and limbs; at night, the fragments of white marble gleamed in the moonlight. At the OKW, where the city Kommandant now had his HQ (someone named Käther had replaced Reynmann, then two days later, Käther had in turn been dismissed to make way for Weidling), they often made me wait for hours before finally granting me a few useless fragments of information. To avoid being too much in the way, I waited with my driver in my car, beneath a cement roof in the courtyard, I watched, as they scurried about, overexcited, haggard officers, exhausted soldiers dawdling so as not to go back under fire too quickly, Hitlerjugend greedy for glory come to beg for a few *Panzerfäuste*, lost *Volkssturm* waiting for orders. One night, I was searching through my pockets for a cigarette when I came across Helene's letter, pocketed at Hohenlychen and forgotten since then. I tore open the envelope and read the letter as I smoked. It was a brief, direct declaration: she didn't understand my attitude, she wrote, she didn't want to understand it, she wanted to know if I wished to join her, she asked if I was planning on marrying her. The honesty and frankness of this letter overwhelmed me; but it was much too late, and I threw the crumpled paper out of the lowered car window into a puddle.

The noose was tightening. The Adlon had closed its doors; my only diversion was drinking schnapps at the Kurfürstenstrasse, or at Wannsee with Thomas, who, laughing, filled me in on the most recent events. Müller now was looking for a mole: an enemy agent, apparently in the entourage of a high-ranking SS official. Schellenberg saw in this a conspiracy to destabilize Himmler, and so Thomas had to follow the developments of the affair. The situation was degenerating into vaudeville: Speer, who had lost the Führer's confidence, had returned, dodging Sturmoviks to land his crate on the Ost-West-Achse, to beg for his *grace*;

Göring had been stripped of all his offices and placed under arrest in
Bavaria, for having somewhat hastily anticipated the death of his lord
and master; the more sober people, von Ribbentrop and the military,
were laying low or evacuating toward the Americans; the countless can-
didates for suicide were putting the finishing touches on their final
scene. Our soldiers kept conscientiously getting themselves killed, a
French battalion from the Charlemagne Division somehow found a way
to enter Berlin on the twenty-fourth to reinforce the Nordland Division, and the administrative center of the Reich was now defended only
by Finns, Estonians, Dutchmen, and young Parisian toughs. Elsewhere,
people were keeping a cool head: a powerful army, it was said, was on
the way to save Berlin and cast the Russians beyond the Oder, but at
the Bendlerstrasse my interlocutors remained perfectly vague about the
position and progression of the divisions, and the promised Wenck offensive was taking just as long to materialize as the one by Steiner's Waffen-SS, a few days earlier. As for me, to tell the truth, I wasn't much
tempted by *Götterdämmerung*, and I would have prefered to be somewhere else, to reflect calmly on my situation. It wasn't so much that I
was afraid of dying, believe me, I had few reasons to keep on living, after all, but the idea of being killed in this way, somewhat at the mercy
of events, by a shell or a stray bullet, displeased me exceedingly, I would
have liked to sit down and contemplate things rather than let myself be
carried away by this black current. But such a choice was not offered
me, I had to serve, like everyone else, and since it was necessary, I did
it loyally, I collected and transmitted this useless information that seemed
to serve only one purpose, to keep me in Berlin. As for our enemies,
they remained supremely indifferent to all this commotion and kept advancing.

Soon the Kurfürstenstrasse too had to be evacuated. The remaining
officers were dispersed; Müller withdrew to his emergency HQ, in the
crypt of the Dreifaltigkeitskirche on Mauerstrasse. The Bendlerstrasse
was practically on the front line, the liaisons had become very complicated: to reach the building, I had to thread my way through the rubble to the edge of the Tiergarten, then continue on foot, guided
through basements and ruins by *Kellerkinder*, filthy little orphans who
knew every nook and crany. The thunder of the bombardments was like
a living thing, a multifaceted and tireless assault on hearing; but when
the immense silence of the pauses descended, it was worse. Entire sections of the city were burning, giant phosphorous fires that sucked in
the air and provoked violent storms that fed the flames even more.
Heavy, violent, brief rains sometimes extinguished a few fires, but

mostly intensified the smell of burning. A few planes were still trying to land on the Ost-West-Achse; twelve Ju-52s transporting SS cadets were shot down on approach, one after the other. Wenck's army, according to the information they deigned to pass on to me, seemed to have vanished into the woodworks somewhere to the south of Potsdam. On April 27, it was very cold out, and after a violent Soviet assault on the Potsdamer Platz, driven back by the Leibstandarte AH, there were several hours of quiet. When I returned to the church on Mauerstrasse to report to Müller, I was told he was in one of the annexes of the Ministry of the Interior, and that I should join him there. I found him in a large, almost bare room with water-stained walls, in the company of Thomas and thirty or so officers from the SD and the *Staatspolizei*. Müller had us wait for half an hour, but only five more men arrived (he had summoned fifty in all). Then we all lined up, at ease, for a brief speech: the day before, after a telephone discussion with Obergruppenführer Kaltenbrunner, the Führer had decided to honor the RSHA for its services and its staunch loyalty. He had asked that the German Cross in Gold be bestowed on ten officers remaining in Berlin who had particularly distinguished themselves during the war. The list had been drawn up by Kaltenbrunner; the ones who didn't hear their names called should not be disappointed, since the honor fell upon them too. Then Müller read the list, at the head of which he himself figured; I wasn't surprised to hear Thomas's name; but to my astonishment, Müller named me too, second to last. What could I have done to be distinguished in this way? I wasn't in Kaltenbrunner's good books, far from it. Thomas, across the room, gave me a quick wink; already we were regrouping to go to the chancellery. In the car, Thomas explained the business to me: among the people they had still been able to find in Berlin, I was one of the few, along with him, who had served at the front, and that's what had counted. The trip to the chancellery along the Wilhelmstrasse had gotten difficult, the water mains had burst, the street was flooded, corpses were floating in the water and swayed gently as our cars went by; we had to finish our trip on foot, soaking wet up to our knees. Müller led us into the ruins of the *Auswärtiges Amt*: from there, an underground tunnel led to the Führer's bunker. In this tunnel too water was flowing, up to our ankles. Some Waffen-SS from the Leibstandarte were guarding the entrance to the bunker: they let us pass, but took our service pistols. We were led through a first bunker and then, via a spiral staircase streaming with water, to a second one, even lower down. We waded through the stream from the AA, at the bottom of the steps it soaked the red carpets of a wide hallway, where they had us sit down along a wall, on wooden school chairs. In front of us, a general from the Wehrmacht was shouting to another, who wore a Gener-aloberst's epaulettes: "We're all going to drown down here!" The Gen-eraloberst was trying to calm him down and assured him a pump was on the way. An abominable stench of urine filled the bunker, mixed with the musty effluvia of mildew, sweat, and wet wool, which they had tried in vain to mask with disinfectant. We were kept waiting for a while; officers came and went, crossing the waterlogged carpets with loud *thwacks* before disappearing into another room in the back, or climbing the spiral staircase; the room resounded with the continuous throbbing of a diesel generator. Two elegant young officers walked by, talking animatedly; behind them emerged my old friend Dr. Hohenegg. I leaped up and seized his arm, overjoyed at seeing him there. He took me by the hand and led me into a room where several Waffen-SS were playing cards or sleeping on bunk beds. "I was sent here as a backup doctor for the Führer," he explained gloomily. His bald, sweating head gleamed beneath the yellowish lightbulb.—"And how is he doing?"— "Oh, not very well. But I'm not looking after him, they've entrusted me with the children of our dear Propaganda Minister. They're in the first bunker," he added, pointing to the ceiling. He looked around and went on in a low voice: "It's something of a waste of time: as soon as I find their mother alone, she swears to God that she's going to poison them all and then commit suicide herself. The poor kids don't suspect a thing, they're charming, it breaks my heart, let me tell you. But our limping Mephistopheles has his mind firmly made up to form an honor guard to accompany his master to Hell. All the better for him."—"So that's where we're at, then?"—"Certainly. That fat Bormann, who doesn't much like the idea, has tried to get *him* to leave, but *he* refused. In my humble opinion, there's not much time left."—"And you, my dear Doktor?" I asked, smiling. I really was happy to see him again. "Me? *Carpe diem*, as the British public school boys say. We're having a party tonight. Upstairs, in the chancellery, so as not to disturb *him*. Come if you can. It'll be full of lusty young virgins who would rather offer their maidenhood to a German, whatever his appearance, than to a hairy, stinking Kalmyk." He patted his paunch: "At my age, you don't turn down offers like that. Afterward," his eyebrows went up comically on his egg-shaped skull—"afterward we'll see."—"Doktor," I said solemnly, "you are wiser than I am."—"I never doubted it for an instant, Obersturmbannführer. But I don't have your mad luck."—"In any case, believe me, I'm delighted to see you again."—"Me too, me too!" We were back in the hallway already. "Come if you can!" he said before scurrying away on his squat legs.

Soon afterward, they had us go into the back room. We pushed back the map-covered tables ourselves and lined up against the wall, our feet in the wet carpet. The two generals who had just been shouting about the water went and stood at attention in front of a door opposite us; on one of the tables, an adjutant was preparing the boxes with the medals. Then the door opened and the Führer appeared. All of us stiffened simultaneously, launched our arms into the air, and bellowed our salute. The two generals were also saluting. The Führer tried to raise his arm in response but it was shaking too much. Then he came forward with a hesitant, jerky, unstable step. Bormann, buttoned up tight in his brown uniform, emerged from the room behind him. I had never seen the Führer so close up. He wore a simple gray uniform and cap; his face looked yellow, haggard, puffy, his eyes remained fixed on one spot, inert, then began blinking violently; a drop of spittle stood out at the corner of his mouth. When he tottered, Bormann held out his hairy paw and supported him by the elbow. He leaned on the corner of a table and gave a brief, somewhat disjointed speech that included Frederick the Great, eternal glory, and the Jews. Then he went over to Müller. Bormann followed him like a shadow; the adjutant was holding open a box with a medal. The Führer took it slowly between his fingers, placed it without pinning it on Müller's right pocket, shook his hand, calling him "My good Müller, my faithful Müller," and patted his arm. I kept my head straight but watched from the corner of my eye. The ceremony was repeated for the next man: Müller barked out his name, rank, and service, then the Führer decorated him. Thomas was decorated next. As the Führer approached me—I was almost at the end of the line—my attention was caught by his nose. I had never noticed how broad and ill-proportioned this nose was. In profile, the little moustache was less distracting and the nose could be seen more clearly: it had a wide base and flat bridges, a little break in the bridge emphasized the tip; it was clearly a Slavonic or Bohemian nose, nearly Mongolo-Ostic. I don't know why this detail fascinated me, but I found it almost scandalous. The Führer approached and I kept observing him. Then he was in front of me. I saw with surprise that his cap scarcely reached my eyes; and yet I am not tall. He muttered his compliment and groped for the medal. His foul, fetid breath overwhelmed me: it was too much to take. So I leaned forward and bit into his bulbous nose, drawing blood. Even today I would be unable to tell you why I did this: I just couldn't restrain myself. The Führer let out a shrill cry and leaped back into Bormann's arms. There was an instant when no one moved. Then several men lay into me. I was struck and thrown to the ground; rolled into a ball on the wet carpet, I tried to protect myself from the kicks as well as I could. Everyone was shouting, the Führer was bellowing. Finally they pulled me back to my feet. My cap had fallen; I at least wanted to adjust my tie, but they held my arms firmly. Bormann was pushing the Führer toward his room and shouting: "Shoot him!" Thomas, behind the crowd, was observing me in silence, looking both disappointed and mocking. They dragged me toward a door at the back of the room. Then Müller interrupted in his loud, harsh voice: "Wait! I want to question him first. Take him to the crypt."

Trevor-Roper, I know, never breathed a word about this episode, nor has Bullock, nor any of the historians who have studied the Führer's last days. Yet it did take place, I assure you. This silence of the chroniclers is understandable: Müller disappeared, killed or gone over to the Russians a few days later; Bormann certainly died trying to flee Berlin; the two generals must have been Krebs and Burgdorf, who committed suicide; the adjutant must be dead too. As for the RSHA officers who witnessed the incident, I don't know what became of them, but one can easily imagine, given their service record, that the ones who survived the war must not have bragged about being decorated by the Führer in person three days before his death. So it's entirely possible that this minor incident indeed escaped the attention of researchers (but perhaps some trace of it remains in the Soviet archives?). I was dragged to the surface up a long stairway that opened onto the chancellery gardens. The magnificent building lay in ruins, gutted by bombs and shells, but a fragrant smell of jasmine and hyacinth filled the cool air. I was brutally pushed into a car and driven to the nearby church; there, they led me down into the bunker and threw me unceremoniously into a concrete room, bare and wet. Puddles dotted the ground; the walls were sweating; and the lock on the heavy metal door plunged me into absolute, uterine darkness: even with my eyes open wide, not the slightest ray of light filtered through. I remained like this for several hours, wet and cold. Then they came to get me. They tied me to a chair, I blinked, the light hurt me; Müller in person interrogated me; they beat me with truncheons, on my ribs, shoulders, and arms, Müller too came over and boxed me with his big peasant's fists. I tried to explain that my thoughtless gesture meant nothing, that I hadn't premeditated it, that I had just gone blank, but Müller wouldn't believe me, he saw a carefully prepared conspiracy, he wanted me to name my accomplices. No matter how much I protested, he wouldn't give up: when Müller set his mind on something, he knew how to stick to it. Finally they threw me back into my cell, where I remained lying in the puddles, waiting for the pain to subside. I must have fallen asleep like this, my head half in the water. I woke up chilled to the bone and twisted with cramps; the door was opening, another man was being shoved in. I just had time to glimpse

an SS officer's uniform, without medals or insignia. In the darkness, I
heard him swearing in a Bavarian dialect: "Isn't there a dry place in
here?"—"Try near the walls," I murmured politely.—"Who're you?"
His voice barked vulgarly, though in a cultivated tone. "Me? I'm Obersturmbannführer Dr. Aue, from the SD. And you?" His voice became
calmer: "My apologies, Obersturmbannführer. I'm Gruppenführer
Fegelein. Ex-Gruppenführer Fegelein," he added with a rather pointed
irony. I knew him by name: he had replaced Wolff as the Reichsführer's liaison officer to the Führer; before, he had commanded an SS cavalry division in Russia, chasing partisans and Jews in the Pripet marshes.
At the Reichsführung, he was said to be ambitious, a gambler, a good-
looking braggart. I leaned up on my elbows: "And what brings you
here, ex-Gruppenführer?"—"Oh, it's a misunderstanding. I'd had a little to drink and I was at home, with a girl; those lunatics in the bunker
thought I wanted to desert. Another one of Bormann's tricks, I'll bet.
They've all gone mad over there; their Walhalla business is not for me,
thanks. But it should get sorted out, my sister-in-law will take care of
it." I didn't know who he was talking about, but I didn't say anything.
It was only when I read Trevor-Roper, years later, that I understood:
Fegelein had married the sister of Eva Braun, whose existence I was unaware of at the time, like pretty much everyone else. This highly diplomatic marriage, unfortunately, proved of little help to him: despite his
connections, his charm, and his easy tongue, Fegelein was shot the following night in the chancellery gardens (this too, I only learned much
later). "And you, Obersturmbannführer?" Fegelein asked. Then I told
him my misadventure. "Ah!" he exclaimed. "That was smart. So that's
why they're all in such a bad mood. I thought that Müller was going to
tear my head off, the brute."—"Oh, he hit you too?"—"Yes. He got it
into his head that the girl I was with is a British spy. I don't know what's
gotten into him all of a sudden."—"It's true," I said, remembering
Thomas's words: "Gruppenführer Müller is looking for a spy, a mole."—
"That's possible," he muttered. "But it has nothing to do with me."—
"Excuse me," I interrupted, "do you know what time it is?"—"Not
exactly. It must be around midnight, one o'clock?"—"Then we should
get some sleep," I suggested pleasantly.—"I'd have preferred my bed,"
Fegelein grumbled.—"I can only agree." I dragged myself on the
ground against the wall and dozed off; my hips were still in the water,
but it was better than my head. I slept well and had pleasant dreams; I
emerged from them regretfully, but I was being kicked in the ribs. "Get
up!" a voice shouted. I stood up with difficulty. Fegelein was sitting by
the door, his arms around his knees; when I went out, he smiled at me
timidly and made a little sign with his hand. They took me up to the

church: two men in civilian clothes were waiting, policemen, one of them with a revolver in his hand; there were also SS men in uniform with them. The policeman with the revolver took me by the arm, pulled me into the street, and shoved me into an Opel; the others got in too. "Where are we going?" I asked the policeman who was driving the barrel of the revolver into my ribs. "Shut your face!" he barked. The car started off, turned onto Mauerstrasse, went about a hundred meters; I heard a high-pitched whistle; an enormous explosion lifted the car and threw it onto its side. The policeman, beneath me, pulled the trigger, I think: I remember having the impression that his shot killed one of the men in front. The other policeman, covered in blood, had fallen inert on top of me. I kicked and elbowed my way out of the overturned car through the rear window, cutting myself a little on the way. Other shells were falling nearby, projecting huge showers of bricks and earth. I was deafened, my ears were ringing. I collapsed onto the sidewalk and lay there for a minute, stunned. The policeman tumbled out behind me and rolled heavily onto my legs. With one hand I found a brick and struck his head with it. We rolled together in the rubble, coated with red brick dust and mud; I hit him with all my strength, but it's not easy to knock out a man with a brick, especially if this brick has already burned. At the third or fourth blow, it crumbled in my hand. I cast around for another one, or for a stone, but the man knocked me over and began strangling me. The blood running down his face traced furrows in the red dust covering it, his eyes were mad, rolling wildly. My hand finally found a cobblestone and I slammed it up and sideways into him. He collapsed on top of me. I freed myself and pounded at his head till his skull burst, leaking brains mixed with dust and hair. Then I stood up, still deafened. I looked for his revolver, but he must have left it in the car, one wheel of which was still spinning in the air. The three other men inside looked dead. For now the shells had stopped falling. I began to run limping down Mauerstrasse.

I had to find somewhere to hide. Around me there were only ministries or government buildings, almost all of them in ruins. I turned down Leipzigstrasse and went into the lobby of an apartment house. Bare or stockinged feet floated in front of me, turning slowly. I raised my head: several people, including children and women, were hanging from the stairway railing, their arms dangling. I found the entrance to the basement and opened it: a gust of putrefaction, shit, and vomit assailed me, the basement was full of water and swollen corpses. I closed the door and tried to go upstairs: after the first landing, the staircase opened onto the void. I headed back down, around the hanged people, and went out. It had begun to rain lightly, I heard explosions everywhere around me. In front of me was the entrance to a U-Bahn station, Stadtmitte on the C line. I ran down the steps, went through the gates, and kept going down into the darkness, guiding myself with one hand on the wall. The tiles were wet, water was welling out of the ceiling and streaming down the vault. Sounds of muffled voices rose from the platform. It was littered with bodies, I couldn't see if they were dead, sleeping or just lying there, I stumbled over them, people were shouting, children crying or moaning. A train with broken windows, lit by wavering candles, was standing at the platform: inside, some Waffen-SS with French insignia were standing at attention, and a tall Brigadeführer in a black leather coat, with his back turned to me, was solemnly handing out decorations to them. I didn't want to disturb them, I went quietly by and jumped down onto the tracks, landing in cold water that came up to my calves. I wanted to head north, but I was disoriented; I tried to remember the direction of the trains when I used to take this line, but I didn't even know what platform I had stumbled upon, everything was confused. To one side, in the tunnel, there was a little light: I went that way, wading in the water that hid the tracks, stumbling over invisible obstacles. At the end of the platform several trains were lined up, also lit by candlelight, a makeshift hospital, crowded with wounded, shouting, swearing, groaning. I walked alongside these cars without anyone noticing me, and groped my way forward, using the wall to guide me. The water rose, reached midcalf. I stopped and plunged my hand into it: it seemed to be flowing slowly toward me. I continued. A floating body bumped against my legs. I could scarcely feel my feet, numb from the cold. In front, I thought I saw a gleam of light, and I seemed to hear other noises besides the lapping of the water. Finally I reached a station lit by a single candle. The water came up to my knees now. Here too there were a lot of people. I called out: "Please, what station is this?"—"Kochstrasse," someone replied amiably. I had gone in the wrong direction, I was heading toward the Russian lines. I turned around and headed back down the tunnel toward Stadtmitte. In front of me I could make out the lights of the U-Bahn hospital. On the tracks, next to the last car, stood two human figures, one quite tall, the other shorter. A flashlight switched on and blinded me; as I was hiding my eyes, a familiar voice grunted: "Hello, Aue. How's it going?"—"You've come at the right time," a second, reedier voice said. "We were just looking for you." It was Clemens and Weser. Another flashlight turned on and they came toward me; I waded backward. "We wanted to talk with you," said Clemens. "About your mother."—"Ah, meine Herren!" I exclaimed. "Do you really think now is a good time?"—"It's always a good time to talk about important things," said the slightly rougher, higher-pitched voice of Weser. I retreated some more but found myself backed against the wall; cold water seeped through the cement and froze my shoulders. "What else do you want with me?" I squealed. "My case has been closed for a long time now!"—"By corrupt, dishonest judges," Clemens said.—"You wriggled your way out with your intrigues," said Weser. "Now all that's over."—"Don't you think it's up to the Reichsführer or to Obergruppenführer Breithaupt to decide that?" The latter was the head of the *SS-Gericht*.—"Breithaupt was killed a few days ago in a car accident," Clemens said phlegmatically. "As for the Reichsführer, he's far away."—"No," Weser added, "now, it's really just you and us."—"But what do you want?"—"We want justice," Clemens said coldly. They had walked up to me and were surrounding me, aiming their flashlights at my face; I had already noticed that they were holding automatics.

"Listen," I stammered, "all this is a huge misunderstanding. I am innocent."—"Innocent?" Weser curtly interrupted. "We'll see about that."—"We're going to tell you how it happened," Clemens began. The powerful light from the flashlights dazed me, his big voice seemed to emanate from this harsh light. "You took the night train from Paris to Marseille. In Marseille, on April twenty-sixth, you had someone issue you a pass for the Italian zone. The next day, you went to Antibes. There, you presented yourself at the house and they welcomed you as a son, as the genuine son that you are. That night, you dined with the family and afterward you slept in one of the upstairs bedrooms, next to the twins' room, opposite the bedroom of your mother and Herr Moreau. Then it was the twenty-eighth."—"Hey," Weser interrupted. "It's the twenty-eighth of April, today. What a coincidence."—"Meine Herren," I said, trying to sound confident, "you're raving."—"Shut your face," Clemens roared. "I'll go on. During the day, we don't really know what you did. We know you cut some wood, and that you left the axe in the kitchen instead of putting it back in the storeroom. Then you walked into town and bought your return ticket. You were wearing civilian clothes, no one noticed you. Then you came back." Weser went on: "Afterward, there are some things we're not sure about. Maybe you talked with Herr Moreau, with your mother. Maybe you had words. We're not sure. We're not sure about the time, either. But we do know that you found yourself alone with Herr Moreau. Then you took the axe in the kitchen, where you'd left it, you returned to the living room, and you killed him."—"We're even willing to believe that you weren't thinking of it when you left the axe," Clemens went on, "that you left the axe there by chance, that you didn't premeditate anything, that it just happened like that. But once you began, you certainly went all the way." Weser continued: "That's for sure. He must have been quite surprised when you laid into his chest with the axe. It went in with the sound of crushed wood and he fell gurgling, his mouth full of blood, taking the axe down with him. You put your foot on his shoulder for leverage and you pulled out the axe and swung again, but you got the angle wrong and the axe bounced back, just breaking a few ribs. Then you stepped back, aimed more carefully, and brought the axe down on his throat. It went through the Adam's apple and you clearly heard the cracking when it crushed his spinal column. He vomited dark flows of blood in one last great heave all over you, it was gushing from his neck too and you were covered with it, and then in front of you his eyes went dull and his blood emptied out through his half-severed neck, you watched his eyes go out like those of a sheep whose throat's just been cut on the grass."—"Meine Herren," I said forcefully, "you are completely insane." Clemens took up: "We don't know if the twins saw that. In any case, they saw you go upstairs. You left the body and the axe there and you went upstairs, covered in blood."—"We don't know why you didn't kill them," said Weser. "You could have, easily. But you didn't. Maybe you didn't want to, maybe you wanted to, but too late, and they'd run away. Maybe you wanted to and then changed your mind. Maybe you already knew they were your sister's children."— "We went by her place, in Pomerania," Clemens grunted. "We found some letters, some documents. There were some very interesting things, among others the children's documents. But we already knew who they were." I let out a hysterical little laugh: "I was there, you know. I was in the woods, I saw you."—"Actually," Weser went on imperturbably, "we thought so. But we didn't want to insist. We said to ourselves that we'd find you sooner or later. And you see, we did find you, in fact."—"Let's go on with our story," said Clemens. "You went upstairs, covered in blood. Your mother was standing there waiting for you, either at the top of the staircase, or in front of the door to her room. She was wearing a nightgown, your old mother. She spoke to you, looking into your eyes. What she said, we don't know. The twins listened to everything, but they didn't tell anyone. She must have reminded you how she had carried you in her womb, then fed you at her breast, how she had wiped your ass and washed you while your father was chasing whores God knows where. Maybe she showed you her breast."—"Not very likely," I spat out with a bitter laugh. "I was allergic to her milk, I never breastfed."—"Too bad for you," Clemens continued without batting an eye. "Maybe then she stroked your chin, your cheek, she called you her child. But you weren't moved: you owed her your love, but you thought only about your hatred. You closed your eyes so you'd stop seeing hers and you took her neck in your hands and you squeezed."—"You're mad!" I shouted. "You're making all this up!"—"Not at all," Weser said sardonically. "Of course, it's a reconstruction. But it agrees with the facts."—"Afterward," Clemens continued in his calm bass voice, "you went into the bathroom and got undressed. You threw your clothes into the bathtub, washed yourself, cleaned off all the blood, and returned to your bedroom, naked."—"There, we can't say," Weser commented. "Maybe you engaged in perverted acts, maybe you just slept. At dawn, you got up, put on your uniform, and left. You took the bus, then the train, you returned to Paris and then to Berlin. On April thirtieth, you sent a telegram to your sister. She went to Antibes, buried your mother and her husband, then she left again as soon as possible, with the boys. Maybe she had already guessed."—"Listen," I babbled, "you've lost your minds. The judges said you had no evidence. Why would I have done that? What would be the motive? You always have to have a motive."—"We don't know," Weser said calmly. "But actually it's all the same to us. Maybe you wanted Moreau's money. Maybe you're a sex fiend. Maybe your wound messed up your head. Maybe it was just an old family hatred, that's pretty common, and you wanted to take advantage of the war to settle your accounts on the sly, thinking it would hardly be noticed among so many other deaths. Maybe you simply went mad."—"But what are you after, damn it!" I shouted again.—"We told you," Clemens murmured: "we want justice."—"The city is burning!" I shouted. "There aren't any more courthouses! All the judges are dead or gone. How do you plan on judging me?"—"We've already judged you," Weser said in a voice that was so quiet that I could hear the water streaming by. "We found you guilty."—"You?" I sniggered. "You're cops. You don't have the right to judge."—"Given the circumstances," Clemens's big voice rumbled, "we'll take that right."—"Then," I said sadly, "even if you are right, you're no better than I."

At that moment, I heard a great din coming from Kochstrasse. People were shouting, running, splashing frantically. A man passed by crying, "The Russians! The Russians are in the tunnel!"—"Shit," Clemens belched. He and Weser aimed their flashlights toward the station; German soldiers were surging back, firing randomly; I could see the muzzle flashes of machine guns, bullets whistled by, cracked against the walls or hit the water with soft little *thwacks*. Men were yelling, falling into the water. Clemens and Weser, lit by their flashlights, calmly raised their pistols and began firing round after round at the enemy. The whole tunnel echoed with cries, gunshots, the sounds of water. From the other side, machine-gun fire volleyed back. Clemens and Weser made to

switch off their flashlights; just then, in a fleeting burst of light, I saw
Weser catch a bullet under the chin, rise as if lifted up, and then fall
straight backward in a huge splash. Clemens bellowed, "Weser! Shit!"
But his light had gone out and, holding my breath, I dove underwater.
Guiding myself by holding onto the tracks rather than swimming, I
headed toward the cars of the makeshift hospital. When my head
emerged from the water, bullets were whistling around me, patients
screamed in panic, I heard French voices, curt orders. "Don't shoot,
guys!" I shouted in French. A hand seized my collar, dragged me, dripping, toward the platform. "You're one of ours?" went a cocky voice. I
was breathing hard and coughing, I had swallowed water. "No, no, German," I said. The man let off a volley of rounds next to my head, deafening me just as Clemens's voice resounded: "Aue! You son of a bitch!
I'll get you!" I hoisted myself onto the platform and, striking out with
hands and elbows at the panicking refugees to clear a path for myself,
found the stairs, which I fled up four at a time.

The street was deserted, except for three foreign Waffen-SS men
charging toward Zimmerstrasse with a heavy machine gun and some
Panzerfäuste, paying no attention to me or to the other civilians escaping from the U–Bahn entrance. I started in the opposite direction, running north up Friedrichstrasse, between burning buildings, corpses,
burned-out cars. I reached Unter den Linden. A large fountain of water was gushing from a blown water main, spraying the bodies and the
rubble. At the corner two grizzled old men were walking along, they
seemed not to be paying any attention to the racket of the artillery and
the heavy mortar shells. One of them wore the armband of the blind;
the other was guiding him. "Where are you going?" I asked, panting.—
"We don't know," the blind man replied.—"Where are you coming
from?" I asked again.—"We don't know that, either." They sat down
on a crate among the ruins and piles of rubble. The blind man leaned
on his cane. The other stared about him with wild eyes, plucking at his
friend's sleeve. I turned my back to them and went on. The avenue, for
as far as I could see, seemed completely deserted. Opposite stood the
building that housed the offices of Dr. Mandelbrod and Herr Leland. It
had been hit a few times but didn't look ruined. One of the main doors
was hanging from a hinge, I pushed it open with my shoulder and entered the lobby, full of marble slabs and moldings fallen from the walls.
Soldiers must have camped here: I noticed traces of a campfire, empty
cans, nearly dry excrement. But the lobby was deserted. I pushed open
the emergency stairway and ran up. At the top floor, the stairs opened
onto a hallway that led to the beautiful reception room before Mandelbrod's office. Two of the amazons were sitting there, one on the sofa,

the other in an armchair, their heads leaning to the side or backward, their eyes wide open, a thin stream of blood running from their temples and the corners of their lips; each one held a small automatic pistol with a mother-of-pearl handle in her hand. A third girl was lying in front of the double padded doors. Cold with horror, I went over to look at them close up, I brought my face to theirs, without touching them. They were perfectly turned out, their hair pulled back, clear gloss made their full lips shine, mascara still outlined a crown of long black eyelashes around their empty eyes; their nails, on the pistol butts, were carefully manicured and painted. No breath raised their chests under the ironed suits. No matter how much I scrutinized their pretty faces, I was incapable of distinguishing one from the other, of recognizing Hilde from Helga or Hedwig; yet they weren't triplets. I stepped over the one who was lying across the doorway and entered the office. Three other girls were lying dead on the sofa and the carpet; Mandelbrod and Leland were at the back of the room, in front of the large shattered bay window, near a mountain of leather suitcases and trunks. Outside, behind them, a fire was roaring, they were paying no attention to the spirals of smoke invading the room. I went up to them, looked at the bags, and asked: "You're planning on going on a trip?" Mandelbrod, who was holding a cat on his lap and stroking it, smiled slightly in the ripples of fat that drowned his features. "Exactly," he said in his beautiful voice. "Would you like to come with us?" I counted the trunks and suitcases out loud: "Nineteen," I said, "not bad. You're going far?"—"To begin with, Moscow," said Mandelbrod. "Afterward, we'll see." Leland, wearing a long navy blue trenchcoat, was sitting on a little chair next to Mandelbrod; he was smoking a cigarette, with a glass ashtray on his knees, and he looked at me without saying anything. "I see," I said. "And you really think you can take all that?"—"Oh, of course," Mandelbrod smiled. "It's already arranged. We're just waiting for them to come get us."—"The Russians? Our men are still holding the area, I should warn you."—"We know that," Leland said, blowing out a long puff of smoke. "The Soviets told us they'd be here tomorrow, without fail."—"A very cultivated colonel," Mandelbrod added. "He told us not to worry, he'd personally take care of us. The fact is, you see, we still have a lot of work to do."—"And the girls?" I asked, waving my hand toward the bodies.—"Ah, the poor little things didn't want to come with us. Their attachment to the fatherland was too strong. They didn't want to understand that some values are even more important."—"The Führer has failed," Leland said coldly. "But the ontological war that he began isn't over. Who else besides Stalin can finish the job?"—"When we offered them our services," Mandelbrod

whispered as he stroked his cat, "they were immediately very interested. They know that they'll need men like us, after this war, that they
can't allow the Western powers to walk off with the cream of the crop.
If you come with us, I can guarantee you a good position, with all the
advantages."—"You can keep doing what you do so well," said Leland.—"You're crazy!" I exclaimed. "You're all crazy! Everyone's gone
mad in this city." Already I was backing to the door, past the gracefully
slumped bodies of the girls. "Except for me!" I shouted before escaping. Leland's last words reached me at the door: "If you change your
mind, come back to see us!"

Unter den Linden was still empty; here and there, a shell struck a
façade or a pile of rubble. My ears were still ringing from the Frenchman's machine-gun volley. I began running toward the Brandenburg
Gate. I had to get out of the city at all costs, it had become a monstrous
trap. My information was already a day old, but I knew that the only
way out was to go through the Tiergarten and then by the Ost-West-
Achse down to the Adolf-Hitler-Platz; then I'd see. The day before, that
side of the city still wasn't sealed off, some Hitlerjugend still held the
bridge over the Havel, Wannsee was in our hands. If I can reach
Thomas's place, I said to myself, I'm saved. The Pariser Platz, in front
of the still relatively intact Gate, was strewn with overturned, wrecked,
burned-out vehicles; in the ambulances, charred corpses still wore on
their extremities white casts made of plaster of Paris, which doesn't
burn. I heard a powerful rumbling noise: a Russian tank passed behind
me, sweeping wrecked cars in front of it; several Waffen-SS were
perched on top, they must have captured it. It stopped right next to me,
fired, then started off in a clatter of treads; one of the Waffen-SS observed me indifferently. The tank turned right into the Wilhelmstrasse
and disappeared. A little farther on, down Unter den Linden, between
the lampposts and the rows of shredded trees, I glimpsed a human shape
through the smoke, a man in civilian clothes with a hat. I began running again and, threading between the obstacles, went through the
Gate, black with smoke, riddled with bullets and shrapnel.

Beyond lay the Tiergarten. I left the road and dove into the trees.
Aside from the whirring of flying mortar shells and distant explosions,
the park was strangely silent. The *Nebelkrähe*, those hooded crows
whose hoarse cries always resound through the Tiergarten, had all left,
fleeing the constant shelling for a safer place: no Sperrkommando in the
sky, no flying court-martial for birds. How lucky they are, and they
don't even know it. Corpses sprawled among the trees; and all along the
pathways, sinister, swayed the hanged. It began to rain again, a light rain
through which the sun still shone. The bushes in the flowerbeds had

blossomed, the smell of rose bushes mingled with that of corpses. From time to time I turned around: between the trees, I seemed to glimpse the silhouette following me. A dead soldier was still holding his Schmeisser; I grabbed it, aimed it at the silhouette, pulled the trigger; but the weapon was jammed and I threw it furiously into a bush. I had hoped not to stray too far from the main road, but on that side I saw movement, vehicles, and I moved deeper into the park. To my right, the Victory Column rose above the trees, hidden by its protective coverings and still obstinately standing. In front of me several pools of water blocked the path: instead of heading back toward the road, I decided to skirt round them toward the canal, where I used to go, a very long time ago, prowling the night in search of pleasure. From there, I said to myself, I'll cut through the zoo and go lose myself in Charlottenburg. I crossed the canal over the bridge where I had had that curious altercation with Hans P., one night. Beyond, the wall of the zoo had collapsed in several places, and I climbed up over the rubble. Sustained fire came from the large bunker, light cannon shots and machine-gun volleys.

This part of the zoo was completely flooded: the bombardments had ripped open the Aquarium and the fish tanks had burst, pouring out tons of water, strewing the lanes with dead fish, crayfish, crocodiles, jellyfish, a panting dolphin that, lying on its side, contemplated me with a worried eye. I waded forward, around the baboon island where babies clutched with minuscule hands the stomachs of their panicking mothers, I wove between parrots, dead monkeys, a giraffe whose long neck hung over a railing, bleeding bears. I entered a half-destroyed building: in a large cage, an immense black gorilla was sitting, dead, a bayonet stuck in its chest. A river of black blood flowed between the bars and mingled with the pools of water. This gorilla looked surprised, astonished; its wrinkled face, its open eyes, its enormous hands, seemed frighteningly human to me, as if it were on the point of talking to me. Beyond this building stretched a long enclosed pond: a hippopotamus was floating in the water, dead, the fin of a mortar shell stuck in its back; another one was lying on a platform, riddled with shrapnel, dying in long, heavy gasps. The water overflowing from the pool was soaking the clothes of two Waffen-SS lying there; a third one rested, leaning against a cage, his eyes blank, his machine gun across his legs. I wanted to go on but I heard bursts of Russian voices, mixed with the trumpeting of a panic-stricken elephant. I hid behind a bush and then turned back to go around the cages across a kind of little bridge. Clemens barred my path, his feet in a puddle at the end of the footbridge, his wet hat still dripping with rainwater, his automatic in his hand. I raised my hands, as in the movies. "You made me run," Clemens panted. "Weser is dead.

But I got you."—"Kriminalkommissar Clemens," I hissed, out of breath from running, "don't be ridiculous. The Russians are a hundred meters away. They'll hear your gunshot."—"I should drown you in a pool, you piece of shit," he belched, "sew you up in a bag and drown you. But I don't have time."—"You haven't even shaved, Kriminalkommissar Clemens," I bellowed, "and you want to pass judgment on me!" He gave an abrupt laugh. A gunshot rang out, his hat came down over his face, and he fell like a block across the bridge, his head in a puddle of water. Thomas stepped out from behind a cage, a carbine in his hands, a large, delighted smile on his lips. "As usual, I arrive just in time," he said happily. He glanced at Clemens's massive body. "What did he want with you?"—"He was one of those two cops. He wanted to kill me."—"Stubborn guy. Still for the same business?"—"Yes. I don't know, they've gone mad."—"You haven't been very smart, either," he said to me severely. "They're looking for you everywhere. Müller is furious." I shrugged and looked around. It had stopped raining, the sun shone through the clouds and made the wet leaves on the trees and the patches of water in the lanes glisten. I could still make out a few scraps of Russian voices: they must have moved a little farther off, behind the monkey enclosure. The elephant trumpeted again. Thomas, his carbine leaning on the railing of the little bridge, had crouched down next to Clemens's body; he had pocketed the policeman's automatic and was rummaging through his clothes. I passed behind him and looked to that side, but there was no one. Thomas had turned toward me and was waving a thick wad of reichsmarks: "Look at that," he said, laughing. "A gold mine, your cop." He put the bills in his pocket and kept searching. Next to him, I saw a thick iron bar, torn from a nearby cage by an explosion. I picked it up, weighed it, then brought it down with all my strength on the nape of Thomas's neck. I heard his vertebrae crack and he toppled over like a log, across Clemens's body. I dropped the bar and contemplated the bodies. Then I turned Thomas over, his eyes were still open, and unbuttoned his tunic. I undid my own and quickly switched jackets with him before turning him onto his stomach again. I inspected the pockets: along with the automatic and Clemens's banknotes were Thomas's papers, those of the Frenchman from the STO, and some cigarettes. I found the keys to his house in his pants pocket; my own papers had stayed in my jacket.

The Russians had moved farther on. In the lane a little elephant came trotting toward me, followed by three chimpanzees and an ocelot. They went around the bodies and over the bridge without slowing down, leaving me alone. I was feverish, my mind was coming apart. But I still remember perfectly the two bodies lying on top of each other in the puddles, on the footbridge, and the animals moving off. I was sad but didn't really know why. I felt all at once the entire weight of the past, of the pain of life and of inalterable memory, I remained alone with the dying hippopotamus, a few ostriches, and the corpses, alone with time and grief and the sorrow of remembering, the cruelty of my existence and of my death still to come. The Kindly Ones were on to me.

GLOSSARY

AA (*Auswärtiges Amt*, "Department of the Exterior"): Foreign Office, headed by Joachim von Ribbentrop.

ABWEHR: Military intelligence service. Its full name was *Amt Ausland/ Abwehr im Oberkommando der Wehrmacht*, "Foreign Office/Defense for the Armed Forces High Command."

AMT: Office.

ARBEITSEINSATZ (*"work operation"*): Department in charge of organizing forced labor of inmates in concentration camps.

AOK (*Armeeoberkommando*): The headquarters of an army, which controlled a certain number of divisions. At all levels (Army, Division, Regiment, etc.), the organization of military headquarters included, among other things, a Chief of Staff; a Ia (pronounced "One-a," *"Eins-a,"* in German), the general officer in charge of operations; a Ib (*Eins-b*) or quartermaster in charge of supplies; and a Ic/AO (*Eins-c/AO*), the officer in charge of military intelligence, or *Abwehroffizier*.

BERÜCK: Commander of the rear zone of an Army Group.

EINSATZ: Action, operation.

EINSATZGRUPPE ("action group" of the SP and SD): Deployed for the first time in 1938, for the Anschluss and the occupation of Czechoslovakia, these SS groups were in charge of dealing with the most urgent security tasks until permanent police *Stelle* ("offices") could be set up. The system was formalized for Poland in September 1939. For the invasion of the USSR, following a formal agreement between the Reich Security Main Office (RSHA) and the Wehrmacht, an Einsatzgruppe was posted to each Army Group (with a fourth, Einsatzgruppe D, attached directly to the Eleventh Army for the Crimea and the Romanian occupation zone). Each Einsatzgruppe was made up of a *Gruppenstab*, or general staff, and several *Einsatzkommandos* (Ek) or *Son-*

derkommandos (Sk). Each Kommando was in turn subdivided into a general staff (the *Kommandostab*), with support personnel (drivers, interpreters, etc.) and several *Teilkommandos*. The general staffs of the Groups and the Kommandos reproduced the organization of the RSHA: thus there was a Leiter I or *Verwaltungsführer* (personnel and administration), a Leiter II (Supply), a Leiter III (SD), IV (Gestapo), and V (Kripo). One of them, usually the Leiter III or IV, also served as Chief of Staff.

GAULEITER: Nazi Germany was divided into administrative regions called *Gaue*. Each *Gau* was supervised by a Gauleiter, a member of the National Socialist Party (NSDAP) appointed by Hitler, to whom he reported.

GESTAPO (*Geheime Staatspolizei*, "Secret State Police"): Directed by SS-Gruppenführer Heinrich Müller, from 1939 till the end of the war. See RSHA.

GOLDFASANEN (*"Golden Pheasants"*): Pejorative term for civil servants in the *Ostministerium*, because of their yellowish-brown uniforms, and for other Nazi functionaries.

GFP (*Geheime Feldpolizei*, "Secret Military Police"): Branch of the Wehrmacht in charge of military security in the theater of operations, especially in the fight against partisans. Most of the officers in the GFP had been recruited from the German police and so belonged to the Security Police (SP) or else the SS; still, this service of military security remained distinct from the services of the RSHA.

HÄFTLING (*plural Häftlinge*): Inmate.

HIWI (*Hilfswillige*, "voluntary workers"): Native auxiliaries of the Wehrmacht, usually recruited from prisoners' camps, and employed in the rear for transport, supplies, hard labor, etc.

HONVÉD: The Hungarian army.

HSSPF (*Höhere SS- und Polizeiführer*, "Supreme Head of the SS and the Police"): To ensure coordination of all SS offices or suboffices at the regional level, in 1937 Himmler established the HSSPFs, who, in principle, had all SS groups in their zone under their orders. In Germany, the Reichsführer-SS appointed one of them for each *Wehrkreis* ("defense region," defined by the Wehrmacht), and, later on, one for each occupied country, who sometimes had under his orders, as in occupied Poland (the "Generalgouvernement"), several SSPFs. In Soviet Russia, during the invasion of 1941, Himmler appointed an HSSPF for each of the three Army Groups, North, Center, and South.

IKL (*Inspektion der Konzentrationslager*, "Inspectorate for Concentration Camps"): The first concentration camp, the one in Dachau, was created on March 20, 1933, followed by many others. In June 1934, following "the Röhm putsch" and the elimination of leaders of the SA, the camps were placed under the direct control of the SS, which then created the IKL, based in Oranienburg, under the command of SS-Obergruppen-führer Theodor Eicke, the commander of Dachau, to whom Himmler gave the mission of reorganizing all the camps. The "Eicke system," which was put in place in 1934 and which lasted until the first years of the war, aimed at the psychological, and sometimes physical, destruction of opponents of the regime; forced labor, at the time, was used only as torture. But in the beginning of 1942, when Germany was intensifying its war effort following the stalemate of the offensive in the USSR, Himmler decided that this system was not adapted to the new situation, which required a maximum use of the inmates' labor force; in March 1942, the IKL was made subordinate to the Economy and Administration Main Office (WVHA) as Amtsgruppe D, with four departments: D I, central office; D II, the *Arbeitseinsatz*, in charge of forced labor; D III, sanitary and medical department; and D IV, department in charge of administration and finance. This reorganization had limited success: Pohl, the head of the WVHA, never managed fully to reform the IKL or to renew its managerial staff, and the tension between the political-police function and the economic function of the camps, aggravated by the extermination function assigned to two camps under the control of the WVHA (KL Auschwitz and KL Lublin, better known as Maidanek), existed until the collapse of the Nazi regime.

KGF (*Kriegsgefangener*): Prisoner of war.

KL (*Konzentrationslager*, "concentration camp," often incorrectly called KZ by the inmates): The daily management of a KL was the responsibility of a department overseen by the Kommandant of the camp, the Abteilung III, run by a *Schutzhaftlagerführer* or *Lagerführer* ("head of preventive detention camp") and his adjunct. The office in charge of the organization of inmate labor, the *Arbeitseinsatz*, was attached to this department under the designation IIIa. The other departments were respectively: I, Kommandantur; II, *Politische Abteilung* ("Political Department," or representatives in the camp of the SP); IV, administration; V, medical and sanitary (for the SS in the camp as well as for the inmates); VI, training and upkeep of the troops; and VII, guard troop of the SS. All these offices were administered by SS officers or noncoms, but the majority of the work was carried out by inmate-functionaries, often called the "privileged ones."

KRIPO(*Kriminalpolizei*,"Criminal Police"): Headed by SS-Gruppen-führer Arthur Nebe from 1937 to July 1944. See also RSHA.

LEBENSBORN: The "Fount of Life" society, established by the SS in 1936 and attached directly to the personal staff of the Reichsführer-SS, in charge of managing orphanages as well as maternity hospitals for members or companions of members of the SS. The *Lebensborn*, in or-der to encourage a higher birth rate among the SS, guaranteed confi-dentiality about childbirth for unmarried women.

LEITER: Head of an office or branch.

MISCHLINGE: Mixed race, mixed-blood. This term was part of the legal vocabulary of the National Socialist racial laws, which defined this status according to the number of non-Aryan ancestors.

NKVD (*Narodnyi Komissariat Vnutrennikh Del*, "People's Commissariat for Internal Affairs"): The main Soviet security agency during the time of the Second World War, an organism that succeeded the Cheka and the OGPU, and was the ancestor of the KGB.

NSV (*Nationalsozialistische Volkswohlfahrt*): National Socialist People's Welfare Association.

OKH (*Oberkommando des Heeres*, "Army High Command"): Whereas the OKH was in principle subordinate to the High Command of the Armed Forces (OKW), in practice it commanded the entirety of oper-ations on the Eastern Front while the OKW controlled operations on all the other fronts. Hitler took direct command of the OKH in De-cember 1941, after dismissing Generalfeldmarschall Walter von Brau-chitsch.

OKHG (*Oberkommando der Heeresgruppe*): The headquarters of an Army Group, which controlled several armies.

OKW (*Oberkommando der Wehrmacht*, "High Command of the Armed Forces"): Created in February 1938 by Hitler to replace the War Min-istry and placed directly under his command. In principle, the OKW controlled the OKH (the Army), the *Luftwaffe* (the Air Force, com-manded by Reichsmarschall Hermann Göring), and the *Kriegsmarine* (the Navy, commanded by Grand Admiral Karl Dönitz). Its Chief of Staff was Field Marshall Wilhelm Keitel.

ORPO (*Hauptamt Ordnungspolizei*, "Main Office of the Order Police"): Organism integrated into the SS in June 1936 under the command of SS-Oberstgruppenführer Kurt Daluege and grouping together the gendarmerie and the various forces of uniformed police (*Gemeindepolizei, Schutzpolizei* or Schupo, etc.). Police battalions from the Orpo were deployed on numerous occasions to commit wholesale massacres in the context of the "Final Solution."

OSTMINISTERIUM: Common name for *Reichsministerium für die besetzten Ostgebiete*, "Ministry for the Occupied Territories in the East," headed by the Nazi ideologue Alfred Rosenberg, author of *The Myth of the Twentieth Century.*

OUN (*Organizatsiya Ukrainskikh Natsionalistiv*): "Organization of Ukrainian Nationalists."

PERSÖNLICHER STAB DES REICHSFÜHRER-SS: Personal staff of the Reichsführer-SS, Heinrich Himmler.

REVIER: Hospital or infirmary. In some concentration camps, it was called the HKB, *Häftlingskrankenbau* or "hospital for inmates."

RKF (*Reichskommissariat für die Festigung deutschen Volkstums*, "Reichskommissariat for the Strengthening of the Germandom"): The destructive tasks given to the *Einsatzgruppen*, in Poland at the end of 1939, and especially beginning with the invasion of the USSR, were organically linked with a set of "positive" tasks also entrusted to the Reichsführer-SS: the repatriation of *Volksdeutschen* ("racial Germans" from the USSR and the Banat) and the settlement of German colonies in the East. To carry out these tasks, Himmler created the RKF within the SS, and was appointed its Reichskommissar. The two sectors of activities, destruction of Jews and Germanification, were closely linked both conceptually and on the organizational level: thus, when the region of Zamosc was chosen as a primary objective for Germanization, Himmler gave this task to the head of the SS and of the Police (SSPF) of the district of Lublin, SS-Gruppenführer Odilo Globocnik, who also commanded Einsatz Reinhard, a structure set up to administer the three extermination camps in Treblinka, Sobibor, and Belzec, and the Orpo battalions deployed to commit massacres in the region.

ROLLBAHN: Wehrmacht units in charge of transport and supplies for troops (the term also designated the main military supply roads in the East).

RSHA (*Reichssicherheitshauptamt*, "Reich Security Main Office"): Upon the Seizure of Power, on January 30, 1933, the SS sought to extend its privileges in terms of security functions. After a long internal struggle, mainly against Göring, Himmler managed, in June 1936, to take control of all the German police forces, the new political police as well as the criminal police and the ordinary police grouped together in the Orpo. These police forces nonetheless remained State institutions, financed by the budget of the Reich, whose employees remained functionaries, subject to the rules of recruitment and promotion of the State bureaucracy. To legitimize this bureaucratically incoherent state of affairs, the Reichsführer was appointed Chief of the German Police within the Ministry of the Interior. The Kripo (Criminal Police) was joined to the Gestapo to form a Security Police (SP), which remained a government structure; the Security Service (SD), however, continued to function within the SS. The SP and the SD were thus joined through "personal union": SS-Obergruppenführer Reinhard Heydrich became officially *Chef der Sicherheitspolizei und des SD*, a position, like that of his leader Heinrich Himmler, straddling the Party and the State.

In 1939, just after the invasion of Poland, an attempt was made to officialize this curious situation by creating a bastard structure: the RSHA, which was supposed to regroup the SP and the SD into a single organization. This reorganization was in fact carried out successfully: all the administrative services of the different structures were fused into an Amt I (personnel) and an Amt II (budget, administration, organization); the SD was divided into an Amt III (*SD-Inland*, or "Interior") and an Amt VI (*SD-Ausland*, or "External"); the Gestapo was rebaptized Amt IV, with the pompous designation of *Gegnererforschung und -bekämpfung* ("Investigation and Struggle Against Adversaries"); and the Kripo became Amt V under the name *Verbrechensbekämpfung* ("Struggle Against Criminals"). An Amt VII was also created for "Ideological Research and Evaluation," *Weltanschauliche Forschung und Auswertung*. But none of this was ever legalized: the ministerial bureaucracy was opposed to the amalgamation of State administrations and Party organizations; it was out of the question to finance the SD out of the Reich's budget. Thus, even if the RSHA existed in actual fact, it had no letterhead, and it was forbidden to use the term in correspondence; Heydrich officially remained "Chief of the SP and the SD."

The structure of the RSHA was reproduced at all the regional levels, *Oberabschnitt, Abschnitt*, etc.: in each district there was an Amt III, an Amt IV, and an Amt V, all under the responsibility of an *Inspekteur der SP und des SD* (IdS). After the beginning of the war, the same structures were established in the occupied territories, where the *Inspekteur* became a *Befehlshaber* ("Commander") *der SP und des SD* (BdS), who sometimes had under his orders several *Kommandeur der SP und des SD* (KdS). The Orpo followed the same scheme, with IdO, BdO, and KdO.

SA (*Sturmabteilung*, "Stormtroops"): Paramilitary units of the National Socialist Party (NSDAP) who played a major role during the rise to power of the Party and just after the Seizure of Power in January 1933. In June 1934, with the support of the SS and the Wehrmacht, Hitler liquidated the leaders of the SA, including its chief, Ernst Röhm. The SA continued to exist until the fall of the regime, but no longer played any political role.

SD (*Hauptamt Sicherheitsdienst*, "Main Office of the Security Service"): SS structure created in the autumn of 1931 under command of Reinhard Heydrich. See also RSHA.

SP (*Hauptamt Sicherheitspolizei*, "Main Office of the Security Police"): Sometimes called Sipo. See also RSHA.

SPIESS: Familiar term designating the noncom in charge of a company, usually a *Hauptfeldwebel* (Sergeant-Major).

SS (*Schutzstaffel*, "Protection Detachment"): The first SS units were formed within the National Socialist Party in the summer of 1925, initially as bodyguards for the Führer, Adolf Hitler, who was already seeking to create a counterweight to the SA. Heinrich Himmler was appointed *Reichsführer-SS*, "Supreme Leader of the SS," on January 6, 1929. The SS became completely independent of the SA in the fall of 1930 and played a major role in the elimination of its leaders in June 1934.

STO (*Service du travail obligatoire*): Program instituted in France by the German occupants to send forcibly recruited workers to Germany.

VOLKSDEUTSCHEN: Unlike *Reichsdeutschen*, these were Germans who had been living for several generations abroad, most of them in homogeneous communities.

WVHA (*Wirtschafts-Verwaltungshauptamt*, "Economy and Administration Main Office"): This SS structure was created in the beginning of 1942 to regroup the administrative–economic branch of the SS, the branches in charge of matters of construction and supplies, the economic enterprises of the SS, and the Inspectorate for Concentration Camps (IKL). Headed by SS-Obergruppenführer Oswald Pohl, Himmler's economic éminence grise, the WVHA included five *Amtsgruppe*, or "groups of offices": Amtsgruppe A, *Truppenverwaltung* ("Troop Administration"), and Amtsgruppe B, *Truppenwirtschaft* ("Troop Finance"), managing all questions of administration and supply for the Waffen-SS (the fighting units of the SS) as well as the concentration camp guards;

Amtsgruppe C, *Bauweisen* ("Construction"), including all technical services of the SS linked to building; the Amtsgruppe D was the rebaptized IKL; as for the Amtsgruppe W, *Wirtschaftliche Unternehmungen* ("Economic Enterprises"), it covered the immense SS economic empire, which included firms in sectors as diverse as construction, armaments, mineral water, textiles, and publishing.

TABLE OF GERMAN RANKS WITH APPROXIMATE AMERICAN EQUIVALENTS

SS	Wehrmacht	Police	American Army
Reichsführer-SS	—	—	—
—	Generalfeldmarschall	—	General of the Armies
SS-Oberstgruppenführer	Generaloberst	Generaloberst der Polizei	General
SS-Obergruppenführer	General .	General der.Polizei	Lieutenant General
SS-Gruppenführer	Generalleutnant	Generalleutnant d.P.	—
SS-Brigadeführer	Generalmajor	Generalmajor d.P.	Brigadier General
SS-Oberführer	—	—	—
SS-Standartenführer	Oberst	Oberst d.P.	Colonel
SS-Obersturmbannführer	Oberstleutnant	Oberstleutnant d.P.	Lieutenant-Colonel
SS-Sturmbannführer	Major	Major d.P.	Major
SS-Hauptsturmführer	Hauptmann	Hauptmann d.P.	Captain
SS-Obersturmführer	Oberleutnant	Oberleutnant d.P.	Lieutenant
SS-Untersturmführer	Leutnant	Leutnant d.P.	Second Lieutenant
SS-Sturmscharführer	Hauptfeldwebel	Meister	Sergeant-Major
SS-Stabsscharführer	Stabsfeldwebel	—	Master Sergeant
SS-Hauptscharführer	Oberfeldwebel	—	Sergeant First Class
SS-Obersharführer	Feldwebel	—	Staff Sergeant
SS-Scharführer	Unterfeldwebel	Hauptwachtmeister	Sergeant
SS-Unterscharführer	Unteroffizier	Rev. O.Wachtmeister	Corporal
SS-Rottenführer	Stabsgefreiter	Oberwachtmeister	Specialist
	Obergefreiter		—
	Gefreiter	Wachtmeister	—
SS-Sturmmann	Oberschütze	Rottwachtmeister	Private First Class
SS-Oberschütze	Schütze	Unterwachtmeister	Private
SS-Schütze	Gemeiner, Landser	Anwärter	Private Recruit